THE COMPLETE ILLUSTRATED STORIES

OF

HANS CHRISTIAN ANDERSEN

THE COMPLETE ILLUSTRATED STORIES

OF

HANS CHRISTIAN ANDERSEN

TRANSLATED BY

H. W. DULCKEN, PH.D.

WITH TWO HUNDRED AND NINETY ILLUSTRATIONS BY A. W. BAYES

ENGRAVED BY DALZIEL BROTHERS

CHANCELLOR
PRESS

First published in Great Britain in 1989
by George Routledge & Sons under the title
Stories for the Household

This facsimile edition published in 1983 by
Chancellor Press
Michelin House
81 Fulham Road
London SW3 6RB

Reprinted 1984, 1985, 1987, 1989, 1990

ISBN 0907 486266

Printed in Italy by OFSA S.p.A., Milan

CONTENTS.

CONTENTS.

THE OLD WOMAN HANGS THE SHILLING ROUND THE CHILD'S NECK.

THE SILVER SHILLING.

THERE was once a Shilling. He came out quite bright from the Mint, and sprang up, and rang out, "Hurrah! now I'm off into the wide world." And into the wide world he certainly went.

The child held him with soft warm hands; the miser clutched him in a cold avaricious palm; the old man turned him goodness knows how many times before parting with him; while careless youth rolled him lightly away. The Shilling was of silver, and had very little copper about him: he had been now a whole year in the world—that is to say, in the country in which he had been struck. But one day he started on his foreign travels; he was the last native coin in the purse borne by his travelling master. The gentleman was himself not aware that he still had this coin until he came across it by chance.

"Why, here's a shilling from home left to me," he said. "Well, he can make the journey with me."

And the Shilling rattled and jumped for joy as it was thrust back into the purse. So here it lay among strange companions, who came and went, each making room for a successor; but the Shilling from home always remained in the bag; which was a distinction for it.

Several weeks had gone by, and the Shilling had travelled far out into the world without exactly knowing where he was, though he learned from the other coins that they were French or Italian. One said they were in such and such a town, another that they had reached such and such a spot; but the Shilling could form no idea of all this. He who has his head, in a bag sees nothing; and this was the case with the Shilling. But one day, as he lay there, he noticed that the purse was not shut, and so he crept forward to the opening, to take a look around. He ought not to have done so; but he was inquisitive, and people often have to pay for that. He slipped out into the fob: and when the purse was taken out at night the Shilling remained behind, and was sent out into the passage with the clothes. There he fell upon the floor: no one heard it, no one saw it.

Next morning the clothes were carried back into the room; the gentleman put them on, and continued his journey, while the Shilling remained behind. The coin was found, and was required to go into service again, so he was sent out with three other coins.

"It is a pleasant thing to look about one in the world," thought the Shilling, "and to get to know strange people and foreign customs."

And now began the history of the Shilling, as told by himself.

"'Away with him, he's bad—no use.' These words went through and through me," said the Shilling. "I knew I sounded well and had been properly coined. The people were certainly mistaken. They could not mean me! but, yes, they did mean me. I was the one of whom they said, 'He's bad—he's no good.' 'I must get rid of that fellow in the dark,' said the man who had received me; and I was passed at night, and abused in the day-time. 'Bad—no good' was the cry: 'we must make haste and get rid of him.'

"And I trembled in the fingers of the holder each time I was to be secretly passed on as a coin of the country.

"What a miserable shilling I am! Of what use is my silver to me, my value, my coinage, if all these things are looked on as worthless? In the eyes of the world one has only the value the world chooses to put upon one. It must be terrible indeed to have a bad conscience, and to creep along on evil ways, if I, who am quite innocent, can feel so badly because I am only thought guilty.

"Each time I was brought out I shuddered at the thought of the eyes that would look at me, for I knew that I should be rejected and flung back upon the table, like an impostor and a cheat. Once I came into the hands of a poor old woman, to whom I was paid for a hard day's work, and she could not get rid of me at all. No one would accept me, and I was a perfect worry to the old dame.

"'I shall certainly be forced to deceive some one with this shilling,' she said; 'for, with the best will in the world, I can't hoard up a false shilling. The rich baker shall have him; he will be able to bear the loss —but it's wrong in me to do it, after all.'

"'And I must lie heavy on that woman's conscience too,' sighed I. 'Am I really so much changed in my old age?'

"And the woman went her way to the rich baker; but he knew too well what kind of shillings would pass to take me, and he threw me back at the woman, who got no bread for me. And I felt miserably low

THE MOTHER TRIES THE SHILLING.

to think that I should be the cause of distress to others—I who had been in my young days so proudly conscious of my value and of the correctness of my mintage. I became as miserable as a poor shilling can be whom no one will accept; but the woman took me home again and looked at me with a friendly, hearty face, and said,

"'No, I will not deceive any one with thee. I will bore a hole through thee, that every one may see thou art a false thing. And yet—it just occurs to me—perhaps this is a lucky shilling; and the thought comes so strongly upon me that I am sure it must be true! I will make a hole through the shilling, and pass a string through the hole, and hang the coin round the neck of my neighbour's little boy for a lucky shilling.'

"So she bored a hole through me. It is certainly not agreeable to have a hole bored through one; but many things can be borne when the intention is good. A thread was passed through the hole, and I became a kind of medal, and was hung round the neck of the little child; and the child smiled at me, and kissed me, and I slept all night on its warm, innocent neck.

"When the morning came, the child's mother took me up in her fingers and looked at me, and she had her own thoughts about me, I could feel that very well. She brought out a pair of scissors, and cut the string through.

"'A lucky shilling!' she said. 'Well, we shall soon see that.'

"And she laid me in vinegar, so that I turned quite green. Then she plugged up the hole, and carried me, in the evening twilight, to the lottery collector, to buy a lottery ticket that should bring her luck.

"How miserably wretched I felt! There was a stinging feeling in me, as if I should crumble to bits. I knew that I should be called false and thrown down—and before a crowd of shillings and other coins, too, who lay there with an image and superscription of which they might be proud. But I escaped that disgrace, for there were many people in the collector's room—he had a great deal to do, and I went rattling down into the box among the other coins. Whether my ticket won anything or not I don't know; but this I do know, that the very next morning I was recognized as a bad shilling, and was sent out to deceive and deceive again. That is a very trying thing to bear when one knows one has a good character, and of that I *am* conscious.

"For a year and a day I thus wandered from house to house and from hand to hand, always abused, always unwelcome; no one trusted me; and I lost confidence in the world and in myself. It was a heavy time. At last, one day a traveller, a strange gentleman, arrived, and I was passed to him, and he was polite enough to accept me for current coin; but he wanted to pass me on, and again I heard the horrible cry, 'No use—false!'

"'I received it as a good coin,' said the man, and he looked closely at me: suddenly he smiled all over his face; and I had never seen that expression before on any face that looked at me. 'Why, whatever is that?' he said. 'That's one of our own country coins, a good honest shilling from my home, and they've bored a hole through him, and they call him false. Now, this is a curious circumstance. I must keep him and take him home with me.'

"A glow of joy thrilled through me when I heard myself called a good honest shilling; and now I was to be taken home, where each and every one would know me, and be sure that I was real silver and properly coined. I could have thrown out sparks for very gladness; but, after all, it's not in my nature to throw out sparks, for that's the property of steel, not of silver.

"I was wrapped up in clean white paper, so that I should not be confounded with the other coins, and spent; and on festive occasions, when fellow-countrymen met together, I was shown about, and they spoke very well of me: they said I was interesting—and it is wonderful how interesting one can be without saying a single word.

"And at last I got home again. All my troubles were ended, joy came back to me, for I was of good silver, and had the right stamp, and I had no more disagreeables to endure, though a hole had been bored through me, as through a false coin; but that does not matter if one is not really false. One must wait for the end, and one will be righted at last—that's my belief," said the Shilling.

THE OLD BELL OF MARBACH.

THE OLD CHURCH BELL.

IN the German land of Wurtemberg, where the acacias bloom by the high road, and the apple trees and pear trees bend in autumn under their burden of ripe fruit, lies the little town of Marbach. Although this place can only be ranked among the smaller towns, it is charmingly situated on the Neckar stream, that flows on and on, hurrying past villages and old castles and green vineyards, to pour its waters into the proud Rhine.

It was late in autumn. The leaves still clung to the grape-vine, but they were already tinged with red. Rainy gusts swept over the country, and the cold autumn winds increased in violence and roughness. It was no pleasant time for poor folk.

The days became shorter and gloomier; and if it was dark out in the

open air, in the little old-fashioned houses it was darker still.   One of
these houses was built with its gable end towards the street, and stood
there, with its small narrow windows, humble and poor enough in appearance; the family was poor, too, that inhabited the little house, but good
and industrious, and rich in a treasure of piety concealed in the depth of
the heart.   And they expected that God would soon give them another
child : the hour had come, and the mother lay in pain and sorrow.   Then
from the church tower opposite the deep rich sound of the bell came to
her.   It was a solemn hour, and the song of the bell filled the heart of
the praying woman with trustfulness and faith ; the thoughts of her
inmost heart soared upward towards the Almighty, and in the same hour
she gave birth to a son.   Then she was filled with a great joy, and the
bell in the tower opposite seemed to be ringing to spread the news of
her happiness over town and country.   The clear child-eyes looked at
her, and the infant's hair gleamed like gold.   Thus was the little one
ushered into the world with the ringing of the church bell on the dark
November day.   The mother and father kissed it, and wrote in their
Bible : "On the 10th of November, 1759, God gave us a son ;" and soon
afterwards the fact was added that the child had been baptized under the
name of " Johann Christoph Friedrich."

And what became of the little fellow, the poor boy in the pretty town
of Marbach ? Ah, at that time no one knew what would become of him,
not even the old church bell that had sung at his birth, hanging so high
in the tower, over him who was one day himself to sing the beautiful
" Lay of the Bell."

Well, the boy grew older, and the world grew older with him.   His
parents certainly removed to another town, but they had left dear friends
in little Marbach ; and thus it was that mother and son one day arose
and drove over to Marbach on a visit.   The lad was only six years old,
but he already knew many things out of the Bible, and many a pious
psalm ; and many an evening he had sat on his little stool, listening while
his father read aloud from " Gellert's Fables," or from the lofty " Mes-
siah " of Klopstock ; and he and his sister, who was his senior by two
years, had wept hot tears of pity for Him who died on the cross that
we might live eternally.

At the time of this first visit to Marbach the little town had not
greatly changed ; and indeed they had not long left it.   The houses stood,
as on the day of the family's departure, with their pointed gables, projecting walls, the higher storeys leaning over the lower, and their tiny
windows ; but there were new graves in the churchyard ; and there, in
the grass, hard by the wall, lay the old bell.   It had fallen from its
position, and had sustained such damage that it could sound no more,
and accordingly a new bell had been put in its place.

Mother and son went into the churchyard.   They stopped where the
old bell lay, and the mother told the boy how for centuries this had been
a very useful bell, and had rung at christenings, at weddings, and at
burials ; how it had spoken at one time to tell of feasts and of rejoicings,
at another to spread the alarm of fire ; and how it had, in fact, sung the

whole life of man. And the boy never forgot what his mother told him that day. It resounded and echoed at intervals in his heart, until, when he was grown a man, he was compelled to sing it. The mother told him also how the bell had sung of faith and comfort to her in the time of her peril, that it had sung at the time when he, her little son, was born And the boy gazed, almost with a feeling of devotion, at the great old bell; and he bent over it and kissed it, as it lay all rusty and broken among the long grass and nettles.

The old bell was held in kindly remembrance by the boy, who grew up in poverty, tall and thin, with reddish hair and freckled face;—yes, that's how he looked; but he had a pair of eyes, clear and deep as the deepest water. And what fortune had he? Why, good fortune, enviable fortune. We find him graciously received into the military school, and even in the department where sons of people in society were taught, and was that not honour and fortune enough? And they educated him to the words of command, "Halt! march! front!" and on such a system much might be expected.

Meanwhile the old church bell had been almost completely forgotten. But it was to be presumed that the bell would find its way into the furnace, and what would become of it then? It was impossible to say, and equally impossible to tell what sounds would come forth from the bell that kept echoing through the young heart of the boy from Marbach; but that bell was of bronze, and kept sounding so loud that it must at last be heard out in the wide world; and the more cramped the space within the school walls, and the more deafening the dreary shout of "March! halt! front!" the louder did the sound ring through the youth's breast; and he sang what he felt in the circle of his companions and the sound was heard beyond the boundaries of the principality. But it was not for this they had given him a presentation to the military school, and board, and clothing. Had he not been already numbered and destined to be a certain wheel in the great watchwork to which we all belong as pieces of practical machinery? How imperfectly do we understand ourselves! and how, then, shall others, even the best men, understand us? But it is the pressure that forms the precious stone. There was pressure enough here; but would the world be able, some day, to recognize the jewel?

In the capital of the prince of the country, a great festival was being celebrated. Thousands of candles and lamps gleamed brightly, and rockets flew towards the heavens in streams of fire. The splendour of that day yet lives in the remembrance of men, but it lives through him, the young scholar of the military school, who was trying in sorrow and tears to escape unperceived from the land: he was compelled to leave all—mother, native country, those he loved—unless he could resign himself to sink into the stream of oblivion among his fellows.

The old bell was better off than he, for the bell would remain peaceably by the churchyard wall in Marbach, safe, and almost forgotten. The wind whistled over it, and might have told a fine tale of him at whose birth the bell had sounded, and over whom the wind had but now blown cold in the forest of a neighbouring land, where he had sunk down, exhausted by fatigue, with his whole wealth, his only hope for the future, the written pages of his tragedy " Fiesco :" the wind might have told of the youth's only patrons, men who were artists, and who yet slunk away to amuse themselves at skittles while his play was being read : the wind could have told of the pale fugitive, who sat for weary weeks and months in the wretched tavern, where the host brawled and drank, and coarse boozing was going on while he sang of the ideal. Heavy days, dark days ! The heart must suffer and endure for itself the trials it is to sing.

Dark days and cold nights also passed over the old bell. The iron frame did not feel them, but the bell within the heart of man is affected by gloomy times. How fared it with the young man ? How fared it

REMOVING THE BELL.

with the old bell ? The bell was carried far away, farther than its sound could have been heard from the lofty tower in which it had once hung. And the youth ? The bell in his heart sounded farther than his eye should ever see or his foot should ever wander ; it is sounding and sounding on, over the ocean, round the whole earth. But let us first speak of the belfry bell. It was carried away from Marbach, was sold for old metal, and destined for the melting furnace in Bavaria. But when and how did this happen ? In the capital of Bavaria, many years after the bell had fallen from the tower, there was a talk of its being melted down, to be used in the manufacture of a memorial in honour of one of the great ones of the German land. And behold how suitable this was—how strangely and wonderfully things happened in the world ! In Denmark, on one of those green islands where the beech woods rustle, and the many Hun's Graves are to be seen, quite a poor boy had been born. He had been accustomed to walk about in wooden shoes, and to carry a dinner wrapped in an old handkerchief to his father, who carved figure-heads on the ship-builder's wharves; but this poor lad had become the pride of his country, for *Thorwaldsen* knew how to hew marble blocks into such glorious shapes as made the whole world wonder, and to him had been awarded the honourable commission that he should fashion of clay a noble form that was to be cast in bronze —a statue of him whose name the father in Marbach had inscribed in the old Bible as Johann Christoph Friedrich.

And the glowing metal flowed into the mould. The old belfry bell— of whose home and of whose vanished sounds no one thought—this very old bell flowed into the mould, and formed the head and bust of the figure that was soon to be unveiled, which now stands in Stuttgard, before the old palace—a representation of him who once walked to and fro there, striving and suffering, harassed by the world without—he, the boy of Marbach, the pupil of the "Karlschule," the fugitive, Germany's great immortal poet, who sang of the liberator of Switzerland and of the Heaven-inspired Maid of Orleans.

It was a beautiful sunny day; flags were waving from roofs and steeples in the royal city of Stuttgard; the bells rang for joy and festivity; one bell alone was silent, but it gleamed in another form in the bright sunshine—it gleamed from the head and breast of the statue of honour. On that day, exactly one hundred years had elapsed since the day on which the bell at Marbach had sung comfort and peace to the suffering mother, when she bore her son, in poverty, in the humble cottage — him who was afterwards to become the rich man, whose treasures enriched the world, the poet who sang of the noble virtues of woman, who sang of all that was great and glorious—Johann Christoph Friedrich Schiller.

THE SNAIL AND THE ROSE TREE.

AROUND the garden ran a hedge of hazels; beyond this hedge lay fields and meadows, wherein were cows and sheep; but in the midst of the garden stood a blooming Rose Tree; and under this Rose Tree lived a Snail, who had a good deal in his shell—namely, himself.

"Wait till my time comes!" he said: "I shall do something more than produce roses, bear nuts, or give milk, like the Rose Tree, the hazel bush, and the cows!"

"I expect a great deal of you," said the Rose Tree. "But may I ask when it will appear?"

"I take my time," replied the Snail. "*You*'re always in such a hurry. You don't rouse people's interest by suspense."

When the next year came, the Snail lay almost in the same spot, in the sunshine under the Rose Tree, which again bore buds that bloomed into roses, until the snow fell and the weather became raw and cold; then the Rose Tree bowed its head and the Snail crept into the ground.

A new year began; and, the roses came out, and the Snail came out also.

"You're an old Rose Tree now!" said the Snail. "You must make haste and come to an end, for you have given the world all that was in you: whether it was of any use is a question that I have had no time to consider; but so much is clear and plain, that you have done nothing at all for your own development, or you would have produced something else. How can you answer for that? In a little time you will be nothing at all but a stick. Do you understand what I say?"

"You alarm me!" replied the Rose Tree. "I never thought of that at all."

THE MAIDEN AND THE ROSE.

"No, you have not taken the trouble to consider anything. Have you ever given an account to yourself, why you bloomed, and how it is that your blooming comes about—why it is thus, and not otherwise?"

"No," answered the Rose Tree. "I bloomed in gladness, because I could not do anything else. The sun shone and warmed me, and the air refreshed me. I drank the pure dew and the fresh rain, and I lived, I breathed. Out of the earth there arose a power within me, from above there came down a strength: I perceived a new ever-increasing happiness, and consequently I was obliged to bloom over and over again; that was my life; I could not do otherwise."

"You have led a very pleasant life," observed the Snail.

"Certainly. Everything I have was given to me," said the Rose Tree. "But more still was given to you. You are one of those deep thoughtful characters, one of those highly gifted spirits, which will cause the world to marvel."

"I've no intention of doing anything of the kind," cried the Snail.

"The world is nothing to me. What have I to do with the world? I have enough of myself and in myself."

"But must we not all, here on earth, give to others the best that we have, and offer what lies in our power? Certainly I have only given roses. But you—you who have been so richly gifted—what have you given to the world? what do you intend to give?"

"What have I given—what do I intend to give? I spit at it. It's worth nothing. It's no business of mine. Continue to give your roses, if you like: you can't do anything better. Let the hazel bush bear nuts, and the cows and ewes give milk: they have their public; but I have mine within myself—I retire within myself, and there I remain. The world is nothing to me."

THE YOUNG CHILD'S KISS.

And so saying the Snail retired into his house, and closed up the entrance after him.

"That is very sad!" said the Rose Tree. "I cannot creep into myself, even if I wish it—I must continue to produce roses. They drop their leaves, and are blown away by the wind. But I saw how a rose was laid in the matron's hymn-book, and one of my roses had a place on the bosom of a fair young girl, and another was kissed by the lips of a child in the full joy of life. That did me good; it was a real blessing. That's my remembrance—my life!"

And the Rose Tree went on blooming in innocence, while the Snail lay and idled away his time in his house—the world did not concern him.

And years rolled by.

The Snail had become dust in the dust, and the Rose Tree was earth in the earth; the rose of remembrance in the hymn-book was faded, but in the garden bloomed fresh rose trees, and under the trees lay new snails; and these still crept into their houses, and spat at the world, for it did not concern them.

Suppose we begin the story again, and read it right through. It will never alter.

LITTLE IDA'S FLOWERS.

"My poor flowers are quite dead!" said little Ida. "They were so pretty yesterday, and now all the leaves hang withered. Why do they do that?" she asked the student, who sat on the sofa; for she liked him very much. He knew the prettiest stories, and could cut out the most amusing pictures—hearts, with little ladies in them who danced, flowers, and great castles in which one could open the doors: he was a merry student. "Why do the flowers look so faded to-day?" she asked again, and showed him a nosegay, which was quite withered.

"Do you know what's the matter with them?" said the student. "The flowers have been at a ball last night, and that's why they hang their heads."

"But flowers cannot dance!" cried little Ida.

"Oh, yes," said the student, "when it grows dark, and we are asleep, they jump about merrily. Almost every night they have a ball."

"Can children go to this ball?"

"Yes," said the student, "quite little daisies, and lilies of the valley."

"Where do the beautiful flowers dance?" asked little Ida.

"Have you not often been outside the town-gate, by the great castle, where the king lives in summer, and where the beautiful garden is with all the flowers? You have seen the swans, which swim up to you when you want to give them bread crumbs? There are capital balls there, believe me."

"I was out there in the garden yesterday, with my mother," said Ida; "but all the leaves were off the trees, and there was not one flower left. Where are they? In the summer I saw so many."

"They are within, in the castle," replied the student. "You must know, as soon as the king and all the court go to town, the flowers run out of the garden into the castle, and are merry. You should see that. The two most beautiful roses seat themselves on the throne, and then they are king and queen; all the red coxcombs range themselves on either side, and stand and bow; they are the chamberlains. Then all the pretty flowers come, and there is a great ball. The blue violets represent little naval cadets: they dance with hyacinths and crocuses, which they call young ladies; the tulips and the great tiger-lilies are old ladies who keep watch that the dancing is well done, and that everything goes on with propriety."

THE STUDENT TELLING LITTLE IDA THE STORY OF THE FLOWERS.

"But," asked little Ida, "is nobody there who hurts the flowers, for dancing in the king's castle?"

"There is nobody who really knows about it," answered the student. "Sometimes, certainly, the old steward of the castle comes at night, and he has to watch there. He has a great bunch of keys with him; but as soon as the flowers hear the keys rattle they are quite quiet, hide behind the long curtains, and only poke their heads out. Then the old steward says, 'I smell that there are flowers here,' but he cannot see them."

"That is famous!" cried little Ida, clapping her hands. "But should not I be able to see the flowers?"

"Yes," said the student; "only remember, when you go out again, to peep through the window; then you will see them. That is what I did to-day. There was a long yellow lily lying on the sofa and stretching herself. She was a court lady."

" Can the flowers out of the Botanical Garden get there ?   Can they go the long distance ? "

" Yes, certainly ;" replied the student, "if they like they can fly. Have you not seen the beautiful butterflies, red, yellow, and white ? They almost look like flowers ; and that is what they have been.   They have flown off their stalks high into the air, and have beaten it with their leaves, as if these leaves were little wings, and thus they flew. And because they behaved themselves well, they got leave to fly about in the day-time too, and were not obliged to sit still upon their stalks at home ; and thus at last the leaves became real wings.   That you have seen yourself.   It may be, however, that the flowers in the Botanical Garden have never been in the king's castle, or that they don't know of the merry proceedings there at night.   Therefore I will tell you something : he will be very much surprised, the botanical professor, who lives close by here.   You know him, do you not ?   When you come into his garden, you must tell one of the flowers that there is a great ball yonder in the castle.   Then that flower will tell it to all the rest, and then they will fly away : when the professor comes out into the garden, there will not be a single flower left, and he won't be able to make out where they are gone."

" But how can one flower tell it to another?   For, you know, flowers cannot speak."

" That they cannot, certainly," replied the student ; "but then they make signs.   Have you not noticed that when the wind blows a little, the flowers nod at one another, and move all their green leaves ?   They can understand that just as well as we when we speak together."

" Can the professor understand these signs ?" asked Ida.

" Yes, certainly.   He came one morning into his garden, and saw a great stinging-nettle standing there, and making signs to a beautiful red carnation with its leaves.   It was saying, 'You are so pretty, and I love you with all my heart.'   But the professor does not like that kind of thing, and he directly slapped the stinging-nettle upon its leaves, for those are its fingers ; but he stung himself, and since that time he has not dared to touch a stinging-nettle."

" That is funny," cried little Ida ; and she laughed.

" How can any one put such notions into a child's head ?" said the tiresome privy councillor, who had come to pay a visit, and was sitting on the sofa.   He did not like the student, and always grumbled when he saw him cutting out the merry funny pictures—sometimes a man hanging on a gibbet and holding a heart in his hand, to show that he stole hearts ; sometimes an old witch riding on a broom, and carrying her husband on her nose.   The councillor could not bear this, and then he said, just as he did now, " How can any one put such notions into a child's head ?   Those are stupid fancies ! "

But to little Ida, what the student told about her flowers seemed very droll ; and she thought much about it.   The flowers hung their heads, for they were tired because they had danced all night ; they were certainly ill.   Then she went with them to her other toys, which stood on a pretty little table, and the whole drawer was full of beautiful things. In the doll's bed lay her doll Sophy, asleep; but little Ida said to her, "You must really get up, Sophy, and manage to lie in the drawer for to-night. The poor flowers are ill, and they must lie in your bed; perhaps they will then get well again."

And she at once took the doll out; but the doll looked cross, and did not say a single word; for she was cross because she could not keep her own bed.

Then Ida laid the flowers in the doll's bed, pulled the little coverlet quite up over them, and said they were to lie still and be good, and she would make them some tea, so that they might get well again, and be able to get up to-morrow. And she drew the curtains closely round the little bed, so that the sun should not shine in their eyes. The whole evening through she could not help thinking of what the student had told her. And when she was going to bed herself, she was obliged first to look behind the curtain which hung before the windows where her mother's beautiful flowers stood—hyacinths as well as tulips; then she whispered, "I know you're going to the ball to-night!" But the flowers made as if they did not understand a word, and did not stir a leaf; but still little Ida knew what she knew.

When she was in bed she lay for a long time thinking how pretty it must be to see the beautiful flowers dancing out in the king's castle. "I wonder if my flowers have really been there?" And then she fell asleep. In the night she awoke again: she had dreamed of the flowers, and of the student with whom the councillor found fault. It was quite quiet in the bed-room where Ida lay; the night-lamp burned on the table, and father and mother were asleep.

"I wonder if my flowers are still lying in Sophy's bed?" she thought to herself. "How I should like to know it!" She raised herself a little, and looked at the door, which stood ajar; within lay the flowers and all her playthings. She listened, and then it seemed to her as if she heard some one playing on the piano in the next room, but quite softly and prettily, as she had never heard it before.

"Now all the flowers are certainly dancing in there!" thought she. "Oh, how glad I should be to see it!" But she dared not get up, for she would have disturbed her father and mother.

"If they would only come in!" thought she. But the flowers did not come, and the music continued to play beautifully; then she could not bear it any longer, for it was too pretty; she crept out of her little bed, and went quietly to the door, and looked into the room. Oh, how splendid it was, what she saw!

There was no night-lamp burning, but still it was quite light: the moon shone through the window into the middle of the floor; it was almost like day. All the hyacinths and tulips stood in two long rows in the room; there were none at all left at the window. There stood the empty flower-pots. On the floor all the flowers were dancing very gracefully round each other, making perfect turns, and holding each other by the long green leaves as they swang round. But at the piano sat a great yellow lily, which little Ida had certainly seen in summer, for she remembered how the student had said, " How like that one is to Miss Lina." Then he had been laughed at by all ; but now it seemed really to little Ida as if the long yellow flower looked like the young lady ; and it had just her manners in playing—sometimes bending its long yellow face to one side, sometimes to the other, and nodding in tune to the charming music! No one noticed little Ida. Then she saw a great blue crocus hop into the middle of the table, where the toys stood, and go to the doll's bed and pull the curtains aside; there lay the sick flowers, but they got up directly, and nodded to the others, to say that they wanted to dance too. The old chimney-sweep doll, whose under lip was broken off, stood up and bowed to the pretty flowers : these did not look at all ill now; they jumped down to the others, and were very merry.

Then it seemed as if something fell down from the table. Ida looked that way. It was the birch rod which was jumping down! it seemed almost as if it belonged to the flowers. At any rate it was very neat ; and a little wax doll, with just such a broad hat on its head as the councillor wore, sat upon it. The birch rod hopped about among the flowers on its three stilted legs, and stamped quite loud, for it was dancing the mazourka; and the other flowers could not manage that dance, because they were too light, and unable to stamp like that.

The wax doll on the birch rod all at once became quite great and long, turned itself over the paper flowers, and said, " How can one put such things in a child's head? those are stupid fancies!" and then the wax doll was exactly like the councillor with the broad hat, and looked just as yellow and cross as he. But the paper flowers hit him on his thin legs, and then he shrank up again, and became quite a little wax doll. That was very amusing to see; and little Ida could not restrain her laughter. The birch rod went on dancing, and the councillor was obliged to dance too ; it was no use, he might make himself great and long, or remain the little yellow wax doll with the big black hat. Then the other flowers put in a good word for him, especially those who had lain in the doll's bed, and then the birch rod gave over. At the same moment there was a loud knocking at the drawer, inside where Ida's doll, Sophy, lay with many other toys. The chimney-sweep ran to the edge of the table, lay flat down on his stomach, and began to pull the drawer out a little. Then Sophy raised herself, and looked round quite astonished.

" There must be a ball here," said she ; " why did nobody tell me ? "

" Will you dance with me ? " asked the chimney-sweep.

" You are a nice sort of fellow to dance ! " she replied, and turned her back upon him.

Then she seated herself upon the drawer, and thought that one of the flowers would come and ask her ; but not one of them came. Then she coughed, " Hem! hem! hem!" but for all that not one came. The chimney-sweep now danced all alone, and that was not at all so bad.

As none of the flowers seemed to notice Sophy, she let herself fall down from the drawer straight upon the floor, so that there was a great noise. The flowers now all came running up, to ask if she had not hurt herself; and they were all very polite to her, especially the flowers that had lain in her bed. But she had not hurt herself at all; and Ida's flowers all thanked her for the nice bed, and were kind to her, took her into the middle of the room, where the moon shone in, and danced with her; and all the other flowers formed a circle round her. Now Sophy was glad, and said they might keep her bed; she did not at all mind lying in the drawer.

But the flowers said, "We thank you heartily, but in any way we cannot live long. To-morrow we shall be quite dead. But tell little Ida she is to bury us out in the garden, where the canary lies; then we shall wake up again in summer, and be far more beautiful."

"No, you must not die," said Sophy; and she kissed the flowers.

Then the door opened, and a great number of splendid flowers came dancing in. Ida could not imagine whence they had come; these must certainly all be flowers from the king's castle yonder. First of all came two glorious roses, and they had little gold crowns on; they were a king and a queen. Then came the prettiest stocks and carnations; and they bowed in all directions. They had music with them. Great poppies and peonies blew upon pea pods till they were quite red in the face. The blue hyacinths and the little white snowdrops rang just as if they had been bells. That was wonderful music! Then came many other flowers, and danced all together; the blue violets and the pink primroses, daisies and the lilies of the valley. And all the flowers kissed one another. It was beautiful to look at!

At last the flowers wished one another goodnight; then little Ida, too, crept to bed, where she dreamed of all she had seen.

When she rose next morning, she went quickly to the little table, to see if the little flowers were still there. She drew aside the curtains of the little bed; there were they all, but they were quite faded, far more than yesterday. Sophy was lying in the drawer where Ida had laid her; she looked very sleepy.

"Do you remember what you were to say to me?" asked little Ida.

But Sophy looked quite stupid, and did not say a single word.

"You are not good at all!" said Ida. "And yet they all danced with you."

Then she took a little paper box, on which were painted beautiful birds, and opened it, and laid the dead flowers in it.

"That shall be your pretty coffin," said she, "and when my cousins come to visit me by and bye, they shall help me to bury you outside in the garden, so that you may grow again in summer, and become more beautiful than ever."

These cousins were two merry boys. Their names were Gustave and Adolphe; their father had given them two new crossbows, and they had brought these with them to show to Ida. She told them about the poor flowers which had died, and then they got leave to bury them. The two boys went first, with their crossbows on their shoulders, and little Ida followed with the dead flowers in the pretty box. Out in the garden a little grave was dug. Ida first kissed the flowers, and then laid them in the earth in the box, and Adolphe and Gustave shot with their crossbows over the grave, for they had neither guns nor cannons.

THE TINDER-BOX.

THERE came a soldier marching along the high road—*one, two! one, two!* He had his knapsack on his back and a sabre by his side, for he had been in the wars, and now he wanted to go home. And on the way he met with an old witch: she was very hideous, and her under lip hung down upon her breast. She said, " Good evening, soldier. What a fine sword you have, and what a big knapsack! You 're a proper soldier! Now you shall have as much money as you like to have."

" I thank you, you old witch!" said the soldier.

" Do you see that great tree ?" quoth the witch; and she pointed to a tree which stood beside them. " It 's quite hollow inside. You must climb to the top, and then you 'll see a hole, through which you can let yourself down and get deep into the tree. I 'll tie a rope round your body, so that I can pull you up again when you call me."

" What am I to do down in the tree ?" asked the soldier.

" Get money," replied the witch. " Listen to me. When you come down to the earth under the tree, you will find yourself in a great hall: it is quite light, for above three hundred lamps are burning there. Then you will see three doors; these you can open, for the keys are hanging there. If you go into the first chamber, you 'll see a great chest in the middle of the floor; on this chest sits a dog, and he 's got a pair of eyes as big as two tea-cups. But you need not care for that. I 'll give you my blue-checked apron, and you can spread it out upon the floor; then go up quickly and take the dog, and set him on my apron; then open the chest, and take as many shillings as you like. They are of copper: if you prefer silver, you must go into the second chamber. But there sits a dog with a pair of eyes as big as mill-wheels. But do not you care for that. Set him upon my apron, and take some of the money. And if you want gold, you can have that too — in fact, as much as you can carry—if you go into the third chamber. But the dog that sits on the money-chest there has two eyes as big as round towers. He is a fierce dog, you may be sure; but you needn't be afraid, for all that. Only set him on my apron, and he won't hurt you; and take out of the chest as much gold as you like."

" That 's not so bad," said the soldier. " But what am I to give you, you old witch? for you will not do it for nothing, I fancy."

" No," replied the witch, " not a single shilling will I have. You shall only bring me an old tinder-box which my grandmother forgot when she was down there last."

" Then tie the rope round my body," cried the soldier.

THE WITCH INDUCES THE SOLDIER TO CLIMB THE TREE.

"Here it is," said the witch, "and here's my blue-checked apron."

Then the soldier climbed up into the tree, let himself slip down into the hole, and stood, as the witch had said, in the great hall where the three hundred lamps were burning.

Now he opened the first door. Ugh! there sat the dog with eyes as big as tea-cups, staring at him. "You're a nice fellow!" exclaimed the soldier; and he set him on the witch's apron, and took as many copper shillings as his pockets would hold, and then locked the chest, set the dog on it again, and went into the second chamber. Aha! there sat the dog with eyes as big as mill-wheels.

"You should not stare so hard at me," said the soldier; "you might strain your eyes." And he set the dog upon the witch's apron. And when he saw the silver money in the chest, he threw away all the copper money he had, and filled his pockets and his knapsack with silver only. Then he went into the third chamber. Oh, but that was horrid! The dog there really had eyes as big as towers, and they turned round and round in his head like wheels.

"Good evening!" said the soldier; and he touched his cap, for he had never seen such a dog as that before. When he had looked at him a little more closely, he thought, "That will do," and lifted him down to the floor, and opened the chest. Mercy! what a quantity of gold was there! He could buy with it the whole town, and the sugar sucking-pigs of the cake woman, and all the tin soldiers, whips, and rocking-horses in the whole world. Yes, that was a quantity of money! Now the soldier threw away all the silver coin with which he had filled his pockets and his knapsack, and took gold instead: yes, all his pockets, his knapsack, his boots, and his cap were filled, so that he could scarcely walk. Now indeed he had plenty of money. He put the dog on the chest, shut the door, and then called up through the tree, "Now pull me up, you old witch."

"Have you the tinder-box?" asked the witch.

"Plague on it!" exclaimed the soldier, "I had clean forgotten that." And he went and brought it.

The witch drew him up, and he stood on the high road again, with pockets, boots, knapsack, and cap full of gold.

"What are you going to do with the tinder-box?" asked the soldier.

"That's nothing to you," retorted the witch. "You've had your money—just give me the tinder-box."

"Nonsense!" said the soldier. "Tell me directly what you're going to do with it, or I'll draw my sword and cut off your head."

"No!" cried the witch.

So the soldier cut off her head. There she lay! But he tied up all his money in her apron, took it on his back like a bundle, put the tinder-box in his pocket, and went straight off towards the town.

That was a splendid town! And he put up at the very best inn, and asked for the finest rooms, and ordered his favourite dishes, for now he was rich, as he had so much money. The servant who had to clean his boots certainly thought them a remarkably old pair for such a rich gentleman; but he had not bought any new ones yet. The next day he procured proper boots and handsome clothes. Now our soldier had become a fine gentleman; and the people told him of all the splendid things which were in their city, and about the king, and what a pretty princess the king's daughter was.

"Where can one get to see her?" asked the soldier.

"She is not to be seen at all," said they all together; she lives in a great copper castle, with a great many walls and towers round about it; no one but the king may go in and out there, for it has been prophesied that she shall marry a common soldier, and the king can't bear that."

"I should like to see her," thought the soldier; but he could not get leave to do so. Now he lived merrily, went to the theatre, drove in the king's garden, and gave much money to the poor; and this was very kind of him, for he knew from old times how hard it is when one has not a shilling. Now he was rich, had fine clothes, and gained many

THE PRINCESS ARRIVES ON THE DOG'S BACK.

friends, who all said he was a rare one, a true cavalier; and that pleased the soldier well. But as he spent money every day and never earned any, he had at last only two shillings left; and he was obliged to turn out of the fine rooms in which he had dwelt, and had to live in a little garret under the roof, and clean his boots for himself, and mend them with a darning-needle. None of his friends came to see him, for there were too many stairs to climb.

It was quite dark one evening, and he could not even buy himself a candle, when it occurred to him that there was a candle-end in the tinder-box which he had taken out of the hollow tree into which the witch had helped him. He brought out the tinder-box and the candle-end; but as soon as he struck fire and the sparks rose up from the flint, the door flew open, and the dog who had eyes as big as a couple of tea-cups, and whom he had seen in the tree, stood before him, and said,

"What are my lord's commands?"

"What is this?" said the soldier. "That's a famous tinder-box, if

I can get everything with it that I want! Bring me some money," said he to the dog; and *whisk!* the dog was gone, and *whisk!* he was back again, with a great bag full of shillings in his mouth.

Now the soldier knew what a capital tinder-box this was. If he struck it once, the dog came who sat upon the chest of copper money; if he struck it twice, the dog came who had the silver; and if he struck it three times, then appeared the dog who had the gold. Now the soldier moved back into the fine rooms, and appeared again in handsome clothes; and all his friends knew him again, and cared very much for him indeed.

Once he thought to himself, "It is a very strange thing that one cannot get to see the princess. They all say she is very beautiful; but what is the use of that, if she has always to sit in the great copper castle with the many towers? Can I not get to see her at all? Where is my tinder-box?" And so he struck a light, and *whisk!* came the dog with eyes as big as tea-cups.

"It is midnight, certainly," said the soldier, "but I should very much like to see the princess, only for one little moment."

And the dog was outside the door directly, and, before the soldier thought it, came back with the princess. She sat upon the dog's back and slept; and every one could see she was a real princess, for she was so lovely. The soldier could not refrain from kissing her, for he was a thorough soldier. Then the dog ran back again with the princess. But when morning came, and the king and queen were drinking tea, the princess said she had had a strange dream the night before, about a dog and a soldier—that she had ridden upon the dog, and the soldier had kissed her.

"That would be a fine history!" said the Queen.

So one of the old court ladies had to watch the next night by the princess's bed, to see if this was really a dream, or what it might be.

The soldier had a great longing to see the lovely princess again; so the dog came in the night, took her away, and ran as fast as he could. But the old lady put on water-boots, and ran just as fast after him. When she saw that they both entered a great house, she thought, "Now I know where it is;" and with a bit of chalk she drew a great cross on the door. Then she went home and lay down, and the dog came up with the princess; but when he saw that there was a cross drawn on the door where the soldier lived, he took a piece of chalk too, and drew crosses on all the doors in the town. And that was cleverly done, for now the lady could not find the right door, because all the doors had crosses upon them.

In the morning early came the King and the Queen, the old court lady and all the officers, to see where it was the princess had been. "Here it is!" said the King, when he saw the first door with a cross upon it. "No, my dear husband, it is there!" said the Queen, who descried another door which also showed a cross. "But there is one, and there is one!" said all, for wherever they looked there were crosses on the doors. So they saw that it would avail them nothing if they searched on.

But the Queen was an exceedingly clever woman, who could do more than ride in a coach. She took her great gold scissors, cut a piece of silk into pieces, and made a neat little bag; this bag she filled with fine wheat flour, and tied it on the princess's back; and when that was done, she cut a little hole in the bag, so that the flour would be scattered along all the way which the princess should take.

In the night the dog came again, took the princess on his back, and ran with her to the soldier, who loved her very much, and would gladly have been a prince, so that he might have her for his wife. The dog did not notice at all how the flour ran out in a stream from the castle to the windows of the soldier's house, where he ran up the wall with the princess. In the morning the King and the Queen saw well enough where their daughter had been, and they took the soldier and put him in prison.

There he sat. Oh, but it was dark and disagreeable there! And they said to him, "To-morrow you shall be hanged." That was not amusing to hear, and he had left his tinder-box at the inn. In the morning he could see, through the iron grating of the little window, how the people were hurrying out of the town to see him hanged. He heard the drums beat and saw the soldiers marching. All the people were running out, and among them was a shoemaker's boy with leather apron and slippers, and he gallopped so fast that one of his slippers flew off, and came right against the wall where the soldier sat looking through the iron grating.

"Halloo, you shoemaker's boy! you needn't be in such a hurry," cried the soldier to him: "it will not begin till I come. But if you will run to where I lived, and bring me my tinder-box, you shall have four shillings; but you must put your best leg foremost."

The shoemaker's boy wanted to get the four shillings, so he went and brought the tinder-box, and—well, we shall hear now what happened.

Outside the town a great gallows had been built, and round it stood the soldiers and many hundred thousand people. The king and queen sat on a splendid throne, opposite to the judges and the whole council. The soldier already stood upon the ladder; but as they were about to put the rope round his neck, he said that before a poor criminal suffered his punishment an innocent request was always granted to him. He wanted very much to smoke a pipe of tobacco, and it would be the last pipe he should smoke in the world. The king would not say "No" to this; so the soldier took his tinder-box, and struck fire. One—two—three!—and there suddenly stood all the dogs—the one with eyes as big as tea-cups, the one with eyes as large as mill-wheels, and the one whose eyes were as big as round towers.

"Help me now, so that I may not be hanged," said the soldier.

And the dogs fell upon the judge and all the council, seized one by the leg and another by the nose, and tossed them all many feet into the air, so that they fell down and were all broken to pieces.

"I won't!" cried the King; but the biggest dog took him and the Queen, and threw them after the others. Then the soldiers were afraid, and the people cried, "Little soldier, you shall be our king, and marry the beautiful princess!"

So they put the soldier into the king's coach, and all the three dogs darted on in front and cried "Hurrah!" and the boys whistled through

their fingers, and the soldiers presented arms.   The princess came out
of the copper castle, and became queen, and she liked that well enough.
The wedding lasted a week, and the three dogs sat at the table too, and
opened their eyes wider than ever at all they saw.

GREAT CLAUS AND LITTLE CLAUS.

THERE lived two men in one village, and they had the same name—
each was called Claus; but one had four horses, and the other only a
single horse.   To distinguish them from each other, folks called him who
had four horses Great Claus, and the one who had only a single horse
Little Claus.   Now we shall hear what happened to each of them, for
this is a true story.

The whole week through Little Claus was obliged to plough for Great
Claus, and to lend him his one horse; then Great Claus helped him out
with all his four, but only once a week, and that on a holiday.   Hurrah!
how Little Claus smacked his whip over all five horses, for they were as
good as his own on that one day.   The sun shone gaily, and all the bells
in the steeples were ringing; the people were all dressed in their best,
and were going to church, with their hymn-books under their arms, to
hear the clergyman preach, and they saw Little Claus ploughing with
five horses; but he was so merry that he smacked his whip again and
again, and cried, " Gee up, all my five!"

"You must not talk so," said Great Claus, "for only the one horse is
yours."

But when no one was passing Little Claus forgot that he was not to
say this, and he cried, "Gee up, all my horses!"

"Now, I must beg of you to let that alone." cried Great Claus, "for
if you say it again, I shall hit your horse on the head, so that it will fall
down dead, and then it will be all over with him."

"I will certainly not say it any more," said Little Claus.

But when people came by soon afterwards, and nodded "good day"
to him, he became very glad, and thought it looked very well, after all,
that he had five horses to plough his field; and so he smacked his whip
again, and cried, "Gee up, all my horses!"

"I'll 'gee up' your horses!" said Great Claus.   And he took the
hatchet and hit the only horse of Little Claus on the head, so that it fell
down, and was dead immediately.

"Oh, now I haven't any horse at all!" said Little Claus, and began
to cry.

Then he flayed the horse, and let the hide dry in the wind, and put it
in a sack and hung it over his shoulder, and went to the town to sell
his horse's skin.

He had a very long way to go, and was obliged to pass through a great
dark wood, and the weather became dreadfully bad.   He went quite

LITTLE CLAUS DEPLORING THE DEATH OF HIS HORSE.

astray, and before he got into the right way again it was evening, and it was too far to get home again or even to the town before nightfall.

Close by the road stood a large farm-house. The shutters were closed outside the windows, but the light could still be seen shining out over them.

"I may be able to get leave to stop here through the night," thought Little Claus; and he went and knocked.

The farmer's wife opened the door; but when she heard what he wanted she told him to go away, declaring that her husband was not at home, and she would not receive strangers.

"Then I shall have to lie outside," said Little Claus. And the farmer's wife shut the door in his face.

Close by stood a great haystack, and between this and the farm-house was a little outhouse thatched with straw.

"Up there I can lie," said Little Claus, when he looked up at the roof; "that is a capital bed. I suppose the stork won't fly down and bite me in the legs." For a living stork was standing on the roof, where he had his nest.

Now little Claus climbed up to the roof of the shed, where he lay, and turned round to settle himself comfortably. The wooden shutters did not cover the windows at the top, and he could look straight into the room. There was a great table, with the cloth laid, and wine and roast meat and a glorious fish upon it. The farmer's wife and the clerk were seated at table, and nobody besides. She was filling his glass, and he was digging his fork into the fish, for that was his favourite dish.

"If one could only get some too!" thought Little Claus, as he stretched out his head towards the window. Heavens! what a glorious cake he saw standing there! Yes, certainly, that *was* a feast.

Now he heard some one riding along the high road. It was the woman's husband, who was coming home. He was a good man enough, but he had the strange peculiarity that he could never bear to see a clerk. If a clerk appeared before his eyes he became quite wild. And that was the reason why the clerk had gone to the wife to wish her good day, because he knew that her husband was not at home; and the good woman therefore put the best fare she had before him. But when they heard the man coming they were frightened, and the woman begged the clerk to creep into a great empty chest which stood there; and he did so, for he knew the husband could not bear the sight of a clerk. The woman quickly hid all the excellent meat and wine in her baking-oven; for if the man had seen that, he would have been certain to ask what it meant.

"Ah, yes!" sighed Little Claus, up in his shed, when he saw all the good fare put away.

"Is there any one up there?" asked the farmer; and he looked up at Little Claus. "Who are you lying there? Better come with me into the room."

And Little Claus told him how he had lost his way, and asked leave to stay there for the night.

"Yes, certainly," said the peasant, "but first we must have something to live on."

The woman received them both in a very friendly way, spread the cloth on a long table, and gave them a great dish of porridge. The farmer was hungry, and ate with a good appetite; but Little Claus could not help thinking of the capital roast meat, fish, and cake, which he knew were in the oven. Under the table, at his feet, he had laid the sack with the horse's hide in it; for we know that he had come out to sell it in the town. He could not relish the porridge, so he trod upon the sack, and the dry skin inside crackled quite loudly.

"Why, what have you in your sack?" asked the farmer.

"Oh, that's a magician," answered Little Claus. "He says we are not to eat porridge, for he has conjured the oven full of roast meat, fish, and cake."

"Wonderful!" cried the farmer; and he opened the oven in a hurry, and found all the dainty provisions which his wife had hidden there, but which, as he thought, the wizard had conjured forth. The woman dared not say anything, but put the things at once on the table; and so they both ate of the meat, the fish, and the cake. Now Little Claus again trod on his sack, and made the hide creak.

" What does he say now ? " said the farmer.

" He says," replied Claus, " that he has conjured three bottles of wine for us, too, and that they are standing there in the corner behind the oven."

Now the woman was obliged to bring out the wine which she had hidden, and the farmer drank it and became very merry. He would have been very glad to see such a conjuror as Little Claus had there in the sack.

" Can he conjure the demon forth ? " asked the farmer. " I should like to see him, for now I am merry."

" Oh, yes," said Little Claus, " my conjuror can do anything that I ask of him.—Can you not ? " he added, and trod on the hide, so that it crackled. " He says ' Yes.' But the demon is very ugly to look at: we had better not see him."

" Oh, I 'm not at all afraid. Pray, what will he look like ? "

" Why, he 'll look the very image of a clerk."

" Ha ! " said the farmer, " that *is* ugly ! You must know, I can't bear the sight of a clerk. But it doesn't matter now, for I know that he 's a demon, so I shall easily stand it. Now I have courage, but he must not come too near me."

" Now I will ask my conjuror," said Little Claus ; and he trod on the sack and held his ear down.

" What does he say ? "

" He says you may go and open the chest that stands in the corner, and you will see the demon crouching in it ; but you must hold the lid so that he doesn't slip out."

" Will you help me to hold him ? " asked the farmer. And he went to the chest where the wife had hidden the real clerk, who sat in there and was very much afraid. The farmer opened the lid a little way and peeped in underneath it.

" Hu ! " he cried, and sprang backward. " Yes, now I 've seen him, and he looked exactly like our clerk. Oh, that was dreadful ! "

Upon this they must drink. So they sat and drank until late into the night.

" You must sell me that conjuror," said the farmer. " Ask as much as you like for him : I 'll give you a whole bushel of money directly."

" No, that I can't do," said Little Claus : " only think how much use I can make of this conjuror."

" Oh, I should so much like to have him ! " cried the farmer ; and he went on begging.

" Well," said Little Claus, at last, " as you have been so kind as to give me shelter for the night, I will let it be so. You shall have the conjuror for a bushel of money ; but I must have the bushel heaped up."

" That you shall have," replied the farmer. " But you must take the chest yonder away with you. I will not keep it in my house an hour. One cannot know,—perhaps he may be there still."

Little Claus gave the farmer his sack with the dry hide in it, and got in exchange a whole bushel of money, and that heaped up. The farmer also gave him a big truck, on which to carry off his money and chest.

"Farewell!" said Little Claus; and he went off with his money and the big chest, in which the clerk was still sitting.

On the other side of the wood was a great deep river. The water rushed along so rapidly that one could scarcely swim against the stream. A fine new bridge had been built over it. Little Claus stopped on the centre of the bridge, and said quite loud, so that the clerk could hear it,

"Ho, what shall I do with this stupid chest? It's as heavy as if stones were in it. I shall only get tired if I drag it any farther, so I'll throw it into the river: if it swims home to me, well and good; and if it does not, it will be no great matter."

And he took the chest with one hand, and lifted it up a little, as if he intended to throw it into the river.

"No! let be!" cried the clerk from within the chest; "let me out first!"

"Hu!" exclaimed Little Claus, pretending to be frightened, "he's in there still! I must make haste and throw him into the river, that he may be drowned."

"Oh, no, no!" screamed the clerk. "I'll give you a whole bushel-full of money if you'll let me go."

"Why, that's another thing!" said Little Claus; and he opened the chest.

The clerk crept quickly out, pushed the empty chest into the water, and went to his house, where Little Claus received a whole bushel-full of money. He had already received one from the farmer, and so now he had his truck loaded with money.

"See, I've been well paid for the horse," he said to himself when he had got home to his own room, and was emptying all the money into a heap in the middle of the floor. "That will vex Great Claus when he hears how rich I have grown through my one horse; but I won't tell him about it outright."

So he sent a boy to Great Claus to ask for a bushel measure.

"What can he want with it?" thought Great Claus. And he smeared some tar underneath the measure, so that some part of whatever was measured should stick to it. And thus it happened; for when he received the measure back, there were three new eight-shilling pieces adhering thereto.

"What's this?" cried Great Claus; and he ran off at once to Little Claus. "Where did you get all that money from?"

"Oh, that's for my horse's skin. I sold it yesterday evening."

"That's really being well paid," said Great Claus. And he ran home in a hurry, took an axe, and killed all his four horses; then he flayed them, and carried off their skins to the town."

"Hides! hides! who'll buy any hides?" he cried through the streets.

GREAT CLAUS BEATEN BY THE SHOEMAKERS AND TANNERS.

All the shoemakers and tanners came running, and asked how much he wanted for them.

"A bushel of money for each!" said Great Claus.

"Are you mad?" said they. "Do you think we have money by the bushel?"

"Hides! hides!" he cried again; and to all who asked him what the hides would cost he replied, "A bushel of money."

"He wants to make fools of us," they all exclaimed. And the shoemakers took their straps, and the tanners their aprons, and they began to beat Great Claus.

"Hides! hides!" they called after him, jeeringly. "Yes, we'll tan your hide for you till the red broth runs down. Out of the town with him!" And Great Claus made the best haste he could, for he had never yet been thrashed as he was thrashed now.

"Well," said he when he got home, "Little Claus shall pay for this. I'll kill him for it."

Now, at Little Claus's the old grandmother had died. She had been very harsh and unkind to him, but yet he was very sorry, and took the dead woman and laid her in his warm bed, to see if she would not come to life again. There he intended she should remain all through the night, and he himself would sit in the corner and sleep on a chair, as he had often done before. As he sat there, in the night the door opened, and Great Claus came in with his axe. He knew where Little Claus's bed stood; and, going straight up to it, he hit the old grandmother on the head, thinking she was Little Claus.

"D'ye see," said he, "you shall not make a fool of me again." And then he went home.

"That's a bad fellow, that man," said Little Claus. "He wanted to kill me. It was a good thing for my old grandmother that she was dead already. He would have taken her life."

And he dressed his grandmother in her Sunday clothes, borrowed a horse of his neighbour, harnessed it to a car, and put the old lady on the back seat, so that she could not fall out when he drove. And so they trundled through the wood. When the sun rose they were in front of an inn; there Little Claus pulled up, and went in to have some refreshment.

The host had very, very much money; he was also a very good man, but exceedingly hot, as if he had pepper and tobacco in him.

"Good morning," said he to Little Claus. "You've put on your Sunday clothes early to-day."

"Yes," answered Little Claus; "I'm going to town with my old grandmother: she's sitting there on the car without. I can't bring her into the room—will you give her a glass of mead? But you must speak very loud, for she can't hear well."

"Yes, that I'll do," said the host. And he poured out a great glass of mead, and went out with it to the dead grandmother, who had been placed upright in the carriage.

"Here's a glass of mead from your son," quoth mine host. But the dead woman replied not a word, but sat quite still. "Don't you hear?" cried the host, as loud as he could, "here is a glass of mead from your son!"

Once more he called out the same thing, but as she persisted in not hearing him, he became angry at last, and threw the glass in her face, so that the mead ran down over her nose, and she tumbled backwards into the car, for she had only been put upright, and not bound fast.

"Hallo!" cried Little Claus, running out at the door, and seizing the host by the breast; "you've killed my grandmother now! See, there's a big hole in her forehead."

"Oh, here's a misfortune!" cried the host, wringing his hands. "That all comes of my hot temper. Dear Little Claus, I'll give you a bushel of money, and have your grandmother buried as if she were my own; only keep quiet, or I shall have my head cut off, and that would be so very disagreeable!"

So Little Claus again received a whole bushel of money, and the host buried the old grandmother as if she had been his own. And when Little Claus came home with all his money, he at once sent his boy to Great Claus to ask to borrow a bushel measure.

"What's that?" said Great Claus. "Have I not killed him? I must go myself and see to this." And so he went over himself with the bushel to Little Claus.

"Now, where did you get all that money from?" he asked; and he opened his eyes wide when he saw all that had been brought together.

"You killed my grandmother, and not me," replied Little Claus; "and I've been and sold her, and got a whole bushel of money for her."

"That's really being well paid," said Great Claus; and he hastened home, took an axe, and killed his own grandmother directly. Then he put her on a carriage, and drove off to the town with her, to where the apothecary lived, and asked him if he would buy a dead person.

"Who is it, and where did you get him from?" asked the apothecary.

"It's my grandmother," answered Great Claus. "I've killed her to get a bushel of money for her."

"Heaven save us!" cried the apothecary, "you're raving! Don't say such things, or you may lose your head." And he told him earnestly what a bad deed this was that he had done, and what a bad man he was, and that he must be punished. And Great Claus was so frightened that he jumped out of the surgery straight into his carriage, and whipped the horses, and drove home. But the apothecary and all the people thought him mad, and so they let him drive whither he would.

"You shall pay for this!" said Great Claus, when he was out upon the high road: "yes, you shall pay me for this, Little Claus!" And directly he got home he took the biggest sack he could find, and went over to Little Claus, and said, "Now, you've tricked me again! First I killed my horses, and then my old grandmother! That's all your fault; but you shall never trick me any more." And he seized Little Claus round the body, and thrust him into the sack, and took him upon his back, and called out to him, "Now I shall go off with you and drown you."

It was a long way that he had to travel before he came to the river, and Little Claus was not too light to carry. The road led him close to a church: the organ was playing, and the people were singing so beautifully! Then Great Claus put down his sack, with Little Claus in it, close to the church door, and thought it would be a very good thing to go in and hear a psalm before he went farther; for Little Claus could not get out, and all the people were in church; and so he went in.

"Ah, yes! yes!" sighed Little Claus in the sack. And he turned and twisted, but he found it impossible to loosen the cord. Then there came by an old drover with snow-white hair, and a great staff in his hand: he was driving a whole herd of cows and oxen before him, and they stumbled against the sack in which Little Claus was confined, so that it was overthrown.

"Oh, dear!" sighed Little Claus, "I'm so young yet, and am to go to heaven directly!"

"And I, poor fellow," said the drover, "am so old already, and can't get there yet!"

"Open the sack," cried Little Claus; "creep into it instead of me, and you will get to heaven directly."

"With all my heart," replied the drover; and he untied the sack, out of which Little Claus crept forth immediately.

"But will you look after the cattle?" said the old man; and he crept into the sack at once, whereupon Little Claus tied it up, and went his way with all the cows and oxen.

Soon afterwards Great Claus came out of the church. He took the sack on his shoulders again, although it seemed to him as if the sack had become lighter; for the old drover was only half as heavy as Little Claus.

"How light he is to carry now! Yes, that is because I have heard a psalm."

So he went to the river, which was deep and broad, threw the sack with the old drover in it into the water, and called after him, thinking that it was little Claus, "You lie there! Now you shan't trick me any more!"

Then he went home; but when he came to a place where there was a cross road, he met little Claus driving all his beasts.

"What's this?" cried great Claus. "Have I not drowned you?"

"Yes," replied Little Claus, "you threw me into the river less than half an hour ago."

"But wherever did you get all those fine beasts from?" asked Great Claus.

"These beasts are sea-cattle," replied Little Claus. "I'll tell you the whole story,—and thank you for drowning me, for now I'm at the top of the tree. I am really rich! How frightened I was when I lay huddled in the sack, and the wind whistled about my ears when you threw me down from the bridge into the cold water! I sank to the bottom immediately; but I did not knock myself, for the most splendid soft grass grows down there. Upon that I fell; and immediately the sack was opened, and the loveliest maiden, with snow-white garments and a green wreath upon her wet hair, took me by the hand, and said, 'Are you come, Little Claus? Here you have some cattle to begin with. A mile farther along the road there is a whole herd more, which I will give to you.' And now I saw that the river formed a great highway for the people of the sea. Down in its bed they walked and drove directly from the sea, and straight into the land, to where the river ends. There it was so beautifully full of flowers and of the freshest grass; the fishes, which swam in the water, shot past my ears, just as here the birds in the air. What pretty people there were there, and what fine cattle pasturing on mounds and in ditches!"

"But why did you come up again to us directly?" asked Great Claus. "I should not have done that, if it is so beautiful down there."

"Why," replied Little Claus, "in that I just acted with good policy. You heard me tell you that the sea-maiden said, 'A mile farther along the road'—and by the road she meant the river, for she can't go anywhere else—'there is a whole herd of cattle for you.' But I know what bends the stream makes—sometimes this way, sometimes that; there's a long way to go round: no, the thing can be managed in a shorter way by coming here to the land, and driving across the fields towards the river again. In this manner I save myself almost half a mile, and get all the quicker to my sea-cattle!"

"Oh, you are a fortunate man!" said Great Claus. "Do you think I should get some sea-cattle too if I went down to the bottom of the river?"

"Yes, I think so," replied Little Claus. "But I cannot carry you in the sack as far as the river; you are too heavy for me! But if you will go there, and creep into the sack yourself, I will throw you in with a great deal of pleasure."

"Thanks!" said Great Claus; "but if I don't get any sea-cattle when I am down there, I shall beat you, you may be sure!"

"Oh, no; don't be so fierce!"

And so they went together to the river. When the beasts, which were thirsty, saw the stream, they ran as fast as they could to get at the water. "See how they hurry!" cried Little Claus. "They are longing to get back to the bottom."

"Yes, but help me first!" said Great Claus, "or else you shall be beaten."

And so he crept into the great sack, which had been laid across the back of one of the oxen.

"Put a stone in, for I'm afraid I shan't sink else," said Great Claus.

"That can be done," replied Little Claus; and he put a big stone into the sack, tied the rope tightly, and pushed against it. *Plump!* There lay Great Claus in the river, and sank at once to the bottom.

"I'm afraid he won't find the cattle!" said Little Claus; and then he drove homeward with what he had.

THE PRINCESS ON THE PEA.

THERE was once a Prince who wanted to marry a princess; but she was to be a *real* princess. So he travelled about, all through the world, to find a real one, but everywhere there was something in the way. There were princesses enough, but whether they were *real* princesses he could not quite make out: there was always something that did not seem quite right. So he came home again, and was quite sad; for he wished so much to have a real princess.

One evening a terrible storm came on. It lightened and thundered, the rain streamed down; it was quite fearful! Then there was a knocking at the town gate, and the old King went out to open it.

It was a Princess who stood outside the gate. But, mercy! how she looked, from the rain and the rough weather! The water ran down

THE PRINCESS COMPLAINING OF THE PEA IN HER BED.

from her hair and her clothes; it ran in at the points of her shoes, and out at the heels; and yet she declared that she was a real princess.

"Yes, we will soon find that out," thought the old Queen. But she said nothing, only went into the bed-chamber, took all the bedding off, and put a pea on the flooring of the bedstead; then she took twenty mattresses and laid them upon the pea, and then twenty eider-down beds upon the mattresses. On this the Princess had to lie all night. In the morning she was asked how she had slept.

"Oh, miserably!" said the Princess. "I scarcely closed my eyes all night long. Goodness knows what was in my bed. I lay upon something hard, so that I am black and blue all over. It is quite dreadful!"

Now they saw that she was a real princess, for through the twenty mattresses and the twenty eider-down beds she had felt the pea. No one but a real princess could be so delicate.

So the Prince took her for his wife, for now he knew that he had a true princess; and the pea was put in the museum, and it is there now, unless somebody has carried it off.

Look you, this is a true story.

THUMBELINA AND THE TOADS.

THUMBELINA.

THERE was once a woman who wished for a very little child; but she did not know where she should procure one. So she went to an old witch, and said,

"I do so very much wish for a little child! can you not tell me where I can get one?"

"Oh! that could easily be managed," said the witch. "There you have a barleycorn: that is not of the kind which grows in the countryman's field, and which the chickens get to eat. Put that into a flower-pot, and you shall see what you shall see."

"Thank you," said the woman; and she gave the witch twelve shillings, for that is what it cost.

Then she went home and planted the barleycorn, and immediately there grew up a great handsome flower, which looked like a tulip; but the leaves were tightly closed, as though it were still a bud.

"That is a beautiful flower," said the woman; and she kissed its yellow and red leaves. But just as she kissed it the flower opened with a pop. It was a real tulip, as one could now see; but in the middle of the flower there sat upon the green velvet stamens a little maiden, delicate and graceful to behold. She was scarcely half a thumb's length in height, and therefore she was called Thumbelina.

A neat polished walnut-shell served Thumbelina for a cradle, blue violet-leaves were her mattresses, with a rose-leaf for a coverlet. There she slept at night; but in the day-time she played upon the table, where the woman had put a plate with a wreath of flowers around it, whose stalks stood in water; on the water swam a great tulip-leaf, and on this the little maiden could sit, and row from one side of the plate to the other, with two white horse-hairs for oars. That looked pretty indeed!

She could also sing, and, indeed, so delicately and sweetly, that the like had never been heard.

Once as she lay at night in her pretty bed, there came an old Toad creeping through the window, in which one pane was broken. The Toad was very ugly, big, and damp: it hopped straight down upon the table, where Thumbelina lay sleeping under the rose-leaf.

"That would be a handsome wife for my son," said the Toad; and she took the walnut-shell in which Thumbelina lay asleep, and hopped with it through the window down into the garden.

There ran a great broad brook; but the margin was swampy and soft, and here the Toad dwelt with her son. Ugh! he was ugly, and looked just like his mother. "Croak! croak! brek kek-kex!" that was all he could say when he saw the graceful little maiden in the walnut-shell.

"Don't speak so loud, or she will awake;" said the old Toad. "She might run away from us, for she is as light as a bit of swan's-down. We will put her out in the brook upon one of the broad water-lily leaves. That will be just like an island for her, she is so small and light. Then she can't get away, while we put the state room under the marsh in order, where you are to live and keep house together."

Out in the brook there grew many water-lilies with broad green leaves, which looked as if they were floating on the water. The leaf which lay farthest out was also the greatest of all, and to that the old Toad swam out and laid the walnut-shell upon it with Thumbelina. The little tiny Thumbelina woke early in the morning, and when she saw where she was, she began to cry very bitterly; for there was water on every side of the great green leaf, and she could not get to land at all. The old Toad sat down in the marsh, decking out her room with rushes and yellow weed—it was to be made very pretty for the new daughter-in-law; then she swam out, with her ugly son, to the leaf on which Thumbelina was. They wanted to take her pretty bed, which was to be put in the bridal chamber before she went in there herself. The old Toad bowed low before her in the water, and said,

"Here is my son; he will be your husband, and you will live splendidly together in the marsh."

"Croak! croak! brek-kek-kex!" was all the son could say.

Then they took the delicate little bed, and swam away with it; but Thumbelina sat all alone upon the green leaf and wept, for she did not like to live at the nasty Toad's, and have her ugly son for a husband. The little fishes swimming in the water below had both seen the Toad, and had also heard what she said; therefore they stretched forth their heads, for they wanted to see the little girl. So soon as they saw her they considered her so pretty that they felt very sorry she should have to go down to the ugly Toad. No, that must never be! They assembled together in the water around the green stalk which held the leaf on which the little maiden stood, and with their teeth they gnawed away the stalk, and so the leaf swam down the stream; and away went Thumbelina far away, where the Toad could not get at her.

Thumbelina sailed by many cities, and the little birds which sat in

the bushes saw her, and said, "What a lovely little girl!" The leaf
swam away with them, farther and farther; so Thumbelina travelled
out of the country.

A graceful little white butterfly always fluttered round her, and at
last alighted on the leaf. Thumbelina pleased him, and she was very
glad of this, for now the Toad could not reach them; and it was so
beautiful where she was floating along—the sun shone upon the water,
and the water glistened like the most splendid gold. She took her
girdle and bound one end of it round the butterfly, fastening the other
end of the ribbon to the leaf. The leaf now glided onward much faster,
and Thumbelina too, for she stood upon the leaf.

There came a big Cockchafer flying up; and he saw her, and immediately clasped his claws round her slender waist, and flew with her up
into a tree. The green leaf went swimming down the brook, and the
butterfly with it; for he was fastened to the leaf, and could not get away
from it.

Mercy! how frightened poor little Thumbelina was when the Cockchafer flew with her up into the tree! But especially she was sorry for
the fine white butterfly whom she had bound fast to the leaf, for, if he
could not free himself from it, he would be obliged to starve. The
Cockchafer, however, did not trouble himself at all about this. He
seated himself with her upon the biggest green leaf of the tree, gave
her the sweet part of the flowers to eat, and declared that she was very
pretty, though she did not in the least resemble a cockchafer. Afterwards came all the other cockchafers who lived in the tree to pay a visit:
they looked at Thumbelina, and said,

"Why, she has not even more than two legs!—that has a wretched
appearance."

"She has not any feelers!" cried another.

"Her waist is quite slender—fie! she looks like a human creature—
how ugly she is!" said all the lady cockchafers.

And yet Thumbelina was very pretty. Even the Cockchafer who had
carried her off saw that; but when all the others declared she was ugly,
he believed it at last, and would not have her at all—she might go
whither she liked. Then they flew down with her from the tree, and set
her upon a daisy, and she wept, because she was so ugly that the cockchafers would have nothing to say to her; and yet she was the loveliest
little being one could imagine, and as tender and delicate as a rose-leaf.

The whole summer through poor Thumbelina lived quite alone in the
great wood. She wove herself a bed out of blades of grass, and hung
it up under a shamrock, so that she was protected from the rain; she
plucked the honey out of the flowers for food, and drank of the dew
which stood every morning upon the leaves. Thus summer and autumn
passed away; but now came winter, the cold long winter. All the birds
who had sung so sweetly before her flew away; trees and flowers shed
their leaves; the great shamrock under which she had lived shrivelled
up, and there remained nothing of it but a yellow withered stalk; and
she was dreadfully cold, for her clothes were torn, and she herself was

so frail and delicate—poor little Thumbelina! she was nearly frozen. It began to snow, and every snow-flake that fell upon her was like a whole shovel-full thrown upon one of us, for we are tall, and she was only an inch long. Then she wrapped herself in a dry leaf, and that tore in the middle, and would not warm her—she shivered with cold.

Close to the wood into which she had now come lay a great corn-field, but the corn was gone long ago; only the naked dry stubble stood up out of the frozen ground. These were just like a great forest for her to wander through; and, oh! how she trembled with cold. Then she arrived at the door of the Field Mouse. This mouse had a little hole under the stubble. There the Field Mouse lived, warm and comfortable, and had a whole room-full of corn—a glorious kitchen and larder. Poor Thumbelina stood at the door just like a poor beggar girl, and begged for a little bit of a barleycorn, for she had not had the smallest morsel to eat for the last two days

"You poor little creature," said the Field Mouse—for after all she was a good old Field Mouse—" come into my warm room and dine with me."

As she was pleased with Thumbelina, she said, "If you like you may stay with me through the winter, but you must keep my room clean and neat, and tell me little stories, for I am very fond of those."

And Thumbelina did as the kind old Field Mouse bade her, and had a very good time of it.

"Now we shall soon have a visitor," said the Field Mouse. "My neighbour is in the habit of visiting me once a week. He is even better off than I am, has great rooms, and a beautiful black velvety fur. If you could only get him for your husband you would be well provided for. You must tell him the prettiest stories you know."

But Thumbelina did not care about this; she thought nothing of the neighbour, for he was a Mole. He came and paid his visits in his black velvet coat. The Field Mouse told how rich and how learned he was, and how his house was more than twenty times larger than hers; that he had learning, but that he did not like the sun and beautiful flowers, for he had never seen them.

Thumbelina had to sing, and she sang " Cockchafer, fly away," and " When the parson goes afield." Then the Mole fell in love with her, because of her delicious voice; but he said nothing, for he was a sedate man.

A short time before, he had dug a long passage through the earth from his own house to theirs; and Thumbelina and the Field Mouse obtained leave to walk in this passage as much as they wished. But he begged them not to be afraid of the dead bird which was lying in the passage. It was an entire bird, with wings and a beak. It certainly must have died only a short time before, and was now buried just where the Mole had made his passage.

The Mole took a bit of decayed wood in his mouth, and it glimmered like fire in the dark ; and then he went first and lighted them through the long dark passage. When they came where the dead bird lay, the

Mole thrust up his broad nose against the ceiling, so that a great hole was made, through which the daylight could shine down. In the middle of the floor lay a dead Swallow, his beautiful wings pressed close against his sides, and his head and feet drawn back under his feathers: the poor bird had certainly died of cold. Thumbelina was very sorry for this; she was very fond of all the little birds, who had sung and twittered so prettily before her through the summer; but the Mole gave him a push with his crooked legs, and said, "Now he doesn't pipe any more. It must be miserable to be born a little bird. I'm thankful that none of my children can be that: such a bird has nothing but his 'tweet-tweet,' and has to starve in the winter!"

"Yes, you may well say that, as a clever man," observed the Field Mouse. "Of what use is all this 'tweet-tweet' to a bird when the winter comes? He must starve and freeze. But they say that's very aristocratic."

Thumbelina said nothing; but when the two others turned their backs on the bird, she bent down, put the feathers aside which covered his head, and kissed him upon his closed eyes.

"Perhaps it was he who sang so prettily before me in the summer," she thought. "How much pleasure he gave me, the dear beautiful bird!"

The Mole now closed up the hole through which the daylight shone in, and accompanied the ladies home. But at night Thumbelina could not sleep at all; so she got up out of her bed, and wove a large beautiful carpet of hay, and carried it and spread it over the dead bird, and laid the thin stamens of flowers, soft as cotton, and which she had found in the Field Mouse's room, at the bird's sides, so that he might lie soft in the ground.

"Farewell, you pretty little bird!" said she. "Farewell! and thanks to you for your beautiful song in the summer, when all the trees were green, and the sun shone down warmly upon us." And then she laid the bird's head upon her heart. But the bird was not dead; he was only lying there torpid with cold; and now he had been warmed, and came to life again.

In autumn all the swallows fly away to warm countries; but if one happens to be belated, it becomes so cold that it falls down as if dead, and lies where it fell, and then the cold snow covers it.

Thumbelina fairly trembled, she was so startled; for the bird was large, very large, compared with her, who was only an inch in height. But she took courage, laid the cotton closer round the poor bird, and brought a leaf that she had used as her own coverlet, and laid it over the bird's head.

The next night she crept out to him again—and now he was alive, but quite weak; he could only open his eyes for a moment, and look at Thumbelina, who stood before him with a bit of decayed wood in her hand, for she had not a lantern.

"I thank you, you pretty little child," said the sick Swallow; "I have been famously warmed. Soon I shall get my strength back again, and I shall be able to fly about in the warm sunshine."

" Oh," she said, " it is so cold without. It snows and freezes. Stay in your warm bed, and I will nurse you."

Then she brought the Swallow water in the petal of a flower; and the Swallow drank, and told her how he had torn one of his wings in a thorn bush, and thus had not been able to fly so fast as the other swallows, which had sped away, far away, to the warm countries. So at last he had fallen to the ground, but he could remember nothing more, and did not know at all how he had come where she had found him.

The whole winter the Swallow remained there, and Thumbelina nursed and tended him heartily. Neither the Field Mouse nor the Mole heard anything about it, for they did not like the poor Swallow. So soon as the spring came, and the sun warmed the earth, the Swallow bade Thumbelina farewell, and she opened the hole which the Mole had made in the ceiling. The sun shone in upon them gloriously, and the Swallow asked if Thumbelina would go with him ; she could sit upon his back, and they would fly away far into the green wood. But Thumbelina knew that the old Field Mouse would be grieved if she left her.

" No, I cannot !" said Thumbelina.

" Farewell, farewell, you good, pretty girl !" said the Swallow; and he flew out into the sunshine. Thumbelina looked after him, and the tears came into her eyes, for she was heartily and sincerely fond of the poor Swallow.

" Tweet-weet! tweet-weet !" sang the bird, and flew into the green forest. Thumbelina felt very sad. She did not get permission to go out into the warm sunshine. The corn which was sown in the field over the house of the Field Mouse grew up high into the air ; it was quite a thick wood for the poor girl, who was only an inch in height.

" You are betrothed now, Thumbelina," said the Field Mouse. " My neighbour has proposed for you. What great fortune for a poor child like you ! Now you must work at your outfit, woollen and linen clothes both ; for you must lack nothing when you have become the Mole's wife."

Thumbelina had to turn the spindle, and the Mole hired four spiders to weave for her day and night. Every evening the Mole paid her a visit ; and he was always saying that when the summer should draw to a close, the sun would not shine nearly so hot, for that now it burned the earth almost as hard as a stone. Yes, when the summer should have gone, then he would keep his wedding day with Thumbelina. But she was not glad at all, for she did not like the tiresome Mole. Every morning when the sun rose, and every evening when it went down, she crept out at the door ; and when the wind blew the corn ears apart, so that she could see the blue sky, she thought how bright and beautiful it was out here, and wished heartily to see her dear Swallow again. But the Swallow did not come back ; he had doubtless flown far away, in the fair green forest. When autumn came on, Thumbelina had all her outfit ready.

" In four weeks you shall celebrate your wedding," said the Field Mouse to her.

But Thumbelina wept, and declared she would not have the tiresome Mole.

"Nonsense," said the Field Mouse; "don't be obstinate, or I will bite you with my white teeth. He is a very fine man whom you will marry. The Queen herself has not such a black velvet fur; and his kitchen and cellar are full. Be thankful for your good fortune."

Now the wedding was to be held. The Mole had already come to fetch Thumbelina; she was to live with him, deep under the earth, and never to come out into the warm sunshine, for that he did not like. The poor little thing was very sorrowful; she was now to say farewell to the glorious sun, which, after all, she had been allowed by the Field Mouse to see from the threshold of the door.

THUMBELINA'S JOURNEY ON THE SWALLOW'S BACK.

"Farewell, thou bright sun!" she said, and stretched out her arms towards it, and walked a little way forth from the house of the Field Mouse, for now the corn had been reaped, and only the dry stubble stood in the fields. "Farewell!" she repeated, twining her arms round a little red flower which still bloomed there. "Greet the little Swallow from me, if you see her again."

"Tweet-weet! tweet-weet!" a voice suddenly sounded over her head. She looked up; it was the little Swallow, who was just flying by. When he saw Thumbelina he was very glad; and Thumbelina told him how loth she was to have the ugly Mole for her husband, and that she was to live deep under the earth, where the sun never shone. And she could not refrain from weeping.

"The cold winter is coming now," said the Swallow; "I am going to fly far away into the warm countries. Will you come with me? You can sit upon my back, then we shall fly from the ugly Mole and his dark room—away, far away, over the mountains, to the warm countries, where the sun shines warmer than here, where it is always summer, and there are lovely flowers. Only fly with me, you dear little Thumbelina, you who have saved my life when I lay frozen in the dark earthy passage."

"Yes, I will go with you!" said Thumbelina, and she seated herself on the bird's back, with her feet on his outspread wing, and bound her girdle fast to one of his strongest feathers; then the Swallow flew up into the air over forest and over sea, high up over the great mountains, where the snow always lies; and Thumbelina felt cold in the bleak air, but then she hid under the bird's warm feathers, and only put out her little head to admire all the beauties beneath her.

At last they came to the warm countries. There the sun shone far brighter than here; the sky seemed twice as high; in ditches and on the hedges grew the most beautiful blue and green grapes; lemons and oranges hung in the woods; the air was fragrant with myrtles and balsams, and on the roads the loveliest children ran about, playing with the gay butterflies. But the Swallow flew still farther, and it became more and more beautiful. Under the most glorious green trees by the blue lake stood a palace of dazzling white marble, from the olden time. Vines clustered around the lofty pillars; at the top were many swallows' nests, and in one of these the Swallow lived who carried Thumbelina.

"That is my house," said the Swallow; "but it is not right that you should live there. It is not yet properly arranged by a great deal, and you will not be content with it. Select for yourself one of the splendid flowers which grow down yonder, then I will put you into it, and you shall have everything as nice as you can wish."

"That is capital," cried she, and clapped her little hands.

A great marble pillar lay there, which had fallen to the ground and had been broken into three pieces; but between these pieces grew the most beautiful great white flowers. The Swallow flew down with Thumbelina, and set her upon one of the broad leaves. But what was the little maid's surprise? There sat a little man in the midst of the flower, as white and transparent as if he had been made of glass: he wore the neatest of gold crowns on his head, and the brightest wings on his shoulders; he himself was not bigger than Thumbelina. He was the angel of the flower. In each of the flowers dwelt such a little man or woman, but this one was king over them all.

"Heavens! how beautiful he is!" whispered Thumbelina to the Swallow.

The little prince was very much frightened at the Swallow; for it was quite a gigantic bird to him, who was so small. But when he saw Thumbelina, he became very glad; she was the prettiest maiden he had ever seen. Therefore he took off his golden crown, and put it upon her, asked her name, and if she would be his wife, and then she should be queen of all the flowers. Now this was truly a different kind of man to the son of the Toad, and the Mole with the black velvet fur. She therefore said, "Yes" to the charming prince. And out of every flower came a lady or a lord, so pretty to behold that it was a delight : each one brought Thumbelina a present; but the best gift was a pair of beautiful wings which had belonged to a great white fly; these were fastened to Thumbelina's back, and now she could fly from flower to flower. Then there was much rejoicing; and the little Swallow sat above them in her nest, and was to sing the marriage song, which she accordingly did as well as she could; but yet in her heart she was sad, for she was so fond, oh ! so fond of Thumbelina, and would have liked never to part from her.

" You shall not be called Thumbelina," said the Flower Angel to her ; " that is an ugly name, and you are too fair for it—we will call you Maia."

" Farewell, farewell ! " said the little Swallow, with a heavy heart; and she flew away again from the warm countries, far away back to Denmark. There she had a little nest over the window of the man who can tell fairy tales. Before him she sang, " Tweet-weet ! tweet-weet ! " and from him we have the whole story.

THE NAUGHTY BOY.

THERE was once an old poet—a very good old poet. One evening, as he sat at home, there was dreadfully bad weather without. The rain streamed down : but the old poet sat comfortably by his stove, where the fire was burning and the roasting apples were hissing.

" There won't be a dry thread left on the poor people who are out in this weather ! " said he, for he was a good old poet.

" Oh, open to me ! I am cold and quite wet," said a little child outside ; and it cried, and knocked at the door, while the rain streamed down, and the wind made all the casements rattle.

" You poor little creature ! " said the poet ; and he went to open the door. There stood a little boy ; he was quite naked, and the water ran in streams from his long fair curls. He was shivering with cold, and had he not been let in, he would certainly have perished in the bad weather.

" You little creature ! " said the poet, and took him by the hand, " come to me, and I will warm you. You shall have wine and an apple, for you are a capital boy."

And so he was. His eyes sparkled like two bright stars, and though the water ran down from his fair curls, they fell in beautiful ringlets. He looked like a little angel-child, but was white with cold and trembled all over. In his hand he carried a famous bow, but it looked quite spoiled by the wet; all the colours in the beautiful arrows had been blurred together by the rain.

The old poet sat down by the stove, took the little boy on his knees, pressed the water out of the long curls, warmed his hands in his own, and made him some sweet whine-whey ; then the boy recovered himself,

THE OLD POET SHOT THROUGH THE HEART BY CUPID.

and his cheeks grew red, and he jumped to the floor and danced round the old poet.

"You are a merry boy," said the old poet. "What is your name?"

"My name is Cupid," he replied; "don't you know me? There lies my bow—I shoot with that, you may believe me! See, now the weather is clearing up outside, and the moon shines."

"But your bow is spoiled," said the old poet.

"That would be a pity," replied the little boy; and he took the bow and looked at it. "Oh, it is quite dry, and has suffered no damage; the string is quite stiff—I will try it!" Then he bent it, and laid an arrow across, aimed, and shot the good old poet straight through the heart. "Do you see now that my bow was not spoiled?" said he, and laughed out loud and ran away. What a naughty boy to shoot at the old poet in that way, who had admitted him into the warm room, and been so kind to him, and given him the best wine and the best apple!

The good poet lay upon the floor and wept; he was really shot straight into the heart. "Fie!" he cried, "what a naughty boy this Cupid is! I shall tell that to all good children, so that they may take care, and never play with him, for he will do them a hurt!"

All good children, girls and boys, to whom he told this, took good heed of this naughty Cupid; but still he tricked them, for he is very cunning. When the students come out from the lectures, he runs at their side with a book under his arm, and has a black coat on. They cannot recognize him at all. And then they take his arm and fancy he is a student too; but he thrusts the arrow into their breasts. Yes, he is always following people! He sits in the great chandelier in the theatre and burns brightly, so that the people think he is a lamp; but afterwards they see their error. He runs about in the palace garden and on the promenades. Yes, he once shot your father and your mother straight through the heart! Only ask them, and you will hear what they say. Oh, he is a bad boy, this Cupid; you must never have anything to do with him. He is after every one. Only think, once he shot an arrow at old grandmamma; but that was a long time ago. The wound has indeed healed long since, but she will never forget it. Fie on that wicked Cupid! But now you know him, and what a naughty boy he is.

THE TRAVELLING COMPANION.

POOR John was in great tribulation, for his father was very ill, and could not get well again. Except these two, there was no one at all in the little room: the lamp on the table was nearly extinguished, and it was quite late in the evening.

"You have been a good son, John," said the sick father. "Providence will help you through the world." And he looked at him with mild earnest eyes, drew a deep breath, and died: it was just as if he slept. But John wept; for now he had no one in the world, neither father nor mother, neither sister nor brother. Poor John! He lay on his knees before the bed, kissed his dead father's hand, and shed very many bitter tears; but at last his eyes closed, and he went to sleep, lying with his head against the hard bed-post.

Then he dreamed a strange dream: he saw the sun and moon shine upon him, and he beheld his father again, fresh and well, and he heard his father laugh as he had always laughed when he was very glad. A beautiful girl, with a golden crown upon her long shining hair, gave him her hand; and his father said, "Do you see what a bride you have gained? She is the most beautiful in the whole world!" Then he awoke, and all the splendour was gone. His father was lying dead and cold in the bed, and there was no one at all with them. Poor John!

In the next week the dead man was buried. The son walked close behind the coffin, and could now no longer see the good father who had loved him so much. He heard how they threw the earth down upon the coffin, and stopped to see the last corner of it; but the next shovel-full of earth hid even that; then he felt just as if his heart would burst into pieces, so sorrowful was he. Around him they were singing a psalm; those were sweet holy tones that arose, and the tears came into John's eyes; he wept, and that did him good in his sorrow. The sun shone magnificently on the green trees, just as it would have said, "You may no longer be sorrowful, John! Do you see how beautiful the sky is? Your father is up there, and prays to the Father of all that it may be always well with you."

JOHN AT THE DEATH-BED OF HIS FATHER

"I will always do right, too," said John, "then I shall go to heaven to my father; and what joy that will be when we see each other again! How much I shall then have to tell him! and he will show me so many things, and explain to me the glories of heaven, just as he taught me here on earth. Oh, how joyful that will be!"

He pictured that to himself so plainly, that he smiled, while the tears were still rolling down his cheeks. The little birds sat up in the chestnut trees, and twittered, "Tweet-weet! tweet-weet!" They were joyful and merry, though they had been at the burying, but they seemed to know that the dead man was now in heaven; that he had wings, far larger and more beautiful than theirs; that he was now happy, because he had been a good man upon earth, and they were glad at it. John saw how they flew from the green tree out into the world, and he felt inclined to fly too. But first he cut out a great cross of wood to put on his father's grave; and when he brought it there in the evening the grave was decked with sand and flowers; strangers had done this, for they were all very fond of the good father who was now dead.

Early next morning John packed his little bundle, and put in his belt his whole inheritance, which consisted of fifty dollars and a few silver shillings; with this he intended to wander out into the world. But first he went to the churchyard, to his father's grave, to say a prayer and to bid him farewell.

Out in the field where he was walking all the flowers stood fresh and beautiful in the warm sunshine; and they nodded in the wind, just as if they would have said, "Welcome to the green wood! Is it not fine here?" But John turned back once more to look at the old church, in which he had been christened when he was a little child, and where he had been every Sunday with his father at the service, and had sung his psalm; then, high up in one of the openings of the tower, he saw the ringer standing in his little pointed red cap, shading his face with his bent arm, to keep the sun from shining in his eyes. John nodded a farewell to him, and the little ringer waved his red cap, laid his hand on his heart, and kissed his hand to John a great many times, to show that he wished the traveller well and hoped he would have a prosperous journey.

John thought what a number of fine things he would get to see in the great splendid world; and he went on farther—farther than he had ever been before. He did not know the places at all through which he came, nor the people whom he met. Now he was far away in a strange region.

The first night he was obliged to lie down on a haystack in the field to sleep, for he had no other bed. But that was very nice, he thought; the king could not be better off. There was the whole field, with the brook, the haystack, and the blue sky above it; that was certainly a beautiful sleeping-room. The green grass with the little red and white flowers was the carpet; the elder bushes and the wild rose hedges were garlands of flowers; and for a wash-hand basin he had the whole brook with the clear fresh water; and the rushes bowed before him and wished him "good evening" and "good morning." The moon was certainly a great night-lamp, high up under the blue ceiling, and that lamp would never set fire to the curtains with its light. John could sleep quite safely, and he did so, and never woke until the sun rose and all the little birds were singing around, "Good morning! good morning! Are you not up yet?"

The bells were ringing for church; it was Sunday. The people went to hear the preacher, and John followed them, and sang a psalm and heard God's word. It seemed to him just as if he was in his own church, where he had been christened and had sung psalms with his father.

Out in the churchyard were many graves, and on some of them the grass grew high. Then he thought of his father's grave, which would at last look like these, as he could not weed it and adorn it. So he sat down and plucked up the long grass, set up the wooden crosses which had fallen down, and put back in their places the wreaths which the wind had blown away from the graves; for he thought, " Perhaps some one will do the same to my father's grave, as I cannot do it."

Outside the churchyard gate stood an old beggar, leaning upon his crutch. John gave him the silver shillings which he had, and then went away, happy and cheerful, into the wide world. Towards evening the weather became terribly bad. He made haste to get under shelter, but dark night soon came on; then at last he came to a little church, which lay quite solitary on a small hill.

" Here I will sit down in a corner," said he, and went in; " I am quite tired and require a little rest." Then he sat down, folded his hands, and said his evening prayer; and before he was aware of it he was asleep and dreaming, while it thundered and lightened without.

When he woke it was midnight; but the bad weather had passed by, and the moon shone in upon him through the windows. In the midst of the church stood an open coffin with a dead man in it who had not yet been buried. John was not at all timid, for he had a good conscience; and he knew very well that the dead do not harm any one. The living, who do evil, are bad men. Two such living bad men stood close by the dead man, who had been placed here in the church till he should be buried. They had an evil design against him, and would not let him rest quietly in his coffin, but were going to throw him out before the church door—the poor dead man!

" Why will you do that?" asked John; " that is bad and wicked. Let him rest, for mercy's sake."

" Nonsense!" replied the bad men; " he has cheated us. He owed us money and could not pay it, and now he's dead into the bargain, and we shall not get a penny! So we mean to revenge ourselves famously: he shall lie like a dog outside the church door!"

" I have not more than fifty dollars," cried John, " that is my whole inheritance; but I will gladly give it you, if you will honestly promise me to leave the poor dead man in peace. I shall manage to get on without the money; I have hearty strong limbs, and Heaven will always help me."

" Yes," said these ugly bad men, " if you will pay his debt we will do nothing to him, you may depend upon that!" And then they took the money he gave them, laughed aloud at his good nature, and went their way. But he laid the corpse out again in the coffin, and folded its hands, took leave of it, and went away contentedly through the great forest.

All around, wherever the moon could shine through between the trees, he saw the graceful little elves playing merrily. They did not let him disturb them; they knew that he was a good innocent man; and it is only the bad people who never get to see the elves. Some of them were not larger than a finger's breadth, and had fastened up their long yellow hair with golden combs: they were rocking themselves, two and two, on the great dew-drops that lay on the leaves and on the high grass; sometimes the drop rolled away, and then they fell down between the long grass-stalks, and that occasioned much laughter and noise among the other little creatures. It was charming. They sang, and John recognized quite plainly the pretty songs which he had learned as a little boy. Great coloured spiders, with silver crowns on their heads, had to spin long hanging bridges and palaces from hedge to hedge ; and as the tiny dew-drops fell on these they looked like gleaming glass in the moonlight. This continued until the sun rose. Then the little elves crept into the flower-buds, and the wind caught their bridges and palaces, which flew through the air in the shape of spider's webs.

John had just come out of the wood, when a strong man's voice called out behind him, " Halloo, comrade ! whither are you journeying ? "

" Into the wide world ! " he replied. " I have neither father nor mother, and am but a poor lad ; but Providence will help me."

" I am going out into the wide world, too," said the strange man : " shall we two keep one another company ? "

" Yes, certainly," said John ; and so they went on together. Soon they became very fond of each other, for they were both good men. But John saw that the stranger was much more clever than himself. He had travelled through almost the whole world, and knew how to tell of almost everything that existed.

The sun already stood high when they seated themselves under a great tree to eat their breakfast ; and just then an old woman came up. Oh, she was very old, and walked quite bent, leaning upon a crutch-stick ; upon her back she carried a bundle of firewood which she had collected in the forest. Her apron was untied, and John saw that three great stalks of fern and some willow twigs looked out from within it. When she was close to them, her foot slipped ; she fell and gave a loud scream, for she had broken her leg, the poor old woman !

John directly proposed that they should carry the old woman home to her dwelling ; but the stranger opened his knapsack, took out a little box, and said that he had a salve there which would immediately make her leg whole and strong, so that she could walk home herself, as if she had never broken her leg at all. But for that he required that she should give him the three rods which she carried in her apron.

" That would be paying well ! " said the old woman, and she nodded her head in a strange way. She did not like to give away the rods, but then it was not agreeable to lie there with a broken leg. So she gave him the wands ; and as soon as he had only rubbed the ointment on her leg, the old mother arose, and walked much better than before—such was the power of this ointment. But then it was not to be bought at the chemist's.

" What do you want with the rods ? " John asked his travelling companion.

" They are three capital fern brooms," replied he. " I like those very much, for I am a whimsical fellow."

And they went on a good way.

" See how the sky is becoming overcast," said John, pointing straight before them. " Those are terribly thick clouds."

" No," replied his travelling companion, " those are not clouds, they are mountains—the great glorious mountains, on which one gets quite up over the clouds, and into the free air. Believe me, it is delicious ! To-morrow we shall certainly be far out into the world."

But that was not so near as it looked ; they had to walk for a whole day before they came to the mountains, where the black woods grew straight up towards heaven, and there were stones almost as big as a whole town. It might certainly be hard work to get quite across them, and for that reason John and his comrade went into the inn to rest themselves well, and gather strength for the morrow's journey.

Down in the great common room in the inn many guests were assembled, for a man was there exhibiting a puppet-show. He had just put up his little theatre, and the people were sitting round to see the play. Quite in front a fat butcher had taken his seat in the very best place ; his great bulldog, who looked very much inclined to bite, sat at his side, and made big eyes, as all the rest were doing too.

Now the play began ; and it was a very nice play, with a king and a queen in it ; they sat upon a beautiful throne, and had gold crowns on their heads and long trains to their clothes, for their means admitted of that. The prettiest of wooden dolls with glass eyes and great moustaches stood at all the doors, and opened and shut them so that fresh air might come into the room. It was a very pleasant play, and not at all mournful. But—goodness knows what the big bulldog can have been thinking of !—just as the queen stood up and was walking across the boards, as the fat butcher did not hold him, he made a spring upon the stage, and seized the queen round her slender waist so that it cracked again. It was quite terrible !

The poor man who managed the play was very much frightened and quite sorrowful about his queen, for she was the daintiest little doll he possessed, and now the ugly bulldog had bitten off her head. But afterwards, when the people went away, the stranger said that he would put her to rights again ; and then he brought out his little box, and rubbed the doll with the ointment with which he had cured the old woman when she broke her leg. As soon as the doll had been rubbed, she was whole again ; yes, she could even move all her limbs by herself ; it was no longer necessary to pull her by her string. The doll was like a living person, only that she could not speak. The man who had the little puppet-show was very glad, now he had not to hold this doll any more. She could dance by herself, and none of the others could do that.

When night came on, and all the people in the inn had gone to bed, there was some one who sighed so fearfully, and went on doing it so long, that they all got up to see who this could be. The man who had shown the play went to his little theatre, for it was there that somebody was sighing. All the wooden dolls lay mixed together, the king and all his followers ; and it was they who sighed so pitiably, and stared with their glass eyes ; for they wished to be rubbed a little as the queen had been, so that they might be able to move by themselves. The queen at once sank on her knees, and stretched forth her beautiful crown, as if she

begged, "Take this from me, but rub my husband and my courtiers!"
Then the poor man, the proprietor of the little theatre and the dolls,
could not refrain from weeping, for he was really sorry for them. He
immediately promised the travelling companion that he would give him
all the money he should receive the next evening for the representation
if the latter would only anoint four or five of his dolls. But the comrade
said he did not require anything at all but the sword the man wore by
his side; and, on receiving this, he anointed six of the dolls, who immediately began to dance so gracefully that all the girls, the living human
girls, fell a dancing too. The coachman and the cook danced, the waiter
and the chambermaid, and all the strangers, and the fire-shovel and
tongs; but these latter fell down just as they made their first leaps
Yes, it was a merry night!

THE BULLDOG WORRIES THE PUPPET.

Next morning John went away from them all with his travelling companion, up on to the high mountains, and through the great pine woods.
They came so high up that the church steeples under them looked at
last like little blueberries among all the green; and they could see very
far, many, many miles away, where they had never been. So much
splendour in the lovely world John had never seen at one time before.
And the sun shone warm in the fresh blue air, and among the mountains
he could hear the huntsmen blowing their horns so gaily and sweetly
that tears came into his eyes, and he could not help calling out, "How
kind has Heaven been to us all, to give us all the splendour that is in
this world!"

The travelling companion also stood there with folded hands, and
looked over the forest and the towns into the warm sunshine. At the
same time there arose lovely sounds over their heads: they looked up,
and a great white swan was soaring in the air, and singing as they had

never heard a bird sing till then. But the song became weaker and weaker; he bowed his head and sank quite slowly down at their feet, where he lay dead, the beautiful bird!

"Two such splendid wings," said the travelling companion, "so white and large, as those which this bird has, are worth money; I will take them with me. Do you see that it was good I got a sabre?"

And so, with one blow, he cut off both the wings of the dead swan, for he wanted to keep them.

. They now travelled for many, many miles over the mountains, till at last they saw a great town before them with hundreds of towers, which glittered like silver in the sun. In the midst of the town was a splendid marble palace, roofed with pure red gold. And there the King lived.

John and the travelling companion would not go into the town at once, but remained in the inn outside the town, that they might dress themselves; for they wished to look nice when they came out into the streets. The host told them that the King was a very good man, who never did harm to any one; but his daughter, yes, goodness preserve us! she was a bad Princess. She possessed beauty enough—no one could be so pretty and so charming as she was—but of what use was that? She was a wicked witch, through whose fault many gallant Princes had lost their lives. She had given permission to all men to seek her hand. Any one might come, be he Prince or beggar: it was all the same to her. He had only to guess three things she had just thought of, and about which she questioned him. If he could do that she would marry him, and he was to be King over the whole country when her father should die; but if he could not guess the three things, she caused him to be hanged or to have his head cut off! Her father, the old King, was very sorry about it; but he could not forbid her to be so wicked, because he had once said that he would have nothing to do with her lovers; she might do as she liked. Every time a Prince came, and was to guess to gain the Princess, he was unable to do it, and was hanged or lost his head. He had been warned in time, you see, and might have given over his wooing. The old King was so sorry for all this misery and woe, that he used to lie on his knees with all his soldiers for a whole day in every year, praying that the Princess might become good; but she would not, by any means. The old women who drank brandy used to colour it quite black before they drank it, they were in such deep mourning—and they certainly could not do more.

"The ugly Princess!" said John; "she ought really to have the rod; that would do her good. If I were only the old King she should be punished!"

Then they heard the people outside shouting "Hurrah!" The Princess came by; and she was really so beautiful that all the people forgot how wicked she was, and that is why they cried "Hurrah!" Twelve beautiful virgins, all in white silk gowns, and each with a golden tulip in her hand, rode on coal-black steeds at her side. The Princess herself had a snow-white horse, decked with diamonds and rubies. Her riding-habit was all of cloth of gold, and the whip she held in her hand looked like a sunbeam; the golden crown on her head was just like little stars out of the sky, and her mantle was sewn together out of more than a thousand beautiful butterflies' wings. In spite of this, she herself was much more lovely than all her clothes.

When John saw her, his face became as red as a drop of blood, and he could hardly utter a word. The Princess looked just like the beautiful lady with the golden crown, of whom he had dreamt on the night when his father died. He found her so enchanting that he could not help loving her greatly. It could not be true that she was a wicked witch, who caused people to be hanged or beheaded if they could not guess the riddles she put to them.

JOHN AND HIS COMPANION SEE THE PRINCESS RIDING BY.

"Every one has permission to aspire to her hand, even the poorest beggar. I will really go to the castle, for I cannot help doing it!"

They all told him not to attempt it, for certainly he would fare as all the rest had done. His travelling companion too tried to dissuade him; but John thought it would end well. He brushed his shoes and his coat, washed his face and his hands, combed his nice fair hair, and then went quite alone into the town and to the palace.

"Come in!" said the old King, when John knocked at the door.

John opened it, and the old King came towards him in a dressing-gown and embroidered slippers; he had the crown on his head, and the sceptre in one hand and the orb in the other. " Wait a little ! " said he, and put the orb under his arm, so that he could reach out his hand to John. But as soon as he learned that his visitor was a suitor, he began to weep so violently that both the sceptre and the orb fell to the ground, and he was obliged to wipe his eyes with his dressing-gown. Poor old King !

" Give it up ! " said he. " You will fare badly, as all the others have done. Well, you shall see ! "

Then he led him out into the Princess's pleasure garden. There was a terrible sight ! In every tree there hung three or four Kings' sons who had wooed the Princess, but had not been able to guess the riddles she proposed to them. Each time that the breeze blew all the skeletons rattled, so that the little birds were frightened, and never dared to come into the garden. All the flowers were tied up to human bones, and in the flower-pots skulls stood and grinned. That was certainly a strange garden for a Princess.

" Here you see it," said the old King. " It will chance to you as it has chanced to all these whom you see here ; therefore you had better give it up. You will really make me unhappy, for I take these things very much to heart."

John kissed the good old King's hand, and said it would go well, for that he was quite enchanted with the beautiful Princess.

Then the Princess herself came riding into the courtyard, with all her ladies ; and they went out to her and wished her good morning. She was beautiful to look at, and she gave John her hand. And he cared much more for her then than before—she could certainly not be a wicked witch, as the people asserted. Then they betook themselves to the hall, and the little pages waited upon them with preserves and gingerbread nuts. But the old King was quite sorrowful ; he could not eat anything at all. Besides, gingerbread nuts were too hard for him.

It was settled that John should come to the palace again the next morning ; then the judges and the whole council would be assembled, and would hear how he succeeded with his answers. If it went well, he should come twice more ; but no one had yet come who had succeeded in guessing right the first time ; and if he did not manage better than they he must die.

John was not at all anxious as to how he should fare. On the contrary, he was merry, thought only of the beautiful Princess, and felt quite certain that he should be helped ; but *how* he did not know, and preferred not to think of it. He danced along on the road returning to the inn, where his travelling companion was waiting for him.

John could not leave off telling how polite the Princess had been to him, and how beautiful she was. He declared he already longed for the next day, when he was to go into the palace and try his luck in guessing.

But the travelling companion shook his head and was quite downcast. " I am so fond of you ! " said he. " We might have been together a long time yet, and now I am to lose you already ! You poor dear

John! I should like to cry, but I will not disturb your merriment on the last evening, perhaps, we shall ever spend together. We will be merry, very merry! To-morrow, when you are gone, I can weep undisturbed."

All the people in the town had heard directly that a new suitor for the Princess had arrived; and there was great sorrow on that account. The theatre remained closed; the women who sold cakes tied bits of crape round their sugar men, and the King and the priests were on their knees in the churches. There was great lamentation; for John would not, they all thought, fare better than the other suitors had fared.

Towards evening the travelling companion mixed a great bowl of punch, and said to John, "Now we will be very merry, and drink to the health of the Princess." But when John had drunk two glasses, he became so sleepy that he found it impossible to keep his eyes open, and he sank into a deep sleep. The travelling companion lifted him very gently from his chair, and laid him in the bed; and when it grew to be dark night, he took the two great wings which he had cut off the swan, and bound them to his own shoulders. Then he put in his pocket the longest of the rods he had received from the old woman who had fallen and broken her leg; and he opened the window and flew away over the town, straight towards the palace, where he seated himself in a corner under the window which looked into the bed-room of the Princess.

All was quiet in the whole town. Now the clock struck a quarter to twelve, the window was opened, and the Princess came out in a long white cloak, and with black wings, and flew away across the town to a great mountain. But the travelling companion made himself invisible, so that she could not see him at all, and flew behind her, and whipped the Princess with his rod, so that the blood almost came wherever he struck. Oh, that was a voyage through the air! The wind caught her cloak, so that it spread out on all sides like a great sail, and the moon shone through it.

"How it hails! how it hails!" said the Princess at every blow she got from the rod; and it served her right. At last she arrived at the mountain, and knocked there. There was a rolling like thunder, and the mountain opened, and the Princess went in. The travelling companion followed her, for no one could see him—he was invisible. They went through a great long passage, where the walls shone in quite a peculiar way: there were more than a thousand glowing spiders running up and down the walls and gleaming like fire. Then they came into a great hall built of silver and gold; flowers as big as sunflowers, red and blue, shone on the walls; but no one could pluck these flowers, for the stems were ugly poisonous snakes, and the flowers were streams of fire pouring out of their mouths. The whole ceiling was covered with shining glowworms and sky-blue bats, flapping their thin wings. It looked quite terrific! In the middle of the floor was a throne, carried by four skeleton horses, with harness of fiery red spiders; the throne itself was of milk-white glass, and the cushions were little black mice, biting each other's tails. Above it was a canopy of pink spider's web, trimmed with the prettiest little green flies, which gleamed like jewels. On the throne sat an old magician, with a crown on his ugly head and a sceptre in his hand. He kissed the Princess on the forehead, made her sit down beside him on the costly throne, and then the music began. Great black grasshoppers played on jews'-harps, and the owl beat her wings upon her body, because she hadn't a drum. That was a strange concert! Little black goblins with a Jack-o'-lantern light on their caps danced about in the hall. But no one could see the travelling companion: he had placed himself just behind the throne, and heard and saw everything. The courtiers, who now came in, were very grand and noble; but he who could see it all knew very well what it all meant. They were nothing more than broomsticks with heads of cabbages on them, which the magician had animated by his power, and to whom he had given embroidered clothes. But that did not matter, for, you see, they were only wanted for show.

After there had been a little dancing, the Princess told the magician that she had a new suitor, and therefore she inquired of him what she should think of to ask the suitor when he should come to-morrow to the palace.

"Listen!" said the magician, "I will tell you that: you must choose something very easy, for then he won't think of it. Think of one of your shoes. That he will not guess. Let him have his head cut off: but don't forget, when you come to me to-morrow night, to bring me his eyes, for I'll eat them."

The Princess courtesied very low, and said she would not forget the eyes. The magician opened the mountain, and she flew home again; but the travelling companion followed her, and beat her again so hard with the rod that she sighed quite deeply about the heavy hail-storm, and hurried as much as she could to get back into the bed-room through the open window. The travelling companion, for his part, flew back to the inn, where John was still asleep, took off his wings, and then lay down upon the bed, for he might well be tired.

It was quite early in the morning when John awoke. The travelling companion also got up, and said he had had a wonderful dream in the night, about the Princess and her shoe; and he therefore begged John to ask if the Princess had not thought about her shoe. For it was this he had heard from the magician in the mountain.

"I may just as well ask about that as about anything else," said John. "Perhaps it is quite right, what you have dreamed. But I will bid you farewell; for, if I guess wrong, I shall never see you more."

Then they embraced each other, and John went into the town and to the palace. The entire hall was filled with people: the judges sat in their arm-chairs and had eider-down pillows behind their heads, for they had a great deal to think about. The old King stood up, and wiped his eyes with a white pocket handkerchief. Now the Princess came in. She was much more beautiful than yesterday, and bowed to all in a very affable manner; but to John she gave her hand, and said, "Good morning to you."

Now John was to guess what she had thought of. Oh, how lovingly she looked at him! But as soon as she heard the single word " shoe " pronounced, she became as white as chalk in the face, and trembled all over. But that availed her nothing, for John had guessed right!

Wonderful! How glad the old King was! He threw a somersault beautiful to behold. And all the people clapped their hands in honour of him and of John, who had guessed right the first time!

The travelling companion was very glad too, when he heard how well matters had gone. But John felt very grateful; and he was sure he should receive help the second and third time, as he had been helped the first. The next day he was to guess again.

The evening passed just like that of yesterday. While John slept the travelling companion flew behind the Princess out to the mountain, and beat her even harder than the time before, for now he had taken two rods. No one saw him, and he heard everything. The Princess was to think of her glove; and this again he told to John as if it had been a dream. Thus John could guess well, which caused great rejoicing in the palace. The whole court threw somersaults, just as they had seen the King do the first time; but the Princess lay on the sofa, and would not say a single word. Now, the question was, if John could guess properly the third time. If he succeeded, he was to have the beautiful Princess and inherit the whole kingdom after the old King's death. If he failed, he was to lose his life, and the magician would eat his beautiful blue eyes.

That evening John went early to bed, said his prayers, and went to sleep quite quietly. But the travelling companion bound his wings to his back and his sword by his side, and took all three rods with him, and so flew away to the palace.

It was a very dark night. The wind blew so hard that the tiles flew off from the roofs, and the trees in the garden where the skeletons hung bent like reeds before the storm. The lightning flashed out every minute, and the thunder rolled just as if it were one peal lasting the whole night. Now the window opened, and the Princess flew out. She was as pale as death; but she laughed at the bad weather, and declared it was not bad enough yet. And her white cloak fluttered in the wind like a great sail; but the travelling companion beat her with the three rods, so that the blood dripped upon the ground, and at last she could scarcely fly any farther. At length, however, she arrived at the mountain.

" It hails and blows dreadfully!" she said. " I have never been out in such weather."

" One may have too much of a good thing," said the magician. " I shall think of something of which he has never thought, or he must be a greater conjuror than I. But now we will be merry." And he took the Princess by the hands, and they danced about with all the little goblins and Jack-o'-lanterns that were in the room. The red spiders jumped just as merrily up and down the walls: it looked as if fiery flowers were spurting out. The owl played the drum, the crickets piped, and the black grasshoppers played on the jew's-harp. It was a merry ball.

When they had danced long enough the Princess was obliged to go home, for she might be missed in the palace. The magician said he would accompany her, then they would have each other's company on the way.

Then they flew away into the bad weather, and the travelling companion broke his three rods across their backs. Never had the magician been out in such a hail-storm. In front of the palace he said good-bye to the Princess, and whispered to her at the same time, " Think of my head." But the travelling companion heard it; and just at the moment when the Princess slipped through the window into her bedroom, and the magician was about to turn back, he seized him by his long beard, and with his sabre cut off the ugly conjuror's head just by the shoulders, so that the magician did not even see him. The body he threw out into the sea to the fishes; but the head he only dipped into the water, and then tied it in his silk handkerchief, took it with him into the inn, and then lay down to sleep.

Next morning he gave John the handkerchief, and told him not to untie it until the Princess asked him to tell her thoughts.

There were so many people in the great hall of the palace, that they stood as close together as radishes bound together in a bundle. The council sat in the chairs with the soft pillows, and the old King had new clothes on; the golden crown and sceptre had been polished, and everything looked quite stately. But the Princess' was very pale, and had a coal-black dress on, as if she were going to be buried.

" Of what have I thought?" she asked John. And he immediately untied the handkerchief, and was himself quite frightened when he saw the ugly magician's head. All present shuddered, for it was terrible to look upon; but the Princess sat just like a statue, and would not utter a single word. At length she stood up, and gave John her hand, for he had guessed well. She did not look at any one, only sighed aloud, and said, " Now you are my lord!—this evening we will hold our wedding."

" I like that!" cried the old King. " Thus I will have it."

All present cried " Hurrah!" The soldiers' band played music in the streets, the bells rang, and the cake-women took off the black crape from their sugar dolls, for joy now reigned around; three oxen roasted whole, and stuffed with ducks and fowls, were placed in the middle of the market, that every one might cut himself a slice; the fountains ran with the best wine; and whoever bought a penny cake at a baker's got six biscuits into the bargain, and the biscuits had raisins in them.

In the evening the whole town was illuminated; the soldiers fired off the cannon, and the boys let off crackers; and there was eating and drinking, clinking of glasses, and dancing, in the palace. All the noble gentlemen and pretty ladies danced with each other, and one could hear, a long distance off, how they sang—

> " Here are many pretty girls, who all love to dance;
> See, they whirl like spinning-wheels, retire and advance.
> Turn, my pretty maiden, do, till the sole falls from your shoe."

DEATH OF THE MAGICIAN.

But still the Princess was a witch, and did not like John. That occurred to the travelling companion; and so he gave John three feathers out of the swan's wings, and a little bottle with a few drops in it, and told John that he must put a large tub of water before the Princess's bed; and when the Princess was about to get into bed, he should give her a little push, so that she should fall into the tub; and then he must dip her three times, after he had put in the feathers and poured in the drops; she would then lose her magic qualities, and love him very much.

John did all that the travelling companion had advised him to do. The Princess screamed out loudly while he dipped her in the tub, and struggled under his hands in the form of a great coal-black swan with fiery eyes. When she came up the second time above the water, the swan was white, with the exception of a black ring round her neck. John let the water close for the third time over the bird, and in the same moment it was again changed to the beautiful Princess. She was more beautiful even than before, and thanked him, with tears in her lovely eyes, that he had freed her from the magic spell.

The next morning the old King came with his whole court, and then there was great congratulation till late into the day.   Last of all came the travelling companion; he had his staff in his hand and his knapsack on his back.   John kissed him many times, and said he must not depart, he must remain with the friend of whose happiness he was the cause. But the travelling companion shook his head, and said mildly and kindly,

"No, now my time is up. I have only paid my debt. Do you remember the dead man whom the bad people wished to injure?   You gave all you possessed in order that he might have rest in his grave.   I am that man."

And in the same moment he vanished.

The wedding festivities lasted a whole month. John and the Princess loved each other truly, and the old King passed many pleasant days, and let their little children ride on his knees and play with his sceptre. And John afterwards became King over the whole country.

THE EMPEROR'S NEW CLOTHES.

MANY years ago there lived an Emperor, who cared so enormously for new clothes that he spent all his money upon them, that he might be very fine.   He did not care about his soldiers, nor about the theatre, and only liked to drive out and show his new clothes. He had a coat for every hour of the day; and just as they say of a king, "He is in council," one always said of him, "The Emperor is in the wardrobe."

In the great city in which he lived it was always very merry; every day a number of strangers arrived there.   One day two cheats came: they gave themselves out as weavers, and declared that they could weave the finest stuff any one could imagine. Not only were their colours and patterns, they said, uncommonly beautiful, but the clothes made of the stuff possessed the wonderful quality that they became invisible to any one who was unfit for the office he held, or was incorrigibly stupid.

"Those would be capital clothes!" thought the Emperor. "If I wore those, I should be able to find out what men in my empire are not fit for the places they have; I could distinguish the clever from the stupid. Yes, the stuff must be woven for me directly!"

And he gave the two cheats a great deal of cash in hand, that they might begin their work at once.

As for them, they put up two looms, and pretended to be working; but they had nothing at all on their looms. They at once demanded the finest silk and the costliest gold; this they put into their own pockets, and worked at the empty looms till late into the night.

"I should like to know how far they have got on with the stuff," thought the Emperor. But he felt quite uncomfortable when he

THE EMPEROR INSPECTING THE INVISIBLE STUFF.

thought that those who were not fit for their offices could not see it. He believed, indeed, that he had nothing to fear for himself, but yet he preferred first to send some one else to see how matters stood. All the people in the whole city knew what peculiar power the stuff possessed, and all were anxious to see how bad or how stupid their neighbours were.

"I will send my honest old Minister to the weavers," thought the Emperor. "He can judge best how the stuff looks, for he has sense, and no one understands his office better than he."

Now the good old Minister went out into the hall where the two cheats sat working at the empty looms.

"Mercy preserve us!" thought the old Minister, and he opened his eyes wide. "I cannot see anything at all!" But he did not say this.

Both the cheats begged him to be kind enough to come nearer, and asked if he did not approve of the colours and the pattern. Then they pointed to the empty loom, and the poor old Minister went on opening his eyes; but he could see nothing, for there was nothing to see.

" Mercy!" thought he, " can I indeed be so stupid? I never thought that, and not a soul must know it. Am I not fit for my office?—No, it will never do for me to tell that I could not see the stuff."

" Do you say nothing to it?" said one of the weavers.

" Oh, it is charming,—quite enchanting!" answered the old Minister, as he peered through his spectacles. " What a fine pattern, and what colours! Yes, 1 shall tell the Emperor that I am very much pleased with it."

" Well, we are glad of that," said both the weavers; and then they named the colours, and explained the strange pattern. The old Minister listened attentively, that he might be able to repeat it when the Emperor came. And he did so.

Now the cheats asked for more money, and more silk and gold, which they declared they wanted for weaving. They put all into their own pockets, and not a thread was put upon the loom; but they continued to work at the empty frames as before.

The Emperor soon sent again, dispatching another honest statesman, to see how the weaving was going on, and if the stuff would soon be ready. He fared just like the first: he looked and looked, but, as there was nothing to be seen but the empty looms, he could see nothing.

" Is not that a pretty piece of stuff?" asked the two cheats; and they displayed and explained the handsome pattern which was not there at all.

" I am not stupid!" thought the man,—" it must be my good ,office, for which I am not fit. It is funny enough, but I must not let it be noticed." And so he praised the stuff which he did not see, and expressed his pleasure at the beautiful colours and the charming pattern. " Yes, it is enchanting," he said to the Emperor.

All the people in the town were talking of the gorgeous stuff. The Emperor wished to see it himself while it was still upon the loom. With a whole crowd of chosen men, among whom were also the two honest statemen who had already been there, he went to the two cunning cheats, who were now weaving with might and main without fibre or thread.

" Is that not splendid?" said the two old statesmen, who had already been there once. " Does not your Majesty remark the pattern and the colours?" And then they pointed to the empty loom, for they thought that the others could see the stuff.

" What's this?" thought the Emperor. " I can see nothing at all! That is terrible. Am I stupid? Am I not fit to be Emperor? That would be the most dreadful thing that could happen to me.—Oh, it is *very* pretty!" he said aloud. " It has our exalted approbation." And he nodded in a contented way, and gazed at the empty loom, for he would not say that he saw nothing. The whole suite whom he had with him looked and looked, and saw nothing, any more than the rest; but, like the Emperor, they said, " That *is* pretty!" and counselled him to wear these splendid new clothes for the first time at the great procession that was presently to take place. " It is splendid, tasteful, excellent!" went from mouth to mouth. On all sides there seemed to be genera, rejoicing, and the Emperor gave the cheats the title of Imperial Court Weavers.

The whole night before the morning on which the procession was to take place the cheats were up, and had lighted more than sixteen candles. The people could see that they were hard at work, completing the Emperor's new clothes. They pretended to take the stuff down from the loom; they made cuts in the air with great scissors; they sewed with needles without thread; and at last they said, " Now the clothes are ready!"

The Emperor came himself with his noblest cavaliers; and the two cheats lifted up one arm as if they were holding something, and said, " See, here are the trousers! here is the coat! here is the cloak!" and so on. " It is as light as a spider's web: one would think one had nothing on; but that is just the beauty of it."

" Yes," said all the cavaliers; but they could not see anything, for nothing was there.

" Does your Imperial Majesty please to condescend to undress?" said the cheats; "then we will put you on the new clothes here in front of the great mirror."

The Emperor took off his clothes, and the cheats pretended to put on him each new garment as it was ready; and the Emperor turned round and round before the mirror.

" Oh, how well they look! how capitally they fit!" said all. " What a pattern! what colours! That *is* a splendid dress!"

" They are standing outside with the canopy which is to be borne above your Majesty in the procession!" announced the head master of the ceremonies.

" Well, I am ready," replied the Emperor. " Does it not suit me well?" · And then he turned again to the mirror, for he wanted it to appear as if he contemplated his adornment with great interest.

The chamberlains, who were to carry the train, stooped down with their hands towards the floor, just as if they were picking up the mantle; then they pretended to be holding something up in the air. They did not dare to let it be noticed that they saw nothing.

So the Emperor went in procession under the rich canopy, and every one in the streets said, " How incomparable are the Emperor's new clothes! what a train he has to his mantle! how it fits him!" No one would let it be perceived that he could see nothing, for that would have shown that he was not fit for his office, or was very stupid. No clothes of the Emperor's had ever had such a success as these.

" But he has nothing on!" a little child cried out at last.

" Just hear what that innocent says!" said the father; and one whispered to another what the child had said.

" But he has nothing on!" said the whole people at length. That touched the Emperor, for it seemed to him that they were right; but he thought within himself, " I must go through with the procession." And the chamberlains held on tighter than ever, and carried the train which did not exist at all.

THE GOLOSHES OF FORTUNE.

I.

A Beginning.

IN a house in Copenhagen, not far from the King's New Market, a company—a very large company—had assembled, having received invitations to an evening party there. One-half of the company already sat at the card tables, the other half awaited the result of the hostess's question, " What shall we do now ? " They had progressed so far, and the entertainment began to take some degree of animation. Among other subjects the conversation turned upon the Middle Ages. Some considered that period much more interesting than our own times : yes, Councillor Knap defended this view so zealously that the lady of the house went over at once to his side ; and both loudly exclaimed against Oersted's treatise in the Almanac on old and modern times, in which the chief advantage is given to our own day. The councillor considered the times of the Danish King Hans as the noblest and happiest age.

While the conversation takes this turn, only interrupted for a moment by the arrival of a newspaper, which contained nothing worth reading, we will betake ourselves to the antechamber, where the cloaks, sticks, and goloshes had found a place. Here sat two maids—an old one and a young one. One would have thought they had come to escort their mistresses home ; but, on looking at them more closely, the observer could see that they were not ordinary servants : their shapes were too graceful for that, their complexions too delicate, and the cut of their dresses too uncommon. They were two fairies. The younger was not Fortune, but lady's-maid to one of her ladies of the bed-chamber, who carry about the more trifling gifts of Fortune. The elder one looked somewhat more gloomy—she was Care, who always goes herself in her own exalted person to perform her business, for thus she knows that it is well done.

They were telling each other where they had been that day. The messenger of Fortune had only transacted a few unimportant affairs, as, for instance, she had preserved a new bonnet from a shower of rain, had procured an honest man a bow from a titled Nobody, and so on ; but what she had still to relate was something quite extraordinary.

" I can likewise tell," said she, " that to-day is my birthday ; and in honour of it a pair of goloshes has been entrusted to me, which I am to bring to the human race. These goloshes have the property that every one who puts them on is at once transported to the time and place in which he likes best to be—every wish in reference to time, place, and circumstance is at once fulfilled ; and so for once man can be happy here below !"

"Believe me," said Care, "he will be very unhappy, and will bless the moment when he can get rid of the goloshes again."

THE GOLOSHES LEFT AT THE DOOR.

"What are you thinking of ? " retorted the other. "Now I shall put them at the door. Somebody will take them by mistake, and become the happy one ! "

You see, that was the dialogue they held.

II.

What happened to the Councillor.

It was late. Councillor Knap, lost in contemplation of the times of King Hans, wished to get home ; and fate willed that instead of his own goloshes he should put on those of Fortune, and thus went out into East Street. But by the power of the goloshes he had been put back three hundred years—into the days of King Hans ; and therefore he put his foot into mud and mire in the street, because in those days there was not any pavement.

"Why, this is horrible—how dirty it is here!" said the councillor. "The good pavement is gone, and all the lamps are put out."

The moon did not yet stand high enough to give much light, and the air was tolerably thick, so that all objects seemed to melt together in the darkness. At the next corner a lamp hung before a picture of the Madonna, but the light it gave was as good as none; he only noticed it when he stood just under it, and his eyes fell upon the painted figure.

"That is probably a museum of art," thought he, "where they have forgotten to take down the sign."

A couple of men in the costume of those past days went by him.

"How they look!" he said. "They must come from a masquerade."

Suddenly there was a sound of drums and fifes, and torches gleamed brightly. The councillor started. And now he saw a strange procession go past. First came a whole troop of drummers, beating their instruments very dexterously; they were followed by men-at-arms, with longbows and crossbows. The chief man in the procession was a clerical lord. The astonished councillor asked what was the meaning of this, and who the man might be.

"That is the Bishop of Zealand."

"What in the world has come to the bishop?" said the councillor, with a sigh, shaking his head. "This could not possibly be the bishop!"

Ruminating on this, and without looking to the right or to the left, the councillor went through the East Street, and over the Highbridge Place. The bridge which led to the Palace Square was not to be found; he perceived the shore of a shallow water, and at length encountered two people, who sat in a boat.

"Do you wish to be ferried over to the Holm, sir?" they asked.

"To the Holm!" repeated the councillor, who did not know, you see, in what period he was. "I want to go to Christian's Haven and to Little Turf Street."

The men stared at him.

"Pray tell me where the bridge is?" said he. "It is shameful that no lanterns are lighted here; and it is as muddy, too, as if one were walking in a marsh." But the longer he talked with the boatmen the less could he understand them. "I don't understand your Bornholm talk," he at last cried, angrily, and turned his back upon them. He could not find the bridge, nor was there any paling. "It is quite scandalous how things look here!" he said—never had he thought his own times so miserable as this evening. "I think it will be best if I take a cab," thought he. But where were the cabs?—not one was to be seen. "I shall have to go back to the King's New Market, where there are many carriages standing, otherwise I shall never get as far as Christian's Haven."

Now he went towards East Street, and had almost gone through it when the moon burst forth.

"What in the world have they been erecting here?" he exclaimed, when he saw the East Gate, which in those days stood at the end of East Street.

THE COUNCILLOR IS ALARMED.

In the meantime, however, he found a passage open, and through this he came out upon our New Market; but it was a broad meadow. Single bushes stood forth, and across the meadow ran a great canal or stream. A few miserable wooden booths for Dutch skippers were erected on the opposite shore.

"Either I behold a *Fata Morgana*, or I am tipsy," sighed the coun‐ cillor. "What can that be? what can that be?"

He turned back, in the full persuasion that he must be ill. In walk‐ ing up the street he looked more closely at the houses; most of them were built of laths, and many were only thatched with straw.

"No, I don't feel well at all!" he lamented. "And yet I only drank one glass of punch! But I cannot stand that; and besides, it was very foolish to give us punch and warm salmon. I shall mention that to our hostess—the agent's lady. Suppose I go back, and say how I feel? But that looks ridiculous, and it is a question if they will be up still."

He looked for the house, but could not find it.

"That is dreadful!" he cried; "I don't know East Street again. Not one shop is to be seen ; old, miserable, tumble-down huts are all I see, as if I were at Roeskilde or Ringstedt.   Oh, I am ill!   It's no use to make ceremony.   But where in all the world is the agent's house ?   It is no longer the same ; but within there are people up still.   I certainly must be ill!''

He now reached a half-open door, where the light shone through a chink.   It was a tavern of that date—a kind of beer-house.   The room had the appearance of a Dutch wine shop ; a number of people, consisting of seamen, citizens of Copenhagen, and a few scholars, sat in deep conversation over their jugs, and paid little attention to the new comer.

"I beg pardon," said the councillor to the hostess, "but I feel very unwell ; would you let them get me a fly to go to Christian's Haven ? "

The woman looked at him and shook her head ; then she spoke to him in German.

The councillor now supposed that she did not understand Danish, so he repeated his wish in the German language.   This, and his costume, convinced the woman that he was a foreigner.   She soon understood that he felt unwell, and therefore brought him a jug of water. It certainly tasted a little of sea water, though it had been taken from the spring outside.

The councillor leaned his head on his hand, drew a deep breath, and thought of all the strange things that were happening about him.

"Is that to-day's number of the ' Day ' ? " he said, quite mechanically, for he saw that the woman was putting away a large sheet of paper.

She did not understand what he meant, but handed him the leaf : it was a woodcut representing a strange appearance in the air which had been seen in the city of Cologne.

"That is very old! " said the councillor, who became quite cheerful at sight of this antiquity.   "How did you come by this strange leaf ? That is very interesting, although the whole thing is a fable.   Now-a-days these appearances are explained to be northern lights that have been seen ; probably they arise from electricity."

Those who sat nearest to him and heard his speech, looked at him in surprise, and one of them rose, took off his hat respectfully, and said, with a very grave face,

" You must certainly be a very learned man, sir! "

" Oh, no! " replied the councillor ; " I can only say a word or two about things one ought to understand."

" *Modestia* is a beautiful virtue," said the man.   "Moreover, I must say to your speech, ' *mihi secus videtur ;*' yet I will gladly suspend my *judicium.*"

" May I ask with whom I have the pleasure of speaking ? " asked the councillor.

" I am a bachelor of theology," replied the man.

This answer sufficed for the councillor ; the title corresponded with the garb.

"Certainly," he thought, "this must be an old village schoolmaster, a queer character, such as one finds sometimes over in Jutland."

"This is certainly not a *locus docendi*," began the man; "but I beg you to take the trouble to speak. You are doubtless well read in the ancients?"

"Oh, yes," replied the councillor. "I am fond of reading useful old books; and am fond of the modern ones, too, with the exception of the 'Every-day Stories,' of which we have enough, in all conscience."

"Every-day Stories?" said the bachelor, inquiringly.

"Yes, I mean the new romances we have now."

"Oh!" said the man, with a smile, "they are very witty, and are much read at court. The King is especially partial to the romance by Messieurs Iffven and Gaudian, which talks about King Arthur and his knights of the Round Table. He has jested about it with his noble lords.

"That I have certainly not yet read," said the councillor: "that must be quite a new book published by Heiberg."

"No," retorted the man, "it is not published by Heiberg, but by Godfrey von Gehmen.*

"Indeed! is he the author?" asked the councillor. "That is a very old name: was not that the name of about the first printer who appeared in Denmark?"

"Why, he *is* our first printer," replied the man.

So far it had gone well. But now one of the men began to speak of a pestilence which he said had been raging a few years ago: he meant the plague of 1484. The councillor supposed that he meant the cholera, and so the conversation went on tolerably. The Freebooters' War of 1490 was so recent that it could not escape mention. The English pirates had taken ships from the very wharves, said the man; and the councillor, who was well acquainted with the events of 1801, joined in manfully against the English. The rest of the talk, however, did not pass over so well; every moment there was a contradiction. The good bachelor was terribly ignorant, and the simplest assertion of the councillor seemed too bold or too fantastic. They looked at each other, and when it became too bad, the bachelor spoke Latin, in the hope that he would be better understood; but it was of no use.

"How are you now?" asked the hostess, and she plucked the councillor by the sleeve.

Now his recollection came back: in the course of the conversation he had forgotten everything that had happened.

"Good heavens! where am I?" he said, and he felt dizzy when he thought of it.

"We'll drink claret, mead, and Bremen beer," cried one of the guests, "and you shall drink with us."

Two girls came in. One of them had on a cap of two colours. They poured out drink and bowed: the councillor felt a cold shudder running all down his back. "What's that? what's that?" he cried; but he was obliged to drink with them. They took possession of the good man

---

* The first printer and publisher in Denmark, under King Hans.

quite politely. He was in despair, and when one said that he was tipsy he felt not the slightest doubt regarding the truth of the statement, and only begged them to procure him a droschky. Now they thought he was speaking Muscovite.

Never had he been in such rude vulgar company.

" One would think the country was falling back into heathenism," was his reflection. " This is the most terrible moment of my life."

But at the same time the idea occurred to him to bend down under the table, and then to creep to the door. He did so; but just as he had reached the entry the others discovered his intention. They seized him by the feet; and now the goloshes, to his great good fortune, came off, and—the whole enchantment vanished.

The councillor saw quite plainly, in front of him, a lamp burning, and behind it a great building; everything looked familiar and splendid. It was East Street, as we know it now. He lay with his legs turned towards a porch, and opposite to him sat the watchman asleep.

" Good heavens! have I been lying here in the street dreaming?" he exclaimed. " Yes, this is East Street sure enough! how splendidly bright and gay! It is terrible what an effect that one glass of punch must have had on me!"

Two minutes afterwards he was sitting in a fly, which drove him out to Christian's Haven. He thought of the terror and anxiety he had undergone, and praised from his heart the happy present, our own time, which, with all its shortcomings, was far better than the period in which he had been placed a short time before.

III.

The Watchman's Adventures.

" On my word, yonder lies a pair a goloshes!" said the watchman. " They must certainly belong to the lieutenant who lives upstairs. They are lying close to the door."

The honest man would gladly have rung the bell and delivered them, for upstairs there was a light still burning; but he did not wish to disturb the other people in the house, and so he let it alone.

" It must be very warm to have a pair of such things on," said he. " How nice and soft the leather is "! They fitted his feet very well. " How droll it is in the world! Now, he might lie down in his warm bed, and yet he does not! There he is pacing up and down the room. He is a happy man! He has neither wife nor children, and every evening he is at a party. Oh, I wish I were he, then I should be a happy man!"

As he uttered the wish, the goloshes he had put on produced their effect, and the watchman was transported into the body and being of the lieutenant. Then he stood up in the room, and held a little pink paper in his fingers, on which was a poem, a poem written by the lieu-

tenant himself. For who is there who has not once in his life had a
poetic moment? and at such a moment, if one writes down one's
thoughts, there is poetry.

Yes, people write poetry when they are in love; but a prudent man
does not print such poems. The lieutenant was in love—and poor—
that's a triangle, or, so to speak, the half of a broken square of happiness. The lieutenant felt that very keenly, and so he laid his head
against the window-frame and sighed a deep sigh.

"The poor watchman in the street yonder is far happier than I. He
does not know what I call want. He has a home, a wife, and children,
who weep at his sorrow and rejoice at his joy. Oh! I should be happier
than I am, could I change my being for his, and pass through life with
his humble desires and hopes. Yes, he is happier than I!"

THE WATCHMAN THINKS OF GOING TO THE MOON.

In that same moment the watchman became a watchman again; for
through the power of the goloshes of Fortune he had assumed the personality of the lieutenant; but then we know he felt far less content,
and preferred to be just what he had despised a short time before. So
the watchman became a watchman again.

"That was an ugly dream," said he, "but droll enough. It seemed
to me that I was the lieutenant up yonder, and that it was not pleasant
at all. I was without the wife and the boys, who are now ready to half
stifle me with kisses."

He sat down again and nodded. The dream would not go quite out
of his thoughts. He had the goloshes still on his feet. A falling star
glided down along the horizon.

"There went one," said he, "but for all that, there are enough left.
I should like to look at those things a little nearer, especially the moon,
for that won't vanish under one's hands. The student for whom my wife

washes says that when we die we fly from one star to another. That's not true, but it would be very nice. If I could only make a little spring up there, then my body might lie here on the stairs for all I care."

Now there are certain assertions we should be very cautious of making in this world, but doubly careful when we have goloshes of Fortune on our feet. Just hear what happened to the watchman.

So far as we are concerned, we all understand the rapidity of dispatch by steam; we have tried it either in railways, or in steamers across the sea. But this speed is as the crawling of the sloth or the march of the snail in comparison with the swiftness with which light travels. That flies nineteen million times quicker. Death is an electric shock we receive in our hearts, and on the wings of electricity the liberated soul flies away. The sunlight requires eight minutes and a few seconds for a journey of more than ninety-five millions of miles; on the wings of electric power the soul requires only a few moments to accomplish the same flight. The space between the orbs of the universe is, for her, not greater than, for us, the distances between the houses of our friends dwelling in the same town and even living close together. Yet this electric shock costs us the life of the body here below, unless, like the watchman, we have the magic goloshes on.

In a few seconds the watchman had traversed the distance of two hundred and sixty thousand miles to the moon, which body, as we know, consists of a much lighter material than that of our earth, and is, as we should say, soft as new-fallen snow. He found himself on one of the many ring mountains with which we are familiar from Dr. Mâdler's great map of the moon. Within the ring a great bowl-shaped hollow went down to the depth of a couple of miles. At the base of the hollow lay a town, of whose appearance we can only form an idea by pouring the white of an egg into a glass of water: the substance here was just as soft as white of egg, and formed similar towers, and cupolas, and terraces like sails, transparent and floating in the thin air. Our earth hung over his head like a great dark red ball.

He immediately became aware of a number of beings, who were certainly what we call " men," but their appearance was very different from ours. If they had been put up in a row and painted, one would have said, " That's a beautiful arabesque!" They had also a language, but no one could expect that the soul of the watchman should understand it. But the watchman's soul did understand it, for our souls have far greater abilities than we suppose. Does not its wonderful dramatic talent show itself in our dreams? Then every one of our acquaintances appears speaking in his own character and with his own voice, in a way that not one of us could imitate in our waking hours. How does our soul bring back to us people of whom we have not thought for many years? Suddenly they come into our souls with their smallest peculiarities about them. In fact, it is a fearful thing, that memory which our souls possess: it can reproduce every sin, every bad thought. And then, it may be asked, shall we be able to give an account of every idle word that has been in our hearts and on our lips?

Thus the watchman's soul understood the language of the people in the moon very well. They disputed about this earth, and doubted if it could be inhabited; the air, they asserted, must be too thick for a sensible moon-man to live there. They considered that the moon alone was peopled; for that, they said, was the real body in which the old-world people dwelt. They also talked of politics.

But let us go down to the East Street, and see how it fared with the body of the watchman.

He sat lifeless upon the stairs. His pike had fallen out of his hand, and his eyes stared up at the moon, which his honest body was wondering about.

"What's o'clock, watchman?" asked a passer-by. But the man who didn't answer was the watchman. Then the passengers tweaked him quite gently by the nose, and then he lost his balance. There lay the body stretched out at full length—the man was dead. All his comrades were very much frightened: dead he was, and dead he remained. It was reported, and it was discussed, and in the morning the body was carried out to the hospital.

That would be a pretty jest for the soul if it should chance to come back, and probably seek its body in the East Street, and not find it! Most likely it would go first to the police and afterwards to the address office, that inquiries might be made from thence respecting the missing goods; and then it would wander out to the hospital. But we may console ourselves with the idea that the soul is most clever when it acts upon its own account; it is the body that makes it stupid.

As we have said, the watchman's body was taken to the hospital, and brought into the washing-room; and naturally enough the first thing they did there was to pull off the goloshes; and then the soul had to come back. It took its way directly towards the body, and in a few seconds there was life in the man. He declared that this had been the most terrible night of his life; he would not have such feelings again, not for a shilling; but now it was past and over.

The same day he was allowed to leave; but the goloshes remained at the hospital.

IV.

A Great Moment.—A very Unusual Journey.

Every one who belongs to Copenhagen knows the look of the entrance to the Frederick's Hospital in Copenhagen; but as, perhaps, a few will read this story who do not belong to Copenhagen, it becomes necessary to give a short description of it.

The hospital is separated from the street by a tolerably high railing, in which the thick iron rails stand so far apart, that certain very thin inmates are said to have squeezed between them, and thus paid their little visits outside the premises. The part of the body most difficult to get through was the head; and here, as it often happens in the world, small heads were the most fortunate. This will be sufficient as an introduction.

One of the young volunteers, of whom one could only say in one sense that he had a great head, had the watch that evening. The rain was pouring down; but in spite of this obstacle he wanted to go out, only for a quarter of an hour. It was needless, he thought, to tell the porter of his wish, especially if he could slip through between the rails. There lay the goloshes which the watchman had forgotten. It never occurred to him in the least that they were goloshes of Fortune. They would do him very good service in this rainy weather, and he pulled them on. Now the question was whether he could squeeze through the bars; till now he had never tried it. There he stood.

"I wish to goodness I had my head outside!" cried he. And immediately, though his head was very thick and big, it glided easily and quickly through. The goloshes must have understood it well; but now the body was to slip through also, and that could not be done.

"I'm too fat," said he. "I thought my head was the thickest. I shan't get through."

Now he wanted to pull his head back quickly, but he could not manage it: he could move his neck, but that was all. His first feeling was one of anger, and then his spirits sank down to zero. The goloshes of Fortune had placed him in this terrible condition, and, unfortunately, it never occurred to him to wish himself free. No: instead of wishing, he only strove, and could not stir from the spot. The rain poured down; not a creature was to be seen in the street; he could not reach the gate bell, and how was he to get loose? He foresaw that he would have to remain here until the morning, and then they would have to send for a blacksmith, to file through the iron bars. But such a business is not to be done quickly. The whole charity school would be upon its legs; the whole sailors' quarter close by would come up and see him standing in the pillory; and a fine crowd there would be.

"Hu!" he cried, "the blood's rising to my head, and I shall go mad! Yes, I'm going mad! If I were free, most likely it would pass over."

That's what he ought to have said at first. The very moment he had uttered the thought his head was free; and now he rushed in, quite dazed with the fright the goloshes of Fortune had given him. But we must not think the whole affair was over; there was much worse to come yet.

The night passed away, and the following day too, and nobody sent for the goloshes. In the evening a display of oratory was to take place in an amateur theatre in a distant street. The house was crammed; and among the audience was the volunteer from the hospital, who appeared to have forgotten his adventure of the previous evening. He had the goloshes on, for they had not been sent for; and as it was dirty in the streets, they might do him good service. A new piece was recited: it was called "My Aunt's Spectacles." These were spectacles which, when any one put them on in a great assembly of people, made all present look like cards, so that one could prophesy from them all that would happen in the coming year.

The idea struck him : he would have liked to possess such a pair of spectacles. If they were used rightly, they would perhaps enable the wearer to look into people's hearts; and that, he thought, would be more interesting than to see what was going to happen in the next year ; for future events would be known in time, but the people's thoughts never.

"Now I'll look at the row of ladies and gentlemen on the first bench : if one could look directly into their hearts ! yes, that must be a hollow, a sort of shop. How my eyes would wander about in that shop ! In every lady's, yonder, I should doubtless find a great milliner's warehouse: with this one here the shop is empty, but it would do no harm to have it cleaned out. But would there really be such shops ? Ah, yes ! " he continued, sighing, " I know one in which all the goods are first-rate, but there's a servant in it already ; that's the only drawback in the whole shop ! From one and another the word would be ' Please to step in ! ' Oh that I might only step in, like a neat little thought, and slip through their hearts !"

That was the word of command for the goloshes. The volunteer shrivelled up, and began to take a very remarkable journey through the hearts of the first row of spectators. The first heart through which he passed was that of a lady ; but he immediately fancied himself in the Orthopædic Institute, in the room where the plaster casts of deformed limbs are kept hanging against the walls ; the only difference was, that these casts were formed in the institute when the patients came in, but here in the heart they were formed and preserved after the good persons had gone away. For they were casts of female friends, whose bodily and mental faults were preserved here.

Quickly he had passed into another female heart. But this seemed to him like a great holy church ; the white dove of innocence fluttered over the high altar. Gladly would he have sunk down on his knees ; but he was obliged to go away into the next heart. Still, however, he heard the tones of the organ, and it seemed to him that he himself had become another and a better man. He felt himself not unworthy to enter into the next sanctuary, which showed itself in the form of a poor garret, containing a sick mother. But through the window the warm sun streamed in, and two sky-blue birds sang full of childlike joy, while the sick mother prayed for a blessing on her daughter.

Now he crept on his hands and knees through an over-filled butcher's shop. There was meat, and nothing but meat, wherever he went. It was the heart of a rich respectable man, whose name is certainly to be found in the address book.

Now he was in the heart of this man's wife : this heart was an old dilapidated pigeon-house. The husband's portrait was used as a mere weathercock : it stood in connection with the doors, and these doors opened and shut according as the husband turned.

Then he came into a cabinet of mirrors, such as we find in the castle of Rosenburg ; but the mirrors magnified in a great degree. In the middle of the floor sat, like a Grand Lama, the insignificant *I* of the proprietor, astonished in the contemplation of his own greatness.

Then he fancied himself transported into a narrow needle-case full of pointed needles; and he thought, "This must decidedly be the heart of an old maid!" But that was not the case. It was a young officer, wearing several orders, and of whom one said, "He's a man of intellect and heart."

Quite confused was the poor volunteer when he emerged from the heart of the last person in the first row. He could not arrange his thoughts, and fancied it must be his powerful imagination which had run away with him.

"Gracious powers!" he sighed, "I must certainly have a great tendency to go mad. It is also unconscionably hot in here: the blood is rising to my head!"

THE VOLUNTEER TRIES A BLISTER.

And now he remembered the great event of the last evening, how his head had been caught between the iron rails of the hospital.

"That's where I must have caught it," thought he. "I must do something at once. A Russian bath might be very good. I wish I were lying on the highest board in the bath-house."

And there he lay on the highest board in the vapour bath; but he was lying there in all his clothes, in boots and goloshes, and the hot drops from the ceiling were falling on his face.

"Hi!" he cried, and jumped down to take a plunge bath.

The attendant uttered a loud cry on seeing a person there with all his clothes on. The volunteer had, however, enough presence of mind to whisper to him, "It's for a wager!" But the first thing he did when he got into his own room was to put a big blister on the nape of his neck, and another on his back, that they might draw out his madness.

Next morning he had a very sore back; and that was all he had got by the goloshes of Fortune.

V.

The Transformation of the Copying Clerk.

The watchman, whom we surely have not yet forgotten, in the mean-time thought of the goloshes, which he had found and brought to the hospital. He took them away; but as neither the lieutenant nor any one in the street would own them, they were taken to the police office.

"They look exactly like my own goloshes," said one of the copying gentlemen, as he looked at the unowned articles and put them beside his own. "More than a shoemaker's eye is required to distinguish them from one another."

"Mr. Copying Clerk," said a servant, coming in with some papers.

The copying clerk turned and spoke to the man: when he had done this, he turned to look at the goloshes again; he was in great doubt if the right-hand or the left-hand pair belonged to him.

"It must be those that are wet," he thought. Now here he thought wrong, for these were the goloshes of Fortune; but why should not the police be sometimes mistaken? He put them on, thrust his papers into his pocket, and put a few manuscripts under his arm, for they were to be read at home, and abstracts to be made from them. But now it was Sunday morning, and the weather was fine. "A walk to Frede-ricksburg would do me good," said he; and he went out accordingly.

There could not be a quieter, steadier person than this young man. We grant him his little walk with all our hearts; it will certainly do him good after so much sitting. At first he only walked like a vegeta-ting creature, so the goloshes had no opportunity of displaying their magic power.

In the avenue he met an acquaintance, one of our younger poets, who told him that he was going to start, next day, on a summer trip.

"Are you going away again already?" asked the copying clerk. "What a happy, free man you are! You can fly wherever you like; we others have a chain to our foot."

"But it is fastened to the bread tree!" replied the poet. "You need not be anxious for the morrow; and when you grow old you get a pension."

"But you are better off, after all," said the copying clerk. "It must be a pleasure to sit and write poetry. Everybody says agreeable things to you, and then you are your own master. Ah, you should just try it, poring over the frivolous affairs in the court."

The poet shook his head; the copying clerk shook his head also: each retained his own opinion; and thus they parted.

"They are a strange race, these poets!" thought the copying clerk. "I should like to try and enter into such a nature—to become a poet myself. I am certain I should not write such complaining verses as the rest. What a splendid spring day for a poet! The air is so remarkably clear, the clouds are so beautiful, and the green smells so sweet. For many years I have not felt as I feel at this moment."

We already notice that he has become a poet. To point this out would, in most cases, be what the Germans call "mawkish." It is a foolish fancy to imagine a poet different from other people, for among the latter there may be natures more poetical than those of many an acknowledged poet. The difference is only that the poet has a better spiritual memory: his ears hold fast the feeling and the idea until they are embodied clearly and firmly in words; and the others cannot do that. But the transition from an every-day nature to that of a poet is always a transition, and as such it must be noticed in the copying clerk.

"What glorious fragrance!" he cried. "How it reminds me of the violets at Aunt Laura's! Yes, that was when I was a little boy. I have not thought of that for a long time. The good old lady! She lies yonder, by the canal. She always had a twig or a couple of green shoots in the water, let the winter be as severe as it might. The violets bloomed, while I had to put warm farthings against the frozen window-panes to make peep-holes. That was a pretty view. Out in the canal the ships were frozen in, and deserted by the whole crew; a screaming crow was the only living creature left. Then, when the spring breezes blew, it all became lively: the ice was sawn asunder amid shouting and cheers, the ships were tarred and rigged, and then they sailed away to strange lands. I remained here, and must always remain, and sit at the police office, and let others take passports for abroad. That's my fate. Oh, yes!" and he sighed deeply. Suddenly he paused. "Good Heaven! what is come to me? I never thought or felt as I do now. It must be the spring air: it is just as dizzying as it is charming!" He felt in his pockets for his papers. "These will give me something else to think of," said he, and let his eyes wander over the first leaf. There he read: "'*Dame Sigbirth; an original tragedy in five acts.*' What is that? And it is my own hand. Have I written this tragedy? '*The Intrigue on the Promenade; or, the Day of Penance.—Vaudeville.*' But where did I get that from? It must have been put into my pocket. Here is a letter. Yes, it was from the manager of the theatre; the pieces were rejected, and the letter is not at all politely worded. H'm! H'm!" said the copying clerk, and he sat down upon a bench: his thoughts were elastic; his head was quite soft. Involuntarily he grasped one of the nearest flowers; it was a common little daisy. What the botanists require several lectures to explain to us, this flower told in a minute. It told the glory of its birth; it told of the strength of the sunlight, which spread out the delicate leaves and made them give out fragrance. Then he thought of the battles of life, which likewise awaken feelings in our breasts. Air and light are the lovers of the flower, but light is the favoured one. Towards the light it turned, and only when the light vanished the flower rolled her leaves together and slept in the embrace of the air.

"It is light that adorns me!" said the Flower.

"But the air allows you to breathe," whispered the poet's voice.

Just by him stood a boy, knocking with his stick upon the marshy ground. The drops of water spurted up among the green twigs, and the copying clerk thought of the millions of infusoria which were cast up on high with the drops, which was the same to them, in proportion to their size, as it would be to us if we were hurled high over the region of clouds. And the copying clerk thought of this, and of the great change which had taken place within him; he smiled. "I sleep and dream! It is wonderful, though, how naturally one can dream, and yet know all the time that it is a dream. I should like to be able to remember it all clearly to-morrow when I wake. I seem to myself quite unusually excited. What a clear appreciation I have of everything, and how free I feel! But I am certain that if I remember anything of it to-morrow, it will be nonsense. That has often been so with me before. It is with all the clever famous things one says and hears in dreams, as with the money of the elves under the earth; when one receives it, it is rich and beautiful, but looked at by daylight, it is nothing but stones and dried leaves. Ah!" he sighed, quite plaintively, and gazed at the chirping birds, as they sprang merrily from bough to bough, "they are much better off than I. Flying is a noble art. Happy he who is born with wings. Yes, if I could change myself into anything, it should be into a lark."

In a moment his coat-tails and sleeves grew together and formed wings; his clothes became feathers, and his goloshes claws. He noticed it quite plainly, and laughed inwardly. "Well, now I can see that I am dreaming, but so wildly I have never dreamed before." And he flew up into the green boughs and sang; but there was no poetry in the song, for the poetic nature was gone. The goloshes, like every one who wishes to do any business thoroughly, could only do one thing at a time. He wished to be a poet, and he became one. Then he wished to be a little bird, and, in changing thus, the former peculiarity was lost.

"That is charming!" he said. "In the day-time I sit in the police office among the driest of law papers; at night I can dream that I am flying about, as a lark in the Fredericksburg Garden. One could really write quite a popular comedy upon it."

Now he flew down into the grass, turned his head in every direction, and beat with his beak upon the bending stalks of grass, which, in proportion to his size, seemed to him as long as palm branches of Northern Africa.

It was only for a moment, and then all around him became as the blackest night. It seemed to him that some immense substance was cast over him; it was a great cap, which a sailor boy threw over the bird. A hand came in and seized the copying clerk by the back and wings in a way that made him whistle. In his first terror he cried aloud, "The impudent rascal! I am copying clerk at the police office!" But that sounded to the boy only like "piep! piep!" and he tapped the bird on the beak and wandered on with him.

In the alley the boy met with two other boys, who belonged to the educated classes, socially speaking; but, according to abilities, they ranked in the lowest class in the school. These bought the bird for a few Danish shillings; and so the copying clerk was carried back to Copenhagen.

"It's a good thing that I am dreaming," he said, " or I should become really angry. First I was a poet, and now I'm a lark! Yes, it must have been the poetic nature which transformed me into that little creature. It is a miserable state of things, especially when one falls into the hands of boys. I should like to know what the end of it will be."

The boys carried him into a very elegant room. A stout smiling lady received them. But she was not at all gratified to see the common field bird, as she called the lark, coming in too. Only for one day she would consent to it; but they must put the bird in the empty cage which stood by the window.

THE COPYING CLERK CHANGES HANDS.

"Perhaps that will please Polly," she added, and laughed at a great Parrot swinging himself proudly in his ring in the handsome brass cage.

"It's Polly's birthday," she said, simply, "so the little field bird shall congratulate him."

Polly did not answer a single word; he only swung proudly to and fro. But a pretty Canary bird, who had been brought here last summer out of his warm fragrant fatherland, began to sing loudly.

"Screamer!" said the lady; and she threw a white handkerchief over the cage.

"Piep! piep!" sighed he; "here's a terrible snow-storm." And thus sighing, he was silent.

The copying clerk, or, as the lady called him, the field bird, was placed in a little cage close to the Canary, and not far from the Parrot. The only human words which Polly could say, and which often sounded very comically, were "*Come, let's be men now!*" Everything else that he screamed out was just as unintelligible as the song of the Canary bird, except for the copying clerk, who was now also a bird, and who understood his comrades very well.

"I flew under the green palm tree and the blossoming almond tree!" sang the Canary. "I flew with my brothers and sisters over the beautiful flowers and over the bright sea, where the plants waved in the depths. I also saw many beautiful parrots, who told the merriest stories."

"Those were wild birds," replied the Parrot. "They had no education. Let us be men now! Why don't you laugh? If the lady and all the strangers could laugh at it, so can you. It is a great fault to have no taste for what is pleasant. No, let us be men now."

"Do you remember the pretty girls who danced under the tents spread out beneath the blooming trees? Do you remember the sweet fruits and the cooling juice in the wild plants?"

"Oh, yes!" replied the Parrot; "but here I am far better off. I have good care and genteel treatment. I know I've a good head, and I don't ask for more. Let us be men now. You are what they call a poetic soul. I have thorough knowledge and wit. You have genius, but no prudence. You mount up into those high natural notes of yours, and then you get covered up. That is never done to me; no, no, for I cost them a little more. I make an impression with my beak, and can cast wit round me. Now let us be men!"

"O my poor blooming fatherland!" sang the Canary. "I will praise thy dark green trees and thy quiet bays, where the branches kiss the clear watery mirror; I'll sing of the joy of all my shining brothers and sisters, where the plants grow by the desert springs."

"Now, pray leave off these dismal tones," cried the Parrot. "Sing something at which one can laugh! Laughter is the sign of the highest mental development. Look if a dog or a horse can laugh! No: they can cry; but laughter—that is given to men alone. Ho! ho! ho!" screamed Polly, and finished the jest with "Let us be men now."

"You little grey Northern bird," said the Canary; "so you have also become a prisoner. It is certainly cold in your woods, but still liberty is there. Fly out! they have forgotten to close your cage; the upper window is open. Fly! fly!"

Instinctively the copying clerk obeyed, and flew forth from his prison. At the same moment the half opened door of the next room creaked, and stealthily, with fierce sparkling eyes, the house cat crept in, and made chase upon him. The Canary fluttered in its cage, the Parrot flapped its wings, and cried "Let us be men now." The copying clerk felt mortally afraid, and flew through the window, away over the houses and streets; at last he was obliged to rest a little.

The house opposite had a homelike look: one of the windows stood open, and he flew in. It was his own room: he perched upon the table.

"Let us be men now," he broke out, involuntarily imitating the Parrot; and in the same moment he was restored to the form of the copying clerk; but he was sitting on the table.

"Heaven preserve me!" he cried. "How could I have come here

and fallen so soundly asleep? That was an unquiet dream, too, that I had. The whole thing was great nonsense."

VI.

The Best that the Goloshes brought.

On the following day, quite early in the morning, as the clerk still lay in bed, there came a tapping at his door: it was his neighbour who lodged on the same floor, a young theologian; and he came in.

"Lend me your goloshes," said he. "It is very wet in the garden, but the sun shines gloriously, and I should like to smoke a pipe down there."

He put on the goloshes, and was soon in the garden, which contained a plum tree and an apple tree. Even a little garden like this is highly prized in the midst of great cities.

The theologian wandered up and down the path; it was only six o'clock, and a post-horn sounded out in the street.

"Oh, travelling! travelling!" he cried out, "that's the greatest happiness in all the world. That's the highest goal of my wishes. Then this disquietude that I feel would be stilled. But it would have to be far away. I should like to see beautiful Switzerland, to travel through Italy, to——"

Yes, it was a good thing that the goloshes took effect immediately, for he might have gone too far even for himself, and for us others too. He was travelling; he was in the midst of Switzerland, packed tightly with eight others in the interior of a diligence. He had a headache and a weary feeling in his neck, and his feet had gone to sleep, for they were swollen by the heavy boots he had on. He was hovering in a condition between sleeping and waking. In his right-hand pocket he had his letter of credit, in his left-hand pocket his passport, and a few louis d'or were sewn into a little bag he wore on his breast. Whenever he dozed off, he dreamed he had lost one or other of these possessions; and then he would start up in a feverish way, and the first movement his hand made was to describe a triangle from left to right, and towards his breast, to feel whether he still possessed them or not. Umbrellas, hats, and walking sticks swang in the net over him, and almost took away the prospect, which was impressive enough: he glanced out at it, and his heart sang what one poet at least, whom we know, has sung in Switzerland, but has not yet printed:

"'Tis a prospect as fine as heart can desire,
　Before me Mont Blanc the rough:
'Tis pleasant to tarry here and admire,
　If only you've money enough."

Great, grave, and dark was all nature around him. The pine woods looked like little mosses upon the high rocks, whose summits were lost in cloudy mists; and then it began to snow, and the wind blew cold.

"Hu!" he sighed; "if we were only on the other side of the Alps, then it would be summer, and I should have got money on my letter of credit: my anxiety about this prevents me from enjoying Switzerland. Oh, if I were only at the other side!"

And then he was on the other side, in the midst of Italy, between Florence and Rome. The lake Thrasymene lay spread out in the evening light, like flaming gold among the dark blue hills. Here, where Hannibal beat Flaminius, the grape-vines held each other by their green fingers; pretty half naked children were keeping a herd of coal-black pigs under a clump of fragrant laurels by the way-side. If we could reproduce this scene accurately, all would cry, " Glorious Italy!" But neither the theologian nor any of his travelling companions in the carriage of the vetturino thought this.

Poisonous flies and gnats flew into the carriage by thousands. In vain they beat the air frantically with a myrtle branch—the flies stung them nevertheless. There was not one person in the carriage whose face was not swollen and covered with stings. The poor horses looked miserable, the flies tormented them wofully, and it only mended the matter for a moment when the coachman dismounted and scraped them clean from the insects that sat upon them in great swarms. Now the sun sank down; a short but icy coldness pervaded all nature; it was like the cold air of a funeral vault after the sultry summer day; and all around the hills and clouds put on that remarkable green tone which we notice on some old pictures, and consider unnatural unless we have ourselves witnessed a similar play of colour. It was a glorious spectacle; but the stomachs of all were empty and their bodies exhausted, and every wish of the heart turned towards a resting-place for the night; but how could that be won? To descry this resting-place all eyes were turned more eagerly to the road than towards the beauties of nature.

The way now led through an olive wood: he could have fancied himself passing between knotty willow trunks at home. Here, by the solitary inn, a dozen crippled beggars had taken up their positions: the quickest among them looked, to quote an expression of Marryat's, like the eldest son of Famine, who had just come of age. The others were either blind or had withered legs, so that they crept about on their hands, or they had withered arms with fingerless hands. This was misery in rags indeed. "*Eccellenza, miserabili!*" they sighed, and stretched forth their diseased limbs. The hostess herself, in untidy hair, and dressed in a dirty blouse, received her guests. The doors were tied up with string; the floor of the room was of brick, and half of it was grubbed up; bats flew about under the roof, and the smell within——

"Yes, lay the table down in the stable," said one of the travellers. "There, at least, one knows what one is breathing."

The windows were opened, so that a little fresh air might find its way in; but quicker than the air came the withered arms and the continual whining, "*Miserabili, Eccellenza!*" On the walls were many inscriptions; half of them were against "*La bella Italia.*"

The supper was served. It consisted of a watery soup, seasoned with pepper and rancid oil. This last dainty played a chief part in the salad; musty eggs and roasted cocks'-combs were the best dishes. Even the wine had a strange taste—it was a dreadful mixture.

At night the boxes were placed against the doors. One of the travellers kept watch while the rest slept. The theologian was the sentry. Oh, how close it was in there! The heat oppressed him, the gnats buzzed and stung, and the *miserabili* outside moaned in their dreams.

"Yes, travelling would be all very well," said the theologian, "if one had no body. If the body could rest, and the mind fly! Wherever I go, I find a want that oppresses my heart: it is something better than the present moment that I desire. Yes, something better—the best; but what is that, and where is it? In my own heart I know very well what I want: I want to attain to a happy goal, the happiest of all!"

And so soon as the word was spoken he found himself at home. The long white curtains hung down from the windows, and in the middle of the room stood a black coffin; in this he was lying in the quiet sleep of death: his wish was fulfilled—his body was at rest and his spirit roaming. "Esteem no man happy who is not yet in his grave," were the words of Solon; here their force was proved anew.

Every corpse is a sphinx of immortality; the sphinx here also in the black sarcophagus answered, what the living man had laid down two days before:

> "Thou strong, stern Death! Thy silence waketh fear
> Thou leavest mould'ring gravestones for thy traces.
> Shall not the soul see Jacob's ladder here?
> No resurrection type but churchyard grasses?
> The deepest woes escape the world's dull eye:
> Thou that alone on duty's path hast sped,
> Heavier those duties on thy heart would lie
> Than lies the earth now on thy coffined head."

Two forms were moving to and fro in the room. We know them both. They were the Fairy of Care and the Ambassadress of Happiness. They bent down over the dead man.

"Do you see?" said Care. "What happiness have your goloshes brought to men?"

"They have at least brought a permanent benefit to him who slumbers here," replied Happiness.

"Oh, no!" said Care. "He went away of himself, he was not summoned. His spirit was not strong enough to lift the treasures which he had been destined to lift. I will do him a favour."

And she drew the goloshes from his feet; then the sleep of death was ended, and the awakened man raised himself up. Care vanished, and with her the goloshes disappeared too: doubtless she looked upon them as her property.

THE HARDY TIN SOLDIER.

THERE were once five and twenty tin soldiers; they were all brothers, for they had all been born of one old tin spoon. They shouldered their muskets, and looked straight before them: their uniform was read and blue, and very splendid. The first thing they had heard in the world, when the lid was taken off their box, had been the words "Tin soldiers!" These words were uttered by a little boy, clapping his hands: the soldiers had been given to him, for it was his birthday; and now he put them upon the table. Each soldier was exactly like the rest; but one of them had been cast last of all, and there had not been enough tin to finish him; but he stood as firmly upon his one leg as the others on their two; and it was just this Soldier who became re-markable.

On the table on which they had been placed stood many other play-things, but the toy that attracted most attention was a neat castle of cardboard.   Through the little windows one could see straight into the hall.   Before the castle some little trees were placed round a little looking-glass, which was to represent a clear lake.   Waxen swans swam on this lake, and were mirrored in it.   This was all very pretty; but the prettiest of all was a little lady, who stood at the open door of the castle: she was also cut out in paper, but she had a dress of the clearest gauze, and a little narrow blue ribbon over her shoulders, that looked like a scarf; and in the middle of this ribbon was a shining tinsel rose as big as her whole face.   The little lady stretched out both her arms, for she was a dancer; and then she lifted one leg so high that the Tin Soldier could not see it at all, and thought that, like himself, she had but one leg.

"That would be the wife for me," thought he; "but she is very grand. She lives in a castle, and I have only a box, and there are five and twenty of us in that.   It is no place for her.   But I must try to make acquaintance with her."

And then he lay down at full length behind a snuff-box which was on the table; there he could easily watch the little dainty lady, who continued to stand on one leg without losing her balance.

When the evening came, all the other tin soldiers were put into their box, and the people in the house went to bed.   Now the toys began to play at "visiting," and at "war," and "giving balls."   The tin soldiers rattled in their box, for they wanted to join, but could not lift the lid. The nutcracker threw somersaults, and the pencil amused itself on the table: there was so much noise that the canary woke up, and began to speak too, and even in verse.   The only two who did not stir from their places were the Tin Soldier and the dancing lady: she stood straight up on the point of one of her toes, and stretched out both her arms; and he was just as enduring on his one leg; and he never turned his eyes away from her.

Now the clock struck twelve—and, bounce!—the lid flew off the snuff-box; but there was not snuff in it, but a little black Goblin: you see it was a trick.

"Tin Soldier!" said the Goblin, "don't stare at things that don't concern you."

But the Tin Soldier pretended not to hear him.

"Just you wait till to-morrow!" said the Goblin.

But when the morning came, and the children got up, the Tin Soldier was placed in the window; and whether it was the Goblin or the draught that did it, all at once the window flew open, and the Soldier fell head over heels out of the third storey.   That was a terrible passage!   He put his leg straight up, and stuck with his helmet downwards and his bayonet between the paving-stones.

The servant-maid and the little boy came down directly to look for him, but though they almost trod upon him they could not see him.   If the Soldier had cried out "Here I am!" they would have found him; but he did not think it fitting to call out loudly, because he was in uniform.

Now it began to rain; the drops soon fell thicker, and at last it came down in a complete stream. When the rain was past, two street boys came by.

"Just look!" said one of them, "there lies a tin soldier. He must come out and ride in the boat."

And they made a boat out of a newspaper, and put the Tin Soldier in the middle of it; and so he sailed down the gutter, and the two boys ran beside him and clapped their hands. Goodness preserve us! how the waves rose in that gutter, and how fast the stream ran! But then it had been a heavy rain. The paper boat rocked up and down, and sometimes turned round so rapidly that the Tin Soldier trembled; but he remained firm, and never changed countenance, and looked straight before him, and shouldered his musket.

All at once the boat went into a long drain, and it became as dark as if he had been in his box.

"Where am I going now?" he thought. "Yes, yes, that's the Goblin's fault. Ah! if the little lady only sat here with me in the boat, it might be twice as dark for what I should care."

Suddenly there came a great Water Rat, which lived under the drain. "Have you a passport?" said the Rat. "Give me your passport."

But the Tin Soldier kept silence, and held his musket tighter than ever.

The boat went on, but the Rat came after it. Hu! how he gnashed his teeth, and called out to the bits of straw and wood,

"Hold him! hold him! he hasn't paid toll—he hasn't shown his passport!"

But the stream became stronger and stronger. The Tin Soldier could see the bright daylight where the arch ended; but he heard a roaring noise, which might well frighten a bolder man. Only think—just where the tunnel ended, the drain ran into a great canal; and for him that would have been as dangerous as for us to be carried down a great waterfall.

Now he was already so near it that he could not stop. The boat was carried out, the poor Tin Soldier stiffening himself as much as he could, and no one could say that he moved an eyelid. The boat whirled round three or four times, and was full of water to the very edge—it must sink. The Tin Soldier stood up to his neck in water, and the boat sank deeper and deeper, and the paper was loosened more and more; and now the water closed over the Soldier's head. Then he thought of the pretty little dancer, and how he should never see her again; and it sounded in the soldier's ears:

> "Farewell, farewell, thou warrior brave,
> For this day thou must die!"

And now the paper parted, and the Tin Soldier fell out; but at that moment he was snapped up by a great fish.

Oh, how dark it was in that fish's body! It was darker yet than in the drain tunnel; and then it was very narrow too. But the Tin Soldier remained unmoved, and lay at full length shouldering his musket.

The fish swam to and fro; he made the most wonderful movements, and then became quite still. At last something flashed through him like lightning. The daylight shone quite clear, and a voice said aloud, "The Tin Soldier!" The fish had been caught, carried to market, bought, and taken into the kitchen, where the cook cut him open with a large knife. She seized the Soldier round the body with both her hands, and carried him into the room, where all were anxious to see the remarkable man who had travelled about in the inside of a fish; but the Tin Soldier was not at all proud. They placed him on the table, and there—no! What curious things may happen in the world! The Tin Soldier was in the very room in which he had been before! he saw the same children, and the same toys stood on the table; and there was the pretty castle with the graceful little dancer. She was still balancing herself on one leg, and held the other extended in the air. She was hardy too. That moved the Tin Soldier: he was very nearly weeping tin tears, but that would not have been proper. He looked at her, but they said nothing to each other.

Then one of the little boys took the Tin Soldier and flung him into the stove. He gave no reason for doing this. It must have been the fault of the Goblin in the snuff-box.

The Tin Soldier stood there quite illuminated, and felt a heat that was terrible; but whether this heat proceeded from the real fire or from love he did not know. The colours had quite gone off from him; but whether that had happened on the journey, or had been caused by grief, no one could say. He looked at the little lady, she looked at him, and he felt that he was melting; but he still stood firm, shouldering his musket. Then suddenly the door flew open, and the draught of air caught the dancer, and she flew like a sylph just into the stove to the Tin Soldier, and flashed up in a flame, and she was gone. Then the Tin Soldier melted down into a lump, and when the servant-maid took the ashes out next day, she found him in the shape of a little tin heart. But of the dancer nothing remained but the tinsel rose, and that was burned as black as a coal.

THE STORY OF A MOTHER.

A MOTHER sat by her little child: she was very sorrowful, and feared that it would die. Its little face was pale, and its eyes were closed. The child drew its breath with difficulty, and sometimes so deeply as if it were sighing; and then the mother looked more sorrowfully than before on the little creature.

Then there was a knock at the door, and a poor old man came in, wrapped up in something that looked like a great horse-cloth, for that keeps warm; and he required it, for it was cold winter. Without, everything was covered with ice and snow, and the wind blew so sharply that it cut one's face.

THE MOTHER WATCHING HER SICK CHILD.

And as the old man trembled with cold, and the child was quiet for a moment, the mother went and put some beer on the stove in a little pot, to warm it for him. The old man sat down and rocked the cradle, and the mother seated herself on an old chair by him, looked at her sick child that drew its breath so painfully, and seized the little hand.

"You think I shall keep it, do you not?" she asked. "The good God will not take it from me!"

And the old man—he was *Death*—nodded in such a strange way, that it might just as well mean *yes* as *no*. And the mother cast down her eyes, and tears rolled down her cheeks.   Her head became heavy: for three days and three nights she had not closed her eyes; and now she slept, but only for a minute; then she started up and shivered with cold.

"What is that?" she asked, and looked round on all sides; but the old man was gone, and her little child was gone; he had taken it with him.   And there in the corner the old clock was humming and whirring; the heavy leaden weight ran down to the floor—plump!—and the clock stopped.

But the poor mother rushed out of the house crying for her child.

Out in the snow sat a woman in long black garments, and she said, "Death has been with you in your room; I saw him hasten away with your child: he strides faster than the wind, and never brings back what he has taken away."

"Only tell me which way he has gone," said the mother.   "Tell me the way, and I will find him."

"I know him," said the woman in the black garments; "but before I tell you, you must sing me all the songs that you have sung to your child.   I love those songs; I have heard them before.   I am Night, and I saw your tears when you sang them."

"I will sing them all, all!" said the mother.   "But do not detain me, that I may overtake him, and find my child."

But Night sat dumb and still.   Then the mother wrung her hands, and sang and wept.   And there were many songs, but yet more tears, and then Night said, "Go to the right into the dark fir wood; for I saw Death take that path with your little child."

Deep in the forest there was a cross road, and she did not know which way to take.   There stood a Blackthorn Bush, with not a leaf nor a blossom upon it; for it was in the cold winter-time, and icicles hung from the twigs.

"Have you not seen Death go by, with my little child?"

"Yes," replied the Bush, "but I shall not tell you which way he went unless you warm me on your bosom.   I'm freezing to death here, I'm turning to ice."

And she pressed the Blackthorn Bush to her bosom, quite close, that it might be well warmed.   And the thorns pierced into her flesh, and her blood oozed out in great drops.   But the Blackthorn shot out fresh green leaves, and blossomed in the dark winter night: so warm is the heart of a sorrowing mother!   And the Blackthorn Bush told her the way that she should go.

Then she came to a great Lake, on which there were neither ships nor boat.   The Lake was not frozen enough to carry her, nor sufficiently open to allow her to wade through, and yet she must cross it if she was to find her child.   Then she laid herself down to drink the Lake; and that was impossible for any one to do.   But the sorrowing mother thought that perhaps a miracle might be wrought.

"No, that can never succeed," said the Lake.   "Let us rather see how we can agree.   I'm fond of collecting pearls, and your eyes are the two clearest I have ever seen: if you will weep them out into me I will carry you over into the great green-house, where Death lives and cultivates flowers and trees; each of these is a human life."

"Oh, what would I not give to get my child!" said the afflicted mother; and she wept yet more, and her eyes fell into the depths of the lake, and became two costly pearls. But the lake lifted her up, as if she sat in a swing, and she was wafted to the opposite shore, where stood a wonderful house, miles in length. One could not tell if it was a mountain containing forests and caves, or a place that had been built. But the poor mother could not see it, for she had wept her eyes out.

"Where shall I find Death, who went away with my little child?" she asked.

"He has not arrived here yet," said an old grey-haired woman, who was going about and watching the hothouse of Death. "How have you found your way here, and who helped you?"

"The good God has helped me," she replied. "He is merciful, and you will be merciful too. Where shall I find my little child?"

"I do not know it," said the old woman, "and you cannot see. Many flowers and trees have faded this night, and death will soon come and transplant them. You know very well that every human being has his tree of life, or his flower of life, just as each is arranged. They look like other plants, but their hearts beat. Children's hearts can beat too. Think of this. Perhaps you may recognize the beating of your child's heart. But what will you give me if I tell you what more you must do?"

"I have nothing more to give," said the afflicted mother. "But I will go for you to the ends of the earth."

"I have nothing for you to do there," said the old woman, "but you can give me your long black hair. You must know yourself that it is beautiful, and it pleases me. You can take my white hair for it, and that is always something."

"Do you ask for nothing more?" asked she. "I will give you that gladly." And she gave her beautiful hair, and received in exchange the old woman's white hair.

And then they went into the great hothouse of death, where flowers and trees were growing marvellously intertwined. There stood the fine hyacinths under glass bells, some quite fresh, others somewhat sickly; water-snakes were twining about them, and black crabs clung tightly to the stalks. There stood gallant palm trees, oaks, and plantains, and parsley and blooming thyme. Each tree and flower had its name; each was a human life: the people were still alive, one in China, another in Greenland, scattered about in the world. There were great trees thrust into little pots, so that they stood quite crowded, and were nearly bursting the pots; there was also many a little weakly flower in rich earth, with moss round about it, cared for and tended. But the sorrowful mother bent down over all the smallest plants, and heard the human heart beating in each, and out of millions she recognized that of her child.

"That is it!" she cried, and stretched out her hands over a little crocus flower, which hung down quite sick and pale.

"Do not touch the flower," said the old dame; "but place yourself here; and when Death comes—I expect him every minute—then don't let him pull up the plant, but threaten him that you will do the same to the other plants; then he 'll be frightened. He has to account for them all; not one may be pulled up till he receives commission from Heaven."

And all at once there was an icy cold rush through the hall, and the blind mother felt that Death was arriving.

"How did you find your way hither?" said he. "How have you been able to come quicker than I?"

"I am a mother," she answered.

And Death stretched out his long hands towards the little delicate flower; but she kept her hands tight about it, and held it fast; and yet she was full of anxious care lest he should touch one of the leaves. Then Death breathed upon her hands, and she felt that his breath was colder than the icy wind; and her hands sank down powerless.

"You can do nothing against me," said Death.

"But the merciful God can," she replied.

"I only do what He commands," said Death. "I am His gardener. I take all His trees and flowers, and transplant them into the great Paradise gardens, in the unknown land. But how they will flourish there, and how it is there, I may not tell you."

"Give me back my child," said the mother; and she implored and wept. All at once she grasped two pretty flowers with her two hands, and called to Death, "I 'll tear off all your flowers, for I am in despair."

"Do not touch them," said Death. "You say you are so unhappy, and now you would make another mother just as unhappy!"

"Another mother?" said the poor woman; and she let the flowers go.

"There are your eyes for you," said Death. "I have fished them up out of the lake; they gleamed up quite brightly. I did not know that they were yours. Take them back—they are clearer now than before—and then look down into the deep well close by. I will tell you the names of the two flowers you wanted to pull up, and you will see what you were about to frustrate and destroy."

And she looked down into the well, and it was a happiness to see how one of them became a blessing to the world, how much joy and gladness she diffused around her. And the woman looked at the life of the other, and it was made up of care and poverty, misery and woe.

"Both are the will of God," said Death.

"Which of them is the flower of misfortune, and which the blessed one?" she asked.

"That I may not tell you," answered Death; "but this much you shall hear, that one of these two flowers is that of your child. It was the fate of your child that you saw—the future of your own child."

Then the mother screamed aloud for terror.

"Which of them belongs to my child? Tell me that! Release the innocent child! Let my child free from all that misery! Rather carry it away! Carry it into God's kingdom! Forget my tears, forget my entreaties, and all that I have done!"

" I do not understand you," said Death. " Will you have your child back, or shall I carry it to that place that you know not ? "

Then the mother wrung her hands, and fell on her knees, and prayed to the good God.

" Hear me not when I pray against Thy will, which is at all times the best! Hear me not! hear me not!" And she let her head sink down on her bosom.

And Death went away with her child into the unknown land.

THE DAISY.

Now YOU shall hear!

Out in the country, close by the road-side, there was a country house: you yourself have certainly once seen it. Before it is a little garden with flowers, and a paling which is painted. Close by it, by the ditch, in the midst of the most beautiful green grass, grew a little Daisy. The sun shone as warmly and as brightly upon it as on the great splendid garden flowers, and so it grew from hour to hour. One morning it stood in full bloom, with its little shining white leaves spreading like rays round the little yellow sun in the centre. It never thought that no man would notice it down in the grass, and that it was a poor despised floweret; no, it was very merry, and turned to the warm sun, looked up at it, and listened to the Lark carolling high in the air.

The little Daisy was as happy as if it were a great holiday, and yet it was only a Monday. All the children were at school; and while they sat on their benches learning, it sat on its little green stalk, and learned also from the warm sun, and from all around, how good God is. And the Daisy was very glad that everything it silently felt was sung so loudly and charmingly by the Lark. And the Daisy looked up with a kind of respect to the happy bird who could sing and fly; but it was not at all sorrowful because it could not fly and sing also.

" I can see and hear," it thought: "the sun shines on me, and the forest kisses me. Oh, how richly have I been gifted!"

Within the palings stood many stiff, aristocratic flowers — the less scent they had the more they flaunted. The peonies blew themselves out to be greater than the roses, but size will not do it; the tulips had the most splendid colours, and they knew that, and held themselves bolt upright, that they might be seen more plainly. They did not notice the little Daisy outside there, but the Daisy looked at them the more, and thought, " How rich and beautiful they are! Yes, the pretty bird flies across to them and visits them. I am glad that I stand so near them, for at any rate I can enjoy the sight of their splendour!" And just as she thought that—" keevit!"—down came flying the Lark, but not down to the peonies and tulips — no, down into the grass to the lowly Daisy, which started so with joy that it did not know what to think.

The little bird danced round about it, and sang,

" Oh, how soft the grass is! and see what a lovely little flower, with gold in its heart and silver on its dress!"

For the yellow point in the Daisy looked like gold, and the little leaves around it shone silvery white.

How happy was the little Daisy — no one can conceive how happy! The bird kissed it with his beak, sang to it, and then flew up again into the blue air. A quarter of an hour passed, at least, before the Daisy could recover itself. Half ashamed, and yet inwardly rejoiced, it looked at the other flowers in the garden; for they had seen the honour and happiness it had gained, and must understand what a joy it was. But the tulips stood up twice as stiff as before, and they looked quite peaky in the face and quite red, for they had been vexed. The peonies were quite wrong-headed : it was well they could not speak, or the Daisy would have received a good scolding. The poor little flower could see very well that they were not in a good humour, and that hurt it sensibly. At this moment there came into the garden a girl with a great sharp shining knife; she went straight up to the tulips, and cut off one after another of them.

" Oh!" sighed the little Daisy, " this is dreadful; now it is all over with them."

Then the girl went away with the tulips. The Daisy was glad to stand out in the grass, and to be only a poor little flower; it felt very grateful; and when the sun went down it folded its leaves and went to sleep, and dreamed all night long about the sun and the pretty little bird.

Next morning, when the flower again happily stretched out all its white leaves, like little arms, towards the air and the light, it recognized the voice of the bird, but the song he was singing sounded mournfully. Yes, the poor Lark had good reason to be sad : he was caught, and now sat in a cage close by the open window. He sang of free and happy roaming, sang of the young green corn in the fields, and of the glorious journey he might make on his wings high through the air. The poor Lark was not in good spirits, for there he sat a prisoner in a cage.

The little Daisy wished very much to help him. But what was it to do? Yes, that was difficult to make out. It quite forgot how everything was beautiful around, how warm the sun shone, and how splendidly white its own leaves were. Ah! it could think only of the imprisoned bird, and how it was powerless to do anything for him.

Just then two little boys came out of the garden. One of them carried in his hand the knife which the girl had used to cut off the tulips. They went straight up to the little Daisy, which could not at all make out what they wanted.

" Here we may cut a capital piece of turf for the Lark," said one of the boys; and he began to cut off a square patch round about the Daisy, so that the flower remained standing in its piece of grass.

" Tear off the flower!" said the other boy.

And the Daisy trembled with fear, for to be torn off would be to lose

THE LITTLE BOYS CUT THE TURF WITH THE DAISY ON IT.

its life; and now it wanted particularly to live, as it was to be given with the piece of turf to the captive Lark.

"No, let it stay," said the other boy; "it makes such a nice ornament."

And so it remained, and was put into the Lark's cage. But the poor bird complained aloud of his lost liberty, and beat his wings against the wires of his prison; and the little Daisy could not speak—could say no consoling word to him, gladly as it would have done so. And thus the whole morning passed.

"Here is no water," said the captive Lark. "They are all gone out, and have forgotten to give me anything to drink. My throat is dry and burning. It is like fire and ice within me, and the air is so close. Oh, I must die! I must leave the warm sunshine, the fresh green, and all the splendour that God has created!"

And then he thrust his beak into the cool turf to refresh himself a little with it. Then the bird's eye fell upon the Daisy, and he nodded to it, and kissed it with his beak, and said,

"You also must wither in here, you poor little flower. They have given you to me with the little patch of green grass on which you grow, instead of the whole world which was mine out there! Every little blade of grass shall be a great tree for me, and every one of your fragrant leaves a great flower. Ah, you only tell me how much I have lost!"

"If I could only comfort him!" thought the little Daisy.

It could not stir a leaf; but the scent which streamed forth from its delicate leaves was far stronger than is generally found in these flowers; the bird also noticed that, and though he was fainting with thirst, and in his pain plucked up the green blades of grass, he did not touch the flower.

The evening came, and yet nobody appeared to bring the poor bird a drop of water. Then he stretched out his pretty wings and beat the air frantically with them; his song changed to a mournful piping, his little head sank down towards the flower, and the bird's heart broke with want and yearning. Then the flower could not fold its leaves, as it had done on the previous evening, and sleep; it drooped, sorrowful and sick, towards the earth.

Not till the next morning did the boys come; and when they found the bird dead they wept—wept many tears—and dug him a neat grave, which they adorned with leaves of flowers. The bird's corpse was put into a pretty red box, for he was to be royally buried — the poor bird! While he was alive and sang they forgot him, and let him sit in his cage and suffer want; but now that he was dead he had adornment and many tears.

But the patch of turf with the Daisy on it was thrown out into the high road: no one thought of the flower that had felt the most for the little bird, and would have been so glad to console him.

A GREAT GRIEF.

This story really consists of two parts; the first part might be left out, but it gives us a few particulars, and these are useful.

We were staying in the country at a gentleman's seat, where it happened that the master was absent for a few days. In the meantime there arrived from the next town a lady; she had a pug dog with her, and came, she said, to dispose of shares in her tan-yard. She had her papers with her, and we advised her to put them in an envelope, and to write thereon the address of the proprietor of the estate, "General War-Commissary Knight," &c.

She listened to us attentively, seized the pen, paused, and begged us to repeat the direction slowly. We complied, and she wrote; but in the midst of the "General War . . . . ." she stuck fast, sighed deeply, and said, "I am only a woman!" Her Puggie had seated itself on the ground while she wrote, and growled; for the dog had come with her for amusement and for the sake of its health; and then the bare floor ought not to be offered to a visitor. His outward appearance was characterized by a snub nose and a very fat back.

"He doesn't bite," said the lady; "he has no teeth. He is like one of the family, faithful and grumpy; but the latter is my grandchildren's fault, for they have teazed him: they play at wedding, and want to give him the part of the bridesmaid, and that's too much for him, poor old fellow."

WAITING TO SEE PUGGIE'S GRAVE.

And she delivered her papers, and took Puggie upon her arm. And this is the first part of the story, which might have been left out.

PUGGIE DIED!! That's the second part.

It was about a week afterwards we arrived in the town, and put up at the inn. Our windows looked into the tan-yard, which was divided into two parts by a partition of planks; in one half were many skins and hides, raw and tanned. Here was all the apparatus necessary to carry on a tannery, and it belonged to the widow. Puggie had died in the morning, and was to be buried in this part of the yard: the grandchildren of the widow (that is, of the tanner's widow, for Puggie had never been married) filled up the grave, and it was a beautiful grave— it must have been quite pleasant to lie there.

The grave was bordered with pieces of flower-pots and strewn over with sand; quite at the top they had stuck up half a beer bottle, with the neck upwards, and that was not at all allegorical.

The children danced round the grave, and the eldest of the boys among them, a practical youngster of seven years, made the proposition that there should be an exhibition of Puggie's burial-place for all who lived in the lane; the price of admission was to be a trouser button, for every boy would be sure to have one, and each might also give one for a little girl. This proposal was adopted by acclamation.

And all the children out of the lane—yes, even out of the little lane at the back—flocked to the place, and each gave a button. Many were noticed to go about on that afternoon with only one brace; but then they had seen Puggie's grave, and the sight was worth much more.

But in front of the tan-yard, close to the entrance, stood a little girl clothed in rags, very pretty to look at, with curly hair, and eyes so blue and clear that it was a pleasure to look into them. The child said not a word, nor did she cry; but each time the little door was opened she gave a long, long look into the yard. She had not a button—that she knew right well, and therefore she remained standing sorrowfully outside, till all the others had seen the grave and had gone away; then she sat down, held her little brown hands before her eyes, and burst into tears: this girl alone had not seen Puggie's grave. It was a grief as great to her as any grown person can experience.

We saw this from above; and, looked at from above, how many a grief of our own and of others can make us smile! That is the story, and whoever does not understand it may go and purchase a share in the tan-yard from the widow.

THE JUMPER.

The Flea, the Grasshopper, and the Skipjack once wanted to see which of them could jump highest; and they invited the whole world, and whoever else would come, to see the grand sight. And there the three famous jumpers were met together in the room.

"Yes, I'll give my daughter to him who jumps highest," said the King, "for it would be mean to let these people jump for nothing."

The Flea stepped out first. He had very pretty manners, and bowed in all directions, for he had young ladies' blood in his veins, and was accustomed to consort only with human beings; and that was of great consequence.

Then came the Grasshopper: he was certainly much heavier, but he had a good figure, and wore the green uniform that was born with him. This person, moreover, maintained that he belonged to a very old family in the land of Egypt, and that he was highly esteemed there. He had just come from the field, he said, and had been put into a card house three storeys high, and all made of picture cards with the figures turned inwards. There were doors and windows in the house, cut in the body of the Queen of Hearts.

THE THREE CANDIDATES.

"I sing so," he said, "that sixteen native crickets who have chirped from their youth up, and have never yet had a card house of their own, would become thinner than they are with envy if they were to hear me."

Both of them, the Flea and the Grasshopper, took care to announce who they were, and that they considered themselves entitled to marry a Princess.

The Skipjack said nothing, but it was said of him that he thought all the more; and directly the Yard Dog had smelt at him he was ready to assert that the Skipjack was of good family, and formed from the breast-bone of an undoubted goose. The old councillor, who had received three medals for holding his tongue, declared that the Skipjack possessed the gift of prophecy: one could tell by his bones whether there would be a severe winter or a mild one; and that's more than one can always tell from the breast-bone of the man who writes the almanack.

"I shall not say anything more," said the old King. "I only go on quietly, and always think the best."

Now they were to take their jump. The Flea sprang so high that no one could see him; and then they asserted that he had not jumped at all. That was very mean. The Grasshopper only sprang half as high, but he sprang straight into the King's face, and the King declared that was horribly rude. The Skipjack stood a long time considering; at last people thought that he could not jump at all.

"I only hope he's not become unwell," said the Yard Dog, and then he smelt at him again.

"Tap!" he sprang with a little crooked jump just into the lap of the Princess, who sat on a low golden stool.

Then the King said, "The highest leap was taken by him who jumped up to my daughter; for therein lies the point; but it requires head to achieve that, and the Skipjack has shown that he has a head."

And so he had the Princess.

"I jumped highest, after all," said the Flea. "But it's all the same. Let her have the goose-bone with its lump of wax and bit of stick. I jumped at the highest; but in this world a body is required if one wishes to be seen."

And the Flea went into foreign military service, where it is said he was killed.

The Grasshopper seated himself out in the ditch, and thought and considered how things happened in the world. And he too said, "Body is required! body is required!" And then he sang his own melancholy song, and from that we have gathered this story, which they say is not true, though it's in print.

THE SHIRT COLLAR.

THERE was once a rich cavalier whose whole effects consisted of a Bootjack and a Hair-brush, but he had the finest Shirt Collar in the world, and about this Shirt Collar we will tell a story.

The Collar was now old enough to think of marrying, and it happened that he was sent to the wash together with a Garter.

"My word!" exclaimed the Shirt Collar. "I have never seen anything so slender and delicate, so charming and genteel. May I ask your name?"

"I shall not tell you that," said the Garter.

"Where is your home?" asked the Shirt Collar.

But the Garter was of rather a retiring nature, and it seemed such a strange question to answer.

"I presume you are a girdle?" said the Shirt Collar—"a sort of under girdle? I see that you are useful as well as ornamental, my little lady."

"You are not to speak to me," said the Garter. "I have not, I think, given you any occasion to do so."

"Oh! when one is as beautiful as you are," cried the Shirt Collar, "I fancy that is occasion enough."

"Go!" said the Garter; "don't come so near me: you look to me quite like a man."

"I am a fine cavalier, too," said the Shirt Collar. "I possess a boot-jack and a hair-brush."

THE SHIRT COLLAR IN ITS GLORY.

And that was not true at all, for it was his master who owned these things, but he was boasting.

"Don't come too near me," said the Garter; "I'm not used to that."

"Affectation!" cried the Shirt Collar.

And then they were taken out of the wash, and starched, and hung over a chair in the sunshine, and then laid on the ironing-board; and now came the hot Iron.

"Mrs. Widow!" said the Shirt Collar, "little Mrs. Widow, I'm getting quite warm; I 'm being quite changed; I 'm losing all my creases; you 're burning a hole in me! Ugh! I propose to you."

" You old rag!" said the Iron, and rode proudly over the Shirt Collar, for it imagined that it was a steam boiler, and that it ought to be out on the railway, dragging carriages. " You old rag!" said the Iron.

The Shirt Collar was a little frayed at the edges, therefore the Paper Scissors came to smooth away the frayed places.

" Ho, ho!" said the Shirt Collar; " I presume you are a first-rate dancer. How you can point your toes! no one in the world can do that like you."

" I know that," said the Scissors.

" You deserve to be a countess," said the Shirt Collar. " All that I possess consists of a genteel cavalier, a bootjack, and a comb. If I had only an estate!"

" What! do you want to marry?" cried the Scissors; and they were angry, and gave such a deep cut that the Collar had to be cashiered.

" I shall have to propose to the Hair-brush," thought the Shirt Collar. " It is wonderful what beautiful hair you have, my little lady. Have you never thought of engaging yourself?"

" Yes, you can easily imagine that," replied the Hair-brush. " I am engaged to the Bootjack."

" Engaged!" cried the Shirt Collar.

Now there was no one left to whom he could offer himself, and so he despised love-making.

A long time passed, and the Shirt Collar was put into the sack of a paper dealer. There was a terribly ragged company, and the fine ones kept to themselves, and the coarse ones to themselves, as is right. They all had much to tell, but the Shirt Collar had most of all, for he was a terrible Jack Brag.

" I have had a tremendous number of love affairs," said the Shirt Collar. " They would not leave me alone; but I was a fine cavalier, a starched one. I had a bootjack and a hair-brush that I never used: you should only have seen me then, when I was turned down. I shall never forget my first love; it was a girdle; and how delicate, how charming, how genteel it was! And my first love threw herself into a washing-tub, and all for me! There was also a widow who stood desperately fond of me, but I let her stand alone till she turned quite black. Then there was a dancer who gave me the wound from which I still suffer—she was very hot tempered. My own hair-brush was in love with me, and lost all her hair from neglected love. Yes, I 've had many experiences of this kind; but I am most sorry for the Garter—I mean for the girdle, that jumped into the wash-tub for love of me. I 've a great deal on my conscience. It 's time I was turned into white paper."

And to that the Shirt Collar came. All the rags were turned into white paper, but the Shirt Collar became the very piece of paper we see here, and upon which this story has been printed, and that was done because he boasted so dreadfully about things that were not at all true. And this we must remember, so that we may on no account do the same, for we cannot know at all whether we shall not be put into the rag bag and manufactured into white paper, on which our whole history, even the most secret, shall be printed, so that we shall be obliged to run about and tell it, as the Shirt Collar did.

OLE LUK-OIE'S VISIT.

OLE LUK-OIE.

THERE's nobody in the whole world who knows so many stories as Ole Luk-Oie. He can tell capital histories.

Towards evening, when the children still sit nicely at table, or upon their stools, Ole Luk-Oie comes. He comes up the stairs quite softly, for he walks in his socks: he opens the door noiselessly, and *whisk !* he squirts sweet milk in the children's eyes, a small, small stream, but enough to prevent them from keeping their eyes open; and thus they cannot see him. He creeps just among them, and blows softly upon their necks, and this makes their heads heavy. Yes, but it doesn't hurt them, for Ole Luk-Oie is very fond of the children; he only wants them to be quiet, and that they are not until they are taken to bed: they are to be quiet that he may tell them stories

When the children sleep, Ole Luk-Oie sits down upon their bed. He is well dressed: his coat is of silk, but it is impossible to say of what colour, for it shines red, green, and blue, according as he turns. Under each arm he carries an umbrella: the one with pictures on it he spreads over the good children, and then they dream all night the most glorious stories; but on his other umbrella nothing at all is painted: this he spreads over the naughty children, and these sleep in a dull way, and when they awake in the morning they have not dreamed of anything.

Now we shall hear how Ole Luk-Oie, every evening through one whole week, came to a little boy named Hjalmar, and what he told him. There are seven stories, for there are seven days in the week.

MONDAY.

" Listen," said Ole Luk-Oie in the evening, when he had put Hjalmar to bed; " now I 'll clear up."

And all the flowers in the flower-pots became great trees, stretching out their long branches under the ceiling of the room and along the walls, so that the whole room looked like a beauteous bower; and all the twigs were covered with flowers, and each flower was more beautiful than a rose, and smelt so sweet that one wanted to eat it—it was sweeter than jam. The fruit gleamed like gold, and there were cakes bursting with raisins. It was incomparably beautiful. But at the same time a terrible wail sounded from the table drawer, where Hjalmar's school-book lay.

" Whatever can that be ?" said Ole Luk-Oie; and he went to the table, and opened the drawer. It was the slate which was suffering from convulsions, for a wrong number had got into the sum, so that it was nearly falling in pieces; the slate pencil tugged and jumped at its string, as if it had been a little dog who wanted to help the sum; but he could not. And thus there was a great lamentation in Hjalmar's copy-book; it was quite terrible to hear. On each page the great letters stood in a row, one underneath the other, and each with a little one at its side; that was the copy; and next to these were a few more letters which thought they looked just like the first; and these Hjalmar had written; but they lay down just as if they had tumbled over the pencil lines on which they were to stand.

" See, this is how you should hold yourselves," said the Copy. " Look, sloping in this way, with a powerful swing !"

" Oh, we should be very glad to do that," replied Hjalmar's Letters, " but we cannot; we are too weakly."

" Then you must take medicine," said Ole Luk-Oie.

" Oh, no," cried they; and they immediately stood up so gracefully that it was beautiful to behold.

" Yes, now we cannot tell any stories," said Ole Luk-Oie; " now I must exercise them. One, two! one two !" and thus he exercised the Letters; and they stood quite slender, and as beautiful as any copy can be. But when Ole Luk-Oie went away, and Hjalmar looked at them next morning, they were as weak and miserable as ever.

TUESDAY.

As soon as Hjalmar was in bed, Ole Luk-Oie touched all the furniture in the room with his little magic squirt, and they immediately began to converse together, and each one spoke of itself, with the exception of the spittoon, which stood silent, and was vexed that they should be so vain as to speak only of themselves, and think only of themselves, without any regard for him who stood so modestly in the corner for every one's use.

Over the chest of drawers hung a great picture in a gilt frame—it was a landscape. One saw therein large old trees, flowers in the grass, and a broad river which flowed round about a forest, past many castles, and far out into the wide ocean.

Ole Luk-Oie touched the painting with his magic squirt, and the birds in it began to sing, the branches of the trees stirred, and the clouds began to move across it; one could see their shadows glide over the landscape.

Now Ole Luk-Oie lifted little Hjalmar up to the frame, and put the boy's feet into the picture, just in the high grass; and there he stood; and the sun shone upon him through the branches of the trees. He ran to the water, and seated himself in a little boat which lay there; it was painted red and white, the sails gleamed like silver, and six swans, each with a gold circlet round its neck and a bright blue star on its forehead, drew the boat past the great wood, where the trees tell of robbers and witches, and the flowers tell of the graceful little elves, and of what the butterflies have told them.

Gorgeous fishes, with scales like silver and gold, swam after their boat; sometimes they gave a spring, so that it splashed in the water; and birds, blue and red, little and great, flew after them in two long rows; the gnats danced, and the cockchafers said, "Boom! boom!" They all wanted to follow Hjalmar, and each one had a story to tell.

That *was* a pleasure voyage. Sometimes the forest was thick and dark, sometimes like a glorious garden full of sunlight and flowers; and there were great palaces of glass and of marble; on the balconies stood Princesses, and these were all little girls whom Hjalmar knew well—he had already played with them. Each one stretched forth her hand, and held out the prettiest sugar heart which ever a cake-woman could sell; and Hjalmar took hold of each sugar heart as he passed by, and the Princess held fast, so that each of them got a piece—she the smaller share, and Hjalmar the larger. At each palace little Princes stood sentry. They shouldered golden swords, and caused raisins and tin soldiers to shower down: one could see that they were real Princes. Sometimes Hjalmar sailed through forests, sometimes through great halls or through the midst of a town. He also came to the town where his nurse lived, who had carried him in her arms when he was quite a little boy, and who had always been so kind to him; and she nodded and beckoned, and sang the pretty verse she had made herself and had sent to Hjalmar.

> "I've loved thee, and kissed thee, Hjalmar, dear boy;
> I've watched thee waking and sleeping;
> May the good Lord guard thee in sorrow, in joy,
> And have thee in His keeping."

And all the birds sang too, the flowers danced on their stalks, and the old trees nodded, just as if Ole Luk-Oie had been telling stories to *them*.

WEDNESDAY.

How the rain was streaming down without! Hjalmar could hear it in his sleep; and when Ole Luk-Oie opened a window, the water stood quite up to the window-sill: there was quite a lake outside, and a noble ship lay close by the house.

"If thou wilt sail with me, little Hjalmar," said Ole Luk-Oie, "thou canst voyage to-night to foreign climes, and be back again to-morrow."

And Hjalmar suddenly stood in his Sunday clothes upon the glorious ship, and immediately the weather became fine, and they sailed through the streets, and steered round by the church; and now everything was one great wild ocean. They sailed on until land was no longer to be seen, and they saw a number of storks, who also came from their home, and were travelling towards the hot countries: these storks flew in a row, one behind the other, and they had already flown far—far! One of them was so weary that his wings would scarcely carry him farther: he was the very last in the row, and soon remained a great way behind the rest; at last he sank, with outspread wings, deeper and deeper; he gave a few more strokes with his pinions, but it was of no use; now he touched the rigging of the ship with his feet, then he glided down from the sail, and—bump!—he stood upon the deck.

Now the cabin boy took him and put him into the hencoop with the Fowls, Ducks, and Turkeys; the poor Stork stood among them quite embarrassed.

"Just look at the fellow!" said all the Fowls.

And the Turkey-cock swelled himself up as much as ever he could, and asked the Stork who he was; and the Ducks walked backwards and quacked to each other, "Quackery! quackery!"

And the Stork told them of hot Africa, of the pyramids, and of the ostrich, which runs like a wild horse through the desert; but the Ducks did not understand what he said, and they said to one another,

"We're all of the same opinion, namely, that he's stupid."

"Yes, certainly he's stupid," said the Turkey-cock; and he gobbled.- Then the Stork was quite silent, and thought of his Africa.

"Those are wonderful thin legs of yours," said the Turkey-cock. "Pray, how much do they cost a yard?"

"Quack! quack! quack!" grinned all the Ducks; but the Stork pretended not to hear it at all.

"You may just as well laugh too," said the Turkey-cock to him, "for that was very wittily said. Or was it, perhaps, too high for you? Yes, yes, he isn't very penetrating. Let us continue to be interesting among ourselves."

And then he gobbled, and the Ducks quacked, "Gick! gack! gick! gack!" It was terrible how they made fun among themselves.

But Hjalmar went to the hencoop, opened the back door, and called to the Stork; and the Stork hopped out to him on to the deck. Now he had rested, and it seemed as if he nodded at Hjalmar, to thank him. Then he spread his wings, and flew away to the warm countries; but the Fowls clucked, and the Ducks quacked, and the Turkey-cock became fiery red in the face.

"To-morrow we shall make songs of you," said Hjalmar; and so saying he awoke, and was lying in his linen bed. It was a wonderful journey that Ole Luk-Oie had caused him to take that night.

THURSDAY.

"I tell you what," said Ole Luk-Oie, "you must not be frightened. Here you shall see a little Mouse," and he held out his hand with the pretty little creature in it. "It has come to invite you to a wedding. There are two little Mice here who are going to enter into the marriage state to-night. They live under the floor of your mother's store-closet : that is said to be a charming dwelling-place !"

"But how can I get through the little mouse-hole in the floor ?" asked Hjalmar.

"Let me manage that," said Ole Luk-Oie. "I will make you small."

And he touched Hjalmar with his magic squirt, and the boy began to shrink and shrink, until he was not so long as a finger.

"Now you may borrow the uniform of a tin soldier : I think it would fit you, and it looks well to wear a uniform when one is in society."

"Yes, certainly," said Hjalmar.

And in a moment he was dressed like the spiciest of tin soldiers.

"Will your honour not be kind enough to take a seat in your mamma's thimble ?" asked the Mouse. "Then I shall have the honour of drawing you."

"Will the young lady really take so much trouble ?" cried Hjalmar.

And thus they drove to the mouse's wedding. First they came into a long passage beneath the boards, which was only just so high that they could drive through it in the thimble ; and the whole passage was lit up with rotten wood.

"Is there not a delicious smell here ?" observed the Mouse. "The entire road has been greased with bacon rinds, and there can be nothing more exquisite."

Now they came into the festive hall. On the right hand stood all the little lady mice ; and they whispered and giggled as if they were making fun of each other ; on the left stood all the gentlemen mice, stroking their whiskers with their fore paws ; and in the centre of the hall the bridegroom and bride might be seen standing in a hollow cheese rind, and kissing each other terribly before all the guests ; for this was the betrothal, and the marriage was to follow immediately.

More and more strangers kept flocking in. One mouse was nearly treading another to death ; and the happy couple had stationed them-selves just in the doorway, so that one could neither come in nor go out. Like the passage, the room had been greased with bacon rinds, and that was the entire banquet ; but for the dessert a pea was produced, in which a mouse belonging to the family had bitten the name of the betrothed

OLE LUK-OIE TAKES HJALMAR TO SEE A WEDDING.

pair—that is to say, the first letter of the name: that was something quite out of the common way.

All the mice said it was a beautiful wedding, and that the entertainment had been very agreeable. And then Hjalmar drove home again: he had really been in grand company; but he had been obliged to crawl, to make himself little, and to put on a tin soldier's uniform.

FRIDAY.

"It is wonderful how many grown-up people there are who would be glad to have me!" said Ole Luk-Oie; "especially those who have done something wrong. 'Good little Ole,' they say to me, 'we cannot close our eyes, and so we lie all night and see our evil deeds, which sit on the bedstead like ugly little goblins, and throw hot water over us; will you not come and drive them away, so that we may have a good sleep?'— and then they sigh deeply—'we would really be glad to pay for it.

Good night, Ole; the money lies on the window-sill.' But I do nothing for money," says Ole Luk-Oie.

"What shall we do this evening?" asked Hjalmar.

"I don't know if you care to go to another wedding to-night. It is of a different kind from that of yesterday. Your sister's great doll, that looks like a man, and is called Hermann, is going to marry the doll Bertha. Moreover, it is the dolls' birthday, and therefore they will receive very many presents."

"Yes, I know that," replied Hjalmar. "Whenever the dolls want new clothes my sister lets them either keep their birthday or celebrate a wedding; that has certainly happened a hundred times already."

"Yes, but to-night is the hundred and first wedding; and when number one hundred and one is past, it is all over; and that is why it will be so splendid. Only look!"

And Hjalmar looked at the table. There stood the little cardboard house with the windows illuminated, and in front of it all the tin soldiers were presenting arms. The bride and bridegroom sat quite thoughtful, and with good reason, on the floor, leaning against a leg of the table. And Ole Luk-Oie, dressed up in the grandmother's black gown, married them to each other. When the ceremony was over, all the pieces of furniture struck up the following beautiful song, which the pencil had written for them. It was sung to the melody of the soldiers' tattoo.

"Let the song swell like the rushing wind,
In honour of those who this day are joined.
Although they stand here so stiff and blind,
Because they are both of a leathery kind.
Hurrah! hurrah! though they're deaf and blind,
Let the song swell like the rushing wind."

And now they received presents—but they had declined to accept provisions of any kind, for they intended to live on love.

"Shall we now go into a summer lodging, or start on a journey?" asked the bridegroom.

And the Swallow, who was a great traveller, and the old yard Hen, who had brought up five broods of chickens, were consulted on the subject. And the Swallow told of the beautiful warm climes, where the grapes hung in ripe heavy clusters, where the air is mild, and the mountains glow with colours unknown here.

"But you have not our brown cole there!" objected the Hen. "I was once in the country, with my children, in one summer that lasted five weeks. There was a sand pit, in which we could walk about and scratch; and we had the *entrée* to a garden where brown cole grew: it was so hot there that one could scarcely breathe; and then we have not all the poisonous animals that infest these warm countries of yours, and we are free from robbers. He is a villain who does not consider our country the most beautiful—he certainly does not deserve to be here!" And then the Hen wept, and went on: "I have also travelled. I rode in a coop above twelve miles; and there is no pleasure at all in travelling!"

" Yes, the Hen is a sensible woman ! " said the doll Bertha. " I don't think anything of travelling among mountains, for you only have to go up, and then down again. No, we will go into the sand pit beyond the gate, and walk about in the cabbage garden."

And so it was settled.

SATURDAY.

" Am I to hear some stories now ? " asked little Hjalmar, as soon as Ole Luk-Oie had set him to sleep.

" This evening we have no time for that," replied Ole Luk-Oie ; and he spread his finest umbrella over the lad. " Only look at these China-men ! "

And the whole umbrella looked like a great China dish, with blue trees and pointed bridges with little Chinamen upon them, who stood there nodding their heads.

" We must have the whole world prettily decked out for to-morrow morning," said Ole Luk-Oie, " for that will be a holiday—it will be Sunday. I will go to the church steeples to see that the little church goblins are polishing the bells, that they may sound sweetly. I will go out into the field, and see if the breezes are blowing the dust from the grass and leaves ; and, what is the greatest work of all, I will bring down all the stars, to polish them. I take them in my apron ; but first each one must be numbered, and the holes in which they are to be placed up there must be numbered likewise, so that they may be placed in the same grooves again · otherwise they would not sit fast, and we should have too many shooting stars, for one after another would fall down."

" Hark ye ! Do you know, Mr. Ole Luk-Oie," said an old Portrait which hung on the wall where Hjalmar slept, " I am Hjalmar's great-grandfather ? I thank you for telling the boy stories ; but you must not confuse his ideas. The stars cannot come down and be polished ! The stars are world-orbs, just like our own earth, and that is just the good thing about them."

" I thank you, old great-grandfather," said Ole Luk-Oie, " I thank you ! You are the head of the family. You are the ancestral head ; but I am older than you ! I am an old heathen : the Romans and Greeks called me the Dream God. I have been in the noblest houses, and am admitted there still ! I know how to act with great people and with small ! Now you may tell your own story ! " And Ole Luk-Oie took his umbrella, and went away.

" Well, well ! May one not even give an opinion now-a-days ? " grumbled the old Portrait. And Hjalmar awoke.

SUNDAY.

" Good evening ! " said Ole Luk-Oie ; and Hjalmar nodded, and then ran and turned his great-grandfather's Portrait against the wall, that it might not interrupt them, as it had done yesterday.

"Now you must tell me stories; about the five green peas that lived in one shell, and about the cock's foot that paid court to the hen's foot, and of the darning-needle who gave herself such airs because she thought herself a working-needle."

"There may be too much of a good thing!" said Ole Luk-Oie. "You know that I prefer showing you something. I will show you my own brother. His name, like mine, is Ole Luk-Oie, but he never comes to any one more than once; and he takes him to whom he comes upon his horse, and tells him stories. He only knows two. One of these is so exceedingly beautiful that no one in the world can imagine it, and the other so horrible and dreadful that it cannot be described."

And then Ole Luk-Oie lifted little Hjalmar up to the window, and said,

"There you will see my brother, the other Ole Luk-Oie. They also call him Death! Do you see, he does not look so terrible as they make him in the picture-books, where he is only a skeleton. No, that is silver embroidery that he has on his coat; that is a splendid hussar's uniform; a mantle of black velvet flies behind him over the horse. See how he gallops along!"

And Hjalmar saw how this Ole Luk-Oie rode away, and took young people as well as old upon his horse. Some of them he put before him, and some behind; but he always asked first, "How stands it with the mark-book?" "Well," they all replied. "Yes, let me see it myself," he said. And then each one had to show him the book; and those who had "very well" and "remarkably well" written in their books, were placed in front of his horse, and a lovely story was told to them; while those who had "middling" or "tolerably well," had to sit up behind, and hear a very terrible story indeed. They trembled and wept, and wanted to jump off the horse, but this they could not do, for they had all, as it were, grown fast to it.

"But Death is a most splendid Ole Luk-Oie," said Hjalmar. "I am not afraid of him!"

"Nor need you be," replied Ole Luk-Oie; "but see that you have a good mark-book!"

"Yes, that is improving!" muttered the great-grandfather's Picture. "It is of some use giving one's opinion." And now he was satisfied.

You see, that is the story of Ole Luk-Oie; and now he may tell you more himself, this evening!

JACK THE DULLARD.

AN OLD STORY TOLD ANEW.

FAR in the interior of the country lay an old baronial hall, and in it lived an old proprietor, who had two sons, which two young men thought themselves too clever by half. They wanted to go out and woo the

King's daughter; for the maiden in question had publicly announced that she would choose for her husband that youth who could arrange his words best.

So these two geniuses prepared themselves a full week for the wooing —this was the longest time that could be granted them; but it was enough, for they had had much preparatory information, and everybody knows how useful that is. One of them knew the whole Latin dictionary by heart, and three whole years of the daily paper of the little town into the bargain; and so well, indeed, that he could repeat it all either backwards or forwards, just as he chose. The other was deeply read in the corporation laws, and knew by heart what every corporation ought to know; and accordingly he thought he could talk of affairs of state, and put his spoke in the wheel in the council. And he knew one thing more: he could embroider braces with roses and other flowers, and with arabesques, for he was a tasty, light-fingered fellow.

"I shall win the Princess!" So cried both of them. Therefore their old papa gave to each a handsome horse. The youth who knew the dictionary and newspaper by heart had a black horse, and he who knew all about the corporation laws received a milk-white steed. Then they rubbed the corners of their mouths with fish-oil, so that they might become very smooth and glib. All the servants stood below in the courtyard, and looked on while they mounted their horses; and just by chance the third son came up. For the proprietor had really three sons, though nobody counted the third with his brothers, because he was not so learned as they, and indeed he was generally known as "Jack the Dullard."

"Hallo!" said Jack the Dullard, "where are you going? I declare you have put on your Sunday clothes!"

"We're going to the King's court, as suitors to the King's daughter. Don't you know the announcement that has been made all through the country?" And they told him all about it.

"My word! I'll be in it too!" cried Jack the Dullard: and his two brothers burst out laughing at him, and rode away.

"Father dear," said Jack, "I must have a horse too. I do feel so desperately inclined to marry! If she accepts me, she accepts me; and if she won't have me, I'll have her; but she *shall* be mine!"

"Don't talk nonsense," replied the old gentleman. "You shall have no horse from me. You don't know how to speak—you can't arrange your words. Your brothers are very different fellows from you."

"Well," quoth Jack the Dullard, "if I can't have a horse, I'll take the billy-goat, who belongs to me, and he can carry me very well!"

And so said, so done. He mounted the billy-goat, pressed his heels into its sides, and galloped down the high street like a hurricane.

"Hei, houp! that was a ride! Here I come!" shouted Jack the Dullard, and he sang till his voice echoed far and wide.

But his brothers rode slowly on in advance of him. They spoke not a word, for they were thinking about the fine extempore speeches they would have to bring out, and these had to be cleverly prepared beforehand.

JACK'S INTRODUCTION TO THE PRINCESS.

"Hallo!" shouted Jack the Dullard. "Here am I! Look what I have found on the high road." And he showed them what it was, and it was a dead crow.

"Dullard!" exclaimed the brothers, "what are you going to do with that?"

"With the crow? why, I am going to give it to the Princess."

"Yes, do so," said they; and they laughed, and rode on.

"Hallo, here I am again! Just see what I have found now: you don't find that on the high road every day!"

And the brothers turned round to see what he could have found now

"Dullard!" they cried, "that is only an old wooden shoe, and the upper part is missing into the bargain; are you going to give that also to the Princess?"

"Most certainly I shall," replied Jack the Dullard; and again the brothers laughed and rode on, and thus they got far in advance of him; but——

"Hallo—hop rara!" and there was Jack the Dullard again. "It is getting better and better," he cried. "Hurrah! it is quite famous."

" Why, what have you found this time ? " inquired the brothers.

" Oh," said Jack the Dullard, " I can hardly tell you. How glad the Princess will be ! "

" Bah ! " said the brothers ; " that is nothing but clay out of the ditch."

" Yes, certainly it is," said Jack the Dullard ; " and clay of the finest sort. See, it is so wet, it runs through one's fingers." And he filled his pocket with the clay.

But his brothers gallopped on till the sparks flew, and consequently they arrived a full hour earlier at the town gate than could Jack. Now at the gate each suitor was provided with a number, and all were placed in rows immediately on their arrival, six in each row, and so closely packed together that they could not move their arms ; and that was a prudent arrangement, for they would certainly have come to blows, had they been able, merely because one of them stood before the other.

All the inhabitants of the country round about stood in great crowds around the castle, almost under the very windows, to see the Princess receive the suitors ; and as each stepped into the hall, his power of speech seemed to desert him, like the light of a candle that is blown out. Then the Princess would say, " He is of no use ! away with him out of the hall ! "

At last the turn came for that brother who knew the dictionary by heart ; but he did not know it now ; he had absolutely forgotten it altogether ; and the boards seemed to re-echo with his footsteps, and the ceiling of the hall was made of looking-glass, so that he saw himself standing on his head ; and at the window stood three clerks and a head clerk, and every one of them was writing down every single word that was uttered, so that it might be printed in the newspapers, and sold for a penny at the street corners. It was a terrible ordeal, and they had moreover made such a fire in the stove, that the room seemed quite red hot.

" It is dreadfully hot here ! " observed the first brother.

" Yes," replied the Princess, " my father is going to roast young pullets to-day."

" Baa ! " there he stood like a baa-lamb. He had not been prepared for a speech of this kind, and had not a word to say, though he intended to say something witty. " Baa ! "

" He is of no use ! " said the Princess. " Away with him ! "

And he was obliged to go accordingly. And now the second brother came in.

" It is terribly warm here ! " he observed.

" Yes, we 're roasting pullets to day," replied the Princess.

" What—what were you—were you pleased to ob——" stammered he —and all the clerks wrote down, " pleased to ob——"

" He is of no use ! " said the Princess. " Away with him ! "

Now came the turn of Jack the Dullard. He rode into the hall on his goat.

" Well, it 's most abominably hot here."

" Yes, because I 'm roasting young pullets," replied the Princess.

"Ah, that's lucky!" exclaimed Jack the Dullard, "for I suppose you'll let me roast my crow at the same time?"

"With the greatest pleasure," said the Princess. "But have you anything you can roast it in? for I have neither pot nor pan."

"Certainly I have!" said Jack. "Here's a cooking utensil with a tin handle."

And he brought out the old wooden shoe, and put the crow into it.

"Well, that *is* a famous dish!" said the Princess. "But what shall we do for sauce?"

"Oh, I have that in my pocket," said Jack: "I have so much of it that I can afford to throw some away;" and he poured some of the clay out of his pocket.

"I like that!" said the Princess. "You can give an answer, and you have something to say for yourself, and so you shall be my husband. But are you aware that every word we speak is being taken down, and will be published in the paper to-morrow? Look yonder, and you will see in every window three clerks and a head clerk; and the old head clerk is the worst of all, for he can't understand anything."

But she only said this to frighten Jack the Dullard; and the clerks gave a great crow of delight, and each one spurted a blot out of his pen on to the floor.

"Oh, those are the gentlemen, are they?" said Jack; "then I will give the best I have to the head clerk." And he turned out his pockets, and flung the wet clay full in the head clerk's face.

"That was very cleverly done," observed the Princess. "I could not have done that; but I shall learn in time."

And accordingly Jack the Dullard was made a king, and received a crown and a wife, and sat upon a throne. And this report we have wet from the press of the head clerk and the corporation of printers—but *they* are not to be depended upon in the least!

THE BEETLE.

THE Emperor's favourite horse was shod with gold. It had a golden shoe on each of its feet.

And why was this?

He was a beautiful creature, with delicate legs, bright intelligent eyes, and a mane that hung down over his neck like a veil. He had carried his master through the fire and smoke of battle, and heard the bullets whistling around him, had kicked, bitten, and taken part in the fight when the enemy advanced, and had sprung with his master on his back over the fallen foe, and had saved the crown of red gold, and the life of the Emperor, which was more valuable than the red gold; and that is why the Emperor's horse had golden shoes.

And a Beetle came creeping forth.

" First the great ones," said he, " and then the little ones ; but greatness is not the only thing that does it." And so saying, he stretched out his thin legs.

" And pray what do you want ? " asked the smith.

" Golden shoes, to be sure," replied the Beetle.

" Why, you must be out of your senses," cried the smith. " Do you want to have golden shoes too ? "

" Golden shoes ? certainly," replied the Beetle. " Am I not just as good as that big creature yonder, that is waited on, and brushed, and has meat and drink put before him ? Don't I belong to the imperial stable ? "

" But *why* is the horse to have golden shoes ? Don't you understand that ? " asked the smith.

" Understand ? I understand that it is a personal slight offered to myself," cried the Beetle. " It is done to annoy me, and therefore I am going into the world to seek my fortune."

" Go along ! " said the smith.

" You 're a rude fellow ! " cried the Beetle ; and then he went out of the stable, flew a little way, and soon afterwards found himself in a beautiful flower garden, all fragrant with roses and lavender.

" Is it not beautiful here ? " asked one of the little Lady-Birds that flew about, with their delicate wings and their red-and-black shields on their backs. " How sweet it is here—how beautiful it is ! "

" I 'm accustomed to better things," said the Beetle. " Do you call *this* beautiful ? Why, there is not so much as a dung-heap."

Then he went on, under the shadow of a great stack, and found a Caterpillar crawling along.

" How beautiful the world is ! " said the Caterpillar : " the sun is so warm, and everything so enjoyable ! And when I go to sleep, and die, as they call it, I shall wake up as a butterfly, with beautiful wings to fly with."

" How conceited you are ! " exclaimed the Beetle. " *You* fly about as a butterfly, indeed ! I 've come out of the stable of the Emperor, and no one there, not even the Emperor's favourite horse—that by the way wears my cast-off golden shoes—has any such idea. To have wings to fly ! why, we can fly now ; " and he spread his wings and flew away. " I don't want to be annoyed, and yet I am annoyed," he said, as he flew off.

Soon afterwards he fell down upon a great lawn. For awhile he lay there and feigned slumber ; at last he fell asleep in earnest.

Suddenly a heavy shower of rain came falling from the clouds. The Beetle woke up at the noise, and wanted to escape into the earth, but could not. He was tumbled over and over : sometimes he was swimming on his stomach, sometimes on his back, and as for flying, that was out of the question ; he doubted whether he should escape from the place with his life. He therefore remained lying where he was.

When the weather had moderated a little, and the Beetle had rubbed the water out of his eyes, he saw something gleaming. It was linen that had been placed there to bleach. He managed to make his way up to it, and crept into a fold of the damp linen. Certainly the place was not so comfortable to lie in as the warm stable; but there was no better to be had, and therefore he remained lying there for a whole day and a whole night, and the rain kept on during all the time. Towards morning he crept forth: he was very much out of temper about the climate.

On the linen two Frogs were sitting. Their bright eyes absolutely gleamed with pleasure.

"Wonderful weather this!" one of them cried. "How refreshing! And the linen keeps the water together so beautifully. My hind legs seem to quiver as if I were going to swim."

"I should like to know," said the second, "if the swallow, who flies so far round, in her many journeys in foreign lands ever meets with a better climate than this. What delicious dampness! It is really as if one were lying in a wet ditch. Whoever does not rejoice in this, certainly does not love his fatherland."

"Have you been in the Emperor's stable?" asked the Beetle; "there the dampness is warm and refreshing. That's the climate for me; but I cannot take it with me on my journey. Is there never a muck-heap, here in the garden, where a person of rank, like myself, can feel himself at home, and take up his quarters?"

But the Frogs either did not or would not understand him.

"I never ask a question twice!" said the Beetle, after he had already asked this one three times without receiving any answer.

Then he went a little farther, and stumbled against a fragment of pottery, that certainly ought not to have been lying there; but as it was once there, it gave a good shelter against wind and weather. Here dwelt several families of Earwigs; and these did not require much, only sociality. The female members of the community were full of the purest maternal affection, and accordingly each one considered her own child the most beautiful and cleverest of all.

"Our son has engaged himself," said one mother. "Dear, innocent boy! His greatest hope is that he may creep one day into a clergyman's ear. It's very artless and lovable, that; and being engaged will keep him steady. What joy for a mother!"

"Our son," said another mother, "had scarcely crept out of the egg, when he was already off on his travels. He's all life and spirits; he'll run his horns off! What joy that is for a mother! Is it not so, Mr. Beetle?" for she knew the stranger by his horny coat.

"You are both quite right," said he; so they begged him to walk in; that is to say, to come as far as he could under the bit of pottery.

"Now, you also see *my* little earwig," observed a third mother and a fourth; "they are lovely little things, and highly amusing. They are never ill-behaved, except when they are uncomfortable in their inside; but, unfortunately, one is very subject to that at their age."

Thus each mother spoke of her baby; and the babies talked among themselves, and made use of the little nippers they have in their tails to nip the beard of the Beetle.

"Yes, they are always busy about something, the little rogues!" said the mothers; and they quite beamed with maternal pride; but the Beetle felt bored by that, and therefore he inquired how far it was to the nearest muck-heap.

"That is quite out in the big world, on the other side of the ditch," answered an Earwig. "I hope none of my children will go so far, for it would be the death of me."

"But I shall try to get so far," said the Beetle; and he went off without taking formal leave; for that is considered the polite thing to do. And by the ditch he met several friends; Beetles, all of them.

"Here we live," they said. "We are very comfortable here. Might we ask you to step down into this rich mud? You must be fatigued after your journey."

"Certainly," replied the Beetle. "I have been exposed to the rain, and have had to lie upon linen, and cleanliness is a thing that greatly exhausts me. I have also pains in one of my wings, from standing in a draught under a fragment of pottery. It is really quite refreshing to be among one's companions once more."

"Perhaps you come from a muck-heap?" observed the oldest of them.

"Indeed, I come from a much higher place," replied the Beetle. "I came from the Emperor's stable, where I was born with golden shoes on my feet. I am travelling on a secret embassy. You must not ask me any questions, for I can't betray my secret."

With this the Beetle stepped down into the rich mud. There sat three young maiden Beetles; and they tittered, because they did not know what to say.

"Not one of them is engaged yet," said their mother; and the Beetle maidens tittered again, this time from embarrassment.

"I have never seen greater beauties in the royal stables," exclaimed the Beetle, who was now resting himself.

"Don't spoil my girls," said the mother; "and don't talk to them, please, unless you have serious intentions. But of course your intentions are serious, and therefore I give you my blessing."

"Hurrah!" cried all the other Beetles together; and our friend was engaged. Immediately after the betrothal came the marriage, for there was no reason for delay.

The following day passed very pleasantly, and the next in tolerable comfort; but on the third it was time to think of food for the wife, and perhaps also for children.

"I have allowed myself to be taken in," said our Beetle to himself. "And now there's nothing for it but to take *them* in, in turn."

So said, so done. Away he went, and he stayed away all day, and stayed away all night; and his wife sat there, a forsaken widow.

"Oh," said the other Beetles. "this fellow whom we received into our family is nothing more than a thorough vagabond. He has gone away, and has left his wife a burden upon our hands."

"Well, then, she shall be unmarried again, and sit here among my daughters," said the mother. "Fie on the villain who forsook her!"

THE SCHOLARS FIND THE BEETLE.

In the meantime the Beetle had been journeying on, and had sailed across the ditch on a cabbage leaf. In the morning two persons came to the ditch. When they saw him, they took him up, and turned him over and over, and looked very learned, especially one of them—a boy.

"Allah sees the black beetle in the black stone and in the black rock. Is not that written in the Koran?" Then he translated the Beetle's name into Latin, and enlarged upon the creature's nature and history. The second person, an older scholar, voted for carrying him home. He said they wanted just such good specimens; and this seemed an uncivil speech to our Beetle, and in consequence he flew suddenly out of the speaker's hand. As he had now dry wings, he flew a tolerable distance, and reached a hotbed, where a sash of the glass roof was partly open, so he quietly slipped in and buried himself in the warm earth.

"Very comfortable it is here," said he.

Soon after he went to sleep, and dreamed that the Emperor's favourite horse had fallen, and had given him his golden shoes, with the promise that he should have two more.

That was all ery charming. When the Beetle woke up, he crept forth and looked around him. What splendour was in the hothouse! In the background great palm trees growing up on high; the sun made them look transparent; and beneath them what a luxuriance of green, and of beaming flowers, red as fire, yellow as amber, or white as fresh-fallen snow!

"This is an incomparable plenty of plants," cried the Beetle. "How good they will taste when they are decayed! A capital store-room this! There must certainly be relations of mine living here. I will just see if I can find any one with whom I may associate. I'm proud, certainly, and I'm proud of being so.".

And so he prowled about in the earth, and thought what a pleasant dream that was about the dying horse, and the golden shoes he had inherited.

Suddenly a hand seized the Beetle, and pressed him, and turned him round and round.

The gardener's little son and a companion had come to the hotbed, had espied the Beetle, and wanted to have their fun with him. First he was wrapped in a vine leaf, and then put into warm trousers pocket. He cribbled and crabbled about there with all his might; but he got a good pressing from the boy's hand for this, which served as a hint to him to keep quiet. Then the boy went rapidly towards the great lake that lay at the end of the garden. Here the Beetle was put in an old broken wooden shoe, on which a little stick was placed upright for a mast, and to this mast the Beetle was bound with a woollen thread. Now he was a sailor, and had to sail away.

The lake was not very large, but to the Beetle it seemed an ocean; and he was so astonished at its extent, that he fell over on his back and kicked out with his legs.

The little ship sailed away. The current of the water seized it; but whenever it went too far from the shore, one of the boys turned up his trousers and went in after it, and brought it back to the land. But at length, just as it went merrily out again, the two boys were called away, and very harshly, so that they hurried to obey the summons, ran away from the lake, and left the little ship to its fate. Thus it drove away from the shore, farther and farther into the open sea: it was terrible work for the Beetle, for he could not get away in consequence of being bound to the mast.

Then a Fly came and paid him a visit.

"What beautiful weather!" said the Fly. "I'll rest here, and sun myself. You have an agreeable time of it."

"You speak without knowing the facts," replied the Beetle. "Don't you see that I'm a prisoner?"

"Ah! but I'm not a prisoner," observed the Fly; and he flew away accordingly.

"Well, now I know the world," said the Beetle to himself. "It is an abominable world. I'm the only honest person in it. First, they refuse me my golden shoes; then I have to lie on wet linen, and to stand in the draught; and, to crown all, they fasten a wife upon me. Then, when I 've taken a quick step out into the world, and found out how one can have it there, and how I wished to have it, one of those human boys comes and ties me up, and leaves me to the mercy of the wild waves, while the Emperor's favourite horse prances about proudly in golden shoes. That is what annoys me more than all. But one must not look for sympathy in this world! My career has been very interesting; but what's the use of that, if nobody knows it? The world does not deserve to be made acquainted with my history, for it ought to have given me golden shoes, when the Emperor's horse was shod, and I stretched out my feet to be shod too. If I had received golden shoes, I should have become an ornament to the stable. Now the stable has lost me, and the world has lost me. It is all over!"

But all was not over yet. A boat, in which there were a few young girls, came rowing up.

"Look, yonder is an old wooden shoe sailing along," said one of the girls.

"There 's a little creature bound fast to it," said another.

The boat came quite close to our Beetle's ship, and the young girls fished him out of the water. One of them drew a small pair of scissors from her pocket, and cut the woollen thread, without hurting the Beetle; and when she stepped on shore, she put him down on the grass.

"Creep, creep—fly, fly—if thou canst," she said. "Liberty is a splendid thing."

And the Beetle flew up, and straight through the open window of a great building; there he sank down, tired and exhausted, exactly on the mane of the Emperor's favourite horse, who stood in the stable when he was at home, and the Beetle also. The Beetle clung fast to the mane, and sat there a short time to recover himself.

"Here I 'm sitting on the Emperor's favourite horse—sitting on him just like the Emperor himself!" he cried. "But what was I saying? Yes, now I remember. That 's a good thought, and quite correct. The smith asked me why the golden shoes were given to the horse. Now I 'm quite clear about the answer. They were given to the horse on *my* account."

And now the Beetle was in a good temper again.

"Travelling expands the mind rarely," said he.

The sun's rays came streaming into the stable, and shone upon him, and made the place lively and bright.

"The world is not so bad, upon the whole," said the Beetle; "but one must know how to take things as they come."

WHAT THE OLD MAN DOES IS ALWAYS RIGHT

I will tell you the story which was told to me when I was a little boy. Every time I thought of the story, it seemed to me to become more and more charming; for it is with stories as it is with many people—they become better as they grow older.

I take it for granted that you have been in the country, and seen a very old farm-house with a thatched roof, and mosses and small plants growing wild upon the thatch. There is a stork's nest on the summit of the gable; for we can't do without the stork. The walls of the house are sloping, and the windows are low, and only one of the latter is made so that it will open. The baking-oven sticks out of the wall like a little fat body. The elder tree hangs over the paling, and beneath its branches, at the foot of the paling, is a pool of water in which a few ducks are disporting themselves. There is a yard dog too, who barks at all comers.

Just such a farm-house stood out in the country; and in this house dwelt an old couple—a peasant and his wife. Small as was their property, there was one article among it that they could do without—a horse, which made a living out of the grass it found by the side of the high road. The old peasant rode into the town on this horse; and often his neighbours borrowed it of him, and rendered the old couple some service in return for the loan of it. But they thought it would be best if they sold the horse, or exchanged it for something that might be more useful to them. But what might this *something* be?

"You'll know that best, old man," said the wife. "It is fair-day to-day, so ride into town, and get rid of the horse for money, or make a good exchange: whichever you do will be right to me. Ride off to the fair."

And she fastened his neckerchief for him, for she could do that better than he could; and she tied it in a double bow, for she could do that very prettily. Then she brushed his hat round and round with the palm of her hand, and gave him a kiss. So he rode away upon the horse that was to be sold or to be bartered for something else. Yes, the old man knew what he was about.

The sun shone hotly down, and not a cloud was to be seen in the sky. The road was very dusty, for many people who were all bound for the fair were driving, or riding, or walking upon it. There was no shelter anywhere from the sunbeams.

Among the rest, a man was trudging along, and driving a cow to the fair. The cow was as beautiful a creature as any cow can be.

"She gives good milk, I'm sure," said the peasant. "That would be a very good exchange—the cow for the horse.

"Hallo, you there with the cow!" he said; "I tell you what—I fancy a horse costs more than a cow, but I don't care for that; a cow would be more useful to me. If you like, we'll exchange."

"To be sure I will," said the man; and they exchanged accordingly.

So that was settled, and the peasant might have turned back, for he had done the business he came to do; but as he had once made up his mind to go to the fair, he determined to proceed, merely to have a look at it; and so he went on to the town with his cow.

Leading the animal, he strode sturdily on; and after a short time, he overtook a man who was driving a sheep. It was a good fat sheep, with a fine fleece on its back.

"I should like to have that fellow," said our peasant to himself. "He would find plenty of grass by our palings, and in the winter we could keep him in the room with us. Perhaps it would be more practical to have a sheep instead of a cow. Shall we exchange?"

The man with the sheep was quite ready, and the bargain was struck. So our peasant went on in the high road with his sheep.

Soon he overtook another man, who came into the road from a field, carrying a great goose under his arm.

"That's a heavy thing you have there. It has plenty of feathers and plenty of fat, and would look well tied to a string, and paddling in the water at our place. That would be something for my old woman; she could make all kinds of profit out of it. How often she has said, 'If we only had a goose!' Now, perhaps, she can have one; and, if possible, it shall be hers. Shall we exchange? I'll give you my sheep for your goose, and thank you into the bargain."

The other man had not the least objection; and accordingly they exchanged, and our peasant became proprietor of the goose.

By this time he was very near the town. The crowd on the high road became greater and greater; there was quite a crush of men and cattle. They walked in the road, and close by the palings; and at the barrier they even walked into the toll-man's potato-field, where his own fowl was strutting about with a string to its leg, lest it should take fright at the crowd, and stray away, and so be lost. This fowl had short tail-feathers, and winked with both its eyes, and looked very cunning. "Cluck, cluck!" said the fowl. What it thought when it said this I cannot tell you; but directly our good man saw it, he thought, "That's the finest fowl I've ever seen in my life! Why, it's finer than our parson's brood hen. On my word, I should like to have that fowl. A fowl can always find a grain or two, and can almost keep itself. I think it would be a good exchange if I could get that for my goose.

"Shall we exchange?" he asked the toll-taker.

"Exchange!" repeated the man; "well, that would not be a bad thing."

And so they exchanged; the toll-taker at the barrier kept the goose, and the peasant carried away the fowl.

Now, he had done a good deal of business on his way to the fair, and he was hot and tired. He wanted something to eat, and a glass of brandy to drink; and soon he was in front of the inn. He was just about to step in, when the hostler came out, so they met at the door. The hostler was carrying a sack.

"What have you in that sack?" asked the peasant.

" Rotten apples," answered the hostler ; " a whole sack-full of them—
enough to feed the pigs with."

" Why, that 's terrible waste !   I should like to take them to my old
woman at home.   Last year the old tree by the turf-hole only bore a
single apple, and we kept it in the cupboard till it was quite rotten and
spoiled.   ' It was always property,' my old woman said ; but here she
could see a quantity of property—a whole sack-full.   Yes, I shall be glad
to show them to her."

" What will you give me for the sack-full ?" asked the hostler.

" What will I give ?   I will give my fowl in exchange."

And he gave the fowl accordingly, and received the apples, which he
carried into the guest-room.   He leaned the sack carefully by the stove,
and then went to the table.   But the stove was hot : he had not thought
of that.   Many guests were present—horse dealers, ox-herds, and two
Englishmen—and the two Englishmen were so rich that their pockets
bulged out with gold coins, and almost burst ; and they could bet, too,
as you shall hear.

Hiss-s-s ! hiss-s-s !   What was that by the stove ?   The apples were
beginning to roast !

" What is that ?"

" Why, do you know—" said our peasant.

And he told the whole story of the horse that he had changed for a
cow, and all the rest of it, down to the apples.

" Well, your old woman will give it you well when you get home !"
said one of the two Englishmen.   " There will be a disturbance."

" What ?—give me what ?" said the peasant.   " She will kiss me, and
say, ' What the old man does is always right.' "

" Shall we wager ?" said the Englishman.   " We 'll wager coined gold
by the ton—a hundred pounds to the hundredweight !"

" A bushel will be enough," replied the peasant.   " I can only set the
bushel of apples against it ; and I 'll throw myself and my old woman
into the bargain—and I fancy that 's piling up the measure."

" Done—taken ! "

And the bet was made.   The host's carriage came up, and the Englishmen got in, and the peasant got in ; away they went, and soon they
stopped before the peasant's hut.

" Good evening, old woman."

" Good evening, old man."

" I 've made the exchange."

" Yes, you understand what you 're about," said the woman.

And she embraced him, and paid no attention to the stranger guests,
nor did she notice the sack.

" I got a cow in exchange for the horse," said he.

" Heaven be thanked !" said she.   " What glorious milk we shall now
have, and butter and cheese on the table !   That was a most capital exchange ! "

" Yes, but I changed the cow for a sheep."

" Ah, that 's better still ! " cried the wife.   " You always think of

THE OLD MAN RELATES HIS SUCCESS.

everything: we have just pasture enough for a sheep. Ewe's-milk and cheese, and woollen jackets and stockings! The cow cannot give those, and her hairs will only come off. How you think of everything!"

"But I changed away the sheep for a goose."

"Then this year we shall really have roast goose to eat, my dear old man. You are always thinking of something to give me pleasure. How charming that is! We can let the goose walk about with a string to her leg, and she'll grow fatter still before we roast her."

"But I gave away the goose for a fowl," said the man.

" A fowl ?   That *was* a good exchange ! " replied the woman.   " The fowl will lay eggs and hatch them, and we shall have chickens : we shall have a whole poultry-yard !   Oh, that 's just what I was wishing for."

" Yes, but I exchanged the fowl for a sack of shrivelled apples."

" What !—I must positively kiss you for that," exclaimed the wife. " My dear, good husband !   Now I 'll tell you something.   Do you know, you had hardly left me this morning, before I began thinking how I could give you something very nice this evening.   I thought it should be pancakes with savoury herbs.   I had eggs, and bacon too ; but I wanted herbs.   So I went over to the schoolmaster's—they have herbs there, I know—but the schoolmistress is a mean woman, though she looks so sweet.   I begged her to lend me a handful of herbs. ' Lend ! ' she answered me ; ' nothing at all grows in our garden, not even a shrivelled apple.   I could not even lend you a shrivelled apple, my dear woman.'   But now *I* can lend *her* ten, or a whole sack-full.   That I 'm very glad of ; that makes me laugh ! "   And with that she gave him a sounding kiss.

" I like that ! " exclaimed both the Englishmen together.   " Always going down-hill, and always merry ; that 's worth the money."

So they paid a hundredweight of gold to the peasant, who was not scolded, but kissed.

Yes, it always pays, when the wife sees and always asserts that her husband knows best, and that whatever he does is right.

You see, that is my story.   I heard it when I was a child ; and now you have heard it too, and know that " What the old man does is always right."

OLE THE TOWER-KEEPER.

" In the world it 's always going up and down—and now I can't go up any higher ! "   So said Ole the tower-keeper.   " Most people have to try both the ups and the downs ; and, rightly considered, we all get to be watchmen at last, and look down upon life from a height."

Such was the speech of Ole, my friend, the old tower-keeper, a strange talkative old fellow, who seemed to speak out everything that came into his head, and who for all that had many a serious thought deep in his heart.   Yes, he was the child of respectable people, and there were even some who said that he was the son of a privy councillor, or that he might have been ; he had studied too, and had been assistant teacher and deputy clerk ; but of what service was all that to him ?   In those days he lived in the clerk's house, and was to have everything in the house, to be at free quarters, as the saying is ; but he was still, so to speak, a fine young gentlemen.   He wanted to have his boots cleaned with patent blacking, and the clerk could only afford ordinary grease ; and upon that point they split—one spoke of stinginess, the other of vanity, and the blacking became the black cause of enmity between them, and at last they parted.

This is what he demanded of the world in general—namely, patent blacking—and he got nothing but grease. Accordingly he at last drew back from all men, and became a hermit; but the church tower is the only place in a great city where hermitage, office, and bread can be found together. So he betook himself up thither, and smoked his pipe as he made his solitary rounds. He looked upward and downward, and had his own thoughts, and told in his way of what he read in books and in himself. I often lent him books, good books; and you may know a man by the company he keeps. He loved neither the English governess-novels, nor the French ones, which he called a mixture of empty wind and raisin-stalks: he wanted biographies and descriptions of the wonders of the world. I visited him at least once a year, generally directly after New Year's-day, and then he always spoke of this and that which the change of the year had put into his head.

I will tell the story of three of these visits, and will reproduce his own words whenever I can remember them.

FIRST VISIT.

Among the books which I had lately lent Ole, was one which had greatly rejoiced and occupied him. It was a geological book, containing an account of the boulders.

"Yes, they're rare old fellows, those boulders!" he said; "and to think that we should pass them without noticing them! And over the street pavement, the paving-stones, those fragments of the oldest remains of antiquity, one walks without ever thinking about them. I have done the very thing myself. But now I look respectfully at every paving-stone. Many thanks for the book! It has filled me with thought, and has made me long to read more on the subject. The romance of the earth is, after all, the most wonderful of all romances. It's a pity one can't read the first volumes of it, because they're written in a language that we don't understand. One must read in the different strata, in the pebble-stones, for each separate period. Yes, it is a romance, a very wonderful romance, and we all have our place in it. We grope and ferret about, and yet remain where we are, but the ball keeps turning, without emptying the ocean over us; the clod on which we move about, holds, and does not let us through. And then it's a story that has been acting for thousands upon thousands of years, and is still going on. My best thanks for the book about the boulders. Those are fellows indeed! they could tell us something worth hearing, if they only knew how to talk. It's really a pleasure, now and then to become a mere nothing, especially when a man is as highly placed as I am. And then to think that we all, even with patent lacquer, are nothing more than insects of a moment on that ant-hill the earth, though we may be insects with stars and garters, places and offices! One feels quite a

novice beside these venerable million-year-old boulders. On last New
Year's-eve I was reading the book, and had lost myself in it so completely, that I forgot my usual New Year's diversion, namely, the wild
hunt to Amack. Ah, you don't know what that is!

"The journey of the witches on broomsticks is well enough known—
that journey is taken on St. John's-eve, to the Brocken; but we have a
wild journey also, which is national and modern, and that is the journey
to Amack on the night of the New Year. All indifferent poets and
poetesses, musicians, newspaper writers, and artistic notabilities, I mean
those who are no good, ride in the New Year's-night through the air to

THE RIDE TO AMACK.

Amack. They sit backwards on their painting brushes or quill pens,
for steel pens won't bear them, they're too stiff. As I told you, I see
that every New Year's-night, and could mention the majority of the
riders by name, but I should not like to draw their enmity upon myself,
for they don't like people to talk about their ride to Amack on quill
pens. I've a kind of niece, who is a fishwife, and who, as she tells me,
supplies three respectable newspapers with the terms of abuse and vitu-
peration they use, and she has herself been at Amack as an invited
guest; but she was carried out thither, for she does not own a quill pen,
nor can she ride. She has told me all about it. Half of what she said
is not true, but the other half gives us information enough. When she
was out there, the festivities began with a song: each of the guests had
written his own song, and each one sang his own song, for he thought
that the best, and it was all one, all the same melody. Then those came

marching up, in little bands, who are only busy with their mouths.
There were ringing bells that sang alternately; and then came the little
drummers that beat their tattoo in the family circle; and acquaintance
was made with those who write without putting their names, which here
means as much as using grease instead of patent blacking; and then
there was the beadle with his boy, and the boy was the worst off, for in
general he gets no notice taken of him; then too there was the good
street-sweeper with his cart, who turns over the dust-bin, and calls it
'good, very good, remarkably good.' And in the midst of the pleasure
that was afforded by the mere meeting of these folks, there shot up out
of the great dirt-heap at Amack a stem, a tree, an immense flower, a
great mushroom, a perfect roof, which formed a sort of warehouse for the
worthy company, for in it hung everything they had given to the world
during the Old Year. Out of the tree poured sparks like flames of fire;
these were the ideas and thoughts, borrowed from others, which they
had used, and which now got free and rushed away like so many fireworks. They played at 'the stick burns,' and the young poets played
at 'heart-burns,' and the witlings played off their jests, and the jests
rolled away with a thundering sound, as if empty pots were being
shattered against doors. 'It was very amusing!' my niece said; in
fact, she said many things that were very malicious but very amusing,
but I won't mention them, for a man must be good-natured and not a
carping critic. But you will easily perceive that when a man once
knows the rights of the journey to Amack, as I know them, it's quite
natural that on the New Year's-night one should look out to see the
wild chase go by. If in the New Year I miss certain persons who used
to be there, I am sure to notice others who are new arrivals; but this
year I omitted taking my look at the guests. I bowled away on the
boulders, rolled back through millions of years, and saw the stones
break loose high up in the North, saw them drifting about on icebergs,
long before Noah's ark was constructed, saw them sink down to the
bottom of the sea, and reappear with a sand-bank, with that one that
peered forth from the flood and said, 'This shall be Zealand!' I saw
them become the dwelling-place of birds that are unknown to us, and
then became the seat of wild chiefs of whom we know nothing, until
with their axes they cut their Runic signs into a few of these stones,
which then came into the calendar of time. But as for me, I had gone
quite beyond all lapse of time, and had become a cipher and a nothing.
Then three or four beautiful falling stars came down, which cleared the
air, and gave my thoughts another direction. You know what a falling
star is, do you not? The learned men are not at all clear about it. I
have my own ideas about shooting stars, as the common people in many
parts call them, and my idea is this: How often are silent thanksgivings
offered up for one who has done a good and noble action! the thanks
are often speechless, but they are not lost for all that. I think these
thanks are caught up, and the sunbeams bring the silent, hidden thankfulness over the head of the benefactor; and if it be a whole people that
has been expressing its gratitude through a long lapse of time, the

thankfulness appears as a nosegay of flowers, and at length falls in the form of a shooting star over the good man's grave. I am always very much pleased when I see a shooting star, especially in the New Year's-night, and then find out for whom the gift of gratitude was intended. Lately a gleaming star fell in the south-west, as a tribute of thanks-giving to many, many! 'For whom was that star intended?' thought I. It fell, no doubt, on the hill by the Bay of Flensberg, where the Danebrog waves over the graves of Schleppegrell, Läslöes, and their comrades. One star also fell in the midst of the land, fell upon Sorö, a flower on the grave of Holberg, the thanks of the year from a great many—thanks for his charming plays!

"It is a great and pleasant thought to know that a shooting star falls upon our graves: on mine certainly none will fall—no sunbeam brings thanks to me, for here there is nothing worthy of thanks. I shall not get the patent lacquer," said Ole; "for my fate on earth is only grease, after all."

SECOND VISIT.

It was New Year's-day, and I went up on the tower. Ole spoke of the toasts that were drunk on the transition from the Old Year into the New, from one grave into the other, as he said. And he told me a story about the glasses, and this story had a very deep meaning. It was this:

"When on the New Year's-night the clock strikes twelve, the people at the table rise up, with full glasses in their hands, and drain these glasses, and drink success to the New Year. They begin the year with the glass in their hands; that is a good beginning for topers. They begin the New Year by going to bed, and that's a good beginning for drones. Sleep is sure to play a great part in the New Year, and the glass like-wise. Do you know what dwells in the glass?" asked Ole. "I will tell you—there dwell in the glass, first, health, and then pleasure, then the most complete sensual delight; and misfortune and the bitterest woe dwell in the glass also. Now suppose we count the glasses—of course I count the different degrees in the glasses for different people.

"You see, the *first glass*, that's the glass of health, and in that the herb of health is found growing; put it up on the beam in the ceiling, and at the end of the year you may be sitting in the arbour of health.

"If you take the *second glass*—from this a little bird soars upwards, twittering in guileless cheerfulness, so that a man may listen to his song and perhaps join in 'Fair is life! no downcast looks! Take courage and march onward!'

"Out of the *third glass* rises a little winged urchin, who cannot cer-tainly be called an angel-child, for there is goblin blood in his veins, and he has the spirit of a goblin; not wishing to hurt or harm you, indeed, but very ready to play off tricks upon you. He'll sit at your ear and whisper merry thoughts to you; he'll creep into your heart and warm you, so that you grow very merry and become a wit, so far as the wits of the others can judge.

" In the *fourth glass* is neither herb, bird, nor urchin : in that glass is the pause drawn by reason, and one may never go beyond that sign.

" Take the *fifth glass*, and you will weep at yourself, you will feel such a deep emotion ; or it will affect you in a different way. Out of the glass there will spring with a bang Prince Carnival, nine times and extravagantly merry : he 'll draw you away with him, you 'll forget your dignity, if you have any, and you 'll forget more than you should or ought to forget. All is dance, song, and sound ; the masks will carry you away with them, and the daughters of vanity, clad in silk and satin, will come with loose hair and alluring charms ; but tear yourself away if you can !

" The *sixth glass !* Yes, in that glass sits a demon, in the form of a little, well-dressed, attractive and very fascinating man, who thoroughly understands you, agrees with you in everything, and becomes quite a second self to you. He has a lantern with him, to give you light as he accompanies you home. There is an old legend about a saint who was allowed to choose one of the seven deadly sins, and who accordingly chose drunkenness, which appeared to him the least, but which led him to commit all the other six. The man's blood is mingled with that of the demon—it is the sixth glass, and with that the germ of all evil shoots up within us ; and each one grows up with a strength like that of the grains of mustard seed, and shoots up into a tree, and spreads over the whole world ; and most people have no choice but to go into the oven, to be re-cast in a new form.

" That 's the history of the glasses," said the tower-keeper Ole, " and it can be told with lacquer or only with grease ; but I give it you with both ! "

THIRD VISIT.

On this occasion I chose the general " moving-day " for my visit to Ole, for on that day it is anything but agreeable down in the streets in the town ; for they are full of sweepings, shreds, and remnants of all sorts, to say nothing of the cast-off rubbish in which one has to wade about. But this time I happened to see two children playing in this wilderness of sweepings. They were playing at " going to bed," for the occasion seemed especially favourable for this sport : they crept under the straw, and drew an old bit of ragged curtain over themselves by way of coverlet. " It was splendid ! " they said ; but it was a little too strong for me, and besides, I was obliged to mount up on my visit to Ole.

" It 's moving-day to-day," he said ; " streets and houses are like a dust-bin, a large dust-bin ; but I 'm content with a cartload. I may get something good out of that, and I really did get something good out of it, once. Shortly after Christmas I was going up the street ; it was rough weather, wet and dirty ; the right kind of weather to catch cold in. The dustman was there with his cart, which was full, and looked like a sample of streets on moving-day. At the back of the cart stood a fir tree, quite green still, and with tinsel on its twigs : it had been used on Christmas-eve, and now it was thrown out into the street, and the dustman had stood it up at the back of his cart. It was droll to look at, or you may say it was mournful—all depends on what you think of when you see it; and I thought about it, and thought this and that of many things that were in the cart: or I might have done so, and that comes to the same thing. There was an old lady's glove too: I wonder what that was thinking of? Shall I tell you? The glove was lying there, pointing with its little finger at the tree. 'I'm sorry for the tree,' it thought; 'and I was also at the feast, where the chandeliers glittered. My life was, so to speak, a ball-night: a pressure of the hand, and I burst! My memory keeps dwelling upon that, and I have really nothing else to live for!' This is what the glove thought, or what it might have thought. 'That's a stupid affair with yonder fir tree,' said the Potsherds. You see, potsherds think everything is stupid. 'When one is in the dust-cart,' they said, 'one ought not to give one's self airs and wear tinsel. I know that I have been useful in the world, far more useful than such a green stick.' That was a view that might be taken, and I don't think it quite a peculiar one; but for all that the fir tree looked very well: it was like a little poetry in the dust-heap; and truly there is dust enough in the streets on moving-day. The way is difficult and troublesome then, and I feel obliged to run away out of the confusion; or if I am on the tower, I stay there and look down, and it is amusing enough.

"There are the good people below, playing at 'changing houses.' They toil and tug away with their goods and chattels, and the household goblin sits in an old tub and moves with them; all the little griefs of the lodging and the family, and the real cares and sorrows, move with them out of the old dwelling into the new; and what gain is there for them or for us in the whole affair? Yes, there was written long ago the good old maxim: 'Think on the great moving-day of death!' That is a serious thought: I hope it is not disagreeable to you that I should have touched upon it? Death is the most certain messenger, after all, in spite of his various occupations. Yes, Death is the omnibus conductor, and he is the passport writer, and he countersigns our service-book, and he is director of the savings bank of life. Do you understand me? All the deeds of our life, the great and the little alike, we put into this savings bank; and when Death calls with his omnibus, and we have to step in, and drive with him into the land of eternity, then on the frontier he gives us our service-book as a pass. As a provision for the journey, he takes this or that good deed we have done, and lets it accompany us; and this may be very pleasant or very terrific. Nobody has ever escaped this omnibus journey: there is certainly a talk about *one* who was not allowed to go—they call him the Wandering Jew: he has to ride behind the omnibus. If he had been allowed to get in he would have escaped the clutches of the poets.

"Just cast your mind's eye into that great omnibus. The society is mixed, for King and beggar, genius and idiot, sit side by side: they must go without their property and money; they have only the service-book

THE REJECTED TRAVELLER.

and the gift out of the saving's bank with them. But which of our deeds is selected and given to us? Perhaps quite a little one, one that we have forgotten, but which has been recorded—small as a pea, but the pea can send out a blooming shoot. The poor bumpkin, who sat on a low stool in the corner, and was jeered at and flouted, will perhaps have his worn-out stool given him as a provision; and the stool may become a litter in the land of eternity, and rise up then as a throne, gleaming like gold and blooming as an arbour. He who always lounged about, and drank the spiced draught of pleasure, that he might forget the wild things he had done here, will have his barrel given to him on the journey, and will have to drink from it as they go on; and the drink is bright and clear, so that the thoughts remain pure, and all good and noble feelings are awakened, and he sees and feels what in life he could not or would not see; and then he has within him the punishment, the *gnawing worm*, which will not die through time incalculable. If on the glasses there stood written '*oblivion*,' on the barrel '*remembrance*' is inscribed.

"When I read a good book, an historical work, I always think at last of the poetry of what I am reading, and of the omnibus of death, and wonder which of the hero's deeds Death took out of the savings bank for him, and what provisions he got on the journey into eternity. There was once a French King—I have forgotten his name, for the names of good people are sometimes forgotten, even by me, but it will come back some day; there was a King who, during a famine, became the benefactor of his people; and the people raised to his memory a monument of snow, with the inscription, 'Quicker than this melts didst thou bring help!'" I fancy that Death, looking back upon the monument, gave him a single snow-flake as provision, a snow-flake that never melts, and this flake floated over his royal head, like a white butterfly, into the land of eternity. Thus too, there was a Louis XI. I have remembered *his* name, for one remembers what is bad—a trait of him often comes into my thoughts, and I wish one could say the story is not true. He had his lord high constable executed, and he could execute him, right or wrong; but he had the innocent children of the constable, one seven and the other eight years old, placed under the scaffold so that the warm blood of their father spurted over them, and then he had them sent to the Bastille, and shut up in iron cages, where not even a coverlet was given them to protect them from the cold. And King Louis sent the executioner to them every week, and had a tooth pulled out of the head of each, that they might not be too comfortable; and the elder of the boys said, 'My mother would die of grief if she knew that my younger brother had to suffer so cruelly; therefore pull out two of my teeth, and spare him.' The tears came into the hangman's eyes, but the King's will was stronger than the tears; and every week two little teeth were brought to him on a silver plate; he had demanded them, and he had them. I fancy that Death took these two teeth out of the savings bank of life, and gave them to Louis XI., to carry with him on the great journey into the land of immortality: they fly before him like two flames of fire; they shine and burn, and they bite him, the innocent children's teeth.

"Yes, that's a serious journey, the omnibus ride on the great moving-day! And when is it to be undertaken? That's just the serious part of it. Any day, any hour, any minute, the omnibus may draw up. Which of our deeds will Death take out of the savings bank, and give to us as provision? Let us think of the moving-day that is not marked in the calendar."

GOOD HUMOUR.

My father left me the best inheritance; to wit—good humour. And who was my father? Why, that has nothing to do with the humour. He was lively and stout, round and fat; and his outer and inner man were in direct contradiction to his calling. And pray what was he by profession and calling in civil society? Yes, if this were to be written down and printed in the very beginning of a book, it is probable that many when they read it would lay the book aside, and say, "It looks so uncomfortable; I don't like anything of that sort." And yet my father was neither a horse slaughterer nor an executioner; on the contrary, his office placed him at the head of the most respectable gentry of the town; and he held his place by right, for it was his right place. He had to go first before the bishop even, and before the Princes of the Blood. He always went first—for he was the driver of the hearse!

There, now it's out! And I will confess that when people saw my father sitting perched up on the omnibus of death, dressed in his long, wide, black cloak, with his black-bordered three-cornered hat on his head—and then his face, exactly as the sun is drawn, round and jocund—it was difficult for them to think of the grave and of sorrow. The face said, "It doesn't matter, it doesn't matter; it will be better than one thinks."

You see, I have inherited my good humour from him, and also the habit of going often to the churchyard, which is a good thing to do if it be done in the right spirit; and then I take in the "Intelligencer," just as he used to do.

I am not quite young. I have neither wife, nor children, nor a library; but, as aforesaid, I take in the "Intelligencer," and that's my favourite newspaper, as it was also my father's. It is very useful, and contains everything that a man needs to know—such as who preaches in the church and in the new books. And then what a lot of charity, and what a number of innocent, harmless verses are found in it! Advertisements for husbands and wives, and requests for interviews—all quite simple and natural. Certainly, one may live merrily and be contentedly buried if one takes in the "Intelligencer." And, as a concluding advantage, by the end of his life a man will have such a capital store of paper, that he may use it as a soft bed, unless he prefers to rest upon wood-shavings.

The newspaper and my walk to the churchyard were always my most exciting occupations—they were like bathing-places for my good humour.

The newspaper every one can read for himself. But please come with me to the churchyard; let us wander there where the sun shines and the trees grow green. Each of the narrow houses is like a closed book, with the back placed uppermost, so that one can only read the title and judge what the book contains, but can tell nothing about it; but I know something of them. I heard it from my father, or found it out myself. I have it all down in my record that I wrote out for my own use and pleasure: all that lie here, and a few more, too, are chronicled in it.

Now we are in the churchyard.

Here, behind this white railing, where once a rose tree grew—it is gone now, but a little evergreen from the next grave stretches out its green fingers to make a show—there rests a very unhappy man; and yet, when he lived, he was in what they call a good position. He had enough to live upon, and something over; but worldly cares, or, to speak more correctly, his artistic taste, weighed heavily upon him. If in the evening he sat in the theatre to enjoy himself thoroughly, he would be quite put out if the machinist had put too strong a light into one side of the moon, or if the sky-pieces hung down over the scenes when they ought to have hung behind them, or when a palm tree was introduced into a scene representing the Berlin Zoological Gardens, or a cactus in a view of the Tyrol, or a beech tree in the far north of Norway. As if that was of any consequence. Is it not quite immaterial? Who would fidget about such a trifle? It's only make-believe, after all, and every one is expected to be amused. Then sometimes the public applauded too much to suit his taste, and sometimes too little. "They're like wet wood this evening," he would say; "they won't kindle at all!" And then he would look round to see what kind of people they were; and sometimes he would find them laughing at the wrong time, when they ought not to have laughed, and that vexed him; and he fretted, and was an unhappy man, and at last fretted himself into his grave.

Here rests a very happy man. That is to say, a very grand man. He was of high birth, and that was lucky for him, for otherwise he would never have been anything worth speaking of; and nature orders all that very wisely, so that it's quite charming when we think of it. He used to go about in a coat embroidered back and front, and appeared in the saloons of society just like one of those costly, pearl-embroidered bell-pulls, which have always a good, thick, serviceable cord behind them to do the work. He likewise had a good stout cord behind him, in the shape of a substitute, who did his duty, and who still continues to do it behind another embroidered bell-pull. Everything is so nicely managed, it's enough to put one into a good humour.

Here rests—well, it's a very mournful reflection—here rests a man who spent sixty-seven years considering how he should get a good idea. The object of his life was to say a good thing, and at last he felt convinced in his own mind that he had got one, and was so glad of it that he died of pure joy at having caught an idea at last. Nobody derived any benefit from it, and nobody even heard what the good thing was. Now, I can fancy that this same good thing won't let him lie quiet in his grave; for let us suppose that it is a good thing which can only be brought out at breakfast if it is to make an effect, and that he, according to the received opinion concerning ghosts, can only rise and walk at midnight. Why, then the good thing would not suit the time, and the

THE CHURCHYARD NARRATION.

man must carry his good idea down with him again. What an unhappy man he must be!

Here rests a remarkably stingy woman. During her lifetime she used to get up at night and mew, so that the neighbours might think she kept a cat—she was so remarkably stingy.

Here is a maiden of another kind. When the canary bird of the heart begins to chirp, reason puts her fingers in her ears. The maiden was going to be married, but—well, it's an every-day story, and we will let the dead rest.

Here sleeps a widow who carried melody in her mouth and gall in her heart. She used to go out for prey in the families round about; and the prey she hunted was her neighbours' faults, and she was an indefatigable hunter.

Here's a family sepulchre. Every member of this family held so firmly to the opinions of the rest, that if all the world, and the newspapers into the bargain, said of a certain thing it is so and so, and the little boy came home from school and said, "I've learned it thus and thus," they declared his opinion to be the only true one, because he belonged to the family. And it is an acknowledged fact, that if the yard cock of the family crowed at midnight, they would declare it was morning, though the watchmen and all the clocks in the city were crying out that it was twelve o'clock at night.

The great poet Goëthe concludes his "Faust" with the words "may be continued;" and our wanderings in the churchyard may be continued too. If any of my friends, or my non-friends, go on too fast for me, I go out to my favourite spot, and select a mound, and bury him or her there—bury that person who is yet alive; and there those I bury must stay till they come back as new and improved characters. I inscribe their life and their deeds, looked at in my fashion, in my record; and that's what all people ought to do. They ought not to be vexed when any one goes on ridiculously, but bury him directly, and maintain their good humour, and keep to the "Intelligencer," which is often a book written by the people with its hand guided.

When the time comes for me to be bound with my history in the boards of the grave, I hope they will put up as my epitaph, "A good humoured one." And that's my story.

"IT'S QUITE TRUE!"

"THAT is a terrible affair!" said a Hen; and she said it in a quarter of the town where the occurrence had not happened. "That is a terrible affair in the poultry-house. I cannot sleep alone to-night! It is quite fortunate that there are many of us on the roost together!" And she told a tale, at which the feathers of the other birds stood on end, and the cock's comb fell down flat. It's quite true!

But we will begin at the beginning; and the beginning begins in a poultry-house in another part of the town. The sun went down, and the fowls jumped up on their perch to roost. There was a Hen, with white feathers and short legs, who laid her right number of eggs, and was a respectable hen in every way; as she flew up on to the roost she pecked herself with her beak, and a little feather fell out.

"There it goes!" said she; "the more I peck myself the handsomer I grow!" And she said it quite merrily, for she was a joker among the hens, though, as I have said, she was very respectable; and then she went to sleep.

It was dark all around; hen sat by hen, but the one that sat next to the merry Hen did not sleep: she heard and she didn't hear, as one should do in this world if one wishes to live in quiet; but she could not refrain from telling it to her next neighbour.

"Did you hear what was said here just now? I name no names; but here is a hen who wants to peck her feathers out to look well. If I were a cock I should despise her."

And just above the Hens sat the Owl, with her husband and her little owlets; the family had sharp ears, and they all heard every word that the neighbouring Hen had spoken, and they rolled their eyes, and the Mother-Owl clapped her wings and said,

"Don't listen to it! But I suppose you heard what was said there? I heard it with my own ears, and one must hear much before one's ears

THE OWLS TELL THE PIGEONS THE DREADFUL NEWS.

fall off. There is one among the fowls who has so completely forgotten what is becoming conduct in a hen that she pulls out all her feathers, and then lets the cock see her."

"*Prenez garde aux enfants*," said the Father-Owl. "That's not fit for the children to hear."

"I'll tell it to the neighbour owl; she's a very proper owl to associate with." And she flew away.

"Hoo! hoo! to-whoo!" they both screeched in front of the neighbour's dovecot to the doves within. "Have you heard it? Have you heard it? Hoo! hoo! there's a hen who has pulled out all her feathers for the sake of the cock. She'll die with cold, if she's not dead already."

"Coo! coo! Where, where?" cried the Pigeons.

"In the neighbour's poultry-yard. I've as good as seen it myself. It's hardly proper to repeat the story, but it's quite true!"

"Believe it! believe every single word of it!" cooed the Pigeons, and they cooed down into their own poultry-yard. "There's a hen, and some say that there are two of them that have plucked out all their feathers, that they may not look like the rest, and that they may attract the cock's attention. That's a bold game, for one may catch cold and die of a fever, and they are both dead."

"Wake up! wake up!" crowed the Cock, and he flew up on to the plank; his eyes were still very heavy with sleep, but yet he crowed. "Three hens have died of an unfortunate attachment to a cock. They have plucked out all their feathers. That's a terrible story. I won't keep it to myself; let it travel farther."

"Let it travel farther!" piped the Bats; and the fowls clucked and the cocks crowed, "Let it go farther! let it go farther!" And so the story travelled from poultry-yard to poultry-yard, and at last came back to the place from which it had gone forth.

"Five fowls," it was told, "have plucked out all their feathers to show which of them had become thinnest out of love to the cock; and then they have pecked each other, and fallen down dead, to the shame and disgrace of their families, and to the great loss of the proprietor."

And the Hen who had lost the little loose feather, of course did not know her own story again; and as she was a very respectable Hen, she said,

"I despise those fowls; but there are many of that sort. One ought not to hush up such a thing, and I shall do what I can that the story may get into the papers, and then it will be spread over all the country, and that will serve those fowls right, and their families too."

It was put into the newspaper; it was printed; and it's quite true *that one little feather may swell till it becomes five fowls.*

CHILDREN'S PRATTLE.

AT the rich merchant's there was a children's party; rich people's children and grand people's children were there. The merchant was a learned man: he had once gone through the college examination, for his honest father had kept him to this, his father who had at first only been a cattle dealer, but always an honest and industrious man. The trade had brought money, and the merchant had managed to increase the store. Clever he was, and he had also a heart, but there was less said of his heart than of his money. At the merchant's, grand people went in and out—people of blood, as it is called, and people of intellect, and people who had both of these, and people who had neither. Now there was a children's party there, and children's prattle, and children speak frankly from the heart. Among the rest there was a beautiful little girl, but the little one was terribly proud; but the servants had taught her that, not her parents, who were far too sensible people. Her father was a groom of the bed-chamber, and that is a very grand office, and she knew it.

"I am a child of the bed-chamber," she said.

Now she might just as well have been a child of the cellar, for nobody can help his birth; and then she told the other children that she was "well born," and said that no one who was not well born could get on far in the world: it was of no use to read and to be industrious, if one was not well born one could not achieve anything.

"And those whose names end with 'sen,'" said she, "they cannot be anything at all. One must put one's arms akimbo and make the elbows quite pointed, and keep them at a great distance, these 'sen!'"

THE POOR BOY AT THE DOOR.

And she stuck out her pretty little arms, and made the elbows quite pointed, to show how it was to be done, and her little arms were very pretty. She was a sweet little girl.

But the little daughter of the merchant became very angry at this speech, for her father's name was Petersen, and she knew that the name ended in "sen;" and therefore she said, as proudly as ever she could,

"But my papa can buy a hundred dollars' worth of bon-bons, and throw them to the children! Can your papa do that?"

"Yes, but my papa," said an author's little daughter, "my papa can put your papa and everybody's papa into the newspaper. All people are afraid of him, my mamma says, for it is my father who rules in the paper."

And the little maiden looked exceedingly proud, as though she had been a real Princess, who is expected to look proud.

But outside at the door, which was ajar, stood a poor boy, peeping through the crack of the door. He was of such lowly station that he was not even allowed to enter the room. He had turned the spit for the cook, and she had allowed him to stand behind the door, and to look at the well-dressed children who were making a merry day within, and for him that was a great deal.

" Oh, to be one of them !" thought he ; and then he heard what was said, which was certainly calculated to make him very unhappy. His parents at home had not a penny to spare to buy a newspaper, much less could they write one ; and what was worst of all, his father's name, and consequently his own, ended completely in 'sen,' and so he could not turn out well. That was terrible. But, after all, he had been born, and very well born as it seemed to him ; that could not be otherwise.

And that is what was done on that evening.

Many years have elapsed since then, and in the course of years children become grown-up persons.

In the town stood a splendid house; it was filled with all kinds of beautiful objects and treasures, and all people wished to see it; even people who dwelt out of town came in to see it. Which of the children of whom we have told might call this house his own ? To know that is very easy. No, no ; it is not so very easy. The house belonged to the poor little boy who had stood on that night behind the door, and he had become something great, although his name ended in " sen,"—Thorwaldsen.

And the three other children ? the children of *blood* and of money, and of spiritual pride ? Well, they had nothing wherewith to reproach each other—they turned out well enough, for they had been well dowered by nature ; and what they had thought and spoken on that evening long ago was mere *children's prattle*.

THE FLYING TRUNK.

THERE was once a merchant, who was so rich that he could pave the whole street with gold, and almost have enough left for a little lane. But he did not do that; he knew how to employ his money differently. When he spent a shilling he got back a crown, such a clever merchant was he ; and this continued till he died.

His son now got all this money ; and he lived merrily, going to the masquerade every evening, making kites out of dollar notes, and playing at ducks and drakes on the sea coast with gold pieces instead of pebbles. In this way the money might soon be spent, and indeed it was so. At last he had no more than four shillings left, and no clothes to wear but a pair of slippers and an old dressing-gown. Now his friends did not trouble themselves any more about him, as they could not walk with him in the street, but one of them, who was good natured, sent him an old trunk, with the remark, "Pack up!" Yes, that was all very well, but he had nothing to pack, therefore he seated himself in the trunk.

That was a wonderful trunk. So soon as any one pressed the lock, the trunk could fly. He pressed it, and, *whirr!* away flew the trunk

THE MERCHANT'S SON VISITS THE PRINCESS.

with him through the chimney and over the clouds, farther and farther away. But as often as the bottom of the trunk cracked a little he was in great fear lest it might go to pieces, and then he would have flung a fine somersault! In that way he came to the land of the Turks. He hid the trunk in a wood under some dry leaves, and then went into the town. He could do that very well, for among the Turks all the people went dressed like himself in dressing-gown and slippers. Then he met a nurse with a little child.

" Here, you Turkish nurse," he began, " what kind of a great castle is that close by the town, in which the windows are so high up ? "

" There dwells the Sultan's daughter," replied she. " It is prophesied that she will be very unhappy respecting a lover ; and therefore nobody may go to her, unless the Sultan and Sultana are there too."

" Thank you !" said the merchant's son ; and he went out into the forest, seated himself in his trunk, flew on the roof, and crept through the window into the Princess's room.

She was lying asleep on the sofa, and she was so beautiful that the merchant's son was compelled to kiss her. Then she awoke, and was very much startled ; but he said he was a Turkish angel who had come down to her through the air, and that pleased her.

They sat down side by side, and he told her stories about her eyes ; he told her they were the most glorious dark lakes, and that thoughts were swimming about in them like mermaids. And he told her about her forehead ; that it was a snowy mountain with the most splendid halls and pictures. And he told her about the stork who brings the lovely little children.

Yes, those were fine histories ! Then he asked the Princes if she would marry him, and she said " Yes," directly.

" But you must come here on Saturday," said she. " Then the Sultan and the Sultana will be here to tea. They will be very proud that I am to marry a Turkish angel. But take care that you know a very pretty story, for both my parents are very fond indeed of stories. My mother likes them high-flown and moral, but my father likes them merry, so that one can laugh."

" Yes, I shall bring no marriage gift but a story," said he ; and so they parted. But the Princess gave him a sabre, the sheath embroidered with gold pieces, and that was very useful to him.

Now he flew away, bought a new dressing-gown, and sat in the forest and made up a story ; it was to be ready by Saturday, and that was not an easy thing.

By the time he had finished it Saturday had come. The Sultan and his wife and all the court were at the Princess's to tea. He was received very graciously.

" Will you relate us a story ?" said the Sultana ; " one that is deep and edifying."

" Yes, but one that we can laugh at," said the Sultan.

" Certainly," he replied ; and began. And now listen well.

" There was once a bundle of Matches, and these Matches were particularly proud of their high descent. Their genealogical tree, that is to say, the great fir tree of which each of them was a little splinter, had been a great old tree out in the forest. The Matches now lay between a Tinder-Box and an old iron Pot ; and they were telling about the days of their youth. ' Yes, when we were upon the green boughs,' they said, ' then we really were upon the green boughs ! Every morning and evening there was diamond tea for us, I mean dew ; we had sunshine all day long whenever the sun shone, and all the little birds had to tell stories. We could see very well that we were rich, for the other trees were only dressed out in summer, while our family had the means to wear green dresses in the winter as well. But then the woodcutter came, like a great revolution, and our family was broken up. The head of the family got an appointment as mainmast in a first-rate ship, which could sail round the world if necessary; the other branches went to other places, and now we have the office of kindling a light for the vulgar herd. That 's how we grand people came to be in the kitchen.'

" ' My fate was of a different kind,' said the iron Pot which stood next to the Matches. 'From the beginning, ever since I came into the world, there has been a great deal of scouring and cooking done in me. I look after the practical part, and am the first here in the house. My only pleasure is to sit in my place after dinner, very clean and neat, and to carry on a sensible conversation with my comrades. But except the Water-Pot, which sometimes is taken down into the courtyard, we always live within our four walls. Our only newsmonger is the Market Basket; but he speaks very uneasily about the government and the people. Yes, the other day there was an old pot that fell down from fright, and burst. He 's liberal, I can tell you!' 'Now you 're talking too much,' the Tinder-Box interrupted, and the steel struck against the flint, so that sparks flew out. 'Shall we not have a merry evening?'

" ' Yes, let us talk about who is the grandest,' said the Matches.

" ' No, I don't like to talk about myself,' retorted the Pot. . 'Let us get up an evening entertainment. I will begin. I will tell a story from real life, something that every one has experienced, so that we can easily imagine the situation, and take pleasure in it. On the Baltic, by the Danish shore—'

" ' That 's a pretty beginning!' cried all the Plates. 'That will be a story we shall like.'

" ' Yes, it happened to me in my youth, when I lived in a quiet family where the furniture was polished, and the floors scoured, and new curtains were put up every fortnight.'

" ' What an interesting way you have of telling a story!' said the Carpet Broom. 'One can tell directly that a man is speaking who has been in woman's society. There 's something pure runs through it.'

"And the pot went on telling his story, and the end was as good as the beginning.

"All the Plates rattled with joy, and the Carpet Broom brought some green parsley out of the dust-hole, and put it like a wreath on the Pot, for he knew that it would vex the others. 'If I crown him to-day,' it thought, 'he will crown me to-morrow.'

" ' Now I 'll dance,' said the Fire Tongs, and they danced. Preserve us! how that implement could lift up one leg! The old chair-cushion burst to see it. 'Shall I be crowned too?' thought the Tongs; and indeed a wreath was awarded.

" ' They 're only common people, after all!' thought the Matches.

Now the Tea-Urn was to sing; but she said she had taken cold, and could not sing unless she felt boiling within. But that was only affectation; she did not want to sing, except when she was in the parlour with the grand people.

"In the window sat an old Quill Pen, with which the maid generally wrote: there was nothing remarkable about this pen, except that it had been dipped too deep into the ink, but she was proud of that. 'If the Tea-Urn won't sing,' she said 'she may leave it alone. Outside hangs a nightingale in a cage, and he can sing. He hasn't had any education, but this evening we'll say, nothing about that.'

"'I think it very wrong,' said the Tea Kettle—he was the kitchen singer, and half-brother to the Tea-Urn—'that that rich and foreign bird should be listened to! Is that patriotic? Let the Market Basket decide.'

"'I am vexed,' said the Market Basket. 'No one can imagine how much I am secretly vexed. Is that a proper way of spending the evening? Would it not be more sensible to put the house in order? Let each one go to his own place, and I would arrange the whole game. That would be quite another thing.'

"'Yes, let us make a disturbance,' cried they all. Then the door opened and the maid came in, and they all stood still; not one stirred. But there was not one pot among them who did not know what he could do, and how grand he was. 'Yes, if I had liked,' each one thought, 'it might have been a very merry evening.'

"The servant girl took the Matches and lighted the fire with them. Mercy! how they sputtered and burst out into flame! 'Now every one can see,' thought they, 'that we are the first. How we shine! what a light!'—and they burned out."

"That was a capital story," said the Sultana. "I feel myself quite carried away to the kitchen, to the Matches. Yes, now thou shalt marry our daughter."

"Yes, certainly," said the Sultan, "thou shalt marry our daughter on Monday."

And they called him *thou*, because he was to belong to the family.

The wedding was decided on, and on the evening before it the whole city was illuminated. Biscuits and cakes were thrown among the people, the street boys stood on their toes, called out "Hurrah!" and whistled on their fingers. It was uncommonly splendid.

"Yes, I shall have to give something as a treat," thought the merchant's son. So he bought rockets and crackers, and every imaginable sort of firework, put them all into his trunk, and flew up into the air.

"Crack!" how they went, and how they went off! All the Turks hopped up with such a start that their slippers flew about their ears; such a meteor they had never yet seen. Now they could understand that it must be a Turkish angel who was going to marry the Princess.

What stories people tell! Every one whom he asked about it had seen it in a separate way; but one and all thought it fine.

"I saw the Turkish angel himself," said one. "He had eyes like glowing stars, and a beard like foaming water."

"He flew in a fiery mantle," said another; "the most lovely little cherub peeped forth from among the folds."

Yes, they were wonderful things that he heard; and on the following day he was to be married.

Now he went back to the forest to rest himself in his trunk. But what had become of that? A spark from the fireworks had set fire to it, and the trunk was burned to ashes. He could not fly any more, and could not get to his bride.

She stood all day on the roof waiting; and most likely she is waiting still. But he wanders through the world telling fairy tales; but they are not so merry as that one he told about the Matches.

THE ANGELS DISCOURSING ABOUT THE CHILD.

THE LAST PEARL.

WE are in a rich, a happy house; all are cheerful and full of joy, master, servants, and friends of the family; for on this day an heir, a son had been born, and mother and child were doing exceedingly well.

The burning lamp in the bed-chamber had been partly shaded, and the windows were guarded by heavy curtains of some costly silken fabric. The carpet was thick and soft as a mossy lawn, and everything invited to slumber—was charmingly suggestive of repose; and the nurse found that, for she slept; and here she might sleep, for everything was good and blessed. The guardian spirit of the house leaned against the head of the bed; over the child at the mother's breast there spread as it were a net of shining stars in endless number, and each star was a pearl of happiness. All the good stars of life had brought their gifts to the new-born one; here sparkled health, wealth, fortune, and love—in short, everything that man can wish for on earth.

"Everything has been presented here," said the guardian spirit.

"No, not everything," said a voice near him, the voice of the child's *good angel*. "One fairy has not yet brought her gift; but she will do so·some day; even if years should elapse first, she will bring her gift. The *last pearl* is yet wanting."

"Wanting! here nothing may be wanting; and if it should be the case, let me go and seek the powerful fairy; let us betake ourselves to her!"

"She comes! she will come some day unsought! Her pearl may not be wanting; it must be there, so that the complete crown may be won."

"Where is she to be found? Where does she dwell? Tell it me, and I will procure the pearl."

"You will do that?" said the good angel of the child. "I will lead you to her directly, wherever she may be. She has no abiding-place—sometimes she rules in the Emperor's palace, sometimes you will find her in the peasant's humble cot; she goes by no person without leaving a trace: she brings two gifts to all, be it a world or a trifle! To this child also she must come. You think the time is equally long, but not equally profitable. Come, let us go for this pearl, the last pearl in all this wealth."

And hand in hand they floated towards the spot where the fairy was now lingering.

It was a great house, with dark windows and empty rooms, and a peculiar stillness reigned therein; a whole row of windows had been opened, so that the rough air could penetrate at its pleasure: the long white hanging curtains moved to and fro in the current of wind.

In the middle of the room was placed an open coffin, and in this coffin lay the corpse of a woman, still in the bloom of youth, and very beautiful. Fresh roses were scattered over her, so that only the delicate folded hands and the noble face, glorified in death by the solemn look of consecration and entrance to the better world, were visible.

Around the coffin stood the husband and the children, a whole troop: the youngest child rested on the father's arm, and all bade their mother the last farewell; the husband kissed her hand, the hand which now was as a withered leaf, but which a short time ago had been working and striving in diligent love for them all. Tears of sorrow rolled over their cheeks, and fell in heavy drops to the floor; but not a word was spoken. The silence which reigned here expressed a world of grief. With silent footsteps and with many a sob they quitted the room.

A burning light stands in the room, and the long red wick peers out high above the flame that flickers in the current of air. Strange men come in, and lay the lid on the coffin over the dead one, and drive the nails firmly in, and the blows of the hammer resound through the house, and echo in the hearts that are bleeding.

"Whither art thou leading me?" asked the guardian spirit. "Here dwells no fairy whose pearl might be counted amongst the best gifts for life!"

"Here she lingers; here in this sacred hour," said the angel, and pointed to a corner of the room; and there, where in her lifetime the mother had taken her seat amid flowers and pictures; there from whence, like the beneficent fairy of the house, she had greeted husband, children, and friends; from whence, like the sunbeams she had spread joy and cheerfulness, and been the centre and the heart of all—there sat a strange woman, clad in long garments. It was "the Chastened Heart," now mistress and mother here in the dead lady's place. A hot tear rolled down into her lap, and formed itself into a pearl glowing with all the colours of the rainbow. The angel seized it, and the pearl shone like a star of sevenfold radiance.

The pearl of Chastening, the last, which must not be wanting! it heightens the lustre and the meaning of the other pearls. Do you see the sheen of the rainbow—of the bow that unites heaven and earth? A bridge has been built between this world and the heaven beyond. Through the earthly night we gaze upward to the stars, looking for perfection. Contemplate it, the pearl of Chastening, for it hides within itself the wings that shall carry us to the better world.

THE STORKS.

On the last house in a little village stood a Stork's nest. The Mother-Stork sat in it with her four young ones, who stretched out their heads with the pointed black beaks, for their beaks had not yet turned red. A little way off stood the Father-Stork, all alone on the ridge of the roof, quite upright and stiff; he had drawn up one of his legs, so as not to be quite idle while he stood sentry. One would have thought he had been carved out of wood, so still did he stand. He thought, "It must look very grand, that my wife has a sentry standing by her nest. They can't tell that it is her husband. They certainly think I have been commanded to stand here. That looks so aristocratic!" And he went on standing on one leg.

Below in the street a whole crowd of children were playing; and when they caught sight of the Storks, one of the boldest of the boys, and afterwards all of them, sang the old verse about the Storks. But they only sang it just as he could remember it:

> "Stork, stork, fly away;
> Stand not on one leg to-day.
> Thy dear wife is in the nest,
> Where she rocks her young to rest.

" The first he will be hanged,
    The second will be hit,
The third he will be shot,
    And the fourth put on the spit."

" Just hear what those boys are saying !" said the little Stork-children. " They say we 're to be hanged and killed."

" You 're not to care for that !" said the Mother-Stork. " Don't listen to it, and then it won't matter."

But the boys went on singing, and pointed at the Storks mockingly with their fingers ; only one boy, whose name was Peter, declared that it was a sin to make a jest of animals, and he would not join in it at all.

The Mother-Stork comforted her children. " Don't you mind it at all," she said ; " see how quiet your father stands, though it 's only on one leg."

" We are very much afraid," said the young Storks : and they drew their heads far back into the nest.

Now to-day, when the children came out again to play, and saw the Storks, they sang their song :

" The first he will be hanged,
    The second will be hit——"

" Shall we be hanged and beaten ?" asked the young Storks.

" No, certainly not," replied the mother. " You shall learn to fly ; I 'll exercise you ; then we shall fly out into the meadows and pay a visit to the frogs ; they will bow before us in the water, and sing ' Co-ax ! co-ax !' and then we shall eat them up. That will be a real pleasure."

" And what then ?" asked the young Storks.

" Then all the Storks will assemble, all that are here in the whole country, and the autumn exercises begin : then one must fly well, for that is highly important, for whoever cannot fly properly will be thrust dead by the general's beak ; so take care and learn well when the exercising begins."

" But then we shall be killed, as the boys say :—and only listen, now they 're singing again."

" Listen to me, and not to them," said the Mother-Stork. " After the great review we shall fly away to the warm countries, far away from here, over mountains and forests. We shall fly to Egypt, where there are three covered houses of stone, which curl in a point and tower above the clouds ; they are called pyramids, and are older than a stork can imagine. There is a river in that country which runs out of its bed, and then all the land is turned to mud. One walks about in the mud, and eats frogs."

" Oh !" cried all the young ones.

" Yes ! It is glorious there ! One does nothing all day long but eat ; and while we are so comfortable over there, here there is not a green leaf on the trees ; here it is so cold that the clouds freeze to pieces, and fall down in little white rags ! "

It was the snow that she meant, but she could not explain it in any other way.

THE BOYS MOCKING THE STORKS.

"And do the naughty boys freeze to pieces?" asked the young Storks.

"No, they do not freeze to pieces; but they are not far from it, and must sit in the dark room and cower. You, on the other hand, can fly about in foreign lands, where there are flowers, and the sun shines warm."

Now some time had elapsed, and the nestlings had grown so large that they could stand upright in the nest and look far around; and the Father-Stork came every day with delicious frogs, little snakes, and all kinds of stork-dainties as he found them. Oh! it looked funny when he performed feats before them! He laid his head quite back upon his tail, and clapped with his beak as if he had been a little clapper; and then he told them stories, all about the marshes.

"Listen! now you must learn to fly," said the Mother-Stork one day; and all the four young ones had to go out on the ridge of the roof. Oh, how they tottered! how they balanced themselves with their wings, and yet they were nearly falling down.

"Only look at me," said the mother. "Thus you must hold your heads! Thus you must pitch your feet! One, two! one, two! That's what will help you on in the world."

Then she flew a little way, and the young ones made a little clumsy leap. Bump!—there they lay, for their bodies were too heavy.

"I will not fly!" said one of the young Storks, and crept back into the nest; "I don't care about getting to the warm countries."

"Do you want to freeze to death here, when the winter comes? Are the boys to come and hang you, and singe you, and roast you? Now I'll call them."

"Oh, no!" cried the young Stork, and hopped out on to the roof again like the rest.

On the third day they could actually fly a little, and then they thought they could also soar and hover in the air. They tried it, but—bump!—down they tumbled, and they had to shoot their wings again quickly enough. Now the boys came into the street again, and sang their song:

"*Stork, stork, fly away!*"

"Shall we fly down and pick their eyes out?" asked the young Storks.

"No," replied the mother, "let them alone. Only listen to me, that's far more important. One, two, three!—now we fly round to the right. One, two, three!—now to the left round the chimney! See, that was very good! the last kick with the feet was so neat and correct that you shall have permission to-morrow to fly with me to the marsh! Several nice stork families go there with their young: show them that mine are the nicest, and that you can start proudly; that looks well, and will get you consideration."

"But are we not to take revenge on the rude boys?" asked the young Storks.

"Let them scream as much as they like. You will fly up to the clouds, and get to the land of the pyramids, when they will have to shiver, and not have a green leaf or a sweet apple."

"Yes, we will revenge ourselves!" they whispered to one another; and then the exercising went on.

Among all the boys down in the street, the one most bent upon singing the teasing song was he who had begun it, and he was quite a little boy. He could hardly be more than six years old. The young Storks certainly thought he was a hundred, for he was much bigger than their mother and father; and how should they know how old children and grown-up people can be? Their revenge was to come upon this boy, for it was he who had begun, and he always kept on. The young Storks were very angry; and as they grew bigger they were less inclined to bear it: at last their mother had to promise them that they should be revenged, but not till the last day of their stay.

"We must first see how you behave at the grand review. If you get through badly, so that the general stabs you through the chest with his beak, the boys will be right, at least in one way. Let us see."

"Yes, you shall see!" cried the young Storks; and then they took

all imaginable pains. They practised every day, and flew so neatly and
so lightly that it was a pleasure to see them.

Now the autumn came on; all the Storks began to assemble, to fly
away to the warm countries while it is winter here. That *was* a review.
They had to fly over forests and villages, to show how well they could
soar, for it was a long journey they had before them. The young Storks
did their part so well that they got as a mark, "Remarkably well, with
frogs and snakes." That was the highest mark; and they might eat
the frogs and snakes; and that is what they did.

"Now we will be revenged!" they said.

"Yes, certainly!" said the Mother-Stork. "What I have thought of
will be the best. I know the pond in which all the little mortals lie
till the stork comes and brings them to their parents. The pretty little
babies lie there and dream so sweetly as they never dream afterwards.
All parents are glad to have such a child, and all children want to have
a sister or a brother. Now we will fly to the pond, and bring one for
each of the children who have not sung the naughty song and laughed
at the storks."

"But he who began to sing—that naughty, ugly boy!" screamed the
young Storks; "what shall we do with him?"

"There is a little dead child in the pond, one that has dreamed itself
to death; we will bring that for him. Then he will cry because we
have brought him a little dead brother. But that good boy—you have
not forgotten him, the one who said, 'It is wrong to laugh at animals!'
for him we will bring a brother and a sister too. And as his name is
Peter, all of you shall be called Peter too."

And it was done as she said; all the storks were named Peter, and
so they are all called even now.

GRANDMOTHER.

GRANDMOTHER is very old; she has many wrinkles, and her hair is
quite white; but her eyes, which are like two stars, and even more
beautiful, look at you mildly and pleasantly, and it does you good to
look into them. And then she can tell the most wonderful stories; and
she has a gown with great flowers worked in it, and it is of heavy silk,
and it rustles. Grandmother knows a great deal, for she was alive
before father and mother, that's quite certain! Grandmother has a
hymn-book with great silver clasps, and she often reads in that book;
in the middle of the book lies a rose, quite flat and dry; it is not as
pretty as the roses she has standing in the glass, and yet she smiles at it
most pleasantly of all, and tears even come into her eyes. I wonder
why Grandmother looks at the withered flower in the old book in that
way? Do you know? Why, each time that Grandmother's tears fall
upon the rose, its colours become fresh again; the rose swells and fills

GRANDMOTHER LOOKING AT THE WITHERED FLOWER.

the whole room with its fragrance; the walls sink as if they were but mist, and all around her is the glorious green wood, where in summer the sunlight streams through the leaves of the trees; and Grandmother —why, she is young again, a charming maid with light curls and full blooming cheeks, pretty and graceful, fresh as any rose; but the eyes, the mild blessed eyes, they have been left to Grandmother. At her side sits a young man, tall and strong: he gives the rose to her, and she smiles; Grandmother cannot smile thus now!—yes, now she smiles! But now he has passed away, and many thoughts and many forms of the past; and the handsome young man is gone, and the rose lies in the hymn-book, and Grandmother sits there again, an old woman, and glances down at the withered rose that lies in the book.

Now Grandmother is dead. She had been sitting in her arm-chair, and telling a long, long, capital tale; and she said the tale was told now, and she was tired; and she leaned her head back to sleep awhile. One could hear her breathing as she slept; but it became quieter and more quiet, and her countenance was full of happiness and peace: it seemed as if a sunshine spread over her features; and she smiled again, and then the people said she was dead.

She was laid in the black coffin; and there she lay shrouded in the white linen folds, looking beautiful and mild, though her eyes were closed; but every wrinkle had vanished, and there was a smile around her mouth; her hair was silver-white and venerable; and we did not feel at all afraid to look at the corpse of her who had been the dear good Grandmother. And the hymn-book was placed under her head, for she had wished it so, and the rose was still in the old book; and then they buried Grandmother.

On the grave, close by the churchyard wall, they planted a rose tree; and it was full of roses; and the nightingale flew singing over the flowers and over the grave. In the church the finest psalms sounded from the organ—the psalms that were written in the old book under the dead one's head. The moon shone down upon the grave, but the dead one was not there. Every child could go safely, even at night, and pluck a rose there by the churchyard wall. A dead person knows more than all we living ones. The dead know what a terror would come upon us, if the strange thing were to happen that they appeared among us: the dead are better than we all; the dead return no more. The earth has been heaped over the coffin, and it is earth that lies in the coffin; and the leaves of the hymn-book are dust, and the rose, with all its recollections, has returned to dust likewise. But above there bloom fresh roses; the nightingale sings and the organ sounds, and the remembrance lives of the old Grandmother with the mild eyes that always looked young. *Eyes can never die!* Ours will once behold Grandmother again, young and beautiful, as when for the first time she kissed the fresh red rose that is now dust in the grave.

THE UGLY DUCKLING.

IT was glorious out in the country. It was summer, and the cornfields were yellow, and the oats were green; the hay had been put up in stacks in the green meadows, and the stork went about on his long red legs, and chattered Egyptian, for this was the language he had learned from his good mother. All around the fields and meadows were great forests, and in the midst of these forests lay deep lakes. Yes, it was really glorious out in the country. In the midst of the sunshine there lay an old farm, surrounded by deep canals, and from the wall down to the water grew great burdocks, so high that little children could stand upright under the loftiest of them. It was just as wild there as in the deepest wood. Here sat a Duck upon her nest, for she had to hatch her young ones; but she was almost tired out before the little ones came; and then she so seldom had visitors. The other ducks liked better to swim about in the canals than to run up to sit down under a burdock, and cackle with her.

At last one egg-shell after another burst open. "Piep! piep!" it cried, and in all the eggs there were little creatures that stuck out their heads.

"Rap! rap!" they said; and they all came rapping out as fast as they could, looking all round them under the green leaves; and the mother let them look as much as they chose, for green is good for the eyes.

"How wide the world is!" said the young ones, for they certainly had much more room now than when they were in the eggs.

"Do you think this is all the world?" asked the mother. "That extends far across the other side of the garden, quite into the parson's field, but I have never been there yet. I hope you are all together," she continued, and stood up. "No, I have not all. The largest egg still lies there. How long is that to last? I am really tired of it." And she sat down again.

"Well, how goes it?" asked an old Duck who had come to pay her a visit.

"It lasts a long time with that one egg," said the Duck who sat there. "It will not burst. Now, only look at the others; are they not the prettiest ducks one could possibly see? They are all like their father: the bad fellow never comes to see me."

"Let me see the egg which will not burst," said the old visitor. "Believe me, it is a turkey's egg. I was once cheated in that way, and had much anxiety and trouble with the young ones, for they are afraid of the water. I could not get them to venture in. I quacked and clucked, but it was no use. Let me see the egg. Yes, that's a turkey's egg! Let it lie there, and teach the other children to swim."

"I think I will sit on it a little longer," said the Duck. "I've sat so long now that I can sit a few days more."

"Just as you please," said the old Duck; and she went away.

At last the great egg burst. "Piep! piep!" said the little one, and crept forth. It was very large and very ugly. The Duck looked at it. "It's a very large duckling," said she; "none of the others look like that: can it really be a turkey chick? Now we shall soon find it out. It must go into the water, even if I have to thrust it in myself."

The next day the weather was splendidly bright, and the sun shone on all the green trees. The Mother-Duck went down to the water with all her little ones. Splash she jumped into the water. "Quack! quack!" she said, and one duckling after another plunged in. The water closed over their heads, but they came up in an instant, and swam capitally; their legs went of themselves, and there they were all in the water. The ugly grey Duckling swam with them.

"No, it's not a turkey," said she; "look how well it can use its legs, and how upright it holds itself. It is my own child! On the whole it's quite pretty, if one looks at it rightly. Quack! quack! come with me, and I'll lead you out into the great world, and present you in the poultry-yard; but keep close to me, so that no one may tread on you, and take care of the cats!"

THE DUCKLING TEASED BY THE GOOSE.

And so they came into the poultry-yard. There was a terrible riot going on in there, for two families were quarrelling about an eel's head, and the cat got it after all.

"See, that's how it goes in the world!" said the Mother-Duck; and she whetted her beak, for she, too, wanted the eel's head. "Only use your legs," she said. "See that you can bustle about, and bow your heads before the old duck yonder. She's the grandest of all here; she's of Spanish blood—that's why she's so fat; and do you see, she has a red rag round her leg; that's something particularly fine, and the greatest distinction a duck can enjoy: it signifies that one does not want to lose her, and that she's to be recognized by man and beast. Shake yourselves—don't turn in your toes; a well brought-up duck turns its toes quite out, just like father and mother, so! Now bend your necks and say 'Rap!'"

And they did so; but the other ducks round about looked at them, and said quite boldly,

"Look there! now we're to have these hanging on as if there were not enough of us already! And—fie!—how that Duckling yonder looks; we won't stand that!" And one duck flew up immediately, and bit it in the neck.

"Let it alone," said the mother; "it does no harm to any one."

"Yes, but it's too large and peculiar," said the Duck who had bitten it; "and therefore it must be buffeted."

"Those are pretty children that the mother has there," said the old Duck with the rag round her leg. "They're all pretty but that one; that was a failure. I wish she could alter it."

"That cannot be done, my lady," replied the Mother-Duck: "It is not pretty, but it has a really good disposition, and swims as well as any other; I may even say it swims better. I think it will grow up pretty, and become smaller in time; it has lain too long in the egg, and therefore is not properly shaped." And then she pinched it in the neck, and smoothed its feathers. "Moreover, it is a drake," she said, "and therefore it is not of so much consequence. I think he will be very strong: he makes his way already."

"The other ducklings are graceful enough," said the old Duck. "Make yourself at home; and if you find an eel's head, you may bring it me."

And now they were at home. But the poor Duckling which had crept last out of the egg, and looked so ugly, was bitten and pushed and jeered, as much by the ducks as by the chickens.

"It is too big!" they all said. And the turkey-cock, who had been born with spurs, and therefore thought himself an emperor, blew himself up like a ship in full sail, and bore straight down upon it; then he gobbled, and grew quite red in the face. The poor Duckling did not know where it should stand or walk; it was quite melancholy because it looked ugly, and was scoffed at by the whole yard.

So it went on the first day; and afterwards it became worse and worse. The poor Duckling was hunted about by every one; even its brothers and sisters were quite angry with it, and said, "If the cat would only catch you, you ugly creature!" And the mother said, "If you were only far away!" And the ducks bit it, and the chickens beat it, and the girl who had to feed the poultry kicked at it with her foot.

Then it ran and flew over the fence, and the little birds in the bushes flew up in fear.

"That is because I am so ugly!" thought the Duckling; and it shut its eyes, but flew on farther; thus it came out into the great moor, where the wild ducks lived. Here it lay the whole night long; and it was weary and downcast.

Towards morning the wild ducks flew up, and looked at their new companion.

"What sort of a one are you?" they asked; and the Duckling turned in every direction, and bowed as well as it could. "You are remarkably ugly!" said the Wild Ducks. "But that is very indifferent to us, so long as you do not marry into our family."

Poor thing! it certainly did not think of marrying, and only hoped to obtain leave to lie among the reeds and drink some of the swamp water

Thus it lay two whole days; then came thither two wild geese, or, properly speaking, two wild ganders It was not long since each had crept out of an egg, and that 's why they were so saucy.

"Listen, comrade," said one of them. "You 're so ugly that I like you. Will you go with us, and become a bird of passage? Near here, in another moor, there are a few sweet lovely wild geese, all unmarried, and all able to say 'Rap!' You've a chance of making your fortune, ugly as you are!"

"Piff! paff!" resounded through the air; and the two ganders fell down dead in the swamp, and the water became blood-red. "Piff! paff!" it sounded again, and whole flocks of wild geese rose up from the reeds. And then there was another report. A great hunt was going on. The hunters were lying in wait all round the moor, and some were even sitting up in the branches of the trees, which spread far over the reeds. The blue smoke rose up like clouds among the dark trees, and was wafted far away across the water; and the hunting dogs came— splash, splash!—into the swamp, and the rushes and the reeds bent down on every side. That was a fright for the poor Duckling! It turned its head, and put it under its wing; but at that moment a frightful great dog stood close by the Duckling. His tongue hung far out of his mouth and his eyes gleamed horrible and ugly; he thrust out his nose close against the Duckling, showed his sharp teeth, and—splash, splash! —on he went, without seizing it.

"Oh, Heaven be thanked!" sighed the Duckling. "I am so ugly, that even the dog does not like to bite me!"

And so it lay quite quiet, while the shots rattled through the reeds and gun after gun was fired. At last, late in the day, silence was restored; but the poor Duckling did not dare to rise up; it waited several hours before it looked round, and then hastened away out of the moor as fast as it could. It ran on over field and meadow; there was such a storm raging that it was difficult to get from one place to another.

Towards evening the Duck came to a little miserable peasant's hut. This hut was so dilapidated that it did not know on which side it should fall; and that 's why it remained standing. The storm whistled round the Duckling in such a way that the poor creature was obliged to sit down, to stand against it; and the tempest grew worse and worse. Then the Duckling noticed that one of the hinges of the door had given way, and the door hung so slanting that the Duckling could slip through the crack into the room; and it did so.

Here lived a woman, with her Tom Cat and her Hen. And the Tom Cat, whom she called Sonnie, could arch his back and purr, he could even give out sparks; but for that one had to stroke his fur the wrong way. The Hen had quite little short legs, and therefore she was called Chickabiddy-shortshanks; she laid good eggs, and the woman loved her as her own child.

In the morning the strange Duckling was at once noticed, and the Tom Cat began to purr, and the Hen to cluck.

"What's this?" said the woman, and looked all round; but she could not see well, and therefore she thought the Duckling was a fat duck that had strayed. "This is a rare prize!" she said. "Now I shall have duck's eggs. I hope it is not a drake. We must try that."

And so the Duckling was admitted on trial for three weeks; but no eggs came. And the Tom Cat was master of the house, and the Hen was the lady, and always said "We and the world!" for she thought they were half the world, and by far the better half. The Duckling thought one might have a different opinion, but the Hen would not allow it.

"Can you lay eggs?" she asked.

"No."

"Then you 'll have the goodness to hold your tongue."

And the Tom Cat said, "Can you curve your back, and purr, and give out sparks?"

"No."

"Then you cannot have any opinion of your own when sensible people are speaking."

And the Duckling sat in a corner and was melancholy; then the fresh air and the sunshine streamed in; and it was seized with such a strange longing to swim on the water, that it could not help telling the Hen of it.

"What are you thinking of?" cried the Hen. "You have nothing to do, that's why you have these fancies. Purr or lay eggs, and they will pass over."

"But it is so charming to swim on the water!" said the Duckling, "so refreshing to let it close above one's head, and to dive down to the bottom."

"Yes, that must be a mighty pleasure, truly," quoth the Hen. "I fancy you must have gone crazy. Ask the Cat about it,—he's the cleverest animal I know,—ask him if he likes to swim on the water, or to dive down: I won't speak about myself. Ask our mistress, the old woman; no one in the world is cleverer than she. Do you think she has any desire to swim, and to let the water close above her head?"

"You don't understand me," said the Duckling.

"We don't understand you? Then pray who is to understand you? You surely don't pretend to be cleverer than the Tom Cat and the woman—I won't say anything of myself. Don't be conceited, child, and be grateful for all the kindness you have received. Did you not get into a warm room, and have you not fallen into company from which you may learn something? But you are a chatterer, and it is not pleasant to associate with you. You may believe me, I speak for your good. I tell you disagreeable things, and by that one may always know one's true friends! Only take care that you learn to lay eggs, or to purr and give out sparks!"

"I think I will go out into the wide world," said the Duckling.

"Yes, do go," replied the Hen.

And the Duckling went away. It swam on the water, and dived, but it was slighted by every creature because of its ugliness.

Now came the autumn. The leaves in the forest turned yellow and

THE FOUR SWANS.

brown; the wind caught them so that they danced about, and up in
the air it was very cold. The clouds hung low, heavy with hail and
snow-flakes, and on the fence stood the raven, crying, "Croak! croak!"
for mere cold; yes, it was enough to make one feel cold to think of
this. The poor little Duckling certainly had not a good time. One
evening—the sun was just setting in his beauty—there came a whole
flock of great handsome birds out of the bushes; they were dazzlingly
white, with long flexible necks; they were swans. They uttered a
very peculiar cry, spread forth their glorious great wings, and flew
away from that cold region to warmer lands, to fair open lakes. They
mounted so high, so high! and the ugly little Duckling felt quite
strangely as it watched them. It turned round and round in the water
like a wheel, stretched out its neck towards them, and uttered such a
strange loud cry as frightened itself. Oh! it could not forget those
beautiful, happy birds; and so soon as it could see them no longer,
it dived down to the very bottom, and when it came up again, it was

quite beside itself. It knew not the name of those birds, and knew not whither they were flying; but it loved them more than it had ever loved any one. It was not at all envious of them. How could it think of wishing to possess such loveliness as they had? It would have been glad if only the ducks would have endured its company—the poor ugly creature!

And the winter grew cold, very cold! The Duckling was forced to swim about in the water, to prevent the surface from freezing entirely; but every night the hole in which it swam about became smaller and smaller. It froze so hard that the icy covering crackled again; and the Duckling was obliged to use its legs continually to prevent the hole from freezing up. At last it become exhausted, and lay quite still, and thus froze fast into the ice.

Early in the morning a peasant came by, and when he saw what had happened, he took his wooden shoe, broke the ice-crust to pieces, and carried the Duckling home to his wife. Then it came to itself again. The children wanted to play with it; but the Duckling thought they would do it an injury, and in its terror fluttered up into the milk-pan, so that the milk spurted down into the room. The woman clasped her hands, at which the Duckling flew down into the butter-tub, and then into the meal-barrel and out again. How it looked then! The woman screamed, and struck at it with the fire-tongs; the children tumbled over one another, in their efforts to catch the Duckling; and they laughed and screamed finely! Happily the door stood open, and the poor creature was able to slip out between the shrubs into the newly-fallen snow; and there it lay quite exhausted.

But it would be too melancholy if I were to tell all the misery and care which the Duckling had to endure in the hard winter. It lay out on the moor among the reeds, when the sun began to shine again and the larks to sing: it was a beautiful spring.

Then all at once the Duckling could flap its wings: they beat the air more strongly than before, and bore it strongly away; and before it well knew how all this happened, it found itself in a great garden, where the elder trees smelt sweet, and bent their long green branches down to the canal that wound through the region. Oh, here it was so beautiful, such a gladness of spring! and from the thicket came three glorious white swans; they rustled their wings, and swam lightly on the water. The Duckling knew the splendid creatures, and felt oppressed by a peculiar sadness.

"I will fly away to them, to the royal birds! and they will kill me, because I, that am so ugly, dare to approach them. But it is of no consequence! Better to be killed by *them* than to be pursued by ducks. and beaten by fowls, and pushed about by the girl who takes care of the poultry-yard, and to suffer hunger in winter!" And it flew out into the water, and swam towards the beautiful swans: these looked at it, and came sailing down upon it with outspread wings. "Kill me!" said the poor creature, and bent its head down upon the water, expecting nothing but death. But what was this that it saw in the clear water? It beheld its own image; and, lo! it was no longer a clumsy dark grey bird, ugly and hateful to look at, but—a swan!

It matters nothing if one is born in a duck-yard, if one has only lain in a swan's egg.

It felt quite glad at all the need and misfortune it had suffered, now it realized its happiness in all the splendour that surrounded it. And the great swans swam round it, and stroked it with their beaks.

Into the garden came little children, who threw bread and corn into the water; and the youngest cried, "There is a new one!" and the other children shouted joyously, "Yes, a new one has arrived!" And they clapped their hands and danced about, and ran to their father and mother; and bread and cake were thrown into the water; and they all said, "The new one is the most beautiful of all! so young and handsome!" and the old swans bowed their heads before him.

Then he felt quite ashamed, and hid his head under his wings, for he did not know what to do; he was so happy, and yet not at all proud. He thought how he had been persecuted and despised; and now he heard them saying that he was the most beautiful of all birds. Even the elder tree bent its branches straight down into the water before him, and the sun shone warm and mild. Then his wings rustled, he lifted his slender neck, and cried rejoicingly from the depths of his heart,

"I never dreamed of so much happiness when I was still the ugly Duckling!"

THE LOVELIEST ROSE IN THE WORLD.

ONCE there reigned a Queen, in whose garden were found the most glorious flowers at all seasons and from all the lands in the world; but especially she loved roses, and therefore she possessed the most various kinds of this flower, from the wild dog-rose, with the apple-scented green leaves, to the most splendid Provence rose. They grew against the earth walls, wound themselves round pillars and window-frames, into the passages, and all along the ceiling in all the halls. And the roses were various in fragrance, form, and colour.

But care and sorrow dwelt in these halls: the Queen lay upon a sick-bed, and the doctors declared that she must die.

"There is still one thing that can serve her," said the wisest of them. "Bring her the loveliest rose in the world, the one which is the expression of the brightest and purest love; for if that is brought before her eyes ere they close, she will not die."

And young and old came from every side with roses, the loveliest that bloomed in each garden; but they were not the right sort. The flower was to be brought out of the garden of Love; but what rose was it there that expressed the highest and purest love?

And the poets sang of the loveliest rose in the world, and each one named his own; and intelligence was sent far round the land to every heart that beat with love, to every class and condition, and to every age.

"No one has till now named the flower," said the wise man. "No one has pointed out the place where it bloomed in its splendour. They are not the roses from the coffin of Romeo and Juliet, or from the Walburg's grave, though these roses will be ever fragrant in song. They are not the roses that sprouted forth from Winkelried's blood-stained lances, from the blood that flows in a sacred cause from the breast of the hero who dies for his country; though no death is sweeter than

THE WISE MAN VISITS THE SICK QUEEN.

this, and no rose redder than the blood that flows then. Nor is it that wondrous flower, to cherish which man devotes, in a quiet chamber, many a sleepless night, and much of his fresh life—the magic flower of science."

"I know where it blooms," said a happy mother, who came with her pretty child to the bed-side of the Queen. "I know where the loveliest rose of the world is found! The rose that is the expression of the highest and purest love springs from the blooming cheeks of my sweet child when, strengthened by sleep, it opens its eyes and smiles at me with all its affection!"

"Lovely is this rose; but there is still a lovelier," said the wise man.

"Yes, a far lovelier one," said one of the women. "I have seen it, and a loftier, purer rose does not bloom. I saw it on the cheeks of the Queen. She had taken off her golden crown, and in the long dreary night she was carrying her sick child in her arms: she wept, kissed it, and prayed for her child as a mother prays in the hour of her anguish."

"Holy and wonderful in its might is the white rose of grief; but it is not the one we seek."

"No, the loveliest rose of the world I saw at the altar of the Lord," said the good old Bishop. "I saw it shine as if an angel's face had appeared. The young maidens went to the Lord's Table, and renewed the promise made at their baptism, and roses were blushing, and pale roses shining on their fresh cheeks. A young girl stood there; she looked with all the purity and love of her young spirit up to heaven: that was the expression of the highest and the purest love."

"May she be blessed!" said the wise man; "but not one of you has yet named to me the loveliest rose of the world."

Then there came into the room a child, the Queen's little son. Tears stood in his eyes and glistened on his cheeks: he carried a great open book, and the binding was of velvet, with great silver clasps.

"Mother!" cried the little boy, "only hear what I have read."

And the child sat by the bed-side, and read from the book of Him who suffered death on the Cross to save men, and even those who were not yet born.

"Greater love there is not——"

And a roseate hue spread over the cheeks of the Queen, and her eyes gleamed, for she saw that from the leaves of the book there bloomed the loveliest rose, that sprang from the blood of CHRIST shed on the Cross.

"I see it!" she said: "he who beholds this, the loveliest rose on earth, shall never die."

HOLGER DANSKE.

"IN Denmark there lies a castle named Kronenburg. It lies close by the Oer Sound, where the ships pass through by hundreds every day —English, Russian, and likewise Prussian ships. And they salute the old castle with cannons—'Boom!' And the castle answers with a 'Boom!' for that's what the cannons say instead of 'Good day' and 'Thank you!' In winter no ships sail there, for the whole sea is covered with ice quite across to the Swedish coast; but it has quite the look of a high road. There wave the Danish flag and the Swedish flag, and Danes and Swedes say 'Good day' and 'Thank you!' to each other, not with cannons, but with a friendly grasp of the hand; and one gets white bread and biscuits from the other—for strange fare tastes best. But the most beautiful of all is the old Kronenburg; and here it is that Holger Danske sits in the deep dark cellar, where nobody goes. He is clad in iron and steel, and leans his head on his strong arm; his long beard hangs down over the marble table, and has grown into it. He sleeps and dreams, but in his dreams he sees everything that happens up here in Denmark. Every Christmas-eve comes an angel, and tells him that what he has dreamed is right, and that he may go to sleep in quiet, for that Denmark is not yet in any real danger; but when once such a danger comes, then old Holger Danske will rouse himself, so that the table shall burst when he draws out his beard! Then he will come forth and strike, so that it shall be heard in all the countries in the world."

An old grandfather sat and told his little grandson all this about Holger Danske; and the little boy knew that what his grandfather told him was true. And while the old man sat and told his story, he carved an image which was to represent Holger Danske, and to be fastened to the prow of a ship; for the old grandfather was a carver of figure-heads, that is, one who cuts out the figures fastened to the front of ships, and from which every ship is named. And here he had cut out Holger Danske, who stood there proudly with his long beard, and held the broad battle-sword in one hand, while with the other he leaned upon the Danish arms.

And the old grandfather told so much about distinguished men and women, that it appeared at last to the little grandson as if he knew as much as Holger Danske himself, who, after all, could only dream; and when the little fellow was in his bed, he thought so much of it, that he actually pressed his chin against the coverlet, and fancied he had a long beard that had grown fast to it.

But the old grandfather remained sitting at his work, and carved away at the last part of it; and this was the Danish coat of arms. When he had done, he looked at the whole, and thought of all he had read and heard, and that he had told this evening to the little boy; and he nodded, and wiped his spectacles, and put them on again, and said,

"Yes, in my time Holger Danske will probably not come; but the boy in the bed yonder may get to see him, and be there when the push really comes."

And the old grandfather nodded again: and the more he looked at Holger Danske the more plain did it become to him that it was a good image he had carved. It seemed really to gain colour, and the armour appeared to gleam like iron and steel; the hearts in the Danish arms became redder and redder, and the lions with the golden crowns on their heads leaped up.*

"That's the most beautiful coat of arms there is in the world!" said the old man. "The lions are strength, and the heart is gentleness and love!"

And he looked at the uppermost lion, and thought of King Canute, who bound great England to the throne of Denmark; and he looked at the second lion, and thought of Waldemar, who united Denmark and conquered the Wendish lands; and he glanced at the third lion, and remembered Margaret, who united Denmark, Sweden, and Norway. But while he looked at the red hearts, they gleamed more brightly than before; they became flames, and his heart followed each of them.

---

* The Danish arms consist of three lions between nine hearts.

HOLGER DANSKE.

The first heart led him into a dark narrow prison: there sat a prisoner, a beautiful woman, the daughter of King Christian IV., Eleanor Ulfeld;* and the flame, which was shaped like a rose, attached itself to her bosom and blossomed, so that it became one with the heart of her, the noblest and best of all Danish women.

And his spirit followed the second flame, which led him out upon the sea, where the cannons thundered and the ships lay shrouded in smoke; and the flame fastened itself in the shape of a ribbon of honour on the breast of Hvitfeld, as he blew himself and his ship into the air, that he might save the fleet.†

And the third flame led him to the wretched huts of Greenland, where

---

* This highly gifted Princess was the wife of Corfitz Ulfeld, who was accused of high treason. Her only crime was the most faithful love to her unhappy consort; but she was compelled to pass twenty-two years in a horrible dungeon, until her persecutor, Queen Sophia Amelia, was dead.

† In the naval battle in Kjoge Bay between the Danes and the Swedes, in 1710, Hvitfeld's ship, the Danebrog, took fire. To save the town of Kjoge, and the Danish fleet which was being driven by the wind towards his vessel, he blew himself and his whole crew into the air.

the preacher Hans Egede * wrought, with love in every word and deed: the flame was a star on his breast, another heart in the Danish arms.

And the spirit of the old grandfather flew on before the waving flames, for his spirit knew whither the flames desired to go. In the humble room of the peasant woman stood Frederick VI., writing his name with chalk on the beam.† The flame trembled on his breast, and trembled in his heart; in the peasant's lowly room his heart too became a heart in the Danish arms. And the old grandfather dried his eyes, for he had known King Frederick with the silvery locks and the honest blue eyes, and had lived for him: he folded his hands, and looked in silence straight before him. Then came the daughter-in-law of the old grandfather, and said it was late, he ought now to rest; and the supper table was spread.

"But it is beautiful. what you have done, grandfather!" said she. "Holger Danske, and all our old coat of arms! It seems to me just as if I had seen that face before!"

"No, that can scarcely be," replied the old grandfather; "but I have seen it, and I have tried to carve it in wood as I have kept it in my memory. It was when the English lay in front of the wharf, on the Danish second of April,‡ when we showed that we were old Danes. In the Denmark, on board which I was, in Steen Bille's squadron, I had a man at my side — it seemed as if the bullets were afraid of him! Merrily he sang old songs, and shot and fought as if he were something more than a man. I remember his face yet; but whence he came, and whither he went, I know not—nobody knows. I have often thought he might have been old Holger Danske himself, who had swum down from the Kronenburg, and aided us in the hour of danger: that was my idea, and there stands his picture."

And the statue threw its great shadow up against the wall, and even over part of the ceiling; it looked as though the real Holger Danske were standing behind it, for the shadow moved; but this might have been because the flame of the candle did not burn steadily. And the daughter-in-law kissed the old grandfather, and led him to the great arm-chair by the table; and she and her husband, who was the son of the old man, and father of the little boy in the bed, sat and ate their supper; and the grandfather spoke of the Danish lions and of the Danish hearts, of strength and of gentleness; and quite clearly did he explain that there was another strength besides the power that lies in the sword; and he pointed to the shelf on which were the old books, where stood the plays of Holberg, which had been read so often, for they

---

* Hans Egede went to Greenland in 1721, and toiled there during fifteen years among incredible hardships and privations. Not only did he spread Christianity, but exhibited in himself a remarkable example of a Christian man.

† On a journey on the west coast of Jutland, the King visited an old woman. When he had already quitted her house, the woman ran after him, and begged him, as a remembrance, to write his name upon a beam; the King turned back, and complied. During his whole lifetime he felt and worked for the peasant class; therefore the Danish peasants begged to be allowed to carry his coffin to the royal vault at Roeskilde, four Danish miles from Copenhagen.

‡ On the 2nd of April, 1801, occurred the sanguinary naval battle between the Danes and the English. under Sir Hyde Parker and Nelson.

were very amusing; one could almost fancy one recognized the people of bygone days in them.

"See, he knew how to strike too," said the grandfather: "he scourged the foolishness and prejudice of the people so long as he could "—and the grandfather nodded at the mirror, above which stood the calendar, with the "Round Tower" * on it, and said, "Tycho Brahe was also one who used the sword, not to cut into flesh and bone, but to build up a plainer way among all the stars of heaven. And then *he* whose father belonged to my calling, the son of the old figure-head carver, he whom we have ourselves seen with his silver hairs and his broad shoulders, he whose name is spoken of in all lands! Yes, *he* was a sculptor; *I* am only a carver. Yes, Holger Danske may come in many forms, so that one hears in every country in the world of Denmark's strength. Shall we now drink the health of Bertel?" †

But the little lad in the bed saw plainly the old Kronenburg with the Oer Sound, the real Holger Danske, who sat deep below, with his beard grown through the marble table, dreaming of all that happens up here. Holger Danske also dreamed of the little humble room where the carver sat; he heard all that passed, and nodded in his sleep, and said,

"Yes, remember me, ye Danish folk; remember me. I shall come in the hour of need."

And without by the Kronenburg shone the bright day, and the wind carried the notes of the hunting-horn over from the neighbouring land; the ships sailed past, and saluted—"Boom! boom!" and from the Kronenburg came the reply, "Boom! boom!" But Holger Danske did not awake, however loudly they shot, for it was only "Good day" and "Thank you!" There must be another kind of shooting before he awakes; but he will awake, for there is faith in Holger Danske.

THE PUPPET SHOWMAN.

On board the steamer was an elderly man with such a merry face that, if it did not belie him, he must have been the happiest fellow in creation. And, indeed, he declared he was the happiest man; I heard it out of his own mouth. He was a Dane, a travelling theatre director. He had all his company with him in a large box, for he was proprietor of a puppet-show. His inborn cheerfulness, he said, had been *purified* by a Poly-technic candidate, and the experiment had made him completely happy. I did not at first understand all this, but afterwards he explained the whole story to me, and here it is. He told me:

"It was in the little town of Slagelse I gave a representation in the hall of the posting-house, and had a brilliant audience, entirely a juvenile

---

* The astronomical observatory at Copenhagen.
† Bertel Thorwaldsen.

one, with the exception of two respectable matrons. All at once a person in black, of student-like appearance, came into the room and sat down ; he laughed aloud at the telling parts, and applauded quite appropriately. That was quite an unusual spectator for me! I felt anxious to know who he was, and I heard he was a candidate from the Polytechnic Institution in Copenhagen, who had been sent out to instruct the folks in the provinces. Punctually at eight o'clock my performance closed ; for children must go early to bed, and a manager must consult the convenience of his public. At nine o'clock the candidate commenced his lecture, with experiments, and now I formed part of *his* audience. It was wonderful to hear and to see. The greater part of it was beyond my scope; but still it made me think that if we men can find out so much, we must be surely intended to last longer than the little span until we are hidden away in the earth. They were quite miracles in a small way that he showed, and yet everything flowed as naturally as water! At the time of Moses and the prophets such a man would have been received among the sages of the land ;, in the middle ages they would have burned him at a stake. All night long I could not go to sleep. And the next evening, when I gave another performance, and the candidate was again present, I felt fairly overflowing with humour. I once heard from a player that when he acted a lover he always thought of one particular lady among the audience ; he only played for her, and forgot all the rest of the house ; and now the Polytechnic candidate was my 'she,' my only auditor, for whom alone I played. And when the performance was over, all the puppets were called before the curtain, and the Polytechnic candidate invited me into his room to take a glass of wine ; and he spoke of my comedies, and I of his science ; and I believe we were both equally pleased. But I had the best of it, for there was much in what he did of which he could not always give me an explanation. For instance, that a piece of iron that falls through a spiral should become magnetic. Now, how does that happen ? The spirit comes upon it ; but whence does it come ? It is as with people in this world ; they are made to tumble through the spiral of this world, and the spirit comes upon them, and there stands a Napoleon, or a Luther, or a person of that kind. 'The whole world is a series of miracles,' said the candidate ; 'but we are so accustomed to them that we call them every-day matters.' And he went on explaining things to me until my skull seemed lifted up over my brain, and I declared that if I were not an old fellow I would at once visit the Polytechnic Institution, that I might learn to look at the sunny side of the world, though I am one of the happiest of men. 'One of the happiest!' said the candidate, and he seemed to take real pleasure in it. 'Are you happy ? ' 'Yes,' I replied, 'and they welcome me in all the towns where I come with my company ; but I certainly have *one* wish, which sometimes lies like lead, like an Alp, upon my good humour: I should like to become a real theatrical manager, the director of a real troupe of men and women ! ' 'I see,' he said, 'you would like to have life breathed into your puppets, so that they might be real actors, and you

THE ANIMATED PUPPETS.

their director; and would you then be quite happy?' He did not believe it; but I believed it, and we talked it over all manner of ways without coming any nearer to an agreement; but we clanked our glasses together, and the wine was excellent. There was some magic in it, or I should certainly have become tipsy. But that did not happen; I retained my clear view of things, and somehow there was sunshine in the room, and sunshine beamed out of the eyes of the Polytechnic candidate. It made me think of the old stories of the gods, in their eternal youth, when they still wandered upon earth and paid visits to the mortals; and I said so to him, and he smiled, and I could have sworn he was one of the ancient gods in disguise, or that, at any rate, he belonged to the family! and certainly he must have been something of the kind, for my highest wish was to have been fulfilled, the puppets were to be gifted with life, and I was to be director of a real company. We drank to my success and clinked our glasses. He packed all my dolls into a box, bound the box on my back, and then let me fall through a spiral. I heard myself tumbling, and then I was lying on the floor—I know that quite well—and the whole company sprang out of the box. The spirit had come upon all of us: all the puppets had become distinguished artists, so they said themselves, and I was the director. All was ready for the first representation; the whole company wanted to speak to me, and the public also. The dancing lady said the house would fall down if she did not keep it up by standing on one leg; for she was the great genius, and begged to be treated as such. The lady who acted the queen wished to be treated off the stage as a queen, or else she should get out of practice. The man who was only employed to deliver a letter gave himself just as many airs as the first lover, for he declared the little ones were just as important as the great ones, and all were of equal consequence, considered as an artistic whole. The hero would only play parts composed of nothing but points; for those brought him down the applause. The prima donna would only play in a red light; for she declared that a blue one did not suit her complexion. It was like a company of flies in a bottle; and I was in the bottle with them, for I was the director. My breath stopped and my head whirled round; I was as miserable as a man can be. It was quite a novel kind of men among whom I now found myself. I only wished I had them all in the box again, and that I had never been a director at all; so I told them roundly that after all they were nothing but puppets; and then they killed me. I found myself lying on my bed in my room; and how I got there, and how I got away at all from the Polytechnic candidate, he may perhaps know, for I don't. The moon shone upon the floor where the box lay open, and the dolls all in a confusion together—great and small all scattered about; but I was not idle. Out of bed I jumped, and into the box they had all to go, some on their heads, some on their feet, and I shut down the lid and seated myself upon the box. 'Now you'll just have to stay there,' said I, 'and I shall beware how I wish you flesh and blood again.' I felt quite light; my good humour had come back, and I was the happiest of mortals. The Polytechnic student had fully purified me. I sat as happy as a king, and went to sleep on the box. The next morning—strictly speaking it was noon, for I slept wonderfully late that day—I was still sitting there, happy and conscious that my former wish had been a foolish one. I inquired for the Polytechnic candidate, but he was gone, like the Greek and Roman gods; and from that time I've been the happiest of men. I am a happy director: none of my company ever grumble, nor my public either, for they are always merry. I can put my pieces together just as I please. I take out of every comedy what pleases me best, and no one is angry at it. Pieces that are neglected now-a-days by the great public, but which it used to run after thirty years ago, and at which it used to cry till the tears ran down its cheeks, these pieces I now take up: I put them before the little ones, and the little ones cry just as papa and mamma used to cry thirty years ago; but I shorten them, for the youngsters don't like a long palaver; what they want is something mournful, but quick."

THE PIGS AT HOME IN THE OLD STATE COACH.

THE PIGS.

CHARLES DICKENS once told us about a pig, and since that time we are in a good humour if we only hear one grunt. St. Antony took the pig under his protection; and when we think of the prodigal son we always associate with him the idea of feeding swine; and it was in front of a pig-sty that a certain carriage stopped in Sweden, about which I am going to talk. The farmer had his pig-sty built out towards the high road, close by his house, and it was a wonderful pig-sty. It was an old state carriage. The seats had been taken out and the wheels taken off, and so the body of the old coach lay on the ground, and four pigs were shut up inside it. I wonder if these were the first that had ever been there? That point could not certainly be determined; but that it had been a real state coach everything bore witness, even to the damask rag that hung down from the roof; everything spoke of better days.

"Humph! humph!" said the occupants; and the coach creaked and groaned, for it had come to a mournful end. "The beautiful has departed," it sighed—or at least it might have done so.

We came back in autumn. The coach was there still, but the pigs were gone. They were playing the grand. lords out in the woods. Blossoms and leaves were gone from all the trees, and storm and rain ruled, and gave them neither peace nor rest; and the birds of passage had flown.

"The beautiful has departed! This was the glorious green wood, but the song of the birds and the warm sunshine are gone! gone!"

Thus said the mournful voice that creaked in the lofty branches of the trees, and it sounded like a deep-drawn sigh, a sigh from the bosom of the wild rose tree, and of him who sat there; it was the Rose King. Do you know him? He is all beard, the finest reddish-green beard; he is easily recognized. Go up to the wild rose bushes, and when in autumn all the flowers have faded from them, and only the wild hips remain, you will often find under them a great red-green moss flower; and that is the Rose King. A little green leaf grows up out of his head, and that's his feather. He is the only man of his kind on the rose bush; and he it was who sighed.

"Gone, gone! The beautiful is gone! The roses have faded, and the leaves fall down. It's wet here; it's boisterous here. The birds who used to sing are dumb, and the pigs go out hunting for acorns, and they are the lords of the forest."

The nights were cold and the days were misty; but, for all that, the raven sat on the branch and sang, "Good, good!"

Raven and crow sat on the high bough; and they had a large family, who all said, "Good, good!" and the majority is always right.

Under the high trees, in the hollow, was a great puddle, and here the pigs reclined, great and small. They found the place so inexpressibly lovely. "Oui! oui!" they all exclaimed. That was all the French they knew, but even that was something; and they were so clever and so fat.

The old ones lay quite still, and reflected; the young ones were very busy, and were not quiet a moment. One little porker had a twist in his tail like a ring, and this ring was his mother's pride: she thought all the rest were looking at the ring, and thinking only of the ring; but that they were not doing; they were thinking of themselves and of what was useful, and what was the use of the wood. They had always heard that the acorns they ate grew at the roots of the trees, and accordingly they had grubbed up the ground; but there came quite a little pig—it's always the young ones who come out with their new-fangled notions— who declared that the acorns fell down from the branches, for one had just fallen down on his head, and the idea had struck him at once, afterwards he had made observations, and now was quite certain on the point. The old ones put their heads together.

"Umph!" they said, "umph! The glory has departed: the twittering of the birds is all over; we want fruit; whatever's good to eat is good, and we eat everything."

"Oui! oui!" chimed in all the rest.

But the mother now looked at her little porker, the one with the ring in his tail.

"One must not overlook the beautiful," she said.

"Good! good!" cried the Crow, and flew down from the tree to try and get an appointment as nightingale; for some one must be appointed; and the Crow obtained the office directly.

" Gone ! gone ! " sighed the Rose King. " All the beautiful is gone ! "

It was boisterous, it was grey, cold, and windy ; and through the forest and over the field swept the rain in long dark streaks. Where is the bird who sang ? where are the flowers upon the meadow, and the sweet berries of the wood ? Gone ! gone !

Then a light gleamed from the forester's house. It was lit up like a star, and threw its long ray among the trees. A song sounded forth out of the house. Beautiful children played there round the old grandfather. He sat with the Bible on his knee, and read of the Creator and of a better world, and spoke of spring that would return, of the forest that would array itself in fresh green, of the roses that would bloom, the nightingale that would sing, and of the beautiful that would reign in its glory again.

But the Rose King heard it not, for he sat in the cold, damp weather, and sighed, " Gone ! gone ! " And the pigs were the lords of the forest, and the old Mother Sow looked proudly at her little porker with the twist in his tail.

" There is always somebody who has a soul for the beautiful ! " she said.

THE PRISONER.

A PICTURE FROM THE FORTRESS WALL.

It is autumn : we stand on the fortress wall, and look out over the sea ; we look at the numerous ships, and at the Swedish coast on the other side of the Sound, which rises far above the mirror of waters in the evening glow ; behind us the wood stands sharply out ; mighty trees surround us, the yellow leaves flutter down from the branches. Below, at the foot of the wall, stand gloomy houses fenced in with palisades; in these it is very narrow and dismal, but still more dismal is it behind the grated loopholes in the wall, for there sit the prisoners, the worst criminals.

A ray of the sinking sun shoots into the bare cell of one of the captives. The sun shines upon the good and the evil. The dark stubborn criminal throws an impatient look at the cold ray. A little bird flies towards the grating. The bird twitters to the wicked as to the just. He only utters his short "tweet! tweet!" but he perches upon the grating, claps his wings, pecks a feather from one of them, puffs himself out, and sets his feathers on end on his neck and breast; and the bad chained man looks at him: a milder expression comes into the criminal's hard face; in his breast there swells up a thought—a thought he himself cannot rightly analyse; but the thought has to do with the sunbeam, with the scent of violets which grow luxuriantly in spring at the foot of the wall. Now the horns of the chasseur soldiers sound merry and full. The little bird starts, and flies away; the sunbeam gradually vanishes, and again it is dark in the room, and dark in the heart of the bad man; but still the sun has shone into that heart, and the twittering of the bird has touched it!

Sound on, ye glorious strains of the hunting-horns! Continue to sound, for the evening is mild, and the surface of the sea, smooth as a mirror, heaves slowly and gently.

IN THE DUCK-YARD.

A DUCK arrived from Portugal. Some said she came from Spain, but that's all the same. At any rate she was called the Portuguese, and laid eggs, and was killed and cooked, and that was *her* career. But the ducklings which crept forth from her eggs were afterwards also called Portuguese, and there is something in that. Now, of the whole family there was only one left in the duck-yard, a yard to which the chickens had access likewise, and where the cock strutted about in a very aggressive manner.

"He annoys me with his loud crowing!" observed the Portuguese Duck. "But he's a handsome bird, there's no denying that, though he is not a drake. He ought to moderate his voice, but that's an art inseparable from polite education, like that possessed by the little singing birds over in the lime trees in the neighbour's garden. How charmingly they sing! There's something quite pretty in their warbling. I call it Portugal. If I had only such a little singing bird, I'd be a mother to him, kind and good, for that's in my blood, my Portuguese blood!"

And while she was still speaking, a little Singing Bird came head over heels from the roof into the yard. The cat was behind him, but the

Bird escaped with a broken wing, and that's how he came tumbling into the yard.

"That's just like the cat; she's a villain!" said the Portuguése Duck. "I remember her ways when I had children of my own. That such a creature should be allowed to live, and to wander about upon the roofs! I don't think they do such things in Portugal!"

And she pitied the little Singing Bird, and the other Ducks who were not of Portuguese descent pitied him too.

"Poor little creature!" they said, as one after another came up. "We certainly can't sing," they said, "but we have a sounding board, or something of the kind, within us ; we can feel that, though we don't talk of it."

"But I can talk of it," said the Portuguese Duck ; "and I'll do something for the little fellow, for that's my duty!" And she stepped into the water-trough, and beat her wings upon the water so heartily, that the little Singing Bird was almost drowned by the bath he got, but the Duck meant it kindly. "That's a good deed," she said: "the others may take example by it."

"Piep!" said the little Bird: one of his wings was broken, and he found it difficult to shake himself; but he quite understood that the bath was kindly meant. "You are very kind-hearted, madam," he said; but he did not wish for a second bath.

"I have never thought about my heart," continued the Portuguese Duck, "but I know this much, that I love all my fellow-creatures except the cat; but nobody can expect me to love her, for she ate up two of my ducklings. But pray make yourself at home, for one can make oneself comfortable. I myself am from a strange country, as you may see from my bearing and from my feathery dress. My drake is a native of these parts, he's not of my race ; but for all that I'm not proud! If any one here in the yard can understand you, I may assert that I am that person."

"She's quite full of Portulak," said a little common Duck, who was witty ; and all the other common Ducks considered the word *Portulak* quite a good joke, for it sounded like Portugal ; and they nudged each other and said "Rapp!" It was too witty! And all the other Ducks now began to notice the little Singing Bird.

"The Portuguese has certainly a greater command of language," they said. "For our part, we don't care to fill our beaks with such long words, but our sympathy is just as great. If we don't do anything for you, we march about with you everywhere ; and we think that the best thing we can do."

"You have a lovely voice," said one of the oldest. "It must be a great satisfaction to be able to give so much pleasure as you are able to impart. I certainly am no great judge of your song, and consequently I keep my beak shut ; and even that is better than talking nonsense to you, as others do."

"Don't plague him so," interposed the Portuguese Duck: "he requires rest and nursing. My little Singing Bird, do you wish me to prepare another bath for you?"

" Oh, no! pray let me be dry!" was the little Bird's petition.

" The water cure is the only remedy for me when I am unwell," quoth the Portuguese. " Amusement is beneficial too. The neighbouring fowls will soon come to pay their visit. There are two Cochin Chinese among them. They wear feathers on their legs, are well educated, and have been brought from afar, consequently they stand higher than the others in my regard."

And the Fowls came, and the Cock came; to-day he was polite enough to abstain from being rude.

" You are a true Singing Bird," he said, " and you do as much with your little voice as can possibly be done with it. But one requires a little more shrillness, that every hearer may hear that one is a male."

THE LITTLE SINGING BIRD RECEIVES DISTINGUISHED PATRONAGE.

The two Chinese stood quite enchanted with the appearance of the Singing Bird. He looked very much rumpled after his bath, so that he seemed to them to have quite the appearance of a little Cochin China fowl.

" He's charming," they cried, and began a conversation with him, speaking in whispers, and using the most aristocratic Chinese dialect.

" We are of your race," they continued. " The Ducks, even the Portuguese, are swimming birds, as you cannot fail to have noticed. You do not know us yet; very few know us, or give themselves the trouble to make our acquaintance—not even any of the fowls, though we are born to occupy a higher grade on the ladder than most of the rest. But that does not disturb us: we quietly pursue our path amid the others, whose principles are certainly not ours; for we look at things on the favourable side, and only speak of what is good, though it is difficult sometimes to find something when nothing exists. Except us two and the Cock. there's no one in the whole poultry-yard who is at once talented and polite. It cannot even be said of the inhabitants of the duck-yard. We warn you, little Singing Bird: don't trust that one yonder with the short tail-feathers, for she's cunning. The pied one there, with the crooked stripes on her wings, is a strife-seeker, and lets nobody have the last word, though she's always in the wrong. The fat duck yonder speaks evil of every one, and that's against our principles: if we have nothing good to tell, we should hold our beaks. The Portuguese is the only one who has any education, and with whom one can associate, but she is passionate, and talks too much about Portugal."

"I wonder what those two Chinese are always whispering to one another about?" whispered one Duck to her friend. "They annoy me— we have never spoken to them."

Now the Drake came up. He thought the little Singing Bird was a sparrow.

"Well, I don't understand the difference," he said; "and indeed it's all the same thing. He's only a plaything, and if one has them, why one has them."

"Don't attach any value to what he says," the Portuguese whispered. "He's very respectable in business matters; and with him business takes precedence of everything. But now I shall lie down for a rest. One owes that to oneself, that one may be nice and fat when one is to be embalmed with apples and plums."

And accordingly she lay down in the sun, and winked with one eye; and she lay very comfortably, and she felt very comfortable, and she slept very comfortably.

The little Singing Bird busied himself with his broken wing. At last he lay down too, and pressed close to his protectress: the sun shone warm and bright, and he had found a very good place.

But the neighbour's fowls were awake. They went about scratching up the earth; and, to tell the truth, they had paid the visit simply and solely to find food for themselves. The Chinese were the first to leave the duck-yard, and the other fowls soon followed them. The witty little Duck said of the Portuguese that the old lady was becoming a ducky dotard. At this the other Ducks laughed and cackled aloud. "Ducky dotard," they whispered; "that's too witty!" and then they repeated the former joke about Portulak, and declared that it was vastly amusing. And then they lay down.

They had been lying asleep for some time, when suddenly something was thrown into the yard for them to eat. It came down with such a thwack, that the whole company started up from sleep and clapped their wings. The Portuguese awoke too, and threw herself over on the other side, pressing the little Singing Bird very hard as she did so.

"Piep!" he cried; "you trod very hard upon me, madam."

"Well, why do you lie in my way?" the Duck retorted. "You must not be so touchy. I have nerves of my own, but yet I never called out 'Piep!'"

"Don't be angry," said the little Bird; "the 'piep' came out of my beak unawares."

The Portuguese did not listen to him, but began eating as fast as she could, and made a good meal. When this was ended, and she lay down again, the little Bird came up, and wanted to be amiable, and sang:

> "Tillee-lilly lee,
> Of the good spring-time
> I'll sing so fine
> As far away I flee."

"Now I want to rest after my dinner," said the Portuguese. "You must conform to the rules of the house while you're here. I want to sleep now."

The little Singing Bird was quite taken aback, for he had meant it kindly. When Madam afterwards awoke, he stood before her again with a little corn that he had found, and laid it at her feet; but as she had not slept well, she was naturally in a very bad humour.

"Give that to a chicken!" she said, "and don't be always standing in my way."

"Why are you angry with me?" replied the little Singing Bird. "What have I done?"

"Done!" repeated the Portuguese Duck: "your mode of expression is not exactly genteel; a fact to which I must call your attention."

"Yesterday it was sunshine here," said the little Bird, "but to-day it's cloudy and the air is close."

"You don't know much about the weather, I fancy," retorted the Portuguese. "The day is not done yet. Don't stand there looking so stupid."

"But you are looking at me just as the wicked eyes looked when I fell into the yard yesterday."

"Impertinent creature!" exclaimed the Portuguese Duck, "would you compare me with the cat, that beast of prey? There's not a drop of malicious blood in me. I've taken your part, and will teach you good manners."

And so saying, she bit off the Singing Bird's head, and he lay dead on the ground.

"Now, what's the meaning of this?" she said, "could he not bear even that? Then certainly he was not made for this world. I've been like a mother to him, I know that, for I've a good heart."

Then the neighbour's Cock stuck his head into the yard, and crowed with steam-engine power.

"You'll kill me with your crowing!" she cried. "It's all your fault. He's lost his head, and I am very near losing mine."

"There's not much lying where he fell!" observed the Cock.

"Speak of him with respect," retorted the Portuguese Duck, "for he had song, manners, and education. He was affectionate and soft, and that's as good in animals as in your so-called human beings."

And all the Ducks came crowding round the little dead Singing Bird. Ducks have strong passions, whether they feel envy or pity; and as there was nothing here to envy, pity manifested itself, even in the two Chinese.

"We shall never get such a singing bird again; he was almost a

Chinese," they whispered; and they wept with a mighty clucking sound, and all the fowls clucked too, but the Ducks went about with the redder eyes.

"We've hearts of our own," they said; "nobody can deny that."

"Hearts!" repeated the Portuguese, "yes, that we have, almost as much as in Portugal."

"Let us think of getting something to satisfy our hunger," said the Drake, "for that's the most important point. If one of our toys is broken, why, we have plenty more!"

THE RED SHOES.

THERE was once a little girl; a very nice pretty little girl. But in summer she had to go barefoot, because she was poor, and in winter she wore thick wooden shoes, so that her little instep became quite red, altogether red.

In the middle of the village lived an old shoemaker's wife: she sat, and sewed, as well as she could, a pair of little shoes, of old strips of red cloth; they were clumsy enough, but well meant, and the little girl was to have them. The little girl's name was Karen.

On the day when her mother was buried she received the red shoes and wore them for the first time. They were certainly not suited for mourning; but she had no others, and therefore thrust her little bare feet into them and walked behind the plain deal coffin.

Suddenly a great carriage came by, and in the carriage sat an old lady: she looked at the little girl and felt pity for her, and said to the clergyman,

"Give me the little girl, and I will provide for her."

Karen thought this was for the sake of the shoes; but the old lady declared they were hideous; and they were burned. But Karen herself was clothed neatly and properly: she was taught to read and to sew, and the people said she was agreeable. But her mirror said, "You are much more than agreeable; you are beautiful."

Once the Queen travelled through the country, and had her little daughter with her; and the daughter was a Princess. And the people flocked towards the castle, and Karen too was among them; and the little Princess stood in a fine white dress at a window, and let herself be gazed at. She had neither train nor golden crown, but she wore splendid red morocco shoes; they were certainly far handsomer than those the shoemaker's wife had made for little Karen. Nothing in the world can compare with red shoes!

Now Karen was old enough to be confirmed: new clothes were made for her, and she was to have new shoes. The rich shoemaker in the town took the measure of her little feet; this was done in his own house, in his little room, and there stood great glass cases with neat shoes and shining boots. It had quite a charming appearance, but the old lady could not see well, and therefore took no pleasure in it. Among the shoes stood a red pair, just like those which the Princess had worn. How beautiful they were ! The shoemaker also said they had been made for a Count's child, but they had not fitted.

"That must be patent leather," observed the old lady, "the shoes shine so ! "

"Yes, they shine!" replied Karen; and they fitted her, and were bought. But the old lady did not know that they were red; for she would never have allowed Karen to go to her confirmation in red shoes; and that is what Karen did.

Every one was looking at her shoes. And when she went across the church porch, towards the door of the choir, it seemed to her as if the old pictures on the tombstones, the portraits of clergymen and clergymen's wives, in their stiff collars and long black garments, fixed their eyes upon her red shoes. And she thought of her shoes only, when the priest laid his hand upon her head and spoke holy words. And the organ pealed solemnly, the children sang with their fresh sweet voices, and the old precentor sang too; but Karen thought only of her red shoes.

In the afternoon the old lady was informed by every one that the shoes were red; and she said it was naughty and unsuitable, and that when Karen went to church in future, she should always go in black shoes, even if they were old.

Next Sunday was Sacrament Sunday. And Karen looked at the black shoes, and looked at the red ones—looked at them again—and put on the red ones.

The sun shone gloriously; Karen and the old lady went along the foot-path through the fields. and it was rather dusty.

By the church door stood an old invalid soldier with a crutch and a long beard; the beard was rather red than white, for it was red altogether; and he bowed down almost to the ground, and asked the old lady if he might dust her shoes. And Karen also stretched out her little foot.

"Look, what pretty dancing-shoes!" said the old soldier. "Fit so tightly when you dance ! "

And he tapped the soles with his hand. And the old lady gave the soldier an alms, and went into the church with Karen.

And every one in the church looked at Karen's red shoes, and all the pictures looked at them. And while Karen knelt in the church she only thought of her red shoes; and she forgot to sing her psalm, and forgot to say her prayer.

Now all the people went out of church, and the old lady stepped into her carriage. Karen lifted up her foot to step in too; then the old soldier said,

"Look, what beautiful dancing-shoes ! "

And Karen could not resist: she was obliged to dance a few steps; and when she once began, her legs went on dancing. It was just as

KAREN AND THE OLD SOLDIER.

though the shoes had obtained power over her. She danced round the corner of the church—she could not help it; the coachman was obliged to run behind her and seize her: he lifted her into the carriage, but her feet went on dancing, so that she kicked the good old lady violently. At last they took off her shoes, and her legs became quiet.

At home the shoes were put away in a cupboard; but Karen could not resist looking at them.

Now the old lady became very ill, and it was said she would not recover. She had to be nursed and waited on; and this was no one's duty so much as Karen's. But there was to be a great ball in the town, and Karen was invited. She looked at the old lady who could not recover; she looked at the red shoes, and thought there would be no harm in it. She put on the shoes, and that she might very well do; but they went to the ball and began to dance.

But when she wished to go to the right hand, the shoes danced to the left, and when she wanted to go upstairs the shoes danced downwards, down into the street and out at the town gate. She danced, and was obliged to dance, straight out into the dark wood.

There was something glistening up among the trees, and she thought it was the moon, for she saw a face. But it was the old soldier with the red beard: he sat and nodded, and said,

"Look, what beautiful dancing-shoes!"

Then she was frightened, and wanted to throw away the red shoes; but they clung fast to her. And she tore off her stockings; but the shoes had grown fast to her feet. And she danced and was compelled to go dancing over field and meadow, in rain and sunshine, by night and by day; but it was most dreadful at night.

She danced out into the open churchyard; but the dead there do not dance; they have far better things to do. She wished to sit down on the poor man's grave, where the bitter fern grows; but there was no peace nor rest for her. And when she danced towards the open church door, she saw there an angel in long white garments, with wings that reached from his shoulders to his feet; his countenance was serious and stern, and in his hand he held a sword that was broad and gleaming.

"Thou shalt dance!" he said—"dance on thy red shoes, till thou art pale and cold, and till thy body shrivels to a skeleton. Thou shalt dance from door to door; and where proud, haughty children dwell, shalt thou knock, that they may hear thee, and be afraid of thee! Thou shalt dance, dance!"

"Mercy!" cried Karen.

But she did not hear what the angel answered, for the shoes carried her away—carried her through the door on to the field, over stock and stone, and she was always obliged to dance.

One morning she danced past a door which she knew well. There was a sound of psalm-singing within, and a coffin was carried out, adorned with flowers. Then she knew that the old lady was dead, and she felt that she was deserted by all, and condemned by the angel of heaven.

She danced, and was compelled to dance—to dance in the dark night. The shoes carried her on over thorn and brier; she scratched herself till she bled; she danced away across the heath to a little lonely house. Here she knew the executioner dwelt; and she tapped with her fingers on the panes, and called,

"Come out, come out! I cannot come in, for I must dance!"

And the executioner said,

"You probably don't know who I am? I cut off the bad people's heads with my axe, and mark how my axe rings!"

"Do not strike off my head," said Karen, "for if you do I cannot repent of my sin. But strike off my feet with the red shoes!"

And then she confessed all her sin, and the executioner cut off her feet with the red shoes; but the shoes danced away with the little feet over the fields and into the deep forest.

And he cut her a pair of wooden feet, with crutches, and taught her a psalm, which the criminals always sing; and she kissed the hand that had held the axe, and went away across the heath.

"Now I have suffered pain enough for the red shoes," said she. "Now I will go into the church, that they may see me."

And she went quickly towards the church door; but when she came there the red shoes danced before her, so that she was frightened, and turned back.

The whole week through she was sorrowful, and wept many bitter tears; but when Sunday came, she said,

"Now I have suffered and striven enough! I think that I am just as good as many of those who sit in the church and carry their heads high."

And then she went boldly on; but she did not get farther than the churchyard gate before she saw the red shoes dancing along before her: then she was seized with terror, and turned back, and repented of her sin right heartily.

KAREN'S RELEASE.

And she went to the parsonage, and begged to be taken there as a servant. She promised to be industrious, and to do all she could; she did not care for wages, and only wished to be under a roof and with good people. The clergyman's wife pitied her, and took her into her service. And she was industrious and thoughtful. Silently she sat and listened when in the evening the pastor read the Bible aloud. All the little ones were very fond of her; but when they spoke of dress and splendour and beauty she would shake her head.

Next Sunday they all went to church, and she was asked if she wished to go too; but she looked sadly, with tears in her eyes, at her crutches. And then the others went to hear God's word; but she went alone into her little room, which was only large enough to contain her bed and a chair. And here she sat with her hymn-book; and as she read it with a pious mind, the wind bore the notes of the organ over to her from the church; and she lifted up her face, wet with tears, and said,

"O Lord, help me!"

Then the sun shone so brightly; and before her stood the angel in the white garments, the same she had seen that night at the church door. But he no longer grasped the sharp sword: he held a green branch covered with roses; and he touched the ceiling, and it rose up high, and wherever he touched it a golden star gleamed forth; and he touched the walls, and they spread forth widely, and she saw the organ which was pealing its rich sounds; and she saw the old pictures of clergymen and their wives; and the congregation sat in the decorated seats, and sang from their hymn-books. The church had come to the poor girl in her narrow room, or her chamber had become a church. She sat in the chair with the rest of the clergyman's people; and when they had finished the psalm, and looked up, they nodded and said,

" That was right, that you came here, Karen."

" It was mercy!" said she.

And the organ sounded its glorious notes; and the children's voices singing in chorus sounded sweet and lovely; the clear sunshine streamed so warm through the window upon the chair in which Karen sat; and her heart became so filled with sunshine, peace, and joy, that it broke. Her soul flew on the sunbeams to heaven; and there was nobody who asked after the RED SHOES!

SOUP ON A SAUSAGE-PEG.

I.

" THAT was a remarkably fine dinner yesterday," observed an old Mouse of the female sex to another who had not been at the festive gathering. " I sat number twenty-one from the old Mouse King, so that I was not badly placed. Should you like to hear the order of the banquet? The courses were very well arranged—mouldy bread, bacon rind, tallow candle, and sausage — and then the same dishes over again from the beginning: it was just as good as having two banquets in succession. There was as much joviality and agreeable jesting as in the family circle. Nothing was left but the pegs at the ends of the sausages. And the discourse turned upon these; and at last the expression, 'Soup on sausage rinds,' or, as they have the proverb in the neighbouring country, 'Soup on a sausage-peg,' was mentioned. Every one had heard the proverb, but no one had ever tasted the sausage-peg soup, much less prepared it. A capital toast was drunk to the inventor of the soup, and it was said he deserved to be a relieving officer. Was not that witty? And the old Mouse King stood up, and promised that the young female mouse who could best prepare that soup should be his queen; and a year was allowed for the trial."

" That was not at all bad," said the other Mouse; " but how does one prepare this soup?"

"Ah, how is it prepared? That is just what all the young female mice, and the old ones too, are asking. They would all very much like to be queen; but they don't want to take the trouble to go out into the world to learn how to prepare the soup, and that they would certainly have to do. But every one has not the gift of leaving the family circle and the chimney corner. In foreign parts one can't get cheese rinds and bacon every day. No, one must bear hunger, and perhaps be eaten up alive by a cat."

Such were probably the considerations by which the majority were deterred from going out into the wide world and gaining information. Only four Mice announced themselves ready to depart. They were young and brisk, but poor. Each of them wished to proceed to one of the four quarters of the globe, and then it would become manifest which of them was favoured by fortune. Every one took a sausage-peg, so as to keep in mind the object of the journey. The stiff sausage-peg was to be to them as a pilgrim's staff.

It was at the beginning of May that they set out, and they did not return till the May of the following year; and then only three of them appeared. The fourth did not report herself, nor was there any intelligence of her, though the day of trial was close at hand.

"Yes, there's always some drawback in even the pleasantest affair," said the Mouse King.

And then he gave orders that all mice within a circuit of many miles should be invited. They were to assemble in the kitchen, where the three travelled Mice would stand up in a row, while a sausage-peg, shrouded in crape, was set up as a memento of the fourth, who was missing. No one was to proclaim his opinion till the Mouse King had settled what was to be said. And now let us hear.

II

What the first little Mouse had seen and learned in her travels.

"When I went out into the wide world," said the little Mouse, "I thought, as many think at my age, that I had already learned everything; but that was not the case. Years must pass before one gets so far. I went to sea at once. I went in a ship that steered towards the north. They had told me that the ship's cook must know how to manage things at sea; but it is easy enough to manage things when one has plenty of sides of bacon, and whole tubs of salt pork, and mouldy flour. One has delicate living on board; but one does not learn to prepare soup on a sausage-peg. We sailed along for many days and nights; the ship rocked fearfully, and we did not get off without a wetting. When we at last reached the port to which we were bound, I left the ship; and it was high up in the far north.

"It is a wonderful thing, to go out of one's own corner at home, and sail in a ship, where one has a sort of corner too, and then suddenly to

find oneself hundreds of miles away in a strange land. I saw great
pathless forests of pine and birch, which smelt so strong that I sneezed,
and thought of sausage. There were great lakes there too. When I
came close to them the waters were quite clear, but from a distance they
looked black as ink. Great swans floated upon them: I thought at first
they were spots of foam, they lay so still; but then I saw them walk
and fly, and I recognized them. They belong to the goose family—one
can see that by their walk; for no one can deny his parentage. I kept
with my own kind. I associated with the forest and field mice, who, by
the way, know very little, especially as regards cookery, though this was
the very subject that had brought me abroad. The thought that soup
might be boiled on a sausage-peg was such a startling statement to
them, that it flew at once from mouth to mouth through the whole
forest. They declared the problem could never be solved; and little did
I think that there, on the very first night, I should be initiated into the
method of its preparation. It was in the height of summer, and that,
the mice said, was the reason why the wood smelt so strongly, and why
the herbs were so fragrant, and the lakes so transparent and yet so
dark, with their white swimming swans.

"On the margin of the wood, among three or four houses, a pole as
tall as the mainmast of a ship had been erected, and from its summit
hung wreaths and fluttering ribbons: this was called a maypole. Men
and maids danced round the tree, and sang as loudly as they could, to
the violin of the fiddler. There were merry doings at sundown and in
the moonlight, but I took no part in them—what has a little mouse to
do with a May dance? I sat in the soft moss and held my sausage-
peg fast. The moon threw its beams especially upon one spot, where
a tree stood, covered with moss so exceedingly fine, I may almost venture
to say it was as fine as the skin of the Mouse King; but it was of a
green colour, and that is a great relief to the eye.

"All at once, the most charming little people came marching forth.
They were only tall enough to reach to my knee. They looked like men,
but were better proportioned: they called themselves elves, and had
delicate clothes on, of flower leaves trimmed with the wings of flies and
gnats, which had a very good appearance. Directly they appeared, they
seemed to be seeking for something—I know not what; but at last
some of them came towards me, and the chief pointed to my sausage-
peg, and said, 'That is just such a one as we want—it is pointed—it is
capital!' and the longer he looked at my pilgrim's staff the more delighted he became.

"'I will lend it,' I said, 'but not to keep.'

"'Not to keep!' they all repeated; and they seized the sausage-peg,
which I gave up to them, and danced away to the spot where the fine
moss grew; and here they set up the peg in the midst of the green.
They wanted to have a maypole of their own, and the one they now had
seemed cut out for them; and they decorated it so that it was beautiful
to behold.

"First, little spiders spun it round with gold thread, and hung it all

THE ELVES APPLY FOR THE LOAN OF THE SAUSAGE-PEG.

over with fluttering veils and flags, so finely woven, bleached so snowy white in the moonshine, that they dazzled my eyes. They took colours from the butterfly's wing, and strewed these over the white linen, and flowers and diamonds gleamed upon it, so that I did not know my sausage-peg again: there is not in all the world such a maypole as they had made of it. And now came the real great party of elves. They were quite without clothes, and looked as genteel as possible; and they invited me to be present at the feast; but I was to keep at a certain distance, for I was too large for them.

"And now began such music! It sounded like thousands of glass bells, so full, so rich, that I thought the swans were singing. I fancied also that I heard the voice of the cuckoo and the blackbird, and at last the whole forest seemed to join in. I heard children's voices, the sound of bells, and the song of birds; the most glorious melodies — and all came from the elves' maypole, namely, my sausage-peg. I should never have believed that so much could come out of it; but that depends very much upon the hands into which it falls. I was quite touched. I wept, as a little mouse may weep, with pure pleasure.

"The night was far too short; but it is not longer up yonder at that season. In the morning dawn the breeze began to blow, the mirror of the forest lake was covered with ripples, and all the delicate veils and flags fluttered away in the air. The waving garlands of spider's web, the hanging bridges and balustrades, and whatever else they are called, flew away as if they were nothing at all. Six elves brought me back my sausage-peg, and asked me at the same time if I had any wish that they could gratify; so I asked them if they could tell me how soup was made on a sausage-peg.

"'How *we* do it?' asked the chief of the elves, with a smile. 'Why, you have just seen it. I fancy you hardly know your sausage-peg again?'

"'You only mean that as a joke,' I replied. And then I told them in so many words, why I had undertaken a journey, and what great hopes were founded on the operation at home. 'What advantage,' I asked, 'can accrue to our Mouse King, and to our whole powerful state, from the fact of my having witnessed all this festivity? I cannot shake it out of the sausage-peg, and say, "Look, here is the peg, now the soup will come." That would be a dish that could only be put on the table when the guests had dined.'

"Then the elf dipped his little finger into the cup of a blue violet and said to me,

"'See here! I will anoint your pilgrim's staff; and when you go back to your country, and come to the castle of the Mouse King, you have but to touch him with the staff, and violets will spring forth and cover its whole surface, even in the coldest winter-time. And so I think I've given you something to carry home, and a little more than something!'"

But before the little Mouse said what this "something more" was, she stretched her staff out towards the King, and in very truth the most beautiful bunch of violets burst forth; and the scent was so powerful that the Mouse King incontinently ordered the mice who stood nearest the chimney to thrust their tails into the fire and create a smell of burning, for the odour of the violets was not to be borne, and was not of the kind he liked.

"But what was the 'something more,' of which you spoke?" asked the Mouse King.

"Why," the little Mouse answered, "I think it is what they call effect!" and herewith she turned the staff round, and lo! there was not a single flower to be seen upon it; she only held the naked skewer, and lifted this up, as a musical conductor lifts his *bâton*. "'Violets,' the elf said to me, 'are for sight, and smell, and touch. Therefore it yet remains to provide for hearing and taste!'"

And now the little Mouse began to beat time; and music was heard, not such as sounded in the forest among the elves, but such as is heard in the kitchen. There was a bubbling sound of boiling and roasting; and all at once it seemed as if the sound were rushing through every chimney, and pots or kettles were boiling over. The fire-shovel hammered upon the brass kettle, and then, on a sudden, all was quiet again. They heard the quiet subdued song of the tea-kettle, and it was wonderful to hear —they could not quite tell if the kettle were beginning to sing or leaving off; and the little pot simmered, and the big pot simmered, and neither cared for the other: there seemed to be no reason at all in the pots. And the little Mouse flourished her *bâton* more and more wildly; the pots foamed, threw up large bubbles, boiled over, and the wind roared and whistled through the chimney. Oh! it became so terrible that the little Mouse lost her stick at last.

"That was a heavy soup!" said the Mouse King. "Shall we not soon hear about the preparation?"

"That was all," said the little Mouse, with a bow.

"That all! Then we should be glad to hear what the next has to relate," said the Mouse King.

III.

What the second little Mouse had to tell.

"I was born in the palace library," said the second Mouse. "I and several members of our family never knew the happiness of getting into the dining-room, much less into the store-room; on my journey, and here to day, are the only times I have seen a kitchen. We have indeed often been compelled to suffer hunger in the library, but we get a good deal of knowledge. The rumour penetrated even to us, of the royal prize offered to those who could cook soup upon a sausage-peg; and it was my old grandmother who thereupon ferreted out a manuscript, which she certainly could not read, but which she had heard read out, and in which it was written: 'Those who are poets can boil soup upon a sausage-peg.' She asked me if I were a poet. I felt quite innocent on the subject, and then she told me I must go out, and manage to become one. I again asked what was requisite in that particular, for it was as difficult for me to find that out as to prepare the soup; but grandmother had heard a good deal of reading, and she said that three things was especially necessary: 'Understanding, imagination, feeling—if you can manage to obtain these three, you are a poet, and the sausage-peg affair will be quite easy to you.'

"And I went forth, and marched towards the west, away into the wide world, to become a poet.

"Understanding is the most important thing in every affair. I knew that, for the two other things are not held in half such respect, and consequently I went out first to seek understanding. Yes, where does he dwell? 'Go to the ant and be wise,' said the great King of the Jews; I knew that from my library experience; and I never stopped till I came to the first great ant-hill, and there I placed myself on the watch, to become wise.

"The ants are a respectable people. They are understanding itself.

Everything with them is like a well-worked sum, that comes right. To
work and to lay eggs, they say, is to live while you live, and to provide
for posterity ; and accordingly that is what they do. They were divided
into the clean and the dirty ants. The rank of each is indicated by a
number, and the ant queen is number ONE ; and her view is the only
correct one, she is the receptacle of all wisdom ; and that was important
for me to know. She spoke so much, and it was all so clever, that it
sounded to me like nonsense. She declared her ant-hill was the loftiest
thing in the world ; though close by it grew a tree, which was certainly
loftier, much loftier, that could not be denied, and therefore it was never
mentioned. One evening an ant had lost herself upon the tree ; she
had crept up the stem—not up to the crown, but higher than any ant
had climbed until then ; and when she turned, and came back home, she
talked of something far higher than the ant-hill that she had found in
her travels ; but the other ants considered that an insult to the whole
community, and consequently she was condemned to wear a muzzle, and
to continual solitary confinement. But a short time afterwards another
ant got on the tree, and made the same journey and the same discovery :
and this one spoke with emphasis, and distinctly, as they said ; and as,
moreover, she was one of the pure ants and very much respected, they
believed her ; and when she died they erected an egg-shell as a memorial
of her, for they had a great respect for the sciences. I saw," continued
the little Mouse, "that the ants are always running to and fro with
their eggs on their backs. One of them once dropped her egg ; she
exerted herself greatly to pick it up again, but she could not succeed.
Then two others came up, and helped her with all their might, inso-
much that they nearly dropped their own eggs over it ; but then they
certainly at once relaxed their exertions, for each should think of himself first—the ant queen had declared that by so doing they exhibited at
once heart and understanding.

"'These two qualities,' she said, 'place us ants on the highest step
among all reasoning beings. Understanding is seen among us all in
predominant measure, and I have the greatest share of understanding.'
And so saying, she raised herself on her hind legs, so that she was easily
to be recognized. I could not be mistaken, and I ate her up. We were
to go to the ants to learn wisdom—and I had got the queen !

I now proceeded nearer to the before-mentioned lofty tree. It was
an oak, and had a great trunk and a far-spreading top, and was very
old. I knew that a living being dwelt here, a Dryad as it is called, who
is born with the tree, and dies with it. I had heard about this in the
library ; and now I saw an oak tree and an oak girl. She uttered a
piercing cry when she saw me so near. Like all females, she was very
much afraid of mice ; and she had more ground for fear than others,
for I might have gnawn through the stem of the tree on which her life
depended. I accosted the maiden in a friendly and honest way, and
bade her take courage. And she took me up in her delicate hand ; and
when I had told her my reason for coming out into the wide world,
she promised me that perhaps on that very evening I should have one

of the two treasures of which I was still in quest. She told me that Phantasus, the genius of imagination, was her very good friend, that he was beautiful as the god of love, and that he rested many an hour under the leafy boughs of the tree, which then rustled more strongly than ever over the pair of them. He called her his dryad, she said, and the tree his tree, for the grand gnarled oak was just to his taste, with its root burrowing so deep in the earth and the stem and crown rising so high out in the fresh air, and knowing the beating snow, and the sharp wind, and the warm sunshine as they deserve to be known. ' Yes,' the Dryad continued, ' the birds sing aloft there in the branches, and tell each other of strange countries they have visited; and on the only dead bough the stork has built a nest which is highly ornamental, and, moreover, one gets to hear something of the land of the pyramids. All that is very pleasing to Phantasus; but it is not enough for him : I myself must talk to him, and tell him of life in the woods, and must revert to my childhood, when I was little, and the tree such a delicate thing that a stinging-nettle overshadowed it—and I have to tell everything, till now that the tree is great and strong. Sit you down under the green thyme, and pay attention; and when Phantasus comes, I shall find an opportunity to pinch his wings, and to pull out a little feather. Take the pen—no better is given to any poet—and it will be enough for you !'

"And when Phantasus came the feather was plucked, and I seized it," said the little Mouse. "I put it in water, and held it there till it grew soft. It was very hard to digest, but I nibbled it up at last. It is very easy to gnaw oneself into being a poet, though there are many things one must do. Now I had these two things, imagination and understanding, and through these I knew that the third was to be found in the library; for a great man has said and written that there are romances whose sole and single use is that they relieve people of their superfluous tears, and that they are, in fact, a sort of sponges sucking up human emotion. I remembered a few of these old books, which had always looked especially palatable, and were much thumbed and very greasy, having evidently absorbed a great deal of feeling into themselves.

"I betook myself back to the library, and, so to speak, devoured a whole novel—that is, the essence of it, the interior part, for I left the crust or binding. When I had digested this, and a second one in addition, I felt a stirring within me, and I ate a bit of a third romance, and now I was a poet. I said so to myself, and told the others also. I had headache, and chestache, and I can't tell what aches besides. I began thinking what kind of stories could be made to refer to a sausage-peg; and many pegs, and sticks, and staves, and splinters came into my mind —the ant queen must have had a particularly fine understanding. I remembered the man who took a white stick in his mouth, by which means he could render himself and the stick invisible; I thought of stick hobby-horses, of ' stock rhymes,' of ' breaking the staff ' over an offender, and goodness knows how many phrases more concerning sticks stocks, staves, and pegs. All my thoughts ran upon sticks, staves, and pegs ; and when one is a poet (and I am a poet, for I have worked most terribly hard to become one) a person can make poetry on these subjects. I shall therefore be able to wait upon you every day with a poem or a history—and that's the soup I have to offer."

"Let us hear what the third has to say," was now the Mouse King's command.

"Peep! peep!" cried a small voice at the kitchen door, and a little Mouse—it was the fourth of the Mice who had contended for the prize, the one whom they looked upon as dead—shot in like an arrow. She toppled the sausage-peg with the crape covering over in a moment. She had been running day and night, and had travelled on the railway, in the goods train, having watched her opportunity, and yet she had almost come too late. She pressed forward, looking very much rumpled, and she had lost her sausage-peg, but not her voice, for she at once took up the word, as if they had been waiting only for her, and wanted to hear none but her, and as if everything else in the world were of no consequence. She spoke at once, and spoke fully : she had appeared so suddenly that no one found time to object to her speech or to her, while she was speaking. And now let us hear what she said.

IV.

What the fourth Mouse, who spoke before the third had spoken, had to tell.

"I BETOOK myself immediately to the largest town," she said ; "the name has escaped me—I have a bad memory for names. From the railway I was carried, with some confiscated goods, to the council-house, and when I arrived there, I ran into the dwelling of the gaoler. The gaoler was talking of his prisoners, and especially of one, who had spoken unconsidered words. These words had given rise to others, and these latter had been written down and recorded.

"'The whole thing is soup on a sausage-peg,' said the gaoler ; 'but the soup may cost him his neck.'

"Now, this gave me an interest in the prisoner," continued the Mouse, "and I watched my opportunity and slipped into his prison— for there's a mouse-hole to be found behind every locked door. The prisoner looked pale, and had a great beard and bright sparkling eyes. The lamp flickered and smoked, but the walls were so accustomed to that, that they grew none the blacker for it. The prisoner scratched pictures and verses in white upon the black ground, but I did not read them. I think he found it tedious, and I was a welcome guest. He lured me with bread crumbs, with whistling, and with friendly words : he was glad to see me, and gradually I got to trust him, and we became good friends. He let me run upon his hand, his arm, and into his sleeve, he let me creep about in his beard, and called me his little friend. I

THE GAOLER'S GRANDDAUGHTER TAKES PITY ON THE LITTLE MOUSE.

really got to love him, for these things are reciprocal. I forgot my
mission in the wide world, forgot my sausage-peg: that I had placed in
a crack in the floor—it's lying there still. I wished to stay where I was,
for if I went away the poor prisoner would have no one at all, and
that's having *too* little, in this world. *I* stayed, but *he* did not stay.
He spoke to me very mournfully the last time, gave me twice as much
bread and cheese as usual, and kissed his hand to me; then he went
away, and never came back. I don't know his history.

"'Soup on a sausage-peg!' said the gaoler, to whom I now went;
but I should not have trusted him. He took me in his hand, certainly,
but he popped me into a cage, a treadmill. That's a horrible engine, in
which you go round and round without getting any farther; and people
laugh at you into the bargain.

"The gaoler's granddaughter was a charming little thing, with a mass
of curly hair that shone like gold, and such merry eyes, and such a
smiling mouth!

"'You poor little mouse,' she said, as she peeped into my ugly cage;
and she drew out the iron rod, and forth I jumped to the window board,
and from thence to the roof spout. Free! free! I thought only of
that, and not of the goal of my journey.

"It was dark, and night was coming on. I took up my quarters in an old tower, where dwelt a watchman and an owl. That is a creature like a cat, who has the great failing that she eats mice. But one may be mistaken, and so was I, for this was a very respectable, well-educated old owl: she knew more than the watchman, and as much as I. The young owls were always making a racket; but 'Go and make soup on a sausage peg' were the hardest words she could prevail on herself to utter, she was so fondly attached to her family. Her conduct inspired me with so much confidence, that from the crack in which I was crouching I called out 'peep!' to her. This confidence of mine pleased her hugely, and she assured me I should be under her protection, and that no creature should be allowed to do me wrong; she would reserve me for herself, for the winter, when there would be short commons.

"She was in every respect a clever woman, and explained to me how the watchman could only 'whoop' with the horn that hung at his side, adding, 'He is terribly conceited about it, and imagines he's an owl in the tower. Wants to do great things, but is very small—soup on a sausage-peg!'

"I begged the owl to give me the recipe for this soup, and then she explained the matter to me.

"'Soup on a sausage-peg,' she said, 'was only a human proverb, and was to be understood thus: Each thinks his own way the best, but the whole signifies nothing.'

"'Nothing!' I exclaimed. I was quite struck. Truth is not always aggreeable, but truth is above everything; and that's what the old owl said. I now thought about it, and readily perceived that if I brought what was *above everything* I brought something far beyond soup on a sausage-peg. So I hastened away, that I might get home in time, and bring the highest and best, that is above everything—namely, *the truth*. The mice are an enlightened people, and the King is above them all. He is capable of making me Queen, for the sake of truth."

"Your truth is a falsehood," said the Mouse who had not yet spoken. "I can prepare the soup, and I mean to prepare it."

V.

How it was prepared.

"I DID not travel," the third Mouse said. "I remained in my country —that's the right thing to do. There's no necessity for travelling; one can get everything as good here. I stayed at home. I've not learned what I know from supernatural beings, or gobbled it up, or held converse with owls. I have what I know through my own reflections. Will you make haste and put that kettle upon the fire? So—now water must be poured in—quite full—up to the brim! So—now more fuel—make up the fire, that the water may boil—it must boil over and over! So—I now throw the peg in. Will the King now be pleased to dip his tail in the boiling water, and to stir it round with the said tail? The longer the King stirs it, the more powerful will the soup become. It costs nothing at all—no further materials are necessary, only stir it round!"

"Cannot any one else do that?" asked the Mouse King.

"No," replied the Mouse. "The power is contained only in the tail of the Mouse King."

And the water boiled and bubbled, and the Mouse King stood close beside the kettle—there was almost danger in it—and he put forth his tail, as the mice do in the dairy, when they skim the cream from a pan of milk, afterwards licking their creamy tails; but his tail only penetrated into the hot steam, and then he sprang hastily down from the hearth.

THE MOUSE KING UNDERSTANDS HOW THE SOUP IS MADE.

"Of course—certainly you are my Queen," he said. "We'll adjourn the soup question till our golden wedding in fifty years' time, so that the poor of my subjects, who will then be fed, may have something to which they can look forward with pleasure for a long time."

And soon the wedding was held. But many of the mice said, as they were returning home, that it could not be really called soup on a sausage-peg, but rather soup on a mouse's tail. They said that some of the stories had been very cleverly told; but the whole thing might have been different. "*I* should have told it so—and so—and so!"

Thus said the critics, who are always wise—after the fact.

And this story went out into the wide world, everywhere; and opinions varied concerning it, but the story remained as it was. And that's the best in great things and in small, so also with regard to soup on a sausage-peg—not to expect any thanks for it.

THE WICKED PRINCE.

THERE was once a wicked Prince. His aim and object was to conquer all the countries in the world, and to inspire all men with fear. He went about with fire and sword, and his soldiers trampled down the corn in the fields, and set fire to the peasants' houses, so that the red flames licked the leaves from the trees, and the fruit hung burned on the black charred branches. With her naked baby in her arms, many a poor mother took refuge behind the still smoking walls of her burned house; but even here the soldiers sought for their victims, and if they found them, it was new food for their demoniac fury: evil spirits could not have raged worse than did these soldiers; but the Prince thought their deeds were right, and that it must be so. Every day his power increased; his name was feared by all, and fortune accompanied him in all his actions. From conquered countries he brought vast treasures home, and in his capital was heaped an amount of wealth unequalled in any other place. And he caused gorgeous palaces, churches, and halls to be built, and every one who saw those great buildings and these vast treasures cried out respectfully, "What a great Prince!" They thought not of the misery he had brought upon other lands and cities; they heard not all the sighs and all the moanings that arose from among the ruins of demolished towns.

The Prince looked upon his gold, and upon his mighty buildings, and his thoughts were like those of the crowd.

"What a great Prince am I! But," so his thought ran on, "I must have more, far more! No power may be equal to mine, much less exceed it!"

And he made war upon all his neighbours, and overcame them all. The conquered Kings he caused to be bound with fetters of gold to his chariot, and thus he drove through the streets of his capital; when he banqueted, those Kings were compelled to kneel at his feet, and at the feet of his courtiers, and receive the broken pieces which were thrown to them from the table.

At last the Prince caused his own statue to be set up in the open squares and in the royal palaces, and he even wished to place it in the churches before the altars; but here the priests stood up against him, and said,

"Prince, thou art mighty, but Heaven is mightier, and we dare not fulfil thy commands."

"Good: then," said the Prince, "I will vanquish Heaven likewise."

And in his pride and impious haughtiness he caused a costly ship to be built, in which he could sail through the air: it was gay and glaring to behold, like the tail of a peacock, and studded and covered with thousands of eyes; but each eye was the muzzle of a gun. The Prince sat in the midst of the ship, and needed only to press on a spring, and a thousand bullets flew out on all sides, while the gun barrels were

re-loaded immediately. Hundreds of eagles were harnessed in front of
the ship, and with the speed of an arrow they flew upwards towards
the sun. How deep the earth lay below them! With its mountains
and forests, it seemed but a field through which the plough had drawn
its furrows, and along which the green bank rose covered with turf;
soon it appeared only like a flat map with indistinct lines; and at last it
lay completely hidden in mist and cloud. Ever higher flew the eagles,
up into the air; then one of the innumerable angels appeared. The
wicked Prince hurled thousands of bullets against him; but the bullets
sprang back from the angel's shining pinions, and fell down like com-

THE PRIESTS EXHORTING THE WICKED PRINCE.

mon hail-stones; but a drop of blood, one single drop, fell from one of
the white wing-feathers, and this drop fell upon the ship in which the
Prince sat, and burned its way deep into the ship, and weighing like a
thousand hundredweight of lead, dragged down the ship in headlong
fall towards the earth; the strongest pinions of the eagles broke; the
wind roared round the Prince's head, and the aroused clouds—formed
from the smoke of burned cities—drew themselves together in threatening shapes, like huge sea crabs stretching forth their claws and nippers
towards him, and piled themselves up in great overshadowing rocks,
with crushing fragments rolling down them, and then to fiery dragons,
till the Prince lay half dead in the ship, which at last was caught with
a terrible shock in the thick branches of a forest.

"I will conquer Heaven!" said the Prince. "I have sworn it, and
my will *must* be done!"

And for seven years he caused his men to work at making ships for sailing through the air, and had thunderbolts made of the hardest steel, for he wished to storm the fortress of Heaven; out of all his dominions he gathered armies together, so that when they were drawn up in rank and file they covered a space of several miles. The armies went on board the ships, and the Prince approached his own vessel. Then there was sent out against him a swarm of gnats, a single swarm of little gnats. The swarm buzzed round the Prince, and stung his face and hands: raging with anger, he drew his sword and struck all round him; but he only struck the empty air, for he could not hit the gnats. Then he commanded his people to bring costly hangings, and to wrap them around him, so that no gnat might further sting him; and the servants did as he commanded them. But a single gnat had attached itself to the inner side of the hangings, and crept into the ear of the Prince, and stung him. It burned like fire, and the poison penetrated to his brain: like a madman he tore the hangings from his body and hurled them far away, tore his clothes and danced about naked before the eyes of his rude, savage soldiers, who now jeered at the mad Prince who wanted to overcome Heaven, and who himself was conquered by one single little gnat.

THE SHEPHERDESS
AND THE CHIMNEY-SWEEPER.

HAVE you ever seen a very old wooden cupboard, quite black with age, and ornamented with carved foliage and arabesques? Just such a cupboard stood in a parlour: it had been a legacy from the great-grandmother, and was covered from top to bottom with carved roses and tulips. There were the quaintest flourishes upon it, and from among these peered forth little stags' heads with antlers. In the middle of the cupboard door an entire figure of a man had been cut out: he was certainly ridiculous to look at, and he grinned, for you could not call it laughing: he had goat's legs, little horns on his head, and a long beard. The children in the room always called him the Billygoat-legs-Major-and Lieutenant-General-War-Commander-Sergeant; that was a difficult name to pronounce, and there are not many who obtain this title; but it was something to have cut him out. And there he was! He was always looking at the table under the mirror, for on this table stood a lovely little Shepherdess made of china. Her shoes were gilt, her dress was adorned with a red rose, and besides this she had a golden hat and a shepherd's crook: she was very lovely. Close by her stood a little Chimney-Sweeper, black as a coal, and also made of porcelain: he was as clean and neat as any other man, for it was only make-believe that he was a sweep; the china-workers might just as well have made a prince of him, if they had been so minded.

There he stood very nattily with his ladder, and with a face as white and pink as a girl's; and that was really a fault, for he ought to have been a little black. He stood quite close to the Shepherdess: they had both been placed where they stood; but as they had been placed there they had become engaged to each other. They suited each other well. Both were young people, both made of the same kind of china, and both were brittle.

THE OLD CHINAMAN AND THE YOUNG COUPLE.

Close to them stood another figure, three times greater than they. This was an old Chinaman, who could nod. He was also of porcelain, and declared himself to be the grandfather of the little Shepherdess; but he could not prove his relationship. He declared he had authority over her, and that therefore he had nodded to Mr. Billygoat-legs-Lieutenant-and-Major-General-War-Commander-Sergeant, who was wooing her for his wife.

"Then you will get a husband!" said the old Chinaman, "a man who I verily believe is made of mahogany. He can make you Billygoat-legs-Lieutenant-and-Major-General-War-Commander-Sergeant's lady: he has the whole cupboard full of silver plate, which he hoards up in secret drawers."

"I won't go into the dark cupboard!" said the little Shepherdess. "I have heard tell that he has eleven porcelain wives in there."

"Then you may become the twelfth," cried the Chinaman. "This night, so soon as it rattles in the old cupboard, you shall be married, as true as I am an old Chinaman!"

And with that he nodded his head and fell asleep. But the little Shepherdess wept and looked at her heart's beloved, the porcelain Chimney-Sweeper.

"I should like to beg of you," said she, "to go out with me into the wide world, for we cannot remain here."

"I'll do whatever you like," replied the little Chimney-Sweep. "Let us start directly! I think I can keep you by exercising my profession."

"If we were only safely down from the table!" said she. "I shall not be happy until we are out in the wide world."

And he comforted her, and showed her how she must place her little foot upon the carved corners and the gilded foliage at the foot of the table; he brought his ladder, too, to help her, and they were soon together upon the floor. But when they looked up at the old cupboard there was great commotion within: all the carved stags were stretching out their heads, rearing up their antlers, and turning their necks; and the Billygoat-legs-Lieutenant-and-Major-General-War-Commander-Sergeant sprang high in the air, and called across to the old Chinaman,

"Now they're running away! now they're running away!"

Then they were a little frightened, and jumped quickly into the drawer of the window-seat. Here were three or four packs of cards which were not complete, and a little puppet-show, which had been built up as well as it could be done. There plays were acted, and all the ladies, diamonds, clubs, hearts, and spades, sat in the first row, fanning themselves; and behind them stood all the knaves, showing that they had a head above and below, as is usual in playing-cards. The play was about two people who were not to be married to each other, and the Shepherdess wept, because it was just like her own history.

"I cannot bear this!" said she. "I must go out of the drawer."

But when they arrived on the floor, and looked up at the drawer, the old Chinaman was awake and was shaking over his whole body—for below he was all one lump.

"Now the old Chinaman's coming!" cried the little Shepherdess; and she fell down upon her porcelain knee, so startled was she.

"I have an idea," said the Chimney-Sweeper. "Shall we creep into the great *pot-pourri* vase, which stands in the corner? Then we can lie on roses and lavender, and throw salt in his eyes if he comes."

"That will be of no use," she replied. "Besides, I know that the old

Chinaman and the *pot-pourri* vase were once engaged to each other, and
a kind of liking always remains when people have stood in such a relation
to each other. No, there's nothing left for us but to go out into the
wide world."

"Have you really courage to go into the wide world with me?"
asked the Chimney-Sweeper. "Have you considered how wide the
world is, and that we can never come back here again?"

"I have," replied she.

And the Chimney-Sweeper looked fondly at her, and said,

"My way is through the chimney. If you have really courage to
creep with me through the stove—through the iron fire-box as well as
up the pipe, then we can get out into the chimney, and I know how to
find my way through there. We'll mount so high that they can't catch
us, and quite at the top there's a hole that leads out into the wide world."

And he led her to the door of the stove.

"It looks very black there," said she; but still she went with him,
through the box and through the pipe, where it was pitch-dark night.

"Now we are in the chimney," said he; "and look, look! up yonder
a beautiful star is shining."

And it was a real star in the sky, which shone straight down upon
them, as if it would show them the way. And they clambered and
crept: it was a frightful way, and terribly steep; but he supported her
and helped her up; he held her, and showed her the best places where
she could place her little porcelain feet; and thus they reached the
edge of the chimney, and upon that they sat down, for they were desperately tired, as they well might be.

The sky with all its stars was high above, and all the roofs of the
town deep below them. They looked far around—far, far out into the
world. The poor Shepherdess had never thought of it as it really was:
she leaned her little head against the Chimney-Sweeper, then she wept so
bitterly that the gold ran down off her girdle.

"That is too much," she said. "I cannot bear that. The world is
too large! If I were only back upon the table below the mirror! I
shall never be happy until I am there again. Now I have followed you
out into the wide world, you may accompany me back again if you
really love me."

And the Chimney-Sweeper spoke sensibly to her—spoke of the old
Chinaman and of the Billygoat-legs-Lieutenant-and-Major-General-War-
Commander-Sergeant; but she sobbed bitterly and kissed her little
Chimney-Sweeper, so that he could not help giving way to her, though
it was foolish.

And so with much labour they climbed down the chimney again.
And they crept through the pipe and the fire-box. That was not pleasant
at all. And there they stood in the dark stove; there they listened
behind the door, to find out what was going on in the room. Then it
was quite quiet: they looked in—ah! there lay the old Chinaman in the
middle of the floor! He had fallen down from the table as he was pursuing them, and now he lay broken into three pieces; his back had come

off all in one piece, and his head had rolled into a corner. The Billy-goat-legs-Lieutenant-and-Major-General-War-Commander-Sergeant stood where he had always stood, considering.

" That is terrible ! " said the little Shepherdess. " The old grandfather has fallen to pieces, and it is our fault. I shall never survive it ! " And then she wrung her little hands.

" He can be mended ! he can be mended ! " said the Chimney-Sweeper. " Don't be so violent. If they glue his back together and give him a good rivet in his neck he will be as good as new, and may say many a disagreeable thing to us yet."

" Do you think so ? " cried she.

So they climbed back upon the table where they used to stand.

" You see, we have come to this," said the Chimney-Sweeper : "we might have saved ourselves all the trouble we have had."

" If the old grandfather was only riveted ! " said the Shepherdess. " I wonder if that is dear ? "

And he was really riveted. The family had his back cemented, and a great rivet was passed through his neck : he was as good as new, only he could no longer nod.

" It seems you have become proud since you fell to pieces," said the Billygoat-legs-Lieutenant-and-Major-General-War-Commander-Sergeant. " I don't think you have any reason to give yourself such airs. Am I to have her, or am I not ? "

And the Chimney-Sweeper and the little Shepherdess looked at the old Chinaman most piteously, for they were afraid he might nod. But he could not do that, and it was irksome to him to tell a stranger that he always had a rivet in his neck. And so the porcelain people remained together, and loved one another until they broke.

TWO BROTHERS.

ON one of the Danish islands where the old Thingstones, the seats of justice of our forefathers, are found in the fields, and great trees tower in the beech woods, there lies a little town, whose low houses are covered with red tiles. In one of these houses wondrous things were brewed over glowing coals on the open hearth ; there was a boiling in glasses, a mixing and a distilling, and herbs were cut up and bruised in mortars, and an elderly man attended to all this.

" One must only do the right thing," said he ; "yes, the right thing. One must learn the truth about every created particle, and keep close to this truth."

In the room with the good housewife sat her two sons, still small, but with grown-up thoughts. The mother had always spoken to them of right and justice, and had exhorted them to hold truth fast, declaring that it was as the countenance of the Almighty in this world.

THE TWO BROTHERS IN THEIR BED-ROOM.

The elder of the boys looked roguish and enterprising. It was his
delight to read of the forces of nature, of the sun and of the stars; no
fairy tale pleased him so much as these. Oh! how glorious it must be,
he thought, to go out on voyages of discovery, or to find out how the
wings of birds could be imitated, and then to fly through the air! yes,
to find that out would be the right thing: father was right, and mother
was right—truth keeps the world together.

The younger brother was quieter, and quite lost himself in books.
When he read of Jacob clothing himself in sheep-skins, to be like Esau
and to cheat his brother of his birthright, his little fist would clench in
anger against the deceiver: when he read of tyrants, and of all the
wickedness and wrong that is in the world, the tears stood in his eyes,
and he was quite filled with the thoughts of the right and truth which
must and will at last be triumphant. One evening he already lay in
bed, but the curtains were not yet drawn close, and the light streamed
in upon him: he had taken the book with him to bed, because he
wanted to finish reading the story of Solon.

And his thoughts lifted and carried him away marvellously, and it seemed to him that his bed became a ship, careering onward with swelling sails. Did he dream? or what was happening to him? It glided onward over the rolling waters and the great ocean of time, and he heard the voice of Solon. In a strange tongue, and yet intelligible to him, he heard the Danish motto, "With law the land is ruled."

And the Genius of the human race stood in the humble room, and bent down over the bed, and printed a kiss on the boy's forehead.

" Be thou strong in fame, and strong in the battle of life! With the truth in thy breast, fly thou towards the land of truth!"

The elder brother was not yet in bed; he stood at the window gazing out at the mists that rose from the meadows. They were not elves dancing there, as the old nurse had told him; he knew better: they were vapours, warmer than the air, and consequently they mounted. A shooting star gleamed athwart the sky, and the thoughts of the boy were roused from the mists of the earth to the shining meteor. The stars of heaven twinkled, and golden threads seemed to hang from them down upon the earth.

"Fly with me!" it sang and sounded in the boy's heart; and the mighty genius, swifter than the bird, than the arrow, than anything that flies with earthly means, carried him aloft to the region where rays stretching from star to star bind the heavenly bodies to each other; our earth revolved in the thin air; the cities on its surface seemed quite close together; and through the sphere it sounded, "What is near, what is far to men, when the mighty genius of mind lifts them up?"

And again the boy stood at the window and gazed forth, and the younger brother lay in his bed, and their mother called them by their names, "Anders Sandoe" and "Hans Christian."

Denmark knows them, and the world knows them—the two brothers OERSTED.

THE OLD STREET LAMP.

DID you ever hear the story of the old Street Lamp? It is not very remarkable, but it may be listened to for once in a way.

It was a very honest old Lamp, that had done its work for many, many years, but which was now to be pensioned off. It hung for the last time to its post, and gave light to the street. It felt as an old dancer at the theatre, who is dancing for the last time, and who to-morrow will sit forgotten in her garret. The Lamp was in great fear about the morrow, for it knew that it was to appear in the council-house, and to be inspected by the mayor and the council, to see if it were fit for further service or not.

And then it was to be decided whether it was to show its light in future for the inhabitants of some suburb, or in the country in some manufactory: perhaps it would have to go at once into an iron foundry to be melted down. In this last case anything might be made of it; but the question whether it would remember, in its new state, that it had been a Street Lamp, troubled it terribly. Whatever might happen, this much was certain, that it would be separated from the watchman and his wife, whom it had got to look upon as quite belonging to its family. When the Lamp had been hung up for the first time the watchman was a young sturdy man: it happened to be the very evening on which he entered on his office. Yes, that was certainly a long time ago, when it first became a Lamp and he a watchman. The wife was a little proud in those days. Only in the evening, when she went by, she deigned to glance at the Lamp; in the day-time never. But now, in these latter years, when all three, the watchman, his wife, and the Lamp, had grown old, the wife had also tended it, cleaned it, and provided it with oil. The two old people were thoroughly honest; never had they cheated the Lamp of a single drop of the oil provided for it.

It was the Lamp's last night in the street, and to-morrow it was to go to the council-house;—those were two dark thoughts! No wonder that it did not burn brightly. But many other thoughts passed through its brain. On what a number of events had it shone—how much it had seen! Perhaps as much as the mayor and the whole council had beheld. But it did not give utterance to these thoughts, for it was a good honest old Lamp, that would not willingly hurt any one, and least of all those in authority. Many things passed through its mind, and at times its light flashed up. In such moments it had a feeling that it, too, would be remembered.

"There was that handsome young man—it is certainly a long while ago—he had a letter on pink paper with a gilt edge. It was so prettily written, as if by a lady's hand. Twice he read it, and kissed it, and looked up to me with eyes which said plainly, 'I am the happiest of men!' Only he and I know what was written in this first letter from his true love. Yes, I remember another pair of eyes. It is wonderful how our thoughts fly about! There was a funeral procession in the street: the young beautiful lady lay in the decorated hearse, in a coffin adorned with flowers and wreaths; and a number of torches quite darkened my light. The people stood in crowds by the houses, and all followed the procession. But when the torches had passed from before my face, and I looked round, a single person stood leaning against my post, weeping. I shall never forget the mournful eyes that looked up to me!"

This and similar thoughts occupied the old Street Lantern, which shone to-night for the last time.

The sentry relieved from his post, at least knows who is to succeed him, and may whisper a few words to him; but the Lamp did not know its successor; and yet it might have given a few useful hints with respect to rain and fog, and some information as to how far the rays of the moon lit up the pavement, from what direction the wind usually came, and much more of the same kind.

On the bridge of the gutter stood three persons who wished to introduce themselves to the Lamp, for they thought the Lamp itself could appoint its successor. The first was a herring's head, that could gleam with light in the darkness. He thought it would be a great saving of oil if they put him up on the post. Number two was a piece of rotten wood, which also glimmers in the dark. He conceived himself descended from an old stem, once the pride of the forest. The third person was a glow-worm. Where this one had come from the Lamp could not imagine; but there it was, and it could give light. But the rotten wood and the herring's head swore by all that was good that it only gave light at certain times, and could not be brought into competition with themselves.

The old Lamp declared that not one of them gave sufficient light to fill the office of a street lamp; but not one of them would believe this. When they heard that the Lamp had not the office to give away, they were very glad of it, and declared that the Lamp was too decrepit to make a good choice.

At the same moment the Wind came careering from the corner of the street, and blew through the air-holes of the old Street Lamp.

"What's this I hear?" he asked. "Are you to go away to-morrow? Do I see you for the last time? Then I must make you a present at parting. I will blow into your brain-box in such a way that you shall be able in future not only to remember everything you have seen and heard, but that you shall have such light within you as shall enable you to see all that is read of or spoken of in your presence."

"Yes, that is really much, very much!" said the old Lamp. "I thank you heartily. I only hope I shall not be melted down."

"That is not likely to happen at once," said the Wind. "Now I will blow a memory into you: if you receive several presents of this kind, you may pass your old days very agreeably."

"If I am only not melted down!" said the Lamp again. "Or should I retain my memory even in that case?"

"Be sensible, old Lamp," said the Wind. And he blew, and at that moment the Moon stepped forth from behind the clouds.

"What will you give the old Lamp?" asked the Wind.

"I'll give nothing," replied the Moon. "I am on the wane, and the lamps never lighted me; but, on the contrary, I've often given light for the lamps."

And with these words the Moon hid herself again behind the clouds, to be safe from further importunity.

A drop now fell upon the Lamp, as if from the roof; but the drop explained that it came from the clouds, and was a present—perhaps the best present possible.

"I shall penetrate you so completely that you shall receive the faculty, if you wish it, to turn into rust in one night, and to crumble into dust."

The Lamp considered this a bad present, and the Wind thought so too.

"Does no one give more? does no one give more?" it blew as loud as it could.

THE OLD STREET LAMP IN GOOD QUARTERS.

Then a bright shooting star fell down, forming a long bright stripe.

"What was that?" cried the Herring's Head. "Did not a star fall? I really think it went into the Lamp! Certainly if such high-born personages try for this office, we may say good-night and betake ourselves home."

And so they did, all three. But the old Lamp shed a marvellous strong light around.

"That was a glorious present," it said. "The bright stars which I have always admired, and which shine as I could never shine though I shone with all my might, have noticed me, a poor old lamp, and have sent me a present, by giving me the faculty that all I remember and see as clearly as if it stood before me, shall also be seen by all whom I love. And in this lies the true pleasure; for joy that we cannot share with others is only half enjoyed."

"That sentiment does honour to your heart," said the Wind. "But for that wax lights are necessary. If these are not lit up in you, your rare faculties will be of no use to others. Look you, the stars did not think of that; they take you and every other light for wax. But I will go down." And he went down.

" Good heavens! wax lights!" exclaimed the Lamp. " I never had those till now, nor am I likely to get them!—If I am only not melted down!"

The next day—yes, it will be best that we pass over the next day. The next evening the Lamp was resting in a grandfather's chair. And guess where! In the watchman's dwelling. He had begged as a favour of the mayor and the council that he might keep the Street Lamp, in consideration of his long and faithful service, for he himself had put up and lit the lantern for the first time on the first day of entering on his duties four and twenty years ago. He looked upon it as his child, for he had no other. And the Lamp was given to him.

Now it lay in the great arm-chair by the warm stove. It seemed as if the Lamp had grown bigger, now that it occupied the chair all alone.

The old people sat at supper, and looked kindly at the old Lamp, to whom they would willingly have granted a place at their table.

Their dwelling was certainly only a cellar two yards below the foot-way, and one had to cross a stone passage to get into the room. But within it was very comfortable and warm, and strips of list had been nailed to the door. Everything looked clean and neat, and there were curtains round the bed and the little windows. On the window-sill stood two curious flower-pots, which sailor Christian had brought home from the East or West Indies. They were only of clay, and represented two elephants. The backs of these creatures had been cut off; and instead of them there bloomed from within the earth with which one elephant was filled, some very excellent chives, and that was the kitchen garden; out of the other grew a great geranium, and that was the flower gar-den. On the wall hung a great coloured print representing the Con-gress of Vienna. There you had all the Kings and Emperors at once. A clock with heavy weights went "tick! tick!" and in fact it always went too fast; but the old people declared this was far better than if it went too slow. They ate their supper, and the Street Lamp lay, as I have said, in the arm-chair close beside the stove. It seemed to the Lamp as if the whole world had been turned round. But when the old watchman looked at it, and spoke of all that they two had gone through in rain and in fog, in the bright short nights of summer and in the long winter nights, when the snow beat down, and one longed to be at home in the cellar, then the old Lamp found its wits again. It saw everything as clearly as if it was happening then; yes, the Wind had kindled a capital light for it.

The old people were very active and industrious; not a single hour was wasted in idleness. On Sunday afternoon some book or other was brought out; generally a book of travels. And the old man read aloud about Africa, about the great woods, with elephants running about wild; and the old woman listened intently, and looked furtively at the clay elephants which served for flower-pots.

" I can almost imagine it to myself!" said she.

And the Lamp wished particularly that a wax candle had been there, and could be lighted up in it ; for then the old woman would be able to see everything to the smallest detail, just as the Lamp saw it—the tall trees with great branches all entwined, the naked black men on horseback, and whole droves of elephants crashing through the reeds with their broad clumsy feet.

" Of what use are all my faculties if I can't obtain a wax light ? " sighed the Lamp. " They have only oil and tallow candles, and that 's not enough."

One day a great number of wax candle ends came down into the cellar : the larger pieces were burned, and the smaller ones the old woman used for waxing her thread. So there were wax candles enough ; but no one thought of putting a little piece into the Lamp.

" Here I stand with my rare faculties ! " thought the Lamp. " I carry everything within me, and cannot let them partake of it ; they don't know that I am able to cover these white walls with the most gorgeous tapestry, to change them into noble forests, and all that they can possibly wish."

The Lamp, however, was kept neat and clean, and stood all shining in a corner, where it caught the eyes of all.   Strangers considered it a bit of old rubbish ; but the old people did not care for that ; they loved the Lamp.

One day—it was the old watchman's birthday—the old woman approached the Lantern, smiling to herself, and said,

" I 'll make an illumination to-day, in honour of my old man ! "

And the Lamp rattled its metal cover, for it thought, " Well, at last there will be a light within me."   But only oil was produced, and no wax light appeared.   The Lamp burned throughout the whole evening, but now understood, only too well, that the gift of the stars would be a hidden treasure for all its life.   Then it had a dream : for one possessing its rare faculties to dream was not difficult.   It seemed as if the old people were dead, and that itself had been taken to the iron foundry to be melted down.   It felt as much alarmed as on that day when it was to appear in the council-house to be inspected by the mayor and council.   But though the power had been given to it to fall into rust and dust at will, it did not use this power.   It was put into the furnace, and turned into an iron candlestick, as fair a candlestick as you would desire—one on which wax lights were to be burned.   It had received the form of an angel holding a great nosegay ; and the wax light was to be placed in the middle of the nosegay.

The candlestick had a place assigned to it on a green writing table.   The room was very comfortable ; many books stood round about the walls, which were hung with beautiful pictures ; it belonged to a poet.   Everything that he wrote or composed showed itself round about him.   Nature appeared sometimes in thick dark forests, sometimes in beautiful meadows, where the storks strutted about, sometimes again in a ship sailing on the foaming ocean, or in the blue sky with all its stars.

" What faculties lie hidden in me ! " said the old Lamp, when it awoke.

"I could almost wish to be melted down! But, no! that must not be so long as the old people live. They love me for myself; they have cleaned me and brought me oil. I am as well off now as the whole Congress, in looking at which they also take pleasure."

And from that time it enjoyed more inward peace; and the honest old Street Lamp had well deserved to enjoy it.

BY THE ALMSHOUSE WINDOW.

NEAR the grass-covered rampart which encircles Copenhagen lies a great red house; balsams and other flowers greet us from the long rows of windows in the house, whose interior is sufficiently poverty-stricken; and poor and old are the people who inhabit it. The building is the Warton Almshouse.

Look! at the window there leans an old maid: she plucks the withered leaf from the balsam, and looks at the grass-covered rampart, on which many children are playing. What is the old maid thinking of? A whole life drama is unfolding itself before her inward gaze.

"The poor little children, how happy they are, how merrily they play and romp together! What red cheeks and what angels' eyes! but they have no shoes nor stockings. They dance on the green rampart, just on the place where, according to the old story, the ground always sank in, and where a sportive frolicsome child had been lured by means of flowers, toys, and sweetmeats into an open grave ready dug for it, and which was afterwards closed over the child; and from that moment, the old story says, the ground gave way no longer, the mound remained firm and fast, and was quickly covered with fine green turf. The little people who now play on that spot know nothing of the old tale, else would they fancy they heard the child crying deep below the earth, and the dew-drops on each blade of grass would be to them tears of woe Nor do they know anything of the Danish King, who here, in the face of the coming foe, took an oath before all his trembling courtiers that he would hold out with the citizens of his capital, and die here in his nest: they know nothing of the men who have fought here, or of the women who from here have drenched with boiling water the enemy, clad in white, and 'biding in the snow to surprise the city.

"No! the poor little ones are playing with light childish spirits. Play on, play on, thou little maiden! Soon the years will come—yes, those glorious years. The priestly hands have been laid on the candidates for confirmation; hand in hand they walk on the green rampart: thou hast a white frock on—it has cost thy mother much labour, and yet it is only cut down for thee out of an old larger dress! You will also wear a red shawl; and what if it hang too far down? People will only see how large, how very large it is. You are thinking of your dress, and of the Giver of all good; so glorious is it to wander on the green rampart.

" And the years roll by ; they have no lack of dark days, but you have your cheerful young spirit, and you have gained *a friend*, you know not how. You met, Oh, how often ! You walk together on the rampart in the fresh spring, on the high days and holidays, when all the world come out to walk upon the ramparts, and all the bells of the church steeples seem to be singing a song of praise for the coming spring.

THE OLD PENSIONER.

" Scarcely have the violets come forth, but there on the rampart, just opposite the beautiful Castle of Rosenberg, there is a tree bright with the first green buds. - Every year this tree sends forth fresh green shoots. Alas ! it is not so with the human heart ! Dark mists, more in number than those that cover the northern skies, cloud the human heart. Poor child—thy friend's bridal chamber is a black coffin, and thou becomest an old maid. From the almshouse window behind the balsams thou shalt look on the merry children at play, and shalt see thy own history renewed."

And that is the life drama that passes before the old maid while she looks out upon the rampart, the green sunny rampart, where the children with their red cheeks and bare shoeless feet are rejoicing merrily, like the other free little birds.

THE LOVERS.

A WHIP-TOP and a little Ball were together in a drawer among some other toys; and the Top said to the Ball,

"Shall we not be bridegroom and bride, as we live together in the same box?"

But the Ball, which had a coat of morocco leather, and was just as conceited as any fine lady, would make no answer to such a proposal.

Next day the little boy came to whom the toys belonged: he painted the top red and yellow, and hammered a brass nail into it; and it looked splendid when the top turned round!

"Look at me!" he cried to the little Ball. "What do you say now? Shall we not be engaged to each other? We suit one another so well! You jump and I dance! No one could be happier than we two should be."

"Indeed? Do you think so?" replied the little Ball. "Perhaps you do not know that my papa and my mamma were morocco slippers, and that I have a Spanish cork inside me?"

"Yes, but I am made of mahogany," said the Top; "and the mayor himself turned me. He has a turning lathe of his own, and it amuses him greatly."

"Can I depend upon that?" asked the little Ball.

"May I never be whipped again if it is not true!" replied the Top.

"You can speak well for yourself," observed the Ball, "but I cannot grant your request. I am as good as engaged to a swallow: every time I leap up into the air she puts her head out of her nest and says, 'Will you?' And now I have silently said 'Yes,' and that is as good as half engaged; but I promise I will never forget you."

"Yes, that will be much good!" said the Top.

And they spoke no more to each other.

Next day the Ball was taken out by the boy. The Top saw how it flew high into the air, like a bird; at last one could no longer see it. Each time it came back again, but gave a high leap when it touched the earth, and that was done either from its longing to mount up again, or because it had a Spanish cork in its body. But the ninth time the little Ball remained absent, and did not come back again; and the boy sought and sought, but it was gone.

THE MAID FINDS THE WHIP-TOP.

"I know very well where it is!" sighed the Top. "It is in the swallow's nest, and has married the swallow!"

The more the Top thought of this, the more it longed for the Ball. Just because it could not get the Ball, its love increased; and the fact that the Ball had chosen another, formed a peculiar feature in the case. So the Top danced round and hummed, but always thought of the little Ball, which became more and more beautiful in his fancy. Thus several years went by, and now it was an old love.

And the Top was no longer young! But one day he was gilt all over; never had he looked so handsome; he was now a golden Top, and sprang till he hummed again. Yes, that was something worth seeing! But all at once he sprang too high, and—he was gone!

They looked and looked, even in the cellar, but he was not to be found. Where could he be?

He had jumped into the dust-box, where all kinds of things were lying: cabbage stalks, sweepings, and dust that had fallen down from the roof.

" Here 's a nice place to lie in !   The gliding will soon leave me here. Among what a rabble have I alighted!"

And then he looked sideways at a long leafless cabbage stump, and at a curious round thing that looked like an old apple ; but it was not an apple—it was an old Ball, which had lain for years in the gutter on the roof, and was quite saturated with water.

" Thank goodness, here comes one of us, with whom one can talk !" said the little Ball, and looked at the gilt Top.   " I am really morocco, worked by maidens' hands, and have a Spanish cork within me ; but no one would think it, to look at me.   I was very nearly marrying a swallow, but I fell into the gutter on the roof, and have lain there full five years, and become quite wet through.   You may believe me, that 's a long time for a young girl."

But the Top said nothing.   He thought of his old love ; and the more he heard, the clearer it became to him that this was she.

Then came the servant-girl, and wanted to turn out the dust-box. " Aha ! there 's a gilt top !" she cried.

And so the Top was brought again to notice and honour, but nothing was heard of the little Ball.   And the Top spoke no more of his old love ; for that dies away when the beloved object has lain for five years in a roof-gutter and got wet through ; yes, one does not know her again when one meets her in the dust-box.

THE BELL.

At evening, in the narrow streets of the great city, when the sun went down and the clouds shone like gold among the chimneys, there was frequently heard, sometimes by one, and sometimes by another, a strange tone, like the sound of a church bell ; but it was only heard for a moment at a time, for in the streets there was a continual rattle of carriages, and endless cries of men and women—and that is a sad interruption.   Then people said, " Now the evening bell sounds, now the sun is setting."

Those who were walking outside the city, where the houses stood farther from each other, with gardens and little fields between, saw the evening sky looking still more glorious, and heard the sound of the bell far more clearly.   It was as though the tones came from a church, deep in the still quiet fragrant wood, and people looked in that direction, and became quite meditative.

Now a certain time passed, and one said to another, " Is there not a church out yonder in the wood ?   That bell has a peculiarly beautiful sound !   Shall we not go out and look at it more closely ? "   And rich people drove out, and poor people walked ; but the way seemed marvellously long to them ; and when they came to a number of willow trees that grew on the margin of the forest, they sat down and looked up to

THE PRINCE GOES IN SEARCH OF THE BELL.

the long branches, and thought they were now really in the green wood. The pastrycook from the town came there too, and pitched his tent; but another pastrycook came and hung up a bell just over his own tent, a bell, in fact, that had been tarred so as to resist the rain, but it had no clapper. And when the people went home again, they declared the whole affair had been very romantic, and that meant much more than merely that they had taken tea. Three persons declared that they had penetrated into the wood to where it ended, and that they had always heard the strange sound of bells, but it had appeared to them as if it came from the town. One of the three wrote a song about it, and said that the sound was like the song of a mother singing to a dear good child; no melody could be more beautiful than the sound of that bell.

The Emperor of that country was also informed of it, and promised that the person who could really find out whence the sound came should have the title of Bell-finder, even if it should turn out not to be a bell.

Many went to the forest, on account of the good entertainment there; but there was only one who came back with a kind of explanation. No one had penetrated deep enough into the wood, nor had he; but he said that the sound came from a very great owl in a hollow tree; it was an owl of wisdom, that kept knocking its head continually against the tree, but whether the sound came from the owl's head, or from the trunk of the tree, he could not say with certainty. He was invested with the title of Bell-finder, and every year wrote a short treatise upon the owl; and people were just as wise after reading his works as they were before.

On a certain day a confirmation was held. The old clergyman had spoken well and impressively, and the candidates for confirmation were quite moved. It was an important day for them; for from being children they became grown-up people, and the childish soul was as it were to be transformed to that of a more sensible person. The sun shone gloriously as the confirmed children marched out of the town, and from the wood the great mysterious bell sounded with peculiar strength. They at once wished to go out to it, and all felt this wish except three. One of these desired to go home, to try on her ball dress; the second was a poor boy, who had borrowed the coat and boots in which he was confirmed from the son of his landlord, and he had to give them back at an appointed time; the third said he never went to a strange place unless his parents went with him, that he had always been an obedient son, and would continue to be so, even after he was confirmed, and they were not to laugh at him. But they did laugh at him, nevertheless.

So these three did not go, but the others trotted on. The sun shone, and the birds sang, and the young people sang too, and held each other by the hand, for they had not yet received any office, and were all alike before Heaven on that day. But two of the smallest soon became weary and returned to the town, and two little girls sat down to bind wreaths, and did not go with the rest. And when the others came to the willow trees where the pastrycook lived, they said, "Well, now we are out here, the bell does not really exist—it is only an imaginary thing."

Then suddenly the bell began to ring in the forest with such a deep and solemn sound that four or five determined to go still deeper into the wood. The leaves hung very close, and it was really difficult to get forward; lilies of the valley and anemones grew thick, and blooming convolvulus and blackberry bushes stretched in long garlands from tree to tree, where the nightingales sang and the sunbeams played. It was splendid; but the path was not practicable for girls—they would have torn their clothes. There lay great blocks of stone covered with mosses of all colours; the fresh spring water gushed forth, and it sounded strangly, almost like "luck, luck."

"That cannot be the bell!" said one of the party, and he laid himself down and listened. "That should be properly studied!"

And he remained there, and let the others go on.

They came to a house built of the bark of trees and of twigs: a great tree laden with wild apples stretched out its branches over the dwelling, as though it would pour its whole blessing upon the roof, which was covered with blooming roses, the long branches turned about the gables. And from the gable hung a little bell. Could that be the bell they had heard ? They all agreed that it was, except one: this dissentient said that the bell was far too small and too delicate to be heard at such a distance, and that they were quite different sounds that had so deeply moved the human heart. He who spoke thus was a King's son, and the others declared that a person of that kind always wanted to be wiser than every one else.

Therefore they let him go alone, and as he went his mind was more and more impressed with the solitude of the forest, but still he heard the little bell, at which the others were rejoicing ; and sometimes, when the wind carried towards him sounds from the pastrycook's abode, he could hear how the party there were singing at their tea. But the deep tones of the bell sounded louder still ; sometimes it was as if an organ were playing to it ; the sound came from the left, the side in which the heart is placed.

Now there was a rustling in the bushes, and a little boy stood before the Prince, a boy with wooden shoes, and such a short jacket that one could plainly see what long wrists he had. They knew one another. The boy was the youngster who had been confirmed that day, and had not been able to come with the rest because he had to go home and give up the borrowed coat and boots to his landlord's son. This he had done, and had then wandered away alone in his poor clothes and his wooden shoes, for the bell sounded so invitingly, he had been obliged to come out.

" We can go together," said the Prince.

But the poor lad in the wooden shoes was quite embarrassed. He pulled at the short sleeves of his jacket, and said he was afraid he could not come quickly enough ; besides, he thought the bell must be sought on the right hand, for there the place was great and glorious.

" But then we shall not meet at all," said the Prince ; and he nodded to the poor boy, who went away into the darkest, deepest part of the forest, where the thorns tore his shabby garments and scratched his face, his feet, and his hands. The Prince also had two or three brave rents, but the sun shone bright on his path ; and it is he whom we will follow, for he was a brisk companion.

" I must and will find the bell," said he, " though I have to go to the end of the world."

Ugly apes sat up in the trees, and grinned and showed their teeth. " Shall we beat him ?" said they. " Shall we smash him ? He's a King's son !"

But he went contentedly farther and farther into the forest, where the most wonderful trees grew : there stood white star-lilies with blood-red stamens, sky-blue tulips that glittered in the breeze, and apple trees whose apples looked completely like great shining soap bubbles : only think how those trees must have gleamed in the sunbeams ! All around lay the most beautiful green meadows, where hart and hind played in the grass, and noble oaks and beech trees grew there ; and when the bark of any tree split, grass and long climbing plants grew out of the rifts ; there were also great wooded tracts with quiet lakes, on which white swans floated and flapped their wings. The Prince often stood still and listened; often he thought that the bell sounded upwards to him from one of the deep lakes; but soon he noticed that the sound did not come from thence, but that the bell was sounding deeper in the wood.

Now the sun went down. The sky shone red as fire; it became quite quiet in the forest, and he sank on his knees, sang his evening hymn, and said,

"I shall never find what I seek, now the sun is going down, and the night, the dark night, is coming. But perhaps I can once more see the round sun before he disappears beneath the horizon. I will climb upon the rocks, for they are higher than the highest trees."

And he seized hold of roots and climbing plants, and clambered up the wet stones, where the water snakes writhed and the toads seemed to be barking at him; but he managed to climb up before the sun, which he could see from this elevation, had quite set. Oh, what splendour! The sea, the great glorious sea, which rolled its great billows towards the shore, lay stretched out before him, and the sun stood aloft like a great flaming altar, there where the sea and sky met; everything melted together in glowing colours; the wood sang, and his heart sang too. All nature was a great holy church, in which trees and floating clouds were the pillars and beams, flowers and grass the velvet carpet, and the heavens themselves the vaulted roof. The red colours faded up there when the sun sank to rest; but millions of stars were lighted up and diamond lamps glittered, and the Prince stretched forth his arms towards heaven, towards the sea, and towards the forest. Suddenly there came from the right hand the poor lad who had been confirmed, with his short jacket and his wooden shoes: he had arrived here at the same time, and had come his own way. And they ran to meet each other, and each took the other's hand in the great temple of nature and of poetry. And above them sounded the holy invisible bell; and blessed spirits surrounded them and floated over them, singing a rejoicing song of praise!

LITTLE TUK'S MARVELLOUS RIDE.

LITTLE TUK.

YES, that was little Tuk. His name was not really Tuk; but when he could not speak plainly, he used to call himself so. It was to mean "Charley;" and it does very well if one only knows it. Now, he was to take care of his little sister Gustava, who was much smaller than he, and at the same time he was to learn his lesson; but these two things would not suit well together. The poor boy sat there with his little sister on his lap, and sang her all kinds of songs that he knew, and every now and then he gave a glance at the geography-book that lay open before him; by to-morrow morning he was to know all the towns in Zealand by heart, and to know everything about them that one can well know.

Now his mother came home, for she had been out, and took little Gustava in her arms. Tuk ran quickly to the window, and read so zealously that he had almost read his eyes out, for it became darker and darker; but his mother had no money to buy candles.

"There goes the old washerwoman out of the lane yonder," said his mother, as she looked out of the window. "The poor woman can hardly drag herself along, and now she has to carry the pail of water from the well. Be a good boy, Tuk, and run across, and help the old woman. Won't you?"

And Tuk ran across quickly, and helped her; but when he came back into the room it had become quite dark. There was nothing said about a candle, and now he had to go to bed, and his bed was an old settle. There he lay, and thought of his geography lesson, and of Zealand, and of all the master had said. He ought certainly to have read it again, but he could not do that. So he put the geography-book under his pillow, because he had heard that this is a very good way to learn one's lesson; but one cannot depend upon it. There he lay, and thought and thought; and all at once he fancied some one kissed him upon his eyes and mouth. He slept, and yet he did not sleep; it was just as if the old washerwoman were looking at him with her kind eyes, and saying,

"It would be a great pity if you did not know your lesson to-morrow. You have helped me, therefore now I will help you; and Providence will help us both."

All at once the book began to crawl, crawl about under Tuk's pillow.

"Kikeliki! Put! put!" It was a Hen that came crawling up, and she came from Kjöge. "I'm a Kjöge hen!"* she said.

And then she told him how many inhabitants were in the town, and about the battle that had been fought there, though that was really hardly worth mentioning.

"Kribli, kribli, plumps!" Something fell down: it was a wooden bird, the Parrot from the shooting match at Prästöe. He said that there were just as many inhabitants yonder as he had nails in his body; and he was very proud. "Thorwaldsen lived close to me.† Plumps! Here I lie very comfortably."

But now little Tuk no longer lay in bed; on a sudden he was on horseback. Gallop, gallop! hop, hop! and so he went on. A splendidly-attired knight, with flowing plume, held him on the front of his saddle, and so they went riding on through the wood of the old town of Wordingborg, and that was a great and very busy town. On the King's castle rose high towers, and the radiance of lights streamed from every window; within was song and dancing, and King Waldemar and the young gaily-dressed maids of honour danced together. Now the morning came on, and so soon as the sun appeared the whole city and the King's castle suddenly sank down, one tower falling after another; and at last only one remained standing on the hill where the castle had formerly been; ‡ and the town was very small and poor, and the school-

---

* Kjoge, a little town on Kjoge Bay. Lifting up children by putting the two hands to the sides of their heads is called "showing them Kjoge hens."
† Prastoe, a still smaller town. A few hundred paces from it lies the estate of Nysoe, where Thorwaldsen usually lived while he was in Denmark, and where he executed many immortal works.
‡ Wordingborg, in King Waldemar's time a considerable town, now a place of no importance Only a lonely tower and a few remains of a wall show where the castle once stood.

boys came with their books under their arms, and said, "Two thousand inhabitants;" but that was not true, for the town had not so many.

And little Tuk lay in his bed, as if he dreamed, and yet as if he did not dream; but some one stood close beside him.

"Little Tuk! little Tuk!" said the voice. It was a seaman, quite a little personage, as small as if he had been a cadet; but he was not a cadet. "I'm to bring you a greeting from Corsör; * that is a town which is just in good progress — a lively town that has steamers and mail coaches. In times past they used always to call it ugly, but that is now no longer true.

"'I lie by the sea shore,' said Corsör. 'I have high roads and pleasure gardens; and I gave birth to a poet who was witty and entertaining, and that cannot be said of all of them. I wanted once to fit out a ship that was to sail round the world; but I did not do that, though I might have done it. But I smell deliciously, for close to my gates the loveliest roses bloom."

Little Tuk looked, and it seemed red and green before his eyes; but when the confusion of colour had a little passed by, it changed all at once into a wooded declivity close by a bay, and high above it stood a glorious old church with two high pointed towers. Out of this hill flowed springs of water in thick columns, so that there was a continual splashing, and close by sat an old King with a golden crown upon his white head: that was King Hroar of the springs, close by the town of Roeskilde, as it is now called. And up the hill into the old church went all the Kings and Queens of Denmark, hand in hand, all with golden crowns; and the organ played, and the springs plashed. Little Tuk saw all and heard all.

"Don't forget the towns," † said King Hroar.

At once everything had vanished, and whither? It seemed to him like turning a leaf in a book. And now stood there an old peasant woman, who came from Soröe, where grass grows in the market-place; she had an apron of grey cotton thrown over her head and shoulders, and the apron was very wet; it must have been raining.

"Yes, that it has!" said she; and she knew many pretty things out of Holberg's plays, and about Waldemar and Absalom. But all at once she cowered down, and wagged her head as if she were about to spring. "Koax!" said she; "it is wet! it is wet! There is a very agreeable death-silence in Soröe!" ‡ Now she changed all at once into a frog— "Koax!"—and then she became an old woman again. "One must dress according to the weather," she said. "It is wet! it is wet! My town

---

* Corsor, on the Great Belt, used to be called the most tiresome of Danish towns before the establishment of steamers: for in those days travellers had often to wait there for a favourable wind. The poet Baggesen was born there.

† Roeskilde (Roesquelle, *Rose-spring*, falsely called Rothschild), once the capital of Denmark. The town took its name from King Hroar and from the many springs in the vicinity. In the beautiful cathedral most of the Kings and Queens of Denmark are buried. In Roeskilde the Danish Estates used to assemble.

‡ Soroe, a very quiet little town, in a fine situation, surrounded by forests and lakes. Holberg, the Moliere of Denmark, here founded a noble academy. The poets Hanch and Ingman were professors here.

is just like a bottle: one goes in at the cork, and must come out again at the rock. In old times I had capital fish, and now I've fresh red-cheeked boys in the bottom of the bottle, and they learn wisdom—Hebrew, Greek.—Koax!"

That sounded just like the croak of the frogs, or the sound of some one marching across the moor in great boots; always the same note, so monotonous and wearisome that little Tuk fairly fell asleep, and that could not hurt him at all.

But even in this sleep came a dream, or whatever it was. His little sister Gustava with the blue eyes and the fair curly hair was all at once a tall slender maiden, and without having wings she could fly; and now they flew over Zealand, over the green forests and the blue lakes.

"Do you hear the cock crow, little Tuk? Kikeliki! The fowls are flying up out of Kjöge! You shall have a poultry-yard—a great, great poultry-yard! You shall not suffer hunger nor need; and you shall hit the bird, as the saying is; you shall become a rich and happy man. Your house shall rise up like King Waldemar's tower, and shall be richly adorned with marble statues, like those of Prästöe. You understand me well. Your name shall travel with fame round the whole world, like the ship that was to sail from Corsör."

"Don't forget the towns," said King Hroar. "You will speak well and sensibly, little Tuk; and when at last you descend to your grave, you shall sleep peacefully—"

"As if I lay in Soröe," said Tuk, and he awoke. It was bright morning, and he could not remember his dream. But that was not necessary, for one must not know what is to happen.

Now he sprang quickly out of his bed, and read his book, and all at once he knew his whole lesson. The old washerwoman, too, put her head in at the door, nodded to him in a friendly way, and said,

"Thank you, you good child, for your help. May your beautiful dreams come true!"

Little Tuk did not know at all what he had dreamed, but there was One above who knew it.

THE FLAX.

The Flax stood in blossom; it had pretty little blue flowers, delicate as a moth's wings, and even more delicate. The sun shone on the Flax, and the rain clouds moistened it, and this was just as good for it as it is for little children when they are washed, and afterwards get a kiss from their mother; they become much prettier, and so did the Flax.

"The people say that I stand uncommonly well," said the Flax, "and that I'm fine and long, and shall make a capital piece of linen. How happy I am! I'm certainly the happiest of beings. How well I am off! And I may come to something! How the sunshine gladdens, and

THE MOTHER SPINNING THE FLAX.

the rain tastes good and refreshes me! I'm wonderfully happy; I'm the happiest of beings."

"Yes, yes, yes!" said the Hedge-stake. "You don't know the world, but we do, for we have knots in us;" and then it creaked out mournfully,

> "Snip-snap-snurre,
> Bassellurre!
> The song is done."

"No, it is not done," said the Flax. "To-morrow the sun will shine, or the rain will refresh us. I feel that I'm growing, I feel that I'm in blossom! I'm the happiest of beings."

But one day the people came and took the Flax by the head and pulled it up by the root. That hurt; and it was laid in water as if they were going to drown it, and then put on the fire as if it was going to be roasted. It was quite fearful!

"One can't always have good times," said the Flax. "One must make one's experiences, and so one gets to know something."

But bad times certainly came. The Flax was moistened and roasted, and broken and hackled. Yes, it did not even know what the operations were called that they did with it. It was put on the spinning-wheel — whirr! whirr! whirr! — it was not possible to collect one's thoughts.

"I have been uncommonly happy!" it thought in all its pain. "One must be content with the good one has enjoyed! Contented! contented! Oh!" And it continued to say that when it was put into the loom, and till it became a large beautiful piece of linen. All the flax, to the last stalk, was used in making one piece.

"But this is quite remarkable! I should never have believed it! How favourable fortune is to me! The Hedge-stake was well informed, truly, with its

> 'Snip-snap-snurre,
> Bassellurre!'

The song is not done by any means. Now it's beginning in earnest. That's quite remarkable! If I've suffered something, I've been made into something! I'm the happiest of all! How strong and fine I am, how white and long! That's something different from being a mere plant: even if one bears flowers, one is not attended to, and only gets watered when it rains. Now I'm attended to and cherished; the maid turns me over every morning, and I get a shower bath from the watering-pot every evening. Yes, the clergyman's wife has even made a speech about me, and says I'm the best piece in the whole parish. I cannot be happier!"

Now the Linen was taken into the house, and put under the scissors: how they cut and tore it, and then pricked it with needles! That was not pleasant; but twelve pieces of body linen of a kind not often mentioned by name, but indispensable to all people, were made of it—a whole dozen!

"Just look! Now something has really been made of me! So, that was my destiny. That's a real blessing. Now I shall be of some use in the world, and that's right, that's a true pleasure! We've been made into twelve things, but yet we're all one and the same; we're just a dozen: how remarkably charming that is!"

Years rolled on, and now they would hold together no longer.

"It must be over one day," said each piece. "I would gladly have held together a little longer, but one must not expect impossibilities."

They were now torn into pieces and fragments. They thought it was all over now, for they were hacked to shreds, and softened and boiled; yes, they themselves did not know all that was done to them; and then they became beautiful white paper.

"Now, that is a surprise, and a glorious surprise!" said the Paper. "Now I'm finer than before, and I shall be written on: that is remarkable good fortune."

And really the most beautiful stories and verses were written upon it, and only once there came a blot; that was certainly remarkable good fortune. And the people heard what was upon it; it was sensible and good, and made people much more sensible and better : there was a great blessing in the words that were on this Paper.

"That is more than I ever imagined when I was a little blue flower in the fields. How could I fancy that I should ever spread joy and knowledge among men? I can't yet understand it myself, but it is really so. I have done nothing myself but what I was obliged with my weak powers to do for my own preservation, and yet I have been promoted from one joy and honour to another. Each time when I think ' the song is done,' it begins again in a higher and better way. Now I shall certainly be sent about to journey through the world, so that all people may read me. That cannot be otherwise ; it's the only probable thing. I've splendid thoughts, as many as I had pretty flowers in the old times. I'm the happiest of beings."

But the Paper was not sent on its travels, it was sent to the printer, and everything that was written upon it was set up in type for a book, or rather for many hundreds of books, for in this way a very far greater number could derive pleasure and profit from the book than if the one paper on which it was written had run about the world, to be worn out before it had got half way.

"Yes, that is certainly the wisest way," thought the Written Paper. "I really did not think of that. I shall stay at home, and be held in honour, just like an old grandfather ; and I am really the grandfather of all these books. Now something can be effected ; I could not have wandered about thus. He who wrote all this looked at me ; every word flowed from his pen right into me. I am the happiest of all."

Then the Paper was tied together in a bundle, and thrown into a tub that stood in the wash-house.

"It's good resting after work," said the Paper. "It is very right that one should collect one's thoughts. Now I'm able for the first time to think of what is in me, and to know oneself is true progress. What will be done with me now? At any rate I shall go forward again : I'm always going forward, I've found that out."

Now, one day all the Paper was taken out and laid by on the hearth ; it was to be burned, for it might not be sold to hucksters to be used for covering for butter and sugar, they said. And all the children in the house stood round about, for they wanted to see the Paper burn, that flamed up so prettily, and afterwards one could see many red sparks among the ashes, careering here and there. One after another faded out quick as the wind, and that they called "seeing the children come out of school," and the last spark was the schoolmaster : one of them thought he had already gone, but at the next moment there came another spark. "There goes the schoolmaster!" they said. Yes, they all knew about it ; they should have known who it was who went there : we shall get to know it, but they did not. All the old Paper, the whole bundle, was laid upon the fire, and it was soon alight. "Ugh!" it said, and burst out into bright flame. Ugh! that was not very agreeable, but when the whole was wrapped in bright flames these mounted up higher than the Flax had ever been able to lift its little blue flowers, and glittered as the white Linen had never been able to glitter. All the written letters turned for a moment quite red, and all the words and thoughts turned to flame.

" Now I 'm mounting straight up to the sun," said a voice in the flame ; and it was as if a thousand voices said this in unison ; and the flames mounted up through the chimney and out at the top, and more delicate than the flames, invisible to human eyes, little tiny beings floated there, as many as there had been blossoms on the Flax. They were lighter even than the flame from which they were born ; and when the flame was extinguished, and nothing remained of the Paper but black ashes, they danced over it once more, and where they touched the black mass the little red sparks appeared. The children came out of school, and the schoolmaster was the last of all. That was fun ! and the children sang over the dead ashes—

> "Snip-snap-snurre,
> Bassellurre!
> The song is done."

But the little invisible beings all said,
" The song is never done, that is the best of all. I know it, and there-fore I 'm the happiest of all."
· But the children could neither hear that nor understand it, nor ought they, for children must not know everything.

THE GIRL WHO TROD ON THE LOAF.

The story of the girl who trod on the loaf to avoid soiling her shoes, and of the misfortune that befell this girl, is well known. It has been written, and even printed.

The girl's name was Ingé : she was a poor child, but proud and pre-sumptuous ; there was a bad foundation in her, as the saying is. When she was quite a little child, it was her delight to catch flies, and tear off their wings, so as to convert them into creeping things. Grown older, she would take cockchafers and beetles, and spit them on pins. Then she pushed a green leaf or a little scrap of paper towards their feet, and the poor creatures seized it, and held it fast, and turned it over and over, struggling to get free from the pin.

" The cockchafer is reading," Ingé would say. " See how he turns the leaf round and round !"

With years she grew worse rather than better ; but she was pretty, and that was her misfortune ; otherwise she would have been more sharply reproved than she was.

" Your headstrong will requires something strong to break it !" her own mother often said. " As a little child, you used to trample on my apron ; but I fear you will one day trample on my heart."

And that is what she really did.

INGÉ TURNS BACK AT THE SIGHT OF HER POOR MOTHER.

She was sent into the country, into service in the house of rich people, who kept her as their own child, and dressed her in corresponding style. She looked well, and her presumption increased.

When she had been there about a year, her mistress said to her. "You ought once to visit your parents, Ingé."

And Ingé set out to visit her parents, but it was only to show herself in her native place, and that the people there might see how grand she had become; but when she came to the entrance of the village, and the young husbandmen and maids stood there chatting, and her own mother appeared among them, sitting on a stone to rest, and with a faggot of sticks before her that she had picked up in the wood, then Ingé turned back, for she felt ashamed that she, who was so finely dressed, should have for a mother a ragged woman, who picked up wood in the forest.

She did not turn back out of pity for her mother's poverty, she was only angry.

And another half-year went by, and her mistress said again, "You ought to go to your home, and visit your old parents, Ingé. I'll make you a present of a great wheaten loaf that you may give to them : they will certainly be glad to see you again."

And Ingé put on her best clothes, and her new shoes, and drew her skirts around her, and set out, stepping very carefully, that she might be clean and neat about the feet; and there was no harm in that. But when she came to the place where the footway led across the moor, and where there was mud and puddles, she threw the loaf into the mud, and trod upon it to pass over without wetting her feet. But as she stood there with one foot upon the loaf and the other uplifted to step farther, the loaf sank with her, deeper and deeper, till she disappeared altogether, and only a great puddle, from which the bubbles rose, remained where she had been.

And that's the story.

But whither did Ingé go? She sank into the moor ground, and went down to the moor woman, who is always brewing there. The moor woman is cousin to the elf maidens, who are well enough known, of whom songs are sung, and whose pictures are painted; but concerning the moor woman it is only known that when the meadows steam in summer-time it is because she is brewing. Into the moor woman's brewery did Ingé sink down; and no one can endure that place long. A box of mud is a palace compared with the moor woman's brewery. Every barrel there has an odour that almost takes away one's senses; and the barrels stand close to each other; and wherever there is a little opening among them, through which one might push one's way, the passage becomes impracticable from the number of damp toads and fat snakes who sit out their time there. Among this company did Ingé fall; and all the horrible mass of living creeping things was so icy cold, that she shuddered in all her limbs, and became stark and stiff. She continued fastened to the loaf, and the loaf drew her down as an amber button draws a fragment of straw.

The moor woman was at home, and on that day there were visitors in the brewery. These visitors were old Bogey and his grandmother, who came to inspect it; and Bogey's grandmother is a venomous old woman, who is never idle : she never rides out to pay a visit without taking her work with her; and, accordingly, she had brought it on the day in question. She sewed biting leather to be worked into men's shoes, and which makes them wander about unable to settle anywhere. She wove webs of lies, and strung together hastily-spoken words that had fallen to the ground; and all this was done for the injury and ruin of mankind. Yes, indeed, she knew how to sew, to weave, and to string, this old grandmother!

Catching sight of Ingé, she put up her double eye-glass, and took another look at the girl.

"That's a girl who has ability!" she observed, "and I beg you will give me the little one as a memento of my visit here. She 'll make a capital statue to stand in my grandson's antechamber."

And Ingé was given up to her, and this is how Ingé came into Bogey's domain. People don't always go there by the direct path, but they can get there by roundabout routes if they have a tendency in that direction.

That was a never-ending antechamber. The visitor became giddy who looked forward, and doubly giddy when he looked back, and saw a whole crowd of people, almost utterly exhausted, waiting till the gate of mercy should be opened to them—they had to wait a long time! Great fat waddling spiders spun webs of a thousand years over their feet, and these webs cut like wire, and bound them like bronze fetters; and, moreover, there was an eternal unrest working in every heart—a miserable unrest. The miser stood there, and had forgotten the key of his strong box, and he knew the key was sticking in the lock. It would take too long to describe the various sorts of torture that were found there together. Ingé felt a terrible pain while she had to stand there as a statue, for she was tied fast to the loaf.

"That's the fruit of wishing to keep one's feet neat and tidy," she said to herself. "Just look how they're all staring at me!"

Yes, certainly, the eyes of all were fixed upon her, and their evil thoughts gleamed forth from their eyes, and they spoke to one another, moving their lips, from which no sound whatever came forth: they were very horrible to behold.

"It must be a great pleasure to look at me!" thought Ingé, "and indeed I have a pretty face and fine clothes." And she turned her eyes for she could not turn her head; her neck was too stiff for that. But she had not considered how her clothes had been soiled in the moor woman's brewhouse. Her garments were covered with mud; a snake had fastened in her hair, and dangled down her back; and out of each fold of her frock a great toad looked forth, croaking like an asthmatic poodle. That was very disconcerting. "But all the rest of them down here look horrible," she observed to herself, and derived consolation from the thought.

The worst of all was the terrible hunger that tormented her. But could she not stoop and break off a piece of the loaf on which she stood? No, her back was too stiff, her hands and arms were benumbed, and her whole body was like a pillar of stone; only she was able to turn her eyes in her head, to turn them quite round, so that she could see backwards: it was an ugly sight. And then the flies came up, and crept to and fro over her eyes, and she blinked her eyes, but the flies would not go away, for they could not fly: their wings had been pulled out, so that they were converted into creeping insects: it was horrible torment added to the hunger, for she felt empty, quite, entirely empty.

"If this lasts much longer," she said, "I shall not be able to bear it." But she had to bear it, and it lasted on and on.

Then a hot tear fell down upon her head, rolled over her face and neck, down on to the loaf on which she stood; and then another tear rolled down, followed by many more. Who might be weeping for Ingé? Had she not still a mother in the world? The tears of sorrow which a mother weeps for her child always make their way to the child; but they do not relieve it, they only increase its torment. And now to bear this unendurable hunger, and yet not to be able to touch the loaf on which she stood! She felt as if she had been feeding on herself, and had become like a thin hollow reed that takes in every sound, for she heard everything that was said of her up in the world, and all that she heard was hard and evil. Her mother, indeed, wept much and sorrowed for her, but for all that she said, "A haughty spirit goes before a fall. That was thy ruin, Ingé. Thou hast sorely grieved thy mother."

Her mother and all on earth knew of the sin she had committed; knew that she had trodden upon the loaf, and had sunk and disappeared; for the cowherd had seen it from the hill beside the moor.

"Greatly hast thou grieved thy mother, Ingé," said the mother; "yes, yes, I thought it would be thus."

"Oh that I never had been born!" thought Ingé; "it would have been far better. But what use is my mother's weeping now?"

And she heard how her master and mistress, who had kept and cherished her like kind parents, now said she was a sinful child, and did not value the gifts of God, but trampled them under her feet, and that the gates of mercy would only open slowly to her.

"They should have punished me," thought Ingé, "and have driven out the whims I had in my head."

She heard how a complete song was made about her, a song of the proud girl who trod upon the loaf to keep her shoes clean, and she heard how the song was sung everywhere.

"That I should have to bear so much evil for that!" thought Ingé; "the others ought to be punished, too, for their sins. Yes, then there would be plenty of punishing to do. Ah, how I'm being tortured!"

And her heart became harder than her outward form.

"Here in this company one can't even become better," she said, "and I don't want to become better! Look, how they're all staring at me!" And her heart was full of anger and malice against all men. "Now they've something to talk about at last up yonder. Ah, how I'm being tortured!"

And then she heard how her story was told to the little children, and the little ones called her the godless Ingé, and said she was so naughty and ugly that she must be well punished.

Thus, even the children's mouths spoke hard words of her.

But one day, while grief and hunger gnawed her hollow frame, and she heard her name mentioned and her story told to an innocent child, a little girl, she became aware that the little one burst into tears at the tale of the haughty, vain Ingé.

"But will Ingé never come up here again?" asked the little girl.

And the reply was, "She will never come up again."

"But if she were to say she was sorry, and to beg pardon, and say she would never do so again?"

" Yes, then she might come; but she will not beg pardon," was the reply.

" I should be *so* glad if she would," said the little girl; and she was quite inconsolable. " I 'll give my doll and all my playthings if she may only come up. It 's too dreadful—poor Ingé !"

And these words penetrated to Ingé's inmost heart, and seemed to do her good. It was the first time any one had said, " Poor Ingé," without adding anything about her faults : a little innocent child was weeping and praying for mercy for her. It made her feel quite strangely, and she herself would gladly have wept, but she could not weep, and that was a torment in itself.

While years were passing above her, for where she was there was no change, she heard herself spoken of more and more seldom. At last one day a sigh struck on her ear : " Ingé, Ingé, how you have grieved me ! I said how it would be !" It was the last sigh of her dying mother.

Occasionally she neard her name spoken by her former employers, and they were pleasant words when the woman said, " Shall I ever see thee again, Ingé ? One knows not what may happen."

But Ingé knew right well that her good mistress would never come to the place where she was.

And again time went on—a long, bitter time. Then Ingé heard her name pronounced once more, and saw two bright stars that seemed gleaming above her. They were two gentle eyes closing upon earth. So many years had gone by since the little girl had been inconsolable and wept about " poor Ingé," that the child had become an old woman, who' was now to be called home to heaven; and in the last hour of existence, when the events of the whole life stand at once before us, the old woman remembered how as a child she had cried heartily at the story of Ingé.

And the eyes of the old woman closed, and the eye of her soul was opened to look upon the hidden things. She, in whose last thoughts Ingé had been present so vividly, saw how deeply the poor girl had sunk, and burst into tears at the sight ; in heaven she stood like a child, and wept for poor Ingé. And her tears and prayers sounded like an echo in the dark empty space that surrounded the tormented captive soul, and the unhoped-for love from above conquered her, for an angel was weeping for her. Why was this vouchsafed to her ? The tormented soul seemed to gather in her thoughts every deed she had done on earth, and she, Ingé, trembled and wept such tears as she had never yet wept. She was filled with sorrow about herself : it seemed as though the gate of mercy could never open to her ; and while in deep penitence she acknowledged this, a beam of light shot radiantly down into the depths to her, with a greater force than that of the sunbeam which melts the snow man the boys have built up ; and quicker than the snow-flake melts, and becomes a drop of water that falls on the warm lips of a child, the stony form of Ingé was changed to mist, and a little bird soared with the speed of lightning upward into the world of men. But

the bird was timid and shy towards all things around; he was ashamed
of himself, ashamed to encounter any living thing, and hurriedly sought
to conceal himself in a dark hole in an old crumbling wall; there he
sat cowering, trembling through his whole frame, and unable to utter a
sound, for he had no voice.   Long he sat there before he could rightly
see all the beauty around him; for it was beautiful.   The air was fresh
and mild, the moon cast its mild radiance over the earth; trees and
bushes exhaled fragrance, and it was right pleasant where he sat, and
his coat of feathers was clean and pure.   How all creation seemed to
speak of beneficence and love! The bird wanted to sing of the thoughts
that stirred in his breast, but he could not; gladly would he have sung

THE BIRD.

as the cuckoo and the nightingale sang in spring-time.   But Heaven,
that hears the mute song of praise of the worm, could hear the notes of
praise which now trembled in the breast of the bird, as David's psalms
were heard before they had fashioned themselves into words and song.

For weeks these toneless songs stirred within the bird; at last, the
holy Christmas-time approached.   The peasant who dwelt near set up a
pole by the old wall, with some ears of corn bound to the top, that the
birds of heaven might have a good meal, and rejoice in the happy,
blessed time.

And on Christmas morning the sun arose and shone upon the ears of
corn, which were surrounded by a number of twittering birds.   Then
out of the hole in the wall streamed forth the voice of another bird, and
the bird soared forth from his hiding-place; and in heaven it was well
known what bird this was.

It was a hard winter.   The ponds were covered with ice, and the
beasts of the field and the birds of the air were stinted for food.   Our
little bird soared away over the high road, and in the ruts of the sledge

he found here and there a grain of corn, and at the halting-places some crumbs. Of these he ate only a few, but he called all the other hungry sparrows around him, that they, too, might have some food. He flew into the towns, and looked round about; and wherever a kind hand had strewn bread on the window-sill for the birds, he only ate a single crumb himself, and gave all the rest to the other birds.

In the course of the winter, the bird had collected so many bread crumbs, and given them to the other birds, that they equalled the weight of the loaf on which Ingé had trod to keep her shoes clean; and when the last bread crumb had been found and given, the grey wings of the bird became white, and spread far out.

"Yonder is a sea swallow, flying away across the water," said the children when they saw the white bird. Now it dived into the sea, and now it rose again into the clear sunlight. It gleamed white; but no one could tell whither it went, though some asserted that it flew straight into the sun.

THE MONEY-PIG.

IN the nursery a number of toys lay strewn about: high up, on the wardrobe, stood the money-box, made of clay and purchased of the potter, and it was in the shape of a little pig; of course the pig had a slit in its back, and this slit had been so enlarged with a knife that whole dollar pieces could slip through; and, indeed, two such had slipped into the box, besides a number of pence. The money-pig was stuffed so full that it could no longer rattle, and that is the highest point of perfection a money-pig can attain. There it stood upon the cupboard, high and lofty, looking down upon everything else in the room. It knew very well that what it had in its stomach would have bought all the toys, and that 's what we call having self-respect.

The others thought of that too, even if they did not exactly express it, for there were many other things to speak of. One of the drawers was half pulled out, and there lay a great handsome Doll, though she was somewhat old, and her neck had been mended. She looked out and said,

"Now we 'll play at men and women, for that is always something!"

And now there was a general uproar, and even the framed prints on the walls turned round and showed that there was a wrong side to them; but they did not do it to protest against the proposal.

It was late at night; the moon shone through the window-frames and afforded the cheapest light. The game was now to begin, and all, even the children's Go-Cart, which certainly belonged to the coarser play-things, were invited to take part in the sport.

"Each one has his own peculiar value," said the Go-Cart: "we cannot all be noblemen. There must be some who do the work, as the saying is."

The money-pig was the only one who received a written invitation, for he was of high standing, and they were afraid he would not accept a verbal message. Indeed, he did not answer to say whether he would come, nor did he come : if he was to take a part, he must enjoy the sport from his own home ; they were to arrange accordingly, and so they did.

The little toy theatre was now put up in such a way that the money-pig could look directly in. They wanted to begin with a comedy, and afterwards there was to be a tea party and a discussion for mental improvement, and with this latter part they began immediately. The rocking-horse spoke of training and race, the Go-Cart of railways and steam power, for all this belonged to their profession, and it was quite

THE PARTY OF TOYS.

right they should talk of it. The clock talked politics—ticks—ticks—and knew what was the time of day, though it was whispered he did not go correctly ; the bamboo cane stood there, stiff and proud, for he was conceited about his brass ferule and his silver top, for being thus bound above and below ; and on the sofa lay two worked cushions, pretty and stupid. And now the play began.

All sat and looked on, and it was requested that the audience should applaud and crack and stamp according as they were gratified. But the riding-whip said he never cracked for old people, only for young ones who were not yet married.

"I crack for everything," said the Cracker.

And these were the thoughts they had while the play went on. The piece was worthless, but it was well played ; all the characters turned their painted side to the audience, for they were so made that they should only be looked at from that side, and not from the other; and all played wonderfully well, coming out quite beyond the lamps, because the wires were a little too long, but that only made them come out the more. The darned Doll was quite exhausted with excitement—so thoroughly exhausted that she burst at the darned place in her neck, and the money-pig was so enchanted in his way that he formed the resolution to do something for one of the players, and to remember him in his will as the one who should be buried with him in the family vault, when matters were so far advanced.

It was true enjoyment, such true enjoyment that they quite gave up the thoughts of tea, and only carried out the idea of mental recreation. That's what they called playing at men and women; and there was nothing wrong in it, for they were only playing; and each one thought of himself and of what the money-pig might think; and the money-pig thought farthest of all, for he thought of making his will and of his burial. And when might this come to pass? Certainly far sooner than was expected. Crack! it fell down from the cupboard—fell on the ground, and was broken to pieces; and the pennies hopped and danced in comical style: the little ones turned round like tops, and the bigger ones rolled away, particularly the one great silver dollar who wanted to go out into the world. And he came out into the world, and they all succeeded in doing so. And the pieces of the money-pig were put into the bust-bin; but the next day a new money-pig was standing on the cupboard: it had not yet a farthing in its stomach, and therefore could not rattle, and in this it was like the other. And that was a beginning —and with that we will make an end.

THE DARNING-NEEDLE.

THERE was once a Darning-Needle, who thought herself so fine, she imagined she was an embroidering-needle.

"Take care, and mind you hold me tight!" she said to the Fingers which took her out. "Don't let me fall! If I fall on the ground I shall certainly never be found again, for I am so fine!"

"That's as it may be," said the Fingers; and they grasped her round the body.

"See, I'm coming with a train!" said the Darning-Needle, and she drew a long thread after her, but there was no knot in the thread.

The Fingers pointed the needle just at the cook's slipper, in which the upper leather had burst, and was to be sewn together.

"That's vulgar work," said the Darning-Needle. "I shall never get through. I'm breaking! I'm breaking!" And she really broke. "Did I not say so?" said the Darning-Needle; "I'm too fine!"

"Now it's quite useless," said the Fingers; but they were obliged to hold her fast, all the same; for the cook dropped some sealing-wax upon the needle, and pinned her handkerchief together with it in front.

"So, now I'm a breast-pin!" said the Darning-Needle. "I knew very well that I should come to honour: when one is something, one comes to something!"

And she laughed quietly to herself—and one can never see when a darning-needle laughs. There she sat, as proud as if she was in a state coach, and looked all about her.

"May I be permitted to ask if you are of gold?" she inquired of the pin, her neighbour. "You have a very pretty appearance, and a peculiar head, but it is only little. You must take pains to grow, for it's not every one that has sealing-wax dropped upon him."

And the Darning-Needle drew herself up so proudly that she fell out of the handkerchief right into the sink, which the cook was rinsing out.

"Now we're going on a journey," said the Darning-Needle.—"If I only don't get lost!"

But she really was lost.

"I'm too fine for this world," she observed, as she lay in the gutter. "But I know who I am, and there's always something in that!"

So the Darning-Needle kept her proud behaviour, and did not lose her good humour. And things of many kinds swam over her, chips and straws and pieces of old newspapers.

"Only look how they sail!" said the Darning-Needle. "They don't know what is under them! I'm here, I remain firmly here. See, there goes a chip thinking of nothing in the world but of himself—of a chip! There's a straw going by now. How he turns! how he twirls about! Don't think only of yourself, you might easily run up against a stone. There swims a bit of newspaper. What's written upon it has long been forgotten, and yet it gives itself airs. I sit quietly and patiently here. I know who I am, and I shall remain what I am."

One day something lay close beside her that glittered splendidly; then the Darning-Needle believed that it was a diamond; but it was a Bit of broken Bottle; and because it shone, the Darning-Needle spoke to it, introducing herself as a breast-pin.

"I suppose you are a diamond?" she observed.

"Why, yes, something of that kind."

And then each believed the other to be a very valuable thing; and they began speaking about the world, and how very conceited it was.

"I have been in a lady's box," said the Darning-Needle, "and this lady was a cook. She had five fingers on each hand, and I never saw anything so conceited as those five fingers. And yet they were only there that they might take me out of the box and put me back into it."

"Were they of good birth?" asked the Bit of Bottle.

"No, indeed," replied the Darning-Needle, "but very haughty. There were five brothers, all of the finger family. They kept very proudly together, though they were of different lengths: the outermost, the thumbling, was short and fat; he walked out in front of the ranks, and only had one joint in his back, and could only make a single bow,

THE COOK WITH THE DARNING NEEDLE.

but he said that if he were hacked off from a man, that man was useless for service in war. Dainty-mouth, the second finger, thrust himself into sweet and sour, pointed to sun and moon, and gave the impression when they wrote. Longman, the third, looked at all the others over his shoulder. Goldborder, the fourth, went about with a golden belt round his waist; and little Playman did nothing at all, and was proud of it. There was nothing but bragging among them, and therefore I went away."

"And now we sit here and glitter!" said the Bit of Bottle.

At that moment more water came into the gutter, so that it overflowed, and the Bit of Bottle was carried away.

"So, he is disposed of," observed the Darning-Needle. "I remain here, I am too fine. But that's my pride, and my pride is honourable." And proudly she sat there, and had many great thoughts. "I could almost believe I had been born of a sunbeam, I'm so fine! It really appears to me as if the sunbeams were always seeking for me under the water. Ah! I'm so fine that my mother cannot find me. If I had my old eye, which broke off, I think I should cry; but, no, I should not do that : it's not genteel to cry."

One day a couple of street boys lay grubbing in the gutter, where they sometimes found old nails, farthings, and similar treasures. It was dirty work, but they took great delight in it.

" Oh ! " cried one, who had pricked himself with the Darning-Needle, " there's a fellow for you ! "

" I'm not a fellow, I'm a young lady ! " said the Darning-Needle.

But nobody listened to her. The sealing-wax had come off, and she had turned black ; but black makes one look slender, and she thought herself finer even than before.

" Here comes an egg-shell sailing along ! " said the boys ; and they stuck the Darning-Needle fast in the egg-shell.

" White walls, and black myself ! that looks well," remarked the Darning-Needle. " Now one can see me. I only hope I shall not be sea-sick ! " But she was not sea-sick at all. " It is good against sea-sick-ness, if one has a steel stomach, and does not forget that one is a little more than an ordinary person ! Now my sea-sickness is over. The finer one is, the more one can bear."

" Crack ! " went the egg-shell, for a hand-barrow went over her.

" Good Heavens, how it crushes one ! " said the Darning-Needle. " I'm getting sea-sick now,—I'm quite sick."

But she was not really sick, though the hand-barrow went over her ; she lay there at full length, and there she may lie.

THE FIR TREE.

Out in the forest stood a pretty little Fir Tree. It had a good place ; it could have sunlight, air there was in plenty, and all around grew many larger comrades — pines as well as firs. But the little Fir Tree wished ardently to become greater. It did not care for the warm sun and the fresh air ; it took no notice of the peasant children, who went about talking together, when they had come out to look for strawberries and raspberries. Often they came with a whole pot-full, or had strung berries on a straw ; then they would sit down by the little Fir Tree and say, " How pretty and small that one is ! " and the Tree did not like to hear that at all.

Next year he had grown a great joint, and the following year he was longer still, for in fir trees one can always tell by the number of rings they have how many years they have been growing.

" Oh, if I were only as great a tree as the others ! " sighed the little Fir, " then I would spread my branches far around, and look out from my crown into the wide world. The birds would then build nests in my boughs, and when the wind blew I could nod just as grandly as the others yonder."

It took no pleasure in the sunshine, in the birds, and in the red clouds that went sailing over him morning and evening.

When it was winter, and the snow lay all around, white and sparkling, a hare would often come jumping along, and spring right over the little Fir Tree. Oh! this made him so angry. But two winters went by, and when the third came the little Tree had grown so tall that the hare was obliged to run round it.

"Oh! to grow, to grow, and become old; that's the only fine thing in the world," thought the Tree.

In the autumn woodcutters always came and felled a few of the largest trees; that was done this year too, and the little Fir Tree, that was now quite well grown, shuddered with fear, for the great stately trees fell to the ground with a crash, and their branches were cut off, so that the trees looked quite naked, long, and slender—they could hardly be recognized. But then they were laid upon waggons, and horses dragged them away out of the wood. Where were they going? What destiny awaited them?

In the spring, when the swallows and the Stork came, the Tree asked them, "Do you know where they were taken? Did you not meet them?"

The swallows knew nothing about it, but the Stork looked thoughtful, nodded his head, and said,

"Yes, I think so. I met many new ships when I flew out of Egypt; on the ships were stately masts; I fancy that these were the trees. They smelt like fir. I can assure you they're stately—very stately."

"Oh that I were only big enough to go over the sea! What kind of thing is this sea, and how does it look?"

"It would take too long to explain all that," said the Stork, and he went away.

"Rejoice in thy youth," said the Sunbeams; "rejoice in thy fresh growth, and in the young life that is within thee."

And the wind kissed the Tree, and the dew wept tears upon it; but the Fir Tree did not understand that.

When Christmas-time approached, quite young trees were felled, sometimes trees which were neither so old nor so large as this Fir Tree, that never rested but always wanted to go away. These young trees, which were almost the most beautiful, kept all their branches; they were put upon waggons, and horses dragged them away out of the wood.

"Where are they all going?" asked the Fir Tree. "They are not greater than I—indeed, one of them was much smaller. Why do they keep all their branches? Whither are they taken?"

"We know that! We know that!" chirped the Sparrows. "Yonder in the town we looked in at the windows. We know where they go. Oh! they are dressed up in the greatest pomp and splendour that can be imagined. We have looked in at the windows, and have perceived that they are planted in the middle of the warm room, and adorned with the most beautiful things—gilt apples, honey-cakes, playthings, and many hundreds of candles."

"And then?" asked the Fir Tree, and trembled through all its branches. "And then? What happens then?"

"Why, we have not seen anything more. But it was incomparable."

"Perhaps I may be destined to tread this glorious path one day!" cried the Fir Tree rejoicingly. "That is even better than travelling across the sea. How painfully I long for it! If it were only Christmas now! Now I am great and grown up, like the rest who were led away last year. Oh, if I were only on the carriage! If I were only in the warm room, among all the pomp and splendour! And then? Yes, then something even better will come, something far more charming, or else why should they adorn me so? There must be something grander, something greater still to come; but what? Oh! I'm suffering, I'm longing! I don't know myself what is the matter with me!"

"Rejoice in us," said Air and Sunshine. "Rejoice in thy fresh youth here in the woodland."

But the Fir Tree did not rejoice at all, but it grew and grew; winter and summer it stood there, green, dark green. The people who saw it said, "That's a handsome tree!" and at Christmas-time it was felled before any one of the others. The axe cut deep into its marrow, and the tree fell to the ground with a sigh: it felt a pain, a sensation of faintness, and could not think at all of happiness, for it was sad at parting from its home, from the place where it had grown up: it knew that it should never again see the dear old companions, the little bushes and flowers all around—perhaps not even the birds. The parting was not at all agreeable.

The Tree only came to itself when it was unloaded in a yard, with other trees, and heard a man say,

"This one is famous; we only want this one!"

Now two servants came in gay liveries, and carried the Fir Tree into a large beautiful saloon. All around the walls hung pictures, and by the great stove stood large Chinese vases with lions on the covers; there were rocking-chairs, silken sofas, great tables covered with picture-books, and toys worth a hundred times a hundred dollars, at least the children said so. And the Fir Tree was put into a great tub filled with sand; but no one could see that it was a tub, for it was hung round with green cloth, and stood on a large many-coloured carpet. Oh, how the Tree trembled! What was to happen now? The servants, and the young ladies also, decked it out. On one branch they hung little nets, cut out of coloured paper; every net was filled with sweetmeats; golden apples and walnuts hung down as if they grew there, and more than a hundred little candles, red, white, and blue, were fastened to the different boughs Dolls that looked exactly like real people—the Tree had never seen such before—swung among the foliage, and high on the summit of the Tree was fixed a tinsel star. It was splendid, particularly splendid.

"This evening," said all, "this evening it will shine."

"Oh," thought the Tree, "that it were evening already! Oh that the lights may be soon lit up! When may that be done? I wonder if trees will come out of the forest to look at me? Will the sparrows fly against the panes? Shall I grow fast here, and stand adorned in summer and winter?"

Yes, he did not guess badly. But he had a complete backache from mere longing, and the backache is just as bad for a Tree as the headache for a person.

At last the candles were lighted. What a brilliance, what splendour! The Tree trembled so in all its branches that one of the candles set fire to a green twig, and it was scorched.

"Heaven preserve us!" cried the young ladies; and they hastily put the fire out.

Now the Tree might not even tremble. Oh, that was terrible! It was so afraid of setting fire to some of its ornaments, and it was quite bewildered with all the brilliance. And now the folding doors were thrown open, and a number of children rushed in as if they would have overturned the whole Tree; the older people followed more deliberately. The little ones stood quite silent, but only for a minute; then they shouted till the room rang: they danced gleefully round the Tree, and one present after another was plucked from it.

"What are they about?" thought the Tree. "What's going to be done?"

And the candles burned down to the twigs, and as they burned down they were extinguished, and then the children received permission to plunder the Tree. Oh! they rushed in upon it, so that every branch cracked again: if it had not been fastened by the top and by the golden star to the ceiling, it would have fallen down.

The children danced about with their pretty toys. No one looked at the Tree except one old man, who came up and peeped among the branches, but only to see if a fig or an apple had not been forgotten.

"A story! a story!" shouted the children: and they drew a little fat man towards the Tree; and he sat down just beneath it,—"for then we shall be in the green wood," said he, "and the tree may have the advantage of listening to my tale. But I can only tell one. Will you hear the story of Ivede-Avede, or of Klumpey-Dumpey, who fell down stairs, and still was raised up to honour and married the Princess?"

"Ivede-Avede!" cried some, "Klumpey-Dumpey!" cried others, and there was a great crying and shouting. Only the Fir Tree was quite silent, and thought, "Shall I not be in it? shall I have nothing to do in it?" But he had been in the evening's amusement, and had done what was required of him.

And the fat man told about Klumpey-Dumpey, who fell down stairs, and yet was raised to honour and married the Princess. And the children clapped their hands, and cried, "Tell another! tell another!" for they wanted to hear about Ivede-Avede; but they only got the story of Klumpey-Dumpey. The Fir Tree stood quite silent and thoughtful; never had the birds in the wood told such a story as that. Klumpey-Dumpey fell down stairs, and yet came to honour and married the Princess!

"Yes, so it happens in the world!" thought the Fir Tree, and believed it must be true, because that was such a nice man who told it. "Well, who can know? Perhaps I shall fall down stairs too, and marry a Princess!" And it looked forward with pleasure to being adorned again, the next evening, with candles and toys, gold and fruit. "To-morrow I shall not tremble," it thought. "I will rejoice in all my splendour. To-morrow I shall hear the story of Klumpey-Dumpey again, and, perhaps, that of Ivede-Avede too."

And the Tree stood all night quiet and thoughtful.

In the morning the servants and the chambermaid came in.

"Now my splendour will begin afresh," thought the Tree. But they dragged him out of the room, and up stairs to the garret, and here they put him in a dark corner where no daylight shone.

"What 's the meaning of this?" thought the Tree. "What am I to do here? What is to happen?"

And he leaned against the wall, and thought, and thought. And he had time enough, for days and nights went by, and nobody came up; and when at length some one came, it was only to put some great boxes in a corner. Now the Tree stood quite hidden away, and the supposition was that it was quite forgotten.

"Now it 's winter outside," thought the Tree. "The earth is hard and covered with snow, and people cannot plant me; therefore I suppose I 'm to be sheltered here until spring comes. How considerate that is! How good people are! If it were only not so dark here, and so terribly solitary!—not even a little hare! That was pretty out there in the wood, when the snow lay thick and the hare sprang past; yes, even when he jumped over me; but then I did not like it. It is terribly lonely up here!"

"Piep! piep!" said a little Mouse, and crept forward, and then came another little one. They smelt at the Fir Tree, and then slipped among the branches.

"It 's horribly cold," said the two little Mice, "or else it would be comfortable here. Don't you think so, you old Fir Tree?"

"I 'm not old at all," said the Fir Free. "There are many much older than I."

"Where do you come from?" asked the Mice. "And what do you know?" They were dreadfully inquisitive. "Tell us about the most beautiful spot on earth. Have you been there? Have you been in the store-room, where cheeses lie on the shelves, and hams hang from the ceiling, where one dances on tallow candles, and goes in thin and comes out fat?"

"I don't know that!" replied the Tree; "but I know the wood, where the sun shines, and where the birds sing."

And then it told all about its youth.

And the little Mice had never heard anything of the kind; and they listened and said,

"What a number of things you have seen! How happy you must have been!"

"I?" said the Fir Tree; and it thought about what it had told.

THE CHILDREN AND THE FIR TREE.

"Yes, those were really quite happy times." But then he told of the Christmas-eve, when he had been hung with sweetmeats and candles.

"Oh!" said the little Mice, "how happy you have been, you old Fir Tree!"

"I'm not old at all," said the Tree. "I only came out of the wood this winter. I'm only rather backward in my growth."

"What splendid stories you can tell!" said the little Mice.

And next night they came with four other little Mice, to hear what the Tree had to relate; and the more it said, the more clearly did it remember everything, and thought, "Those were quite merry days! But they may come again. Klumpey-Dumpey fell down stairs, and yet he married the Princess. Perhaps I may marry a Princess too!" And then the Fir Tree thought of a pretty little birch tree that grew out in the forest: for the Fir Tree, that birch was a real Princess.

"Who's Klumpey-Dumpey?" asked the little Mice.

And then the Fir Tree told the whole story. It could remember every single word; and the little Mice were ready to leap to the very top of the tree with pleasure. Next night a great many more Mice came, and on Sunday two Rats even appeared; but these thought the story was not pretty, and the little Mice were sorry for that, for now they also did not like it so much as before.

"Do you only know one story?" asked the Rats.

"Only that one," replied the Tree. "I heard that on the happiest evening of my life; I did not think then how happy I was."

"That's a very miserable story. Don't you know any about bacon and tallow candles—a store-room story?"

"No," said the Tree.

"Then we'd rather not hear you," said the Rats.

And they went back to their own people. The little Mice at last stayed away also; and then the Tree sighed and said,

"It was very nice when they sat round me, the merry little Mice, and listened when I spoke to them. Now that's past too. But I shall remember to be pleased when they take me out."

But when did that happen? Why, it was one morning that people came and rummaged in the garret: the boxes were put away, and the Tree brought out; they certainly threw him rather roughly on the floor, but a servant dragged him away at once to the stairs, where the daylight shone.

"Now life is beginning again!" thought the Tree.

It felt the fresh air and the first sunbeams, and now it was out in the courtyard. Everything passed so quickly that the Tree quite forgot to look at itself, there was so much to look at all round. The courtyard was close to a garden, and here everything was blooming; the roses hung fresh and fragrant over the little paling, the linden trees were in blossom, and the swallows cried, "Quinze-wit! quinze-wit! my husband's come!" But it was not the Fir Tree that they meant.

"Now I shall live!" said the Tree, rejoicingly, and spread its branches far out; but, alas! they were all withered and yellow; and it lay in the corner among nettles and weeds. The tinsel star was still upon it, and shone in the bright sunshine.

In the courtyard a couple of the merry children were playing, who had danced round the tree at Christmas-time, and had rejoiced over it. One of the youngest ran up and tore off the golden star.

"Look what is sticking to the ugly old fir tree," said the child, and he trod upon the branches till they cracked again under his boots.

And the Tree looked at all the blooming flowers and the splendour of the garden, and then looked at itself, and wished it had remained in the dark corner of the garret; it thought of its fresh youth in the wood, of the merry Christmas-eve, and of the little Mice which had listened so pleasantly to the story of Klumpey-Dumpey.

"Past! past!" said the old Tree. "Had I but rejoiced when I could have done so! Past! past!"

And the servant came and chopped the Tree into little pieces; a whole bundle lay there. it blazed brightly under the great brewing copper, and it sighed deeply, and each sigh was like a little shot: and the children who were at play there ran up and seated themselves at the fire, looked into it, and cried, " Puff! puff!" But at each explosion, which was a deep sigh, the tree thought of a summer day in the woods, or of a winter night there, when the stars beamed; he thought of Christmas-eve and of Klumpey-Dumpey, the only story he had ever heard or knew how to tell; and then the Tree was burned.

The boys played in the garden, and the youngest had on his breast a golden star, which the Tree had worn on its happiest evening. Now that was past, and the Tree's life was past, and the story is past too: past! past!—and that's the way with all stories.

THE SWINEHERD.

THERE was once a poor Prince, who had a kingdom which was quite small, but still it was large enough that he could marry upon it, and that is what he wanted to do.

Now, it was certainly somewhat bold of him to say to the Emperor's daughter, "Will you have me?" But he did venture it, for his name was famous far and wide: there were hundreds of Princesses who would have been glad to say yes; but did *she* say so? Well, we shall see.

On the grave of the Prince's father there grew a rose bush, a very beautiful rose bush. It bloomed only every fifth year, and even then it bore only a single rose, but what a rose that was! It was so sweet that whoever smelt at it forgot all sorrow and trouble. And then he had a nightingale, which could sing as if all possible melodies were collected in its little throat. This rose and this nightingale the Princess was to have, and therefore they were put into great silver vessels and sent to her.

The Emperor caused the presents to be carried before him into the great hall where the Princess was playing at "visiting" with her maids of honour, and when she saw the great silver vessels with the presents in them, she clapped her hands with joy.

"If it were only a little pussy-cat!" said she.

But then came out the rose bush with the splendid rose.

"Oh, how pretty it is made!" said all the court ladies.

"It is more than pretty," said the Emperor, "it is charming."

But the Princess felt it, and then she almost began to cry.

"Fie, papa!" she said, "it is not artificial, it's a *natural* rose!"

"Fie," said all the court ladies, "it's a natural one!"

"Let us first see what is in the other vessel before we get angry," said the Emperor. And then the nightingale came out; it sang so beautifully that they did not at once know what to say against it.

"*Superbe! charmant!*" said the maids of honour, for they all spoke French as badly as possible.

"How that bird reminds me of the late Emperor's musical snuff-box," said an old cavalier. "Yes, it is the same tone, the same expression."

"Yes," said the Emperor; and then he wept like a little child at the remembrance of his dead father.

"I really hope it is not a natural bird," said the Princess.

"Yes, it is a natural bird," said they who had brought it.

"Then let the bird fly away," said the Princess; and she would by no means allow the Prince to come.

But the Prince was not to be frightened. He stained his face brown and black, drew his hat down over his brows, and knocked at the door.

"Good day, Emperor," he said: "could I not be employed here in the castle?"

"Yes," replied the Emperor, "but there are so many who ask for an appointment, that I do not know if it can be managed; but I'll bear you in mind. But it just occurs to me that I want some one who can keep the pigs, for we have many pigs here, very many."

So the Prince was appointed the Emperor's swineherd. He received a miserable small room down by the pig-sty, and here he was obliged to stay; but all day long he sat and worked, and when it was evening he had finished a neat little pot, with bells all round it, and when the pot boiled these bells rang out prettily and played the old melody—

> "Oh, my darling Augustine,
> All is lost, all is lost."

But the cleverest thing about the whole arrangement was, that by holding one's finger in the smoke, one could at once smell what provisions were being cooked at every hearth in the town. That was quite a different thing from the rose.

Now the Princess came with all her maids of honour, and when she heard the melody she stood still and looked quite pleased; for she, too, could play "Oh, my darling Augustine," on the piano. It was the only thing she could play, but then she played it with one finger.

"Why, that is what I play!" she cried. "He must be an educated swineherd! Harkye: go down and ask the price of the instrument."

So one of the maids of honour had to go down; but first she put on a pair of pattens.

"What do you want for the pot?" inquired the lady.

"I want ten kisses from the Princess," replied the swineherd.

"Heaven preserve us!" exclaimed the maid of honour.

"Well, I won't sell it for less," said the swineherd.

"And what did he say?" asked the Princess.

"I don't like to repeat it," replied the lady.

"Well, you can whisper it in my ear." And the lady whispered it to her.—"He is very rude," declared the Princess; and she went away. But when she had gone a little way, the bells sounded so prettily—

> "Oh, my darling Augustine,
> All is lost, all is lost."

"Harkye," said the Princess: "ask him if he will take ten kisses from my maids of honour."

THE SWINEHERD RECEIVING PAYMENT.

"I'm much obliged," replied the swineherd: "ten kisses from the Princess, or I shall keep my pot."

"How tiresome that is!" cried the Princess. "But at least you must stand before me, so that nobody sees it."

And the maids of honour stood before her, and spread out their dresses, and then the swineherd received ten kisses, and she received the pot.

Then there was rejoicing! All the evening and all the day long the pot was kept boiling; there was not a kitchen hearth in the whole town of which they did not know what it had cooked, at the shoemaker's as well as the chamberlain's. The ladies danced with pleasure, and clapped their hands.

"We know who will have sweet soup and pancakes for dinner, and who has hasty pudding and cutlets; how interesting that is!"

"Very interesting!" said the head lady-superintendent.

"Yes, but keep counsel, for I'm the Emperor's daughter."

"Yes, certainly," said all.

The swineherd, that is to say, the Prince—but of course they did not know but that he was a regular swineherd—let no day pass by without doing something, and so he made a rattle; when any person swung this rattle, he could play all the waltzes, hops, and polkas that have been known since the creation of the world.

"But that is *superbe!*" cried the Princess, as she went past. "l have never heard a finer composition. Harkye: go down and ask what the instrument costs; but I give no more kisses."

"He demands a hundred kisses from the Princess," said the maid of honour who had gone down to make the inquiry.

"I think he must be mad!" exclaimed the Princess; and she went away; but when she had gone a little distance she stood still. "One must encourage art," she observed. "I am the Emperor's daughter! Tell him he shall receive ten kisses, like last time, and he may take the rest from my maids of honour."

"Ah, but we don't like to do it!" said the maids of honour.

"That's all nonsense!" retorted the Princess, "and if I can allow myself to be kissed, you can too; remember, I give you board and wages."

And so the maids of honour had to go down to him again.

"A hundred kisses from the Princess," said he, "or each shall keep his own."

"Stand before me," said she then; and all the maids of honour stood before her while he kissed the Princess.

"What is that crowd down by the pig-sty?" asked the Emperor, who had stepped out to the balcony. He rubbed his eyes, and put on his spectacles. "Why, those are the maids of honour, at their tricks, yonder; I shall have to go down to them."

And he pulled up his slippers behind, for they were shoes that he had trodden down at heel. Gracious mercy, how he hurried! So soon as he came down in the courtyard, he went quite softly, and the maids of honour were too busy counting the kisses, and seeing fair play, to notice the Emperor. Then he stood on tiptoe.

"What's that?" said he, when he saw that there was kissing going on; and he hit them on the head with his slipper, just as the swineherd was taking the eighty-sixth kiss.

"Be off!" said the Emperor, for he was angry.

And the Princess and the swineherd were both expelled from his dominions. So there she stood and cried, the rain streamed down, and the swineherd scolded.

"Oh, miserable wretch that I am!" said the Princess; "if I had only taken the handsome Prince! Oh, how unhappy I am!"

Then the swineherd went behind a tree, washed the stains from his face, threw away the shabby clothes, and stepped forth in his princely attire, so handsome that the Princess was fain to bow before him.

"I have come to this, that I despise you," said he. "You would not have an honest Prince; you did not value the rose and the nightingale, but for a plaything you kissed the swineherd, and now you have your reward."

And then he went into his kingdom and shut the door in her face. So now she might stand outside and sing—

"Oh, my darling Augustine,
All is lost, all is lost."

SOMETHING.

" I WANT to be something!" said the eldest of five brothers. " I want to do something in the world. I don't care how humble my position may be in society, if I only effect some good, for that will really be something. I 'll make bricks, for they are quite indispensable things, and then I shall truly have done something."

" But that *something* will not be enough!" quoth the second brother. " What you intend doing is just as much as nothing at all. It is journeyman's work, and can be done by a machine. No, I would rather be a bricklayer at once, for that *is* something real; and that 's what I will be. That brings rank : as a bricklayer one belongs to a guild, and is a citizen, and has one's own flag and one's own house of call. Yes, and if all goes well, I will keep journeymen. I shall become a master bricklayer, and my wife will be a master's wife—that is what *I* call something."

" That 's nothing at all!" said the third. " That is beyond the pale of the guild, and there are many of those in a town that stand far above the mere master artizan. You may be an honest man ; but as a ' master ' you will after all only belong to those who are ranked among common men. I know something better than that. I will be an architect, and will thus enter into the territory of art and speculation. I shall be reckoned among those who stand high in point of intellect. I shall certainly have to serve up from the pickaxe, so to speak ; so I must begin as a carpenter's apprentice, and must go about as an assistant, in a cap, though I am accustomed to wear a silk hat. I shall have to fetch beer and spirits for the common journeymen, and they will call me ' thou,' and that is insulting ! But I shall imagine to myself that the whole thing is only acting, and a kind of masquerade. To-morrow—that is to say, when I have served my time—I shall go my own way, and the others will be nothing to me. I shall go to the academy, and get instructions in drawing, and shall be called an architect. *That 's something !* I may get to be called ' sir,' and even ' worshipful sir,' or even get a handle at the front or at the back of my name, and shall go on building and building, just as those before me have built. That will always be a thing to remember, and that 's what *I* call something !"

" But I don't care at all for *that* something," said the fourth. " *I* won't sail in the wake of others, and be a copyist. I will be a genius, and will stand up greater than all the rest of you together. I shall be the creator of a new style, and will give the plan of a building suitable to the climate and the material of the country, for the nationality of the people, for the development of the age—and an additional storey for my own genius."

" But supposing the climate and the material are bad," said the fifth, " that would be a disastrous circumstance, for these two exert a great influence ! Nationality, moreover, may expand itself until it becomes affectation, and the development of the century may run wild with your work, as youth often runs wild. I quite realize the fact that none of you will be anything real, however much you may believe in yourselves. But, do what you like, I will not resemble you : I shall keep on the outside of things, and criticise whatever you produce. To every work there is attached something that is not right—something that has gone wrong ; and I will ferret that out and find fault with it ; and *that* will be doing *something !*"

And he kept his word ; and everybody said concerning this fifth brother, " There is certainly something in him ; he has a good head, but he does nothing." And by that very means they thought *something* of him !

Now, you see, this is only a little story ; but it will never end so long as the world lasts.

But what became of the five brothers ? Why, this is *nothing*, and not *something*.

Listen, it is a capital story.

The eldest brother, he who manufactured bricks, soon became aware of the fact that every brick, however small it might be, produced for him a little coin, though this coin was only copper ; and many copper pennies laid one upon the other can be changed into a shining dollar ; and wherever one knocks with such a dollar in one's hand, whether at the baker's, or the butcher's, or the tailor's—wherever it may be, the door flies open, and the visitor is welcomed, and gets what he wants. You see, that is what comes of bricks. Some of those belonging to the eldest brother certainly crumbled away, or broke in two, but there was a use even for these.

On the high rampart, the wall that kept out the sea, Margaret, the poor woman, wished to build herself a little house. All the faulty bricks were given to her, and a few perfect ones into the bargain, for the eldest brother was a good-natured man, though he certainly did not achieve anything beyond the manufacture of bricks. The poor woman put together the house for herself. It was little and narrow, and the single window was quite crooked. The door was too low, and the thatched roof might have shown better workmanship. But after all it was a shelter ; and from the little house you could look far across the sea, whose waves broke vainly against the protecting rampart on which it was built. The salt billows spurted their spray over the whole house, which was still standing when he who had given the bricks for its erection had long been dead and buried.

The second brother knew better how to build a wall, for he had served an apprenticeship to it. When he had served his time and passed his examination, he packed his knapsack and sang the journey-man's song:

"While I am young I'll wander, from place to place I'll roam,
And everywhere build houses, until I come back home;
And youth will give me courage, and my true love won't forget:
Hurrah then for a workman's life! I'll be a master yet!"

And he carried his idea into effect. When he had come home and become a master, he built one house after another in the town. He built a whole street; and when the street was finished and became an ornament to the place, the houses built a house for him in return, that was to be his own. But how can houses build a house? If you ask them they will not answer you, but people will understand what is meant by the expression, and say, "Certainly, it was the street that built his house for him." It was little, and the floor was covered with clay; but when he danced with his bride upon this clay floor, it seemed to become polished oak; and from every stone in the wall sprang forth a flower, and the room was gay, as if with the costliest paper-hanger's work. It was a pretty house, and in it lived a happy pair. The flag of the guild fluttered before the house, and the journeymen and apprentices shouted hurrah! Yes, he certainly was *something!* And at last he died; and *that* was something too.

Now came the architect, the third brother, who had been at first a carpenter's apprentice, had worn a cap, and served as an errand boy, but had afterwards gone to the academy, and risen to become an architect, and to be called "honoured sir." Yes, if the houses of the street had built a house for the brother who had become a bricklayer, the street now received its name from the architect, and the handsomest house in it became his property. *That* was something, and *he* was something; and he had a long title before and after his name. His children were called *genteel* children, and when he died his widow was "a widow of rank," and *that* is something!—and his name always remained at the corner of the street, and lived on in the mouth of every one as the street's name — and *that* was something!

Now came the genius of the family, the fourth brother, who wanted to invent something new and original, and an additional storey on the top of it for himself. But the top storey tumbled down, and he came tumbling down with it, and broke his neck. Nevertheless he had a splendid funeral, with guild flags and music, poems in the papers, and flowers strewn on the paving-stones in the street; and three funeral orations were held over him, each one longer than the last, which would have rejoiced him greatly, for he always liked it when people talked about him; a monument also was erected over his grave. It was only one storey high, but still it was *something*.

Now he was dead, like the three other brothers; but the last, the one who was a critic, outlived them all: and that was quite right, for by this means he got the last word, and it was of great importance to him to have the last word. The people always said he had a good head of his own. At last his hour came, and he died, and came to the gates of

Paradise. There souls always enter two and two, and he came up with another soul that wanted to get into Paradise too; and who should this be but old Dame Margaret from the house upon the sea wall.

"I suppose this is done for the sake of contrast, that I and this wretched soul should arrive here at exactly the same time," said the critic. "Pray, who are you, my good woman?" he asked. "Do you want to get in here too?"

And the old woman courtesied as well as she could: she thought it must be St. Peter himself talking to her.

"I'm a poor old woman of a very humble family," she replied. "I'm old Margaret that lived in the house on the sea wall."

"Well, and what have you done? What have you accomplished down there?"

"I have really accomplished nothing at all in the world: nothing that I can plead to have the doors here opened to me. It would be a real mercy to allow me to slip in through the gate."

"In what manner did you leave the world?" asked he, just for the sake of saying something; for it was wearisome work standing there and saying nothing.

"Why, I really don't know how I left it. I was sick and miserable during my last years, and could not well bear creeping out of bed, and going out suddenly into the frost and cold. It was a hard winter, but I have got out of it all now. For a few days the weather was quite calm, but very cold, as your honour must very well know. The sea was covered with ice as far as one could look. All the people from the town walked out upon the ice, and I think they said there was a dance there, and skating. There was beautiful music and a great feast there too; the sound came into my poor little room, where I lay ill. And it was towards the evening; the moon had risen beautifully, but was not yet in its full splendour; I looked from my bed out over the wide sea, and far off, just where the sea and sky join, a strange white cloud came up. I lay looking at the cloud, and I saw a little black spot in the middle of it, that grew larger and larger; and now I knew what it meant, for I am old and experienced, though this token is not often seen. I knew it, and a shuddering came upon me. Twice in my life I have seen the same thing; and I knew there would be an awful tempest, and a spring flood, which would overwhelm the poor people who were now drinking and dancing and rejoicing — young and old, the whole city had issued forth: who was to warn them, if no one saw what was coming yonder, or knew, as I did, what it meant? I was dreadfully alarmed, and felt more lively than I had done for a long time. I crept out of bed, and got to the window, but could not crawl farther, I was so exhausted. But I managed to open the window. I saw the people outside running and jumping about on the ice; I could see the beautiful flags that waved in the wind. I heard the boys shouting 'hurrah!' and the servant men and maids singing. There were all kinds of merriment going on. But the white cloud with the black spot! I cried out as loud as I could, but no one heard me; I was too far from the people. Soon the storm would

burst, and the ice would break, and all who were upon it would be lost
without remedy. They could not hear me, and I could not come out to
them. Oh, if I could only bring them ashore! Then kind Heaven
inspired me with the thought of setting fire to my bed, and rather to
let the house burn down, than that all those people should perish so
miserably. I succeeded in lighting up a beacon for them. The red
flame blazed up on high, and I escaped out of the door, but fell down
exhausted on the threshold, and could get no farther. The flames
rushed out towards me, flickered through the window, and rose high
above the roof. All the people on the ice yonder beheld it, and ran as

DAME MARGERY FIRES HER BED FOR A BEACON

fast as they could, to give aid to a poor old woman who, they thought,
was being burned to death. Not one remained behind. I heard them
coming; but I also became aware of a rushing sound in the air; I heard
a rumbling like the sound of heavy artillery; the spring flood was lifting
the covering of ice, which presently cracked and burst into a thousand
fragments. But the people succeeded in reaching the sea wall—I saved
them all! But I fancy I could not bear the cold and the fright, and so
I came up here to the gates of Paradise. I am told they are opened to
poor creatures like me—and now I have no house left down upon the
rampart: not that I think this will give me admission here."

Then the gates of heaven were opened, and the angel led the old
woman in. She left a straw behind her, a straw that had been in her
bed when she set it on fire to save the lives of many; and this straw

had been changed into the purest gold—into gold that grew and grew, and spread out into beauteous leaves and flowers.

"Look, this is what the poor woman brought," said the angel to the critic. "What dost *thou* bring? I know that thou hast accomplished nothing—thou hast not made so much as a single brick. Ah, if thou couldst only return, and effect at least as much as that! Probably the brick, when thou hadst made it, would not be worth much; but if it were made with a good will, it would at least be *something*. But thou canst not go back, and I can do nothing for thee!"

Then the poor soul, the old dame who had lived on the dyke, put in a petition for him. She said,

"His brother gave me the bricks and the pieces out of which I built up my house, and that was a great deal for a poor woman like me. Could not all those bricks and pieces be counted as a single brick in his favour? It was an act of mercy. He wants it now; and is not this the very fountain of mercy?"

Then the angel said,

"Thy brother, him whom thou hast regarded as the least among you all, he whose honest industry seemed to thee as the most humble, hath given thee this heavenly gift. Thou shalt not be turned away. It shall be vouchsafed to thee to stand here without the gate, and to reflect, and repent of thy life down yonder; but thou shalt not be admitted until thou hast in earnest accomplished *something*."

"I could have said that in better words!" thought the critic, but he did not find fault aloud; and for him, after all, that was "SOMETHING!"

A LEAF FROM THE SKY.

HIGH up yonder, in the thin clear air, flew an angel with a flower from the heavenly garden. As he was kissing the flower, a very little leaf fell down into the soft soil in the midst of the wood, and immediately took root, and sprouted, and sent forth shoots among the other plants.

"A funny kind of slip that," said the Plants.

And neither Thistle or Stinging-Nettle would recognize the stranger. "That must be a kind of garden plant," said they.

And they sneered; and the plant was despised by them as being a thing out of the garden.

"Where are you coming?" cried the lofty Thistles, whose leaves are all armed with thorns. "You give yourself a good deal of space. That's all nonsense—we are not here to support you!" they grumbled.

And winter came, and snow covered the plant; but the plant imparted to the snowy covering a lustre as if the sun was shining upon it from below as from above. When spring came, the plant appeared as a blooming object, more beautiful than any production of the forest.

THE POOR GIRL'S TREASURE.

And now appeared on the scene the botanical professor, who could
show what he was in black and white. He inspected the plant and
tested it, but found it was not included in his botanical system; and he
could not possibly find out to what class it belonged.

"That must be some subordinate species," he said. "I don't know
it. It's not included in any system."

"Not included in any system!" repeated the Thistles and the Nettles.
The great trees that stood round about saw and heard it; but they

said not a word, good or bad, which is the wisest thing to do for people who are stupid.

There came through the forest a poor innocent girl.   Her heart was pure, and her understanding was enlarged by faith.   Her whole inheritance was an old Bible; but out of its pages a voice said to her, "If people wish to do us evil, remember how it was said of Joseph. They imagined evil in their hearts, but God turned it to good.   If we suffer wrong—if we are misunderstood and despised—then we may recall the words of Him who was purity and goodness itself, and who forgave and prayed for those who buffeted and nailed Him to the cross."

The girl stood still in front of the wonderful plant, whose great leaves exhaled a sweet and refreshing fragrance, and whose flowers glittered like a coloured flame in the sun; and from each flower there came a sound as though it concealed within itself a deep fount of melody that thousands of years could not exhaust.   With pious gratitude the girl looked on this beautiful work of the Creator, and bent down one of the branches towards herself to breathe in its sweetness; and a light arose in her soul.   It seemed to do her heart good; and gladly would she have plucked a flower, but she could not make up her mind to break one off, for it would soon fade if she did so.   Therefore the girl only took a single leaf, and laid it in her Bible at home; and it lay there quite fresh, always green, and never fading.

Among the pages of the Bible it was kept; and, with the Bible, it was laid under the young girl's head when, a few weeks afterwards, she lay in her coffin, with the solemn calm of death on her gentle face, as if the earthly remains bore the impress of the truth that she now stood before her Creator.

But the wonderful plant still bloomed without in the forest.   It was almost like a tree to look upon; and all the birds of passage bowed before it.

"That's giving itself foreign airs now," said the Thistles and the Burdocks; "we never behave like that here."

And the black snails actually spat at the flower.

Then came the swineherd.   He was collecting thistles and shrubs, to burn them for the ashes.   The wonderful plant was placed bodily in his bundle.

"It shall be made useful," he said; and so said, so done.

But soon afterwards, the King of the country was troubled with a terrible depression of spirits.   He was busy and industrious, but that did him no good.   They read him deep and learned books, and then they read from the lightest and most superficial that they could find; but it was of no use.   Then one of the wise men of the world, to whom they had applied, sent a messenger to tell the King that there was one remedy to give him relief and to cure him.   He said ·

"In the King's own country there grows in a forest a plant of heavenly origin.   Its appearance is thus and thus.   It cannot be mistaken."

"I fancy it was taken up in my bundle, and burned to ashes long ago," said the swineherd; "but I did not know any better."

"You did not know any better! Ignorance of ignorances!"

And those words the swineherd might well take to himself, for they were meant for him, and for no one else.

Not another leaf was to be found; the only one lay in the coffin of the dead girl, and no one knew anything about that.

And the King himself, in his melancholy, wandered out to the spot in the wood.

"Here is where the plant stood," he said; "it is a sacred place."

And the place was surrounded with a golden railing, and a sentry was posted there.

The botanical professor wrote a long treatise upon the heavenly plant. For this he was gilded all over, and this gilding suited him and his family very well. And indeed that was the most agreeable part of the whole story. But the King remained as low-spirited as before; but that he had always been, at least so the sentry said.

THE DROP OF WATER.

Of course you know what is meant by a magnifying glass—one of those round spectacle-glasses that make everything look a hundred times bigger than it is? When any one takes one of these and holds it to his eye, and looks at a drop of water from the pond yonder, he sees above a thousand wonderful creatures that are otherwise never discerned in the water. But they are there, and it is no delusion. It almost looks like a great plate-full of spiders jumping about in a crowd. And how fierce they are! They tear off each other's legs and arms and bodies, before and behind; and yet they are merry and joyful in their way.

Now, there was once an old man whom all the people called Kribble-Krabble, for that was his name. He always wanted the best of everything, and when he could not manage it otherwise, he did it by magic.

There he sat one day, and held his magnifying glass to his eye, and looked at a drop of water that had been taken out of a puddle by the ditch. But what a kribbling and crabbling was there! All the thousands of little creatures hopped and sprang and tugged at one another, and ate each other up.

"That is horrible!" said old Kribble-Krabble. "Can one not persuade them to live in peace and quietness, so that each one may mind his own business?"

And he thought it over and over, but it would not do, and so he had recourse to magic.

"I must give them colour, that they may be seen more plainly," said he; and he poured something like a little drop of red wine into the drop of water, but it was witches' blood from the lobes of the ear, the finest kind, at ninepence a drop. And now the wonderful little creatures were pink all over: it looked like a whole town of naked wild men.

"What have you there?" asked another old magician, who had no name—and that was the best thing about him.

"Yes, if you can guess what it is," said Kribble-Krabble, "I'll make you a present of it."

But it is not so easy to find out if one does not know.

And the magician who had no name looked through the magnifying

THE TWO MAGICIANS.

glass. It looked really like a great town reflected there, in which all the people were running about without clothes. It was terrible! But it was still more terrible to see how one beat and pushed the other, and bit and hacked, and tugged and mauled him. Those at the top were being pulled down, and those at the bottom were struggling upwards.

"Look! look! his leg is longer than mine! Bah! Away with it! There is one who has a little bruise. It hurts him, but it shall hurt him still more."

And they hacked away at him, and they pulled at him, and ate him up, because of the little bruise. And there was one sitting as still as any little maiden, and wishing only for peace and quietness. But now she had to come out, and they tugged at her, and pulled her about, and ate her up.

"That's funny!" said the magician.

"Yes; but what do you think it is?" said Kribble-Krabble. ".Can you find that out?"

"Why, one can see that easily enough," said the other. "That's Paris, or some other great city, for they're all alike. It's a great city!"

"It's a drop of puddle water!" said Kribble-Krabble.

THE DUMB BOOK.

BY the high road in the forest lay a lonely peasant's hut; the road went right through the farm-yard. The sun shone down, and all the windows were open. In the house was bustle and movement; but in the garden, in an arbour of blossoming elder, stood an open coffin. A dead man had been carried out here, and he was to be buried this morning. Nobody stood by the coffin and looked sorrowfully at the dead man; no one shed a tear for him: his face was covered with a white cloth, and under his head lay a great thick book, whose leaves consisted of whole sheets of blotting paper, and on each leaf lay a faded flower. It was a complete herbanum, gathered by him in various places; it was to be buried with him, for so he had wished it. With each flower a chapter in his life was associated.

"Who is the dead man?" we asked; and the answer was:

"The Old Student. They say he was once a brisk lad, and studied the old languages, and sang, and even wrote poems. Then something happened to him that made him turn his thoughts to brandy, and take to it; and when at last he had ruined his health, he came out here into the country, where somebody paid for his board and lodging. He was as gentle as a child, except when the dark mood came upon him; but when it came he became like a giant, and then ran about in the woods like a hunted stag; but when we once got him home again, and prevailed with him so far that he opened the book with the dried plants, he often sat whole days, and looked sometimes at one plant and sometimes at another, and at times the tears rolled over his cheeks: Heaven knows what he was thinking of. But he begged us to put the book into the coffin, and now he lies there, and in a little while the lid will be nailed down, and he will have his quiet rest in the grave."

The face-cloth was raised, and there was peace upon the features of the dead man, and a sunbeam played upon it; a swallow shot with arrowy flight into the arbour, and turned rapidly, and twittered over the dead man's head.

THE POWER OF THE BOOK.

What a strange feeling it is—and we have doubtless all experienced
it—that of turning over old letters of the days of our youth!—a new
life seems to come up with them, with all its hopes and sorrows. How
many persons with whom we were intimate in those days, are as it were
dead to us! and yet they are alive, but for a long time we have not
thought of them—of them whom we then thought to hold fast for ages,
and with whom we were to share sorrow and joy.

Here the withered oak-leaf in the book reminded the owner of the
friend, the school-fellow, who was to be a friend for life: he fastened the
green leaf in the student's cap in the green wood, when the bond was
made "for life:" where does he live now? The leaf is preserved, but
the friendship has perished! And here is a foreign hothouse plant, too
delicate for the gardens of the North; the leaves almost seem to keep

their fragrance still. She gave it to him, the young lady in the noble-man's garden. Here is the water rose, which he plucked himself, and moistened with salt tears—the rose of the sweet waters. And here is a nettle—what tale may its leaves have to tell? What were his thoughts when he plucked it and kept it? Here is a lily of the valley from the solitudes of the forest. Here's an evergreen from the flower-pot of the tavern; and here's a naked sharp blade of grass.

The blooming elder waves its fresh fragrant blossoms over the dead man's head, and the swallow flies past again. "Pee-wit! pee-wit!" And now the men come with nails and hammers, and the lid is laid over the dead man, that his head may rest upon the dumb book—vanished and scattered!

THE JEWISH GIRL.

AMONG the children in a charity school sat a little Jewish girl. She was a good, intelligent child, the quickest in all the school; but she had to be excluded from one lesson, for she was not allowed to take part in the scripture-lesson, for it was a Christian school.

In that hour the girl was allowed to open the geography-book, or to do her sum for the next day; but that was soon done; and when she had mastered her lesson in geography, the book indeed remained open before her, but the little one read no more in it: she listened silently to the words of the Christian teacher, who soon became aware that she was listening more intently than almost any of the other children.

"Read your book, Sara," the teacher said, in mild reproof; but her dark beaming eye remained fixed upon him; and once when he addressed a question to her, she knew how to answer better than any of the others could have done. She had heard and understood, and had kept his words in her heart.

When her father, a poor honest man, first brought the girl to the school, he had stipulated that she should be excluded from the lessons on the Christian faith. But it would have caused disturbance, and perhaps might have awakened discontent in the minds of the others, if she had been sent from the room during the hours in question, and con-sequently she stayed; but this could not go on any longer.

The teacher betook himself to her father, and exhorted him either to remove his daughter from the school, or to consent that Sara should become a Christian.

"I can no longer be a silent spectator of the gleaming eyes of the child, and of her deep and earnest longing for the words of the Gospel," said the teacher.

Then the father burst into tears.

"I know but little of the commandment given to my fathers," he said; "but Sara's mother was steadfast in the faith, a true daughter of

Israel, and I vowed to her as she lay dying that our child should never be baptized. I must keep my vow, for it is even as a covenant with God Himself."

And accordingly the little Jewish maiden quitted the Christian school.

Years have rolled on.

In one of the smallest provincial towns there dwelt, as a servant in a humble household, a maiden who held the Mosaic faith. Her hair was black as ebony, her eye dark as night, and yet full of splendour and light, as is usual with the daughters of Israel. It was Sara. The expression in the countenance of the now grown-up maiden was still that of the child sitting upon the school-room bench and listening with thoughtful eyes to the words of the Christian teacher.

Every Sunday there pealed from the church the sounds of the organ and the song of the congregation. The strains penetrated into the house where the Jewish girl, industrious and faithful in all things, stood at her work.

"Thou shalt keep holy the Sabbath-day," said a voice within her, the voice of the Law; but her Sabbath-day was a working day among the Christians, and that seemed unfortunate to her. But then the thought arose in her soul: "Doth God reckon by days and hours?" And when this thought grew strong within her, it seemed a comfort that on the Sunday of the Christians the hour of prayer remained undisturbed; and when the sound of the organ and the songs of the congregation sounded across to her as she stood in the kitchen at her work, then even that place seemed to become a sacred one to her. Then she would read in the Old Testament, the treasure and comfort of her people, and it was only in this one she could read; for she kept faithfully in the depths of her heart the words the teacher had spoken when she left the school, and the promise her father had given to her dying mother, that she should never receive Christian baptism, or deny the faith of her ancestors. The New Testament was to be a sealed book to her; and yet she knew much of it, and the Gospel echoed faintly among the recollections of her youth.

One evening she was sitting in a corner of the living-room. Her master was reading aloud; and she might listen to him, for it was not the Gospel that he read, but an old story-book, therefore she might stay. The book told of a Hungarian knight who was taken prisoner by a Turkish pasha, who caused him to be yoked with his oxen to the plough, and driven with blows of the whip till the blood came, and he almost sank under the pain and ignominy he endured. The faithful wife of the knight at home parted with all her jewels, and pledged castle and land. The knight's friends amassed large sums, for the ransom demanded was almost unattainably high; but it was collected at last, and the knight was freed from servitude and misery. Sick and exhausted, he reached his home. But soon another summons came to war against the foes of Christianity: the knight heard the cry, and he could stay no longer, for he had neither peace nor rest. He caused himself to be lifted on his

SARA LISTENING TO THE SINGING IN THE CHURCH.

war-horse; and the blood came back to his cheek, his strength appeared to return, and he went forth to battle and to victory. The very same pasha who had yoked him to the plough became his prisoner, and was dragged to his castle. But not an hour had passed when the knight stood before the captive pasha, and said to him,

"What dost thou suppose awaiteth thee?"

"I know it," replied the Turk. "Retribution."

"Yes, the retribution of the Christian!" resumed the knight. "The doctrine of Christ commands us to forgive our enemies, and to love our fellow-man, for it teaches us that God is love. Depart in peace, depart to thy home: I will restore thee to thy dear ones; but in future be mild and merciful to all who are unfortunate."

Then the prisoner broke out into tears, and exclaimed,

" How could I believe in the possibility of such mercy ? Misery and torment seemed to await me, they seemed inevitable ; therefore I took poison, which I secretly carried about me, and in a few hours its effects will slay me. I must die—there is no remedy ! But before I die, do thou expound to me the teaching which includes so great a measure of love and mercy, for it is great and godlike ! Grant me to hear this teaching, and to die a Christian ! " And his prayer was fulfilled.

That was the legend which the master read out of the old story-book. All the audience listened with sympathy and pleasure ; but Sara, the Jewish girl, sitting alone in her corner, listened with a burning heart ; great tears came into her gleaming black eyes, and she sat there with a gentle and lowly spirit as she had once sat on the school bench, and felt the grandeur of the Gospel ; and the tears rolled down over her cheeks.

But again the dying words of her mother rose up within her :

" Let not my daughter become a Christian," the voice cried ; and together with it arose the words of the Law : " Thou shalt honour thy father and thy mother."

" I am not admitted into the community of the Christians," she said ; " they abuse me for being a Jew girl—our neighbour's boys hooted me last Sunday, when I stood at the open church door, and looked in at the flaming candles on the altar, and listened to the song of the congregation. Ever since I sat upon the school bench I have felt the force of Christianity, a force like that of a sunbeam, which streams into my soul, however firmly I may shut my eyes against it. But I will not pain thee in thy grave, O my mother, I will not be unfaithful to the oath of my father, I will not read the Bible of the Christians. I have the religion of my people, and to that will I hold ! "

And years rolled on again.

The master died. His widow fell into poverty ; and the servant girl was to be dismissed. But Sara refused to leave the house : she became the staff in time of trouble, and kept the household together, working till late in the night to earn the daily bread through the labour of her hands ; for no relative came forward to assist the family, and the widow became weaker every day, and lay for months together on the bed of sickness. Sara worked hard, and in the intervals sat kindly ministering by the sick-bed : she was gentle and pious, an angel of blessing in the poverty-stricken house.

" Yonder on the table lies the Bible," said the sick woman to Sara. " Read me something from it, for the night appears to be so long—oh, so long !—and my soul thirsts for the word of the Lord."

And Sara bowed her head. She took the book, and folded her hands over the Bible of the Christians, and opened it, and read to the sick woman. Tears stood in her eyes, which gleamed and shone with ecstacy. and light shone in her heart.

" O my mother," she whispered to herself ; " thy child may not re-ceive the baptism of the Christians, or be admitted into the congregation —thou hast willed it so, and I shall respect thy command : we will remain in union together here on earth; but beyond this earth there is a higher union, even union in God! He will be at our side, and lead us through the valley of death. It is He that descendeth upon the earth when it is athirst, and covers it with fruitfulness. I understand it—I know not how I came to learn the truth; but it is through Him, through Christ!"

And she started as she pronounced the sacred name, and there came upon her a baptism as of flames of fire, and her frame shook, and her limbs tottered so that she sank down fainting, weaker even than the sick woman by whose couch she had watched.

"Poor Sara!" said the people; "she is overcome with night watching and toil!"

They carried her out into the hospital for the sick poor. There she died; and from thence they carried her to the grave, but not to the churchyard of the Christians, for yonder was no room for the Jewish girl; outside, by the wall, her grave was dug.

But God's sun, that shines upon the graves of the Christians, throws its beams also upon the grave of the Jewish girl beyond the wall; and when the psalms are sung in the churchyard of the Christians, they echo likewise over her lonely resting-place; and she who sleeps beneath is included in the call to the resurrection, in the name of Him who spake to His disciples:

"John baptized you with water, but I will baptize you with the Holy Ghost!"

THE ELDER TREE MOTHER.

THERE was once a little boy who had caught cold; he had gone out and got wet feet; no one could imagine how it had happened, for it was quite dry weather. Now his mother undressed him, put him to bed, and had the tea-urn brought in to make him a good cup of elder tea, for that warms well. At the same time there also came in at the door the friendly old man who lived all alone at the top of the house, and was very solitary. He had neither wife nor children, but he was very fond of little children, and knew so many stories that it was quite delightful.

"Now you are to drink your tea," said the mother, "and then perhaps you will hear a story."

"Ah! if one only could tell a new one!" said the old man, with a friendly nod. "But where did the little man get his feet wet?" he asked.

"Yes," replied the mother, "no one can tell how that came about."

"Shall I have a story?" asked the boy.

"Yes, if you can tell me at all accurately—for I must know that first—how deep the gutter is in the little street through which you go to school."

" Just half way up to my knee," answered the boy, " that is, if I put my feet in the deep hole."

" You see, that's how we get our feet wet," said the old gentleman. " Now I ought certainly to tell you a story ; but I don't know any more."

" You can make up one directly," answered the little boy. " Mother says that everything you look at can be turned into a story, and that you can make a tale of everything you touch."

" Yes, but those stories and tales are worth nothing! No, the real ones come of themselves. They knock at my forehead and say, ' Here I am!'"

" Will there soon be a knock?" asked the little boy, and the mother laughed, and put elder tea in the pot, and poured hot water upon it.

" A story ! a story !"

" Yes, if a story would come of itself ; but that kind of thing is very grand; it only comes when it's in the humour.—Wait!" he cried all at once; " here we have it. Look you; there's one in the tea-pot now."

And the little boy looked across at the tea-pot. The lid raised itself more and more, and the elder flowers came forth from it, white and fresh ; they shot forth long fresh branches even out of the spout, they spread abroad in all directions, and became larger and larger ; there was the most glorious elder bush—in fact, quite a great tree. It penetrated even to the bed, and thrust the curtains aside; how fragrant it was, and how it bloomed! And in the midst of the tree sat an old, pleasant-looking woman in a strange dress. It was quite green, like the leaves of the elder tree, and bordered with great white elder blossoms ; one could not at once discern whether this border was of stuff or of living green and real flowers.

" What is the woman's name ?" the little boy asked.

" The Romans and Greeks," replied the old man, " used to call her a Dryad ; but we don't understand that : out in the sailor's suburb we have a better name for her ; there she's called Elder Tree Mother, and it is to her you must pay attention : only listen, and look at that glorious elder tree.

" Just such a great blooming tree stands outside ; it grew there in the corner of a poor little yard, and under this tree two old people sat one afternoon in the brightest sunshine. It was an old, old sailor, and his old, old wife ; they had great grandchildren, and were soon to celebrate their golden wedding ;* but they could not quite make out the date, and the Elder Tree Mother sat in the tree and looked pleased, just as she does here. ' I know very well when the golden wedding is to be,' said she ; but they did not hear it—they were talking of old times.

" ' Yes, do you remember,' said the old seaman, ' when we were quite little, and ran about and played together! it was in the very same yard where we are sitting now, and we planted little twigs in the yard, and made a garden.'

The golden wedding is celebrated in several countries of the Continent, by the two wedded pairs who survive to see the fiftieth anniversary of their marriage-day.

THE OLD NEIGHBOUR VISITS THE LITTLE BOY.

"'Yes,' replied the old woman, 'I remember it very well: we watered the twigs, and one of them was an elder twig; that struck root, shot out other green twigs, and has become a great tree, under which we old people sit.'

"'Surely,' said he; 'and yonder in the corner stood a butt of water; there I swam my boat; I had cut it out myself. How it could sail! But I certainly soon had to sail elsewhere myself.'

"'But first we went to school and learned something,' said she, 'and then we were confirmed; we both cried, but in the afternoon we went hand in hand to the round tower, and looked out into the wide world, over Copenhagen and across the water; then we went out to Fredericksberg, where the King and Queen were sailing in their splendid boats upon the canals.'

"'But I was obliged to sail elsewhere, and that for many years, far away on long voyages.'

"'Yes, I often cried about you,' she said. 'I thought you were dead and gone, and lying down in the deep waters. rocked by the waves.

Many a night I got up to look if the weathercock was turning. Yes, it turned indeed; but you did not come. I remember so clearly how the rain streamed down from the sky. The man with the cart who fetched away the dust came to the place where I was in service. I went down with him to the dust-bin, and remained standing in the doorway. What wretched weather it was! And just as I stood there the postman came up and gave me a letter. It was from you! How that letter had travelled about! I tore it open and read; I laughed and wept at once, I was so glad. There it stood written that you were in the warm countries where the coffee-beans grow. You told me so much, and I read it all while the rain was streaming down, and I stood by the dust-bin. Then somebody came and clasped me round the waist.'

" 'And you gave him a terrible box on the ear—one that sounded?'

" 'I did not know that it was you. You had arrived just as quickly as your letter. And you were so handsome; but that you are still. You had a large yellow silk handkerchief in your pocket, and a hat on your head. You were so handsome! And, gracious! what weather it was, and how the street looked!'

" 'Then we were married,' said he; 'do you remember? And then when our first little boy came, and then Marie, and Neils, and Peter, and Jack, and Christian?'

" 'Yes; and how all of these have grown up to be respectable people, and every one likes them.'

" 'And their children have had little ones in their turn,' said the old sailor. ' Yes, those are children's children! They 're of the right sort. It was, if I don't mistake, at this very season of the year that we were married?'

" 'Yes; this is the day of your golden wedding,' said the Elder Tree Mother, putting out her head just between the two old people; and they thought it was a neighbour nodding to them, and they looked at each other, and took hold of one another's hands.

" Soon afterwards came their children and grandchildren; these knew very well that it was the golden wedding-day; they had already brought their congratulations in the morning, but the old people had forgotten it, while they remembered everything right well that had happened years and years ago.

" And the elder tree smelt so sweet, and the sun that was just setting shone just in the faces of the old couple, so that their cheeks looked quite red; and the youngest of their grandchildren danced about them, and cried out quite gleefully that there was to be a feast this evening, for they were to have hot potatoes; and the Elder Mother nodded in the tree, and called out ' hurrah!' with all the rest."

" But that was not a story," said the little boy who had heard it told.

" Yes, so you understand it," replied the old man; " but let us ask the Elder Mother about it."

" That was not a story," said the Elder Mother; " but now it comes; but of truth the strangest stories are formed, otherwise my beautiful elder tree could not have sprouted forth out of the tea-pot."

And then she took the little boy out of bed, and laid him upon her bosom, and the blossoming elder branches wound round them, so that they sat as it were in the thickest arbour, and this arbour flew with them through the air. It was indescribably beautiful. Elder Mother all at once became a pretty young girl; but her dress was still of the green stuff with the white blossoms that Elder Mother had worn; in her bosom she had a real elder blossom, and on her head a wreath of elder flowers; her eyes were so large and blue, they were beautiful to look at She and the boy were of the same age, and they kissed each other and felt similar joys.

Hand in hand they went forth out of the arbour, and now they stood in the beauteous flower garden of home. The father's staff was tied up near the fresh grass-plot, and for the little boy there was life in that staff. As soon as they seated themselves upon it, the polished head turned into a noble neighing horse's head, with a flowing mane, and four slender legs shot forth; the creature was strong and spirited, and they rode at a gallop round the grass-plot—hurrah!

"Now we're going to ride many miles away," said the boy; "we'll ride to the nobleman's estate, where we went last year!"

And they rode round and round the grass-plot, and the little girl, who, as we know, was no one else but Elder Mother, kept crying out,

"Now we're in the country! Do you see the farm-house, with the great baking-oven standing out of the wall like an enormous egg by the way-side? The elder tree spreads its branches over it, and the cock walks about, scratching for his hens; look how he struts! Now we are near the church; it lies high up on the hill, under the great oak trees, one of which is half dead. Now we are at the forge, where the fire burns and the half-clad men beat with their hammers, so that the sparks fly far around. Away, away to the splendid nobleman's seat!"

And everything that the little maiden mentioned, as she sat on the stick behind him, flew past them, and the little boy saw it all, though they were only riding round and round the grass-plot. Then they played in the side walk, and scratched up the earth to make a little garden; and she took elder flowers out of her hair and planted them, and they grew just like those that the old people had planted when they were little, as has been already told. They went hand in hand just as the old people had done in their childhood; but not to the high tower, or to the Fredericksberg Garden. No, the little girl took hold of the boy round the body, and then they flew far away out into the country.

And it was spring, and summer came, and autumn, and winter, and thousands of pictures were mirrored in the boy's eyes and heart, and the little maiden was always singing to him.

He will never forget that; and throughout their whole journey the elder tree smelt so sweet, so fragrant: he noticed the roses and the fresh beech trees; but the elder tree smelt stronger than all, for its flowers hung round the little girl's heart, and he often leaned against them as they flew onward.

"Here it is beautiful in spring!" said the little girl.

And they stood in the green beech wood, where the thyme lay spread in fragrance at their feet, and the pale pink anemones looked glorious among the vivid green.

" Oh, that it were always spring in the merry green wood ! "

" Here it is beautiful in summer ! " said she.

And they passed by old castles of knightly days, castles whose high walls and pointed turrets were mirrored in the canals, where swans swam about, and looked down the old shady avenues. In the fields the corn waved like a sea, in the ditches yellow and red flowers were growing, and in the hedges wild hops and blooming convolvulus. In the evening the moon rose round and large, and the haystacks in the meadows smelt sweet.

" Here it is beautiful in autumn ! " said the little girl.

And the sky seemed twice as lofty and twice as blue as before, and the forest was decked in the most gorgeous tints of red, yellow, and green. The hunting dogs raced about ; whole flocks of wild ducks flew screaming over the Hun's Graves, on which bramble bushes twined over the old stones. The sea was dark blue, and covered with ships with white sails ; and in the barns sat old women, girls, and children, picking hops into a large tub : the young people sang songs, and the older ones told tales of magicians and goblins. It could not be finer anywhere.

" Here it is beautiful in winter ! " said the little girl.

And all the trees were covered with hoar frost, so that they looked like white trees of coral. The snow crumbled beneath one's feet, as if every one had new boots on ; and one shooting star after another fell from the sky. In the room the Christmas tree was lighted up, and there were presents, and there was happiness. In the country people's farm-houses the violin sounded, and there were merry games for apples ; and even the poorest child said, " It is beautiful in winter ! "

Yes, it was beautiful ; and the little girl showed the boy everything ; and still the blossoming tree smelt sweet, and still waved the red flag with the white cross, the flag under which the old seaman had sailed. The boy became a youth, and was to go out into the wide world, far away to the hot countries where the coffee grows. But when they were to part the little girl took an elder blossom from her breast, and gave it to him to keep. It was laid in his hymn-book, and in the foreign land, when he opened the book, it was always at the place where the flower of remembrance lay ; and the more he looked at the flower the fresher it became, so that. he seemed, as it were, to breathe the forest air of home ; then he plainly saw the little girl looking out with her clear blue eyes from between the petals of the flower, and then she whispered, " Here it is beautiful in spring, summer, autumn, and winter ! " and hundreds of pictures glided through his thoughts.

Thus many years went by, and now he was an old man, and sat with his old wife under the blossoming elder tree : they were holding each other by the hand, just as the great-grandmother and great-grandfather had done outside ; and, like these, they spoke of old times and of the golden wedding. The little maiden with the blue eyes and with the elder blossoms in her hair sat up in the tree, and nodded to both of them, and said, "To-day is our golden wedding-day!" and then she took two flowers out of her hair and kissed them, and they gleamed first like silver and then like gold, and when she laid them on the heads of the old people each changed into a golden crown. There they both sat, like a King and a Queen, under the fragrant tree which looked quite like an elder bush, and he told his old wife of the story of the Elder Tree Mother, as it had been told to him when he was quite a little boy, and they both thought that the story in many points resembled their own, and those parts they liked the best.

"Yes, thus it is!" said the little girl in the tree. "Some call me Elder Tree Mother, others the Dryad, but my real name is Remembrance: it is I who sit in the tree that grows on and on, and I can think back and tell stories. Let me see if you have still your flower."

THE BOY AND HIS MOTHER.

And the old man opened his hymn-book; there lay the elder blossom as fresh as if it had only just been placed there; and Remembrance nodded, and the two old people with the golden crowns on their heads sat in the red evening sunlight, and they closed their eyes, and—and—the story was finished.

The little boy lay in his bed and did not know whether he had been dreaming or had heard a tale told; the tea-pot stood on the table, but no elder bush was growing out of it, and the old man who had told about it was just going out of the door, and indeed he went.

"How beautiful that was!" said the little boy. "Mother, I have been in the hot countries."

"Yes, I can imagine that!" replied his mother. "When one drinks two cups of hot elder tea one very often gets into the hot countries!" And she covered him up well, that he might not take cold. "You have slept well while I disputed with him as to whether it was a story or a fairy tale."

"And where is the Elder Tree Mother?" asked the little lad.

"She's in the tea pot," replied his mother; "and there she may stay."

TWO MAIDENS.

HAVE you ever seen a maiden? I mean what our paviours call a maiden, a thing with which they ram down the paving-stones in the roads. A maiden of this kind is made altogether of wood, broad below, and girt round with iron rings; at the top she is narrow, and has a stick passed across through her waist; and this stick forms the arms of the maiden.

In the shed stood two Maidens of this kind. They had their place among shovels, hand-carts, wheelbarrows, and measuring tapes; and to

THE TWO MAIDENS.

all this company the news had come that the Maidens were no longer to be called "maidens," but "hand-rammers;" which word was the newest and the only correct designation among the paviours for the thing we all know from the old times by the name of "the maiden."

Now, there are among us human creatures certain individuals who are known as "emancipated women;" as, for instance, principals of institutions, dancers who stand professionally on one leg, milliners, and sick nurses; and with this class of emancipated women the two Maidens in the shed associated themselves. They were "maidens" among the paviour folk, and determined not to give up this honourable appellation, and let themselves be miscalled rammers.

"Maiden is a human name, but hand-rammer is a *thing*, and we won't be called *things*—that's insulting us."

"My lover would be ready to give up his engagement," said the youngest, who was betrothed to a paviour's hammer; and the hammer is the thing which drives great piles into the earth, like a machine, and therefore does on a large scale what ten maidens effect in a similar way. "He wants to marry me as a Maiden, but whether he would have me, were I a hand-rammer, is a question; so I won't have my name changed."

"And I," said the elder one, "would rather have both my arms broken off."

But the Wheelbarrow was of a different opinion; and the Wheelbarrow was looked upon as of some consequence, for he considered himself a quarter of a coach, because he went about upon one wheel.

"I must submit to your notice," he said, "that the name 'maiden' is common enough, and not nearly so refined as 'hand-rammer,' or 'stamper,' which latter has also been proposed, and through which you would be introduced into the category of seals; and only think of the great stamp of state, which impresses the royal seal that gives effect to the laws! No, in your case I would surrender my maiden name."

"No, certainly not!" exclaimed the elder. "I am too old for that."

"I presume you have never heard of what is called 'European necessity?'" observed the honest Measuring Tape. "One must be able to adapt oneself to time and circumstances, and if there is a law that the 'maiden' is to be called 'hand-rammer,' why, she must be called 'hand-rammer,' and no pouting will avail, for everything has its measure."

"No; if there must be a change," said the younger, "I should prefer to be called 'Missy,' for that reminds one a little of maidens."

"But I would rather be chopped to chips," said the elder.

At last they all went to work. The Maidens rode—that is, they were put in a wheelbarrow, and that was a distinction; but still they were called "hand-rammers."

"Mai——!" they said, as they were bumped upon the pavement. "Mai——!" and they were very nearly pronouncing the whole word "maiden;" but they broke off short, and swallowed the last syllable; for after mature deliberation they considered it beneath their dignity to protest. But they always called each other "maiden," and praised the good old days in which everything had been called by its right name, and those who were maidens were called maidens. And they remained as they were; for the hammer really broke off his engagement with the younger one, for nothing would suit him but he must have a maiden for his bride.

THE FARM-YARD COCK AND THE WEATHERCOCK.

THERE were two Cocks—one on the dunghill, the other on the roof. Both were conceited; but which of the two effected most? Tell us your opinion; but we shall keep our own nevertheless.

The poultry-yard was divided by a partition of boards from another yard, in which lay a manure-heap, whereon lay and grew a great Cucumber, which was fully conscious of being a forcing-bed plant.

"That's a privilege of birth," the Cucumber said to herself. "Not all can be born cucumbers; there must be other kinds too. The fowls, the ducks, and all the cattle in the neighbouring yard are creatures too. I now look up to the Yard Cock on the partition. He certainly is of much greater consequence than the Weathercock, who is so highly placed, and who can't even creak, much less crow; and he has neither hens nor chickens, and thinks only of himself, and perspires verdigris. But the Yard Cock—he's something like a cock! His gait is like a dance, his crowing is music; and wherever he comes, it is known directly. What a trumpeter he is! If he would only come in here! Even if he were to eat me up, stalk and all, it would be quite a blissful death," said the Cucumber.

In the night the weather became very bad. Hens, chickens, and even the Cock himself sought shelter. The wind blew down the partition between the two yards with a crash; the tiles came tumbling down, but the Weathercock sat firm. He did not even turn round; he could not turn round, and yet he was young and newly cast, but steady and sedate. He had been "born old," and did not at all resemble the birds that fly beneath the vault of heaven, such as the sparrows and the swallows. He despised those, considering them piping birds of trifling stature—ordinary song birds. The pigeons, he allowed, were big and shining, and gleamed like mother-o'-pearl, and looked like a kind of weathercocks; but then they were fat and stupid, and their whole endeavour was to fill themselves with food.

"Moreover, they are tedious things to converse with," said the Weathercock.

The birds of passage had also paid a visit to the Weathercock, and told him tales of foreign lands, of airy caravans, and exciting robber stories; of encounters with birds of prey; and that was interesting for the first time, but the Weathercock knew that afterwards they always repeated themselves, and that was tedious.

"They are tedious, and all is tedious," he said. "No one is fit to associate with, and one and all of them are wearisome and stupid. The world is worth nothing," he cried. "The whole thing is a stupidity."

The Weathercock was what is called "used up;" and that quality would certainly have made him interesting in the eyes of the Cucumber if she had known it; but she had only eyes for the Yard Cock, who had now actually come into her own yard.

The wind had blown down the plank, but the storm had passed over.

"What do you think of *that* crowing?" the Yard Cock inquired of his hens and chickens. "It was a little rough — the elegance was wanting."

And hens and chickens stepped upon the muck-heap, and the Cock strutted to and fro on it like a knight.

"Garden plant!" he cried out to the Cucumber; and in this one

word she understood his deep feeling, and forgot that he was pecking at
her and eating her up—a happy death!

And the hens came, and the chickens came, and when one of them
runs the rest run also; and they clucked and chirped, and looked at the
Cock, and were proud that he was of their kind.

"Cock-a-doodle-doo!" he crowed. "The chickens will grow up large
fowls if I make a noise in the poultry-yard of the world."

And hens and chickens clucked and chirped, and the Cock told them
a great piece of news:

"A cock can lay an egg; and do you know what there is in that egg?
In that egg lies a basilisk. No one can stand the sight of a basilisk.

THE WEATHERCOCK.

Men know that, and now you know it too—you know what is in me,
and what a Cock of the world I am."

And with this the Yard Cock flapped his wings, and made his comb
swell up, and crowed again; and all of them shuddered—all the hens
and the chickens; but they were proud that one of their people should
be such a cock of the world. They clucked and chirped, so that the
Weathercock heard it; and he heard it, but he never stirred.

"It's all stupid stuff!" said a voice within the Weathercock. "The
Yard Cock does not lay eggs, and I am too lazy to lay any. If I liked,
I could lay a wind-egg; but the world is not worth a wind-egg. And
now I don't like even to sit here any longer."

And with this the Weathercock broke off; but he did not kill the
Yard Cock, though he intended to do so, as the hens declared. And
what does the moral say?—"Better to crow than to be 'used up' and
break off."

THE OLD GRAVESTONE.

In a little provincial town, in the time of the year when people say "the evenings are drawing in," there was one evening quite a social gathering in the home of a father of a family. The weather was still mild and warm. The lamp gleamed on the table; the long curtains hung down in folds before the open windows, by which stood many flower-pots; and outside, beneath the dark blue sky, was the most beautiful moonshine. But they were not talking about this. They were talking about the old great stone which lay below in the court-yard, close by the kitchen door, and on which the maids often laid the cleaned copper kitchen utensils that they might dry in the sun, and where the children were fond of playing. It was, in fact, an old grave-stone.

"Yes," said the master of the house, "I believe the stone comes from the old convent churchyard; for from the church yonder, the pulpit, the memorial boards, and the gravestones were sold. My father bought the latter, and they were cut in two to be used as paving-stones; but that old stone was kept back, and has been lying in the courtyard ever since."

"One can very well see that it is a gravestone," observed the eldest of the children; "we can still decipher on it an hour-glass and a piece of an angel; but the inscription which stood below it is quite effaced, except that you may read the name of *Preben*, and a great *S* close behind it, and a little farther down the name of *Martha*. But nothing more can be distinguished, and even that is only plain when it has been raining, or when we have washed the stone."

"On my word, that must be the gravestone of Preben Schwane and his wife!"

These words were spoken by an old man; so old, that he might well have been the grandfather of all who were present in the room.

"Yes, they were one of the last pairs that were buried in the old churchyard of the convent. They were an honest old couple. I can remember them from the days of my boyhood. Every one knew them, and every one esteemed them. They were the oldest pair here in the town. The people declared that they had more than a tub-full of gold; and yet they went about very plainly dressed, in the coarsest stuffs, but always with splendidly clean linen. They were a fine old pair, Preben and Martha! When both of them sat on the bench at the top of the steep stone stairs in front of the house, with the old linden tree spreading its branches above them, and nodded at one in their kind gentle way, it seemed quite to do one good. They were very kind to the poor; they fed them and clothed them; and there was judgment in their benevolence and true Christianity. The old woman died first: that day is still quite clear before my mind. I was a little boy, and had accompanied my father over there, and we were just there when she fell

PREBEN SCHWANE AND HIS WIFE MARTHA.

asleep. The old man was very much moved, and wept like a child.
The corpse lay in the room next to the one where we sat; and he spoke
to my father and to a few neighbours who were there, and said how
lonely it would be now in his house, and how good and faithful she (his
dead wife) had been, how many years they had wandered together
through life, and how it had come about that they came to know each
other and to fall in love. I was, as I have told you, a boy, and only
stood by and listened to what the others said; but it filled me with
quite a strange emotion to listen to the old man, and to watch how his
cheeks gradually flushed red when he spoke of the days of their courtship, and told how beautiful she was, and how many little innocent
pretexts he had invented to meet her. And then he talked of the
wedding-day, and his eyes gleamed; he seemed to talk himself back
into that time of joy. And yet she was lying in the next room—dead
—an old woman; and he was an old man, speaking of the past days of
hope! Yes, yes, thus it is! Then I was but a child, and now I am

old—as old as Preben Schwane was then. Time passes away, and all things change. I can very well remember the day when she was buried, and how Preben Schwane walked close behind the coffin. A few years before, the couple had caused their gravestone to be prepared, and their names to be engraved on it, with the inscription, all but the date. In the evening the stone was taken to the churchyard, and laid over the grave; and the year afterwards it was taken up, that old Preben Schwane might be laid to rest beside his wife. They did not leave behind them anything like the wealth people had attributed to them: what there was went to families distantly related to them—to people of whom, until then, one had known nothing. The old wooden house, with the seat at the top of the steps, beneath the lime tree, was taken down by the corporation; it was too old and rotten to be left standing. Afterwards, when the same fate befell the convent church, and the graveyard was levelled, Preben and Martha's tombstone was sold, like everything else, to any one who would buy it; and that is how it has happened that this stone was not hewn in two, as many another has been, but that it still lies below in the yard as a scouring-bench for the maids and a plaything for the children. The high road now goes over the resting-place of old Preben and his wife. No one thinks of them any more."

And the old man who had told all this shook his head scornfully.

"Forgotten! Everything will be forgotten!" he said.

And then they spoke in the room of other things; but the youngest child, a boy with great serious eyes, mounted up on a chair behind the window-curtains, and looked out into the yard, where the moon was pouring its radiance over the old stone—the old stone that had always appeared to him so tame and flat, but which lay there now like a great leaf out of a book of chronicles. All that the boy had heard about old Preben and his wife seemed concentrated in the stone; and he gazed at it, and looked at the pure bright moon and up into the clear air, and it seemed as though the countenance of the Creator was beaming over His world.

"Forgotten! Everything will be forgotten!" was repeated in the room.

But in that moment an invisible angel kissed the boy's forehead, and whispered to him:

"Preserve the seed-corn that has been entrusted to thee, that it may bear fruit. Guard it well! Through thee, my child, the obliterated inscription on the old tombstone shall be chronicled in golden letters to future generations! The old pair shall wander again arm in arm through the streets, and smile, and sit with their fresh healthy faces under the lime tree on the bench by the steep stairs, and nod at rich and poor. The seed-corn of this hour shall ripen in the course of time to a blooming poem. The beautiful and the good shall not be forgotten; it shall live on in legend and in song."

THE OLD BACHELOR'S NIGHTCAP.

THERE is a street in Copenhagen that has this strange name—
"Hysken Sträde." Whence comes this name and what is its meaning?
It is said to be German; but injustice has been done to the Germans in
this matter, for it would have to be "Häuschen," and not "Hysken."
For here stood, once upon a time, and indeed for a great many years, a
few little houses, which were principally nothing more than wooden
booths, just as we see now in the market-places at fair-time. They
were, perhaps a little larger, and had windows; but the panes consisted
of horn or bladder, for glass was then too expensive to be used in every
house. But then we are speaking of a long time ago—so long since,
that grandfather and great-grandfather, when they talked about them,
used to speak of them as "the old times"—in fact, it is several centuries
ago.

The rich merchants in Bremen and Lubeck carried on trade with
Copenhagen. They did not reside in the town themselves, but sent

their clerks, who lived in the wooden booths in the Häuschen Street, and sold beer and spices. The German beer was good, and there were many kinds of it, as there were, for instance, Bremen, and Prussinger, and Sous beer, and even Brunswick mumm; and quantities of spices were sold—saffron, and aniseed, and ginger, and especially pepper. Yes, pepper was the chief article here; and so it happened that the German clerks got the nickname "pepper gentry;" and there was a condition made with them in Lubeck and in Bremen, that they would not marry at Copenhagen, and many of them became very old. They had to care for themselves, and to look after their own comforts, and to put out their own fires—when they had any; and some of them became very solitary old boys, with eccentric ideas and eccentric habits. From them all unmarried men, who have attained a certain age, are called in Denmark "pepper gentry;" and this must be understood by all who wish to comprehend this history.

The "pepper gentleman" becomes a butt for ridicule, and is continually told that he ought to put on his nightcap, and draw it down over his eyes, and do nothing but sleep. The boys sing,

> "Cut, cut wood,
> Poor bachelor so good.
> Go, take your nightcap, go to rest,
> For 't is the nightcap suits you best!"

Yes, that's what they sing about the "pepperer"—thus they make game of the poor bachelor and his nightcap, and turn it into ridicule, just because they know very little about either. Ah, that kind of nightcap no one should wish to earn! And why not?—We shall hear.

In the old times the "Housekin Street" was not paved, and the people stumbled out of one hole into another, as in a neglected byeway; and it was narrow too. The booths leaned side by side, and stood so close together that in the summer-time a sail was often stretched from one booth to its opposite neighbour, on which occasion the fragrance of pepper, saffron, and ginger became doubly powerful. Behind the counters young men were seldom seen. The clerks were generally old boys; but they did not look like what we should fancy them, namely, with wig, and nightcap, and plush small-clothes, and with waistcoat and coat buttoned up to the chin. No, grandfather's great-grandfather may look like that, and has been thus portrayed, but the "pepper gentry" had no superfluous means, and accordingly did not have their portraits taken; though, indeed, it would be interesting now to have a picture of one of them, as he stood behind the counter or went to church on holy days. His hat was high-crowned and broad-brimmed, and sometimes one of the youngest clerks would mount a feather. The woollen shirt was hidden behind a broad clean collar, the close jacket was buttoned up to the chin, and the cloak hung loose over it; and the trousers were tucked into the broad-toed shoes, for the clerks did not wear stockings. In their girdles they sported a dinner-knife and spoon, and a larger knife was placed there also for the defence of the owner; and this weapon was often very necessary. Just so was

Anthony, one of the oldest clerks, clad on high days and holy days, except that, instead of a high-crowned hat, he wore a low bonnet, and under it a knitted cap (a regular nightcap), to which he had grown so accustomed that it was always on his head; and he had two of them— nightcaps, of course. The old fellow was a subject for a painter. He was as thin as a lath, had wrinkles clustering round his eyes and mouth, and long bony fingers, and bushy grey eyebrows: over the left eye hung quite a tuft of hair, and that did not look very handsome, though it made him very noticeable. People knew that he came from Bremen; but that was not his native place, though his master lived there. His own native place was in Thuringia, the town of Eisenach, close by the Wartburg. Old Anthony did not speak much of this, but he thought of it all the more.

The old clerks of the Häuschen Street did not often come together. Each one remained in his booth, which was closed early in the evening; and then it looked dark enough in the street: only a faint glimmer of light forced its way through the little horn-pane in the roof; and in the booth sat, generally on his bed, the old bachelor, his German hymn-book in his hand, singing an evening psalm in a low voice; or he went about in the booth till late into the night, and busied himself about all sorts of things. It was certainly not an amusing life. To be a stranger in a strange land is a bitter lot: nobody cares for you, unless you happen to get in anybody's way.

Often when it was dark night outside, with snow and rain, the place looked very gloomy and lonely. No lamps were to be seen, with the exception of one solitary light hanging before the picture of the Virgin that was fastened against the wall. The plash of the water against the neighbouring rampart at the castle wharf could be plainly heard. Such evenings are long and dreary, unless people devise some employment for themselves. There is not always packing or unpacking to do, nor can the scales be polished or paper bags be made continually; and, failing these, people should devise other employment for themselves. And that is just what old Anthony did; for he used to mend his clothes and put pieces on his boots. When he at last sought his couch, he used from habit to keep his nightcap on. He drew it down a little closer; but soon he would push it up again, to see if the light had been properly extinguished. He would touch it, press the wick together, and then lie down on the other side, and draw his nightcap down again; but then a doubt would come upon him, if every coal in the little fire-pan below had been properly deadened and put out—a tiny spark might have been left burning, and might set fire to something and cause damage. And therefore he rose from his bed, and crept down the ladder, for it could scarcely be called a stair. And when he came to the fire-pan not a spark was to be discovered, and he might just go back again. But often, when he had gone half of the way back, it would occur to him that the shutters might not be securely fastened; yes, then his thin legs must carry him downstairs once more. He was cold, and his teeth chattered in his mouth when he crept back again to bed:

for the cold seems to become doubly severe when it knows it cannot stay much longer. He drew up the coverlet closer around him, and pulled down the nightcap lower over his brows, and turned his thoughts away from trade and from the labours of the day. But that did not procure him agreeable entertainment; for now old thoughts came and put up their curtains, and these curtains have sometimes pins in them, with which one pricks oneself, and one cries out " Oh !" and they prick into one's flesh and burn so, that the tears sometimes come into one's eyes ; and that often happened to old Anthony—hot tears. The largest pearls streamed forth, and fell on the coverlet or on the floor, and then they sounded as if one of his heart-strings had broken. Sometimes again they seemed to rise up in flame, illuminating a picture of life that never faded out of his heart. If he then dried his eyes with his night-cap, the tear and the picture were indeed crushed, but the source of the tears remained, and welled up afresh from his heart. The pictures did not come up in the order in which the scenes had occurred in reality, for very often the most painful would come together ; then again the most joyful would come, but these had the deepest shadows of all.

The beech woods of Denmark are acknowledged to be fine, but the woods of Thuringia arose far more beautiful in the eyes of Anthony. More mighty and more venerable seemed to him the old oaks around the proud knightly castle, where the creeping plants hung down over the stony blocks of the rock ; sweeter there bloomed the flowers of the apple tree than in the Danish land. This he remembered very vividly. A glittering tear rolled down over his cheek ; and in this tear he could plainly see two children playing—a boy and a girl. The boy had red cheeks, and yellow curling hair, and honest blue eyes. He was the son of the merchant Anthony—it was himself. The little girl had brown eyes and black hair, and had a bright clever look. She was the burgo-master's daughter Molly. The two were playing with an apple. They shook the apple, and heard the pips rattling in it. Then they cut the apple in two, and each of them took a half ; they divided even the pips, and ate them all but one, which the little girl proposed that they should lay in the earth.

" Then you shall see," she said, " what will come out. It will be something you don't at all expect. A whole apple tree will come out, but not directly."

And she put the pip in a flower-pot, and both were very busy and eager about it. The boy made a hole in the earth with his finger, and the little girl dropped the pip in it, and they both covered it with earth.

" Now, you must not take it out to-morrow to see if it has struck root," said Molly. " That won't do at all. I did it with my flowers ; but only twice. I wanted to see if they were growing — and I didn't know any better then—and the plants withered."

Anthony took away the flower-pot, and every morning, the whole winter through, he looked at it ; but nothing was to be seen but the black earth. At length, however, the spring came, and the sun shone warm again ; and two little green leaves came up out of the pot.

"Those are for me and Molly," said the boy. "That's beautiful—that's marvellously beautiful!"

Soon a third leaf made its appearance. Whom did that represent? Yes, and there came another, and yet another. Day by day and week by week they grew larger, and the plant began to take the form of a real tree. And all this was now mirrored in a single tear, which was wiped away and disappeared; but it might come again from its source in the heart of old Anthony.

In the neighbourhood of Eisenach a row of stony mountains rises up.

IMPERTINENT MOLLY.

One of these mountains is round in outline, and lifts itself above the rest, naked and without tree, bush, or grass. It is called the Venus Mount. In this mountain dwells Lady Venus, one of the deities of the heathen times. She is also called Lady Holle; and every child in and around Eisenach has heard about her. She it was who lured Tannhauser, the noble knight and minstrel, from the circle of the singers of the Wartburg into her mountain.

Little Molly and Anthony often stood by this mountain; and once Molly said,

"You may knock and say, 'Lady Holle, open the door—Tannhauser s here!'"

But Anthony did not dare. Molly, however, did it, though she only said the words "Lady Holle, Lady Holle!" aloud and distinctly; the rest she muttered so indistinctly that Anthony felt convinced she had not really said anything; and yet she looked as bold and saucy as possible—as saucy as when she sometimes came round him with other little girls in the garden, and all wanted to kiss him because he did not like to be kissed and tried to keep them off; and she was the only one who dared to kiss him in spite of his resistance.

"*I* may kiss him!" she would say proudly.

That was her vainity; and Anthony submitted, and thought no more about it.

How charming and how teazing Molly was! It was said that Lady Holle in the mountain was beautiful also, but that her beauty was like that of a tempting fiend. The greatest beauty and grace was possessed by Saint Elizabeth, the patron of the country, the pious Princess of Thuringia, whose good actions have been immortalized in many places in legends and stories. In the chapel her picture was hanging, surrounded by silver lamps; but it was not in the least like Molly.

The apple tree which the two children had planted grew year by year, and became taller and taller—so tall, that it had to be transplanted into the garden, into the fresh air, where the dew fell and the sun shone warm. And the tree developed itself strongly, so that it could resist the winter. And it seemed as if, after the rigour of the cold season was past, it put forth blossoms in spring for very joy. In the autumn it brought two apples—one for Molly and one for Anthony. It could not well have produced less.

The tree had grown apace, and Molly grew like the tree. She was as fresh as an apple blossom: but Anthony was not long to behold this flower. All things change! Molly's father left his old home, and Molly went with him, far away. Yes, in our time steam has made the journey they took a matter of a few hours, but then more than a day and a night were necessary to go so far eastward from Eisenach to the farthest border of Thuringia, to the city which is still called Weimar.

And Molly wept, and Anthony wept; but all their tears melted into one, and this tear had the rosy, charming hue of joy. For Molly told him she loved him—loved him more than all the splendours of Weimar.

One, two, three years went by, and during this period two letters were received. One came by a carrier, and a traveller brought the other. The way was long and difficult, and passed through many windings by towns and villages.

Often had Molly and Anthony heard of Tristram and Iseult, and often had the boy applied the story to himself and Molly, though the name Tristram was said to mean "born in tribulation," and that did not apply to Anthony, nor would he ever be able to think, like Tristram, "She has forgotten me." But, indeed, Iseult did not forget her faithful knight; and when both were laid to rest in the earth, one on each side of the church, the linden trees grew from their graves over the church roof, and there encountered each other in bloom. Anthony thought that was beautiful, but mournful; but it could not become mournful between him and Molly: and he whistled a song of the old minnesinger, Walter of the Vogelverde:

> " Under the lindens
> Upon the heath."

And especially that passage appeared charming to him:

> "From the forest, down in the vale,
> Sang her sweet song the nightingale."

This song was often in his mouth, and he sang and whistled it in the moonlight night, when he rode along the deep hollow way on horseback to get to Weimar and visit Molly. He wished to come unexpectedly, and he came unexpectedly.

He was made welcome with full goblets of wine, with jovial company, fine company, and a pretty room and a good bed were provided for him; and yet his reception was not what he had dreamed and fancied it would be. He could not understand himself — he could not understand the others; but *we* can understand it. One may be admitted into a house and associate with a family without becoming one of them. One may converse together as one would converse in a post-carriage, and know one another as people know each other on a journey, each incommoding the other and wishing that either oneself or the good neighbour were away. Yes, that was the kind of thing Anthony felt.

" I am an honest girl," said Molly, " and I myself will tell you what it is. Much has changed since we were children together — changed inwardly and outwardly. Habit and will have no power over our hearts. Anthony, I should not like to have an enemy in you, now that I shall soon be far away from here. Believe me, I entertain the best wishes for you; but to feel for you what I know now one may feel for a man, has never been the case with me. You must reconcile yourself to this. Farewell, Anthony !"

And Anthony bade her farewell. No tear came into his eye, but he felt that he was no longer Molly's friend. Hot iron and cold iron alike take the skin from our lips, and we have the same feeling when we kiss it: and he kissed himself into hatred as into love.

Within twenty-four hours Anthony was back in Eisenach, though certainly the horse on which he rode was ruined.

" What matter!" he said: " I am ruined too; and I will destroy everything that can remind me of her, or of Lady Holle, or Venus the heathen woman ! I will break down the apple tree and tear it up by the roots, so that it shall never bear flower or fruit more!"

But the apple tree was not broken down, though he himself was broken down, and bound on a couch by fever. What was it that raised him up again? A medicine was presented to him which had strength to do this — the bitterest of medicines, that shakes up body and spirit together. Anthony's father ceased to be the richest of merchants. Heavy days—days of trial—were at the door; misfortune came rolling into the house like great waves of the sea. The father became a poor man. Sorrow and suffering took away his strength. Then Anthony had to think of something else besides nursing his love-sorrows and his anger against Molly. He had to take his father's place—to give orders, to help, to act energetically, and at last to go out into the world and earn his bread.

Anthony went to Bremen. There he learned what poverty and hard living meant; and these sometimes make the heart hard, and sometimes soften it, even too much.

How different the world was, and how different the people were from what he had supposed them to be in his childhood! What were the minne-singer's songs to him now?—an echo, a vanishing sound! Yes. that is what he thought sometimes; but again the songs would sound in his soul, and his heart became gentle.

"God's will is best!" he would say then. "It was well that I was not permitted to keep Molly's heart—that she did not remain true to me. What would it have led to now, when fortune has turned away from me? She quitted me before she knew of this loss of prosperity, or had any notion of what awaited me. That was a mercy of Providence towards me. Everything has happened for the best. It was not her fault — and I have been so bitter, and have shown so much rancour towards her!"

And years went by. Anthony's father was dead, and strangers lived in the old house. But Anthony was destined to see it again. His rich employer sent him on commercial journeys, and his duty led him into his native town of Eisenach. The old Wartburg stood unchanged on the mountain, with "the monk and the nun" hewn out in stone. The great oaks gave to the scene the outlines it had possessed in his childish days. The Venus Mount glimmered grey and naked over the valley. He would have been glad to cry, "Lady Holle, Lady Holle, unlock the door, and I shall enter and remain in my native earth!"

That was a sinful thought, and he blessed himself to drive it away. Then a little bird out of the thicket sang clearly, and the old minne-song came into his mind:

> "From the forest, down in the vale,
> Sang her sweet song the nightingale."

And here in the town of his childhood, which he thus saw again through tears, much came back into his remembrance. The paternal house stood as in the old times; but the garden was altered, and a field-path led over a portion of the old ground, and the apple tree that he had not broken down stood there, but outside the garden, on the farther side of the path. But the sun threw its rays on the apple tree as in the old days, the dew descended gently upon it as then, and it bore such a burden of fruit that the branches were bent down towards the earth.

"That flourishes!" he said. "The tree can grow!"

Nevertheless, one of the branches of the tree was broken. Mischievous hands had torn it down towards the ground; for now the tree stood by the public way.

"They break its blossoms off without a feeling of thankfulness — they steal its fruit and break the branches. One might say of the tree as has been said of some men — 'It was not sung at his cradle that it should come thus.' How brightly its history began, and what has it come to? Forsake and forgotten—a garden tree by the hedge, in the field, and on the public way! There it stands unprotected, plundered, and broken! It has certainly not died, but in the course of years the number of blossoms will diminish; at last the fruit will cease altogether; and at last—at last all will be over!"

Such were Anthony's thoughts under the tree; such were his thoughts during many a night in the lonely chamber of the wooden house in the distant land—in the Häuschen Street in Copenhagen, whither his rich employer, the Bremen merchant, had sent him, first making it a condition that he should not marry.

"Marry! Ha, ha!" he laughed bitterly to himself.

Winter had set in early; it was freezing hard. Without, a snowstorm was raging, so that every one who could do so remained at home; thus, too, it happened that those who lived opposite to Anthony did not notice that for two days his house had not been unlocked, and that he did not show himself; for who would go out unnecessarily in such weather?

They were grey, gloomy days; and in the house, whose windows were not of glass, twilight only alternated with dark night. Old Anthony had not left his bed during the two days, for he had not the strength to rise; he had for a long time felt in his limbs the hardness of the weather. Forsaken by all, lay the old bachelor, unable to help himself. He could scarcely reach the water-jug that he had placed by his bed-side, and the last drop it contained had been consumed. It was not fever, nor sickness, but old age that had struck him down. Up yonder, where his couch was placed, he was overshadowed as it were by continual night. A little spider, which, however, he could not see, busily and cheerfully span its web around him, as if it were weaving a little crape banner that should wave when the old man closed his eyes.

The time was very slow, and long, and dreary. Tears he had none to shed, nor did he feel pain. The thought of Molly never came into his mind. He felt as if the world and its noise concerned him no longer—as if he were lying outside the world, and no one were thinking of him. For a moment he felt a sensation of hunger—of thirst. Yes, he felt them both. But nobody came to tend him—nobody. He thought of those who had once suffered want; of Saint Elizabeth, as she had once wandered on earth; of her, the saint of his home and of his childhood, the noble Duchess of Thuringia, the benevolent lady who had been accustomed to visit the lowliest cottages, bringing to the inmates refreshment and comfort. Her pious deeds shone bright upon his soul. He thought of her as she had come to distribute words of comfort, binding up the wounds of the afflicted and giving meat to the hungry, though her stern husband had chidden her for it. He thought of the legend told of her, how she had been carrying the full basket containing food and wine, when her husband, who watched her footsteps, came forth and asked angrily what she was carrying, whereupon she answered, in fear and trembling, that the basket contained roses which she had plucked in the garden; how he had torn away the white cloth from the basket, and a miracle had been performed for the pious lady; for bread and wine, and everything in the basket, had been transformed into roses!

Thus the saint's memory dwelt in Anthony's quiet mind; thus she stood bodily before his downcast face, before his warehouse in the simple booth in the Danish land. He uncovered his head, and looked

THE OPPOSITE NEIGHBOUR LOOKS AFTER OLD ANTHONY.

into her gentle eyes, and everything around him was beautiful and roseate. Yes, the roses seemed to unfold themselves in fragrance. There came to him a sweet, peculiar odour of apples, and he saw a blooming apple tree, which spread its branches above him---it was the tree which Molly and he had planted together.

And the tree strewed down its fragrant leaves upon him, cooling his burning brow. The leaves fell upon his parched lips, and were like strengthening bread and wine; and they fell upon his breast, and he felt reassured and calm, and inclined to sleep peacefully.

"Now I shall sleep," he whispered to himself. "Sleep is refreshing. To-morrow I shall be upon my feet again, and strong and well—glorious, wonderful! That apple tree, planted in true affection, now stands before me in heavenly radiance——"

And he slept.

The day afterwards—it was the third day that his shop had remained closed—the snow-storm had ceased, and a neighbour from the opposite house came over towards the booth where dwelt old Anthony, who had not yet shown himself. Anthony lay stretched upon his bed—dead—with his old cap clutched tightly in his two hands! They did not put that cap on his head in his coffin, for he had a new white one.

Where were now the tears that he had wept? What had become of the pearls? They remained in the nightcap—and the true ones do not come out in the wash—they were preserved in the nightcap, and in time forgotten; but the old thoughts and the old dreams still remained in the "bachelor's nightcap." Don't wish for such a cap for yourself. It would make your forehead very hot, would make your pulse beat feverishly, and conjure up dreams which appear like reality. The first who wore that identical cap afterwards felt all that at once, though it was half a century afterwards; and that man was the burgomaster himself, who, with his wife and eleven children, was well and firmly established, and had amassed a very tolerable amount of wealth. He was immediately seized with dreams of unfortunate love, of bankruptcy, and of heavy times.

"Hallo! how the nightcap burns!" he cried, and tore it from his head.

And a pearl rolled out, and another, and another, and they sounded and glittered.

"This must be gout," said the burgomaster. "Something dazzles my eyes!"

They were tears, shed half a century before by old Anthony from Eisenach.

Every one who afterwards put that nightcap upon his head had visions and dreams which excited him not a little. His own history was changed into that of Anthony, and became a story; in fact, many stories. But some one else may tell *them*. We have told the first. And our last word is—don't wish for "the Old Bachelor's Nightcap."

A ROSE FROM THE GRAVE OF HOMER.

ALL the songs of the East tell of the love of the nightingale to the rose; in the silent starlit nights the winged songster serenades his fragrant flower.

Not far from Smyrna, under the lofty plantains, where the merchant drives his loaded camels, that proudly lift their long necks and tramp over the holy ground, I saw a hedge of roses. Wild pigeons flew among the branches of the high trees, and their wings glistened, while a sunbeam glided over them, as if they were of mother-o'-pearl.

The rose hedge bore a flower which was the most beautiful among all, and the nightingale sang to her of his woes; but the Rose was silent—not a dew-drop lay, like a tear of sympathy, upon her leaves: she bent down over a few great stones.

"Here rests the greatest singer of the world!" said the Rose: "over his tomb will I pour out my fragrance, and on it I will let fall my leaves when the storm tears them off. He who sang of Troy became earth, and from that earth I have sprung. I, a rose from the grave of Homer, am too lofty to bloom for a poor nightingale!"

And the nightingale sang himself to death.

THE ROSE TREASURED BY THE POET.

The camel driver came with his loaded camels and his black slaves: his little son found the dead bird, and buried the little songster in the grave of the great Homer. And the Rose trembled in the wind. The evening came, and the Rose wrapped her leaves more closely together, and dreamed thus:

"It was a fair sunshiny day; a crowd of strangers drew near, for they had undertaken a pilgrimage to the grave of Homer. Among the strangers was a singer from the North, the home of clouds and of the Northern Light. He plucked the Rose, placed it in a book, and carried it away into another part of the world, to his distant fatherland. The Rose faded with grief, and lay in the narrow book, which he opened in his home, saying, 'Here is a rose from the grave of Homer.'"

This the flower dreamed; and sne awoke and trembled in the wind. A drop of dew fell from the leaves upon the singer's grave. The sun rose, and the Rose glowed more beauteous than before; it was a hot day, and she was in her own warm Asia. Then footsteps were heard, and Frankish strangers came, such as the Rose had seen in her dream; and among the strangers was a poet from the North: he plucked the Rose, pressed a kiss upon her fresh mouth, and carried her away to the home of the clouds and of the Northern Light.

Like a mummy the flower corpse now rests in his "Iliad," and, as in a dream, she hears him open the book and say, "Here is a rose from the grave of Homer."

THE WIND TELLS ABOUT WALDEMAR DAA AND HIS DAUGHTERS.

WHEN the wind sweeps across the grass, the field has a ripple like a pond, and when it sweeps across the corn the field waves to and fro like a high sea. That is called the wind's dance; but the wind does not dance only, he also tells stories; and how loudly he can sing out of his deep chest, and how different it sounds in the tree-tops in the forest, and through the loopholes and clefts and cracks in walls! Do you see how the wind drives the clouds up yonder, like a frightened flock of sheep? Do you hear how the wind howls down here through the open valley, like a watchman blowing his horn? With wonderful tones he whistles and screams down the chimney and into the fireplace! The fire crackles and flares up, and shines far into the room, and the little place is warm and snug, and it is pleasant to sit there listening to the sounds. Let the Wind speak, for he knows plenty of stories and fairy tales, many more than are known to any of us. Just hear what the Wind can tell.

"Huh—uh—ush! roar along!" That is the burden of the song.

"By the shores of the Great Belt, one of the straits that unite the Cattegat with the Baltic, lies an old mansion with thick red walls," says the Wind. "I know every stone in it; I saw it when it still belonged to the castle of Marsk Stig on the promontory. But it had to be pulled down, and the stone was used again for the walls of a new mansion in another place, the baronial mansion of Borreby, which still stands by the coast.

"I knew them, the noble lords and ladies, the changing races that dwelt there, and now I'm going to tell about Waldemar Daa and his daughters. How proudly he carried himself—he was of royal blood! He could do more than merely hunt the stag and empty the wine-can. 'It *shall* be done,' he was accustomed to say.

"His wife walked proudly in gold-embroidered garments over the polished marble floors. The tapestries were gorgeous, the furniture was expensive and artistically carved. She had brought gold and silver plate with her into the house, and there was German beer in the cellar. Black fiery horses neighed in the stables. There was a wealthy look about the house of Borreby at that time, when wealth was still at home there.

"Four children dwelt there also; three delicate maidens, Ida, Joanna, and Anna Dorothea: I have never forgotten their names.

"They were rich people, noble people, born in affluence, nurtured in affluence.

"Huh—sh! roar along!" sang the Wind; and then he continued:

"I did not see here, as in other great noble houses, the high-born lady sitting among her woman in the great hall turning the spinning-wheel: here she swept the sounding chords of the cithern, and sang to the

THE HOME OF WALDEMAR DAA.

sound, but not always old Danish melodies, but songs of a strange land. It was 'live and let live' here: stranger guests came from far and near, the music sounded, the goblets clashed, and I was not able to drown the noise," said the Wind. "Ostentation, and haughtiness, and splendour, and display, and rule were there, but the fear of the Lord was not there.

"And it was just on the evening of the first day of May," the Wind continued. "I came from the west, and had seen how the ships were being crushed by the waves, with all on board, and flung on the west coast of Jutland. I had hurried across the heath, and over Jutland's wood-girt eastern coast, and over the Island of Fünen, and now I drove over the Great Belt, groaning and sighing.

"Then I lay down to rest on the shore of Seeland, in the neighbourhood of the great house of Borreby, where the forest, the splendid oak orest, still rose.

"The young men-servants of the neighbourhood were collecting branches and brushwood under the oak trees; the largest and driest they could find they carried into the village, and piled them up in a heap, and set them on fire; and men and maids danced, singing in a circle round the blazing pile.

"I lay quite quiet," continued the Wind; "but I silently touched a branch, which had been brought by the handsomest of the men-servants, and the wood blazed up brightly, blazed up higher than all the rest; and now he was the chosen one, and bore the name of Street-goat, and might choose his Street-lamb first from among the maids; and there was mirth and rejoicing, greater than I had ever heard before in the halls of the rich baronial mansion.

"And the noble lady drove towards the baronial mansion, with her three daughters, in a gilded carriage drawn by six horses. The daughters were young and fair — three charming blossoms, rose, lily, and pale hyacinth. The mother was a proud tulip, and never acknowledged the salutation of one of the men or maids who paused in their sport to do her honour: the gracious lady seemed a flower that was rather stiff in the stalk.

"Rose, lily, and pale hyacinth; yes, I saw them all three.! Whose lambkins will they one day become? thought I; their Street-goat will be a gallant knight, perhaps a Prince. Huh—sh! hurry along! hurry along!

"Yes, the carriage rolled on with them, and the peasant people resumed their dancing. They rode that summer through all the villages round about. But in the night, when I rose again," said the Wind, "the very noble lady lay down, to rise again no more: that thing came upon her which comes upon all—there is nothing new in that.

"Waldemar Daa stood for a space silent and thoughtful. 'The proudest tree can be bowed without being broken,' said a voice within him. His daughters wept, and all the people in the mansion wiped their eyes; but Lady Daa had driven away—and I drove away too, and rushed along, huh—sh!'" said the Wind.

"I returned again; I often returned again over the Island of Fünen and the shores of the Belt, and I sat down by Borreby, by the splendid oak wood; there the heron made his nest, and wood pigeons haunted the place, and blue ravens, and even the black stork. It was still spring; some of them were yet sitting on their eggs, others had already hatched their young. But how they flew up, how they cried! The axe sounded, blow upon blow: the wood was to be felled. Waldemar Daa wanted to build a noble ship, a man-of-war, a three-decker, which the King would be sure to buy; and therefore the wood must be felled, the landmark of the seamen, the refuge of the birds. The hawk startled up and flew away, for its nest was destroyed; the heron and all the birds of the forest became homeless, and flew about in fear and in anger: I could well understand how they felt. Crows and ravens croaked aloud as if in scorn. 'Crack! crack! the nest cracks, cracks, cracks!'

"Far in the interior of the wood, where the noisy swarm of labourers were working, stood Waldemar Daa and his three daughters; and all laughed at the wild cries of the birds; only one, the youngest, Anna Dorothea, felt grieved in her heart; and when they made preparations to fell a tree that was almost dead, and on whose naked branches the black stork had built his nest, whence the little storks were stretching out their heads, she begged for mercy for the little things, and tears came into her eyes. Therefore the tree with the black stork's nest was left standing. The tree was not worth speaking of.

"There was a great hewing and sawing, and a three-decker was built. The architect was of low origin, but of great pride; his eyes and forehead told how clever he was, and Waldemar Daa was fond of listening to him, and so was Waldemar's daughter Ida, the eldest, who was now fifteen years old; and while he built a ship for the father, he was building for himself an airy castle, into which he and Ida were to go as a married couple—which might indeed have happened, if the castle with stone walls, and ramparts, and moats had remained. But in spite of his wise head, the architect remained but a poor bird; and, indeed, what business has a sparrow to take part in a dance of peacocks? Huh—sh! I careered away, and he careered away too, for he was not allowed to stay; and little Ida very soon got over it, because she was obliged to get over it.

"The proud black horses were neighing in the stable; they were worth looking at, and accordingly they *were* looked at. The admiral, who had been sent by the King himself to inspect the new ship and take measures for its purchase, spoke loudly in admiration of the beautiful horses.

"I heard all that," said the Wind. "I accompanied the gentlemen through the open door, and strewed blades of straw like bars of gold before their feet. Waldemar Daa wanted to have gold, and the admiral wished for the proud black horses, and that is why he praised them so much; but the hint was not taken, and consequently the ship was not bought. It remained on the shore covered over with boards, a Noan's ark that never got to the water—Huh—sh! rush away! away!—and that was a pity.

"In the winter, when the fields were covered with snow, and the water with large blocks of ice that I blew up on to the coast," continued the Wind, "crows and ravens came, all as black as might be, great flocks of them, and alighted on the dead, deserted, lonely ship by the shore, and croaked in hoarse accents of the wood that was no more; of the many pretty birds' nests destroyed, and the little ones left without a home; and all for the sake of that great bit of lumber, that proud ship that never sailed forth.

"I made the snow-flakes whirl, and the snow lay like a great lake high around the ship, and drifted over it. I let it hear my voice, that it might know what a storm has to say. Certainly I did my part towards teaching it seamanship. Huh—sh! push along!

"And the winter passed away; winter and summer, both passed away, and they are still passing away, even as I pass away; as the snow whirls along, and the apple blossom whirls along, and the leaves fall—away! away! away!—and men are passing away too!

IN THE WOOD.

"But the daughters were still young, and little Ida was a rose, as fair to look upon as on the day when the architect saw her. I often seized her long brown hair, when she stood in the garden by the apple tree, musing, and not heeding how I strewed blossoms on her hair, and loosened it, while she was gazing at the red sun and the golden sky, through the dark underwood and the trees of the garden.

"Her sister was bright and slender as a lily. Joanna had height and deportment, but was like her mother, rather stiff in the stalk. She was very fond of walking through the great hall, where hung the portraits of her ancestors. The women were painted in dresses of silk and velvet, with a tiny little hat, embroidered with pearls, on their plaited hair. They were handsome women. The gentlemen were represented clad in steel, or in costly cloaks lined with squirrel's skin; they wore little ruffs, and swords at their sides, but not buckled to their hips. Where would Joanna's picture find its place on that wall some day? and how would *he* look, her noble lord and husband? This is what she thought of, and of this she spoke softly to herself. I heard it as I swept into the long hall and turned round to come out again.

"Anna Dorothea, the pale hyacinth, a child of fourteen, was quiet and thoughtful; her great deep blue eyes had a musing look, but the childlike smile still played around her lips: I was not able to blow it away, nor did I wish to do so.

"We met in the garden, in the hollow lane, in the field and meadow; she gathered herbs and flowers which she knew would be useful to her father in concocting the drinks and drops he distilled. Waldemar Daa was arrogant and proud, but he was also a learned man, and knew a great deal. That was no secret, and many opinions were expressed concerning it. In his chimney there was fire even in summer-time. He would lock the door of his room, and for days the fire would be poked and raked; but of this he did not talk much—the forces of nature must be conquered in silence; and soon he would discover the art of making the best thing of all—the red gold.

"That is why the chimney was always smoking, therefore the flames crackled so frequently. Yes, I was there too," said the Wind. " 'Let it go,' I sang down through the chimney: 'it will end in smoke, air, coals and ashes! You will burn yourself! Hu-uh-ush! drive away! drive away!' But Waldemar Daa did *not* drive it away.

"The splendid black horses in the stable—what became of them? what became of the old gold and silver vessels in cupboards and chests, the cows in the fields, and the house and home itself? Yes, they may melt, may melt in the golden crucible, and yet yield no gold.

"Empty grew the barns and store-rooms, the cellars and magazines. The servants decreased in number, and the mice multiplied. Then a window broke, and then another, and I could get in elsewhere besides at the door," said the Wind. " 'Where the chimney smokes the meal is being cooked,' the proverb says. But here the chimney smoked that devoured all the meals, for the sake of the red gold.

"I blew through the courtyard gate like a watchman blowing his horn," the Wind went on, " but no watchman was there. I twirled the weathercock round on the summit of the tower, and it creaked like the snoring of the warder, but no warder was there; only mice and rats were there. Poverty laid the table-cloth; poverty sat in the wardrobe and in the larder; the door fell off its hinges, cracks and fissures made their appearance, and I went in and out at pleasure; and that is how I know all about it.

"Amid smoke and ashes, amid sorrow and sleepless nights, the hair and beard of the master turned grey, and deep furrows showed themselves around his temples; his skin turned pale and yellow, as his eyes looked greedily for the gold, the desired gold.

"I blew the smoke and ashes into his face and beard: the result of his labour was debt instead of pelf. I sung through the burst window-panes and the yawning clefts in the walls. I blew into the chests of drawers belonging to the daughters, wherein lay the clothes that had become faded and threadbare from being worn over and over again. That was not the song that had been sung at the children's cradle. The lordly life had changed to a life of penury. I was the only one who rejoiced aloud in that castle," said the Wind. "I snowed them up, and they say snow keeps people warm. They had no wood, and the forest from which they might have brought it was cut down. It was a biting frost. I rushed in through loopholes and passages, over gables and roofs, that I might be brisk. They were lying in bed because of the cold, the three high-born daughters, and their father was crouching under his leathern coverlet. Nothing to bite, nothing to break, no fire on the hearth—there was a life for high-born people! Huh-sh! let it go! But that is what my Lord Daa could *not* do--he could *not* let it go.

"'After winter comes spring,' he said. 'After want, good times will come: one must not lose patience; one must learn to wait! Now my house and lands are mortgaged, it is indeed high time; and the gold will soon come. At Easter!'

"I heard how he spoke thus, looking at a spider's web. 'Thou cunning little weaver, thou dost teach me perseverance. Let them tear thy web, and thou wilt begin it again, and complete it. Let them destroy it again, and thou wilt resolutely begin to work again—again! That is what we must do, and that will repay itself at last.'

"It was the morning of Easter-day. The bells sounded from the neighbouring church, and the sun seemed to rejoice in the sky. The master had watched through the night in feverish excitement, and had been melting and cooling, distilling and mixing. I heard him sighing like a soul in despair; I heard him praying, and I noticed how he held his breath. The lamp was burned out, but he did not notice it. I blew at the fire of coals, and it threw its red glow upon his ghastly white face, lighting it up with a glare, and his sunken eyes looked forth wildly out of their deep sockets—but they became larger and larger, as though they would burst.

"Look at the alchymic glass! It glows in the crucible, red-hot, and pure and heavy! He lifted it with a trembling hand, and cried with a trembling voice, 'Gold! gold!'

"He was quite dizzy—I could have blown him down," said the Wind; "but I only fanned the glowing coals, and accompanied him through the door to where his daughters sat shivering. His coat was powdered with ashes, and there were ashes in his beard and in his tangled hair. He stood straight up, and held his costly treasure on high, in the brittle glass. 'Found, found!—Gold, gold!' he shouted, and again held aloft the glass to let it flash in the sunshine; but his hand trembled, and the alchymic glass fell clattering to the ground, and broke into a thousand pieces; and the last bubble of his happiness had burst! Hu-uh-ush! rushing away!—and I rushed away from the gold-maker's house.

"Late in autumn, when the days are short, and the mist comes and strews cold drops upon the berries and leafless branches, I came back in fresh spirits, rushed through the air, swept the sky clear, and snapped the dry twigs—which is certainly no great labour, but yet it must be done. Then there was another kind of sweeping clean at Waldemar Daa's, in the mansion of Borreby. His enemy, Owe Rainel. of Basnäs, was there with the mortgage of the house and everything it contained in his pocket. I drummed against the broken window-panes, beat against the old rotten doors, and whistled through cracks and rifts—huh-sh! Mr. Owe Rainel did not like staying there. Ida and Anna Dorothea wept bitterly; Joanna stood pale and proud, and bit her thumb till it bled—but what could that avail? Owe Rainel offered to allow Waldemar Daa to remain in the mansion till the end of his life, but no thanks were given him for his offer. I listened to hear what occurred. I saw the ruined gentleman lift his head and throw it back prouder than ever, and I rushed against the house and the old lime trees with such force, that one of the thickest branches broke, one that was not decayed; and the branch remained lying at the entrance as a broom when any one wanted to sweep the place out. and a grand sweeping out there was—I thought it would be so.

"It was hard on that day to preserve one's composure; but their will was as hard as their fortune.

"There was nothing they could call their own except the clothes they wore: yes, there was one thing more—the alchymist's glass, a new one that had lately been bought, and filled with what had been gathered up from the ground of the treasure which promised so much but never kept its promise. Waldemar Daa hid the glass in his bosom, and taking his stick in his hand, the once rich gentleman passed with his daughters out of the house of Borreby. I blew cold upon his heated cheeks, I stroked his grey beard and his long white hair, and I sang as well as I could,—'Huh-sh! gone away! gone away!' And that was the end of the wealth and splendour.

"Ida walked on one side of the old man, and Ann Dorothea on the other. Joanna turned round at the entrance—why? Fortune would not turn because she did so. She looked at the old walls of what had once been the castle of Marsk Stig, and perhaps she thought of his daughters:

"'The eldest gave the youngest her hand.
And forth they went to the far-off land.'

Was she thinking of this old song? Here were three of them, and

LEAVING THE OLD HOME.

their father was with them too. They walked along the road on which
they had once driven in their splendid carriage—they walked forth as
beggars, with their father, and wandered out into the open field, and
into a mud hut, which they rented for a dollar and a half a year—into
their new house with the empty rooms and empty vessels. Crows and
magpies fluttered above them, and cried, as if in contempt, 'Craw!
craw! out of the nest! craw! craw!' as they had done in the wood at
Borreby when the trees were felled.

"Daa and his daughters could not help hearing it. I blew about
their ears, for what use would it be that they should listen?

"And they went to live in the mud hut on the open field, and I
wandered away over moor and field, through bare bushes and leafless
forests, to the open waters, the free shores, to other lands—huh-uh-ush!
away, away!—year after year!"

And how did Waldemar Daa and his daughters prosper? The Wind
tell us:

"The one I saw last, yes, for the last time, was Anna Dorothea, the pale hyacinth: then she was old and bent, for it was fifty years afterwards. She lived longer than the rest; she knew all.

"Yonder on the heath, by the Jutland town of Wiborg, stood the fine new house of the canon, built of red bricks with projecting gables; the smoke came up thickly from the chimney. The canon's gentle lady and her beautiful daughters sat in the bay window, and looked over the hawthorn hedge of the garden towards the brown heath. What were they looking at? Their glances rested upon the stork's nest without, and on the hut, which was almost falling in; the roof consisted of moss and houseleek, in so far as a roof existed there at all—the stork's nest covered the greater part of it, and that alone was in proper condition, for it was kept in order by the stork himself.

"That is a house to be looked at, but not to be touched: I must deal gently with it," said the Wind. "For the sake of the stork's nest the hut has been allowed to stand, though it was a blot upon the landscape. They did not like to drive the stork away, therefore the old shed was left standing, and the poor woman who dwelt in it was allowed to stay: she had the Egyptian bird to thank for that; or was it perchance her reward, because she had once interceded for the nest of its black brother in the forest of Borreby? At that time she, the poor woman, was a young child, a pale hyacinth in the rich garden. She remembered all that right well, did Anna Dorothea.

"'Oh! oh!' Yes, people can sigh like the wind moaning in the rushes and reeds. 'Oh! oh!' she sighed, 'no bells sounded at thy burial, Waldemar Daa! The poor schoolboys did not even sing a psalm when the former lord of Borreby was laid in the earth to rest! Oh, everything has an end, even misery. Sister Ida became the wife of a peasant. That was the hardest trial that befell our father, that the husband of a daughter of his should be a miserable serf, whom the proprietor could mount on the wooden horse for punishment! I suppose he is under the ground now. And thou, Ida? Alas, alas! it is not ended yet, wretch that I am! Grant me that I may die, kind Heaven!'

"That was Anna Dorothea's prayer in the wretched hut which was left standing for the sake of the stork.

"I took pity on the fairest of the sisters," said the Wind. "Her courage was like that of a man, and in man's clothes she took service as a sailor on board of a ship. She was sparing of words, and of a dark countenance, but willing at her work. But she did not know how to climb; so I blew her overboard before anybody found out that she was a woman, and, according to my thinking, that was well done!" said the Wind.

"On such an Easter morning as that on which Waldemar Daa had fancied that he had found the red gold, I heard the tones of a psalm under the stork's nest, among the crumbling walls—it was Anna Dorothea's last song.

"There was no window, only a hole in the wall. The sun rose up like a mass of gold, and looked through. What a splendour he diffused! Her eyes and her heart were breaking—but that they would have done, even if the sun had not shone that morning on Anna Dorothea.

"The stork covered her hut till her death. I sang at her grave!" said the Wind. "I sang at her father's grave; I know where his grave is, and where hers is, and nobody else knows it.

"New times, changed times! The old high road now runs through cultivated fields; the new road winds among the trim ditches, and soon the railway will come with its train of carriages, and rush over the graves which are forgotten like the names—hu-ush! passed away! passed away!

"That is the story of Waldemar Daa and his daughters. Tell it better, any of you, if you know how," said the Wind, and turned away —and he was gone.

FIVE OUT OF ONE SHELL.

THERE were five peas in one shell: they were green, and the pod was green, and so they thought all the world was green; and that was just as it should be! The shell grew, and the peas grew; they accommodated themselves to circumstances, sitting all in a row. The sun shone without, and warmed the husk, and the rain made it clear and transparent; it was mild and agreeable in the bright day and in the dark night, just as it should be, and the peas as they sat there became bigger and bigger, and more and more thoughtful, for something they must do.

"Are we to sit here everlastingly?" asked one. "I'm afraid we shall become hard by long sitting. It seems to me there must be something outside—I have a kind of inkling of it."

And weeks went by. The peas became yellow, and the pod also.

"All the world's turning yellow," said they; and they had a right to say it.

Suddenly they felt a tug at the shell. The shell was torn off, passed through human hands, and glided down into the pocket of a jacket, in company with other full pods.

"Now we shall soon be opened!" they said; and that is just what they were waiting for.

"I should like to know who of us will get farthest!" said the smallest of the five. "Yes, now it will soon show itself."

"What is to be will be," said the biggest.

"Crack!" the pod burst, and all the five peas rolled out into the bright sunshine. There they lay in a child's hand. A little boy was clutching them, and said they were fine peas for his pea-shooter; and he put one in directly and shot it out.

"Now I'm flying out into the wide world, catch me if you can!" And he was gone.

" I," said the second, " I shall fly straight into the sun. That's a shell worth looking at, and one that exactly suits me." And away he went.

" We'll go to sleep wherever we arrive," said the two next, " but we shall roll on all the same." And they certainly rolled and tumbled down on the ground before they got into the pea-shooter; but they were put in for all that. " We shall go farthest," said they.

" What is to happen will happen," said the last, as he was shot forth out of the pea-shooter; and he flew up against the old board under the garret window, just into a crack which was filled up with moss and soft mould; and the moss closed round him; there he lay, a prisoner indeed, but not forgotten by provident nature.

" What is to happen will happen," said he.

Within, in the little garret, lived a poor woman, who went out in the day to clean stoves, chop wood small, and to do other hard work of the same kind, for she was strong and industrious too. But she always remained poor; and at home in the garret lay her half-grown only daughter, who was very delicate and weak; for a whole year she had kept her bed, and it seemed as if she could neither live nor die.

" She is going to her little sister," the woman said. " I had only the two children, and it was not an easy thing to provide for both, but the good God provided for one of them by taking her home to Himself; now I should be glad to keep the other that was left me; but I suppose they are not to remain separated, and my sick girl will go to her sister in heaven."

But the sick girl remained where she was. She lay quiet and patient all day long while her mother went to earn money out of doors. It was spring, and early in the morning, just as the mother was about to go out to work, the sun shone mildly and pleasantly through the little window, and threw its rays across the floor; and the sick girl fixed her eyes on the lowest pane in the window.

" What may that green thing be that looks in at the window? It is moving in the wind."

And the mother stepped to the window, and half opened it. " Oh!" said she, " on my word, that is a little pea which has taken root here, and is putting out its little leaves. How can it have got here into the crack? That is a little garden with which you can amuse yourself."

And the sick girl's bed was moved nearer to the window, so that she could always see the growing pea; and the mother went forth to her work.

" Mother, I think I shall get well," said the sick child in the evening. " The sun shone in upon me to-day delightfully warm. The little pea is prospering famously, and I shall prosper too, and get up, and go out into the warm sunshine."

" God grant it!" said the mother, but she did not believe it would be so; but she took care to prop with a little stick the green plant which had given her daughter the pleasant thoughts of life, so that it might not be broken by the wind; she tied a piece of string to the window-sill and to the upper part of the frame, so that the pea might have

THE POOR WOMAN AND HER SICK DAUGHTER.

something round which it could twine, when it shot up: and it did shoot up indeed—one could see how it grew every day.

"Really, here is a flower coming!" said the woman one day; and now she began to cherish the hope that her sick daughter would recover. She remembered that lately the child had spoken much more cheerfully than before, that in the last few days she had risen up in bed of her own accord, and had sat upright, looking with delighted eyes at the little garden in which only one plant grew. A week afterwards the invalid for the first time sat up for a whole hour. Quite happy, she sat there in the warm sunshine; the window was opened, and outside before it stood a pink pea blossom, fully blown. The sick girl bent down and gently kissed the delicate leaves. This day was like a festival.

"The Heavenly Father Himself has planted that pea, and caused it to prosper, to be a joy to you, and to me also, my blessed child!" said the glad mother; and she smiled at the flower, as if it had been a good angel.

But about the other peas? Why, the one who flew out into the wide world and said, "Catch me if you can," fell into the gutter on the roof, and found a home in a pigeon's crop; the two lazy ones got just as far, for they, too, were eaten up by pigeons, and thus, at any rate, they were of some real use; but the fourth, who wanted to go up into the sun, fell into the sink, and lay there in the dirty water for weeks and weeks, and swelled prodigiously.

"How beautifully fat I'm growing!" said the Pea. "I shall burst at last; and I don't think any pea can do more than that. I'm the most remarkable of all the five that were in the shell."

And the Sink said he was right.

But the young girl at the garret window stood there with gleaming eyes, with the roseate hue of health on her cheeks, and folded her thin hands over the pea blossom, and thanked Heaven for it.

"I," said the Sink, "stand up for my own pea."

THE METAL PIG.

IN the city of Florence, not far from the *Piazza del Granduca*, there runs a little cross street, I think it is called *Porta Rosa*. In this street, in front of a kind of market hall where vegetables are sold, there lies a Pig artistically fashioned of metal. The fresh clear water pours from the jaws of the creature, which has become a blackish-green from age; only the snout shines as if it had been polished, and indeed it has been, by many hundreds of children and *lazzaroni*, who seize it with their hands, and place their mouths close to the mouth of the animal, to drink. It is a perfect picture to see the well-shaped creature clasped by a half naked boy, who lays his red lips against its jaw.

Every one who comes to Florence can easily find the place; he need only ask the first beggar he meets for the Metal Pig, and he will find it.

It was late on a winter evening. The mountains were covered with snow; but the moon shone, and moonlight in Italy is just as good as the light of a murky Northern winter's day; nay, it is better, for the air shines and lifts us up, while in the North the cold grey leaden covering seems to press us downwards to the earth—the cold damp earth, which will once press down our coffin.

In the Grand Duke's palace garden, under a penthouse roof, where a thousand roses bloom in winter, a little ragged boy had been sitting all day long, a boy who might serve as a type of Italy, pretty and smiling, and yet suffering. He was hungry and thirsty, but no one gave him anything; and when it became dark, and the garden was to be closed, the porter turned him out. Long he stood musing on the bridge that spans the Arno, and looked at the stars, whose light glittered in the water between him and the splendid marble bridge of *Della Trinitá*.

He took the way towards the Metal Pig, half knelt down, clasped his arms round it, put his mouth against its shining snout, and drank the fresh water in deep draughts. Close by lay a few leaves of salad and one or two chestnuts; these were his supper. No one was in the street

THE METAL PIG.

but himself—it belonged to him alone and; he boldly sat down on the Pig's back, bent forward, so that his curly head rested on the head of the animal, and before he was aware fell asleep.

It was midnight. The Metal Pig stirred, and he heard it say quite distinctly, "You little boy, hold tight, for now I am going to run," and away it ran with him. This was a wonderful ride. First they got to the *Piazza del Granduca*, and the metal horse which carries the Duke's statue neighed aloud, the painted coats of arms on the old council-house looked like transparent pictures, and Michael Angelo's "David" swang his sling: there was a strange life stirring among them. The metal groups representing persons, and the rape of the Sabines, stood there as if they were alive: a cry of mortal fear escaped them, and resounded over the splendid square.

By the *Palazzo Degli Uffizi*, in the arcade, where the nobility assemble for the Carnival amusements, the Metal Pig stopped. "Hold tight," said the creature, "for now we are going up stairs." The little boy spoke not a word, for he was half frightened half delighted.

They came into a long gallery where the boy had already been. The walls shone with pictures; here stood statues and busts, all in the most charming light, as if it had been broad day; but the most beautiful of all was when the door of a side room opened: the little boy could remember the splendour that was there, but on this night everything shone in the most glorious colours.

Here stood a beautiful woman, as radiant in beauty as nature and the greatest master of sculpture could make her: she moved her graceful limbs, dolphins sprang at her feet, and immortality shone out of her eyes. The world calls her the Venus de Medici. By her side are statues in which the spirit of life has been breathed into the stone; they are handsome unclothed men. One was sharpening a sword, and was called the Grinder; the Wrestling Gladiators formed another group; and the sword was sharpened, and they strove for the goddess of beauty.

The boy was dazzled by all this pomp: the walls gleamed with bright colours, and everything was life and movement.

What splendour, what beauty shone from hall to hall! and the little boy saw everything plainly, for the Metal Pig went step by step from one picture to another through all this scene of magnificence. Each fresh glory effaced the last. One picture only fixed itself firmly in his soul especially, through the very happy children introduced into it, for these the little boy fancied he had greeted in the daylight.

Many persons pass by this picture with indifference, and yet it contains a treasure of poetry. It represents the Saviour descending into hell. But these are not the damned whom the spectator sees around him, they are heathen. The Florentine Agniolo Bronzino painted this picture. Most beautiful is the expression on the faces of the children, —the full confidence that they will get to heaven: two little beings are already embracing, and one little one stretches out his hand towards another who stands below him, and points to himself as if he were saying, "I am going to heaven!" The older people stand uncertain, hoping, but bowing in humble adoration before the Lord Jesus. The boy's eyes rested longer on this picture than on any other. The Metal Pig stood still before it. A low sigh was heard: did it come from the picture or from the animal? The boy lifted up his hands towards the smiling children; then the Pig ran away with him, away through the open vestibule.

"Thanks and blessings to you, you dear thing!" said the little boy, and caressed the Metal Pig, as it sprang down the steps with him.

"Thanks and blessings to yourself," replied the Metal Pig. "I have helped you, and you have helped me, for only with an innocent child on my back do I receive power to run! Yes, you see, I may even step into the rays of the lamp in front of the picture of the Madonna, only I may not go into the church. But from without, when you are with me, I may look in through the open door. Do not get down from my back; if you do so, I shall lie dead as you see me in the day-time at the *Porta Rosa*."

" I will stay with you, my dear creature!" cried the child.

So they went in hot haste through the streets of Florence, out into the place before the church of *Santa Croce*. The folding doors flew open, and lights gleamed out from the altar through the church into the deserted square.

A wonderful blaze of light streamed forth from a monument in the left aisle, and a thousand moving stars seemed to form a glory round it. A coat of arms shone upon the grave, a red ladder in a blue field seemed to glow like fire. It was the grave of Galileo. The monument is unadorned, but the red ladder is a significant emblem, as if it were that of art, for in art the way always leads up a burning ladder, towards heaven. The prophets of mind soar upwards towards heaven, like Elias of old.

To the right, in the aisle of the church, every statue on the richly carved sarcophagi seemed endowed with life. Here stood Michael Angelo, there Dante with the laurel wreath round his brow, Alfieri and Machiavelli; for here the great men, the pride of Italy, rest side by side.* It is a glorious church, far more beautiful than the marble cathedral of Florence, though not so large.

It seemed as if the marble vestments stirred, as if the great forms raised their heads higher and looked up, amid song and music, to the bright altar glowing with colour, where the white-clad boys swing the golden censers; and the strong fragrance streamed out of the church into the open square.

The boy stretched forth his hand towards the gleaming light, and in a moment the Metal Pig resumed its headlong career: he was obliged to cling tightly; and the wind whistled about his ears; he heard the church door creak on its hinges as it closed; but at the same moment his senses seemed to desert him, he felt a cold shudder pass over him, and awoke.

It was morning, and he was still sitting on the Metal Pig, which stood where it always stood on the *Porta Rosa,* and he had slipped half off its back.

Fear and trembling filled the soul of the boy at the thought of her whom he called mother, and who had yesterday sent him forth to bring money; for he had none, and was hungry and thirsty. Once more he clasped his arms round the neck of his metal horse, kissed its lips, and nodded farewell to it. Then he wandered away into one of the narrowest streets, where there was scarcely room for a laden ass. A great iron-clamped door stood ajar; he passed through it, and climbed up a brick stair with dirty walls and a rope for a balustrade, till he came to

---

* Opposite to the grave of Galileo is the tomb of Michael Angelo. On the monument his bust is displayed, with three figures, representing Sculpture, Painting, and Architecture. Close by is a monument to Dante, whose corpse is interred at Ravenna; on this monument Italy is represented pointing to a colossal statue of the poet, while Poetry weeps over his loss. A few paces farther on is Alfieri's monument, adorned with laurel, the lyre, and dramatic masks: Italy weeps at his grave. Machiavelli here closes the series of celebrated men.

an open gallery hung with rags; from here a flight of stairs led down
into the court, where there was a fountain, and great iron wires led up
to the different storeys, and many water-buckets hung side by side, and
at times the roller creaked, and one of the buckets would dance into the
air, swaying so that the water splashed out of it down into the courtyard. A second ruinous brick staircase here led upwards. Two Russian
sailors were running briskly down, and almost overturned the poor boy:
they were going home from their nightly carouse. A large woman, no
longer young, followed them.

"What do you bring home?" she asked the boy.

"Don't be angry," he pleaded. "I received nothing—nothing at
all." And he seized the mother's dress, and would have kissed it.

They went into the little room. I will not describe it, but only say that
there stood in it an earthern pot with handles, made for holding fire, and
called a *marito*. This pot she took in her arms, warmed her fingers, and
pushed the boy with her elbow.

"Certainly you must have brought some money?" said she.

The boy wept, and she struck him with her foot, so that he cried
aloud.

"Will you be silent, or I'll break your screaming head!"

And she brandished the fire-pot which she held in her hand. The boy
crouched down to the earth with a scream of terror. Then a neighbour
stepped in, also with a *marito* in her arms.

"Felicita," she said, "what are you doing to the child?"

"The child is mine," retorted Felicita. "I can murder him if I like,
and you too, Giannina."

And she swung her fire-pot. The other lifted up hers in self-defence,
and the two pots clashed together with such fury that fragments, fire, and
ashes flew about the room; but at the same moment the boy rushed out
at the door, sped across the courtyard, and fled from the house. The poor
child ran till he was quite out of breath. He stopped by the church,
whose great doors had opened to him the previous night, and went in.
Everything was radiant. The boy knelt down at the first grave on the
right hand, the grave of Michael Angelo, and soon he sobbed aloud.
People came and went, and Mass was performed; but no one noticed the
boy, only an elderly citizen stood still, looked at him, and then went
away like the rest.

Hunger and thirst tormented the child; he was quite faint and ill,
and he crept into a corner between the marble monuments, and went to
sleep. Towards evening he was awakened by a tug at his sleeve; he
started up, and the same citizen stood before him.

"Are you ill? Where do you live? Have you been here all day?"
were three of the many questions the old man asked of him.

He answered, and the old man took him into his little house, close by,
in a back street. They came into a glover's workshop, where a woman
sat sewing busily. A little white Spitz dog, so closely shaven that his
pink skin could be seen, frisked about on the table and gambolled before
the boy.

" Innocent souls soon make acquaintance," said the woman.

And she caressed the boy and the dog. The good people gave the child food and drink, and said he should be permitted to stay the night with them ; and next day Father Guiseppe would speak to his mother. A little simple bed was assigned to him, but for him who had often slept on the hard stones it was a royal couch ; and he slept sweetly, and dreamed of the splendid pictures and of the Metal Pig.

Father Guiseppe went out next morning : the poor child was not glad of this, for he knew that the object of the errand was to send him back to his mother. He wept, and kissed the merry little dog, and the woman nodded approvingly at both.

What news did Father Guiseppe bring home ? He spoke a great deal with his wife, and she nodded and stroked the boy's cheek.

"He is a capital lad!" said she. " He may become an accomplished glove-maker, like you ; and look what delicate fingers he has ! Madonna intended him for a glove-maker."

And the boy stayed in the house, and the woman herself taught him to sew : he ate well, slept well, and became merry, and began to tease Bellissima, as the little dog was called ; but the woman grew angry at this, and scolded and threatened him with her finger. This touched the boy's heart, and he sat thoughtful in his little chamber. This chamber looked upon the street in which skins were dried ; there were thick bars of iron before his window. He could not sleep, for the Metal Pig was always present in his thoughts, and suddenly he heard outside a pit-pat. That must be the Pig! He sprang to the window, but nothing was to be seen—it had passed by already.

"Help the gentleman to carry his box of colours," said the woman next morning to the boy, when their young neighbour the artist passed by, carrying a paint-box and a large rolled canvas.

The boy took the box and followed the painter ; they betook themselves to the gallery, and mounted the same staircase which he remembered well from the night when he had ridden on the Metal Pig. He recognized the statues and pictures, the beautiful marble Venus, and the Venus that lived in the picture ; and again he saw the Madonna, and the Saviour, and St. John.

They stood still before the picture by Bronzino, in which Christ is descending into hell, and the children smiling around him in the sweet expectation of heaven. The poor child smiled too, for he felt as if his heaven were here.

" Go home now," said the painter, when the boy had stood until the other had set up his easel.

"May I see you paint?" asked the boy. " May I see you put the picture upon this white canvas ? "

" I am not going to paint yet," replied the man ; and he brought out a piece of white chalk. His hand moved quickly ; his eye measured the great picture, and though nothing appeared but a thin line, the figure of the Saviour stood there, as in the coloured picture.

" Why don't you go ? " said the painter.

And the boy wandered home silently, and seated himself on the table and learned to sew gloves.

But all day long his thoughts were in the picture gallery; and so it came that he pricked his fingers, and was awkward; but he did not tease Bellissima. When evening came, and when the house door stood open, he crept out: it was cold but starlight, a bright beautiful evening. Away he went through the already deserted streets, and soon came to the Metal Pig. He bent down on it, kissed its shining mouth, and seated himself on its back.

"You happy creature!" he said; "how I have longed for you! We must take a ride to-night."

The Metal Pig lay motionless, and the fresh stream gushed forth from its mouth. The little boy sat astride on its back: then something tugged at his clothes. He looked down, and there was Bellissima—little smooth-shaven Bellissima—barking as if she would have said, "Here am I too: why are you sitting there?" A fiery dragon could not have terrified the boy so much as did the little dog in this place. Bellissima in the street, and not *dressed*, as the old lady called it! What would be the end of it? The dog never came out in winter, except attired in a little lamb-skin, which had been cut out and made into a coat for him; it was made to fasten with a red ribbon round the little dog's neck and body, and was adorned with bows and with bells. The dog looked almost like a little kid, when in winter he got permission to patter out with his mistress. Bellissima was outside, and not dressed! what would be the end of it? All his fancies were put to flight; yet the boy kissed the Metal Pig once more, and then took Bellissima on his arm: the little thing trembled with cold, therefore the boy ran as fast as he could.

"What are you running away with there?" asked two police soldiers whom he met, and at whom Bellissima barked. "Where have you stolen that pretty dog?" they asked, and they took it away from him.

"Oh, give it back to me!" cried the boy despairingly.

"If you have not stolen him, you may say at home that the dog may be sent for from the watch-house." And they told him where the watch-house was, and went away with Bellissima.

Here was a terrible calamity! The boy did not know whether he should jump into the Arno, or go home and confess everything; they would certainly kill him, he thought.

"But I will gladly be killed; then I shall die and get to heaven," he reasoned. And he went home, principally with the idea of being killed.

The door was locked, and he could not reach the knocker; no one was in the street, but a stone lay there, and with this he thundered at the door.

"Who is there?" cried somebody from within.

"It is I," said he. "The dog is gone. Open the door, and then kill me!"

There was quite a panic. Madame was especially concerned for poor Bellissima. She immediately looked at the wall, where the dog's dress usually hung, and there was the little lamb-skin.

" Bellissima in the watch-house!" she cried aloud. " You bad boy! How did you entice her out? She 'll be frozen, the poor delicate little thing! among those rough soldiers."

The father was at once dispatched—the woman lamented and the boy wept. All the inhabitants of the house came together, and among the rest the painter: he took the boy between his knees and questioned him; and in broken sentences he heard the whole story about the Metal Pig and the gallery, which was certainly rather incomprehensible.

The painter consoled the little fellow, and tried to calm the old lady's anger; but she would not be pacified until the father came in with Bellissima, who had been among the soldiers; then there was great rejoicing; and the painter caressed the boy, and gave him a hand-full of pictures.

Oh, those were capital pieces — such funny heads! — and truly the Metal Pig was there among them, bodily. Oh, nothing could be more

THE OFFICERS SEIZE THE DOG.

superb! By means of a few strokes it was made to stand there on the paper, and even the house that stood behind it was sketched in.

Oh for the ability to draw and paint! He who could do this could conjure up the whole world around him!

On the first leisure moment of the following day, the little fellow seized the pencil, and on the back of one of the pictures he attempted to copy the drawing of the Metal Pig, and he succeeded!—it was certainly rather crooked, rather up and down, one leg thick and another thin; but still it was to be recognized, and he rejoiced himself at it. The pencil would not quite work as it should do, that he could well observe; but on the next day a second Metal Pig was drawn by the side of the first, and this looked a hundred times better; and the third was already so good that every one could tell what it was meant for.

But the glove-making prospered little, and the orders given in the town were executed but slowly; for the Metal Pig had taught him that all pictures may be drawn on paper; and Florence is a picture-book for any one who chooses to turn over its pages. On the *Piazza del Trinitá* stands a slender pillar, and upon it the goddess of justice, blindfolded and with her scales in her hand. Soon she was placed on the paper, and it was the little glove-maker's boy who placed her there. The collection of pictures increased, but as yet it only contained representations of lifeless objects, when one day Bellissima came gambolling before him.

" Stand still ! " said he, " then you shall be made beautiful and put into my collection."

But Bellissima would not stand still, so she had to be bound fast; her head and tail were tied and she barked and jumped, and the string had to be pulled tight; and then the signora came in.

" You wicked boy !—The poor creature ! " was all she could utter.

And she pushed the boy aside, thrust him away with her foot, forbade him to enter her house again, and called him a most ungrateful good-for-nothing and a wicked boy; and then weeping, she kissed her little half strangled Bellissima.

At this very moment the painter came down stairs, and here is the turning-point of the story.

In the year 1834 there was an exhibition in the Academy of Arts at Florence. Two pictures, placed side by side, collected a number of spectators. The smaller of the two represented a merry little boy who sat drawing, with a little white Spitz dog, curiously shorn, for his model; but the animal would not stand still, and was therefore bound by a string fastened to its head and its tail. There was a truth and life in this picture that interested every one. The painter was said to be a young Florentine, who had been found in the streets in his childhood, had been brought up by an old glove-maker, and had taught himself to draw. It was further said that a painter, now become famous, had discovered this talent just as the boy was to be sent away for tying up the favourite little dog of Madame, and using it as a model.

The glove-maker's boy had become a great painter: the picture proved this, and still more the larger picture that stood beside it. Here was represented only one figure, a handsome boy, clad in rags, asleep in the streets, and leaning against the Metal Pig in the *Porta Rosa* street. All the spectators knew the spot. The child's arms rested upon the head of the Pig; the little fellow was fast asleep, and the lamp before the picture of the Madonna threw a strong effective light on the pale delicate face of the child—it was a beautiful picture ! A great gilt frame surrounded it, and on one corner of the frame a laurel wreath had been hung; but a black band wound unseen among the green leaves, and a streamer of crape hung down from it. For within the last few days the young artist had—died !

THE MAGIC MIRROR.

THE SNOW QUEEN.

IN SEVEN STORIES.

FIRST STORY.

Which treats of the Mirror and Fragments.

LOOK you, now we're going to begin. When we are at the end of the story we shall know more than we do now, for he was a bad goblin. He was one of the very worst, for he was a demon. One day he was in very good spirits, for he had made a mirror which had this peculiarity, that everything good and beautiful that was reflected in it shrank together into almost nothing, but that whatever was worthless and looked ugly became prominent and looked worse than ever. The most lovely landscapes seen in this mirror looked like boiled spinach, and the best people became hideous, or stood on their heads and had no bodies; their faces were so distorted as to be unrecognizable, and a single freckle was shown spread out over nose and mouth. That was very amusing, the demon said. When a good pious thought passed through any person's mind, these were again shown in the mirror, so that the demon chuckled at his artistic invention. Those who visited the goblin school—for he kept a goblin school—declared everywhere that a wonder had been wrought. For now, they asserted, one could see, for the first time, how the world and the people in it really looked. Now they wanted to fly up to heaven, to sneer and scoff at the angels themselves. The higher they flew with the mirror, the more it grinned; they could scarcely hold it fast. They flew higher and higher, and then the mirror trembled so terribly amid its grinning that it fell down out of their hands to the earth, where it was shattered into a hundred million million and more fragments. And now this mirror occasioned much more unhappiness than before; for some of the fragments were scarcely so large as a barleycorn, and these flew about in the world, and whenever they flew into any one's eye they stuck there, and those people saw everything wrongly, or had only eyes for the bad side of a thing, for every little fragment of the mirror had retained the same power which the whole glass possessed. A few persons even got a fragment of the mirror into their hearts, and that was terrible indeed, for such a heart became a block of ice. A few fragments of the mirror were so large that they were used as window-panes, but it was a bad thing to look at one's friends through these panes; other pieces were made into spectacles, and then it went badly when people put on these spectacles to see rightly and to be just; and then the demon laughed till his paunch shook, for it tickled him so. But without, some little fragments of glass still floated about in the air—and now we shall hear.

SECOND STORY.

A Little Boy and a Little Girl.

In the great town, where there are many houses and so many people that there is not room enough for every one to have a little garden, and where consequently most persons are compelled to be content with some flowers in flower-pots, were two poor children who possessed a garden somewhat larger than a flower-pot. They were not brother and sister, but they loved each other quite as much as if they had been. Their parents lived just opposite each other in two garrets, there where the roof of one neighbour's house joined that of another; and where the water-pipe ran between the two houses was a little window; one had only to step across the pipe to get from one window to the other.

The parents of each child had a great box, in which grew kitchen herbs that they used, and a little rose bush; there was one in each box, and they grew famously. Now, it occurred to the parents to place the boxes across the pipe, so that they reached from one window to another, and looked quite like two embankments of flowers. Pea plants hung down over the boxes, and the rose bushes shot forth long twigs, which clustered round the windows and bent down towards each other: it was almost like a triumphal arch of flowers and leaves. As the boxes were very high, and the children knew that they might not creep upon them, they often obtained permission to step out upon the roof behind the boxes, and to sit upon their little stools under the roses, and there they could play capitally.

In the winter there was an end of this amusement. The windows were sometimes quite frozen all over. But then they warmed copper shillings on the stove, and held the warm coins against the frozen pane; and this made a capital peep-hole, so round, so round! and behind it gleamed a pretty mild eye at each window; and these eyes belonged to

GERDA AND KAY.

the little boy and the little girl. His name was Kay and the little girl's was Gerda.

In the summer they could get to one another at one bound; but in the winter they had to go down and up the long staircase, while the snow was pelting without.

"Those are the white bees swarming," said the old grandmother.

"Have they a Queen-bee?" asked the little boy. For he knew that there is one among the real bees.

"Yes, they have one," replied grandmamma. "She always flies where they swarm thickest. She is the largest of them all, and never remains quiet upon the earth; she flies up again into the black cloud. Many a midnight she is flying through the streets of the town, and looks in at the windows, and then they freeze in such a strange way, and look like flowers."

"Yes, I've seen that!" cried both the children; and now they knew that it was true.

"Can the Snow Queen come in here?" asked the little girl.

"Only let her come," cried the boy; "I'll set her upon the warm stove, and then she'll melt."

But grandmother smoothed his hair, and told some other tales.

In the evening, when little Kay was at home and half undressed, he clambered upon the chair by the window, and looked through the little hole. A few flakes of snow were falling outside, and one of them, the largest of them all, remained lying on the edge of one of the flower-boxes. The snow-flake grew larger and larger, and at last became a maiden clothed in the finest white gauze, put together of millions of starry flakes. She was beautiful and delicate, but of ice—of shining, glittering ice. Yet she was alive; her eyes flashed like two clear stars, but there was no peace or rest in them. She nodded towards the window, and beckoned with her hand. The little boy was frightened, and sprang down from the chair; then it seemed as if a great bird flew by outside, in front of the window.

Next day there was a clear frost, and then the spring came; the sun shone, the green sprouted forth, the swallows built nests, the windows were opened, and the little children again sat in their garden high up in the roof, over all the floors.

How splendidly the roses bloomed this summer! The little girl had learned a psalm, in which mention was made of roses; and, in speaking of roses, she thought of her own; and she sang it to the little boy, and he sang, too,—

"The roses will fade and pass away,
But we the Christ-child shall see one day."

And the little ones held each other by the hand, kissed the roses, looked at God's bright sunshine, and spoke to it, as if the Christ-child were there. What splendid summer days those were! How beautiful it was without, among the fresh rose bushes, which seemed as if they would never leave off blooming!

Kay and Gerda sat and looked at the picture-book of beasts and birds. Then it was, while the clock was just striking twelve on the church tower, that Kay said,

"Oh! something struck my heart and pricked me in the eye."

The little girl fell upon his neck; he blinked his eyes. No, there was nothing at all to be seen.

"I think it is gone," said he; but it was not gone. It was just one of those glass fragments which sprang from the mirror—the magic mirror that we remember well, the ugly glass that made everything great and good which was mirrored in it to seem small and mean, but in which the mean and the wicked things were brought out in relief, and every fault was noticeable at once. Poor little Kay had also received a splinter just in his heart, and that will now soon become like a lump of ice. It did not hurt him now, but the splinter was still there.

"Why do you cry?" he asked. "You look ugly like that. There's nothing the matter with me. Oh, fie!" he suddenly exclaimed, "that rose is worm-eaten, and this one is quite crooked. After all, they're ugly roses. They're like the box in which they stand."

And then he kicked the box with his foot, and tore both the roses off.

"Kay, what are you about?" cried the little girl.

And when he noticed her fright he tore off another rose, and then sprang in at his own window, away from pretty little Gerda.

When she afterwards came with her picture-book, he said it was only fit for babies in arms; and when grandmother told stories he always came in with a *but;* and when he could manage it, he would get behind her, put on a pair of spectacles, and talk just as she did; he could do that very cleverly, and the people laughed at him. Soon he could mimic the speech and the gait of everybody in the street. Everything that was peculiar or ugly about him Kay could imitate; and people said, "That boy must certainly have a remarkable head." But it was the glass that stuck deep in his heart; so it happened that he even teased little Gerda, who loved him with all her heart.

His games now became quite different from what they were before; they became quite sensible. One winter's day when it snowed he came out with a great burning-glass, held up the blue tail of his coat, and let the snow-flakes fall upon it.

"Now look at the glass, Gerda," said he.

And every flake of snow was magnified, and looked like a splendid flower, or a star with ten points: it was beautiful to behold.

"See how clever that is," said Kay. "That's much more interesting than real flowers; and there is not a single fault in it—they're quite regular until they begin to melt."

Soon after Kay came in thick gloves, and with his sledge upon his back. He called up to Gerda, "I've got leave to go into the great square, where the other boys play," and he was gone.

In the great square the boldest among the boys often tied their sledges to the country people's carts, and thus rode with them a good way. They went capitally. When they were in the midst of their playing there came a great sledge. It was painted quite white, and in it sat somebody wrapped in a rough white fur, and with a white rough cap on his head. The sledge drove twice round the square, and Kay bound his little sledge to it, and so he drove on with it. It went faster and faster, straight into the next street. The man who drove turned round and nodded in a friendly way to Kay; it was as if they knew one another: each time when Kay wanted to cast loose his little sledge, the stranger nodded again, and then Kay remained where he was, and thus they drove out at the town gate. Then the snow began to fall so rapidly that the boy could not see a hand's breadth before him, but still he drove on. Now he hastily dropped the cord, so as to get loose from the great sledge, but that was no use, for his sledge was fast bound to the other, and they went on like the wind. Then he called out quite loudly, but nobody heard him; and the snow beat down, and the sledge flew onward; every now and then it gave a jump, and they seemed to be flying over hedges and ditches. The boy was quite frightened. He wanted to say his prayer, but could remember nothing but the multiplication table.

The snow-flakes became larger and larger; at last they looked like great white fowls. All at once they sprang aside and the great sledge stopped, and the person who had driven it rose up. The fur and the cap were made altogether of ice. It was *a lady*, tall and slender, and brilliantly white: it was the Snow Queen.

"We have driven well!" said she. "But why do you tremble with cold? Creep into my fur."

And she seated him beside her in her own sledge, and wrapped the fur round him, and he felt as if he sank into a snow-drift.

"Are you still cold?" asked she, and then she kissed him on the forehead.

Oh, that was colder than ice; it went quite through to his heart, half of which was already a lump of ice: he felt as if he were going to die; but only for a moment; for then he seemed quiet well, and he did not notice the cold all about him.

"My sledge! don't forget my sledge."

That was the first thing he thought of; and it was bound fast to one of the white chickens, and this chicken flew behind him with the sledge upon its back. The Snow Queen kissed Kay again, and then he had forgotten little Gerda, his grandmother, and all at home.

"Now you shall have no more kisses," said she, "for if you did I should kiss you to death."

Kay looked at her. She was so beautiful, he could not imagine a more sensible or lovely face; she did not appear to him to be made of ice now as before, when she sat at the window and beckoned to him. In his eyes she was perfect; he did not feel at all afraid. He told her that he could do mental arithmetic as far as fractions, that he knew the number of square miles, and the number of inhabitants in the country. And she always smiled, and then it seemed to him that what he knew was not enough, and he looked up into the wide sky, and she flew with him high up upon the black cloud, and the storm blew and whistled; it seemed as though the wind sang old songs. They flew over woods and lakes, over sea and land: below them roared the cold wind, the wolves howled, the snow crackled; over them flew the black screaming crows; but above all the moon shone bright and clear, and Kay looked at the long, long winter night; by day he slept at the feet of the Queen.

THIRD STORY.

The Flower Garden of the Woman who could Conjure.

BUT how did it fare with little Gerda when Kay did not return? What could have become of him? No one knew, no one could give information. The boys only told that they had seen him bind his sledge to another very large one, which had driven along the street and out at the town gate. Nobody knew what had become of him; many tears were shed, and little Gerda especially wept long and bitterly: then she said he was dead—he had been drowned in the river which flowed close by their school. Oh, those were very dark long winter days! But now spring came, with warmer sunshine.

"Kay is dead and gone," said little Gerda.

"I don't believe it," said the Sunshine.

"He is dead and gone," said she to the Sparrows.

"We don't believe it," they replied; and at last little Gerda did not believe it herself.

"I will put on my new red shoes," she said one morning, "those that Kay has never seen; and then I will go down to the river, and ask for him."

It was still very early; she kissed the old grandmother, who was still asleep, put on her red shoes, and went quite alone out of the town gate towards the river.

"Is it true that you have taken away my little playmate from me? I will give you my red shoes if you will give him back to me!"

And it seemed to her as if the waves nodded quite strangely; and then she took her red shoes, that she liked best of anything she possessed, and threw them both into the river; but they fell close to the shore, and the little wavelets carried them back to her, to the land. It seemed as if the river would not take from her the dearest things she possessed because he had not her little Kay; but she thought she had not thrown the shoes far enough out; so she crept into a boat that lay among the reeds; she went to the other end of the boat, and threw the shoes from thence into the water; but the boat was not bound fast, and at the movement she made it glided away from the shore. She noticed it, and hurried to get back, but before she reached the other end the boat was a yard from the bank, and it drifted away faster than before.

Then little Gerda was very much frightened, and began to cry; but no one heard her except the Sparrows, and they could not carry her to land; but they flew along by the shore, and sang, as if to console her, "Here we are! here we are!" The boat drove on with the stream, and little Gerda sat quite still, with only her stockings on her feet; her little red shoes floated along behind her, but they could not come up to the boat, for that made more way.

It was very pretty on both shores. There were beautiful flowers, old trees, and slopes with sheep and cows; but not *one* person was to be seen.

"Perhaps the river will carry me to little Kay," thought Gerda.

And then she became more cheerful, and rose up, and for many hours she watched the charming green banks; then she came to a great cherry orchard, in which stood a little house with remarkable blue and red windows; it had a thatched roof, and without stood two wooden soldiers, who presented arms to those who sailed past.

Gerda called to them, for she thought they were alive, but of course they did not answer. She came quite close to them; the river carried the boat towards the shore.

Gerda called still louder, and then there came out of the house an old woman leaning on a crutch: she had on a great velvet hat, painted over with the finest flowers.

"You poor little child!" said the old woman, "how did you manage to come on the great rolling river, and to float thus far out into the world?"

And then the old woman went quite into the water, seized the boat with her crutch-stick, drew it to land, and lifted little Gerda out. And Gerda was glad to be on dry land again, though she felt a little afraid of the strange old woman.

"Come and tell me who you are, and how you came here," said the old lady. And Gerda told her everything; and the old woman shook her head, and said, "Hem! hem!" And when Gerda had told everything, and asked if she had not seen little Kay, the woman said that he had not yet come by, but that he probably would soon come. Gerda was not to be sorrowful, but to look at the flowers and taste the cherries, for they were better than any picture-book, for each one of them could tell a story. Then she took Gerda by the hand and led her into the little house, and the old woman locked the door.

The windows were very high, and the panes were red, blue, and yellow; the daylight shone in a remarkable way, with different colours. On the table stood the finest cherries, and Gerda ate as many of them as she liked, for she had leave to do so. While she was eating them, the old lady combed her hair with a golden comb, and the hair hung in ringlets of pretty yellow round the friendly little face, which looked as blooming as a rose.

"I have long wished for such a dear little girl as you," said the old lady. "Now you shall see how well we shall live with one another."

And as the ancient dame combed her hair, Gerda forgot her adopted brother Kay more and more; for this old woman could conjure, but she was not a wicked witch. She only practised a little magic for her own amusement, and wanted to keep little Gerda. Therefore she went into the garden, stretched out her crutch towards all the rose bushes, and, beautiful as they were, they all sank into the earth, and one could not tell where they had stood. The old woman was afraid that if the little girl saw roses, she would think of her own, and remember little Kay, and run away.

Now Gerda was led out into the flower-garden. What fragrance was there, and what loveliness! Every conceivable flower was there in full bloom; there were some for every season: no picture-book could be gayer and prettier. Gerda jumped high for joy, and played till the sun went down behind the high cherry trees; then she was put into a lovely bed with red silk pillows stuffed with blue violets, and she slept there, and dreamed as gloriously as a Queen on her wedding-day.

One day she played again with the flowers in the warm sunshine; and thus many days went by. Gerda knew every flower; but, as many as there were of them, it still seemed to her as if one were wanting, but

GERDA AND THE STRANGE WOMAN.

which one she did not know. One day she sat looking at the old lady's hat with the painted flowers, and the prettiest of them all was a rose. The old lady had forgotten to efface it from her hat when she caused the others to disappear. But so it always is when one does not keep one's wits about one.

"What, are there no roses here?" cried Gerda.

And she went among the beds, and searched and searched, but there was not one to be found. Then she sat down and wept: her tears fell just upon a spot where a rose-bud lay buried, and when the warm tears moistened the earth, the tree at once sprouted up as blooming as when it had sunk; and Gerda embraced it, and kissed the Roses, and thought of the beautiful roses at home, and also of little Kay.

"Oh, how I have been detained!" said the little girl. "I wanted to seek for little Kay! Do you not know where he is?" she asked the Roses. "Do you think he is dead?"

"He is not dead," the Roses answered. "We have been in the ground. All the dead people are there, but Kay is not there."

"Thank you," said little Gerda; and she went to the other flowers, looked into their cups, and asked, "Do you not know where little Kay is?"

But every flower stood in the sun thinking only of her own story or fancy tale: Gerda heard many, many of them; but not one knew anything of Kay.

And what did the Tiger-Lily say?

"Do you hear the drum 'Rub-dub'? There are only two notes, always 'rub-dub!' Hear the morning song of the women, hear the call of the priests. The Hindoo widow stands in her long red mantle on the funeral pile; the flames rise up around her and her dead husband; but the Hindoo woman is thinking of the living one here in the circle, of him whose eyes burn hotter than flames, whose fiery glances have burned in her soul more ardently than the flames themselves, which are soon to burn her body to ashes. Can the flame of the heart die in the flame of the funeral pile?"

"I don't understand that at all!" said little Gerda.

"That's my story," said the Lily.

What says the Convolvulus?

"Over the narrow road looms an old knightly castle: thickly the ivy grows over the crumbling red walls, leaf by leaf up to the balcony, and there stands a beautiful girl; she bends over the balustrade and glances up the road. No rose on its branch is fresher than she; no apple blossom wafted onward by the wind floats more lightly along. How her costly silks rustle! 'Comes he not yet?'"

"Is it Kay whom you mean?" asked little Gerda.

"I'm only speaking of a story—my dream," replied the Convolvulus.

What said the little Snowdrop?

"Between the trees a long board hangs by ropes; that is a swing. Two pretty little girls, with clothes white as snow and long green silk ribbons on their hats, are sitting upon it, swinging; their brother, who is greater than they, stands in the swing, and has slung his arm round the rope to hold himself, for in one hand he has a little saucer, and in the other a clay pipe; he is blowing bubbles. The swing flies, and the bubbles rise with beautiful changing colours; the last still hangs from the pipe-bowl, swaying in the wind. The swing flies on: the little black dog, light as the bubbles, stands up on his hind legs and wants to be taken into the swing; it flies on, and the dog falls, barks, and grows angry, for he is teased, and the bubble bursts. A swinging board and a bursting bubble—that is my song."

"It may be very pretty, what you're telling, but you speak it so mournfully, and you don't mention little Kay at all."

What do the Hyacinths say?

"There were three beautiful sisters, transparent and delicate. The dress of one was red, that of the second blue, and that of the third quite white; hand in hand they danced by the calm lake in the bright moonlight. They were not elves, they were human beings. It was so sweet and fragrant there! The girls disappeared in the forest, and the sweet fragrance became stronger: three coffins, with the three beautiful maidens lying in them, glided from the wood-thicket across the lake; the glow-worms flew gleaming about them like little hovering lights. Are the dancing girls sleeping, or are they dead? The flower-scent says they are dead and the evening bell tolls their knell."

"You make me quite sorrowful," said little Gerda. "You scent so strongly, I cannot help thinking of the dead maidens. Ah! is little Kay really dead? The roses have been down in the earth, and they say no."

"Kling! klang!" tolled the Hyacinth Bells. "We are not tolling for little Kay—we don't know him; we only sing our song, the only one we know."

And Gerda went to the Buttercup, gleaming forth from the green leaves.

"You are a little bright sun," said Gerda. "Tell me, if you know, where I may find my companion."

And the Buttercup shone so gaily, and looked back at Gerda. What song might the Buttercup sing? It was not about Kay.

"In a little courtyard the clear sun shone warm on the first day of spring. The sunbeams glided down the white wall of the neighbouring house; close by grew the first yellow flower, glancing like·gold in the bright sun's ray. The old grandmother sat out of doors in her chair; her granddaughter, a poor handsome maidservant, was coming home for a short visit: she kissed her grandmother. There was gold, heart's gold, in that blessed kiss, gold in the mouth, gold in the south, gold in the morning hour. See, that's my little story," said the Buttercup.

"My poor old grandmother!" sighed Gerda. "Yes, she is surely longing for me and grieving for me, just as she did for little Kay. But I shall soon go home and take Kay with me. There is no use of my asking the flowers, they only know their own song, and give me no information." And then she tied her little frock round her, that she might run the faster; but the Jonquil struck against her leg as she sprang over it, and she stopped to look at the tall yellow flower, and asked, "Do you, perhaps, know anything of little Kay?"

And she bent quite down to the flower, and what did it say?

"I can see myself! I can see myself!" said the Jonquil. "Oh! oh! how I smell! Up in the little room in the gable stands a little dancing girl: she stands sometimes on one foot, sometimes on both; she seems to tread on all the world. She's nothing but an ocular delusion: she pours water out of a tea-pot on a bit of stuff—it is her boddice. 'Cleanliness is a fine thing,' she says; her white frock hangs on a hook; it has been washed in the tea-pot too, and dried on the roof: she puts it on and ties her saffron handkerchief round her neck, and the dress looks all the whiter. Point your toes! look how she seems to stand on a stalk. I can see myself! I can see myself!"

"I don't care at all about that," said Gerda. "You need not tell me that."

And then she ran to the end of the garden. The door was locked, but she pressed against the rusty lock, and it broke off, the door sprang open, and little Gerda ran with naked feet out into the wide world. She looked back three times, but no one was there to pursue her; at last she could run no longer, and seated herself on a great stone, and when she looked round the summer was over—it was late in autumn: one could not notice that in the beautiful garden, where there was always sunshine, and the flowers of every season always bloomed.

"Alas! how I have loitered!" said little Gerda. "Autumn has come. I may not rest again."

And she rose up to go on. Oh! how sore and tired her little feet were. All around it looked cold and bleak; the long willow leaves were quite yellow, and the dew fell down like water; one leaf after another dropped; only the sloe-thorn still bore fruit, but the sloes were sour, and set the teeth on edge. Oh! how grey and gloomy it looked, the wide world!

FOURTH STORY.

The Prince and Princess.

Gerda was compelled to rest again; then there came hopping across the snow, just opposite the spot where she was sitting, a great Crow. This Crow stopped a long time to look at her, nodding its head—now it said, "Krah! krah! Good day! good day!" It could not pronounce better, but it felt friendly towards the little girl, and asked where she was going all alone in the wide world. The word "alone" Gerda understood very well, and felt how much it expressed; and she told the Crow the whole story of her life and fortunes, and asked if it had not seen Kay.

And the Crow nodded very gravely, and said,

"That may be! that may be!"

"What, do you think so?" cried the little girl, and nearly pressed the Crow to death, she kissed it so.

"Gently, gently!" said the Crow. "I think I know: I believe it may be little Kay, but he has certainly forgotten you, with the Princess."

"Does he live with a Princess?" asked Gerda.

"Yes; listen," said the Crow. "But it's so difficult for me to speak your language. If you know the Crow's language, I can tell it much better."

"No, I never learned it," said Gerda; "but my grandmother understood it, and could speak the language too. I only wish I had learned it."

"That doesn't matter," said the Crow. "But it will go badly."

And then the Crow told what it knew.

"In the country in which we now are lives a Princess who is quite wonderfully clever, but then she has read all the newspapers in the world, and has forgotten them again, she is so clever. Lately she was sitting on the throne—and that's not so pleasant as is generally supposed —and she began to sing a song, and it was just this, ' Why should I not marry yet ?' You see, there was something in that," said the Crow. "And so she wanted to marry, but she wished for a husband who could answer when he was spoken to, not one who only stood and looked handsome, for that was wearisome. And so she had all her maids of

GERDA AND THE CROW.

honour summoned, and when they heard her intention they were very glad. ' I like that,' said they ; ' I thought the very same thing the other day.' You may be sure that every word I am telling you is true," added the Crow. " I have a tame sweetheart who goes about freely in the castle, and she told me everything."

Of course the sweetheart was a crow, for one crow always finds out another, and birds of a feather flock together.

" Newspapers were published directly, with a border of hearts and the Princess's initials. One could read in them that every young man who was good looking might come to the castle and speak with the Princess, and him who spoke so that one could hear he was at home there, and who spoke best, the Princess would choose for her husband. Yes, yes," said the Crow, "you may believe me. It's as true as I sit here. Young men came flocking in; there was a great crowding and much running to and fro, but no one succeeded the first or second day. They could all speak well when they were out in the streets, but when they entered at the palace gates, and saw the guards standing in their silver lace, and went up the staircase, and saw the lackeys in their golden liveries, and the great lighted halls, they became confused. And when they stood before the throne itself, on which the Princess sat, they could do nothing but repeat the last word she had spoken, and she did not care to hear her own words again. It was just as if the people in there had taken some narcotic and fallen asleep, till they got into the street again, for not till then were they able to speak. There stood a whole row of them, from the town gate to the palace gate. I went out myself to see it," said the Crow. "They were hungry and thirsty, but in the palace they did not receive so much as a glass of lukewarm water. A few of the wisest had brought bread and butter with them, but they would not share with their neighbours, for they thought, 'Let him look hungry, and the Princess won't have him.'"

"But Kay, little Kay?" asked Gerda. "When did he come? Was he among the crowd?"

"Wait, wait! We're just coming to him. It was on the third day that there came a little personage, without horse or carriage, walking quite merrily up to the castle; his eyes sparkled like yours, he had fine long hair, but his clothes were shabby."

"That was Kay!" cried Gerda, rejoicingly. "Oh, then I have found him!" And she clapped her hands.

"He had a little knapsack on his back," observed the Crow.

"No, that must certainly have been his sledge," said Gerda, "for he went away with a sledge."

"That may well be," said the Crow, "for I did not look to it very closely. But this much I know from my tame sweetheart, that when he passed under the palace gate and saw the Life Guards in silver, and mounted the staircase and saw the lackeys in gold, he was not in the least embarrassed. He nodded, and said to them, 'It must be tedious work standing on the stairs—I'd rather go in.' The halls shone full of lights; privy councillors and Excellencies walked about with bare feet, and carried golden vessels; any one might have become solemn; and his boots creaked most noisily, but he was not embarrassed."

"That is certainly Kay!" cried Gerda. "He had new boots on; I've heard them creak in grandmother's room."

"Yes, certainly they creaked," resumed the Crow. "And he went boldly in to the Princess herself, who sat on a pearl that was as big as a spinning-wheel; and all the maids of honour with their attendants, and the attendants' attendants, and all the cavaliers with their followers, and the followers of their followers, who themselves kept a page apiece, were standing round; and the nearer they stood to the door, the prouder they looked. The followers' followers' pages, who always went in slippers, could hardly be looked at, so proudly did they stand in the doorway!"

"That must be terrible!" faltered little Gerda. "And yet Kay won the Princess?"

"If I had not been a crow, I would have married her myself, notwithstanding that I am engaged. They say he spoke as well as I can when I speak the crows' language; I heard that from my tame sweetheart. He was merry and agreeable; he had not come to marry, but only to hear the wisdom of the Princess; and he approved of her, and she of him."

"Yes, certainly that was Kay!" said Gerda. "He was so clever, he could do mental arithmetic up to fractions. Oh! won't you lead me to the castle too?"

"That's easily said," replied the Crow. "But how are we to manage it? I'll talk it over with my tame sweetheart; she can probably advise us; for this I must tell you—a little girl like yourself will never get leave to go completely in."

"Yes, I shall get leave," said Gerda. "When Kay hears that I'm there he'll come out directly, and bring me in."

"Wait for me yonder at the grating," said the Crow; and it wagged its head and flew away.

It was already late in the evening when the Crow came back.

"Rax! rax!" it said. "I'm to greet you kindly from my sweetheart, and here's a little loaf for you. She took it from the kitchen. There's plenty of bread there, and you must be hungry. You can't possibly get into the palace, for you are barefoot, and the guards in silver and the lackeys in gold would not allow it. But don't cry; you shall go up. My sweetheart knows a little back staircase that leads up to the bed-room, and she knows where she can get the key."

And they went into the garden, into the great avenue, where one leaf was falling down after another; and when the lights were extinguished in the palace one after the other, the Crow led Gerda to a back door, which stood ajar.

Oh, how Gerda's heart beat with fear and longing! It was just as if she had been going to do something wicked; and yet she only wanted to know if it was little Kay. Yes, it must be he. She thought so deeply of his clear eyes and his long hair, she could fancy she saw how he smiled as he had smiled at home when they sat among the roses. He would certainly be glad to see her; to hear what a long distance she had come for his sake; to know how sorry they had all been at home when he did not come back. Oh, what a fear and what a joy that was!

Now they were on the staircase. A little lamp was burning upon a cupboard, and in the middle of the floor stood the tame Crow turning her head on every side and looking at Gerda, who courtesied as her grandmother had taught her to do.

"My betrothed has spoken to me very favourably of you, my little lady," said the tame Crow. "Your history, as it may be called, is very moving. Will you take the lamp? then I will precede you. We will go the straight way, and then we shall meet nobody."

" I feel as if some one were coming after us," said Gerda, as something rushed by her: it seemed like a shadow on the wall; horses with flying manes and thin legs, hunters, and ladies and gentlemen on horseback.

"These are only dreams," said the Crow; "they are coming to carry the high masters' thoughts out hunting. That's all the better, for you may look at them the more closely, in bed. But I hope, when you are taken into favour and get promotion, you will show a grateful heart."

"Of that we may be sure!" observed the Crow from the wood.

Now they came into the first hall: it was hung with rose-coloured satin, and artificial flowers were worked on the walls; and here the dreams already came flitting by them, but they moved so quickly that Gerda could not see the high-born lords and ladies. Each hall was more splendid than the last; yes, one could almost become bewildered! Now they were in the bed-chamber. Here the ceiling was like a great palm tree with leaves of glass, of costly glass, and in the middle of the floor two beds hung on a thick stalk of gold, and each of them looked like a lily. One of them was white, and in that lay the Princess; the other was red, and in that Gerda was to seek little Kay. She bent one of the red leaves aside, and then she saw a little brown neck. Oh, that was Kay! She called out his name quite loud, and held the lamp towards him. The dreams rushed into the room again on horseback— he awoke, turned his head, and—it was not little Kay!

The Prince was only like him in the neck; but he was young and good looking, and the Princess looked up, blinking, from the white lily, and asked who was there. Then little Gerda wept, and told her whole history, and all that the Crows had done for her.

"You poor child!" said the Prince and Princess.

And they praised the Crows, and said that they were not angry with them at all, but the Crows were not to do it again. However, they should be rewarded.

"Will you fly out free?" asked the Princess, "or will you have fixed positions as court crows, with the right to everything that is left in the kitchen?"

And the two Crows bowed, and begged for fixed positions, for they thought of their old age, and said, "It is so good to have some provisions for one's old days," as they called them.

And the Prince got up out of his bed, and let Gerda sleep in it, and he could not do more than that. She folded her little hands, and thought, "How good men and animals are!" and then she shut her eyes and went quietly to sleep. All the dreams came flying in again, looking like angels, and they drew a little sledge, on which Kay sat nodding; but all this was only a dream, and therefore it was gone again as soon as she awoke.

The next day she was clothed from head to foot in velvet; and an offer was made her that she should stay in the castle and enjoy pleasant times; but she only begged for a little carriage, with a horse to draw it, and a pair of little boots; then she would drive out into the world and seek for Kay.

And she received not only boots, but a muff likewise, and was neatly dressed; and when she was ready to depart a coach made of pure gold stopped before the door. Upon it shone like a star the coat of arms of the Prince and Princess; coachman, footmen, and outriders—for there were outriders too—sat on horseback with gold crowns on their heads. The Prince and Princess themselves helped her into the carriage, and wished her all good fortune. The forest Crow, who was now married, accompanied her the first three miles; he sat by Gerda's side, for he could not bear riding backwards: the other Crow stood in the doorway flapping her wings; she did not go with them, for she suffered from headache, that had come on since she had obtained a fixed position and was allowed to eat too much. The coach was lined with sugar-biscuits, and in the seat there were gingerbread-nuts and fruit.

"Farewell, farewell!" cried the Prince and Princess; and little Gerda wept, and the Crow wept. So they went on for the first three miles; and then the Crow said good bye, and that was the heaviest parting of all. The Crow flew up on a tree, and beat his black wings as long as he could see the coach, which glittered like the bright sunshine.

FIFTH STORY.

The Little Robber Girl.

THEY drove on through the thick forest, but the coach gleamed like a torch, that dazzled the robbers' eyes, and they could not bear it.

"That is gold! that is gold!" cried they, and rushed forward, and seized the horses, killed the postilions, the coachman, and the footmen, and then pulled little Gerda out of the carriage.

"She is fat—she is pretty—she is fed with nut-kernels!" said the old robber woman, who had a very long matted beard, and shaggy eyebrows that hung down over her eyes. "She's as good as a little pet lamb; how I shall relish her!"

And she drew out her shining knife, that gleamed in a horrible way.

"Oh!" screamed the old woman at the same moment; for her own daughter who hung at her back bit her ear in a very naughty and spiteful manner. "You ugly brat!" screamed the old woman; and she had not time to kill Gerda.

"She shall play with me!" said the little robber girl. "She shall give me her muff and her pretty dress, and sleep with me in my bed!"

And then the girl gave another bite, so that the woman jumped high up, and turned right round, and all the robbers laughed, and said,

"Look how she dances with her calf."

"I want to go into the carriage," said the little robber girl.

And she would have her own way, for she was spoiled, and very obstinate; and she and Gerda sat in the carriage, and drove over stock and stone deep into the forest. The little robber girl was as big as Gerda, but stronger and more broad shouldered; and she had a brown skin;

her eyes were quite black, and they looked almost mournful. She clasped little Gerda round the waist, and said,

"They shall not kill you as long as I am not angry with you. I suppose you are a Princess?"

"No," replied Gerda. And she told all that had happened to her, and how fond she was of little Kay.

The robber girl looked at her seriously, nodded slightly, and said,

"They shall not kill you even if I do get angry with you, for then I will do it myself."

And then she dried Gerda's eyes, and put her two hands into the beautiful muff that was so soft and warm.

Now the coach stopped, and they were in the courtyard of a robber castle. It had burst from the top to the ground; ravens and crows flew out of the great holes, and big bulldogs—each of which looked as if he could devour a man—jumped high up, but they did not bark, for that was forbidden.

In the great old smoky hall, a bright fire burned upon the stone floor; the smoke passed along under the ceiling, and had to seek an exit for itself. A great cauldron of soup was boiling and hares and rabbits were roasting on the spit.

"You shall sleep to-night with me and all my little animals," said the robber girl.

They got something to eat and drink, and then went to a corner, where straw and carpets were spread out. Above these sat on laths and perches more than a hundred pigeons, that all seemed asleep, but they turned a little when the two little girls came.

"All these belong to me," said the little robber girl; and she quickly seized one of the nearest, held it by the feet, and shook it so that it flapped its wings. "Kiss it!" she cried, and beat it in Gerda's face. "There sit the wood rascals," she continued, pointing to a number of laths that had been nailed in front of a hole in the wall. "Those are wood rascals, those two; they fly away directly if one does not keep them well locked up. And here's my old sweetheart 'Ba.'" And she pulled out by the horn a Reindeer, that was tied up, and had a polished copper ring round its neck. "We're obliged to keep him tight too, or he'd run away from us. Every evening I tickle his neck with a sharp knife, and he's very frightened at that."

And the little girl drew a long knife from a cleft in the wall, and let it glide over the Reindeer's neck; the poor creature kicked out its legs, and the little robber girl laughed, and drew Gerda into bed with her.

"Do you keep the knife while you're asleep?" asked Gerda, and looked at it in rather a frightened way.

"I always sleep with my knife," replied the robber girl. "One does not know what may happen. But now tell me again what you told me just now about little Kay, and why you came out into the wide world."

And Gerda told it again from the beginning; and the Wood Pigeons cooed above them in their cage, and the other pigeons slept. The little robber girl put her arm round Gerda's neck, held her knife in the other

GERDA PREPARING TO START.

hand, and slept so that one could hear her; but Gerda could not close
her eyes at all—she did not know whether she was to live or die.

The robbers sat round the fire, sang and drank, and the old robber
woman tumbled about. It was quite terrible for a little girl to behold.

Then the Wood Pigeons said, "Coo! coo! we have seen little Kay. A
white owl was carrying his sledge: he sat in the Snow Queen's carriage,
which drove close by the forest as we lay in our nests. She blew upon
us young pigeons, and all died except us two. Coo! coo!"

"What are you saying there?" asked Gerda. "Whither was the Snow
Queen travelling? Do you know anything about it?"

"She was probably journeying to Lapland, for there they have always
ice and snow. Ask the Reindeer that is tied to the cord."

"There is ice and snow yonder, and it is glorious and fine," said the
Reindeer. "There one may run about free in great glittering plains.
There the Snow Queen has her summer tent; but her strong castle is up
towards the North Pole, on the island that's called Spitzbergen."

"Oh, Kay, little Kay!" cried Gerda.

" You must lie still," exclaimed the robber girl, " or I shall thrust my knife into your body."

In the morning Gerda told her all that the Wood Pigeons had said, and the robber girl looked quite serious, and nodded her head and said,

" That's all the same, that's all the same !"

" Do you know where Lapland is ? " she asked the Reindeer.

" Who should know better than I?" the creature replied, and its eyes sparkled in its head. " I was born and bred there; I ran about there in the snow fields."

" Listen !" said the robber girl to Gerda. " You see all our men have gone away. Only mother is here still, and she'll stay; but towards noon she drinks out of the big bottle, and then she sleeps for a little while; then I 'll do something for you."

Then she sprang out of bed, and clasped her mother round the neck and pulled her beard, crying

" Good morning, my own old nanny-goat." And her mother filliped her nose till it was red and blue ; and it was all done for pure love.

When the mother had drunk out of her bottle and had gone to sleep upon it, the robber girl went to the Reindeer, and said,

" I should like very much to tickle you a few times more with the knife, for you are very funny then; but it's all the same. I 'll loosen your cord and help you out, so that you may run to Lapland; but you must use your legs well, and carry this little girl to the palace of the Snow Queen, where her playfellow is. You 've heard what she told me, for she spoke loud enough, and you were listening."

The Reindeer sprang up high for joy. The robber girl lifted little Gerda on its back, and had the forethought to tie her fast, and even to give her own little cushion as a saddle.

" There are your fur boots for you," she said, " for it 's growing cold; but I shall keep the muff, for that's so very pretty. Still, you shall not be cold, for all that: here's my mother's big muffles—they 'll just reach up to your elbows. Now you look just like my ugly mother."

And Gerda wept for joy.

" I can't bear to see you whimper," said the little robber girl. " No, you just ought to look very glad. And here are two loaves and a ham for you, now you won't be hungry."

These were tied on the Reindeer's back. The little robber girl opened the door, coaxed in all the big dogs, and then cut the rope with her sharp knife, and said to the Reindeer,

" Now run, but take good care of the little girl."

And Gerda stretched out her hands with the big muffles towards the little robber girl, and said, " Farewell ! "

And the Reindeer ran over stock and stone, away through the great forest, over marshes and steppes, as quick as it could go. The wolves howled and the ravens croaked. " Hiss ! hiss !" it went in the air. It seemed as if the sky were flashing fire.

" Those are my old Northern Lights," said the Reindeer. " Look how they glow !" And then it ran on faster than ever, day and night.

SIXTH STORY.

The Lapland Woman and the Finland Woman.

At a little hut they stopped. It was very humble; the roof sloped down almost to the ground, and the door was so low that the family had to creep on their stomachs when they wanted to go in or out. No one was in the house but an old Lapland woman, cooking fish by the light of a train-oil lamp; and the Reindeer told Gerda's whole history, but it related its own first, for this seemed to the Reindeer the more important of the two. Gerda was so exhausted by the cold that she could not speak.

"Oh, you poor things," said the Lapland woman, "you 've a long way to run yet! You must go more than a hundred miles into Finmark, for the Snow Queen is there, staying in the country, and burning Bengal lights every evening. I 'll write a few words on a dried cod, for I have no paper, and I 'll give you that as a letter to the Finland woman; she can give you better information than I."

And when Gerda had been warmed and refreshed with food and drink, the Lapland woman wrote a few words on a dried codfish, and telling Gerda to take care of these, tied her again on the Reindeer, and the Reindeer sprang away. Flash! flash! it went high in the air; the whole night long the most beautiful blue Northern Lights were burning.

And then they got to Finmark, and knocked at the chimney of the Finland woman, for she had not even a hut.

There was such a heat in the chimney that the woman herself went about almost naked. She at once loosened little Gerda's dress and took off the child's mufflers and boots; otherwise it would have been too hot for her to bear. Then she laid a piece of ice on the Reindeer's head, and read what was written on the codfish; she read it three times, and when she knew it by heart, she popped the fish into the soup-cauldron, for it was eatable, and she never wasted anything.

Now the Reindeer first told his own history, and then little Gerda's; and the Finland woman blinked with her clever eyes, but said nothing.

"You are very clever," said the Reindeer: "I know you can tie all the winds of the world together with a bit of twine: if the seaman unties one knot, he has a good wind; if he loosens the second, it blows hard; but if he unties the third and the fourth, there comes such a tempest that the forests are thrown down. Won't you give the little girl a draught, so that she may get twelve men's power, and overcome the Snow Queen?"

"Twelve men's power!" repeated the Finland woman. "Great use that would be!"

And she went to a bed, and brought out a great rolled-up fur, and unrolled it; wonderful characters were written upon it, and the Finland woman read until the water ran down over her forehead.

But the Reindeer again begged so hard for little Gerda, and Gerda looked at the Finland woman with such beseeching eyes full of tears, that she began to blink again with her own, and drew the Reindeer into a corner, and whispered to him, while she laid fresh ice upon his head,

"Little Kay is certainly at the Sea Queen's, and finds everything there to his taste and liking, and thinks it the best place in the world; but that is because he has a splinter of glass in his eye, and a little fragment in his heart; but these must be got out, or he will never be a human being again, and the Sea Queen will keep her power over him."

"But cannot you give something to little Gerda, so as to give her power over all this?"

GERDA TRAVELLING IN LAPLAND.

"I can give her no greater power than she possesses already: don't you see how great that is? Don't you see how men and animals are obliged to serve her, and how she gets on so well in the world, with her naked feet? She cannot receive her power from us: it consists in this, that she is a dear innocent child. If she herself cannot penetrate to the Snow Queen and get the glass out of little Kay, we can be of no use! Two miles from here the Snow Queen's garden begins; you can carry the little girl thither: set her down by the great bush that stands with its red berries in the snow. Don't stand gossipping, but make haste, and get back here!"

And then the Finland woman lifted little Gerda on the Reindeer, which ran as fast as it could.

"Oh, I haven't my boots! I haven't my mufflers!" cried Gerda.

She soon noticed that in the cutting cold; but the Reindeer dare not stop: it ran till it came to the bush with the red berries; there it set Gerda down, and kissed her on the mouth, and great bright tears ran over the creature's cheeks; and then it ran back, as fast as it could. There stood poor Gerda without shoes, without gloves, in the midst of the terrible cold Finmark.

She ran forward as fast as possible; then came a whole regiment of snow-flakes; but they did not fall down from the sky, for that was quite bright, and shone with the Northern Light: the snow-flakes ran along the ground, and the nearer they came the larger they grew. Gerda still remembered how large and beautiful the snow-flakes had appeared when she looked at them through the burning-glass. But here they were certainly far longer and much more terrible—they were alive They were the advanced posts of the Snow Queen, and had the strangest shapes. A few looked like ugly great porcupines; others like knots formed of snakes, which stretched forth their heads; and others like little fat bears, whose hair stood on end: all were brilliantly white, all were living snow-flakes.

Then little Gerda said her prayer; and the cold was so great that she could see her own breath, which went forth out of her mouth like smoke. The breath became thicker and thicker, and formed itself into little angels, who grew and grew whenever they touched the earth; and all had helmets on their heads and shields and spears in their hands; their number increased more and more, and when Gerda had finished her prayer a whole legion stood round about her, and struck with their spears at the terrible snow-flakes, so that these were shattered into a thousand pieces; and little Gerda could go forward afresh, with good courage. The angels stroked her hands and feet, and then she felt less how cold it was, and hastened on to the Snow Queen's palace.

But now we must see what Kay is doing. He certainly was not thinking of little Gerda, and least of all that she was standing in front of the palace.

SEVENTH STORY.

Of the Snow Queen's Castle, and what happened there at last.

THE walls of the palace were formed of the drifting snow, and the windows and doors of the cutting winds. There were more than a hundred halls, all blown together by the snow: the greatest of these extended for several miles; the strong Northern Light illumined them all, and how great and empty, how icily cold and shining they all were! Never was merriment there, not even a little bear's ball, at which the storm could have played the music, while the bears walked about on their hind legs and showed off their pretty manners; never any little sport of mouth-slapping or bars-touch; never any little coffee gossip among the young lady white foxes. Empty, vast, and cold were the halls of the Snow Queen. The Northern Lights flamed so brightly that one could count them where they stood highest and lowest. In the midst of this immense empty snow hall was a frozen lake, which had burst into a thousand pieces; but each piece was like the rest, so that it was a perfect work of art; and in the middle of the lake sat the Snow Queen when she was at home, and then she said that she sat in the mirror of reason, and that this was the only one, and the best in the world.

Little Kay was quite blue with cold—indeed, almost black; but he did not notice it, for she had kissed the cold shudderings away from him, and his heart was like a lump of ice. He dragged a few sharp flat pieces of ice to and fro, joining them together in all kinds of ways, for he wanted to achieve something with them. It was just like when we have little tablets of wood, and lay them together to form figures— what we call the Chinese game. Kay also went and laid figures, and, indeed, very artistic ones. That was the icy game of reason. In his eyes these figures were very remarkable and of the highest importance; that was because of the fragment of glass sticking in his eye. He laid out the figures so that they formed a word—but he could never manage to lay down the word as he wished to have it—the word "Eternity." And the Snow Queen had said,

"If you can find out this figure, you shall be your own master, and I will give you the whole world and a new pair of skates."

But he could not.

"Now I'll hasten away to the warm lands," said the Snow Queen. "I will go and look into the black pots·" these were the volcanoes, Etna and Vesuvius, as they are called. "I shall make them a little white! That's necessary; that will do the grapes and lemons good."

And the Snow Queen flew away, and Kay sat quite alone in the great icy hall that was miles in extent, and looked at his pieces of ice, and thought so deeply that cracks were heard inside him: one would have thought that he was frozen.

Then it happened that little Gerda stepped through the great gate into the wide hall. Here reigned cutting winds, but she prayed a prayer, and the winds lay down as if they would have gone to sleep; and she stepped into the great empty cold halls, and beheld Kay: she knew him, and flew to him and embraced him, and held him fast, and called out,

"Kay, dear little Kay! at last I have found you!"

But he sat quite still, stiff and cold. Then little Gerda wept hot tears, that fell upon his breast; they penetrated into his heart, they thawed the lump of ice, and consumed the little piece of glass in it. He looked at her, and she sang:

> "Roses bloom and roses decay,
> But we the Christ-child shall see one day."

Then Kay burst into tears; he wept so that the splinter of glass came out of his eye. Now he recognized her, and cried rejoicingly,

"Gerda, dear Gerda! where have you been all this time? And where have I been ?" And he looked all around him. "How cold it is here! how large and void!"

And he clung to Gerda, and she laughed and wept for joy. It was so glorious that even the pieces of ice round about danced for joy; and when they were tired and lay down, they formed themselves just into the letters of which the Snow Queen had said that if he found them out he should be his own master, and she would give him the whole world and a new pair of skates.

And Gerda kissed his cheeks, and they became blooming; she kissed his eyes, and they shone like her own; she kissed his hands and feet,

GERDA AND KAY RETURNING HOME

and he became well and merry. The Snow Queen might now come home; his letter of release stood written in shining characters of ice.

And they took one another by the hand, and wandered forth from the great palace of ice. They spoke of the grandmother, and of the roses on the roof; and where they went the winds rested and the sun burst forth; and when they came to the bush with the red berries, the Reindeer was standing there waiting: it had brought another young reindeer, which gave the children warm milk, and kissed them on the mouth. Then they carried Kay and Gerda, first to the Finnish woman, where they warmed themselves thoroughly in the hot room, and received instructions for their journey home, and then to the Lapland woman. who had made their new clothes and put their sledge in order.

The Reindeer and the young one sprang at their side, and followed them as far as the boundary of the country.   There the first green sprouted forth, and there they took leave of the two reindeers and the Lapland woman.   "Farewell!" said all.   And the first little birds began to twitter, the forest was decked with green buds, and out of it on a beautiful horse (which Gerda knew, for it was the same that had drawn her golden coach) a young girl came riding, with a shining red cap on her head and a pair of pistols in the holsters.   This was the little robber girl, who had grown tired of staying at home, and wished to go first to the north, and if that did not suit her, to some other region. She knew Gerda at once, and Gerda knew her too; and it was a right merry meeting.

"You are a fine fellow to gad about!" she said to little Kay.   "I should like to know if you deserve that one should run to the end of the world after you?"

But Gerda patted her cheeks, and asked after the Prince and Princess.

"They 've gone to foreign countries," said the robber girl.

"But the Crow?" said Gerda.

"Why, the Crow is dead," answered the other.   "The tame one has become a widow, and goes about with an end of black worsted thread round her leg.   She complains most lamentably, but it 's all talk.   But now tell me how you have fared, and how you caught him."

And Gerda and Kay told their story.

"Snipp-snapp-snurre-purre-base llurre!" said the robber girl.

And she took them both by the hand, and promised that if she ever came through their town, she would come up and pay them a visit. And then she rode away into the wide world.   But Gerda and Kay went hand in hand, and as they went it became beautiful spring, with green and with flowers.   The church bells sounded, and they recognized the high steeples and the great town: it was the one in which they lived; and they went to the grandmother's door, and up the stairs, and into the room, where everything remained in its usual place.   The big clock was going "Tick! tack!" and the hands were turning; but as they went through the rooms they noticed that they had become grown-up people. The roses out on the roof gutter were blooming in at the open window, and there stood the little children's chairs, and Kay and Gerda sat each upon their own, and held each other by the hand.   They had forgotten the cold empty splendour at the Snow Queen's like a heavy dream.   The grandmother was sitting in God's bright sunshine, and read aloud out of the Bible, "Except ye become as little children, ye shall in no wise enter into the kingdom of God."

And Kay and Gerda looked into each other's eyes, and all at once they understood the old song—

> "Roses bloom and roses decay,
> But we the Christ–child shall see one day."

There they both sat, grown up, and yet children—children in heart— and it was summer, warm delightful summer.

THE NIGHTINGALE.

In China, you must know, the Emperor is a Chinaman, and all whom he has about him are Chinamen too. It happened a good many years ago, but that's just why it's worth while to hear the story, before it is forgotten. The Emperor's palace was the most splendid in the world; it was made entirely of porcelain, very costly, but so delicate and brittle that one had to take care how one touched it. In the garden were to be seen the most wonderful flowers, and to the costliest of them silver bells were tied, which sounded, so that nobody should pass by without noticing the flowers. Yes, everything in the Emperor's garden was admirably arranged. And it extended so far, that the gardener himself did not know where the end was. If a man went on and on, he came into a glorious forest with high trees and deep lakes. The wood extended straight down to the sea, which was blue and deep; great ships could sail to beneath the branches of the trees; and in the trees lived a Nightingale, which sang so splendidly that even the poor fisherman, who had many other things to do, stopped still and listened, when he had gone out at night to throw out his nets, and heard the Nightingale.

"How beautiful that is!" he said; but he was obliged to attend to his property, and thus forgot the bird. But when in the next night the bird sang again, and the fisherman heard it, he exclaimed again, "How beautiful that is!"

From all the countries of the world travellers came to the city of the Emperor, and admired it, and the palace, and the garden, but when they heard the Nightingale, they said, "That is the best of all!"

And the travellers told of it when they came home; and the learned men wrote many books about the town, the palace, and the garden. But they did not forget the Nightingale; that was placed highest of all; and those who were poets wrote most magnificent poems about the Nightingale in the wood by the deep lake.

The books went through all the world, and a few of them once came to the Emperor. He sat in his golden chair, and read, and read: every moment he nodded his head, for it pleased him to peruse the masterly descriptions of the city, the palace, and the garden. "But the Nightingale is the best of all," it stood written there.

"What's that?" exclaimed the Emperor. "I don't know the Nightingale at all! Is there such a bird in my empire, and even in my garden? I've never heard of that. To think that I should have to learn such a thing for the first time from books!"

And hereupon he called his cavalier. This cavalier was so grand that if any one lower in rank than himself dared to speak to him, or to ask him any question, he answered nothing but "P!"—and that meant nothing.

"There is said to be a wonderful bird here called a Nightingale!" said the Emperor. "They say it is the best thing in all my great empire. Why have I never heard anything about it?"

"I have never heard him named," replied the cavalier. "He has never been introduced at court."

"I command that he shall appear this evening, and sing before me," said the Emperor. "All the world knows what I possess, and I do not know it myself!"

"I have never heard him mentioned," said the cavalier. "I will seek for him. I will find him."

But where was he to be found? The cavalier ran up and down all the staircases, through halls and passages, but no one among all those whom he met had heard talk of the nightingale. And the cavalier ran back to the Emperor, and said that it must be a fable invented by the writers of books.

"Your Imperial Majesty cannot believe how much is written that is fiction, besides something that they call the black art."

"But the book in which I read this," said the Emperor, "was sent to me by the high and mighty Emperor of Japan, and therefore it cannot be a falsehood. I will hear the Nightingale! It must be here this evening! It has my imperial favour; and if it does not come, all the court shall be trampled upon after the court has supped!"

"Tsing-pe!" said the cavalier; and again he ran up and down all the staircases, and through all the halls and corridors; and half the court ran with him, for the courtiers did not like being trampled upon.

Then there was a great inquiry after the wonderful Nightingale, which all the world knew excepting the people at court.

At last they met with a poor little girl in the kitchen, who said,

"The Nightingale? I know it well; yes, it can sing gloriously. Every evening I get leave to carry my poor sick mother the scraps from the table. She lives down by the strand, and when I get back and am tired, and rest in the wood, then I hear the Nightingale sing. And then the water comes into my eyes, and it is just as if my mother kissed me!"

"Little kitchen girl," said the cavalier, "I will get you a place in the kitchen, with permission to see the Emperor dine, if you will lead us to the Nightingale, for it is announced for this evening."

So they all went out into the wood where the Nightingale was accustomed to sing; half the court went forth. When they were in the midst of their journey a cow began to low.

"Oh!" cried the court pages, "now we have it! That shows a wonderful power in so small a creature! I have certainly heard it before."

"No, those are cows lowing!" said the little kitchen girl. "We are a long way from the place yet."

Now the frogs began to croak in the marsh.

"Glorious!" said the Chinese court preacher. "Now I hear it—it sounds just like little church bells."

"No, those are frogs!" said the little kitchenmaid. "But now I think we shall soon hear it."

THE COURTIERS FIND THE NIGHTINGALE.

And then the Nightingale began to sing.

"That is it!" exclaimed the little girl. "Listen, listen! and yonder it sits."

And she pointed to a little grey bird up in the boughs.

"Is it possible?" cried the cavalier. "I should never have thought it looked like that! How simple it looks! It must certainly have lost its colour at seeing such grand people around."

"Little Nightingale!" called the little kitchenmaid, quite loudly, "our gracious Emperor wishes you to sing before him."

"With the greatest pleasure!" replied the Nightingale, and began to sing most delightfully.

"It sounds just like glass bells!" said the cavalier. "And look at its little throat, how it's working! It's wonderful that we should never have heard it before. That bird will be a great success at court."

"Shall I sing once more before the Emperor?" asked the Nightingale, for it thought the Emperor was present.

" My excellent little Nightingale," said the cavalier, " I have great pleasure in inviting you to a court festival this evening, when you shall charm his Imperial Majesty with your beautiful singing."

" My song sounds best in the green wood ! " replied the Nightingale; still it came willingly when it heard what the Emperor wished.

The palace was festively adorned. The walls and the flooring, which were of porcelain, gleamed in the rays of thousands of golden lamps. The most glorious flowers, which could ring clearly, had been placed in the passages. There was a running to and fro, and a thorough draught, and all the bells rang so loudly that one could not hear one-self speak.

In the midst of the great hall, where the Emperor sat, a golden perch had been placed, on which the Nightingale was to sit. The whole court was there, and the little cook-maid had got leave to stand behind the door, as she had now received the title of a real court cook. All were in full dress, and all looked at the little grey bird, to which the Emperor nodded.

And the Nightingale sang so gloriously that the tears came into the Emperor's eyes, and the tears ran down over his cheeks; and then the Nightingale sang still more sweetly, that went straight to the heart. The Emperor was so much pleased that he said the Nightingale should have his golden slipper to wear round its neck. But the Nightingale declined this with thanks, saying it had already received a sufficient reward.

" I have seen tears in the Emperor's eyes—that is the real treasure to me. An Emperor's tears have a peculiar power. I am rewarded enough ! " And then it sang again with a sweet glorious voice.

" That's the most amiable coquetry I ever saw ! " said the ladies who stood round about, and then they took water in their mouths to gurgle when any one spoke to them. They thought they should be nightin-gales too. And the lackeys and chambermaids reported that they were satisfied too; and that was saying a good deal, for they are the most difficult to please. In short, the Nightingale achieved a real success.

It was now to remain at court, to have its own cage, with liberty to go out twice every day and once at night. Twelve servants were appointed when the Nightingale went out, each of whom had a silken string fastened to the bird's leg, and which they held very tight. There was really no pleasure in an excursion of that kind.

The whole city spoke of the wonderful bird, and when two people met, one said nothing but " Nightin," and the other said "gale ; " and then they sighed, and understood one another. Eleven pedlers' children were named after the bird, but not one of them could sing a note.

One day the Emperor received a large parcel, on which was written " The Nightingale."

" There we have a new book about this celebrated bird," said the Emperor.

But it was not a book, but a little work of art, contained in a box, an artificial nightingale, which was to sing like a natural one, and was

THE NIGHTINGALE SINGING BEFORE THE EMPEROR.

brilliantly ornamented with diamonds, rubies, and sapphires. So soon as the artificial bird was wound up, he could sing one of the pieces that he really sang, and then his tail moved up and down, and shone with

silver and gold. Round his neck hung a little ribbon, and on that was
written, "The Emperor of China's nightingale is poor compared to that
of the Emperor of Japan."

"That is capital!" said they all, and he who had brought the artificial
bird immediately received the title, Imperial Head-Nightingale-Bringer.

"Now they must sing together; what a duet that will be!"

And so they had to sing together; but it did not sound very well, for
the real Nightingale sang in its own way, and the artificial bird sang
waltzes.

"That's not his fault," said the playmaster; "he's quite perfect, and
very much in my style."

Now the artificial bird was to sing alone. He had just as much
success as the real one, and then it was much handsomer to look at—it
shone like bracelets and breast-pins.

Three and thirty times over did it sing the same piece, and yet was
not tired. The people would gladly have heard it again, but the
Emperor said that the living Nightingale ought to sing something now.
But where was it? No one had noticed that it had flown away out of
the open window, back to the green wood.

"But what is become of that?" said the Emperor.

And all the courtiers abused the Nightingale, and declared that it
was a very ungrateful creature.

"We have the best bird, after all," said they.

And so the artificial bird had to sing again, and that was the thirty-
fourth time that they listened to the same piece. For all that they did
not know it quite by heart, for it was so very difficult. And the playmaster praised the bird particularly; yes, he declared that it was better
than a nightingale, not only with regard to its plumage and the many
beautiful diamonds, but inside as well.

"For you see, ladies and gentlemen, and above all, your Imperial
Majesty, with a real nightingale one can never calculate what is coming,
but in this artificial bird everything is settled. One can explain it; one
can open it and make people understand where the waltzes come from,
how they go, and how one follows up another."

"Those are quite our own ideas," they all said.

And the speaker received permission to show the bird to the people
on the next Sunday. The people were to hear it sing too, the Emperor
commanded; and they did hear it, and were as much pleased as if they
had all got tipsy upon tea, for that's quite the Chinese fashion; and
they all said, "Oh!" and held up their forefingers and nodded. But
the poor fisherman, who had heard the real Nightingale, said,

"It sounds pretty enough, and the melodies resemble each other, but
there's something wanting, though I know not what!"

The real Nightingale was banished from the country and empire. The
artificial bird had its place on a silken cushion close to the Emperor's
bed; all the presents it had received, gold and precious stones, were
ranged about it; in title it had advanced to be the High Imperial After-
Dinner-Singer, and in rank to number one on the left hand; for the

Emperor considered that side the most important on which the heart is placed, and even in an Emperor the heart is on the left side; and the playmaster wrote a work of five and twenty volumes about the artificial bird; it was very learned and very long, full of the most difficult Chinese words; but yet all the people declared that they had read it and understood it, for fear of being considered stupid, and having their bodies trampled on.

So a whole year went by. The Emperor, the court, and all the other Chinese knew every little twitter in the artificial bird's song by heart. But just for that reason it pleased them best—they could sing with it themselves, and they did so. The street boys sang, "Tsi-tsi-tsi-glug-glug!" and the Emperor himself sang it too. Yes, that was certainly famous.

But one evening, when the artificial bird was singing its best, and the Emperor lay in bed listening to it, something inside the bird said, "Whizz!" Something cracked. "Whir-r-r!" All the wheels ran round, and then the music stopped.

The Emperor immediately sprang out of bed, and caused his body physician to be called; but what could *he* do? Then they sent for a watchmaker, and after a good deal of talking and investigation, the bird was put into something like order; but the watchmaker said that the bird must be carefully treated, for the barrels were worn, and it would be impossible to put new ones in in such a manner that the music would go. There was a great lamentation; only once in a year was it permitted to let the bird sing, and that was almost too much. But then the playmaster made a little speech, full of heavy words, and said this was just as good as before—and so of course it was as good as before.

Now five years had gone by, and a real grief came upon the whole nation. The Chinese were really fond of their Emperor, and now he was ill, and could not, it was said, live much longer. Already a new Emperor had been chosen, and the people stood out in the street and asked the cavalier how their old Emperor did.

"P!" said he, and shook his head.

Cold and pale lay the Emperor in his great gorgeous bed; the whole court thought him dead, and each one ran to pay homage to the new ruler. The chamberlains ran out to talk it over, and the ladies'-maids had a great coffee party. All about, in all the halls and passages, cloth had been laid down so that no footstep could be heard, and therefore it was quiet there, quite quiet. But the Emperor was not dead yet: stiff and pale he lay on the gorgeous bed with the long velvet curtains and the heavy gold tassels; high up, a window stood open, and the moon shone in upon the Emperor and the artificial bird.

The poor Emperor could scarcely breathe; it was just as if something lay upon his chest: he opened his eyes, and then he saw that it was Death who sat upon his chest, and had put on his golden crown, and held in one hand the Emperor's sword, and in the other his beautiful banner. And all around, from among the folds of the splendid velvet curtains, strange heads peered forth; a few very ugly, the rest quite lovely and mild. These were all the Emperor's bad and good deeds, that stood before him now that Death sat upon his heart.

"Do you remember this?" whispered one to the other, "Do you remember that?" and then they told him so much that the perspiration ran from his forehead.

"I did not know that!" said the Emperor. "Music! music! the great Chinese drum!" he cried, "so that I need not hear all they say!"

And they continued speaking, and Death nodded like a Chinaman to all they said.

"Music! music!" cried the Emperor. "You little precious golden bird, sing, sing! I have given you gold and costly presents; I have even hung my golden slipper around your neck—sing now, sing!"

But the bird stood still; no one was there to wind him up, and he could not sing without that; but Death continued to stare at the Emperor with his great hollow eyes, and it was quiet, fearfully quiet.

Then there sounded from the window, suddenly, the most lovely song. It was the little live Nightingale, that sat outside on a spray. It had heard of the Emperor's sad plight, and had come to sing to him of comfort and hope. And as it sang the spectres grew paler and paler; the blood ran quicker and more quickly through the Emperor's weak limbs; and even Death listened, and said,

"Go on, little Nightingale, go on!"

"But will you give me that splendid golden sword? Will you give me that rich banner? Will you give me the Emperor's crown?"

And Death gave up each of these treasures for a song. And the Nightingale sang on and on; and it sang of the quiet churchyard where the white roses grow, where the elder blossom smells sweet, and where the fresh grass is moistened by the tears of survivors. Then Death felt a longing to see his garden, and floated out at the window in the form of a cold white mist.

"Thanks! thanks!" said the Emperor. "You heavenly little bird! I know you well. I banished you from my country and empire, and yet you have charmed away the evil faces from my couch, and banished Death from my heart! How can I reward you?"

"You have rewarded me!" replied the Nightingale. "I have drawn tears from your eyes, when I sang the first time—I shall never forget that. Those are the jewels that rejoice a singer's heart. But now sleep and grow fresh and strong again. I will sing you something."

And it sang, and the Emperor fell into a sweet slumber. Ah! how mild and refreshing that sleep was! The sun shone upon him through the windows, when he awoke refreshed and restored: not one of his servants had yet returned, for they all thought he was dead; only the Nightingale still sat beside him and sang.

"You must always stay with me," said the Emperor. "You shall sing as you please; and I'll break the artificial bird into a thousand pieces."

"Not so," replied the Nightingale. "It did well as long as it could; keep it as you have done till now. I cannot build my nest in the palace to dwell in it, but let me come when I feel the wish; then I will sit in the evening on the spray yonder by the window, and sing you something, so that you may be glad and thoughtful at once. I will sing of those who are happy and of those who suffer. I will sing of good and of evil that remains hidden round about you. The little singing bird flies far around, to the poor fisherman, to the peasant's roof, to every one who dwells far away from you and from your court. I love your heart more than your crown, and yet the crown has an air of sanctity about it. I will come and sing to you—but one thing you must promise me."

"Everything!" said the Emperor; and he stood there in his imperial robes, which he had put on himself, and pressed the sword which was heavy with gold to his heart.

"One thing I beg of you: tell no one that you have a little bird who tells you everything. Then it will go all the better."

And the Nightingale flew away.

The servants came in to look to their dead Emperor, and—yes, there he stood, and the Emperor said "Good morning!"

THE NEIGHBOURING FAMILIES.

ONE would really have thought that something important was going on by the duck-pond; but nothing was going on. All the ducks lying quietly upon the water, or standing on their heads in it—for they could do that—swam suddenly to the shore. One could see the traces of their feet on the wet earth, and their quacking sounded far and wide. The water, lately clear and bright as a mirror, was quite in a commotion. Before, every tree, every neighbouring bush, the old farm-house with the holes in the roof and the swallow's nest, and especially the great rose bush covered with flowers, had been mirrored in it. This rose bush covered the wall and hung over the water, in which everything appeared as in a picture, only that everything stood on its head; but when the water was set in motion everything swam away, and the picture was gone. Two feathers, which the fluttering ducks had lost, floated to and fro, and all at once they took a start, as if the wind were coming; but the wind did not come, so they had to be still, and the water became quiet and smooth again. The Roses mirrored themselves in it again; they were beautiful, but they did not know it, for no one had told them. The sun shone among the delicate leaves; everything breathed in the sweet fragrance, and all felt as we feel when we are filled with the thought of our greatest happiness.

"How beautiful is life!" said each Rose. "Only one thing I wish, that I were able to kiss the sun, because it is so bright and so warm. The roses, too, in the water yonder, our images, I should like to kiss, and the pretty birds in the nests. There are some up yonder too; they thrust out their heads and pipe quite feebly: they have no feathers like their father and mother. They are good neighbours, below and above. How beautiful is life!"

The young ones above and below: those below are certainly only shadows in the water—mere Sparrows; their parents were Sparrows too; they had taken possession of the empty swallow's nest of last year, and kept house in it as if it had been their own.

"Are those ducks' children swimming yonder?" asked the young Sparrows, when they noticed the ducks' feathers upon the water.

"If you must ask questions, ask sensible ones," replied their mother. "Don't you see that they are feathers? living clothes, stuff like I wear

THE DUCK-POND.

and like you will wear; but ours is finer. I wish, by the way, we had those up here in our own nest, for they keep one warm. I wonder what the ducks were so frightened at. Not at us, certainly, though I said 'piep' to you rather loudly. The thick-headed roses ought to know it, but they know nothing; they only look at one another and smell. I'm very tired of those neighbours."

"Just listen to those darling birds up there," said the Roses. "They begin to want to sing, but are not able yet. But it will be managed in time. What a pleasure that must be! It's nice to have such merry neighbours."

Suddenly two horses came gallopping up to water. A peasant boy rode on one, and he had taken off all his clothes, except his big broad straw hat. The boy whistled like a bird, and rode into the pond where it was deepest, and when he came past the rose bush he plucked a rose, and put it upon his hat. And now he thought he looked very fine, and rode on. The other Roses looked after their sister, and said to each other, "Whither may she be journeying?" but they did not know.

"I should like to go out into the world," said one; "but it's beautiful, too, here at home among the green leaves. All day the sun shines warm and bright, and in the night-time the sky is more beautiful still; we can see that through all the little holes in it."

They meant the stars, but they knew no better.

"We make it lively about the house," said the Mother-Sparrow; "and 'the swallow's nest brings luck,' people say, so they're glad to see us. But the neighbours! Such a rose bush climbing up the wall causes damp. It will most likely be taken away; and then, at least, corn will perhaps grow here. The roses are fit for nothing but to be looked at, or at most one may be stuck on a hat. Every year, I know from my mother, they fall off. The farmer's wife preserves them, and puts salt among them; then they get a French name that I neither can nor will pronounce, and are put upon the fire to make a good smell. You see, *that*'s their life. They're only for the eye and the nose. Now you know it."

When the evening came, and the gnats played in the warm air and the red clouds, the nightingale came and sang to the Roses, saying that the beautiful was like sunshine to the world, and that the beautiful lived for ever. But the Roses thought the nightingale was singing of itself, and indeed one might easily have thought so; they never imagined that the song was about them. But they rejoiced greatly in it, and wondered whether all the little Sparrows might become nightingales.

"I understood the song of that bird very well," said the young Sparrows, "only one word was not clear. What is *the beautiful?*"

"That's nothing at all," replied the Mother-Sparrow; "that's only an outside affair. Yonder, at the nobleman's seat, where the pigeons have their own house, and have corn and peas strewn before them every day, —I've been there myself and dined with them; for tell me what company you keep, and I'll tell you who you are—yonder at the nobleman's seat there are two birds with green necks and a crest upon their head, they can spread out their tails like a great shell, and then it plays with various colours, so that the sight makes one's eyes ache. These birds are called peacocks, and that's *the beautiful*. They should only be plucked a little, then they would look no better than all the rest of us. I should have plucked them myself if they had not been so large."

"I'll pluck them," piped the little Sparrow who had no feathers yet.

In the farm-house dwelt two young married people; they loved each other well, were industrious and active, and everything in their home looked very pretty. On Sunday morning the young wife came out, plucked a hand-full of the most beautiful roses, and put them into a glass of water, which she put upon the cupboard.

"Now I see that it is Sunday," said the husband, and he kissed his little wife.

They sat down, read their hymn-book, and held each other by the hand; and the sun shone on the fresh roses and the young couple.

"This sight is really too wearisome," said the Mother-Sparrow, who could look from the nest into the room; and she flew away.

The same thing happened the next Sunday, for every Sunday fresh roses were placed in the glass; but the rose bush bloomed as beautiful as ever.

The young Sparrow had feathers now, and wanted to fly out too, but the mother would not allow it, and they were obliged to stay at home. She flew alone; but, however it may have happened, before she was aware of it, she was entangled in a noose of horse-hair which some boys had fastened to the branches. The horse-hair wound itself fast round her legs, as fast as if it would cut the leg through. What pain, what a fright she was in!

The boys came running up, and seized the bird; and indeed, roughly enough.

"It's only a Sparrow," said they; but they did not let her go, but took her home with them. And whenever she cried, they tapped her on the beak.

In the farm-house stood an old man, who understood making soap for shaving and washing, in cakes as well as in balls. He was a merry, wandering old man. When he saw the Sparrow, which the boys had brought, and for which they said they did not care, he said,

"Shall we make it very beautiful?"

The Mother-Sparrow felt an icy shudder pass through her.

Out of the box, in which were the most brilliant colours, the old man took a quantity of shining gold leaf, and the boys were sent for some white of egg, with which the Sparrow was completely smeared; the gold leaf was stuck upon that, and there was the Mother-Sparrow gilded all over. She did not think of the adornment, but trembled all over. And the soap-man tore off a fragment from the red lining of his old jacket, cut notches in it, so that it looked like a cock's comb, and stuck it on the bird's head.

"Now you shall see the gold jacket fly," said the old man; and he released the Sparrow, which flew away in deadly fear, with the sunlight shining upon her.

How it glittered! All the sparrows, and even a crow, a knowing old boy, were startled at the sight; but still they flew after her, to know what kind of strange bird this might be.

Driven by fear and horror, she flew homeward; she was nearly sinking powerless to the earth; the flock of pursuing birds increased, and some even tried to peck at her.

"Look at her! look at her!" they all cried.

"Look at her! look at her!" cried the young ones, when the Mother-Sparrow approached the nest. "That must be a young peacock. He glitters with all colours. It quite hurts one's eyes, as mother told us. Piep! that's *the beautiful!*"

And now they pecked at the bird with their little beaks, so that she could not possibly get into the nest; she was so much exhausted that she could not even say "Piep!" much less "I am your mother!"

The other birds also fell upon the Sparrow, and plucked off feather after feather till she fell bleeding into the rose bush.

"You poor creature!" said all the Roses: "be quiet, and we will hide you. Lean your head against us."

The Sparrow spread out her wings once more, then drew them tight to her body, and lay dead by the neighbouring family, the beautiful fresh Roses.

THE PAINTER SKETCHING THE ROSE BUSH.

"Piep!" sounded from the nest. "Where can our mother be? It's quite inexplicable. It cannot be a trick of hers, and mean that we're to shift for ourselves: she has left us the house as an inheritance, but to which of us shall it belong when we have families of our own?"

"Yes, it won't do for you to stay with me when I enlarge my establishment with a wife and children," observed the smallest.

"I shall have more wives and children than you!" cried the second.

"But I am the eldest!" said the third.

Now they all became excited. They struck out with their wings, hacked with their beaks, and flump! one after another was thrust out of the nest. There they lay with their anger, holding their heads on one side, and blinking with the eye that looked upwards. That was their way to look so stupid.

They could fly a little; by practice they improved, and at last they fixed upon a sign by which they should know each other when they met later in the world. This sign was to be the cry of "Piep!" with a scratching of the left foot three times against the ground.

The young sparrow that had remained behind in the nest made itself as broad as it possibly could, for it was the proprietor. But the proprietorship did not last long. In the night the red fire burst through the window, the flames seized upon the roof, the dry straw blazed brightly up, and the whole house was burned, and the young sparrow too; but the two others who wanted to marry managed to escape with their lives.

When the sun rose again, and everything looked as much refreshed as if nature had had a quiet sleep, there remained of the farm-house nothing but a few charred beams, leaning against the chimney that was now its own master. Thick smoke still rose from among the fragments, but without stood the rose bush quite unharmed, and every flower, every twig was immersed in the clear water.

"How beautifully those roses bloom before the ruined house!" cried a passer by. "I cannot imagine a more agreeable picture: I must have that."

And the traveller took out of his portfolio a little book with white leaves: he was a painter, and with his pencil he drew the smoking house, the charred beams, and the overhanging chimney, which bent more and more; quite in the foreground appeared the blooming rose bush, which presented a charming sight, and indeed for its sake the whole picture had been made.

Later in the day, the two Sparrows that had been born here came by. "Where is the house?" asked they. "Where is the nest? Piep! All is burned, and our strong brother is burned too. That's what he has got by keeping the nest to himself. The Roses have escaped well enough—there they stand yet, with their red cheeks. They certainly don't mourn at their neighbour's misfortune. I won't speak to them, it's so ugly here, that's my opinion." And it flew up and away.

On a beautiful sunny autumn day, when one could almost have believed it was the middle of summer, there hopped about in the clean dry courtyard of the nobleman's seat, in front of the great steps, a number of pigeons, black, and white, and variegated, all shining in the sunlight. The old Mother-Pigeons said to their young ones,

"Stand in groups, stand in groups, for that looks much better."

"What are those little grey creatures, that run about behind us?" asked an old Pigeon, with red and green in her eyes. "Little grey ones, little grey ones!" she cried.

"They are sparrows, good creatures. We have always had the reputation of being kind, so we will allow them to pick up the corn with us.

They don't interrupt conversation, and they make such very pretty courtesies."

Yes, they courtesied three times each with the left leg, and said, "Piep." By that they recognized each other as the Sparrows from the nest by the burned house.

"Here's very good eating," said the Sparrows.

The Pigeons strutted round one another, bulged out their chests mightily, and had their own secret views and opinions on things in general.

"Do you see that pouter pigeon?" said one, speaking to the others. "Do you see that one, swallowing the peas? She takes too many, and the best, moreover. Curoo! curoo! How she lifts up her crest, the ugly spiteful thing! Curoo! curoo!"

And all their eyes sparkled with spite.

"Stand in groups, stand in groups! Little grey ones, little grey ones! Curoo! curoo!"

So their beaks went on and on, and so they will go on when a thousand years are gone.

The Sparrows feasted bravely. They listened attentively, and even stood in the ranks of the Pigeons, but it did not suit them well. They were satisfied, and so they quitted the Pigeons, exchanged opinions concerning them, slipped under the garden railings, and when they found the door of the garden open, one of them, who was over-fed, and consequently valorous, hopped on the threshold.

"Piep!" said he, "I may venture that."

"Piep!" said the other, "so can I, and something more too."

And he hopped right into the room. No one was present; the third Sparrow saw that, and hopped still farther into the room, and said,

"Everything or nothing! By the way, this is a funny man's-nest; and what have they put up there? What's that?"

Just in front of the Sparrows the roses were blooming; they were mirrored in the water, and the charred beams leaned against the toppling chimney.

"Why, what is this? How came this in the room in the nobleman's seat?"

And then these Sparrows wanted to fly over the chimney and the roses, but flew against a flat wall. It was all a picture, a great beautiful picture, that the painter had completed from a sketch.

"Piep!" said the Sparrows, "it's nothing, it only looks like something. Piep! that's *the beautiful!* Can you understand it? *I* can't."

And they flew away, for some people came into the room.

Days and years went by. The Pigeons had often cooed, not to say growled, the spiteful things; the Sparrows had suffered cold in winter, and lived riotously in summer; they were all betrothed or married, or whatever you like to call it. They had little ones, and of course each thought his own the handsomest and the cleverest: one flew this way, another that, and when they met they knew each other by their "Piep!" and the three courtesies with the left leg. The eldest had remained a

maiden Sparrow, with no nest and no young ones.   Her great idea was
to see a town, therefore she flew to Copenhagen.

There was to be seen a great house painted with many colours, close
by the castle and by the canal, in which latter swam many ships laden
with apples and pottery.   The windows were broader below than at
the top, and when the Sparrows looked through, every room appeared
to them like a tulip with the most beautiful colours and shades.   But
in the middle of the tulip were white people, made of marble; a few
certainly were made of plaster, but in the eyes of a sparrow that's all
the same.   Upon the roof stood a metal carriage, with metal horses
harnessed to it, and the Goddess of Victory, also of bronze, driving.
It was THORWALDSEN'S MUSEUM.

"How it shines! how it shines!" said the little maiden Sparrow.
"I suppose that's what they call *the beautiful*.   Piep!   But this is
greater than the peacock!"

It still remembered what, in its days of childhood, the Mother-Sparrow had declared to be the greatest among the beautiful.   The Sparrow
flew down into the courtyard.   There everything was very splendid:
upon the walls palms and branches were painted; in the midst of the
court stood a great blooming rose tree, spreading out its fresh branches,
covered with many roses, over a grave.   Thither the maiden Sparrow
flew, for there she saw many of her own kind.   "Piep!" and three
courtesies with the left leg—that salutation it had often made throughout
the summer, and nobody had replied, for friends who are once parted
don't meet every day; and now this form of greeting had become quite
a habit with it.   But to-day two old Sparrows and a young one replied
"Piep!" and courtesied three times, each with the left leg.

"Ah! good day! good day!"   They were two old ones from the nest,
and a little one belonging to the family.   "Do we meet here again?
It's a grand place, but there's not much to eat.   This is *the beautiful!*
Piep!"

And many people came out of the side chambers where the glorious
marble statues stood, and approached the grave where slept the great
master who had formed these marble images.   All stood with radiant
faces by Thorwaldsen's grave, and some gathered up the fallen rose
leaves and kept them.   They had come from afar: one from mighty
England, others from Germany and France.   The most beautiful among
the ladies plucked one of the roses and hid it in her bosom.   Then the
Sparrows thought that the roses ruled here, and that the whole house
had been built for their sake; that appeared to them to be too much;
but as all the people showed their love for the roses, they would not be
behindhand.   "Piep!" they said, and swept the ground with their tails,
and glanced with one eye at the roses; and they had not looked long at
the flowers before they recognized them as old neighbours.   And so
the roses really were.   The painter who had sketched the rose bush by
the ruined house had afterwards received permission to dig it up, and
had given it to the architect, for nowhere could more beautiful roses be
found.   And the architect had planted it upon Thorwaldsen's grave,

where it bloomed, an image of the beautiful, and gave its red fragrant leaves to be carried into distant lands as mementoes.

"Have you found a situation here in the town?" asked the Sparrows.

And the Roses nodded; they recognized their brown neighbours, and were glad to see them again. "How glorious it is to live and bloom, to see old faces again, and cheerful faces every day!"

"Piep!" said the Sparrows. "Yes, these are truly our old neighbours; we remember their origin by the pond. Piep! how they've got on! Yes, some people succeed while they're asleep. Why, yonder is a withered leaf—I see it quite plainly!"

And they pecked at it till the leaf fell. But the tree stood there greener and fresher than ever; the Roses bloomed in the sunshine by Thorwaldsen's grave, and were associated with his immortal name.

THE LITTLE MATCH GIRL.

It was terribly cold; it snowed and was already almost dark, and evening came on, the last evening of the year. In the cold and gloom a poor little girl, bare headed and barefoot, was walking through the streets. When she left her own house she certainly had had slippers on; but of what use were they? They were very big slippers, and her mother had used them till then, so big were they. The little maid lost them as she slipped across the road, where two carriages were rattling by terribly fast. One slipper was not to be found again, and a boy had seized the other, and run away with it. He thought he could use it very well as a cradle, some day when he had children of his own. So now the little girl went with her little naked feet, which were quite red and blue with the cold. In an old apron she carried a number of matches, and a bundle of them in her hand. No one had bought anything of her all day, and no one had given her a farthing.

Shivering with cold and hunger she crept along, a picture of misery, poor little girl! The snow-flakes covered her long fair hair, which fell in pretty curls over her neck; but she did not think of that now. In all the windows lights were shining, and there was a glorious smell of roast goose, for it was New Year's-eve. Yes, she thought of that!

In a corner formed by two houses, one of which projected beyond the other, she sat down, cowering. She had drawn up her little feet, but she was still colder, and she did not dare to go home, for she had sold no matches, and did not bring a farthing of money. From her father she would certainly receive a beating, and besides, it was cold at home, for they had nothing over them but a roof through which the wind whistled, though the largest rents had been stopped with straw and rags.

Her little hands were almost benumbed with the cold. Ah! a match might do her good, if she could only draw one from the bundle, and rub it against the wall. and warm her hands at it. She drew one out.

THE PEOPLE FIND THE LITTLE MATCH GIRL.

R-r-atch! how it sputtered and burned! It was a warm bright flame, like a little candle, when she held her hands over it; it was a wonderful little light! It really seemed to the little girl as if she sat before a great polished stove, with bright brass feet and a brass cover. How the fire burned! how comfortable it was! but the little flame went out, the stove vanished, and she had only the remains of the burned match in her hand.

A second was rubbed against the wall. It burned up, and when the light fell upon the wall it became transparent like a thin veil, and she could see through it into the room. On the table a snow-white cloth was spread; upon it stood a shining dinner service; the roast goose smoked gloriously, stuffed with apples and dried plums. And what was still more splendid to behold, the goose hopped down from the dish, and waddled along the floor, with a knife and fork in its breast, to the little girl. Then the match went out, and only the thick, damp, cold wall was before her. She lighted another match. Then she was sitting under a beautiful Christmas tree; it was greater and more ornamented than the one she had seen through the glass door at the rich merchant's. Thousands of candles burned upon the green branches, and coloured pictures like those in the print shops looked down upon them. The little girl stretched forth her hand towards them; then the match went out. The Christmas lights mounted higher. She saw them now as stars in the sky: one of them fell down, forming a long line of fire.

"Now some one is dying," thought the little girl, for her old grandmother, the only person who had loved her, and who was now dead, had told her that when a star fell down a soul mounted up to God.

She rubbed another match against the wall; it became bright again, and in the brightness the old grandmother stood clear and shining, mild and lovely.

"Grandmother!" cried the child, "Oh! take me with you! I know you will go when the match is burned out. You will vanish like the warm fire, the warm food, and the great glorious Christmas tree!"

And she hastily rubbed the whole bundle of matches, for she wished to hold her grandmother fast. And the matches burned with such a glow that it became brighter than in the middle of the day; grandmother had never been so large or so beautiful. She took the little girl in her arms, and both flew in brightness and joy above the earth, very, very high, and up there was neither cold, nor hunger, nor care—they were with God!

But in the corner, leaning against the wall, sat the poor girl with red cheeks and smiling mouth, frozen to death on the last evening of the Old Year. The New Year's sun rose upon a little corpse! The child sat there, stiff and cold, with the matches of which one bundle was burned. "She wanted to warm herself," the people said. No one imagined what a beautiful thing she had seen, and in what glory she had gone in with her grandmother to the New Year's-day.

THE ELF-HILL.

A few great Lizards race nimbly about in the clefts of an old tree; they could understand each other very well, for they spoke the lizards' language.

"How it grumbles and growls in the old elf-hill!" said one Lizard. "I've not been able to close my eyes for two nights, because of the noise; I might just as well lie and have the tooth-ache, for then I can't sleep either."

"There's something wrong in there," said the other Lizard. "They let the hill stand on four red posts till the cock crows at morn. It is regularly aired, and the elf girls have learned new dances. There's something going on."

"Yes, I have spoken with an earthworm of my acquaintance," said the third Lizard "The earthworm came straight out of the hill, where he had been grubbing in the ground night and day: he had heard much. He can't see, the miserable creature, but he understands how to toss about and listen. They expect some friends in the elf-hill—grand strangers; but who they are the earthworm would not tell, and perhaps, indeed, he did not know. All the Will-o'-the-wisps are ordered to hold a torch dance, as it is called; and silver and gold, of which there is enough in the elf-hill, is being polished and put out in the moonshine."

"Who may these strangers be?" asked all the Lizards. "What can be going on there? Hark, how it hums! Hark, how it murmurs!"

At the same moment the elf-hill opened, and an old elf maid,* hollow behind, came tripping out. She was the old Elf King's housekeeper. She was a distant relative of the royal family, and wore an amber heart on her forehead. Her legs moved so rapidly—trip, trip! Gracious! how she could trip! straight down to the sea, to the night Raven.

"You are invited to the elf-hill for this evening," said she; "but will you do me a great service and undertake the invitations? You must do something, as you don't keep any house yourself. We shall have some very distinguished friends, magicians who have something to say; and so the old Elf King wants to make a display."

"Who's to be invited?" asked the night Raven.

"To the great ball the world may come, even men, if they can talk in their sleep, or do something that falls in our line. But at the first feast there's to be a strict selection; we will have only the most distinguished. I have had a dispute with the Elf King, for I declared that we could not even admit ghosts. The merman and his daughters must be invited first. They may not be very well pleased to come on the dry land, but they shall have a wet stone to sit upon, or something still better, and then I think they won't refuse for this time. All the old demons of the first class, with tails, and the wood demon and his gnomes we must have; and then I think we may not leave out the grave pig, the death horse,† and the church twig: they certainly belong to the clergy, and are not reckoned among our people. But that's only their office: they are closely related to us, and visit us diligently."

"Croak!" said the night Raven, and flew away to give the invitations.

The elf girls were already dancing on the elf-hill, and they danced with shawls which were woven of mist and moonshine; and that looks very pretty for those who like that sort of thing. In the midst, below the elf-hill, the great hall was splendidly decorated; the floor had been washed with moonshine, and the walls rubbed with witches' salve, so that they glowed like tulips in the light. In the kitchen, plenty of frogs were turning on the spit, snail-skins with children's fingers in them, and salads of mushroom spawn, damp mouse muzzles, and hemlock; beer brewed by the marsh witch, gleaming saltpetre wine from grave cellars:

---

* A prevailing superstition regarding the elf maid, or *elle maid*, is, that she is fair to look at in front, but behind she is hollow, like a mask.

† It is a popular superstition in Denmark, that under every church that is built, a living horse must be buried; the ghost of this horse is the death horse, that limps every night on three legs to the house where some one is to die. Under a few churches a living pig was buried, and the ghost of this was called the grave pig.

THE ELF KING'S FEAST.

everything very grand; and rusty nails and church window glass among the sweets.

The old Elf King had one of his crowns polished with powdered slate pencil; it was slate pencil from the first form, and it's very difficult for the Elf King to get first form slate pencil! In the bed-room, curtains were hung up, and fastened with snail slime. Yes, there was a grumbling and murmuring there!

"Now we must burn horse-hair and pig's bristles as incense here," said the Elf King, "and then I think I shall have done my part."

"Father dear!" said the youngest of the daughters, "shall I hear now who the distinguished strangers are?"

"Well," said he, "I suppose I must tell it now. Two of my daughters must hold themselves prepared to be married; two will certainly be married. The old gnome from Norway yonder, he who lives in the Dovre mountains, and possesses many rock castles of field stones, and a gold mine which is better than one thinks, is coming with his two sons, who want each to select a wife. The old gnome is a true old honest Norwegian veteran, merry and straightforward. I know him from old days, when we drank brotherhood with one another. He was down here to fetch his wife; now she is dead,—she was a daughter of the King of the Chalk-rocks of Moen. He took his wife upon chalk, as the saying is. Oh, how I long to see the old Norwegian gnome! The lads, they say, are rather rude, forward lads; but perhaps they are belied, and they'll be right enough when they grow older. Let me see that you can teach them manners."

"And when will they come?" asked the daughters.

"That depends on wind and weather," said the Elf King. "They travel economically: they come when there's a chance by a ship. I wanted them to go across Sweden, but the old one would not incline to that wish. He does not advance with the times, and I don't like that."

Then two Will-o'-the-wisps came hopping up, one quicker than the other, and so one of them arrived first.

"They're coming! they're coming!" they cried.

"Give me my crown, and let me stand in the moonshine," said the Elf King.

And the daughters lifted up their shawls and bowed down to the earth.

There stood the old gnome of Dovre, with the crown of hardened ice and polished fir cones; moreover, he wore a bear-skin and great warm boots. His sons, on the contrary, went bare necked, and with trousers without braces, for they were strong men.

"Is that an acclivity?" asked the youngest of the lads; and he pointed to the elf-hill. "In Norway yonder we should call it a hole."

"Boys!" said the old man, "holes go down, mounds go up. Have you no eyes in your heads?"

The only thing they wondered at down here, they said, was that they could understand the language without difficulty.

"Don't give yourselves airs," said the old man. "One would think you were home nurtured."

And then they went into the elf-hill, where the really grand company were assembled, and that in such haste that one might almost say they had been blown together. But for each it was nicely and prettily arranged. The sea folks sat at table in great washing tubs: they said it was just as if they were at home. All observed the ceremonies of the table except the two young Northern gnomes, and they put their legs up on the table; but they thought all that suited them well.

"Your feet off the table-cloth!" cried the old gnome.

And they obeyed, but not immediately. Their ladies they tickled with pine cones that they had brought with them, and then took off their boots for their own convenience, and gave them to the ladies to hold. But the father, the old Dovre gnome, was quite different from them : he told such fine stories of the proud Norwegian rocks, and of the waterfalls which rushed down with white foam and with a noise like thunder and the sound of organs ; he told of the salmon that leaps up against the falling waters when the Reck plays upon the golden harp ; he told of shining winter nights, when the sledge bells sound, and the lads run with burning torches over the ice, which is so transparent that they see the fishes start beneath their feet. Yes ! he could tell it so finely that one saw what he described : it was just as if the sawmills were going, as if the servants and maids were singing songs and dancing the kalling dance. Hurrah ! all at once the old gnome gave the old elf girl a kiss : that *was* a kiss ! and yet they were nothing to each other.

Now the elf maidens had to dance, nimbly, and also with stamping steps, and that suited them well ; then came the artistic and solo dance. Wonderful how they could use their legs ! one hardly knew where they began and where they ended, which were their arms and which their legs—they were all mingled together like wood shavings ; and then they whirled round till the death horse and the grave pig turned giddy and were obliged to leave the table.

" Prur ! " said the old gnome ; " that 's a strange fashion of using one's legs. But what can they do more than dance, stretch out their limbs, and make a whirlwind ? "

" You shall soon know ! " said the Elf King.

And then he called forward the youngest of his daughters. She was as light and graceful as moonshine ; she was the most delicate of all the sisters. She took a white shaving in her mouth, and then she was quite gone : that was her art.

But the old gnome said he should not like his wife to possess this art, and he did not think that his boys cared for it.

The other could walk under herself, just as if she had a shadow, and the gnome people had none. The third daughter was of quite another kind ; she had served in the brewhouse of the moor witch, and knew how to stuff elder-tree knots with glow-worms.

" She will make a good housewife," said the old gnome ; and then he winked a health with his eyes, for he did not want to drink too much.

Now came the fourth : she had a great harp to play upon, and when she struck the first chord all lifted up their left feet, for the gnomes are left-legged ; and when she struck the second chord, all were compelled to do as she wished.

" That 's a dangerous woman ! " said the old gnome ; but both the sons went out of the hill, for they had had enough of it.

" And what can the next daughter do ? " asked the Old Gnome.

" I have learned to love what is Norwegian," said she, " and I will never marry unless I can go to Norway."

But the youngest sister whispered to the old King, " That 's only because she has heard in a Norwegian song, that when the world sinks down the cliffs of Norway will remain standing like monuments, and so she wants to get up there, because she is afraid of sinking down."

"Ho! ho!" said the old gnome, "was it meant in that way? But what can the seventh and last do?"

"The sixth comes before the seventh!" said the Elf King, for he could count. But the sixth would not come out.

"I can only tell people the truth!" said she. "Nobody cares for me, and I have enough to do to sew my shroud."

Now came the seventh and last, and what could she do? Why, she could tell stories, as many as she wished.

"Here are all my fingers," said the old gnome; "tell me one for each."

And she took him by the wrist, and he laughed till it clucked within him; and when she came to the ring finger, which had a ring round its waist, just as if it knew there was to be a wedding, the old gnome said,

"Hold fast what you have: the hand is yours; I'll have you for my own wife."

And the elf girl said that the story of the ring finger and of little Peter Playman, the fifth, were still wanting.

"We'll hear those in winter," said the Gnome, "and we'll hear about the pine tree, and about the birch, and about the spirits' gifts, and about the biting frost. You shall tell your tales, for no one up there knows how to do that well; and then we'll sit in the stone chamber where the pine logs burn, and drink mead out of the horns of the old Norwegian Kings—Reck has given me a couple; and when we sit there, and the Nix comes on a visit, she'll sing you all the songs of the shepherds in the mountains. That will be merry. The salmon will spring in the waterfall, and beat against the stone walls, but he shall not come in."

"Yes, it's very good living in Norway; but where are the lads?"

Yes, where were they? They were running about in the fields, and blowing out the Will-o'-the-wisps, which had come so good naturedly for the torch dance.

"What romping about is that?" said the old gnome. "I have taken a mother for you, and now you may take one of the aunts."

But the lads said that they would rather make a speech and drink brotherhood—they did not care to marry; and they made speeches, and drank brotherhood, and tipped up their glasses on their nails, to show they had emptied them. Afterwards they took their coats off and lay down on the table to sleep, for they made no ceremony. But the old gnome danced about the room with his young bride, and he changed boots with her, for that's more fashionable than exchanging rings.

"Now the cock crows," said the old elf girl who attended to the housekeeping. "Now we must shut the shutters, so that the sun may not burn us."

And the hill shut itself up. But outside, the Lizards ran up and down in the cleft tree, and one said to the other,

"Oh, how I like that old Norwegian gnome!"

"I like the lads better," said the Earthworm. But he could not see, the miserable creature.

THE FIELD OF BUCKWHEAT.

THE BUCKWHEAT.

OFTEN, after a thunder-storm, when one passes a field in which buck-wheat is growing, it appears quite blackened and singed. It is just as if a flame of fire had passed across it; and then the countryman says, "It got that from lightning." But whence has it received that? I will tell you what the sparrow told me about it, and the sparrow heard it from an old Willow Tree which stood by a Buckwheat field, and still stands there. It is quite a great venerable Willow Tree, but crippled and old: it is burst in the middle, and grass and brambles grow out of the cleft; the tree bends forward, and the branches hang quite down to the ground, as if they were long green hair.

On all the fields round about corn was growing, not only rye and barley, but also oats, yes, the most capital oats, which when ripe looks like a number of little yellow canary birds sitting upon a spray. The corn stood smiling, and the richer an ear was, the deeper did it bend in pious humility.

But there was also a field of Buckwheat, and this field was exactly opposite to the old Willow Tree. The Buckwheat did not bend at all, like the rest of the grain, but stood up proudly and stiffly.

"I'm as rich as any corn ear," said he. "Moreover, I'm very much handsomer: my flowers are beautiful as the blossoms of the apple tree: it's quite a delight to look upon me and mine. Do you know anything more splendid than we are, you old Willow Tree?"

And the Willow Tree nodded his head, just as if he would have said, "Yes, that's true enough!"

But the Buckwheat spread itself out from mere vainglory, and said, "The stupid tree! he's so old that the grass grows in his body."

Now a terrible storm came on: all the field flowers folded their leaves together or bowed their little heads while the storm passed over them, but the Buckwheat stood erect in its pride.

"Bend your head like us," said the Flowers.

"I've not the slightest cause to do so," replied the Buckwheat.

"Bend your head as we do," cried the various Crops. "Now the storm comes flying on. He has wings that reach from the clouds just down to the earth, and he'll beat you in halves before you can cry for mercy."

"Yes, but I won't bend," quoth the Buckwheat.

"Shut up your flowers and bend your leaves," said the old Willow Tree. "Don't look up at the lightning when the cloud bursts: even men do not do that, for in the lightning one may look into heaven, but the light dazzles even men; and what would happen to us, if we dared do so—we, the plants of the field, that are much less worthy than they?"

"Much less worthy!" cried the Buckwheat. "Now I'll just look straight up into heaven."

And it did so, in its pride and vainglory. It was as if the whole world were on fire, so vivid was the lightning.

When afterwards the bad weather had passed by, the flowers and the crops stood in the still, pure air, quite refreshed by the rain; but the Buckwheat was burned coal-black by the lightning, and it was now like a dead weed upon the field.

And the old Willow Tree waved its branches in the wind, and great drops of water fell down out of the green leaves, just as if the tree wept.

And the Sparrows asked, "Why do you weep? Here everything is so cheerful: see how the sun shines, see how the clouds sail on. Do you not breathe the scent of flowers and bushes? Why do you weep, Willow Tree?"

And the Willow Tree told them of the pride of the Buckwheat, of its vainglory, and of the punishment which always follows such sin.

I, who tell you this tale, have heard it from the sparrows. They told it me one evening when I begged them to give me a story.

THE OLD HOUSE.

Down yonder, in the street, stood an old, old house. It was almost three hundred years old, for one could read as much on the beam, on which was carved the date of its erection, surrounded by tulips and trailing hops. There one could read entire verses in the characters of olden times, and over each window a face had been carved in the beam, and these faces made all kinds of grimaces. One storey projected a long way above the other, and close under the roof was a leaden gutter with a dragon's head. The rain water was to run out of the dragon's mouth, but it ran out of the creature's body instead, for there was a hole in the pipe.

All the other houses in the street were still new and neat, with large window-panes and smooth walls. One could easily see that they would have nothing to do with the old house. They thought perhaps, "How long is that old rubbish-heap to stand there, a scandal to the whole street? The parapet stands so far forward that no one can see out of our windows what is going on in that direction. The staircase is as broad as a castle staircase, and as steep as if it led to a church tower. The iron railing looks like the gate of a family vault, and there are brass bosses upon it. It's too ridiculous!"

Just opposite stood some more new neat houses that thought exactly like the rest; but here at the window sat a little boy, with fresh red cheeks, with clear sparkling eyes, and he was particularly fond of the old house, in sunshine as well as by moonlight. And when he looked down at the wall where the plaster had fallen off, then he could sit and fancy all kinds of pictures—how the street must have appeared in old times, with parapets, open staircases, and pointed gables; he could see soldiers with halberds, and roof-gutters running about in the form of dragons and griffins. That was just a good house to look at; and in it lived an old man who went about in leather knee-smalls, and wore a coat with great brass buttons, and a wig which one could at once see was a real wig. Every morning an old man came to him, to clean his rooms and run on his errands. With this exception the old man in the leather knee-smalls was all alone in the old house. Sometimes he came to one of the windows and looked out, and the little boy nodded to him, and the old man nodded back, and thus they became acquainted and became friends, though they had never spoken to one another; but, indeed, that was not at all necessary.

The little boy heard his parents say, "The old man opposite is very well off, but he is terribly lonely."

Next Sunday the little boy wrapped something in a piece of paper, went with it to the house door, and said to the man who ran errands for the old gentleman,

"Harkye: will you take this to the old gentleman opposite for me? I have two tin soldiers; this is one of them, and he shall have it, because I know that he is terribly lonely."

And the old attendant looked quite pleased, and nodded, and carried the Tin Soldier into the old house. Afterwards he was sent over, to ask if the little boy would not like to come himself and pay a visit. His parents gave him leave; and so it was that he came to the old house.

The brass bosses on the staircase shone much more brightly than usual; one would have thought they had been polished in honour of his visit. And it was just as if the carved trumpeters—for on the doors there were carved trumpeters, standing in tulips — were blowing with all their might; their cheeks looked much rounder than before. Yes, they blew "Tan-ta-ra-ra! the little boy's coming! tan-ta-ra-ra!" and then the door opened. The whole of the hall was hung with old portraits of knights in armour and ladies in silk gowns; and the armour rattled and the silk dresses rustled; and then came a staircase that went up a great way and down a little way, and then one came to a balcony which was certainly in a very rickety state, with long cracks and great holes; but out of all these grew grass and leaves, for the whole balcony, the courtyard, and the wall were overgrown with so much green that it looked like a garden, but it was only a balcony. Here stood old flower-pots that had faces with asses' ears; but the flowers grew just as they chose. In one pot pinks were growing over on all sides; that is to say, the green stalks, sprout upon sprout, and they said quite plainly, "The air has caressed me and the sun has kissed me, and promised me a little flower for next Sunday, a little flower next Sunday!"

And then they came to a room where the walls were covered with pig-skin, and golden flowers had been stamped on the leather.

> "Flowers fade fast,
> But pig-skin will last,"

said the walls. And there stood chairs with quite high backs, with carved work and elbows on each side.

"Sit down!" said they. "Oh, how it cracks inside me! Now I shall be sure to have the gout, like the old cupboard. Gout in my back, ugh!"

And then the little boy came to the room where the old man sat.

"Thank you for the Tin Soldier, my little friend," said the old man, "and thank you for coming over to me."

"Thanks! thanks!" or "Crick! crack!" said all the furniture; there were so many pieces that they almost stood in each other's way to see the little boy.

And in the middle, on the wall, hung a picture, a beautiful lady, young and cheerful in appearance, but dressed just like people of the old times, with powder in her hair and skirts that stuck out stiffly. She said neither thanks nor crack, but looked down upon the little boy with her mild eyes; and he at once asked the old man,

"Where did you get her from?"

"From the dealer opposite," replied the old man. "Many pictures are always hanging there. No one knew them or troubled himself about them, for they are all buried. But many years ago I knew this lady, and now she's been dead and gone for half a century."

And under the picture hung, behind glass, a nosegay of withered flowers; they were certainly also half a century old — at least they looked it; and the pendulum of the great clock went to and fro, and the hands turned round, and everything in the room grew older still, but no one noticed it.

"They say at home," said the little boy, "that you are always terribly solitary."

"Oh," answered the old man, "old thoughts come, with all that they bring, to visit me; and now you are coming too, I'm very well off."

And then he took from a shelf a book with pictures: there were long processions of wonderful coaches, such as one never sees at the present day, soldiers like the knave of clubs, and citizens with waving flags. The tailors had a flag with shears on it held by two lions, and the shoemakers a flag without boots, but with an eagle that had two heads; for among the shoemakers everything must be so arranged that they can say, "There's a pair." Yes, that was a picture-book! And the old man went into the other room, to fetch preserves, and apples, and nuts. It was really glorious in that old house.

"I can't stand it," said the Tin Soldier, who stood upon the shelf. "It is terribly lonely and dull here. When a person has been accustomed to family life, one cannot get accustomed to their existence here. I cannot stand it! The day is long enough, but the evening is longer still! Here it is not at all like in your house opposite, where your father and mother were always conversing cheerfully together, and you and all the other dear children made a famous noise. How solitary it is here at the old man's! Do you think he gets any kisses? Do you think he gets friendly looks, or a Christmas tree? He'll get nothing but a grave! I cannot stand it!"

"You must not look at it from the sorrowful side," said the little boy. "To me all appears remarkably pretty, and all the old thoughts, with all they bring with them, come to visit here."

"Yes, but I don't see them, and don't know them," objected the Tin Soldier. "I can't bear it!"

"You must bear it," said the little boy.

And the old man came with the pleasantest face and with the best of preserved fruits and apples and nuts; and then the little boy thought no more of the Tin Soldier. Happy and delighted, the youngster went home; and days went by, weeks went by, and there was much nodding from the boy's home across to the old house and back; and then the little boy went over there again.

And the carved trumpeters blew, "Tanta-ra-ra! tanta-ra-ra! there's the little boy, tanta-ra-ra!" and the swords and armour on the old pictures rattled, and the silken dresses rustled, and the leather told tales, and the old chairs had the gout in their backs. Ugh! it was just like the first time, for over there one day or one hour was just like another.

"I can't stand it!" said the Tin Soldier. "I've wept tears of tin. It's too dreamy here. I had rather go to war and lose my arms and legs; at any rate, that's a change. I cannot stand it! Now I know what it means to have a visit from one's old thoughts and all they bring with them. I've had visits from my own, and you may believe me, that's no pleasure in the long run. I was very nearly jumping down from the shelf. I could see you all in the house opposite as plainly as if you had been here. It was Sunday morning, and you children were all standing round the table singing the psalm you sing every morning. You were standing reverently with folded hands, and your father and mother were just as piously disposed; then the door opened, and your little sister Maria, who is not two years old yet, and who always dances when she hears music or song, of whatever description they may be, was brought in. She was not to do it, but she immediately began to dance, though she could not get into right time, for the song was too slow, so she first stood on one leg and bent her head quite over in front, but it was not long enough. You all stood very quietly, though that was rather difficult; but I laughed inwardly, and so I fell down from the table and got a bruise which I have still; for it was not right of one to laugh. But all this, and all the rest that I have experienced, now passes by my inward vision, and those must be the old thoughts with every-thing they bring with them. Tell me, do you still sing on Sundays? Tell me something about little Maria. And how is my comrade and brother tin soldier? Yes, he must be very happy. I can't stand it!"

"You have been given away," said the little boy. "You must stay where you are. Don't you see that?"

And the old man came with a box in which many things were to be seen: little rouge-pots and scent-boxes; and old cards, so large and so richly gilt as one never sees them in these days; and many little boxes were opened, likewise the piano; and in this were painted landscapes, inside the lid. But the piano was quite hoarse when the old man played upon it; and then he nodded to the picture that he had bought at the dealer's, and the old man's eyes shone quite brightly.

"I'll go to the war! I'll go to the war!" cried the Tin Soldier, as loud as he could; and he threw himself down on the floor.

Where had he gone? The old man searched, the little boy searched, but he was gone, and could not be found.

"I shall find him," said the old man.

But he never found him: the flooring was so open and full of holes, that the Tin Soldier had fallen through a crack, and there he lay as in an open grave.

And the day passed away, and the little boy went home; and the week passed by, and many weeks passed by. The windows were quite frozen up, and the little boy had to sit and breathe upon the panes, to make a peep-hole to look at the old house; and snow had blown among all the carving and the inscriptions, and covered the whole staircase, as if no one were in the house at all. And, indeed, there *was* no one in the house, for the old man had died!

DISAPPEARANCE OF THE TIN SOLDIER.

In the evening a carriage stopped at the door, and in that he was laid, in his coffin; he was to rest in a family vault in the country. So he was carried away; but no one followed him on his last journey, for all his friends were dead. And the little boy kissed his hand after the coffin as it rolled away.

A few days later, and there was an auction in the old house; and the little boy saw from his window how the old knights and ladies, the flower-pots with the long ears, the chairs and the cupboards were carried away. One was taken here, and then there: *her* portrait, that had been bought by the dealer, went back into his shop, and there it was hung; for no one cared for the old picture.

In the spring the house itself was pulled down, for the people said it was old rubbish. One could look from the street straight into the room with the leather wall-covering, which was taken down, ragged and torn; and the green of the balcony hung straggling over the beams, that threatened to fall in altogether. And now a clearance was made.

"That does good!" said a neighbour.

And a capital house was built, with large windows and smooth white walls; but in front of the place where the old house had really stood, a little garden was planted, and by the neighbour's wall tall vine shoots clambered up. In front of the garden was placed a great iron railing with an iron door; and it had a stately look. The people stopped in front, and looked through. And the sparrows sat down in dozens upon the vine branches, and chattered all at once as loud as they could; but not about the old house, for they could not remember that, for many years had gone by—so many, that the little boy had grown to be a man, a thorough man, whose parents rejoiced in him. And he had just married, and was come with his wife to live in the house, in front of which was the garden; and here he stood next to her while she planted a field flower which she considered very pretty; she planted it with her little hand, pressing the earth close round it with her fingers. "Ah, what was that?" She pricked herself. Out of the soft earth something pointed was sticking up. Only think! that was the Tin Soldier, the same that had been lost up in the old man's room, and had been hidden among old wood and rubbish for a long time, and had lain in the ground many a year. And the young wife first dried the Soldier in a green leaf, and then with her fine handkerchief, that smelt so deliciously. And the Tin Soldier felt just as if he were waking from a fainting fit.

"Let me see him," said the young man. And then he smiled and shook his head. "Yes, it can scarcely be the same; but it reminds me of an affair with a Tin Soldier which I had when I was a little boy."

And then he told his wife about the old house, and the old man, and of the Tin Soldier he had sent across to the old man whom he had thought so lonely; and the tears came into the young wife's eyes for the old house and the old man.

"It is possible, after all, that it may be the same Tin Soldier," said she. "I will take care of him, and remember what you have told me; but you must show me the old man's grave."

"I don't know where that is," replied he, "and no one knows it. All his friends were dead; none tended his grave, and I was but a little boy."

"Ah, how terribly lonely he must have been!" said she.

"Yes, horribly lonely," said the Tin Soldier; "but it is glorious not to be forgotten."

"Glorious!" repeated a voice close to them.

But nobody except the Tin Soldier perceived that it came from a rag of the pig's-leather hangings, which was now devoid of all gilding. It looked like wet earth, but yet it had an opinion, which it expressed thus:

> "Gilding fades fast,
> Pig-skin will last!"

But the Tin Soldier did not believe that.

THE GRAND OLD SNAILS.

THE HAPPY FAMILY.

THE biggest leaf here in the country is certainly the burdock leaf. Put one in front of your waist and it's just like an apron, and if you lay it upon your head it is almost as good as an umbrella, for it is quite remarkably large. A burdock never grows alone; where there is one tree there are several more. It's splendid to behold! and all this splendour is snails' meat. The great white snails, which the grand people in old times used to have made into fricassees, and when they had eaten them they would say, "H'm, how good that is!" for they had the idea that it tasted delicious. These snails lived on burdock leaves, and that's why burdocks were sown.

Now there was an old estate, on which people ate snails no longer. The snails had died out, but the burdocks had not. These latter grew and grew in all the walks and on all the beds—there was no stopping them; the place became a complete forest of burdocks. Here and there stood an apple or plum tree; but for this, nobody would have thought a garden had been there. Everything was burdock, and among the burdocks lived the two last ancient Snails.

They did not know themselves how old they were, but they could very well remember that there had been a great many more of them, that they had descended from a foreign family, and that the whole forest had been planted for them and theirs. They had never been away from home, but it was known to them that something existed in the world called the *ducal palace*, and that there one was boiled, and one became black, and was laid upon a silver dish; but what was done afterwards they did not know. Moreover, they could not imagine what that might be, being boiled and laid upon a silver dish; but it was stated to be fine, and particularly grand! Neither the cockchafer, nor the toad, nor the earthworm, whom they questioned about it, could give them any information, for none of their own kind had ever been boiled and laid on silver dishes.

The old white Snails were the grandest in the world; they knew that! The forest was there for their sake, and the ducal palace too, so that they might be boiled and laid on silver dishes.

They led a very retired and happy life, and as they themselves were childless, they had adopted a little common snail, which they brought up as their own child. But the little thing would not grow, for it was only a common snail, though the old people, and particularly the mother, declared one could easily see how he grew. And when the father could not see it, she requested him to feel the little snail's shell, and he felt it, and acknowledged that she was right.

One day it rained very hard.

" Listen, how it 's drumming on the burdock leaves, rum-dum-dum! rum-dum-dum!" said the Father-Snail.

"That 's what I call drops," said the mother. " It 's coming straight down the stalks. You 'll see it will be wet here directly. I 'm only glad that we have our good houses, and that the little one has his own. There has been more done for us than for any other creature; one can see very plainly that we are the grand folks of the world! We have houses from our birth, and the burdock forest has been planted for us: I should like to know how far it extends, and what lies beyond it."

" There 's nothing," said the Father-Snail, " that can be better than here at home; I have nothing at all to wish for."

" Yes," said the mother, " I should like to be taken to the ducal palace and boiled, and laid upon a silver dish; that has been done to all our ancestors, and you may be sure it 's quite a distinguished honour."

" The ducal palace has perhaps fallen in," said the Father-Snail, " or the forest of burdocks may have grown over it, so that the people can't get out at all. You need not be in a hurry—but you always hurry so, and the little one is beginning just the same way. Has he not been creeping up that stalk these three days? My head quite aches when I look up at him."

" You must not scold him," said the Mother-Snail. " He crawls very deliberately We shall have much joy in him; and we old people have nothing else to live for. But have you ever thought where we shall get a wife for him? Don't you think that farther in the wood there may be some more of our kind?"

" There may be black snails there, I think," said the old man, " black snails without houses! but they 're too vulgar. And they 're conceited, for all that. But we can give the commission to the ants: they run to and fro, as if they had business; they 're sure to know of a wife for our young gentleman."

" I certainly know the most beautiful of brides," said one of the Ants; " but I fear she would not do, for she is the Queen!"

"That does not matter," said the two old Snails. "Has sне a house?"

"She has a castle!" replied the Ant. "The most beautiful ant's castle, with seven hundred passages."

"Thank you," said the Mother-Snail; "our boy shall not go into an ant-hill. If you know of nothing better, we 'll give the commission to the white gnats; they fly far about in rain and sunshine, and they know the burdock wood, inside and outside."

"We have a wife for him," said the Gnats. "A hundred man-steps from here a little snail with a house is sitting on a gooseberry bush, she is quite alone, and old enough to marry. It 's only a hundred man-steps from here."

"Yes, let her come to him," said the old people. "He has a whole burdock forest, and she has only a bush."

And so they brought the little maiden snail. Eight days passed before she arrived, but that was the rare circumstance about it, for by this one could see that she was of the right kind.

And then they had a wedding. Six glow-worms lighted as well as they could: with this exception it went very quietly, for the old snail people could not bear feasting and dissipation. But a capital speech was made by the Mother-Snail. The father could not speak, he was so much moved. Then they gave the young couple the whole burdock forest for an inheritance, and said, what they had always said, namely—that it was the best place in the world, and that the young people, if they lived honourably, and increased and multiplied, would some day be taken with their children to the ducal palace, and boiled black, and laid upon a silver dish. And when the speech was finished, the old people crept into their houses and never came out again, for they slept.

The young snail pair now ruled in the forest, and had a numerous progeny. But as the young ones were never boiled and put into silver dishes, they concluded that the ducal palace had fallen in, and that all the people in the world had died out. And as nobody contradicted them, they must have been right. And the rain fell down upon the burdock leaves to play the drum for them, and the sun shone to colour the burdock forest for them; and they were happy, very happy—the whole family was happy, uncommonly happy!

THE ROSE-ELF.

In the midst of the garden grew a rose bush, which was quite covered with roses; and in one of them, the most beautiful of all, there dwelt an elf. He was so tiny that no human eye could see him. Behind every leaf in the rose he had a bed-room. He was as well formed and beautiful as any child could be, and had wings that reached from his shoulders to his feet. Oh, what a fragrance there was in his rooms! and how clear and bright were the walls! They were made of the pale pink rose leaves.

The whole day he rejoiced in the warm sunshine, flew from flower to flower, danced on the wings of the flying butterfly, and measured how many steps he would have to take to pass along all the roads and cross-roads that are marked out on a single hidden leaf. What we call veins on the leaf were to him high roads and cross-roads. Yes, those were long roads for him! Before he had finished his journey the sun went down, for he had begun his work too late!

It became very cold, the dew fell, and the wind blew : now the best thing to be done was to come home. He made what haste he could, but the rose had shut itself up, and he could not get in; not a single rose stood open. The poor little elf was very much frightened. He had never been out at night before; he had always slumbered sweetly and comfortably behind the warm rose leaves. Oh, it certainly would be the death of him.

At the other end of the garden there was, he knew, an arbour of fine honeysuckle. The flowers looked like great painted horns, and he wished to go down into one of them to sleep till the next day.

He flew thither. Silence! two people were in there—a handsome young man and a young girl. They sat side by side, and wished that they need never part. They loved each other better than a good child loves its father and mother.

"Yet we must part!" said the young man. "Your brother does not like us, therefore he sends me away on an errand so far over mountains and seas. Farewell, my sweet bride, for that you shall be!"

And they kissed each other, and the young girl wept, and gave him a rose. But, before she gave it him, she impressed a kiss so firmly and closely upon it that the flower opened. Then the little elf flew into it, and leaned his head against the delicate fragrant walls. Here he could plainly hear them say "Farewell! farewell!" and he felt that the rose was placed on the young man's heart. Oh, how that heart beats! the little elf could not go to sleep, it thumped so.

But not long did the rose rest undisturbed on that breast. The man took it out, and as he went lonely through the wood, he kissed the flower so often and so fervently that the little elf was almost crushed. He could feel through the leaf how the man's lips burned, and the rose itself had opened, as if under the hottest noonday sun.

Then came another man, gloomy and wicked; he was the bad brother

THE GIRL AND THE FLOWER-POT.

of the pretty maiden. He drew out a sharp knife, and while the other kissed the rose the bad man stabbed him to death, and then, cutting off his head, buried both head and body in the soft earth under the linden tree.

"Now he's forgotten and gone!" thought the wicked brother; "he will never come back again. He was to have taken a long journey over mountains and seas. One can easily lose one's life, and he has lost his. He cannot come back again, and my sister dare not ask news of him from me."

Then with his feet he shuffled dry leaves over the loose earth, and went home in the dark night. But he did not go alone, as he thought; the little elf accompanied him. The elf sat in a dry, rolled-up linden leaf that had fallen on the wicked man's hair as he dug. The hat was now placed over the leaf, and it was very dark in the hat, and the elf trembled with fear and with anger at the evil deed.

In the morning hour the bad man got home; he took off his hat, and went into his sister's bed-room. There lay the beautiful blooming girl,

dreaming of him whom she loved from her heart, and of whom she now
believed that he was going across the mountains and through the forests.
And the wicked brother bent over her, and laughed hideously, as only a
fiend can laugh.   Then the dry leaf fell out of his hair upon the coverlet; but he did not remark it, and he went out to sleep a little himself
in the morning hour.   But the elf slipped forth from the withered leaf,
placed himself in the ear of the sleeping girl, and told her, as in a
dream, the dreadful history of the murder; described to her the place
where her brother had slain her lover and buried his corpse; told her
of the blooming linden tree close by it, and said,

"That you may not think it is only a dream that I have told you,
you will find on your bed a withered leaf."

And she found it when she awoke.   Oh, what bitter tears she wept!
The window stood open the whole day: the little elf could easily get
out to the roses and all the other flowers, but he could not find it in
his heart to quit the afflicted maiden.   In the window stood a plant, a
monthly rose bush: he seated himself in one of the flowers, and looked
at the poor girl.   Her brother often came into the room, and, in spite
of his wicked deed, he always seemed cheerful, but she dared not say a
word of the grief that was in her heart.

As soon as the night came, she crept out of the house, went to the
wood, to the place where the linden tree stood, removed the leaves from
the ground, turned up the earth, and immediately found him who had
been slain.   Oh, how she wept, and prayed that she might die also!

Gladly would she have taken the corpse home with her, but that
she could not do.   Then she took the pale head with the closed eyes,
kissed the cold mouth, and shook the earth out of the beautiful hair.
"That I will keep," she said.   And when she had laid earth upon the
dead body, she took the head, and a little sprig of the jasmine that
bloomed in the wood where he was buried, home with her.

As soon as she came into her room, she brought the greatest flower-
pot she could find: in this she laid the dead man's head, strewed earth
upon it, and then planted the jasmine twig in the pot.

"Farewell! farewell!" whispered the little elf: he could endure it
no longer to see all this pain, and therefore flew out to his rose in the
garden.   But the rose was faded; only a few pale leaves clung to the
wild bush.

"Alas! how soon everything good and beautiful passes away!" sighed
the elf.

At last he found another rose, and this became his house; behind
its delicate fragrant leaves he could hide himself and dwell.

Every morning he flew to the window of the poor girl, and she was
always standing weeping by the flower-pot.   The bitter tears fell upon
the jasmine spray, and every day, as the girl became paler and paler,
the twig stood there fresher and greener, and one shoot after another
sprouted forth, little white buds burst out, and these she kissed.   But
the bad brother scolded his sister, and asked if she had gone mad   He
could not bear it, and could not imagine why she was always weeping

over the flower-pot. He did not know what closed eyes were there, what red lips had there faded into earth. And she bowed her head upon the flower-pot, and the little elf o: the rose bush found her slumbering there. Then he seated himself in her ear, told her of the evening in the arbour, of the fragrance of the rose, and the love of the elves. And she dreamed a marvellously sweet dream, and while she dreamed her life passed away. She had died a quiet death, and she was in heaven, with him whom she loved.

And the jasmine opened its great white bells. They smelt quite peculiarly sweet; it could not weep in any óther way over the dead one.

But the wicked brother looked at the beautiful blooming plant, and took it for himself as an inheritance, and put it in his sleeping-room, close by his bed, for it was glorious to look upon and its fragrance was sweet and lovely. The little Rose-elf followed, and went from flower to flower—for in each dwelt a little soul—and told of the murdered young man, whose head was now earth beneath the earth, and told of the evil brother and of the poor sister.

"We know it!" said each soul in the flowers, "we know it: have we not sprung from the eyes and lips of the murdered man? We know it! we know it!"

And then they nodded in a strange fashion with their heads.

The Rose-elf could not at all understand how they could be so quiet, and he flew out to the bees that were gathering honey, and told them the story of the wicked brother. And the bees told it to their Queen, and the Queen commanded that they should all kill the murderer next morning. But in the night—it was the first night that followed upon the sister's death—when the brother was sleeping in his bed, close to the fragrant jasmine, each flower opened, and invisible, but armed with poisonous spears, the flower-souls came out and seated themselves in his ear, and told him bad dreams, and then flew across his lips and pricked his tongue with the poisonous spears.

"Now we have avenged the dead man!" they said, and flew back into the jasmine's white bells.

When the morning came and the windows of the bed-chamber were opened, the Rose-elf and the Queen Bee and the whole swarm of bees rushed in to kill him.

But he was dead already. People stood around his bed, and said, "The scent of the jasmine has killed him!" Then the Rose-elf understood the revenge of the flowers, and told it to the Queen and to the bees, and the Queen hummed with the whole swarm around the flower-pot. The bees were not to be driven away. Then a man carried away the flower-pot, and one of the bees stung him in the hand, so that he let the pot fall, and it broke in pieces.

Then they beheld the whitened skull, and knew that the dead man on the bed was a murderer.

And the Queen Bee hummed in the air, and sang of the revenge of the bees, and of the Rose-elf, and said that behind the smallest leaf there dwells ONE who can bring the evil to light, and repay it.

THE SHADOW.

In the hot countries the sun burns very strongly; there the people become quite mahogany brown, and in the very hottest countries they are even burned into negroes. But this time it was only to the hot countries that a learned man out of the cold regions had come. He thought he could roam about there just as he had been accustomed to do at home; but he soon altered his opinion. He and all sensible people had to remain at home, where the window-shutters and doors were shut all day long, and it looked as if all the inmates were asleep or had gone out. The narrow street with the high houses in which he lived was, however, built in such a way that the sun shone upon it from morning till evening; it was really quite unbearable! The learned man from the cold regions was a young man and a clever man: it seemed to him as if he was sitting in a glowing oven that exhausted him greatly, and he became quite thin; even his Shadow shrivelled up and became much smaller than it had been at home; the sun even took the Shadow away, and it did not return till the evening when the sun went down. It was really a pleasure to see this. So soon as a light was brought into the room the Shadow stretched itself quite up the wall, farther even than the ceiling, so tall did it make itself; it was obliged to stretch to get strength again. The learned man went out into the balcony to stretch himself, and so soon as the stars came out in the beautiful clear sky, he felt himself reviving. On all the balconies in the streets — and in the hot countries there is a balcony to every window — young people now appeared, for one must breathe fresh air, even if one has got used to becoming mahogany brown; then it became lively above and below; the tinkers and tailors—by which we mean all kinds of people—sat below in the street; then tables and chairs were brought out, and candles burned, yes, more than a thousand candles; one talked and then sang, and the people walked to and fro; carriages drove past, mules trotted, " Kling-ling-ling !" for they had bells on their harness; dead people were buried with solemn songs; the church bells rang, and it was indeed very lively in the street. Only in one house, just opposite to that in which the learned man dwelt, it was quite quiet, and yet somebody lived there, for there were flowers upon the balcony, blooming beautifully in the hot sun, and they could not have done this if they had not been watered, so that some one must have watered them; therefore, there must be people in that house. Towards evening the door was half opened, but it was dark, at least in the front room; farther back, in the interior, music was heard. The strange learned man thought this music very lovely, but it was quite possible that he only imagined this, for out there in the hot countries he found everything requisite, if only there had been no sun. The stranger's landlord said that he did not know who had taken the opposite house—one saw nobody there, and so far as the music was concerned, it seemed very monotonous to him.

"It was just," he said, "as if some one sat there, always practising a piece that he could not manage—always the same piece. He seemed to say, 'I shall manage it, after all;' but he did not manage it, however long he played."

Will the stranger awake at night? He slept with the balcony door open: the wind lifted up the curtain before it, and he fancied that a wonderful radiance came from the balcony of the house opposite; all the flowers appeared like flames of the most gorgeous colours, and in the midst, among the flowers, stood a beautiful slender maiden: it seemed as if a radiance came from her also. His eyes were quite dazzled; but he had only opened them too wide just when he awoke out of his sleep. With one leap he was out of bed; quite quietly he crept behind the curtain; but the maiden was gone, the splendour was gone, the flowers gleamed no longer, but stood there as beautiful as ever. The door was ajar, and from within sounded music, so lovely, so charming, that one fell into sweet thought at the sound. It was just like magic work. But who lived there? Where was the real entrance? for towards the street and towards the lane at the side the whole ground floor was shop by shop, and the people could not always run through there.

One evening the stranger sat upon his balcony; in the room just behind him a light was burning, and so it was quite natural that his Shadow fell upon the wall of the opposite house; yes, it sat just among the flowers on the balcony, and when the stranger moved his Shadow moved too.

"I think my Shadow is the only living thing we see yonder," said the learned man. "Look how gracefully it sits among the flowers. The door is only ajar, but the Shadow ought to be sensible enough to walk in and look round, and then come back and tell me what it has seen.

"Yes, you would thus make yourself very useful," said he, as if in sport. "Be so good as to slip in. Now, will you go?" And then he nodded at the Shadow, and the Shadow nodded back at him. "Now go, but don't stay away altogether."

And the stranger stood up, and the Shadow on the balcony opposite stood up too, and the stranger moved round, and if any one had noticed closely he would have remarked how the Shadow went away in the same moment, straight through the half-opened door of the opposite house, as the stranger returned into his room and let the curtain fall.

Next morning the learned man went out to drink coffee and read the papers.

"What is this?" said he, when he came out into the sunshine. "I have no Shadow! So it really went away yesterday evening, and did not come back: that's very tiresome."

And that fretted him, but not so much because the Shadow was gone as because he knew that there was a story of a man without a shadow. All the people in the house knew this story, and if the learned man came home and told his own history, they would say that it was only an imitation, and he did not choose them to say that of him. So he would not speak of it at all, and that was a very sensible idea of his.

In the evening he again went out on his balcony: he had placed the light behind him, for he knew that a shadow always wants its master for a screen, but he could not coax it forth. He made himself little, he made himself long, but there was no shadow, and no shadow came. He said, " Here, here ! " but that did no good.

That was vexatious, but in the warm countries everything grows very quickly, and after the lapse of a week he remarked to his great joy that a new shadow was growing out of his legs when he went into the sunshine, so that the root must have remained behind. After three weeks he had quite a respectable shadow, which, when he started on his return to the North, grew more and more, so that at last it was so long and great that he could very well have parted with half of it.

When the learned man got home he wrote books about what is true in the world, and what is good, and what is pretty; and days went by, and years went by, many years.

He was one evening sitting in his room when there came a little quiet knock at the door. " Come in ! " said he; but nobody came. Then he opened the door, and there stood before him such a remarkably thin man that he felt quite uncomfortable. This man was, however, very respectably dressed; he looked like a man of standing.

" Whom have I the honour to address ? " asked the professor.

" Ah ! " replied the genteel man, " I thought you would not know me; I have become so much a body that I have got real flesh and clothes. You never thought to see me in such a condition. Don't you know your old Shadow ? You certainly never thought that I would come again. Things have gone remarkably well with me since I was with you last. I've become rich in every respect: if I want to buy myself free from servitude I can do it ! "

And he rattled a number of valuable charms, which hung by his watch, and put his hand upon the thick gold chain he wore round his neck ; and how the diamond rings glittered on his fingers ! and everything was real !

" No, I cannot regain my self-possession at all ! " said the learned man. " What 's the meaning of all this ? "

" Nothing common," said the Shadow. " But you yourself don't belong to common folks; and I have, as you very well know, trodden in your footsteps from my childhood upwards. So soon as I found that I was experienced enough to find my way through the world alone, I went away. I am in the most brilliant circumstances ; but I was seized with a kind of longing to see you once more before you die, and I wanted to see these regions once more, for one always holds by one's fatherland. I know that you have got another shadow: have I anything to pay to it, or to you ? You have only to tell me."

" Is it really you ? " said the learned man. " Why, that is wonderful ! I should never have thought that I should ever meet my old Shadow as a man ! "

" Only tell me what I have to pay," said the Shadow, " for I don't like to be in any one's debt."

" How can you talk in that way ? " said the learned man. " Of what debt can there be a question here? You are as free as any one! I am exceedingly pleased at your good fortune! Sit down, old friend, and tell me a little how it has happened, and what you saw in the warm countries, and in the house opposite ours."

"Yes, that I will tell you," said the Shadow; and it sat down. "But then you must promise me never to tell any one in this town,

THE VISIT OF THE SHADOW.

when you meet me, that I have been your Shadow! I have the intention of engaging myself to be married; I can do more than support a family."

"Be quite easy," replied the learned man; "I will tell nobody who you really are. Here's my hand. I promise it, and my word's as good as my bond."

"A Shadow's word in return!" said the Shadow, for he was obliged to talk in that way. But, by the way, it was quite wonderful how complete a man he had become. He was dressed all in black, and wore the very finest black cloth, polished boots, and a hat that could be crushed together till it was nothing but crown and rim, besides what we have already noticed of him, namely, the charms, the gold neck-chain, and the diamond rings. The Shadow was indeed wonderfully well clothed; and it was just this that made a complete man of him.

"Now I will tell you," said the Shadow; and then he put down his polished boots as firmly as he could on the arm of the learned man's new shadow that lay like a poodle dog at his feet. This was done perhaps from pride, perhaps so that the new shadow might stick to his feet; but the prostrate shadow remained quite quiet, so that it might listen well, for it wanted to know how one could get free and work up to be one's own master.

"Do you know who lived in the house opposite to us?" asked the Shadow. "That was the most glorious of all; it was Poetry! I was there for three weeks, and that was just as if one had lived there a thousand years, and could read all that has been written and composed. For this I say, and it is truth, I have seen everything, and I know everything!"

"Poetry!" cried the learned man. "Yes, she often lives as a hermit in great cities. Poetry! Yes, I myself saw her for one single brief moment, but sleep was heavy on my eyes: she stood on the balcony, gleaming as the Northern Light gleams, flowers with living flames. Tell me! tell me! You were upon the balcony. You went through the door, and then——"

"Then I was in the ante-room," said the Shadow. "You sat opposite, and were always looking across at the ante-room. There was no light; a kind of semi-obscurity reigned there; but one door after another in a whole row of halls and rooms stood open, and there it was light; and the mass of light would have killed me if I had got as far as to where the maiden sat. But I was deliberate, I took my time; and that's what one must do."

"And what didst thou see then?" asked the learned man.

"I saw everything, and I will tell you what; but—it is really not pride on my part—as a free man, and with the acquirements I possess, besides my good position and my remarkable fortune, I wish you would say *you* to me."

"I beg your pardon," said the learned man. "This *thou* is an old habit, and old habits are difficult to alter. You are perfectly right, and I will remember it. But now tell me everything you saw."

"Everything," said the Shadow; "for I saw everything, and I know everything."

"How did things look in the inner room?" asked the learned man. "Was it there as in a cool grave? Was it there like in a holy temple? Were the chambers like the starry sky, when one stands on the high mountains?"

"Everything was there." said the Shadow. "I was certainly not quite inside; I remained in the front room, in the half darkness; but I stood there remarkably well. I saw everything and know everything. I have been in the ante-room at the Court of Poetry."

"But what did you see? Did all the gods of antiquity march through the halls? Did the old heroes fight there? Did lovely children play there, and relate their dreams?"

"I tell you that I have been there, and so you will easily understand that I saw everything that was to be seen. If *you* had got there you would not have remained a man; but I became one, and at the same time I learned to understand my inner being and the relation in which I stood to Poetry. Yes, when I was with you I did not think of these things; but you know that whenever the sun rises or sets I am wonderfully great. In the moonshine I was almost more noticeable than you yourself. I did not then understand my inward being; in the ante-room it was revealed to me. I became a man! I came out ripe. But you were no longer in the warm countries. I was ashamed to go about as a man in the state I was then in: I required boots, clothes, and all this human varnish by which a man is known. I hid myself; yes, I can confide a secret to you—you will not put it into a book. I hid myself under the cake-woman's gown; the woman had no idea how much she concealed. Only in the evening did I go out: I ran about the streets by moonlight; I stretched myself quite long up the wall: that tickled my back quite agreeably. I ran up and down, looked through the highest windows into the halls and through the roof, where nobody could see, and I saw what nobody saw and what nobody ought to see. On the whole it is a bad world: I should not like to be a man if I were not allowed to be of some consequence. I saw the most incomprehensible things going an among men, and women, and parents, and 'dear incomparable children.' I saw what no one else knows, but what they all would be very glad to know, namely, bad goings on at their neighbours'. If I had written a newspaper, how it would have been read! But I wrote directly to the persons interested, and there was terror in every town to which I came. They were so afraid of me that they were remarkably fond of me. The professor made me a professor; the tailor gave me new clothes (I am well provided); the coining superintendent coined money for me; the women declared I was handsome: and thus I became the man I am. And now, farewell! Here is my card; I live on the sunny side, and am always at home in rainy weather."

And the Shadow went away.

"That was very remarkable," said the learned man.

Years and days passed by, and the Shadow came again.

"How goes it?" he asked.

"Ah!" said the learned man, "I'm writing about the true, the good, and the beautiful; but nobody cares to hear of anything of the kind: I am quite in despair, for I take that to heart."

"That I do not," said the Shadow. "I'm becoming fat and hearty, and that's what one must try to become. You don't understand the world, and you're getting ill. You must travel. I'll make a journey this summer; will you go too? I should like to have a travelling companion; will you go with me as my shadow? I shall be very happy to take you, and I 'll pay the expenses."

" I suppose you travel very far?" said the learned man.

" As you take it," replied the Shadow. " A journey will do you a great deal of good. Will you be my shadow?—then you shall have everything on the journey for nothing."

" That 's too strong!" said the learned man.

" But it 's the way of the world," said the Shadow, "and so it will remain!" And he went away.

The learned man was not at all fortunate. Sorrow and care pursued him, and what he said of the true and the good and the beautiful was as little valued by most people as a nutmeg would be by a cow. At last he became quite ill.

" You really look like a shadow!" people said; and a shudder ran through him at these words, for he attached a peculiar meaning to them.

" You must go to a watering-place!" said the Shadow, who came to pay him a visit. " There 's no other help for you. I 'll take you with me, for the sake of old acquaintance. I 'll pay the expenses of the journey, and you shall make a description of it, and shorten time for me on the way. I want to visit a watering-place. My beard doesn't grow quite as it should, and that is a kind of illness; and a beard I must have. Now, be reasonable and accept my proposal: we shall travel like comrades."

And they travelled. The Shadow was master now, and the master was shadow: they drove together, they rode together, and walked side by side, and before and behind each other, just as the sun happened to stand. The Shadow always knew when to take the place of honour. The learned man did not particularly notice this, for he had a very good heart, and was moreover particularly mild and friendly. Then one day the master said to the Shadow,

" As we have in this way become travelling companions, and have also from childhood's days grown up with one another, shall we not drink brotherhood? That sounds more confidential."

" You 're saying a thing there," said the Shadow, who was now really the master, " that is said in a very kind and straightforward way. I will be just as kind and straightforward. You, who are a learned gentleman, know very well how wonderful nature is. There are some men who cannot bear to smell brown paper, they become sick at it; others shudder to the marrow of their bones if one scratches with a nail upon a pane of glass; and I for my part have a similar feeling when any one says ' thou ' to me; I feel myself, as I did in my first position with you, oppressed by it. You see that this is a feeling, not pride. I cannot let you say ' thou ' * to me, but I will gladly say ' thou ' to you; and thus your wish will be at any rate partly fulfilled."

---

* On the Continent, people who have "drunk brotherhood" address each other as " thou," in preference to the more ceremonious " you."

And now the Shadow addressed his former master as "thou."

"That's rather strong," said the latter, "that I am to say 'you,' while he says 'thou.'" But he was obliged to submit to it.

They came to a bathing-place, where many strangers were, and among them a beautiful young Princess, who had this disease, that she saw too sharply, which was very disquieting. She at once saw that the new arrival was a very different personage from all the rest.

"They say he is here to get his beard to grow; but I see the real reason—he can't throw a shadow."

She had now become inquisitive, and therefore she at once began a conversation with the strange gentleman on the promenade. As a Princess, she was not obliged to use much ceremony, therefore she said outright to him at once,

"Your illness consists in this, that you can't throw a shadow."

"Your Royal Highness must be much better," replied the Shadow. "I know your illness consists in this, that you see too sharply; but you have got the better of that. I have a very unusual shadow: don't you see the person who always accompanies me? Other people have a common shadow, but I don't love what is common. One often gives one's servants finer cloth for their liveries than one wears oneself, and so I have let my shadow deck himself out like a separate person; yes, you see I have even given him a shadow of his own. That cost very much, but I like to have something peculiar."

"How!" said the Princess, "can I really have been cured? This is the best bathing-place in existence; water has wonderful power now-a-days. But I'm not going away from here yet, for now it begins to be amusing. The foreign Prince—for he must be a Prince—pleases me remarkably well. I only hope his beard won't grow, for if it does he'll go away."

That evening the Princess and the Shadow danced together in the great ball-room. She was light, but he was still lighter; never had she seen such a dancer. She told him from what country she came, and he knew the country—he had been there, but just when she had been absent. He had looked through the windows of her castle, from below as well as from above; he had learned many circumstances, and could therefore make allusions, and give replies to the Princess, at which she marvelled greatly. She thought he must be the cleverest man in all the world, and was inspired with great respect for all his knowledge. And when she danced with him again, she fell in love with him, and the Shadow noticed that particularly, for she looked him almost through and through with her eyes. They danced together once more, and she was nearly telling him, but she was discreet: she thought of her country, and her kingdom, and of the many people over whom she was to rule.

"He is a clever man," she said to herself, "and that is well, and he dances capitally, and that is well too; but has he well-grounded knowledge? That is just as important, and he must be examined."

And she immediately put such a difficult question to him, that she could not have answered it herself; and the Shadow made a wry face.

"You cannot answer me that," said the Princess.

" I learned that in my childhood," replied the Shadow, "and I believe my very shadow, standing yonder by the door, could answer it."

"Your shadow!" cried the Princess: "that would be very remarkable."

" I do not assert as quite certain that he can do so," said the Shadow, " but I am almost inclined to believe it. But your Royal Highness will allow me to remind you that he is so proud of passing for a man, that, if he is to be in a good humour, and he should be so to answer rightly, he must be treated just like a man."

" I like that," said the Princess.

And now she went to the learned man at the door; and she spoke with him of sun and moon, of the green forests, and of people near and far off; and the learned man answered very cleverly and very well.

" What a man that must be, who has such a clever shadow!" she thought. " It would be a real blessing for my country and for my people if I chose him; and I 'll do it!"

And they soon struck a bargain—the Princess and the Shadow; but no one was to know anything of it till she had returned to her kingdom.

" No one—not even my shadow," said the Shadow; and for this he had especial reasons.

And they came to the country where the Princess ruled, and where was her home.

" Listen, my friend," said the Shadow to the learned man. " Now I am as lucky and powerful as any one can become, I 'll do something particular for you. You shall live with me in my palace, drive with me in the royal carriage, and have a hundred thousand dollars a year; but you must let yourself be called a shadow by every one, and may never say that you were once a man; and once a year, when I sit on the balcony and show myself, you must lie at my feet as it becomes my shadow to do. For I will tell you I 'm going to marry the Princess, and this evening the wedding will be held."

" Now, that 's too strong!" said the learned man. " I won't do it; I won't have it. That would be cheating the whole country and the Princess too. I 'll tell everything—that I 'm the man and you are the Shadow, and that you only wear men's clothes!"

" No one would believe that," said the Shadow. " Be reasonable, or I 'll call the watch."

" I 'll go straight to the Princess," said the learned man.

" But I 'll go first," said the Shadow; "and you shall go to prison."

And that was so; for the sentinels obeyed him of whom they knew that he was to marry the Princess.

" You tremble," said the Princess, when the Shadow came to her. " Has anything happened? You must not be ill to-day, when we are to have our wedding."

" I have experienced the most terrible thing that can happen," said the Shadow. " Only think!—such a poor shallow brain cannot bear much—only think! my shadow has gone mad: he fancies he has become a man, and—only think!—that I am his shadow."

" This is terrible ! " said the Princess. " He 's locked up, I hope ? "

" Certainly. I 'm afraid he will never recover."

" Poor shadow ! " cried the Princess, " he 's very unfortunate. It would really be a good action to deliver him from his little bit of life. And when I think how prone the people are, now-a-days, to take the part of the low against the high, it seems to me quite necessary to put him quietly out of the way."

" That 's certainly very hard, for he was a faithful servant," said the Shadow ; and he pretended to sigh.

" You 've a noble character," said the Princess, and she bowed before him.

In the evening the whole town was illuminated, and cannon were fired—bang !—and the soldiers presented arms. That *was* a wedding ! The Princess and the Shadow stepped out on the balcony to show themselves and receive another cheer.

The learned man heard nothing of all this festivity, for he had already been executed.

THE ANGEL.

WHENEVER a good child dies, an angel from heaven comes down to earth and takes the dead child in his arms, spreads out his great white wings, and flies away over all the places the child has loved, and picks quite a hand-full of flowers, which he carries up to the Almighty, that they may bloom in heaven more brightly than on earth. And the Father presses all the flowers to His heart ; but He kisses the flower that pleases Him best, and the flower is then endowed with a voice, and can join in the great chorus of praise !

" See "—this is what an angel said, as he carried a dead child up to heaven, and the child heard, as if in a dream, and they went on over the regions of home where the little child had played, and they came through gardens with beautiful flowers—" which of these shall we take with us to plant in heaven ? " asked the angel.

Now there stood near them a slender, beautiful rose bush ; but a wicked hand had broken the stem, so that all the branches, covered with half-opened buds, were hanging around, quite withered.

" The poor rose bush ! " said the child. " Take it, that it may bloom up yonder."

And the angel took it, and kissed the child, and the little one half opened his eyes. They plucked some of the rich flowers, but also took with them the despised buttercup and the wild pansy.

" Now we have flowers," said the child.

And the angel nodded, but he did not yet fly upwards to heaven. It was night and quite silent. They remained in the great city ; they floated about there in a small street, where lay whole heaps of straw.

THE SICK BOY AND THE LITTLE FLOWER.

ashes, and sweepings, for it had been removal-day. There lay fragments of plates, bits of plaster, rags, and old hats, and all this did not look well. And the angel pointed amid all this confusion to a few fragments of a flower-pot, and to a lump of earth which had fallen out, and which was kept together by the roots of a great dried field flower, which was of no use, and had therefore been thrown out into the street.

"We will take that with us," said the angel. "I will tell you why, as we fly onward.

"Down yonder in the narrow lane, in the low cellar, lived a poor sick boy; from his childhood he had been bedridden. When he was at his best he could go up and down the room a few times, leaning on crutches; that was the utmost he could do. For a few days in summer the sunbeams would penetrate for a few hours to the ground of the cellar, and when the poor boy sat there and the sun shone on him, and he looked at the red blood in his three fingers, as he held them up before his face, he would say, 'Yes, to-day he has been out!' He knew the forest with its beautiful vernal green only from the fact that the neighbour's son brought him the first green branch of a beech tree, and he held that up over his head, and dreamed he was in the beech wood where the sun shone and the birds sang. On a spring day the neighbour's boy also brought him field flowers, and among these was, by chance, one to which the root was hanging; and so it was planted in a flower-pot, and placed by the bed, close to the window. And the flower had been planted by a fortunate hand; and it grew, threw out new shoots, and bore flowers every year. It became as a splendid flower garden to the sickly boy— his little treasure here on earth. He watered it, and tended it, and took care that it had the benefit of every ray of sunlight, down to the last that struggled in through the narrow window; and the flower itself was woven into his dreams, for it grew for him and gladdened his eyes, and spread its fragrance about him; and towards it he turned in death, when the Father called him. He has now been with the Almighty for a year; for a year the flower has stood forgotten in the window, and is withered; and thus, at the removal, it has been thrown out into the dust of the street. And this is the flower, the poor withered flower, which we have taken into our nosegay; for this flower has given more joy than the richest flower in a Queen's garden!"

"But how do you know all this?" asked the child which the angel was carrying to heaven.

"I know it," said the angel, "for I myself was that little boy who walked on crutches! I know my flower well!"

And the child opened his eyes and looked into the glorious happy face of the angel; and at the same moment they entered the regions where there is peace and joy. And the Father pressed the dead child to His bosom, and then it received wings like the angel, and flew hand in hand with him. And the Almighty pressed all the flowers to His heart; but He kissed the dry withered field flower, and it received a voice and sang with all the angels hovering around—some near, and some in wider circles, and some in infinite distance, but all equally happy. And they all sang, little and great, the good happy child, and the poor field flower that had lain there withered, thrown among the dust, in the rubbish of the removal-day, in the narrow dark lane.

TWELVE BY THE MAIL.

It was bitterly cold; the sky gleamed with stars, and not a breeze was stirring.

Bump! an old pot was thrown at the neighbours' house doors. Bang! bang! went the gun; for they were welcoming the New Year. It was New Year's-eve! The church clock was striking twelve!

Tan-ta-ra-ra! the mail came lumbering up. The great carriage stopped at the gate of the town. There were twelve persons in it; all the places were taken.

"Hurrah! hurrah!" sang the people in the houses of the town, for the New Year was being welcomed, and as the clock struck they stood up with the filled glass in their hand, to drink success to the new comer.

"Happy New Year!" was the cry. "A pretty wife, plenty of money, and no sorrow or care!"

This wish was passed round, and then glasses were clashed together till they rang again, and in front of the town gate the post-carriage stopped with the strange guests, the twelve travellers.

THE ARRIVAL OF THE MAIL.

And who were these strangers? Each of them had his passport and his luggage with him; they even brought presents for me and for you and for all the people of the little town. Who are they? What did they want? and what did they bring with them?

"Good morning!" they cried to the sentry at the town gate.

"Good morning!" replied the sentry, for the clock struck twelve.

"Your name and profession?" the sentry inquired of the one who alighted first from the carriage.

"See yourself, in the passport," replied the man. "I am myself!" And a capital fellow he looked, arrayed in a bear-skin and fur boots. "I am the man on whom many persons fix their hopes. Come to me to-morrow, and I'll give you a New Year's present. I throw pence and dollars among the people, I even give balls, thirty-one balls; but I cannot devote more than thirty-one nights to this. My ships are frozen in, but in my office it is warm and comfortable. I'm a merchant. My name is JANUARY, and I only carry accounts with me.".

Now the second alighted. He was a merry companion; he was a theatre director, manager of the masque balls, and all the amusements one can imagine. His luggage consisted of a great tub.

"We'll dance the cat out of the tub at carnival-time," said he. "I'll prepare a merry tune for you and for myself too. I have not a very long time to live—the shortest, in fact, of my whole family, for I only

THE PASSENGERS DISMOUNTING.

become twenty-eight days old. Sometimes they pop me in an extra day, but I trouble myself very little about that. Hurrah!"

"You must not shout so!" said the sentry.

"Certainly, I may shout!" retorted the man. "I'm Prince Carnival, travelling under the name of FEBRUARY!"

The third now got out. He looked like Fasting itself, but carried his nose very high, for he was related to the "Forty Knights," and was a weather prophet. But that's not a profitable office, and that's why he praised fasting. In his button-hole he had a little bunch of violets, but they were very small.

"MARCH! MARCH!" the fourth called after him, and slapped him on the shoulder. "Do you smell nothing? Go quickly into the guard-room; there they're drinking punch, your favourite drink! I can smell it already out here. Forward, Master MARCH!"

But it was not true; the speaker only wanted to let him feel the influence of his own name, and make an APRIL fool of him; for with that the fourth began his career in the town. He looked very jovial, did little work, but had the more holidays.

"If it were only a little more steady in the world!" said he; "but sometimes one is in a good humour, sometimes in a bad one, according to circumstances; now rain, now sunshine. I am a kind of house and office-letting agent, also a manager of funerals. I can laugh or cry, according to circumstances. Here in this box I have my summer wardrobe, but it would be very foolish to put it on. Here I am now! On Sundays I go out walking in shoes and silk stockings, and with a muff!"

After him, a lady came out of the carriage. She called herself Miss MAY. She wore a summer costume and overshoes, a light green dress, and anemones in her hair, and she was so scented with wild thyme that the sentry had to sneeze.

"God bless you!" she said, and that was her salutation.

How pretty she was! and she was a singer, not a theatre singer nor a ballad singer, but a singer of the woods, or she roamed through the gay green forest, and sang there for her own amusement.

"Now comes the young dame!" said those in the carriage.

And the young dame stepped out, delicate, proud, and pretty. It was easy to see that she was Mistress JUNE, accustomed to be served by drowsy marmots. She gave a great feast on the longest day of the year, that the guests might have time to partake of the many dishes at her table. She, indeed, kept her own carriage; but still she travelled in the mail with the rest, because she wanted to show that she was not high-minded. But she was not without protection; her elder brother JULY was with her.

He was a plump young fellow, clad in summer garments, and with a Panama hat. He had but little baggage with him, because it was cumbersome in the great heat; therefore he had only provided himself with swimming trousers, and those are not much.

Then came the mother herself, Madam AUGUST, wholesale dealer in fruit, proprietress of a large number of fishponds, and land cultivator, in a great crinoline; she was fat and hot, could use her hands well, and would herself carry out beer to the workmen in the fields.

"In the sweat of thy face shalt thou eat bread," said she: "that is written in the *Book*. Afterwards come the excursions, dance and playing in the greenwood, and the harvest feasts!"

She was a thorough housewife.

After her, a man came out of the coach, a painter, Mr. Master-colourer SEPTEMBER. The forest had to receive him; the leaves were to change their colours, but how beautifully! when he wished it; soon the wood gleamed with red, yellow, and brown. The master whistled like the black magpie, was a quick workman, and wound the brown green hop plants round his beer-jug. That was an ornament for the jug, and he had a good idea of ornament. There he stood with his colour-pot, and that was his whole luggage.

A landed proprieter followed him, one who cared for the ploughing and preparing of the land, and also for field sports. Squire OCTOBER brought his dog and his gun with him, and had nuts in his game-bag. " Crack! crack! " He had much baggage, even an English plough; and he spoke of farming, but one could scarcely hear what he said, for the coughing and gasping of his neighbour.

It was NOVEMBER who coughed so violently as he got out. He was very much plagued by a cold; he was continually having recourse to his pocket-handkerchief, and yet, he said, he was obliged to accompany the servant girls, and initiate them into their new winter service. He said he should get rid of his cold when he went out wood-cutting, and had to saw and split wood, for he was sawyer-master to the firewood guild. He spent his evenings cutting the wooden soles for skates, for he knew, he said, that in a few weeks there would be occasion to use these amusing shoes.

At length appeared the last passenger, old Mother DECEMBER, with her fire-stool. The old lady was cold, but her eyes glistened like two bright stars. She carried on her arm a flower-pot, in which a little fir tree was growing.

" This tree I will guard and cherish, that it may grow large by Christmas-eve, and may reach from the ground to the ceiling, and may rear itself upward with flaming candles, golden apples, and little carved figures. The fire-stool warms like a stove. I bring the story-book out of my pocket and read aloud, so that all the children in the room become quite quiet; but the little figures on the trees become lively, and the little waxen angel on the top spreads out his wings of gold leaf, flies down from his green perch, and kisses great and small in the room, yes, even the poor children who stand out in the passage and in the street, singing the carol about the Star of Bethlehem.

" Well, now the coach may drive away! " said the sentry: " we have the whole twelve. Let the chaise drive up."

" First let all the twelve come in to me," said the captain on duty, " one after the other. The passports I will keep here. Each of them is available for a month; when that has passed, I shall write their behaviour on each passport. Mr. January, have the goodness to come here."

And Mr. January stepped forward.

" When a year is passed I think I shall be able to tell you what the twelve have brought to me, and to you, and to all of us. Now I do not know it, and they don't know it themselves, probably, for we live in strange times."

———◆———

MY POST OF OBSERVATION.

WHAT THE MOON SAW.

INTRODUCTION.

I⊤ is a strange thing, that when I feel most fervently and most deeply, my hands and my tongue seem alike tied, so that I cannot rightly describe or accurately portray the thoughts that are rising within me; and yet I am a painter: my eye tells me as much as that, and all my friends who have seen my sketches and fancies say the same.

I am a poor lad, and live in one of the narrowest of lanes; but I do not want for light, as my room is high up in the house, with an extensive prospect over the neighbouring roofs. During the first few days I went to live in the town, I felt low-spirited and solitary enough. Instead of the forest and the green hills of former days, I had here only a forest of chimney-pots to look out upon. And then I had not a single friend; not one familiar face greeted me.

So one evening I sat at the window, in a desponding mood; and presently I opened the casement and looked out. Oh, how my heart leaped up with joy! Here was a well-known face at last—a round, friendly countenance, the face of a good friend I had known at home. In fact, it was the MOON that looked in upon me. He was quite unchanged, the dear old Moon, and had the same face exactly that he used to show when he peered down upon me through the willow trees on the moor. I kissed my hand to him over and over again, as he shone far into my little room; and he, for his part, promised me that every evening, when he came abroad, he would look in upon me for a few moments. This promise he has faithfully kept. It is a pity that he can only stay such a short time when he comes. Whenever he appears, he tells me of one thing or another that he has seen on the previous night or on that same evening.

" Just paint the scenes I describe to you "—this is what he said to me—" and you will have a very pretty picture-book."

I have followed his injunction for many evenings. I could make up a new "Thousand and One Nights," in my own way, out of these pictures, but the number might be too great, after all. The pictures I have here given have not been chosen at random, but follow in their proper order, just as they were described to me. Some great gifted painter, or some poet or musician, may make something more of them if he likes; what I have given here are only hasty sketches, hurriedly put upon the paper, with some of my own thoughts interspersed; for the Moon did not come to me every evening—a cloud sometimes hid his face from me.

FIRST EVENING.

"'LAST night"—I am quoting the Moon's own words—" last night I was gliding through the cloudless Indian sky. My face was mirrored in the waters of the Ganges, and my beams strove to pierce through the thick intertwining boughs of the bananas, arching beneath me like the tortoise's shell. Forth from the thicket tripped a Hindoo maid, light as a gazelle, beautiful as Eve. Airy and ethereal as a vision, and yet sharply defined amid the surrounding shadows, stood this daughter of Hindostan: I could read on her delicate brow the thought that had brought her hither. The thorny creeping plants tore her sandals, but for all that she came rapidly forward. The deer that had come down to the river to quench their thirst, sprang by with a startled bound, for in her hand the maiden bore a lighted lamp. I could see the blood in her delicate finger-tips, as she spread them for a screen before the dancing flame. She came down to the stream, and set the lamp upon the water, and let it float away. The flame flickered to and fro, and seemed ready to expire; but still the lamp burned on, and the girl's black sparkling eyes, half veiled behind their long silken lashes, followed it with a gaze of earnest intensity. She well knew that if the lamp continued to burn so long as she could keep it in sight, her betrothed was still alive ; but if the lamp was suddenly extinguished, he

THE INDIAN GIRL.

was dead. And the lamp burned bravely on, and she fell on her knees, and prayed. Near her in the grass lay a speckled snake, but she heeded it not—she thought only of Bramah and of her betrothed. 'He lives!' she shouted joyfully, 'he lives!' And from the mountains the echo came back upon her, 'he lives!'"

SECOND EVENING.

"YESTERDAY," said the Moon to me, "I looked down upon a small courtyard surrounded on all sides by houses. In the courtyard sat a clucking hen with eleven chickens; and a pretty little girl was running and jumping around them. The hen was frightened, and screamed, and spread out her wings over the little brood. Then the girl's father came out and scolded her; and I glided away and thought no more of the matter.

"But this evening, only a few minutes ago, I looked down into the same courtyard. Everything was quiet. But presently the little girl came forth again, crept quietly to the hen-house, pushed back the bolt, and slipped into the apartment of the hen and chickens. They cried out loudly, and came fluttering down from their perches, and ran about in dismay, and the little girl ran after them. I saw it quite plainly,

THE LITTLE GIRL AND THE CHICKENS.

for I looked through a hole in the hen-house wall. I was angry with the wilful child, and felt glad when her father came out and scolded her more violently than yesterday, holding her roughly by the arm: she held down her head, and her blue eyes were full of large tears. 'What are you about here?' he asked. She wept and said, 'I wanted to kiss the hen and beg her pardon for frightening her yesterday; but I was afraid to tell you.'

"And the father kissed the innocent child's forehead, and I kissed her on the mouth and eyes."

THIRD EVENING.

"In the narrow street round the corner yonder—it is so narrow that my beams can only glide for a minute along the walls of the house, but in that minute I see enough to learn what the world is made of—in that narrow street I saw a woman. Sixteen years ago that woman was a child, playing in the garden of the old parsonage in the country. The hedges of rose bushes were old, and the flowers were faded. They straggled wild over the paths, and the ragged branches grew up among the boughs of the apple trees; here and there were a few roses still in bloom—not so fair as the queen of flowers generally appears, but still they had colour and scent too. The clergyman's little daughter appeared to me a far lovelier rose, as she sat on her stool under the straggling hedge, hugging and caressing her doll with the battered pasteboard cheeks.

"Ten years afterwards I saw her again. I beheld her in a splendid ball-room : she was the beautiful bride of a rich merchant. I rejoiced at her happiness, and sought her on calm quiet evenings—ah, nobody thinks of my clear eye and my silent glance! Alas! my rose ran wild, like the rose bushes in the garden of the parsonage. There are tragedies in every-day life, and to-night I saw the last act of one.

"She was lying in bed in a house in that narrow street; she was sick unto death, and the cruel landlord came up, and tore away the thin coverlet, her only protection against the cold. 'Get up!' said he; 'your face is enough to frighten one. Get up and dress yourself. Give me money, or I'll turn you out into the street! Quick—get up!' She answered, 'Alas! death is gnawing at my heart. Let me rest.' But he forced her to get up and bathe her face, and put a wreath of roses in her hair; and he placed her in a chair at the window, with a candle burning beside her, and went away.

"I looked at her, and she was sitting motionless, with her hands in her lap. The wind caught the open window and shut it with a crash, so that a pane came clattering down in fragments; but still she never moved. The curtain caught fire, and the flames played about her face; and then I saw that she was dead. There at the window sat the dead woman, preaching a sermon against *sin*—my poor faded rose out of the parsonage garden!"

FOURTH EVENING.

"THIS evening I saw a German play acted," said the Moon. "It was in a little town. A stable had been turned into a theatre; that is to say, the stable had been left standing, and had been turned into private boxes, and all the timber work had been covered with coloured paper. A little iron chandelier hung beneath the ceiling, and that it might be made to disappear into the ceiling, as it does in great theatres, when the *ting-ting* of the prompter's bell is heard, a great inverted tub had been placed just above it.

"'*Ting-ting!*' and the little iron chandelier suddenly rose at least half a yard and disappeared in the tub; and that was the sign that the play was going to begin. A young nobleman and his lady, who happened to be passing through the little town, were present at the performance, and consequently the house was crowded. But under the chandelier was a vacant space like a little crater: not a single soul sat there, for the tallow was dropping, drip, drip! I saw everything, for it was so warm in there that every loophole had been opened. The male and female servants stood outside, peeping through the chinks, although a real policeman was inside, threatening them with a stick. Close by the orchestra could be seen the noble young couple in two old arm-chairs, which were usually occupied by his worship the mayor and his lady;

THE PLAY IN A STABLE.

but these latter were to-day obliged to content themselves with wooden forms, just as if they had been ordinary citizens; and the lady observed quietly to herself, 'One sees, now, that there is rank above rank;' and this incident gave an air of extra festivity to the whole proceedings. The chandelier gave little leaps, the crowd got their knuckles rapped, and I, the Moon, was present at the performance from beginning to end."

FIFTH EVENING.

"YESTERDAY," began the Moon, "I looked down upon the turmoil of Paris. My eye penetrated into an apartment of the Louvre. An old grandmother, poorly clad — she belonged to the working class — was following one of the under servants into the great empty throne-room, for this was the apartment she wanted to see—that she was resolved to see; it had cost her many a little sacrifice and many a coaxing word to penetrate thus far. She folded her thin hands, and looked round with an air of reverence, as if she had been in a church.

" 'Here it was!' she said, 'here!' And she approached the throne, from which hung the rich velvet fringed with gold lace. 'There,' she exclaimed, 'there!' and she knelt and kissed the purple carpet. I think she was actually weeping.

" 'But it was not *this very* velvet!' observed the footman, and a smile played about his mouth.

" 'True, but it was this very place,' replied the woman, 'and it must have looked just like this.'

" 'It looked so, and yet it did not,' observed the man: 'the windows were beaten in, and the doors were off their hinges, and there was blood upon the floor.'

" 'But for all that you can say, my grandson died upon the throne of France. Died!' mournfully repeated the old woman.

" I do not think another word was spoken, and they soon quitted the hall. The evening twilight faded, and my light shone doubly vivid upon the rich velvet that covered the throne of France.

" Now, who do you think this poor woman was? Listen, I will tell you a story.

" It happened, in the Revolution of July, on the evening of the most brilliantly victorious day, when every house was a fortress, every window a breastwork. The people stormed the Tuileries. Even women and children were to be found among the combatants. They penetrated into the apartments and halls of the palace. A poor half-grown boy in a ragged blouse fought among the older insurgents. Mortally wounded with several bayonet thrusts, he sank down. This happened in the throne-room. They laid the bleeding youth upon the throne of France, wrapped the velvet round his wounds, and his blood streamed forth upon the imperial purple. There was a picture! the splendid hall, the fighting groups! A torn flag lay upon the ground, the tricolor was waving above the bayonets, and on the throne lay the poor lad with the pale glorified countenance, his eyes turned towards the sky, his limbs writhing in the death agony, his breast bare, and his poor tattered clothing half hidden by the rich velvet embroidered with silver lilies. At the boy's cradle a prophecy had been spoken: 'He will die on the throne of France!' The mother's heart had fondly imagined a second Napoleon.

" My beams have kissed the wreath of *immortelles* on his grave, and this night they kissed the forehead of the old grandame, while in a dream the picture floated before her which thou mayest draw — the poor boy on the throne of France."

SIXTH EVENING.

" I 've been in Upsala," said the Moon: " I looked down upon the great plain covered with coarse grass, and upon the barren fields. I mirrored my face in the Tyris river, while the steamboat drove the fish into the rushes. Beneath me floated the waves, throwing long shadows on the so-called graves of Odin, Thor, and Friga. In the scanty turf that covers the hill-side, names have been cut.* There is no monument here, no memorial on which the traveller can have his name carved, no rocky wall on whose surface he can get it painted; so visitors have the turf cut away for that purpose. The naked earth peers through in the form of great letters and names; these form a network over the whole hill. Here is an immortality, which lasts till the fresh turf grows!

" Up on the hill stood a man, a poet. He emptied the mead horn with the broad silver rim, and murmured a name. He begged the winds not to betray him, but I heard the name. I knew it. A count's coronet sparkles above it, and therefore he did not speak it out. I smiled, for I knew that a poet's crown adorned his own name. The nobility of Eleanora d'Este is attached to the name of Tasso. And I also know where the Rose of Beauty blooms!"

Thus spake the Moon, and a cloud came between us. May no cloud separate the poet from the rose!

SEVENTH EVENING.

"Along the margin of the shore stretches a forest of firs and beeches, and fresh and fragrant is this wood; hundreds of nightingales visit it every spring. Close beside it is the sea, the ever-changing sea, and between the two is placed the broad high road. One carriage after another rolls over it; but I did not follow them, for my eye loves best to rest upon one point. A Hun's Grave † lies there, and the sloe and blackthorn grow luxuriantly among the stones. Here is true poetry in nature.

" And how do you think men appreciate this poetry ? I will tell you what I heard there last evening and during the night.

" First, two rich landed proprietors came driving by. 'Those are glorious trees!' said the first. 'Certainly; there are ten loads of firewood in each,' observed the other: 'it will be a hard winter, and last year we got fourteen dollars a load'—and they were gone. 'The road here is wretched,' observed another man who drove past. 'That's the fault of those horrible trees,' replied his neighbour; 'there is no free current of air; the wind can only come from the sea'—and they were

---

* Travellers on the Continent have frequent opportunities of seeing how universally this custom prevails among travellers. In some places on the Rhine, pots of paint and brushes are offered by the natives to the traveller desirous of "immortalizing" himself.

† Large mounds similar to the " barrows" found in Britain, are thus designated in Germany and the North.

gone. The stage coach went rattling past. All the passengers were asleep at this beautiful spot. The postillion blew his horn, but he only thought, 'I can play capitally. It sounds well here. I wonder if those in there like it?'—and the stage coach vanished. Then two young fellows came gallopping up on horseback. There's youth and spirit in the blood here! thought I; and, indeed, they looked with a smile at the moss-grown hill and thick forest. 'I should not dislike a walk here with the miller's Christine,' said one—and they flew past.

THE POOR GIRL RESTS ON THE HUN'S GRAVE.

"The flowers scented the air; every breath of air was hushed: it seemed as if the sea were a part of the sky that stretched above the deep valley. A carriage rolled by. Six people were sitting in it. Four of them were asleep; the fifth was thinking of his new summer coat, which would suit him admirably; the sixth turned to the coachman and asked him if there were anything remarkable connected with yonder heap of stones. 'No,' replied the coachman, 'it's only a heap of stones; but the trees are remarkable.' 'How so?' 'Why, I'll tell you how they are very remarkable. You see, in winter, when the snow lies very deep, and has hidden the whole road so that nothing is to be seen, those trees serve me for a landmark. I steer by them, so as not to drive into the sea; and you see that is why the trees are remarkable.'

"Now came a painter. He spoke not a word, but his eyes sparkled.

He began to whistle. At this the nightingales sang louder than ever. 'Hold your tongues!' he cried, testily; and he made accurate notes of all the colours and transitions—blue, and lilac, and dark brown. 'That will make a beautiful picture,' he said. He took it in just as a mirror takes in a view; and as he worked he whistled a march of Rossini. And last of all came a poor girl. She laid aside the burden she carried and sat down to rest upon the Hun's Grave. Her pale handsome face was bent in a listening attitude towards the forest. Her eyes brightened, she gazed earnestly at the sea and the sky, her hands were folded, and I think she prayed, 'Our Father.' She herself could not understand the feeling that swept through her, but I know that this minute, and the beautiful natural scene, will live within her memory for years, far more vividly and more truly than the painter could portray it with his colours on paper. My rays followed her till the morning dawn kissed her brow."

EIGHTH EVENING.

HEAVY clouds obscured the sky, and the Moon did not make his appearance at all. I stood in my little room, more lonely than ever, and looked up at the sky where he ought to have shown himself. My thoughts flew far away, up to my great friend, who every evening told me such pretty tales, and showed me pictures. Yes, he has had an experience indeed. He glided over the waters of the Deluge, and smiled on Noah's ark just as he lately glanced down upon me, and brought comfort and promise of a new world that was to spring forth from the old. When the Children of Israel sat weeping by the waters of Babylon, he glanced mournfully upon the willows where hung the silent harps. When Romeo climbed the balcony, and the promise of true love fluttered like a cherub toward heaven, the round Moon hung, half hidden among the dark cypresses, in the lucid air. He saw the captive giant at St. Helena, looking from the lonely rock across the wide ocean, while great thoughts swept through his soul. Ah! what tales the Moon can tell. Human life is like a story to him. To-night I shall not see thee again, old friend. To-night I can draw no picture of the memories of thy visit. And, as I looked dreamily towards the clouds, the sky became bright. There was a glancing light, and a beam from the Moon fell upon me. It vanished again, and dark clouds flew past; but still it was a greeting, a friendly good night offered to me by the Moon.

NINTH EVENING.

THE air was clear again. Several evenings had passed, and the Moon was in the first quarter. Again he gave me an outline for a sketch. Listen to what he told me.

" I have followed the polar bird and the swimming whale to the eastern coast of Greenland. Gaunt ice-covered rocks and dark clouds hung over a valley, where dwarf willows and barberry bushes stood clothed in green. The blooming lychnis exhaled sweet odours. My light was faint, my face pale as the water lily that, torn from its stem, has been drifting for weeks with the tide. The crown-shaped Northern Light burned fiercely in the sky. Its ring was broad, and from its circumference the rays shot like whirling shafts of fire across the whole sky, flashing in changing radiance from green to red. The inhabitants of that icy region were assembling for dance and festivity; but accustomed to this glorious spectacle, they scarcely deigned to glance at it. ' Let us leave the souls of the dead to their ball-play with the heads of the walruses,' they thought in their superstition, and they turned their whole attention to the song and dance. In the midst of the circle, and divested of his furry cloak, stood a Greenlander, with a small pipe, and he played and sang a song about catching the seal, and the chorus around chimed in with, ' *Eia, Eia, Ah.*' And in their white furs they danced about in the circle, till you might fancy it was a polar bear's ball.

"And now a Court of Judgment was opened. Those Greenlanders who had quarrelled stepped forward, and the offended person chanted forth the faults of his adversary in an extempore song, turning them sharply into ridicule, to the sound of the pipe and the measure of the dance. The defendant replied with satire as keen, while the audience laughed and gave their verdict.

The rocks heaved, the glaciers melted, and great masses of ice and snow came crashing down, shivering to fragments as they fell : it was a glorious Greenland summer night. A hundred paces away, under the open tent of hides, lay a sick man. Life still flowed through his warm blood, but still he was to die ; he himself felt it, and all who stood round him knew it also ; therefore his wife was already sewing round him the shroud of furs, that she might not afterwards be obliged to touch the dead body. And she asked, ' Wilt thou be buried on the rock, in the firm snow ? I will deck the spot with thy *kayak*, and thy arrows, and the *angekokk* shall dance over it. Or wouldst thou rather be buried in the sea ?' ' In the sea,' he whispered, and nodded with a mournful smile. ' Yes, it is a pleasant summer tent, the sea,' observed the wife. ' Thousands of seals sport there, the walrus shall lie at thy feet, and the hunt will be safe and merry !' And the yelling children tore the outspread hide from the window-hole, that the dead man might be carried to the ocean, the billowy ocean, that had given him food in life, and that now, in death, was to afford him a place of rest. For his monument, he had the floating, ever-changing icebergs, whereon the seal sleeps, while the storm bird flies round their gleaming summits."

TENTH EVENING.

"I KNEW an old maid," said the Moon. "Every winter she wore a wrapper of yellow satin, and it always remained new, and was the only

THE OLD MAID.

fashion she followed. In summer she always wore the same straw hat, and I verily believe the very same grey-blue dress.

"She never went out, except across the street to an old female friend; and in later years she did not even take this walk, for the old friend was dead. In her solitude my old maid was always busy at the window, which was adorned in summer with pretty flowers, and in winter with cress, grown upon felt. During the last months I saw her no more at the window, but she was still alive. I knew that, for I had not yet seen her begin the 'long journey,' of which she often spoke with her friend. 'Yes, yes,' she was in the habit of saying, 'when I come to die, I shall take a longer journey than I have made my whole life long. Our family vault is six miles from here. I shall be carried there, and shall sleep there among my family and relatives.' Last night a van stopped at the house. A coffin was carried out, and then I knew that she was dead. They placed straw round the coffin, and the van drove away. There slept the quiet old lady, who had not gone out of her house once for the last year. The van rolled out through the town gate as briskly as if it were going for a pleasant excursion. On the high road the pace was quicker yet. The coachman looked nervously round every now and then—I fancy he half expected to see her sitting on the coffin, in her yellow satin wrapper. And because he was startled, he foolishly lashed his horses, while he held the reins so tightly that the poor beasts were in a foam: they were young and fiery. A hare jumped across the road and startled them, and they fairly ran away. The old sober maiden, who had for years and years moved quietly round and round in a dull circle, was now, in death, rattled over stock and stone on the public highway. The coffin in its covering of straw tumbled out of the van, and was left on the high road, while horses, coachman, and carriage flew past in wild career. The lark rose up carolling from the field, twittering her morning lay over the coffin, and presently perched upon it, picking with her beak at the straw covering, as though she would tear it up. The lark rose up again, singing gaily, and I withdrew behind the red morning clouds."

ELEVENTH EVENING.

"I WILL give you a picture of Pompeii," said the Moon. "I was in the suburb in the Street of Tombs, as they call it, where the fair monuments stand, in the spot where, ages ago, the merry youths, their temples bound with rosy wreaths, danced with the fair sisters of Laïs. Now, the stillness of death reigned around. German mercenaries, in the Neapolitan service, kept guard, played cards, and diced; and a troop of strangers from beyond the mountains came into the town, accompanied by a sentry. They wanted to see the city that had risen from the grave illumined by my beams; and I showed them the wheel-ruts in the streets paved with broad lava slabs; I showed them the names on the doors, and the signs that hung there yet: they saw in the little court-yard the basins of the fountains, ornamented with shells; but no jet of water gushed upwards, no songs sounded forth from the richly-painted chambers, where the bronze dog kept the door.

"It was the City of the Dead; only Vesuvius thundered forth his ever-lasting hymn, each separate verse of which is called by men an eruption. We went to the temple of Venus, built of snow-white marble, with its high altar in front of the broad steps, and the weeping willows sprouting freshly forth among the pillars. The air was transparent and blue, and black Vesuvius formed the background, with fire ever shooting forth from it, like the stem of the pine tree. Above it stretched the smoky cloud in the silence of the night, like the crown of the pine, but in a blood-red illumination. Among the company was a lady singer, a real and great singer. I have witnessed the homage paid to her in the greatest cities of Europe. When they came to the tragic theatre, they all sat down on the amphitheatre steps, and thus a small part of the house was occupied by an audience, as it had been many centuries ago. The stage still stood unchanged, and its walled side-scenes, and the two arches in the background, through which the beholders saw the same scene that had been exhibited in the old times—a scene painted by nature herself, namely, the mountains between Sorrento and Amalfi. The singer gaily mounted the ancient stage, and sang. The place inspired her, and she reminded me of a wild Arab horse, that rushes headlong on with snorting nostrils and flying mane—her song was so light and yet so firm. Anon I thought of the mourning mother beneath the cross at Golgotha, so deep was the expression of pain. And, just as it had done thousands of years ago, the sound of applause and delight now filled the theatre. 'Happy, gifted creature!' all the hearers exclaimed. Five minutes more, and the stage was empty, the company had vanished, and not a sound more was heard—all were gone. But the ruins stood unchanged, as they will stand when centuries shall have gone by, and when none shall know of the momentary applause and of the triumph of the fair songstress; when all will be forgotten and gone. and even for me this hour will be but a dream of the past."

TWELFTH EVENING.

"I LOOKED through the windows of an editor's house," said the Moon. "It was somewhere in Germany. I saw handsome furniture, many books, and a chaos of newspapers. Several young men were present: the editor himself stood at his desk, and two little books, both by young authors, were to be noticed. 'This one has been sent to me,' said he. 'I have not read it yet; what think *you* of the contents?' 'Oh,' said the person addressed—he was a poet himself—'it is good enough; a little broad, certainly; but, you see, the author is still young. The verses might be better, to be sure; the thoughts are sound, though there is certainly a good deal of commonplace among them. But what will you have? You can't be always getting something new. That he 'll turn out anything great I don't believe, but you may safely praise him. He is well read, a remarkable Oriental scholar, and has a good judgment. It was he who wrote that nice review of my "Reflections on Domestic Life." We must be lenient towards the young man.'

"'But he is a complete hack!' objected another of the gentlemen. 'Nothing is worse in poetry than mediocrity, and he certainly does not go beyond that.'

"'Poor fellow!' observed a third, 'and his aunt is so happy about him. It was she, Mr. Editor, who got together so many subscribers for your last translation.'

"'Ah, the good woman! Well, I have noticed the book briefly. Undoubted talent—a welcome offering—a flower in the garden of poetry —prettily brought out—and so on. But this other book—I suppose the author expects me to purchase it? I hear it is praised. He has genius, certainly: don't you think so?'

"'Yes, all the world declares as much,' replied the poet, 'but it has turned out rather wildly. The punctuation of the book, in particular, is very eccentric.'

" ' It will be good for him if we pull him to pieces, and anger him a little, otherwise he will get too good an opinion of himself.'

" ' But that would be unfair,' objected the fourth. ' Let us not carp at little faults, but rejoice over the real and abundant good that we find here : he surpasses all the rest.'

" ' Not so. If he be a true genius, he can bear the sharp voice of censure. There are people enough to praise him. Don't let us quite turn his head.'

" ' Decided talent,' wrote the editor, ' with the usual carelessness. That he can write incorrect verses may be seen in page 25, where there are two false quantities. We recommend him to study the ancients, etc.'

" I went away," continued the Moon, " and looked through the windows in the aunt's house. There sat the be-praised poet, the *tame* one ; all the guests paid homage to him, and he was happy.

" I sought the other poet out, the *wild* one ; him also I found in a great assembly at his patron's, where the tame poet's book was being discussed.

" ' I shall read yours also,' said Mæcenas ; ' but to speak honestly—you know I never hide my opinion from you—I don't expect much from it, for you are much too wild, too fantastic. But it must be allowed that, as a man, you are highly respectable.'

" A young girl sat in a corner ; and she read in a book these words :

" ' In the dust lies genius and glory,
But ev'ry-day talent will *pay*.
It 's only the old, old story,
But the piece is repeated each day.' "

THIRTEENTH EVENING.

THE Moon said, " Beside the woodland path there are two small farm-houses. The doors are low, and some of the windows are placed quite high, and others close to the ground ; and whitethorn and barberry bushes grow around them. The roof of each house is overgrown with moss and with yellow flowers and houseleek. Cabbage and potatoes are the only plants cultivated in the gardens, but out of the hedge there grows a willow tree, and under this willow tree sat a little girl, and she sat with her eyes fixed upon the old oak tree between the two huts.

" It was an old withered stem. It had been sawn off at the top, and a stork had built his nest upon it ; and he stood in this nest clapping with his beak. A little boy came and stood by the girl's side : they were brother and sister.

" ' What are you looking at ?' he asked.

" ' I 'm watching the stork,' she replied : ' our neighbour told me that he would bring us a little brother or sister to-day ; let us watch to see it come !'

" ' The stork brings no such things,' the boy declared, ' you may be sure of that. Our neighbour told me the same thing, but she laughed when she said it, and so I asked her if she could say " On my honour,"

WATCHING THE STORK.

and she could not; and I know by that that the story about the storks is not true, and that they only tell it to us children for fun.'

"'But where do the babies come from, then?' asked the girl.

"'Why, an angel from heaven brings them under his cloak, but no man can see him; and that's why we never know when he brings them.'

"At that moment there was a rustling in the branches of the willow tree, and the children folded their hands and looked at one another: it was certainly the angel coming with the baby. They took each other's hand, and at that moment the door of one of the houses opened, and the neighbour appeared.

"'Come in, you two,' she said. 'She what the stork has brought. It is a little brother.'

"And the children nodded gravely at one another, for they had felt quite sure already that the baby was come."

FOURTEENTH EVENING.

"I was gliding over the Lüneburg Heath," the Moon said. "A lonely hut stood by the wayside, a few scanty bushes grew near it, and a nightingale who had lost his way sang sweetly. He died in the coldness of the night: it was his farewell song that I heard.

"The morning dawn came glimmering red. I saw a caravan of emigrant peasant families who were bound to Hamburgh, there to take ship for America, where fancied prosperity would bloom for them. The mothers carried their little children at their backs, the elder ones tottered by their sides, and a poor starved horse tugged at a cart that bore their scanty effects. The cold wind whistled, and therefore the little girl nestled closer to the mother, who, looking up at my decreasing disc, thought of the bitter want at home, and spoke of the heavy taxes they had not been able to raise. The whole caravan thought of the same thing; therefore, the rising dawn seemed to them a message from the sun, of fortune that was to gleam brightly upon them. They heard the dying nightingale sing: it was no false prophet, but a harbinger of fortune. The wind whistled, therefore they did not understand that the nightingale sang, 'Far away over the sea! Thou hast paid the long passage with all that was thine, and poor and helpless shalt thou enter Canaan. Thou must sell thyself, thy wife, and thy children. But your griefs shall not last long. Behind the broad fragrant leaves lurks the goddess of death, and her welcome kiss shall breathe fever into thy blood. Fare away, fare away, over the heaving billows.' And the caravan listened well pleased to the song of the nightingale, which seemed to promise good fortune. Day broke through the light clouds; country people went across the heath to church: the black-gowned women with their white head-dresses looked like ghosts that had stepped forth from the church pictures. All around lay a wide dead plain, covered with faded brown heath, and black charred spaces between the white sand hills. The women carried hymn books, and walked into the church. Oh, pray, pray for those who are wandering to find graves beyond the foaming billows."

FIFTEENTH EVENING.

"I know a Pulcinella," * the Moon told me. "The public applaud vociferously directly they see him. Every one of his movements is comic, and is sure to throw the house into convulsions of laughter; and yet there is no art in it all—it is complete nature. When he was yet a little boy, playing about with other boys, he was already Punch. Nature had intended him for it, and had provided him with a hump on

---

* The comic or grotesque character of the Italian ballet, from which the English "Punch" takes his origin.

PULCINELLA ON COLUMBINE'S GRAVE.

his back, and another on his breast; but his inward man, his mind, on the contrary, was richly furnished. No one could surpass him in depth of feeling or in readiness of intellect. The theatre was his ideal world. If he had possessed a slender well-shaped figure, he might have been the first tragedian on any stage: the heroic, the great, filled his soul; and yet he had to become a Pulcinella. His very sorrow and melancholy did but increase the comic dryness of his sharply-cut features, and increased the laughter of the audience, who showered plaudits on their favourite. The lovely Columbine was indeed kind and cordial to him; but she preferred to marry the Harlequin. It would have been too ridiculous if beauty and ugliness had in reality paired together.

"When Pulcinella was in very bad spirits, she was the only one who could force a hearty burst of laughter, or even a smile from him: first she would be melancholy with him, then quieter, and at last quite cheerful and happy. 'I know very well what is the matter with you,' she said; 'yes, you're in love!' And he could not help laughing. 'I and Love!' he cried, 'that would have an absurd look. How the public would shout!' 'Certainly, you are in love,' she continued; and added with a comic pathos, 'and I am the person you are in love with.' You see, such a thing may be said when it is quite out of the question—and, indeed, Pulcinella burst out laughing, and gave a leap into the air, and his melancholy was forgotten.

"And yet she had only spoken the truth. He *did* love her, love her adoringly, as he loved what was great and lofty in art. At her wedding he was the merriest among the guests, but in the stillness of night he wept: if the public had seen his distorted face then, they would have applauded rapturously.

"And a few days ago, Columbine died. On the day of the funeral, Harlequin was not required to show himself on the boards, for he was a disconsolate widower. The director had to give a very merry piece, that the public might not too painfully miss the pretty Columbine and the agile Harlequin. Therefore Pulcinella had to be more boisterous and extravagant than ever; and he danced and capered, with despair in his heart; and the audience yelled, and shouted, '*bravo! bravissimo!*' Pulcinella was actually called before the curtain. He was pronounced inimitable.

"But last night the hideous little fellow went out of the town, quite alone, to the deserted churchyard. The wreath of flowers on Columbine's grave was already faded, and he sat down there. It was a study for a painter. As he sat with his chin on his hands, his eyes turned up towards me, he looked like a grotesque monument—a Punch on a grave—peculiar and whimsical! If the people could have seen their favourite, they would have cried as usual, '*Bravo, Pulcinella! bravo, bravissimo!*'"

SIXTEENTH EVENING.

HEAR what the Moon told me. "I have seen the cadet who had just been made an officer put on his handsome uniform for the first time; I have seen the young bride in her wedding dress, and the Princess girl-wife happy in her gorgeous robes; but never have I seen a felicity equal to that of a little girl of four years old, whom I watched this evening. She had received a new blue dress and a new pink hat; the splendid attire had just been put on, and all were calling for a candle, for my rays, shining in through the windows of the room, were not bright enough for the occasion, and further illumination was required. There stood the little maid, stiff and upright as a doll, her arms stretched painfully straight out away from the dress, and her fingers apart; and, Oh, what happiness beamed from her eyes and from her whole countenance! 'To-morrow you shall go out in your new clothes,' said her mother; and the little one looked up at her hat and down at her frock, and smiled brightly. 'Mother,' she cried, 'what will the little dogs think when they see me in these splendid new things?'"

SEVENTEENTH EVENING.

" I HAVE spoken to you of Pompeii," said the Moon; " that corpse of a city, exposed in the view of living towns: I know another sight still more strange, and this is not the corpse, but the spectre of a city. Whenever the jetty fountains splash into the marble basins, they seem to me to be telling the story of the floating city. Yes, the spouting water may tell of her, the waves of the sea may sing of her fame! On the surface of the ocean a mist often rests, and that is her widow's veil. The Bridegroom of the Sea is dead, his palace and his city are his mausoleum! Dost thou know this city? She has never heard the rolling of wheels or the hoof-tread of horses in her streets, through which the fish swim, while the black gondola glides spectrally over the green water. I will show you the place," continued the Moon, " the largest square in it, and you will fancy yourself transported into the city of a fairy tale. The grass grows rank among the broad flagstones, and in the morning twilight thousands of tame pigeons flutter around the solitary lofty tower. On three sides you find yourself surrounded by cloistered walks. In these the silent Turk sits smoking his long pipe; the handsome Greek leans against the pillar, and gazes at the upraised trophies and lofty masts, memorials of power that is gone. The flags hang down like mourning scarves. A girl rests there: she has put down her heavy pails filled with water, the yoke with which she has carried them rests on one of her shoulders, and she leans against the mast of victory. That is not a fairy palace you see before you yonder, but a church: the gilded domes and shining orbs flash back my beams; the glorious bronze horses up yonder have made journeys, like the bronze horse in the fairy tale: they have come hither, and gone hence, and have returned again. Do you notice the variegated splendour of the walls and windows? It looks as if Genius had followed the caprices of a child, in the adornment of these singular temples. Do you see the winged lion on the pillar? The gold glitters still, but his wings are tied—the lion is dead, for the King of the Sea is dead; the great halls stand desolate, and where gorgeous paintings hung of yore, the naked wall now peers through. The *lazzarone* sleeps under the arcade, whose pavement in old times was to be trodden only by the feet of the high nobility. From the deep wells, and perhaps from the prisons by the Bridge of Sighs, rise the accents of woe, as at the time when the tambourine was heard in the gay gondolas, and the golden ring was cast from the Bucentaur to Adria, the Queen of the Seas. Adria! shroud thyself in mists; let the veil of thy widowhood shroud thy form, and clothe in the weeds of woe the mausoleum of thy bridegroom — the marble, spectral Venice!"

EIGHTEENTH EVENING.

"I LOOKED down upon a great theatre," said the Moon. "The house was crowded, for a new actor was to make his first appearance that night. My rays glided over a little window in the wall, and I saw a painted face with the forehead pressed against the panes. It was the hero of the evening. The knightly beard curled crisply about the chin; but there were tears in the man's eyes, for he had been hissed off, and indeed with reason. The poor Incapable! But Incapables cannot be admitted into the empire of Art. He had deep feeling, and loved his art enthusiastically, but the art loved not him. The prompter's bell sounded; '*the hero enters with a determined air*,' so ran the stage direction in his part, and he had to appear before an audience who turned him into ridicule. When the piece was over, I saw a form wrapped in a mantle creeping down the steps: it was the vanquished knight of the evening. The scene-shifters whispered to one another, and I followed the poor fellow home to his room. To hang oneself is to die a mean death, and poison is not always at hand, I know; but he thought of both. I saw how he looked at his pale face in the glass, with eyes half closed, to see if he should look well as a corpse. A man may be very unhappy, and yet exceedingly affected. He thought of death, of suicide; I believe he pitied himself, for he wept bitterly; and when a man has had his cry out he doesn't kill himself.

"Since that time a year had rolled by. Again a play was to be acted, but in a little theatre, and by a poor strolling company. Again I saw the well-remembered face, with the painted cheeks and the crisp beard. He looked up at me and smiled; and yet he had been hissed off only a minute before — hissed off from a wretched theatre by a miserable audience. And to-night a shabby hearse rolled out of the town gate. It was a suicide—our painted, despised hero. The driver of the hearse was the only person present, for no one followed except my beams. In a corner of the churchyard the corpse of the suicide was shovelled into the earth, and nettles will soon be rankly growing over his grave, and the sexton will throw thorns and weeds from the other graves upon it."

NINETEENTH EVENING.

"I COME from Rome," said the Moon. "In the midst of the city, upon one of the seven hills, lie the ruins of the imperial palace. The wild fig tree grows in the clefts of the wall, and covers the nakedness thereof with its broad grey-green leaves; trampling among heaps of rubbish, the ass treads upon green laurels, and rejoices over the rank thistles. From this spot, whence the eagles of Rome once flew abroad, whence they 'came, saw, and conquered,' our door leads into a little mean house, built of clay between two pillars; the wild vine hangs like a mourning garland over the crooked window. An old woman and her little granddaughter live there: they rule now in the palace of the Cæsars, and show to strangers the remains of its past glories. Of the splendid throne-hall only a naked wall yet stands, and a black cypress throws its dark shadow on the spot where the throne once stood. The dust lies several feet deep on the broken pavement; and the little maiden, now the daughter of the imperial palace, often sits there on her stool when the evening bells ring. The keyhole of the door close by she calls her turret window; through this she can see half Rome, as far as the mighty cupola of St. Peter's.

" On this evening, as usual, stillness reigned around; and in the full beam of my light came the little granddaughter. On her head she carried an earthen pitcher of antique shape filled with water. Her feet were bare, her short frock and her white sleeves were torn. I kissed her pretty round shoulders, her dark eyes, and black shining hair. She mounted the stairs; they were steep, having been made up of rough blocks of broken marble and the capital of a fallen pillar. The coloured lizards slipped away, startled, from before her feet, but she was not frightened at them. Already she lifted her hand to pull the door-bell— a hare's foot fastened to a string formed the bell-handle of the imperial palace. She paused for a moment— of what might she be thinking? Perhaps of the beautiful Christ-child, dressed in gold and silver, which was down below in the chapel, where the silver candlesticks gleamed so bright, and where her little friends sang the hymns in which she also could join? I know not. Presently she moved again—she stumbled; the earthen vessel fell from her head, and broke on the marble steps. She burst into tears. The beautiful daughter of the imperial palace wept over the worthless broken pitcher; with her bare feet she stood there weeping, and dared not pull the string, the bell-rope of the imperial palace!"

TWENTIETH EVENING.

It was more than a fortnight since the Moon had shone. Now he stood once more, round and bright, above the clouds, moving slowly onward. Hear what the Moon told me.

" From a town in Fezzan I followed a caravan. On the margin of the sandy desert, in a salt plain, that shone like a frozen lake, and was only covered in spots with light drifting sand, a halt was made. The eldest of the company — the water gourd hung at his girdle, and on his head was a little bag of unleavened bread — drew a square in the sand with his staff, and wrote in it a few words out of the Koran, and then the whole caravan passed over the consecrated spot. A young merchant, a child of the East, as I could tell by his eye and his figure, rode pensively forward on his white snorting steed. Was he thinking, perchance, of his fair young wife? It was only two days ago that the camel, adorned with furs and with costly shawls, had carried her, the beauteous bride, round the walls of the city, while drums and cymbals had sounded, the women sang, and festive shots, of which the bridegroom fired the greatest number, resounded round the camel; and now he was journeying with the caravan across the desert.

"For many nights I followed the train. I saw them rest by the well-side among the stunted palms; they thrust the knife into the breast of the camel that had fallen, and roasted its flesh by the fire. My beams cooled the glowing sands, and showed them the black rocks, dead islands in the immense ocean of sand. No hostile tribes met them in their pathless route, no storms arose, no columns of sand whirled destruction over the journeying caravan. At home the beautiful wife prayed for her husband and her father. 'Are they dead?' she asked of my golden crescent; 'Are they dead?' she cried to my full disc. Now the desert lies behind them. This evening they sit beneath the lofty palm trees, where the crane flutters round them with its long wings, and the pelican watches them from the branches of the mimosa. The luxuriant herbage is trampled down, crushed by the feet of elephants. A troop of negroes are returning from a market in the interior of the land; the women, with copper buttons in their black hair, and decked out in clothes dyed with indigo, drive the heavily-laden oxen, on whose backs slumber the naked black children. A negro leads a young lion which he has bought by a string. They approach the caravan; the young merchant sits pensive and motionless, thinking of his beautiful wife, dreaming, in the land of the blacks, of his white fragrant lily beyond the desert. He raises his head, and——"

But at this moment a cloud passed before the Moon, and then another. I heard nothing more from him this evening.

TWENTY-FIRST EVENING.

"I LOOKED down on Tyrol," said the Moon, "and my beams caused the dark pines to throw long shadows upon the rocks. I looked at the pictures of St. Christopher carrying the Infant Jesus that are painted there upon the walls of the houses, colossal figures reaching from the ground to the roof. St. Florian was represented pouring water on the burning house, and the Lord hung bleeding on the great cross by the way-side. To the present generation these are old pictures, but I saw when they were put up, and marked how one followed the other. On the brow of the mountain yonder is perched, like a swallow's nest, a lonely convent of nuns. Two of the sisters stood up in the tower tolling the bell; they were both young, and therefore their glances flew over the mountain out into the world. A travelling coach passed by below, the postillion wound his horn, and the poor nuns looked after the carriage for a moment with a mournful glance, and a tear gleamed in the eyes of the younger one. And the horn sounded faintly and more faint, and the convent bell drowned its expiring echoes."

THE LITTLE GIRL'S TROUBLE.

TWENTY-SECOND EVENING.

"I saw a little girl weeping," said the Moon: "she was weeping over the depravity of the world. She had received a most beautiful doll as a present. Oh, that was a glorious doll, so fair and delicate! She did not seem created for the sorrows of this world. But the brothers of the little girl, those great naughty boys, had set the doll high up in the branches of a tree, and had run away.

"The little girl could not reach up to the doll, and could not help her down, and that is why she was crying. The doll must certainly have been crying too, for she stretched out her arms among the green branches, and looked quite mournful. Yes, these are the troubles of life of which the little girl had often heard tell. Alas, poor doll! it began to grow dark already; and suppose night were to come on completely! Was she to be left sitting there alone on the bough all night long? No, the little maid could not make up her mind to that. 'I'll stay with you,' she said, although she felt anything but happy in her mind. She could almost fancy she distinctly saw little gnomes, with their high-crowned hats, sitting in the bushes; and farther back in the long walk, tall spectres appeared to be dancing. They came nearer and nearer, and stretched out their hands towards the tree on which the doll sat; they laughed scornfully, and pointed at her with their fingers. Oh, how frightened the little maid was! 'But if one has not done anything wrong,' she thought, 'nothing evil can harm one. I wonder if I have done anything wrong?' And she considered. 'Oh, yes! I laughed at the poor duck with the red rag on her leg; she limped along so funnily, I could not help laughing; but it's a sin to laugh at animals.' And she looked up at the doll. 'Did you laugh at the duck, too?' she asked; and it seemed as if the doll shook her head."

TWENTY-THIRD EVENING.

HEAR what the Moon told me. "Some years ago, here in Copenhagen, I looked through the window of a mean little room. The father and mother slept, but the little son was not asleep. I saw the flowered cotton curtains of the bed move, and the child peep forth. At first, I thought he was looking at the great clock, which was gaily painted in red and green. At the top sat a cuckoo, below hung the heavy leaden weights, and the pendulum with the polished disc of metal went to and fro, and said 'tick, tick.' But no, he was not looking at the clock, but at his mother's spinning-wheel, that stood just underneath it. That was the boy's favourite piece of furniture, but he dared not touch it, for if he meddled with it he got a rap on the knuckles. For hours together, when his mother was spinning, he would sit quietly by her side, watching the murmuring spindle and the revolving wheel, and as he sat he thought of many things. Oh, if he might only turn the wheel himself! Father and mother were asleep: he looked at them, and looked at the spinning-wheel, and presently a little naked foot peered out of the bed, and then a second foot, and then two little white legs. There he stood. He looked round once more, to see if father and mother were still asleep —yes, they slept; and now he crept *softly, softly*, in his short little nightgown, to the spinning-wheel, and began to spin. The thread flew from the wheel, and the wheel whirled faster and faster. I kissed his fair hair and his blue eyes, it was such a pretty picture.

"At that moment the mother awoke. The curtain shook; she looked forth, and fancied she saw a gnome or some other kind of little spectre. 'In Heaven's name!' she cried, and aroused her husband in a frightened way. He opened his eyes, rubbed them with his hands, and looked at the brisk little lad. 'Why, that is Bertel,' said he. And my eye quitted the poor room, for I have so much to see. At the same moment I looked at the halls of the Vatican, where the marble gods are enthroned. I shone upon the group of the Laocoon; the stone seemed to sigh. I pressed a silent kiss on the lips of the Muses, and they seemed to stir and move. But my rays lingered longest about the Nile group with the colossal god. Leaning against the Sphinx, he lies there thoughtful and meditative, as if he were thinking on the rolling centuries; and little love-gods sport with him and with the crocodiles. In the horn of plenty sits with folded arms a little tiny love-god contemplating the

LITTLE BERTEL'S AMBITION.

great solemn river-god, a true picture of the boy at the spinning-wheel, —the features were exactly the same. Charming and lifelike stood the little marble form, and yet the wheel of the year has turned more than a thousand times since the time when it sprang forth from the stone. Just as often as the boy in the little room turned the spinning-wheel had the great wheel murmured, before the age could again call forth marble gods equal to those he afterwards formed.

"Years have passed since all this happened," the Moon went on to say. " Yesterday I looked upon a bay on the eastern coast of Denmark. Glorious woods are there, and high trees, an old knightly castle with red walls, swans floating in the ponds, and in the background appears, among orchards, a little town with a church. Many boats, the crews all furnished with torches, glided over the silent expanse—but these fires had not been kindled for catching fish, for everything had a festive look. Music sounded, a song was sung, and in one of the boats a man stood erect, to whom homage was paid by the rest, a tall sturdy man, wrapped in a cloak. He had blue eyes and long white hair. I knew him, and thought of the Vatican, and of the group of the Nile, and the old marble gods. I thought of the simple little room where little Bertel sat in his nightshirt by the spinning-wheel. The wheel of time has turned, and new gods have come forth from the stone. From the boats there arose a shout : ' Hurrah ! hurrah for Bertel Thorwaldsen !' "

TWENTY-FOURTH EVENING.

" I WILL now give you a picture from Frankfort," said the Moon. " I especially noticed one building there. It was not the house in which Goethe was born, nor the old council-house, through whose grated windows peered the horns of the oxen that were roasted and given to the people when the Emperors were crowned. No, it was a private house, plain in appearance, and painted green. It stood near the old Jews' Street. It was Rothschild's house.

" I looked through the open door. The staircase was brilliantly lighted : servants carrying wax candles in massive silver candlesticks stood there, and bowed low before an aged woman, who was being brought down stairs in a litter. The proprietor of the house stood bare headed, and respectfully imprinted a kiss on the hand of the old woman. She was his mother. She nodded in a friendly manner to him and to the servants, and they carried her into the dark narrow street, into a little house, that was her dwelling. Here her children had been born, from hence the fortune of the family had arisen. If she deserted the despised street and the little house, fortune would also desert her children. That was her firm belief."

The Moon told me no more ; his visit this evening was far too short. But I thought of the old woman in the narrow despised street. It would have cost her but a word, and a brilliant house would have arisen for her on the banks of the Thames—a word, and a villa would have been prepared in the Bay of Naples.

" If I deserted the lowly house, where the fortunes of my sons first began to bloom, fortune would desert them !" It was a superstition, but a superstition of such a class, that he who knows the story and has seen this picture, need have only two words placed under the picture to make him understand it ; and these two words are : " A mother."

TWENTY-FIFTH EVENING.

" It was yesterday, in the morning twilight "—these are the words the Moon told me—" in the great city no chimney was yet smoking—and it was just at the chimneys that I was looking. Suddenly a little head emerged from one of them, and then half a body, the arms resting on the rim of the chimney-pot. ' Ya-hip! ya-hip!' cried a voice. It was the little chimney-sweeper, who had for the first time in his life crept through a chimney and stuck out his head at the top. ' Ya-hip! ya-hip!'

THE LITTLE CHIMNEY-SWEEPER.

Yes, certainly that was a very different thing from creeping about in the dark narrow chimneys! the air blew so fresh, and he could look over the whole city towards the green wood. The sun was just rising. It shone round and great, just in his face, that beamed with triumph, though it was very prettily blacked with soot.

" ' The whole town can see me now,' he exclaimed, ' and the moon can see me now, and the sun too. Ya-hip! ya-hip!' And he flourished his broom in triumph "

TWENTY-SIXTH EVENING.

" Last night I looked down upon a town in China," said the Moon. " My beams irradiated the naked walls that form the streets there. Now and then, certainly, a door is seen, but it is locked, for what does the

Chinaman care about the outer world? Close wooden shutters covered the windows behind the walls of the houses; but through the windows of the temple a faint light glimmered. I looked in, and saw the quaint decorations within. From the floor to the ceiling pictures are painted in the most glaring colours, and richly gilt—pictures representing the deeds of the gods here on earth. In each niche statues are placed, but they are almost entirely hidden by the coloured drapery and the banners that hang down. Before each idol (and they are all made of tin) stood a little altar of holy water, with flowers and burning wax lights on it. Above all the rest stood Fo, the chief deity, clad in a garment of yellow silk, for yellow is here the sacred colour. At the foot of the altar sat a living being, a young priest. He appeared to be praying, but in the

PRETTY PU.

midst of his prayer he seemed to fall into deep thought, and this must have been wrong, for his cheeks glowed and he held down his head. Poor Soui-hong! Was he, perhaps, dreaming of working in the little flower garden behind the high street wall? And did that occupation seem more agreeable to him than watching the wax lights in the temple? Or did he wish to sit at the rich feast, wiping his mouth with silver paper between each course? Or was his sin so great that, if he dared utter it, the Celestial Empire would punish it with death? Had his thoughts ventured to fly with the ships of the barbarians, to their homes in far distant England? No, his thoughts did not fly so far, and yet they were sinful, sinful as thoughts born of young hearts, sinful here in the temple, in the presence of Fo and the other holy gods.

"I know whither his thoughts had strayed. At the farther end of the city, on the flat roof paved with porcelain, on which stood the handsome vases covered with painted flowers, sat the beauteous Pu, of the little roguish eyes, of the full lips, and of the tiny feet. The tight shoe pained her, but her heart pained her still more. She lifted her graceful round arm, and her satin dress rustled. Before her stood a glass bowl containing four goldfish. She stirred the bowl carefully with a slender lacquered stick, very slowly, for she, too, was lost in thought. Was she thinking, perchance, how the fishes were richly clothed in gold, how they lived calmly and peacefully in their crystal world, how they were regularly fed, and yet how much happier they might be if they were free? Yes, that she could well understand, the beautiful Pu. Her thoughts wandered away from her home, wandered to the temple, but not for the sake of holy things. Poor Pu! Poor Soui-hong!

"Their earthly thoughts met, but my cold beam lay between the two like the sword of the cherub."

TWENTY-SEVENTH EVENING.

"THE air was calm," said the Moon; "the water was as transparent as the pure ether through which I was gliding, and deep below the surface I could see the strange plants that stretched up their long arms towards me like the gigantic trees of the forest. The fishes swam to and fro above their tops. High in the air a flight of wild swans were winging their way, one of which sank lower and lower, with wearied pinions, his eyes following the airy caravan, that melted farther and farther into the distance. With outspread wings he sank slowly, as a soap bubble sinks in the still air, till he touched the water. At length his head lay back between his wings, and silently he lay there, like a white lotus flower upon the quiet lake. And a gentle wind arose, and crisped the quiet surface, which gleamed like the clouds that poured along in great broad waves; and the swan raised his head, and the glowing water splashed like blue fire over his breast and back. The morning dawn illuminated the red clouds, the swan rose strenghthened, and flew towards the rising sun, towards the bluish coast whither the caravan had gone; but he flew all alone, with a longing in his breast. Lonely he flew over the blue swelling billows."

TWENTY-EIGHTH EVENING.

"I WILL give you another picture of Sweden," said the Moon. "Among dark pine woods, near the melancholy banks of the Stoxen, lies the old convent church of Wreta. My rays glided through the grating into the roomy vaults, where kings sleep tranquilly in great stone coffins. On the wall, above the grave of each, is placed the emblem of earthly grandeur, a kingly crown; but it is made only of wood, painted and gilt, and is hung on a wooden peg driven into the wall. The worms have gnawn the gilded wood, the spider has spun her web from the crown down to the sand, like a mourning banner, frail and transient as the grief of mortals. How quietly they sleep! I can remember them quite plainly. I still see the bold smile on their lips, that so strongly and plainly expressed joy or grief. When the steamboat winds along like a magic snail over the lakes, a stranger often comes to the church, and visits the burial vault; he asks the names of the kings, and they have a dead and forgotten sound. He glances with a smile at the worm-eaten crowns, and if he happens to be a pious, thoughtful man, something of melancholy mingles with the smile. Slumber on, ye dead ones! The Moon thinks of you, the Moon at night sends down his rays into your silent kingdom, over which hangs the crown of pine wood."

TWENTY-NINTH EVENING.

"Close by the high road," said the Moon, "is an inn, and opposite to it is a great waggon-shed, whose straw roof was just being re-thatched. I looked down between the bare rafters and through the open loft into the comfortless space below. The turkey-cock slept on the beam, and the saddle rested in the empty crib. In the middle of the shed stood a travelling carriage; the proprietor was inside, fast asleep, while the horses were being watered. The coachman stretched himself, though I am very sure that he had been most comfortably asleep half the last stage. The door of the servants' room stood open, and the bed looked as if it had been turned over and over; the candle stood on the floor, and had burned deep down into the socket. The wind blew cold through the shed: it was nearer to the dawn than to midnight. In the wooden frame on the ground slept a wandering family of musicians. The father and mother seemed to be dreaming of the burning liquor that remained in the bottle. The little pale daughter was dreaming too, for her eyes were wet with tears. The harp stood at their heads, and the dog lay stretched at their feet."

THIRTIETH EVENING.

"It was in a little provincial town," the Moon said; "it certainly happened last year, but that has nothing to do with the matter. I saw it quite plainly. To-day I read about it in the papers, but there it was not half so clearly expressed. In the tap-room of the little inn sat the bear leader, eating his supper; the bear was tied up outside, behind the wood pile—poor Bruin, who did nobody any harm, though he looked grim enough. Up in the garret three little children were playing by the light of my beams; the eldest was perhaps six years old, the youngest certainly not more than two. Tramp! tramp!—somebody was coming up stairs: who might it be? The door was thrust open—it was Bruin, the great, shaggy Bruin! He had got tired of waiting down in the courtyard, and had found his way to the stairs. I saw it all," said the

THE BEAR PLAYING AT SOLDIERS WITH THE CHILDREN.

Moon. "The children were very much frightened at first at the great shaggy animal; each of them crept into a corner, but he found them all out, and smelt at them, but did them no harm. 'This must be a great dog,' they said, and began to stroke him. He lay down upon the ground, the youngest boy clambered on his back, and, bending down a little head of golden curls, played at hiding in the beast's shaggy skin. Presently the eldest boy took his drum, and beat upon it till it rattled again: the bear rose up on its hind legs and began to dance. It was a charming sight to behold. Each boy now took his gun, and the bear was obliged to have one too, and he held it up quite properly. Here was a capital playmate they had found! and they began marching— one, two; one, two.

"Suddenly some one came to the door, which opened, and the mother of the children appeared. You should have seen her in her dumb terror, with her face as white as chalk, her mouth half open, and her eyes fixed in a horrified stare. But the youngest boy nodded to her in great glee, and called out in his infantile prattle, 'We're playing at soldiers.' And then the bear leader came running up."

THIRTY-FIRST EVENING.

THE wind blew stormy and cold, the clouds flew hurriedly past; only for a moment now and then did the Moon become visible. He said, "I looked down from the silent sky upon the driving clouds, and saw the great shadows chasing each other across the earth. I looked upon a prison. A closed carriage stood before it; a prisoner was to be carried away. My rays pierced through the grated window towards the wall: the prisoner was scratching a few lines upon it, as a parting token; but he did not write words, but a melody, the outpouring of his heart. The door was opened, and he was led forth, and fixed his eyes upon my round disc. Clouds passed between us, as if he were not to see my face, nor I his. He stepped into the carriage, the door was closed, the whip cracked, and the horses gallopped off into the thick forest, whither my rays were not able to follow him; but as I glanced through the grated window, my rays glided over the notes, his last farewell engraved on the prison wall—where words fail, sounds can often speak. My rays could only light up isolated notes, so the greater part of what was written there will ever remain dark to me. Was it the death-hymn he wrote there? Were these the glad notes of joy? Did he drive away to meet his death, or hasten to the embraces of his beloved? The rays of the Moon do not read all that is written by mortals."

THIRTY-SECOND EVENING.

"I LOVE the children," said the Moon, "especially the quite little ones—they are so droll. Sometimes I peep into the room, between the curtain and the window-frame, when they are not thinking of me. It gives me pleasure to see them dressing and undressing. First, the little round naked shoulder comes creeping out of the frock, then the arm; or I see how the stocking is drawn off, and a plump little white leg makes its appearance, and a little white foot that is fit to be kissed, and I kiss it too.

"But about what I was going to tell you. This evening I looked through a window, before which no curtain was drawn, for nobody lives opposite. I saw a whole troop of little ones, all of one family, and among them was a little sister. She is only four years old, but can say her prayers as well as any of the rest. The mother sits by her bed every evening, and hears her say her prayers; and then she has a kiss, and the mother sits by the bed till the little one has gone to sleep, which generally happens as soon as ever she can close her eyes.

" This evening the two elder children were a little boisterous. One of them hopped about on one leg in his long white nightgown, and the other stood on a chair surrounded by the clothes of all the children, and declared he was acting Grecian statues. The third and fourth laid the clean linen carefully in the box, for that is a thing that has to be done; and the mother sat by the bed of the youngest, and announced to all the rest that they were to be quiet, for little sister was going to say her prayers.

" I looked in, over the lamp, into the little maiden's bed, where she lay under the neat white coverlet, her hands folded demurely and her little face quite grave and serious. She was praying the Lord's Prayer aloud. But her mother interrupted her in the middle of her prayer. 'How is it,' she asked, 'that when you have prayed for daily bread, you always add something I cannot understand? You must tell me what that is.' The little one lay silent, and looked at her mother in embarrassment. 'What is it you say after *our daily bread?*' 'Dear mother, don't be angry: I only said, *and plenty of butter on it.*' "

THE STORY OF THE YEAR.

It was far in January, and a terrible fall of snow was pelting down. The snow eddied through the streets and lanes; the window-panes seemed plastered with snow on the outside; snow plumped down in masses from the roofs: and a sudden hurry had seized on the people, for they ran, and jostled, and fell into each other's arms, and as they clutched each other fast for a moment, they felt that they were safe at least for that length of time. Coaches and horses seemed frosted with sugar. The footmen stood with their backs against the carriages, so as to turn their faces from the wind. The foot passengers kept in the shelter of the carriages, which could only move slowly on in the deep snow; and when the storm at last abated, and a narrow path was swept clean alongside the houses, the people stood still in this path when they met, for none liked to take the first step aside into the deep snow to let the other pass him. Thus they stood silent and motionless, till, as if by tacit consent, each sacrificed one leg, and stepping aside, buried it in the deep snow-heap.

Towards evening it grew calm. The sky looked as if it had been swept, and had become more lofty and transparent. The stars looked as if they were quite new, and some of them were amazingly bright and pure. It froze so hard that the snow creaked, and the upper rind of snow might well have grown hard enough to bear the Sparrows in the morning dawn. These little birds hopped up and down where the sweeping had been done; but they found very little food, and were not a little cold.

" Piep !" said one of them to another; " they call this a new year, and it is worse than the last! We might just as well have kept the old one. I 'm dissatisfied, and I 've a right to be so."

" Yes; and the people ran about and fired off shots to celebrate the New Year," said a shivering little Sparrow; " and they threw pans and pots against the doors, and were quite boisterous with joy because the Old Year was gone. I was glad of it too, because I hoped we should have had warm days; but that has come to nothing—it freezes much harder than before. People have made a mistake in reckoning the time !"

" That they have !" a third put in, who was old, and had a white poll: " they 've something they call the calendar—it 's an invention of their own—and everything is to be arranged according to that; but it won't do. When spring comes, then the year begins, and I reckon according to that."

" But when will spring come ? " the others inquired.

" It will come when the stork comes back. But his movements are very uncertain, and here in town no one knows anything about it: in the country they are better informed. Shall we fly out there and wait? There, at any rate, we shall be nearer to spring."

" Yes, that may be all very well," observed one of the Sparrows, who had been hopping about for a long time, chirping, without saying anything decided. " I 've found a few comforts here in town, which I am afraid I should miss out in the country. Near this neighbourhood, in a courtyard, there lives a family of people, who have taken the very sensible notion of placing three or four flower-pots against the wall, with their mouths all turned inwards, and the bottom of each pointing outwards. In each flower-pot a hole has been cut, big enough for me to fly in and out at it. I and my husband have built a nest in one of those pots, and have brought up our young family there. The family of people of course made the whole arrangement that they might have the pleasure of seeing us, or else they would not have done it. To please themselves they also strew crumbs of bread; and so we have food, and are in a manner provided for. So I think my husband and I will stay where we are, although we are very dissatisfied—but we shall stay."

" And we will fly into the country to see if spring is not coming !"

And away they flew.

Out in the country it was hard winter, and the glass was a few degrees lower than in the town. The sharp winds swept across the snow-covered fields. The farmer, muffled in warm mittens, sat in his sledge, and beat his arms across his breast to warm himself, and the whip lay across his knees. The horses ran till they smoked again. The snow creaked, and the Sparrows hopped about in the ruts, and shivered, " Piep ! when will spring come ? it is very long in coming !"

" Very long," sounded from the next snow-covered hill, far over the field. It might be the echo which was heard; or perhaps the words were spoken by yonder wonderful old man, who sat in wind and weather high on the heap of snow. He was quite white, attired like a peasant in a coarse white coat of frieze; he had long white hair, and was quite pale, with big blue eyes.

"Who is that old man yonder?" asked the Sparrows.

"I know who he is," quoth an old Raven, who sat on the fence-rail, and was condescending enough to acknowledge that we are all like little birds in the sight of Heaven, and therefore was not above speaking to the Sparrows, and giving them information. "I know who the old man

THE STORKS BRINGING BACK THE SPRING.

is. It is Winter, the old man of last year. He is not dead, as the calendar says, but is guardian to little Prince Spring, who is to come. Yes, Winter bears sway here. Ugh! the cold makes you shiver, does it not, you little ones?"

"Yes. Did I not tell the truth?" said the smallest Sparrow: "the calendar is only an invention of man, and is not arranged according to nature! They ought to leave these things to us, who are born cleverer than they."

And one week passed away, and two passed away. The frozen lake lay hard and stiff, looking like a sheet of lead, and damp icy mists lay brooding over the land; the great black crows flew about in long rows, but silently; and it seemed as if nature slept. Then a sunbeam glided along over the lake, and made it shine like burnished tin. The snowy covering on the field and on the hill did not glitter as it had done; but the white form, Winter himself, still sat there, his gaze fixed unswervingly upon the south. He did not notice that the snowy carpet seemed to sink as it were into the earth, and that here and there a little grass-green patch appeared, and that all these patches were crowded with Sparrows, which cried, "Kee-wit! kee-wit! Is spring coming now?"

"Spring!" The cry resounded over field and meadow, and through the black-brown woods, where the moss still glimmered in bright green upon the tree trunks; and from the south the first two storks came flying through the air. On the back of each sat a pretty little child—one was a girl and the other a boy. They greeted the earth with a kiss, and wherever they set their feet, white flowers grew up from beneath the snow. Then they went hand in hand to the old ice man, Winter, clung to his breast embracing him, and in a moment they, and he, and all the region around were hidden in a thick damp mist, dark and heavy, that closed over all like a veil. Gradually the wind rose, and now it rushed roaring along, and drove away the mist with heavy blows, so that the sun shone warmly forth, and Winter himself vanished, and the beautiful children of Spring sat on the throne of the year.

"That's what I call spring," cried each of the Sparrows. "Now we shall get our rights, and have amends for the stern winter."

Wherever the two children turned, green buds burst forth on bushes and trees, the grass shot upwards, and the corn-fields turned green and became more and more lovely. And the little maiden strewed flowers all around. Her apron, which she held up before her, was always full of them; they seemed to spring up there, for her lap continued full, however zealously she strewed the blossoms around; and in her eagerness she scattered a snow of blossoms over apple trees and peach trees, so that they stood in full beauty before their green leaves had fairly come forth.

And she clapped her hands, and the boy clapped his, and then flocks of birds came flying up, nobody knew whence, and they all twittered and sang, "Spring has come."

That was beautiful to behold. Many an old granny crept forth over the threshold into the sunshine, and tripped gleefully about, casting a glance at the yellow flowers which shone everywhere in the fields, just as they used to do when she was young. The world grew young again to her, and she said, "It is a blessed day out here to-day!"

The forest still wore its brown-green dress, made of buds; but the thyme was already there, fresh and fragrant; there were violets in plenty, anemones and primroses came forth, and there was sap and strength in every blade of grass. That was certainly a beautiful carpet on which no one could resist sitting down, and there accordingly the young spring pair sat hand in hand, and sang and smiled, and grew on.

A mild rain fell down upon them from the sky, but they did not notice it, for the rain-drops were mingled with their own tears of joy. They kissed each other, and were betrothed as people that should marry, and in the same moment the verdure of the woods was unfolded, and when the sun rose, the forest stood there arrayed in green.

SUMMER TIME.

And hand in hand the betrothed pair wandered under the pendent ocean of fresh leaves, where the rays of the sun gleamed through the interstices in lovely, ever-changing hues. What virgin purity, what refreshing balm in the delicate leaves! The brooks and streams rippled clearly and merrily among the green velvety rushes and over the coloured pebbles. All nature seemed to say, "There is plenty, and there shall be plenty always!" And the cuckoo sang and the lark carolled: it was a charming spring; but the willows had woolly gloves over their blossoms: they were desperately careful, and that is wearisome.

And days went by and weeks went by, and the heat came as it were whirling down. Hot waves of air came through the corn, that became yellower and yellower. The white water-lily of the North spread its great green leaves over the glassy mirror of the woodland lakes, and the fishes sought out the shady spots beneath; and at the sheltered side of the wood, where the sun shone down upon the walls of the farm-house, warming the blooming roses, and the cherry trees, which hung full of juicy black berries, almost hot with the fierce beams, there sat the lovely wife of Summer, the same being whom we have seen as a child and as a bride; and her glance was fixed upon the black gathering clouds, which in wavy outlines—blue-black and heavy—were piling themselves up, like mountains, higher and higher. They came from three sides, and growing like a petrified sea, they came swooping towards the forest, where every sound had been silenced as if by magic. Every breath of air was hushed, every bird was mute. There was a seriousness — a suspense throughout all nature; but in the highways and lanes, foot passengers, and riders, and men in carriages were hurrying on to get under shelter. Then suddenly there was a flashing of light, as if the sun were burst forth—flaming, burning, all-devouring! And the darkness returned amid a rolling crash. The rain poured down in streams, and there was alternate darkness and blinding light; alternate silence and deafening clamour. The young, brown, feathery reeds on the moor moved to and fro in long waves, the twigs of the woods were hidden in a mist of waters, and still came darkness and light, and still silence and roaring followed one another; the grass and corn lay beaten down and swamped, looking as though they could never raise themselves again. But soon the rain fell only in gentle drops, the sun peered through the clouds, the water-drops glittered like pearls on the leaves, the birds sang, the fishes leaped up from the surface of the lake, the gnats danced in the sunshine, and yonder on the rock, in the salt heaving sea water, sat Summer himself—a strong man with sturdy limbs and long dripping hair—there he sat, strengthened by the cool bath, in the warm sunshine. All nature round about was renewed, everything stood luxuriant, strong and beautiful; it was summer, warm, lovely summer.

And pleasant and sweet was the fragrance that streamed upwards from the rich clover-field, where the bees swarmed round the old ruined place of meeting: the bramble wound itself around the altar stone, which, washed by the rain, glittered in the sunshine; and thither flew the Queen-bee with her swarm, and prepared wax and honey. Only Summer saw it, he and his strong wife; for them the altar table stood covered with the offerings of nature.

And the evening sky shone like gold, shone as no church dome can shine; and in the interval between the evening and the morning red there was moonlight: it was summer.

And days went by, and weeks went by. The bright scythes of the reapers gleamed in the corn-fields; the branches of the apple trees bent down, heavy with red-and-yellow fruit. The hops smelt sweetly, hanging in large clusters; and under the hazel bushes where hung great bunches of nuts, rested a man and woman—Summer and his quiet consort.

"What wealth!" exclaimed the woman: "all around a blessing is diffused, everywhere the scene looks homelike and good; and yet—I know not why—I long for peace and rest—I know not how to express it. Now they are already ploughing again in the field. The people want to gain more and more. See, the storks flock together, and follow at a little distance behind the plough—the bird of Egypt that carried us through the air. Do you remember how we came as children to this land of the North? We brought with us flowers, and pleasant sunshine, and green to the woods; the wind has treated them roughly, and they have become dark and brown like the trees of the South, but they do not, like them, bear fruit."

"Do you wish to see the golden fruit?" said Summer: "then rejoice."

And he lifted his arm, and the leaves of the forest put on hues of red and gold, and beauteous tints spread over all the woodland. The rose bush gleamed with scarlet hips; the elder branches hung down with great heavy bunches of dark berries; the wild chestnuts fell ripe from their dark husks; and in the depths of the forests the violets bloomed for the second time.

But the Queen of the Year became more and more silent, and paler and paler.

"It blows cold," she said, "and night brings damp mists. I long for the land of my childhood."

And she saw the storks fly away, one and all; and she stretched forth her hands towards them. She looked up at the nests, which stood empty. In one of them the long-stalked cornflower was growing; in another, the yellow mustard-seed, as if the nest were only there for its protection; and the Sparrows were flying up into the storks' nests.

"Piep! where has the master gone? I suppose he can't bear it when the wind blows, and that therefore he has left the country. I wish him a pleasant journey!"

The forest leaves became more and more yellow, leaf fell down upon leaf, and the stormy winds of autumn howled. The year was now far advanced, and the Queen of the Year reclined upon the fallen yellow leaves, and looked with mild eyes at the gleaming star, and her husband stood by her. A gust swept through the leaves, which fell again in a shower, and the Queen was gone, but a butterfly, the last of the season, flew through the cold air.

The wet fogs came, an icy wind blew, and the long dark nights drew on apace. The Ruler of the Year stood there with locks white as snow. but he knew not it was his hair that gleamed so white—he thought snow-flakes were falling from the clouds; and soon a thin covering of snow was spread over the fields.

And then the church bells rang for the Christmas-time.

"The bells ring for the new-born," said the Ruler of the Year. "Soon the new King and Queen will be born; and I shall go to rest, as my wife has done—to rest in the gleaming star."

And in the fresh green fir wood, where the snow lay, stood the Angel of Christmas, and consecrated the young trees that were to adorn his feast.

"May there be joy in the room and under the green boughs," said the Ruler of the Year. In a few weeks he had become a very old man, white as snow. "My time for rest draws near, and the young pair of the year shall now receive my crown and sceptre."

"But the might is still thine," said the Angel of Christmas; "the might and not the rest. Let the snow lie warmly upon the young seed. Learn to bear it, that another receives homage while thou yet reignest.

Learn to bear being forgotten while thou art yet alive. The hour of thy release will come when spring appears."

"And when will spring come?" asked Winter.

"It will come when the stork returns."

And with white locks and snowy beard, cold, bent, and hoary, but strong as the wintry storm and firm as ice, old Winter sat on the snowy drift on the hill, looking towards the south, where he had before sat and gazed. The ice cracked, the snow creaked, the skaters skimmed to and fro on the smooth lakes, ravens and crows contrasted picturesquely with the white ground, and not a breath of wind stirred. And in the quiet air old Winter clenched his fists, and the ice was fathoms thick between land and land.

Then the Sparrows came again out of the town, and asked, "Who is that old man yonder?"

And the Raven sat there again, or a son of his, which comes to quite the same thing, and answered them and said, "It is Winter, the old man of last year. He is not dead, as the almanack says, but he is the guardian of Spring, who is coming."

"When will spring come?" asked the Sparrows. "Then we shall have good times and a better rule. The old one was worth nothing."

And Winter nodded in quiet thought at the leafless forest, where every tree showed the graceful form and bend of its twigs; and during the winter sleep the icy mists of the clouds came down, and the ruler dreamed of his youthful days, and of the time of his manhood; and towards the morning dawn the whole wood was clothed in glittering hoar frost. That was the summer dream of Winter, and the sun scattered the hoar frost from the boughs.

"When will spring come?" asked the Sparrows.

"The spring!" sounded like an echo from the hills on which the snow lay. The sun shone warmer, the snow melted, and the birds twittered, "Spring is coming!"

And aloft through the air came the first stork, and the second followed him. A lovely child sat on the back of each, and they alighted on the field, kissed the earth, and kissed the old silent man, and he disappeared, shrouded in the cloudy mist. And the story of the year was done.

"That is all very well," said the Sparrows; "it is very beautiful too, but it is not according to the almanack, and therefore it is irregular."

THE RACERS.

A PRIZE, or rather two prizes, had been appointed—a great one and a little one—for the greatest swiftness, not in a single race, but for swiftness throughout an entire year.

"I got the first prize!" said the Hare; "there must be justice when relations and good friends are among the prize committee; but that the Snail should have received the second prize, I consider almost an insult to myself."

"No!" declared the Fence-rail, who had been witness at the distribution of prizes, "reference must also be had to industry and perseverance. Many respectable people said so, and I understood it well. The Snail certainly took half a year to get across the threshold of the door; but he did himself an injury and broke his collar-bone in the haste he was compelled to make. He devoted himself entirely to his work, and he ran with his house on his back! All that is very charming, and that's how he got the second prize."

"I might certainly have been considered too," said the Swallow. "I should think that no one appeared swifter in flying and soaring than myself, and how far I have been around—far—far—far!"

"Yes, that's just your misfortune," said the Fence-rail. "You're too fond of fluttering. You must always be journeying about into far countries when it begins to be cold here. You've no love of fatherland in you. You cannot be taken into account."

"But if I lay in the moor all through the winter?" said the Swallow. "Suppose I slept through the whole time; shouldn't I be taken into account then?"

"Bring a certificate from the old moor hen that you have slept away half the time in your fatherland, and you shall be taken into account."

"I deserved the first prize, and not the second," said the Snail. "I know so much at least, that the Hare only ran from cowardice, because he thought each time there was danger in delay. I, on the other hand, made my running the business of my life, and have become a cripple in the service. If any one was to have the first prize, I should have had it; but I don't understand chattering and boasting; on the contrary, 1 despise it!"

And the Snail looked quite haughty.

"I am able to depose with word and oath that each prize, at least my vote for each, was given after proper consideration," observed the old Boundary-post in the wood, who had been a member of the college of judges. "I always go on with due consideration, with order, and calculation. Seven times before I have had the honour to be present at the distribution of prizes and to give my vote; but not till to-day have 1 carried out my will. I always went to the first prize from the beginning of the alphabet, and to the second from the end. Be kind enough to give me your attention, and I will explain to you how one begins at the beginning. The eighth letter from A is H, and there we have the Hare, and so I awarded him the first prize; the eighth letter from the end of the alphabet is S, and therefore the Snail received the second prize. Next time, I will have its turn for the first prize, and R for the second: there must be due order and calculation in everything! One must have a certain starting-point!"

"I should certainly have voted for myself, if I had not been among the judges," said the Mule, who had been one of the committee. "One must not only consider the rapidity of advance, but every other quality also that is found—as for example, how much a candidate is able to draw; but I would not have put that prominently forward this time, nor the sagacity of the Hare in his flight, or the cunning with which he suddenly takes a leap to one side to bring people on a false track, so that they may not know where he has hidden himself. No! there is something else on which many lay great stress, and which one may not leave out of the calculation. I mean what is called the beautiful. On the beautiful I particularly fixed my eyes; I looked at the beautiful well-grown ears of the Hare: it's quite a pleasure to see how long they are; it almost seemed to me as if I saw myself in the days of my childhood. And so I voted for the Hare."

THE RACERS.

"But," said the Fly, "I'm not going to talk, I'm only going to say that I have overtaken more than one hare. Quite lately I crushed the hind legs of one. I was sitting on the engine in front of a railway train—I often do that, for thus one can best notice one's own swiftness. A young hare ran for a long time in front of the engine; he had no idea that I was present; but at last he was obliged to give in and spring aside—and then the engine crushed his hind legs, for I was upon it. The hare lay there, but I rode on. That certainly was conquering him! But I don't count upon getting the prize!"

"It certainly appears to me," thought the Wild Rose—but she did not say it, for it is not her nature to give her opinion, though it would have been quite as well if she had done so—" it certainly appears to me that the sunbeam ought to have had the first prize and the second too. The sunbeam flies with intense rapidity along the enormous path from the sun to ourselves, and arrives in such strength that all nature awakes at it; such beauty does it possess that all we roses blush and exhale fragrance in its presence. Our worshipful judges do not appear to have noticed this at all. If I were the sunbeam, I would give each of them a sunstroke—but that would only make them mad, and that they may become as things stand. I say nothing," thought the Wild Rose. " May peace reign in the forest! It is glorious to blossom, to scent, and to live—to live in song and legend. The sunbeam will outlive us all."

" What's the first prize?" asked the Earthworm, who had overslept the time, and only came up now.

" It consists in a free admission to a cabbage garden," replied the Mule. " I proposed that as the prize. The Hare was decided to have won it, and therefore I as an active and reflective member took especial notice of the advantage of him who was to get it: now the Hare is provided for. The Snail may sit upon the fence and lick up moss and sunshine, and has further been appointed one of the first umpires in the racing. That's worth a great deal, to have some one of talent in the thing men call a committee. I must say I expect much from the future —we have made a very good beginning."

SHE WAS GOOD FOR NOTHING.

The mayor stood at the open window. His shirt-frill was very fine and so were his ruffles; he had a breast-pin stuck in his frill, and was uncommonly smooth shaven—all his own work; certainly he had given himself a slight cut, but he had stuck a bit of newspaper on the place.

" Harkye, youngster!" he cried.

The youngster in question was no other than the son of the poor washerwoman, who was just going past the house; and he pulled off his cap respectfully. The peak of the said cap was broken in the middle, for the cap was arranged so that it could be rolled up and crammed into his pocket. In his poor, but clean and well-mended attire, with heavy wooden shoes on his feet, the boy stood there, as humble and abashed as if he stood opposite the King himself. ·

" You're a good boy," said Mr. Mayor. " You're a civil boy. I suppose your mother is rinsing clothes down yonder in the river? I suppose you are to carry that thing to your mother that you have in your pocket? That's a bad affair with your mother. How much have you got in it?"

" Half a quartern," stammered the boy, in a frightened voice.

" And this morning she had just as much," the mayor continued.

" No," replied the boy, " it was yesterday."

THE MAYOR AND THE WASHERWOMAN'S SON.

"Two halves make a whole. She's good for nothing! It's a sad thing with that kind of people! Tell your mother that she ought to be ashamed of herself; and mind you don't become a drunkard—but you will become one, though. Poor child—there, go!"

Accordingly the boy went on his way. He kept his cap in his hand, and the wind played with his yellow hair, so that great locks of it stood up straight. He turned down by the street corner, into the little lane that led to the river, where his mother stood by the washing bench, beating the heavy linen with the mallet. The water rolled quickly along, for the flood-gates at the mill had been drawn up, and the sheets were caught by the stream, and threatened to overturn the bench. The washerwoman was obliged to lean against the bench to support it.

"I was very nearly sailing away," she said. "It is a good thing that you are come, for I have need to recruit my strength a little. For six hours I've been standing in the water. Have you brought anything for me?"

The boy produced the bottle, and the mother put it to her mouth, and took a little.

"Ah, how that revives one!" said she: "how it warms! It is as good as a hot meal, and not so dear. And you, my boy! you look quite pale. You are shivering in your thin clothes—to be sure it is autumn. Ugh! how cold the water is! I hope I shall not be ill. But no, I shall not be that! Give me a little more, and you may have a sip too, but only a little sip, for you must not accustom yourself to it, my poor dear child!"

And she stepped up to the bridge on which the boy stood, and came ashore. The water dripped from the straw matting she had wound round her, and from her gown.

"I work and toil as much as ever I can," she said, "but I do it willingly, if I can only manage to bring you up honestly and well, my boy."

As she spoke, a somewhat older woman came towards them. She was poor enough to behold, lame of one leg, and with a large false curl hanging down over one of her eyes, which was a blind one. The curl was intended to cover the eye, but it only made the defect more striking. This was a friend of the laundress. She was called among the neighbours, "Lame Martha with the curl."

"Oh, you poor thing! How you work, standing there in the water!" cried the visitor. "You really require something to warm you; and yet malicious folks cry out about the few drops you take!"

And in a few minutes' time the mayor's late speech was reported to the laundress; for Martha had heard it all, and she had been angry that a man could speak as he had done to a woman's own child, about the few drops the mother took; and she was the more angry, because the mayor on that very day was giving a great feast, at which wine was drunk by the bottle —good wine, strong wine.

"A good many will take more than they need—but that's not called drinking. *They* are good; but *you* are good for nothing!" cried Martha, indignantly.

"Ah, so he spoke to you, my child?" said the washerwoman; and her lips trembled as she spoke. "So he says you have a mother who is good for nothing? Well, perhaps he's right, but he should not have said it to the child. Still, I have had much misfortune from that house."

"You were in service there when the mayor's parents were alive, and lived in that house. That is many years ago: many bushels of salt have been eaten since then, and we may well be thirsty;" and Martha smiled. "The mayor has a great dinner party to-day. The guests were to have been put off, but it was too late, and the dinner was already cooked. The footman told me about it. A letter came a little while ago, to say that the younger brother had died in Copenhagen."

"Died!" repeated the laundress—and she became pale as death.

"Yes, certainly," said Martha. "Do you take that so much to heart?

Well, you must have known him years ago, when you were in service in the house."

"Is he dead? He was such a good, worthy man! There are not many like him." And the tears rolled down her cheeks. "Good gracious! everything is whirling around me—it was too much for me. I feel quite ill." And she leaned against the plank.

"Good gracious, you are ill indeed!" exclaimed the other woman. "Come, come, it will pass over presently. But no, you really look seriously ill. The best thing will be for me to lead you home."

"But my linen yonder—"

"I will take care of that. Come, give me your arm. The boy can stay here and take care of it, and I'll come back and finish the washing; that's only a trifle."

The laundress's limbs shook under her. "I have stood too long in the cold water," she said faintly, "and I have eaten and drunk nothing since this morning. The fever is in my bones. O kind Heaven, help me to get home! My poor child!" And she burst into tears.

The boy wept too, and soon he was sitting alone by the river, beside the damp linen. The two women could make only slow progress. The laundress dragged her weary limbs along, and tottered through the lane and round the corner into the street where stood the house of the mayor; and just in front of his mansion she sank down on the pavement. Many people assembled round her, and Lame Martha ran into the house to get help. The mayor and his guests came to the window.

"That's the washerwoman!" he said. "She has taken a glass too much. She is good for nothing. It's a pity for the pretty son she has. I really like the child very well; but the mother is good for nothing."

Presently the laundress came to herself, and they led her into her poor dwelling, and put her to bed. Kind Martha heated a mug of beer for her, with butter and sugar, which she considered the best medicine; and then she hastened to the river, and rinsed the linen—badly enough, though her will was good. Strictly speaking, she drew it ashore, wet as it was, and laid it in a basket.

Towards evening she was sitting in the poor little room with the laundress. The mayor's cook had given her some roasted potatoes and a fine fat piece of ham, for the sick woman, and Martha and the boy discussed these viands while the patient enjoyed the smell, which she pronounced very nourishing.

And presently the boy was put to bed, in the same bed in which his mother lay; but he slept at her feet, covered with an old quilt made up of blue and white patches.

Soon the patient felt a little better. The warm beer had strengthened her, and the fragrance of the provisions pleased her also.

"Thanks, you kind soul," she said to Martha. "I will tell you all when the boy is asleep. I think he has dropped off already. How gentle and good he looks, as he lies there with his eyes closed. He does not know what his mother has suffered, and Heaven grant he may never know it. I was in service at the councillor's, the father of the mayor. It happened that the youngest of the sons, the student, came home. I was young then, a wild girl, but honest, that I may declare in the face of Heaven. The student was merry and kind, good and brave. Every drop of blood in him was good and honest. I have not seen a better man on this earth. He was the son of the house, and I was only a maid, but we formed an attachment to each other, honestly and honourably. And he told his mother of it, for she was in his eyes as a Deity on earth; and she was wise and gentle. He went away on a journey, but before he started he put his gold ring on my finger; and directly he was gone my mistress called me. With a firm yet gentle seriousness she spoke to me, and it seemed as if Wisdom itself were speaking. She showed me clearly, in spirit and in truth, the difference there was between him and me.

"'Now he is charmed with your pretty appearance,' she said, 'but your good looks will leave you. You have not been educated as he has. You are not equals in mind, and there is the misfortune. I respect the poor,' she continued: 'in the sight of God they may occupy a higher place than many a rich man can fill; but here on earth we must beware of entering a false track as we go onward, or our carriage is upset, and we are thrown into the road. I know that a worthy man wishes to marry you—an artisan—I mean Erich the glovemaker. He is a widower without children, and is well to do. Think it over.'

"Every word she spoke cut into my heart like a knife, but I knew that my mistress was right, and that knowledge weighed heavily upon me. I kissed her hand, and wept bitter tears, and I wept still more when I went into my room and threw myself on my bed. It was a heavy night that I had to pass through. Heaven knows what I suffered and how I wrestled! The next Sunday I went to the Lord's house, to pray for strength and guidance. It seemed like a Providence, that as I stepped out of church Erich came towards me. And now there was no longer a doubt in my mind. We were suited to each other in rank and in means, and he was even then a thriving man. Therefore I went up to him, took his hand, and said, 'Are you still of the same mind towards me?' 'Yes, ever and always,' he replied. 'Will you marry a girl who honours and respects, but who does not love you—though that may come later?' I asked again. 'Yes, it will come!' he answered. And upon this we joined hands. I went home to my mistress. I wore the gold ring that her son had given me at my heart. I could not put it on my finger in the day-time, but only in the evening when I went to bed. I kissed the ring again and again, till my lips almost bled, and then I gave it to my mistress, and told her the banns were to be put up next week for me and the glovemaker. Then my mistress put her arms round me and kissed me. *She* did not say that I was good for nothing; but perhaps I was better then than I am now, though the misfortunes of life had not yet found me out. In a few weeks we were married; and for the first year the world went well with us: we had a journeyman and an apprentice, and you, Martha, lived with us as our servant."

"Oh, you were a dear, good mistress," cried Martha. "Never shall I forget how kind you and your husband were!"

"Yes, those were our good years, when you were with us. We had not any children yet. The student I never saw again.—Yes, though, I saw him, but he did not see me. He was here at his mother's funeral. I saw him stand by the grave. He was pale as death, and very downcast, but that was for his mother; afterwards, when his father died, he was away in a foreign land, and did not come back hither. I know that he never married; I believe he became a lawyer. He had forgotten me, and even if he had seen me again, he would not have known me, I look so ugly. And that is very fortunate."

And then she spoke of her days of trial, and told how misfortune had come as it were swooping down upon them.

"We had five hundred dollars," she said; "and as there was a house in the street to be bought for two hundred, and it would pay to pull it down and build a new one, it was bought. The builder and carpenter calculated the expense, and the new house was to cost ten hundred and twenty. Erich had credit, and borrowed the money in the chief town, but the captain who was to bring it was shipwrecked, and the money was lost with him.

"Just at that time my dear sweet boy who is sleeping yonder was born. My husband was struck down by a long heavy illness: for three quarters of a year I was compelled to dress and undress him. We went back more and more, and fell into debt. All that we had was sold, and my husband died. I have worked, and toiled, and striven, for the sake of the child, and scrubbed staircases, washed linen, clean and coarse alike, but I was not to be better off, such was God's good will. But He will take me to Himself in His own good time, and will not forsake my boy."

And she fell asleep.

Towards morning she felt much refreshed, and strong enough, as she thought, to go back to her work. She had just stepped again into the cold water, when a trembling and faintness seized her: she clutched at the air with her hand, took a step forward, and fell down. Her head rested on the bank, and her feet were still in the water; her wooden shoes, with a wisp of straw in each, which she had worn, floated down the stream, and thus Martha found her on coming to bring her some coffee.

In the meantime a messenger from the mayor's house had been dispatched to her poor lodging to tell her "to come to the mayor immediately, for he had something to tell her." It was too late! A barber-surgeon was brought to open a vein in her arm; but the poor woman was dead.

"She has drunk herself to death!" said the mayor.

In the letter that brought the news of his brother's death, the contents of the will had been mentioned, and it was a legacy of six hundred dollars to the glovemaker's widow, who had once been his mother's maid. The money was to be paid, according to the mayor's discretion, in larger or smaller sums, to her or to her child.

"There was some fuss between my brother and her," said the mayor.

"It's a good thing that she is dead; for now the boy will have the whole, and I will get him into a house among respectable people. He may turn out a reputable working man."

And Heaven gave its blessing to these words.

So the mayor sent for the boy, promised to take care of him, and added that it was a good thing the lad's mother was dead, inasmuch as she had been good for nothing.

They bore her to the churchyard, to the cemetery of the poor, and Martha strewed sand upon her grave, and planted a rose tree upon it, and the boy stood beside her.

"My dear mother!" he cried, as the tears fell fast. "Is it true what they said, that she was good for nothing?"

"No, she was good for much!" replied the old servant, and she looked up indignantly. "I knew it many a year ago, and more than all since last night. I tell you she was worth much, and the Lord in heaven knows it is true, let the world say as much as it chooses, 'She was good for nothing.'"

IN A THOUSAND YEARS.

YES, in a thousand years people will fly on the wings of steam through the air, over the ocean! The young inhabitants of America will become visitors of old Europe. They will come over to see the monuments and the great cities, which will then be in ruins, just as we in our time make pilgrimages to the tottering splendours of Southern Asia. In a thousand years they will come!

The Thames, the Danube, and the Rhine still roll their course, Mont Blanc stands firm with its snow-capped summit, and the Northern Lights gleam over the lands of the North; but generation after generation has become dust, whole rows of the mighty of the moment are forgotten, like those who already slumber under the hill on which the rich trader whose ground it is has built a bench, on which he can sit and look out across his waving corn-fields.

"To Europe!" cry the young sons of America; "to the land of our ancestors, the glorious land of monuments and fancy—to Europe!"

The ship of the air comes. It is crowded with passengers, for the transit is quicker than by sea. The electro-magnetic wire under the ocean has already telegraphed the number of the aërial caravan. Europe is in sight: it is the coast of Ireland that they see, but the passengers are still asleep; they will not be called till they are exactly over England. There they will first step on European shore, in the land of Shakespeare as the educated call it; in the land of politics, the land of machines, as it is called by others.

Here they stay a whole day. That is all the time the busy race can devote to the whole of England and Scotland. Then the journey is continued through the tunnel under the English Channel, to France, the land of Charlemagne and Napoleon. Molière is named: the learned men talk of the classic school of remote antiquity: there is rejoicing and shouting for the names of heroes, poets, and men of science, whom our time does not know, but who will be born after our time in Paris, the centre of Europe, and elsewhere.

The air steamboat flies over the country whence Columbus went forth, where Cortez was born, and where Calderon sang dramas in sounding verse. Beautiful black-eyed women live still in the blooming valleys, and the oldest songs speak of the Cid and the Alhambra.

Then through the air, over the sea, to Italy, where once lay old, everlasting Rome. It has vanished! The Campagna lies desert: a single ruined wall is shown as the remains of St. Peter's, but there is a doubt if this ruin be genuine.

THE SHIP OF THE AIR.

Next to Greece, to sleep a night in the grand hotel at the top of Mount Olympus, to say that they have been there; and the journey is continued to the Bosphorus, to rest there a few hours, and see the place where Byzantium lay; and where the legend tells that the harem stood in the time of the Turks, poor fishermen are now spreading their nets.

Over the remains of mighty cities on the broad Danube, cities which we in our time know not, the travellers pass; but here and there, on the rich sites of those that time shall bring forth, the caravan sometimes descends, and departs thence again.

Down below lies Germany, that was once covered with a close net of railways and canals, the region where Luther spoke, where Goethe sang, and Mozart once held the sceptre of harmony. Great names shine there, in science and in art, names that are unknown to us. One day devoted to seeing Germany, and one for the North, the country of Oersted and Linnæus, and for Norway, the land of the old heroes and the young

Normans. Iceland is visited on the journey home : the geysers burn no more, Hecla is an extinct volcano, but the rocky island is still fixed in the midst of the foaming sea, a continual monument of legend and poetry.

"There is really a great deal to be seen in Europe," says the young American, "and we have seen it in a week, according to the directions of the great traveller" (and here he mentions the name of one of his contemporaries) "in his celebrated work, 'How to See all Europe in a Week.'"

"THERE IS A DIFFERENCE."

IT was in the month of May. The wind still blew cold, but bushes and trees, field and meadow, all alike said the spring had come. There was store of flowers even in the wild hedges ; and there spring carried on his affairs, and preached from a little apple tree, where one branch hung fresh and blooming, covered with delicate pink blossoms that were just ready to open. The Apple Tree Branch knew well enough how beautiful he was, for the knowledge is inherent in the leaf as well as in the blood; and consequently the Branch was not surprised when a nobleman's carriage stopped opposite to him on the road, and the young countess said that an apple branch was the loveliest thing one could behold, a very emblem of spring in its most charming form. And the Branch was most carefully broken off, and she held it in her delicate hand, and sheltered it with her silk parasol. Then they drove to the castle, where there were lofty halls and splendid apartments. Pure white curtains fluttered round the open windows, and beautiful flowers stood in shining transparent vases; and in one of these, which looked as if it had been cut out of fresh-fallen snow, the Apple Branch was placed among some fresh light twigs of beech. It was charming to behold. But the Branch became proud; and this was quite like human nature.

People of various kinds came through the room, and according to their rank they might express their admiration. A few said nothing at all, and others again said too much, and the Apple Tree Branch soon got to understand that there was a difference among plants.

"Some are created for beauty, and some for use; and there are some which one can do without altogether," thought the Apple Branch.

And as he stood just in front of the open window, from whence he could see into the garden and across the fields, he had flowers and plants enough to contemplate and to think about, for there were rich plants and humble plants—some very humble indeed.

"Poor despised herbs!" said the Apple Branch. "There is certainly a difference! And how unhappy they must feel, if indeed that kind *can* feel like myself and my equals. Certainly there is a difference, and distinctions must be made, or we should all be equal."

And the Apple Branch looked down with a species of pity, especially upon a certain kind of flower of which great numbers are found in the fields and in ditches. No one bound them into a nosegay, they were too common; for they might be found even among the paving-stones, shooting up everywhere like the rankest weeds, and they had the ugly name of "dandelion," or "dog-flower."

"Poor despised plants!" said the Apple Branch. "It is not your fault that you received the ugly name you bear. But it is with plants as with men—there must be a difference!"

"A difference?" said the Sunbeam; and he kissed the blooming Apple Branch, and saluted in like manner the yellow dandelions out in the field —all the brothers of the Sunbeam kissed them, the poor flowers as well as the rich.

Now the Apple Branch had never thought of the boundless benefi-cence of Providence in creation towards everything that lives and moves and has its being; he had never thought how much that is beautiful and good may be hidden, but not forgotten; but that, too, was quite like human nature.

The Sunbeam, the ray of light, knew better, and said,

"You don't see far and you don't see clearly. What is the despised plant that you especially pity?"

"The dandelion," replied the Apple Branch. "It is never received into a nosegay; it is trodden under foot. There are too many of them; and when they run to seed, they fly away like little pieces of wool over the roads, and hang and cling to people's dress. They are nothing but weeds—but it is right there should be weeds too. Oh, I'm really very thankful that I was not created one of those flowers."

But there came across the fields a whole troop of joyful children, the youngest of whom was so small that it was carried by the rest, and when it was set down in the grass among the yellow flowers it laughed aloud with glee, kicked out with its little legs, rolled about and plucked the yellow flowers, and kissed them in its pretty innocence. The elder children broke off the flowers with their tall stalks, and bent the stalks round into one another, link by link, so that a whole chain was made; first a necklace, and then a scarf to hang over their shoulders and tie round their waists, and then a chaplet to wear on the head: it was quite a gala of green links and yellow flowers. The eldest children carefully gathered the stalks on which hung the white feathery ball, formed by the flower that had run to seed; and this loose, airy wool-flower, which is a beautiful object, looking like the finest snowy down, they held to their mouths, and tried to blow away the whole head at one breath; for their grandmother had said that whoever could do this would be sure to get new clothes before the year was out. So on this occasion the despised flower was actually raised to the rank of a prophet or augur.

"Do you see?" said the Sunbeam. "Do you see the beauty of those flowers? do you see their power?"

"Yes—over children," replied the Apple Branch.

THE CHILDREN AND THE DANDELIONS.

And now an old woman came into the field, and began to dig with a blunt shaftless knife round the root of the dandelion plant, and pulled it up out of the ground. With some of the roots she intended to make tea for herself; others she was going to sell for money to the druggist.

"But beauty is a higher thing!" said the Apple Tree Branch. "Only the chosen few can be admitted into the realm of beauty. There is a difference among plants, just as there is a difference among men."

And then the Sunbeam spoke of the boundless love of the Creator, as manifested in the creation, and of the just distribution of things in time and in eternity.

"Yes, yes, that is your opinion," the Apple Branch persisted.

But now some people came into the room, and the beautiful young countess appeared, the lady who had placed the Apple Branch in the transparent vase in the sunlight. She carried in her hand a flower, or something of the kind. The object, whatever it might be, was hidden by three or four great leaves, wrapped around it like a shield, that no draught or gust of wind should injure it; and it was carried more carefully than the Apple Bough had ever been. Very gently the large leaves were now removed, and lo, there appeared the fine feathery seed crown of the despised dandelion! This it was that the lady had plucked with the greatest care, and had carried home with every precaution, so that not one of the delicate feathery darts that form its downy ball should be blown away. She now produced it, quite uninjured, and admired its beautiful form, its peculiar construction, and its airy beauty, which was to be scattered by the wind.

"Look, with what singular beauty Providence has invested it," she said. "I will paint it, together with the Apple Branch, whose beauty all have admired; but this humble flower has received just as much from Heaven in a different way; and, various as they are, both are children of the kingdom of beauty."

And the Sunbeam kissed the humble flower, and he kissed the blooming Apple Branch, whose leaves appeared covered with a roseate blush.

EVERYTHING IN ITS RIGHT PLACE.

It is more than a hundred years ago.

Behind the wood, by the great lake, stood the old baronial mansion. Round about it lay a deep moat, in which grew reeds and grass. Close by the bridge, near the entrance-gate, rose an old willow tree that bent over the reeds.

Up from the hollow lane sounded the clang of horns and the trampling of horses; therefore the little girl who kept the geese hastened to drive her charges away from the bridge, before the hunting company should come galloping up. They drew near with such speed that the girl was obliged to climb up in a hurry, and perch herself on the coping-stone of the bridge, lest she should be ridden down. She was still half a child, and had a pretty light figure, and a gentle expression in her face, with two clear blue eyes. The noble baron took no note of this, but as he galloped past the little goose-herd, he reversed the whip he held in his hand, and in rough sport gave her such a push in the chest with the butt-end, that she fell backwards into the ditch.

"Everything in its place!" he cried; "into the puddle with you!" And he laughed aloud, for this was intended for wit, and the company joined in his mirth: the whole party shouted and clamoured, and the dogs barked their loudest.

Fortunately for herself, the poor girl in falling seized one of the hanging branches of the willow tree, by means of which she kept herself suspended over the muddy water, and as soon as the baron and his company had disappeared through the castle-gate, the girl tried to scramble up again; but the bough broke off at the top, and she would have fallen backward among the reeds, if a strong hand from above had not at that moment seized her. It was the hand of a pedler, who had seen from a short distance what had happened, and who now hurried up to give aid.

"Everything in its right place!" he said, mimicking the gracious baron; and he drew the little maiden up to the firm ground. He would have restored the broken branch to the place from which it had been torn, but "everything in its place" cannot always be managed, and therefore he stuck the piece in the ground. "Grow and prosper till you can furnish a good flute for them up yonder," he said; for he would have liked to play the "rogue's march" for my lord the baron and my lord's whole family. And then he betook himself to the castle, but not into the ancestral hall, he was too humble for that! He went to the servants' quarters, and the men and maids turned over his stock of goods, and bargained with him; and from above, where the guests were at table, came a sound of roaring and screaming that was intended for song, and indeed they did their best. Loud laughter, mingled with the barking and howling of dogs, sounded through the windows, for there was feasting and carousing up yonder. Wine and strong old ale foamed in the jugs and glasses, and the dogs sat with their masters and dined with

THE GOOSE-GIRL ON THE BRIDGE.

them. They had the pedler summoned up stairs, but only to make fun of him. The wine had mounted into their heads, and the sense had flown out. They poured wine into a stocking, that the pedler might drink with them, but that he must drink quickly; that was considered a rare jest, and was a cause of fresh laughter. And then whole farms, with oxen and peasants too, were staked on a card, and lost and won.

"Everything in its right place!" said the pedler, when he had at last made his escape out of what he called "the Sodom and Gomorrah up yonder." "The open high road is my right place," he said; "I did not feel at all happy there."

And the little maiden who sat keeping the geese nodded at him in a friendly way, as he strode along beside the hedges.

And days and weeks went by; and it became manifest that the willow branch which the pedler had stuck into the ground by the castle moat remained fresh and green, and even brought forth new twigs. The little goose-girl saw that the branch must have taken root, and rejoiced greatly at the circumstance: for this tree, she said, was now her tree.

The tree certainly came forward well; but everything else belonging to the castle went very rapidly back, what with feasting and gambling—for these two are like wheels, upon which no man can stand securely.

Six years had not passed away before the noble lord passed out of the castle gate, a beggared man, and the mansion was bought by a rich dealer; and this purchaser was the very man who had once been made a jest of there, for whom wine had been poured into a stocking; but honesty and industry are good winds to speed a vessel; and now the dealer was possessor of the baronial estate. But from that hour no more card-playing was permitted there.

"That is bad reading," said he: "when the Evil One saw a Bible for the first time, he wanted to put a bad book against it, and invented card-playing."

The new proprietor took a wife, and who might that be but the goose-girl, who had always been faithful and good, and looked as beautiful and fine in her new clothes as if she had been born a great lady. And how did all this come about? That is too long a story for our busy time, but it really happened, and the most important part is to come.

It was a good thing now to be in the old mansion. The mother managed the domestic affairs, and the father superintended the estate, and it seemed as if blessings were streaming down. Where rectitude enters in, prosperity is sure to follow. The old house was cleaned and painted, the ditches were cleared and fruit trees planted. Everything wore a bright cheerful look, and the floors were as polished as a draught board. In the long winter evenings the lady sat at the spinning-wheel with her maids, and every Sunday evening there was a reading from the Bible by the Councillor of Justice himself — this title the dealer had gained, though it was only in his old age. The children grew up—for children had come—and they received the best education, though all had not equal abilities, as we find indeed in all families.

In the meantime the willow branch at the castle gate had grown to be a splendid tree, which stood there free and self-sustained. "That is our genealogical tree," the old people said, and the tree was to be honoured and respected—so they told all the children, even those who had not very good heads.

And a hundred years rolled by.

It was in our own time. The lake had been converted to moorland, and the old mansion had almost disappeared. A pool of water and the ruins of some walls, this was all that was left of the old baronial castle, with its deep moat; and here stood also a magnificent old willow, with pendent boughs, which seemed to show how beautiful a tree may be if left to itself. The main stem was certainly split from the root to the crown, and the storm had bowed the noble tree a little; but it stood firm for all that, and from every cleft into which wind and weather had carried a portion of earth, grasses and flowers sprang forth: especially near the top, where the great branches parted, a sort of hanging garden had been formed of wild raspberry bush, and even a small quantity of mistletoe had taken root, and stood, slender and graceful, in the midst of the old willow which was mirrored in the dark water. A field-path led close by the old tree.

High by the forest hill, with a splendid prospect in every direction, stood the new baronial hall, large and magnificent, with panes of glass so clearly transparent, that it looked as if there were no panes there at all. The grand flight of steps that led to the entrance looked like a bower of roses and broad-leaved plants. The lawn was as freshly green as if each separate blade of grass were cleaned morning and evening. In the hall hung costly pictures; silken chairs and sofas stood there, so easy that they looked almost as if they could run by themselves; there were tables of great marble slabs, and books bound in morocco and gold. Yes, truly, people of rank lived here: the baron with his family.

All things here corresponded with each other. The motto was still "Everything in its right place;" and therefore all the pictures which had been put up in the old house for honour and glory, hung now in the passage that led to the servants' hall: they were considered as old lumber, and especially two old portraits, one representing a man in a pink coat and powdered wig, the other a lady with powdered hair and holding a rose in her hand, and each surrounded with a wreath of willow leaves. These two pictures were pierced with many holes, because the little barons were in the habit of setting up the old people as a mark for their crossbows. The pictures represented the Councillor of Justice and his lady, the founders of the present family.

"But they did not properly belong to our family," said one of the little barons. "He was a dealer, and she had kept the geese. They were not like papa and mamma."

The pictures were pronounced to be worthless; and as the motto was "Everything in its right place," the great-grandmother and great-grandfather were sent into the passage that led to the servants' hall.

The son of the neighbouring clergyman was tutor in the great house. One day he was out walking with his pupils, the little barons and their eldest sister, who had just been confirmed; they came along the field-path past the old willow, and as they walked on the young lady bound a wreath of field flowers, "Everything in its right place," and the flowers formed a pretty whole. At the same time she heard every word that was spoken, and she liked to hear the clergyman's son talk of the power of nature and of the great men and women in history. She had a good hearty disposition, with true nobility of thought and soul, and a heart full of love for all that God hath created.

The party came to a halt at the old willow tree. The youngest baron insisted on having such a flute cut for him from it as he had had made of other willows. Accordingly the tutor broke off a branch.

"Oh, don't do that!" cried the young baroness; but it was done already. "That is our famous old tree," she continued, "and I love it dearly. They laugh at me at home for this, but I don't mind. There is a story attached to this tree."

And she told what we all know about the tree, about the old mansion, the pedler and the goose-girl, who had met for the first time in this spot,

THE OLD WILLOW TREE.

and had afterwards become the founders of the noble family to which
the young barons belonged.

"They would not be ennobled, the good old folks!" she said. "They
kept to the motto, 'Everything in its right place;' and accordingly they
thought it would be out of place for them to purchase a title with money.
My grandfather, the first baron, was their son. He is said to have been
a very learned man, very popular with princes and princesses, and a
frequent guest at the court festivals. The others at home love him best;
but, I don't know how, there seems to me something about that first
pair that draws my heart towards them. How comfortable, how patri-
archal it must have been in the old house, where the mistress sat at the
spinning-wheel among her maids, and the old master read aloud from
the Bible!"

"They were charming, sensible people," said the clergyman's son.

And with this the conversation naturally fell upon nobles and citizens.
The young man scarcely seemed to belong to the citizen class, so well
did he speak concerning the purpose and meaning of nobility. He said,

"It is a great thing to belong to a family that has distinguished itself, and thus to have, as it were, in one's blood, a spur that urges one on to make progress in all that is good. It is delightful to have a name that serves as a card of admission into the highest circles. Nobility means that which is great and noble: it is a coin that has received a stamp to indicate what it is worth. It is the fallacy of the time, and many poets have frequently maintained this fallacy, that nobility of birth is accompanied by foolishness, and that the lower you go among the poor, the more does everything around you shine. But that is not my view, for I consider it entirely false. In the higher classes many beautiful and kindly traits are found. My mother told me one of this kind, and I could tell you many others.

"My mother was on a visit to a great family in town. My grandmother, I think, had been housekeeper to the count's mother. The great nobleman and my mother were alone in the room, when the former noticed that an old woman came limping on crutches into the courtyard. Indeed, she was accustomed to come every Sunday, and carry away a gift with her. 'Ah, there is the poor old lady,' said the nobleman: 'walking is a great toil to her;' and before my mother understood what he meant, he had gone out of the room and run down the stairs, to save the old woman the toilsome walk, by carrying to her the gift she had come to receive.

"Now, that was only a small circumstance, but, like the widow's two mites in the Scripture, it has a sound that finds an echo in the depths of the heart in human nature; and these are the things the poet should show and point out; especially in these times should he sing of it, for that does good, and pacifies and unites men. But where a bit of mortality, because it has a genealogical tree and a coat of arms, rears up like an Arabian horse, and prances in the street, and says in the room, 'People out of the street have been here,' when a commoner has been — that is nobility in decay, and become a mere mask — a mask of the kind that Thespis created; and people are glad when such an one is turned into satire."

This was the speech of the clergyman's son. It was certainly rather long, but then the flute was being finished while he made it.

At the castle there was a great company. Many guests came from the neighbourhood and from the capital. Many ladies, some tastefully and others tastelessly dressed, were there, and the great hall was quite full of people. The clergymen from the neighbourhood stood respectfully congregated in a corner, which made it look almost as if there were to be a burial there. But it was not so, for this was a party of pleasure, only that the pleasure had not yet begun.

A great concert was to be performed, and consequently the little baron had brought in his willow flute; but he could not get a note out of it, nor could his papa, and therefore the flute was worth nothing. There was instrumental music and song, both of the kind that delight the performers most—quite charming!

"You are a performer?" said a cavalier—his father's son and nothing else—to the tutor. "You play the flute and make it too—that's genius. That should command, and should have the place of honour!"

"No, indeed," replied the young man, "I only advance with the times, as every one is obliged to do."

"Oh, you will enchant us with the little instrument, will you not?" And with these words he handed to the clergyman's son the flute cut from the willow tree by the pool, and announced aloud that the tutor was about to perform a solo on that instrument.

Now, they only wanted to make fun of him, that was easily seen; and therefore the tutor would not play, though indeed he could do so very well; but they crowded round him and importuned him so strongly, that at last he took the flute and put it to his lips.

That was a wonderful flute! A sound, as sustained as that which is emitted by the whistle of a steam engine, and much stronger, echoed far over courtyard, garden, and wood, miles away into the country; and simultaneously with the tone came a rushing wind that roared, "Everything in its right place!" And papa flew as if carried by the wind straight out of the hall and into the shepherd's cot; and the shepherd flew, not into the hall, for there he could not come — no, but into the room of the servants, among the smart lackeys who strutted about there in silk stockings; and the proud servants were struck motionless with horror at the thought that such a personage dared to sit down to table with them.

But in the hall the young baroness flew up to the place of honour at the top of the table, where she was worthy to sit; and the young clergyman's son had a seat next to her; and there the two sat as if they were a newly-married pair. An old count of one of the most ancient families in the country remained untouched in his place of honour; for the flute was just, as men ought to be. The witty cavalier, the son of his father and nothing else, who had been the cause of the flute-playing, flew head-over-heels into the poultry-house—but not alone.

For a whole mile round about the sounds of the flute were heard, and singular events took place. A rich banker's family, driving along in a coach and four, was blown quite out of the carriage, and could not even find a place on the footboard at the back. Two rich peasants who in our times had grown too high for their corn-fields, were tumbled into the ditch. It was a dangerous flute, that: luckily, it burst at the first note; and that was a good thing, for then it was put back into the owner's pocket. "Everything in its right place."

The day afterwards not a word was said about this marvellous event; and thence has come the expression, "pocketing the flute." Everything was in its usual order, only that the two old portraits of the dealer and the goose-girl hung on the wall in the banqueting-hall. They had been blown up yonder, and as one of the real connoisseurs said they had been painted by a master's hand, they remained where they were, and were restored. "Everything in its right place."

And to that it will come; for *hereafter* is long—longer than this story.

THE GOBLIN AND THE HUCKSTER.

THERE was once a regular student: he lived in a garret, and nothing at all belonged to him; but there was also once a regular huckster: he lived on the ground floor, and the whole house was his; and the Goblin kept with him, for on the huckster's table on Christmas-eve there was always a dish of plum porridge, with a great piece of butter floating in the middle. The huckster could accomplish that, and consequently the Goblin stuck to the huckster's shop, and that was very interesting.

One evening the student came through the back door to buy candles and cheese for himself. He had no one to send, and that's why he came himself. He procured what he wanted and paid for it, and the huckster and his wife both nodded a "good evening" to him; and the woman was one who could do more than merely nod—she had an immense power of tongue! And the student nodded too, and then suddenly stood still, reading the sheet of paper in which the cheese had been wrapped. It was a leaf torn out of an old book, a book that ought not to have been torn up, a book that was full of poetry.

"Yonder lies some more of the same sort," said the huckster: "I gave an old woman a little coffee for the books; give me two groschen, and you shall have the remainder."

"Yes," said the student, "give me the book instead of the cheese: I can eat my bread and butter without cheese. It would be a sin to tear the book up entirely. You are a capital man, a practical man, but you understand no more about poetry than does that cask yonder."

Now, that was an insulting speech, especially towards the cask; but the huckster laughed and the student laughed, for it was only said in fun. But the Goblin was angry that any one should dare to say such things to a huckster who lived in his own house and sold the best butter.

When it was night, and the shop was closed and all were in bed, the Goblin came forth, went into the bed-room, and took away the good lady's tongue; for she did not want that while she was asleep; and whenever he put this tongue upon any object in the room, the said object acquired speech and language, and could express its thoughts and feelings as well as the lady herself could have done; but only one object could use it at a time, and that was a good thing, otherwise they would have interrupted each other.

And the Goblin laid the tongue upon the Cask in which the old newspapers were lying.

"Is it true," he asked, "that you don't know what poetry means?"

"Of course I know it," replied the Cask: "poetry is something that always stands at the foot of a column in the newspapers, and is sometimes cut out. I dare swear I have more of it in me than the student, and I'm only a poor tub compared to the huckster."

Then the Goblin put the tongue upon the coffee-mill, and, mercy! how it began to go! And he put it upon the butter-cask, and on the cash-box: they were all of the waste-paper Cask's opinion, and the opinion of the majority must be respected.

"Now I shall tell it to the student!"

And with these words the Goblin went quite quietly up the back stairs to the garret, where the student lived. The student had still a candle burning, and the Goblin peeped through the keyhole, and saw that he was reading in the torn book that he had carried up out of the shop down stairs.

But how light it was in his room! Out of the book shot a clear beam, expanding into a thick stem, and into a mighty tree, which grew upward and spread its branches far over the student. Each leaf was fresh, and every blossom was a beautiful female head, some with dark sparkling eyes, others with wonderfully clear blue orbs; every fruit was a gleaming star, and there was a glorious sound of song in the student's room.

Never had the little Goblin imagined such splendour, far less had he ever seen or heard anything like it. He stood still on tiptoe, and peeped in till the light went out in the student's garret. Probably the student blew it out, and went to bed; but the little Goblin remained standing there nevertheless, for the music still sounded on, soft and beautiful—a splendid cradle song for the student who had lain down to rest.

"This is an incomparable place," said the Goblin: "I never expected such a thing! I should like to stay here with the student."

And then the little man thought it over—and he was a sensible little man too—but he sighed, "The student has no porridge!" And then he went down again to the huckster's shop: and it was a very good thing that he got down there again at last, for the Cask had almost worn out the good woman's tongue, for it had spoken out at one side everything that was contained in it, and was just about turning itself over, to give it out from the other side also, when the Goblin came in, and restored the tongue to its owner. But from that time forth the whole shop, from the cashbox down to the firewood, took its tone from the Cask, and paid him such respect, and thought so much of him, that when the huckster afterwards read the critical articles on theatricals and art in the newspaper, they were persuaded the information came from the Cask itself.

But the Goblin could no longer sit quietly and contentedly listening to all the wisdom down there: so soon as the light glimmered from the garret in the evening, he felt as if the rays were strong cables drawing him up, and he was obliged to go and peep through the keyhole; and there a feeling of greatness rolled around him, such as we feel beside the ever-heaving sea when the storm rushes over it, and he burst into tears! He did not know himself why he was weeping, but a peculiar feeling of pleasure mingled with his tears. How wonderfully glorious it must be to sit with the student under the same tree! But that might not be—he was obliged to be content with the view through the keyhole, and to be glad of that. There he stood on the cold landing-place, with the autumn wind blowing down from the loft-hole: it was cold, very cold; but the little mannikin only felt that when the light in the room was extinguished and the tones in the tree died away. Ha! then he shivered, and crept down again to his warm corner, where it was homely and comfortable.

And when Christmas came, and brought with it the porridge and the great lump of butter, why, then he thought the huckster the better man.

But in the middle of the night the Goblin was awakened by a terrible tumult and knocking against the window-shutters. People rapped noisily without, and the watchman blew his horn, for a great fire had broken out—the whole street was full of smoke and flame. Was it in the house itself or at a neighbour's? Where was it? Terror seized on all. The huckster's wife was so bewildered that she took her gold earrings out of her ears and put them in her pocket, that at any rate she might save something; the huckster ran up for his share-papers, and the maid for her black silk mantilla, for she had found means to purchase one. Each wanted to save the best thing they possessed; the

Goblin wanted to do the same thing, and in a few leaps he was up the stairs and into the room of the student, who stood quite quietly at the open window, looking at the conflagration that was raging in the house of the neighbour opposite. The Goblin seized upon the wonderful book which lay upon the table, popped it into his red cap, and held the cap tight with both hands. The great treasure of the house was saved; and now he ran up and away, quite on to the roof of the house, on to the chimney. There he sat, illuminated by the flames of the burning house opposite, both hands pressed tightly over his cap, in which the treasure lay; and now he knew the real feelings of his heart, and knew to whom it really belonged. But when the fire was extinguished, and the Goblin could think calmly again, why, then . . . . .

"I must divide myself between the two," he said; "I can't quite give up the huckster, because of the porridge!"

Now, that was spoken quite like a human creature. We all of us visit the huckster for the sake of the porridge.

THE BOND OF FRIENDSHIP.

We have before taken little journeys together, and now we want to take a longer one. Whither? To Sparta, to Mycene, to Delphi? There are a hundred places at whose names the heart beats with the desire of travel. On horseback we go up the mountain paths, through brake and through brier. A single traveller makes an appearance like a whole caravan. He rides forward with his guide, a pack-horse carries trunks, a tent, and provisions, and a few armed soldiers follow as a guard. No inn with warm beds awaits him at the end of his tiring day's journey: the tent is often his dwelling-place. In the great wild region the guide cooks him a pillau of rice, fowls, and curry for his supper. A thousand gnats swarm round the tent. It is a boisterous night, and to-morrow the way will lead across swollen streams; take care that you are not washed away!

What is your reward for undergoing these hardships? The fullest, richest reward. Nature manifests herself here in all her greatness; every spot is historical, and the eye and the thoughts are alike delighted. The poet may sing it, the painter portray it in rich pictures; but the air of reality which sinks deep into the soul of the spectator, and remains there, neither painter nor poet can produce.

In many little sketches I have endeavoured to give an idea of a small part of Athens and its environs; but how colourless the picture seems! How little does it exhibit Greece, the mourning genius of beauty, whose past greatness and whose sorrow the stranger never forgets!

The lonely herdsmen yonder on the hills would, perhaps, by a simple recital of an event in his life, better enlighten the stranger who wishes

THE GREEK MOTHER'S SONG.

in a few features to behold the land of the Hellenes, than any picture
could do.

"Then," says my Muse, "let him speak."

A custom, a good, peculiar custom, shall be the subject of the mountain shepherd's tale.   It is called

THE BOND OF FRIENDSHIP.

Our rude house was put together of clay; but the door-posts were
columns of fluted marble found near the spot where the house was
erected.   The roof reached almost down to the ground.   It was now
dark brown and ugly, but it had originally consisted of blooming olive
and fresh laurel branches brought from beyond the mountain.   Around
our dwelling was a narrow gorge, whose walls of rock rose steeply
upwards, and showed naked and black, and round their summits often
hung clouds, like white living figures.   Never did I hear a singing bird
there, never did the men there dance to the sound of the bagpipe; but
the spot was sacred from the old times: even its name reminded of this,
for it was called Delphi!   The dark solemn mountains were all covered
with snow; the highest, which gleamed the longest in the red light of
evening, was Parnassus; the brook which rolled from it near our house
was once sacred also.   Now the ass sullies it with its feet, but the
stream rolls on and on, and becomes clear again.   How I can remember
every spot in the deep holy solitude!   In the midst of the hut a fire

was kindled, and when the hot ashes lay there red and glowing, the bread was baked in them. When the snow was piled so high around our hut as almost to hide it, my mother appeared most cheerful: then she would hold my head between her hands, and sing the songs she never sang at other times, for the Turks our masters would not allow it. She sang:

"On the summit of Olympus, in the forest of dwarf firs, lay an old stag. His eyes were heavy with tears; he wept blue and even red tears; and there came a roebuck by, and said, 'What ails thee, that thou weepest those blue and red tears?' And the stag answered. 'The Turk has come to our city: he has wild dogs for the chase, a goodly pack.' 'I will drive them away across the islands,' cried the young roebuck, 'I will drive them away across the islands into the deep sea!' But before evening sank down the roebuck was slain, and before night the stag was hunted and dead."

And when my mother sang thus, her eyes became moist, and on the long eyelashes hung a tear; but she hid it, and baked our black bread in the ashes. Then I would clench my fist and cry,

"We will kill the Turks!"

But she repeated from the song the words,

"I will drive them across the islands into the deep sea. But before evening sank down the roebuck was slain, and before the night came the stag was hunted and dead."

For several days and nights we had been lonely in our hut, when my father came home. I knew he would bring me shells from the Gulf of Lepanto, or perhaps even a bright gleaming knife. This time he brought us a child, a little half-naked girl, that he carried under his sheep-skin cloak. It was wrapped in a fur, and all that the little creature possessed when this was taken off, and she lay in my mother's lap, were three silver coins, fastened in her dark hair. My father told us that the Turks had killed the child's parents; and he told so much about them that I dreamed of the Turks all night. He himself had been wounded, and my mother bound up his arm. The wound was deep, and the thick sheep-skin was stiff with frozen blood. The little maiden was to be my sister. How radiantly beautiful she looked! Even my mother's eyes were not more gentle than hers. Anastasia, as she was called, was to be my sister, because her father had been united to mine by the old custom which we still keep. They had sworn brotherhood in their youth, and chosen the most beautiful and virtuous girl in the neighbourhood to consecrate their bond of friendship. I often heard of the strange good custom.

So now the little girl was my sister. She sat in my lap, and I brought her flowers and the feathers of the mountain birds: we drank together of the waters of Parnassus, and dwelt together for many a year under the laurel roof of the hut, while my mother sang winter after winter of the stag who wept red tears. But as yet I did not understand that it was my own countrymen whose many sorrows were mirrored in those tears.

One day there came three Frankish men. Their dress was different from ours. They had tents and beds with them on their horses, and more than twenty Turks, all armed with swords and muskets, accompanied them; for they were friends of the pasha, and had letters from him commanding an escort for them. They only came to see our mountains, to ascend Parnassus amid the snow and the clouds, and to look at the strange black steep rock near our hut. They could not find room in it, nor could they endure the smoke that rolled along the ceiling and found its way out at the low door; therefore they pitched their tents on the small space outside our dwelling, roasted lambs and birds, and poured out strong sweet wine, of which the Turks were not allowed to partake.

When they departed, I accompanied them for some distance, carrying my little sister Anastasia, wrapped in a goat-skin, on my back. One of the Frankish gentlemen made me stand in front of a rock, and drew me, and her too, as we stood there, so that we looked like one creature. I never thought of it before, but Anastasia and I were really one. She was always sitting in my lap or riding in the goat-skin at my back, and when I dreamed, she appeared in my dreams.

Two nights afterwards, other men, armed with knives and muskets, came into our tent. They were Albanians, brave men, my mother told me. They only stayed a short time. My sister Anastasia sat on the knee of one of them, and when they were gone she had not three, but only two silver coins in her hair. They wrapped tobacco in strips of paper and smoked it. I remember they were undecided as to the road they were to take.

But they had to make a choice. They went, and my father went with them. Soon afterwards we heard the sound of firing. The noise was renewed, and soldiers rushed into our hut, and took my mother, and myself, and my sister Anastasia prisoners. They declared that the robbers had been entertained by us, and that my father had acted as the robbers' guide, and therefore we must go with them. Presently I saw the corpses of the robbers brought in; I saw my father's corpse too. I cried and cried till I fell asleep. When I awoke, we were in prison, but the room was not worse than ours in our own house. They gave me onions to eat, and musty wine poured from a tarry cask, but we had no better fare at home.

How long we were kept prisoners I do not know; but many days and nights went by. When we were set free it was the time of the holy Easter feast. I carried Anastasia on my back, for my mother was ill, and could only move slowly, and it was a long way till we came down to the sea, to the Gulf of Lepanto. We went into a church that gleamed with pictures painted on a golden ground. They were pictures of angels, and very beautiful; but it seemed to me that our little Anastasia was just as beautiful. In the middle of the floor stood a coffin filled with roses. "The Lord Christ is pictured there in the form of a beautiful rose," said my mother; and the priest announced. "Christ is risen!" All the people kissed each other: each one had a burning taper in his hand, and I received one myself, and so did little Anastasia.   The bagpipes sounded, men danced hand in hand from the church, and outside the women were roasting the Easter lamb.   We were invited to partake, and I sat by the fire ; a boy, older than myself, put his arms round my neck, kissed me, and said, " Christ is risen! " and thus it was that for the first time I met Aphtanides.

My mother could make fishermen's nets, for which there was a good demand here in the bay, and we lived a long time by the side of the sea, the beautiful sea, that tasted like tears, and in its colours reminded me of the song of the stag that wept—for sometimes its waters were red, and sometimes green or blue.

Aphtanides knew how to manage our boat, and I often sat in it, with my little Anastasia, while it glided on through the water, swift as a bird flying through the air.   Then, when the sun sank down, the mountains were tinted with a deeper and deeper blue, one range seemed to rise behind the other, and behind them all stood Parnassus with its snow-crowned summit.   The mountain-top gleamed in the evening rays like glowing iron, and it seemed as though the light came from within it ; for long after the sun had set, the mountain still shone through the clear blue air.   The white water birds touched the surface of the sea with their wings, and all here was as calm and quiet as among the black rocks at Delphi.   I lay on my back in the boat, Anastasia leaned against me, and the stars above us shone brighter than the lamps in our church. They were the same stars, and they stood exactly in the same positions above me, as when I had sat in front of our hut at Delphi; and at last I almost fancied I was back there.   Suddenly there was a splash in the water, and the boat rocked violently.   I cried out in horror, for Anastasia had fallen into the water; but in a moment Aphtanides had sprung in after her, and was holding her up to me !   We dried her clothes as well as we could, remaining on the water till they were dry ; for no one was to know what a fright we had had for our little adopted sister, in whose life Aphtanides now had a part.

The summer came.   The sun burned so hot that the leaves turned yellow on the trees.   I thought of our cool mountains, and of the fresh water they contained ; my mother, too, longed for them ; and one evening we wandered home.   What peace, what silence !   We walke ! on through the thick thyme, still fragrant though the sun had scorched its leaves.   Not a single herdsman did we meet, not one solitary hut did we pass.   Everything was quiet and deserted; but a shooting star announced that in heaven there was yet life.   I know not if the clear blue air gleamed with light of its own, or if the radiance came from the stars ; but we could see the outlines of the mountains quite plainly. My mother lighted a fire, roasted some roots she had brought with her, and I and my little sister slept among the thyme, without fear of the ugly Smidraki,* from whose throat fire spurts forth, or of the wolf and

* According to the Greek superstition, this is a monster generated from the unopened entrails of slaughtered sheep, which are thrown away in the fields.

THE FRIENDS AT LEPANTO.

jackal; for my mother sat beside us, and I considered her presence protection enough for us.

We reached our old home; but the hut was a heap of ruins, and a new one had to be built. A few women lent my mother their aid, and in a few days walls were raised, and covered with a new roof of olive branches. My mother made many bottle-cases of bark and skins; I kept the little flock of the priests,* and Anastasia and the little tortoises were my playmates.

Once we had a visit from our beloved Aphtanides, who said he had greatly longed to see us, and who stayed with us two whole happy days.

A month afterwards he came again, and told us that he was going in a ship to Corfu and Patras, but must bid us good bye first; and he had brought a large fish for our mother. He had a great deal to tell, not only of the fishermen yonder in the Gulf of Lepanto, but also of Kings and heroes, who had once possessed Greece, just as the Turks possess it now.

I have seen a bud on a rose bush gradually unfold in days and weeks, till it became a rose, and hung there in its beauty, before I was aware how large and beautiful and red it had become; and the same thing I now saw in Anastasia. She was now a beautiful grown girl, and I

---

* A peasant who can read often becomes a priest; he is then called " very holy Sir," and the lower orders kiss the ground on which he has stepped.

had become a stout stripling   The wolf-skins that covered my mother's and Anastasia's bed, I had myself taken from wolves that had fallen beneath my shots.

Years had gone by, when one evening Aphtanides came in, slender as a reed, strong and brown.   He kissed us all, and had much to tell of the fortifications of Malta, of the great ocean, and of the marvellous sepulchres of Egypt.   It sounded strange as a legend of the priests, and I looked up to him with a kind of veneration.

" How much you know! " I exclaimed ; " what wonders you can tell of ! "

" But you have told me the finest thing, after all," he replied.   " You told me of a thing that has never been out of my thoughts—of the good old custom of the bond of friendship, a custom I should like to follow. Brother, let you and I go to church, as your father and Anastasia's went before us : your sister Anastasia is the most beautiful and most innocent of girls ; she shall consecrate us !   No people has such grand old customs as we Greeks."

Anastasia blushed like a young rose, and my mother kissed Aphtanides.

A couple of miles from our house, there where loose earth lies on the hill and a few scattered trees give a shelter, stood the little church ; a silver lamp hung in front of the altar.

I had put on my best clothes : the white fustanella fell in rich folds round my hips, the red jacket fitted tight and close, the tassel on my fez cap was silver, and in my girdle gleamed a knife and my pistols. Aphtanides was clad in the blue garb worn by Greek sailors ; on his chest hung a silver plate with the figure of the Virgin Mary ; his scarf was as costly as those worn by rich lords.   Every one could see that we were about to go through a solemn ceremony.   We stepped into the little simple church, where the evening sunlight, streaming through the door, gleamed on the burning lamp and the pictures on golden ground. We knelt down on the altar steps, and Anastasia came before us.   A long white garment hung loose over her graceful form ; on her white neck and bosom hung a chain, covered with old and new coins, forming a kind of collar.   Her black hair was fastened in a knot, and confined by a head-dress made of silver and gold coins that had been found in an old temple.   No Greek girl had more beautiful ornaments than she. Her countenance glowed, and her eyes were like two stars.

We all three prayed silently ; and then she said to us,

" Will you be friends in life and in death ? "

" Yes," we replied.

" Will you, whatever may happen, remember this : my brother is a part of myself.   My secrets are his, my happiness is his.   Self-sacrifice, patience—everything in me belongs to him as to me ? "

And we again answered, " Yes."

Then she joined our hands and kissed us on the forehead, and we again prayed silently.   Then the priest came through the door near the altar, and blessed us all three ; and a song, sung by the other holy men, sounded from behind the altar screen, and the bond of eternal friendship was concluded. When we rose, I saw my mother standing by the church door weeping heartily.

How cheerful it was now, in our little hut, and by the springs of Delphi! On the evening before his departure, Aphtanides sat thoughtful with me on the declivity of a mountain; his arm was flung round my waist, and mine was round his neck: we spoke of the sorrows of Greece, and of the men whom the country could trust. Every thought of our souls lay clear before each of us, and I seized his hand.

"One thing thou must still know, one thing that till now has been a secret between myself and Heaven. My whole soul is filled with love! with a love stronger than the love I bear to my mother and to thee!"

"And whom do you love?" asked Aphtanides, and his face and neck grew red as fire.

"I love Anastasia," I replied—and his hand trembled in mine, and he became pale as a corpse. I saw it; I understood the cause; and I believe *my* hand trembled. I bent towards him, kissed his forehead, and whispered, "I have never spoken of it to her, and perhaps she does not love me. Brother, think of this: I have seen her daily; she has grown up beside me, and has become a part of my soul!"

"And she shall be thine!" he exclaimed, "thine! I may not deceive thee, nor will I do so. I also love her; but to-morrow I depart. In a year we shall see each other once more, and then you will be married, will you not? I have a little gold of my own: it shall be thine. Thou must, thou shalt take it."

And we wandered home silently across the mountains. It was late in the evening when we stood at my mother's door.

Anastasia held the lamp upwards as we entered: my mother was not there. She gazed at Aphtanides with a beautifully mournful gaze.

"To-morrow you are going from us," she said: "I am very sorry for it."

"Sorry!" he repeated, and in his voice there seemed a trouble as great as the grief I myself felt. I could not speak, but he seized her hand, and said, "Our brother yonder loves you, and he is dear to you, is he not? His very silence is a proof of his affection."

Anastasia trembled and burst into tears. Then I saw no one but her, thought of none but her, and threw my arms round her, and said, "I love thee!" She pressed her lips to mine, and flung her arms round my neck; but the lamp had fallen to the ground, and all was dark around us—dark as in the heart of poor Aphtanides.

Before daybreak he rose, kissed us all, said farewell, and went away. He had given all his money to my mother for us. Anastasia was my betrothed, and a few days afterwards she became my wife.

THE BOTTLE-NECK.

IN a narrow crooked street, among other abodes of poverty, stood an especially narrow and tall house built of timber, which time had knocked about in such fashion that it seemed to be out of joint in every direction. The house was inhabited by poor people, and the deepest poverty was apparent in the garret lodging in the gable, where, in front of the only window, hung an old bent birdcage, which had not even a proper water-glass, but only a Bottle-neck reversed, with a cork stuck in the mouth, to do duty for one. An old maid stood by the window: she had hung the cage with green chickweed; and a little chaffinch hopped from perch to perch, and sang and twittered merrily enough.

"Yes, it's all very well for you to sing," said the Bottle-neck; that is to say, it did not pronounce the words as we can speak them, for a bottle-neck can't speak; but that's what he thought to himself in his own mind, like when we people talk quietly to ourselves. "Yes, it's all very well for you to sing, you that have all your limbs uninjured. You ought to feel what it's like to lose one's body, and to have only mouth and neck left, and to be hampered with work into the bargain, as in my case; and then I'm sure you would not sing. But after all it is well that there should be somebody at least who is merry. I've no reason to sing, and, moreover, I can't sing. Yes, when I was a whole bottle, I sang out well if they rubbed me with a cork. They used to call me a perfect lark, a magnificent lark! Ah, when I was out at a picnic with the tanner's family, and his daughter was betrothed! Yes, I remember it as if it had happened only yesterday. I have gone through a great deal, when I come to recollect. I've been in the fire and the water, have been deep in the black earth, and have mounted higher than most of the others; and now I'm hanging here, outside the birdcage, in the air and the sunshine! Oh, it would be quite worth while to hear my history; but I don't speak aloud of it, because I can't."

And now the Bottle-neck told its story, which was sufficiently remarkable. It told the story to itself, or only thought it in its own mind; and the little bird sang his song merrily, and down in the street there was driving and hurrying, and every one thought of his own affairs, or perhaps of nothing at all; and only the Bottle-neck thought. It thought of the flaming furnace in the manufactory, where it had been blown into life; it still remembered that it had been quite warm, that it had glanced into the hissing furnace, the home of its origin, and had felt a great desire to leap directly back again; but that gradually it had become cooler, and had been very comfortable in the place to which it was taken. It had stood in a rank with a whole regiment of brothers and sisters, all out of the same furnace; some of them had certainly been blown into champagne bottles, and others into beer bottles, and that makes a difference. Later, out in the world, it may well happen that a beer bottle may contain the most precious wine, and a champagne bottle be filled with blacking; but even in decay there is always something left by which people can see what one has been—nobility is nobility, even when filled with blacking.

All the bottles were packed up, and our bottle was among them. At that time it did not think to finish its career as a bottle-neck, or that it should work its way up to be a bird's glass, which is always an honourable thing, for one is of some consequence, after all. The bottle did not again behold the light of day till it was unpacked with the other bottles in the cellar of the wine merchant, and rinsed out for the first time; and that was a strange sensation. There it lay, empty and without a cork, and felt strangely unwell, as if it wanted something, it could not tell what. At last it was filled with good costly wine, and was provided with a cork, and sealed down. A ticket was placed on it marked " first quality; " and it felt as if it had carried off the first prize at an examination; for, you see, the wine was good and the bottle was good. When one is young, that's the time for poetry! There was a singing and sounding within it, of things which it could not understand—of green sunny mountains, whereon the grape grows, where many vine dressers, men and women, sing and dance and rejoice. " Ah, how beautiful is life! " There was a singing and sounding of all this in the bottle, as in a young poet's brain; and many a young poet does not understand the meaning of the song that is within him.

One morning the bottle was bought, for the tanner's apprentice was dispatched for a bottle of wine—" of the best." And now it was put in the provision basket, with ham and cheese and sausages; the finest butter and the best bread were put into the basket too—the tanner's daughter herself packed it. She was young and very pretty; her brown eyes laughed, and round her mouth played a smile as elegant as that in her eyes. She had delicate hands, beautifully white, and her neck was whiter still; you saw at once that she was one of the most beautiful girls in the town: and still she was not engaged.

The provision basket was in the lap of the young girl when the family drove out into the forest. The bottle-neck looked out from the folds of the white napkin. There was red wax upon the cork, and the bottle looked straight into the girl's face. It also looked at the young sailor who sat next to the girl. He was a friend of old days, the son of the portrait painter. Quite lately he had passed with honour through his examination as mate, and to-morrow he was to sail away in a ship, far off to a distant land. There had been much talk of this while the basket was being packed; and certainly the eyes and mouth of the tanner's pretty daughter did not wear a very joyous expression just then.

The young people sauntered through the green wood, and talked to one another. What were they talking of? No, the bottle could not hear that, for it was in the provision basket. A long time passed before it was drawn forth; but when that happened, there had been pleasant things going on, for all were laughing, and the tanner's daughter laughed too; but she spoke less than before, and her cheeks glowed like two roses.

The father took the full bottle and the corkscrew in his hand. Yes, it's a strange thing to be drawn thus, the first time! The Bottle-neck could never afterwards forget that impressive moment; and indeed there was quite a convulsion within him when the cork flew out, and a great throbbing as the wine poured forth into the glasses.

"Health to the betrothed pair!" cried the papa. And every glass was emptied to the dregs, and the young mate kissed his beautiful bride.

"Happiness and blessing!" said the two old people, the father and mother. And the young man filled the glasses again.

"Safe return, and a wedding this day next year!" he cried; and when the glasses were emptied, he took the bottle, raised it on high, and said, "Thou hast been present at the happiest day of my life, thou shalt never serve another!"

And so saying, he hurled it high into the air. The tanner's daughter did not then think that she should see the bottle fly again; and yet it was to be so. It then fell into the thick reeds on the margin of a little woodland lake; and the Bottle-neck could remember quite plainly how it lay there for some time.

"I gave them wine, and they gave me marsh water," he said; "but it was all meant for the best."

He could no longer see the betrothed couple and the cheerful old people; but for a long time he could hear them rejoicing and singing. Then at last came two peasant boys, and looked into the reeds; they spied out the bottle, and took it up; and now it was provided for.

At their home, in the wooden cottage, the eldest of three brothers, who was a sailor, and about to start on a long voyage, had been the day before to take leave. The mother was just engaged in packing up various things he was to take with him upon his journey, and which the father was going to carry into the town that evening to see his son once more, to give him a farewell greeting from the lad's mother and himself, and a little bottle of medicated brandy had already been wrapped up in a parcel, when the boys came in with the larger and stronger bottle which they had found. This bottle would hold more than the little one, and they pronounced that the brandy would be capital for a bad digestion, inasmuch as it was mixed with medical herbs. The draught that was now poured into the bottle was not so good as the red wine with which it had once been filled; these were bitter drops, but even these are sometimes good. The new big bottle was to go, and not the little one; and so the bottle went travelling again. It was taken on board for Peter Jensen, in the very same ship in which the young mate sailed. But he did not see the bottle; and, indeed, he would not have known it, or thought it was the same one out of which they had drunk a health to the betrothed pair and to his own happy return.

Certainly it had no longer wine to give, but still it contained something that was just as good. Accordingly, whenever Peter Jensen brought it out, it was dubbed by his messmates The Apothecary. It contained the best medicine, medicine that strengthened the weak, and it gave liberally so long as it had a drop left. That was a pleasant time,

THE BOTTLE IS PRESENT ON A JOYOUS OCCASION.

and the bottle sang when it was rubbed with the cork; and it was called the Great Lark, "Peter Jensen's Lark."

Long days and months rolled on, and the bottle already stood empty in a corner, when it happened—whether on the passage out or home the bottle could not tell, for it had never been ashore—that a storm arose; great waves came careering along, darkly and heavily, and lifted and tossed the ship to and fro. The mainmast was shivered, and a wave started one of the planks, and the pumps became useless. It was black night. The ship sank; but at the last moment the young mate wrote on a leaf of paper, "God's will be done! We are sinking!" He wrote the name of his betrothed, and his own name, and that of the ship, and put the leaf in an empty bottle that happened to be at hand: he corked it firmly down, and threw it out into the foaming sea. He knew not that it was the very bottle from which the goblet of joy and hope had once been filled for him; and now it was tossing on the waves with his last greeting and the message of death.

The ship sank, and the crew sank with her. The bottle sped on like a bird, for it bore a heart, a loving letter, within itself. And the sun rose and set; and the bottle felt as at the time when it first came into being in the red gleaming oven—it felt a strong desire to leap back into the light.

It experienced calms and fresh storms; but it was hurled against no rock, and was devoured by no shark; and thus it drifted on for a year and a day, sometimes towards the north, sometimes towards the south,

just as the current carried it.   Beyond this it was its own master, but
one may grow tired even of that.

The written page, the last farewell of the bridegroom to his betrothed,
would only bring sorrow if it came into her hands; but where were the
hands, so white and delicate, which had once spread the cloth on the
fresh grass in the green wood, on the betrothal day?   Where was the
tanner's daughter?   Yes, where was the land, and which land might be
nearest to her dwelling?   The bottle knew not; it drove onward and
onward, and was at last tired of wandering, because that was not in its
way; but yet it had to travel until at last it came to land—to a strange
land.   It understood not a word of what was spoken here, for this was
not the language it had heard spoken before; and one loses a good deal
if one does not understand the language.

The bottle was fished out and examined on all sides.   The leaf of
paper within it was discovered, and taken out, and turned over and over,
but the people did not understand what was written thereon.   They saw
that the bottle must have been thrown overboard, and that something
about this was written on the paper, but what were the words?   That
question remained unanswered, and the paper was put back into the
bottle, and the latter was deposited in a great cupboard in a great room
in a great house.

Whenever strangers came, the paper was brought out and turned
over and over, so that the inscription, which was only written in pencil,
became more and more illegible, so that at last no one could see that
there were letters on it.   And for a whole year more the bottle remained
standing in the cupboard; and then it was put into the loft, where it
became covered with dust and cobwebs.   Ah, how often it thought of
the better days, the times when it had poured forth red wine in the
green wood, when it had been rocked on the waves of the sea, and when
it had carried a secret, a letter, a parting sigh, safely enclosed in its
bosom.

For full twenty years it stood up in the loft; and it might have remained there longer, but that the house was to be rebuilt.   The roof
was taken off, and then the bottle was noticed, and they spoke about
it, but it did not understand their language; for one cannot learn a
language by being shut up in a loft, even if one stays there twenty years.

"If I had been down in the room," thought the Bottle, "I might
have learned it."

It was now washed and rinsed, and indeed this was requisite.   It felt
quite transparent and fresh, and as if its youth had been renewed in
this its old age; but the paper it had carried so faithfully had been
destroyed in the washing.

The bottle was filled with seeds, though it scarcely knew what they
were.   It was corked and well wrapped up.   No light nor lantern was
it vouchsafed to behold, much less the sun or the moon; and yet, it
thought, when one goes on a journey one ought to see something; but
though it saw nothing, it did what was most important—it travelled to
the place of its destination, and was there unpacked.

"What trouble they have taken over yonder with that bottle!" it heard people say; "and yet it is most likely broken." But it was not broken.

The bottle understood every word that was now said; this was the language it had heard at the furnace, and at the wine merchant's, and in the forest, and in the ship, the only good old language it understood: it had come back home, and the language was as a salutation of welcome to it. For very joy it felt ready to jump out of people's hands; hardly did it notice that its cork had been drawn, and that it had been emptied and carried into the cellar, to be placed there and forgotten. There's no place like home, even if it's in a cellar! It never occurred to the bottle to think how long it would lie there, for it felt comfortable, and accordingly lay there for years. At last people came down into the cellar to carry off all the bottles, and ours among the rest.

Out in the garden there was a great festival. Flaming lamps hung like garlands, and paper lanterns shone transparent, like great tulips. The evening was lovely, the weather still and clear, the stars twinkled; it was the time of the new moon, but in reality the whole moon could be seen as a bluish grey disc with a golden rim round half its surface, which was a very beautiful sight for those who had good eyes.

The illumination extended even to the most retired of the garden walks; at least so much of it, that one could find one's way there. Among the leaves of the hedges stood bottles, with a light in each; and among them was also the bottle we know, and which was destined one day to finish its career as a bottle-neck, a bird's drinking-glass. Everything here appeared lovely to our bottle, for it was once more in the green wood, amid joy and feasting, and heard song and music, and the noise and murmur of a crowd, especially in that part of the garden where the lamps blazed and the paper lanterns displayed their many colours. Thus it stood, in a distant walk certainly, but that made it the more important; for it bore its light, and was at once ornamental and useful, and that is as it should be: in such an hour one forgets twenty years spent in a loft, and it is right one should do so.

There passed close to it a pair, like the pair who had walked together long ago in the wood, the sailor and the tanner's daughter; the bottle seemed to experience all that over again. In the garden were walking not only the guests, but other people who were allowed to view all the splendour; and among these latter came an old maid who seemed to stand alone in the world. She was just thinking, like the bottle, of the green wood, and of a young betrothed pair—of a pair which concerned her very nearly, a pair in which she had an interest, and of which she had been a part in that happiest hour of her life—the hour one never forgets, if one should become ever so old a maid. But she did not know our bottle, nor did the bottle recognize the old maid: it is thus we pass each other in the world, meeting again and again, as these two met, now that they were together again in the same town.

From the garden the bottle was dispatched once more to the wine merchant's, where it was filled with wine, and sold to the aëronaut, who was to make an ascent in his balloon on the following Sunday. A great crowd had assembled to witness the sight; military music had been provided, and many other preparations had been made. The bottle saw everything from a basket in which it lay next to a live rabbit, which latter was quite bewildered because he knew he was to be taken up into the air, and let down again in a parachute; but the bottle knew nothing of the "up" or the "down;" it only saw the balloon swelling up bigger and bigger, and at last, when it could swell no more, beginning to rise, and to grow more and more restless. The ropes that held it were cut, and the huge machine floated aloft with the aëronaut and the basket containing the bottle and the rabbit, and the music sounded, and all the people cried, "Hurrah!"

"This is a wonderful passage, up into the air!" thought the Bottle; "this is a new way of sailing: at any rate, up here we cannot strike upon anything."

Thousands of people gazed up at the balloon, and the old maid looked up at it also; she stood at the open window of the garret, in which hung the cage with the little chaffinch, who had no water-glass as yet, but was obliged to be content with an old cup. In the window stood a myrtle in a pot; and it had been put a little aside that it might not fall out, for the old maid was leaning out of the window to look, and she distinctly saw the aëronaut in the balloon, and how he let down the rabbit in the parachute, and then drank to the health of all the spectators, and at length hurled the bottle high in the air; she never thought that this was the identical bottle which she had already once seen thrown aloft in honour of her and of her friend on the day of rejoicing in the green wood, in the time of her youth.

The bottle had no respite for thought, for it was quite startled at thus suddenly reaching the highest point in its career. Steeples and roofs lay far, far beneath, and the people looked like mites.

But now it began to descend with a much more rapid fall than that of the rabbit; the bottle threw somersaults in the air, and felt quite young, and quite free and unfettered; and yet it was half full of wine, though it did not remain so long. What a journey! The sun shone on the bottle, all the people were looking at it; the balloon was already far away, and soon the bottle was far away too, for it fell upon a roof and broke; but the pieces had got such an impetus that they could not stop themselves, but went jumping and rolling on till they came down into the courtyard and lay there in smaller pieces yet; the Bottle-neck only managed to keep whole, and that was cut off as clean as if it had been done with a diamond.

"That would do capitally for a bird-glass," said the cellarmen; but they had neither a bird nor a cage; and to expect them to provide both because they had found a bottle-neck that might be made available for a glass, would have been expecting too much; but the old maid in the garret, perhaps it might be useful to her; and now the Bottle-neck was taken up to her, and was provided with a cork. The part that had been uppermost was now turned downwards, as often happens when changes take place; fresh water was poured into it, and it was fastened to the cage of the little bird, which sang and twittered right merrily.

"Yes, it 's very well for you to sing," said the Bottle-neck.

And it was considered remarkable for having been in the balloon—for that was all they knew of its history. Now it hung there as a bird-glass, and heard the murmuring and noise of the people in the street below, and also the words of the old maid in the room within. An old friend had just come to visit her, and they talked—not of the Bottle-neck, but about the myrtle in the window.

"No, you certainly must not spend a dollar for your daughter's bridal wreath," said the old maid. "You shall have a beautiful little nosegay

THE MYRTLE TREE.

from me, full of blossoms. Do you see how splendidly that tree has come on? yes, that has been raised from a spray of the myrtle you gave me on the day after my betrothal, and from which I was to have made my own wreath when the year was past; but that day never came! The eyes closed that were to have been my joy and delight through life. In the depths of the sea he sleeps sweetly, my dear one! The myrtle has become an old tree, and I become a yet older woman; and when it faded at last, I took the last green shoot, and planted it in the ground, and it has become a great tree; and now at length the myrtle will serve at the wedding—as a wreath for your daughter."

There were tears in the eyes of the old maid. She spoke of the beloved of her youth, of their betrothal in the wood; many thoughts came to her, but the thought never came, that quite close to her, before the very window, was a remembrance of those times—the neck of the bottle which had shouted for joy when the cork flew out with a bang on the betrothal day. But the Bottle-neck did not recognize her, for he was not listening to what this old maid said — and still that was because he was thinking of her.

IB AND CHRISTINE.

Not far from the clear stream Gudenau, in North Jutland, in the forest which extends by its banks and far into the country, a great ridge of land rises and stretches along like a wall through the wood. By this ridge, westward, stands a farm-house, surrounded by poor land; the sandy soil is seen through the spare rye and wheat-ears that grow upon it. Some years have elapsed since the time of which we speak. The people who lived here cultivated the fields, and moreover kept three sheep, a pig, and two oxen; in fact, they supported themselves quite comfortably, for they had enough to live on if they took things as they came. Indeed, they could have managed to save enough to keep two horses; but, like the other peasants of the neighbourhood, they said, "The horse eats itself up" — that is to say, it eats as much as it earns. Jeppe-Jäns cultivated his field in summer. In the winter he made wooden shoes, and then he had an assistant, a journeyman, who understood as well as he himself did how to make the wooden shoes strong, and light, and graceful. They carved shoes and spoons, and that brought in money. It would have been wronging the Jeppe-Jänses to call them poor people.

Little Ib, a boy seven years old, the only child of the family, would sit by, looking at the workmen, cutting at a stick, and occasionally cutting his finger. But one day Ib succeeded so well with two pieces of wood, that they really looked like little wooden shoes; and these he wanted to give to little Christine. And who was little Christine? She was the boatman's daughter, and was graceful and delicate as a gentleman's child; had she been differently dressed, no one would have imagined that she came out of the hut on the neighbouring heath. There lived her father, who was a widower, and supported himself by carrying firewood in his great boat out of the forest to the estate of Silkeborg, with its great eel-pond and eel-weir, and sometimes even to the distant little town of Randers. He had no one who could take care of little Christine, and therefore the child was almost always with him in his boat, or in the forest among the heath plants and barberry bushes. Sometimes, when he had to go as far as the town, he would bring little Christine, who was a year younger than Ib, to stay at the Jeppe-Jänses.

Ib and Christine agreed very well in every particular: they divided their bread and berries when they were hungry, they dug in the ground together for treasures, and they ran, and crept, and played about everywhere. And one day they ventured together up the high ridge, and a long way into the forest; once they found a few snipe's eggs there, and that was a great event for them.

Ib had never been on the heath where Christine's father lived, nor had he ever been on the river. But even this was to happen; for Christine's father once invited him to go with them, and on the evening before the excursion, he followed the boatman over the heath to the house of the latter.

Next morning early, the two children were sitting high up on the pile of firewood in the boat, eating bread and whistleberries. Christine's father and his assistant propelled the boat with staves. They had the current with them, and swiftly they glided down the stream, through the lakes it forms in its course, and which sometimes seemed shut in by reeds and water plants, though there was always room for them to pass, and though the old trees bent quite forward over the water, and the old oaks bent down their bare branches, as if they had turned up their sleeves, and wanted to show their knotty naked arms. Old elder trees, which the stream had washed away from the bank, clung with their fibrous roots to the bottom of the stream, and looked like little wooded islands. The water-lilies rocked themselves on the river. It was a splendid excursion; and at last they came to the great eel-weir, where the water rushed through the flood-gates; and Ib and Christine thought this was beautiful to behold.

In those days there was no manufactory there, nor was there any town: only the old great farm-yard, with its scanty fields, with few servants and a few head of cattle, could be seen there; and the rushing of the water through the weir and the cry of the wild ducks were the only signs of life in Silkeborg. After the firewood had been unloaded, the father of Christine bought a whole bundle of eels and a slaughtered sucking-pig, and all was put into a basket and placed in the stern of the boat. Then they went back again up the stream; but the wind was favourable, and when the sails were hoisted it was as good as if two horses had been harnessed to the boat.

When they had arrived at a point in the stream where the assistant-boatman dwelt, a little way from the bank, the boat was moored, and the two men landed, after exhorting the children to sit still. But the children did not do that, or at least they obeyed only for a very short time. They must be peeping into the basket in which the eels and the sucking-pig had been placed, and they must needs pull the sucking-pig out, and take it in their hands, and feel and touch it all over; and as both wanted to hold it at the same time, it came to pass that they let it fall into the water, and the sucking-pig drifted away with the stream — and here was a terrible event!

Ib jumped ashore, and ran a little distance along the bank, and Christine sprang after him.

"Take me with you!" she cried.

And in a few minutes they were deep in the thicket, and could no longer see either the boat or the bank. They ran on a little farther, and then Christine fell down on the ground and began to cry; but Ib picked her up.

"Follow me!" he cried. "Yonder lies the house."

But the house was not yonder. They wandered on and on, over the dry, rustling, last year's leaves, and over fallen branches that crackled beneath their feet. Soon they heard a loud piercing scream. They stood still and listened, and presently the scream of an eagle sounded through the wood It was an ugly scream, and they were frightened at it; but before them, in the thick wood, the most beautiful blueberries grew in wonderful profusion. They were so inviting that the children could not do otherwise than stop; and they lingered for some time, eating the blueberries till they had quite blue mouths and blue cheeks. Now again they heard the cry they had heard before.

"We shall get into trouble about the pig," said Christine.

"Come, let us go to our house," said Ib; "it is here in the wood."

And they went forward. They presently came to a wood, but it did not lead them home; and darkness came on, and they were afraid. The wonderful stillness that reigned around was interrupted now and then by the shrill cries of the great horrid owl and of the birds that were strange to them. At last they both lost themselves in a thicket. Christine cried, and Ib cried too; and after they had bemoaned themselves for a time, they threw themselves down on the dry leaves, and went fast asleep.

The sun was high in the heavens when the two children awoke. They were cold; but in the neighbourhood of this resting-place, on the hill, the sun shone through the trees, and there they thought they would warm themselves; and from there Ib fancied they would be able to see his parents' house. But they were far away from the house in question, in quite another part of the forest. They clambered to the top of the rising ground, and found themselves on the summit of a slope running down to the margin of a transparent lake. They could see fish in great numbers in the pure water illumined by the sun's rays. This spectacle was quite a sudden surprise for them; but close beside them grew a nut bush covered with the finest nuts; and now they picked the nuts, and cracked them, and ate the delicate young kernels, which had only just become perfect. But there was another surprise and another fright in store for them. Out of the thicket stepped a tall old woman: her face was quite brown, and her hair was deep black and shining. The whites of her eyes gleamed like a negro's; on her back she carried a bundle, and in her hand she bore a knotted stick. She was a gipsy. The children did not at once understand what she said. She brought three nuts out of her pocket, and told them that in these nuts the most beautiful, the loveliest things were hidden, for they were wishing-nuts.

Ib looked at her, and she seemed so friendly, that he plucked up courage and asked her if she would give him the nuts; and the woman gave them to him, and gathered some more for herself, a whole pocketfull, from the nut bush.

And Ib and Christine looked at the wishing-nuts with great eyes.

"Is there a carriage with a pair of horses in this nut?" he asked.

"Yes, there's a golden carriage with two horses," answered the woman.

"Then give me the nut," said little Christine.

And Ib gave it to her, and the strange woman tied it in her pocket-handkerchief for her.

"Is there in this nut a pretty little neckerchief, like the one Christine wears round her neck?" inquired Ib.

IB AND CHRISTINE MEET THE GIPSY.

"There are ten neckerchiefs in it," answered the woman. "There are beautiful dresses in it, and stockings, and a hat with a veil."

"Then I will have that one too," cried little Christine.

And Ib gave her the second nut also. The third was a little black thing.

"That one you can keep," said Christine; "and it is a pretty one too."

"What is in it?" inquired Ib.

"The best of all things for you," replied the gipsy woman.

And Ib held the nut very tight. The woman promised to lead the children into the right path, so that they might find their way home; and now they went forward, certainly in quite a different direction from the path they should have followed. But that is no reason why we should suspect the gipsy woman of wanting to steal the children. In the wild wood-path they met the forest bailiff, who knew Ib; and by his help, Ib and Christine both arrived at home, where their friends had been very anxious about them. They were pardoned and forgiven, although they had indeed both deserved "to get into trouble;" firstly, because they had let the sucking-pig fall into the water, and secondly, because they had run away.

Christine was taken back to her father on the heath, and Ib remained in the farm-house on the margin of the wood by the great ridge. The first thing he did in the evening was to bring forth out of his pocket the little black nut, in which "the best thing of all" was said to be enclosed. He placed it carefully in the crack of the door, and then shut the door so as to break the nut; but there was not much kernel in it. The nut looked as if it were filled with tobacco or black rich earth; it was what we call hollow, or worm-eaten.

"Yes, that's exactly what I thought," said Ib. "How could the very best thing be contained in this little nut? And Christine will get just as little out of her two nuts, and will have neither fine clothes nor the golden carriage."

And winter came on, and the new year began; indeed, several years went by.

Ib was at last to be confirmed; and for this reason he went during a whole winter to the clergyman, far away in the nearest village, to prepare. About this time the boatman one day visited Ib's parents, and told them that Christine was now going into service, and that she had been really fortunate in getting a remarkably good place, and falling into worthy hands.

"Only think!" he said; "she is going to the rich innkeeper's, in the inn at Herning, far towards the west, many miles from here. She is to assist the hostess in keeping the house; and afterwards, if she takes to it well, and stays to be confirmed there, the people are going to adopt her as their own daughter."

And Ib and Christine took leave of one another. People called them "the betrothed;" and at parting, the girl showed Ib that she had still the two nuts which he had given her long ago, during their wanderings in the forest; and she told him, moreover, that in a drawer she had carefully kept the little wooden shoes which he had carved as a present for her in their childish days. And thereupon they parted.

Ib was confirmed. But he remained in his mother's house, for he had become a clever maker of wooden shoes, and in summer he looked after the field. He did it all alone, for his mother kept no farm-servant, and his father had died long ago.

Only seldom he got news of Christine from some passing postillion or eel-fisher. But she was well off at the rich innkeeper's; and after she had been confirmed, she wrote a letter to her father, and sent a kind message to Ib and his mother; and in the letter there was mention made of certain linen garments and a fine new gown, which Christine had received as a present from her employers. This was certainly good news.

Next spring, there was a knock one day at the door of our Ib's old mother, and behold, the boatman and Christine stepped into the room. She had come on a visit to spend a day : a carriage had to come from the Herning Inn to the next village, and she had taken the opportunity to see her friends once again. She looked as handsome as a real lady, and she had a pretty gown on, which had been well sewn, and made expressly for her. There she stood, in grand array, and Ib was in his working clothes. He could not utter a word : he certainly seized her hand, and held it fast in his own, and was heartily glad ; but he could not get his tongue to obey him. Christine was not embarrassed, however, for she went on talking and talking, and, moreover, kissed Ib on his mouth in the heartiest manner.

"Did you know me again directly, Ib ?" she asked ; but even afterwards, when they were left quite by themselves, and he stood there still holding her hand in his, he could only say,

"You look quite like a real lady, and I am so uncouth. How often I have thought of you, Christine, and of the old times ! "

And arm in arm they sauntered up the great ridge, and looked across the stream towards the heath, towards the great hills overgrown with bloom. It was perfectly silent ; but by the time they parted it had grown quite clear to him that Christine must be his wife. Had they not, even in their childhood, been called the betrothed pair ? To him they seemed to be really engaged to each other, though neither of them had spoken a word on the subject. Only for a few more hours could they remain together, for Christine was obliged to go back into the next village, from whence the carriage was to start early next morning for Herning. Her father and Ib escorted her as far as the village. It was a fair moonlight evening, and when they reached their destination, and Ib still held Christine's hand in his own, he could not make up his mind to let her go. His eyes brightened, but still the words came halting over his lips. Yet they came from the depths of his heart, when he said,

" If you have not become too grand, Christine, and if you can make up your mind to live with me in my mother's house as my wife, we must become a wedded pair some day ; but we can wait awhile yet."

" Yes, let us wait for a time, Ib," she replied ; and he kissed her lips. " I confide in you, Ib," said Christine ; " and I think that I love you— but I will sleep upon it."

And with that they parted. And on the way home Ib told the boatman that he and Christine were as good as betrothed ; and the boatman declared he had always expected it would turn out so ; and he went home with Ib, and remained that night in the young man's house ; but nothing further was said of the betrothal.

A year passed by, in the course of which two letters were exchanged between Ib and Christine. The signature was prefaced by the words, " Faithful till death ! " One day the boatman came in to Ib, and brought him a greeting from Christine. What he had further to say was brought out in somewhat hesitating fashion, but it was to the effect that Christine was almost more than prosperous, for she was a pretty girl, courted and loved. The son of the host had been home on a visit; he was employed in the office of some great institution in Copenhagen; and he was very much pleased with Christine, and she had taken a fancy to him: his parents were ready to give their consent, but Christine was very anxious to retain Ib's good opinion; "and so she had thought of refusing this great piece of good fortune," said the boatman.

At first Ib said not a word, but he became as white as the wall, and slightly shook his head. Then he said slowly,

"Christine must not refuse this advantageous offer."

"Then do you write a few words to her," said the boatman.

And Ib sat down to write; but he could not manage it well: the words would not come as he wished them; and first he altered, and then he tore up the page; but the next morning a letter lay ready to be sent to Christine, and it contained the following words:

"I have read the letter you have sent to your father, and gather from it that you are prospering in all things, and that there is a prospect of higher fortune for you. Ask your heart, Christine, and ponder well the fate that awaits you, if you take me for your husband; what I possess is but little. Do not think of me, or my position, but think of your own welfare. You are bound to me by no promise, and if in your heart you have given me one, I release you from it. May all treasures of happiness be poured out upon you, Christine. Heaven will console me in its own good time.   "Ever your sincere friend,   "Ib."

And the letter was dispatched, and Christine duly received it.

In the course of that November her banns were published in the church on the heath, and in Copenhagen, where her bridegroom lived; and to Copenhagen she proceeded, under the protection of her future mother-in-law, because the bridegroom could not undertake the journey into Jutland on account of his various occupations. On the journey, Christine met her father in a certain village, and here the two took leave of one another. A few words were mentioned concerning this fact, but Ib made no remark upon it: his mother said he had grown very silent of late; indeed, he had become very pensive, and thus the three nuts came into his mind which the gipsy woman had given him long ago, and of which he had given two to Christine. Yes, it seemed right—they were wishing-nuts, and in one of them lay a golden carriage with two horses, and in the other very elegant clothes; all those luxuries would now be Christine's in the capital. Her part had thus come true. And to him, Ib, the nut had offered only black earth. The gipsy woman had said this was "the best of all for him." Yes, it was right—that also was coming true. The black earth was the best for him. Now he understood clearly what had been the woman's meaning. In the black earth, in the dark grave, would be the best happiness for him.

And once again years passed by, not very many, but they seemed long years to Ib. The old innkeeper and his wife died, and the whole of their property, many thousands of dollars, came to the son. Yes, now Christine could have the golden carriage and plenty of fine clothes.

During the two long years that followed no letter came from Christine; and when her father at length received one from her, it was not written in prosperity, by any means. Poor Christine! neither she nor her husband had understood how to keep the money together, and there seemed to be no blessing with it, because they had not sought it.

And again the weather bloomed and faded. The winter had swept for many years across the heath, and over the ridge beneath which Ib dwelt, sheltered from the rough winds. The spring sun shone bright, and Ib guided the plough across his field, when one day it glided over what appeared to be a fire stone. Something like a great black ship came out of the ground, and when Ib took it up it proved to be a piece of metal; and the place from which the plough had cut the stone gleamed brightly with ore. It was a great golden armlet of ancient workmanship that he had found. He had disturbed a " Hun's Grave," and discovered the costly treasure buried in it. Ib showed what he had found to the clergyman, who explained its value to him, and then he betook himself to the local judges, who reported the discovery to the keeper of the museum, and recommended Ib to deliver up the treasure in person.

" You have found in the earth the best thing you could find," said the judge.

" The best thing! " thought Ib. " The very best thing for me, and found in the earth! Well, if that is the best, the gipsy woman was correct in what she prophesied to me."

So Ib travelled with the ferry-boat from Aarhus to Copenhagen. To him, who had but once or twice passed beyond the river that rolled by his home, this seemed like a voyage across the ocean. And he arrived in Copenhagen.

The value of the gold he had found was paid over to him; it was a large sum—six hundred dollars. And Ib of the heath wandered about in the great capital.

On the day on which he had settled to go back with the captain, Ib lost his way in the streets, and took quite a different direction from the one he intended to follow. He had wandered into the suburb of Christianshaven, into a poor little street. Not a human being was to be seen. At last a very little girl came out of one of the wretched houses. Ib inquired of the little one the way to the street which he wanted; but she looked shyly at him, and began to cry bitterly. He asked her what ailed her, but could not understand what she said in reply. But as they went along the street together, they passed beneath the light of a lamp; and when the light fell on the girl's face, he felt a strange and sharp emotion, for Christine stood bodily before him, just as he remembered her from the days of his childhood.

And he went with the little maiden into the wretched house, and ascended the narrow, crazy staircase, which led to a little attic chamber in the roof. The air in this chamber was heavy and almost suffocating: no light was burning; but there was heavy sighing and moaning in one corner.   Ib struck a light with the help of a match.   It was the mother of the child who lay sighing on the miserable bed.

"Can I be of any service to you?" asked Ib.   "This little girl has brought me up here, but I am a stranger in this city.   Are there no neighbours or friends whom I could call to you?"   And he raised the sick woman's head, and smoothed her pillow.

It was Christine of the heath!

For years her name had not been mentioned yonder, for the mention of her would have disturbed Ib's peace of mind, and rumour had told nothing good concerning her.   The wealth which her husband had in-

LITTLE CHRISTINE.

herited from his parents had made him proud and arrogant.   He had given up his certain appointment, had travelled for half a year in foreign lands, and on his return had incurred debts, and yet lived in an expensive fashion.   His carriage had bent over more and more, so to speak, until at last it turned over completely.   The many merry companions and table-friends he had entertained declared it served him right, for he had kept house like a madman; and one morning his corpse was found in the canal.

The icy hand of death was already on Christine.   Her youngest child, only a few weeks old, expected in prosperity and born in misery, was already in its grave, and it had come to this with Christine herself, that she lay sick to death and forsaken, in a miserable room, amid a poverty that she might well have borne in her childish days, but which now oppressed her painfully, since she had been accustomed to better things. It was her eldest child, also a little Christine, that here suffered hunger and poverty with her, and whom Ib had now brought home.

" I am unhappy at the thought of dying and leaving the poor child here alone," she said. " Ah, what is to become of the poor thing ? " And not a word more could she utter.

And Ib brought out another match, and lighted up a piece of candle he found in the room, and the flame illumined the wretched dwelling. And Ib looked at the little girl, and thought how Christine had looked when she was young; and he felt that for her sake he would be fond of this child, which was as yet a stranger to him. The dying woman gazed at him, and her eyes opened wider and wider—did she recognize him ? He never knew, for no further word passed over her lips.

And it was in the forest by the river Gudenau, in the region of the heath. The air was thick and dark, and there were no blossoms on the heath plant; but the autumn tempests whirled the yellow leaves from the wood into the stream, and out over the heath towards the hut of the boatman, in which strangers now dwelt; but beneath the ridge, safe beneath the protection of the high trees, stood the little farm, trimly whitewashed and painted, and within it the turf blazed up cheerily in the chimney; for within was sunlight, the beaming sunlight of a child's two eyes; and the tones of the spring birds sounded in the words that came from the child's rosy lips: she sat on Ib's knee, and Ib was to her both father and mother, for her own parents were dead, and had vanished from her as a dream vanishes alike from children and grown men. Ib sat in the pretty neat house, for he was a prosperous man, while the mother of the little girl rested in the churchyard at Copenhagen, where she had died in poverty.

Ib had money, and was said to have provided for the future. He had won gold out of the black earth, and he had a Christine for his own, after all.

THE SNOW MAN.

" IT 's so wonderfully cold that my whole body crackles !" said the Snow Man. " This is a kind of wind that can blow life into one; and how the gleaming one up yonder is staring at me." He meant the sun, which was just about to set. " It shall not make *me* wink — I shall manage to keep the pieces."

He had two triangular pieces of tile in his head instead of eyes. His mouth was made of an old rake, and consequently was furnished with teeth.

He had been born amid the joyous shouts of the boys, and welcomed by the sound of sledge bells and the slashing of whips.

The sun went down, and the full moon rose, round, large, clear, and beautiful in the blue air.

"There it comes again from the other side," said the Snow Man. He intended to say the sun is showing himself again. "Ah! I have cured him of staring. Now let him hang up there and shine, that I may see myself. If I only knew how I could manage to move from this place, I should like so much to move. If I could, I would slide along yonder on the ice, just as I see the boys slide; but I don't understand it; I don't know how to run."

"Away! away!" barked the old Yard Dog. He was quite hoarse, and could not pronounce the genuine "bow, wow." He had got the hoarseness from the time when who as an indoor dog, and lay by the fire. "The sun will teach you to run! I saw that last winter in your predecessor, and before that in *his* predecessor. Away! away!—and away they all go."

"I don't understand you, comrade," said the Snow Man. "That thing up yonder is to teach me to run?" He meant the moon. "Yes, it was running itself, when I saw it a little while ago, and now it comes creeping from the other side."

"You know nothing at all," retorted the Yard Dog. "But then you've only just been patched up. What you see yonder is the moon, and the one that went before was the sun. It will come again to-morrow, and will teach you to run down into the ditch by the wall. We shall soon have a change of weather; I can feel that in my left hind leg, for it pricks and pains me: the weather is going to change."

"I don't understand him," said the Snow Man; "but I have a feeling that he's talking about something disagreeable. The one who stared so just now, and whom he called the sun, is not my friend. I can feel that."

"Away! away!" barked the Yard Dog; and he turned round three times, and then crept into his kennel to sleep.

The weather really changed. Towards morning, a thick damp fog lay over the whole region; later there came a wind, an icy wind. The cold seemed quite to seize upon one; but when the sun rose, what splendour! Trees and bushes were covered with hoar frost, and looked like a complete forest of coral, and every twig seemed covered with gleaming white buds. The many delicate ramifications, concealed in summer by the wreath of leaves, now made their appearance: it seemed like a lace-work, gleaming white. A snowy radiance sprang from every twig. The birch waved in the wind—it had life, like the rest of the trees in summer. It was wonderfully beautiful. And when the sun shone, how it all gleamed and sparkled, as if diamond dust had been strewn everywhere, and big diamonds had been dropped on the snowy carpet of the earth! or one could imagine that countless little lights were gleaming, whiter than even the snow itself.

"That is wonderfully beautiful," said a young girl, who came with a young man into the garden. They both stood still near the Snow Man, and contemplated the glittering trees. "Summer cannot show a more beautiful sight," said she; and her eyes sparkled.

"And we can't have such a fellow as this in summer-time," replied the young man, and he pointed to the Snow Man. "He is capital."

The girl laughed, nodded at the Snow Man, and then danced away over the snow with her friend—over the snow that cracked and crackled under her tread as if she were walking on starch.

"Who were those two?" the Snow Man inquired of the Yard Dog. "You've been longer in the yard than I. Do you know them?"

"Of course I know them," replied the Yard Dog. "She has stroked me, and he has thrown me a meat bone. I don't bite those two."

"But what are they?" asked the Snow Man.

"Lovers!" replied the Yard Dog. "They will go to live in the same kennel, and gnaw at the same bone. Away! away!"

THE SNOW MAN AND THE YARD DOG.

"Are they the same kind of beings as you and I?" asked the Snow Man.

"Why, they belong to the master," retorted the Yard Dog. "People certainly know very little who were only born yesterday. I can see that in you. I have age and information. I know every one here in the house, and I know a time when I did not lie out here in the cold, fastened to a chain. Away! away!"

"The cold is charming," said the Snow Man. "Tell me, tell me.—But you must not clank with your chain, for it jars within me when you do that."

"Away! away!" barked the Yard Dog. "They told me I was a pretty little fellow: then I used to lie in a chair covered with velvet, up in master's house, and sit in the lap of the mistress of all. They used to kiss my nose, and wipe my paws with an embroidered handkerchief. I was called 'Ami—dear Ami—sweet Ami.' But afterwards I grew too big for them, and they gave me away to the housekeeper. So I came to live in the basement storey. You can look into that from where you are standing, and you can see into the room where I was master; for I was master at the housekeeper's. It was certainly a smaller place than up stairs, but I was more comfortable, and was not continually taken hold of and pulled about by children as I had been. I received just as good food as ever, and even better. I had my own cushion, and there was a stove, the finest thing in the world at this season. I went under the stove, and could lie down quite beneath it. Ah! I still dream of that stove. Away! away!"

"Does a stove look so beautiful?" asked the Snow Man. "Is it at all like me?"

"It's just the reverse of you. It's as black as a crow, and has a long neck and a brazen drum. It eats firewood, so that the fire spurts out of its mouth. One must keep at its side, or under it, and there one is very comfortable. You can see it through the window from where you stand."

And the Snow Man looked and saw a bright polished thing with a brazen drum, and the fire gleamed from the lower part of it. The Snow Man felt quite strangely: an odd emotion came over him, he knew not what it meant, and could not account for it; but all people who are not snow men know the feeling.

"And why did you leave her?" asked the Snow Man, for it seemed to him that the stove must be of the female sex. "How could you quit such a comfortable place?"

"I was obliged," replied the Yard Dog. "They turned me out of doors, and chained me up here. I had bitten the youngest young master in the leg, because he kicked away the bone I was gnawing. 'Bone for bone,' I thought. They took that very much amiss, and from that time I have been fastened to a chain and have lost my voice. Don't you hear how hoarse I am? Away! away! I can't talk any more like other dogs. Away! away! that was the end of the affair."

But the Snow Man was no longer listening to him. He was looking in at the housekeeper's basement lodging, into the room where the stove stood on its four iron legs, just the same size as the Snow Man himself.

"What a strange crackling within me!" he said. "Shall I ever get in there? It is an innocent wish, and our innocent wishes are certain to be fulfilled. I must go in there and lean against her, even if I have to break through the window."

"You will never get in there," said the Yard Dog; "and if you approach the stove you'll melt away—away!"

"I am as good as gone," replied the Snow Man. "I think I am breaking up."

The whole day the Snow Man stood looking in through the window. In the twilight hour the room became still more inviting: from the stove came a mild gleam, not like the sun nor like the moon; no, it was only as the stove can glow when he has something to eat. When the room door opened, the flame started out of his mouth; this was a habit the stove had. The flame fell distinctly on the white face of the Snow Man, and gleamed red upon his bosom.

"I can endure it no longer," said he; "how beautiful it looks when it stretches out its tongue!"

The night was long; but it did not appear long to the Snow Man, who stood there lost in his own charming reflections, crackling with the cold.

In the morning the window-panes of the basement lodging were covered with ice. They bore the most beautiful ice-flowers that any snow man could desire; but they concealed the stove. The window-panes would not thaw; he could not see the stove, which he pictured to himself as a lovely female being. It crackled and whistled in him and around him; it was just the kind of frosty weather a snow man must thoroughly enjoy. But he did not enjoy it; and, indeed, how could he enjoy himself when he was stove-sick?

"That's a terrible disease for a Snow Man," said the Yard Dog. "I have suffered from it myself, but I got over it. Away! away!" he barked; and he added, "the weather is going to change."

And the weather did change; it began to thaw.

The warmth increased, and the Snow Man decreased. He said nothing and made no complaint—and that's an infallible sign.

One morning he broke down. And, behold, where he had stood, something like a broomstick remained sticking up out of the ground. It was the pole round which the boys had built him up.

"Ah! now I can understand why he had such an intense longing," said the Yard Dog. "Why, there's a shovel for cleaning out the stove fastened to the pole. The Snow Man had a stove-rake in his body, and that's what moved within him. Now he has got over that too. Away! away!"

And soon they had got over the winter.

"Away! away!" barked the hoarse Yard Dog; but the girls in the house sang:

> "Green thyme! from your house come out;
> Willow, your woolly fingers stretch out;
> Lark and cuckoo cheerfully sing,
> For in February is coming the spring.
> And with the cuckoo I'll sing too,
> Come thou, dear sun, come out, cuckoo!"

And nobody thought any more of the Snow Man.

THE THORNY ROAD OF HONOUR.

An old story yet lives of the 'Thorny Road of Honour," of a marksman, who indeed attained to rank and office, but only after a lifelong and weary strife against difficulties. Who has not, in reading this story, thought of his own strife, and of his own numerous "difficulties"? The story is very closely akin to reality; but still it has its harmonious explanation here on earth, while reality often points beyond the confines of life to the regions of eternity. The history of the world is like a magic lantern that displays to us, in light pictures upon the dark ground of the present, how the benefactors of mankind, the martyrs of genius, wandered along the thorny road of honour.

From all periods, and from every country, these shining pictures display themselves to us: each only appears for a few moments, but each represents a whole life, sometimes a whole age, with its conflicts and victories. Let us contemplate here and there one of the company of martyrs—the company which will receive new members until the world itself shall pass away.

We look down upon a crowded amphitheatre. Out of the " Clouds " of Aristophanes, satire and humour are pouring down in streams upon the audience; on the stage Socrates, the most remarkable man in Athens, he who had been the shield and defence of the people against the thirty tyrants, is held up mentally and bodily to ridicule—Socrates, who saved Alcibiades and Xenophon in the turmoil of battle, and whose genius soared far above the gods of the ancients. He himself is present; he has risen from the spectator's bench, and has stepped forward, that the laughing Athenians may well appreciate the likeness between himself and the caricature on the stage: there he stands before them, towering high above them all.

Thou juicy, green, poisonous hemlock, throw thy shadow over Athens —not thou, olive tree of fame!

Seven cities contended for the honour of giving birth to Homer— that is to say, they contended after his death! Let us look at him as he was in his life-time. He wanders on foot through the cities, and recites his verses for a livelihood; the thought for the morrow turns his hair grey! He, the great seer, is blind, and painfully pursues his way—the sharp thorn tears the mantle of the king of poets. His song yet lives, and through that alone live all the heroes and gods of antiquity.

One picture after another springs up from the east, from the west, far removed from each other in time and place, and yet each one forming a portion of the thorny road of honour, on which the thistle indeed displays a flower, but only to adorn the grave.

The camels pass along under the palm trees; they are richly laden with indigo and other treasures of price, sent by the ruler of the land to him whose songs are the delight of the people, the fame of the country: he whom envy and falsehood have driven into exile has been found, and the caravan approaches the little town in which he has taken refuge. A poor corpse is carried out of the town gate, and the funeral procession causes the caravan to halt. The dead man is he whom they have been sent to seek—Firdusi—who has wandered the thorny road of honour even to the end.

The African, with blunt features, thick lips, and woolly hair, sits on the marble steps of the palace in the capital of Portugal, and begs: he is the submissive slave of Camoens, and but for him, and for the copper coins thrown to him by the passers by, his master, the poet of the "Lusiad," would die of hunger. Now, a costly monument marks the grave of Camoens.

There is a new picture.

Behind the iron grating a man appears, pale as death, with long unkempt beard.

THE KING OF POETS.

"I have made a discovery," he says, "the greatest that has been made for centuries; and they have kept me locked up here for more than twenty years!"

Who is the man?

"A madman," replies the keeper of the madhouse. "What whimsical ideas these lunatics have! He imagines that one can propel things by means of steam."

It is Solomon de Cares, the discoverer of the power of steam, whose theory, expressed in dark words, is not understood by Richelieu — and he dies in the madhouse!

Here stands Columbus, whom the street boys used once to follow and jeer, because he wanted to discover a new world—and he *has* discovered it. Shouts of joy greet him from the breasts of all, and the clash of bells sounds to celebrate his triumphant return; but the clash of the bells of envy soon drowns the others. The discoverer of a world, he who lifted the American gold land from the sea, and gave it to his King—he is rewarded with iron chains. He wishes that these chains may be placed in his coffin, for they witness to the world of the way in which a man's contemporaries reward good service.

One picture after another comes crowding on; the thorny path of honour and of fame is over-filled.

Here in dark night sits the man who measured the mountains in the moon; he who forced his way out into the endless space, among stars and planets; he, the mighty man who understood the spirit of nature, and felt the earth moving beneath his feet — Galileo. Blind and deaf he sits — an old man thrust through with the spear of suffering, and amid the torments of neglect, scarcely able to lift his foot—that foot with which, in the anguish of his soul, when men denied the truth, he stamped upon the ground with the exclamation, "*Yet* it moves!"

Here stands a woman of childlike mind, yet full of faith and inspiration; she carries the banner in front of the combating army, and brings victory and salvation to her fatherland. The sound of shouting arises, and the pile flames up: they are burning the witch, Joan of Arc. Yes, and a future century jeers at the White Lily. Voltaire, the satyr of human intellect, writes "*La Pucelle.*"

At the *Thing* or Assembly at Viborg, the Danish nobles burn the laws of the King—they flame up high, illuminating the period and the law-giver, and throw a glory into the dark prison tower, where an old man is growing grey and bent. With his finger he marks out a groove in the stone table. It is the popular King who sits there, once the ruler of three kingdoms, the friend of the citizen and the peasant: it is Christian the Second. Enemies wrote his history. Let us remember his improvements of seven and twenty years, if we cannot forget his crime.

A ship sails away, quitting the Danish shores; a man leans against the mast, casting a last glance towards the Island Hueen. It is Tycho Brahé. He raised the name of Denmark to the stars, and was rewarded with injury, loss, and sorrow. He is going to a strange country.

"The vault of heaven is above me everywhere," he says, "and what do I want more?"

And away sails the famous Dane, the astronomer, to live honoured and free in a strange land.

"Ay, free, if only from the unbearable sufferings of the body!" comes in a sigh through time, and strikes upon our ear. What a picture! Griffenfeldt, a Danish Prometheus, bound to the rocky island of Munkholm.

We are in America, on the margin of one of the largest rivers; an innumerable crowd has gathered, for it is said that a ship is to sail against wind and weather, bidding defiance to the elements; the man who thinks he can solve the problem is named Robert Fulton. The ship begins its passage, but suddenly it stops. The crowd begins to laugh and whistle and hiss—the very father of the man whistles with the rest. "Conceit! Foolery!" is the cry. "It has happened just as he deserved: put the crack-brain under lock and key!"

Then suddenly a little nail breaks, which had stopped the machine for a few moments; and now the wheels turn again, the floats break the force of the waters, and the ship continues its course—and the beam of the steam engine shortens the distance between far lands from hours into minutes.

O human race, canst thou grasp the happiness of such a minute of consciousness, this penetration of the soul by its mission, the moment in which all dejection, and every wound—even those caused by own fault—is changed into health and strength and clearness—when discord is converted to harmony—the minute in which men seem to recognize the manifestation of the heavenly grace in one man, and feel how this one imparts it to all?

Thus the thorny path of honour shows itself as a glory, surrounding the earth with its beams: thrice happy he who is chosen to be a wanderer there, and, without merit of his own, to be placed between the builder of the bridge and the earth, between Providence and the human race!

On mighty wings the spirit of history floats through the ages, and shows—giving courage and comfort, and awakening gentle thoughts—on the dark nightly background, but in gleaming pictures, the thorny path of honour; which does not, like a fairy tale, end in brilliancy and joy here on earth, but stretches out beyond all time, even into eternity!

THE CHILD IN THE GRAVE.

THERE was mourning in the house, sorrow in every heart. The youngest child, a boy four years old, the joy and hope of his parents, had died. There still remained to them two daughters, the elder of whom was about to be confirmed—good, charming girls both; but the child that one has lost always seems the dearest; and here it was the youngest, and a son. It was a heavy trial. The sisters mourned as young hearts can, and were especially moved at the sight of their parents' sorrow. The father was bowed down, and the mother completely struck down by the great grief. Day and night she had been busy about the sick child, and had tended, lifted, and carried it; she had felt how it was a part of herself. She could not realize that the child was dead, and that it must be laid in a coffin and sleep in the ground. She thought God *could not* take this child from her; and when it was so, nevertheless, and there could be no more doubt on the subject, she said in her feverish pain,

"God did not know it. He has heartless servants here on earth, who do according to their own liking, and hear not the prayers of a mother."

In her grief she fell away from God, and then there came dark thoughts, thoughts of death, of everlasting death—that man was but dust in the dust, and that with this life all was ended. But these thoughts gave her no stay, nothing on which she could take hold; and she sank into the fathomless abyss of despair.

In her heaviest hours she could weep no more, and she thought not of the young daughters who were still left to her. The tears of her husband fell upon her forehead, but she did not look at him. Her thoughts were with the dead child; her whole thought and being were fixed upon it, to call back every remembrance of the little one, every innocent childish word it had uttered.

The day of the funeral came. For nights before the mother had not slept; but in the morning twilight she now slept, overcome by weariness; and in the meantime the coffin was carried into a distant room, and there nailed down, that she might not hear the blows of the hammer.

When she awoke, and wanted to see her child, the husband said,

"We have nailed down the coffin. It was necessary to do so."

"When God is hard towards me, how should men be better?" she said, with sobs and groans.

The coffin was carried to the grave. The disconsolate mother sat with her young daughters. She looked at her daughters, and yet did not see them, for her thoughts were no longer busy at the domestic hearth. She gave herself up to her grief, and grief tossed her to and fro as the sea tosses a ship without compass or rudder. So the day of the funeral passed away, and similar days followed, of dark, wearying pain. With moist eyes and mournful glances, the sorrowing daughters and the afflicted husband looked upon her who would not hear their words of comfort; and, indeed, what words of comfort could they speak to her, when they themselves were heavily bowed down?

It seemed as though she knew sleep no more; and yet he would now have been her best friend, who would have strengthened her body, and poured peace into her soul. They persuaded her to seek her couch, and she lay still there, like one who slept. One night her husband was listening, as he often did, to her breathing, and fully believed that she had now found rest and relief. He folded his arms and prayed, and soon sank into a deep healthy sleep; and thus he did not notice that his wife arose, threw on her clothes, and silently glided from the house, to go where her thoughts always lingered—to the grave which held her child. She stepped through the garden of the house, and over the fields, where a path led to the churchyard. No one saw her on her walk—she had seen nobody, for her eyes were fixed upon the one goal of her journey.

It was a lovely starlight night; the air was still mild; it was in the beginning of September. She entered the churchyard, and stood by the little grave, which looked like a great nosegay of fragrant flowers. She

THE MOTHER AT THE GRAVE.

sat down, and bowed her head low over the grave, as if she could have seen her child through the intervening earth, her little boy, whose smile rose so vividly before her—the gentle expression of whose eyes, even on the sick bed, she could never forget. How eloquent had that glance been, when she had bent over him and seized his delicate hand, which he had no longer strength to raise! As she had sat by his crib, so she now sat by his grave, but here her tears had free course, and fell thick upon the grave.

"Thou wouldst gladly go down and be with thy child," said a voice quite close to her, a voice that sounded so clear and deep, it went straight to her heart.

She looked up, and near her stood a man wrapped in a black cloak, with a hood drawn closely down over his face. But she glanced keenly up, and saw his face under his hood. It was stern, but yet awakened confidence, and his eyes beamed with the radiance of youth.

"Down to my child!" she repeated; and a despairing supplication spoke out of her words.

"Darest thou follow me?" asked the form. "I am Death."

And she bowed her head in acquiescence. Then suddenly it seemed as though all the stars were shining with the radiance of the full moon;

she saw the varied colours of the flowers on the grave, and the covering of earth was gradually withdrawn like a floating drapery ; and she sank down, and the apparition covered her with a black cloak ; night closed around her, the night of death, and she sank deeper than the sexton's spade can penetrate, and the churchyard was as a roof over her head.

A corner of the cloak was removed, and she stood in a great hall which spread wide and pleasantly around. It was twilight. But in a moment her child appeared, and was pressed to her heart, smiling at her in greater beauty than he had ever possessed. She uttered a cry, but it was inaudible. A glorious swelling strain of music sounded in the distance, and then near to her, and then again in the distance : never had such tones fallen on her ear ; they came from beyond the great dark curtain which separated the hall from the great land of eternity beyond.

"My sweet darling mother," she heard her child say.

It was the well-known, much-loved voice, and kiss followed kiss in boundless felicity ; and the child pointed to the dark curtain.

" It is not so beautiful on earth. Do you see, mother — do you see them all ? Oh, that is happiness !"

But the mother saw nothing which the child pointed out—nothing but the dark night. She looked with earthly eyes, and could not see as the child saw, which God had called to Himself. She could hear the sounds of the music, but she heard not the word—*the Word* in which she was to believe.

" Now I can fly, mother — I can fly with all the other happy children into the presence of the Almighty. I would fain fly ; but, if you weep as you are weeping now, I might be lost to you—and yet I would go so gladly. May I not fly ? And you will come to me soon — will you not, dear mother ?"

" Oh, stay ! stay !" entreated the mother. " Only one moment more — only once more I should wish to look at thee, and kiss thee, and press thee in my arms."

And she kissed and fondled the child. Then her name was called from above — called in a plaintive voice. What might this mean ?

"Hearest thou ?" asked the child. " It is my father who calls thee."

And in a few moments deep sighs were heard, as of weeping children.

" They are my sisters," said the child. " Mother, you surely have not forgotten them ? "

And then she remembered those she had left behind. A great terror came upon her. She looked out into the night, and above her dim forms were flitting past. She seemed to recognize a few more of these. They floated through the Hall of Death towards the dark curtain, and there they vanished. Would her husband and her daughter thus flit past ? No, their sighs and lamentations still sounded from above :—and she had been nearly forgetting them for the sake of him who was dead !

" Mother, now the bells of heaven are ringing," said the child. " Mother, now the sun is going to rise."

And an overpowering light streamed in upon her. The child had vanished, and she was borne upwards. It became cold round about her, and she lifted up her head, and saw that she was lying in the church-yard, on the grave of her child.

But the Lord had been a stay unto her feet, in a dream, and a light to her spirit; and she bowed her knees and prayed for forgiveness that she had wished to keep back a soul from its immortal flight, and that she had forgotten her duties towards the living who were left to her.

And when she had spoken those words, it was as if her heart were lightened. Then the sun burst forth, and over her head a little bird sang out, and the church bells sounded for early service. Everything was holy around her, and her heart was chastened. She acknowledged the goodness of God, she acknowledged the duties she had to perform, and eagerly she went home. She bent over her husband, who still slept; her warm devoted kiss awakened him, and heart-felt words of love came from the lips of both. And she was gentle and strong, as a wife can be; and from her came the consoling words,

> " God's will is always the best."

Then her husband asked her,
" From whence hast thou all at once derived this strength — this feeling of consolation ? "

And she kissed him, and kissed her children, and said,
' They came from God, through the child in the grave."

IN THE UTTERMOST PARTS OF THE SEA.

GREAT ships had been sent up towards the North Pole, to explore the most distant coasts, and to try how far men might penetrate up yonder. For more than a year they had already been pushing their way among ice, and snow, and mist, and their crews had endured many hard-ships; and now the winter was come, and the sun had entirely disap-peared from those regions. For many many weeks there would now be a long night. All around, as far as the eye could reach, was a single field of ice; the ships had been made fast to it, and the snow had piled itself up in great masses, and of these huts had been built in the form of bee-hives, some of them spacious as the old " Hun's Graves," others only containing room enough to hold two or four men. But it was not dark, for the Northern Lights flamed red and blue, like a great continual firework; and the snow glistened and gleamed, so that the night here was one long, flaming, twilight hour. When the gleam was brightest, the natives came in crowds, wonderful to behold in their rough, hairy, fur dresses; and they rode in sledges formed of blocks of ice, and brought with them furs and peltry in great bundles, so that the snow houses were furnished with warm carpets; and, in turn, the furs also served for coverlets when the sailors went to bed under their roofs of snow, while outside it froze in far different fashion than here with us in the winter. In our regions it was still the late autumn-time ; and they thought of that up yonder, and often pictured to themselves the yellow leaves on the trees of home. The clock showed that it was evening, and time to go to sleep ; and in the huts two men had already stretched themselves out, seeking rest. The younger of these had his best, dearest treasure, that he had brought from home — the Bible, which his grandmother had given him on his departure. Every night the sacred volume rested beneath his head, and he knew from his childish years what was written in it. Every day he read in the book, and often the holy words came into his mind where it is written, " If I take the wings of the morning, and flee into the uttermost parts of the sea, even there Thou art with me, and Thy right hand shall uphold me ;" and, under the

THE YOUNG SAILOR'S TREASURE.

influence of the eternal Word and of the true faith, he closed his eyes, and sleep came upon him, and dreams—the manifestation of Providence to the spirit. The soul lived and was working while the body was enjoying its rest : he felt this life, and it seemed to him as if dear old well-known melodies were sounding, as if the mild breezes of summer were playing around him ; and over his bed he beheld a brightness, as if something were shining in through the crust of snow. He lifted up his head, and behold, the bright gleam was no ripple down from the snowy roof, but came from the mighty pinions of an angel, into whose beaming face he was gazing. As if from the cup of a lily the angel arose from among the leaves of the Bible, and stretching out his arm, the walls of the snow hut sank down around, as though they had been a light airy veil of mist ; the green meadows and hills of home, and its ruddy woods, lay spread around him in the quiet sunshine of a beauteous autumn day ; the nest of the stork was empty, but ripe fruit still clung to the wild apple tree, although the leaves had fallen ; the red hips gleamed, and the magpie whistled in the green cage over the window of the peasant's cottage that was his home; the magpie whistled the tune that had been taught him, and the grandmother hung green food around the cage, as he, the grandson, had been accustomed to do; and the daughter of the blacksmith, very young and fair, stood by the well drawing water, and nodded to the granddame, and the old woman nodded to her, and showed her a letter that had come from a long way off. That very morning the letter had arrived from the cold regions of the North—there where the grandson was resting in the hand of God. And they smiled and they wept; and he, far away among the ice and snow, under the pinions of the angel, he, too, smiled and wept with them in spirit, for he saw them and heard them. And from the letter they read aloud the words of Holy Writ, that in the uttermost parts of the sea His right hand would be a stay and a safety. And the sound of a beauteous hymn welled up all around; and the angel spread his wings like a veil over the sleeping youth. The vision had fled, and it grew dark in the snow hut; but the Bible rested beneath his head, and faith and hope dwelt in his soul. God was with him; and he carried *home* about with him in his heart, even in the uttermost parts of the sea.

UNDER THE WILLOW TREE.

THE region round the little town of Kjöge is very bleak and bare. The town certainly lies by the sea shore, which is always beautiful, but just there it might be more beautiful than it is: all around are flat fields, and it is a long way to the forest. But when one is very much at home in a place, one always finds something beautiful, and something that one longs for in the most charming spot in the world that is strange to us. We confess that, by the utmost boundary of the little town, where some humble gardens skirt the streamlet that falls into the sea, it must be very pretty in summer; and this was the opinion of the two children from neighbouring houses, who were playing there, and forcing their way through the gooseberry bushes to get to one another. In one of the gardens stood an elder tree, and in the other an old willow, and under the latter especially the children were very fond of playing: they were allowed to play there, though, indeed, the tree stood close beside the stream, and they might easily have fallen into the water. But the eye of God watches over the little ones; if it did not, they would be badly off. And, moreover, they were very careful with respect to the water; in fact, the boy was so much afraid of it, that they could not lure him into the sea in summer, when the other children were splashing about in the waves. Accordingly, he was famously jeered and mocked at, and had to bear the jeering and mockery as best he could. But once Joanna, the neighbour's little girl, dreamed she was sailing in a boat, and Knud waded out to join her till the water rose, first to his neck, and afterwards closed over his head, so that he disappeared altogether. From the time when little Knud heard of this dream, he would no longer bear the teasing of the other boys. He might go into the water now, he said, for Joanna had dreamed it. He certainly never carried the idea into practice, but the dream was his great guide for all that.

Their parents, who were poor people, often took tea together, and Knud and Joanna played in the gardens and on the high road, where a row of willows had been planted beside the skirting ditch; these trees, with their polled tops, certainly did not look beautiful, but they were not put there for ornament, but for use. The old willow tree in the garden was much handsomer, and therefore the children were fond of sitting under it. In the town itself there was a great market-place, and at the time of the fair this place was covered with whole streets of tents and booths, containing silk ribbons, boots, and everything that a person could wish for. There was great crowding, and generally the weather was rainy; but it did not destroy the fragrance of the honey-cakes and the gingerbread, of which there was a booth quite full; and the best of it was, that the man who kept this booth came every year to lodge during the fair-time in the dwelling of little Knud's father. Consequently there came a present of a bit of gingerbread every now and then, and of course Joanna received her share of the gift. But perhaps the most charming thing of all was that the gingerbread dealer knew all sorts of tales, and could even relate histories about his own gingerbread cakes; and one evening, in particular, he told a story about them which made such a deep impression on the children that they never forgot it; and for that reason it is perhaps advisable that we should hear it too, more especially as the story is not long.

"On the shop-board," he said, "lay two gingerbread cakes, one in the shape of a man with a hat, the other of a maiden without a bonnet; both their faces were on the side that was uppermost, for they were to be looked at on that side, and not on the other; and, indeed, most people have a favourable side from which they should be viewed. On the left side the man wore a bitter almond—that was his heart; but the maiden, on the other hand, was honey-cake all over. They were placed as samples on the shop-board, and remaining there a long time, at last they fell in love with one another, but neither told the other, as they should have done if they had expected anything to come of it.

"'He is a man, and therefore he must speak first,' she thought; but she felt quite contented, for she knew her love was returned.

"His thoughts were far more extravagant, as is always the case with a man. He dreamed that he was a real street boy, that he had four pennies of his own, and that he purchased the maiden and ate her up. So they lay on the shop-board for weeks and weeks, and grew dry and hard, but the thoughts of the maiden became ever more gentle and maidenly.

"'It is enough for me that I have lived on the same table with him,' she said, and—crack!—she broke in two.

THE NAUGHTY BOY WHO ATE THE GINGERBREAD MAIDEN.

"'If she had only known of my love, she would have kept together a little longer,' he thought.

"And that is the story, and here they are, both of them," said the baker in conclusion. "They are remarkable for their curious history, and for their silent love, which never came to anything. And there they are for you!" and, so saying, he gave Joanna the man who was yet entire, and Knud got the broken maiden; but the children had been so much impressed by the story that they could not summon courage to eat the lovers up.

On the following day they went out with them to the churchyard, and sat down by the church wall, which is covered, winter and summer, with the most luxuriant ivy as with a rich carpet. Here they stood the two cake figures up in the sunshine among the green leaves, and told the story to a group of other children; they told them of the silent love which led to nothing. It was called *love* because the story was so lovely, on that they all agreed. But when they turned to look again at the gingerbread pair, a big boy, out of mischief, had eaten up the broken maiden. The children cried about this, and afterwards—probably that the poor lover might not be left in the world lonely and desolate—they ate him up too; but they never forgot the story.

The children were always together by the elder tree and under the willow, and the little girl sang the most beautiful songs with a voice that was clear as a bell. Knud, on the other hand, had not a note of music in him, but he knew the words of the songs, and that, at least, was something. The people of Kjöge, even to the rich wife of the fancy-shop keeper, stood still and listened when Joanna sang. "She has a very sweet voice, that little girl," they said.

Those were glorious days, but they could not last for ever. The neighbours were neighbours no longer. The little maiden's mother was dead, and the father intended to marry again, in the capital, where he had been promised a living as a messenger, which was to be a very lucrative office. And the neighbours separated regretfully, the children weeping heartily, but the parents promised that they should at least write to one another once a year.

And Knud was bound apprentice to a shoemaker, for the big boy could not be allowed to run wild any longer; and moreover he was confirmed.

Ah, how gladly on that day of celebration would he have been in Copenhagen with little Joanna! but he remained in Kjöge, and had never yet been to Copenhagen, though the little town is only five Danish miles distant from the capital; but far across the bay, when the sky was clear, Knud had seen the towers in the distance, and on the day of his confirmation he could distinctly see the golden cross on the principal church glittering in the sun.

Ah, how often his thoughts were with Joanna! Did she think of him? Yes. Towards Christmas there came a letter from her father to the parents of Knud, to say that they were getting on very well in Copenhagen, and especially might Joanna look forward to a brilliant future on the strength of her fine voice. She had been engaged in the theatre in which people sing, and was already earning some money, out of which she sent her dear neighbours of Kjöge a dollar for the merry Christmas-eve. They were to drink her health, she had herself added in a postscript; and in the same postscript there stood further, "A kind greeting to Knud."

The whole family wept; and yet all this was very pleasant—those were joyful tears that they shed. Knud's thoughts had been occupied every day with Joanna; and now he knew that she also thought of him; and the nearer the time came when his apprenticeship would be over, the more clearly did it appear to him that he was very fond of Joanna, and that she must be his wife; and when he thought of this, a smile came upon his lips, and he drew the thread twice as fast as before, and pressed his foot hard against the knee-strap. He ran the awl far into his finger, but he did not care for that. He determined not to play the dumb lover, as the two gingerbread cakes had done: the story should teach him a lesson.

And now he was a journeyman, and his knapsack was packed ready for his journey: at length, for the first time in his life, he was to go to Copenhagen, where a master was already waiting for him. How glad Joanna would be! She was now seventeen years old, and he nineteen.

Already in Kjöge he had wanted to buy a gold ring for her; but he recollected that such things were to be had far better in Copenhagen. And now he took leave of his parents, and on a rainy day, late in the autumn, went forth on foot out of the town of his birth. The leaves were falling down from the trees, and he arrived at his new master's in the metropolis wet to the skin. Next Sunday he was to pay a visit to Joanna's father. The new journeyman's clothes were brought forth, and the new hat from Kjöge was put on, which became Knud very well, for till this time he had only worn a cap. And he found the house he sought, and mounted flight after flight of stairs until he became almost giddy. It was terrible to him to see how people lived piled up one over the other in the dreadful city.

Everything in the room had a prosperous look, and Joanna's father received him very kindly. To the new wife he was a stranger, but she shook hands with him, and gave him some coffee.

"Joanna will be glad to see you," said the father: "you have grown quite a nice young man. You shall see her presently. She is a girl who rejoices my heart, and, please God, she will rejoice it yet more. She has her own room now, and pays us rent for it."

And the father knocked quite politely at the door, as if he were a visitor, and then they went in.

But how pretty everything was in that room! such an apartment was certainly not to be found in all Kjöge: the Queen herself could not be more charmingly lodged. There were carpets, there were window curtains quite down to the floor, and around were flowers and pictures, and a mirror into which there was almost danger that a visitor might step, for it was as large as a door; and there was even a velvet chair.

Knud saw all this at a glance; and yet he saw nothing but Joanna. She was a grown maiden, quite different from what Knud had fancied her, and much more beautiful. In all Kjöge there was not a girl like her. How graceful she was, and with what an odd unfamiliar glance she looked at Knud! But that was only for a moment, and then she rushed towards him as if she would have kissed him. She did not really do so, but she came very near it. Yes, she was certainly rejoiced at the arrival of the friend of her youth! The tears were actually in her eyes; and she had much to say, and many questions to put concerning all, from Knud's parents down to the elder tree and the willow, which she called Elder-mother and Willow-father, as if they had been human beings; and indeed they might pass as such, just as well as the gingerbread cakes; and of these she spoke too, and of their silent love, and how they had lain upon the shop-board and split in two — and then she laughed very heartily; but the blood mounted into Knud's cheeks, and his heart beat thick and fast. No, she had not grown proud at all. And it was through her—he noticed it well—that her parents invited him to stay the whole evening with them; and she poured out the tea and gave him a cup with her own hands; and afterwards she took a book and read aloud to them, and it seemed to Knud that what she read was all about himself and his love, for it matched so well with his thoughts; and then she sang a simple song, but through her singing it became like a history, and seemed to be the outpouring of her very heart. Yes, certainly she was fond of Knud. The tears coursed down his cheeks — he could not restrain them, nor could he speak a single word: he seemed to himself as if he were struck dumb; and yet she pressed his hand, and said,

"You have a good heart, Knud—remain always as you are now."

That was an evening of matchless delight to Knud; to sleep after it was impossible, and accordingly Knud did not sleep.

At parting, Joanna's father had said, "Now, you won't forget us altogether! Don't let the whole winter go by without once coming to see us again;" and therefore he could very well go again the next Sunday, and resolved to do so. But every evening when working hours were over — and they worked by candlelight there — Knud went out through the town: he went into the street in which Joanna lived, and looked up at her window; it was almost always lit up, and one evening he could see the shadow of her face quite plainly on the curtain — and that was a grand evening for him. His master's wife did not like his galivanting abroad every evening, as she expressed it, and she shook her head; but the master only smiled.

"He is only a young fellow," he said.

But Knud thought to himself: "On Sunday I shall see her, and I shall tell her how completely she reigns in my heart and soul, and that she must be my little wife. I know I am only a poor journeyman shoemaker, but I shall work and strive — yes, I shall tell her so. Nothing comes of silent love: I have learned that from the cakes."

And Sunday came round, and Knud sallied forth; but, unluckily, they were all invited out for that evening, and were obliged to tell him so. Joanna pressed his hand, and said,

"Have you ever been to the theatre? You must go once. I shall sing on Wednesday, and if you have time on that evening, I will send you a ticket; my father knows where your master lives."

How kind that was of her! And on Wednesday at noon he received a sealed paper, with no words written in it; but the ticket was there, and in the evening Knud went to the theatre for the first time in his life. And what did he see? He saw Joanna, and how charming and how beautiful she looked! She was certainly married to a stranger, but that was all in the play—something that was only make-believe, as Knud knew very well. If it had been real, he thought, she would never have had the heart to send him a ticket that he might go and see it. And all the people shouted and applauded, and Knud cried out "hurrah!"

KNUD'S DISAPPOINTMENT.

Even the King smiled at Joanna, and seemed to delight in her. Ah, how small Knud felt! but then he loved her so dearly, and thought that she loved him too; but it was for the man to speak the first word, as the gingerbread maiden in the child's story had taught him; and there was a great deal for him in that story.

So soon as Sunday came, he went again. He felt as if he were going into a church. Joanna was alone, and received him—it could not have happened more fortunately.

"It is well that you are come," she said. "I had an idea of sending my father to you, only I felt a presentiment that you would be here this evening; for I must tell you that I start for France on Friday: I must go there, if I am to become efficient."

It seemed to Knud as if the whole room were whirling round and round with him. He felt as if his heart would presently burst; no tear rose to his eyes, but still it was easy to see how sorrowful he was.

"You honest, faithful soul!" she exclaimed.

And these words of hers loosened Knud's tongue. He told her how constantly he loved her, and that she must become his wife; and as he said this, he saw Joanna change colour and turn pale. She let his hand fall, and answered, seriously and mournfully,

"Knud, do not make yourself and me unhappy. I shall always be a good sister to you, one in whom you may trust, but I shall never be anything more."

And she drew her white hand over his hot forehead.

"Heaven gives us strength for much," she said, "if we only endeavour to do our best."

At that moment the stepmother came into the room; and Joanna said quickly,

"Knud is quite inconsolable because I am going away. Come, be a man," she continued, and laid her hand upon his shoulder; and it seemed as if they had been talking of the journey, and nothing else. "You are a child," she added; "but now you must be good and reasonable, as you used to be under the willow tree, when we were both children."

But Knud felt as if the whole world had slid out of its course, and his thoughts were like a loose thread fluttering to and fro in the wind. He stayed, though he could not remember if she had asked him to stay; and she was kind and good, and poured out his tea for him, and sang to him. It had not the old tone, and yet it was wonderfully beautiful, and made his heart feel ready to burst. And then they parted. Knud did not offer her his hand, but she seized it, and said,

"Surely you will shake hands with your sister at parting, old playfellow!"

And she smiled through the tears that were rolling over her cheeks, and she repeated the word "brother"—and certainly there was good consolation in that—and thus they parted.

She sailed to France, and Knud wandered about the muddy streets of Copenhagen. The other journeymen in the workshop asked him why he went about so gloomily, and told him he should go and amuse himself with them, for he was a young fellow.

And they went with him to the dancing-rooms. He saw many handsome girls there, but certainly not one like Joanna; and here, where he thought to forget her, she stood more vividly than ever before the eyes of his soul. "Heaven gives us strength for a great deal, if we only try to do our best," she had said; and holy thoughts came into his mind, and he folded his hands. The violins played, and the girls danced round in a circle; and he was quite startled, for it seemed to him as if he were in a place to which he ought not to have brought Joanna—for she was there with him, in his heart; and accordingly he went out. He ran through the streets, and passed by the house where she had dwelt; it was dark there, dark everywhere, and empty, and lonely. The world went on in its course, but Knud pursued his lonely way, unheedingly.

The winter came, and the streams were frozen. Everything seemed to be preparing for a burial. But when spring returned, and the first steamer was to start, a longing seized him to go away, far, far into the world, but not to France. So he packed his knapsack, and wandered far into the German land, from city to city, without rest or peace; and it was not till he came to the glorious old city of Nuremberg that he could master his restless spirit; and in Nuremberg, therefore, he decided to remain.

Nuremberg is a wonderful old city, and looks as if it were cut out of an old picture-book. The streets seem to stretch themselves along just as they please. The houses do not like standing in regular ranks.

Gables with little towers, arabesques, and pillars, start out over the pathway, and from the strange peaked roofs water-spouts, formed like dragons or great slim dogs, extend far over the street.

Here in the market-place stood Knud, with his knapsack on his back. He stood by one of the old fountains that are adorned with splendid bronze figures, scriptural and historical, rising up between the gushing jets of water. A pretty servant-maid was just filling her pails, and she gave Knud a refreshing draught; and as her hand was full of roses, she gave him one of the flowers, and he accepted it as a good omen.

From the neighbouring church the strains of the organ were sounding: they seemed to him as familiar as the tones of the organ at home at Kjöge; and he went into the great cathedral. The sunlight streamed in through the stained glass windows, between the two lofty slender pillars. His spirit became prayerful, and peace returned to his soul.

And he sought and found a good master in Nuremberg, with whom he stayed, and in whose house he learned the German language.

The old moat round the town has been converted into a number of little kitchen gardens; but the high walls are standing yet, with their heavy towers. The ropemaker twists his ropes on a gallery or walk built of wood, inside the town wall, where elder bushes grow out of the clefts and cracks, spreading their green twigs over the little low houses that stand below; and in one of these dwelt the master with whom Knud worked; and over the little garret window at which Knud sat the elder waved its branches.

Here he lived through a summer and a winter; but when the spring came again he could bear it no longer. The elder was in blossom, and its fragrance reminded him so of home, that he fancied himself back in the garden at Kjöge; and therefore Knud went away from his master, and dwelt with another, farther in the town, over whose house no elder bush grew.

His workshop was quite close to one of the old stone bridges, by a low water-mill, that rushed and foamed always. Without, rolled the roaring stream, hemmed in by houses, whose old decayed gables looked ready to topple down into the water. No elder grew here—there was not even a flower-pot with its little green plant; but just opposite the workshop stood a great old willow tree, that seemed to cling fast to the house, for fear of being carried away by the water, and which stretched forth its branches over the river, just as the willow at Kjöge spread its arms across the streamlet by the gardens there.

Yes, he had certainly gone from the "Elder-mother" to the "Willow-father." The tree here had something, especially on moonlight evenings, that went straight to his heart—and that something was not in the moonlight, but in the old tree itself.

Nevertheless, he could not remain. Why not? Ask the willow tree, ask the blooming elder! And therefore he bade farewell to his master in Nuremberg, and journeyed onward.

To no one did he speak of Joanna—in his secret heart he hid his sorrow; and he thought of the deep meaning in the old childish story of the two cakes. Now he understood why the man had a bitter almond in his breast—he himself felt the bitterness of it; and Joanna, who was always so gentle and kind, was typified by the honey-cake. The strap of his knapsack seemed so tight across his chest that he could scarcely breathe; he loosened it, but was not relieved. He saw but half the world around him; the other half he carried about him and within himself. And thus it stood with him.

Not till he came in sight of the high mountains did the world appear freer to him; and now his thoughts were turned without, and tears came into his eyes.

The Alps appeared to him as the folded wings of the earth; how if they were to unfold themselves, and display their variegated pictures of black woods, foaming waters, clouds, and masses of snow? At the last day, he thought, the world will lift up its great wings, and mount upwards towards the sky, and burst like a soap-bubble in the glance of the Highest!

"Ah," sighed he, "that the Last Day were come!"

Silently he wandered through the land, that seemed to him as an orchard covered with soft turf. From the wooden balconies of the houses the girls who sat busy with their lace-making nodded at him; the summits of the mountains glowed in the red sun of the evening; and when he saw the green lakes gleaming among the dark trees, he thought of the coast by the Bay of Kjöge, and there was a longing in his bosom, but it was pain no more.

There where the Rhine rolls onward like a great billow, and bursts, and is changed into snow-white, gleaming, cloud-like masses, as if clouds were being created there, with the rainbow fluttering like a loose band above them; there he thought of the water-mill at Kjöge, with its rushing, foaming water.

Gladly would he have remained in the quiet Rhenish town, but here too were too many elder trees and willows, and therefore he journeyed on, over the high, mighty mountains, through shattered walls of rock, and on roads that clung like swallows' nests to the mountain-side. The waters foamed on in the depths, the clouds were below him, and he strode on over thistles, Alpine roses, and snow, in the warm summer sun; and saying farewell to the lands of the North, he passed on under the shade of blooming chestnut trees, and through vineyards and fields of maize. The mountains were a wall between him and all his recollections; and he wished it to be so.

Before him lay a great glorious city which they called *Milano*, and here he found a German master who gave him work. They were an old pious couple, in whose workshop he now laboured. And the two old people became quite fond of the quiet journeyman, who said little, but worked all the more, and led a pious Christian life. To himself also it seemed as if Heaven had lifted the heavy burden from his heart.

His favourite pastime was to mount now and then upon the mighty marble church, which seemed to him to have been formed of the snow of his native land, fashioned into roofs, and pinnacles, and decorated open halls: from every corner and every point the white statues smiled upon him. Above him was the blue sky, below him the city and the wide-spreading Lombard plains, and towards the north the high mountains clad with perpetual snow; and he thought of the church at Kjöge, with its red ivy-covered walls, but he did not long to go thither: here, beyond the mountains, he would be buried.

He had dwelt here a year, and three years had passed away since he left his home, when one day his master took him into the city, not to the circus where riders exhibited, but to the opera, where was a hall worth seeing. There were seven storeys, from each of which beautiful silken curtains hung down, and from the ground to the dizzy height of the roof sat elegant ladies, with bouquets of flowers in their hands, as if they were at a ball, and the gentlemen were in full dress, and many of them decorated with gold and silver. It was as bright there as in the brilliant sunshine, and the music rolled gloriously through the building. Everything was much more splendid than in the theatre at Copenhagen, but then Joanna had been there, and——could it be? Yes, it was like magic—she was here also! for the curtain rose, and Joanna appeared, dressed in silk and gold, with a crown upon her head: she sang as he thought none but angels could sing, and came far forward, quite to the front of the stage, and smiled as only Joanna could smile, and looked straight down at Knud. Poor Knud seized his master's hand, and called out aloud, " Joanna!" but no one heard but the master, who nodded his head, for the loud music sounded above everything.

" Yes, yes, her name is Joanna," said the master.

And he drew forth a printed playbill, and showed Knud her name—for the full name was printed there.

No, it was not a dream! All the people applauded and threw wreaths and flowers to her, and every time she went away they called her back, so that she was always going and coming.

In the street the people crowded round her carriage, and drew it away in triumph. Knud was in the foremost row, and shouted as joyously as any; and when the carriage stopped before her brilliantly lighted house, Knud stood close beside the door of the carriage. It flew open, and she stepped out: the light fell upon her dear face, as she smiled, and made a kindly gesture of thanks, and appeared deeply moved. Knud looked straight into her face, and she looked into his, but she did not know him. A man with a star glittering on his breast gave her his arm—and it was whispered about that the two were engaged.

Then Knud went home and packed his knapsack. He was determined to go back to his own home, to the elder and willow trees—ah, under the willow tree! A whole life is sometimes lived through in a single hour.

The old couple begged him to remain, but no words could induce him to stay. It was in vain they told him that winter was coming, and pointed out that snow had already fallen in the mountains; he said he could march on, with his knapsack on his back, in the wake of the slow-moving carriage, for which they would have to clear a path.

So he went away towards the mountains, and marched up them and down them. His strength was giving way, but still he saw no village, no house; he marched on towards the north. The stars gleamed above him, his feet stumbled, and his head grew dizzy. Deep in the valley stars were shining too, and it seemed as if there were another sky below him. He felt he was ill. The stars below him became more and more numerous, and glowed brighter and brighter, and moved to and fro. It was a little town whose lights beamed there; and when he understood that, he exerted the remains of his strength, and at last reached the shelter of a humble inn.

That night and the whole of the following day he remained there, for his body required rest and refreshment. It was thawing, and there was rain in the valley. But early on the second morning came a man with an organ, who played a tune of home; and now Knud could stay no longer. He continued his journey towards the north, marching onward for many days with haste and hurry, as if he were trying to get home before all were dead there; but to no one did he speak of his longing, for no one would have believed in the sorrow of his heart, the deepest a human heart can feel. Such a grief is not for the world, for it is not amusing; nor is it even for friends; and moreover he had no friends— a stranger, he wandered through strange lands towards his home in the North.

It was evening. He was walking on the public high road. The frost began to make itself felt, and the country soon became flatter, containing mere field and meadow. By the road-side grew a great willow tree. Everything reminded him of home, and he sat down under the tree: he felt very tired, his head began to nod, and his eyes closed in slumber, but still he was conscious that the tree stretched its arm above him; and in his wandering fancy the tree itself appeared to be an old, mighty man — it seemed as if the "Willow-father" himself had taken up his tired son in his arms, and were carrying him back into the land of home, to the bare bleak shore of Kjöge, to the garden of his childhood. Yes, he dreamed it was the willow tree of Kjöge that had travelled out into the world to seek him, and that now had found him, and had led him back into the little garden by the streamlet, and there stood Joanna, in all her splendour, with the golden crown on her head, as he had seen her last, and she called out "Welcome!" to him.

And before him stood two remarkable shapes, which looked much more human than he remembered them to have been in his childhood: they had changed also, but they were still the two cakes that turned the right side towards him, and looked very well.

"We thank you," they said to Knud. "You have loosened our tongues, and have taught us that thoughts should be spoken out freely, or nothing will come of them; and now something has indeed come of it—we are betrothed."

Then they went hand in hand through the streets of Kjöge, and they looked very respectable in every way: there was no fault to find with them. And they went on straight towards the church, and Knud and

KNUD AT REST—UNDER THE WILLOW TREE.

Joanna followed them; they also were walking hand in hand; and the church stood there as it had always stood, with its red walls, on which the green ivy grew; and the great door of the church flew open, and the organ sounded, and they walked up the long aisle of the church.

"Our master first," said the cake couple, and made room for Joanna and Knud, who knelt by the altar, and she bent her head over him, and tears fell from her eyes, but they were icy cold, for it was the ice around her heart that was melting—melting by his strong love; and the tears fell upon his burning cheeks, and he awoke, and was sitting under the old willow tree in the strange land, in the cold wintry evening: an icy hail was falling from the clouds and beating on his face.

"That was the most delicious hour of my life!" he said, "and it was but a dream. Oh, let me dream again!"

And he closed his eyes once more, and slept and dreamed.

Towards morning there was a great fall of snow. The wind drifted the snow over him, but he slept on. The villagers came forth to go to church, and by the road-side sat a journeyman. He was dead—frozen to death under the willow tree!

CHARMING.

ALFRED the sculptor—you know him? We all know him: he won the great gold medal, and got a travelling scholarship, went to Italy, and then came back to his native land. He was young in those days, and indeed he is young yet, though he is ten years older than he was then.

After his return he visited one of the little provincial towns on the island of Seeland. The whole town knew who the stranger was, and one of the richest persons gave a party in honour of him, and all who were of any consequence, or possessed any property, were invited. It was quite an event, and all the town knew of it without its being announced by beat of drum. Apprentice boys, and children of poor people, and even some of the poor people themselves, stood in front of the house, and looked at the lighted curtain; and the watchman could fancy that *he* was giving a party, so many people were in the streets. There was quite an air of festivity about, and in the house was festivity also, for Mr. Alfred the sculptor was there.

He talked, and told anecdotes, and all listened to him with pleasure and a certain kind of awe; but none felt such respect for him as did the elderly widow of an official: she seemed, so far as Mr. Alfred was concerned, like a fresh piece of blotting paper, that absorbed all that was spoken, and asked for more. She was very appreciative and incredibly ignorant—a kind of female Caspar Hauser.

"I should like to see Rome," she said. "It must be a lovely city, with all the strangers who are continually arriving there. Now, do give us a description of Rome. How does the city look when you come in by the gate?"

"I cannot very well describe it," replied the sculptor. "A great open place, and in the midst of it an obelisk, which is a thousand years old."

"An organist!" exclaimed the lady, who had never met with the word *obelisk*.

A few of the guests could hardly keep from laughing, nor could the sculptor quite keep his countenance; but the smile that rose to his lips faded away, for he saw, close by the inquisitive dame, a pair of dark blue eyes—they belonged to the daughter of the speaker, and any one who has such a daughter cannot be silly! The mother was like a fountain of questions, and the daughter, who listened but never spoke, might pass for the beautiful Naiad of the fountain. How charming she was! She was a study for the sculptor to contemplate, but not to converse with; and, indeed, she did not speak, or only very seldom.

"Has the Pope a large family?" asked the lady.

And the young man considerately answered, as if the question had been better put,

"No, he does not come of a great family."

"That's not what I mean," the widow persisted. "I mean, has he a wife and children?"

"The Pope is not allowed to marry," said the gentleman.

"I don't like that," was the lady's comment.

She certainly might have put more sensible questions; but if she had not spoken in just the manner she used, would her daughter have leaned so gracefully upon her shoulder, looking straight out with the almost mournful smile upon her face?

Then Mr. Alfred spoke again, and told of the glory of colour in Italy, of the purple hills, the blue Mediterranean, the azure sky of the South, whose brightness and glory was only to be surpassed in the North by a maiden's deep blue eyes. And this he said with a peculiar application; but she who should have understood his meaning, looked as if she were quite unconscious of it, and that again was charming!

"Italy!" sighed a few of the guests.

"Oh, to travel!" sighed others.

"Charming! charming!" chorused they all.

"Yes, if I win a hundred thousand dollars in the lottery," said the head tax-collector's lady, "then we will travel. I and my daughter, and you, Mr. Alfred; you must be our guide. We'll all three travel together, and one or two good friends more." And she nodded in such a friendly way at the company, that each one might imagine he or she was the person who was to be taken to Italy. "Yes, we will go to Italy! but not to those parts where there are robbers—we'll keep to Rome, and to the great high roads where one is safe."

And the daughter sighed very quietly. And how much may lie in one little sigh, or be placed in it! The young man placed a great deal in it. The two blue eyes, lit up that evening in honour of him, must conceal treasures—treasures of the heart and mind—richer than all the glories of Rome; and when he left the party that night he had lost *his* heart—lost it completely, to the young lady.

The house of the head tax-collector's widow was now the one which Mr. Alfred the sculptor most assiduously frequented; and it was understood that his visits were not intended for that lady, though he and she were the people who kept up the conversation: he came for the daughter's sake. They called her Kala. Her name was really Calen Malena, and these two names had been contracted into the one name, Kala. She was beautiful; but a few said she was rather dull, and probably slept late of a morning.

"She has always been accustomed to that," her mother said. "She's a beauty, and they always are easily tired. She sleeps rather late, but that makes her eyes so clear."

What a power lay in the depths of those dark blue eyes! "Still waters run deep." The young man felt the truth of this proverb, and his heart had sunk into the depths. He spoke and told his adventures, and the mamma was as simple and eager in her questioning as on the first evening of their meeting.

It was a pleasure to hear Alfred describe anything. He spoke of

Naples, of excursions to Mount Vesuvius, and showed coloured prints of several of the eruptions. And the head tax-collector's widow had never heard of them before, or taken time to consider the question.

"Good heavens!" she exclaimed. "So that is a burning mountain! But is it not dangerous to the people round about?"

"Whole cities have been destroyed," he answered; "for instance, Pompeii and Herculaneum."

"But the poor people!—And you saw all that with your own eyes?"

"No, I did not see any of the eruptions represented in these pictures, but I will show you a picture of my own of an eruption I saw."

He laid a pencil sketch upon the table, and mamma, who had been absorbed in the contemplation of the highly coloured prints, threw a glance at the pale drawing, and cried in astonishment,

"Did you see it throw up white fire?"

For a moment Alfred's respect for Kala's mamma suffered a sudden diminution; but, dazzled by the light that illumined Kala, he soon found it quite natural that the old lady should have no eye for colour. After all, it was of no consequence, for Kala's mamma had the best of all things—namely, Kala herself.

And Alfred and Kala were betrothed, which was natural enough, and the betrothal was announced in the little newspaper of the town. Mamma purchased thirty copies of the paper, that she might cut out the paragraph and send it to their friends and acquaintances. And the betrothed pair were happy, and the mother-in-law elect was happy too, for it seemed like connecting herself with Thorwaldsen.

"For you are a continuation of Thorwaldsen," she said to Alfred.

And it seemed to Alfred that mamma had in this instance said a clever thing. Kala said nothing; but her eyes shone, her lips smiled, her every movement was graceful: yes, she was beautiful; that cannot be too often repeated.

Alfred undertook to take a bust of Kala and of his mother-in-law. They sat to him accordingly, and saw how he moulded and smoothed the soft clay with his fingers.

"I suppose it's only on our account," said mamma-in-law, "that you undertake this commonplace work, and don't leave your servant to do all that sticking together."

"It is necessary that I should mould the clay myself," he replied.

"Ah, yes, you are so very polite," retorted mamma; and Kala silently pressed his hand, still soiled by the clay.

And he unfolded to both of them the loveliness of nature in creation, pointing out how the living stood higher in the scale than the dead creature, how the plant was developed beyond the mineral, the animal beyond the plant, and man beyond the animal. He strove to show them how mind and beauty become manifest in outward form, and how it was the sculptor's task to seize that beauty and to manifest it in his works.

Kala stood silent, and nodded approbation of the expressed thought, while mamma-in-law made the following confession:

"It's difficult to follow all that. But I manage to hobble after you

KALA'S BUST.

with my thoughts, though they whirl round and round, but I contrive
to hold them fast."

And Kala's beauty held Alfred fast, filled his whole soul, and seized
and mastered him. Beauty gleamed forth from Kala's every feature—
gleamed from her eyes, lurked in the corners of her mouth, and in every
movement of her fingers. Alfred the sculptor saw this: he spoke only
of her, thought only of her, and the two became one; and thus it may
be said that she spoke much, for he and she were one, and he was
always talking of her.

Such was the betrothal; and now came the wedding, with bridesmaids
and wedding presents, all duly mentioned in the wedding speech.

Mamma-in-law had set up Thorwaldsen's bust at the end of the table,
attired in a dressing-gown, for he was to be a guest; such was her whim.
Songs were sung and cheers were given, for it was a gay wedding,
and they were a handsome pair. "Pygmalion received his Galatea,"
so one of the songs said.

"Ah, that's your mythologics," said mamma-in-law.

Next day the youthful pair started for Copenhagen, where they were to live. Mamma-in-law accompanied them, "to take care of the commonplace," as she said, meaning the domestic economy. Kala was like a doll in a doll's house, all was so bright, so new, and so fine. There they sat, all three; and as for Alfred, to use a proverb that will describe his position, we may say that he sat like the friar in the goose-yard.

The magic of form had enchanted him. He had looked at the case, and cared not to inquire what the case contained, and that omission brings unhappiness, much unhappiness, into married life; for the case may be broken and the gilt may come off, and then the purchaser may repent his bargain. In a large party it is very disagreeable to observe that one's buttons are giving way, and that there are no buckles to fall back upon; but it is worse still in a great company to become aware that wife and mother-in-law are talking nonsense, and that one cannot depend upon oneself for a happy piece of wit to carry off the stupidity of the thing.

The young married pair often sat hand in hand, he speaking and she letting fall a word here and there—the same melody, the same clear, bell-like sounds. It was a mental relief when Sophy, one of her friends, came to pay a visit.

Sophy was not pretty. She was certainly free from bodily deformity, though Kala always asserted she was a little crooked; but no eye save a friend's would have remarked it. She was a very sensible girl, and it never occurred to her that she might become at all dangerous here. Her appearance was like a pleasant breath of air in the doll's house; and air was certainly required there, as they all acknowledged. They felt they wanted airing, and consequently they came out into the air, and mamma-in-law and the young couple travelled to Italy.

"Thank Heaven that we are in our own four walls again," was the exclamation of mother and daughter when they came home a year after.

"There's no pleasure in travelling," said mamma-in-law. "To tell the truth, it's very wearisome—I beg pardon for saying so. I found the time hang heavy, although I had my children with me; and it's expensive work, travelling, very expensive! And all those galleries one has to see, and the quantity of things you are obliged to run after! You must do it for decency's sake, for you're sure to be asked when you come back; and then you're sure to be told that you've omitted to see what was best worth seeing. I got tired at last of those endless Madonnas: one seemed to be turning a Madonna oneself!"

"And what bad living you get!" said Kala.

"Yes," replied mamma, "no such thing as an honest meat soup. It's miserable trash, their cookery."

And the travelling fatigued Kala: she was always fatigued, that was the worst of it. Sophy was taken into the house, where her presence was a real advantage.

Mamma-in-law acknowledged that Sophy understood both housewifery and art, though a knowledge of the latter could not be expected from a person of her limited means; and she was, moreover, an honest, faithful girl: she showed that thoroughly while Kala lay sick—fading away.

Where the case is everything, the case should be strong, or else all is over. And all *was* over with the case—Kala died.

"She was beautiful," said mamma; "she was quite different from the antiques, for they are so damaged. A beauty ought to be perfect, and Kala was a perfect beauty."

Alfred wept, and mamma wept, and both of them wore mourning. The black dress suited mamma very well, and she wore mourning the longest. Moreover, she had soon to experience another grief in seeing Alfred marry again—marry Sophy, who had no appearance at all.

"He's gone to the very extreme," cried mamma-in-law; "he has gone from the most beautiful to the ugliest, and has forgotten his first wife. Men have no endurance. My husband was of a different stamp, and he died before me."

"Pygmalion received his Galatea," said Alfred: "yes, that's what they said in the wedding song. I had once really fallen in love with the beautiful statue, which awoke to life in my arms; but the kindred soul which Heaven sends down to us, the angel who can feel and sympathize with and elevate us, I have not found and won till now. You came, Sophy, not in the glory of outward beauty, though you are fair, fairer than is needful. The chief thing remains the chief. You came to teach the sculptor that his work is but clay and dust, only an outward form in a fabric that passes away, and that we must seek the essence, the internal spirit. Poor Kala! ours was but wayfarers' life. Yonder, where we shall know each other by sympathy, we shall be half strangers."

"That was not lovingly spoken," said Sophy, "not spoken like a true Christian. Yonder, where there is no giving in marriage, but where, as you say, souls attract each other by sympathy; there where everything beautiful developes itself and is elevated, her soul may acquire such completeness that it may sound more harmoniously than mine; and you will then once more utter the first rapturous exclamation of your love, 'Beautiful—most beautiful!'"

THE BISHOP OF BÖRGLUM AND HIS WARRIORS.

Our scene is laid in Northern Jutland, in the so-called "wild moor." We hear what is called the "Wester-wow-wow"—the peculiar roar of the North Sea as it breaks against the western coast of Jutland. It rolls and thunders with a sound that penetrates for miles into the land; and we are quite near the roaring. Before us rises a great mound of sand—a mountain we have long seen, and towards which we are wending our way, driving slowly along through the deep sand. On this mountain of sand is a lofty old building—the convent of Börglum. In one of its wings (the larger one) there is still a church. And at this convent we now arrive in the late evening hour; but the weather is clear in the bright June night around us, and the eye can range far, far over field and moor to the Bay of Aalborg, over heath and meadow, and far across the deep blue sea.

Now we are there, and roll past between barns and other farm buildings; and at the left of the gate we turn aside to the old Castle Farm, where the lime trees stand in lines along the walls, and, sheltered from the wind and weather, grow so luxuriantly that their twigs and leaves almost conceal the windows.

We mount the winding staircase of stone, and march through the long passages under the heavy roof-beams. The wind moans very strangely here, both within and without. It is hardly known how, but the people say—yes, people say a great many things when they are frightened or want to frighten others — they say that the old dead choir-men glide silently past us into the church, where mass is sung. They can be heard in the rushing of the storm, and their singing brings up strange thoughts in the hearers — thoughts of the old times into which we are carried back.

On the coast a ship is stranded; and the bishop's warriors are there, and spare not those whom the sea has spared. The sea washes away the blood that has flowed from the cloven skulls. The stranded goods belong to the bishop, and there is a store of goods here. The sea casts up tubs and barrels filled with costly wine for the convent cellar, and in the convent is already good store of beer and mead. There is plenty in the kitchen—dead game and poultry, hams and sausages; and fat fish swim in the ponds without.

The Bishop of Börglum is a mighty lord. He has great possessions, but still he longs for more — everything must bow before the mighty Olaf Glob. His rich cousin at Thyland is dead, and his widow is to have the rich inheritance. But how comes it that one relation is always harder towards another than even strangers would be? The widow's husband had possessed all Thyland, with the exception of the Church property. Her son was not at home. In his boyhood he had already started on a journey, for his desire was to see foreign lands and strange people. For years there had been no news of him. Perhaps he had long been laid in the grave, and would never come back to his home, to rule where his mother then ruled.

" What has a woman to do with rule ? " said the bishop.

He summoned the widow before a law court; but what did he gain thereby ? The widow had never been disobedient to the law, and was strong in her just rights.

Bishop Olaf of Börglum, what dost thou purpose ? What writest thou on yonder smooth parchment, sealing it with thy seal, and intrusting it to the horsemen and servants, who ride away—far away—to the city of the Pope ?

It is the time of falling leaves and of stranded ships, and soon icy winter will come.

JENS GLOB MEETS HIS MOTHER.

Twice had icy winter returned before the bishop welcomed the horsemen and servants back to their home. They came from Rome with a
papal decree—a ban, or bull, against the widow who had dared to offend
the pious bishop. "Cursed be she and all that belongs to her. Let
her be expelled from the congregation and the Church. Let no man
stretch forth a helping hand to her, and let friends and relations avoid
her as a plague and a pestilence!"

"What will not bend must break," said the Bishop of Börglum.

And all forsake the widow; but she holds fast to her God. He is her helper and defender.

One servant only — an old maid — remained faithful to her; and, with the old servant, the widow herself followed the plough; and the crop grew, although the land had been cursed by the Pope and by the bishop.

"Thou child of perdition, I will yet carry out my purpose!" cried the Bishop of Börglum. "Now will I lay the hand of the Pope upon thee, to summon thee before the tribunal that shall condemn thee!"

Then did the widow yoke the two last oxen that remained to her to a waggon, and mounted up on the waggon, with her old servant, and travelled away across the heath out of the Danish land. As a stranger she came into a foreign country, where a strange tongue was spoken and where new customs prevailed. Farther and farther she journeyed, to where green hills rise into mountains, and the vine clothes their sides. Strange merchants drive by her, and they look anxiously after their waggons laden with merchandise. They fear an attack from the armed followers of the robber-knights. The two poor women, in their humble vehicle drawn by two black oxen, travel fearlessly through the dangerous sunken road and through the darksome forest. And now they were in Franconia. And there met them a stalwart knight, with a train of twelve armed followers. He paused, gazed at the strange vehicle, and questioned the women as to the goal of their journey and the place whence they came. Then one of them mentioned Thyland in Denmark, and spoke of her sorrows — of her woes — which were soon to cease, for so Divine Providence had willed it. For the stranger knight is the widow's son! He seized her hand, he embraced her, and the mother wept. For years she had not been able to weep, but had only bitten her lips till the blood started.

It is the time of falling leaves and of stranded ships, and soon will icy winter come.

The sea rolled wine-tubs to the shore for the bishop's cellar. In the kitchen the deer roasted on the spit before the fire. At Börglum it was warm and cheerful in the heated rooms, while cold winter raged without, when a piece of news was brought to the bishop: "Jens Glob, of Thyland, has come back, and his mother with him." Jens Glob laid a complaint against the bishop, and summoned him before the temporal and the spiritual court.

"That will avail him little," said the bishop. "Best leave off thy efforts, knight Jens."

Again it is the time of falling leaves, of stranded ships—icy winter comes again, and the "white bees" are swarming, and sting the traveller's face till they melt.

"Keen weather to-day!" say the people, as they step in.

Jens Glob stands so deeply wrapped in thought that he singes the skirt of his wide garment.

" Thou Börglum bishop," he exclaims, " I shall subdue thee after all!
Under the shield of the Pope, the law cannot reach thee; but Jens
Glob shall reach thee !"

Then he writes a letter to his brother-in-law, Olaf Hase, in Salling-
land, and prays that knight to meet him on Christmas-eve, at mass, in
the church at Widberg.   The bishop himself is to read the mass, and
consequently will journey from Börglum to Thyland; and this is known
to Jens Glob.

Moorland and meadow are covered with ice and snow.   The marsh
will bear horse and rider, the bishop with his priests and armed men.
They ride the shortest way, through the waving reeds, where the wind
moans sadly.

Blow thy brazen trumpet, thou trumpeter clad in fox-skin! it sounds
merrily in the clear air.   So they ride on over heath and moorland —
over what is the garden of Fata Morgana in the hot summer, though
now icy, like all the country—towards the church of Widberg.

The wind is blowing his trumpet too—blowing it harder and harder.
He blows up a storm — a terrible storm — that increases more and
more.   Towards the church they ride, as fast as they may through the
storm.   The church stands firm, but the storm careers on over field and
moorland, over land and sea.

Börglum's bishop reaches the church; but Olaf Hase will scarce do
so, hard as he may ride.   He journeys with his warriors on the farther
side of the bay, to help Jens Glob, now that the bishop is to be summoned before the judgment seat of the Highest.

The church is the judgment hall; the altar is the council table.   The
lights burn clear in the heavy brass candelabra.   The storm reads out
the accusation and the sentence, roaming in the air over moor and
heath, and over the rolling waters.   No ferry-boat can sail over the bay
in such weather as this.

Olaf Hase makes halt at Ottesworde.   There he dismisses his warriors,
presents them with their horses and harness, and gives them leave to
ride home and greet his wife.   He intends to risk his life alone in the
roaring waters; but they are to bear witness for him that it is not his
fault if Jens Glob stands without reinforcement in the church at Widberg.   The faithful warriors will not leave him, but follow him out into
the deep waters.   Ten of them are carried away; but Olaf Hase and
two of the youngest men reach the farther side.   They have still four
miles to ride.

It is past midnight.   It is Christmas.   The wind has abated.   The
church is lighted up; the gleaming radiance shines through the window-
frames, and pours out over meadow and heath.   The mass has long been
finished, silence reigns in the church, and the wax is heard dropping
from the candles to the stone pavement.   And now Olaf Hase arrives.

In the forecourt Jens Glob greets him kindly, and says,

" I have just made an agreement with the bishop."

" Sayest thou so?" replied Olaf Hase.   " Then neither thou nor the
bishop shall quit this church alive."

And the sword leaps from the scabbard, and Olaf Hase deals a blow that makes the panel of the church door, which Jens Glob hastily closes between them, fly in fragments.

"Hold, brother! First hear what the agreement was that I made. I have slain the bishop and his warriors and priests. They will have no word more to say in the matter, nor will I speak again of all the wrong that my mother has endured."

The long wicks of the altar lights glimmer red; but there is a redder gleam upon the pavement, where the bishop lies with cloven skull, and his dead warriors around him, in the quiet of the holy Christmas night.

And four days afterwards the bells toll for a funeral in the convent of Börglum. The murdered bishop and the slain warriors and priests are displayed under a black canopy, surrounded by candelabra decked with crape. There lies the dead man, in the black cloak wrought with silver; the crosier in the powerless hand that was once so mighty. The incense rises in clouds, and the monks chant the funeral hymn. It sounds like a wail—it sounds like a sentence of wrath and condemnation that must be heard far over the land, carried by the wind—sung by the wind—the wail that sometimes is silent, but never dies; for ever again it rises in song, singing even into our own time this legend of the Bishop of Börglum and his hard nephew. It is heard in the dark night by the frightened husbandman, driving by in the heavy sandy road past the convent of Börglum. It is heard by the sleepless listener in the thickly-walled rooms at Börglum. And not only to the ear of superstition is the sighing and the tread of hurrying feet audible in the long echoing passages leading to the convent door that has long been locked. The door still seems to open, and the lights seem to flame in the brazen candlesticks; the fragrance of incense arises; the church gleams in its ancient splendour; and the monks sing and say the mass over the slain bishop, who lies there in the black silver-embroidered mantle, with the crosier in his powerless hand; and on his pale proud forehead gleams the red wound like fire, and there burn the worldly mind and the wicked thoughts.

Sink down into his grave — into oblivion — ye terrible shapes of the times of old!

Hark to the raging of the angry wind, sounding above the rolling sea! A storm approaches without, calling aloud for human lives. The sea has not put on a new mind with the new time. This night it is a horrible pit to devour up lives, and to-morrow, perhaps, it may be a glassy mirror—even as in the old time that we have buried. Sleep sweetly, if thou canst sleep!

Now it is morning.

The new time flings sunshine into the room. The wind still keeps up mightily. A wreck is announced—as in the old time.

During the night, down yonder by Lökken, the little fishing village with the red-tiled roofs—we can see it up here from the window—a ship has come ashore. It has struck, and is fast imbedded in the sand;

but the rocket apparatus has thrown a rope on board, and formed a bridge from the wreck to the mainland; and all on board are saved, and reach the land, and are wrapped in warm blankets; and to-day they are invited to the farm at the convent of Börglum. In comfortable rooms they encounter hospitality and friendly faces. They are addressed in the language of their country, and the piano sounds for them with melodies of their native land; and before these have died away, the chord has been struck, the wire of thought that reaches to the land of the sufferers announces that they are rescued. Then their anxieties are dispelled; and at even they join in the dance at the feast given in the great hall at Börglum. Waltzes and Styrian dances are given, and Danish popular songs, and melodies of foreign lands in these modern times.

Blessed be thou, new time! Speak thou of summer and of purer gales! Send thy sunbeams gleaming into our hearts and thoughts! On thy glowing canvas let them be painted—the dark legends of the rough hard times that are past!

THE BUTTERFLY.

THE Butterfly wished for a bride; and, as may well be imagined, he wanted to select a very pretty one from among the flowers; therefore he threw a critical glance at all the flower-beds, and found that every flower sat quietly and demurely on her stalk, just as a maiden ought to sit before she is engaged; but there were a great many of them, and the choice threatened to become wearisome. The Butterfly did not care to take much trouble, and consequently he flew off on a visit to the daisies. The French call this floweret "Marguerite," and they know that Marguerite can prophecy, when lovers pluck off its leaves, and ask of every leaf they pluck some question concerning their lovers. "Heartily? Painfully? Loves me much? A little? Not at all?" and so on. Every one asks in his own language. The Butterfly came to Marguerite too, to inquire; but he did not pluck off her leaves: he kissed each of them, for he considered that most is to be done with kindness.

"Darling Marguerite daisy!" he said to her, "you are the wisest woman among the flowers. Pray, pray tell me, shall I get this one or that? Which will be my bride? When I know that, I will directly fly to her and propose for her."

But Marguerite did not answer him. She was angry that he had called her a "woman," when she was yet a girl; and there is a great difference. He asked for the second and for the third time, and when she remained dumb, and answered him not a word, he would wait no longer, but flew away to begin his wooing at once.

It was in the beginning of spring; the crocus and the snowdrop were blooming around.

"They are very pretty," thought the Butterfly. "Charming little lasses, but a little too much of the schoolgirl about them." Like all young lads, he looked out for the elder girls.

Then he flew off to the anemones. These were a little too bitter for his taste; the violet somewhat too sentimental; the lime blossoms were too small, and, moreover, they had too many relations; the apple blossoms—they looked like roses, but they bloomed to-day, to fall off to-morrow, to fall beneath the first wind that blew; and he thought that a marriage with them would last too short a time. The Pease Blossom pleased him best of all: she was white and red, and graceful and delicate, and belonged to the domestic maidens who look well, and at the same time are useful in the kitchen. He was just about to make

THE BUTTERFLY IN SEARCH OF A BRIDE.

his offer, when close by the maiden he saw a pod at whose end hung a withered flower.

"Who is that?" he asked.

"That is my sister," replied the Pease Blossom.

"Oh, indeed; and you will get to look like her!" he said.

And away he flew, for he felt quite shocked.

The honeysuckle hung forth blooming from the hedge, but there was a number of girls like that, with long faces and sallow complexions. No, he did not like her.

But which one did he like?

The spring went by, and the summer drew towards its close; it was autumn, but he was still undecided.

And now the flowers appeared in their most gorgeous robes, but in vain—they had lost the fresh fragrant air of youth. But the heart demands fragrance, even when it is no longer young, and there is very little of that to be found among the dahlias and dry chrysanthemums, therefore the Butterfly turned to the Mint on the ground.

You see, this plant has no blossom; but indeed it is blossom all over, full of fragrance from head to foot, with flower scent in every leaf.

"I shall take her," said the Butterfly.

And he made an offer for her.

But the Mint stood silent and stiff, listening to him. At last she said, "Friendship, if you please, but nothing more. I am old, and you are old, but we may very well live for one another; but as to marrying—no—don't let us appear ridiculous at our age."

And thus it happened that the Butterfly had no wife at all. He had been too long choosing, and that is a bad plan. So the Butterfly became what we call an old bachelor.

It was late in autumn, with rain and cloudy weather. The wind blew cold over the backs of the old willow trees, so that they creaked again. It was no weather to be flying about in summer clothes, nor, indeed, was the Butterfly in the open air. He had got under shelter by chance, where there was fire in the stove and the heat of summer. He could live well enough, but he said,

"It's not enough merely to live. One must have freedom, sunshine, and a little flower."

And he flew against the window-frame, and was seen and admired, and then stuck upon a pin and placed in the box of curiosities; they could not do more for him.

"Now I am perched on a stalk, like the flowers," said the Butterfly. "It certainly is not very pleasant. It must be something like being married, for one is stuck fast."

And he consoled himself in some measure with the thought.

"That's very poor comfort," said the potted Plants in the room.

"But," thought the Butterfly, "one cannot well trust these potted Plants. They've had too much to do with mankind."

ANNE LISBETH.

ANNE LISBETH had a colour like milk and blood; young, fresh, and merry, she looked beautiful, with gleaming white teeth and clear eyes; her footstep was light in the dance, and her mind was lighter still. And what came of it all? Her son was an ugly brat! Yes, he was not pretty; so he was put out to be nursed by the labourer's wife. Anne Lisbeth was taken into the count's castle, and sat there in the splendid room arrayed in silks and velvets; not a breath of wind might blow upon her, and no one was allowed to speak a harsh word to her. No, that might not be, for she was nurse to the count's child, which was delicate and fair as a prince, and beautiful as an angel; and how she loved this child! Her own boy was provided for at the labourer's, where the mouth boiled over more frequently than the pot, and where, in general, no one was at home to take care of the child. Then he would cry; but what nobody knows, that nobody cares for; and he would cry till he was tired, and then he fell asleep; and in sleep one feels neither hunger nor thirst. A capital invention is sleep.

With years, just as weeds shoot up, Anne Lisbeth's child grew, but yet they said his growth was stunted; but he had quite become a member of the family in which he dwelt; they had received money to keep him. Anne Lisbeth was rid of him for good. She had become a town lady, and had a comfortable home of her own; and out of doors she wore a bonnet when she went out for a walk; but she never walked out to see the labourer—that was too far from the town; and indeed she had nothing to go for: the boy belonged to the labouring people, and she said he could eat his food, and he should do something to earn his food, and consequently he kept Matz's red cow. He could already tend cattle and make himself useful.

The big dog, by the yard gate of the nobleman's mansion, sits proudly in the sunshine on the top of the kennel, and barks at every one who goes by; if it rains he creeps into his house, and there he is warm and dry. Anne Lisbeth's boy sat in the sunshine on the fence of the field, and cut out a pole-pin. In the spring he knew of three strawberry plants that were in blossom, and would certainly bear fruit, and that was his most hopeful thought; but they came to nothing. He sat out in the rain in foul weather, and was wet to the skin, and afterwards the cold wind dried the clothes on his back. When he came to the lordly farm-yard he was hustled and cuffed, for the men and maids declared he was horribly ugly; but he was used to that—loved by nobody!

That was how it went with Anne Lisbeth's boy; and how could it go otherwise? It was, once for all, his fate to be loved by nobody.

Till now a "land crab," the land at last threw him overboard. He went to sea in a wretched vessel, and sat by the helm, while the skipper sat over the grog-can. He was dirty and ugly, half frozen and half starved: one would have thought he had never had enough; and that really was the case.

It was late in autumn, rough, wet, windy weather; the wind cut cold through the thickest clothing, especially at sea; and out to sea went a wretched boat, with only two men on board, or, properly speaking, with only a man and a half, the skipper and his boy. It had only been a kind of twilight all day, and now it became dark, and it was bitterly cold. The skipper drank a dram, which was to warm him from within. The bottle was old, and the glass too; it was whole at the top, but the foot was broken off, and therefore it stood upon a little carved block of wood painted blue. "A dram comforts one, and two are better still," thought the skipper. The boy sat at the helm, which he held fast in his hard seamed hands: he was ugly, and his hair was matted, and he looked crippled and stunted; he was the field labourer's boy, though in the church register he was entered as Anne Lisbeth's son.

The wind cut its way through the rigging, and the boat cut through the sea. The sail blew out, filled by the wind, and they drove on in wild career. It was rough and wet around and above, and it might come worse still. Hold! what was that? what struck there? what burst yonder? what seized the boat? It heeled, and lay on its beam ends! Was it a waterspout? Was it a heavy sea coming suddenly down? The boy at the helm cried out aloud, "Heaven help us!" The boat had struck on a great rock standing up from the depths of the sea, and it sank like an old shoe in a puddle; it sank "with man and mouse," as the saying is; and there were mice on board, but only one man and a half, the skipper and the labourer's boy. No one saw it but the

ANNE LISBETH'S BOY.

swimming seagulls, and the fishes down yonder, and even they did not see it rightly, for they started back in terror when the water rushed into the ship, and it sank. There it lay scarce a fathom below the surface, and those two were provided for, buried and forgotten! Only the glass with the foot of blue wood did not sink, for the wood kept it up; the glass drifted away, to be broken and cast upon the shore—where and when? But, indeed, that is of no consequence. It had served its time, and it had been loved, which Anne Lisbeth's boy had not been. But in heaven no soul will be able to say, "Never loved!"

Anne Lisbeth had lived in the city for many years. She was called Madame, and felt her dignity, when she remembered the old "noble" days in which she had driven in the carriage, and had associated with countesses and baronesses. Her beautiful noble-child was the dearest angel, the kindest heart; he had loved her so much, and she had loved him in return; they had kissed and loved each other, and the boy had been her joy, her second life. Now he was so tall, and was fourteen years old, handsome and clever: she had not seen him since she carried him in her arms; for many years she had not been in the count's palace, for indeed it was quite a journey thither.

"I must once make an effort and go," said Anne Lisbeth. "I must go to my darling, to my sweet count's child. Yes, he certainly must long to see me too, the young count; he thinks of me and loves me as in those days when he flung his angel arms round my neck and cried 'Anne Liz.!' It sounded like music. Yes, I must make an effort and see him again."

She drove across the country in a grazier's cart, and then got out and continued her journey on foot, and thus reached the count's castle. It was great and magnificent as it had always been, and the garden looked the same as ever; but all the people there were strangers to her; not one of them knew Anne Lisbeth, and they did not know of what consequence she had once been there, but she felt sure the countess would let them know it, and her darling boy too. How she longed to see him!

Now Anne Lisbeth was at her journey's end. She was kept waiting a considerable time, and for those who wait time passes slowly. But before the great people went to table she was called in and accosted very graciously. She was to see her sweet boy after dinner, and then she was to be called in again.

How tall and slender and thin he had grown! But he had still his beautiful eyes and the angel-sweet mouth! He looked at her, but he said not a word: certainly he did not know her. He turned round, and was about to go away, but she seized his hand and pressed it to her mouth.

"Good, good!" said he; and with that he went out of the room— he who filled her every thought—he whom she had loved best, and who was her whole earthly pride.

Anne Lisbeth went out of the castle into the open highway, and she felt very mournful: he had been so cold and strange to her, had not a word nor a thought for her, he whom she had once carried day and night, and whom she still carried in her dreams.

A great black raven shot down in front of her on to the high road, and croaked and croaked again.

"Ha!" she said, "what bird of ill omen art thou?"

She came past the hut of the labourer; the wife stood at the door, and the two women spoke to one another.

"You look well," said the woman. "You are plump and fat; you're well off."

"Oh, yes," answered Anne Lisbeth.

"The boat went down with them," continued the woman. "Hans skipper and the boy were both drowned. There's an end of them. I always thought the boy would be able to help me out with a few dollars. He'll never cost *you* anything more, Anne Lisbeth."

" So they were drowned ? " Anne Lisbeth repeated ; and then nothing more was said on the subject.

Anne Lisbeth was very low-spirited because her count-child had shown no disposition to talk with her who loved him so well, and who had journeyed all that way to get a sight of him ; and the journey had cost money too, though the pleasure she had derived from it was not great. Still she said not a word about this. She would not relieve her heart by telling the labourer's wife about it, lest the latter should think she did not enjoy her former position at the castle. Then the raven screamed again, and flew past over her once more.

ANNE LISBETH AT THE LABOURER'S COTTAGE.

" The black wretch ! " said Ann Lisbeth ; " he 'll end by frightening me to-day."

She had brought coffee and chicory with her, for she thought it would be a charity towards the poor woman to give them to her to boil a cup of coffee, and then she herself would take a cup too. The woman prepared the coffee, and in the meantime Anne Lisbeth sat down upon a chair and fell asleep. There she dreamed of something she had never dreamed before : singularly enough, she dreamed of her own child that had wept and hungered there in the labourer's hut, had been hustled about in heat and in cold, and was now lying in the depths of the sea, Heaven knows where. She dreamed she was sitting in the hut, where the woman was busy preparing the coffee—she could smell the roasting coffee beans. But suddenly it seemed to her that there stood on the threshold a beautiful young form, as beautiful as the count's child; and this apparition said to her,

" The world is passing away! Hold fast to me, for you are my mother after all.   You have an angel in heaven.   Hold me fast! "

And the child-angel stretched out its hand to her; and there was a terrible crash, for the world was going to pieces, and the angel was raising himself above the earth, and holding her by the sleeve so tightly, it seemed to her, that she was lifted up from the ground; but, on the other hand, something heavy hung at her feet and dragged her down, and it seemed to her that hundreds of women clung to her, and cried,

" If thou art to be saved, we must be saved too! Hold fast! hold fast! "

And then they all hung on to her; but there were too many of them, and—*ritsch! ratsch!*—the sleeve tore, and Anne Lisbeth fell down in horror—and awoke.   And, indeed, she was on the point of falling over, with the chair on which she sat: she was so startled and alarmed that she could not recollect what it was she had dreamed, but she remembered that it had been something dreadful.

The coffee was taken, and they had a chat together; and then Anne Lisbeth went away towards the little town where she was to meet the carrier, and to drive back with him to her own home.   But when she came to speak to him, he said he should not be ready to start before the evening of the next day.   She began to think about the expense and the length of the way, and when she considered that the route by the sea shore was shorter by two miles than the other, and that the weather was clear and the moon shone, she determined to make her way on foot, and to start at once, that she might be at home by next day.

The sun had set, and the evening bells, tolled in the towers of the village churches, still sounded through the air; but no, it was not the bells, but the cry of the frogs in the marshes.   Now they were silent, and all around was still; not a bird was heard, for they were all gone to rest; and even the owl seemed to be at home: deep silence reigned on the margin of the forest and by the sea shore.   As Anne Lisbeth walked on she could hear her own footsteps on the sand; there was no sound of waves in the sea; everything out in the deep waters had sunk to silence. All was quiet there, the living and the dead creatures of the sea.

Anne Lisbeth walked on "thinking of nothing at all," as the saying is, or rather, her thoughts wandered; but thoughts had not wandered away from her, for they are never absent from us, they only slumber. But those that have not yet stirred come forth at their time, and begin to stir sometimes in the heart and sometimes in the head, and seem to come upon us as if from above.

It is written that a good deed bears its fruit of blessing, and it is also written that sin is death.   Much has been written and much has been said which one does not know or think of in general; and thus it was with Anne Lisbeth. But it may happen that a light arises within one, and that the forgotten things may approach.

All virtues and all vices lie in our hearts. They are in mine and in thine; they lie there like little grains of seed; and then from without comes a ray of sunshine or the touch of an evil hand, or may be you turn the corner and go to the right or to the left, and that may be decisive; for the little seed-corn perhaps is stirred, and it swells and shoots up. and it bursts, and pours its sap into all your blood, and then your career has commenced. There are tormenting thoughts, which one does not feel when one walks on with slumbering senses, but they are there, fermenting in the heart. Anne Lisbeth walked on thus with her senses half in slumber, but the thoughts were fermenting within her. From one Shrove Tuesday to the next there comes much that weighs upon the heart—the reckoning of a whole year: much is forgotten, sins against Heaven in word and in thought, against our neighbour, and against our own conscience. We don't think of these things, and Anne Lisbeth did not think of them. She had committed no crime against the law of the land, she was very respectable, an honoured and well-placed person. that she knew. And as she walked along by the margin of the sea, what was it she saw lying there? An old hat, a man's hat. Now, where might that have been washed overboard? She came nearer, and stopped to look at the hat. Ha! what was lying yonder? She shuddered; but it was nothing save a heap of sea grass and tangle flung across a long stone; but it looked just like a corpse; it was only sea grass and tangle, and yet she was frightened at it, and as she turned away to walk on much came into her mind that she had heard in her childhood — old superstitions of spectres by the sea shore, of the ghosts of drowned but unburied people whose corpses have been washed up on to the desert shore. The body, she had heard, could do harm to none, but the spirit could pursue the lonely wanderer, and attach itself to him, and demand to be carried to the churchyard that it might rest in consecrated ground. "Hold fast! hold fast!" the spectre would then cry; and while Anne Lisbeth murmured the words to herself, her whole dream suddenly stood before her just as she had dreamed it, when the mothers clung to her and had repeated this word amid the crash of the world, when her sleeve was torn and she slipped out of the grasp of her child, who wanted to hold her up in that terrible hour. Her child, her own child, which she had never loved, now lay buried in the sea, and might rise up like a spectre from the waters, and cry, "Hold fast! carry me to consecrated earth." And as these thoughts passed through her mind, fear gave speed to her feet, so that she walked on faster and faster; fear came upon her like the touch of a cold wet hand that was laid upon her heart, so that she almost fainted; and as she looked out across the sea, all there grew darker and darker; a heavy mist came rolling onward, and clung round bush and tree, twisting them into fantastic shapes. She turned round. and glanced up at the moon, which had risen behind her. It looked like a pale, rayless surface; and a deadly weight appeared to cling to her limbs. "Hold fast!" thought she; and when she turned round a second time and looked at the moon, its white face seemed quite close to her, and the mist hung like a pale garment from her shoulders. " Hold fast ! carry me to consecrated earth ! " sounded in her ears in strange hollow tones. The sound did not come from frogs or ravens ; she saw no sign of any such creatures. " A grave ! dig me a grave ! " was repeated quite loud. Yes, it was the spectre of her child, the child that lay in the ocean, and whose spirit could have no rest until it was carried to the churchyard, and until a grave had been dug for it in consecrated ground. Thither she would go, and there she would dig ; and she went on in the direction of the church, and the weight on her heart seemed to grow lighter, and even to vanish altogether ; but when she turned to go home by the shortest way, it returned. " Hold fast ! hold fast ! " and the words came quite clear, though they were like the croak of a frog or the wail of a bird, " A grave ! dig me a grave ! "

The mist was cold and damp ; her hands and face were cold and damp with horror ; a heavy weight again seized her and clung to her, and in her mind a great space opened for thoughts that had never before been there.

Here in the North the beech wood often buds in a single night, and in the morning sunlight it appears in its full glory of youthful green ; and thus in a single instant can the consciousness unfold itself of the sin that has been contained in the thoughts, words, and works of our past life. It springs up and unfolds itself in a single second when once the conscience is awakened ; and God wakens it when we least expect it. Then we find no excuse for ourselves—the deed is there, and bears witness against us ; the thoughts seem to become words, and to sound far out into the world. We are horrified at the thought of what we have carried within us, and have not stifled over what we have sown in our thoughtlessness and pride. The heart hides within itself all the virtues and likewise all the vices, and they grow even in the shallowest ground.

Anne Lisbeth now experienced all the thoughts we have clothed in words. She was overpowered by them, and sank down, and crept along for some distance on the ground. " A grave ! dig me a grave ! " it sounded again in her ears ; and she would gladly have buried herself if in the grave there had been forgetfulness of every deed. It was the first hour of her awakening—full of anguish and horror. Superstition alternately made her shudder with cold and made her blood burn with the heat of fever. Many things of which she had never liked to speak came into her mind. Silent as the cloud shadows in the bright moonshine, a spectral apparition flitted by her : she had heard of it before. Close by her galloped four snorting steeds, with fire spurting from their eyes and nostrils ; they dragged a red-hot coach, and within it sat the wicked proprietor who had ruled here a hundred years ago. The legend said that every night at twelve o'clock he drove into his castle yard and out again. There ! there ! He was not pale, as dead men are said to be, but black as a coal. He nodded at Anne Lisbeth and beckoned to her. " Hold fast ! hold fast ! then you may ride again in a nobleman's carriage, and forget your own child ! "

ANNE LISBETH FOUND ON THE SEA SHORE.

She gathered herself up, and hastened to the churchyard; but the black crosses and the black ravens danced before her eyes, and she could not distinguish one from the other. The ravens croaked, as the raven had done that she saw in the day-time, but now she understood what they said. "I am the raven-mother! I am the raven-mother!" each raven croaked, and Anne Lisbeth now understood that the name also applied to her; and she fancied she should be transformed into a black bird, and be obliged to cry what they cried, if she did not dig the grave.

And she threw herself on the earth, and with her hands dug a grave in the hard ground, so that the blood ran from her fingers.

"A grave! dig me a grave!" it still sounded; she was fearful that the cock might crow, and the first red streak appear in the east, before she had finished her work, and then she would be lost.

And the cock crowed, and day dawned in the east, and the grave was only half dug. An icy hand passed over her head and face and down towards her heart.

"Only half a grave!" a voice wailed, and fled away.

Yes, it fled away over the sea—it was the ocean spectre; and exhausted and overpowered, Anne Lisbeth sank to the ground, and her senses forsook her.

It was bright day when she came to herself, and two men were raising her up; but she was not lying in the churchyard, but on the sea shore, where she had dug a deep hole in the sand, and cut her hand against a broken glass, whose sharp stem was stuck in a little painted block of wood. Anne Lisbeth was in a fever. Conscience had shuffled the cards of superstition, and had laid out these cards, and she fancied she had only half a soul, and that her child had taken the other half down into the sea. Never would she be able to swing herself aloft to the mercy of Heaven till she had recovered this other half, which was now held fast in the deep water. Anne Lisbeth got back to her former home, but was no longer the woman she had been: her thoughts were confused like a tangled skein; only one thread, only one thought she had disentangled, namely, that she must carry the spectre of the sea shore to the churchyard, and dig a grave for him, that thus she might win back her soul.

Many a night she was missed from her home; and she was always found on the sea shore, waiting for the spectre. In this way a whole year passed by; and then one night she vanished again, and was not to be found; the whole of the next day was wasted in fruitless search.

Towards evening, when the clerk came into the church to toll the vesper bell, he saw by the altar Anne Lisbeth, who had spent the whole day there. Her physical forces were almost exhausted, but her eyes gleamed brightly, and her cheeks had a rosy flush. The last rays of the sun shone upon her, and gleamed over the altar on the bright buckles of the Bible which lay there, opened at the words of the prophet Joel: "Rend your hearts, and not your garments, and turn unto the Lord!" That was just a chance, the people said, as many things happen by chance.

In the face of Anne Lisbeth, illumined by the sun, peace and rest were to be seen. She said she was happy, for now she had conquered. Last night the spectre of the shore, her own child, had come to her, and had said to her,

"Thou hast dug me only half a grave, but thou hast now, for a year and a day, buried me altogether in thy heart, and it is there that a mother can best hide her child!"

And then he gave her her lost soul back again, and brought her here into the church.

"Now I am in the house of God," she said, "and in that house we are happy."

And when the sun had set, Anne Lisbeth's soul had risen to that region where there is no more anguish, and Anne Lisbeth's troubles were over.

THE LAST DREAM OF THE OLD OAK TREE.

A CHRISTMAS TALE.

In the forest, high up on the steep shore, hard by the open sea coast, stood a very old Oak Tree. It was exactly three hundred and sixty-five years old, but that long time was not more for the Tree than just as many days would be to us men. We wake by day and sleep through the night, and then we have our dreams: it is different with the Tree, which keeps awake through three seasons of the year, and does not get its sleep till winter comes. Winter is its time for rest, its night after the long day which is called spring, summer, and autumn.

On many a warm summer day the Ephemera, the fly that lives but for a day, had danced around his crown—had lived, enjoyed, and felt happy; and then rested for a moment in quiet bliss the tiny creature, on one of the great fresh Oak leaves; and then the Tree always said,

"Poor little thing! Your whole life is but a single day! How very short! It's quite melancholy."

"Melancholy! Why do you say that?" the Ephemera would then always reply. "It's wonderfully bright, warm, and beautiful all around me, and that makes me rejoice."

"But only one day, and then it's all done!"

"Done!" repeated the Ephemera. "What's the meaning of *done?* Are you *done*, too?"

"No; I shall perhaps live for thousands of your days, and my day is whole seasons long! It's something so long, that you can't at all manage to reckon it out."

"No? then I don't understand you. You say you have thousands of my days; but I have thousands of moments, in which I can be merry and happy. Does all the beauty of this world cease when you die?"

"No," replied the Tree; "it will certainly last much longer — far longer than I can possibly think."

"Well, then, we have the same time, only that we reckon differently."

And the Ephemera danced and floated in the air, and rejoiced in her delicate wings of gauze and velvet, and rejoiced in the balmy breezes laden with the fragrance of the meadows and of wild roses and elder flowers, of the garden hedges, wild thyme, and mint, and daisies; the scent of these was all so strong that the Ephemera was almost intoxicated. The day was long and beautiful, full of joy and of sweet feeling, and when the sun sank low the little fly felt very agreeably tired of all its happiness and enjoyment. The delicate wings would not carry it any more, and quietly and slowly it glided down upon the soft grass blade, nodded its head as well as it could nod, and went quietly to sleep —and was dead.

"Poor little Ephemera!" said the Oak. "That was a terribly short life!"

And on every summer day the same dance was repeated, the same question and answer, and the same sleep. The same thing was repeated through whole generations of Ephemera, and all of them felt equally merry and equally happy.

The Oak stood there awake through the spring morning, the noon of summer, and the evening of autumn; and its time of rest, its night, was coming on apace. Winter was approaching.

Already the storms were singing their "good night! good night!" Here fell a leaf, and there fell a leaf.

"We'll rock you, and dandle you! Go to sleep! go to sleep! We sing you to sleep, we shake you to sleep, but it does you good in your old twigs, does it not? They seem to crack for very joy. Sleep sweetly! sleep sweetly! It's your three hundred and sixty-fifth night. Properly speaking, you're only a stripling as yet! Sleep sweetly! The clouds strew down snow, there will be quite a coverlet, warm and protecting, around your feet. Sweet sleep to you, and pleasant dreams!"

And the old Oak Tree stood there, denuded of all its leaves, to sleep through the long winter, and to dream many a dream, always about something that had happened to it, just as in the dreams of men.

The great Oak had once been small—indeed, an acorn had been its cradle. According to human computation, it was now in its fourth century. It was the greatest and best tree in the forest; its crown towered far above all the other trees, and could be descried from afar across the sea, so that it served as a landmark to the sailors: the Tree had no idea how many eyes were in the habit of seeking it. High up in its green summit the wood pigeon built her nest, and the cuckoo sat in its boughs and sang his song; and in autumn, when the leaves looked like thin plates of copper, the birds of passage came and rested there, before they flew away across the sea; but now it was winter, and the Tree stood there leafless, so that every one could see how gnarled and crooked the branches were that shot forth from its trunk. Crows and rooks came and took their seat by turns in the boughs, and spoke of the hard times which were beginning, and of the difficulty of getting a living in winter.

It was just at the holy Christmas-time, when the Tree dreamed its most glorious dream.

The Tree had distinct feeling of the festive time, and fancied he heard the bells ringing from the churches all around; and yet it seemed as if it were a fine summer's day, mild and warm. Fresh and green he spread out his mighty crown; the sunbeams played among the twigs and the leaves; the air was full of the fragrance of herbs and blossoms; gay butterflies chased each other to and fro. The ephemeral insects danced as if all the world were created merely for them to dance and be merry in. All that the Tree had experienced for years and years, and that had happened around him, seemed to pass by him again, as in a festive pageant. He saw the knights of ancient days ride by with their noble dames on gallant steeds, with plumes waving in their bonnets and falcons on their wrists. The hunting horn sounded, and the dogs barked.

THE LOVERS AT THE OLD OAK TREE.

He saw hostile warriors in coloured jerkins and with shining weapons, with spear and halbert, pitching their tents and striking them again. The watch-fires flamed up anew, and men sang and slept under the branches of the Tree. He saw loving couples meeting near his trunk, happily, in the moonshine; and they cut the initials of their names in the grey-green bark of his stem. Once—but long years had rolled by since then—citherns and Æolian harps had been hung up on his boughs by merry wanderers; now they hung there again, and once again they sounded in tones of marvellous sweetness. The wood pigeons cooed, as if they were telling what the Tree felt in all this, and the cuckoo called out to tell him how many summer days he had yet to live.

Then it appeared to him as if new life were rippling down into the remotest fibre of his root, and mounting up into his highest branches, to the tops of the leaves. The Tree felt that he was stretching and spreading himself, and through his root he felt that there was life and motion even in the ground itself. He felt his strength increase, he grew higher, his stem shot up unceasingly, and he grew more and more, his crown became fuller and spread out; and in proportion as the Tree grew, he felt his happiness increase, and his joyous hope that he should reach even higher—quite up to the warm brilliant sun.

Already had he grown high up above the clouds, which floated past beneath his crown like dark troops of passage-birds, or like great white swans. And every leaf of the Tree had the gift of sight, as if it had eyes wherewith to see: the stars became visible in broad daylight, great and sparkling; each of them sparkled like a pair of eyes, mild and clear. They recalled to his memory well-known gentle eyes, eyes of children, eyes of lovers, who had met beneath his boughs.

It was a marvellous spectacle, and one full of happiness and joy! And yet amid all this happiness the Tree felt a longing, a yearning desire that all other trees of the wood beneath him, and all the bushes, and herbs, and flowers, might be able to rise with him, that they too might see this splendour and experience this joy. The great majestic Oak was not quite happy in his happiness, while he had not them all, great and little, about him; and this feeling of yearning trembled through his every twig, through his every leaf, warmly and fervently as through a human heart.

The crown of the Tree waved to and fro, as if he sought something in his silent longing, and he looked down. Then he felt the fragrance of thyme, and soon afterwards the more powerful scent of honeysuckle and violets; and he fancied he heard the cuckoo answering him.

Yes, through the clouds the green summits of the forest came peering up, and under himself the Oak saw the other trees, as they grew and raised themselves aloft. Bushes and herbs shot up high, and some tore themselves up bodily by the roots to rise the quicker. The birch was the quickest of all. Like a white streak of lightning, its slender stem shot upwards in a zigzag line, and the branches spread around it like green gauze and like banners; the whole woodland natives, even to the brown-plumed rushes, grew up with the rest, and the birds came too, and sang; and on the grass blade that fluttered aloft like a long silken ribbon into the air, sat the grasshopper cleaning his wings with his leg; the May beetles hummed, and the bees murmured, and every bird sang in his appointed manner; all was song and sound of gladness up into the high heaven.

" But the little blue flower by the water-side, where is that ? " said the Oak ; " and the purple bell-flower and the daisy ? " for, you see, the old Oak Tree wanted to have them all about him.

" We are here ! we are here ! " was shouted and sung in reply.

" But the beautiful thyme of last summer—and in the last year there was certainly a place here covered with lilies of the valley ! and the wild apple tree that blossomed so splendidly ! and all the glory of the wood that came year by year—if that had only just been born, it might have been here now ! "

" We are here ! we are here ! " replied voices still higher in the air. It seemed as if they had flown on before.

" Why, that is beautiful, indescribably beautiful ! " exclaimed the old

Oak Tree, rejoicingly. "I have them all around me, great and small; not one has been forgotten! How can so much happiness be imagined? How can it be possible?"

"In heaven, in the better land, it can be imagined, and it is possible!" the reply sounded through the air.

And the old Tree, who grew on and on, felt how his roots were tearing themselves free from the ground.

"That's right! that's better than all!" said the Tree. "Now no fetters hold me! I can fly up now, to the very highest, in glory and in light! And all my beloved ones are with me, great and small—all of them, all!"

That was the dream of the old Oak Tree; and while he dreamed thus a mighty storm came rushing over land and sea—at the holy Christmas-tide. The sea rolled great billows towards the shore, and there was a cracking and crashing in the tree—his root was torn out of the ground in the very moment while he was dreaming that his root freed itself from the earth. He fell. His three hundred and sixty-five years were now as the single day of the Ephemera.

On the morning of the Christmas festival, when the sun rose, the storm had subsided. From all the churches sounded the festive bells, and from every hearth, even from the smallest hut, arose the smoke in blue clouds, like the smoke from the altars of the druids of old at the feast of thanks offerings. The sea became gradually calm, and on board a great ship in the offing, that had fought successfully with the tempest, all the flags were displayed, as a token of joy suitable to the festive day.

"The Tree is down—the old Oak Tree, our landmark on the coast!" said the sailors. "It fell in the storm of last night. Who can replace it? No one can."

This was the funeral oration, short but well meant, that was given to the Tree, which lay stretched on the snowy covering on the sea shore; and over its prostrate form sounded the notes of a song from the ship, a carol of the joys of Christmas, and of the redemption of the soul of man by His blood, and of eternal life.

> "Sing, sing aloud, this blessed morn—
> It is fulfilled—and He is born,
> Oh, joy without compare!
> Hallelujah! Hallelujah!"

Thus sounded the old psalm tune, and every one on board the ship felt lifted up in his own way, through the song and the prayer, just as the old Tree had felt lifted up in its last, its most beauteous dream in the Christmas night.

THE BELL-DEEP.

"Ding-dong! ding-dong!" It sounds up from the "bell-deep" in the Odense-Au. Every child in the old town of Odense, on the island of Fünen, knows the Au, which washes the gardens round about the town, and flows on under the wooden bridges from the dam to the water-mill. In the Au grow the yellow water-lilies and brown feathery reeds; the dark velvety flag grows there, high and thick; old and decayed willows, slanting and tottering, hang far out over the stream beside the monks' meadow and by the bleaching ground; but opposite there are gardens upon gardens, each different from the rest, some with pretty flowers and bowers like little dolls' pleasure grounds, often displaying only cabbage and other kitchen plants; and here and there the gardens cannot be seen at all, for the great elder trees that spread themselves out by the bank, and hang far out over the streaming waters, which are deeper here and there than an oar can fathom. Opposite the old nunnery is the deepest place, which is called the "bell-deep," and there dwells the old water spirit, the "Au-mann." This spirit sleeps through the day while the sun shines down upon the water; but in starry and moonlit nights he shows himself. He is very old: grandmother says that she has heard her own grandmother tell of him; he is said to lead a solitary life, and to have nobody with whom he can converse save the great old church Bell. Once the Bell hung in the church tower; but now there is no trace left of the tower or of the church, which was called St. Alban's.

"Ding-dong! ding-dong!" sounded the Bell, when the tower still stood there; and one evening, while the sun was setting, and the Bell was swinging away bravely, it broke loose and came flying down through the air, the brilliant metal shining in the ruddy beam.

"Ding-dong! ding-dong! Now I'll retire to rest!" sang the Bell, and flew down into the Odense-Au where it is deepest; and that is why the place is called the "bell-deep."

But the Bell got neither rest nor sleep. Down in the Au-mann's haunt it sounds and rings, so that the tones sometimes pierce upward through the waters; and many people maintain that its strains forebode the death of some one; but that is not true, for then the Bell is only talking with the Au-mann, who is now no longer alone.

And what is the Bell telling? It is old, very old, as we have already observed; it was there long before grandmother's grandmother was born; and yet it is but a child in comparison with the Au-mann, who is an old quiet personage, an oddity, with his hose of eel-skin, and his scaly jacket with the yellow lilies for buttons, and a wreath of reed in his hair and seaweed in his beard; but he looks very pretty for all that.

What the Bell tells? To repeat it all would require years and days; for year by year it is telling the old stories, sometimes short ones, sometimes long ones, according to its whim; it tells of old times, of the dark hard times, thus:

"In the church of St. Alban, the monk mounted up into the tower. He was young and handsome, but thoughtful exceedingly. He looked through the loophole out upon the Odense-Au, when the bed of the water was yet broad and the monks' meadow was still a lake: he looked out over it, and over the rampart, and over the nuns' hill opposite, where the convent lay, and the light gleamed forth from the nun's cell; he had known the nun right well, and he thought of her, and his heart beat quicker as he thought. Ding-dong! ding-dong!"

Yes, this was the story the Bell told.

THE AU-MANN LISTENING TO THE BELL.

"Into the tower came also the dapper man-servant of the bishop; and when I, the Bell, who am made of metal, rang hard and loud, and swung to and fro, I might have beaten out his brains. He sat down close under me, and played with two little sticks as if they had been a stringed instrument; and he sang to it. 'Now I may sing it out aloud, though at other times I may not whisper it. I may sing of everything that is kept concealed behind lock and bars. Yonder it is cold and wet. The rats are eating her up alive! Nobody knows of it! Nobody hears of it! Not even now, for the Bell is ringing and singing its loud Ding-dong! ding-dong!'

"There was a King in those days; they called him Canute. He bowed himself before bishop and monk; but when he offended the free peasants

with heavy taxes and hard words, they seized their weapons and put him
to flight like a wild beast.   He sought shelter in the church, and shut
gate and door behind him.   The violent band surrounded the church;
I heard tell of it.   The crows, ravens, and magpies started up in terror
at the yelling and shouting that sounded around.   They flew into the
tower and out again, they looked down upon the throng below, and they
also looked into the windows of the church, and screamed out aloud
what they saw there.   King Canute knelt before the altar in prayer,
his brothers Eric and Benedict stood by him as a guard with drawn
swords; but the King's servant, the treacherous Blake, betrayed his
master; the throng in front of the church knew where they could hit
the King, and one of them flung a stone through a pane of glass, and the
King lay there dead!   The cries and screams of the savage horde and of
the birds sounded through the air, and I joined in it also; for I sang
'Ding-dong! ding-dong!'

" The church bell hangs high and looks far around, and sees the birds
around it, and understands their language; the wind roars in upon it
through windows and loopholes; and the wind knows everything, for he
gets it from the air, which encircles all things, and the church bell understands his tongue, and rings it out into the world, 'Ding-dong! ding-
dong!'

" But it was too much for me to hear and to know; I was not able
any longer to ring it out.   I became so tired, so heavy, that the beam
broke, and I flew out into the gleaming Au where the water is deepest,
and where the Au-mann lives, solitary and alone; and year by year I
tell him what I have heard and what I know.   Ding-dong! ding-dong!"

Thus it sounds complainingly out of the bell-deep in the Odense-Au:
that is what grandmother told us.

But the schoolmaster says that there was not any bell that rung down
there, for that it could not do so; and that no Au-mann dwelt yonder,
for there was no Au-mann at all!   And when all the other church bells
are sounding sweetly, he says that it is not really the bells that are
sounding, but that it is the air itself which sends forth the notes; and
grandmother said to us that the Bell itself said it was the air who told
it him, consequently they are agreed on that point, and this much is sure.

" Be cautious, cautious, and take good heed to thyself," they both say.

The air knows everything.   It is around us, it is in us, it talks of our
thoughts and of our deeds, and it speaks longer of them than does the
Bell down in the depths of the Odense-Au where the Au-mann dwells;
it rings it out into the vault of heaven, far, far out, for ever and ever,
till the heaven bells sound " Ding-dong! ding-dong!"

THE LITTLE SEA MAID.

FAR out in the sea the water is as blue as the petals of the most beautiful corn-flower, and as clear as the purest glass. But it is very deep, deeper than any cable will sound; many steeples must be placed one above the other to reach from the ground to the surface of the water. And down there live the sea people.

Now, you must not believe there is nothing down there but the naked sand; no,—the strangest plants and flowers grow there, so pliable in their stalks and leaves that at the least motion of the water they move just as if they had life. All fishes, great and small, glide among the twigs, just as here the birds do in the trees. In the deepest spot of all lies the Sea King's castle: the walls are of coral and the tall gothic windows of the clearest amber; shells form the roof, and they open and shut according as the water flows. It looks lovely, for in each shell lie gleaming pearls, a single one of which would have great value in a Queen's diadem.

The Sea King below there had been a widower for many years, while his old mother kept house for him. She was a clever woman, but proud of her rank, so she wore twelve oysters on her tail, while the other great people were only allowed to wear six. Beyond this she was deserving of great praise, especially because she was very fond of her granddaughters, the little Sea Princesses. These were six pretty children; but the youngest was the most beautiful of all. Her skin was as clear and as fine as a rose leaf, her eyes were as blue as the deepest sea, but, like all the rest, she had no feet, for her body ended in a fish-tail.

All day long they could play in the castle, down in the halls, where living flowers grew out of the walls. The great amber windows were opened, and then the fishes swam in to them, just as the swallows fly in to us when we open our windows; but the fishes swam straight up to the Princesses, ate out of their hands, and let themselves be stroked.

Outside the castle was a great garden with bright red and dark blue flowers; the fruit glowed like gold, and the flowers like flames of fire; and they continually kept moving their stalks and leaves. The earth itself was the finest sand, but blue as the flame of brimstone. A peculiar blue radiance lay upon everything down there: one would have thought oneself high in the air, with the canopy of heaven above and around, rather than at the bottom of the deep sea. During a calm the sun could be seen; it appeared like a purple flower, from which all light streamed out.

Each of the little Princesses had her own little place in the garden, where she might dig and plant at her good pleasure. One gave her flower-bed the form of a whale; another thought it better to make hers like a little sea woman; but the youngest made hers quite round, like the sun, and had flowers which gleamed red as the sun itself. She was a strange child, quiet and thoughtful; and when the other sisters made a display of the beautiful things they had received out of wrecked ships, she would have nothing beyond the red flowers which resembled the sun, except a pretty marble statue. This was a figure of a charming boy, hewn out of white clear stone, which had sunk down to the bottom of the sea from a wreck. She planted a pink weeping willow beside this statue; the tree grew famously, and hung its fresh branches over the statue towards the blue sandy ground, where the shadow showed violet, and moved like the branches themselves; it seemed as if the ends of the branches and the roots were playing together and wished to kiss each other.

There was no greater pleasure for her than to hear of the world of men above them. The old grandmother had to tell all she knew of ships and towns, of men and animals. It seemed particularly beautiful to her that up on the earth the flowers shed fragrance, for they had none down at the bottom of the sea, and that the trees were green, and that the fishes which one saw there among the trees could sing so loud and clear that it was a pleasure to hear them. What the grandmother called fishes were the little birds; the Princess could not understand them in any other way, for she had never seen a bird.

"When you have reached your fifteenth year," said the grandmother, "you shall have leave to rise up out of the sea, to sit on the rocks in the moonlight, and to see the great ships sailing by. Then you will see forests and towns!"

In the next year one of the sisters was fifteen years of age, but each of the others was one year younger than the next; so that the youngest had full five years to wait before she could come up from the bottom of the sea, and find how our world looked. But one promised to tell the others what she had seen and what she had thought the most beautiful on the first day of her visit; for their grandmother could not tell them enough—there was so much about which they wanted information.

No one was more anxious about these things than the youngest—just that one who had the longest time to wait, and who was always quiet and thoughtful. Many a night she stood by the open window, and looked up through the dark blue water at the fishes splashing with their fins and tails. Moon and stars she could see; they certainly shone quite faintly, but through the water they looked much larger than they appear in our eyes. When something like a black cloud passed among them, she knew that it was either a whale swimming over her head, or a ship with many people: they certainly did not think that a pretty little sea maid was standing down below stretching up her white hands towards the keel of their ship.

Now the eldest Princess was fifteen years old, and might mount up to the surface of the sea.

When she came back, she had a hundred things to tell,—but the finest thing, she said, was to lie in the moonshine on a sand-bank in the quiet sea, and to look at the neighbouring coast, with the large town, where the lights twinkled like a hundred stars, and to hear the music and the noise and clamour of carriages and men, to see the many church steeples, and to hear the sound of the bells. Just because she could not get up to these, she longed for them more than for anything.

Oh, how the youngest sister listened! and afterwards when she stood at the open window and looked up through the dark blue water, she thought of the great city with all its bustle and noise; and then she thought she could hear the church bells ringing, even down to the depth where she was.

In the following year, the second sister received permission to mount upward through the water and to swim whither she pleased. She rose up just as the sun was setting; and this spectacle, she said, was the most beautiful. The whole sky looked like gold, she said, and as to

THE SEA PRINCESSES.

the clouds, she could not properly describe their beauty. They sailed away over her head, purple and violet-coloured, but far quicker than the clouds there flew a flight of wild swans, like a long white veil, over the water towards where the sun stood. She swam towards them; but the sun sank, and the roseate hue faded on the sea and in the clouds.

In the following year the next sister went up. She was the boldest of them all, and therefore she swam up a broad stream that poured its waters into the sea. She saw glorious green hills clothed with vines; palaces and castles shone forth from amid splendid woods; she heard how all the birds sang; and the sun shone so warm that she was often obliged to dive under the water to cool her glowing face. In a little bay she found a whole swarm of little mortals. They were quite naked, and splashed about in the water: she wanted to play with them, but they fled in affright, and a little black animal came—it was a dog, but she had never seen a dog—and it barked at her so terribly that she became frightened, and tried to gain the open sea. But she could never forget the glorious woods, the green hills, and the pretty children, who could swim in the water though they had not fish-tails.

The fourth sister was not so bold: she remained out in the midst of the wild sea, and declared that just there it was most beautiful. One could see for many miles around, and the sky above looked like a bell of glass. She had seen ships, but only in the far distance—they looked like seagulls; and the funny dolphins had thrown somersaults, and the great whales spouted out water from their nostrils, so that it looked like hundreds of fountains all around.

Now came the turn of the fifth sister. Her birthday came in the winter, and so she saw what the others had not seen the first time. The sea looked quite green, and great icebergs were floating about; each one appeared like a pearl, she said, and yet was much taller than the church steeples built by men. They showed themselves in the strangest forms, and shone like diamonds. She had seated herself upon one of the greatest of all, and let the wind play with her long hair; and all the sailing ships tacked about in a very rapid way beyond where she sat; but towards evening the sky became covered with clouds, it thundered and lightened, and the black waves lifted the great iceblocks high up, and let them glow in the red glare. On all the ships the sails were reefed, and there was fear and anguish. But she sat quietly upon her floating iceberg, and saw the forked blue flashes dart into the sea.

Each of the sisters, as she came up for the first time to the surface of the water, was delighted with the new and beautiful sights she saw ; but as they now had permission, as grown-up girls, to go whenever they liked, it became indifferent to them. They wished themselves back again, and after a month had elapsed they said it was best of all down below, for there one felt so comfortably at home.

Many an evening hour the five sisters took one another by the arm and rose up in a row over the water. They had splendid voices, more charming than any mortal could have ; and when a storm was approaching, so that they could apprehend that ships would go down, they swam on before the ships and sang lovely songs, which told how beautiful it was at the bottom of the sea, and exhorted the sailors not to be afraid to come down. But these could not understand the words, and thought it was the storm sighing; and they did not see the splendours below, for if the ships sank they were drowned, and came as corpses to the Sea King's palace.

When the sisters thus rose up, arm in arm, in the evening time, through the water, the little sister stood all alone looking after them ; and she felt as if she must weep; but the sea maid has no tears, and for this reason she suffers far more acutely.

"Oh, if I were only fifteen years old!" said she. "I know I shall love the world up there very much, and the people who live and dwell there."

At last she was really fifteen years old.

"Now, you see, you are grown up," said the grandmother, the old dowager. "Come, let me adorn you like your sisters."

And she put a wreath of white lilies in the little maid's hair, but each flower was half a pearl; and the old lady let eight great oysters attach themselves to the Princess's tail, in token of her high rank.

" But that hurts so! " said the little sea maid.

" Yes, pride must suffer pain," replied the old lady.

Oh, how glad she would have been to shake off all the tokens of rank and lay aside the heavy wreath! Her red flowers in the garden suited her better; but she could not help it. " Farewell! " she said, and then she rose, light and clear as a water-bubble, up through the sea.

The sun had just set when she lifted her head above the sea, but all the clouds still shone like roses and gold, and in the pale red sky the evening stars gleamed bright and beautiful. The air was mild and fresh and the sea quite calm. There lay a great ship with three masts; one single sail only was set, for not a breeze stirred, and around in the shrouds and on the yards sat the sailors. There was music and singing, and as the evening closed in, hundreds of coloured lanterns were lighted up, and looked as if the flags of every nation were waving in the air. The little sea maid swam straight to the cabin window, and each time the sea lifted her up she could look through the panes, which were clear as crystal, and see many people standing within dressed in their best. But the handsomest of all was the young Prince with the great black eyes: he was certainly not much more than sixteen years old; it was his birthday, and that was the cause of all this feasting. The sailors were dancing upon deck; and when the young Prince came out, more than a hundred rockets rose into the air; they shone like day, so that the little sea maid was quite startled, and dived under the water; but soon she put out her head again, and then it seemed just as if all the stars of heaven were falling down upon her. She had never seen such fireworks. Great suns spurted fire all around, glorious fiery fishes flew up into the blue air, and everything was mirrored in the clear blue sea. The ship itself was so brightly lit up that every separate rope could be seen, and the people therefore appeared the more plainly. Oh, how handsome the young Prince was! And he pressed the people's hands and smiled, while the music rang out in the glorious night.

It became late; but the little sea maid could not turn her eyes from the ship and from the beautiful Prince. The coloured lanterns were extinguished, rockets ceased to fly into the air, and no more cannons were fired; but there was a murmuring and a buzzing deep down in the sea; and she sat on the water, swaying up and down, so that she could look into the cabin. But as the ship got more way, one sail after another was spread. And now the waves rose higher, great clouds came up, and in the distance there was lightning. Oh! it was going to be fearful weather, therefore the sailors furled the sails. The great ship flew in swift career over the wild sea: the waters rose up like great black mountains, which wanted to roll over the masts; but like a swan the ship dived into the valleys between these high waves, and then let itself be lifted on high again. To the little sea maid this seemed merry sport, but to the sailors it appeared very differently. The ship groaned and creaked; the thick planks were bent by the heavy blows; the sea broke into the ship; the mainmast snapped in two like a thin reed; and the ship lay over on her side, while the water rushed into the hold. Now the little sea maid saw that the people were in peril; she herself was obliged to take care to avoid the beams and fragments of the ship which were floating about on the waters. One moment it was so pitch dark that not a single object could be descried, but when it lightened it became so bright that she could distinguish every one on board. She looked particularly for the young Prince, and when the ship parted she saw him sink into the sea. Now she was very glad, for now he would come down to her. But then she remembered that people could not live in the water, and that when he got down to her father's palace he would certainly be dead. No, he must not die: so she swam about among the beams and planks that strewed the surface, quite forgetting that one of them might have crushed her. Diving down deep under the water, she again rose high up among the waves, and in this way she at last came to the Prince, who could scarcely swim longer in that stormy sea. His arms and legs began to fail him, his beautiful eyes closed, and he would have died had the little sea maid not come. She held his head up over the water, and then allowed the waves to carry her and him whither they listed.

When the morning came the storm had passed by. Of the ship not a fragment was to be seen. The sun came up red and shining out of the water; it was as if its beams brought back the hue of life to the cheeks of the Prince, but his eyes remained closed. The sea maid kissed his high fair forehead and put back his wet hair, and he seemed to her to be like the marble statue in her little garden: she kissed him again and hoped that he might live.

Now she saw in front of her the dry land—high blue mountains, on whose summits the white snow gleamed as if swans were lying there. Down on the coast were glorious green forests, and a building—she could not tell whether it was a church or a convent—stood there. In its garden grew orange and citron trees, and high palms waved in front of the gate. The sea formed a little bay there; it was quite calm, but very deep. Straight towards the rock where the fine white sand had been cast up, she swam with the handsome Prince, and laid him upon the sand, taking especial care that his head was raised in the warm sunshine.

Now all the bells rang in the great white building, and many young girls came walking through the garden. Then the little sea maid swam farther out between some high stones that stood up out of the water, laid some sea foam upon her hair and neck, so that no one could see her little countenance, and then she watched to see who would come to the poor Prince.

In a short time a young girl went that way. She seemed to be much startled, but only for a moment; then she brought more people, and the sea maid perceived that the Prince came back to life and that he smiled at all around him. But he did not cast a smile at her: he did not know that she had saved him. And she felt very sorrowful; and when he was led away into the great building, she dived mournfully under the water and returned to her father's palace.

She had always been gentle and melancholy, but now she became much more so. Her sisters asked her what she had seen the first time she rose up to the surface, but she would tell them nothing.

Many an evening and many a morning she went up to the place where she had left the Prince. She saw how the fruits of the garden grew ripe and were gathered; she saw how the snow melted on the high mountain; but she did not see the Prince, and so she always returned home more sorrowful still. Then her only comfort was to sit in her

THE SEA MAID SAVES THE PRINCE

little garden, and to wind her arm round the beautiful marble statue that resembled the Prince; but she did not tend her flowers; they grew as if in a wilderness over the paths, and trailed their long leaves and stalks up into the branches of trees, so that it became quite dark there.

At last she could endure it no longer, and told all to one of her sisters, and then the others heard of it too; but nobody knew of it beyond these and a few other sea maids, who told the secret to their intimate friends. One of these knew who the Prince was; she too had seen the festival on board the ship; and she announced whence he came and where his kingdom lay.

"Come, little sister!" said the other Princesses; and, linking their arms together, they rose up in a long row out of the sea, at the place where they knew the Prince's palace lay.

This palace was built of a kind of bright yellow stone, with great marble staircases, one of which led directly down into the sea. Over the roof rose splendid gilt cupolas, and between the pillars which surrounded the whole dwelling stood marble statues which looked as if they were alive. Through the clear glass in the high windows one looked into the glorious halls, where costly silk hangings and tapestries were hung up, and all the walls were decked with splendid pictures, so that it was a perfect delight to see them. In the midst of the greatest of these halls a great fountain plashed; its jets shot high up towards the glass dome in the ceiling, through which the sun shone down upon the water and upon the lovely plants growing in the great basin.

Now she knew where he lived, and many an evening and many a night she spent there on the water. She swam far closer to the land than any of the others would have dared to venture; indeed, she went quite up the narrow channel under the splendid marble balcony, which threw a broad shadow upon the water. Here she sat and watched the young Prince, who thought himself quite alone in the bright moonlight.

Many an evening she saw him sailing, amid the sounds of music, in his costly boat with the waving flags; she peeped up through the green reeds, and when the wind caught her silver-white veil, and any one saw it, he thought it was a white swan spreading out its wings.

Many a night when the fishermen were on the sea with their torches, she heard much good told of the young Prince; and she rejoiced that she had saved his life when he was driven about, half dead, on the wild billows: she thought how quietly his head had reclined on her bosom, and how heartily she had kissed him; but he knew nothing of it, and could not even dream of her.

More and more she began to love mankind, and more and more she wished to be able to wander about among those whose world seemed far larger than her own. For they could fly over the sea in ships, and mount up the high hills far above the clouds, and the lands they possessed stretched out in woods and fields farther than her eyes could reach. There was much she wished to know, but her sisters could not answer all her questions; therefore she applied to the old grandmother; and the old lady knew the upper world, which she rightly called "the countries above the sea," very well.

"If people are not drowned," asked the little sea maid, "can they live for ever? Do they not die as we die down here in the sea?"

"Yes," replied the old lady. "They too must die, and their life is even shorter than ours. We can live to be three hundred years old, but when we cease to exist here, we are turned into foam on the surface of the water, and have not even a grave down here among those we love. We have not an immortal soul; we never receive another life; we are like the green seaweed, which when once cut through can never bloom again. Men, on the contrary, have a soul which lives for ever, which lives on after the body has become dust; it mounts up through the clear air, up to all the shining stars! As we rise up out of the waters and behold all the lands of the earth, so they rise up to unknown glorious places which we can never see."

"Why did we not receive an immortal soul?" asked the little sea maid, sorrowfully. "I would gladly give all the hundreds of years I have to live to be a human being only for one day, and to have a hope of partaking the heavenly kingdom."

"You must not think of that," replied the old lady. "We feel ourselves far more happy and far better than mankind yonder."

"Then I am to die and be cast as foam upon the sea, not hearing the music of the waves, nor seeing the pretty flowers and the red sun? Can I not do anything to win an immortal soul?"

"No!" answered the grandmother. "Only if a man were to love you so that you should be more to him than father or mother; if he should cling to you with his every thought and with all his love, and let the priest lay his right hand in yours with a promise of faithfulness here

THE PRINCE'S PLEASURE BARGE.

and in all eternity, then his soul would be imparted to your body, and you would receive a share of the happiness of mankind. He would give a soul to you and yet retain his own. But that can never come to pass. What is considered beautiful here in the sea—the fish-tail—they would consider ugly on the earth: they don't understand it; there one must have two clumsy supports which they call legs, to be called beautiful."

Then the little sea maid sighed, and looked mournfully upon her fish-tail.

"Let us be glad!" said the old lady. "Let us dance and leap in the three hundred years we have to live. That is certainly long enough; after that we can rest ourselves all the better. This evening we shall have a court ball."

It was a splendid sight, such as is never seen on earth. The walls and the ceiling of the great dancing-saloon were of thick but transparent glass. Several hundreds of huge shells, pink and grass-green, stood on each side in rows, filled with a blue fire which lit up the whole hall and shone through the walls, so that the sea without was quite lit up ; one could see all the innumerable fishes, great and small, swimming towards the glass walls ; of some the scales gleamed with purple, while in others they shone like silver and gold. Through the midst of the hall flowed a broad stream, and on this the sea men and sea women danced to their own charming songs. Such beautiful voices the people of the earth have not. The little sea maid sang the most sweetly of all, and the whole court applauded with hands and tails, and for a moment she felt gay in her heart, for she knew she had the loveliest voice of all in the sea or on the earth. But soon she thought again of the world above her ; she could not forget the charming Prince, or her sorrow at not having an immortal soul like his. Therefore she crept out of her father's palace, and while everything within was joy and gladness, she sat melancholy in her little garden. Then she heard the bugle horn sounding through the waters, and thought, " Now he is certainly sailing above, he on whom my wishes hang, and in whose hand I should like to lay my life's happiness. I will dare everything to win him and an immortal soul. While my sisters dance yonder in my father's palace, I will go to the sea witch of whom I have always been so much afraid : perhaps she can counsel and help me."

Now the little sea maid went out of her garden to the foaming whirlpools behind which the sorceress dwelt. She had never travelled that way before. No flowers grew there, no sea grass ; only the naked grey sand stretched out towards the whirlpools, where the water rushed round like roaring mill-wheels and tore down everything it seized into the deep. Through the midst of these rushing whirlpools she was obliged to pass to get into the domain of the witch ; and for a long way there was no other road except one which led over warm gushing mud : this the witch called her turf-moor. Behind it lay her house in the midst of a singular forest, in which all the trees and bushes were polypes—half animals, half plants. They looked like hundred-headed snakes growing up out of the earth. All the branches were long slimy arms, with fingers like supple worms, and they moved limb by limb from the root to the farthest point ; all that they could seize on in the water they held fast and did not let it go. The little sea maid stopped in front of them quite frightened ; her heart beat with fear, and she was nearly turning back ; but then she thought of the Prince and the human soul, and her courage came back again. She bound her long flying hair closely around her head, so that the polypes might not seize it. She put her hands together on her breast, and then shot forward as a fish shoots through the water, among the ugly polypes, which stretched out their supple arms and fingers after her. She saw that each of them held something it had seized with hundreds of little arms, like strong iron bands. People who had perished at sea and had sunk deep down, looked forth as white skeletons from among the polypes' arms ; ships' oars and chests they also held fast, and skeletons of land animals, and a little sea woman whom they had caught and strangled ; and this seemed the most terrible of all to our little Princess.

Now she came to a great marshy place in the wood, where fat water snakes rolled about, showing their ugly cream-coloured bodies. In the midst of this marsh was a house built of white bones of shipwrecked men; there sat the sea witch feeding a toad out of her mouth, just as a person might feed a little canary-bird with sugar. She called the ugly fat water snakes her little chickens, and allowed them to crawl upwards and all about her.

"I know what you want," said the sea witch. "It is stupid of you, but you shall have your way, for it will bring you to grief, my pretty Princess. You want to get rid of your fish-tail, and to have two supports instead of it, like those the people of the earth walk with, so that the young Prince may fall in love with you, and you may get an immortal soul." And with this the witch laughed loudly and dis-agreeably, so that the toad and the water snakes tumbled down to the ground, where they crawled about. "You come just in time," said the witch: "after to-morrow at sunrise I could not help you until another year had gone by. I will prepare a draught for you, with which you must swim to land to-morrow before the sun rises, and seat yourself there and drink it; then your tail will shrivel up and become what the people of the earth call legs, but it will hurt you—it will seem as if you were cut with a sharp sword. All who see you will declare you to be the prettiest human being they ever beheld. You will keep your graceful walk; no dancer will be able to move so lightly as you; but every step you take will be as if you trod upon sharp knives, and as if your blood must flow. If you will bear all this, I can help you."

"Yes!" said the little sea maid, with a trembling voice; and she thought of the Prince and the immortal soul.

"But, remember," said the witch, "when you have once received a human form, you can never be a sea maid again; you can never return through the water to your sisters or to your father's palace; and if you do not win the Prince's love, so that he forgets father and mother for your sake, is attached to you heart and soul, and tells the priest to join your hands, you will not receive an immortal soul. On the first morning after he has married another your heart will break and you will become foam on the water."

"I will do it," said the little sea maid; but she became as pale as death.

"But you must pay me, too," said the witch; "and it is not a trifle that I ask. You have the finest voice of all here at the bottom of the water; with that you think to enchant him; but this voice you must give to me. The best thing you possess I will have for my costly draught! I must give you my own blood in it, so that the draught may be sharp as a two-edged sword."

"But if you take away my voice," said the little sea maid, "what will remain to me?"

"Your beautiful form," replied the witch, "your graceful walk, and your speaking eyes: with those you can take captive a human heart. Well, have you lost your courage? Put out your little tongue, and then

I will cut it off for my payment, and then you shall have the strong draught."

"It shall be so," said the little sea maid.

And the witch put on her pot to brew the draught.

"Cleanliness is a good thing," said she; and she cleaned out the pot with the snakes, which she tied up in a big knot; then she scratched herself, and let her black blood drop into it. ⋅ The stream rose up in the strangest forms, enough to frighten the beholder. Every moment the witch threw something else into the pot; and when it boiled thoroughly, there was a sound like the weeping of a crocodile. At last the draught was ready. It looked like the purest water.

"There you have it," said the witch.

And she cut off the little sea maid's tongue, so that now the Princess was dumb, and could neither sing nor speak.

She could see her father's palace. The torches were extinguished in the great hall, and they were certainly sleeping within, but she did not dare to go to them, now that she was dumb and was about to quit them for ever. She felt as if her heart would burst with sorrow. She crept into the garden, took a flower from each bed of her sisters, blew a thousand kisses towards the palace, and rose up through the dark blue sea.

The sun had not yet risen when she beheld the Prince's castle and mounted the splendid marble staircase. The moon shone beautifully clear. The little sea maid drank the burning sharp draught, and it seemed as if a two-edged sword went through her delicate body. She fell down in a swoon, and lay as if she were dead. When the sun shone out over the sea she awoke, and felt a sharp pain; but just before her stood the handsome young Prince. He fixed his coal-black eyes upon her, so that she cast down her own, and then she perceived that her fishtail was gone, and that she had the prettiest pair of white feet a little girl could have. But she had no clothes, so she shrouded herself in her long hair. The Prince asked how she came there; and she looked at him mildly, but very mournfully, with her dark blue eyes, for she could not speak. Then he took her by the hand, and led her into the castle. Each step she took was, as the witch had told her, as if she had been treading on pointed needles and knives, but she bore it gladly. At the Prince's right hand she moved on, light as a soap-bubble, and he, like all the rest, was astonished at her graceful swaying movements.

She now received splendid clothes of silk and muslin. In the castle she was the most beautiful creature to be seen; but she was dumb, and could neither sing nor speak. Lovely slaves, dressed in silk and gold, stepped forward, and sang before the Prince and his royal parents; one sang more charmingly than all the rest, and the Prince smiled at her and clapped his hands. Then the little sea maid became sad; she knew that she herself had sung far more sweetly, and thought,

"Oh! he should only know that I have given away my voice for ever to be with him."

Now the slaves danced pretty waving dances to the loveliest music; then the little sea maid lifted her beautiful white arms, stood on the tips

THE SEA MAID DANCING BEFORE THE PRINCE.

of her toes, and glided dancing over the floor as no one had yet danced. At each movement her beauty became more apparent, and her eyes spoke more directly to the heart than the songs of the slaves.

All were delighted, and especially the Prince, who called her his little foundling; and she danced again and again, although every time she touched the earth it seemed as if she were treading upon sharp knives. The Prince said that she should always remain with him, and she received permission to sleep on a velvet cushion before his door

He had a page's dress made for her, that she might accompany him on horseback. They rode through the blooming woods, where the green boughs swept their shoulders and the little birds sang in the fresh leaves. She climbed with the Prince up the high mountains, and although her delicate feet bled so that even the others could see it, she laughed at it herself, and followed him until they saw the clouds sailing beneath them like a flock of birds travelling to distant lands.

At home in the Prince's castle, when the others slept at night, she went out on to the broad marble steps. It cooled her burning feet to stand in the cold sea water, and then she thought of the dear ones in the deep.

Once, in the night-time, her sisters came arm in arm. Sadly they sang as they floated above the water; and she beckoned to them, and they recognized her, and told her how she had grieved them all. Then she visited them every night; and once she saw in the distance her old grandmother, who had not been above the surface for many years, and the Sea King with his crown upon his head. They stretched out their hands towards her, but did not venture so near the land as her sisters.

Day by day the Prince grew more fond of her. He loved her as one loves a dear good child, but it never came into his head to make her his wife; and yet she must become his wife, or she would not receive an immortal soul, and would have to become foam on the sea on his marriage morning.

"Do you not love me best of them all?" the eyes of the little sea maid seemed to say, when he took her in his arms and kissed her fair forehead.

"Yes, you are the dearest to me!" said the Prince, "for you have the best heart of them all. You are the most devoted to me, and are like a young girl whom I once saw, but whom I certainly shall not find again. I was on board a ship which was wrecked. The waves threw me ashore near a holy temple, where several young girls performed the service. The youngest of them found me by the shore and saved my life. I only saw her twice: she was the only one in the world I could love; but you chase her picture out of my mind, you are so like her. She belongs to the holy temple, and therefore my good fortune has sent you to me. We will never part!"

"Ah! he does not know that I saved his life," thought the little sea maid. "I carried him over the sea to the wood where the temple stands. I sat here under the foam and looked to see if any one would come. I saw the beautiful girl whom he loves better than me." And the sea maid sighed deeply—she could not weep. "The maiden belongs to the holy temple," she said, "and will never come out into the world —they will meet no more. I am with him and see him every day; I will cherish him, love him, give up my life for him."

But now they said that the Prince was to marry, and that the beautiful daughter of a neighbouring King was to be his wife, and that was why such a beautiful ship was being prepared. The story was, that the Prince travelled to visit the land of the neighbouring King, but it was done that he might see the King's daughter. A great company was to go with him. The little sea maid shook her head and smiled; she knew the Prince's thoughts far better than any of the others.

"I must travel," he had said to her; "I must see the beautiful Princess: my parents desire it, but they do not wish to compel me to bring her home as my bride. I cannot love her. She is not like the beautiful maiden in the temple, whom you resemble. If I were to choose a bride, I would rather choose you, my dear dumb foundling with the speaking eyes."

And he kissed her red lips and played with her long hair, so that she dreamed of happiness and of an immortal soul.

"You are not afraid of the sea, my dumb child?" said he, when they stood on the superb ship which was to carry him to the country of the neighbouring King; and he told her of storm and calm, of strange fishes in the deep, and of what the divers had seen there. And she smiled at his tales, for she knew better than any one what happened at the bottom of the sea.

In the moonlight night, when all were asleep, except the steersman who stood by the helm, she sat on the side of the ship gazing down through the clear water. She fancied she saw her father's palace. High on the battlements stood her old grandmother, with the silver crown on her head, and looking through the rushing tide up to the vessel's keel. Then her sisters came forth over the water, and looked mournfully at her and wrung their white hands. She beckoned to them, smiled, and wished to tell them that she was well and happy; but the cabin-boy approached her, and her sisters dived down, so that he thought the white objects he had seen were foam on the surface of the water.

The next morning the ship sailed into the harbour of the neighbouring King's splendid city. All the church bells sounded, and from the high towers the trumpets were blown, while the soldiers stood there with flying colours and flashing bayonets. Each day brought some festivity with it; balls and entertainments followed one another; but the Princess was not yet there. People said she was being educated in a holy temple far away, where she was learning every royal virtue. At last she arrived.

The little sea maid was anxious to see the beauty of the Princess, and was obliged to acknowledge it. A more lovely apparition she had never beheld. The Princess's skin was pure and clear, and behind the long dark eyelashes there smiled a pair of faithful dark blue eyes.

"You are the lady who saved me when I lay like a corpse upon the shore!" said the Prince; and he folded his blushing bride to his heart. "Oh, I am too, too happy!" he cried to the little sea maid. "The best hope I could have is fulfilled. You will rejoice at my happiness, for you are the most devoted to me of them all!"

And the little sea maid kissed his hand; and it seemed already to her as if her heart was broken, for his wedding morning was to bring death to her, and change her into foam on the sea.

All the church bells were ringing, and heralds rode about the streets announcing the betrothal. On every altar fragrant oil was burning in gorgeous lamps of silver. The priests swang their censers, and bride and bridegroom laid hand in hand, and received the bishop's blessing. The little sea maid was dressed in cloth of gold, and held up the bride's train; but her ears heard nothing of the festive music, her eye marked not the holy ceremony; she thought of the night of her death, and of all that she had lost in this world.

On the same evening the bride and bridegroom went on board the ship. The cannon roared, all the flags waved; in the midst of the ship a costly tent of gold and purple, with the most beautiful cushions, had been set up, and there the married pair were to sleep in the cool still night.

The sails swelled in the wind and the ship glided smoothly and lightly over the clear sea. When it grew dark, coloured lamps were lighted and the sailors danced merry dances on deck. The little sea maid thought of the first time when she had risen up out of the sea, and beheld a similar scene of splendour and joy; and she joined in the whirling dance, and flitted on as the swallow flits away when he is pursued; and all shouted and admired her, for she had danced so prettily. Her delicate feet were cut as if with knives, but she did not feel it, for her heart was wounded far more painfully. She knew this was the last evening on which she should see him for whom she had left her friends and her home, and had given up her beautiful voice, and had suffered unheard-of pains every day, while he was utterly unconscious of all. It was the last evening she should breathe the same air with him, and behold the starry sky and the deep sea; and everlasting night without thought or dream awaited her, for she had no soul, and could win none. And everything was merriment and gladness on the ship till past midnight, and she laughed and danced with thoughts of death in her heart. The Prince kissed his beautiful bride, and she played with his raven hair, and hand in hand they went to rest in the splendid tent.

It became quiet on the ship; only the helmsman stood by the helm, and the little sea maid leaned her white arms upon the bulwark and gazed out towards the east for the morning dawn—the first ray, she knew, would kill her. Then she saw her sisters rising out of the flood; they were pale, like herself; their long beautiful hair no longer waved in the wind—it had been cut off.

"We have given it to the witch, that we might bring you help, so that you may not die to-night. She has given us a knife; here it is—look! how sharp! Before the sun rises you must thrust it into the heart of the Prince, and when the warm blood falls upon your feet they will grow together again into a fish-tail, and you will become a sea maid again, and come back to us, and live your three hundred years before you become dead salt sea foam. Make haste! He or you must die before the sun rises! Our old grandmother mourns so that her white hair has fallen off, as ours did under the witch's scissors. Kill the Prince and come back! Make haste! Do you see that red streak in the sky? In a few minutes the sun will rise, and you must die!"

And they gave a very mournful sigh, and vanished beneath the waves.

The little sea maid drew back the purple curtain from the tent, and saw the beautiful bride lying with her head on the Prince's breast; and she bent down and kissed his brow, and gazed up to the sky where the morning red was gleaming brighter and brighter; then she looked at the sharp knife, and again fixed her eyes upon the Prince, who in his sleep murmured his bride's name. She only was in his thoughts, and the knife trembled in the sea maid's hands. But then she flung it far away into the waves—they gleamed red where it fell, and it seemed as if drops of blood spurted up out of the water. Once more she looked with half-extinguished eyes upon the Prince; then she threw herself from the ship into the sea, and felt her frame dissolving into foam.

Now the sun rose up out of the sea. The rays fell mild and warm upon the cold sea foam, and the little sea maid felt nothing of death. She saw the bright sun, and over her head sailed hundreds of glorious ethereal beings—she could see them through the white sails of the ship and the red clouds of the sky; their speech was melody, but of such a spiritual kind that no human ear could hear it, just as no human eye could see them, without wings they floated through the air. The little sea maid found that she had a frame like these, and was rising more and more out of the foam.

"Whither am I going?" she asked; and her voice sounded like that of the other beings, so spiritual, that no earthly music could be compared to it

"To the daughters of the air!" replied the others. "A sea maid has no immortal soul, and can never gain one, except she win the love of a mortal. Her eternal existence depends upon the power of another. The daughters of the air have likewise no immortal soul, but they can make themselves one through good deeds. We fly to the hot countries, where the close pestilent air kills men, and there we bring coolness. We disperse the fragrance of the flowers through the air, and spread refreshment and health. After we have striven for three hundred years to accomplish all the good we can bring about, we receive an immortal soul and take part in the eternal happiness of men. You, poor little sea maid, have striven with your whole heart after the goal we pursue; you have suffered and endured; you have by good works raised yourself to the world of spirits, and can gain an immortal soul after three hundred years."

And the little sea maid lifted her glorified eyes towards God's sun, and for the first time she felt them fill with tears. On the ship there was again life and noise. She saw the Prince and his bride searching for her; then they looked mournfully at the pearly foam, as if they knew that she had thrown herself into the waves. Invisible, she kissed the forehead of the bride, fanned the Prince, and mounted with the other children of the air on the rosy cloud which floated through the ether.

After three hundred years we shall thus float into Paradise!

"And we may even get there sooner," whispered a daughter of the air. "Invisibly we float into the houses of men where children are, and for every day on which we find a good child that brings joy to its parents and deserves their love, our time of probation is shortened. The child does not know when we fly through the room; and when we smile with joy at the child's conduct, a year is counted off from the three hundred; but when we see a naughty or a wicked child, we shed tears of grief, and for every tear a day is added to our time of trial."

THE WILD SWANS.

FAR away, where the swallows fly when our winter comes on, lived a King who had eleven sons, and one daughter named Eliza. The eleven brothers were Princes, and each went to school with a star on his breast and his sword by his side. They wrote with pencils of diamond upon slates of gold, and learned by heart just as well as they read: one could see directly that they were Princes. Their sister Eliza sat upon a little stool of plate glass, and had a picture-book which had been bought for the value of half a kingdom.

Oh, the children were particularly well off; but it was not always to remain so.

Their father, who was King of the whole country, married a bad Queen who did not love the poor children at all. On the very first day they could notice this. In the whole palace there was great feasting, and the children were playing there. Then guests came; but instead of the children receiving, as they had been accustomed to do, all the spare cake and all the roasted apples, they only had some sand given them in a tea-cup, and were told that they might make believe that was something good.

The next week the Queen took the little sister Eliza into the country, to a peasant and his wife; and but a short time had elapsed before she told the King so many falsehoods about the poor Princes that he did not trouble himself any more about them.

"Fly out into the world and get your own living," said the wicked Queen. "Fly like great birds without a voice."

But she could not make it so bad for them as she had intended, for they became eleven magnificent wild swans. With a strange cry they flew out of the palace windows, far over the park and into the wood.

It was yet quite early morning when they came by the place where their sister Eliza lay asleep in the peasant's room. Here they hovered over the roof, turned their long necks, and flapped their wings; but no one heard or saw it. They were obliged to fly on, high up towards the clouds, far away into the wide world; there they flew into a great dark wood, which stretched away to the sea shore.

Poor little Eliza stood in the peasant's room and played with a green leaf, for she had no other playthings. And she pricked a hole in the leaf, and looked through it up at the sun, and it seemed to her that she saw her brothers' clear eyes; each time the warm sun shone upon her cheeks she thought of all the kisses they had given her.

Each day passed just like the rest. When the wind swept through the great rose hedges outside the house, it seemed to whisper to them, "What can be more beautiful than you?" But the roses shook their heads and answered, "Eliza!" And when the old woman sat in front of her door on Sunday and read in her hymn-book, the wind turned the leaves and said to the book, "Who can be more pious than you?" and the hymn-book said, "Eliza!" And what the rose bushes and the hymn-book said was the simple truth.

When she was fifteen years old she was to go home. And when the Queen saw how beautiful she was, she became spiteful and filled with hatred towards her. She would have been glad to change her into a wild swan, like her brothers, but she did not dare to do so at once, because the King wished to see his daughter.

Early in the morning the Queen went into the bath, which was built of white marble, and decked with soft cushions and the most splendid tapestry; and she took three toads and kissed them, and said to the first,

"Sit upon Eliza's head when she comes into the bath, that she may become as stupid as you.—Seat yourself upon her forehead," she said to the second, "that she may become as ugly as you, and her father may not know her.—Rest on her heart," she whispered to the third, "that she may receive an evil mind and suffer pain from it."

Then she put the toads into the clear water, which at once assumed a green colour; and calling Eliza, caused her to undress and step into the water. And while Eliza dived, one of the toads sat upon her hair, and the second on her forehead, and the third on her heart; but she did not seem to notice it; and as soon as she rose, three red poppies were floating on the water. If the creatures had not been poisonous, and if the witch had not kissed them, they would have been changed into red roses. But at any rate they became flowers, because they had rested on the girl's head, and forehead, and heart. She was too good and innocent for sorcery to have power over her.

When the wicked Queen saw that, she rubbed Eliza with walnut juice, so that the girl became dark brown, and smeared a hurtful ointment on her face, and let her beautiful hair hang in confusion. It was quite impossible to recognize the pretty Eliza.

When her father saw her he was much shocked, and declared this was not his daughter. No one but the yard dog and the swallows would recognize her; but they were poor animals who had nothing to say in the matter.

Then poor Eliza wept, and thought of her eleven brothers who were all away. Sorrowfully she crept out of the castle, and walked all day over field and moor till she came into the great wood. She did not know whither she wished to go, only she felt very downcast and longed for her brothers: they had certainly been, like herself, thrust forth into the world, and she would seek for them and find them.

She had been only a short time in the wood when the night fell; she quite lost the path, therefore she lay down upon the soft moss, prayed her evening prayer, and leaned her head against the stump of a tree. Deep silence reigned around, the air was mild, and in the grass and in the moss gleamed like a green fire hundreds of glowworms; when she lightly touched one of the twigs with her hand, the shining insects fell down upon her like shooting stars.

The whole night long she dreamed of her brothers. They were children again playing together, writing with their diamond pencils upon their golden slates, and looking at the beautiful picture-book which had cost half a kingdom. But on the slates they were not writing, as they had been accustomed to do, lines and letters, but the brave deeds they had done, and all they had seen and experienced; and in the picture-book everything was alive—the birds sang, and the people went out of the book and spoke with Eliza and her brothers. But when the leaf was turned, they jumped back again directly, so that there should be no confusion.

When she awoke the sun was already standing high. She could certainly not see it, for the lofty trees spread their branches far and wide above her. But the rays played there above like a gauzy veil, there was a fragrance from the fresh verdure, and the birds almost perched upon her shoulders. She heard the plashing of water; it was from a number of springs all flowing into a lake which had the most delightful sandy bottom. It was surrounded by thick growing bushes, but at one part the stags had made a large opening, and here Eliza went down to the water. The lake was so clear, that if the wind had not stirred the branches and the bushes, so that they moved, one would have thought they were painted upon the depths of the lake, so clearly was every leaf mirrored, whether the sun shone upon it or whether it lay in shadow.

When Eliza saw her own face she was terrified—so brown and ugly was she; but when she wetted her little hand and rubbed her eyes and her forehead, the white skin gleamed forth again. Then she undressed and went down into the fresh water: a more beautiful King's daughter than she was could not be found in the world. And when she had dressed herself again and plaited her long hair, she went to the bubbling spring, drank out of her hollow hand, and then wandered far into the wood, not knowing whither she went. She thought of her dear brothers, and thought that Heaven would certainly not forsake her. It is God who lets the wild apples grow, to satisfy the hungry. He showed her a wild apple tree, with the boughs bending under the weight of the fruit. Here she took her midday meal, placing props under the boughs, and then went into the darkest part of the forest. There it was so still that she could hear her own footsteps, as well as the rustling of every dry leaf which bent under her feet. Not one bird was to be seen, not one ray of sunlight could find its way through the great dark boughs of the trees; the lofty trunks stood so close together that when she looked before her it appeared as though she were surrounded by sets of palings one behind the other. Oh, here was a solitude such as she had never before known!

The night came on quite dark. Not a single glowworm now gleamed in the grass. Sorrowfully she lay down to sleep. Then it seemed to her as if the branches of the trees parted above her head, and mild eyes of angels looked down upon her from on high.

When the morning came, she did not know if it had really been so or if she had dreamed it.

She went a few steps forward, and then she met an old woman with berries in her basket, and the old woman gave her a few of them. Eliza asked the dame if she had not seen eleven Princes riding through the wood.

"No," replied the old woman, "but yesterday I saw eleven swans swimming in the river close by, with golden crowns on their heads."

And she led Eliza a short distance farther, to a declivity, and at the foot of the slope a little river wound its way. The trees on its margin stretched their long leafy branches across towards each other, and where their natural growth would not allow them to come together, the roots had been torn out of the ground, and hung, intermingled with the branches, over the water.

ELIZA LOOKING OUT FOR HER BROTHERS, THE WILD SWANS.

Eliza said farewell to the old woman, and went beside the river to the place where the stream flowed out to the great open ocean.

The whole glorious sea lay before the young girl's eyes, but not one sail appeared on its surface, and not a boat was to be seen. How was she to proceed? She looked at the innumerable little pebbles on the shore; the water had worn them all round. Glass, ironstones, everything that was there had received its shape from the water, which was much softer than even her delicate hand.

"It rolls on unweariedly, and thus what is hard becomes smooth. I will be just as unwearied. Thanks for your lesson, you clear rolling waves; my heart tells me that one day you will lead me to my dear brothers."

On the foam-covered sea grass lay eleven white swan feathers, which she collected into a bunch. Drops of water were upon them—whether they were dew-drops or tears nobody could tell. Solitary it was there on the strand, but she did not feel it, for the sea showed continual changes—more in a few hours than the lovely lakes can produce in a whole year. Then a great black cloud came. It seemed as if the sea would say, "I can look angry, too;" and then the wind blew, and the waves turned their white side outward. But when the clouds gleamed red and the winds slept, the sea looked like a rose leaf; sometimes it became green, sometimes white. But however quietly it might rest, there was still a slight motion on the shore; the water rose gently like the breast of a sleeping child.

When the sun was just about to set, Eliza saw eleven wild swans, with crowns on their heads, flying towards the land: they swept along one after the other, so that they looked like a long white band. Then Eliza descended the slope and hid herself behind a bush. The swans alighted near her and flapped their great white wings.

As soon as the sun had disappeared beneath the water, the swans' feathers fell off, and eleven handsome Princes, Eliza's brothers, stood there. She uttered a loud cry, for although they were greatly altered, she knew and felt that it must be they. And she sprang into their arms and called them by their names; and the Princes felt supremely happy when they saw their little sister again; and they knew her, though she was now tall and beautiful. They smiled and wept; and soon they understood how cruel their stepmother had been to them all.

" We brothers," said the eldest, " fly about as wild swans as long as the sun is in the sky, but directly it sinks down we receive our human form again. Therefore we must always take care that we have a resting-place for our feet when the sun sets; for if at that moment we were flying up towards the clouds, we should sink down into the deep as men. We do not dwell here: there lies a land just as fair as this beyond the sea. But the way thither is long; we must cross the great sea, and on our path there is no island where we could pass the night, only a little rock stands forth in the midst of the waves; it is but just large enough that we can rest upon it close to each other. If the sea is rough, the foam spurts far over us, but we thank God for the rock. There we pass the night in our human form: but for this rock we could never visit our beloved native land, for we require two of the longest days in the year for our journey. Only once in each year is it granted to us to visit our home. For eleven days we may stay here and fly over the great wood, from whence we can see the palace in which we were born and in which our father lives, and the high church tower, beneath whose shade our mother lies buried. Here it seems to us as though the bushes and trees were our relatives; here the wild horses career across the steppe, as we have seen them do in our childhood; here the charcoal-burner sings the old songs to which we danced as children; here is our fatherland: hither we feel ourselves drawn, and here we have found you, our dear little sister. Two days more we may stay here; then we must away across the sea to a glorious land, but which is not our native land. How can we bear you away ? for we have neither ship nor boat."

ELIZA AND HER BROTHERS, THE SWANS.

"In what way can I release you?" asked the sister; and they conversed nearly the whole night, only slumbering for a few hours.

She was awakened by the rustling of the swans' wings above her head. Her brothers were again enchanted, and they flew in wide circles and at last far away; but one of them, the youngest, remained behind, and the swan laid his head in her lap, and she stroked his wings; and the whole day they remained together. Towards evening the others came back, and when the sun had gone down they stood there in their own shapes.

"To-morrow we fly far away from here, and cannot come back until a whole year has gone by. But we cannot leave you thus: Have you courage to come with us? My arm is strong enough to carry you in the wood; and should not all our wings be strong enough to fly with you over the sea?"

"Yes, take me with you," said Eliza.

The whole night they were occupied in weaving a net of the pliable willow bark and tough reeds; and it was great and strong. On this net Eliza lay down; and when the sun rose, and her brothers were changed into wild swans, they seized the net with their beaks, and flew with their beloved sister, who was still asleep, high up towards the clouds. The sunbeams fell exactly upon her face, so one of the swans flew over her head, that his broad wings might overshadow her.

They were far away from the shore when Eliza awoke: she was still dreaming, so strange did it appear to her to be carried high through the air and over the sea. By her side lay a branch with beautiful ripe berries and a bundle of sweet-tasting roots. The youngest of the brothers had collected them and placed them there for her. She smiled at him thankfully, for she recognized him; he it was who flew over her and shaded her with his wings.

They were so high that the greatest ship they descried beneath them seemed like a white seagull lying upon the waters. A great cloud stood behind them—it was a perfect mountain; and upon it Eliza saw her own shadow and those of the eleven swans; there they flew on, gigantic in size. Here was a picture, a more splendid one than she had ever yet seen. But as the sun rose higher and the cloud was left farther behind them, the floating shadowy images vanished away.

The whole day they flew onward through the air, like a whirring arrow, but their flight was slower than it was wont to be, for they had their sister to carry. Bad weather came on; the evening drew near; Eliza looked anxiously at the setting sun, for the lonely rock in the ocean could not be seen. It seemed to her as if the swans beat the air more strongly with their wings. Alas! she was the cause that they did not advance fast enough. When the sun went down, they must become men and fall into the sea and drown. Then she prayed a prayer from the depths of her heart; but still she could descry no rock. The dark clouds came nearer in a great black threatening body, rolling forward like a mass of lead, and the lightning burst forth, flash upon flash.

Now the sun just touched the margin of the sea. Eliza's heart trembled. Then the swans darted downwards, so swiftly that she thought they were falling, but they paused again. The sun was half hidden below the water. And now for the first time she saw the little rock beneath her, and it looked no larger than a seal might look, thrusting his head forth from the water. The sun sank very fast; at last it appeared only like a star; and then her foot touched the firm land. The sun was extinguished like the last spark in a piece of burned paper; her brothers were standing around her, arm in arm, but there was not more than just enough room for her and for them. The sea beat against the rock and went over her like small rain; the sky glowed in continual fire, and peal on peal the thunder rolled; but sister and brothers held each other by the hand and sang psalms, from which they gained comfort and courage.

In the morning twilight the air was pure and calm. As soon as the sun rose the swans flew away with Eliza from the island. The sea still ran high, and when they soared up aloft, the white foam looked like millions of white swans swimming upon the water.

When the sun mounted higher, Eliza saw before her, half floating in the air, a mountainous country with shining masses of ice on its water, and in the midst of it rose a castle, apparently a mile long, with row above row of elegant columns, while beneath waved the palm woods and bright flowers as large as mill-wheels. She asked if this was the country to which they were bound, but the swans shook their heads, for what she beheld was the gorgeous, ever-changing palace of Fata Morgana, and into this they might bring no human being. As Eliza gazed at it, mountains, woods, and castle fell down, and twenty proud churches, all nearly alike, with high towers and pointed windows, stood before them. She fancied she heard the organs sounding, but it was the sea she heard. When she was quite near the churches they changed to a fleet sailing beneath her, but when she looked down it was only a sea mist gliding over the ocean. Thus she had a continual change before her eyes, till at last she saw the real land to which they were bound. There arose the most glorious blue mountains, with cedar forests, cities, and palaces. Long before the sun went down she sat on the rock, in front of a great cave overgrown with delicate green trailing plants looking like embroidered carpets.

"Now we shall see what you will dream of here to-night," said the youngest brother; and he showed her to her bed-chamber.

"Heaven grant that I may dream of a way to release you," she replied.

And this thought possessed her mightily, and she prayed ardently for help; yes, even in her sleep she continued to pray. Then it seemed to her as if she were flying high in the air to the cloudy palace of Fata Morgana; and the fairy came out to meet her, beautiful and radiant; and yet the fairy was quite like the old woman who had given her the berries in the wood, and had told her of the swans with golden crowns on their heads.

"Your brothers can be released," said she. "But have you courage and perseverance? Certainly, water is softer than your delicate hands, and yet it changes the shape of stones; but it feels not the pain that your fingers will feel; it has no heart, and cannot suffer the agony and torment you will have to endure. Do you see the stinging-nettle which I hold in my hand? Many of the same kind grow around the cave in which you sleep: those only, and those that grow upon churchyard graves, are serviceable, remember that. Those you must pluck, though they will burn your hands into blisters. Break these nettles to pieces with your feet, and you will have flax; of this you must plait and weave eleven shirts of mail with long sleeves: throw these over the eleven swans, and the charm will be broken. But recollect well, from the moment you begin this work until it is finished, even though it should take years to accomplish, you must not speak. The first word you utter will pierce your brothers' hearts like a deadly dagger. Their lives hang on your tongue. Remember all this!"

And she touched her hand with the nettle; it was like a burning fire, and Eliza woke with the smart. It was broad daylight; and close by the spot where she had slept lay a nettle like the one she had seen in her dream. She fell upon her knees and prayed gratefully, and went forth from the cave to begin her work.

With her delicate hands she groped among the ugly nettles. These stung like fire, burning great blisters on her arms and hands; but she thought she would bear it gladly if she could only release her dear brothers. Then she bruised every nettle with her bare feet and plaited the green flax.

When the sun had set her brothers came, and they were frightened when they found her dumb. They thought it was some new sorcery of their wicked stepmother's; but when they saw her hands, they understood what she was doing for their sake, and the youngest brother wept. And where his tears dropped she felt no more pain, and the burning blisters vanished.

She passed the night at her work, for she could not sleep till she had delivered her dear brothers. The whole of the following day, while the swans were away, she sat in solitude, but never had time flown so quickly with her as now. One shirt of mail was already finished, and now she began the second.

Then a hunting horn sounded among the hills, and she was struck with fear. The noise came nearer and nearer; she heard the barking dogs, and timidly she fled into the cave, bound into a bundle the nettles she had collected and prepared, and sat upon the bundle.

Immediately a great dog came bounding out of the ravine, and then another, and another: they barked loudly, ran back, and then came again. Only a few minutes had gone before all the huntsmen stood before the cave, and the handsomest of them was the King of the country. He came forward to Eliza, for he had never seen a more beautiful maiden.

"How did you come hither, you delightful child?" he asked.

Eliza shook her head, for she might not speak—it would cost her brothers their deliverance and their lives. And she hid her hands under her apron, so that the King might not see what she was suffering.

"Come with me," said he. "You cannot stop here. If you are as good as you are beautiful, I will dress you in velvet and silk, and place the golden crown on your head, and you shall dwell in my richest castle, and rule."

And then he lifted her on his horse. She wept and wrung her hands; but the King said,

"I only wish for your happiness: one day you will thank me for this."

And then he gallopped away among the mountains with her on his horse, and the hunters gallopped at their heels.

When the sun went down, the fair regal city lay before them, with
its churches and cupolas; and the King led her into the castle, where
great fountains plashed in the lofty marble halls, and where walls and
ceilings were covered with glorious pictures. But she had no eyes for
all this—she only wept and mourned. Passively she let the women
put royal robes upon her, and weave pearls in her hair, and draw dainty
gloves over her blistered fingers.

When she stood there in full array, she was dazzlingly beautiful, so
that the Court bowed deeper than ever. And the King chose her for
his bride, although the archbishop shook his head and whispered that
the beauteous fresh maid was certainly a witch, who blinded the eyes
and led astray the heart of the King.

But the King gave no ear to this, but ordered that the music should
sound, and the costliest dishes should be served, and the most beautiful
maidens should dance before them. And she was led through fragrant
gardens into gorgeous halls; but never a smile came upon her lips or
shone in her eyes: there she stood, a picture of grief. Then the King
opened a little chamber close by, where she was to sleep. This chamber was decked with splendid green tapestry, and completely resembled
the cave in which she had been. On the floor lay the bundle of flax
which she had prepared from the nettles, and under the ceiling hung the
shirt of mail she had completed. All these things one of the huntsmen
had brought with him as curiosities.

"Here you may dream yourself back in your former home," said the
King. "Here is the work which occupied you there, and now, in the
midst of all your splendour, it will amuse you to think of that time."

When Eliza saw this that lay so near her heart, a smile played round
her mouth and the crimson blood came back into her cheeks. She
thought of her brothers' deliverance, and kissed the King's hand; and
he pressed her to his heart, and caused the marriage feast to be announced by all the church bells. The beautiful dumb girl out of the
wood became the Queen of the country.

Then the archbishop whispered evil words into the King's ear, but
they did not sink into the King's heart. The marriage was to take
place; the archbishop himself was obliged to place the crown on her
head, and with wicked spite he pressed the narrow circlet so tightly
upon her brow that it pained her. But a heavier ring lay close around
her heart—sorrow for her brothers; she did not feel the bodily pain.
Her mouth was dumb, for a single word would cost her brothers their
lives, but her eyes glowed with love for the kind, handsome King, who
did everything to rejoice her. She loved him with her whole heart,
more and more every day. Oh that she had been able to confide in
him and to tell him of her grief! But she was compelled to be dumb,
and to finish her work in silence. Therefore at night she crept away
from his side, and went quietly into the little chamber which was decorated like the cave, and wove one shirt of mail after another. But
when she began the seventh she had no flax left.

She knew that in the churchyard nettles were growing that she could use; but she must pluck them herself, and how was she to go out there?

"Oh. what is the pain in my fingers to the torment my heart endures?" thought she. "I must venture it, and help will not be denied me!"

With a trembling heart, as though the deed she purposed doing had been evil, she crept into the garden in the moonlight night, and went through the lanes and through the deserted streets to the churchyard. There, on one of the broadest tombstones, she saw sitting a circle of lamias. These hideous wretches took off their ragged garments, as if they were going to bathe; then with their skinny fingers they clawed open the fresh graves, and with fiendish greed they snatched up the corpses and ate the flesh. Eliza was obliged to pass close by them, and they fastened their evil glances upon her; but she prayed silently, and collected the burning nettles, and carried them into the castle.

Only one person had seen her, and that was the archbishop. He was awake while others slept. Now he felt sure his opinion was correct, that all was not as it should be with the Queen; she was a witch, and thus she had bewitched the King and the whole people.

In secret he told the King what he had seen and what he feared; and when the hard words came from his tongue, the pictures of saints in the cathedral shook their heads, as though they could have said, "It is not so! Eliza is innocent!" But the archbishop interpreted this differently — he thought they were bearing witness against her, and shaking their heads at her sinfulness. Then two heavy tears rolled down the King's cheeks; he went home with doubt in his heart, and at night pretended to be asleep; but no quiet sleep came upon his eyes, for he noticed that Eliza got up. Every night she did this, and each time he followed her silently, and saw how she disappeared from her chamber.

From day to day his face became darker. Eliza saw it, but did not understand the reason; but it frightened her—and what did she not suffer in her heart for her brothers? Her hot tears flowed upon the royal velvet and purple; they lay there like sparkling diamonds, and all who saw the splendour wished they were Queens. In the meantime she had almost finished her work. Only one shirt of mail was still to be completed, but she had no flax left, and not a single nettle. Once more, for the last time, therefore, she must go to the churchyard, only to pluck a few hands-full. She thought with terror of this solitary wandering and of the horrible lamias, but her will was firm as her trust in Providence.

Eliza went on, but the King and the archbishop followed her. They saw her vanish into the churchyard through the wicket gate; and when they drew near, the lamias were sitting upon the gravestones as Eliza had seen them; and the King turned aside, for he fancied her among them, whose head had rested against his breast that very evening.

"The people must condemn her," said he.

And the people condemned her to suffer death by fire.

Out of the gorgeous regal halls she was led into a dark damp cell, where the wind whistled through the grated window; instead of velvet and silk they gave her the bundle of nettles which she had collected: on this she could lay her head; and the hard burning coats of mail which she had woven were to be her coverlet. But nothing could have been given her that she liked better. She resumed her work and prayed. Without, the street boys were singing jeering songs about her, and not a soul comforted her with a kind word.

But towards evening there came the whirring of swans' wings close by the grating—it was the youngest of her brothers. He had found his sister, and she sobbed aloud with joy, though she knew that the

ELIZA CARRIED TO EXECUTION.

approaching night would probably be the last she had to live. But now the work was almost finished, and her brothers were here.

Now came the archbishop, to stay with her in her last hour, for he had promised the King to do so. And she shook her head, and with looks and gestures she begged him to depart, for in this night she must finish her work, or else all would be in vain, all her tears, her pain, and her sleepless nights. The archbishop withdrew uttering evil words against her; but poor Eliza knew she was innocent, and continued her work.

It was still twilight; not till an hour afterwards would the sun rise. And the eleven brothers stood at the castle gate, and demanded to be brought before the King. That could not be, they were told, for it was still almost night; the King was asleep, and might not be disturbed. They begged, they threatened, and the sentries came, yes, even the King himself came out, and asked what was the meaning of this. At that

572 The Complete Illustrated Stories

moment the sun rose, and no more were the brothers to be seen, but eleven wild swans flew away over the castle.

All the people came flocking out at the town gate, for they wanted to see the witch burned. The old horse drew the cart on which she sat. They had put upon her a garment of coarse sackcloth. Her lovely hair hung loose about her beautiful head; her cheeks were as pale as death; and her lips moved silently, while her fingers were engaged with the green flax. Even on the way to death she did not interrupt the work she had begun; the ten shirts of mail lay at her feet, and she wrought at the eleventh. The mob derided her.

"Look at the red witch, how she mutters! She has no hymn-book in her hand; no, there she sits with her ugly sorcery—tear it in a thousand pieces!"

And they all pressed upon her, and wanted to tear up the shirts of mail. Then eleven wild swans came flying up, and sat round about her on the cart, and beat with their wings; and the mob gave way before them, terrified.

"That is a sign from heaven! She is certainly innocent!" whispered many. But they did not dare to say it aloud.

Now the executioner seized her by the hand; then she hastily threw the eleven shirts over the swans, and immediately eleven handsome Princes stood there. But the youngest had a swan's wing instead of an arm, for a sleeve was wanting to his shirt — she had not quite finished it.

"Now I may speak!" she said. "I am innocent!"

And the people who saw what happened bowed before her as before a saint; but she sank lifeless into her brothers' arms, such an effect had suspense, anguish, and pain had upon her.

"Yes, she is innocent," said the eldest brother.

And now he told everything that had taken place; and while he spoke a fragrance arose as of millions of roses, for every piece of faggot in the pile had taken root and was sending forth shoots; and a fragrant hedge stood there, tall and great, covered with red roses, and at the top a flower, white and shining, gleaming like a star. This flower the King plucked and placed in Eliza's bosom; and she awoke with peace and happiness in her heart.

And all the church bells rang of themselves, and the birds came in great flocks. And back to the castle such a marriage procession was held as no King had ever seen.

THE MARSH KING'S DAUGHTER.

The storks tell their little ones very many stories, all of the moor and the marsh. These stories are generally adapted to the age and capacity of the hearers. The youngest are content if they are told "Kribble-krabble, plurre-murre" as a story, and find it charming; but the older ones want something with a deeper meaning, or at any rate something relating to the family. Of the two oldest and longest stories that have been preserved among the storks, we are only acquainted with one, namely, that of Moses, who was exposed by his mother on the banks of the Nile, and whom the King's daughter found, and who afterwards became a great man and a prophet. That history is very well known.

The second is not known yet, perhaps because it is quite an inland story. It has been handed down from mouth to mouth, from stork-mamma to stork-mamma, for thousands of years, and each of them has told it better and better; and now we'll tell it best of all.

The first Stork pair who told the story had their summer residence on the wooden house of the Viking, which lay by the wild moor in Wendsyssel: that is to say, if we are to speak out of the abundance of our knowledge, hard by the great moor in the circle of Hjörring, high up by the Skagen, the most northern point of Jutland. The wilderness there is still a great wide moor-heath, about which we can read in the official description of districts. It is said that in old times there was here a sea, whose bottom was upheaved; now the moorland extends for miles on all sides, surrounded by damp meadows, and unsteady shaking swamp, and turfy moor, with blueberries and stunted trees. Mists are almost always hovering over this region, which seventy years ago was still inhabited by the wolves. It is certainly rightly called the "wild moor;" and one can easily think how dreary and lonely it must have been, and how much marsh and lake there was here a thousand years ago. Yes, in detail, exactly the same things were seen then that may yet be beheld. The reeds had the same height, and bore the same kind of long leaves and bluish-brown feathery plumes that they bear now; the birch stood there, with its white bark and its fine loosely-hanging leaves, just as now; and as regards the living creatures that dwelt here—why, the fly wore its gauzy dress of the same cut that it wears now, and the favourite colours of the stork were white picked out with black, and red stockings. The people certainly wore coats of a different cut from those they now wear; but whoever stepped out on the shaking moorland, be he huntsman or follower, master or servant, met with the same fate a thousand years ago that he would meet with to-day. He sank and went down to the Marsh King, as they called him, who ruled below in the great moorland empire. They also called him Gungel King; but we like the name Marsh King better, and by that we'll call him, as the storks did. Very little is known of the Marsh King's rule; but perhaps that is a good thing.

In the neighbourhood of the moorland, hard by the great arm of the German Ocean and the Cattegat, which is called the Lümfjorden, lay the wooden house of the Viking, with its stone water-tight cellars, with its tower and its three projecting storeys. On the roof the Stork had built his nest, and Stork-mamma there hatched the eggs, and felt sure that her hatching would come to something.

One evening Stork-papa stayed out very long, and when he came home he looked very bustling and important.

"I've something very terrible to tell you," he said to the Stork-mamma.

"Let that be," she replied. "Remember that I'm hatching the eggs, and you might agitate me, and I might do them a mischief."

"You must know it," he continued. "She has arrived here — the daughter of our host in Egypt—she has dared to undertake the journey here—and she's gone!"

"She who came from the race of the fairies? Oh, tell me all about it! You know I can't bear to be kept long in suspense when I'm hatching eggs."

"You see, mother, she believed in what the doctor said, and you told me true. She believed that the moor flowers would bring healing to her sick father, and she has flown here in swan's plumage, in company with the other Swan Princesses, who come to the North every year to renew their youth. She has come here, and she is gone!"

"You are much too long-winded!" exclaimed the Stork-Mamma, "and the eggs might catch cold. I can't bear being kept in such suspense!"

"I have kept watch," said the Stork-papa; "and to-night, when I went into the reeds—there where the marsh ground will bear me—three swans came. Something in their flight seemed to say to me, 'Look out! That's not altogether swan; it's only swan's feathers!' Yes, mother, you have a feeling of intuition just as I have; you can tell whether a thing is right or wrong."

"Yes, certainly," she replied; "but tell me about the Princess. I'm sick of hearing of the swan's feathers."

"Well, you know that in the middle of the moor there is something like a lake," continued Stork-papa. "You can see one corner of it if you raise yourself a little. There, by the reeds and the green mud, lay a great elder stump, and on this the three swans sat, flapping their wings and looking about them. One of them threw off her plumage, and I immediately recognized her as our house Princess from Egypt! There she sat, with no covering but her long black hair. I heard her tell the others to pay good heed to the swan's plumage, while she dived down into the water to pluck the flowers which she fancied she saw growing there. The others nodded, and picked up the empty feather dress and took care of it. 'I wonder what they will do with it?' thought I; and perhaps she asked herself the same question. If so, she got an answer — a very practical answer — for the two rose up and flew away with her swan's plumage. 'Do thou dive down!' they cried; 'thou shalt never see Egypt again! Remain thou here in the moor!' And so saying, they tore the swan's plumage into a thousand pieces, so that the feathers whirled about like a snow-storm; and away they flew—the two faithless Princesses!"

"Why, that is terrible!" said Stork-mamma. "I can't bear to hear any more of it. But now tell me what happened next."

"The Princess wept and lamented aloud. Her tears fell fast on the elder stump, and the latter moved, for it was not a regular elder stump,

THE PRINCESS LEFT IN THE MARSH.

but the Marsh King—he who lives and rules in the depths of the moor! I myself saw it — how the stump of the tree turned round, and ceased to be a tree stump; long thin branches grew forth from it like arms. Then the poor child was terribly frightened, and sprang up to flee away. She hurried across to the green slimy ground; but that cannot even carry me, much less her. She sank immediately, and the elder stump dived down too; and it was he who drew her down. Great black bubbles rose up out of the moor-slime, and the last trace of both of them vanished when these burst. Now the Princess is buried in the wild moor, and never more will she bear away a flower to Egypt. Your heart would have burst, mother, if you had seen it."

"You ought not to tell me anything of the kind at such a time as this," said Stork-mamma; "the eggs might suffer by it. The Princess will find some way of escape; some one will come to help her. If it had been you or I, or one of our people, it would certainly have been all over with us."

"But I shall go and look every day to see if anything happens," said Stork-papa.

And he was as good as his word.

A long time had passed, when at last he saw a green stalk shooting up out of the deep moor-ground. When it reached the surface a leaf spread out and unfolded itself broader and broader; close by it, a bud came out. And one morning, when Stork-papa flew over the stalk, the bud opened through the power of the strong sunbeams, and in the cup of the flower lay a beautiful child—a little girl—looking just as if she had risen out of the bath. The little one so closely resembled the Princess from Egypt, that at the first moment the Stork thought it must be the Princess herself; but, on second thoughts, it appeared more probable that it must be the daughter of the Princess and of the Marsh King; and that also explained her being placed in the cup of the water-lily.

"But she cannot possibly be left lying there," thought Stork-papa; "and in my nest there are so many persons already. But stay, I have a thought. The wife of the Viking has no children, and how often has she not wished for a little one! People always say, 'The stork has brought a little one;' and I will do so in earnest this time. I shall fly with the child to the Viking's wife. What rejoicing there will be yonder!"

And Stork-papa lifted the little girl out of the flower-cup, flew to the wooden house, picked a hole with his beak in the bladder-covered window, laid the charming child on the bosom of the Viking's wife, and then hurried up to the Stork-mamma, and told her what he had seen and done; and the little Storks listened to the story, for they were big enough to do so now.

"So you see," he concluded, "the Princess is not dead, for she must have sent the little one up here; and now that is provided for too."

"Ah, I said it would be so from the very beginning!" said the Stork-mamma; "but now think a little of your own family. Our travelling time is drawing on; sometimes I feel quite restless in my wings already. The cuckoo and the nightingale have started, and I heard the quails saying that they were going too, as soon as the wind was favourable. Our young ones will behave well at the exercising, or I am much deceived in them."

The Viking's wife was extremely glad when she woke next morning and found the charming infant lying in her arms. She kissed and caressed it, but it cried violently, and struggled with its arms and legs, and did not seem rejoiced at all. At length it cried itself to sleep, and as it lay there still and tranquil, it looked exceedingly beautiful. The Viking's wife was in high glee: she felt light in body and soul; her heart leapt within her; and it seemed to her as if her husband and his warriors, who were absent, must return quite as suddenly and unexpectedly as the little one had come.

Therefore she and the whole household had enough to do in preparing everything for the reception of her lord. The long coloured curtains of tapestry, which she and her maids had worked, and on which they had woven pictures of their idols, Odin, Thor, and Friga, were hung up; the slaves polished the old shields, that served as ornaments; and cushions were placed on the benches, and dry wood laid on the fireplace in the midst of the hall, so that the flame might be fanned up at a moment's notice. The Viking's wife herself assisted in the work, so that towards evening she was very tired, and went to sleep quickly and lightly.

When she awoke towards morning, she was violently alarmed, for the infant had vanished! She sprang from her couch, lighted a pine torch, and searched all round about; and, behold, in the part of the bed where she had stretched her feet, lay, not the child, but a great ugly frog! She was horror-struck at the sight, and seized a heavy stick to kill the frog, but the creature looked at her with such strange mournful eyes, that she was not able to strike the blow. Once more she looked round the room—the frog uttered a low, wailing croak, and she started, sprang from the couch, and ran to the window and opened it. At that moment the sun shone forth, and flung its beams through the window on the couch and on the great frog; and suddenly it appeared as though the frog's great mouth contracted and became small and red, and its limbs moved and stretched and became beautifully symmetrical, and it was no longer an ugly frog which lay there, but her pretty child!

"What is this?" she said. "Have I had a bad dream? Is it not my own lovely cherub lying there?"

And she kissed and hugged it; but the child struggled and fought like a little wild cat.

Not on this day nor on the morrow did the Viking return, although he certainly was on his way home; but the wind was against him, for it blew towards the south, favourably for the storks. A good wind for one is a contrary wind for another.

When one or two more days and nights had gone, the Viking's wife clearly understood how the case was with her child, that a terrible power of sorcery was upon it. By day it was charming as an angel of light, though it had a wild, savage temper; but at night it became an ugly frog, quiet and mournful, with sorrowful eyes. Here were two natures changing inwardly as well as outwardly with the sunlight. The reason of this was that by day the child had the form of its mother, but the disposition of its father; while, on the contrary, at night the paternal descent became manifest in its bodily appearance, though the mind and heart of the mother then became dominant in the child. Who might be able to loosen this charm that wicked sorcery had worked?

The wife of the Viking lived in care and sorrow about it; and yet her heart yearned towards the little creature, of whose condition she felt she should not dare tell her husband on his return, for he would pro-

bably, according to the custom which then prevailed, expose the child
on the public highway, and let whoever listed take it away. The good
Viking woman could not find it in her heart to allow this, and she
therefore determined that the Viking should never see the child except
by daylight.

One morning the wings of storks were heard rushing over the roof;
more than a hundred pairs of those birds had rested from their exercise
during the previous night, and now they soared aloft, to travel southwards.

" All males here, and ready," they cried ; "and the wives and children too."

" How light we feel ! " screamed the young Storks in chorus : " it
seems to be creeping all over us, down into our very toes, as if we
were filled with frogs. Ah, how charming it is, travelling to foreign
lands ! "

" Mind you keep close to us during your flight," said papa and mamma.
" Don't use your beaks too much, for that tires the chest."

And the Storks flew away.

At the same time the sound of the trumpets rolled across the heath,
for the Viking had landed with his warriors ; they were returning home,
richly laden with spoil, from the Gallic coast, where the people, as in the
land of the Britons, sang in frightened accents :

" Deliver us from the wild Northmen ! "

And life and tumultuous joy came with them into the Viking's castle
on the moorland. The great mead-tub was brought into the hall, the
pile of wood was set ablaze, horses were killed, and a great feast was to
begin. The officiating priest sprinkled the slaves with the warm blood ;
the fire crackled, the smoke rolled along beneath the roof ; but they
were accustomed to that. Guests were invited, and received handsome
gifts : all feuds and all malice were forgotten. And the company drank
deep, and threw the bones of the feast in each others' faces, and this
was considered a sign of good humour. The bard, a kind of minstrel,
but who was also a warrior, and had been on the expedition with the
rest, sang them a song, in which they heard all their warlike deeds
praised, and everything remarkable was specially noticed. Every verse
ended with the burden :

—" Goods and gold, friends and foes will die ; every man must one day die
But a famous name will never die ! "

And with that they beat upon their shields, and hammered the table
in glorious fashion with bones and knives.

The Viking's wife sat upon the high seat in the open hall. She wore
a silken dress and golden armlets, and great amber beads : she was in
her costliest garb. And the bard mentioned her in his song, and sang
of the rich treasure she had brought her rich husband. The latter was
delighted with the beautiful child, which she had seen in the day-time
in all its loveliness ; and the savage ways of the little creature pleased

THE VIKING'S FEAST.

him especially. He declared that the girl might grow up to be a stately heroine, strong and determined as a man. She would not wink her eyes when a practised hand cut off her eyebrows with a sword by way of a jest.

The full mead-barrel was emptied, and a fresh one brought in, for these were people who liked to enjoy all things plentifully. The old proverb was indeed well known, which says, "The cattle know when they should quit the pasture, but a foolish man knoweth not the measure of his own appetite." Yes, they knew it well enough; but one *knows* one thing, and one *does* another. They also knew that "even the welcome guest becomes wearisome when he sitteth long in the house; " but for all that they sat still, for pork and mead are good things; and there was high carousing, and at night the bondmen slept among the warm ashes, and dipped their fingers in the fat grease and licked them. Those were glorious times!

Once more in the year the Viking sallied forth, though the storms of autumn already began to roar: he went with his warriors to the shores of Britain, for he declared that was but an excursion across the water; and his wife stayed at home with the little girl. And thus much is certain, that the poor lady soon got to love the frog with its gentle eyes and its sorrowful sighs, almost better than the pretty child that bit and beat all around her.

The rough damp mist of autumn, which devours the leaves of the forest, had already descended upon thicket and heath. "Birds featherless," as they called the snow, flew in thick masses, and the winter was coming on fast. The sparrows took possession of the storks' nests, and talked about the absent proprietors according to their fashion; but these —the Stork-pair, with all the young ones—what had become of them?

The Storks were now in the land of Egypt, where the sun sent forth warm rays, as it does here on a fine midsummer day. Tamarinds and acacias bloomed in the country all around; the crescent of Mahomet glittered from the cupolas of the temples, and on the slender towers sat many a stork-pair resting after the long journey. Great troops divided the nests, built close together on venerable pillars and in fallen temple arches of forgotten cities. The date-palm lifted up its screen as if it would be a sunshade; the greyish-white pyramids stood like masses of shadow in the clear air of the far desert, where the ostrich ran his swift career, and the lion gazed with his great grave eyes at the marble sphinx which lay half buried in the sand. The waters of the Nile had fallen, and the whole river bed was crowded with frogs; and this spectacle was just according to the taste of the Stork family. The young Storks thought it was optical illusion, they found everything so glorious.

"Yes, it's delightful here; and it's always like this in our warm country," said the Stork-mamma.

And the young ones felt quite frisky on the strength of it

"Is there anything more to be seen?" they asked. "Are we to go much farther into the country?"

"There's nothing further to be seen," answered Stork-mamma. "Behind this delightful region there are luxuriant forests, whose branches are interlaced with one another, while prickly climbing plants close up the paths—only the elephant can force a way for himself with his great feet; and the snakes are too big and the lizards too quick for us. If you go into the desert, you'll get your eyes full of sand when there's a light breeze, but when it blows great guns you may get into the middle of a pillar of sand. It is best to stay here, where there are frogs and locusts. I shall stay here, and you shall stay too."

And there they remained. The parents sat in the nest on the slender

minaret, and rested, and yet were busily employed smoothing and cleaning their feathers, and whetting their beaks against their red stockings.
Now and then they stretched out their necks, and bowed gravely, and
lifted their heads, with their high foreheads and fine smooth feathers,
and looked very clever with their brown eyes. The female young ones
strutted about in the juicy reeds, looked slily at the other young storks.
made acquaintances, and swallowed a frog at every third step, or rolled
a little snake to and fro in their bills, which they thought became them
well, and, moreover, tasted nice. The male young ones began a quarrel.
beat each other with their wings, struck with their beaks, and even
pricked each other till the blood came. And in this way sometimes one
couple was betrothed, and sometimes another, of the young ladies and
gentlemen, and that was just what they wanted, and their chief object
in life: then they took to a new nest, and began new quarrels, for in
hot countries people are generally hot tempered and passionate. But it
was pleasant for all that, and the old people especially were much rejoiced, for all that young people do seems to suit them well. There was
sunshine every day, and every day plenty to eat, and nothing to think
of but pleasure. But in the rich castle at the Egyptian host's, as they
called him, there was no pleasure to be found.

The rich mighty lord reclined on his divan, in the midst of the great
hall of the many-coloured walls, looking as if he were sitting in a tulip;
but he was stiff and powerless in all his limbs, and lay stretched out like
a mummy. His family and servants surrounded him, for he was not
dead, though one could not exactly say that he was alive. The healing
moor flower from the North, which was to have been found and brought
home by her who loved him best, never appeared. His beauteous young
daughter, who had flown in the swan's plumage over sea and land to the
far North, was never to come back. "She is dead!" the two returning
Swan-maidens had said, and they had concocted a complete story, which
ran as follows:

"We three together flew high in the air: a hunter saw us, and shot
his arrow at us; it struck our young companion and friend, and slowly,
singing her farewell song, she sank down, a dying swan, into the woodland lake. By the shore of the lake, under a weeping birch tree, we
laid her in the cool earth. But we had our revenge. We bound fire
under the wings of the swallow who had her nest beneath the huntsman's thatch; the house burst into flames, the huntsman was burned in
the house, and the glare shone over the sea as far as the hanging birch
beneath which she sleeps. Never will she return to the land of Egypt."

And then the two wept. And when Stork-papa heard the story, he
clapped with his beak so that it could be heard a long way off.

"Treachery and lies!" he cried. "I should like to run my beak
deep into their chests."

"And perhaps break it off," interposed the Stork-mamma; "and then
you would look well. Think first of yourself, and then of your family,
and all the rest does not concern you."

"But to-morrow I shall seat myself at the edge of the open cupola,

when the wise and learned men assemble to consult on the sick man's
state : perhaps they may come a little nearer the truth."

And the learned and wise men came together and spoke a great deal,
out of which the Stork could make no sense — and it had no result,
either for the sick man or for the daughter in the swampy waste.   But
for all that we may listen to what the people said, for we have to listen
to a great deal of talk in the world.

But then it will be an advantage to hear what went before, and in
this case we are well informed, for we know just as much about it as
Stork-papa.

"Love gives life ! the highest love gives the highest life :   Only
through love can his life be preserved."

That is what they all said, and the learned men said it was very
cleverly and beautifully spoken.

" That is a beautiful thought !" Stork-papa said immediately.

" I don't quite understand it," Stork-mamma replied ; " and that 's
not my fault, but the fault of the thought.   But let it be as it will,
I 've something else to think of."

And now the learned men had spoken of love to this one and that
one, and of the difference between the love of one's neighbour and love
between parents and children, of the love of plants for the light, when
the sunbeam kisses the ground and the germ springs forth from it,—
everything was so fully and elaborately explained that it was quite
impossible for Stork-papa to take it in, much less to repeat it.   He felt
quite weighed down with thought, and half shut his eyes, and the whole
of the following day he stood thoughtfully upon one leg : it was quite
heavy for him to carry, all that learning.

But one thing Stork-papa understood.   All, high and low, had spoken
out of their inmost hearts, and said that it was a great misfortune for
thousands of people, yes, for the whole country, that this man was lying
sick, and could not get well, and that it would spread joy and pleasure
abroad if he should recover.   But where grew the flower that could
restore him to health ?   They had all searched for it, consulted learned
books, the twinkling stars, the weather and the wind ; they had made
inquiries in every byway of which they could think ; and at length the
wise men and the learned men had said, as we have already told, that
" Love begets life—will restore a father's life ;" and on this occasion they
had surpassed themselves, and said more than they understood.   They
repeated it, and wrote down as a recipe, " Love begets life."   But how
was the thing to be prepared according to the recipe ? that was a point
they could not get over.   At last they were decided upon the point that
help must come by means of the Princess, through her who clave to her
father with her whole soul ; and at last a method had been devised
whereby help could be procured in this dilemma.   Yes, it was already
more than a year ago since the Princess had sallied forth by night, when
the brief rays of the new moon were waning : she had gone out to the
marble sphinx, had shaken the dust from her sandals, and gone onward

THE KING OF EGYPT DECEIVED BY THE PRINCESSES.

through the long passage which leads into the midst of one of the great pyramids, where one of the mighty Kings of antiquity, surrounded by pomp and treasure, lay swathed in mummy cloths. There she was to incline her ear to the breast of the dead King; for thus, said the wise men, it should be made manifest to her where she might find life and health for her father. She had fulfilled all these injunctions, and had seen in a vision that she was to bring home from the deep lake in the northern moorland—the very place had been accurately described to her

—the lotos flower which grows in the depths of the waters, and then her father would regain health and strength.

And therefore she had gone forth in the swan's plumage out of the land of Egypt to the open heath, to the woodland moor. And the Stork-papa and Stork-mamma knew all this; and now we also know it more accurately than we knew it before. We know that the Marsh King had drawn her down to himself, and know that to her loved ones at home she is dead for ever. One of the wisest of them said, as the Stork-mamma said too, " She will manage to help herself;" and at last they quieted their minds with that, and resolved to wait and see what would happen, for they ' new of nothing better that they could do.

"I should like to take away the swan's feathers from the two faithless Princesses," said the Stork-papa; "then, at any rate, they will not be able to fly up again to the wild moor and do mischief. I'll hide the two swan-feather suits up there, till somebody has occasion for them."

"But where do you intend to hide them?" asked Stork-mamma.

"Up in our nest in the moor," answered he. "I and our young ones will take turns in carrying them up yonder on our return, and if that should prove too difficult for us, there are places enough on the way where we can conceal them till our next journey. Certainly, one suit of swan's feathers would be enough for the Princess, but two are always better. In those northern countries no one can have too many wraps."

"No one will thank you for it," quoth Stork-mamma; "but you 're the master. Except at breeding-time, I have nothing to say."

In the Viking's castle by the wild moor, whither the Storks bent their flight when the spring approached, they had given the little girl the name of Helga; but this name was too soft for a temper like that which was associated with her beauteous form. Every month this temper showed itself in sharper outlines; and in the course of years—during which the Storks made the same journey over and over again, in autumn to the Nile, in spring back to the moorland lake—the child grew to be a great girl; and before people were aware of it, she was a beautiful maiden in her sixteenth year. The shell was splendid, but the kernel was harsh and hard; and she was hard, as indeed were most people in those dark, gloomy times. It was a pleasure to her to splash about with her white hands in the blood of the horse that had been slain in sacrifice. In her wild mood she bit off the neck of the black cock the priest was about to offer up; and to her father she said in perfect seriousness,

"If thy enemy should pull down the roof of thy house, while thou wert sleeping in careless safety; if I felt it or heard it, I would not wake thee even if I had the power. I should never do it, for my ears still tingle with the blow that thou gavest me years ago—thou! I have never forgotten it."

But the Viking took her words in jest; for, like all others, he was bewitched with her beauty, and he knew not how temper and form changed in Helga. Without a saddle she sat upon a horse, as if she were part of it, while it rushed along in full career; nor would she spring from the horse when it quarrelled and fought with other horses. Often she would throw herself, in her clothes, from the high shore into the sea, and swim to meet the Viking when his boat steered near home; and she cut her longest lock of hair, and twisted it into a string for her bow.

"Self-achieved is well-achieved," she said.

The Viking's wife was strong of character and of will, according to the custom of the times; but, compared to her daughter, she appeared as a

THE TRANSFORMED PRINCESS.

feeble, timid woman, for she knew that an evil charm weighed heavily upon the unfortunate child.

It seemed as if, out of mere malice, when her mother stood on the threshold or came out into the yard, Helga would often seat herself on the margin of the well, and wave her arms in the air; then suddenly she would dive into the deep well, where her frog nature enabled her to dive and rise, down and up, until she climbed forth again like a cat, and came back into the hall dripping with water, so that the green leaves strewn upon the ground floated and turned in the streams that flowed from her garments.

But there was one thing that imposed a check upon Helga, and that was the evening twilight. When that came she was quiet and thoughtful, and would listen to reproof and advice; and then a secret feeling seemed to draw her towards her mother. And when the sun sank, and the usual transformation of body and spirit took place in her, she would sit quiet and mournful, shrunk to the shape of the frog, her body indeed much larger than that of the animal whose likeness she took, and for that reason much more hideous to behold, for she looked like a wretched dwarf with a frog's head and webbed fingers. Her eyes then assumed a very melancholy expression. She had no voice, and could only utter a hollow croaking that sounded like the stifled sob of a dreaming child. Then the Viking's wife took her on her lap, and forgot the ugly form as she looked into the mournful eyes, and said,

"I could almost wish that thou wert always my poor dumb frog-child; for thou art only the more terrible when thy nature is veiled in a form of beauty."

And the Viking woman wrote Runic characters against sorcery and spells of sickness, and threw them over the wretched child; but she could not see that they worked any good.

"One can scarcely believe that she was ever so small that she could lie in the cup of a water-lily," said Stork-papa, "now she's grown up the image of her Egyptian mother. Ah, we shall never see that poor lady again! Probably she did not know how to help herself, as you and the learned physicians said. Year after year I have flown to and fro, across and across the great moorland, and she has never once given a sign that she was still alive. Yes, I may as well tell you, that every year, when I came here a few days before you, to repair the nest and attend to various matters, I spent a whole night in flying to and fro over the lake, as if I had been an owl or a bat, but every time in vain. The two suits of swan feathers which I and the young ones dragged up here out of the land of the Nile have consequently not been used: we had trouble enough with them to bring them hither in three journeys; and now they lie down here in the nest, and if it should happen that a fire broke out, and the wooden house were burned, they would be destroyed."

"And our good nest would be destroyed too," said Stork-mamma; "but you think less of that than of your plumage stuff and of your Moor Princess. You'd best go down into the mud and stay there with her. You're a bad father to your own children, as I said already when I hatched our first brood. I only hope neither we nor our children will get an arrow in our wings through that wild girl. Helga doesn't know in the least what she does. I wish she would only remember that we have lived here longer than she, and that we have never forgotten our duty, and have given our toll every year, a feather, an egg, and a young one, as it was right we should do. Do you think I can now wander about in the courtyard and everywhere, as I was wont in former days, and as I still do in Egypt, where I am almost the playfellow of the people, and that I can press into pot and kettle as I can yonder? No, I sit up here and am angry at her, the stupid chit! And I am angry at you too. You should have just left her lying in the water-lily, and she would have been dead long ago."

"You are much better than your words," said Stork-papa. "I know you better than you know yourself."

And with that he gave a hop, and flapped his wings heavily twice, stretched out his legs behind him, and flew away, or rather sailed away, without moving his wings. He had already gone some distance when he gave a great *flap!* The sun shone upon his grand plumage, and his head and neck were stretched forth proudly. There was power in it, and dash!

"After all, he's handsomer than any of them," said Stork-mamma to herself; "but I won't tell him so."

Early in that autumn the Viking came home, laden with booty, and bringing prisoners with him. Among these was a young Christian priest, one of those who contemned the gods of the North.

Often in those later times there had been a talk, in hall and chamber, of the new faith that was spreading far and wide in the South, and which, by means of Saint Ansgarius, had penetrated as far as Hedeby on the Schlei. Even Helga had heard of this belief in One who, from love to men and for their redemption, had sacrificed His life; but with her all this had, as the saying is, gone in at one ear and come out at the other. It seemed as if she only understood the meaning of the word "love," when she crouched in a corner of the chamber in the form of a miserable frog; but the Viking's wife had listened to the mighty history that was told throughout the lands, and had felt strangely moved thereby.

On their return from their last voyage, the men told of the splendid temples built of hewn stones, raised for the worship of Him whose worship is love. Some massive vessels of gold, made with cunning art, had been brought home among the booty, and each one had a peculiar fragrance; for they were incense vessels, which had been swung by Christian priests before the altar.

In the deep cellars of the Viking's house the young priest had been immured, his hands and feet bound with strips of bark. The Viking's wife declared that he was beautiful as Bulder to behold, and his misfortune touched her heart; but Helga declared that it would be right to tie ropes to his heels and fasten him to the tails of wild oxen. And she exclaimed,

"Then I would let loose the dogs—hurrah! over the moor and across the swamp! That would be a spectacle for the gods! And yet finer would it be to follow him in his career."

But the Viking would not suffer him to die such a death: he purposed to sacrifice the priest on the morrow, on the death-stone in the grove, as a despiser and foe of the high gods.

For the first time a man was to be sacrificed here.

Helga begged, as a boon, that she might sprinkle the image of the god and the assembled multitude with the blood of the priest. She sharpened her glittering knife, and when one of the great savage dogs, of whom a number were running about near the Viking's abode, ran by her, she thrust the knife into his side, "merely to try its sharpness," as she said. And the Viking's wife looked mournfully at the wild, evil-disposed girl; and when night came on and the maiden exchanged beauty of form for gentleness of soul, she spoke in eloquent words to Helga of the sorrow that was deep in her heart.

The ugly frog, in its monstrous form, stood before her, and fixed its brown eyes upon her face, listening to her words, and seeming to comprehend them with human intelligence.

"Never, not even to my lord and husband, have I allowed my lips to utter a word concerning the sufferings I have to undergo through thee," said the Viking's wife; "my heart is full of woe concerning thee: more powerful, and greater than I ever fancied it, is the love of a mother! But love never entered into thy heart—thy heart that is like the wet, cold moorland plants."

Then the miserable form trembled, and it was as though these words touched an invisible bond between body and soul, and great tears came into the mournful eyes.

"Thy hard time will come," said the Viking's wife; "and it will be terrible to me too. It had been better if thou hadst been set out by the high road, and the night wind had lulled thee to sleep."

And the Viking's wife wept bitter tears, and went away full of wrath and bitterness of spirit, disappearing behind the curtain of furs that hung loose over the beam and divided the hall.

The wrinkled frog crouched in the corner alone. A deep silence reigned all around, but at intervals a half-stifled sigh escaped from its breast, from the breast of Helga. It seemed as though a painful new life were arising in her inmost heart. She came forward and listened; and, stepping forward again, grasped with her clumsy hands the heavy pole that was laid across before the door. Silently and laboriously she pushed back the pole, silently drew back the bolt, and took up the flickering lamp which stood in the ante-chamber of the hall. It seemed as if a strong hidden will gave her strength. She drew back the iron bolt from the closed cellar door, and crept in to the captive. He was asleep; and when he awoke and saw the hideous form, he shuddered as though he had beheld a wicked appariton. She drew her knife, cut the bonds that confined his hands and feet, and beckoned him to follow her.

He uttered some holy names and made the sign of the cross; and when the form remained montionless at his side, he said,

"Who art thou? Whence this animal shape that thou bearest, while yet thou art full of gentle mercy?"

The frog-woman beckoned him to follow, and led him through corridors shrouded with' curtains, into the stables, and there pointed to a horse. He mounted on its back, and she also sprang up before him.

THE FLIGHT.

holding fast by the horse's mane. The prisoner understood her meaning, and in a rapid trot they rode on a way which he would never have
found, out on to the open heath.

He thought not of her hideous form, but felt how the mercy and
loving-kindness of the Almighty were working by means of this monstrous apparition; he prayed pious prayers and sang songs of praise.
Then she trembled. Was it the power of song and of prayer that worked
in her, or was she shuddering at the cold morning twilight that was
approaching? What were her feelings? She raised herself up, and
wanted to stop the horse and to alight; but the Christian priest held
her back with all his strength, and sang a pious song, as if that would
have the power to loosen the charm that turned her into the hideous
semblance of a frog. And the horse gallopped on more wildly than
ever; the sky turned red, the first sunbeam pierced through the clouds,
and as the flood of light came streaming down, the frog changed its
nature. Helga was again the beautiful maiden with the wicked, demo-

niac spirit. He held a beautiful maiden in his arms, but was horrified at the sight: he swung himself from the horse, and compelled it to stand. This seemed to him a new and terrible sorcery; but Helga likewise leaped from the saddle, and stood on the ground. The child's short garment reached only to her knee. She plucked the sharp knife from her girdle, and quick as lightning she rushed in upon the astonished priest.

"Let me get at thee!" she screamed; "let me get at thee, and plunge this knife in thy body! Thou art pale as straw, thou beardless slave!"

She pressed in upon him. They struggled together in a hard strife, but an invisible power seemed given to the Christian captive. He held her fast; and the old oak tree beneath which they stood came to his assistance; for its roots, which projected over the ground, held fast the maiden's feet that had become entangled in it. Quite close to them gushed a spring; and he sprinkled Helga's face and neck with the fresh water, and commanded the unclean spirit to come forth, and blessed her in the Christian fashion; but the water of faith has no power when the well-spring of faith flows not from within.

And yet the Christian showed his power even now, and opposed more than the mere might of a man against the evil that struggled within the girl. His holy action seemed to overpower her: she dropped her hands, and gazed with frightened eyes and pale cheeks upon him who appeared to her a mighty magician learned in secret arts; he seemed to her to speak in a dark Runic tongue, and to be making cabalistic signs in the air. She would not have winked had he swung a sharp knife or a glittering axe against her; but she trembled when he signed her with the sign of the cross on her brow and her bosom, and she sat there like a tame bird with bowed head.

Then he spoke to her in gentle words of the kindly deed she had done for him in the past night, when she came to him in the form of the hideous frog, to loosen his bonds and to lead him out to life and light; and he told her that she too was bound in closer bonds than those that had confined him, and that she should be released by his means. He would take her to Hedeby (Schleswig), to the holy Ansgarius, and yonder in the Christian city the spell that bound her would be loosed. But he would not let her sit before him on the horse, though of her own accord she offered to do so.

"Thou must sit behind me, not before me," he said. "Thy magic beauty hath a power that comes of evil, and I fear it; and yet I feel that the victory is sure to him who hath faith."

And he knelt down and prayed fervently. It seemed as though the woodland scenes were consecrated as a holy church by his prayer. The birds sang as though they belonged to the new congregation, the wild flowers smelt sweet as incense; and while he spoke the horse that had carried them both in headlong career stood still before the tall bramble bushes, and plucked at them, so that the ripe juicy berries fell down upon Helga's hands, offering themselves for her refreshment.

Patiently she suffered the priest to lift her on the horse, and sat like a somnambulist, neither completely asleep nor wholly awake. The

Christian bound two branches together with bark, in the form of a cross, which he held up high as they rode through the forest. The wood became thicker as they went on, and at last became a trackless wilderness.

The wild sloe grew across the way, so that they had to ride round the bushes. The bubbling spring became not a stream but a standing marsh, round which likewise they were obliged to lead the horse. There was strength and refreshment in the cool forest breeze; and no small power lay in the gentle words, which were spoken in faith and in Chris-

THE CHRISTIAN PRIEST'S SPELL.

tian love, from a strong inward yearning to lead the poor lost one into the way of light and life.

They say the rain-drops can hollow the hard stone, and the waves of the sea can smooth and round the sharp edges of the rocks. Thus did the dew of mercy, that dropped upon Helga, smooth what was rough and penetrate what was hard in her. The effects did not yet appear, nor was she aware of them herself; but doth the seed in the bosom of earth know, when the refreshing dew and the quickening sunbeams fall upon it, that it hath within itself the power of growth and blossoming? As the song of the mother penetrates into the heart of the child, and it babbles the words after her, without understanding their import, until they afterwards engender thought, and come forward in due time clearer and more clearly, so here also did the Word work, that is powerful to create.

They rode forth from the dense forest, across the heath, and then again through pathless roads; and towards evening they encountered a band of robbers.

" Where hast thou stolen that beauteous maiden ? " cried the robbers; and they seized the horse's bridle and dragged the two riders from its back. The priest had no weapon save the knife he had taken from Helga, and with this he tried to defend himself. One of the robbers lifted his axe to slay him, but the young priest sprang aside and eluded the blow, which struck deep into the horse's neck, so that the blood spurted forth, and the creature sank down on the ground. Then Helga seemed suddenly to wake up from her long reverie, and threw herself hastily upon the gasping animal. The priest stood before her to protect and defend her, but one of the robbers swung his iron hammer over the Christian's head, and brought it down with such a crash that blood and brains were scattered around, and the priest sank to the earth, dead.

Then the robbers seized beautiful Helga by her white arms and her slender waist; but the sun went down, and its last ray disappeared at that moment, and she was changed into the form of a frog. A white-green mouth spread over half her face, her arms became thin and slimy, and broad hands with webbed fingers spread out upon them like fans. Then the robbers were seized with terror, and let her go. She stood, a hideous monster, among them; and as it is the nature of the frog to do, she hopped up high, and disappeared in the thicket. Then the robbers saw that this must be a bad prank of the spirit Loke, or the evil power of magic, and in great affright they hurried away from the spot.

The full moon was already rising. Presently it shone with splendid radiance over the earth, and poor Helga crept forth from the thicket in the wretched frog's shape. She stood still beside the corpse of the priest and the carcase of the slain horse. She looked at them with eyes that appeared to weep, and from the frog-mouth came forth a croaking like the voice of a child bursting into tears. She leaned first over the one, then over the other, brought water in her hollow hand, which had become larger and more capacious by the webbed skin, and poured it over them; but dead they were, and dead they would remain, she at last understood. Soon the wild beasts would come and tear their dead bodies; but no, that must not be! so she dug up the earth as well as she could, in the endeavour to prepare a grave for them. She had nothing to work with but a stake and her two hands encumbered with the webbed skin that grew between the fingers, and which were torn by the labour, so that the blood flowed over them. At last she saw that her endeavours would not succeed. Then she brought water and washed the dead man's face, and covered it with fresh green leaves; she brought green boughs and laid them upon him, scattering dead leaves in the spaces between. Then she brought the heaviest stones she could carry and laid them over the dead body, stopping up the interstices with moss. And now she thought the grave-hill would be strong and secure. The

HELGA AND THE PRIEST ATTACKED BY ROBBERS.

night had passed away in this difficult work — the sun broke through the clouds, and beautiful Helga stood there in all her loveliness, with bleeding hands, and with the first tears flowing that had ever bedewed her maiden cheeks.

Then in this transformation it seemed as if two natures were striving within her. Her whole frame trembled, and she looked around, as if she had just awoke from a troubled dream. Then she ran towards the slender tree, clung to it for support, and in another moment she had climbed to the summit of the tree, and held fast. There she sat like a startled squirrel, and remained the whole day long in the silent solitude of the wood, where everything is quiet, and, as they say, dead. Butterflies fluttered around in sport, and in the neighbourhood were several ant-hills, each with its hundreds of busy little occupants moving briskly to and fro. In the air danced a number of gnats, swarm upon swarm, and hosts of buzzing flies, ladybirds, gold beetles, and other little winged creatures; the worm crept forth from the damp ground, the moles came out; but except these all was silent around—silent, and, as people say, dead—for they speak of things as they understand them. No one noticed Helga, but some flocks of crows, that flew screaming about the top of the tree on which she sat: the birds hopped close up to her on the twigs with pert curiosity; but when the glance of her eye fell upon them, it was a signal for their flight. But they could not understand her—nor, indeed, could she understand herself.

HELGA IN THE TREE.

When the evening twilight came on, and the sun was sinking, the time of her transformation roused her to fresh activity. She glided down from the tree, and as the last sunbeam vanished she stood in the wrinkled form of the frog, with the torn webbed skin on her hands; but her eyes now gleamed with a splendour of beauty that had scarcely been theirs when she wore her garb of loveliness, for they were a pair of pure, pious, maidenly eyes that shone out of the frog-face. They bore witness of depth of feeling, of the gentle human heart; and the beauteous eyes overflowed in tears, weeping precious drops that lightened the heart.

On the sepulchral mound she had raised there yet lay the cross of boughs, the last work of him who slept beneath. Helga lifted up the cross, in pursuance of a sudden thought that came upon her. She planted it upon the burial mound, over the priest and the dead horse. The sorrowful remembrance of him called fresh tears into her eyes; and in this tender frame of mind she marked the same sign in the sand around the grave; and as she wrote the sign with both her hands, the webbed skin fell from them like a torn glove; and when she washed her hands in the woodland spring, and gazed in wonder at their snowy whiteness, she again made the holy sign in the air between herself and the dead man; then her lips trembled, the holy name that had been preached to her during the ride from the forest came to her mouth, and she pronounced it audibly.

Then the frog-skin fell from her, and she was once more the beauteous maiden. But her head sank wearily, her tired limbs required rest, and she fell into a deep slumber.

Her sleep, however, was short. Towards midnight she awoke. Before her stood the dead horse, beaming and full of life, which gleamed forth from his eyes and from his wounded neck; close beside the creature stood the murdered Christian priest, "more beautiful than Bulder," the Viking woman would have said; and yet he seemed to stand in a flame of fire.

Such gravity, such an air of justice, such a piercing look shone out of his great mild eyes, that their glance seemed to penetrate every corner of her heart. Beautiful Helga trembled at the look, and her remembrance awoke as though she stood before the tribunal of judgment. Every good deed that had been done for her, every loving word that had been spoken, seemed endowed with life: she understood that it had been love that kept her here during the days of trial, during which the creature formed of dust and spirit, soul and earth, combats and struggles; she acknowledged that she had only followed the leading of temper, and had done nothing for herself; everything had been given her, everything had happened as it were by the interposition of Providence. She bowed herself humbly, confessing her own deep imperfection in the presence of the Power that can read every thought of the heart—and then the priest spoke.

"Thou daughter of the moorland," he said, "out of the earth, out of the moor, thou camest; but from the earth thou shalt arise. I come from the land of the dead. Thou, too, shalt pass through the deep valleys into the beaming mountain region, where dwell mercy and completeness. I cannot lead thee to Hedeby, that thou mayest receive Christian baptism; for, first, thou must burst the veil of waters over the deep moorland, and draw forth the living source of thy being and of thy birth; thou must exercise thy faculties in deeds before the consecration can be given thee."

And he lifted her upon the horse, and gave her a golden censer similar to the one she had seen in the Viking's castle. The open wound in the forehead of the slain Christian shone like a diadem. He took the cross from the grave and held it aloft. And now they rode through the air, over the rustling wood, over the hills where the old heroes lay buried, each on his dead war-horse; and the iron figures rose up and galloped forth, and stationed themselves on the summits of the hills. The golden hoop on the forehead of each gleamed in the moonlight and their mantles floated in the night breeze. The dragon that guards buried treasures likewise lifted up his head and gazed after the riders. The gnomes and wood spirits peeped forth from beneath the hills and from between the furrows of the fields, and flitted to and fro with red, blue, and green torches, like the sparks in the ashes of a burned paper.

Over woodland and heath, over river and marsh they fled away, up to the wild moor; and over this they hovered in wide circles. The Christian priest held the cross aloft; it gleamed like gold; and from his lips dropped pious prayers. Beautiful Helga joined in the hymns he sang, like a child joining in its mother's song. She swung the censer, and a wondrous fragrance of incense streamed forth thence, so that the reeds and grass of the moor burst forth into blossom. Every germ came forth from the deep ground. All that had life lifted itself up. A veil of water-lilies spread itself forth like a carpet of wrought flowers, and upon this carpet lay a sleeping woman, young and beautiful. Helga thought it was her own likeness she saw upon the mirror of the calm waters. But it was her mother whom she beheld, the Moor King's wife, the Princess from the banks of the Nile.

The dead priest commanded that the slumbering woman should be lifted upon the horse; but the horse sank under the burden, as though its body had been a cloth fluttering in the wind. But the holy sign gave strength to the airy phantom, and then the three rode from the moor to the firm land.

Then the cock crowed in the Viking's castle, and the phantom shapes dissolved and floated away in air; but mother and daughter stood opposite each other.

"Am I really looking at my own image from beneath the deep waters?" asked the mother.

"Is it myself that I see reflected on the clear mirror?" exclaimed the daughter.

And they approached one another and embraced. The heart of the mother beat quickest, and she understood the quickening pulses.

"My child! thou flower of my own heart! my lotos flower of the deep waters!"

And she embraced her child anew, and wept; and the tears were as a new baptism of life and love to Helga.

"In the swan's plumage came I hither," said the mother, "and here also I threw off my dress of feathers. I sank through the shaking moorland, far down into the black slime, which closed like a wall around me. But soon I felt a fresher stream; a power drew me down, deeper and ever deeper. I felt the weight of sleep upon my eyelids; I slumbered, and dreams hovered round me. It seemed to me that I was again in the pyramid in Egypt, and yet the waving willow trunk that had fright-

HELGA IS TAKEN BACK TO THE MARSH.

ened me up in the moor was ever before me. I looked at the clefts and wrinkles in the stem, and they shone forth in colours and took the form of hieroglyphics: it was the case of the mummy at which I was gazing; at last the case burst, and forth stepped the thousand-year-old King, the mummied form, black as pitch, shining ʰlack as the wood snail or the fat mud of the swamp: whether it was the Marsh King or the mummy of the pyramids I knew not. He seized me in his arms, and I felt as if I must die. When I returned to consciousness a little bird was sitting on my bosom, beating with its wings, and twittering and singing. The bird flew away from me up towards the heavy, dark covering, but a long green band still fastened him to me. I heard and understood his longing tones: 'Freedom! Sunlight! To my father!' Then I thought of my father and the sunny land of my birth, my life, and my love; and I loosened the band and let the bird soar away home to the father. Since that hour I have dreamed no more. I have slept a sleep, a long and heavy sleep, till within this hour; harmony and incense awoke me and set me free."

The green band from the heart of the mother to the bird's wings, where did it flutter now ?. whither had it been wafted ? Only the Stork had seen it. The band was the green stalk, the bow at the end, the beauteous flower, the cradle of the child that had now bloomed into beauty and was once more resting on its mother's heart.

And while the two were locked in each other's embrace, the old Stork flew around them in smaller and smaller circles, and at length shot away in swift flight towards his nest, whence he brought out the swan-feather suits he had preserved there for years, throwing one to each of them, and the feathers closed around them, so that they soared up from the earth in the semblance of two white swans.

"And now we will speak with one another," quoth Stork-papa, "now we·understand each other, though the beak of one bird is differently shaped from that of another. It happens more than fortunately that you came to-night. To-morrow we should have been gone—mother, myself, and the young ones, for we are flying southward. Yes, only look at me ! I am an old friend from the land of the Nile, and mother has a heart larger than her beak. She always declared the Princess would find a way to help herself; and I and the young ones carried the swan's feathers up here.   But how glad I am ! and how fortunate that I 'm here still ! At dawn of day we shall move hence, a great company of storks. We 'll fly first, and do you follow us; thus you cannot miss your way ; moreover, I and the youngsters will keep a sharp eye upon you."

"And the lotos flower which I was to bring with me," said the Egyptian Princess, "she is flying by my side in the swan's plumage ! I bring with me the flower of my heart; and thus the riddle has been read. Homeward! homeward!"

But Helga declared she could not quit the Danish land before she had once more seen her foster-mother, the affectionate Viking woman. Every beautiful recollection, every kind word, every tear that her foster-mother had wept for her, rose up in her memory, and in that moment she almost felt as if she loved the Viking woman best of all.

"Yes, we must go to the Viking's castle," said Stork-papa ; "mother and the youngsters are waiting for us there. How they will turn up their eyes and flap their wings ! Yes, you see, mother doesn't speak much—she 's short and dry, but she means all the better. I 'll begin clapping at once, that they may know we 're coming."

And Stork-papa clapped in first-rate style, and they all flew away towards the Viking's castle.

In the castle every one was sunk in deep sleep. The Viking's wife had not retired to rest until it was late. She was anxious about Helga, who had vanished with the Christian priest three days before: she knew Helga must have assisted him in his flight, for it was the girl's horse that had been missed from the stables ; but how all this had been effected was a mystery to her. The Viking woman had heard of the miracles told of the Christian priest, and which were said to be wrought by him and by those who believed in his words and followed him. Her passing thoughts formed themselves into a dream, and it seemed to her that she

HELGA MEETS WITH HER MOTHER IN THE MARSH.

was still lying awake on her couch, and that deep darkness reigned
without. The storm drew near: she heard the sea roaring and rolling
to the east and to the west, like the waves of the North Sea and the
Cattegat. The immense snake which was believed to surround the span
of the earth in the depths of the ocean was trembling in convulsions;
she dreamed that the night of the fall of the gods had come—Ragnarok,
as the heathen called the last day, when everything was to pass away,
even the great gods themselves. The war-trumpet sounded, and the
gods rode over the rainbow, clad in steel, to fight the last battle. The
winged Valkyrs rode before them, and the dead warriors closed the train.
The whole firmament was ablaze with Northern Lights, and yet the darkness seemed to predominate. It was a terrible hour.

And close by the terrified Viking woman Helga seemed to be crouching on the floor in the hideous frog form, trembling and pressing close to her foster-mother, who took her on her lap and embraced her affectionately, hideous though she was. The air resounded with the blows of clubs and swords, and with the hissing of arrows, as if a hail-storm were passing across it. The hour was come when earth and sky were to burst, the stars to fall, and all things to be swallowed up in Surtur's sea of fire; but she knew that there would be a new heaven and a new earth, that the corn-fields then would wave where now the ocean rolled over the desolate tracts of sand, and that the unutterable God would reign; and up to Him rose Bulder the gentle, the affectionate, delivered from the kingdom of the dead: he came; the Viking woman saw him and recognized his countenance; it was that of the captive Christian priest. "White Christian!" she cried aloud, and with these words she pressed a kiss upon the forehead of the hideous frog-child. Then the frog-skin fell off, and Helga stood revealed in all her beauty, lovely and gentle as she had never appeared, and with beaming eyes. She kissed her foster-mother's hands, blessed her for all the care and affection lavished during the days of bitterness and trial, for the thought she had awakened and cherished in her, for naming the name, which she repeated, " White Christian; " and beauteous Helga arose in the form of a mighty swan, and spread her white wings with a rushing like the sound of a troop of birds of passage winging their way through the air.

The Viking woman awoke, and she heard the same noise without still continuing. She knew it was the time for the storks to depart, and that it must be those birds whose wings she heard. She wished to see them once more, and to bid them farewell as they set forth on their journey. Therefore she rose from her couch and stepped out upon the threshold, and on the top of the gable she saw stork ranged behind stork, and around the castle, over the high trees, flew bands of storks wheeling in wide circles; but opposite the threshold where she stood, by the well where Helga had often sat and alarmed her with her wildness, sat two white swans gazing at her with intelligent eyes. And she remembered her dream, which still filled her soul as if it were reality. She thought of Helga in the shape of a swan, and of the Christian priest; and suddenly she felt her heart rejoice within her.

The swans flapped their wings and arched their necks, as if they would send her a greeting, and the Viking's wife spread out her arms towards them, as if she felt all this, and smiled through her tears, and then stood sunk in deep thought.

Then all the storks arose, flapping their wings and clapping with their beaks, to start on their voyage towards the South.

" We will not wait for the swans," said Stork-mamma: "if they want to go with us they had better come. We can't sit here till the plovers start. It is a fine thing, after all, to travel in this way, in families, not like the finches and partridges, where the male and female birds fly in separate bodies, which appears to me a very unbecoming thing. What are yonder swans flapping their wings for?"

THE DISGUISED PRINCESSES BID FAREWELL TO THE VIKING WOMAN.

"Well, every one flies in his own fashion," said Stork-papa : "the swans in an oblique line, the cranes in a triangle, and the plovers in a snake's line."

"Don't talk about snakes while we are flying up here," said Stork-mamma. "It only puts ideas into the children's heads which can't be gratified."

"Are those the high mountains of which I have heard tell?" asked Helga, in the swan's plumage.

"They are storm clouds driving on beneath us," replied her mother.

"What are yonder white clouds that rise so high?" asked Helga again.

"Those are the mountains covered with perpetual snow which you see yonder," replied her mother.

And they flew across the lofty Alps towards the blue Mediterranean.

"Africa's land! Egypt's strand!" sang, rejoicingly, in her swan's plumage, the daughter of the Nile, as from the lofty air she saw her native land looming in the form of a yellowish wavy stripe of shore.

And all the birds caught sight of it, and hastened their flight.

"I can scent the Nile mud and wet frogs," said Stork-mamma; "I begin to feel quite hungry. Yes; now you shall taste something nice; and you will see the maraboo bird, the crane, and the ibis. They all belong to our family, though they are not nearly so beautiful as we. They give themselves great airs, especially the ibis. He has been quite spoiled by the Egyptians, for they make a mummy of him and stuff him with spices. I would rather be stuffed with live frogs, and so would you, and so you shall. Better have something in one's inside while one is alive than to be made a fuss with after one is dead. That's my opinion, and I am always right."

"Now the storks are come," said the people in the rich house on the banks of the Nile, where the royal lord lay in the open hall on the downy cushions, covered with a leopard-skin, not alive and yet not dead, but waiting and hoping for the lotos flower from the deep moorland in the far North. Friends and servants stood around his couch.

And into the hall flew two beauteous swans. They had come with the storks. They threw off their dazzling white plumage, and two lovely female forms were revealed, as like each other as two dew-drops. They bent over the old, pale, sick man, they put back their long hair, and while Helga bent over her grandfather, his white cheeks reddened, his eyes brightened, and life came back to his wasted limbs. The old man rose up cheerful and well, and daughter and granddaughter embraced him joyfully, as if they were giving him a morning greeting after a long heavy dream.

And joy reigned through the whole house, and likewise in the Storks' nest, though there the chief cause was certainly the good food, especially the numberless frogs, which seemed to spring up in heaps out of the ground; and while the learned men wrote down hastily, in flying characters, a sketch of the history of the two Princesses, and of the flower of health that had been a source of joy for the home and the land, the Stork pair told the story to their family in their own fashion, but not till all had eaten their fill, otherwise the youngsters would have found something more interesting to do than to listen to stories.

"Now, at last, you will become something," whispered Stork-mamma, "there's no doubt about that."

"What should I become?" asked Stork-papa. "What have I done? Nothing at all!"

"You have done more than the rest! But for you and the youngsters the two Princesses would never have seen Egypt again, or have effected the old man's cure. You will turn out something! They must certainly give you a doctor's degree, and our youngsters will inherit it, and so will their children after them, and so on. You already look like an Egyptian doctor—at least in my eyes."

"I cannot quite repeat the words as they were spoken," said Stork-papa, who had listened from the roof to the report of these events made by the learned men, and was now telling it again to his own family. "What they said was so confused, it was so wise and learned, that they immediately received rank and presents: even the head cook received an especial mark of distinction—probably for the soup."

"And what did you receive?" asked Stork-mamma. "Surely they

THE KING OF EGYPT'S RECOVERY.

ought not to forget the most important person of all, and you are certainly he! The learned men have done nothing throughout the whole
affair but used their tongues; but you will doubtless receive what is
due to you."

Late in the night, when the gentle peace of sleep rested upon the
now happy house, there was one who still watched. It was not Stork-
papa, though he stood upon one leg and slept on guard—it was Helga
who watched. She bowed herself forward over the balcony, and looked
into the clear air, gazed at the great gleaming stars, greater and purer

in their lustre than she had ever seen them in the North, and yet the same orbs. She thought of the Viking woman in the wild moorland, of the gentle eyes of her foster-mother, and of the tears which the kind soul had wept over the poor frog-child that now lived in splendour under the gleaming stars, in the beauteous spring air on the banks of the Nile. She thought of the love that dwelt in the breast of the heathen woman, the love that had been shown to a wretched creature, hateful in human form, and hideous in its transformation. She looked at the gleaming stars, and thought of the glory that had shone upon the forehead of the dead man, when she flew with him through the forest and across the moorland; sounds passed through her memory, words she had heard pronounced as they rode onward, and when she was borne wondering and trembling through the air, words from the great Fountain of love that embraces all human kind.

Yes, great things had been achieved and won! Day and night beautiful Helga was absorbed in the contemplation of the great sum of her happiness, and stood in the contemplation of it like a child that turns hurriedly from the giver to gaze on the splendours of the gifts it has received. She seemed to lose herself in the increasing happiness, in contemplation of what might come, of what would come. Had she not been borne by miracle to greater and greater bliss? And in this idea she one day lost herself so completely, that she thought no more of the Giver. It was the exuberance of youthful courage, unfolding its wings for a bold flight! Her eyes were gleaming with courage, when suddenly a loud noise in the courtyard below recalled her thoughts from their wandering flight. There she saw two great ostriches running round rapidly in a narrow circle. Never before had she seen such creatures—great clumsy things they were, with wings that looked as if they had been clipped, and the birds themselves looking as if they had suffered violence of some kind; and now for the first time she heard the legend which the Egyptians tell of the ostrich.

Once, they say, the ostriches were a beautiful, glorious race of birds, with strong large wings; and one evening the larger birds of the forest said to the ostrich. "Brother, shall we fly to-morrow, God willing, to the river to drink?" And the ostrich answered, "I will." At daybreak, accordingly, they winged their flight from thence, flying first up on high, towards the sun, that gleamed like the eye of God—higher and higher, the ostrich far in advance of all the other birds. Proudly the ostrich flew straight towards the light, boasting of his strength, and not thinking of the Giver, or saying, "God willing!" Then suddenly the avenging angel drew aside the veil from the flaming ocean of sunlight, and in a moment the wings of the proud bird were scorched and shrivelled up, and he sank miserably to the ground. Since that time the ostrich has never again been able to raise himself in the air, but flees timidly along the ground, and runs round in a narrow circle. And this is a warning for us men, that in all our thoughts and schemes, in all our doings and devices, we should say, "God willing." And Helga bowed her head thoughtfully and gravely, and looked at the circling

A MESSAGE TO THE VIKING WOMAN.

ostrich, noticing its timid fear, and its stupid pleasure at sight of its own great shadow cast upon the white sunlit wall. And seriousness struck its roots deep into her mind and heart. A rich life in present and future happiness was given and won; and what was yet to come? the best of all, "God willing."

In early spring, when the storks flew again towards the North, beautiful Helga took off her golden bracelet and scratched her name upon it; and beckoning to the Stork-father, she placed the golden hoop around his neck, and begged him to deliver it to the Viking woman, so that the latter might see that her adopted daughter was well, and had not forgotten her.

"That's heavy to carry," thought the Stork-papa, when he had the golden ring round his neck; "but gold and honour are not to be flung into the street. The stork brings good fortune; they'll be obliged to acknowledge that over yonder."

"You lay gold and I lay eggs," said the Stork-mamma. "But with you it's only once in a way, whereas I lay eggs every year; but neither of us is appreciated—that's very disheartening."

" Still one has one's inward consciousness, mother," replied Stork-papa.

"But you can't hang that round your neck," Stork-mamma retorted, "and it won't give you a good wind or a good meal."

The little nightingale, singing yonder in the tamarind tree, will soon be going north too. Helga the fair had often heard the sweet bird sing up yonder by the wild moor; now she wanted to give it a message to carry, for she had learned the language of birds when she flew in the swan's plumage; she had often conversed with stork and with swallow, and she knew the nightingale would understand her. So she begged the little bird to fly to the beech wood on the peninsula of Jutland, where the grave-hill had been reared with stones and branches, and begged the nightingale to persuade all other little birds that they might build their nests around the place, so that the song of birds should resound over that sepulchre for evermore. And the nightingale flew away—and time flew away.

In autumn the eagle stood upon the pyramid, and saw a stately train of richly laden camels approaching, and richly attired armed men on foaming Arab steeds, shining white as silver, with pink trembling nostrils, and great thick manes hanging down almost over their slender legs. Wealthy guests, a royal Prince of Arabia, handsome as a Prince should be, came into the proud mansion on whose roof the storks' nests now stood empty; those who had inhabited the nest were away now in the far North, but they would soon return. And, indeed, they returned on that very day that was so rich in joy and gladness. Here a marriage was celebrated, and fair Helga was the bride, shining in jewels and silk. The bridegroom was the young Arab Prince, and bride and bridegroom sat together at the upper end of the table, between mother and grand-father.

But her gaze was not fixed upon the bridegroom, with his manly sun-browned cheeks, round which a black beard curled; she gazed not at his dark fiery eyes that were fixed upon her—but far away at a gleaming star that shone down from the sky.

Then strong wings were heard beating the air. The storks were coming home, and however tired the old Stork pair might be from the journey, and however much they needed repose, they did not fail to come down at once to the balustrades of the verandah, for they knew what feast was being celebrated. Already on the frontier of the land they had heard that Helga had caused their figures to be painted on the wall—for did they not belong to her history?

"That's very pretty and suggestive," said Stork-papa.

"But it's very little," observed Stork-mamma. "They could not possibly have done less."

And when Helga saw them, she rose and came on to the verandah, to stroke the backs of the Storks. The old pair waved their heads and bowed their necks, and even the youngest among the young ones felt highly honoured by the reception.

And Helga looked up to the gleaming star, which seemed to glow purer and purer ; and between the star and herself there floated a form, purer than the air, and visible through it : it floated quite close to her. It was the spirit of the dead Christian priest ; he too was coming to her wedding feast—coming from heaven.

" The glory and brightness yonder outshines everything that is known on earth ! " he said.

And fair Helga begged so fervently, so beseechingly, as she had never yet prayed, that it might be permitted her to gaze in there for one single moment, that she might be allowed to cast but a single glance into the brightness that beamed in the kingdom of heaven.

Then he bore her up amid splendour and glory. Not only around her, but within her, sounded voices and beamed a brightness that words cannot express.

" Now we must go back ; thou wilt be missed," he said.

" Only one more look ! " she begged. " But one short minute more ! "

" We must go back to the earth. The guests will all depart."

" Only one more look—the last."

And Helga stood again in the verandah ; but the marriage lights without had vanished, and the lamps in the hall were extinguished, and the storks were gone—nowhere a guest to be seen—no bridegroom—all seemed to have been swept away in those few short minutes !

Then a great dread came upon her. Alone she went through the empty great hall into the next chamber. Strange warriors slept yonder. She opened a side door which led into her own chamber, and, as she thought to step in there, she suddenly found herself in the garden ; but yet it had not looked thus here before — the sky gleamed red — the morning dawn was come.

Three minutes only in heaven and a whole night on earth had passed away !

Then she saw the Storks again. She called to them and spoke their language ; and Stork-papa turned his head towards her, listened to her words, and drew near.

" You speak our language," he said ; " what do you wish ? Why do you appear here—you, a strange woman ? "

" It is I—it is Helga—dost thou not know me ? Three minutes ago we were speaking together yonder in the verandah ! "

" That 's a mistake," said the Stork ; " you must have dreamed that ! "

" No, no ! " she persisted. And she reminded him of the Viking's castle, and of the great ocean, and of the journey hither.

Then Stork-papa winked with his eyes, and said,

" Why, that 's an old story, which I heard from the time of my great-grandfather. There certainly was here in Egypt a Princess of that kind from the Danish land, but she vanished on the evening of her wedding-day, many hundred years ago, and never came back ! You may read about it yourself yonder on the monument in the garden ; there you 'll find swans and storks sculptured, and at the top you yourself are cut in white marble ! "

And thus it was. Helga saw it, and understood it, and sank on her knees.

The sun burst forth in glory; and as, in time of yore, the frog shape had vanished in its beams, and the beautiful form had stood displayed, so now in the light a beauteous form, clearer, purer than air—a beam of brightness—flew up into heaven!

The body crumbled to dust, and a faded lotos flower lay on the spot where Helga had stood.

"Well, that's a new ending to the story," said Stork-papa. "I had certainly not expected it. But I like it very well."

"But what will the young ones say to it?" said Stork-mamma.

"Yes, certainly, that's the important point," replied he.

THE PEN AND INKSTAND.

IN the room of a poet, where his Inkstand stood upon the table, it was said, "It is wonderful what can come out of an inkstand. What will the next thing be? It is wonderful!"

"Yes, certainly," said the Inkstand. "It's extraordinary—that's what I always say," he exclaimed to the Pen and to the other articles on the table that were near enough to hear. "It is wonderful what a number of things can come out of me. It's quite incredible. And I really don't myself know what will be the next thing, when that man begins to dip into me. One drop out of me is enough for half a page of paper; and what cannot be contained in half a page? From me all the works of the poet go forth—all these living men, whom people can imagine they have met—all the deep feeling, the humour, the vivid pictures of nature. I myself don't understand how it is, for I am not acquainted with nature, but it certainly is in me. From me all these things have gone forth, and from me proceed the troops of charming maidens, and of brave knights on prancing steeds, and all the lame and the blind, and I don't know what more—I assure you I don't think of anything."

"There you are right," said the Pen; "you don't think at all, for if you did, you would comprehend that you only furnish the fluid. You give the fluid, that I may exhibit upon the paper what dwells in me, and what I would bring to the day. It is the pen that writes. No man doubts that; and, indeed, most people have about as much insight into poetry as an old inkstand."

"You have but little experience," replied the Inkstand. "You've hardly been in service a week, and are already half worn out. Do you fancy you are the poet? You are only a servant; and before you came I knew many of your sort, some of the goose family, and others of English manufacture. I know the quill as well as the steel pen. Many

have been in my service, and I shall have many more when *he* comes—
the man who goes through the motions for me, and writes down what
he derives from me. I should like to know what will be the next thing
he 'll take out of me."

"Inkpot!" exclaimed the Pen.

Late in the evening the poet came home. He had been to a concert,
where he had heard a famous violinist, with whose admirable performances
he was quite enchanted. The player had drawn a wonderful wealth of
tone from the instrument: sometimes it had sounded like tinkling water-
drops, like rolling pearls, sometimes like birds twittering in chorus, and
then again it went swelling on like the wind through the fir trees. The
poet thought he heard his own heart weeping, but weeping melodiously,
like the sound of woman's voice. It seemed as though not only the
strings sounded, but every part of the instrument. It was a wonderful

THE POET.

performance; and difficult as the piece was, the bow seemed to glide
easily to and fro over the strings, and it looked as though every one
might do it. The violin seemed to sound of itself, and the bow to move
of itself—those two appeared to do everything; and the audience forgot
the master who guided them and breathed soul and spirit into them.
The master was forgotten; but the poet remembered him, and named
him, and wrote down his thoughts concerning the subject.

"How foolish it would be of the violin and the bow to boast of their
achievements! And yet we men often commit this folly—the poet, the
artist, the labourer in the domain of science, the general—we all do it.
We are only the instruments which the Almighty uses: to Him alone
be the honour! We have nothing of which we should be proud."

Yes, that is what the poet wrote down. He wrote it in the form of a
parable, which he called "The Master and the Instruments."

" That is what you get, madam," said the Pen to the Inkstand, when the two were alone again. " Did you not hear him read aloud what I have written down ? "

" Yes, what I gave you to write," retorted the Inkstand. " That was a cut at you, because of your conceit. That you should not even have understood that you were being quizzed ! I gave you a cut from within me—surely I must know my own satire ! "

" Ink-pipkin ! " cried the Pen.

" Writing-stick ! " cried the Inkstand.

And each of them felt a conviction that he had answered well ; and it is a pleasing conviction to feel that one has given a good answer—a conviction on which one can sleep ; and accordingly they slept upon it. But the poet did not sleep. Thoughts welled up from within him, like the tones from the violin, falling like pearls, rushing like the storm wind through the forests. He understood his own heart in these thoughts, and caught a ray from the Eternal Master.

To *Him* be all the honour !

A STORY FROM THE SAND-DUNES.

This is a story from the sand-dunes or sand-hills of Jutland ; though it does not begin in Jutland, the northern peninsula, but far away in the south, in Spain. The ocean is the high road between the nations— transport thyself thither in thought to sunny Spain. There it is warm and beautiful, there the fiery pomegranate blossoms flourish among the dark laurels ; from the mountains a cool refreshing wind blows down, upon, and over the orange gardens, over the gorgeous Moorish halls with their golden cupolas and coloured walls : through the streets go children in procession, with candles and with waving flags, and over them, lofty and clear, rises the sky with its gleaming stars. There is a sound of song and of castagnettes, and youths and maidens join in the dance under the blooming acacias, while the mendicant sits upon the hewn marble stone, refreshing himself with the juicy melon, and dreamily enjoying life. The whole is like a glorious dream. And there was a newly married couple who completely gave themselves up to its charm ; moreover, they possessed the good things of this life, health and cheerulness of soul, riches and honour.

" We are as happy as it is possible to be," exclaimed the young couple, from the depths of their hearts. They had indeed but one step more to mount in the ladder of happiness, in the hope that God would give them a child—a son like them in form and in spirit.

The happy child would be welcomed with rejoicing, would be tended with all care and love, and enjoy every advantage that wealth and ease possessed by an influential family could give.

And the days went by like a glad festival.

IN SPAIN.

"Life is a gracious gift of Providence, an almost inappreciable gift!" said the young wife, "and yet they tell us that fulness of joy is found only in the future life, for ever and ever. I cannot compass the thought."

"And perhaps the thought arises from the arrogance of men," said the husband. "It seems a great pride to believe that we shall live for ever, that we shall be as gods. Were these not the words of the serpent, the origin of falsehood?"

"Surely you do not doubt the future life?" exclaimed the young wife; and it seemed as if one of the first shadows flitted over the sunny heaven of her thoughts.

"Faith promises it, and the priests tell us so!" replied the man; "but amid all my happiness, I feel that it is arrogance to demand a continued happiness, another life after this. Has not so much been given us in this state of existence, that we ought to be, that we *must* be, contented with it?"

"Yes, it has been given to *us*," said the young wife, "but to how many thousands is not this life one scene of hard trial? How many have been thrown into this world, as if only to suffer poverty and shame and sickness and misfortune? If there were no life after this, everything on earth would be too unequally distributed, and the Almighty would not be justice itself."

"Yonder beggar," replied the man, "has his joys which seem to him great, and which rejoice him as much as the King is rejoiced in the splendour of his palace. And then, do you not think that the beast of burden, which suffers blows and hunger, and works itself to death, suffers from its heavy fate? The dumb beast might likewise demand a future life, and declare the decree unjust that does not admit it into a higher place of creation."

"HE has said, 'In my Father's house are many mansions,'" replied the young wife: "heaven is immeasurable, as the love of our Maker is immeasurable. Even the dumb beast is His creature; and I firmly believe that no life will be lost, but that each will receive that amount of happiness which he can enjoy, and which is sufficient for him."

"This world is sufficient for me!" said the man, and he threw his arms round his beautiful, amiable wife, and then smoked his cigarette on the open balcony, where the cool air was filled with the fragrance of oranges and pinks. The sound of music and the clatter of castagnettes came up from the road, the stars gleamed above, and two eyes full of affection, the eyes of his wife, looked on him with the undying glance of love.

"Such a moment," he said, "makes it worth while to be born, to fall, and to disappear!" and he smiled.

The young wife raised her hand in mild reproach, and the shadow passed away from her world, and they were happy—quite happy.

Everything seemed to work together for them. They advanced in honour, in prosperity, and in joy. There was a change, indeed, but only a change of place; not in enjoyment of life and of happiness. The young man was sent by his sovereign as ambassador to the Court of Russia. This was an honourable office, and his birth and his acquirements gave him a title to be thus honoured. He possessed a great fortune, and his wife had brought him wealth equal to his own, for she was the only daughter of a rich and respected merchant. One of this merchant's largest and finest ships was to be dispatched during that year to Stockholm, and it was arranged that the dear young people, the daughter and the son-in-law, should travel in it to St. Petersburg. And all the arrangements on board were princely—rich carpets for the feet, and silk and luxury on all sides.

In an old heroic song, "The King's Son of England," it says, "Moreover, he sailed in a gallant ship, and the anchor was gilded with ruddy gold, and each rope was woven through with silk."

And this ship involuntarily rose in the mind of him who saw the vessel from Spain, for here was the same pomp, and the same parting thought naturally arose—the thought:

> "God grant that we all in joy
> Once more may meet again."

And the wind blew fairly seaward from the Spanish shore, and the parting was to be but a brief one, for in a few weeks the voyagers would reach their destination; but when they came out upon the high seas, the wind sank, the sea became calm and shining, the stars of heaven gleamed brightly, and they were festive evenings that were spent in the sumptuous cabin.

At length the voyagers began to wish for wind, for a favouring breeze; but the breeze would not blow, or, if it did arise, it was contrary. Thus weeks passed away, two full months; and then at last the fair wind blew—it blew from the south-west. The ship sailed on the high seas between Scotland and Jutland, and the wind increased just as in the old song of " The King's Son of England."

> "And it blew a storm, and the rain came down,
> And they found not land nor shelter,
> And forth they threw their anchor of gold,
> As the wind blew westward, toward Denmark."

This all happened a long, long while ago. King Christian VII. then sat on the Danish throne, and he was still a young man. Much has happened since that time, much has changed or has been changed. Sea and moorland have been converted into green meadows, heath has become arable land, and in the shelter of the West Jute huts grow apple trees and rose bushes, though they certainly require to be sought for, as they bend beneath the sharp west wind. In Western Jutland one may go back in thought to the old times, farther back than the days when Christian VII. bore rule. As it did then, in Jutland, the brown heath now also extends for miles, with its " Hun's Graves," its aërial spectacles, and its crossing, sandy, uneven roads; westward, where large rivulets run into the bays, extend marshes and meadow land, girdled with lofty sand-hills, which, like a row of Alps, raise their peaked summits towards the ocean, only broken by the high clayey ridges, from which the waves year by year bite out huge mouths-full, so that the impending shores fall down as if by the shock of an earthquake. Thus it is there to-day, and thus it was many, many years ago, when the happy pair were sailing in the gorgeous ship.

It was in the last days of September, a Sunday, and sunny weather; the chiming of the church bells in the Bay of Nissum was wafted along like a chain of sounds. The churches there are erected almost entirely of hewn boulder stones, each like a piece of rock; the North Sea might foam over them, and they would not be overthrown. Most of them are without steeples, and the bells are hung between two beams in the open air. The service was over, and the congregation thronged out into the churchyard, where then, as now, not a tree nor a bush was to be seen; not a single flower had been planted there, nor had a wreath been laid upon the graves. Rough mounds show where the dead have been buried, and rank grass, tossed by the wind, grows thickly over the whole churchyard. Here and there a grave had a monument to show, in the shape of a half-decayed block of wood rudely shaped into the form of a coffin, the said block having been brought from the forest of West Jutland; but the forest of West Jutland is the wild sea itself, where the inhabitants find the hewn beams and planks and fragments which the breakers cast ashore. The wind and the sea fog soon destroy the wood. One of these blocks had been placed by loving hands on a child's grave, and one of the women, who had come out of the church, stepped towards it. She stood still in front of it, and let her glance rest on the discoloured memorial. A few moments afterwards her husband stepped up to her. Neither of them spoke a word, but he took her hand, and they wandered across the brown heath, over moor and meadow, towards the sand-hills; for a long time they thus walked silently side by side.

"That was a good sermon to-day," the man said at length. "If we had not God to look to, we should have nothing!"

"Yes," observed the woman, "He sends joy and sorrow, and He has a right to send them. To-morrow our little boy would have been five years old, if we had been allowed to keep him."

"You will gain nothing by fretting, wife," said the man. "The boy is well provided for. He is there whither we pray to go."

And they said nothing more, but went forward to their house among the sand-hills. Suddenly, in front of one of the houses, where the sea grass did not keep the sand down with its twining roots, there arose what appeared to be a column of smoke rising into the air. A gust of wind swept in among the hills, whirling the particles of sand high in the air. Another, and the strings of fish hung up to dry flapped and beat violently against the wall of the hut; and then all was still again, and the sun shone down hotly.

Man and wife stepped into the house. They had soon taken off their Sunday clothes, and emerging again, they hurried away over the dunes, which stood there like huge waves of sand suddenly arrested in their course, while the sandweeds and the dune grass with its bluish stalks spread a changing colour over them. A few neighbours came up and helped one another to draw the boats higher up on the sand. The wind now blew more sharply than before; it was cutting and cold: and when they went back over the sand-hills, sand and little pointed stones blew into their faces. The waves reared themselves up with their white crowns of foam, and the wind cut off their crests, flinging the foam far around.

The evening came on. In the air was a swelling roar, moaning and complaining like a troop of despairing spirits, that sounded above the hoarse rolling of the sea; for the fisher's little hut was on the very margin. The sand rattled against the window-panes, and every now and then came a violent gust of wind, that shook the house to its foundations. It was dark, but towards midnight the moon would rise.

The air became clearer, but the storm swept in all its gigantic force over the perturbed sea. The fisher people had long gone to bed, but in such weather there was no chance of closing an eye. Presently there was a knocking at the window, and the door was opened, and a voice said,

"There's a great ship fast stranded on the outermost reef."

In a moment the fish people had sprung from their couch and hastily arrayed themselves.

The moon had risen, and it was light enough to make the surrounding objects visible to those who could open their eyes for the blinding clouds of sand. The violence of the wind was terrible, and only by creeping forward between the gusts was it possible to pass among the sand-hills; and now the salt spray flew up from the sea like down, while the ocean foamed like a roaring cataract towards the beach. It required a practised eye to descry the vessel out in the offing. The vessel was a noble brig. The billows now lifted it over the reef, three

SAVED FROM THE WRECK.

or four cables' lengths out of the usual channel. It drove towards the land, struck against the second reef, and remained fixed.

To render assistance was impossible; the sea rolled fairly in upon the vessel, making a clean breach over her. Those on shore fancied they heard the cries of help from on board, and could plainly descry the busy useless efforts made by the stranded crew. Now a wave came rolling onward, falling like a rock upon the bowsprit and tearing it from the brig. The stern was lifted high above the flood. Two people were seen to embrace and plunge together into the sea; in a moment more, and one of the largest waves that rolled towards the sand-hills threw a body upon the shore. It was a woman, and appeared quite dead, said the sailors; but some women thought they discerned signs of life in her, and the stranger was carried across the sand-hills into the fisherman's hut. How beautiful and fair she was! certainly she must be a great lady.

They laid her upon the humble bed that boasted not a yard of linen; but there was a woollen coverlet, and that would keep the occupant warm.

Life returned to her, but she was delirious, and knew nothing of what had happened or where she was; and it was better so, for everything she loved and valued lay buried in the sea. It was with her ship as with the vessel in the song of "The King's Son of England."

> "Alas! it was a grief to see
> How the gallant ship sank speedily."

Portions of wreck and fragments of wood drifted ashore, and they were all that remained of what had been the ship. The wind still drove howling over the coast. For a few moments the strange lady seemed to rest; but she awoke in pain, and cries of anguish and fear came from her lips. She opened her wonderfully beautiful eyes, and spoke a few words, but none understood her.

And behold, as a reward for the pain and sorrow she had undergone, she held in her arms a new-born child, the child that was to have rested upon a gorgeous couch, surrounded by silken curtains, in the sumptuous home. It was to have been welcomed with joy to a life rich in all the goods of the earth; and now Providence had caused it to be born in this humble retreat, and not even a kiss did it receive from its mother.

The fisher's wife laid the child upon the mother's bosom, and it rested on a heart that beat no more, for she was dead. The child who was to be nursed by wealth and fortune, was cast into the world, washed by the sea among the sand-hills, to partake the fate and heavy days of the poor. And here again comes into our mind the old song of the English King's son, in which mention is made of the customs prevalent at that time, when knights and squires plundered those who had been saved from shipwreck.

The ship had been stranded some distance south of Nissum Bay. The hard inhuman days, in which, as we have stated, the inhabitants of the Jutland shores did evil to the shipwrecked, were long past. Affection and sympathy and self-sacrifice for the unfortunate were to be found, as they are to be found in our own time, in many a brilliant example. The dying mother and the unfortunate child would have found succour and help wherever the wind blew them; but nowhere could they have found more earnest care than in the hut of the poor fisherwife, who had stood but yesterday, with a heavy heart, beside the grave which covered her child, which would have been five years old that day if God had spared it to her.

No one knew who the dead stranger was, or could even form a conjecture. The pieces of wreck said nothing on the subject.

Into the rich house in Spain no tidings penetrated of the fate of the daughter and the son-in-law. They had not arrived at their destined post, and violent storms had raged during the past weeks. At last the verdict was given, " Foundered at sea—all lost."

But on the sand-hills near Hunsby, in the fisherman's hut, lived a little scion of the rich Spanish family.

Where Heaven sends food for two, a third can manage to make a meal, and in the depths of the sea is many a dish of fish for the hungry.

And they called the boy Jürgen.

"It must certainly be a Jewish child," the people said, "it looks so swarthy."

"It might be an Italian or a Spaniard," observed the clergyman.

But to the fisherwoman these three nations seemed the same, and she consoled herself with the idea that the child was baptized as a Christian.

The boy throve. The noble blood in his veins was warm, and he became strong on his homely fare. He grew apace in the humble house, and the Danish dialect spoken by the West Jutes became his language. The pomegranate seed from Spanish soil became a hardy plant on the coast of West Jutland. Such may be a man's fate! To this home he clung with the roots of his whole being. He was to have experience of cold and hunger, and the misfortunes and hardships that surrounded the humble, but he tasted also of the poor man's joys.

Childhood has sunny heights for all, whose memory gleams through the whole after life. The boy had many opportunities for pleasure and play. The whole coast, for miles and miles, was full of playthings, for it was a mosaic of pebbles, red as coral, yellow as amber, and others again white and rounded like birds' eggs, and all smoothed and prepared by the sea. Even the bleached fish skeletons, the water plants dried by the wind, seaweed, white, gleaming, and long linen-like bands, waving among the stones, all these seemed made to give pleasure and amusement to the eye and the thoughts; and the boy had an intelligent mind—many and great faculties lay dormant in him. How readily he retained in his mind the stories and songs he heard, and how neat-handed he was! With stones and mussel shells he could put together pictures and ships with which one could decorate the room; and he could cut out his thoughts wonderfully on a stick, his foster-mother said, though the boy was still so young and little! His voice sounded sweetly; every melody flowed at once from his lips. Many chords were attained in his heart which might have sounded out into the world, if he had been placed elsewhere than in the fisherman's hut by the North Sea.

One day another ship was stranded there. Among other things, a chest of rare flower bulbs floated ashore. Some were put into the cooking pots, for they were thought to be eatable, and others lay and shrivelled in the sand, but they did not accomplish their purpose or unfold the richness of colour whose germ was within them. Would it be better with Jürgen? The flower bulbs had soon played their part, but he had still years of apprenticeship before him.

Neither he nor his friends remarked in what a solitary and uniform way one day succeeded another, for there was plenty to do and to see. The sea itself was a great lesson-book, unfolding a new leaf every day, such as calm and storm, breakers and waifs. The visits to the church were festal visits. But among the festal visits in the fisherman's house, one was particularly distinguished. It was repeated twice in the year, and was, in fact, the visit of the brother of Jürgen's foster-mother, the eel breeder from Zjaltring, upon the neighbourhood of the " Bow Hill." He used to come in a cart painted red and filled with eels. The cart was covered and locked like a box, and painted all over with blue and white tulips. It was drawn by two dun oxen, and Jürgen was allowed to guide them.

The eel breeder was a witty fellow, a merry guest, and brought a measure of brandy with him. Every one received a small glass-full, or a cup-full when there was a scarcity of glasses : even Jürgen had as much as a large thimble-full, that he might digest the fat eel, the eel breeder said, who always told the same story over again, and when his hearers laughed he immediately told it over again to the same audience. As, during his childhood, and even later, Jürgen used many expressions from this story of the eel breeder's, and made use of it in various ways, it is as well that we should listen to it too. Here it is :

" The eels went into the bay ; and the mother-eel said to her daughters, who begged leave to go a little way up the bay, ' Don't go too far : the ugly eel spearer might come and snap you all up.' But they went too far ; and of eight daughters only three came back to the eel-mother, and these wept and said, ' We only went a little way before the door, and the ugly eel spearer came directly, and stabbed five of our party to death.' ' They 'll come again,' said the mother-eel. ' Oh, no,' exclaimed the daughters, ' for he skinned them, and cut them in two, and fried them.' ' Oh, they 'll come again,' the mother-eel persisted. ' No,' replied the daughters, ' for he ate them all up.' ' They 'll come again,' repeated the mother-eel. ' But he drank brandy after them,' continued the daughters. ' Ah, then they 'll never come back,' said the mother, and she burst out crying, ' It 's the brandy that buries the eels.'

" And therefore," said the eel breeder, in conclusion, " it is always right to take brandy after eating eels."

And this story was the tinsel thread, the most humorous recollection of Jürgen's life. *He* likewise wanted to go a little way outside the door and up the bay—that is to say, out into the world in a ship ; and his mother said, like the eel breeder, "There are so many bad people— eel spearers ! " But he wished to go a little way past the sand-hills, a little way into the dunes ; and he succeeded in doing so. Four merry days, the happiest of his childhood, unrolled themselves, and the whole beauty and splendour of Jutland, all the joy and sunshine of his home, were concentrated in these. He was to go to a festival—though it was certainly a burial feast.

A wealthy relative of the fisherman's family had died. The farm lay deep in the country, eastward, and a point towards the north, as the saying is. Jürgen's foster-parents were to go, and he was to accompany them from the dunes, across heath and moor. They came to the green meadows where the river Skjärn rolls its course, the river of many eels, where mother-eels dwell with their daughters, who are caught and eaten up by wicked people. But men were said sometimes to have acted no better towards their own fellow men; for had not the knight, Sir Bugge, been murdered by wicked people? and though he was well spoken of, had he not wanted to kill the architect, as the legend tells us, who had built for him the castle with the thick walls and tower, where Jürgen and his parents now stood, and where the river falls into the bay? The wall on the ramparts still remained, and red crumbling fragments lay strewn around. Here it was that Sir Bugge, after the architect had left

THE EEL BREEDER'S VISIT.

him, said to one of his men, " Go thou after him, and say, ' Master, the tower shakes.' If he turns round, you are to kill him, and take from him the money I paid him; but if he does not turn round let him depart in peace." The man obeyed, and the architect never turned round, but called back, " The tower does not shake in the least, but one day there will come a man from the west, in a blue cloak, who will cause it to shake!" And indeed so it chanced, a hundred years later; for the North Sea broke in, and the tower was cast down, but the man who then possessed the castle, Prebjörn Gyldenstjerne, built a new castle higher up, at the end of the meadow, and that stands to this day, and is called Nörre Vosborg.

Past this castle went Jürgen and his foster-parents. They had told him its story during the long winter evenings, and now he saw the lordly castle, with its double moat, and trees, and bushes; the wall, covered with ferns, rose within the moat; but most beautiful of all were the lofty lime trees, which grew up to the highest windows and filled the air with sweet fragrance. In a corner of the garden towards the north-west stood a great bush full of blossom like winter snow amid the summer's green: it was a juniper bush, the first that Jürgen had seen thus in bloom. He never forgot it, nor the lime tree: the child's soul treasured up these remembrances of beauty and fragrance to gladden the old man.

From Nörre Vosborg, where the juniper blossomed, the way went more easily, for they encountered other guests who were also bound for the burial, and were riding in waggons. Our travellers had to sit all together on a little box at the back of the waggon, but even this was preferable to walking, they thought. So they pursued their journey in the waggon across the rugged heath. The oxen which drew the vehicle slipped every now and then, where a patch of fresh grass appeared amid the heather. The sun shone warm, and it was wonderful to behold how in the far distance something like smoke seemed to be rising; and yet this smoke was clearer than the mist; it was transparent, and looked like rays of light rolling and dancing afar over the heath.

"That is Lokeman driving his sheep," said some one; and this was enough to excite the fancy of Jürgen. It seemed to him as if they were now going to enter fairyland, though everything was still real.

How quiet it was! Far and wide the heath extended around them like a beautiful carpet. The heather bloomed and the juniper bushes and the vigorous oak saplings stood up like nosegays from the earth. An inviting place for a frolic, if it were not for the number of poisonous adders of which the travellers spoke, as they did also of the wolves which formerly infested the place, from which circumstance the region was still called the Wolfsborg region. The old man who guided the oxen related how, in the lifetime of his father, the horses had to sustain many a hard fight with the wild beasts that were now extinct; and how he himself, when he went out one morning to bring in the horses, had found one of them standing with its fore feet on a wolf it had killed, after the savage beast had torn and lacerated the legs of the brave horse.

The journey over the heath and the deep sand was only too quickly accomplished. They stopped before the house of mourning, where they found plenty of guests within and without. Waggon after waggon stood ranged in a row, and horses and oxen went out to crop the scanty pasture. Great sand-hills, like those at home by the North Sea, rose behind the house and extended far and wide. How had they come here, miles into the interior of the land, and as large and high as those on the coast? The wind had lifted and carried them hither, and to them also a history was attached.

Psalms were sung, and a few of the old people shed tears; beyond this, the guests were cheerful enough, as it appeared to Jürgen, and there was plenty to eat and drink. Eels there were of the fattest, upon which brandy should be poured to bury them, as the eel breeder said; and certainly his maxim was here carried out.

Jürgen went to and fro in the house. On the third day he felt quite at home, like as in the fisherman's hut on the sand-hills where he had passed his early days. Here on the heath there was certainly an un-heard-of wealth, for the flowers and blackberries and bilberries were to be found in plenty, so large and sweet, that when they were crushed beneath the tread of the passers by, the heath was coloured with their red juice.

Here was a Hun's Grave, and yonder another. Columns of smoke rose into the still air: it was a heath-fire, he was told, that shone so splendidly in the dark evening.

Now came the fourth day, and the funeral festivities were to conclude, and they were to go back from the land-dunes to the sand-dunes.

"Ours are the best," said the old fisherman, Jürgen's foster-father; "these have no strength."

And they spoke of the way in which the sand-dunes had come into the country, and it seemed all very intelligible. This was the explanation they gave:

A corpse had been found on the coast, and the peasants had buried it in the churchyard; and from that time the sand began to fly and the sea broke in violently. A wise man in the parish advised them to open the grave and to look if the buried man was not lying sucking his thumb; for if so, he was a man of the sea, and the sea would not rest until it had got him back. So the grave was opened, and he really was found with his thumb in his mouth. So they laid him upon a cart and harnessed two oxen before it; and as if stung by an adder, the oxen ran away with the man of the sea over heath and moorland to the ocean; and then the sand ceased flying inland, but the hills that had been heaped up still remained there. All this Jürgen heard and treasured in his memory from the happiest days of his childhood, the days of the burial feast. How glorious it was to get out into strange regions and to see strange people! And he was to go farther still. He was not yet fourteen years old when he went out in a ship to see what the world could show him: bad weather, heavy seas, malice, and hard men—these were his experiences, for he became a ship boy. There were cold nights, and bad living, and blows to be endured; then he felt as if his noble Spanish blood boiled within him, and bitter wicked words seethed up to his lips; but it was better to gulp them down, though he felt as the eel must feel when it is flayed and cut up and put into the frying-pan.

"I shall come again!" said a voice within him. He saw the Spanish coast, the native land of his parents. He even saw the town where they had lived in happiness and prosperity; but he knew nothing of his home or race, and his race knew just as little about him.

The poor ship boy was not allowed to land; but on the last day of their stay he managed to get ashore. There were several purchases to be made, and he was to carry them on board.

There stood Jürgen in his shabby clothes, which looked as if they had

been washed in the ditch and dried in the chimney : for the first time
he, the inhabitant of the dunes, saw a great city. How lofty the houses
seemed, and how full of people were the streets! some pushing this
way, some that—a perfect maelstrom of citizens and peasants, monks
and soldiers—a calling and shouting, and jingling of bell-harnessed asses
and mules, and the church bells chiming between song and sound,
hammering and knocking, all going on at once. Every handicraft had
its home in the basements of the houses or in the lanes ; and the sun
shone so hotly, and the air was so close, that one seemed to be in
an oven full of beetles, cockchafers, bees, and flies, all humming and
murmuring together. Jürgen hardly knew where he was or which way
he went. Then he saw just in front of him the mighty portal of the
cathedral ; the lights were gleaming in the dark aisles, and a fragrance

JÜRGEN RESTS AT HIS ANCESTORS' RESIDENCE.

of incense was wafted towards him. Even the poorest beggar ventured
up the steps into the temple. The sailor with whom Jürgen went
took his way through the church, and Jürgen stood in the sanctuary.
Coloured pictures gleamed from their golden ground. On the altar
stood the figure of the Virgin with the child Jesus, surrounded by
lights and flowers; priests in festive garb were chanting, and choir
boys, beautifully attired, swung the silver censer. What splendour,
what magnificence did he see here! It streamed through his soul and
overpowered him; the church and the faith of his parents surrounded
him, and touched a chord in his soul, so that the tears overflowed his
eyes.

From the church they went to the market-place. Here a quantity of
provisions were given him to carry. The way to the harbour was long,
and, tired and overpowered by various emotions, he rested for a few
moments before a splendid house, with marble pillars, statues, and broad
staircases. Here he rested his burden against the wall. Then a liveried

porter came out, lifted up a silver-headed cane, and drove him away—him, the grandson of the house. But no one there knew that, and he just as little as any one. And afterwards he went on board again, and there were hard words and cuffs, little sleep and much work such were his experiences. They say that it is well to suffer in youth, if age brings something to make up for it.

His time for servitude on shipboard had expired, and the vessel lay once more at Ringkjöbing, in Jutland: he came ashore and went home to the sand-dunes by Hunsby; but his foster-mother had died while he was away on his voyage.

A hard winter followed that summer. Snow storms swept over land and sea, and there was a difficulty in getting about. How variously things appeared to be distributed in the world! here biting cold and snow-storms, while in the Spanish land there was burning sunshine and oppressive heat. And yet, when here at home there came a clear frosty day, and Jürgen saw the swans flying in numbers from the sea towards the land, and across to Vosborg, it appeared to him that people could breathe most freely here; and here too was a splendid summer! In imagination he saw the heath bloom and grow purple with rich juicy berries, and saw the elder trees and the lime trees at Vosborg in full blossom. He determined to go there once more.

Spring came on, and the fishery began. Jürgen was an active assistant in this; he had grown in the last year, and was quick at work. He was full of life, he understood how to swim; to tread water, to turn over and tumble in the flood. They often warned him to beware of the troops of dogfish, which could seize the best swimmer, and draw him down and devour him; but such was not Jürgen's fate.

At the neighbour's on the dune was a boy named Martin, with whom Jürgen was very friendly, and the two took service in the same ship to Norway, and also went together to Holland; and they had never had any quarrel; but a quarrel can easily come, for when a person is hot by nature he often uses strong gestures, and that is what Jürgen did one day on board when they had a quarrel about nothing at all. They were sitting behind the cabin door, eating out of a delf plate which they had placed between them. Jürgen held his pocket-knife in his hand, and lifted it against Martin, and at the same time became ashy pale in the face, and his eyes had an ugly look. Martin only said,

"Ah! ha! so you're one of that sort who are fond of using the knife!"

Hardly were the words spoken when Jürgen's hand sank down. He answered not a syllable, but went on eating, and afterwards walked away to his work. When they were resting again, he stepped up to Martin, and said,

"You may hit me in the face! I have deserved it. But I feel as if I had a pot in me that boiled over."

"There let the thing rest," replied Martin.

And after that they were almost doubly as good friends as before; and when afterwards they got back to the dunes and began telling their adventures, this was told among the rest; and Martin said that Jürgen was certainly passionate, but a good fellow for all that.

They were both young and strong, well grown and stalwart; but Jürgen was the cleverer of the two.

In Norway the peasants go into the mountains, and lead out the cattle there to pasture. On the west coast of Jutland, huts have been erected among the sand-hills; they are built of pieces of wreck, and roofed with turf and heather. There are sleeping-places around the walls, and here the fisher people live and sleep during the early spring. Every fisherman has his female helper, his manager, as she is called, whose business consists in baiting the hooks, preparing the warm beer for the fishermen when they come ashore, and getting their dinners cooked when they come back into the hut tired and hungry. Moreover, the managers bring up the fish from the boats, cut them open, prepare them, and have generally a great deal to do.

Jürgen, his father, and several other fishermen and their managers inhabited the same hut; Martin lived in the next one.

One of the girls, Else by name, had known Jürgen from childhood: they were glad to see each other, and in many things were of the same mind; but in outward appearance they were entirely opposite, for he was brown, whereas she was pale and had flaxen hair, and eyes as blue as the sea in sunshine.

One day as they were walking together, and Jürgen held her hand in his very firmly and warmly, she said to him,

"Jürgen, I have something weighing upon my heart! Let me be your manager, for you are like a brother to me, whereas Martin, who has engaged me; he and I are lovers——but you need not tell that to the rest."

And it seemed to Jürgen as if the loose sand were giving way under his feet. He spoke not a word, but only nodded his head, which signified "yes." More was not required; but suddenly he felt in his heart that he detested Martin; and the longer he considered of this—for he had never thought of Else in this way before—the more did it become clear to him that Martin had stolen from him the only being he loved; and now it was all at once plain to him that Else was the being in question.

When the sea is somewhat disturbed, and the fishermen come home in their great boats, it is a sight to behold how they cross the reefs. One of the men stands upright in the bow of the boat, and the others watch him, sitting with the oars in their hands. Outside the reef they appear to be rowing not towards the land, but backing out to sea, till the man standing in the boat gives them the sign that the great wave is coming which is to float them across the reef; and accordingly the boat is lifted—lifted high in the air, so that its keel is seen from the shore; and in the next minute the whole boat is hidden from the eye—neither mast nor keel nor people can be seen, as though the sea had devoured them; but in a few moments they emerge like a great sea animal climbing up the waves, and the oars move as if the creature had legs. The second and the third reef are passed in the same manner; and now the

ELSE AFFIRMS HER PREFERENCE FOR MARTIN.

fishermen jump into the water; every wave helps them, and pushes
the boat well forward, till at length they have drawn it beyond the
range of the breakers.

A wrong order given in front of the reef—the slightest hesitation—
and the boat must founder.

"Then it would be all over with me, and Martin too!" This thought
struck Jürgen while they were out at sea, where his foster-father had
been taken alarmingly ill. The fever had seized him. They were only
a few oars' strokes from the reef, and Jürgen sprang from his seat and
stood up in the bow.

"Father—let me come!" he said; and his eye glanced towards
Martin and across the waves; but while every oar bent with the exertions of the rowers, as the great wave came towering towards them, he
beheld the pale face of his father, and dare not obey the evil impulse
that had seized him. The boat came safely across the reef to land, but
the evil thought remained in his blood, and roused up every little fibre

of bitterness which had remained in his memory since he and Martin had been comrades. But he could not weave the fibres together, nor did he endeavour to do so. He felt that Martin had despoiled him, and this was enough to make him detest his former friend. Several of the fishermen noticed this, but not Martin, who continued obliging and talkative—the latter a little too much.

Jürgen's adopted father had to keep his bed, which became his death-bed, for in the next week he died; and now Jürgen was installed as heir in the little house behind the sand-hills. It was but a little house, certainly, but still it was something, and Martin had nothing of the kind.

"You will not take sea service again, Jürgen?" observed one of the old fishermen. "You will always stay with us, now."

But this was not Jürgen's intention, for he was just thinking of looking about him a little in the world. The eel breeder of Zjaltring had an uncle in Alt-Skage, who was a fisherman, but at the same time a prosperous merchant, who had ships upon the sea; he was said to be a good old man, and it would not be amiss to enter his service. Alt-Skage lies in the extreme north of Jutland, as far removed from the Hunsby dunes as one can travel in that country; and this is just what pleased Jürgen, for he did not want to remain till the wedding of Martin and Else, which was to be celebrated in a few weeks.

The old fisherman asserted that it was foolish now to quit the neighbourhood, for that Jürgen had a home, and Else would probably be inclined to take him rather than Martin.

Jürgen answered so much at random, that it was not easy to understand what he meant; but the old man brought Else to him, and she said,

"You have a home now; that ought to be well considered."

And Jürgen thought of many things. The sea has heavy waves, but there are heavier waves in the human heart. Many thoughts, strong and weak, thronged through Jürgen's brain; and he said to Else,

"If Martin had a house like mine, whom would you rather have?"

"But Martin has no house, and cannot get one."

"But let us suppose he had one."

"Why, then I would certainly take Martin, for that's what my heart tells me; but one can't live upon that."

And Jürgen thought of these things all night through. Something was working within him, he could not understand what it was, but he had a thought that was stronger than his love for Else; and so he went to Martin, and what he said and did there was well considered. He let the house to Martin on the most liberal terms, saying that he wished to go to sea again, because it pleased him to do so. And Else kissed him on the mouth when she heard that, for she loved Martin best.

In the early morning Jürgen purposed to start. On the evening before his departure, when it was already growing late, he felt a wish to visit Martin once more; he started, and among the dunes the old fisher met him, who was angry at his going. The old man made jokes about

Martin, and declared there must be some magic about that fellow, " of whom all the girls were so fond." Jürgen paid no heed to this speech, but said farewell to the old man, and went on towards the house where Martin dwelt. He heard loud talking within. Martin was not alone, and this made Jürgen waver in his determination, for he did not wish to encounter Else ; and on second consideration, he thought it better not to hear Martin thank him again, and therefore he turned back.

On the following morning, before break of day, he fastened his knapsack, took his wooden provision-box in his hand, and went away among the sand-hills towards the coast path. That way was easier to traverse than the heavy sand road, and moreover shorter ; for he intended to go in the first instance to Zjaltring, by Bowberg, where the eel breeder lived, to whom he had promised a visit.

The sea lay pure and blue before him, and mussel shells and sea pebbles, the playthings of his youth, crunched under his feet. While he was thus marching on, his nose suddenly began to bleed : it was a trifling incident, but little things can have great significances. A few large drops of blood fell upon one of his sleeves. He wiped them on and stopped the bleeding, and it seemed to him as if this had cleared and lightened his brain. In the sand the sea eringa was blooming here and there. He broke off a stalk and stuck it in his hat ; he determined to be merry and of good cheer, for he was going into the wide world— " a little way outside the door in front of the bay," as the young eels had said. "Beware of bad people, who will catch you and flay you, cut you in two, and put you in the frying-pan!" he repeated in his mind, and smiled, for he thought he should find his way through the world— good courage is a strong weapon!

The sun already stood high when he approached the narrow entrance to Nissum Bay. He looked back, and saw a couple of horsemen gallopping a long distance behind him, and they were accompanied by other people. But this concerned him nothing.

The ferry was on the opposite side of the bay. Jürgen called to the ferryman, and when the latter came over with the boat, Jürgen stepped in ; but before they had gone half-way across, the men whom he had seen riding so hastily behind him, hailed the ferryman and summoned him to return in the name of the law. Jürgen did not understand the reason of this, but he thought it would be best to turn back, and therefore himself took an oar and returned. The moment the boat touched the shore, the men sprang on board, and, before he was aware, they had bound his hands with a rope.

"Thy wicked deed will cost thee thy life," they said. "It is well that we caught thee."

He was accused of nothing less than murder! Martin had been found dead, with a knife thrust through his neck. One of the fishermen had (late on the previous evening) met Jürgen going towards Martin's house ; and this was not the first time Jürgen had raised his knife against Martin—so they knew that he was the murderer. The town in which the prison was built was a long way off, and the wind was contrary for going there; but not half an hour would be required to get across the bay, and a quarter of an hour would bring them from thence to Nörre Vosborg, a great castle with walls and ditches. One of Jürgen's captors was a fisherman, a brother of the keeper of the castle, and he declared it might be managed that Jürgen should for the present be put into the dungeon at Vosborg, where Long Martha the gipsy had been shut up till her execution.

No attention was paid to the defence made by Jürgen; the few drops of blood upon his shirt-sleeve bore heavy witness against him. But Jürgen was conscious of his innocence, and as there was no chance of immediately righting himself, he submitted to his fate.

The party landed just at the spot where Sir Bugge's castle had stood and where Jürgen had walked with his foster-parents after the burial feast, during the four happiest days of his childhood. He was led by the old path over the meadow to Vosborg; and again the elder blossomed and the lofty lindens smelt sweet, and it seemed but yesterday that he had left the spot.

In the two wings of the castle a staircase reads down to a spot below the entrance, and from thence there is access to a low vaulted cellar. Here Long Martha had been imprisoned, and hence she had been led away to the scaffold. She had eaten the hearts of five children, and had been under the delusion that if she could obtain two more, she would be able to fly and to make herself invisible. In the midst of the cellar roof was a little narrow air-hole, but no window. The blooming lindens could not waft a breath of comforting fragrance into that abode, where all was dark and mouldy. Only a rough bench stood in the prison; but "a good conscience is a soft pillow," and consequently Jürgen could sleep well.

The thick oaken door was locked, and secured on the outside by an iron bar; but the goblin of superstition can creep through a key-hole into the baron's castle just as into the fisherman's hut; and wherefore should he not creep in here, where Jürgen sat thinking of Long Martha and her evil deeds? Her last thought on the night before her execution had filled this space; and all the magic came into Jürgen's mind which tradition asserted to have been practised there in the old times, when Sir Schwanwedel dwelt there. All this passed through Jürgen's mind, and made him shudder; but a sunbeam—a refreshing thought from without—penetrated his heart even here: it was the remembrance of the blooming elder and the fragrant lime trees.

He was not left there long. They carried him off to the town of Ringkjöbing, where his imprisonment was just as hard.

Those times were not like ours. Hard measure was dealt out to the "common" people; and it was just after the days when farms were converted into knights' estates, on which occasions coachmen and servants were often made magistrates, and had it in their power to sentence a poor man, for a small offence, to lose his property and to corporal punishment. Judges of this kind were still to be found; and in Jutland, far from the capital and from the enlightened well-meaning head of the government, the law was still sometimes very loosely administered; and the smallest grievance that Jürgen had to expect was that his case would be protracted.

Cold and cheerless was his abode — and when would this state of things end? He had innocently sunk into misfortune and sorrow— that was his fate. He had leisure now to ponder on the difference of fortune on earth, and to wonder why this fate had been allotted to him; and he felt sure that the question would be answered in the next life— the existence that awaits us when this is over. This faith had grown strong in him in the poor fisherman's hut; that which had never shone into his father's mind, in all the richness and sunshine of Spain, was vouchsafed as a light of comfort in his poverty and distress—a sign of mercy from God that never deceives.

The spring storms began to blow. The rolling and moaning of the North Sea could be heard for miles inland when the wind was lulled, for then it sounded like the rushing of a thousand waggons over a hard road with a mine beneath. Jürgen, in his prison, heard these sounds, and it was a relief to him. No melody could have appealed so directly to his heart as did these sounds of the sea—the rolling sea, the boundless sea, on which a man can be borne across the world before the wind, carrying his own house with him wherever he is driven, just as the snail carries its home even into a strange land.

How he listened to the deep moaning, and how the thought arose in him—"Free! free! How happy to be free, even without shoes and in ragged clothes!" Sometimes, when such thoughts crossed his mind, the fiery nature rose within him, and he beat the wall with his clenched fists.

Weeks, months, a whole year had gone by, when a vagabond—Niels, the thief, called also the horse couper — was arrested; and now the better times came, and it was seen what wrong Jürgen had endured.

In the neighbourhood of Ringkjöbing, at a beer-house, Niels, the thief, had met Martin on the afternoon before Jürgen's departure from home and before the murder. A few glasses were drunk—not enough to cloud any one's brain, but yet enough to loosen Martin's tongue, and he began to boast, and to say that he had obtained a house, and intended to marry; and when Niels asked where he intended to get the money, Martin shook his pocket proudly, and said,

"The money is here, where it ought to be."

This boast cost him his life, for when he went home, Niels went after him, and thrust a knife through his throat, to rob the murdered man of the expected gold, which did not exist.

This was circumstantially explained; but for us it is enough to know that Jürgen was set at liberty. But what amends did he get for having been imprisoned a whole year, and shut out from all communion with men? They told him he was fortunate in being proved innocent, and that he might go. The burgomaster gave him two dollars for travelling expenses, and many citizens offered him provisions and beer — there were still some good men, not all "grind and flay." But the best of all was, that the merchant Brönne of Skjagen, the same into whose service Jürgen intended to go a year since, was just at that time on business in the town of Ringkjöbing. Brönne heard the whole story; and the man had a good heart, and understood what Jürgen must have felt and suffered. He therefore made up his mind to make amends to the poor lad, and convince him that there were still kind folks in the world.

So Jürgen went forth from the prison as if to Paradise, to find freedom, affection, and trust. He was to travel this road now; for no goblet of life is all bitterness: no good man would pour out such measure to his fellow man, and how should God do it, who is love itself?

"Let all that be buried and forgotten," said Brönne the merchant. "Let us draw a thick line through last year; and we will even burn the calendar. And in two days we'll start for dear, friendly, peaceful Skjagen. They call Skjagen an out-of-the-way corner; but it's a good warm chimney-corner, and its windows open towards every part of the world."

That was a journey!—it was like taking fresh breath—out of the cold dungeon air into the warm sunshine! The heath stood blooming in its greatest pride, and the herd-boy sat on the Hun's Grave and blew his pipe, which he had carved for himself out of the sheep's bone. Fata Morgana, the beautiful aërial phenomenon of the desert, showed itself with hanging gardens and swaying forests, and the wonderful cloud phenomenon, called here the "Lokeman driving his flock," was seen likewise.

Up through the land of the Wendels, up towards Skjagen, they went, from whence the men with the long beards (the Longobardi, or Lombards) had emigrated in the days when, in the reign of King Snio, all the children and the old people were to have been killed, till the noble Dame Gambaruk proposed that the younger people had better emigrate. All this was known to Jürgen—thus much knowledge he had; and even if he did not know the land of the Lombards beyond the high Alps, he had an idea how it must be there, for in his boyhood he had been in the south, in Spain. He thought of the southern fruits piled up there; of the red pomegranate blossoms; of the humming, murmuring, and toiling in the great bee-hive of a city he had seen; but, after all, home is best; and Jürgen's home was Denmark.

At length they reached "Wendelskajn," as Skjagen is called in the old Norwegian and Icelandic writings. Then already Old Skjagen, with the western and eastern town, extended for miles, with sand-hills and arable land, as far as the lighthouse near the "Skjagenzweig." Then, as now, the houses were strewn among the wind-raised sand-hills—a desert where the wind sports with the sand, and where the voices of the seamen and the wild swans strike harshly on the ear. In the southwest, a mile from the sea, lies Old Skjagen; and here dwelt merchant Brönne, and here Jürgen was henceforth to dwell. The great house was painted with tar; the smaller buildings had each an overturned boat for a roof; the pig-sty had been put together of pieces of wreck.

JÜRGEN'S BETTER FORTUNE.

There was no fence here, for indeed there was nothing to fence in; but long rows of fishes were hung upon lines, one above the other, to dry in the wind. The whole coast was strewn with spoiled herrings, for there were so many of those fish, that a net was scarcely thrown into the sea before they were caught by cartloads; there were so many, that often they were thrown back into the sea or left to lie on the shore.

The old man's wife and daughter, and his servants too, came rejoicingly to meet him. There was a great pressing of hands, and talking, and questioning. And the daughter, what a lovely face and bright eyes she had!

The interior of the house was roomy and comfortable. Fritters that a King would have looked upon as a dainty dish, were placed on the table; and there was wine from the vineyard of Skjagen—that is, the sea; for there the grapes come ashore ready pressed and prepared in barrels and in bottles.

When the mother and daughter heard who Jürgen was, and how

innocently he had suffered, they looked at him in a still more friendly way; and the eyes of the charming Clara were the friendliest of all. Jürgen found a happy home in Old Skjagen. It did his heart good; and his heart had been sorely tried, and had drunk the bitter goblet of love, which softens or hardens according to circumstances. Jürgen's heart was still soft — it was young, and there was still room in it; and therefore it was well that Mistress Clara was going in three weeks in her father's ship to Christiansand, in Norway, to visit an aunt and to stay there the whole winter.

On the Sunday before her departure they all went to church, to the holy Communion. The church was large and handsome, and had been built centuries before by Scotchmen and Hollanders; it lay at a little distance from the town. It was certainly somewhat ruinous, and the road to it was heavy, through the deep sand; but the people gladly went through the difficulties to get to the house of God, to sing psalms and hear the sermon. The sand had heaped itself up round the walls of the church, but the graves were kept free from it.

It was the largest church north of the Limfjord. The Virgin Mary, with the golden crown on her head and the child Jesus in her arms, stood lifelike upon the altar; the holy Apostles had been carved in the choir; and on the walls hung portraits of the old burgomasters and councillors of Skjagen; the pulpit was of carved work. The sun shone brightly into the church, and its radiance fell on the polished brass chandelier and on the little ship that hung from the vaulted roof.

Jürgen felt as if overcome by a holy, childlike feeling, like that which possessed him when, as a boy, he had stood in the splendid Spanish cathedral; but here the feeling was different, for he felt conscious of being one of the congregation.

After the sermon followed the holy Communion. He partook of the bread and wine, and it happened that he knelt beside Mistress Clara; but his thoughts were so fixed upon Heaven and the holy service, that he did not notice his neighbour until he rose from his knees, and then he saw tears rolling down her cheeks.

Two days later she left Skjagen and went to Norway. He stayed behind, and made himself useful in the house and in the business. He went out fishing, and at that time fish were more plentiful and larger than now. Every Sunday when he sat in the church, and his eye rested on the statue of the Virgin on the altar, his glance rested for a time on the spot where Mistress Clara had knelt beside him, and he thought of her, how hearty and kind she had been to him.

And so the autumn and the winter time passed away. There was wealth here, and a real family life; even down to the domestic animals, who were all well kept. The kitchen glittered with copper and tin and white plates, and from the roof hung hams and beef and winter stores in plenty. All this is still to be seen in many rich farms of the west coast of Jutland: plenty to eat and drink, clean decorated rooms, clever heads, happy tempers, and hospitality prevail there as in an Arab tent.

Never since the famous burial feast had Jürgen spent such a happy time; and yet Mistress Clara was absent. except in the thoughts and memory of all.

In April a ship was to start for Norway, and Jürgen was to sail in it. He was full of life and spirits, and looked so stout and jovial that Dame Brönne declared it did her good to see him.

"And it's a pleasure to see you too, old wife," said the old merchant. "Jürgen has brought life into our winter evenings, and into you too, mother. You look younger this year, and you seem well and bonny. But then you were once the prettiest girl in Wiborg, and that's saying a great deal, for I have always found the Wiborg girls the prettiest of any."

Jürgen said nothing to this, but he thought of a certain maiden of Skjagen; and he sailed to visit that maiden, for the ship steered to Christiansand in Norway, and a favouring wind bore it rapidly to that town.

One morning merchant Brönne went out to the lighthouse that stands far away from Old Skjagen: the coal fire had long gone out and the sun was already high when he mounted the tower. The sand-banks extend under the water a whole mile from the shore. Outside these banks many ships were seen that day; and with the help of his telescope the old man thought he descried his own vessel, the Karen Brönne.

Yes, surely, there she was; and the ship was sailing up with Jürgen and Clara on board. The church and the lighthouse appeared to them as a heron and a swan rising from the blue waters. Clara sat on deck, and saw the sand-hills gradually looming forth: if the wind held she might reach her home in about an hour — so near were they to home and its joys—so near were they to death and its terrors. For a plank in the ship gave way, and the water rushed in. The crew flew to the pumps and attempted to stop the leak, and a signal of distress was hoisted; but they were still a full mile from the shore. Fishing-boats were in sight, but they were still far distant. The wind blew shore-ward, and the tide was in their favour too; but all was insufficient, for the ship sank. Jürgen threw his right arm about Clara and pressed her close to him.

With what a look she gazed in his face! As he threw himself in God's name into the water with her, she uttered a cry; but still she felt safe certain that he would not let her sink.

And now, in the hour of terror and danger, Jürgen experienced what the old song told:

"And written it stood, how the brave King's son
Embraced the bride his valour had won."

How rejoiced he felt that he was a good swimmer! He worked his way onward with his feet and with one hand, while with the other he tightly held the young girl. He rested upon the waves, he trod the water, he practised all the arts he knew, so as to reserve strength enough to reach the shore. He heard how Clara uttered a sigh, and felt a convulsive shudder pass through her, and he pressed her to him closer than ever.

Now and then a wave rolled over her; and he was still a few cables' lengths from the land, when help came in the shape of an approaching boat. But under the water—he could see it clearly—stood a white form gazing at him; a wave lifted him up, and the form approached him : he felt a shock, and it grew dark, and everything vanished from his gaze.

On the sand-reef lay the wreck of a ship, which the sea washed over ; the white figure-head leaned against an anchor, the sharp iron of which extended just to the surface. Jürgen had come in contact with this, and the tide had driven him against it with double force. He sank down fainting with his load, but the next wave lifted him and the young girl aloft again.

The fishermen grasped them and lifted them into the boat. The blood streamed down over Jürgen's face ; he seemed dead, but he still clutched the girl so tightly that they were obliged to loosen her by force from his grasp. And Clara lay pale and lifeless in the boat, that now made for the shore.

All means were tried to restore Clara to life ; but she was dead ! For some time he had been swimming onward with a corpse, and had exerted himself to exhaustion for one who was dead.

Jürgen was still breathing. The fishermen carried him into the nearest house upon the sand-hills. A kind of surgeon who lived there, and who was at the same time a smith and a general dealer, bound up Jürgen's wounds in a temporary way, till a physician could be got next day from the nearest town.

The brain of the sick man was affected. In delirium he uttered wild cries ; but on the third day he lay quiet and exhausted on his couch, and his life seemed to hang by a thread, and the physician said it would be best if this string snapped.

" Let us pray that God may take him to Himself ; he will never be a sane man again ! "

But life would not depart from him—the thread would not snap ; but the thread of memory broke : the thread of all his mental power had been cut through ; and, what was most terrible, a body remained — a living healthy body—that wandered about like a spectre.

Jürgen remained in the house of the merchant Brönne.

" He contracted his illness in his endeavour to save our child," said the old man, " and now he is our son."

People called Jürgen imbecile ; but that was not the right expression. He was like an instrument, in which the strings are loose and will sound no more ; only at times for a few minutes they regained their power, and then they sounded anew : old melodies were heard, snatches of song ; pictures unrolled themselves, and then disappeared again in the mist, and once more he sat staring before him, without a thought. We may believe that he did not suffer, but his dark eyes lost their brightness, and looked only like black clouded glass.

" Poor imbecile Jürgen ! " said the people.

He it was whose life was to have been so pleasant that it would be " presumption and pride " to expect or believe in a higher existence hereafter. All his great mental faculties had been lost; only hard days, pain, and disappointment had been his lot. He was like a rare plant torn from its native soil, and thrown upon the sand, to wither there. And was the image, fashioned in God's likeness, to have no better destination? Was it to be merely the sport of chance? No. The all-loving God would certainly repay him, in the life to come, for what he had suffered and lost here. "The Lord is good to all, and His mercy is over all His works." These words from the Psalms of David, the old pious wife of the merchant repeated in patience and hope, and the prayer of her heart was that Jürgen might soon be summoned to enter into the life eternal.

In the churchyard where the sand blows across the walls, Clara lay buried. It seemed as if Jürgen knew nothing of this—it did not come within the compass of his thoughts, which comprised only fragments of a past time. Every Sunday he went with the old people to church, and sat silent there with vacant gaze. One day, while the Psalms were being sung, he uttered a deep sigh, and his eyes gleamed: they were fixed upon the altar, upon the place where he had knelt with his friend who was dead. He uttered her name, and became pale as death, and tears rolled over his cheeks.

They led him out of the church, and he said to the bystanders that he was well, and had never been ill: he, the heavily afflicted, the waif cast upon the world, remembered nothing of his sufferings. And the Lord our Creator is wise and full of loving-kindness—who can doubt it?

In Spain, where the warm breezes blow over the Moorish cupolas, among the orange trees and laurels, where song and the sound of castagnettes are always heard, sat in the sumptuous house a childish old man, the richest merchant in the place, while children marched in procession through the streets, with waving flags and lighted tapers. How much of his wealth would the old man not have given to be able to press his children to his heart! his daughter, or her child, that had perhaps never seen the light in this world, far less a Paradise.

"Poor child!"

Yes, poor child—a child still, and yet more than thirty years old; for to that age Jürgen had attained in Old Skjagen.

The drifting sand had covered the graves in the churchyard quite up to the walls of the church; but yet the dead must be buried among their relations and loved ones who had gone before them. Merchant Brönne and his wife now rested here with their children, under the white sand.

It was spring-time, the season of storms. The sand-hills whirled up in clouds, and the sea ran high, and flocks of birds flew like clouds in the storms, shrieking across the dunes; and shipwreck followed shipwreck on the reefs of "Skjagensweig" from towards the Hunsby dunes. One evening Jürgen was sitting alone in the room. Suddenly his mind seemed to become clearer, and a feeling of unrest came upon him, which in his younger years had often driven him forth upon the heath and the sand-hills.

" Home! home!" he exclaimed.

No one heard him. He went out of the house towards the dunes. Sand and stones blew into his face and whirled around him. He went on farther and farther, towards the church: the sand lay high around the walls, half over the windows, but the heap had been shovelled away from the door, and the entrance was free and easy to open; and Jürgen went into the church.

The storm went howling over the town of Skjagen. Within the memory of man the sea had not run so high — a terrible tempest! but Jürgen was in the temple of God, and while black night reigned without, a light arose in his soul, a light that was never to be extinguished; he felt the heavy stone which seemed to weigh upon his head burst asunder. He thought he heard the sound of the organ, but it was the storm and the moaning of the sea. He sat down on one of the seats; and behold, the candles were lighted up one by one; a richness was displayed such as he had only seen in the church in Spain; and all the pictures of the old councillors were endued with life, and stepped forth from the walls against which they had stood for centuries, and seated themselves in the entrance of the church. The gates and doors flew open, and in came all the dead people, festively clad, and sat down to the sound of beautiful music, and filled the seats in the church. Then the psalm tune rolled forth like a sounding sea; and his old foster-parents from the Hunsby dunes were here, and the old merchant Brönne and his wife; and at their side, close to Jürgen, sat their friendly, lovely daughter Clara, who gave her hand to Jürgen, and they both went to the altar, where they had once knelt together, and the priest joined their hands and knit them together for life. Then the sound of music was heard again, wonderful, like a child's voice full of joy and expectation, and it swelled on to an organ's sound, to a tempest of full, noble sounds, lovely and elevating to hear, and yet strong enough to burst the stone tombs.

And the little ship that hung down from the roof of the choir came down, and became wonderfully large and beautiful, with silken sails and golden yards, " and every rope wrought through with silk," as the old song said. The married pair went on board, and the whole congregation with them, for there was room and joyfulness for all. And the walls and arches of the church bloomed like the juniper and the fragrant lime trees, and the leaves and branches waved and distributed coolness; then they bent and parted, and the ship sailed through the midst of them, through the sea, and through the air; and every church taper became a star, and the wind sang a psalm tune, and all sang with the wind:

" In love, to glory — no life shall be lost. Full of blessedness and joy. Hallelujah!"

And these words were the last that Jürgen spoke in this world. The thread snapped that bound the immortal soul, and nothing but a dead body lay in the dark church, around which the storm raged, covering it with loose sand.

The next morning was Sunday, and the congregation and their pastor went forth to the service. The road to church had been heavy; the sand made the way almost impassable; and now, when they at last reached their goal, a great hill of sand was piled up before the entrance, and the church itself was buried. The priest spoke a short prayer, and said that God had closed the door of this house, and the congregation must go and build a new one for Him elsewhere.

So they sang a psalm under the open sky, and went back to their homes.

Jürgen was nowhere to be found in the town of Skjagen, or in the dunes, however much they sought for him. It was thought that the waves, which had rolled far up on the sand, had swept him away.

His body lay buried in a great sepulchre, in the church itself. In the storm the Lord's hand had thrown a hand-full of earth on his grave; and the heavy mound of sand lay upon it, and lies there to this day.

The whirling sand had covered the high vaulted passages; white-thorn and wild rose trees grow over the church, over which the wanderer now walks; while the tower, standing forth like a gigantic tombstone over a grave, is to be seen for miles around: no King has a more splendid tombstone. No one disturbs the rest of the dead; no one knew of this, and we are the first who know of this grave — the storm sang the tale to me among the sand-hills.

THE PHŒNIX BIRD.

In the Garden of Paradise, beneath the Tree of Knowledge, bloomed a rose bush. Here, in the first rose, a bird was born: his flight was like the flashing of light, his plumage was beauteous, and his song ravishing.

But when Eve plucked the fruit of the knowledge of good and evil, when she and Adam were driven from Paradise, there fell from the flaming sword of the cherub a spark into the nest of the bird, which blazed up forthwith. The bird perished in the flames; but from the red egg in the nest there fluttered aloft a new one — the one solitary Phœnix bird. The fable tells us that he dwells in Arabia, and that every hundred years he burns himself to death in his nest; but each time a new Phœnix, the only one in the world, rises up from the red egg.

The bird flutters round us, swift as light, beauteous in colour, charming in song. When a mother sits by her infant's cradle, he stands on the pillow, and, with his wings, forms a glory around the infant's head. He flies through the chamber of content, and brings sunshine into it, and the violets on the humble table smell doubly sweet.

But the Phœnix is not the bird of Arabia alone. He wings his way in the glimmer of the Northern Lights over the plains of Lapland, and hops among the yellow flowers in the short Greenland summer. Beneath the copper mountains of Fahlun and England's coal mines, he flies, in the shape of a dusty moth, over the hymn-book that rests on the knees of the pious miner. On a lotus leaf he floats down the sacred waters of the Ganges, and the eye of the Hindoo maid gleams bright when she beholds him.

The Phœnix bird, dost thou not know him? The Bird of Paradise, the holy swan of song! On the car of Thespis he sat in the guise of a chattering raven, and flapped his black wings, smeared with the lees of wine; over the sounding harp of Iceland swept the swan's red beak; on Shakespeare's shoulder he sat in the guise of Odin's raven, and

THE PHŒNIX BIRD.

whispered in the poet's ear "Immortality!" and at the minstrels' feast he fluttered through the halls of the Wartburg.

The Phœnix bird, dost thou not know him? He sang to thee the *Marseillaise*, and thou kissedst the pen that fell from his wing; he came in the radiance of Paradise, and perchance thou didst turn away from him towards the sparrow who sat with tinsel on his wings.

The Bird of Paradise — renewed each century — born in flame, ending in flame! Thy picture, in a golden frame, hangs in the halls of the rich, but thou thyself often fliest around, lonely and disregarded, a myth —"The Phœnix of Arabia."

In Paradise, when thou wert born in the first rose, beneath the Tree of Knowledge, thou receivedst a kiss, and thy right name was given thee—thy name, POETRY.

THE GARDEN OF PARADISE.

ONCE there was a King's son. No one had so many beautiful books as he: everything that had happened in this world he could read there, and could see pictures of it all in lovely copper-plates. Of every people and of every land he could get intelligence; but there was not a word to tell where the Garden of Paradise could be found, and it was just that of which he thought most.

His grandmother had told him, when he was quite little but was to begin to go to school, that every flower in this Paradise Garden was a delicate cake, and the pistils contained the choicest wine; on one of the flowers history was written, and on another geography or tables, so that one had only to eat cake, and one knew a lesson; and the more one ate, the more history, geography, or tables did one learn.

At that time he believed this. But when he became a bigger boy, and learned more and became wiser, he understood well that the splendour in the Garden of Paradise must be of quite a different kind.

"Oh, why did Eve pluck from the Tree of Knowledge? Why did Adam eat the forbidden fruit? If I had been he it would never have happened—then sin would never have come into the world."

That he said then, and he still said it when he was seventeen years old. The Garden of Paradise filled all his thoughts

One day he walked in the wood. He was walking quite alone, for that was his greatest pleasure. The evening came, and the clouds gathered together; rain streamed down as if the sky were one single river from which the water was pouring; it was as dark as it usually is at night in the deepest well. Often he slipped on the smooth grass, often he fell over the smooth stones which peered up out of the wet rocky ground. Everything was soaked with water, and there was not a dry thread on the poor Prince. He was obliged to climb over great blocks of stone, where the water spurted from the thick moss. He was nearly fainting. Then he heard a strange rushing, and saw before him a great illuminated cave. In the midst of it burned a fire, so large that a stag might have been roasted at it. And this was in fact being done. A glorious deer had been stuck, horns and all, upon a spit, and was turning slowly between two felled pine trunks. An elderly woman, large and strongly built, looking like a disguised man, sat by the fire, into which she threw one piece of wood after another.

"Come nearer!" said she. "Sit down by the fire and dry your clothes."

"There's a great draught here!" said the Prince; and he sat down on the ground.

"That will be worse when my sons come home," replied the woman. "You are here in the Cavern of the Winds, and my sons are the four winds of the world: can you understand that?"

"Where are your sons?" asked the Prince.

"It 's difficult to answer when stupid questions are asked," said the woman. "My sons do business on their own account. They play at shuttlecock with the clouds up yonder in the King's hall."

And she pointed upwards.

"Oh, indeed!" said the Prince. "But you speak rather gruffly, by the way, and are not so mild as the women I generally see about me."

"Yes, they have most likely nothing else to do! I must be hard, if I want to keep my sons in order; but I can do it, though they are obstinate fellows. Do you see the four sacks hanging there by the wall? They are just as frightened of those as you used to be of the rod stuck behind the glass. I can bend the lads together, I tell you, and then I pop them into the bag: we don't make any ceremony. There they sit, and may not wander about again until I think fit to allow them. But here comes one of them!"

It was the North Wind, who rushed in with piercing cold; great hailstones skipped about on the floor, and snow-flakes fluttered about. He was dressed in a jacket and trousers of bear-skin; a cap of seal-skin was drawn down over his ears; long icicles hung on his beard, and one hailstone after another rolled from the collar of his jacket.

"Do not go so near the fire directly," said the Prince, "you might get your hands and face frost-bitten."

"Frost-bitten?" repeated the North Wind, and he laughed aloud. "Cold is exactly what rejoices me most! But what kind of little tailor art thou? How did you find your way into the Cavern of the Winds?"

"He is my guest," interposed the old woman, "and if you 're not satisfied with this explanation you may go into the sack: do you understand me?"

You see, that was the right way; and now the North Wind told whence he came and where he had been for almost a month.

"I came from the Polar Sea," said he; "I have been in the bear's icy land with the walrus hunters. I sat and slept on the helm when they went away from the North Cape, and when I awoke now and then, the storm-bird flew round my legs. That 's a comical bird! He gives a sharp clap with his wings, and then holds them quite still and shoots along in full career."

"Don't be too long-winded," said the mother of the Winds. "And so you came to the Bear's Island?"

"It is very beautiful there! There 's a floor for dancing on as flat as a plate. Half-thawed snow, with a little moss, sharp stones, and skeletons of walruses and polar bears lay around, and likewise gigantic arms and legs of a rusty green colour. One would have thought the sun had never shone there. I blew a little upon the mist, so that one could see the hut: it was a house built of wreck-wood and covered with walrus-skins — the fleshy side turned outwards. It was full of green and red, and on the roof sat a live polar bear who was growling. I went to the shore to look after birds' nests, and saw the unfledged nestlings screaming and opening their beaks; then I blew down into their thousand throats, and taught them to shut their mouths. Farther on the huge walruses were splashing like great maggots with pigs' heads and teeth an ell long!"

"You tell your story well, my son," said the old lady. "My mouth waters when I hear you!"

"Then the hunting began! The harpoon was hurled into the walrus's breast, so that a smoking stream of blood spurted like a fountain over the ice. When I thought of my sport, I blew, and let my sailing ships, the big icebergs, crush the boats between them. Oh, how the people whistled and how they cried! but I whistled louder than they. They were obliged to throw the dead walruses and their chests and tackle out upon the ice. I shook the snow-flakes over them, and let them drive south in their crushed boats with their booty to taste salt water. They 'll never come to Bear's Island again!"

"Then you have done a wicked thing!" said the mother of the Winds.

"What good I have done others may tell," replied he. "But here comes a brother from the west. I like him best of all: he tastes of the sea and brings a delicious coolness with him."

"Is that little Zephyr?" asked the Prince.

"Yes, certainly, that is Zephyr," replied the old woman. "But he is not little. Years ago he was a pretty boy, but that 's past now."

He looked like a wild man, but he had a broad-brimmed hat on, to save his face. In his hand he held a club of mahogany, hewn in the American mahogany forests. It was no trifle.

"Where do you come from?" said his mother.

"Out of the forest wilderness," said he, "where the water snake lies in the wet grass, and people don't seem to be wanted."

"What were you doing there?"

"I looked into the deepest river, and watched how it rushed down from the rocks, and turned to spray, and shot up towards the clouds to carry the rainbow. I saw the wild buffalo swimming in the stream, but the stream carried him away. He drifted with the flock of wild ducks that flew up where the water fell down in a cataract. The buffalo had to go down it! That pleased me, and I blew a storm, so that ancient trees were split up into splinters!"

"And have you done nothing else?" asked the old dame.

"I have thrown somersaults in the Savannahs: I have stroked the wild horses and shaken the cocoa-nut palms. Yes, yes, I have stories to tell! But one must not tell all one knows. You know that, old lady."

And he kissed his mother so roughly that she almost tumbled over. He was a terribly wild young fellow!

Now came the South Wind, with a turban on and a flying Bedouin's cloak.

"It 's terribly cold out here!" cried he, and threw some more wood on the fire. "One can feel that the North Wind came first."

"It 's so hot that one could roast a Polar bear here," said the North Wind.

"You 're a Polar bear yourself," retorted the South Wind.

" Do you want to be put in the sack ? " asked the old dame. " Sit upon the stone yonder and tell me where you have been."

" In Africa, mother," he answered. " I was out hunting the lion with the Hottentots in the land of the Kaffirs. Grass grows there in the plains, green as an olive. There the ostrich ran races with me, but I am swifter than he. I came into the desert where the yellow sand lies: it looks there like the bottom of the sea. I met a caravan. The people were killing their last camel to get water to drink, but it was very little they got. The sun burned above and the sand below. The outspread deserts had no bounds. Then I rolled in the fine loose sand, and whirled it up in great pillars. That was a dance! You should have seen how the dromedary stood there terrified, and the merchant drew the caftan over his head. He threw himself down before me, as before Allah, his God. Now they are buried—a pyramid of sand covers them all. When I some day blow that away, the sun will bleach the white bones; then travellers may see that men have been there before them. Otherwise, one would not believe that, in the desert ! "

" So you have done nothing but evil!" exclaimed the mother. " March into the sack ! "

And before he was aware, she had seized the South Wind round the body, and popped him into the bag. He rolled about on the floor ; but she sat down on the sack, and then he had to keep quiet.

" Those are lively boys of yours," said the Prince.

" Yes," she replied, " and I know how to punish them! Here comes the fourth ! "

That was the East Wind, who came dressed like a Chinaman.

" Oh ! do you come from that region ? " said his mother. " I thought you had been in the Garden of Paradise."

" I don't fly there till to-morrow," said the East Wind. " It will be a hundred years to-morrow since I was there. I come from China now, where I danced around the porcelain tower till all the bells jingled again ! In the streets the officials were being thrashed: the bamboos were broken upon their shoulders, yet they were high people, from the first to the ninth grade. They cried, ' Many thanks, my paternal benefactor ! ' but it didn't come from their hearts. And I rang the bells and sang ' Tsing, tsang, tsu ! ' "

" You are foolish," said the old dame. " It is a good thing that you are going into the Garden of Paradise to-morrow : that always helps on your education. Drink bravely out of the spring of Wisdom, and bring home a little bottle-full for me."

" That I will do," said the East Wind. " But why have you clapped my brother South in the bag ? Out with him ! He shall tell me about the Phœnix bird, for about that bird the Princess in the Garden of Paradise always wants to hear, when I pay my visit every hundredth year. Open the sack, then you shall be my sweetest of mothers, and I will give you two pockets-full of tea, green and fresh as I plucked it at the place where it grew ! "

THE EAST WIND TELLING HIS STORY

"Well, for the sake of the tea, and because you are my darling boy,
I will open the sack."

She did so, and the South Wind crept out; but he looked quite downcast, because the strange Prince had seen his disgrace.

"There you have a palm leaf for the Princess," said the South Wind.
"This palm leaf was given me by the Phœnix bird, the only one who is
in the world. With his beak he has scratched upon it a description of
all the hundred years he has lived. Now she may read herself how the
Phœnix bird set fire to her nest, and sat upon it, and was burned to
death like a Hindoo's widow. How the dry branches crackled! What
a smoke and a steam there was! At last everything burst into flame,
and the old Phœnix turned to ashes, but her egg lay red hot in the fire;
it burst with a great bang, and the young one flew out. Now this young
one is ruler over all the birds, and the only Phœnix in the world. It
has bitten a hole in the palm leaf I have given you: that is a greeting
to the Princess."

" Let us have something to eat," said the mother of the Winds.

And now they all sat down to eat of the roasted deer. The Prince sat beside the East Wind, and they soon became good friends.

" Just tell me," said the Prince, " what Princess is that about whom there is so much talk here ? and where does the Garden of Paradise lie ? "

" Ho, ho ! " said the East Wind, " do you want to go there ? Well, then, fly to-morrow with me ! But I must tell you, however, that no man has been there since the time of Adam and Eve. You have read of them in your Bible histories ? "

" Yes," said the Prince.

" When they were driven away, the Garden of Paradise sank into the earth ; but it kept its warm sunshine, its mild air, and all its splendour. The Queen of the Fairies lives there, and there lies the Island of Happiness, where death never comes, and where it is beautiful. Sit upon my back to-morrow, and I will take you with me : I think it can very well be done. But now leave off talking, for I want to sleep."

And then they all went to rest.

In the early morning the Prince awoke, and was not a little astonished to find himself high above the clouds. He was sitting on the back of the East Wind, who was faithfully holding him : they were so high in the air, that the woods and fields, rivers and lakes, looked as if they were painted on a map below them.

" Good morning ! " said the East Wind. " You might very well sleep a little longer, for there is not much to be seen on the flat country under us, unless you care to count the churches. They stand like dots of chalk on the green carpet."

What he called green carpet was field and meadow.

" It was rude of me not to say good bye to your mother and your brothers," said the Prince.

" When one is asleep one must be excused," replied the East Wind.

And then they flew on faster than ever. One could hear it in the tops of the trees, for when they passed over them the leaves and twigs rustled ; one could hear it on the sea and on the lakes, for when they flew by the water rose higher, and the great ships bowed themselves towards the water like swimming swans.

Towards evening, when it became dark, the great towns looked charming, for lights were burning below, here and there ; it was just as when one has lighted a piece of paper, and sees all the little sparks which vanish one after another. And the Prince clapped his hands ; but the East Wind begged him to let that be, and rather to hold fast, otherwise he might easily fall down and get caught on a church spire.

The eagle in the dark woods flew lightly, but the East Wind flew more lightly still. The Cossack on his little horse skimmed swiftly over the surface of the earth, but the Prince skimmed more swiftly still.

" Now you can see the Himalayas," said the East Wind. " That is the highest mountain range in Asia. Now we shall soon get to the Garden of Paradise."

Then they turned more to the south, and soon the air was fragrant with flowers and spices, figs and pomegranates grew wild, and the wild vine bore clusters of red and purple grapes. Here both alighted and stretched themselves on the soft grass, where the flowers nodded to the wind, as though they would have said "Welcome!"

"Are we now in the Garden of Paradise?" asked the Prince.

"Not at all," replied the East Wind. "But we shall soon get there. Do you see the rocky wall yonder, and the great cave, where the vines cluster like a broad green curtain? Through that we shall pass. Wrap yourself in your cloak. Here the sun scorches you, but a step farther it will be icy cold. The bird which hovers past the cave has one wing in the region of summer and the other in the wintry cold."

"So this is the way to the garden of Paradise?" observed the Prince.

They went into the cave. Ugh! but it was icy cold there, but this

THE EAST WIND CARRYING THE YOUNG PRINCE TO THE GARDEN OF PARADISE.

did not last long. The East Wind spread out his wings, and they gleamed like the brightest fire. What a cave was that! Great blocks of stone, from which the water dripped down, hung over them in the strangest shapes; sometimes it was so narrow that they had to creep on their hands and knees, sometimes as lofty and broad as in the open air. The place looked like a number of mortuary chapels, with dumb organ pipes, the organs themselves being petrified.

"We are going through the way of death to the Garden of Paradise, are we not?" inquired the Prince.

The East Wind answered not a syllable, but he pointed forward to where a lovely blue light gleamed upon them. The stone blocks over their heads became more and more like a mist, and at last looked like a white cloud in the moonlight. Now they were in a deliciously mild air, fresh as on the hills, fragrant as among the roses of the valley. There ran a river, clear as the air itself, and the fishes were like silver and gold; purple eels, flashing out blue sparks at every moment, played in the water below; and the broad water-plant leaves shone in the colours of the rainbow; the flower itself was an orange-coloured burning flame, to which the water gave nourishment, as the oil to the burning lamp; a bridge of marble, strong, indeed, but so lightly built that it looked as if made of lace and glass beads, led them across the water to the Island of Happiness, where the Garden of Paradise bloomed.

Were they palm trees that grew here, or gigantic water plants? Such verdant mighty trees the Prince had never beheld; the most wonderful climbing plants hung there in long festoons, as one only sees them illuminated in gold and colours on the margins of gold missal-books or twined among the initial letters. Here were the strangest groupings of birds, flowers, and twining lines. Close by, in the grass, stood a flock of peacocks with their shining starry trains outspread.

Yes, it was really so! But when the Prince touched these, he found they were not birds, but plants; they were great burdocks, which shone like the peacock's gorgeous train. The lion and the tiger sprang to and fro like agile cats among the green bushes, which were fragrant as the blossom of the olive tree; and the lion and the tiger were tame. The wild wood pigeon shone like the most beautiful pearl, and beat her wings against the lion's mane; and the antelope, usually so timid, stood by nodding its head, as if it wished to play too.

Now came the Fairy of Paradise. Her garb shone like the sun, and her countenance was cheerful like that of a happy mother when she is well pleased with her child. She was young and beautiful, and was followed by a number of pretty maidens, each with a gleaming star in her hair. The East Wind gave her the written leaf from the Phœnix bird, and her eyes shone with pleasure.

She took the Prince by the hand and led him into her palace, where the walls had the colour of a splendid tulip leaf when it is held up in the sunlight. The ceiling was a great sparkling flower, and the more one looked up at it, the deeper did its cup appear. The Prince stepped to the window and looked through one of the panes. Here he saw the Tree of Knowledge, with the serpent, and Adam and Eve were standing close by.

"Were they not driven out?" he asked.

And the Fairy smiled, and explained to him that Time had burned in the picture upon that pane, but not as people are accustomed to see pictures. No, there was life in it: the leaves of the trees moved; men came and went as in a dissolving view. And he looked through another pane, and there was Jacob's dream, with the ladder reaching up into heaven, and the angels with great wings were ascending and descending. Yes, everything that had happened in the world lived and moved in the glass panes; such cunning pictures only Time could burn in.

The Fairy smiled, and led him into a great lofty hall, whose walls appeared transparent. Here were portraits, and each face looked fairer than the last. There were to be seen millions of happy ones who smiled and sang, so that it flowed together into a melody; the uppermost were so small that they looked like the smallest rosebud, when it is drawn as a point upon paper. And in the midst of the hall stood a great tree with rich pendent boughs; golden apples, great and small, hung like oranges among the leaves. That was the Tree of Knowledge, of whose fruit Adam and Eve had eaten. From each leaf fell a shining red dew-drop; it was as though the tree wept tears of blood.

"Let us now get into the boat," said the Fairy, "then we will enjoy some refreshment on the heaving waters. The boat rocks, yet does not quit its station; but all the lands of the earth will glide past in our sight."

And it was wonderful to behold how the whole coast moved. There came the lofty snow-covered Alps, with clouds and black pine trees; the horn sounded with its melancholy note, and the shepherd trolled his merry song in the valley. Then the banana trees bent their long hanging branches over the boat; coal-black swans swam on the water, and the strangest animals and flowers showed themselves upon the shore. That was New Holland, the fifth great division of the world, which glided past with a background of blue hills. They heard the song of the priests, and saw the savages dancing to the sound of drums and of bone trumpets. Egypt's pyramids, towering aloft to the clouds, overturned pillars and sphinxes, half buried in the sand, sailed past likewise. The Northern Lights shone over the extinct volcanoes of the Pole—it was a firework that no one could imitate. The Prince was quite happy, and he saw a hundred times more than we can relate here.

"And can I always stay here?" asked he.

"That depends upon yourself," answered the Fairy. "If you do not, like Adam, yield to the temptation to do what is forbidden, you may always remain here."

"I shall not touch the apples on the Tree of Knowledge!" said the Prince. "Here are thousands of fruits just as beautiful as those."

"Search your own heart, and if you are not strong enough, go away with the East Wind that brought you hither. He is going to fly back, and will not show himself here again for a hundred years: the time will pass for you in this place as if it were a hundred hours, but it is a long time for the temptation of sin. Every evening, when I leave you, I shall have to call to you, 'Come with me!' and I shall have to beckon to you with my hand; but stay where you are: do not go with me, or your longing will become greater with every step. You will then come into the hall where the Tree of Knowledge grows; I sleep under its fragrant pendent boughs; you will bend over me, and I must smile; but if you press a kiss upon my mouth, the Paradise will sink deep into the earth and be lost to you. The keen wind of the desert will rush around you, the cold rain drop upon your head, and sorrow and woe will be your portion."

"I shall stay here!" said the Prince.

And the East Wind kissed him on the forehead, and said,

"Be strong, and we shall meet here again in a hundred years. Farewell! farewell!"

And the East Wind spread out his broad wings, and they flashed like sheet lightning in harvest-time, or like the Northern Light in the cold winter.

"Farewell! farewell!" sounded from among the flowers and the trees. Storks and pelicans flew away in rows like fluttering ribbons, and bore him company to the boundary of the garden.

"Now we will begin our dances!" cried the Fairy. "At the end, when I dance with you, when the sun goes down, you will see me beckon to you; you will hear me call to you, ' Come with me;' but do not obey. For a hundred years I must repeat this every evening; every time, when the trial is past, you will gain more strength; at last you will not think of it at all. This evening is the first time. Now I have warned you."

And the Fairy led him into a great hall of white transparent lilies; the yellow stamens in each flower formed a little golden harp, which sounded like stringed instrument and flute. The most beautiful maidens, floating and slender, clad in gauzy mist, glided by in the dance, and sang of the happiness of living, and declared that they would never die, and that the Garden of Paradise would bloom for ever.

And the sun went down. The whole sky shone like gold, which gave to the lilies the hue of the most glorious roses; and the Prince drank of the foaming wine which the maidens poured out for him, and felt a happiness he had never before known. He saw how the background of the hall opened, and the Tree of Knowledge stood in a glory which blinded his eyes; the singing there was soft and lovely as the voice of his dear mother, and it was as though she sang, "My child! my beloved child!"

Then the Fairy beckoned to him, and called out persuasively,

"Come with me! come with me!"

And he rushed towards her, forgetting his promise, forgetting it the very first evening; and still she beckoned and smiled. The fragrance, the delicious fragrance around became stronger, the harps sounded far more lovely, and it seemed as though the millions of smiling heads in the hall, where the tree grew, nodded and sang, "One must know everything—man is the lord of the earth." And they were no longer drops of blood that the Tree of Knowledge wept; they were red shining stars which he seemed to see.

"Come! come!" the quivering voice still cried, and at every step the Prince's cheeks burned more hotly and his blood flowed more rapidly.

"I must!" said he. "It is no sin, it cannot be one. Why not follow beauty and joy? I only want to see her asleep; there will be nothing lost if I only refrain from kissing her; and I will not kiss her: I am strong and have a resolute will!"

And the Fairy threw off her shining cloak and bent back the branches, and in another moment she was hidden among them.

"I have not yet sinned," said the Prince, "and I will not."

And he pushed the boughs aside. There she slept already, beautiful as only a fairy in the Garden of Paradise can be. She smiled in her dreams, and he bent over her, and saw tears quivering beneath her eyelids!

"Do you weep for me?" he whispered. "Weep not, thou glorious woman! Now only I understand the bliss of Paradise! It streams through my blood, through my thoughts; the power of the angel and of increasing life I feel in my mortal body! Let what will happen to me now; one moment like this is wealth enough!"

And he kissed the tears from her eyes—his mouth touched hers.

Then there resounded a clap of thunder so loud and dreadful that no one had ever heard the like, and everything fell down; and the beautifu' Fairy and the charming Paradise sank down, deeper and deeper. The Prince saw it vanish into the black night; like a little bright star it gleamed out of the far distance. A deadly chill ran through his frame, and he closed his eyes and lay for a long time as one dead.

The cold rain fell upon his face, the keen wind roared round his head, and then his senses returned to him.

THE MOTHER OF THE WINDS UPBRAIDS THE PRINCE.

"What have I done?" he sighed. "I have sinned like Adam— sinned so that Paradise has sunk deep down!"

And he opened his eyes, and the star in the distance—the star that gleamed like the Paradise that had sunk down, was the morning star in the sky.

He stood up, and found himself in the great forest, close by the Cave of the Winds, and the mother of the Winds sat by his side: she looked angry, and raised her arm in the air.

"The very first evening!" said she. "I thought it would be so! Yes, if you were my son, you would have to go into the sack!"

"Yes, he shall go in there!" said Death. He was a strong old man, with a scythe in his hand, and with great black wings. "Yes, he shall be laid in his coffin, but not yet: I only register him, and let him wander awhile in the world to expiate his sins and to grow better. But one day I shall come. When he least expects it, I shall clap him in the black coffin, put him on my head, and fly up towards the star. There, too, blooms the garden of Paradise ; and if he is good and pious he will go in there ; but if his thoughts are evil, and his heart still full of sin, he will sink with his coffin deeper than Paradise has sunk, and only every thousandth year I shall fetch him, that he may sink deeper, or that he may attain to the star—the shining star up yonder ! "

THE ICE MAIDEN.

I.

Little Rudy.

Let us visit Switzerland, and wander through the glorious land of mountains, where the forests cling to the steep walls of rock ; let us mount up to the dazzling snow-fields, and then descend into the green valleys through which rivers and brooks are rushing, hurrying on as if they could not reach the sea and disappear there quickly enough. The sun looks hotly down upon the deep valley, and it glares likewise upon the heavy masses of snow, so that they harden in the course of centuries into gleaming blocks of ice, or form themselves into falling avalanches, or become piled up into glaciers. Two such glaciers lie in the broad rocky gorges under the " Schreckhorn" and the " Wetterhorn," by the little mountain town of Grindelwald: they are wonderful to behold, and therefore in the summer-time many strangers come from all parts of the world to see them. The strangers come across the lofty snow-covered mountains, they come through the deep valleys; and in this latter case they must climb for several hours, and, as they climb, the valley seems to be descending behind them, deeper and deeper, and they look down upon it as out of a balloon. Beneath them the clouds often hang like thick heavy veils over the mountain-tops, while a sun-beam still penetrates into the valley, through which the many brown houses lie scattered, making one particular spot stand forth in shining transparent green. Down there the water hums and gushes, while above, it purls and ripples and looks like silver bands fluttering down the mountain.

On both sides of the road that leads up hill, stand wooden houses. Each has its potato patch ; and this is an indispensable appendage, for there are many little mouths in those cottages—plenty of children are there, who can eat up their share right heartily. They peep forth every-where, and gather round the traveller, whether he be on foot or in a carriage. All the children here carry on a trade: the little people offer carved houses for sale, models of those that are built here in the moun-tains. In rain or in sunshine, there are the children offering their wares.

About twenty years ago, a little boy might often be seen standing there, anxious to carry on his trade, but always standing a short distance away from the rest. He would stand there with a very grave face, holding his little box with the carved toys so firmly in both hands that it seemed as if he would not let it go on any account. This appearance of earnestness, together with the fact of his being such a little fellow, often attracted the notice of strangers; so that he was very frequently beckoned forward, and relieved of a great part of his stock, without himself knowing why this preference was shown him. A couple of miles away, in the mountains, lived his grandfather, who carved the pretty little houses; and in the old man's room stood a wooden cupboard filled with things of that kind—carved toys in abundance, nutcrackers, knives and forks, boxes adorned with carved leaves and with jumping chamois, all kinds of things that delight children's eyes; but the boy looked with greater longing at an old rifle that hung from the beam under the ceiling, for his grandfather had promised him that it should be his one day, when he should have grown tall and strong enough to manage it properly.

Young as the boy was, he had to keep the goats; and if ability to climb with his flock makes a good goatherd, then Rudy was certainly an efficient one, for he even climbed a little higher than the goats could mount, and loved to take the birds' nests from the high trees. A bold and courageous child he was, but he was never seen to smile, save when he stood by the foaming waterfall or heard an avalanche crashing down the mountain-side. He never played with the other children, and only came in contact with them when his grandfather sent him down the mountain to deal in carved toys; and this was a business Rudy did not exactly like. He preferred clambering about alone among the mountains, or sitting beside his grandfather and hearing the old man tell stories of the old times, or of the people in the neighbouring town of Meiningen, his birthplace. The old man said that the people who dwelt in that place had not been there from the beginning: they had come into the land from the far north, where their ancestors dwelt, who were called Swedes. And Rudy was very proud of knowing this. But he had others who taught him something, and these others were companions of his belonging to the animal creation. There was a great dog, whose name was Ajola, and who had belonged to Rudy's father; and a Tom Cat was there too; this Tom Cat was an especial crony of Rudy's, for it was Pussy who had taught him to climb.

"Come with me out on the roof," the Cat had said, quite distinctly and plainly, to Rudy; for, you see, children who cannot talk yet, can understand the language of fowls and ducks right well, and cats and dogs speak to them quite as plainly as father and mother can do; but that is only when the children are very little, and then even grandfather's stick will become a perfect horse to them, and can neigh, and in their eyes is furnished with head and legs and tail, all complete. With some children this period ends later than with others, and of such we are accustomed to say that they are very backward, and that they have remained children a long time.   People are in the habit of saying many strange things.

"Come out with me on to the roof,'1 was perhaps the first thing the Cat had said and that Rudy had understood.   "What people say about falling down is all fancy : one does not fall down if one is not afraid. Just you come, and put one of your paws thus and the other thus. Feel your way with your fore paws.   You must have eyes in your head and nimble paws; and if an empty space comes, jump over, and then hold tight, as I do."

And Rudy did so too; consequently he was often found seated on the top of the roof by the Cat; and afterwards he sat with him in the tree-tops, and at last was even seen seated on the window-sills, whither Puss could not come.

"Higher up!" said Tree and Bush.   "Don't you see how we climb ? How high we reach, and how tight we cling, even to the narrowest, loftiest ridge of rock!"

And Rudy climbed to the very summit of the mountain, frequently reaching the top before the sun touched it, and there he drank his morning draught of fresh mountain air, the draught that the bountiful Creator above can prepare, and the recipe for making which, according to the reading of men, consists in mingling the fragrant aroma of the mountain herbs with the scent of the wild thyme and mint of the valley.   All that is heavy is absorbed by the brooding clouds, and then the wind drives them along, and rubs them against the tree-tops, and the spirit of fragrance is infused into the air to make it lighter and fresher, ever fresher.   And this was Rudy's morning draught.

The sunbeams, the blessing-laden daughters of the sun, kissed his cheeks, and Giddiness, who stood lurking by, never ventured to approach him; but the swallows, who had no less than seven nests on his grandfather's roof, flew round about him and his goats, and sang, "We and you! we and you!"   They brought him a greeting from home, from his grandfather, and even from the two fowls, the only birds in the house, but with whom Rudy never became at all intimate.

Small as he was, he had been a traveller, and for such a little fellow he had made no mean journey.   He had been born over in the Canton of Wallis, and had been carried across the high mountains to his present dwelling.   Not long ago he had made a pilgrimage on foot to the "Staubbach" or "Dust Fountain," which flutters through the air like a silver tissue before the snow-covered dazzling white mountain called the "Jungfrau" or "Maiden."   He had also been in the Grindelwald, at the great glacier; but that was a sad story.   His mother had met her death there; and there, said grandfather, little Rudy had lost his childlike cheerfulness.   When the boy was not a year old his mother had written concerning him that he laughed more than he cried, but from the time when he sat in the ice cleft, another spirit came upon him.   His grandfather seldom talked of it, but they knew the story through the whole mountain region.

Rudy's father had been a postillion.   The great dog that lay in grandfather's room had always followed him in his journeys over the Simplon down to the Lake of Geneva. In the valley of the Rhone, in the Canton of Wallis, lived some relatives of Rudy on the father's side. His uncle was a first-rate chamois hunter and a well-known guide. Rudy was only a year old when he lost his father, and the mother now longed to return with her child to her relatives in the Oberland of Berne. Her father lived a few miles from Grindelwald; he was a wood-carver, and earned enough to live on. Thus, in the month of June, carrying her child, and accompanied by two chamois hunters, she set out on her journey home, across the Gemmi towards Grindelwald. They had already gone the greater part of the way, had crossed the high ridge as far as the snow-field, and already caught sight of the valley of home, with all the well-known wooden houses, and had only one great glacier to cross. The snow had fallen freshly, and concealed a cleft which did not indeed reach to the deep ground where the water gushed, but was still more than six feet deep. The young mother, with her child in her arms, stumbled, slipped over the edge, and vanished. No cry was heard, no sigh, but they could hear the crying of the little child. More than an hour elapsed before ropes and poles could be brought up from the nearest house for the purpose of giving help, and after much exertion what appeared to be two corpses were brought forth from the icy cleft. Every means was tried; and the child, but not the mother, was recalled to life; and thus the old grandfather had a daughter's son brought into his house, an orphan, the boy who had laughed more than he cried; but it seemed that a great change had taken place in him, and this change must have been wrought in the glacier cleft, in the cold wondrous ice world, in which, according to the Swiss peasants' belief, the souls of the wicked are shut up until the last day.

The glacier lies stretched out, a foaming body of water stiffened into ice, and as it were pressed together into green blocks, one huge lump piled upon another; from beneath it the rushing stream of melted ice and snow thunders down into the valley, and deep caverns and great clefts extend below. It is a wondrous glass palace, and within dwells the Ice Maiden, the Glacier Queen. She, the death-dealing, the crushing one, is partly a child of air, partly the mighty ruler of the river; thus she is also able to raise herself to the summit of the snow mountain, where the bold climbers are obliged to hew steps in the ice before they can mount; she sails on the slender fir twig down the rushing stream, and springs from one block to another, with her long snow-white hair and her blue-green garment fluttering around her and glittering like the water in the deep Swiss lakes.

"To crush and to hold, mine is the power!" she says. "They have stolen a beautiful boy from me, a boy whom I have kissed, but not kissed to death. He is again among men: he keeps the goats on the mountains, and climb upwards, ever higher, far away from the others, but not from me. He is mine, and I will have him!"

And she gave a commission to the spirit called Giddiness to act for her, for it was too hot for the Ice Maiden, in summer, in the green woods where the wild mint grows ; and Giddiness mounted up, higher and higher ; and his brethren went with him, for he has many brethren, a whole troop of them ; and the Ice Maiden chose the strongest of the many who hover without and within.   These spirits sit on the staircase railing and upon the railing at the summit of the tower ; they run like squirrels along the rocky ridge, they spring over railing and path, and tread the air as a swimmer treads the water, luring their victims forth, and hurling them down into the abyss.   Giddiness and the Ice Maiden both grasp at a man as a polypus grasps at everything that comes near it. And now Giddiness was to seize upon Rudy.

"Yes, but to seize *him*," said Giddiness, "is more than I can do. The cat, that wretched creature, has taught him her tricks.   That child has a particular power which thrusts me away ; I am not able to seize him, this boy, when he hangs by a bough over the abyss.   How gladly would I tickle the soles of his feet, or thrust him head over heels into the air !   But I am not able to do it."

"We shall manage to do it," said the Ice Maiden.   "Thou or I — I shall do it—I !"

"No, no !" sounded a voice around her, like the echo of the church bells among the mountains ; but it was a song ; it was the melting chorus of other spirits of nature — of good affectionate spirits — the Daughters of the Sunshine.   These hover every evening in a wreath about the summits of the mountains ; there they spread forth their roseate wings, which become more and more fiery as the sun sinks, and gleam above the high mountains.   The people call this the "Alpine glow."   And then, when the sun has set, they retire into the mountain summits, into the white snow, and slumber there until the sun rises again, when they appear once more.   They are especially fond of flowers, butterflies, and human beings ; and among these latter they had chosen Rudy as an especial favourite.

"You shall not catch him — you shall not have him," they said.

"I have caught them larger and stronger than he," said the Ice Maiden.

Then the Daughters of the Sun sang a song of the wanderer whose mantle the storm carried away

"The wind took the covering, but not the man.   Ye can seize him, but not hold him, ye children of strength.   He is stronger, he is more spiritual than even we are.   He will mount higher than the sun, our parent.   He possesses the magic word that binds wind and water, so that they must serve him and obey him.   You will but loosen the heavy oppressive weight that holds him down, and he will rise all the higher."

Gloriously swelled the chorus that sounded like the ringing of the church bells.

And every morning the sunbeams pierced through the one little window into the grandfather's house, and shone upon the quiet child. The Daughters of the Sunbeams kissed the boy ; they wanted to thaw and remove the icy kisses which the royal maiden of the glaciers had given him when he lay in the lap of his dead mother in the deep ice cleft, from whence he had been saved as if by a miracle.

RUDY TAKES LEAVE OF HIS GRANDFATHER.

II.

The Journey to the new Home.

RUDY was now eight years old. His uncle, who dwelt beyond the mountains in the Rhone valley, wished that the boy should come to him to learn something and get on in the world; the grandfather saw the justice of this, and let the lad go.

Accordingly Rudy said good bye. There were others besides his grandfather to whom he had to say farewell; and foremost came Ajola, the old dog.

"Your father was the postillion and I was the post dog," said Ajola; "we went to and fro together; and I know some dogs from beyond the mountains, and some people too. I was never much of a talker; but now that we most likely shall not be able to talk much longer together, I will tell you a little more than usual. I will tell you a story that I have kept to myself and ruminated on for a long while. I don't understand it, and you won't understand it, but that does not signify: this much at least I have made out, that things are not quite equally divided in the world, either for dogs or for men. Not all are destined to sit on a lady's lap and to drink milk: *I*'ve not been accustomed to it, but I've seen one of those little lap dogs, driving in the coach, and taking up a passenger's place in it; the lady, who was its mistress, or whose master it was, had a little bottle of milk with her, out of which she gave the dog a drink; and she offered him sweetmeats, but he only sniffed at them, and would not even accept them, and then she ate them up herself. I was running along in the mud beside the carriage, as hungry as a dog can be, chewing my own thoughts, that this could not be quite right; but they say a good many things are going on that are not quite right. Should you like to sit in a lady's lap and ride in a coach? I should be glad if you did. But one can't manage that for oneself. I never could manage it, either by barking or howling."

These were Ajola's words; and Rudy embraced him and kissed him heartily on his wet nose; then the lad took the Cat in his arms, but Puss struggled, saying,

"You're too strong for me, and I don't like to use my claws against you! Clamber away over the mountains, for I have taught you how to climb. Don't think that you can fall, and then you will be sure to maintain your hold."

And so saying the Cat ran away, not wishing Rudy to see that the tears were in his eyes.

The Fowls were strutting about in the room. One of them had lost its tail. A traveller who wanted to be a sportsman had shot the Fowl's tail away, looking upon the bird as a bird of prey.

"Rudy wants to go across the mountains," said one of the Fowls.

"He's always in a hurry," said the other, "and I don't like saying good bye."

And with this they both tripped away.

To the goats he also said farewell; and they bleated "Meek! meek!" and wanted to go with him, which made him feel very sorrowful.

Two brave guides from the neighbourhood, who wanted to go across the mountains to the other side of the Gemmi, took him with them, and he followed them on foot. It was a tough march for such a little fellow, but Rudy was a strong boy, and his courage never gave way.

The swallows flew with them for a little distance. "We and you! we and you!" sang they. The road led across the foaming Lutchine, which pours forth in many little streams from the black cleft of the Grindel glacier, and fallen trunks of trees and blocks of stone serve for a bridge. When they had reached the forest opposite, they began to ascend the slope where the glacier had slipped away from the mountain, and now they strode across and around ice blocks over the glacier. Rudy sometimes had alternately to crawl and to walk for some distance: his eyes gleamed with delight, and he trod so firmly in his spiked climbing-shoes that it seemed as if he wished to leave a trace behind him at every footstep. The black earth which the mountain stream had strewn over the glacier gave the great mass a swarthy look, but the bluish-green glassy ice nevertheless peered through. They had to make circuits round the numerous little lakes which had formed among the great blocks of ice, and now and then they passed close to a great stone that lay tottering on the edge of a crack in the ice, and sometimes the stone would overbalance, and roll crashing down, and a hollow echo sounded forth from the deep dark fissures in the glacier.

Thus they continued climbing. The glacier itself extended upwards like a mighty river of piled-up ice masses, shut in by steep rocks. Rudy thought for a moment of the tale they had told him, how he and his mother had lain in one of these deep, cold-breathing fissures; but soon all such thoughts vanished from him, and the tale seemed to him only like many others of the same kind which he had heard. Now and then, when the men thought the way too toilsome for the little lad, they would reach him a hand; but he did not grow tired, and stood on the smooth ice as safely as a chamois. Now they stepped on the face of the rock, and strode on among the rugged stones; sometimes, again, they marched among the pine trees, and then over the pasture grounds, ever seeing new and changing landscapes. Around them rose snow-clad mountains, whose names the "Jungfrau," the "Mönch," the "Eiger," were known to every child, and consequently to Rudy too. Rudy had never yet been so high; he had never yet stepped on the outspread sea of snow: here it lay with its motionless snowy billows, from which the wind every now and then blew off a flake, as it blows the foam from the waves of the sea. The glaciers stand here, so to speak, hand in hand; each one is a glass palace for the Ice Maiden, whose might and whose desire it is to catch and to bury. The sun shone warm, the snow was dazzlingly white and seemed strewn with bluish sparkling diamonds. Numberless insects, especially butterflies and bees, lay dead upon the snow; they had ventured too high, or the wind had carried them up until they perished in the frosty air. Above the Wetterhorn hung, like a bundle of fine black wool, a threatening cloud; it bowed down, teeming with the weight it bore, the weight of a whirlwind, irresistible when once it bursts forth. The impressions of this whole journey—the night encampment in these lofty regions, the late walk, the deep rocky chasms, where the water has pierced through the blocks of stone by a labour, at the thought of whose duration calculation stands still—all this was indelibly impressed upon Rudy's recollection.

A deserted stone building beyond the snow sea offered them a shelter for the night. Here they found fuel and pine branches, and soon a fire was kindled, and the bed arranged for the night as comfortably as possible. Then the men seated themselves round the fire, smoked their pipes, and drank the warm refreshing drink they had prepared for themselves. Rudy received his share of the supper; and then the men began te'ling stories of the mysterious beings of the Alpine land: of the strange gigantic serpents that lay coiled in the deep lakes; of the marvellous company of spirits that had been known to carry sleeping men by night through the air to the wonderful floating city, Venice; of the wild shepherd who drove his black sheep across the mountain pastures, and how, though no man had seen him, the sound of the bell and the ghostly bleating of the flock had been heard by many. Rudy listened attentively, but without any feeling of fear, for he knew not what fear meant; and while he listened he seemed to hear the hollow, unearthly bleating and lowing; and it became more and more audible, so that presently the men heard it too, and stopped in their talk to listen, and told Rudy he must not go to sleep.

It was a "Föhn," the mighty whirlwind that hurls itself from the mountains into the valley, cracking the trees in its strength as if they were feeble reeds, and carrying the wooden houses from one bank of a river to the other as we move the figures on a chess board.

After the lapse of about an hour, they told Rudy it was all over, and he might go to sleep; and tired out with his long march, he went to sleep on the instant, like a soldier obeying the word of command.

Very early next morning they resumed their journey. This day the sun shone on new mountains for Rudy, on fresh glaciers and new fields of snow: they had entered the Canton of Wallis, and had proceeded beyond the ridge which could be seen from the Grindelwald; but they were still far from the new home. Other charms came in view, new valleys, forests, and mountain paths, and new houses also came into view, and other people. But what strange-looking people were these! They were deformed, and had fat, sallow faces; and from their necks hung heavy, ugly lumps of flesh, like bags: they were *crétins*, dragging themselves languidly along, and looking at the strangers with stupid eyes; the women especially were hideous in appearance. Were the people whom the boy would find in his new home like these?

III.

Uncle.

THANK Heaven! the people in the house of Rudy's uncle, where the boy was now to live, looked like those he had been accustomed to see; only one of them was a *crétin*, a poor idiotic lad, one of those pitiable creatures who wander in their loneliness from house to house in the Canton of Wallis, staying a couple of months with each family. Poor Saperli happened to be at Rudy's uncle's when the boy arrived.

Uncle was still a stalwart huntsman, and, moreover, understood the craft of tub-making; his wife was a little lively woman with a face like a bird's. She had eyes like an eagle, and her neck was covered with a fluffy down.

Everything here was new to Rudy—costume, manners, and habits, and even the language; but to the latter the child's ear would soon adapt itself. There was an appearance of wealth here, compared with grandfather's dwelling. The room was larger, the walls were ornamented with chamois horns, among which hung polished rifles, and over the door was a picture of the Madonna, with fresh Alpine roses and a burning lamp in front of it.

As already stated, uncle was one of the best chamois hunters in the whole country, and one of the most trusted guides. In this household Rudy was now to become the pet child. There was one pet here already in the person of an old blind and deaf hound, who no longer went out hunting as he had been used to do; but his good qualities of former days had not been forgotten, and on the strength of them the creature was looked upon as one of the family and carefully tended. Rudy stroked the dog, who, however, was not willing to make acquaintance with a stranger; but Rudy did not long remain a stranger in that house.

"It is not bad living, here in the Canton of Wallis," said uncle; "and we have chamois here, who don't die so easily as the steinbock; and it is much better here now than in former days. They may say what they like in honour of the old times, but ours are better, after all: the bog has been opened, and a fresh wind blows through our sequestered valley. Something better always comes up when the old is worn out," he continued. And when uncle was in a very communicative mood, he would tell of his youthful years, and of still earlier times, the strong times of his father, when Wallis was, as he expressed it, a closed bog, full of sick people and miserable *crétins*. "But the French soldiers came in," he said, "and they were the proper doctors, for they killed the disease at once, and they killed the people who had it too. They knew all about fighting, did the French, and they could fight in more than one way. Their girls could make conquests too," and then uncle would laugh and nod to his wife, who was a Frenchwoman by birth. "The French hammered away at our stones in famous style! They hammered the Simplon road through the rocks—such a road that I can now say to a child of three years, 'Go to Italy, only keep to the high road,' and the child will arrive safely in Italy if it does not stray from the road."

And then uncle would sing a French song, and cry "Hurrah!" and "Long live Napoleon Bonaparte!"

Here Rudy for the first time heard them tell of France and Lyons, the great town on the Rhone, where his uncle had been.

Not many years were to elapse before Rudy should become an expert chamois hunter; his uncle said he had the stuff for it in him, and accordingly taught him to handle a rifle, to take aim, and shoot; and in the hunting season he took the lad with him into the mountains and let him drink the warm blood of the chamois, which cures the huntsman of giddiness; he also taught him to judge of the various times when the avalanches would roll down the mountains, at noon or at evening, according as the sunbeams had shone upon the place; he taught him to notice the way the chamois sprang, that Rudy might learn to come down firmly on his feet; and told him that where the rocky cleft gave no support for the foot, a man must cling by his elbows, hips, and legs, and that even the neck could be used as a support in case of need. The chamois were clever, he said—they sent out scouts; but the hunter should be more clever still, keep out of the line of scent, and lead them astray; and one day when Rudy was out hunting with uncle, the latter hung his coat and hat on the alpenstock, and the chamois took the coat for a man.

The rocky path was narrow; it was, properly speaking, not a path at all, but merely a narrow shelf beside the yawning abyss. The snow that lay here was half thawed, the stone crumbled beneath the tread, and therefore uncle laid himself down and crept forward. Every fragment that crumbled away from the rock fell down, jumping and rolling from one ledge of rock to another until it was lost to sight in the darkness below. About a hundred paces behind his uncle stood Rudy, on a firm projecting point of rock; and from this station he saw a great "lamb's vulture" circling in the air and hovering over uncle, whom it evidently intended to hurl into the abyss with a blow of its wings, that it might make a prey of him. Uncle's whole attention was absorbed by the chamois which was to be seen, with its young one, on the other side of the cleft. Rudy kept his eyes firmly fixed upon the bird. He knew what the vulture intended to do, and accordingly stood with his rifle ready to fire; when suddenly the chamois leaped up: uncle fired, and the creature fell pierced by the deadly bullet; but the young one sprang away as if it had been accustomed all its life to flee from danger. Startled by the sound of the rifle, the great bird soared away in another direction, and uncle knew nothing of the danger in which he had stood until Rudy informed him of it.

As they were returning homeward, in the best spirits, uncle whistling one of the songs of his youth, they suddenly heard a peculiar noise not far from them; they looked around, and yonder, on the declivity of the mountain, the snowy covering suddenly rose, and began to heave up and down, like a piece of linen stretched on a field when the wind passes beneath it. The snow waves, which had been smooth and hard as marble slabs, now broke to pieces, and the roar of waters sounded like rumbling thunder. An avalanche was falling, not over Rudy and uncle, but near where they stood, not at all far from them.

"Hold fast, Rudy!" cried uncle, "hold fast with all your strength."

And Rudy clung to the trunk of the nearest tree. Uncle clambered up above him, and the avalanche rolled past, many feet from them; but the concussion of the air, the stormy wings of the avalanche, broke trees and shrubs all around as if they had been frail reeds, and scattered the fragments headlong down. Rudy lay crouched upon the earth, the trunk of the tree to which he clung was split through, and the crown hurled far away; and there among the broken branches lay uncle, with his head shattered: his hand was still warm, but his face could no longer be recognized. Rudy stood by him pale and trembling; it was the first fright of his life—the first time he felt a shudder run through him.

Late at night he brought the sorrowful news into his home, which was now a house of mourning. The wife could find no words, no tears for her grief; at last, when the corpse was brought home, her sorrow found utterance. The poor *crétin* crept into his bed, and was not seen during the whole of the next day; but at last, towards evening, he stole up to Rudy.

"Write a letter for me," he said. "Saperli can't write, but Saperli can carry the letter to the post."

"A letter from you?" asked Rudy. "And to whom?"

"To the Lord."

"To *whom* do you say?"

And the simpleton, as they called the *crétin*, looked at Rudy with a moving glance, folded his hands, and said solemnly and slowly,

"To the Saviour! Saperli will send Him a letter, and beg that Saperli may lie dead, and not the man in the house here."

Rudy pressed his hand, and said,

"The letter would not arrive, and it cannot restore him to us."

But it was very difficult to make poor Saperli believe that this was impossible.

"Now thou art the prop of this house," said the widow; and Rudy became, in very truth, the stay of his home.

IV

Babette.

WHO is the best marksman in the Canton of Wallis? The chamois knew well enough, and said to each other, "Beware of Rudy." Who is the handsomest marksman? "Why, Rudy," said the girls; but *they* did not add, "Beware of Rudy." Nor did even the grave mothers pronounce such a warning, for Rudy nodded at them just as kindly as at the young maidens. How quick and merry he was! His cheeks were browned, his teeth regular and white, and his eyes black and shining; he was a handsome lad, and only twenty years old. The icy water could not harm him when he swam; he could turn and twist in the water like a fish, and climb better than any man in the mountains; he could cling like a snail to the rocky ledge, for he had good sinews and muscles of his own; and he showed that in his power of jumping, an art he had learned first from the Cat and afterwards from the goats. Rudy was the safest guide to whom any man could trust himself, and might have amassed a fortune in that calling; his uncle had also taught him the craft of tub-making; but he did not take to that occupation, preferring chamois hunting, which also brought in money. Rudy was what might be called a good match, if he did not look higher than his station. And he was such a dancer, that the girls dreamed of him, and indeed more than one of them carried the thought of him into her waking hours.

"He kissed me once at the dance!" said the schoolmaster's daughter Annette to her dearest girl-friend; but she should not have said that, even to her dearest friend. A secret of that kind is hard to keep—it is like sand in a sieve, sure to run out ; and soon it was known that Rudy, honest lad though he was, kissed his partner in the dance ; and yet he had not kissed the one whom he would have liked best of all to kiss.

" Yes," said an old hunter, " he has kissed Annette. He has begun with A, and will kiss his way through the whole alphabet."

A kiss at the dance was all that the busy tongues could say against him until now: he had certainly kissed Annette, but she was not the beloved one of his heart.

Down in the valley near Bex, among the great walnut trees, by a little brawling mountain stream, lived the rich miller. The dwelling-house was a great building, three storeys high, with little towers, roofed with planks and covered with plates of metal that shone in the sunlight and in the moonlight ; the principal tower was surmounted by a weather-vane, a flashing arrow that had pierced an apple—an emblem of Tell's famous feat. The mill looked pleasant and comfortable, and could be easily drawn and described; but the miller's daughter could neither be drawn nor described,—so, at least, Rudy would have said ; and yet she was portrayed in his heart, where her eyes gleamed so brightly that they had lighted up a fire. This had burst out quite suddenly, as other fires break forth ; and the strangest circumstance of all was, that the miller's daughter, pretty Babette, had no idea of the conquest she had made, for she and Rudy had never exchanged a word together.

The miller was rich, and this wealth of his made Babette very difficult to get at, as if she had been high up in a tree. But nothing is so high that it may not be reached if a man will but climb ; and he will not fall, if he is not afraid of falling. That was a lesson Rudy had brought from his first home.

Now it happened that on one occasion Rudy had some business to do in Bex. It was quite a journey thither, for in those days the railway had not yet been completed. From the Rhone glacier, along the foot of the Simplon, away among many changing mountain heights, the proud valley of Wallis extends, with its mighty river the Rhone, which often overflows its banks and rushes across the fields and high roads, carrying destruction with it. Between the little towns of Sion and St. Maurice the valley makes a bend, like an elbow, and becomes so narrow behind St. Maurice that it only affords room for the bed of the river and a narrow road. An old tower here stands as a sentinel at the boundary of the Canton of Wallis, which ends here. The tower looks across over the stone bridge at the toll-house on the opposite side. There commences the Canton of Waadt, and at a little distance is the first town of that Canton, Bex. At every step the signs of fertility and plenty increase, and the traveller seems to be journeying through a garden of walnut trees and chestnuts ; here and there cypresses appear, and blooming pomegranates ; and the climate has the southern warmth of Italy.

Rudy duly arrived in Bex, and concluded his business there ; then he took a turn in the town ; but not even a miller's lad, much less Babette, did he see there. That was not as it should be.

THE MILLER'S DAUGHTER.

Evening came on; the air was full of the fragrance of the wild thyme and of the blooming lime trees; a gleaming bluish veil seemed to hang over the green mountains; far around reigned a silence—not the silence of sleep or of death; but a stillness as if all nature held its breath, as if it were waiting to have its picture photographed upon the blue sky. Here and there among the trees on the green meadows stood long poles, supporting the telegraphic wires that had been drawn through the quiet valley; against one of these leaned an object, so motionless that it might have been taken for the trunk of a tree; but it was Rudy, who stood as quiet and motionless as all nature around him. He did not sleep, nor was he dead by any means; but just as the records of great events sometimes fly along the telegraph—messages of vital importance to those whom they concern, while the wire gives no sign, by sound or movement, of what is passing over it—so there was passing through the mind of Rudy a thought which was to be the happiness of his whole life and his one absorbing idea from that moment. His eyes were fixed on one point—on a light that gleamed out among the trees from the chamber of the miller where Babette dwelt.   So motionless did Rudy stand here, one might have thought he was taking aim at a chamois, a creature which sometimes stands as if carved out of the rock, till suddenly, if a stone should roll down, it springs away in a headlong career.   And something of this kind happened to Rudy—suddenly a thought rolled into his mind.

" Never falter ! " he cried.   " Pay a visit to the mill, say good evening to the miller and good evening to Babette.   He does not fall down who is not afraid of falling.   Babette must see me, sooner or later, if I am to be her husband."

And Rudy laughed, for he was of good courage, and he strode away towards the mill.   He knew what he wanted ; he wanted to have little Babette.

The river, with its yellowish bed, foamed along, and the willows and lime trees hung over the hurrying waters ; Rudy strode along the path towards the miller's house.   But, as the children's song has it :

> " Nobody was at home to greet him,
>   Only the house cat came to meet him."

The house cat stood on the step and said " Miaw," and arched her back ; but Rudy paid no attention to this address.   He knocked, but no one heard him, no one opened the door to him.   " Miaw ! " said the cat.   If Rudy had been still a child, he would have understood her language, and have known that the cat was saying, " There 's nobody at home here ! " but being a grown man, he must fain go over to the mill to make inquiries, and there he heard the news that the miller had gone far away to Interlaken, and Babette with him : a great shooting match was to come off there ; it would begin to-morrow, and last a full week, and people from all the German Cantons were to be present at it.

Poor Rudy ! he might be said to have chosen an unlucky day for his visit to Bex, and now he might go home.   He turned about accordingly, and marched over St. Maurice and Sion towards his own valley and the mountains of his home ; but he was not discouraged.   When the sun rose next morning his good humour already stood high, for it had never set.

" Babette is at Interlaken, many days' journey from here," he said to himself.   " It is a long way thither if a man travels along the broad high road, but it is not so far if one takes the short cut across the mountains, and the chamois hunter's path is straight forward.   I've been that way already : yonder is my early home, where I lived as a child in grandfather's house, and there 's a shooting match at Interlaken.   I'll be there too, and be the best shot ; and I'll be with Babette too, when once I have made her acquaintance."

With a light knapsack containing his Sunday clothes on his back, and his gun and hunting bag across his shoulder, Rudy mounted the hill by the short cut, which was, nevertheless, tolerably long ; but the shooting match had only begun that day, and was to last a week or more ; and they had told him that the miller and Babette would pass the whole time with their friends at Interlaken. Rudy marched across the Gemmi, intending to descend at Grindelwald.

Fresh and merry, he walked on in the strengthening light mountain air. The valley sank deeper and deeper behind him, and his horizon became more and more extended; here a snowy peak appeared, and there another, and presently the whole gleaming white chain of the Alps could be seen. Rudy knew every peak, and he made straight towards the Schreckhorn, that raised its white-powdered, stony fingers up into the blue air.

At last he had crossed the ridge. The grassy pastures bent down towards the valley of his old home. The air was light and his spirits were light. Mountain and valley bloomed fair with verdure and with flowers, and his heart was filled with the feeling of youth, that recks not of coming age or of death. To live, to conquer, to enjoy, free as a bird!— and light as a bird he felt. And the swallows flew past him, and sang, as they had sang in his childhood, "We and you! we and you!" and all seemed joy and rapid motion.

Below lay the summer-green meadow, studded with brown wooden houses, with the Lutchine rushing and humming among them. He saw the glacier with the grass-green borders and the clouded snow; he looked into the deep crevasses, and beheld the upper and the lower glacier. The church bells sounded across to him, as if they were ringing to welcome him into the valley of home; and his heart beat stronger, and swelled so, that for a moment Babette entirely disappeared, so large did his heart become, and so full of recollections.

He went along again, up on the mountain where he had stood as a child with other little children, offering carved houses for sale. There among the pine trees stood the house of his maternal grandfather; but strangers inhabited it now. Children came running along the road towards him to sell their wares, and one of them offered him an Alpine rose, which Rudy looked upon as a good omen; and he bought the rose, thinking of Babette. Soon he had crossed the bridge where the two branches of the Lutchine join; the woods became thicker here and the walnut trees gave a friendly shade. Now he saw the waving flags, the flags with the white cross in a red field, the national emblem of the Switzer and the Dane, and Interlaken lay before him.

This was certainly a town without equal, according to Rudy's estimate. It was a little Swiss town in its Sunday dress. It did not look like other places, a heavy mass of stone houses, dismal and pretentious; no; here the wooden houses looked as if they had run down into the valley from the hills, and placed themselves in a row beside the clear river that ran so gaily by; they were a little out of order, but nevertheless they formed a kind of street; and the prettiest of all the streets was one that had grown up since Rudy had been here in his boyish days; and it looked to him as if it had been built of all the natty little houses his grandfather had carved, and which used to be kept in the cupboard of the old house. A whole row of such houses seemed to have grown up here like strong chestnut trees; each of them was called an hotel, and had carved work on the windows and doors, and a projecting roof, prettily and tastefully built, and in front of each was a garden separating it from the broad macadamized road. The houses only stood on one side of the road, so that they did not hide the fresh green pastures, in which the cows were walking about with bells round their necks like those which sound upon the lofty Alps. The pasture was surrounded by high mountains, which seemed to have stepped aside in the middle, so that the sparkling snow-covered mountain, the "Jungfrau," the most beautiful of all the Swiss peaks, could be plainly seen.

What a number of richly dressed ladies and gentlemen from foreign lands! what a crowd of people from the various Cantons! Every marksman wore his number displayed in a wreath round his hat. There was music and singing, barrel organs and trumpets, bustle and noise. Houses and bridges were adorned with verses and emblems; flags and banners were waving; the rifles cracked merrily now and again; and in Rudy's ears the sound of the shots was the sweetest music; and in the bustle and tumult he had quite forgotten Babette, for whose sake he had come.

And now the marksmen went crowding to shoot at the target. Rudy soon took up his station among them, and proved to be the most skilful and the most fortunate of all—each time his bullet struck the black spot in the centre of the target.

"Who may that stranger, that young marksman be?" asked many of the bystanders. "He speaks the French they talk in the Canton of Wallis."

"He can also make himself well understood in our German," said others.

"They say he lived as a child in the neighbourhood of Grindelwald," observed one of the marksmen.

And he was full of life, this stranger youth. His eyes gleamed, and his glance and his arm were sure, and that is why he hit the mark so well. Fortune gives courage, but Rudy had courage enough of his own. He had soon assembled a circle of friends round him; who paid him honour, and showed respect for him; and Babette was quite forgotten for the moment. Then suddenly a heavy hand clapped him on the shoulder, and a deep voice addressed him in the French tongue:

"You're from the Canton of Wallis?"

Rudy turned round, and saw a red good-humoured face, belonging to a portly person. The speaker was the rich miller of Bex; and his broad body almost eclipsed the pretty delicate Babette, who, however, soon peeped forth from behind him with her bright dark eyes. It pleased the rich miller that a marksman from his Canton should have shot best, and have won respect from all present. Well, Rudy was certainly a fortunate youth, for the object for whose sake he had come, but whom he had forgotten after his arrival, now came to seek him out.

When fellow-countrymen meet at a long distance from home, they are certain to converse and to make acquaintance with one another. By virtue of his good shooting Rudy had become the first at the marksmen's meeting, just as the miller was the first at home in Bex on the strength of his money and of his good mill; and so the two men shook hands, a thing they had never done before; Babette also held out her hand frankly to Rudy, who pressed it so warmly and gave her such an earnest look that she blushed crimson to the roots of her hair.

The miller talked of the long distance they had come, and of the many huge towns they had seen; according to his idea they had made quite a long journey of it, having travelled by railway, steamboat, and diligence.

"I came the shortest way," observed Rudy. "I walked across the mountains. No road is so high but a man may get over it."

"And break his neck," quoth the miller, with a laugh. "You look just the fellow to break your neck some of these days, so bold as you are, too."

"Oh, a man does not fall unless he thinks he shall fall," observed Rudy.

The relatives of the miller in Interlaken, at whose house he and Babette were staying, invited Rudy to visit them, for he belonged to the same Canton as the rich miller. That was a good offer for Rudy. Fortune was favourable to him, as she always is to him who seeks to win by his own energy, and remembers that " Providence provides us with nuts, but leaves us to crack them."

Rudy sat among the miller's relatives like one of the family. A glass was emptied to the health of the best marksman, and Babette clinked her glass with the rest, and Rudy returned thanks for the toast.

Towards evening they all took a walk on the pretty road by the prosperous hotels under the old walnut trees, and so many people were there, and there was so much pushing, that Rudy was obliged to offer his arm to Babette. He declared he was very glad to have met people from Waadt, for Waadt and Wallis were good neighbour Cantons. He expressed his joy so heartily, that Babette could not help giving him a grateful pressure of the hand. They walked on together as if they had been old friends, and she talked and chattered away; and Rudy thought how charmingly she pointed out the ridiculous and absurd points in the costume and manners of the foreign ladies; not that she did it to make game of them, for they might be very good honourable people, as Babette well knew, for was not her own godmother one of these grand English ladies? Eighteen years ago, when Babette was christened, this lady had been residing in Bex, and had given Babette the costly brooch the girl now wore on her neck. Twice the lady had written, and this year Babette had expected to meet her and her two daughters at Interlaken. "The daughters were old maids, nearly thirty years old," added Babette; but then she herself was only eighteen.

The sweet little mouth never rested for a moment; and everything that Babette said sounded in Rudy's ears like a matter of the utmost importance; and he, on his part, told all he had to tell—how often he had been at Bex, how well he knew the mill, and how often he had seen Babette, though she had probably never noticed him; and how, when he had lately called at the mill, full of thoughts that he could not express, she and her father had been absent—had gone far away, but not so far that a man might not climb over the wall that made the way so long.

He said all that and a great deal more. He said how fond he was of her, and that he had come hither on her account, and not for the sake of the marksmen's meeting.

Babette was quite still while he said all this; it seemed to her as if he valued her far too highly.

And as they wandered on, the sun sank down behind the high rocky wall. The "Jungfrau" stood there in full beauty and splendour, surrounded by the green wreath of the forest-clad hills. Every one stood still to enjoy the glorious sight, and Rudy and Babette rejoiced in it too.

"It is nowhere more beautiful than here!" said Babette,

"Nowhere!" cried Rudy, and he looked at Babette. "To-morrow I must return home," he said, after a silence of a few moments.

"Come and see us at Bex," whispered Babette; "it will please my father."

V.

On the Way Home.

OH, what a load Rudy had to carry when he went homeward across the mountains on the following day!. Yes, he had three silver goblets, two handsome rifles, and a silver coffee-biggin. The coffee-biggin would be useful when he set up housekeeping. But that was not all he had to carry: he bore something mightier and weightier, or rather it bore him, carrying him homewards across the high mountains. The weather was rough, grey, rainy, and heavy; the clouds floated down upon the mountain heights like funereal crape, concealing the sparkling summits. From the woodland valleys the last strokes of the axe sounded upward, and down the declivities of the mountains rolled trunks of trees, which looked like thin sticks from above, but were in reality thick enough to serve as masts for the largest ships. The Lutchine foamed along with its monotonous song, the wind whistled, the clouds sailed onward. Then suddenly a young girl appeared walking beside Rudy: he had not noticed her till now that she was quite close to him. She wanted, like himself, to cross the mountain. The maiden's eyes had a peculiar power: you were obliged to look at them, and they were strange to behold, clear as glass, and deep, deep, unfathomably deep.

"Have you a sweetheart?" asked Rudy, for his thoughts all ran on that subject.

"I have none," replied the girl, with a laugh; but she did not seem to be speaking a true word. "Don't let us make a circuit," she said. "We must keep more to the left, then the way will be shorter."

"Yes, and we shall fall into an ice cleft," said Rudy. "You want to be a guide, and you don't know the way better than that!"

"I know the way well," the girl replied, "and my thoughts are not wandering. Yours are down in the valley, but up here one ought to

THE TEMPTATION.

think of the Ice Maiden: she does not love the human race—so people say."

"I'm not afraid of her," cried Rudy. "She was obliged to give me up when I was still a child, and I shall not give myself up to her now that I am older."

And the darkness increased, the rain fell, and the snow came, and dazzled and gleamed.

"Reach me your hand," said the girl to Rudy; "I will help you to climb."

And he felt the touch of her fingers icy cold upon him.

"*You* help me!" cried Rudy. "I don't want a woman's help yet to show me how to climb."

And he went on faster, away from her. The driving snow closed round him like a mantle, the wind whistled, and behind him he heard the girl laughing and singing in a strange way. He felt sure she was a phantom in the service of the Ice Maiden. Rudy had heard tell of such apparitions when he passed the night on the mountains in his boyish days, during his journey from his grandfather's house.

The snow-fall abated, and the cloud was now below him. He looked back, but nobody was to be seen; but he could hear a singing and whooping that did not seem to proceed from a human voice.

When Rudy at last reached the highest mountain plateau, whence the path led downward into the Rhone valley, he saw in the direction of Chamouny, in a strip of pure blue sky, two bright stars which glittered and twinkled; and he thought of Babette, of himself, and of his good fortune, and the reflection made him quite warm.

VI.

The Visit to the Mill.

"WHAT magnificent things you have brought home!" exclaimed the old aunt; and her strange eagle's eyes flashed, and her thin neck waved to and fro faster than ever in strange contortions. "You have luck, Rudy! I must kiss you, my darling boy!"

And Rudy allowed himself to be kissed, but with an expression in his face which told that he submitted to it as a necessary evil, a little domestic infliction.

"How handsome you are, Rudy!" said the old woman, admiringly.

"Don't put nonsense into my head," replied Rudy, with a laugh; but still he was pleased to hear her say it.

"I repeat it," she cried. "Good luck attends upon you!"

"Perhaps you are right," he observed; and he thought of Babette. Never had he felt such a longing to go down into the deep valley.

"They must have returned," he said to himself. "It is two days beyond the time when they were to have been back. I must go to Bex."

Accordingly Rudy journeyed to Bex, and the people of the mill were at home. He was well received, and the people at Interlaken had sent a kind message of remembrance to him. Babette did not say much: she had grown very silent, but her eyes spoke eloquently, and that was quite enough for Rudy. It seemed as if the miller, who was accustomed to lead the conversation, and who always expected his hearers to laugh at his ideas and jokes because he was the rich miller, it seemed as if he would never tire of hearing Rudy's hunting adventures; and Rudy spoke of the dangers and difficulties the chamois hunters have to encounter on the high mountains, how they have to cling, how they have to clamber over the frail ledges of snow, that are, as it were, glued to the mountain-side by frost and cold, and to clamber across the bridges of snow that stretch across rocky chasms. And the eyes of the brave Rudy flashed while he told of the hunter's life, of the cunning of the chamois and its perilous leaps, of the mighty whirlwind and the rushing avalanches. He noticed clearly enough, that with every fresh narrative he enlisted the miller more and more in his favour; and the old man felt especially interested in what the young hunter told about the lamb's vulture and the royal eagle.

Among other circumstances it was mentioned how, not far off, in the Canton of Wallis, there was an eagle's nest built very cleverly under a steep overhanging rock, and in the nest was an eaglet which could not be captured. An Englishman had a few days before offered Rudy a hand-full of gold pieces if he would procure him the eaglet alive.

"But there is reason in all things," said Rudy: "that eaglet is not to be taken; it would be folly to make the attempt."

And the wine flowed and conversation flowed; but the evening appeared far too short for Rudy, although it was past midnight when he set out to go home after his first visit to the mill.

The lights still gleamed for a short time through the windows of the mill among the green trees, and the Parlour Cat came forth from the open loophole in the roof, and met the Kitchen Cat walking along the rain-spout.

"Do you know the news in the mill?" asked the Parlour Cat. "There's a secret betrothal going on in the house. Father knows nothing about it. Rudy and Babette were treading on each other's paws under the table all the evening. They trod upon me twice, but I would not mew for fear of exciting attention."

"*I* should have mewed," said the Kitchen Cat.

"What will pass in the kitchen would never do for the parlour," retorted the other Cat; "but I'm curious to know what the miller will think about it when he hears of the affair."

Yes, indeed, what would the miller say? That is what Rudy would have liked to know too; and, moreover, he could not bear to remain long in suspense without knowing it. Accordingly, a few days afterwards, when the omnibus rattled across the Rhone bridge between Wallis and Waadt, Rudy sat in the vehicle, in good spirits as usual, and already basking in the sunny prospect of the consent he hoped to gain that very evening.

And when the evening came, and the omnibus was making its way back, Rudy once more sat in it as a passenger; but in the mill the Parlour Cat had some important news to dispense.

"Do you know it, you there out of the kitchen? The miller has been told all about it. There was a fine end to it all. Rudy came here towards evening, and he and Babette had much to whisper and to tell each other, standing in the passage outside the miller's room. I was lying at their feet, but they had neither eyes nor thoughts for me. 'I shall go to your father without more ado,' said Rudy; 'that's the honest way to do it.' 'Shall I go with you?' asked Babette; 'it will give you courage.' 'I've courage enough,' replied Rudy; 'but if you are present he must be kind, whether he likes it or not.' And they went in together. Rudy trod upon my tail most horribly: He's a very awkward fellow, is Rudy. I called out, but neither he nor Babette had ears to hear me. They opened the door, and both went in, and I went on before them; but I sprang up on the back of a chair, for I could not know where Rudy would step. But it was the miller who stepped this time: he stepped out right well. And Rudy had to step out of the door on to the mountain among the chamois; and he may take aim at them now, may Rudy, and not at our Babette."

" But what did they talk about? What did they say?" asked the Kitchen Cat.

"What did they say? Why, they said everything that people are accustomed to say when they come a wooing. 'I love her and she loves me, and if there's milk enough in the pail for one, there's enough for two.' 'But she's perched too high for you,' said the miller. 'She's perched on grist, on golden grist, as you very well know, and you can't reach up to her.' 'Nothing is so high that a man can't reach it, if he has the will,' said Rudy, for he is a bold fellow. 'But you can't reach the eaglet, you said so yourself the other day, and Babette is higher than that.' 'I shall take both of them,' exclaimed Rudy. 'I'll give you Babette when you give me the young eaglet alive,' said the miller, and he laughed till the tears ran down his cheeks. 'But now I must thank you for your visit. Call again to-morrow, and you'll find no-body at home. Good bye to you, Rudy.' And Babette said good bye too, as pitifully as a little kitten that can't see its mother yet. 'Your word is your bond,' cried Rudy. 'Don't cry, Babette: I'll bring you the eaglet!' 'You'll break your neck first, I hope,' said the miller, 'and then we shall be rid of your dangling here!' That's what I call a capital kick!

"And now Rudy is gone, and Babette sits and weeps, but the miller sings German songs that he has learned on his late journey. I don't like to be down-hearted about it, for that can do no good!"

"Well, after all, there's some prospect for him still," observed the Kitchen Cat.

VII.

The Eagle's Nest.

DOWN from the rocky path sounded a fresh song, merry and strong, redolent of courage and good spirits; and the singer was Rudy, who came to seek his friend Vesinand.

"You must help me! We will have Nagli with us. I want to take the eaglet out of the nest on the rock."

"Would you not like to take the black spots out of the moon first?" replied Vesinand. "That would be just as easy. You seem to be in a merry mood."

"Certainly I am, for I hope to be married soon. But let us speak seriously, and I will tell you what it is all about."

And soon Vesinand and Nagli knew what Rudy wanted.

"You're a headstrong fellow," they said. "It can't be done: you will break your neck over it."

"A man does not fall who's not afraid of falling," Rudy persisted.

At midnight they set out with poles, ladders, and ropes; their way led through forest and thicket, over loose rolling stones, ever upward, upward, through the dark night. The water rushed beneath them, water dripped down from above, and heavy clouds careered through the air. The hunters reached the steep wall of rock. Here it was darker than ever. The opposite sides of the chasm almost touched, and the sky could only be seen through a small cleft above them, and around them and beneath them was the great abyss with its foaming waters. The three sat on the rock waiting for the dawning of day, when the eagle should fly forth, for the old bird must be shot before they could think of capturing the young one. Rudy sat on the ground, as silent as if he were a piece of the stone on which he crouched; his rifle he held before him ready cocked; his eyes were fixed on the upper cleft beneath which the eagle's nest lay concealed against the rock. And a long time had those three hunters to wait.

Now there was a rushing, whirring sound above them, and a great soaring object darkened the air. Two guns were pointed, as the black form of the eagle arose from the nest. A shot rang sharply out, for a moment the outstretched wings continued to move, and then the bird sank slowly down, and it seemed with its outstretched wings to fill up the chasm, and threatened to bear down the hunters in its fall. Then the eagle sank down into the abyss, breaking off twigs of trees and bushes in its descent.

And now the hunters began operations. Three of the longest ladders were bound together—those would reach high enough; they were reared on end on the last firm foothold on the margin of the abyss; but they did not reach far enough; and higher up, where the nest lay concealed under the shelter of the projecting crag, the rock was as smooth as a wall. After a short council the men determined that two ladders should be tied together and let down from above into the cleft, and that these should be attached to the three that had been fastened together below. With great labour the two ladders were dragged up and the rope made fast above; then the ladders were passed over the margin of the projecting rock, so that they hung dangling above the abyss. Rudy had already taken his place on the lowest step. It was an icy-cold morning; misty clouds were rising from the dark chasm. Rudy sat as a fly sits on a waving wheat-straw which some nest-building bird has deposited on the edge of a factory chimney; only the fly can spread its wings and escape if the wheat-straw gives way, while Rudy had nothing for it, in such a case, but to break his neck. The wind whistled about him, and below in the abyss thundered the waters from the melting glacier, the palace of the Ice Maiden.

Now he imparted a swaying motion to the ladders, just as a spider sways itself to and fro, when, hanging at the end of its thread, it wishes to seize upon an object; and when Rudy for the fourth time touched the top of the ladder, the highest of the three that had been bound together, he seized it and held it firmly. Then he bound the other two ladders with a strong hand to the first three, so that they reached up to the eagle's nest; but they rattled and swayed as if they had loose hinges.

The five long ladders thus bound together, and standing perpendicularly against the rocky wall, looked like a long swaying reed; and now came the most dangerous part of the business. There was climbing to be done as the cat climbs; but Rudy had learned to climb, and it was the Cat who had taught him. He knew nothing of the Spirit of Giddiness who stood treading the air behind him, and stretching out long arms towards him like the feelers of a polypus. Now he stood upon the highest step of the topmost ladder, and perceived that after all it was not high enough to let him look into the nest: he could only reach up into it with his hand. He felt about to test the firmness of the thick plaited branches that formed the lower part of the nest, and when he had secured a thick, steady piece, he swung himself up by it from the ladder, and leaned against the branch, so that his head and shoulders were above the level of the nest. A stifling stench of carrion streamed towards him, for in the nest lay chamois, birds, and lambs, in a putrid state. The Spirit of Giddiness, that had no power over him, blew the poisonous vapour into his face, to make him sick and trouble his senses; and below, in the black yawning gulf, on the rushing waters, sat the Ice Maiden herself, with her long whitish-green hair, and stared at him with cold deathlike eyes.

"Now I shall catch you!" she thought.

In a corner of the nest he saw the young one, which was not yet fledged, sitting large and stately. Rudy fixed his eyes upon it, held himself fast with all the strength of one hand, while with the other he threw the noose over the young eagle. It was caught—caught alive! Its legs were entangled in the tough noose, and Rudy threw the cord and the bird across his shoulder, so that the creature hung some distance beneath him, while he held fast by a rope they had lowered down to assist him, till his feet touched the topmost round of the ladder.

"Hold fast! Don't fancy you're going to fall, and you won't fall!" It was the old maxim, and he followed it; he held fast and climbed, was convinced that he should not fall, and accordingly he did not fall.

And now a whoop resounded, strong and jubilant, and Rudy stood safe and sound on the firm rock with the captured eaglet.

VIII.

What news the Parlour Cat had to tell.

"Here is what you wished for!" said Rudy, as he entered the house of the miller at Bex.

He set down a great basket on the ground, and lifted the cloth that covered it. Two yellow eyes bordered with black stared forth; they seemed to shoot forth sparks, and gleamed burning and savage, as if they would burn and bite all they looked at. The short strong beak was open, ready to snap, and the neck was red and covered with wattles.

"The young eagle!" cried the miller.

Babette screamed aloud and started back, but she could not turn her eyes from Rudy or from the eagle.

"You're not to be frightened off," observed the miller.

"And you always keep your word," answered Rudy. "Every man has his own character."

"But why did you not break your neck?" asked the miller.

"Because I held fast," replied Rudy; "and I do that still. I hold Babette fast!"

"First see that you get her," said the miller; and he laughed. But his laughter was a good sign, and Babette knew it.

"We must have him out of the basket; his staring is enough to drive one mad. But how did you contrive to get at him?"

And Rudy had to relate the adventure, at which the miller opened his eyes wider and wider.

"With your courage and good fortune you may gain a living for three wives," cried the miller at last.

"Thank you!" said Rudy.

"Still, you have not Babette yet," continued the miller; and he tapped the young huntsman playfully on the shoulder.

"Do you know the latest news from the mill?" the Parlour Cat inquired of the Kitchen Cat. "Rudy has brought us the eaglet, and is going to take Babette away in exchange. They have kissed each other, and let the old man see it. That's as good as a betrothal. The old man behaved quite politely; he drew in his claws, and took his nap, and let the two young ones sit together and purr. They've so much to tell each other that they won't have done till Christmas."

And they had not done till Christmas. The wind tossed up the brown leaves; the snow whirled through the valley and over the high mountains; the Ice Maiden sat in her proud castle, which increases in size during the winter; the rocky walls were covered with a coating of ice, and icicles thick as pine trunks and heavy as elephants hung down, where in the summer the mountain stream spread its misty veil; garlands of ice of whimsical forms hung sparkling on the snow-powdered fir trees. The Ice Maiden rode on the rushing wind over the deepest valleys. The snowy covering reached almost down to Bex, and the Ice Maiden came thither also, and saw Rudy sitting in the mill: this winter he sat much more indoors than was his custom — he sat by Babette. The wedding was to be next summer; his ears often buzzed, his friends spoke so much about it. In the mill there was sunshine — the loveliest Alpine rose bloomed there, the cheerful smiling Babette, beautiful as the spring, the spring that makes all the birds sing of summer and of marriage feasts.

"How those two are always sitting together—close together!" said the Parlour Cat. "I've heard enough of their mewing."

IX.

The Ice Maiden.

SPRING had unfolded its fresh green garland on the walnut and chestnut trees extending from the bridge at St. Maurice to the shore of the Lake of Geneva, along the Rhone that rushes along with headlong speed from its source beneath the green glacier, the ice palace where the Ice Maiden dwells, and whence she soars on the sharp wind up to the loftiest snow-field, there to rest upon her snowy couch: there she sat, and gazed with far-seeing glance into the deep valleys, where the men ran busily to and fro, like ants on the stone that glitters in the sun.

"Ye spirit powers, as the Children of the Sun call you," said the Ice Maiden, "ye are but worms. Let a snowball roll from the mountain, and you and your houses and towns are crushed and swept away!"

And higher she lifted her haughty head, and gazed out far and wide with deadly flashing eyes.

But from the valley there arose a rumbling sound. They were blasting the rocks. Human work was going on. Roads and tunnels for railways were being constructed.

"They 're playing like moles!" she said. "They 're digging passages under the earth, and thence come these sounds like the firing of guns. When I remove one of my castles, it sounds louder than the thunder's roar."

Out of the valley rose a smoke which moved forward like a fluttering veil: it was the waving steam plume of the engine, which on the lately opened road dragged the train, the curling snake, each of whose joints is a carriage. Away it shot, swift as an arrow.

"They 're playing at being masters down yonder, the spirit powers," said the Ice Maiden, "but the power of the forces of nature is greater than theirs."

And she laughed and sang till the valley echoed.

"Yonder rolls an avalanche!" said the people.

But the Children of the Sun sang louder still of HUMAN THOUGHT, the powerful agent that places barriers against the sea, and levels mountains, and fills up valleys—of human thought, that is master of the powers of nature. And at this time there marched across the snow-field where the Ice Maiden rules, a company of travellers. The men had bound themselves to one another with ropes, that they might, as it were, form a heavier body here on the slippery surface of ice on the margin of the deep chasms.

"Insects that you are!" cried the Ice Maiden. "*You* the rulers of the powers of nature!"

And she turned away from the company, and looked contemptuously down into the deep valley, where the long train of carriages was rushing along.

"There they sit, those thinkers! there they sit, in the power of the forces of nature! I see them, all and each of them! One of them sits alone, proud as a King, and yonder they sit in a crowd. Half of them are asleep. And when the steam dragon stops, they alight and go their ways. The thoughts go abroad into the world."

And she laughed again.

"There rolls another avalanche!" said the people in the valley.

"It will not reach us," said two who sat behind the steam dragon. "Two hearts that beat like one," as the song has it. These two were Babette and Rudy ; and the miller was with them too.

"I go as baggage!" he said. "I am here as a necessary appendage."

"There those two sit," said the Ice Maiden. "Many a chamois have I crushed, millions of Alpine roses have I broken to pieces, not even sparing the roots. I 'll wipe them out, these thoughts—these spirit-powers."

And she laughed again.

"There rolls another avalanche!" said the people in the valley below.

X.

Babette's Godmother.

At Montreux, the first of the towns which with Clarens, Ferney, and Crin form a garland round the north-eastern portion of the Lake of Geneva, lived Babette's godmother, a highborn English lady, with her daughters and a young male relative. They had only lately arrived, but the miller had already waited upon them to tell them of Babette's betrothal, and the story of Rudy and the eaglet, and of his visit to Interlaken—in short, the whole story. And the visitors were much pleased to hear it, and showed themselves very friendly towards Rudy, Babette, and the miller, who were all three urgently invited to come, and came accordingly. Babette was to see her godmother, and the lady to make acquaintance with Babette.

By the little town of Villeneuve, at the extremity of the Lake of Geneva, lay the steam ship which in its half-hour's trip to Ferney stops just below Montreux. The coast here has been sung by poets ; here, under the walnut trees, by the deep bluish-green lake, sat Byron, and wrote his melodious verses of the prisoner in the gloomy rocky fortress of Chillon. Yonder, where the weeping willows of Clarens are clearly mirrored in the water, Rousseau wandered, dreaming of Heloise. The Rhone rolls onward among the lofty snow-clad mountains of Savoy : here, not far from its mouth, lies in the lake a little island, so small, that seen from the coast it appears like a ship upon the waters. It is a rock which a lady, about a century ago, caused to be walled round with stone and coated with earth, wherein three acacia trees were planted, which now overshadow the whole island.

Babette was quite delighted with this spot, which seemed to her the prettiest point of all their journey, and she declared that they must land there, for it must be charming there. But the steamer glided past, and was moored, according to custom, at Ferney.

The little party wandered from here among the white sunny walls which surround the vineyards of Montreux, where the fig tree casts its shadow over the peasant's huts and laurels and cypresses grow in the gardens. Half-way up the hill was situated the hotel in which the English lady was staying.

The reception was very hearty. The English lady was a very friendly lady, with a round smiling face : in her childhood her head must have been like one of Raphael's angels ; but she had an old angel's head now, surrounded by curls of silvery white. The daughters were tall, slender, good-looking, ladylike girls. The young cousin whom they had brought with them was dressed in white from head to foot. He had yellow hair, and enough of yellow whisker to have been shared among three or four gentlemen. He immediately showed the very greatest attention to Babette.

Richly bound volumes, music-books, and drawings lay strewn about upon the large table; the balcony door stood open, and they could look out upon the beautiful far-spreading lake, which lay so shining and still that the mountains of Savoy, with their towns, forests, and snowy peaks, were most accurately reproduced on its surface.

Rudy, who was generally frank, cheerful, and ready, felt very uncomfortable here, and he moved as if he were walking on peas spread over a smooth surface. How long and wearisome the time seemed to him! He could have fancied himself on a treadmill! And now they even went out to walk together; that was just as slow and wearisome as the rest. Rudy might have taken one step backward to every two he made forward, and yet have kept up with the others. They went down to Chillon, the old gloomy castle on the rocky island, to see the instruments of torture, the deadly dungeons, the rusty chains fastened to the walls, the stone benches on which men condemned to death had sat, the trap-door through which the unhappy wretches were hurled down to be impaled below upon tipped iron stakes in the water. They called it a pleasure to see all this. It was a place of execution that had been lifted by Byron's song into the domain of poetry. Rudy only associated the prison feeling with it. He leaned against one of the great stone window-panes, and looked out into the deep bluish-green water and over at the little island with the three acacias; thither he wished himself transported, to be free from the whole chattering company. But Babette was in unusually good spirits. She declared she had enjoyed herself immensely, and told Rudy she considered the young cousin a complete gentleman.

"A complete booby!" cried Rudy.

And it was the first time he had said anything she did not like. The Englishman had given her a little book in remembrance of Chillon. It was Byron's poem, "The Prisoner of Chillon," translated into French, so that Babette could read it.

"The book may be good," said Rudy, "but I don't like the combed and curled fellow who gave it you."

"He looked to me like a flour-sack without any flour," said the miller; and he laughed at his own joke.

Rudy laughed too, and said that was just his own opinion.

XI.

The Cousin.

A few days after these events, when Rudy went to pay a visit at the mill, he found the young Englishman there, and Babette was just about to offer her visitor some boiled trout, which she certainly must have decorated with parsley with her own hands, so tempting did they look, —a thing that was not at all necessary. What did the Englishman want here? And what business had Babette to treat him and pet him?

Rudy was jealous; and that pleased Babette, for she liked to become acquainted with all the points of his character, the weak as well as the strong.   Love was still only a game to her, and she played with Rudy's whole heart ; yet he was, we must confess, her happiness, her whole life, her constant thought, the best and most precious possession she had on earth ; but, for all that, the darker his glance became, the more did her eyes laugh, and she would have liked to kiss the fair Englishman with the yellow beard, if her doing this would have made Rudy wild and sent him raging away; for that would show how much he loved her. Now, this was not right of Babette; but she was only nineteen years old.   She did not think much, and least of all did she think that her conduct might be misinterpreted by the young Englishman into something very unworthy of the respectable affianced miller's daughter.

The mill stood just where the high road from Bex leads down under the snow-covered mountain height, which in the language of the country is called "Diablerets."   It was not far from a rushing mountain stream, whose waters were whitish-grey, like foaming soapsuds : it was not this stream that worked the mill; a smaller stream drove round the great wheel—one which fell from the rock some way beyond the main river, and whose power and fall were increased by a stone dam, and by a long wooden trough, which carried it over the level of the great stream. This trough was so full that the water poured over its margin; this wooden margin offered a narrow slippery path for those who chose to walk along it, that they might get to the mill by the shortest cut; and to whom, of all people, should the idea of reaching the mill by this road occur, but to the young Englishman !   Dressed in white, like a miller's man, he climbed over at night, guided by the light that shone from Babette's chamber window; but he had not learned how to climb like Rudy, and consequently was near upon falling headlong into the stream below, but he escaped with a pair of wet coat-sleeves and soiled trousers; and thus, wet and bespattered with mud, he came below Babette's window.   Here he climbed into the old elm tree, and began to imitate the voice of the owl, the only bird whose cry he could manage.   Babette heard the noise, and looked out of her window through the thin curtain; but when she saw the white form, and conjectured who it was, her heart beat with fear and with anger also.   She put out the light in a hurry, saw that all the bolts of the windows were well secured, and then let him whoop and tu-whoo to his heart's content.

It would be dreadful if Rudy were in the mill just now !   But Rudy was not in the mill; no—what was worse still, he stood just under the elm tree.   Presently there were loud and angry voices, and there might be a fight there, and even murder.   Babette opened the window in a fright, and called Rudy by name, begging him to go, and declaring that she would not allow him to remain.

"You won't allow me to remain ? " he shouted.   "Then it 's a planned thing!   You expect good friends, better men than I!   For shame, Babette ! "

"You are odious ! " cried Babette.   "I hate you!   Go, go ! "

THE ENGLISHMAN'S INTRUSION.

"I have not deserved this," he said, and went away, his face burning like fire, and his heart burning as fiercely.

Babette threw herself on her bed and wept.

"So dearly as I love you, Rudy! And that you should think evil of me!"

Then she broke out in anger; and that was good for her, for otherwise she would have suffered too much from her grief; and now she could sleep—could sleep the strengthening sleep of health and youth.

XII.

Evil Powers.

RUDY quitted Bex and took the way towards his home; he went up the mountain, into the fresh cool air, where the snow lay on the ground, where the Ice Maiden ruled. The leafy trees stood far below him and looked like field plants; the pines and bushes all looked tiny from here; the Alpine roses grew beside the snow, that lay in long patches like linen lying to bleach. A blue gentian that stood by his path he crushed with a blow of his rifle-stock.

Higher up still two chamois came in view. Rudy's eyes brightened and his thoughts took a new direction; but he was not near enough to be sure of his aim, so he mounted higher, where nothing but scanty grass grew among the blocks of stone. The chamois were straying quietly along on the snow-field. He hastened his steps till the veil of clouds began to encompass him, and suddenly he found himself in front of a steep wall of rock; and now the rain began to pour down.

He felt a burning thirst, his head was hot, his limbs were cold. He took his hunting flask, but it was empty—he had not thought of filling it when he rushed out upon the mountains. He had never been ill in his life, but now he had warnings of such a condition, for he was weary, and had an inclination to lie down, a longing to go to sleep, though the rain was pouring all around. He tried to collect his faculties, but all objects danced and trembled strangely before his eyes. Then suddenly he beheld what he had never seen in that spot before—a new low-browed house, that leaned against the rock. At the door stood a young girl, and she almost appeared to him like the schoolmaster's daughter Annette, whom he had once kissed at the dance; but it was not Annette, though he felt certain he had seen this girl before; perhaps at Grindelwald on that evening when he returned from the marksmen's feast at Interlaken.

"Whence do you come?" he asked.

"I am at home here. I am keeping my flock," was the reply.

"Your flock! Where does it graze? There is nothing here."

"Much you know about what is here," retorted the girl, with a laugh. "Behind us, lower down, is a glorious pasture: my goats graze there. I tend them carefully. Not one of them do I lose, and what is once mine remains mine."

"You are bold," said Rudy.

"And you too," replied the girl.

"If you have any milk in the house, pray give me some to drink; I am insufferably thirsty."

"I've something better than milk," said the girl, "and I will give you that. Yesterday some travellers were here with their guide, who forgot a bottle of wine of a kind you have probably never tasted. They will not come back to take it away, and I do not drink it, therefore you must drink it."

And the girl brought the wine, and poured it into a wooden cup, which she gave to Rudy.

"That *is* good wine," said he. "I've never tasted any so strong or so fiery!"

And his eyes glistened, and a glowing, life-like feeling streamed through him, as if every care, every pressure, had melted into air, and the fresh bubbling human nature stirred within him.

"Why, this must be Annette!" he cried. "Give me a kiss."

"Then give me the beautiful ring that you wear on your finger."

"My betrothal ring?"

"Yes, that very one," said the girl.

And again she poured wine in the cup, and she put it to his lips, and he drank. The joy of life streamed into his blood: the whole world seemed to be his, and why should he mourn? Everything is made for us to enjoy, that it may make us happy. The stream of life is the stream of enjoyment, and to be carried along by it is happiness. He looked at the young girl — it was Annette, and yet not Annette; still less did it seem like the phantom, the goblin as he called it, which had met him at Grindelwald. The girl here on the mountain looked fresh as the white snow, blooming as an Alpine rose, and swift-footed as a kid; but still she looked as much a mortal as Rudy himself. And he looked in her wonderfully clear eyes, only for a moment he looked into them, and — who shall describe it? — in that moment, whether it was the life of the spirit or death that filled him, he was borne upward, or else he sank into the deep and deadly ice cleft, lower and lower. He saw the icy walls gleaming like blue-green glass, fathomless abysses yawned around, and the water dropped tinkling down like shining bells, clear as pearls, glowing with pale blue flames. The Ice Maiden kissed him — a kiss which sent a shudder from neck to brow; a cry of pain escaped from him; he tore himself away, staggered, and—it was night before his eyes; but soon he opened them again. Evil powers had been playing their sport with him.

Vanished was the Alpine girl, vanished the sheltering hut; the water poured down the naked rocky wall, and snow lay all around. Rudy trembled with cold: he was wet to the skin, and his ring was gone—the betrothal ring which Babette had given him. His rifle lay near him in the snow: he took it up and tried to fire it, but it missed. Damp clouds hovered like masses of snow over the abyss, and Giddiness was there, lying in wait for the powerless prey; and below, in the deep abyss, there was a sound as if a block of stone were falling, crushing in its descent everything that tried to arrest its progress.

But Babette sat in the mill and wept. Rudy had not been there for six days — he who was wrong, and who ought to come and beg her pardon. and whom she loved with her whole heart.

XIII.

In the Mill.

"WHAT a strange thing it is with those people!" said the Parlour Cat to the Kitchen Cat. "They're parted now, Babette and Rudy. She's weeping; and he, I suppose, does not think any more about her."

"I don't like that," said the Kitchen Cat.

"Nor do I," observed the Parlour Cat; "but I won't take it to heart. Babette may betroth herself to the red-beard. But he has not been here either since that night when he wanted to climb on the roof."

Evil powers sport with us and in us: Rudy had experienced that, and had thought much of it. What was all that which had happened to him and around him on the summit of the mountain? Were they spirits he had seen, or had he had a feverish vision? Never until now had he suffered from fever or any other illness. But in judging Babette, he had looked into his own heart also. He had traced the wild whirlwind, the hot wind that had raged there. Would he be able to confess to Babette every thought he had had—thoughts that might become actions in the hour of temptation? He had lost her ring, and through this loss she had won him again. Would she be able to confess to him? He felt as if his heart would burst when he thought of her. What a number of recollections arose within him! He saw her, as if she were standing bodily before him, laughing like a wayward child. Many a sweet word she had spoken out of the fulness of her heart now crept into his breast like a sunbeam, and soon there was nothing but sunshine within him when he thought of Babette.

Yes, she would be able to confess to him, and she should do so. Accordingly he went to the mill, and the confession began with a kiss, and ended in the fact that Rudy was declared to be the sinner. His great fault had been that he had doubted Babette's fidelity—it was quite wicked of him. Such distrust, such headlong anger, might bring sorrow upon them both. Yes, certainly they could; and accordingly Babette read him a short lecture, to her own great contentment, and with charming grace. But in one point she agreed with Rudy: the nephew of her godmother was a booby, and she would burn the book he had given her, for she would not keep the slightest thing that reminded her of him.

"That's all past and gone," said the Parlour Cat. "Rudy is here again, and they understand one another, and that's the greatest happiness, they say."

"I heard from the rats last night," observed the Kitchen Cat, "that the greatest happiness was to eat tallow candles and to have plenty of rancid bacon. Now, whom is one to believe, the rats or the lovers?"

"Neither," said the Parlour Cat; "that's always the safest way."

The greatest happiness of Rudy and Babette—the fairest day, as they called it—the wedding day, now approached rapidly.

But the wedding was not to be celebrated at the church at Bex and in the mill. Babette's godmother wished her godchild to be married from her house, and the service was to be read in the beautiful little church at Montreux. The miller insisted upon having his way in this matter. He alone knew what were the English lady's intentions with respect to her godchild, and declared that the lady intended making such a wedding present, that they were bound to show some sense of obligation. The day was fixed. On the evening before it, they were to travel to Villeneuve, so that they might drive over early to Montreux, that the young English ladies might dress the bride.

" I suppose there will be a wedding feast here in the house ? " said the Parlour Cat : " if not, I wouldn't give a mew for the whole affair."

" Of course there will be a feast here," replied the Kitchen Cat. " Ducks and pigeons have been killed, and a whole buck is hanging against the wall. My mouth waters when I think of it. To-morrow the journey will begin."

Yes, to-morrow. And on this evening Rudy and Babette sat for the last time together in the mill as a betrothed pair.

Without, the Alps were glowing, the evening bells sounded, and the Daughters of the Sunbeams sang, " Let that happen which is best."

XIV.

Visions of the Night.

THE sun had gone down and the clouds lowered among the high mountains in the Rhone valley ; the wind blew from the south—a wind from Africa was passing over the lofty Alps a whirlwind that tore the clouds asunder; and when it had passed by, all was still for a moment; the rent clouds hung in fantastic forms among the forest-clad mountains and over the hurrying Rhone; they hung in shapes like that of the sea monsters of the primeval world, like the roaring eagles of the air, like the leaping frogs of the marshes ; they came down towards the rushing stream, sailing upon it, and yet suspended in air. The river carried down with it an uprooted pine tree, and bubbling eddies rushed on in front of the mass; they were Spirits of Giddiness, more than one of them, that whirled along over the foaming stream. The moon lit up the snow on the mountain-tops, the dark woods, and the wonderful white clouds—the nightly visions, the spirits of the powers of nature. The dwellers in the mountains saw them through the window-panes sailing on in troops in front of the Ice Maiden, who came out of her glacier palace, and sat on the frail ship, the uprooted pine tree : she was carrying the glacier water down the river into the open sea.

" The wedding guests are coming ! " she said ; and she sang the news to the air and to the water.

Visions without, visions within. Babette was dreaming a wonderful dream.

It seemed to her as if she were married to Rudy, and had been his wife for many years. He was absent, chamois hunting, but she was sitting at home in her dwelling, and the young Englishman, he with the yellow beard, was sitting by her. His eyes were so eloquent, his words had such magic power, that when he stretched out his hand to her, she was forced to follow him. They went away together from her home. On they went, ever downwards; and it seemed to Babette as though there lay on her heart a weight that grew heavier and heavier, and this weight was a sin against Heaven and a sin against Rudy. And suddenly she stood forsaken, and her dress was torn by the thorns, and her head had turned grey: she looked upwards in her misery, and on the edge of the rock she caught sight of Rudy: she stretched out her arms to him, but did not dare to call or to beseech him to help her; and, indeed, that would have availed her nothing, for soon she saw that it was not he, but only his hunting coat and his hat, hanging up on the alpenstock in the fashion adopted by the hunters to deceive the chamois. And in her hopeless agony Babette moaned out,

"Oh that I had died on my wedding-day, the happiest day of my life! That would have been a mercy, a great happiness! Then all would have happened for the best! the best that could happen to me and to Rudy; for no one knows what the future will bring!"

And in her God-forsaken despair she threw herself into the abyss, and a string seemed to burst, and a thunder-clap resounded through the mountains!

Babette awoke: the dream was past and effaced from her mind, but she knew that she had dreamed something terrible, and that it was about the young Englishman, whom she had not seen, whom she had not even thought of, for months past. Could he be in Montreux? Should she see him at her wedding? A light shade passed over her delicate mouth and her eyebrows contracted to a frown, but soon there was a smile on her lips and beams of gladness shot from her eyes; for, without, the sun was shining brightly, and it was morning, and she was to be married to Rudy.

Rudy was already in the sitting-room when she entered it, and now they started for Villeneuve. They were both supremely happy, and so was the miller likewise. He laughed, and his face beamed with good-humour. A kind father he was, and an honest man.

"Now we are the masters of the house!" said the Parlour Cat.

XV.

Conclusion.

It was not yet evening when the three happy people entered Villeneuve, where they dined. Thereupon the miller sat in the arm-chair, smoked his pipe, and took a short nap. The betrothed pair went arm in arm out of the town: they walked along the road, under the green-clad rocks, beside the deep blue-green lake; the grey walls and heavy towers of gloomy Chillon were mirrored in the clear flood; the little island of the three acacias lay still nearer to them, looking like a nosegay in the lake.

"It must be charming there!" said Babette.

She felt the greatest desire to go there; and this wish might be immediately fulfilled, for by the shore lay a boat, and it was an easy matter to loosen the rope by which it was fastened. No one was to be seen of whom permission could be asked to use the little vessel, and so they borrowed the boat without ceremony, for Rudy was an expert rower.

THE LOVERS ON THE ISLAND.

The oars cut like fins into the yielding water—the water that is so pliant and yet so strong—that has a back to bear burdens and a mouth to devour—that can smile, the very picture of mildness, and yet can terrify and crush. The water glistened in the wake of the boat, which in a few minutes had carried the two over to the island, where they stepped ashore. There was not more room on the spot than two persons would require for a dance.

Rudy danced round it twice or thrice with Babette; then they sat down, hand in hand, upon the bench under the drooping acacias, looked into each other's eyes; and everything glowed in the radiance of the setting sun. The pine woods on the mountains were bathed in a lilac tint, like that of the blooming heather; and where the trees ended and the naked rock was shown, it glowed as if the stone had been transparent; the clouds in the sky were like red fire, and the whole lake lay like a fresh blushing rose leaf. Gradually the shadows crept up the snow-covered mountains of Savoy, painting them blue-black; but the highest summit gleamed like red lava, and seemed to give a picture from the early history of the mountains' formation, when these masses rose glowing from the depths of the earth and had not yet cooled. Rudy and Babette declared they had never yet beheld such a sunset in the Alps. The snow-covered Dent du Midi was tipped with a radiance like that of the full moon when she first rises above the horizon.

"So much beauty! So much happiness!" they both exclaimed.

"This earth has nothing more to give," said Rudy. "An evening like this seems to comprise a whole life! How often have I felt my happiness as I feel it now, and have thought, 'If everything were to end this moment, how happily I should have lived! How glorious is this world!' And then the day would end, and another began, and the new day seemed more beautiful to me than the last! How immeasurably good is God, Babette!"

"I am happy from the very depth of my heart!" she said.

"This earth can offer me nothing more," said Rudy.

And the evening bells began to sound from the mountains of Savoy and from the Swiss hills, and in the west rose the black Jura range, crowned with a wreath of gold.

"May Heaven grant to thee what is happiest and best!" murmured Babette.

"It will," replied Rudy. "To-morrow I shall have it. To-morrow you will be mine entirely. My own sweet wife!"

"The boat!" exclaimed Babette, suddenly.

The little skiff in which they were to return had broken loose and was drifting away from the island.

"I will bring it back," said Rudy.

And he threw aside his coat, pulled off his boots, jumped into the lake, and swam with powerful strokes towards the boat.

Cold and deep was the clear blue-green ice water from the glacier of the mountain. Rudy looked down into its depths—one glance—and it seemed to him that he saw a golden ring, rolling, shining, sparkling: he thought of his ring of betrothal—and the ring grew larger, and widened into a sparkling circle into which the gleaming glacier shone: deep abysses yawned around, and the water-drops rang like the chiming of bells, and glittered with white flames. In a moment he beheld all this that it has taken many words to describe. Young hunters and young girls, men and women who had at different times sunk down into the crevasses among the glaciers, stood here living, with smiling mouths, and deep below them sounded the church bells of sunken cities. The congregation knelt beneath the church roof, the organ pipes were formed of great icicles, and beneath all the Ice Maiden sat on the clear transparent ground. She raised herself towards Rudy and kissed his feet; then a cold death-like numbness poured through his limbs, and an electric shock—ice and fire mingled! There is no difference to be felt between a sudden touch of these two.

"Mine! mine!" sounded around him and within him. "I kissed thee when thou wert little, kissed thee on thy mouth. Now I kiss thy feet, and thou art mine altogether!"

And he disappeared beneath the clear blue water.

All was silent; the chime of the church bells ceased, the last echoes died away with the last ruddy tints of the evening clouds.

"Thou art mine!" sounded from the depths. "Thou art mine!" sounded from the heights, from the regions of the Infinite.

Glorious! from love to love—to fly from earth to heaven!

A chord broke, a sound of mourning was heard; the icy kiss of Death conquered that which was to pass away; the prologue ended that the true drama of life might begin, and discord was blended into harmony.

Do you call that a sorrowful story?

But poor Babette. Her anguish was unspeakable. The boat drifted farther and farther away. No one on the mainland knew that the betrothed pair had gone over to the little island. The sun went down and it became dark. She stood alone, weeping—despairing. A storm came on: flash after flash lit up the Jura mountains, Switzerland and Savoy; flash upon flash on all sides, the rolling thunder-clap mingling with clap for minutes together. The gleams of lightning were sometimes bright as the sun, showing every separate vine as at noonday, and the next moment all would be shrouded in darkness. The flashes were forked, ring-shaped, wavy; they darted into the lake and glittered on every side, while the rolling of the thunder was redoubled by the echo. On the mainland, people drew the boats high up on the shore; everything that had life hastened to get under shelter; and now the rain came pouring down.

"Where can Rudy and Babette be in this tempest?" said the miller.

Babette sat with folded hands, her head on her knees, speechless with grief; she no longer moaned or wept.

"In the deep waters!" was the one thought in her mind. "He is far down in the lakes as if under the glacier."

And then arose in her the remembrance of what Rudy had told concerning the death of his mother and his own rescue; how he had been borne forth, like a corpse, from the depths of the glacier.

"The Ice Maiden has got him again!"

And a flash of lightning glared like sunshine over the white snow. Babette started up. The whole lake was at this moment like a shining glacier; and there stood the Ice Maiden, majestic, with a bluish-white light upon her, and at her feet lay Rudy's corpse.

"Mine!" she said.

And again there was darkness all around, and the crash of falling waters.

"How cruel!" groaned Babette. "Why must he die when the day of our happiness was about to dawn? O Lord, enlighten my understanding! Send Thy light into my heart! I understand not Thy ways. I grope in darkness, amid the behests of Thy power and Thy wisdom!"

And the light for which she prayed was given to her. A gleam of thought, a ray of light, her dream of the past night in its living reality, flashed through her. She remembered the words, the wish she had uttered, concerning what would be "THE BEST" for her and for Rudy.

"Woe is me! Was it the germ of sin within my heart? Was my dream a vision of a future life, whose strings must be snapped asunder that I might be saved? Wretched that I am!"

And she sat there in the dark night, lamenting. Through the thick darkness Rudy's words seemed to sound, the last words he had spoken on earth, "The earth has nothing more to give me!" They had sounded in the fulness of joy; they echoed now through the depths of distress.

And years have flown by since that time. The lake smiles and its shores smile; the grape-vine is covered with swelling branches; steam boats with waving flags glide along; pleasure boats with full sails flit across the mirror of waters like white butterflies; the railway has been opened past Chillon, and leads deep into the valley of the Rhone. At every station strangers alight, with red-bound guide-books in their hands, and they read of the sights they have come to see. They visit Chillon, and in the lake they behold the little island with three acacias, and in the book they read about the betrothed pair who, on an evening of the year 1856, sailed across thither, and of the death of the bridegroom, and how the despairing cries of the bride were not heard on the shore till the next morning.

But the guide-book has nothing to tell concerning the quiet life of Babette in her father's house — not in the mill, for other people live there now, but in the beautiful house near the station, from whose windows she on many an evening looks across over the chestnut trees towards the snowy mountains on which Rudy once wandered; in the evening she marks the Alpine glow—the Children of the Sun recline on the lofty mountains, and renew the song of the wanderer whose cloak the whirlwind once tore away, taking the garment but not the man.

There is a rosy gleam on the snow of the mountains, a rosy gleam in every heart in which dwells the thought, "God lets that happen which is best for us!" But the cause is not always revealed to us, as it was revealed to Babette in her dream.

THE NORTHERN SWANS FLYING FORTH

THE SWAN'S NEST.

BETWEEN the Baltic and the North Sea there lies an old swan's nest, wherein swans are born and have been born that shall never die.

In olden times a flock of swans flew over the Alps to the green plains around Milan, where it was delightful to dwell: this flight of swans men called *the Lombards*.

Another flock, with shining plumage and honest eyes, soared southward to Byzantium; the swans established themselves there close by the Emperor's throne, and spread their wings over him as shields to protect him. They received the name of *Varangians*.

On the coast of France there sounded a cry of fear, for the bloodstained swans that came from the North with fire under their wings; and the people prayed, "Heaven deliver us from the wild *Northmen*."

On the fresh sward of England stood the Danish swan by the open sea shore, with the crown of three kingdoms on his head; and he stretched out his golden sceptre over the land. The heathens on the Pomeranian coast bent the knee, and the Danish swans came with the banner of the Cross and with the drawn sword.

"That was in the very old times," you say.

In later days two mighty swans have been seen to fly from the nest. A light shone far through the air, far over the lands of the earth; the swan, with the strong beating of his wings, scattered the twilight mists, and the starry sky was seen, and it was as if it came nearer to the earth. That was the swan *Tycho Brahé*.

"Yes, then," you say; "but in our own days?"

We have seen swan after swan soar by in glorious flight. One let his pinions glide over the strings of the golden harp, and it resounded through the North : Norway's mountains seemed to rise higher in the sunlight of former days ; there was a rustling among the pine trees and the birches ; the gods of the North, the heroes, and the noble women showed themselves in the dark forest depths.

We have seen a swan beat with his wings upon the marble crag, so that it burst, and the forms of beauty imprisoned in the stone stepped out to the sunny day, and men in the lands round about lifted up their heads to behold these mighty forms.

We have seen a third swan spinning the thread of thought that is fastened from country to country round the world, so that the word may fly with lightning speed from land to land.

And our Lord loves the old swan's nest between the Baltic and the Northern Sea.   And when the mighty birds come soaring through the air to destroy it, even the callow young stand round in a circle on the margin of the nest, and though their breasts may be struck so that their blood flows, they bear it, and strike with their wings and their claws.

Centuries will pass by, swans will fly forth from the nest, men will see them and hear them in the world, before it shall be said in spirit and in truth, " This is the last swan — the last song from the swan's nest."

THE STONE OF THE WISE MEN.

FAR away in the land of India, far away towards the East, at the end of the world, stood the Tree of the Sun, a noble tree, such as we have never seen and shall probably never see.   The crown stretched out several miles around ; it was really an entire wood ; each of its smallest branches formed, in its turn, a whole tree.   Palms, beech trees, pines, plane trees, and various other kinds grew here, which are found scattered in all other parts of the world : they shot out like small branches from the great boughs, and these large boughs with their windings and knots formed, as it were, valleys and hills, clothed with velvety green and covered with flowers.   Everything was like a wide, blooming meadow, or like the most charming garden.   Here the birds from all quarters of the world assembled together—birds from the primeval forests of America, the rose gardens of Damascus, from the deserts of Africa, in which the elephant and the lion boast of being the only rulers.   The Polar birds came flying hither, and of course the stork and the swallow were not absent ; but the birds were not the only living beings : the stag, the squirrel, the antelope, and a hundred other beautiful and light-footed animals were here at home.   The crown of the tree was a wide-spread fragrant garden, and in the midst of it, where the great boughs raised themselves into a green hill, there stood a castle of crystal, with a view towards every quarter of heaven. Each tower was reared in the form of a lily. Through the stem one could ascend, for within it was a winding stair; one could step out upon the leaves as upon balconies; and up in the calyx of the flower itself was the most beautiful, sparkling round hall, above which no other roof rose but the blue firmament with sun and stars.

Just as much splendour, though in another way, appeared below, in the wide halls of the castle. Here, on the walls, the whole world around was reflected. One saw everything that was done, so that there was no necessity of reading any papers, and indeed papers were not obtainable there. Everything was to be seen in living pictures, if one only wished to see it; for too much is still too much even for the wisest man; and this man dwelt here. His name is very difficult—you will not be able to pronounce it, and therefore it may remain unmentioned. He knew everything that a man on earth can know or can get to know; every invention which had already been or which was yet to be made was known to him; but nothing more, for everything in the world has its limits. The wise King Solomon was only half as wise as he, and yet he was very wise, and governed the powers of nature, and held sway over potent spirits: yes, Death itself was obliged to give him every morning a list of those who were to die during the day. But King Solomon himself was obliged to die too; and this thought it was which often in the deepest manner employed the inquirer, the mighty lord in the castle on the Tree of the Sun. He also, however high he might tower above men in wisdom, must die one day. He knew that he and his children also must fade away like the leaves of the forest, and become dust. He saw the human race fade away like the leaves on the tree; saw new men come to fill their places; but the leaves that fell off never sprouted forth again—they fell to dust or were transformed into other parts of plants.

"What happens to man," the wise man asked himself, "when the angel of death touches him? What may death be? The body is dissolved. And the soul? Yes, what is the soul? whither doth it go? To eternal life, says the comforting voice of religion; but what is the transition? where does one live, and how? Above, in heaven, says the pious man, thither we go. Thither?" repeated the wise man, and fixed his eyes upon the moon and the stars; "up yonder?"

But he saw, from the earthly ball, that above and below were alike changing their position, according as one stood here or there on the rolling globe; and even if he mounted as high as the loftiest mountains of earth rear their heads, to the air which we below call clear and transparent—the pure heaven—a black darkness spread abroad like a cloth, and the sun had a coppery glow and sent forth no rays, and our earth lay wrapped in an orange-coloured mist. How narrow were the limits of the corporeal eye, and how little the eye of the soul could see!—how little did even the wisest know of that which is the most important to us all!

In the most secret chamber of the castle lay the greatest treasure of the earth: the Book of Truth. Leaf for leaf, the wise man read it through : every man may read in this book, but only by fragments. To many an eye the characters seem to tremble, so that the words cannot be put together; on certain pages the writing often seems so pale, so blurred, that only a blank leaf appears. The wiser a man becomes, the more he will read ; and the wisest read most. He knew how to unite the sunlight and the moonlight with the light of reason and of hidden powers; and through this stronger light many things came clearly before him from the page. But in the division of the book whose title is " Life after Death " not even one point was to be distinctly seen. That pained him. Should he not be able here upon earth to obtain a light by which everything should become clear to him that stood written in the Book of Truth ?

Like the wise King Solomon, he understood the language of the animals, and could interpret their talk and their songs. But that made him none the wiser. He found out the forces of plants and metals— the forces to be used for the cure of diseases, for delaying death—but none that could destroy death. In all created things that were within his reach he sought the light that should shine upon the certainty of an eternal life ; but he found it not. The Book of Truth lay before him with leaves that appeared blank. Christianity showed itself to him in the Bible with words of promise of an eternal life ; but he wanted to read it in *his* book ; but here he saw nothing written on the subject.

He had five children—four sons, educated as well as the children of the wisest father could be, and a daughter, fair, mild, and clever, but blind ; yet this appeared no deprivation to her—her father and brothers were outward eyes to her, and the vividness of her feelings saw for her.

Never had the sons gone farther from the castle than the branches of the tree extended, nor had the sister strayed from home. They were happy children in the land of childhood—in the beautiful fragrant Tree of the Sun. Like all children, they were very glad when any history was related to them ; and the father told them many things that other children would not have understood ; but these were just as clever as most grown-up people are among us. He explained to them what they saw in the pictures of life on the castle walls—the doings of men and the march of events in all the lands of the earth ; and often the sons expressed the wish that they could be present at all the great deeds and take part in them ; and their father then told them that out in the world it was difficult and toilsome—that the world was not quite what it appeared to them as they looked forth upon it from their beauteous home. He spoke to them of the true, the beautiful, and the good, and told them that these three held together in the world, and that under the pressure they had to endure they became hardened into a precious stone, clearer than the water of the diamond—a jewel whose splendour had value with God, whose brightness outshone everything, and which was the so-called " Stone of the Wise." He told them how men could attain by investigation to the knowledge of the existence of God, and

THE BOOK OF TRUTH.

that through men themselves one could attain to the certainty that such a jewel as the "Stone of the Wise" existed. This narration would have exceeded the perception of other children, but these children understood it, and at length other children, too, will learn to comprehend its meaning.

They questioned their father concerning the true, the beautiful, and the good; and he explained it to them, told them many things, and told them also that God, when He made man out of the dust of the earth, gave five kisses to His work—fiery kisses, heart kisses—which we now call the five senses. Through these the true, the beautiful, and the good is seen, perceived, and understood; through these it is valued, protected, and furthered. Five senses have been given corporeally and mentally, inwardly and outwardly, to body and soul.

The children reflected deeply upon all these things; they meditated upon them by day and by night. Then the eldest of the brothers dreamed a splendid dream. Strangely enough, the second brother had the same dream, and the third, and the fourth brother likewise; all of them dreamed exactly the same thing—namely, that each went out into the world and found the "Stone of the Wise," which gleamed like a beaming light on his forehead when, in the morning dawn, he rode back on his swift horse over the velvety green meadows of his home into the castle of his father; and the jewel threw such a heavenly light and radiance upon the leaves of the book, that everything was illuminated that stood written concerning the life beyond the grave. But the sister dreamed nothing about going out into the wide world: it never entered her mind. Her world was her father's house.

"I shall ride forth into the wide world," said the eldest brother. "I must try what life is like there, and go to and fro among men. I will practise only the good and the true; with these I will protect the beautiful. Much shall change for the better when I am there."

Now his thoughts were bold and great, as our thoughts generally are at home, before we have gone forth into the world and have encountered wind and rain, and thorns and thistles.

In him and in all his brothers the five senses were highly developed, inwardly and outwardly; but each of them had *one* sense which in keenness and development surpassed the other four. In the case of the eldest this pre-eminent sense was Sight. This was to do him especial service. He said he had eyes for all time, eyes for all nations, eyes that could look into the depths of the earth, where the treasures lie hidden, and deep into the hearts of men, as though nothing but a pane of glass were placed before them: he could read more than we can see on the cheek that blushes or grows pale, in the eye that droops or smiles. Stags and antelopes escorted him to the boundary of his home towards the west, and there the wild swans received him and flew north-west. He followed them. And now he had gone far out into the world—far from the land of his father, that extended eastward to the end of the earth.

But how he opened his eyes in astonishment! Many things were here to be seen; and many things appear very different when a man beholds them with his own eyes, or when he merely sees them in a picture, as the son had done in his father's house, however faithful the picture may be. At the outset he nearly lost his eyes in astonishment at all the rubbish and all the masquerading stuff put forward to represent the beautiful; but he did not quite lose them, and soon found full employment for them. He wished to go thoroughly and honestly to work in the understanding of the beautiful, the true, and the good. But how were these represented in the world? He saw that often the garland that belonged to the beautiful was given to the hideous; that the good was often passed by without notice, while mediocrity was applauded when it should have been hissed off. People looked to the dress, and not to the wearer; asked for a name, and not for desert; and went more by reputation than by service. It was the same thing everywhere.

"I see I must attack these things vigorously," he said, and attacked them with vigour accordingly.

But while he was looking for the truth, came the Evil One, the father of lies. Gladly would the fiend have plucked out the eyes of this Seer; but that would have been too direct: the devil works in a more cunning way. He let him see and seek the true and the good; but while the young man was contemplating them, the Evil Spirit blew one mote after another into each of his eyes; and such a proceeding would be hurtful even to the best sight. Then the fiend blew upon the motes, so that they became beams; and the eyes were destroyed, and the Seer stood like a blind man in the wide world, and had no faith in it: he lost his good opinion of it and himself; and when a man gives up the world and himself, all is over with him.

"Over!" said the wild swan, who flew across the sea towards the

THE END OF THE FIRST BROTHER'S SEARCH.

east. "Over!" twittered the swallows, who likewise flew eastward, towards the Tree of the Sun. That was no good news that they carried to the young man's home.

"I fancy the *Seer* must have fared badly," said the second brother; "but the *Hearer* may have better fortune." For this one possessed the sense of hearing in an eminent degree: he could hear the grass grow, so quick was he to hear.

He took a hearty leave of all at home, and rode away, provided with good abilities and good intentions. The swallows escorted him, and he followed the swans; and he stood far from his home in the wide world.

But he experienced the fact that one may have too much of a good thing. His hearing was *too* fine. He not only heard the grass grow, but could hear every man's heart beat, in sorrow and in joy. The whole world was to him like a great clockmaker's workshop, wherein all the

clocks were going " tick, tick ! " and all the turret clocks striking " ding
dong." It was unbearable. For a long time his ears held out, but at
last all the noise and screaming became too much for one man. There
came blackguard boys of sixty years old—for years alone don't make
men—and raised a tumult at which the Hearer might certainly have
laughed, but for the applause which followed, and which echoed through
every house and street, and was audible even in the country high road.
Falsehood thrust itself forward and played the master ; the bells on
the fool's cap jangled and declared they were church bells ; and the
noise became too bad for the Hearer, and he thrust his fingers into his
ears ; but still he could hear false singing and bad sounds, gossip and
idle words, scandal and slander, groaning and moaning without and
within. Heaven help us ! He thrust his fingers deeper and deeper into
his ears, but at last the drums burst. Now he could hear nothing at
all of the good, the true, and the beautiful, for his hearing was to have
been the bridge by which he crossed. He became silent and suspicious,
trusted no one at last, not even himself, and, no longer hoping to find
and bring home the costly jewel, he gave it up, and gave himself up ;
and that was the worst of all. The birds who winged their flight towards the east brought tidings of this, till the news reached the castle
in the Tree of the Sun.

" *I* will try now ! " said the third brother. " I have a sharp *nose* ! "
Now that was not said in very good taste ; but it was his way, and one
must take him as he was. He had a happy temper, and was a poet, a
real poet: he could sing many things that he could not say, and many
things struck him far earlier than they occurred to others. " I can
smell fire ! " he said ; and he attributed to the sense of smelling, which
he possessed in a very high degree, a great power in the region of the
beautiful.
" Every fragrant spot in the realm of the beautiful has its frequenters,"
he said. " One man feels at home in the atmosphere of the tavern,
among the flaring tallow candles, where the smell of spirits mingles with
the fumes of bad tobacco. Another prefers sitting among the overpowering scent of jessamine, or scenting himself with strong clove oil. This
man seeks out the fresh sea breeze, while that one climbs to the highest
mountain-top and looks down upon the busy little life beneath."
Thus he spake. It seemed to him as if he had already been out in
the world, as if he had already associated with men and known them.
But this experience arose from within himself : it was the poet within
him, the gift of Heaven, and bestowed on him in his cradle.
He bade farewell to his paternal roof in the Tree of the Sun, and
departed on foot through the pleasant scenery of home. Arrived at its
confines, he mounted on the back of an ostrich, which runs faster than
a horse ; and afterwards, when he fell in with the wild swans, he swung
himself on the strongest of them, for he loved change ; and away he
flew over the sea to distant lands with great forests, deep lakes, mighty
mountains, and proud cities ; and wherever he came it seemed as if sun-

THE DEPARTURE OF THE THIRD BROTHER.

shine travelled with him across the fields, for every flower, every bush, every tree exhaled a new fragrance, in the consciousness that a friend and protector was in the neighbourhood, who understood them and knew their value. The crippled rose bush reared up its twigs, unfolded its leaves, and bore the most beautiful roses; every one could see it, and even the black damp Wood Snail noticed its beauty.

"I will give my seal to the flower," said the Snail; "I have spit at it, and I can do no more for it."

"Thus it always fares with the beautiful in this world!" said the poet.

And he sang a song concerning it, sang it in his own way; but nobody listened. Then he gave the drummer twopence and a peacock's feather, and set the song for the drum, and had it drummed in all the streets of the town; and the people heard it, and said, "That's a well-constructed song." Then the poet sang several songs of the beautiful, the true, and the good. His songs were listened to in the tavern, where the tallow candles smoked, in the fresh meadow, in the forest, and on the high seas. It appeared as if this brother was to have better fortune than the two others. But the Evil Spirit was angry at this, and accordingly he set to work with incense powder and incense smoke, which he can prepare so artfully as to confuse an angel, and how much more therefore a poor poet! The Evil One knows how to take that kind of people! He surrounded the poet so completely with incense, that the man lost his head, and forgot his mission and his home, and at last himself—and ended in smoke.

But when the little birds heard of this they mourned, and for three days they sang not one song. The black Wood Snail became blacker still, not for grief, but for envy.

"They should have strewed incense for me," she said, "for it was I who gave him his idea of the most famous of his songs, the drum song of 'The Way of the World;' it was I who spat at the rose! I can bring witness to the fact."

But no tidings of all this penetrated to the poet's home in India, for all the birds were silent for three days; and when the time of mourning was over, their grief had been so deep that they had forgotten for whom they wept. That's the usual way!

"Now I shall have to go out into the world, to disappear like the rest," said the fourth brother.

He had just as good a wit as the third, but he was no poet, though he could be witty. Those two had filled the castle with cheerfulness, and now the last cheerfulness was going away. Sight and hearing have always been looked upon as the two chief senses of men, and as the two that it is most desirable to sharpen; the other senses are looked upon as of less consequence. But that was not the opinion of this son, as he had especially cultivated his *taste* in every respect, and taste is very powerful. It holds sway over what goes into the mouth, and also over what penetrates into the mind; and consequently this brother tasted everything that was stored up in bottles and pots, saying that this was the rough work of his office. Every man was to him a vessel in which something was seething, every country an enormous kitchen, a kitchen of the mind.

"That is no delicacy," he said; and he wanted to go out and try what was delicate. "Perhaps fortune may be more favourable to me than it was to my brothers," he said. "I shall start on my travels. But what conveyance shall I choose? Are air balloons invented yet?" he asked his father, who knew of all inventions that had been made or that were to be made. But air balloons had not yet been invented, nor steam ships, nor railways. "Good: then I shall choose an air balloon," he said; "my father knows how they are made and guided. Nobody has invented them yet, and consequently the people will believe that it is an aërial phantom. When I have used the balloon I will burn it, and for this purpose you must give me a few pieces of the invention that will be made next—I mean chemical matches."

And he obtained what he wanted, and flew away. The birds accompanied him farther than they had flown with the other brothers. They were curious to know what would be the result of the flight, and more of them came sweeping up : they thought he was some new bird ; and he soon had a goodly following. The air became black with birds, they came on like a cloud—like the cloud of locusts over the land of Egypt.

Now he was out in the wide world.

The air balloon descended over one of the greatest cities, and the aëronaut took up his station on the highest point, on the church steeple. The balloon rose again, which it ought not to have done : where it went to is not known, but that was not a matter of consequence, for it was not yet invented. Then he sat on the church steeple. The birds no longer hovered around him, they had got tired of him, and he was tired of them.

All the chimneys in the town were smoking merrily.

"Those are altars erected to thy honour !" said the Wind, who wished to say something agreeable to him.

He sat boldly up there, and looked down upon the people in the street. There was one stepping along, proud of his purse, another of the key he carried at his girdle, though he had nothing to unlock ; one proud of his moth-eaten coat, another of his wasted body.

"Vanity ! I must hasten downward, dip my finger in the pot, and taste !" he said. "But for awhile I will still sit here, for the wind blows so pleasantly against my back. I 'll sit here as long as the wind blows. I 'll enjoy a slight rest. ' It is good to sleep long in the morning, when one has much to do,' says the lazy man. I 'll stop here as long as this wind blows, for it pleases me."

And there he sat, but he was sitting upon the weathercock of the steeple, which kept turning round and round with him, so that he was under the false impression that the same wind still blew ; so he might stay up there a goodly while.

But in India, in the castle in the Tree of the Sun, it was solitary and still, since the brothers had gone away one after the other.

"It goes not well with them," said the father ; "they will never bring the gleaming jewel home ; it is not made for me : they are gone, they are dead !"

And he bent down over the Book of Truth, and gazed at the page on which he should read of life after death ; but for him nothing was to be seen or learned upon it.

The blind daughter was his consolation and joy ; she attached herself with sincere affection to him, and for the sake of his peace and joy she wished the costly jewel might be found and brought home. With kindly longing she thought of her brothers. Where were they ? Where did they live ? She wished sincerely that she might dream of them, but it was strange, not even in dreams could she approach them. But at length, one night she dreamed that the voices of her brothers sounded across to her, calling to her from the wide world, and she could not

refrain, but went far far out, and yet it seemed in her dream that she
was still in her father's house. She did not meet her brothers, but she
felt, as it were, a fire burning in her hand, but it did not hurt her, for
it was the jewel she was bringing to her father.   When she awoke, she
thought for a moment that she still held the stone, but it was the knob
of her distaff that she was grasping.   During the long nights she had
spun incessantly, and round the distaff was turned a thread, finer than
the finest web of the spider; human eyes were unable to distinguish
the separate threads. She had wetted them with her tears, and the
twist was strong as a cable. She rose, and her resolution was taken:
the dream must be made a reality. It was night, and her father slept.
She pressed a kiss upon his hand, and then took her distaff, and fastened
the end of the thread to her father's house. But for this, blind as she
was, she would never have found her way home ; to the thread she must
hold fast, and trust not to herself or to others.   From the Tree of the
Sun she broke four leaves ; these she would confide to wind and weather,
that they might fly to her brothers as a letter and a greeting, in case
she did not meet them in the wide world. How would she fare out
yonder, she, the poor blind child ?   But she had the invisible thread to
which she could hold fast. She possessed a gift which all the others
lacked. This was *thoroughness ;* and in virtue of this it seemed as if she
could see to the tips of her fingers and hear down into her very heart.

And quietly she went forth into the noisy, whirling, wonderful world,
and wherever she went the sky grew bright—she felt the warm ray—the
rainbow spread itself out from the dark world through the blue air.
She heard the song of the birds, and smelt the scent of orange groves
and apple orchards so strongly that she seemed to taste it. Soft tones
and charming songs reached her ear, but also howling and roaring, and
thoughts and opinions sounded in strange contradiction to each other.
Into the innermost depths of her heart penetrated the echoes of human
thoughts and feelings. One chorus sounded darkly—

> "The life of earth is a shadow vain,
> A night created for sorrow ! "

but then came another strain—

> "The life of earth is the scent of the rose,
> With its sunshine and its pleasure."

And if one strophe sounded painfully—

> "Each mortal thinks of himself alone,
> This truth has been shown, how often!"

on the other side the answer pealed forth—

> "A mighty stream of warmest love
> All through the world shall bear us."

She heard, indeed, the words—

> "In the little petty whirl here below,
> Each thing shows mean and paltry;"

THE BLIND GIRL'S MESSENGERS.

but then came also the comfort—

"Many things great and good are achieved,
That the ear of man heareth never."

And if sometimes the mocking strain sounded around her—

"Join in the common cry; with a jest
Destroy the good gifts of the Giver,"

in the blind girl's heart a stronger voice repeated—

"To trust in thyself and in God is best;
His will be done for ever."

And whenever she entered the circle of human kind, and appeared
among young or old, the knowledge of the true, the good, and the beautiful beamed into their hearts.   Whether she entered the study of the
artist, or the festive decorated hall, or the crowded factory, with its
whirring wheels, it seemed as though a sunbeam were stealing in—as if

the sweet string sounded, the flower exhaled its perfume, and a living dew-drop fell upon the exhausted blood.

But the Evil Spirit could not see this and be content. He has more cunning than ten thousand men, and he found out a way to compass his end. He betook himself to the marsh, collected little bubbles of the stagnant water, and passed over them a sevenfold echo of lying words to give them strength. Then he pounded up paid-for heroic poems and lying epitaphs, as many as he could get, boiled them in tears that envy had shed, put upon them rouge he had scraped from faded cheeks, and of these he composed a maiden, with the aspect and gait of the blessed blind girl, the angel of thoroughness; and then the Evil One's plot was in full progress. The world knew not which of the two was the true one; and, indeed, how should the world know?

> "To trust in thyself and in God is best;
> His good will be done for ever,"

sung the blind girl, in full faith. She intrusted the four green leaves from the Tree of the Sun to the winds, as a letter and a greeting to her brothers, and had full confidence that they would reach their destination, and that the jewel would be found which outshines all the glories of the world. From the forehead of humanity it would gleam even to the castle of her father.

"Even to my father's house," she repeated. "Yes, the place of the jewel is on earth, and I shall bring more than the promise of it with me. I feel its glow, it swells more and more in my closed hand. Every grain of truth, were it never so fine, which the sharp wind carried up and whirled towards me, I took up and treasured; I let it be penetrated by the fragrance of the beautiful, of which there is so much in the world, even for the blind. I took the sound of the beating heart engaged in what is good, and added it to the first. All that I bring is but dust, but still it is the dust of the jewel we seek, and in plenty. I have my whole hand full of it."

And she stretched forth her hand towards her father. She was soon at home—she had travelled thither in the flight of thoughts, never having quitted her hold of the invisible thread from the paternal home.

The evil powers rushed with hurricane fury over the Tree of the Sun, pressed with a wind-blast against the open doors, and into the sanctuary where lay the Book of Truth.

"It will be blown away by the wind!" said the father, and he seized the hand she had opened.

"No," she replied, with quiet confidence, "it cannot be blown away; I feel the beam warming my very soul."

And the father became aware of a glancing flame, there where the shining dust poured out of her hand over the Book of Truth, that was to tell of the certainty of an everlasting life; and on it stood one shining word—one only word—"BELIEVE."

And with the father and daughter were again the four brothers. When the green leaf fell upon the bosom of each, a longing for home had seized them and led them back. They had arrived. The birds of passage, and the stag, the antelope, and all the creatures of the forest followed them, for all wished to have a part in their joy.

We have often seen, where a sunbeam bursts through a crack in the door into the dusty room, how a whirling column of dust seems circling round; but this was not poor and insignificant like common dust, for even the rainbow is dead in colour compared with the beauty which showed itself. Thus, from the leaf of the book with the beaming word "*Believe*," arose every grain of truth, decked with the charms of *the beautiful* and *the good*, burning brighter than the mighty pillar of flame that led Moses and the children of Israel through the desert; and from the word "*Believe*" the bridge of *Hope* arose, spanning the distance, even to the immeasurable love in the realms of the Infinite.

THE PSYCHE.

In the fresh morning dawn, in the rosy air gleams a great Star, the brightest Star of the morning. His rays tremble on the white wall, as if he wished to write down on it what he can tell, what he has seen there and elsewhere during thousands of years in our rolling world. Let us hear one of his stories.

"A short time ago"—the Star's "short time ago" is called among men "centuries ago"—"my rays followed a young artist. It was in the city of the Popes, in the world-city Rome. Much has been changed there in the course of time, but the changes have not come so quickly as the change from youth to old age. Then already the palace of the Cæsars was a ruin, as it is now; fig trees and laurels grew among the fallen marble columns, and in the desolate bathing-halls, where the gilding still clings to the wall; the Coliseum was a gigantic ruin; the church bells sounded, the incense sent up its fragrant cloud, and through the streets marched processions with flaming tapers and glowing canopies. Holy Church was there, and art was held as a high and holy thing. In Rome lived the greatest painter in the world, Raphael; there also dwelt the first of sculptors, Michael Angelo. Even the Pope paid homage to these two, and honoured them with a visit : art was recognized and honoured, and was rewarded also. But, for all that, everything great and splendid was not seen and known.

"In a narrow lane stood an old house. Once it had been a temple; a young sculptor now dwelt there. He was young and quite unknown. He certainly had friends, young artists, like himself, young in spirit, young in hopes and thoughts; they told him he was rich in talent, and an artist, but that he was foolish for having no faith in his own power; for he always broke what he had fashioned out of clay, and never completed anything; and a work must be completed if it is to be seen and to bring money.

"'You are a dreamer,' they went on to say to him, 'and that's your misfortune. But the reason of this is, that you have never lived, you have never tasted life, you have never enjoyed it in great wholesome draughts, as it ought to be enjoyed. In youth one must mingle one's own personality with life, that they may become one. Look at the great master Raphael, whom the Pope honours and the world admires: he's no despiser of wine and bread.'

"'And he even appreciates the baker's daughter, the pretty *Fornarina*,' added Angelo, one of the merriest of the young friends.

"Yes, they said a good many things of the kind, according to their age and their reason. They wanted to draw the young artist out with them into the merry wild life, the mad life as it might also be called; and at certain times he felt an inclination for it. He had warm blood, a strong imagination, and could take part in the merry chat, and laugh aloud with the rest; but what they called 'Raphael's merry life' disappeared before him like a vapour when he saw the divine radiance that beamed forth from the pictures of the great master; and when he stood in the Vatican, before the forms of beauty which the masters had hewn out of marble thousands of years since, his breast swelled, and he felt within himself something high, something holy, something elevating, great, and good, and he wished that he could produce similar forms from the blocks of marble. He wished to make a picture of that which was within him, stirring upward from his heart to the realms of the infinite; but how, and in what form? The soft clay was fashioned under his fingers into forms of beauty, but the next day he broke what he had fashioned, according to his wont.

"One day he walked past one of those rich palaces of which Rome has many to show. He stopped before the great open portal, and beheld a garden surrounded by cloistered walks. The garden bloomed with a goodly show of the fairest roses. Great white lilies with green juicy leaves shot upward from the marble basin in which the clear water was splashing; and a form glided past, the daughter of the princely house, graceful, delicate, and wonderfully fair. Such a form of female loveliness he had never before beheld—yet, stay: he had seen it, painted by Raphael, painted as a Psyche, in one of the Roman palaces. Yes, there it had been painted; but here it passed by him in living reality.

"The remembrance lived in his thoughts, in his heart. He went home to his humble room, and modelled a Psyche of clay. It was the rich young Roman girl, the noble maiden; and for the first time he looked at his work with satisfaction. It had a meaning for him, for it was *she*. And the friends who saw his work shouted aloud for joy; they declared that this work was a manifestation of his artistic power, of which they had long been aware, and that now the world should be made aware of it too.

"The clay figure was lifelike and beautiful, but it had not the whiteness or the durability of marble. So they declared that the Psyche must henceforth live in marble. He already possessed a costly block of that stone. It had been lying for years, the property of his parents, in the courtyard. Fragments of glass, climbing weeds, and remains of

THE ROMAN GARDEN.

artichokes had gathered about it and sullied its purity; but under the surface the block was as white as the mountain snow; and from this block the Psyche was to arise."

Now, it happened one morning—the bright Star tells nothing about this, but we know it occurred—that a noble Roman company came into the narrow lane. The carriage stopped at the top of the lane, and the company proceeded on foot towards the house, to inspect the young sculptor's work, for they had heard him spoken of by chance. And who were these distinguished guests? Poor young man! or fortunate young man he might be called. The noble young lady stood in the room and smiled radiantly when her father said to her, "It is your living image." That smile could not be copied, any more than the look could be reproduced, the wonderful look which she cast upon the young artist. It was a fiery look, that seemed at once to elevate and to crush him.

"The Psyche must be executed in marble," said the wealthy patrician. And those were words of life for the dead clay and the heavy block of marble, and words of life likewise for the deeply-moved artist. "When the work is finished I will purchase it," continued the rich noble.

A new era seemed to have arisen in the poor studio. Life and cheerfulness gleamed there, and busy industry plied its work. The beaming Morning Star beheld how the work progressed. The clay itself seemed inspired since *she* had been there, and moulded itself, in heightened beauty, to a likeness of the well-known features.

"Now I know what life is," cried the artist rejoicingly; "it is Love! It is the lofty abandonment of self for the dawning of the beautiful in the soul! What my friends call life and enjoyment is a passing shadow; it is like bubbles among seething dregs, not the pure heavenly wine that consecrates us to life."

The marble block was reared in its place. The chisel struck great fragments from it; the measurements were taken, points and lines were made, the mechanical part was executed, till gradually the stone assumed a human female form, a shape of beauty, and became converted into the Psyche, fair and glorious—a divine being in human shape. The heavy stone appeared as a gliding, dancing, airy Psyche, with the heavenly innocent smile—the smile that had mirrored itself in the soul of the young artist.

The Star of the roseate dawn beheld and understood what was stirring within the young man, and could read the meaning of the changing colour of his cheek, of the light that flashed from his eye, as he stood busily working, reproducing what had been put into his soul from above.

"Thou art a master like those masters among the ancient Greeks," exclaimed his delighted friends: "soon shall the whole world admire thy Psyche."

"*My* Psyche!" he repeated. "Yes, mine. She must be mine. I, too, am an artist, like those great men who are gone. Providence has granted me the boon, and has made me the equal of that lady of noble birth."

And he knelt down and breathed a prayer of thankfulness to Heaven, and then he forgot Heaven for her sake—for the sake of her picture in stone—for the Psyche which stood there as if formed of snow, blushing in the morning dawn.

He was to see her in reality, the living graceful Psyche, whose words sounded like music in his ears. He could now carry the news into the rich palace that the marble Psyche was finished. He betook himself thither, strode through the open courtyard where the waters ran splashing from the dolphin's jaws into the marble basins, where the snowy lilies and the fresh roses bloomed in abundance. He stepped into the great lofty hall, whose walls and ceilings shone with gilding and bright colours and heraldic devices. Gaily dressed serving-men, adorned with trappings like sleigh horses, walked to and fro, and some reclined at their ease upon the carved oak seats, as if they were the masters of the house.

He told them what had brought him to the palace, and was conducted up the shining marble staircase, covered with soft carpets and adorned with many a statue. Then he went on through richly furnished chambers, over mosaic floors, amid gorgeous pictures. All this pomp and luxury seemed to weary him; but soon he felt relieved, for the princely old master of the house received him most graciously, almost heartily; and when he took his leave he was requested to step into the Signora's apartment, for she, too, wished to see him. The servants led him through more luxurious halls and chambers into her room, where she appeared the chief and leading ornament.

She spoke to him. No hymn of supplication, no holy chant could melt his soul like the sound of her voice. He took her hand and lifted it to his lips : no rose was softer, but a fire thrilled through him from this rose—a feeling of power came upon him, and words poured from his tongue—he knew not what he said. Does the crater of the volcano know that glowing lava is pouring from it ? He confessed what he felt for her. She stood before him astonished, offended, proud, with contempt in her face, an expression of disgust, as if she had suddenly touched a cold unclean reptile ; her cheeks reddened, her lips grew white, and her eyes flashed fire, though they were dark as the blackness of night.

" Madman !" she cried, " away ! begone !"

And she turned her back upon him. Her beautiful face wore an expression like that of the stony countenance with the snaky locks.

Like a stricken, fainting man, he tottered down the staircase and out into the street. Like a man walking in his sleep he found his way back to his dwelling. Then he woke up to madness and agony, and seized his hammer, swung it high in the air, and rushed forward to shatter the beautiful marble image. But, in his pain, he had not noticed that his friend Angelo stood beside him ; and Angelo held back his arm with a strong grasp, crying,

" Are you mad ? What are you about ?"

They struggled together. Angelo was the stronger; and, with a deep sigh of exhaustion, the young artist threw himself into a chair.

"What has happened ?" asked Angelo. "Command yourself. Speak!"

But what could he say ? How could he explain ? And as Angelo could make no sense of his friend's incoherent words, he forbore to question him further, and merely said,

" Your blood grows thick from your eternal dreaming. Be a man, as all others are, and don't go on living in ideals, for that is what drives men crazy. A jovial feast will make you sleep quietly and happily. Believe me, the time will come when you will be old, and your sinews will shrink, and then, on some fine sunshiny day, when everything is laughing and rejoicing, you will lie there a faded plant, that will grow no more. I do not live in dreams, but in reality. Come with me: be a man !"

And he drew the artist away with him. At this moment he was able to do so, for a fire ran in the blood of the young sculptor; a change had taken place in his soul; he felt a longing to tear himself away from the

old, the accustomed—to forget, if possible, his own individuality; and
therefore it was that he followed Angelo.

In an out-of-the-way suburb of Rome lay a tavern much visited by
artists. It was built on the ruins of some ancient baths. The great
yellow citrons hung down among the dark shining leaves and covered
a part of the old reddish-yellow walls. The tavern consisted of a vaulted
chamber, almost like a cavern, in the ruins. A lamp burned there before the picture of the Madonna. A great fire gleamed on the hearth,
and roasting and boiling was going on there; without, under the citron
trees and laurels, stood a few covered tables.

The two artists were received by their friends with shouts of welcome. Little was eaten, but much was drunk, and the spirits of the
company rose. Songs were sung and ditties were played on the guitar;
presently the *Saltarello* sounded, and the merry dance began. Two
young Roman girls, who sat as models to the artists, took part in the
dance and in the festivity. Two charming Bacchantes were they; certainly not Psyches—not delicate beautiful roses, but fresh, hearty, glowing carnations.

How hot it was on that day! Even after sun-down it was hot: there
was fire in the blood, fire in every glance, fire everywhere. The air
gleamed with gold and roses, and life seemed like gold and roses.

"At last you have joined us, for once," said his friends. "Now let
yourself be carried by the waves within and around you."

"Never yet have I felt so well, so merry!" cried the young artist.
"You are right, you are all of you right. I was a fool, a dreamer—
man belongs to reality, and not to fancy."

With song and with sounding guitars the young people returned that
evening from the tavern, through the narrow streets; the two glowing
carnations, daughters of the Campagna, went with them.

In Angelo's room, among a litter of coloured sketches (studies) and
glowing pictures, the voices sounded mellower, but not less merrily.
On the ground lay many a sketch that resembled the daughters of the
Campagna, in their fresh hearty comeliness, but the two originals were
far handsomer than their portraits. All the burners of the six-armed
lamp flared and flamed; and the *human* flamed up from within, and
appeared in the glare as if it were divine.

"Apollo! Jupiter! I feel myself raised to your heaven, to your glory!
I feel as if the blossom of life were unfolding itself in my veins at this
moment!"

Yes, the blossom unfolded itself, and then burst and fell, and an evil
vapour arose from it, blinding the sight, leading astray the fancy—the
firework of the senses went out, and it became dark.

He was again in his own room · there he sat down on his bed and
collected his thoughts.

"Fie on thee!" these were the words that sounded out of his mouth
from the depths of his heart. "Wretched man, go, begone!" And a
deep painful sigh burst from his bosom.

"Away! begone!" These, her words, the words of the living Psyche,

THE SCULPTOR AMONG HIS FRIENDS.

echoed through his heart, escaped from his lips. He buried his head in
the pillows, his thoughts grew confused, and he fell asleep.

In the morning dawn he started up, and collected his thoughts anew.
What had happened? Had all the past been a dream? The visit to *her*,
the feast at the tavern, the evening with the purple carnations of the Campagna? No, it was all real—a reality he had never before experienced.

In the purple air gleamed the bright Star, and its beams fell upon
him and upon the marble Psyche. He trembled as he looked at that
picture of immortality, and his glance seemed impure to him. He threw
the cloth over the statue, and then touched it once more to unveil the
form—but he was not able to look again at his own work.

Gloomy, quiet, absorbed in his own thoughts, he sat there through the
long day; he heard nothing of what was going on around him, and no
man guessed what was passing in this human soul.

And days and weeks went by, but the nights passed more slowly
than the days. The flashing Star beheld him one morning as he rose,
pale and trembling with fever, from his sad couch; then he stepped
towards the statue, threw back the covering, took one long sorrowful
gaze at his work, and then, almost sinking beneath the burden, he

dragged the statue out into the garden. In that place was an old dry well, now nothing but a hole: into this he cast the Psyche, threw earth in above her, and covered up the spot with twigs and nettles.

"Away! begone!" Such was the short epitaph he spoke.

The Star beheld all this from the pink morning sky, and its beam trembled upon two great tears upon the pale feverish cheeks of the young man; and soon it was said that he was sick unto death, and he lay stretched upon a bed of pain.

The convent Brother Ignatius visited him as a physician and a friend, and brought him words of comfort, of religion, and spoke to him of the peace and happiness of the Church, of the sinfulness of man, of rest and mercy to be found in heaven.

And the words fell like warm sunbeams upon a teeming soil. The soil smoked and sent up clouds of mist, fantastic pictures, pictures in which there was reality; and from these floating islands he looked across at human life. He found it vanity and delusion—and vanity and delusion it had been to him. They told him that art was a sorcerer, betraying us to vanity and to earthly lusts; that we are false to ourselves, unfaithful to our friends, unfaithful towards Heaven; and that the serpent was always repeating within us, "Eat, and thou shalt become as God."

And it appeared to him as if now, for the first time, he knew himself, and had found the way that leads to truth and to peace. In the Church was the light and the brightness of God—in the monk's cell he should find the rest through which the tree of human life might grow on into eternity.

Brother Ignatius strengthened his longings, and the determination became firm within him. A child of the world became a servant of the Church—the young artist renounced the world, and retired into the cloister.

The brothers came forward affectionately to welcome him, and his inauguration was as a Sunday feast. Heaven seemed to him to dwell in the sunshine of the church, and to beam upon him from the holy pictures and from the cross. And when, in the evening, at the sunset hour, he stood in his little cell, and, opening the window, looked out upon old Rome, upon the desolated temples, and the great dead Coliseum—when he saw all this in its spring garb, when the acacias bloomed, and the ivy was fresh, and roses burst forth everywhere, and the citron and orange were in the height of their beauty, and the palm trees waved their branches — then he felt a deeper emotion than had ever yet thrilled through him. The quiet open Campagna spread itself forth towards the blue snow-covered mountains, which seemed to be painted in the air; all the outlines melting into each other, breathing peace and beauty, floating, dreaming—and all appearing like a dream!

Yes, this world was a dream, and the dream lasts for hours, and may return for hours; but convent life is a life of years—long years, and many years.

From within comes much that renders men impure. He felt the

truth of this. What flames arose up in him at times! What a source of evil, of that which he would not, welled up continually! He mortified his body, but the evil came from within.

One day, after the lapse of many years, he met Angelo, who recognized him.

"Man!" exclaimed Angelo. "Yes, it is thou! Art thou happy now? Thou hast sinned against God, and cast away His boon from thee—hast neglected thy mission in this world! Read the parable of the intrusted talent! The MASTER, who spoke that parable, spoke truth! What hast thou gained? what hast thou found? Dost thou not fashion for thyself a religion and a dreamy life after thine own idea, as almost all do? Suppose all this is a dream, a fair delusion!"

THE PENITENT.

"Get thee away from me, Satan!" said the monk; and he quitted Angelo.

"There is a devil, a personal devil! This day I have seen him!" said the monk to himself. "Once I extended a finger to him, and he took my whole hand. But now," he sighed, "the evil is within me, and it is in yonder man; but it does not bow him down: he goes abroad with head erect, and enjoys his comfort; and I grasped at comfort in the consolations of religion. If it were nothing but a consolation? Supposing everything here were, like the world I have quitted, only a beautiful fancy, a delusion, like the beauty of the evening clouds, like the misty blue of the distant hills!—when you approach them, they are very different! O eternity! Thou actest like the great calm ocean, that beckons us, and fills us with expectation—and when we embark upon thee, we sink, disappear, and cease to be. Delusion! away with it' begone!"

And tearless, but sunk in bitter reflection, he sat upon his hard couch, and then knelt down—before whom ? Before the stone cross fastened to the wall ?—No, it was only habit that made him take this position.

The more deeply he looked into his own heart the blacker did the darkness seem. " Nothing within, nothing without—this life squandered and cast away ! " And this thought rolled and grew like a snowball, until it seemed to crush him.

" I can confide my griefs to none. I may speak to none of the gnawing worm within. My secret is my prisoner; if I let the captive escape, I shall be his ! "

And the godlike power that dwelt within him suffered and strove.

" O Lord, my Lord ! " he cried in his despair, " be merciful, and grant me faith. I threw away the gift thou hadst vouchsafed to me, I left my mission unfulfilled. I lacked strength, and strength thou didst not give me. Immortality—the Psyche in my breast—away with it !—it shall be buried like that Psyche, the best gleam of my life ; never will it arise out of its grave ! "

The Star glowed in the roseate air, the Star that shall surely be extinguished and pass away while the soul still lives on ; its trembling beam fell upon the white wall, but it wrote nothing there upon being made perfect in God, nothing of the hope of mercy, of the reliance on the divine love that thrills through the heart of the believer.

" The Psyche within can never die. Shall it live in consciousness ? Can the incomprehensible happen ? Yes, yes. My being is incomprehensible. Thou art unfathomable, O Lord. Thy whole world is incomprehensible—a wonder-work of power, of glory, and of love."

His eyes gleamed, and then closed in death. The tolling of the church bell was the last sound that echoed above him, above the dead man ; and they buried him, covering him with earth that had been brought from Jerusalem, and in which was mingled the dust of many of the pious dead.

When years had gone by his skeleton was dug up, as the skeletons of the monks who had died before him had been: it was clad in a brown frock, a rosary was put into the bony hand, and the form was placed among the ranks of other skeletons in the cloisters of the convent. And the sun shone without, while within the censers were waved and the Mass was celebrated.

And years rolled by.

The bones fell asunder and became mingled with others. Skulls were piled up till they formed an outer wall around the church ; and there lay also *his* head in the burning sun, for many dead were there, and no one knew their names, and his name was forgotten also. And see, something was moving in the sunshine, in the sightless cavernous eyes ! What might that be ? A sparkling lizard moved about in the skull, gliding in and out through the sightless holes. The lizard now represented all the life left in that head, in which once great thoughts, bright dreams, the love of art and of the glorious had arisen, whence hot tears had rolled down, where hope and immortality had had their being. The lizard sprang away and disappeared, and the skull itself crumbled to pieces and became dust among dust.

Centuries passed away. The bright Star gleamed unaltered, radiant and large, as it had gleamed for thousands of years, and the air glowed red with tints fresh as roses, crimson like blood.

There, where once had stood the narrow lane containing the ruins of the temple, a nunnery was now built; a grave was being dug in the convent garden, for a young nun had died, and was to be laid in the earth this morning. The spade struck against a hard substance: it was a stone, that shone dazzling white. A block of marble soon appeared, a rounded shoulder was laid bare, and now the spade was plied with a more careful hand, and presently a female head was seen, and butterflies' wings. Out of the grave in which the young nun was to be laid they lifted, in the rosy morning, a wonderful statue of a Psyche carved in white marble.

"How beautiful, how perfect it is!" cried the spectators. "A relic of the best period of art."

And who could the sculptor have been? No one knew, no one remembered him, except the bright Star that had gleamed for thousands of years. The Star had seen the course of that life on earth, and knew of the man's trials, of his weakness — in fact, that he had been but human. The man's life had passed away, his dust had been scattered abroad as dust is destined to be; but the result of his noblest striving, the glorious work that gave token of the divine element within him—the Psyche that never dies, that lives beyond posterity—the brightness even of this earthly Psyche remained here after him, and was seen and acknowledged and appreciated.

The bright Morning Star in the roseate air threw its glancing ray downward upon the Psyche, and upon the radiant countenances of the admiring spectators, who here beheld the *image of the soul* portrayed in marble.

What is earthly will pass away and be forgotten, and the Star in the vast firmament knows it. What is heavenly will shine brightly through posterity; and when the ages of posterity are past, the Psyche—the soul—will still live on!

THE STORY OF MY LIFE.

I.

My life is a pretty story, as rich as it was fortunate. If, when I was a boy, and went out poor and alone into the world, a powerful fairy had appeared to me and said, "Choose thy career and thy aim, and then, according as thy mind develops itself, and according to the reasonable progress of our world, thou shalt be led and protected by me," my fate could not have been more happily, more cleverly and prosperously fulfilled. The story of my life will show to the world the truth it has revealed to me: that there is a gracious God who makes all things work together for our good.

My native land, Denmark, is a poetical country, full of folk-lore and old songs, and with a rich history, interwoven with that of Sweden and Norway. The Danish islands have splendid forests of beech and fields of corn and clover; they look like gardens laid out in the grand style. On one of these green islands, Fünen, lies my birthplace, Odense, so called after the heathen god Odin, who, according to the old tradition, lived here; the place is the capital of the island, and is twenty-two miles distant from Copenhagen.

In the year 1805 there lived here, in a poor little room, a young married pair, right faithfully attached to one another. The man was a shoemaker, scarcely two and twenty years of age, a very gifted man, with a truly poetic temperament. His wife was a few years older, knowing nothing of the world or of life, but with a heart full of love. The young man had constructed his own workshop and his own bed, and for this latter piece of furniture he had used as material the wooden scaffolding which had not long before supported the coffin of a certain deceased Count Frampe, when his honour had lain in state shortly before: the remnants of black cloth, still adhering to the boards, were a memorial of this event. Instead of the nobleman's corpse, surrounded by crape and candelabra, there lay on this same bed, on the 2nd of April, 1805, a living, crying babe; and that babe was I, Hans Christian Andersen. They tell me that my father sat by the bed, on the first days of my existence, reading Holberg's works, while I screamed.

"Wilt thou go to sleep? or else listen," he is reported to have said, in jest; but I went on screaming. And in the church where I was christened I screamed too, so that the clergyman, who was of an irritable temperament, declared, "The boy cries like a cat!" an opinion for which my mother never forgave him. But a poor emigrant, Gomar, who stood godfather, consoled her with the axiom that the louder I cried as a child, the better I should sing when I grew older.

A single little room, almost filled up with shoemaker's implements, the great bed, and the crib in which I lay, formed the shelter of my childhood; but the walls were hung with pictures, and over the workshop was a shelf with books and songs; the little kitchen showed a store of shining plates and cooking utensils; and there was a way, up a certain ladder, by which the inhabitants could mount to the loft and so out on to the roof, where in the rain gutter next to the neighbour's house stood a large box full of earth, in which grew kitchen herbs, and which formed the only garden my mother possessed; and in my story, "The Snow Queen," this garden is blooming still.

I was an only child, and was considerably spoiled; but my mother told me that I was far better off than she had been, and that I was cared for like a little nobleman. As a child, she had been turned out by her parents to beg, and when she was not able to do this, she had sat the whole day under a bridge and wept. In old Domenica in the "Improvisatore," and in the mother of the "Fiddler," I have portrayed her individuality under two different aspects.

My father let me have my own way in everything. I possessed his entire affection—he lived for me. On Sundays he made me panoramas, theatres, and transformation pictures; and he would read me pieces out of Holberg's plays and stories from the "Thousand and one Nights;" and those were the only moments in which I remember him as looking really cheerful, for in his position as an artizan he did not feel happy. His parents had been farmers, well to do in the world, but all kinds of misfortunes came upon them. Their cattle died, their farm-house was burned, and at length the man lost his reason. Then the wife went with him to Odense, and apprenticed their clever son to a shoemaker; there was nothing else to be done, though it was the lad's ardent wish to be admitted into the grammar school. Two prosperous citizens had once talked of clubbing together and giving him free board, in order to help him on; but it came to nothing. My poor father never could get his darling wish realized, but it never vanished from his remembrance. I can remember that in my childhood I once saw tears in his eyes when a pupil of the grammar school, who had come to us to order new boots, showed his books and talked of all he was learning.

"That was the way I ought to have gone," said my father.

And then he kissed me eagerly, and spoke not a word more the who.e evening.

He seldom associated with those of his own class. On Sundays he went out into the forest, taking me with him. He would not talk much, but generally sat lost in thought, while I ran about stringing strawberries on a long stalk, or weaving garlands. Only once in the year, in the month of May, when the forest was arrayed in its freshest green, my mother accompanied us; at which times she wore a cotton dress, which she only put on for this occasion and when she took the sacrament, and which was her holiday gown during all the years I can remember. She always carried home a great number of beechen twigs, which were put up behind our glittering stove. Pieces of St. John's wort were stuck into the clefts between the beams, and from their growth we judged whether we were to live a long or short time. Green leaves and pictures adorned our little room, which my mother always kept bright and neat: she had a peculiar pride in having the bed furniture and window-curtains as white as snow.

My father's mother came to our house every day, if only for a few moments, to see her little grandson; for I was the joy and pride of her age. She was a quiet, very amiable old woman, with mild blue eyes and a delicate form. The trials of life had pressed sorely upon her: from being a rich farmer's wife she had sunk into deep poverty, and lived with her afflicted husband in a little cottage, which she had bought with the last small remnant of her fortune. I never saw her weep; but it made a deep impression upon me when I heard her sigh quietly, as she told how her own maternal grandmother had been a lady of noble birth, in the German town of Cassel, and had run away from her home and kindred to marry a "theatre player," as she expressed it; and that now the descendants were suffering for this. I do not remember that she ever mentioned the family name of this grandmother; her own maiden name had been Nommesen. She had the office of attending to a garden at the hospital for the insane; and every Saturday evening she brought a few flowers, which she was allowed to carry home from thence. Those flowers were destined to adorn my mother's bureau; but they were called mine, and I had the privilege of putting them into a glass of water, whereat I rejoiced greatly. All that she could bring, she brought for me, for she loved me with her whole heart, and I understood and appreciated her love.

Twice a year she used to burn the dead rubbish in the garden. On these occasions I used to go to her to the asylum, and lie down upon the great heaps of green leaves and pease stalks: I had many flowers to play with; and another circumstance, to which I attached especial importance, was that I got better fare than I could expect at home. All the harmless lunatics used to walk about freely in the yard; they often came into the garden to see us, and with mingled curiosity and terror I used to listen to them and follow them about; I would even venture with the keepers to visit the dangerous madmen. A long passage

AN ANATOMICAL LECTURE.

led between two rows of their cells. Once the keeper had gone away,
and I lay down on the ground and peeped through the crack below the
door of one of these cells. Within, a naked woman was sitting on a
bed of a straw; her hair hung down over her shoulders, and she sang
in quite a sweet voice. All at once she started up and rushed towards
the door outside which I lay; the little wicket, through which provisions were handed to her, flew open, and she glared down upon me and
stretched out her long arm to seize me. I screamed aloud with terror.
I felt her finger-tips touching my clothes. I was half dead with fright
when the keeper came; and in later years this sight and the impression
it made upon me never departed from my mind.

Close by the spot where the dry plant stalks were burned, some poor
old women had their spinning-room; I often looked in, and soon became
their favourite. Among these people I had a flow of talk which astonished them all. By chance I had heard something of the interior

structure of man, without of course understanding the matter; but the mysterious nature of the subject attracted me, and I used with a piece of chalk to draw all kinds of flourishes on the door, to represent anatomical studies, and my description of the heart and lungs made an immense impression on my audience. They considered me a marvellously clever child, too clever to live long, and they rewarded my eloquence by telling me fairy tales, and a world as rich as that of the "Thousand and One Nights" arose before me. The stories told by the old women and the extravagant figures I saw moving about in the asylum produced such an effect upon me, that I dared scarcely venture out of the house when the evening shadows fell; and accordingly, when the sun went down, I generally got permission to lie down on my parents' bed with the flowered curtains, for my own crib must not thus early take up the space in the narrow room: here in the great bed I lay, absorbed in waking dreams, as if the outer world concerned me not.

Of my insane grandfather I was very much afraid: only once he had spoken to me, and then he had used the ceremonious "you" instead of the usual "thou" in his address. He used to sit carving strange figures out of wood—men with the heads of beasts and beasts with wings; these he would pack in a basket, and then go out into the country, where the peasants' wives were always glad to entertain him, for he gave away the strange toys to them and to their children. One day, when he was coming back to Odense, I heard the street boys calling after him, and in great terror I hid behind the stairs, for I knew that I was of his flesh and blood.

All my immediate surroundings were calculated to kindle my imagination. Odense itself, in those days when no steamboat existed and postal communication was not much developed, was a very different place from what it is now. One could have fancied it was a hundred years ago, for many customs of a bygone period still prevailed. The guilds went about in procession, and before them came their harlequin with bauble and bells. On Carnival Monday the butchers used to lead the fat ox through the streets, bedizened with flowers; a lad in a white garment, with great wings on his shoulders, rode on its back; the seamen went through the streets with music and with all their flags, and at last the two boldest of them wrestled together on a plank between two boats, he being declared the victor who avoided falling into the water. But the event which especially fixed itself in my memory, and was continually freshened by subsequent narrations, was the coming of the Spaniards to Fünen in 1808. I was only three years old at the time, but I can distinctly remember the strange brown men who went clanking about the streets, and the cannon which were fired. I saw the people sleeping on straw in an old ruined church near the hospital; and one day a Spanish soldier took me in his arms, and pressed to my lips a silver image he wore on his breast. I remember that my mother was angry about it, for she said it was "something Catholic;" but I was pleased with the silver image, and with the strange man too, who danced me up, and kissed me, and wept. No doubt he had children of his own at home in Spain. I saw one of his comrades led away to execution for murdering a Frenchman : many years afterwards I wrote my poem, " The Soldier," on this subject ; Chamisso has translated it into German, and it was afterwards incorporated in the illustrated popular book of " Soldiers' Songs."

Scarcely ever did I associate with other boys ; even at school I took no part in their sports, but sat in the room by myself. At home I had toys enough that my father had made for me. My greatest pleasure was to make dolls' clothes, or to spread an apron of my mother's between the wall and two sticks by a currant bush which I had planted in the yard, and to sit beneath it looking at the sunlit leaves. I was a remarkably dreamy child, and sat so often with closed eyes that people thought at last I had weak eyes, though the sense of sight was particulary well developed in me.

Occasionally, at harvest-time, my mother went out to glean in tne fields ; at these times I accompanied her, and we walked like the biblical Ruth over the corn-fields of Boaz. One day we came to a place where the bailiff was notorious as a violent man : we saw him coming with a great whip, and my mother and all the rest ran away ; but I had wooden shoes on, and lost them ; the stubble wounded my naked feet, and I could not run, and consequently remained behind. He raised his whip, but I looked up into his face, and cried involuntarily, " How dare you strike me, when God can see you ? " and the stern man all at once looked at me quite mildly, stroked my cheeks, asked me my name, and gave me some money. When I showed his present to my mother, she said to the rest, " He 's a wonderful child, my Hans Christian ; everybody likes him, and even that bad fellow has given him money."

Thus I grew up pious and superstitious. I had no idea of poverty or want ; my parents had only enough to live on from day to day, and yet I had plenty of everything, and an old woman made up my father's clothes afresh for me. Sometimes I accompanied my parents to the theatre, where the first plays which I saw were acted in German. The " Donau-weibchen " was the favourite piece of the whole town ; but first of all I saw Holberg's " Political Tinker " treated as an opera. The first impression made upon me by the theatre and the assembled audience was by no means a sign that anything poetical was concealed within me ; for my first exclamation, on seeing the multitude of spectators, was, " If we had only as many tubs of butter as there are people here, what a butter-feast we would have ! " The theatre was soon my favourite place. As I could go there but seldom, I made friends with the bill distributor, who gave me a programme every day ; and I would sit with this in a corner, and imagine the whole play, according to the title of the piece and the names of the characters. This was my first unconscious attempt at composition.

My father was fond of reading not only plays and narratives, but history and the Bible : in his quiet mind he pondered over what he had read ; but my mother did not understand him when he tried to expound it, and so he became more and more silent. One day he closed the Bible with the words, "Christ was a man like ourselves; but what a remarkable man!" My mother was frightened at these words, and burst into tears; and in my fear I prayed to God that he would forgive my father this dreadful profanity. "There is no devil except the one in our own hearts," I heard my father say; and again I was afraid for him and for his soul; and accordingly I quite agreed in opinion with my mother and our female neighbours, when one morning my father, who had probably scratched himself with a nail, showed three deep cuts on his arm, that the devil had visited my father in the night to prove that he really existed.

MY FATHER RAMBLES WITH ME INTO THE WOOD.

My father's wanderings into the forest became more frequent — he could get no rest. The events of the war then raging in Germany engrossed his whole attention, and he read of them eagerly in the newspapers. Napoleon was his hero, and the Emperor's rapid rise seemed to him fraught with bright example. Denmark allied herself with France at that time, and nothing but war was talked of. My father took service as a soldier, in the hope of coming home a lieutenant; my mother wept; our neighbours shrugged their shoulders, and declared that it was madness for a man to go out and get shot who had no necessity to take such a step.

On the morning when the corps was to march, I heard my father singing and speaking cheerfully, but his heart was deeply touched: I could tell this by the wild emotion with which he kissed me at parting. I was lying alone in the room, sick of the measles, when the drums beat, and my mother accompanied him weeping as far as the town gate. When they were gone, my old grandmother came in. She looked at me with her mild eyes, and said that it would be well if I died now, but that God's will was always the best. That was one of the first painful mornings I can remember.

The regiment, however, did not march farther than to Holstein: peace was concluded, the volunteer came back to his old workshop, and everything seemed to have returned to its old order. I still played with my dolls, and made them act pieces, always in German, for that was the language of my theatrical experience; but my German was a kind of gibberish I put together myself, and in which only one correct German

MY THEATRE.

word occurred, namely, *besen* (broom), a word which I had caught up from the various expressions my father had brought from Holstein.

"You have profited by my journey," he said, jestingly. "Heaven knows if you will ever get so far; but you must see to it yourself—remember that, Hans Christian."

But my mother declared that so long as she had a word to say, I should stop at home, and not sacrifice my health as he had done.

She spoke the truth—his health had suffered. One morning he woke up in wild delirium, talking of nothing but of campaigns and of Napoleon: he fancied he had received orders from the Emperor, and that he had obtained a command. My mother dispatched me at once,—not to the physician, but to a so-called "wise woman" who dwelt half a mile from Odense. I went to her, and she questioned me, measured one of my arms with a woollen thread, made some strange signs, and at last laid a green twig on my chest; she told me it was a piece of the same kind of tree on which the Saviour had been crucified.

"Now go home," she said, "along the bank of the river: if thy father is to die this time, his spirit will meet thee."

It may well be imagined how frightened I was—I, who was so filled with superstition, and whose imagination was so easily excited.

"And did nothing meet you?" my mother asked, when I came home. I assured her with a beating heart that I had seen nothing.

On the third day my father died. His corpse rested on the bed; I and my mother lay on our knees before it, and all night long a cricket kept chirping.

"He is dead," my mother said to the insect; "you need not call him, the Ice Maiden has carried him off."

And I understood what she meant. I remembered how, in the past winter, when our window-panes were frozen, my father had pointed to them and showed us a figure that resembled a female with outstretched arms. "I fancy she will take me away," he had said, jestingly. Now that he lay dead in his coffin my mother remembered his words, and they came back to my remembrance also.

He was buried in St. Knud's churchyard, to the left of the side door leading to the altar, and my grandmother planted roses upon his grave. Now there are already two other graves in the same place, and the grass grows rank over them.

From the time of my father's death I was left altogether to myself; my mother went out washing for people, and I sat alone at home with my little theatre, worked at clothes for the dolls, and read plays. They tell me that I was always neat and clean in my attire; that I was tall and thin, had long hair of almost a yellow colour, and went bareheaded. In our neighbourhood lived the widow of a clergyman, Madame Bunkeflod, with the sister of her dead husband. These two ladies opened their door to me, and theirs was the first educated house where I was received. The deceased preacher had written poems, and his name was known at that time in Danish literature; his "spinning songs" were in the mouths of the people. In my "Vignettes to Danish Poets" I sang of him whom my contemporaries had forgotten, in the following words:

> "Spindles whirr, wheels revolve,
>   The spinning song sounds free;
> The merry lays of youth are turned
>   To ancient melody."

Here I heard for the first time the word "poet" uttered with a respect as if it designated something sacred. My father had read Holberg's comedies to me; but here they did not speak of these, but of verses, of poetry. "My brother the poet," Bunkeflod's sister would say, and her eyes gleamed. From her I learned that it was a glorious and happy thing to be a poet. Here also I read Shakespeare for the first time: it was certainly only in a bad translation; but the bold pictures he drew, the incidents of blood and slaughter, his witches and spectres, were exactly to my taste. I immediately began to perform Shakespeare on my puppet theatre; I saw Hamlet's ghost, and walked with Lear on the desolate heath. The more persons died in a piece, the more interesting did it appear to me. In those days I wrote my first piece. It was nothing less ambitious than a tragedy, wherein, of course, all the characters died. The plot I took from an old song of Pyramus and Thisbe, but I had extended the story by the introduction of a hermit and his son, both of whom were in love with Thisbe, and committed suicide when she died. Many speeches of the hermit were biblical passages, taken out of the little catechism, especially from the " Duty to One's Neighbour." The piece itself was called " Abor and Elvira."

" It ought to be called ' The *Aborre* (gruff) and the Dummy,' " said our female neighbour, wittily, when, after reading the play with great contentment and satisfaction to all the people in our street, I brought it to her.

I was terribly depressed at this, for I felt that she was making fun of me and of my poem, which all the others praised; and I went mournfully to relate the fact to my mother, who replied, " She only says that because *her* son did not write it," and I was much consoled, and began another piece, in which a King and a Queen were to make their appearance. I could not agree with Shakespeare in making these personages speak the language of ordinary mortals. I inquired of my mother and of several other people how a King really spoke, but could not gain any satisfactory information, for they said it was many years since a King had visited Odense, but they supposed he spoke foreign languages. Accordingly I procured a kind of lexicon in which were German, French, and English words with their Danish translation; and now my trouble was over, for I took a word from each language and inserted it in my piece, in the speeches of the King and Queen. Thus arose a kind of Babylonian dialect, which I considered the only suitable one for such exalted personages. Every one was obliged to hear my play : it was a perfect treat to me to read it, and it never occurred to me that my audience might not experience the same pleasure in listening.

The son of our female neighbour had a situation in a cloth manufactory, and brought home a sum of money every week; but I, on the contrary, as the people declared, went about doing nothing. I was now to go to the factory too, " not for the sake of the money," my mother said, " but that I may know where he is, and what he's doing." My old grandmother took me there, and very melancholy she was on the occasion, for she declared she had never thought to see the day when I should have to associate with the low boys there. Many German workmen were employed in this place : they sang and talked merrily, and many a coarse jest created great laughter. I heard what was said, and have experienced the fact that a child can hear such things with innocent ears, for what they spoke of took no hold upon me. At that time I had a very good high soprano voice, and knew it very well; for when I sang in my parents' little garden, the people in the street would stop and listen, and the high-born strangers in the garden of the Councillor of State, that abutted on ours, would listen at the palings. Consequently, when they asked me in the factory if I could sing, I immediately began, and all the looms stood still, all the workmen listened to

me, and I had to sing and sing again, and the other boys were commis-
sioned to do my work.   I then told them that I could act plays, and
remembered whole scenes of Holberg and Shakespeare.   All there liked
me, and I found the first days in the factory very pleasant; but one day
when I was in full song, and they were talking of the marvellously high
compass of my voice, one of the workmen suddenly called out, "That's
not a boy, but a little girl!" and seized hold of me.   I cried and protested, while the others laughed at the jest; and, shy as a girl, I rushed
out of the house and home to my mother, who at once promised me
that I should never go to the factory again.   I resumed my visits at
Madame Bunkeflod's, for whose birthday I made a pincushion of my
own invention.   I also made acquaintance with another old lady, a
clergyman's widow, to whom I read aloud out of the novels she procured from the circulating library.   One of these books began in somewhat the following way:
    " It was a stormy night—the rain beat against the window-panes," &c.
    " That's a remarkable book," said the old lady.
    And I asked quite innocently how she knew that.
    " I can hear that from the beginning," she replied.   "It will be some-
thing quite extraordinary."
    And I was filled with respectful astonishment at her penetration.
    Once, at harvest-time, my mother went with me many miles from
Odense to a nobleman's seat in the neighbourhood of her birthplace,
Bogense.   The lady there, at whose parents' house she had been in
service, had said that she might pay her a visit.   That was a great journey
for me: we travelled the greater part of the way on foot, and took, I
think, two days to get through it.   Here the country made so powerful
an impression on me, that it was my highest wish to remain there and
become a farmer.   It was just hop-gathering time; and I sat in the barn,
by a great tub, with my mother and many other people, and helped to
pick the hops.   Stories were told, and each related whatever marvellous
adventures had befallen him.   One afternoon I heard an old man saying
how God knew everything that happened and all that would happen.
My thoughts ran entirely on this; and in the evening, when I wandered
away from the yard alone to where there was a deep pond, and had
stepped on some stones in the water near its margin, a question suddenly
came into my head, whether God really knew everything that was to
happen.
    " If He has determined that I am to live," I thought, "and that I am
to become many years old, and if I now jump into the water and drown
myself, then it will not be according to His will."
    And in a moment I was determined to drown myself, and rushed to-
wards the deepest spot.   Then a new thought struck me that this was
the devil seeking to gain power over me; and I gave a great cry, and
fled as if I were pursued, and ran weeping into my mother's arms; but
neither she nor any one else could get me to tell what was the matter.
    " He must have seen a ghost," said one of the women.
    And I myself believed this was the case.

My mother married again. A young artizan was her second husband; but his family, who belonged to the same class as himself, considered that he had made a very disadvantageous match, and neither I nor my mother received permission to visit them. My stepfather was a silent young man, entirely averse from interfering with my education, so I lived entirely for my panorama-box and my puppet theatre, and my great delight was to collect coloured scraps to make into costumes for my company. My mother thought this good practice towards my becoming a tailor, a craft for which she considered me destined by nature; but I declared that I would go on the stage and become a player, a wish that my mother most decidedly opposed, for her only ideas of a "player" were taken from strolling companies and from rope-dancers. No, I must and should become a tailor. The only thing that gave me any consolation with regard to my destined occupation was the prospect it held out to me of procuring plenty of scraps for my puppet theatre.

My love for reading, the many dramatic scenes I knew by heart, and my very good voice, all awakened a kind of attention towards me on the part of many good families in Odense. I was summoned to them, and my strange appearance excited their interest. Among the many into whose houses I came was Colonel Hoeg Guldberg, who with his family showed me very hearty kindness: he even presented me to Prince Christian, the present King.

I grew apace and became a tall boy, and my mother declared that she could no longer let me wander about. I went into the free school, where they taught me religion, arithmetic, and writing; the latter badly enough, and I could scarcely spell a word correctly. Whenever the master's birthday came round, I wove a wreath and wrote a poem for him, which he took half smiling, half with contempt; and the last time he scolded me for my performance. The street boys had also heard from their parents that I was a strange fellow, and went to rich people's houses, and consequently one day I was pursued by a wild horde, who shouted after me, "There goes the play-writer!" I hid myself at home in a corner, shed tears, and prayed. My mother declared that I must be confirmed, that I might be apprenticed to a tailor and learn to do something sensible. She loved me with her whole heart, but did not understand my striving and yearning, nor indeed did I then understand it myself. Those around her always spoke against my way of going on, and grumbled at me. We belonged to St. Knud's parish, and here the candidates for confirmation might report themselves either to the canon or the chaplain. Only the children of those we called the "grand families" and the pupils of the Latin school went to the canon; the poor children resorted to the chaplain. Nevertheless, I reported myself to the canon, who was obliged to accept me, though no doubt he thought my proceeding a piece of vanity, for by joining his class, though I was placed at the bottom of it, I got to stand above all those who went to the chaplain. Still I may hope it was not vanity alone that drove me to this step. I stood in terror of the poor boys, who had jeered at me, and always felt impelled to approach the pupils of the Latin school, whom I considered far better than all the rest. When they were at play in the churchyard, I would stand outside at the paling, peeping in and wishing that I was one of those happy beings; not on account of their play, but of the many books they had to read, and the prospect they had of doing something in the world. Now, at the canon's I could come among them and be like one of themselves, but I cannot now remember one of them, so they must have taken very little notice of me. Every day the feeling grew upon me that I had intruded where I had no right to be; but a young girl, whom I shall have to mention again, and who was considered the grandest of the company, always looked at me in a very friendly way; and one day she even gave me a rose, and I went away quite delighted that there was one, at least, who did not despise and reject me.

An old tailoress came, and altered my dead father's overcoat into a confirmation dress for me. I had never worn such a coat before; and now also, for the first time in my life, I received a pair of boots. My delight on this occasion was very great. My only fear was, that the new boots might not be seen by all; consequently I put them on over my trousers, and thus walked into the church. The boots creaked loudly, and I felt a secret joy at the circumstance, for now the congregation would be sure to hear that they were new. My meditations were disturbed, and I felt, with many a twinge of conscience, that I was thinking quite as much of my new boots as of heavenly things. I prayed earnestly to be forgiven, and then, alas! back went my thoughts to my new boots.

In the foregoing year I had saved a small sum of money. When I counted it, I found it to consist of thirteen rix-bank dollars. I was quite enchanted to find myself the possessor of so large a sum; and as my mother kept insisting upon my being apprenticed to a tailor, I begged and plagued her to allow me to go to Copenhagen, a place I looked upon as the greatest city in the world.

"What do you intend to do there?" asked my mother.

"I intend to become famous," I replied; and I told her what I had read about remarkable men. "First," I said, "they have a great deal of trouble to go through, and then they become famous."

It was a most inexplicable yearning that impelled me onwards. I wept, I begged, and at last my mother yielded; but first she sent for an old dame, a reputed "wise woman," from the hospital, to come and prophecy my future destiny by means of cards and coffee grounds.

"Your son will be a great man," was the verdict of the old dame, "and Odense will one day be illuminated in honour of him."

My mother wept when she heard this, and I received permission to start on my travels. All our neighbours declared to my mother that it was a terrible venture, to allow me at the age of fourteen to go off to Copenhagen, which was so far off—a great puzzling town where I knew nobody.

"You see, he won't leave me any peace," my mother replied. "I have been obliged to consent, though I'm sure he won't get farther than Nyborg. When he sees the wild ocean, I fancy he 'll be afraid and turn back."

During the summer that preceded my confirmation, a portion of the operatic and dramatic company from the Theatre Royal Copenhagen had been in Odense, where they gave a series of operas and tragedies. The whole town had been full of it; and, thanks to a compact I made with the bill distributor, I had witnessed all their performances behind the scenes, and had even appeared on the stage as a page, a shepherd, or in some similar character, and had spoken a few words. My zeal was so great that I always appeared ready dressed for my part when the players came to dress, and this drew their attention towards me; my enthusiasm and my childish ways amused them; they gave me some friendly words, and I looked up to them as to supernatural beings. Then all the praises I had received for my declamation and my voice came to have a meaning for me: the stage was my vocation; this was the career in which I should become a celebrated man, and therefore I must go to Copenhagen. I had heard much about the theatre in Copenhagen, and that there was something performed there called a ballet, which was said to be finer than opera or drama; the dancer, Madame Schall, was especially mentioned as the first performer, and consequently she appeared in my imagination as the queen of all, and in my fancy I regarded her as the person who was to do everything for me if I could only secure her patronage. Full of this thought I went to the old printer Iversen, one of the most respected citizens of Odense, whom I remembered to have often seen in communication with the players during their stay; I felt sure that he must know Madame Schall, and I would beg him to give me a letter of introduction to her, and Providence would take care of the rest.

The old man saw me for the first time. He listened to my request politely enough, but very seriously dissuaded me from carrying out my project, advising me to learn a handicraft.

"That would really be a great sin," I replied.

The air with which I said this evidently surprised him, and it prepossessed him in my favour. He told me that he was not personally acquainted with the dancer, but that he would give me a letter for her. When I received this paper, I fancied myself near the attainment of my object.

My mother packed a small bundle of clothes, and spoke to the postillion, asking him to take me as a cheap passenger to Copenhagen; the fare was to be three rix-bank dollars. The afternoon came, and my mother sorrowfully accompanied me to the town gate. Here my old grandmother was standing; her beautiful hair had lately turned grey; she fell upon my neck and wept, but was unable to utter a word, and I was profoundly sorrowful! Thus we parted. I never saw her again, for she died in the following year. I do not know where her grave is, for she rests in the pauper churchyard.

The postillion blew his horn. It was a fine sunny afternoon, and soon the sun shone into my light childish heart. I rejoiced at every new thing that I saw, and was I not journeying towards the goal of my wishes? But when I reached the Great Belt at Nyborg, and the ship departed from my native island, I felt how lonely and forsaken I was, and that no one was present with me but the Father in heaven. As soon as I set my foot on shore at Seeland, I went behind a shed that stood by the sea, fell on my knees, and begged for help and guidance from above; and then I felt strengthened and ready to trust in God and my good fortune. The whole day and the next night I was carried on through villages and towns, and when we stopped to change horses, I stood by the carriage, gnawing my crust of bread, and fancying I was already far away in the wide world.

II.

IT was on Monday morning, the 5th of September, 1819, when from the heights of Fredericksberg I for the first time beheld Copenhagen. There I alighted, and went with my little bundle through the castle garden, the long avenue and the suburb, into the city. On the evening before my arrival had broken out the great so-called " Jew feud," which extended through several countries of Europe. The whole city was in commotion, the streets were full of people, and the noise and bustle of Copenhagen realized the notion I had formed of what was for me the largest city in the world. With hardly ten dollars in my pocket, I betook myself to one of the smaller inns. My first journey was to the theatre: I walked round the building several times, and almost looked upon it as a home. One of the ticket sellers, who walk about here, noticed me, and asked if I wanted a ticket. I was so utterly inexperienced in the world's ways, that I thought he was offering me one as a present, and accordingly accepted his proposed gift with best thanks. He thought I was making fun of him, and became angry; and, somewhat startled, I quitted the spot which had attracted me more than all the rest of the town. I little thought that in this very building my first dramatic effort would be produced, that was to introduce me to the Danish public, ten years later.

The next day I put on my confirmation suit, of course not forgetting the new boots, which were again drawn up over my trousers; and thus, in my finest array, and on my head a great hat that fell far down over my eyes, I went to the dancer, Madame Schall, to deliver my letter of introduction. Before I rang the bell, I fell on my knees at the door, and prayed that I might find help and protection here. A servant girl came tripping up the stairs with her basket; she smiled kindly at me, gave me a shilling, and ran on. I stared in astonishment at the shilling and at her, for I had my confirmation clothes on, and considered that I looked quite distinguished; how, then, could she imagine that I came to beg? I called after her.

"Keep it, keep it!" she cried, and was gone.

I INTRODUCE MYSELF TO A PATRONESS.

At last I was admitted to the presence of the lady, who looked at me and listened to me with the greatest astonishment. She had not the slightest knowledge of the person who had written the letter I brought, and my whole appearance and demeanour struck her as exceedingly strange. I spoke of my great attachment to the theatre, and to her question in what piece I proposed to act, I replied, "in Cinderella." This piece had been acted by the royal company in Odense, and the chief part had impressed me so powerfully that I could play it from memory. I begged permission to take off my boots, as I should otherwise not be light enough for this part; and then I took my great hat for a tambourine, and began to dance about, and to sing:

"Rank and riches cannot shield us
From our sorrows here below."

My strange gestures and excessive excitability made the lady look upon me as mad, and she got rid of me as soon as she could.

I now went to the director of the theatre to seek an engagement: he looked at me, and pronounced me "too thin for the theatre."

"Oh," I replied, "if I were only engaged at a salary of a hundred bank dollars, I would soon get fat."

The director gravely desired me to leave, observing that he only engaged persons of education.

I now felt utterly downcast: I had nobody who could give me consolation or advice. Then it seemed that to die was the only thing left for me, and the best thing that could happen; but presently my thoughts rose to the Father in heaven, and with the confidence of a child towards its father, they took hold on His providence. I wept out my grief, and then said to myself, When things are at the worst He sends help, for I have read so, and that one must suffer a great deal before one can succeed. Then I went and bought a gallery ticket to see the opera, "Paul and Virginia." The lovers' parting moved me to such a degree that I burst into violent weeping. Two women who sat beside me tried to console me, by reminding me that what I saw was only a play and not reality, and one of them good-naturedly gave me a large sandwich. I had complete confidence in all my fellow-creatures, and told my consolers with the most perfect frankness that I was really not crying about the Paul and Virginia on the stage, but because I looked upon the theatre as my own Virginia, to be parted from whom would make me as unhappy as the parting from his love made Paul. They looked wonderingly at me, but did not seem to understand what I said; so I told them why I had come to Copenhagen, and how I stood alone in the world; and then the kind-hearted woman insisted on giving me more sandwiches, fruit, and cake.

The next morning I paid my reckoning, and found to my discomfiture that my whole remaining wealth consisted of a single dollar; therefore it became necessary that I should make up my mind to return home at once with a skipper, or to try and get apprenticed to some handicraft. The latter seemed the better thing to do; for if I went back to Odense I should have to be apprenticed there, and I felt certain that people would laugh at me if I came home, having done nothing. It was a matter of perfect indifference to me what trade I learned, as I only took the step as a means of earning my bread in Copenhagen. I bought a newspaper, looked through the advertisements, and saw that a carpenter was seeking an apprentice. I applied to the man, who received me kindly, but said that before he decided upon taking me he must receive my certificate of baptism and a certificate of character from Odense; in the meantime I might lodge with him and try how I liked his trade. Next morning at six o'clock I made my appearance in his workshop. I found several journeymen and apprentices, but the master was not there. They talked jovially, and withal loosely. I was as bashful as a girl, and when they noticed that they teazed me unmercifully. Later in the day the coarse jests of the lads went so far that, remembering the scene in the manufactory, I resolved not to stay a day longer in the workshop. Accordingly I went to the master and took leave of him with tears, telling him that I could not bear it: he tried to console me, but I was inconsolable, and turned away.

Now I wandered through the streets. Nobody knew me, and I was quite forsaken. Then I remembered that in a newspaper at Odense I had read of a certain Italian named Siboni, who held the appointment of director of the musical conservatory in Copenhagen. Now, everybody had praised my voice; perhaps he would do something for me; if not, I must try this very evening to find a skipper with whom I might return home. The very thought of going back agitated me violently, and in this condition I betook myself to Siboni. There happened to be a large dinner party at his house. Among the guests were our celebrated composer Weyse and the poet Baggesen. To the housekeeper who opened the door to me I not only related the reason of my coming, but my whole history. She listened with great sympathy, and must have repeated the greater part of what I told her in the dining-room, for I had to wait a long time; and when the door opened, the whole company came out and looked at me. I was asked to sing. Siboni listened attentively; and then I recited some scenes from Holberg and one or two poems; and at last the feeling of my desolate position so overcame me that I burst into tears. And now the whole company applauded.

"I prophesy," said Baggesen, "that he will one day do something. But do not become vain," he continued, addressing me, "when the whole public applauds you."

And he added something about real true nature, and how it was destroyed by age and by contact with men; but I did not quite catch his meaning. Siboni promised to cultivate my voice, and that I should learn enough to obtain an engagement as a singer at the Theatre Royal. I was quite happy; I laughed and wept; and when the housekeeper let me out and noticed the state of excitement I was in, she stroked my cheek, and told me that I was to go next day to Professor Weyse, who intended to be kind to me, and on whom I could depend.

Accordingly I went to Weyse, who had fought his own way up from a poor position. He had been deeply moved by my friendlessness, and had made a collection for me which produced seventy dollars. Then I wrote my first letter to my mother—a joyful letter, declaring that all the fortune in the world had streamed towards me. My mother in her delight showed everybody the letter. Some listened in surprise, and others smiled and wondered what would be the end of it all.

In order to understand Siboni, it was requisite that I should at least learn some German. A Copenhagen lady who had travelled with me from Odense, and who was ready to help me in any way in her power, persuaded one of her friends, a teacher of languages, to give me some German lessons without remuneration; and thus I learned a few German phrases. Siboni opened his house to me, and gave me board and instruction; but half a year afterwards, my voice was either changing, or had been spoiled by my walking about through the whole winter in torn boots and with insufficient clothing. Every prospect of my ever being a distinguished singer was gone. Siboni told me so honestly, and counselled me to return to Odense and learn a handicraft.

And now, after I had painted to my mother in the rich colours of fancy the fortune I had really felt within my grasp, I was to go home to be the general laughingstock! Tortured by this thought, I stood utterly downcast. But in what appeared a great misfortune lay the germ of better things. As I stood once more alone, racking my brain to find what I should do, it came into my mind that there lived here in Copenhagen the poet Guldberg, a brother of that colonel who had shown me so much kindness in Odense. He lived at that time by the new churchyard which he has sung so eloquently in his poems. I wrote to him and told him everything: afterwards I went personally, and found him surrounded by books and tobacco-pipes. The strong hearty man gave me a kindly reception; and as he had seen by my letter how incorrectly I wrote, he promised me some lessons in the Danish language. He also examined me a little in German, and thought it might be well if he gave me a little assistance in that particular also. He devoted to my benefit the profits of a little book he was then publishing. This fact became known, and I think it produced more than a hundred dollars. The excellent Weyse and others also helped me on.

To live in the inn would have been too expensive for me, so I was obliged to seek a private lodging. My inexperience of the world led me to a widow in one of the most notorious streets of Copenhagen. She was inclined to accept me as a lodger; and I had no idea of the kind of world that was busy about me. She was a hard but industrious woman, and she painted the other people in Copenhagen to me in such terrible colours that I fancied her house was the only secure haven for me. I was to pay twenty dollars a month for a room which was in fact only an empty store-room, without window or light, but I had leave to sit in her room. I was to try it for two days first, but the very next day she told me that I must either decide or go. I, who at that time very easily attached myself to any one, had already conceived an affection for my landlady, and felt at home with her; but Weyse had said I must not give more than sixteen dollars a month, for the sum I received from him and Guldberg together came to just this amount; and even then nothing was left for my other requirements. Consequently I felt very mournful; and when my landlady had gone out, I sat down on the sofa and gazed sorrowfully at the portrait of her dead husband. I was still such a child, that when the tears ran down over my cheeks, I touched the eyes of the picture with the drops, that the dead man might feel how sorrowful I was, and soften the heart of his wife. She must have understood that more was not to be extracted from me, for when she came back she told me she would keep me for the sixteen dollars, and I thanked Heaven and the dead husband.

I was now in the very midst of the mysteries of Copenhagen, but I understood them not. In the house where I lived was a friendly young lady, who often wept: her old father came every evening and paid her a visit. I often opened the door to him. He wore a plain coat, was very much muffled up about the neck, and wore his hat pressed down over his forehead. He always took tea with her, and no one was to be present, for he was a shy man: she never seemed to be very glad at his coming. Many years afterwards, when I had gained a different position, and the fashionable world and the so-called "*salon* life" were open to me, I was one evening surprised, in a brilliantly lighted hall, by the entrance of an old gentleman with an order in his button-hole—an old gentleman whom I at once recognized as the father in the shabby coat, whom I had often admitted. I fancy he never suspected that I had opened the door to him when he came to act a part; but in those days I thought of nothing but my own acting. I was still so childish that I played with my puppet theatre and made dolls' clothes; and to procure materials for this purpose I went to the shops and begged remnants of different stuffs and of silk ribbons. I myself did not possess a single shilling, for my landlady took all my money a month in advance; only now and then, when I had executed some commission for her, she would give me a trifle, which was spent in the purchase of paper or of old books of plays. I was now very glad, and doubly so because Professor Guldberg had induced the first comic actor of the theatre, Lindgreen, to give me instruction. He made me study several parts out of Holberg; for instance, Hendrik, and stupid lads,—for which kind of business I was said to show some talent; but my great delight was to play Correggio. I received permission to learn this part on my own account, although Lindgreen asked me with comic gravity if I thought I could get to resemble the great painter. However, I managed to recite the monologue in the picture gallery with so much emotion that the old man clapped me on the shoulder, and said,

"You have feeling, but you must not become an actor. Heaven knows what you should do: speak to Guldberg about it. To learn a little Latin always paves the way to becoming a student."

I a student! Such a thought had never come into my mind. The theatre was nearer to me and attracted me more, but I could always learn Latin. First I spoke of it to the lady who had procured me lessons in German *gratis;* but she told me that Latin was the most expensive language in the world, and that to get lessons in it without paying was a thing impossible. Guldberg, however, managed that one of his friends gave me a few lessons a week from kindness.

The solo dancer, Dahlen, whose wife was at that time one of the first artistes on the Danish stage, opened his house to me. Many an evening I went there, and the gentle, kindly wife was good to me. The husband admitted me into his dancing school, and thus I was brought a step nearer the theatre. There I used to stand the whole morning, with a long stick, stretching my legs; but, in spite of my zeal, Dahlen considered I could never be anything but one of the *corps de ballet.* One advantage, however, I had procured: I was allowed to go behind the scenes in the evening, and even to sit on the back seat of the box belonging to the ballet. I fancied I had my foot already in the theatre, though I had never yet been on the stage.

One evening they gave the operetta, "The Two Little Savoyards." In the market scene everybody could come on, even the scene-shifters, to help to fill up the stage. I heard that, and put a little colour on my cheeks, and went on with the rest, quite happy to have the chance. I was in my usual clothes : I wore the famous confirmation coat, which still held together, though it looked rather shabby, in spite of incessant brushing and careful repairs, and the great hat fell over my nose, as of old. I was quite conscious of these defects, and sought to hide them, but my efforts only made my movements the more angular. Indeed, I could not stand straight, for my waistcoat would have displayed its scanty proportions too plainly against my long meagre form. I felt painfully that I might be made a laughingstock, but for the moment the happiness of appearing in front of the footlights stifled every other thought : my heart beat thick as I stepped on. Then came one of the singers, who had a great deal to say in those days, and who is now quite forgotten ; he took me by the hand, and jeeringly congratulated me on my first appearance.

"Allow me," he said, "to introduce you to the Danish public."

And he dragged me forward towards the lamps. His intention was to raise a laugh at the expense of my ungainly figure. I felt it, and the tears came into my eyes ; I tore myself away, and sorrowfully left the stage. But soon afterwards Dahlen arranged a ballet, "Armida," in which a little part was given to me : I appeared as a demon. From the time of the performance of this ballet dates my acquaintance with the wife of the poet, Professor Heiberg, now the highly honoured artiste of the Danish stage, who then, as a little girl, had a part in the piece. Our names were printed together on the bill. That was an epoch in my life, when my name was for the first time printed : I thought to behold in it a nimbus of immortality. I could not refrain from gazing at the printed name, and took the ballet programme to bed with me in the evening, lay awake at night with a light, and read my name over and over. I was quite happy.

It was now the second year of my residence in Copenhagen. The sum of money that had been collected for me was exhausted, but I felt ashamed to acknowledge my destitute condition. I had removed to the house of a sea captain's widow, where I only had my lodging and coffee in the morning. Those were heavy dark days for me. The woman thought I went out to dine with various families, while I was sitting on a bench in the King's Garden eating a small roll : only on rare occasions I ventured into one of the cheaper eating-houses, and sat down at the most distant table. I was really very forlorn, but I did not feel the full weight of my position. Every person who addressed a friendly word to me I looked upon as a sincere friend. God was with me in my little room, and many an evening, when I had said my prayers, I could ask Him with childish simplicity whether my lot would soon improve. I had a kind of belief that the fortune of New Year's-day would endure for the whole year. It was my highest aim to obtain a part in a drama. New Year's-day came ; the theatre was closed, and only an old half-blind porter sat at the stage entrance, which was quite deserted; with a beating heart I slipped past him, glided among the wings and scenes, and emerged upon the empty stage. There I fell on my knees, but not a single verse could I think of to declaim, but I said my " Our Father " aloud, and then went away, satisfied that inasmuch as I had spoken on the stage on New Year's-day, I should succeed in the course of the year in saying more from the same place—in fact, that a character would be allotted to me.

In the two years I had passed in Copenhagen I had not been out into the country. Only once I had gone into the Zoological Gardens, and had quite lost myself in the contemplation of the crowd and bustle of life. In the third year I came for the first time, on a spring day, among the green trees: it was in the garden of Fredericksberg, the summer residence of Frederick VI. Suddenly I found myself standing beneath the great budding beech trees: the sun shone through the leaves, the air was filled with fragrance, and the birds sang. I was quite overcome, shouted aloud, and threw my arms round one of the trees and kissed it.

" Is he mad ? " exclaimed one of the servants of the palace.

I ran away terrified, and walked quietly and gravely back to the town.

By this time my voice had begun to recover its tone. The teacher of the choir school heard it, offered me a place in the school, and declared his opinion that by singing in the chorus I should attain a greater ease and freedom of movement on the stage. Thus I went over from the dancing school to the singing school, and made my appearance in the chorus, sometimes as a shepherd, sometimes as a warrior. The theatre was my world: I had free entrance to the pit, and consequently it went badly with my Latin. I heard many people say that a knowledge of Latin was not necessary for singing in the chorus, and that one might even become a great actor without it. I quite agreed with this opinion, and several times excused myself from the Latin lessons in the evening, sometimes with good cause, sometimes without. Guldberg heard of it, and for the first time in my life I received a heavy reproof, which I richly deserved, but which crushed me terribly : I believe no malefactor could have suffered more on hearing his sentence of death. I must have expressed my sufferings in my face, for he said, " Don't act; " but it was not acting. I was now to leave off learning Latin. I felt more than ever how much I depended on the kindness of others. At times I had dark heavy thoughts concerning my future, for I was in want of the common necessaries of life, but generally I was as completely careless as a child.

The widow and daughter of the celebrated Danish statesman, Christian Colbjörnsen, were the two first ladies of rank who took a hearty interest in me as a poor lad: they often saw me, and listened to me with sympathy. Madame de Colbjörnsen lived during the summer at Bakkehüs, where the poet Rahbek and his interesting wife also resided. Rahbek never spoke to me, but his friendly and lively lady often chatted with me. I had begun to write another tragedy, and read it to her; but at the very first scenes she cried out,

" Why, there are whole passages which you have copied from Oehlen-schläger and Ingemann ! "

" Yes, but they are so beautiful," I replied, in my simplicity, and read on.

One day, when I was going from her to Madame de Colbjörnsen, she gave me a bunch of roses, and said,

" Will you take those to her ? it will certainly give her pleasure to receive them from the hand of a poet."

The words were spoken half in jest, but it was the first time that any one had used the expression " poet " in connection with my name : the words thrilled through me, and the tears came into my eyes. I know that from this moment the real desire to write seized me : before it had been only a pastime to fill up the intervals of playing with my doll's theatre.

At Bakkehüs lived also Professor Thiele. In those days he was only a young student, but he had already edited the " Danish Popular Stories," and was the author of many pretty poems. He was a man of feeling, enthusiasm, and sympathy. Quietly and attentively he watched my mental development, and now we are friends. He was one of the few who in those days told me the truth and spoke sensibly, when others amused themselves at my cost and appreciated only the comic aspect of my untutored condition. They had given me in sport the title of " the little declaimer," and I had gained a kind of notoriety in this character. People made game of me, and I accepted every smile as a smile of approval. One of my later friends has told me that he saw me by accident for the first time in those days. It was in the drawing-room of a rich merchant, where they had asked me, in sport, to recite one of my own poems ; and he told me I spoke with so much emotion, that ridicule was converted into sympathy.

Every day I heard people say what a good thing it would be for me if I could study ; but nobody took a step to help me, and I found it difficult enough to get a living. Then it occurred to me that I would write a tragedy and submit it for approval to the direction of the Theatre Royal, and with the money it would bring me in I would begin to study. While Guldberg had still been giving me lessons in Danish, I had been writing a tragedy from a German tale entitled " The Chapel in the Forest ; " but this was only looked upon as an exercise in composition, and Guldberg had positively forbidden my sending it into the theatre, nor had I any idea of disobeying. I invented my own plot, and in a fortnight my national tragedy was ready. It was entitled " The Bandits of Wissenberg," (the name of a little village in Fünen). Hardly a word in it was properly spelt ; for I had obtained no help, as it was to be anonymous ; but one person was admitted into the secret—the young lady whom I had first met at Odense during the preparatory lessons for confirmation, the only person who had at that time been friendly and kind to me. By her means I had obtained an introduction to the Colbjörnsens, and from them to the various families who had admitted me into their circles. This young lady paid for the copying of my work in a legible form, and took the necessary steps for bringing it under the notice of the direction. In six weeks the manuscript was returned to me, declined, with a letter which intimated that it was useless to send pieces which, like the present one, betrayed a lack of all elementary education.

It was at the end of the theatrical season of 1823 that I received a letter from the management of the theatre, dismissing me from the ballet and chorus; the letter added, that a continuance in this department could lead to nothing for me, but expressed a wish that my numerous friends might do something for me, and procure me the education, without which the possession of talent was useless. I felt myself thrust out into the wide world, without help and without support. I must write a piece for the theatre, and it *must* be accepted; that was the only course that remained for me. I accordingly wrote another tragedy from a historical tale called " Alfsol." I was delighted with the first part, and immediately betook myself therewith to the Danish translator of Shakespeare, the late Admiral Wulff, who good-naturedly heard me read it; I afterwards received the greatest kindness from his family. I had also introduced myself to our celebrated philosopher Oersted; and his house has remained to me to the present day a beloved home, to which my heart has grown fast, and in which I possess old and unchanging friends. A noted orator, Provost Gutfeldt, was then alive; and he it was who expressed real admiration of my tragedy, which was now completed, and he sent it to the management of the theatre with a letter of recommendation. I wavered between hope and fear. During the past summer I had suffered bitter want, but had never mentioned it: had I spoken, the many who sympathized with me would certainly have come to my assistance; false shame kept me from saying how badly things went with me; but I had one consolation, for in that year I read Scott's works for the first time. A new world opened before me; I forgot everything in its delight, and the lending library had the money destined to pay for my dinners.

Then it was also that I first met one of the most remarkable men of Denmark; one who unites to the greatest efficiency in his office, the noblest and best of hearts—a man to whom I look upon with confidence in everything—in whom I have found a second father, and whose children have been brethren and sisters to me. I mean the Conference Councillor Collin. He was at that time director of the Theatre Royal, and every one said what a good thing it would be if he could be got to interest himself for me. Oersted or Gutfeldt spoke to him about me, and thus it was that I went for the first time to a house that was afterwards to become so dear to me. Before the walls of Copenhagen were enlarged this house lay outside the walls, and was used as a country residence by the Spanish Ambassador; it now stands, a quaint timber building, in one of the principal streets: an old-fashioned wooden balcony leads to the entrance, and a great tree waves its green branches over the courtyard and the pointed gables. It was to be as my father's house to me; and who would not gladly linger over a description of *home?* I saw in Collin only a man of business, for his address was brief and grave: I went away without hope of receiving any help from this quarter; and yet Collin was strongly interested in my welfare, and was working for my good—working silently, as he has wrought for the good of all during his active life. But in those days I did not understand the indifference with which he seems to listen, while in reality his heart is bleeding for the woes of the sorrowful, and he is meditating how he shall best put in action the help that is sure to follow. My beloved play, for which many had loaded me with praise, he mentioned in so cursory a manner, that I was inclined to see in him rather an enemy than a protector. But when a few days had elapsed, I was summoned before the directors of the theatre. Here Rahbek gave me back "Alfsol," as unfitted for the stage; but, he added, there were

MY INTERVIEW WITH COLLIN.

so many grains of gold in the piece, that it was hoped if I studied earnestly, attended a school, and learned what was necessary, I might some day be able to produce works worthy to be acted on the Danish stage. In order to procure me this learning and to provide for my support, Collin had recommended me to King Frederick VI., who had granted me a certain pension for some years, and the directors of the public schools had, through Collin's recommendation, granted me free tuition in the Latin school at Slagelse, where, they told me, a new and active rector had just been appointed. I was almost struck dumb with astonishment: I had never imagined that my career would ever take this direction, and, indeed, I had now no clear idea of the course I was expected to follow. With the first mail coach I was to travel to Slagelse, which lies twelve German miles from Copenhagen. It was the place where the poets Ingemann and Baggesen had been to school. I was to receive a quarterly sum from Collin, to whom I was to look as my guardian; and he was to examine me as to my industry and progress.

I now went for the second time and expressed my thanks to him; and he said to me in a kind and hearty manner,

"Write to me frankly about everything you require, and let me know how you are getting on."

From that day I gained a place in his heart. No father could have been more to me than he was and is; no one has rejoiced more heartily in my subsequent success and fortune; none has more heartily sympathized in my distresses; and I am proud of being able to say that one of the noblest men Denmark can boast feels for me as for his own child. His benefits were conferred without a word or a look that could have made them heavy to accept; and this was not the case with some to whom I had to pay my thanks at this turn in my fate. Several requested me to think of my enormous good fortune, and to remember my poverty, and strictly enjoined the greatest diligence on my part; but Collin's words manifested the heartiness of a father, and he it was to whom I really owed everything. My departure was very suddenly decided on, and I had an affair of my own yet to settle: I had, namely, spoken with an old acquaintance from Odense, who now managed a printing business for a widow, to have "Alfsol" printed, that I might earn some money for myself. But before the printing could be put in hand, I was first to get together a certain number of subscribers, and I had not yet been able to produce them; the piece was in the printing office, which was locked when I went to bring away my manuscript; but a few years afterwards the tragedy suddenly appeared in print, anonymously, without my knowledge and permission, and in its unrevised form.

One beautiful day in autumn I left Copenhagen in the coach, to begin my school life in Slagelse; a young student, who had passed his first examination a month before, and was now journeying to his home in Jutland, to show himself as a student and to visit his parents and friends, sat by me, and rejoiced aloud at the new life that now lay open before him. He assured me that he would be the unhappiest of men if he were in my place, and had to begin now to attend the Latin school. But I travelled with good courage to the little town on the island of Seeland. My mother received a radiant letter from me: my only regret was that my poor father and my old grandmother were not alive, to hear that I was going to be a pupil in the Latin school.

III.

WHEN I arrived, late at night, in the inn at Slagelse, I asked the hostess if there were anything remarkable to be seen in the town.

"Yes," she replied; "there's a new fire engine, and Pastor Bartholm's library."

And those were about all the curiosities of the place. A couple of hussar officers constituted the genteel society. Every one knew what was going on in every house, what scholar had advanced, and who had retrograded, and all such interesting particulars. A private theatre, where the pupils of the Latin school and the servant girls had free admission to the dress rehearsals, formed the chief topic of conversation. The town was far from a wood, and still farther from the sea coast, but the chief high road ran through it, and the post horn sounded from the rolling carriage.

I was put to board in the house of a respectable widow of the better class, and had a little room looking out upon the garden and on the fields; in the school my place was assigned me in the last class but one, among the little boys, for I knew nothing at all.

I was really not unlike a wild bird shut up in a cage; I had the best will in the world to learn, but went groping about, as if I had been thrown into the sea: one wave followed another—grammar, geography, mathematics. I felt overwhelmed by the flood, and terribly afraid that I should never be able to master all this. The rector, who took especial pleasure in ridiculing every one, made me no exception to his rule. To me he appeared as a divinity, whose every word was to be implicitly believed; and when one day I answered his questions badly, and he called me stupid, I communicated the fact to Collin, and added that I feared I did not deserve what was done for me; but he wrote a soothing answer. In some subjects I began to get good marks, and the teachers were heartily kind to me; but although I was making progress, I lost confidence in myself more and more. Still, at one of the earliest examinations, I obtained praise from the rector, and he wrote the commendation in my mark-book. Quite happy at this, I went to spend a few days in Copenhagen. Guldberg, who noticed the improvement in me, received me very kindly, and commended my zeal. His brother in Odense gave me the means, in the following summer, to visit my native place, where I had not been since I had gone forth in search of adventures. I crossed the Belt and went on to Odense on foot. When I approached the town, and saw the lofty old church tower, my heart was softened and I burst into tears, for I deeply felt how Providence had watched over me. My mother was delighted to see me, the Iversen and Guldberg families received me kindly, and in the smaller streets I saw the people open the windows to look out after me, for all had heard how remarkably fortunate I had been; but when one of the chief citizens who had built a high tower on his house took me up there, and I looked out upon the town and the region around, and saw on the square below a few poor women from the hospital, who had known me from a child, pointing up at me, I felt as if I stood upon the very pinnacle of fortune.

But when I got back to Slagelse, all this nimbus and its very remembrance vanished away. I may honestly say I was very industrious, and as soon as it was practicable I moved up into a higher class; but here I felt the burden still greater, and my exertions did not seem to produce sufficient effect. Many an evening when sleep threatened to overcome me, I washed my head with cold water, or jumped about in the little lonely garden till I was broad awake, and could take the book in hand again. The rector was accustomed to fill up his hours of teaching with ironical phrases, nicknames, and satire of not the happiest kind. I felt benumbed by fear when he entered; consequently, my answers often expressed the reverse of what I meant, and my fright was more painful than ever. What was to become of me?

In a moment of despondency, I wrote a letter to the head assistant master, one of those who had been kindest to me. I said in this letter that I considered myself too dull a person to be ever able to study, and asked his advice as to what course I should take; for it seemed to me that the money spent for me in Copenhagen was being thrown away. The excellent man strengthened me with gentle words, and wrote me a hearty comforting letter: he declared that the rector meant well towards me, but that his way was peculiar, that I was making all the progress that could be expected, and that I must not doubt my capabilities. He

MY HOLIDAY.

told me that he himself had begun his studies as a peasant lad of three and twenty, consequently older than I; that my misfortune was, that I required a course different from that followed by the other pupils—a thing not to be done in a school; and that really I was pushing forward, and stood well with masters and fellow-pupils.

Every Sunday we went to church, where we had to hear a very old clergyman preach. My companions employed themselves, during his sermon, in getting by heart their lessons in history and mathematics; I used to learn my lesson in religion, and thought this a less sinful proceeding. The dress rehearsals in the private theatre were points of light in my school life; they took place in a back building where one could hear the cows lowing; the outdoor scene was a representation of the market-place of the town; and this gave the whole affair an air of home, for the people liked to see their own houses painted on the canvas.

On Saturday afternoon it was my delight to go out to the Antvorskov Castle, which had once been a convent, and was then in ruins. I watched the digging out of the old ruined cellars with as much interest as if the place had been a Pompeii. Often too, I wandered out to the cross of St. Anders, on one of the hills near Slagelse. This cross is a relic of the Catholic days of Denmark. St. Anders was a priest in Slagelse, and journeyed to the Holy Land; on the day of his departure for home, he stayed too long, praying on the shore, and the ship sailed away without him. He was walking along the shore in mournful mood, when a man came riding along, and took the holy man behind him on his ass. St. Anders immediately fell into a deep sleep, and when he awoke he heard the bells of Slagelse chiming. He was lying on the " Hvilehöi " (hill of rest), on which the cross now stands : he had got home a year and a day before the ship which had sailed away without him, for an angel had carried him home. I got to love the legend and the place of which it was told ; from here I could see the ocean and Fünen ; here I could live in my fancies, while at home the feeling of duty bound me to my books.

But I was happiest of all when I could go in summer, while the forest was green, to the town of Soröe, which lies in the midst of the forest, surrounded by lakes. Here is an academy founded by the poet Holberg, and everything spoke of the monastic solitude. I paid a visit to the poet Ingemann, who had married a short time before, and was established here as a teacher; already in Copenhagen he had been kind to me, and now his reception of me was heartier than ever. His life appeared to me like a beautiful fairy tale. Flowers and vine leaves wreathed the windows of his house, and the rooms were ornamented with portraits of distinguished poets, and other pictures. We went sailing on the lake, with an æolian harp fixed to the mast of our boat. Ingemann had a wonderful gift of narration, and his amiable wife treated me as an elder sister might have done. How I loved these people ! Our friendship has increased with years, and since that time I have been almost every year a welcome guest there, and have felt that there are people in whose company one seems to grow better, the darkness of life vanishes, and the whole world seems bathed in sunshine.

Among the pupils of the academy were two who could make verses : they heard that I was given to the same pursuit, and cultivated my acquaintance. One of them was Petit, who afterwards translated some of my books, not very accurately, but with the best intention; the other, Carl Bagger, one of the most gifted of Danish *literati*, but one whose works have been harshly judged. His poems are full of life and originality, and his " Life of my Brother " is a genial book, in criticising which our Danish monthly literary periodical has evinced a great lack of judgment. These two youths were very different from me ; life seemed to gallop through their veins, while I was soft and childish.

So far as my behaviour was concerned, I always received the character " remarkably good," in my mark-book ; once, however, it happened that " very good " was substituted ; and so childishly anxious was I, that I wrote to Collin on the subject, assuring him most earnestly that it was not by my fault that I was marked " very good."

The rector had grown tired of his residence in Slagelse. He applied for a similar position in the Latin school at Helsingör, and his application was successful. He informed me of this, and kindly added that I might write to Collin and ask permission to accompany him. I might live in his house, and go immediately and join his family there; by this means I might become a student in a year and a half, which could not be achieved if I stayed behind; he would give me some private lessons in Latin and Greek. On this occasion he wrote himself to Collin. This letter, which was shown to me at a later period, contained the greatest praise of my industry, my progress, and my good abilities, which latter I thought he had entirely denied, and the want of which I so deeply deplored. I had no idea that he judged me so favourably; the consciousness of this would have strengthened and encouraged me, while I felt quite depressed by the continual blame I incurred. Collin's permission was given as a matter of course, and I became an inmate of the rector's house. Unfortunately, it proved an unhappy house for me.

I accompanied the rector to Helsingör, one of the most beautiful points of Denmark, close to the Oeresund, which is here not quite a mile broad, and appears like a broad river rolling between Sweden and Denmark. The ships of all nations sail past by hundreds every day; in winter the ice spreads its broad bridge between the countries; and when the icy covering breaks up in spring it looks like a moving glacier. Nature here produced a strong effect upon me, but I could only look up at it by stealth. When school-time was over, the house door was generally locked; I was obliged to remain in the close school-room and learn my Latin, or to play with the children, or to sit in my little bed-room, and never went out to see anybody. My life in this house continually rises before me in the darkest dreams of my recollection. I was ready to succumb, and my prayer to God every evening was that He would deign to take this cup from me, and give me the rest of the grave. I had not a particle of confidence in myself; I never mentioned in my letters how hard it went with me; and when the rector made a jest of me, and mocked at my feelings, I complained of no one but myself, for I felt sure they would say in Copenhagen,

"He does not like to do anything; the fantastical being cannot reconcile himself to the realities of life."

I am told that my letters to Collin at this period betrayed an anguish of spirit that moved him deeply. My low spirits were attributed to causes within myself, and not to outward influences. In reality my disposition was elastic and singularly impressionable to every gleam of sunshine; but only on the few holidays in the year, when I could go to Copenhagen, did a gleam of this kind cross my path.

What a transition it was, when I passed in a few days from the rector's room into a house in Copenhagen, where I found all the elegance, cleanliness, and comfort of society! The house in question was that of Admiral Wulff, whose lady showed me motherly kindness, and whose children came to meet me with hearty affection. They lived in a compartment of the Amalienberg Palace, and gave me a room looking out upon the square. I well remember the first evening here; Aladdin's words were in my mind, where he is represented as looking down from his rich palace upon the square, and saying, "Here I walked as a poor boy!" And my soul was filled with thankfulness.

During the whole time of my residence at Slagelse I had not written more than four or five poems; two of them, "The Soul," and "To my Mother," are printed in my collected works. During my stay at Helsingör only a single poem was written, "The Dying Child," which was afterwards the best approved and the most widely circulated of all my attempts in verse. I read it to my acquaintances in Copenhagen, and excited some attention; but many only noticed my Fünen pronunciation, which suppresses the letter *d* wherever it occurs. Some few praised me, but from the majority I received a lecture on modesty and a caution against thinking too much of myself—I, who had not the slightest confidence in my own powers! In Wulff's house I met many talented men, and among all, I bowed in spirit with the greatest reverence to one—it was to the poet Adam Oehlenschläger. His praise sounded from every mouth around me, and I looked up to him with pious trust. How happy was I when one evening, in a great illuminated hall, where, painfully conscious of my shabby clothes, I had concealed myself among the curtains, he came up to me, and gave me his hand! I could have dropped on my knees before him. I saw Weyse again, and heard him play an impromptu on the piano; Wulff read parts of his translation of Byron, and Oehlenschläger's young daughter Charlotte astonished me by her bright youthful spirits.

When, after a residence of a few days, I went back from this house to the rector's, I felt the difference very deeply. The rector himself had just returned from Copenhagen, and had heard that I had recited a poem of my own composition; he looked at me with a piercing glance, and desired me to bring him the poem, adding, that he would forgive me if he found a spark of poetry in it. Trembling, I brought "The Dying Child." He read it, pronounced it to be sentimental trash, and poured forth all his anger upon me. If this had been done under the impression that I wasted my time habitually in writing verses, or that mine was a character that required repression, the intention would have been good; but he had no reason to believe that either was the case. From that day my position became more unhappy than ever, and my mental sufferings were so severe that I nearly succumbed beneath them: those were the darkest, the most unhappy days of my life. At last one of the teachers, who was going to Copenhagen, told Collin how badly things went with me; whereupon the latter at once removed me from the rector's house and from the school. When in taking leave of him I thanked him for the good he had done me, the passionate man cursed me, and angrily declared that I should never become a student, that my verses would moulder in the bookseller's warehouse, and that I should end my days in a lunatic asylum. I quitted him in a state of despair. Several years afterwards, when my works were read, and the "Improvisatore" had appeared, I met him in Copenhagen: he held out his hand to me in reconciliation, and said that he had made a mistake and treated

MY POEM CRITICISED

me on a wrong plan, but that now I could afford to let him sail on his own line. Those heavy dark hours were not without their consequent blessings in my later life.

A young man, afterwards very favourably known in Denmark for his zeal for Northern legendary lore and history, now became my tutor. I hired a small garret, which I have described in the "Fiddler," and another little work of mine tells how often the moon looked in to visit me there. I had a certain sum allowed me for my support, and as I must henceforth pay for the instruction I received, it was necessary to economize in some way. Several families gave me a place at their table on certain days, so that the week days were filled up. I became a kind of pensioner, like many another poor student in Copenhagen at the present day; and the variety thus introduced into my life, and the insight I obtained into the private life of many families, was not without its influence on me. I studied industriously. In certain departments I had already distinguished myself at Helsingör, especially in mathematics; in those branches I was therefore left to myself, and all efforts were directed to pushing me on in Latin and Greek; but my excellent tutor also found that much was to be done in a department in which I did not think myself deficient, namely, in religious instruction. He kept strictly to the words of the Bible. I knew these, for, from my first entrance into the school, I had carefully remembered all that was taught and said of the Book. I understood it with the idea that God is Love, and could not comprehend what was in contradiction to this, like the idea of a burning hell, where the fire endures for ever. Free from the terrorism and repression of the school benches, I spoke out my doubts with natural frankness ; my master, one of the noblest and most amiable of men, but who held fast to the letter, often became quite anxious about me : we argued together, while the same bright flame burned in the hearts of both. It was good for me that I fell into the hands of this unspoiled gifted man, whose nature was in some respects as peculiar as my own.

A fault of mine that showed itself very openly was a tendency, not to scoff, but to play with my best feelings, and to look upon intellect as the most valuable thing in the world. The rector had misunderstood my soft demonstrative nature, and my habit of expressing emotion had been turned into ridicule and repressed ; and the change this system wrought in me showed itself now that I was left free to pursue my own path. I did not exactly go from extreme timidity to boisterous hilarity, but I wearied myself with useless striving to appear something that I was not. I jested at feeling, and thought I had rid myself of it altogether, and yet I could be unhappy all day if I encountered a sour face where I had expected to find a friendly one. To the poems that I had written with tears, I now gave ridiculous titles or comic burdens. One I called " The Complaint of the Young Cat," another " The Sick Poet." The few poems I wrote at that time were all of a humorous kind. A complete change had taken place in me : the stunted shrub had been transplanted, and now began to send forth new shoots.

Wulff's eldest daughter, a lively genial girl, understood and even encouraged the humour which appeared in my scattered poems. She possessed my entire confidence, protected me like a good sister, and made a deep impression on me by awakening my sense of the comic.

At this period also a new stream began to run its course through Danish literature. The people began to take interest in what was written, though politics played no part in it.

Heiberg, who had gained for himself the name of a true poet by his charming works " Psyche " and " Walter the Potter," had introduced *vaudeville* to the Danish stage : it was Danish *vaudeville*, blood of our blood, and accordingly was received with acclamation, and almost drove away everything else. Thalia held carnival on the Danish stage, and Heiberg was her prime minister. I made his acquaintance at Oersted's ; an eloquent man, and the hero of the day, he interested me in the highest degree. He entered genially into conversation with me, and I went to call upon him. He considered my humorous poems worthy of a place in his capital weekly periodical, the " Flying Post." A short time before I had succeeded with difficulty in getting my poem, " The Dying Child," printed in a newspaper. No publisher of a journal, though many of them accepted the most miserable trash, would venture to print a work written by a man who went to school. The poem of mine which has become the most popular was accepted with an apology ; Heiberg saw it, and accorded it an honourable place. Two humorous poems of mine made their *début* in his pages under the signature H. I remember well the evening when the " Flying Post " appeared with my first verses in it. I was in a house where they wished me well, but looked upon my poetic talent as something very insignificant, and found some fault in every line I wrote. The master of the house came in with the "Flying Post " in his hand.

" Here are two capital poems. They must be Heiberg's : none but he could have written them."

And my poems were read out amid universal approval. The daughter of the house, who had been admitted to my secret, called out in the joy of her heart that the pieces were mine, and the admirers were silent and looked annoyed. That pained me deeply. One of our secondary *literati*, but a man of rank, who had a good house, one day gave me a place at his table. He mentioned that a new annual was to appear with the new year, and that he had been applied to for a contribution. I happened to say that the only little poem I possessed at the moment was to appear in this work at the request of the editor.

"Then it appears that people of all and every sort are to contribute to this book!" said my host, angrily. " Well, then, he can do without me; and I hardly think I shall give him anything."

My tutor lived at some distance from my lodging. I went to him twice a day. On my way to him my whole thoughts were taken up with my tasks; on my way home I breathed more freely, and all sorts of strange visions of poetry chased each other through my brain, but not one of them was transferred to paper. Only five or six humorous pieces were thrown off in the course of the year; and these disturbed me less when they were once quietly on the paper, than when they were wandering through my head.

In September, 1828, I became a student, and when the examination was over, the thousands of thoughts and ideas which had pursued me on my way to my tutor's flew out into the world like a swarm of bees in my first work, "A Foot Journey to Amak," a humorous book, which fully expressed my state of mind at the time, especially my propensity to turn everything into a jest, and with tears in my eyes to make sport of my feelings. It was a fantastic bit of coloured patchwork. As no bookseller had the courage to publish the little book, I ventured it at my own risk, and in a few days after it had appeared it was out of print. The bookseller Reitzel bought the second edition of me, and afterwards published a third; the book was also reprinted in Sweden. Every one read my book, and I heard nothing but approval; moreover, I was a student, and had thus attained my highest wish. I was giddy with joy, and in this state of feeling wrote my first dramatic work, a little piece in rhymed verse, entitled " The Courtship on St. Nicholas' Steeple; or, What does the Pit say ? "

The piece was a mistake, inasmuch as it satirized something that no longer exists among us, namely, the drama of chivalry ; it also made a little fun of the prevailing enthusiasm for *vaudeville*. The following is a sketch of the plot :

The watchman on St. Nicholas' tower, who always spoke in the character of a castled knight, wanted to marry his daughter to the keeper of a neighbouring church tower; but she was in love with a young tailor, who had just made a pilgrimage to Eulenspielzel's grave, and returned to find the punch-bowl already full, and the consent about to be given. The loving pair took refuge in the tailor's house of call, where dance and merriment reigned; but the watchman carried off his daughter, who thereupon went mad, and declared she would never become sane until her tailor was given to her. The old watchman concluded that Destiny should decide the matter; but where was Destiny to be found? Then suddenly the idea occurs to him that the public is the Pythia he seeks. The public must decide whether she is to marry the tailor or the keeper. Then it was decided that an appeal should be made to the youngest poet, that he might produce the story as a *vaudeville*, that style being so greatly in favour just now; and when the *vaudeville* came to be put on the stage, if the public whistled or hissed, such manifestation was not to be taken as a sign that the young author's work had failed, but simply as the voice of Destiny, saying, "She is to be married to the keeper." If, on the other hand, the *vaudeville* was applauded, it would mean, "She is to marry the tailor." "This speech," the father observed, "must be spoken in prose, that the public might understand it." And now each of the characters fancied himself on the stage, where in a concluding song the lovers begged for the audience to applaud, while the keeper entreated them to whistle, or at least to hiss.

My fellow-students welcomed the piece with acclamation. They were proud of me: I was the second of their comrades who had brought a piece upon the Danish stage in this year; for Arnesen, who was a student with me, had written "The Intrigue in the Popular Theatre," a *vaudeville* that long retained its place in the *repertoire*. We were the two young authors of the October examination, two of the sixteen poets whom this scholastic year had produced, and who were jocularly divided into the twelve greater and the four less.

A happy man was I now: I had poetic courage and youthful spirits; all houses began to be open to me, and I flew from circle to circle. Still I studied valiantly, and accordingly passed successfully in September, 1829, through my *Examen Philologicum et Philosophicum*, and was enabled to publish my first collection of poems, which found a cordial welcome. And now the sun shone bright upon my path in life.

IV.

As yet I had seen but a small part of my native country; to wit, a few places in Fünen and Seeland, and the chalky hills of Moen, one of the most beautiful points of our scenery. The beech forest hangs like a wreath over the white chalky rocks, from which the beholder gazes far out across the Baltic. In the summer of 1830 I wished to devote a portion of my first literary gains to the purpose of visiting Jutland, and becoming better acquainted with my native Fünen. I had no idea what serious consequences this summer excursion would bring, or what a transition was to take place in my inner life.

Jutland, stretching out between the North Sea and the Baltic till it ends in the drifting sands by the reef at Skjagen, possesses a peculiar character: towards the Baltic it presents great forests and hills; towards the North Sea mountains and loose sand; a magnificent lonely aspect; and between these two opposite aspects of nature stretches the brown heath with its wandering gipsies, its screaming birds, its quiet loneliness. The Danish poet Steen-Blicher has portrayed it in his novels. This was the first strange aspect of nature that I had beheld, and it consequently made a deep impression upon me. In the towns where my "Pedestrian Journey" and my humorous poems were known, I was well received. Fünen opened its country life for me, and not far from my birthplace. Odense, I passed several weeks as a welcome guest at the villa of good old Iversen. Poems now shot forth quickly on the paper, but the humorous ones became fewer and fewer. The feeling at which I had often jested now wished to revenge itself on me. On my journey I came to stay in a rich house in one of our smaller towns. Here a new world opened before me, a great world, though it could be contained in the four lines I then wrote:

"Two soft brown eyes mine eyes did see;
Home, fortune, happiness lay there for me;
With the peace of a child, yet a spirit so high,
And the memory will haunt me until I die."

New plans of life arose within me. I determined to give up writing verses, for to what could that lead? I would study and become a clergyman. I had but one thought, and that was of her; but it was self-delusion: she loved another, and she married him. Many years afterwards I understood and felt that here also all was for the best for her and for me. Probably she had no idea how deep my feeling was towards her, and knew not the effect it produced on me. She became a good man's excellent wife, and afterwards a happy mother. God's blessing be upon her!

Till now the element of parody had been the strongest in my writings. Several of my friends disapproved of this, and declared that my activity in this direction could lead to nothing good. Critics took up this line of argument just now, when a deeper feeling had quite effaced from my mind the fault that was attacked. A new collection of poems, "Fancies and Sketches," which appeared with the new year, manifested plainly enough what it was that oppressed my heart. A paraphrase of the feelings of my own breast appeared in a serious *vaudeville* I wrote, entitled "Parting and Meeting," with the one difference, that the love was here represented as mutual. The piece was performed in the theatre five years afterwards.

Among the friends I possessed at Copenhagan in those days, was Orla Lehmann, who afterwards, in the political life of Denmark, rose higher than any one in the favour of the people. Full of active life, eloquent and bold, he attracted me strongly by his character. The German language was much cultivated in his father's house; Heine's poems had been received there, and young Orla was enchanted with them. He lived in the country in the neighbourhood of the castle of Fredericksberg; I went out there to see him, and he came out rejoicing to meet me, repeating one of Heine's pieces, "Thalatta, Thalatta, thou endless sea." Reading Heine together, the afternoon and the evening slipped away; I had to stay there the night. But on this day I had made acquaintance with a poet who seemed to me to be singing out of my very soul. He displaced Hoffman, who, as the "Pedestrian Journey" shows, had hitherto made the deepest impression upon me. In my young days only three authors seem to have mingled with my very blood; they were Sir Walter Scott, Hoffman, and Heine.

I fell more and more into a morbid frame of mind, and felt a desire to seek out the mournful in life, and to linger over its mournful aspects. I became over-sensitive, and remembered the blame, not the praise, that was given me. My late schooling, during which I was forced forward too rapidly, and my desire to appear as an author directly I became a student, explain the fact that my first book, the "Pedestrian Journey," was not free from grammatical errors. I might have paid some one to correct the proof sheets for me, a kind of work that was new to me, and then I should have escaped censure in this respect. These faults were now jeered at, and the critics lingered over them while they hardly mentioned the better part. I know people who only read my poems to find out the faults. For instance, the number of times I had used the word "beautiful," or a similar epithet, was carefully noted. A gentleman, now a clergyman, who at that time wrote *vaudevilles* and critical articles, had the bad taste, in a company where I was present, to go through some of my poems in this spirit, until a little girl of six years, who had listened with astonishment to his depreciation of it all, took the book, and pointed to the word "and" with the remark, "But here's a little word against which you have not yet said anything." He felt the truth of the child's words, and kissed the little maid with a blush on his face.

I suffered much in this state of things; but being still somewhat subdued from the effect of my school life, I took everything without reply. I was too soft, too unpardonably good natured. Every one knew that this was my way, and some became almost cruel on the strength of it. All wanted to teach me; nearly all declared that I was being spoiled by praise, and that therefore *they* were anxious to tell me the truth; accordingly, I heard nothing spoken of but my faults, my real and alleged weaknesses. At times, indeed, the spirit of opposition was kindled within me, and then I declared that I would yet be a poet who should be honoured. But any word of this kind was at once caught up as the manifestation of unbearable vanity on my part, and was diligently repeated as such from house to house. I was a good fellow, so the general verdict said, but one of the most conceited people in the world; and this opinion was held of me at a time when I was often ready to despair of my own ability, and frequently thought, as in the darkest days of my school-time, that the idea of my talent was all self-delusion. I was ready to hold this belief myself, but to hear it uttered in hard and scornful words by others was more than I could always bear, and if at any time I gave vent to a proud, unconsidered word, this was turned into a scourge wherewith I might be chastised. But when used by those we love, such scourges become whips of scorpions.

Collin accordingly gave it as his opinion that I should undertake a little journey, for instance, to Northern Germany, to recreate myself and gain new ideas. In the spring of 1831 I left Denmark for the first time. I saw Lubeck and Hamburg; everything was new and surprising to me. I saw the first mountains, the Harz; the world seemed spreading and widening marvellously around me; my good humour came back to me like a bird of passage. But care is like a flock of sparrows remaining behind to hatch a brood in the nest of the bird of passage; and I did not yet feel quite strengthened.

In Dresden I made the acquaintance of Tieck; Ingemann had given me a letter to him; and one evening I heard him read a play of Shakespeare's. At my departure he wished me success as a poet, and embraced me heartily. This made a very deep impression upon me: I shall never forget the expression in his eyes. I left him with tears, and prayed earnestly to God for strength to tread the path my soul longed to follow —for strength to express what I felt in my heart; and I prayed that when I should see Tieck again, I might be known and valued by him.

Not till many years afterwards, when my later writings had been translated and appreciated in Germany, did we meet again. Then I felt the warm pressure of the hand of him who had given me the initiatory kiss in my second fatherland. In Berlin a letter of Oersted's procured me the acquaintance of Chamisso. The grave man with the flowing locks and the honest eyes opened the door to me himself. He read the letter I brought, and I know not how it was, but we seemed to understand each other at once. I felt full confidence in him, and could speak freely to him, though in bad German. Chamisso, however, understood Danish. I submitted my poems to him, and he was the first who translated some of them into German, and thus introduced them into Germany. In the "Morgenblatt" he spoke of me in the following generous words: "Gifted with wit, humour, and popular *naïveté*, Andersen has moreover at his command notes that awaken deeper echoes. Especially he shows the ability to create little pictures and landscapes by a few light but graphic touches. These pictures are, however, often too local in their nature to appeal to men not born in the poet's fatherland. Perhaps those parts of his works that could be translated, or that have been translated, are least calculated to give a picture of him." Chamisso became my friend for life, and the pleasure he took in the success of my later works is manifest in the letters to me that have been printed in the collected edition of his works.

The little voyage to Germany had a great influence upon me, and my friends in Copenhagen admitted the fact. The impressions of my journey were at once written down by me, and published under the title, "Shadows of Travel." But even if I had really improved, the old petty tendency still remained at home, to find out my faults and to educate me, and I was weak enough to bear this from people who had no right to assume such a position towards me. I seldom jested at the precepts I received, and if I allowed myself to do so, this conduct of mine was ascribed to my boundless vanity, and my friends declared that I would not listen to the advice of sensible people. One of these educationists once asked me if I wrote "Hound" with a small *h*.* It appears he had found a clerical error of this kind in my last book. I replied, laughing, "That I had been speaking of a small hound." My readers will say that these were petty grievances; but continual dropping will wear a hole in a stone. I allude to the matter here, because I feel constrained to protest against the accusation of vanity, which was brought against me when no other fault could be found with my private life, and which I still occasionally encounter, like an old coin that has almost passed out of circulation.

From the end of the year 1828 till the beginning of 1839 I was compelled to support myself solely by my writings. Denmark is a small country. In those days very few books went to Sweden and Norway, and thus my emolument could not be great. I found it difficult to pay my way; doubly difficult, because I was obliged to suit my dress in some measure to the circle in which I was received. To continue producing and producing was ruinous, indeed impossible; accordingly I translated a couple of pieces for the theatre, "La Quarantaine" and "La Reine de Seize Ans;" and as at that time a young composer named Hartmann, a grandson of him who composed the Danish national song, "King Christian stood by the lofty mast," wished to have a text for an opera, I declared myself ready to furnish one. Through Hoffman's writings I had become acquainted with Gozzi's mask comedies. I read "Il Corvo," considered it a capital subject, and in a few weeks had completed my *libretto*, "The Raven." To the ears of my countrymen it will seem strange that it was I who recommended Hartmann, and who pledged myself in my letter to the directors of the theatre for the fact that he was a man of talent, who could furnish something good; for now he takes rank as the first among our living Danish composers. For Bredal, another young composer, I prepared a text from Sir Walter Scott's "Bride of Lammermoor." Both works were produced on the stage, but I was subjected to very harsh criticism as one who had spoiled the works of foreign authors: it seemed to be forgotten that I had ever had any good in me, and I was declared to be a man wholly destitute of ability. The composer Weyse, on the other hand, of whom I have already spoken as my first benefactor, was completely satisfied with my treatment of the subject. He told me that he had long wished to compose an opera on the subject of Sir Walter Scott's "Kenilworth,"

---

* In Danish, as in German, every substantive has a capital initial letter

and asked me to work with him in the production of a book. I did not imagine that I should be entirely outlawed by the critics for this. I required money for my expenses, and this was another reason for undertaking the task; moreover, I felt gratified at the idea of working with Weyse, the most celebrated of our composers. I was glad that he, who had first spoken on my behalf at Siboni's house, was ready to enter into more intimate relations with me. But I had scarcely half finished the *libretto*, when I began to hear myself blamed for making use of a well-known romance. I wished to retire from the task, but Weyse encouraged me, and dissuaded me from drawing back. Afterwards, when I was going abroad, before he had finished the music, I left my fate, so far as the book was concerned, entirely in his hands. Accordingly he interpolated whole stanzas, and the altered *finale* is entirely his. It was a peculiarity with this strange man to like no work that ended mournfully; therefore Amy Robsart was to be made happy with Leicester, and Elizabeth to abandon the Earl and sing the air, " Proud England, I am thine." At first I protested against this, but afterwards yielded, for the piece was written for Weyse. It was brought upon the stage, but only the songs have been printed. Then followed anonymous attacks upon me, coarse letters sent to me by the post, whose concealed writers jeered and abused me. However, in the same year I produced another volume of poems, entitled " The Twelve Months of the Year." This book has afterwards been considered as containing some of my best lyrical pieces, but at the time of its appearance it was a failure.

In those days a certain monthly periodical of literature, now defunct, was in full bloom: at its first appearance it numbered many eminent men among its contributors; but it lacked men who could efficiently express themselves on æsthetic subjects. Unfortunately, every one considered himself competent to express an opinion on matters of that kind; but a man may write most efficiently on medicine, or on the science of education, and may have made himself a name, and yet be a tyro in poetry. And the proof was shown in this case. Gradually the editor found it more and more difficult to get a critic for poetical works, but the man who always showed himself most zealously ready, in speech and writing, to step into the arena of criticism, was the historian and state councillor Molbeck, who has played so prominent a part as a Danish critic that I must be allowed to describe him more closely. He is a painstaking collector, writes Danish very correctly, and his Danish Dictionary is a very meritorious work, whatever its faults may be; but as a poetical critic he is one-sided and partial even to fanaticism. Unfortunately he belongs to that class of scientific men who have only one-sixty-fourth of poetry in their composition, and these are the worst æsthetic judges; and by his censures on Ingemann's romances he has shown how incapable he is of appreciating the works he criticises. He has himself produced a volume of poems of a mediocre kind, " A Pilgrimage through Denmark," written in a weak, florid style, and " A Journey through Germany, France, and Italy," in which the information seems to be derived not from experience but from books. He was sitting in his study, or in the royal library, in which he holds an office, when suddenly he was made director of the theatre and censor of the works offered for acceptance there. He was in bad health, prejudiced, and ill humoured. The consequence may be imagined. Of my first poems he spoke very favourably; but soon my star waned before a rising orb—that of a young lyric poet, Paludan Müller; and as he no longer loved me, he hated me, and that is the whole truth. In the same periodical the very pieces that had been praised were decried by the same critic who had lauded them, now that they appeared in a new and augmented edition. We have a Danish proverb which says, "When the waggon sticks, all hang on to it;" and I now experienced its truth.

It happened, moreover, that a new star arose in Danish literature. Henrik Hertz appeared anonymously with his "Spectral Letters." It was a kind of expulsion of the profane from the Temple. The deceased Baggesen sent polemic letters from Paradise, written in a style very much resembling his own. These letters contained a kind of apotheosis for Heiberg and certain attacks upon Oehlenschläger and Hanch. The old story of my orthographical blunders saw the light once more. My name and my career as a pupil at Slagelse were mentioned in connection with St. Anders. I was satirized, or, if people will have it, chastised.

Hertz's book at that time filled all Denmark. No one was spoken of but he. The anonymous nature of the letters gave additional piquancy to the affair: people were charmed, and with reason. Heiberg, in his "Flying Post" exculpated a few æsthetically unimportant men, but not me. I felt the wound of the sharp knife deeply, and my opponents looked upon me as effectually excluded from the world of culture. Nevertheless, I soon afterwards published a little book, "Vignettes of Danish Poets," in which I characterized living and dead celebrities, devoting a few words to each, but only speaking of their excellences. The book attracted attention: it is still considered one of the best things I have done, but the critics passed it by in silence. Here, as before, it appeared that they passed by those of my writings which were the most successful.

My affairs now stood at the lowest ebb; and just in the year when Hertz had made himself known, and was to receive a pension with which to travel, I had preferred a request for a similar favour. The universal opinion was that I had reached my culminating point: if ever I were to travel, it must be now. I felt, what has afterwards been acknowledged, that travelling would be the best thing for me. In order that I might come into notice, I was told that I must endeavour to obtain a kind of recommendation from some of the chief poets and men of science, for just now many young men of merit were preferring a request similar to mine, and I should find it difficult to make myself heard among them. Accordingly, I procured recommendations, and, so far as I know, I am the only Danish poet who has had to produce vouchers for that fact in his own country. It was remarkable, moreover, that the men who recommended me found I possessed the most various qualifications. Oehlenschläger, for instance, praised my lyrical talent, my *serious* tendency; Ingemann, my power of portraying popular life; Heiberg declared that since Wessel's time he had met with no Danish poet who had more humour than I; Oersted was pleased to observe that all my opponents and my upholders were agreed upon the fact that I was a true poet; and Thiele expressed himself warmly and energetically upon the genius which he said he had seen combating in me against the weight of poverty and adverse circumstances. I received a travelling pension: Hertz got a larger and I a smaller one, and this was just and right.

"Now you must be glad," said my friends. "Take care to appreciate your boundless good fortune. Enjoy the present moment heartily, for it will probably be the only opportunity you will have. You should hear what people say about your intention of travelling, and how we are obliged to defend you, and sometimes we are unable to do so."

That was rather painful to hear. I felt a burning desire to get away, so that I might breathe freely; but care sits firm on the rider's horse. More than one care pressed upon my heart, and though I am unlocking its chambers before the world, one or two doors I must needs keep closed. At my departure my prayer to God was, that I might die far away from Denmark, or that I might return strengthened for labour, and able to produce works which should do me credit and give satisfaction to my good friends.

Now that I was to depart, the picture of those who were dear to me rose warmly in my heart. Among those whom I have already named were two who had an especial influence upon my poetry and my life, and whom I must here mention again. A motherly friend, a woman of unusually cultivated mind, Madame Lässöe, had admitted me into her pleasant family circle. Often she listened with deep sympathy to my sorrows, turned my attention more and more to the beautiful and the poetical in the details of life, and when almost every one had despaired of me as a poet, she kept up my courage; and if in anything that I have written purity of feeling can be traced, it is to this lady especially that I am indebted for it. Another friend of great consequence to me was a son of Collin, Eduard. He had grown up in easy and happy circumstances, and possessed a boldness and decision of character of which I was entirely destitute. I felt that he loved me sincerely, and my whole soft soul flew out to meet him. He was more deliberate and more practical than I, and this made me often misunderstand him. He wished to infuse some of his own spirit into me, who stood like a swaying reed blown to and fro by every wind. In the practical part of life, he, my junior, stood protectingly at my side, helping me in many things, from Latin style to the arrangement of my affairs and the publication of my writings. He has always remained the same, and if a man may number his friends, I must put him in the first rank among mine. When we go from the mountains we begin to see them in their real form, and it is the same with friends.

Over Cassel and the Rhine, I reached Paris; but I retained no vivid impression of what I saw. The idea for a poem was growing more and more firmly in my mind, and as it became clearer to me, I hoped to win my enemies over by it. There is an old Danish popular song, "Agnéte and the Man of the Sea," which accorded with my own state of mind, and which I felt a wish to use as a subject. The song sets forth how the fair maid Agnéte was wandering alone by the sea shore, when a man of the sea came forth out of the waves and lured her down with his honeyed words. She followed him to his home beneath the waters, and in the seven years that she was his wife she bore him seven children. One day she was sitting by the cradle, the church bells sounded down to her through the sea, and she felt a longing to visit the church once more. With her tears and entreaties she moved the man of the sea to lead her upwards: she promised to return immediately. He begged her not to forget his children, and especially the youngest in the cradle: then he stopped her ears and her mouth, and carried her up to the sea shore. But as soon as she entered the church, all the pictures on the wall turned away their faces when they saw the daughter of sin from the depths of the sea. Then she was frightened, and would not go back, although the little children were crying below. I treated the song freely in the lyric and dramatic style. I may aver that the subject seemed to take hold on my very heart, and all the remembrances of our beech woods and of the open sea appeared to melt together in it.

Thus in the midst of bustling Paris the national tones of Denmark surrounded me. I became filled with the deepest gratitude to God, for I felt that everything I had was the gift of His mercy. And I now received a vivid impression from what was passing around me. I witnessed one of the July celebrations at a time when they had the charm of novelty; it was in the year 1833. I was present at the unveiling of the Napoleon statue. I saw the experienced King Louis Philippe, on whom the hand of Providence had so openly manifested itself; his son, the Duke of Orleans, danced merrily and joyously in the charming popular ball in the Hotel de Ville. Accident brought me into contact for the first time with the poet Heine, who then occupied the throne in my world of poesy. When I expressed to him how rejoiced I was at meeting him, and at his friendly reception of me, he replied that this could scarcely be so, for I had not been to visit him. I replied that just because I had such a high appreciation of his powers I had feared that he might find it ridiculous if I, an unknown Danish poet, sought him out; "and," I added, "your smile would have hurt me deeply." He gave a friendly answer. Several years later, when we met again in Paris, I was very kindly received in his house, and was allowed to look into the bright poetic part of his soul. Paul Dupont also made friendly advances towards me, and Victor Hugo received me likewise. During my whole journey to Paris, and in the month that I passed there, I did not hear a single word from home. Could not my friends have found something pleasant to impart to me? At length one day a letter arrived—a big expensive letter: my heart beat with hope and expectation, for it was the first letter I had had. I opened it, and beheld—not a written line, but a Copenhagen newspaper with a satirical poem about me. This had been sent so far to me, unpaid, probably by the anonymous author himself. This hateful piece of malice hurt me deeply. I never found out who was the author; perhaps one of those who afterwards called me friend and pressed my hand. People have sometimes bad thoughts; well, I have mine too.

It is a weakness of my countrymen, that in foreign lands, during their residence in a large city, they live almost entirely in a circle of their own people; they must dine together, meet in the theatre, and see all the sights in each other's company; letters are shown about, news from home is discussed, and at last one hardly knows if one is at home or abroad. I partook of this weakness, and accordingly determined, when I quitted Paris, to board for a month in Switzerland, in some quiet place, and to associate only with Frenchmen, that I might learn their language, a knowledge of which I felt to be in the highest degree important to me.

THE LAMPOON.

In the little town of Locle, in a valley of the Jura mountains, where snow fell in August, and the clouds floated beneath us, I was received by the amiable family of a wealthy clockmaker. They would not hear of my paying anything, I lived among them as a relative; and when the time came to part, the children shed tears. These little people had become my friends, though I did not understand their *patois*, and they would shout into my ears, fancying that I must be deaf, to be so dull. What a stillness, what a silence was there in nature, up yonder, in the evening! We could just hear the bells sounding from the French frontier. A short distance from the town stood a solitary house, white and cleanly. The visitor descending through two cellars came upon noisy mill-wheels, turning in a stream which rushed along here, hidden from the world. On my solitary walks I often visited this place; and here I finished my poem, "Agnéte and the Man of the Sea," which I had begun in Paris. From Locle I sent it home to Denmark, and never was one of my earlier or later works accompanied by greater hopes. But the poem was coldly received. The verdict was, that I was trying to imitate Oehlenschläger, who had once sent masterpieces home. In these last years the poem has, I think, begun to be more generally read, and to find friends. But it was a step in advance: unconsciously to myself, this poem closed my simply lyrical activity. Of late the opinion has been expressed in Denmark that although at its first appearance the piece excited far less attention than was accorded to other and inferior works of mine, the poetry had a deeper and stronger tone. For me, the poem closed an epoch of my life.

V.

On the 5th of September, 1833, I went across the Simplon into Italy. On the anniversary of the day on which, fourteen years before, I had entered Copenhagen, poor and helpless, was I to tread this land of my longing and of my poetic fortune. It seemed here, as it had often happened before, without any premeditation on my part, as though I had especial days of fortune in the year; but fortune has come to me so often, that perhaps I have only chronicled her visits on days that I particularly remembered. All around me was like spring, though the grapes hung in long clusters from tree to tree; never afterwards have I seen Italy in such beauty. I sailed on the Lago Maggiore, visited the cathedral of Milan, passed a few days in Genoa, and from thence undertook the beautiful coast journey to Carrara. In Paris I had seen statues, but my eyes had been closed to them; only in Florence, before the Venus de Medici, it seemed as though a veil fell from them. A new world of art lay open before me: that was the first fruits of my journey. Here I learned to comprehend the beauty of form, the spirit that manifests itself in outlines. The life of the people, the aspect of nature, everything around me was new, and yet seemed so strangely well known, as if I had come into a familiar country where I had passed my childhood. With peculiar quickness I accustomed myself to the new scenes and became familiar with all around, while a deep Northern despondency—it was not home-sickness, but a heavy unhappy feeling—took possession of me. In Rome I received the first news how little the poem, " Agnéte and the Man of the Sea," which I had sent home, was esteemed: in Rome the next letter I received brought me the news that my mother was dead, and I stood all alone in the world.

It was at this time that I met Hertz for the first time, in Rome. In a letter to me, Collin had said that he would be glad to hear that I and Hertz had become friends and associated together; but even without this letter the friendship would have come about, for Hertz held out his hand kindly to me, and expressed his sympathy with my sorrow. Of all with whom I associated there, he was the most completely educated, and we often talked confidentially together, even concerning the attacks which were often made upon my poetry at home. He, who had himself inflicted a wound upon me, spoke the following words, which sank deep into my memory:

"It has been your misfortune that you were obliged to print everything. The public has been able to follow your progress step by step; and I believe that even a Goethe, in your position, would have had the same disagreeables to bear."

His conversation taught me much, and I felt that I had gained a merciful judge the more. In his company I travelled to Naples, where we lived together in one house.

In Rome I also made the acquaintance of Thorwaldsen. Many years before, when I had not long been in Copenhagen, and was walking, a poor lad, through the streets, Thorwaldsen had been there too, having returned for the first time from Italy. We met in the streets. I knew that he was a man distinguished in art, looked at him, and took off my hat; he passed, but suddenly returning, said to me,

"Where have I seen you before? I think we know each other."

"No," I replied, "we do not know each other at all."

In Rome I reminded him of this encounter, and he smiled and pressed my hand, saying,

"We must then already have felt that we should become good friends."

I read my Agnéte to him, and was delighted when he said, in speaking of it,

"Why, it sounds to me as if I heard the rushing of the sea at home in Denmark." And then he embraced me.

One day, when he saw how downcast I was, and I told him of the lampoon that had been sent to me from home, he set his teeth angrily, and said, in a momentary outburst of passion.

"Yes, yes, I know those people! I should have been served just in the same way if I had remained there; I should perhaps not even have got leave to exhibit a model! Heaven be praised that I have not need of them, for they know how to abuse and plague a man."

He begged me to keep my courage up, and then it must and would go well with me; and then he told me of a few dark passages in his own life, how he too had been hurt and misjudged.

After the Carnival I went from Rome to Naples, saw the blue grotto at Capri, which had then just been discovered, visited the temples at Pœstum, and came back to Rome in the Easter week; from thence I went over Florence and Venice to Vienna and Munich.

But at that time I had neither thought nor appreciation for Germany, and when I thought of Denmark, I felt terror and anguish at the apprehension of the evil I expected to encounter there. Italy with its nature and its popular life filled my soul, and I felt a longing for that country. My earlier life, and the later scenes I had beheld, were melted together in my mind into a fiction, which I was constrained to write down, though I felt sure that it would bring me more sorrow than joy in my native land, if necessity should compel me to print it. In Rome, already I had written the first chapters. The work was my novel, "The Improvisatore."

At my first visits to the theatre, when I was a little boy in Odense, where, as I have already stated, the pieces were given in German, I had seen the "Donau-weibchen," and the public had been especially delighted with the actress who played the chief character; she was courted and honoured, and I often thought how happy she must be. Many years afterwards, when I returned to Odense as a student, I saw in a room of the old hospital where the poor widows lived, and where a number of beds stood ranged side by side, a painting of a female in a gilt frame hanging over one of these beds. The picture represented Lessing's Emilia Galotti plucking the rose; but it was a portrait, and it contrasted strangely with the surrounding poverty.

"Whom does it represent?" I asked.

"Oh," said one of the old woman, "that is the face of the German lady, the poor lady who was once an actress."

And now appeared a little ladylike woman with a wrinkled face, and attired in a silk gown that had once been black. This was the once famous singer, whose performance of the "Donau-weibchen" had created such enthusiasm. This made a great impression on me, and frequently came back into my mind. In Naples I heard Malibran for the first time. Her singing and acting surpassed everything I had yet seen and heard; and yet when I saw her I could not help thinking of the poor old singer in the hospital at Odense. I combined the two figures in the character of "Annunciata" in my romance, and Italy was the background for the mingled tissue of truth and fiction.

In August, 1834, I returned to Denmark. At Ingemann's in Sorö, in a little attic room among fragrant lime trees, I wrote the first part of the book, and I finished the work in Copenhagen. Even my best friends were almost giving me up as a poet. It was said, a mistake had been made concerning my talent. With much difficulty I found a publisher for the book, for which I received a very small sum. The "Improvisatore" appeared, was read, went out of print, and was reprinted. The critics were silent, the newspapers made no sign; but I heard it said around me that interest had been excited by my book, and that people were pleased with it.

At last the poet Carl Bagger, who at that time was editor of a paper, wrote the first opinion concerning my work. He began ironically, with the usual diatribe against me: "It was all over with this author—he had gone beyond his mark," &c.; in short, he went through all the usual pipe and tea-cup criticism, and then, suddenly veering round, expressed a warm enthusiasm for me and for my book. Now the people laughed about me; but I wept—it was my nature to do so; I wept myself out and felt warm gratitude towards the Creator and towards my fellow-creatures.

"To Conference Councillor Collin and his noble wife, in whom I have found parents, and to their children, who became my brothers and sisters, who gave me a home in my native country, I here offer the best I have to give." So said the dedication.

Many who had been inimical to me now changed their views; and thus I gained one, as I hope, for life. That one was the poet Hauch, one of the most noble characters I know. He had come back from Italy, after a residence of several years abroad, at the time when the good people of Copenhagen were intoxicated with Heiberg's *vaudevilles*, and when my " Pedestrian Journey " had its success. He stood up against Heiberg, and gave me a thrust here and there : nobody drew his attention to the better among my lyric poems ; they represented me to him as a spoiled obstinate child of fortune. He now read my " Improvisatore," felt that I was capable of better things, and the nobility of his character was shown in a hearty letter which he wrote to me, wherein he acknowledged that he had done me wrong, and offered me the hand of reconciliation. From that day we became friends. Zealously has he tried to do me good, and heartily has he encouraged my every forward step. But so little have many understood his kindness and the confidence that existed between us, that not long since, when he wrote a novel, and introduced in it a fantastic character of a poet, whose vanity brings him to the madhouse, the good people of Denmark declared that he had behaved very unhandsomely towards me, in portraying my weaknesses. Let it not be believed that this is an unsupported assertion or a misunderstanding on my part : Hauch felt himself called upon to write a dissertation upon me as a poet, to show what he really thought of me.

But to return to the " Improvisatore." This book raised my fallen house, brought my friends about me, and achieved something more : for the first time I felt that I had really won favour. The book was translated into German by Kruse, under the long title " Youthful Life and Dreams of an Italian Poet." I expressed my dislike to this title, but Kruse declared it was necessary to excite attention. Bagger had, as I said, been the first to notice the book ; at length, after a considerable time had elapsed, a second critique appeared in a more courteous style than I had been accustomed to hear, but yet one that slurred over the best parts of the book, and lingered over the faults and the incorrectly spelt Italian words. And when Nicolai's well-known book, " Italy as It really Is," happened at that time to come to us, people said it was easy now to estimate the worth of what Andersen had written, for one must go to Nicolai to get a real notion of Italy.

The first real appreciation, or perhaps over-appreciation, of my book came from Germany. Like a rich man, I bowed in joyful gratitude towards the sunshine ; for my heart is grateful : I am not, as the Danish monthly periodical condescended to assert in its critique upon the " Improvisatore," an ungrateful man, who in his book shows no real sense of what his benefactors have done for him. I myself was the poor Antonio who groaned beneath his load ; *I*, the poor boy who had received the bread of charity. From Sweden, also, afterwards, praise came to me ; the Swedish papers contained favourable notices of the work ; and in these last years it has been received with equal kindness in England, where the poetess Mary Howitt translated it ; I am told it has met with similar favour in Holland and in Russia.

There dwells in the public a power greater than the power of critics or of separate ıactions. I felt that I now stood on a better footing at home, and my spirit had moments in which it raised its wings. In these alternations of hope and despondency I wrote my next romance, " O. Z." which is considered by many in Denmark as my best, an opinion in which I do not concur. It portrays characteristic features of city life. Before " O. Z." my first tales and stories appeared; but this is not the place to speak of them. At that time I felt a strong mental desire to write, and fancied I had found my proper sphere in novel writing. In the next year, 1837, " Only a Fiddler " was produced, a book on which I pondered deeply, though the incidents were rapidly put on the paper. My design was to show that talent was not genius, and that when the sunshine of fortune is wanting, talent will perish here on earth, but not the nobler, better nature. This book too won me a public; but the critics would not yet vouchsafe me an encouraging appreciation—forgetting that in process of time the boy grows to be a man, and that knowledge may be acquired in other ways than by following the ordinary beaten track. There was no getting rid of the old established notions. When " O. Z." appeared, the work was revised, sheet by sheet, by a professor of the university who had offered to undertake this work; it was seen by two other competent men; and yet the critics asserted that Andersen's usual grammatical inaccuracies were to be found here, as in his other works. The book was further thrown into the shade by the fact that the " Every-day Stories," published by Heiberg, written in a splendid style, redolent of truth and taste, appeared just at that time; their own value, and the recommendation of the name of Heiberg, who was then the shining star in literature, gave them the first rank.

I had, however, achieved thus much, that people no longer doubted my poetic faculty, whereas, before my journey to Italy, all such powers had been strenuously denied me. But no Danish criticism touched upon the idea which may have been embodied in my romances; it was only after they appeared in the Swedish that some newspapers in that country went deeper into the matter, and took up my works with honest good will. In Germany the same thing was done; and from thence my courage was strengthened to continue. It was not until last year that a man of consequence in Denmark, the poet Hauch, expressed himself in the dissertation I have already mentioned concerning these romances, and in a few words explained their characteristic feature.

In the same year in which the " Fiddler " appeared, 1837, I visited the neighbouring country of Sweden for the first time. I went by the Göta canal to Stockholm. At that time what we now call Scandinavian sympathy was unknown; from the old wars against our neighbours there remained a kind of inherited mistrust: little of Swedish literature was known, and but few Danes considered the fact that a very little practice and pains would enable them to read and understand the Swedish tongue. Tegnér's " Futhcof " and " Axel " were scarcely known, except through translations. I had read a few more Swedish authors, and the unfortunate dead Stagnelius impressed me with his poems even more than Tegnér, who at that time represented poetry in Sweden. I, whose travels had till now always been to the South, and who in quitting Copenhagen had bid farewell to my native tongue, felt almost at home everywhere in Sweden; the languages are so closely allied that two people may speak, each using his native tongue, and each understanding the other. It appeared to me, the Dane, as if the limits of Denmark were widened; the relationship of the nations became more and more prominent in other respects, and I felt how closely allied Dane and Swede and Norwegian are to each other. I met friendly hearty people, and to such I readily attach myself. This journey I count among the most joyous I have made. A stranger to Swedish scenery, I was in the highest degree impressed with the journey to Tröllhätta, and with the very picturesque position of Stockholm. To the uninitiated it will sound fabulous when I say that the steamers from the lakes ascend the mountains, whence the great pine and beech forests may be seen waving below; for the ships are raised or lowered through large flood-gates while the traveller goes on his woodland journey. Not one of the cascades of Switzerland or of Italy, not even the cataract of Ferni, has so majestic an appearance as that of Tröllhätta; such at least was the impression it made upon me.

With this journey, and especially with the last-named place, is associated the memory of an acquaintance of great interest, and one that was not without its influence upon me — I mean that of the Swedish authoress, Frederika Bremer. I had just been conversing with the captain of the steamer and a few fellow-passengers concerning the Swedish authors resident in Stockholm, and I expressed a wish to see and talk with Miss Bremer.

" You will not meet her," said the captain: " she is absent on a visit to Norway."

" She will be sure to come back before I go," I observed, in jest. " I 'm always fortunate on my journeys, and most of my wishes are fulfilled."

" But it will scarcely be the case this time," replied the captain.

A few hours afterwards he came laughing, with the list of the newly embarked passengers in his hand, and called out to me,

" You lucky personage! good fortune certainly attends you. Miss Bremer is here, and is going to Stockholm with us."

I thought he was jesting. He showed me the list, but I was still unconvinced, for I saw no one among the new arrivals who looked like an authoress. Evening came on, and at midnight we were on the great Lake Wener. Next morning I wished to see this great sheet of water, whose shores can hardly be discerned at sunrise, and accordingly left the cabin. At the same moment there emerged from the ladies' cabin another passenger, a lady, neither young nor old, and wrapped in a cloak. I thought, If Miss Bremer is on board, this must be she; and I began a conversation with her. She replied politely, but formally, and would not tell me frankly if she was the authoress of the celebrated novels or not. She asked my name, and recognized it, but owned that she had not read any of my works. On her asking if I had no book of my own with me, I lent her a copy of the " Improvisatore," which I had destined for Beskow She disappeared with the book, and I saw no more of her all the morning. When I met her again, her face glowed and she was as hearty as possible. She pressed my hand, and said that she had read the greater part of the first volume, and that now she knew me. The steamer flew with us across the mountains and through quiet inland lakes into the Baltic, where the islands lie strewn like an archipelago, with wonderful transitions from naked rocks to spots covered with grass, and others clad with forests and houses. The rapids and the rushing tide here render necessary the services of a good pilot; indeed, there are spots at which the passengers are obliged to sit motionless in their places, while the pilot keeps his eyes fixed upon one point: we feel in the ship the hand of powerful Nature seizing our craft for a moment, and then letting it go. Miss Bremer told me many a legend and many a tale connected with one or other of the islands or of the castles upon them. In Stockholm I improved my acquaintance with her, and year by year correspondence has cemented our friendship. She is a noble woman: the great truths of religion and the poetic in the quiet events of life have deeply penetrated her.

The Swedish translations of my romances did not appear until after my tour in Sweden: only my lyrical poems and pedestrian journey were known to a few authors, and these received me in the heartiest way. I found hospitality and saw faces in a holiday dress of smiles, and Sweden and its inhabitants became dear to me. The city itself appeared to me to rival Naples in its position and picturesque appearance: of course the Italian city has the advantage of the Southern air and sunshine, but the aspect of Stockholm is just as attractive: it has some resemblance to Constantinople seen from Pera, but of course the minarets are wanting. A great diversity of colour prevails in the Swedish capital: there are whitewashed buildings, wooden houses painted red, cabins built of turf, with blooming plants; pines and beech trees peer forth among the houses and the churches with their cupolas and towers. The streets in Södermalm rise up with wooden staircases, high out of the Mälar Lake, which is covered with smoking steamers and with boats rowed by women in many-coloured garb.

I had been recommended by Oersted to Berzelius, who procured me a good reception in old Upsala: from thence I returned to Stockholm. City, land, and people became dear to me: as I have said, the boundaries of my home seemed to enlarge, and I felt how nearly the three nations are related. Impressed with this feeling, I wrote a "Scandinavian Song," with a laudatory verse for each of the three nations, in which the best characteristic of each was held forth.

"It seems that the Swedes have made much of him," was the first expression of opinion I heard at home.

Years went by, and the neighbours came to understand one another better. Oehlenschläger, Frederika Bremer, and Tegnér induced them to read each other's authors: they came to value one another, and the foolish remains of the old enmity, which had been founded in ignorance, faded away, and now a fine hearty feeling exists between Swedes and Danes. In Copenhagen a Scandinavian Union was founded, and now my

I MEET FREDERIKA BREMER.

song came into favour, and it was said, "Whatever Andersen has written will live," an opinion just as incorrect as the earlier, which declared my writings to be merely the produce of gratified vanity.

After my return I began diligently to study history and to make myself further acquainted with foreign literature. Still the book which attracted me most strongly was that of Nature, and during my summer visits to country houses in Fünen, especially in Sykkesholm, romantically situate in the midst of a forest, and on the baronial estate of Glorup, whose proprietors accorded me the kindest reception, I certainly learned more in my solitary wanderings than the wisdom of the schools could teach me. Then already, as in later days, Collin's house in Copenhagen was a second home to me, for here I found parents and brothers and sisters. Social life in the best circles was opened to me, and the student life especially interested me, for here the interest of youth was restored to me. Student life in Copenhagen is different from a similar condition in the German towns, and at that time was especially animated. Its highest point of interest for me was in the Students' Union, where professors and students met together, and no line of demarcation is drawn between the older and the younger members. In this union were to be found journals and books of various lands ; once a week an author read out his latest work ; sometimes a concert or a burlesque performance was got up ; and here, it may be said, originated the first Danish popular comedies, in which the events of the day were used in an innocent, but always a witty and amusing manner. Sometimes performances were given in the presence of ladies for the furtherance of some benevolent object, as lately, for instance, to contribute to Thorwaldsen's Museum, to carry out Bissen's statues in marble for the university, and for similar purposes. The professors and students undertook to represent the characters ; I also appeared several times, and gained the conviction that my fear at appearing on the stage far outweighed my dramatic talent, if, indeed, I possessed any. Beyond this, I wrote and arranged several pieces, and thus contributed my share. I have reproduced a few pictures of those days, especially the Students' Union, in the romance, " O. Z." The cheerful and humorous spirit which appears in parts of that work, and of other things I wrote at that period, had its origin in Collin's house, where I was so agreeably influenced that my mental malady never gained the upper hand. Collin's eldest married daughter especially influenced me by her sprightly humour and wit. When a man's spirit is soft and elastic as the surface of the sea, it is sure to mirror his surroundings.

My writings continued to be bought and read in my native land, and thus I received a higher sum for each successive work. But when we consider what narrow bounds enclose the reading world of Denmark, it will easily be believed that my emolument could not be great. Still, I had enough to live upon. Collin—who is one of those men who perform more than they promise—was my helper, my comfort, and my support.

At that time the late Count von Rantzau-Breitenburg, a Holsteiner, was privy state minister in Denmark. A noble, amiable character was his—that of an educated gentleman, with the courtesy of a true knight. He followed accurately the movements of Danish literature. In his youth he had been a great traveller, and had resided long in Spain and Italy. He read my " Improvisatore" in the original, felt himself strongly attracted by the work, and expressed himself warmly in favour of the book at Court and in society. Nor was this all : he sought me out, and became to me a benefactor and a friend.

One morning, as I sat alone in my little room, the friendly man stood before me for the first time. He was one of those men who at once inspire confidence. He invited me to visit him, and asked me frankly if he could be useful to me in any way. I pointed out how irksome it was

MY HOME AT COLLIN'S.

to be compelled to write that I might live; to be always thinking of the morrow, and not to be able to work and develope myself free from care. He pressed my hand in a friendly way, and promised to prove a useful friend to me. Collin and Oersted silently united with him and became my advocates.

For several years an arrangement had existed, under King Frederick VI., which was very honourable to the Danish government—the custom, namely, not only of devoting a considerable sum annually to the use of young artists and *literati* as travelling pensions, but to be devoted to giving certain among them a kind of yearly stipend. All our best poets have partaken of this bounty, as Oehlenschläger, Ingemann, Heiberg, C. Winther, and others. Hertz had just then received a stipend of this sort, and his future had thus been assured. It was my hope and my wish to be made a partaker of this bounty, and I gained my wish. Frederick VI. accorded me a pension of two hundred dollars specie annually. I was filled with joy and thankfulness, for now I was no longer compelled to write that I might live—I had a secure provision in case of sickness—I was less dependent on those around me; and a new era commenced in my life.

VI.

FROM this day a continual sunshine seemed to smile upon my heart. I felt a sense of quiet, of security. When I looked back upon my past life, I could clearly understand that a loving Providence watched over me, and that everything was ordained by a higher power; and the more firmly a man can grasp this idea, the more safe will he feel. Childhood was far behind me, but my youth really began from this time; until now, my life had been a laborious swimming against the stream. The spring-time of my life began; but even spring has its dark days, its storms, before the bright summer comes: these days are sent to develope the fruit that is to ripen.

Whether the fault was on my side or not, there was certainly a party against me. I felt wounded and hurt by several concurrent disagreeables, was uncomfortable at home, and indeed felt ill. Therefore I abandoned my piece, whose representation had been so long delayed, to its fate, and hurried away dispirited and out of health. To make this section of my life clear and intelligible to my readers, I should be obliged to enter in detail into the mysteries of the theatre, to give a sketch of our artistic cliques, and to speak of persons who do not belong to public life. Many a man in my place would have become ill, or have got very angry; and perhaps the latter would have been the wisest course.

Before my departure several of my young friends among the students organized a *fête* for me: among the elder division of those who received me on this occasion were Collin, Oehlenschläger, and Oersted. This was like the breaking in of sunshine upon my clouded spirits; I found heartiness and friendship as I sorrowfully left my native land. It was in October, 1840.

I visited Italy for the second time, and from thence proceeded to Greece and Constantinople. I have told the story of my journey in my own way in "A Poet's Bazaar."

In Holstein I stayed a few days with Count Rantzau-Breitenburg, from whom I had received an invitation, and whose ancestral castle I now saw for the first time. I made acquaintance with the rich Holstein scenery, and then hastened by way of Nuremberg to Munich. I cast a glance at Munich's artist life, but for the most part went my solitary way, sometimes full of life-gladness, at others filled with doubts of my powers. I had a peculiar talent in lingering over the shadowy phases of life, and thoroughly understood the art of tormenting myself.

In the winter-time I crossed the Brenner, stayed a few days in Florence, where I had once resided for some time, and came to Rome for the Christmas holidays. Here I met old friends, saw the wonderful art-treasures once more, and was present at a Carnival and Moccoli.

But not only was I physically ill, Nature around me seemed to be sick likewise: there was no longer the freshness, the repose I had found in my first visit to Rome. There were shocks of earthquake, the Tiber rose and overflowed the streets, fevers were rife in the city and carried off numbers of the inhabitants; (thus Prince Borghese lost his wife and three sons within a few days;) rain and wind raged through the place. In short, it was very uncomfortable, and I received but cold comfort from home. I was told that my play "Raphaella" had been acted, and had passed two or three times quietly across the stage, without attracting a numerous audience, and the management had accordingly withdrawn the piece. Other letters from Copenhagen to my countrymen in Rome made enthusiastic mention of a new work of Heiberg's, a satirical poem called "A Soul after Death." It had just appeared, said the writers, and "Andersen was capitally taken off in it." That was all I heard: the book was capital, and I was made to appear ridiculous in it. Nobody told me what was really said concerning me, and wherein lay the jest which amused them so much. It is doubly painful to be held up to ridicule without knowing what people are laughing at. The news affected me like molten lead poured into a wound, in its power of hurting me. Not until my return did I get a sight of the book, and found on reading it that the mention made of me was far too trivial to be a cause of disturbance. It was simply a jest on my fame, "from Schonen to Hundsrück," which Heiberg did not approve of; and then he represented my "Mulatto" and "Raphaella" as being played in Tartarus, where—and this was the cream of the jest—the captive souls were obliged to see both pieces in one evening, and then were allowed to go quietly to bed. I considered the poetry so good that I was nearly writing to Heiberg to express my thanks; but I slept on the idea, and when I awoke and thought of it again, I feared such an effusion might be misunderstood, and accordingly abstained.

The Danish poet Holst was in Rome at that time: he had this year received a travelling pension. Holst had written an elegy on the death of King Frederick VI., which went from mouth to mouth, and produced an enthusiasm like that called forth by Becker's Rhine song in Germany, which came out at the same time. He lived in Rome in the same house with me, and showed me much sympathy. We travelled together to Naples, where, though it was now March, the sun would not shine heartily, and the snow lay around upon the mountains. There was fever in my veins; I suffered mentally and corporeally, and was soon prostrated by so violent a seizure that a quick blood-letting, which my good Neapolitan host insisted on my instantly undergoing, certainly saved my life.

In a few days my health had manifestly improved, and I embarked on a French war steamer for Greece. Holst accompanied me on board. A new life seemed to open, and indeed did open for me here: if this does not appear in my later writings, it certainly was manifested in my views of life and in my development. When my European home was left behind, it seemed as though a stream of oblivion ran between me and all bitter and mournful thoughts; I felt health in my blood, health in my thoughts, and lifted my head with fresh courage.

Like a new Switzerland with a loftier and a clearer sky, Greece lay stretched out before me. Nature here made a deep solemn impression on my mind; I felt that I was standing on a great battle-field of the world, where nations had fought and perished. No single poem can give an idea of such greatness; every dry river-bed, every hill, every stone have great remembrances to tell of, and how petty seem the unevennesses of life at such a place! A flood of ideas pressed upon me, in such numbers that not one would be brought on the paper. The thought that the godlike has to fight the good fight here on earth—that it is repulsed here, but yet goes on victorious through all time, was what I wished to express, and I found a vehicle in the story of the "Wandering Jew." Already, a year ago, the thought of this subject had arisen in my mind, and at times quite carried me away: like the man who digs for hidden coin, I thought sometimes I could lift a treasure, but it would suddenly vanish before me, and I doubted if I should ever bring it to the day. I felt in how many varied branches of knowledge I must first make progress. Often at home, when I had been compelled to listen to remonstrances concerning my defective studies, I had sat up till late at night reading history, or Hegel's "Philosophy of History." I did not mention it, for I should have been at once desired to devote myself to other studies—as in the case of a well-meaning lady who once told me how it was generally asserted that I had not studied enough. "You haven't any mythology," she said; "in all your poems there's not a single god! You must study mythology, read Racine and Corneille." That was her idea of study: and thus every one had some advice to give me. I had read much and sketched out much for my "Ahasuerus," and I hoped that in Greece I should be able to collect all my notes into something clear and complete.

In Constantinople I passed eleven interesting days. I am generally fortunate in my travels, and thus happened to be in the capital at the celebration of Mahomet's birthday. I saw the great illumination, which seemed to me like a page from the "Thousand and One Nights."

Our Danish consul lives several miles from Constantinople, and I had only an opportunity of seeing him once; but was very warmly received by the Austrian envoy, Baron von Stürmer; in his house I found a German home and German friends.

In August, 1841, I was again in Copenhagen. I wrote down my reminiscences of travel under the title of "A Poet's Bazaar," dividing the work into sections, according to the various countries I had traversed. In several places I had found individuals towards whom, as towards many at home, I felt under obligation. A poet is like a bird; he gives what he has—he gives his song. I wished to give something to each of these kind ones: it was a passing feeling, born, I may honestly say, in a grateful heart. To Count Rantzau-Breitenburg, who lived in Italy and loved the land, and who, in consequence of the "Improvisatore," had become my benefactor and friend, I dedicated the part of the book that related to the peninsula. To Liszt and Thalberg, both of whom had met me in the friendliest manner, I inscribed the part that described the journey on the Danube, because one of them was an

CONSTANTINOPLE.

Austrian, the other a Hungarian. The reasons that induced me to make these dedications will be readily appreciated; but the dedications were looked upon in my own country as new proofs of my vanity. It was asserted that I wished to make a parade of names, and boast of having distinguished persons for my friends. The book has been translated into various languages, dedications and all. I know not how these have been criticised abroad. If I have been judged as in Denmark, I trust this explanation will produce a change of opinion. In Denmark my " Bazaar" procured me the largest sum that I had yet received—a proof that my works were being read. No real criticism appeared except in a few daily journals, and afterwards in a poetical attempt of a young author who, the year before, had written to me expressing his appreciation of my work·and his wish to do me honour, and who now, at his first appearance, hurled his satirical poems at me. I was personally attached to this young man, and am fond of him still ; no doubt he thought more of the pleasantness of sailing in Heiberg's wake than of wounding me.

Thorwaldsen, whose acquaintance I had made in Rome in 1833 and 1834, was expected back in Denmark in the autumn of 1838, and great festive preparations were made for his reception. A flag hoisted on one of the church steeples of Copenhagen was to be the signal to announce the anchoring of the ship that brought him. It was a national festival : boats, decorated with flowers and flags, filled the harbour ; the artists, the sculptors, all had their flags with emblems ; the students displayed a Minerva ; a golden Pegasus had been given to the poets. It was foggy weather, and the ship was not descried till it was close to the town, when all streamed forth to meet it. The poets, who had been invited, I think, on Heiberg's selection, filled their boat, but Oehlenschläger and Heiberg himself had not made their appearance. Suddenly the cannons were heard booming from the ship, which was already casting anchor, and it was to be feared that Thorwaldsen would have disembarked before we could arrive. The wind wafted the notes of song across to us, for the festive reception had begun. I wanted to see it, and called out to the rest, " Let us row across."

" Without Oehlenschläger and Heiberg ? " they asked.

" But they don't come, and all will be over soon."

One of the poets declared that if these two were absent we could not well carry our ensign, and he pointed to the Pagasus. " We 'll throw him into the boat," I said, and took it from the pole ; then we rowed after the rest, and came past in time to see Thorwaldsen step ashore. We found Oehlenschläger and Heiberg in another boat : they came across to us just as the rejoicing began. The people drew Thorwaldsen's carriage through the streets to his house, where all who had the slightest acquaintance with him, or even with a friend of his, crowded round him. In the evening the artists gave him a serenade : the torches gleamed in the garden among the great trees : the rejoicings were real and heartfelt. Young and old hurried in at the open door, and the genial old man pressed those whom he knew to his bosom, kissed them, or shook their hands. There was round Thorwaldsen a halo, which kept me back : my heart beat with joy at seeing him who had been so kind and gentle to me in a foreign land, who had embraced me and declared that we must always remain friends ; but here, amid all this rejoicing, where thousands were watching his every movement, and when I should have been noticed and criticised by them all—criticised, probably, as a vain man, only anxious to show that he knew Thorwaldsen too, and had been kindly treated by him—I withdrew among the crowd and avoided recognition. A few days afterwards, one morning early I paid him a visit, and found in him a friend who expressed his surprise that he had not seen me sooner.

In honour of Thorwaldsen a musico-poetical academy had been founded, and poets designated by Holberg composed and read each a song in praise of the great man who had returned to us. I had written on the subject of Jason who had brought home the golden fleece — Jason Thorwaldsen who went out to win the golden prize of art. A festive banquet and a dance closed the celebration, in which for the first time in Denmark popular life and an earnest interest in the domain of art were exhibited. From this evening I saw Thorwaldsen almost daily in social circles or in his studio ; I often lived for weeks together with him at Nysö, where he seemed to have taken root, and where most of his Danish works were completed. His was a genial, healthy nature, not without humour, and thus Holberg was the poet whom he loved best ; he would not enter into the question of the misery and discord in the world. One morning at Nysö, while he was at work on a statue, I went in and wished him good morning. He seemed disinclined to notice me, so I crept quietly away. At breakfast he was very uncommunicative, and when they asked him to talk, he said in his dry way,

" This morning I have spoken more than I have for many days, and nobody listened to me. There I stood, thinking that Andersen was behind me, for he had bid me good morning, and I told him a long story about Byron and myself. I thought that he might give me a word of reply, and turned round, and, behold—I had been standing for an hour talking to the bare walls."

We all begged him to tell the story once more ; but we only got it very concisely, thus :

" Why, it was in Rome, when I was to make a statue of Byron ; he sat down opposite me, but at once began to put on quite a different expression from the one he usually wore.

" ' Will you not sit still ? ' I said. ' But you must not make such a face.'

" ' That is my usual expression,' said Byron.

" ' Indeed ? ' I said ; and then I gave him the expression I chose, and when the statue was finished, every one pronounced it a likeness. But when Byron saw it, he exclaimed,

" ' It 's not at all like me ! I look far more unhappy than that.'

" He was determined, you see, to be so especially unhappy ! " continued Thorwaldsen, with a humorous look.

The great artist took pleasure, after dinner, in listening to music with half-closed eyes ; and his great delight was, in the evening, to play at Lotto, a game that all the neighbourhood of Nysö was compelled to learn. As we only played for bits of glass, I may relate the fact that the great man was exceedingly anxious to win. He could, with warmth and eagerness, take the part of any one whom he considered wronged : he stood up against injustice and quizzing, even against the lady of the house, who, moreover, regarded him with truly filial feelings of affection, and whose thoughts were always employed in the endeavour to make things agreeable to him. In his company I wrote some of my stories, for instance, " Ole Luk-Oie, the Sandman," and he listened to them with pleasure and interest. In the twilight hour, when the family circle sat in the open garden-room, Thorwaldsen would often come quietly to me, and clap me on the shoulder, with a " Well, are not we little ones to have a story ? " With a simplicity peculiar to him, he gave me the kindest praise, for what he called the truthfulness in my fictions. He liked to hear the same story over and over again; and often, when engaged upon his most glorious works, he would pause with a smile to listen to the story of " The Lovers " or " The Ugly Duckling." I have a knack for improvising little verses and rhymes in my native tongue; this pleased Thorwaldsen, and once when he was modelling Holberg's portrait in clay, at Nysö, he asked me to give him a verse for his work, and I gave him the following:

> " Holberg the Dane shall live no more," Death cried:
> "I break the clay that did his soul contain !"
> "And through my art," thus Thorwaldsen replied,
> " E'en in cold clay shall Holberg live again."

One morning when he was modelling his great work, " The Walk to Golgotha," I went into his studio.

" Now tell me," he said, " do you think that I have dressed Pilate properly ? "

" You must not say anything to him," cried the baroness, who was always with him; " it is right, it is charming; pray, go your way ! "

Thorwaldsen, however, repeated his question.

" Indeed," I replied, " since you ask me, I must confess that Pilate seems to me attired more like an Egyptian than like a Roman."

" So it seemed to me, too," observed Thorwaldsen ; and he thrust his hands into the clay and destroyed the figure.

" Now, it 's your fault that he has destroyed an immortal work ! " cried the baroness, angrily, to me.

" Well, we 'll make another immortal work," said the sculptor, laughing; and he restored Pilate in the form in which the figure now appears in the basrelief in the " Frauenkirche " of Copenhagen.

His last birthday was celebrated there, in the country. I had written a little merry song on the occasion; it was still wet on the paper when we sang it in the morning before his door, to an accompaniment of clanging fire-irons and of barbarous sounds produced by rubbing corks over glass bottles. Thorwaldsen opened his door, appeared in dressing-gown and slippers, and marched about the room, waving his skull cap and joining in the chorus. There was life and humour in the genial old man.

Through my last works and the practice of a wise economy, I had saved a little sum, which I determined to devote to another journey to Paris ; and in the winter of 1843 I went thither, by way of Dusseldorf and Belgium. . . The jovial Alexandre Dumas I usually found in bed, even if it was long past noon: there he would lie, with paper, pens, and ink, writing at his newest drama. One day, when I found him thus, he nodded merrily to me, and said, " Sit down for a minute. I have a visit from my Muse, but she'll go directly." He wrote, talked

ALEXANDRE DUMAS INTRODUCES ME TO RACHEL.

loud, then broke into a cheer, sprang out of bed, and cried, " The third
act is finished!"

I have to thank him for an introduction to Rachel. I had not yet
seen her act, when Alexander Dumas asked me if I should like to make
her acquaintance. One evening, when she was to act Phèdre, he took
me on to the stage of the *Théatre Français*. The play had begun, and
behind the scenes, where a screen formed a kind of room wherein stood
a table with refreshments and a few stools, sat the young girl, who, as
an author has said, knows how to hew living statues out of the marble
blocks of Racine and Corneille. She was thin and slenderly built, and
looked very youthful. There, and still more afterwards in her own
house, she seemed to me a picture of Melancholy, like a young girl who

had just wept out her grief, and has sat down to brood silently over it. She spoke kindly to us, in a deep strong voice. In the course of her conversation with Dumas she forgot me; I stood there unnoticed. Dumas remarked it, said a kind thing of me, and I ventured to put a word into the conversation, though I was painfully conscious of being in the presence of those who perhaps spoke the purest French in all France. I said that I had seen much that was glorious and interesting, but that I had never yet met with a Rachel, and had principally on her account devoted the emolument of my last works to a journey to Paris. When I added an apology for my bad French, she smiled, and said,

"When you say such a polite thing to a Frenchwoman, she is sure to think that you speak well."

When I told her how her fame had resounded in the North, she replied that she intended to come to St. Petersburgh and to Copenhagen.

"If I come to your city," she said, "you must be my protector, for you will be the only friend I have there. But that we may become acquainted, and as you say you have come to Paris chiefly on my account, we must meet more frequently. You will be welcome at my house; I see my friends every Thursday evening. But duty calls me," she added, gave us her hand with a friendly nod, and in a few moments was standing on the stage, great and transformed, with the expression of the Tragic Muse on her face: the thunders of applause penetrated to where we stood. As a Northerner, I cannot accustom myself to the French method of acting tragedy. Rachel plays according to that school, but she appears like Nature personified; she is the French Tragic Muse, and the others are but poor mortals. When Rachel plays, one thinks that all tragedy must be as she acts it: there is truth—nature—but in another manifestation than that to which we are accustomed. In her house I found everything rich and gorgeous—perhaps a little too artificial. The front room was hung with bluish-green, half illuminated by dim lamps, and adorned with statuettes of French authors; in the reception, a purple-red hue predominated on the walls, in the curtains and bookshelves. She was dressed in black, as she is represented in the well-known English engraving. The circle around her consisted of gentlemen, principally artists and men of letters. I heard one or two titles mentioned. Servants in a rich livery announced the names of the guests. Tea was taken, and refreshments were handed round, more in German than in French fashion. Victor Hugo had told me he thought Rachel understood German. I inquired if this were so, and she answered in that language, "I can read it, for I was born in Lorraine: I have German books, too; see here!" and she showed me Grillparger's "Sappho," but then continued the conversation in French. She expressed a desire to play the part of Sappho; then she spoke of Schiller's Maria Stuart, a character she had acted in a French translation.] afterwards saw her in this part, and especially in the last act she showed a quiet tragic feeling worthy of one of the best German actresses. But just this act it was that pleased the French least.

A VISIT TO JENNY LIND.

"My countrymen," she said, "are not used to this style; and yet it is the only one in which the character can be rendered. A woman whose heart is ready to break with grief, and who is about to bid farewell for ever to her friends, must not rage like a maniac."

I must return to the year 1840. One day, in the hotel in which I lived, I saw the name Jenny Lind in the register of strangers who had come from Sweden. I knew already that she was the first singer in Stockholm. I had been in that country in the same year, and had met with honour and kindness there, consequently I thought it would not be considered impertinent if I paid my respects to the young *artiste*. At that time she was not known beyond Sweden, so that I may assume that her name was only familiar to a few in Copenhagen. She received me very politely, but distantly, almost coldly. She told me that, in the course of a journey with her father to the south of Sweden, she had gone for a few days to Copenhagen, to see the city. We parted as strangers from one another, and the impression she left on my mind soon vanished.

In the autumn of 1843 Jenny Lind came again to Copenhagen; one of my friends, the genial ballet master Bournonville, the husband of a Swedish lady, a friend of Jenny Lind, told me of her arrival, and added that she had a kind remembrance of me, and had now read my works. He begged me to go with him, and employ my small powers of persuasion to induce her to appear a few times at the Theatre Royal, and promised me that I should be enchanted with what I would hear. This time I was not received as a stranger: cordially she gave me her hand, and spoke of my writings, and of Miss Frederika Bremer, who was a good friend of hers. Soon the question of her appearance at Copenhagen was mooted, and Jenny Lind expressed great apprehensions on the subject.

"Except in Sweden," she said, "I have never appeared in public. In my own country all are so kind and gentle towards me; and if I were to appear in Copenhagen, and to be hissed! I cannot risk it!"

I said that I certainly could not judge of her powers, inasmuch as I had never heard her sing, nor did I know how she acted; but, judging by the state of feeling in Copenhagen, I felt sure that if she sang and acted tolerably, she would have a success, and that she might certainly risk it. Bournonville's persuasion procured for the good people of Copenhagen one of the greatest treats they had ever enjoyed. Jenny Lind appeared as Alice in "Robert le Diable." It was like a new revelation in the domain of art: the fresh young voice went direct to the hearts of all; here were truth and nature; everything had clearness and meaning. In a concert Jenny Lind sang her Swedish songs: there was a peculiar, a seductive charm about them; all recollection of the concert-room vanished; the popular melodies exerted their spell, sung as they were by a pure voice with the immortal accent of genius. All Copenhagen was in raptures. Jenny Lind was the first *artiste* to whom the students offered a serenade; the torches flashed around the hospitable villa where the song was sung. She expressed her thanks by a few more of the Swedish songs, and I then saw her hurry into the darkest corner and weep out her emotion.

"Yes, yes," she said, "I will exert myself, I will strive. I shall be more efficient than I am now when I come to Copenhagen again."

On the stage she was the great *artiste*, towering above all around her; at home, in her chamber, a gentle young girl with the simple trust and piety of a child. . . . The "Daughter of the Regiment" and the "Sonnambula" are certainly Jenny Lind's greatest parts; no one can portray these two characters as she has portrayed them. The spectator laughs and weeps—the sight does him good—he feels a better man for it; he feels that there is something divine in art. "In the course of centuries," said Mendelssohn to me of Jenny Lind, "a character like hers is only produced once;" and his words expressed my entire conviction. One feels at her appearance on the stage that the holy draught is poured from a pure vessel.

In Berlin I found a hearty welcome, which has since always been repeated, in the house of the minister Savigny, where I made the acquaintance of the wonderfully gifted Bettina* and her clever daughters. I had an hour's conversation with Bettina, during which she charmed me into mute admiration by the wonderful flow of her ideas. Her writings are famous; but another talent which she possesses, namely, that of drawing, has not become so generally known. Here again it is the idea that astonishes us. Thus she showed me a sketch she had made to illustrate an event which had lately happened. A young man had been suffocated by the fumes of a wine cellar. She had represented him descending, half naked, into the vault, where the wine vats, in monstrous shapes, lay grouped around. Bacchantes were dancing around him, and preparing to seize and strangle their victim. I know that

BETTINA'S PORTFOLIO.

Thorwaldsen, to whom she showed her drawings, was astonished at the power they displayed.

It does a man good, in a strange land, to come into a house where kind eyes gleam like festive lamps when he appears, where he may look on a quiet domestic happiness; and such a house was opened to me in the abode of Professor Weiss. But how many new acquaintances, and how many old ones renewed, should I not have to chronicle, were I to tell all! I found Tieck also, whom I had never seen since my first visit to Germany. He was much changed, but the clever gentle eyes were unaltered, and the pressure of his hand was the same; I felt that he was attached to me and wished me well. I was obliged to visit him at Potsdam, where he lived in a comfortable and easy style. From him I heard how graciously the King and Queen of Prussia were disposed

---

* Bettina, the German authoress, was the daughter of Clement Brentano, a German poet of some merit, and one of the founders of the "romantic school" of German poetic literature.

towards me, that they had read my novel "Only a Fiddler," and had inquired of Tieck concerning me. Their Majesties were absent; I had arrived at Berlin the very evening before their departure for Berlin, when the shameful attempt upon the King's life was made.

Over Stettin we went, in stormy weather, to Copenhagen. Well and happy I saw all my loved ones, and then travelled on to Fünen, to pass the bright summer days there. I received a letter from the minister Rantzau-Breitenburg, who was with the King and Queen of Denmark in the bathing-place of Föhr. He wrote that he had the pleasure to announce to me that a gracious invitation to Föhr had been issued for me. This island lies in the German Ocean, not far from the Schleswig coast, near the interesting "Halligens," the islands which Biernatzky has so ably portrayed in his novels. I was thus to behold nature in an aspect altogether new to me. I was delighted at the condescension of my King and Queen, and rejoiced at the prospect of seeing Rantzau again. Alas! it was the last time I saw him.

At my last visit to Berlin I had sought out the brothers Grimm, but our acquaintance did not proceed far. I had brought no letter of recommendation to them, because I had been told (and I had believed it) that if any one in Berlin knew me, it would be the brothers Grimm. Accordingly I sought out their dwelling. The maid asked me with which of the brothers I wanted to speak. I replied,

"With the one who has written most," for I did not know who had been the chief author of the "Stories."

"Jacob is the most learned," said the girl.

"Then take me to him."

I entered the room, and Jacob Grimm, with his intelligent character-istic face, stood before me.

"I come to you without a letter of recommendation, in the hope that my name may not be quite strange to you."

"What is your name?" he asked.

I mentioned it, and Jacob Grimm said, in half embarrassment,

"I don't remember ever to have heard that name. What have you written?"

Now I became quite embarrassed, but mentioned my "Stories."

"I do not know them," he said; "but tell me the names of some other of your writings; I must certainly have heard of them."

I mentioned several titles, but he shook his head. I felt quite unhappy.

"But what must you think of me," I said, "that I come to you and enumerate what I have done? You must know me. There is in Denmark a collection of stories of all nations dedicated to you, and at least one story of mine is contained in that."

Good-naturedly, but with some embarrassment, he answered,

"In truth, I have not read that collection, but I am glad to make your acquaintance. May I take you to my brother William?"

"No, thank you," said I; for I only wished to get away: I had fared badly enough with one brother. I pressed his hand and hurried off.

That same month Jacob Grimm came to Copenhagen. Immediately on his arrival, and still in his travelling clothes, the amiable man hastened to me. He knew me now, and came to me right heartily. I was just standing packing my things for a journey into the provinces, and had only a few minutes to spare; thus our interview was as short as our first meeting in Berlin. Now we met in Berlin as old acquaintances. Jacob Grimm is one of those people to whom one insensibly becomes attached.

One day I was reading one of my stories. In the little circle around me one gentleman was evidently listening with sympathy, and afterwards criticised characteristically and well. It was Jacob's brother, William Grimm.

"I should have known you if you had come to me when you were here the last time," he said.

JACOB GRIMM'S VISIT TO ME.

I saw these two amiable and gifted brothers almost daily: the circles to which I was invited seemed to be theirs also, and it was a joy to me that they listened to my stories and sympathized with me—they, whose names will be remembered as long as popular stories are told. That Grimm had not known me at my first visit to Berlin had put me out so much, that when people talked to me of the kindly reception I had encountered in that city, I used to shake my head doubtfully, and say, "But Grimm did not know me."

It was Professor Hase, and the genial improvisatore Professor Wolff in Jena, whom I had chiefly to thank for the fact that a complete edition of my works appeared in Germany. At my arrival in Leipzic this was arranged for me; a few business hours were mingled with my holiday journey, and the city of booksellers brought me its tribute in the shape of a literary *honorarium*. But it brought me still more. I passed some nappy hours with glorious, genial Mendelssohn; I heard him play over and over again; his bright eyes seemed to pierce into my soul: few men have more of the outward sign of the inward flame than he. A gentle amiable wife and beautiful children spread blessings through his rich well-ordered house. When he quizzed me about the stork, who so often appeared in my stories, there was something childlike and amiable about the genial composer. I also met my fellow-countryman Gade, whose compositions have found such general appreciation in Germany

While I was staying at Marseilles, chance procured me a short interview with one of my friends from the North, Ole Bull. He came from America, and had been received in France with acclamation and serenades, a fact of which I was here a witness. At the *table d'hôte* in the *Hotel des Empereurs*, where we both lodged, we flew to meet one an-

MENDELSSOHN.

other. He told me a thing of which I had no idea; namely, that my works had found many friends in America, that I had been inquired for in the kindest manner, and that the English translations of my works had been reprinted, and spread in a cheap form over the whole country. So my name had flown across the great ocean! I felt quite overwhelmed, and yet glad and happy. Why should such fortune come to me, rather than to thousands of others? I had a feeling, and I still nave it, as if I were a peasant boy on whose shoulders a royal cloak is cast. But it made me happy, and it makes me happy still! Is that vanity, or does the vanity consist in my expressing my happiness?

Ole Bull went away to Algeria, and I to the Pyrenees. By way of Provence, which had quite a Danish look to me, I reached Nismes, where the grandeur of the glorious Roman theatre at once seemed to transport me into Italy. I have never heard the antiquities of Southern France appreciated as their beauty and number deserve. The so-called

THE BAKER POET.

"square house" still stands in all its splendour, like the temple of
Theseus in Athens; Rome has nothing so well preserved to show. In
Nismes lives the baker Reboul, who writes the most charming poems.
Those who do not know him by his works have heard of him through
"Lamartine's Journey to the East." I found his house out, stepped
into the baker's shop, and turned to a man who was standing in his
shirt-sleeves, thrusting loaves into an oven. It was Reboul himself. A
noble countenance full of manly character turned to greet me. When
I told him my name, he was polite enough to say that he knew it from
the "*Revue de Paris*," and begged me to visit him in the middle of the
day, for then he would be able to receive me more worthily. When I
went back I found him in an almost elegant little room, which was
adorned with pictures, statuettes, and books; the latter consisted not
only of French authors, but of translations from the Greek classics. A
picture on the wall represented the subject of his most celebrated poem,
"*L'Ange et l'Enfant.*" He knew from Marmier's "*Chansons du Nord*"
that I had treated the same theme, and I told him that my poem had
been written in my school days. In the morning he had appeared as
the busy baker, but now he was altogether the poet. He spoke eagerly
of the literature of his country, and expressed a wish to see the North,
whose nature and whose literary activity appeared to interest him. It
was with a feeling of great respect that I quitted a man to whom the
Muses have given no small gift, but who has had sense enough, in spite

of the incense that had been burned before him, to keep to his honest work, and who prefers to be the remarkable baker of Nismes, rather than lose himself, after a short reign in Paris, among a hundred other poets.

And now, a few miles on the other side of the mountains, we descend upon Spain, where beauty blooms, where gleam the bright brown eyes. The only poetical picture I retain of the bath " Vernet " in the Pyrenees is the following: In the market, under a glorious old tree, a wandering pedler had spread out all his wares, handkerchiefs, books, and pictures, a complete bazaar; but the earth was his table: all the youth of the place, embrowned by the sun, stood assembled round the precious store; a few old crones peered forth from their open shops; a long procession of bathing visitors, ladies and gentlemen, passed by on horses and donkeys, and two little children, half hidden behind a palisade of planks, were playing at being cocks, and crying " Kikeriki! " with all their might.

Much more comfortably arranged is the fortress of Villefranche, a few miles away, with a castle of the time of Louis XIV. The way leads past this town over Olette to Spain, and here accordingly there is some industry and traffic; many of the houses are conspicuous by their beautiful Moorish marble windows.

And here, amid the fresh nature of the mountains, on the borders of a glorious land, whose beauties and whose wants I am not now to know, I conclude these pages, which are also to be a boundary in my life, for coming years, with their beauties and their wants. Before I quit the Pyrenees these lines will fly to Germany, and a great division of my life will have concluded. I myself shall follow them, and a new and unknown division will begin. What will this new division unroll to me? I cannot tell, but with thankful trust I can look forward. My whole life, with its bright and its dark days, has been for the best. It is like a sea voyage towards a certain goal: I stand at the helm, I have chosen my course; but God rules over storm and sea, and may ordain it otherwise; and if it is so, it will be the best for me. This belief is firmly rooted in my mind, and in this belief I am happy.

The story of my life to this moment lies unrolled before me, more rich and beautiful than I could have imagined it. I feel that I am a child of fortune; nearly all have met me kindly and frankly; very seldom has my trust in my fellow-men been deceived. From the prince to the poorest peasant I have found noble human hearts. Frankly and openly, as if I sat among dear friends, I have here told my own tale — have spoken of my joys and sorrows, have expressed my thankfulness at every encouragement and sign of good will, as I think I might express it, to the Giver of all good. Is this vanity? I think not, for my feeling has been one of humility; my thought was thankfulness to God. I have not told it only because a sketch of my life was required for the collected edition of my works, but because, as I have already said, my life is the best commentary upon my writings.

In a few days I shall bid farewell to the Pyrenees, and go over Switzerland to dear friendly Germany, where so much of joy has been mingled in my life, where I have so many sympathizing friends, where my efforts have been kindly received, and where kindness too will judge of these pages.

When the Christmas tree is lighted up, when, as the saying is, "the white bees swarm," then, God willing, I shall be back in Denmark, among my dear ones, with my heart full of the rich bloom of travel, strengthened in body and soul. Then new works will be committed to paper. Heaven send its blessing upon them! A star of fortune shines above me. Thousands have deserved it more than I; often I cannot understand why this good should have been vouchsafed to me among so many thousands. But if the star should set, even while I am penning these lines, be it so; still I can say it has shone, and I have received a rich portion. Even here what is best will happen. To God and my fellow-creatures, my thanks, my love!

H. C. ANDERSEN.

Vernet in the Pyrenees, July, 1846.

THE MOOR-WOMAN BREWING.

"THE WILL-O'-THE-WISP IS IN THE TOWN," SAYS THE MOOR-WOMAN.

THERE was a man who once knew many stories, but they had slipped away from him—so he said; the Story that used to visit him of its own accord no longer came and knocked at his door: and why did it come no longer? It is true enough that for days and years the man had not thought of it, had not expected it to come and knock; and if he had expected it, it would certainly not have come; for without there was war, and within was the care and sorrow that war brings with it.

The stork and the swallows came back from their long journey, for they thought of no danger; and, behold, when they arrived, the nest was burnt, the habitations of men were burnt, the hedges were all in disorder, and everything seemed gone, and the enemy's horses were stamping in the old graves. Those were hard, gloomy times, but they came to an end.

And now they were past and gone, so people said · and yet no Story came and knocked at the door, or gave any tidings of its presence.

" I suppose it must be dead, or gone away with many other things," said the man.

But the Story never dies. And more than a whole year went by, and he longed—oh, so very much!—for the Story.

" I wonder if the Story will ever come back again, and knock ? "

And he remembered it so well in all the various forms in which it had come to him, sometimes young and charming, like spring itself, sometimes as a beautiful maiden, with a wreath of thyme in her hair, and a beechen branch in her hand, and with eyes that gleamed like deep woodland lakes in the bright sunshine.

Sometimes it had come to him in the guise of a pedlar, and had opened its box and let silver ribbon come fluttering out, with verses and inscriptions of old remembrances.

But it was most charming of all when it came as an old grandmother, with silvery hair, and such large sensible eyes: she knew so well how to tell about the oldest times, long before the Princesses span with the golden spindles, and the dragons lay outside the castles, guarding them. She told with such an air of truth, that black spots danced before the eyes of all who heard her, and the floor became black with human blood ; terrible to see and to hear, and yet so entertaining, because such a long time had passed since it all happened.

" Will it ever knock at my door again ? " said the man ; and he gazed at the door, so that black spots came before his eyes and upon the floor ; he did not know if it was blood, or mourning crape from the dark heavy days.

And as he sat thus, the thought came upon him, whether the Story might not have hidden itself, like the Princess in the old tale ? And he would now go in search of it : if he found it, it would beam in new splendour, lovelier than ever.

" Who knows ? Perhaps it has hidden itself in the straw that balances on the margin of the well. Carefully, carefully ! Perhaps it lies hidden in a certain flower—that flower in one of the great books on the bookshelf."

And the man went and opened one of the newest books, to gain information on this point ; but there was no flower to be found. There he read about Holger Danske ; and the man read that the tale had been invented and put together by a monk in France, that it was a romance, "translated into Danish and printed in that language ; " that Holger Danske had never really lived, and consequently could never come again, as we have sung, and have been so glad to believe. And William Tell was treated just like Holger Danske. These were all only myths—nothing on which we could depend; and yet it is all written in a very learned book.

" Well, I shall believe what I believe ! " said the man : " there grows no plantain where no foot has trod."

And he closed the book and put it back in its place, and went to the fresh flowers at the window: perhaps the story might have hidden itself in the red tulips, with the golden yellow edges, or in the fresh rose, or in the beaming camellia. The sunshine lay among the flowers, but no Story.

The flowers which had been here in the dark troublous time had been much more beautiful; but they had been cut off, one after another, to be woven into wreaths and placed in coffins, and the flag had waved over them! Perhaps the Story had been buried with the flowers; but then the flowers would have known of it, and the coffin would have heard it, and every little blade of grass that shot forth would have told of it. The Story never dies.

Perhaps it has been here once, and has knocked—but who had eyes or ears for it in those times? People looked darkly, gloomily, and almost angrily at the sunshine of spring, at the twittering birds, and all the cheerful green; the tongue could not even bear the old, merry, popular songs, and they were laid in the coffin with so much that our heart held dear. The Story may have knocked without obtaining a hearing; there was none to bid it welcome, and so it may have gone away

"I will go forth and seek it! Out in the country! out in the wood! and on the open sea beach!"

IN SEARCH OF THE STORY.

Out in the country lies an old manor house, with red walls, pointed gables, and a red flag that floats on the tower. The nightingale sings among the finely-fringed beech-leaves, looking at the blooming apple trees of the garden, and thinking that they bear roses. Here the bees are mightily busy in the summer-time, and hover round their queen with their humming song. The autumn has much to tell of the wild chase, of the leaves of the trees, and of the races of men that are passing away together. The wild swans sing at Christmas-time on the open water, while in the old hall the guests by the fire-side gladly listen to songs and to old legends.

Down into the old part of the garden, where the great avenue of wild chestnut trees lures the wanderer to tread its shades, went the man who was in search of the Story; for here the wind had once murmured something to him of " Waldemar Daa and his Daughters." The Dryad in the tree, who was the Story-mother herself, had here told him the " Dream of the old Oak Tree." Here, in the time of the ancestral mother, had stood clipped hedges, but now only ferns and stinging-nettles grew there, hiding the scattered fragments of old sculptured figures; the moss is growing in their eyes, but they can see as well as ever, which was more than the man could do who was in search of the Story, for he could not find it. Where could it be?

The crows flew past him by hundreds across the old trees, and screamed, " Krah! da!—Krah! da!"

And he went out of the garden, and over the grass-plot of the yard, into the alder grove; there stood a little six-sided house, with a poultry-yard and a duck-yard. In the middle of the room sat the old woman, who had the management of the whole, and who knew accurately about every egg that was laid, and about every chicken that could creep out of an egg. But she was not the Story of which the man was in search; that she could attest with a Christian certificate of baptism and of vaccination that lay in her drawer.

Without, not far from the house, is a hill covered with red-thorn and broom: here lies an old grave-stone, which was brought here many years ago from the churchyard of the provincial town, a remembrance of one of the most honoured councillors of the place; his wife and his five daughters, all with folded hands and stiff ruffs, stand round him. One could look at them so long, that it had an effect upon the thoughts, and these reacted upon the stones, as if they were telling of old times; at least it had been so with the man who was in search of the Story.

As he came nearer, he noticed a living butterfly sitting on the fore-head of the sculptured councillor. The butterfly flapped its wings, and flew a little bit farther, and then returned fatigued to sit upon the grave-stone, as if to point out what grew there. Four-leaved shamrocks grew there; there were seven specimens close to each other. When fortune comes, it comes in a heap. He plucked the shamrocks, and put them in his pocket.

" Fortune is as good as red gold, but a new, charming story would be better still," thought the man; but he could not find it here.

And the sun went down, round and large; the meadow was covered with vapour: the moor-woman was at her brewing.

It was evening: he stood alone in his room, and looked out upon the sea, over the meadow, over moor and coast. The moon shone bright, a mist was over the meadow, making it look like a great lake; and, indeed, it was once so, as the legend tells—and in the moonlight the eye realizes these myths.

Then the man thought of what he had been reading in the town, that William Tell and Holger Danske never really lived, but yet live in popular story, like the lake yonder, a living evidence for such myths. Yes, Holger Danske will return again!

As he stood thus and thought, something beat quite strongly against the window. Was it a bird, a bat, or an owl? Those are not let in, even when they knock. The window flew open of itself, and an old woman looked in at the man.

A STRANGE VISITOR.

"What's your pleasure?" said he. "Who are you? You're looking in at the first floor window. Are you standing on a ladder?"

"You have a four-leaved shamrock in your pocket," she replied. "Indeed, you have seven, and one of them is a six-leaved one."

"Who are you?" asked the man again.

"The Moor-woman," she replied. "The Moor-woman who brews. I was at it. The bung was in the cask, but one of the little moor-imps pulled it out in his mischief, and flung it up into the yard, where it beat against the window; and now the beer's running out of the cask, and that won't do good to anybody."

"Pray tell me some more!" said the man.

"Yes, wait a little," answered the Moor-woman. "I've something else to do just now." And she was gone.

The man was going to shut the window, when the woman already stood before him again.

"Now it's done," she said; "but I shall have half the beer to brew over again to-morrow, if the weather is suitable. Well, what have you to ask me? I've come back, for I always keep my word, and you have seven four-leaved shamrocks in your pocket, and one of them is a six-leaved one. That inspires respect, for that's an order that grows beside the sandy way; but that every one does not find. What have you to ask me? Don't stand there like a ridiculous oaf, for I must go back again directly to my bung and my cask."

And the man asked about the Story, and inquired if the Moor-woman had met it in her journevings.

"By the big brewing-vat!" exclaimed the woman, "haven't you got stories enough? I really believe that most people have enough of them. Here are other things to take notice of, other things to examine. Even the children have gone beyond that. Give the little boy a cigar, and the little girl a new crinoline; they like that much better. To listen to stories! No, indeed, there are more important things to be done here, and other things to notice!"

"What do you mean by that?" asked the man. "and what do you know of the world? You don't see anything but frogs and will-o'-the-wisps!"

"Yes, beware of the will-o'-the-wisps," said the Moor-woman, "for they're out—they're let loose—that's what we must talk about! Come to me in the moor, where my presence is necessary, and I will tell you all about it; but you must make haste, and come while your seven four-leaved shamrocks, of which one has six leaves, are still fresh, and the moon stands high!"

And the Moor-woman was gone.

THE MOOR-WOMAN'S REPROOF.

It struck twelve in the town, and before the last stroke had died away, the man was out in the yard, out in the garden, and stood in the meadow. The mist had vanished, and the Moor-woman stopped her brewing.

"You've been a long time coming!" said the Moor-woman. "Witches get forward faster than men, and I'm glad that I belong to the witch folk!"

"What have you to say to me now?" asked the man. "Is it anything about the Story?"

"Can you never get beyond asking about that?" retorted the woman.

"Can you tell me anything about the poetry of the future?" resumed the man.

"Don't get on your stilts," said the crone, "and I'll answer you. You think of nothing but poetry, and only ask about that Story, as if she were the lady of the whole troop. She's the oldest of us all, but she takes precedence of the youngest. I know her well. I've been young, too, and she's no chicken now. I was once quite a pretty elf-maiden, and have danced in my time with the others in the moonlight, and have heard the nightingale, and have gone into the forest and met the Story-maiden, who was always to be found out there, running about. Sometimes she took up her night's lodging in a half-blown tulip, or in a field flower; sometimes she would slip into the church, and wrap herself in the mourning crape that hung down from the candles on the altar."

" You are capitally well-informed," said the man.

"I ought at least to know as much as you," answered the Moor-woman. " Stories and poetry—yes, they're like two yards of the same piece of stuff: they can go and lie down where they like, and one can brew all their prattle, and have it all the better and cheaper. You shall have it from me for nothing. I have a whole cupboard-full of poetry in bottles. It makes essences; and that's the best of it—bitter and sweet herbs. I have everything that people want of poetry, in bottles, so that I can put a little on my handkerchief, on holidays, to smell."

"Why, these are wonderful things that you're telling!" said the man. " You have poetry in bottles?"

"More than you can require," said the woman. "I suppose you know the history of 'the Girl who trod on the Loaf, so that she might not soil her Shoes'? That has been written, and printed too."

"I told that story myself," said the man.

"Yes, then you must know it; and you must know also that the girl sank into the earth directly, to the Moor-woman, just as Old Boguey's grandmother was paying her morning visit to inspect the brewery. She saw the girl gliding down, and asked to have her as a remembrance of her visit, and got her too; while I received a present that's of no use to me—a travelling druggist's shop—a whole cupboard-full of poetry in bottles. Grandmother told me where the cupboard was to be placed, and there it's standing still. Just look! You've your seven four-leaved shamrocks in your pocket, one of which is a six-leaved one, and so you will be able to see it."

And really in the midst of the moor lay something like a great knotted block of alder, and that was the old grandmother's cupboard. The Moor-woman said that this was always open to her and to every one in the land, if they only knew where the cupboard stood. It could be opened either at the front or at the back, and at every side and corner—a perfect work of art, and yet only an old alder stump in appearance. The poets of all lands, and especially those of our own country, had been arranged here; the spirit of them had been extracted, refined, criticised and reno-vated, and then stored up in bottles. With what may be called great aptitude, if it was not genius, the grandmother had taken as it were the flavour of this and of that poet, and had added a little devilry, and then corked up the bottles for use during all future times.

"Pray let me see," said the man.

"Yes, but there are more important things to hear," replied the Moor-woman.

THE MOOR-WOMAN TELLS THE STORY.

"But now we are at the cupboard!" said the man. And he looked
in. "Here are bottles of all sizes. What is in this one? and what in
that one yonder?"

"Here is what they call may-balm," replied the woman: "I have not
tried it myself. But I have not yet told you the 'more important' thing
you were to hear. THE WILL-O'-THE-WISP'S IN THE TOWN! That's
of much more consequence than poetry and stories. I ought, indeed, to
hold my tongue; but there must be a necessity—a fate—a something
that sticks in my throat, and that wants to come out. Take care, you
mortals!"

"I don't understand a word of all this!" cried the man.

"Be kind enough to seat yourself on that cupboard," she retorted,
"but take care you don't fall through and break the bottles—you know
what's inside them. I must tell of the great event. It occurred no
longer ago than the day before yesterday. It did not happen earlier.

It has now three hundred and sixty-three days to run about. I suppose you know how many days there are in a year?"

And this is what the Moor-woman told:

"There was a great commotion yesterday out here in the marsh! There was a christening feast! A little Will-o'-the-Wisp was born here —in fact, twelve of them were born all together; and they have permission, if they choose to use it, to go abroad among men, and to move about and command among them, just as if they were born mortals That was a great event in the marsh, and accordingly all the Will-o'-the-Wisps, male and female, went dancing like little lights across the moor. There are some of them of the dog species, but those are not worth mentioning. I sat there on the cupboard, and had all the twelve little new-born Will-o'-the-Wisps upon my lap: they shone like glow-worms; they already began to hop, and increased in size every moment, so that before a quarter of an hour had elapsed, each of them looked just as large as his father or his uncle. Now, it's an old-established regulation and favour, that when the moon stands just as it did yesterday, and the wind blows just as it blew then, it is allowed and accorded to all Will-o'-the-Wisps—that is, to all those who are born at that minute of time—to become mortals, and individually to exert their power for the space of one year.

"The Will-o'-the-Wisp may run about in the country and through the world, if it is not afraid of falling into the sea, or of being blown out by a heavy storm. It can enter into a person and speak for him, and make all the movements it pleases. The Will-o'-the-Wisp may take whatever form he likes, of man or woman, and can act in their spirit and in their disguise in such a way that he can effect whatever he wishes to do. But he must manage, in the course of the year, to lead three hundred and sixty-five people into a bad way, and in a grand style, too: to lead them away from the right and the truth; and then he reaches the highest point. Such Will-o'-the-Wisps can attain to the honour of being a runner before the devil's state coach; and then he'll wear clothes of fiery yellow, and breathe forth flames out of his throat. That's enough to make a simple Will-o'-the-Wisp smack his lips. But there's some danger in this, and a great deal of work for a Will-o'-the-Wisp who aspires to play so distinguished a part. If the eyes of the man are opened to what he is, and if the man can then blow him away, it's all over with him, and he must come back into the marsh; or if, before the year is up, the Will-o'-the-Wisp is seized with a longing to see his family, and so returns to it and gives the matter up, it is over with him likewise, and he can no longer burn clear, and soon becomes extinguished, and cannot be lit up again; and when the year has elapsed, and he has not led three hundred and sixty-five people away from the truth and from all that is grand and noble, he is condemned to be imprisoned in decayed wood, and to lie glimmering there without being able to move; and that's the most terrible punishment that can be inflicted on a lively Will-o'-the-Wisp.

"Now, all this I know, and all this I told to the twelve little Will-o'-the-Wisps whom I had on my lap, and who seemed quite crazy with joy.

"I told them that the safest and most convenient course was to give up the honour, and do nothing at all; but the little flames would not agree to this, and already fancied themselves clad in fiery yellow clothes, breathing flames from their throats.

"'Stay with us,' said some of the older ones.

"'Carry on your sport with mortals,' said the others.

"'The mortals are drying up our meadows; they've taken to draining. What will our successors do?'

"'We want to flame; we will flame—flame!' cried the new-born Will-o'-the-Wisps.

"And thus the affair was settled.

"And now a ball was given, a minute long; it could not well be shorter. The little elf-maidens whirled round three times with the rest, that they might not appear proud, but they preferred dancing with one another.

"And now the sponsors' gifts were presented, and presents were thrown them. These presents flew like pebbles across the sea-water. Each of the elf-maidens gave a little piece of her veil.

"'Take that,' they said, 'and then you'll know the higher dance, the most difficult turns and twists—that is to say, if you should find them necessary. You'll know the proper deportment, and then you can show yourself in the very pick of society.'

"The night raven taught each of the young Will-o'-the-Wisps to say, 'Goo—goo—good,' and to say it in the right place; and that's a great gift, which brings its own reward.

"The owl and the stork——but they said it was not worth mentioning, and so we won't mention it.

"*King Waldemar's wild chase* was just then rushing over the moor, and when the great lords heard of the festivities that were going on, they sent a couple of handsome dogs, which hunt on the spoom of the wind, as a present; and these might carry two or three of the Will-o'-the-Wisps. A couple of old Alpas, spirits who occupy themselves with Alp-pressing, were also at the feast; and from these the young Will-o'-the-Wisps learned the art of slipping through every key-hole, as if the door stood open before them. These Alpas offered to carry the youngsters to the town, with which they were well acquainted. They usually rode through the atmosphere on their own back hair, which is fastened into a knot, for they love a hard seat; but now they sat sideways on the wild hunting dogs, took the young Will-o'-the-Wisps in their laps, who wanted to go into the town to mislead and entice mortals, and, whisk! away they were. Now, this is what happened last night. To-day the Will-o'-the-Wisps are in the town, and have taken the matter in hand—but where and how? Ah, can you tell me that? Still, I've a lightning conductor in my great toe, and that will always tell me something."

"Why, this is a complete story," exclaimed the man.

"Yes, but it is only the beginning," replied the woman. "Can you tell me how the Will-o'-the-Wisps deport themselves, and how they behave? and in what shapes they have aforetime appeared and led people into crooked paths?"

"I believe," replied the man, "that one could tell quite a romance about the Will-o'-the-Wisps, in twelve parts; or, better still, one might make quite a popular play of them."

"You might write that," said the woman, "but it's best let alone."

"Yes, that's better and more agreeable," the man replied, "for then we shall escape from the newspapers, and not be tied up by them, which is just as uncomfortable as for a Will-o'-the-Wisp to lie in decaying wood, to have to gleam, and not be able to stir."

KING WALDEMAR'S GIFT.

"I don't care about it either way," cried the woman. "Let the rest write, those who can, and those who cannot likewise. I'll give you an old bung from my cask that will open the cupboard where poetry's kept in bottles, and you may take from that whatever may be wanting. But you, my good man, seem to have blotted your hands sufficiently with ink, and to have come to that age of satiety, that you need not be running about every year for stories, especially as there are much more important things to be done. You must have understood what is going on?"

"The Will-o'-the-Wisp is in the town," said the man. "I've heard it, and I have understood it. But what do you think I ought to do? I should be thrashed if I were to go to the people and say, 'Look, yonder goes a Will-o'-the-Wisp in his best clothes!'"

"They also go in undress," replied the woman. "The Will-o'-the-Wisp can assume all kinds of forms, and appear in every place. He goes into the church, but not for the sake of the service; and perhaps he may enter into one or other of the priests. He speaks in the Parliament, not for the benefit of the country, but only for himself. He's an artist with the colour-pot as well as in the theatre; but when he gets all the power into his own hands, then the pot's empty! I chatter and chatter, but it must come out, what's sticking in my throat, to the disadvantage of my own family. But I must now be the woman that will save a good many people. It is not done with my good will, or for the sake of a medal. I do the most insane things I possibly can, and then I tell a poet about it, and thus the whole town gets to know of it directly."

"The town will not take that to heart," observed the man; "that will not disturb a single person; for they will all think I 'm only telling them a story if I say, 'The Will-o'-the-Wisp is in the town, says the Moor-woman. Take care of yourselves!'"

THE WINDMILL.

A WINDMILL stood upon the hill, proud to look at, and it was proud too.

"I am not proud at all," it said, "but I am very much enlightened without and within. I have sun and moon for my outward use, and for inward use too; and into the bargain I have stearine candles, train oil lamps, and tallow candles; I may well say that I 'm enlightened. I am a thinking being, and so well constructed that it 's quite delightful. I have a good windpipe in my chest, and I have four wings that are placed outside my head, just beneath my hat; the birds have only two wings, and are obliged to carry them on their backs. I am a Dutchman by birth, that may be seen by my figure—a flying Dutchman. They are considered supernatural beings, I know, and yet I am quite natural. I have a gallery round my chest, and house-room beneath it; that 's where my thoughts dwell. My strongest thought, who rules and reigns, is called by the others 'the man in the mill.' He knows what he wants, and is lord over the meal and the bran; but he has his companion too, and she calls herself 'Mother.' She is the very heart of me. She does not run about stupidly and awkwardly, for she knows what she wants, she knows what she can do, she 's as soft as a zephyr and as strong as a

EXAMINING THE MILL.

storm; she knows how to begin a thing carefully, and to have her own way. She is my soft temper, and the father is my hard one: they are two, and yet one; they each call the other 'My half.' These two have some little boys, young thoughts, that can grow. The little ones keep everything in order. When, lately, in my wisdom, I let the father and the boys examine my throat and the hole in my chest, to see what was going on there—for something in me was out of order, and it's well to examine one's self—the little ones made a tremendous noise. The youngest jumped up into my hat, and shouted so there that it tickled me. The little thoughts may grow; I know that very well; and out in the world thoughts come too, and not only of my kind, for as far as I can see I cannot discern anything like myself; but the wingless houses, whose throats make no noise, have thoughts too, and these come to my thoughts, and make love to them, as it is called. It's wonderful enough —yes, there are many wonderful things. Something has come over me, or into me,—something has changed in the mill-work: it seems as if the one-half, the father, had altered, and had received a better temper and a more affectionate helpmate—so young and good, and yet the same, only more gentle and good through the course of time. What was bitter has passed away, and the whole is much more comfortable.

"The days go on, and the days come nearer and nearer to clearness and to joy; and then a day will come when it will be over with me: but not over altogether. I must be pulled down that I may be built up again; I shall cease, but yet shall live on. To become quite a different being, and yet remain the same! That's difficult for me to understand, however enlightened I may be with sun, moon, stearine, train oil, and tallow. My old wood-work and my old brick-work will rise again from the dust!

"I will hope that I may keep my old thoughts, the father in the mill, and the mother, great ones and little ones—the family; for I call them all, great and little, the *company of thoughts*, because I must, and cannot refrain from it.

"And I must also remain 'myself,' with my throat in my chest, my wings on my head, the gallery round my body; else I should not know myself, nor could the others know me, and say, 'There's the mill on the hill, proud to look at, and yet not proud at all.'"

That is what the mill said. Indeed, it said much more, but that is the most important part.

And the days came, and the days went, and yesterday was the last day.

Then the mill caught fire. The flames rose up high, and beat out and in, and bit at the beams and planks, and ate them up. The mill fell, and nothing remained of it but a heap of ashes. The smoke drove across the scene of the conflagration, and the wind carried it away.

Whatever had been alive in the mill remained, and what had been gained by it has nothing to do with this story.

The miller's family—one soul, many thoughts, and yet only one—built a new, a splendid mill, which answered its purpose. It was quite like the old one, and people said, "Why, yonder is the mill on the hill, proud to look at!" But this mill was better arranged, more according to the time than the last, so that progress might be made. The old beams had became worm-eaten and spongy—they lay in dust and ashes. The body of the mill did not rise out of the dust as they had believed it would do: they had taken it literally, and all things are *not* to be taken literally.

IN THE NURSERY.

FATHER, and mother, and brothers, and sisters, were gone to the play; only little Anna and her grandpapa were left at home.

"We'll have a play too," he said; "and it may begin immediately."

"But we have no theatre," cried little Anna, "and we have no one to act for us: my old doll cannot, for she is a fright, and my new one cannot, for she must not rumple her new clothes."

"One can always get actors if one makes use of what one has," observed grandpapa.

"Now we'll go into the theatre. Here we will put up a book, there another, and there a third, in a sloping row. Now three on the other side; so, now we have the side-scenes. The old box that lies yonder may be the back stairs; and we'll lay the flooring on top of it. The stage represents a room, as every one may see. Now we want the actors. Let us see what we can find in the plaything-box. First the personages, and then we will get the play ready: one after the other, that will be capital! Here's a pipe-head, and yonder an odd glove; they will do very well for father and daughter."

"But those are only two characters," said little Anna. "Here's my brother's old waistcoat—could not that play in our piece, too?"

"It's big enough, certainly," replied grandpapa. "It shall be the lover. There's nothing in the pockets, and that's very interesting, for that's half of an unfortunate attachment. And here we have the nutcrackers' boots, with spurs to them. Row, dow, dow! how they can stamp and strut! They shall represent the unwelcome wooer, whom the lady does not like. What kind of play will you have now? Shall it be a tragedy, or a domestic drama?"

"A domestic drama, please," said little Anna; "for the others are so fond of that. Do you know one?"

"I know a hundred," said grandpapa. "Those that are most in favour are from the French, but they are not good for little girls. In the meantime, we may take one of the prettiest, for inside they're all very much alike. Now I shake the pen! Cock-a-lorum! So now, here's the play, brin-bran-span new! Now listen to the play-bill."

And grandpapa took a newspaper, and read as if he were reading from it:

THE PIPE-HEAD AND THE GOOD HEAD.

A Family Drama in one Act.

CHARACTERS.

MR. PIPE-HEAD, *a father*,   MR. WAISTCOAT, *a lover*,
MISS GLOVE, *a daughter*,   MR. DE BOOTS, *a suitor*.

"And now we're going to begin. The curtain rises: we have no curtain, so it has risen already. All the characters are there, and so we have them at hand. Now I speak as Papa Pipe-head! he's angry to-day. One can see that he's a coloured meerschaum.

THE COMEDY.

"'Snik, snak, snurre, bassellurre! I'm master of this house! I'm the father of my daughter! Will you hear what I have to say? Mr. de Boots is a person in whom one may see one's face; his upper part is of morocco, and he has spurs into the bargain. Snikke, snakke, snak! He shall have my daughter!'

"Now listen to what the Waistcoat says, little Anna," said grandpapa. "Now the Waistcoat's speaking. The Waistcoat has a lay-down collar, and is very modest; but he knows his own value, and has quite a right to say what he says:

"'I haven't a spot on me! Goodness of material ought to be appreciated. I am of real silk, and have strings to me.'

"'—On the wedding day, but no longer; you don't keep your colour in the wash.' This is Mr. Pipe-head who is speaking. 'Mr. de Boots is water-tight, of strong leather, and yet very delicate; he can creak, and clank with his spurs, and has an Italian physiognomy—'"

"But they ought to speak in verses," said Anna, "for I've heard that's the most charming way of all."

"They can do that too," replied grandpapa; "and if the public de- mands it, they will talk in that way. Just look at little Miss Glove, how she's pointing her fingers!

> "'Could I but have my love,
> Who then so happy as Glove!
> Ah!
> If I from him must part,
> I'm sure 't will break my heart!'
> 'Bah!'

That last word was spoken by Mr. Pipe-head; and now it's Mr. Waist- coat's turn:

> "'O Glove, my own dear,
> Though it cost thee a tear,
> Thou must be mine,
> For Holger Danske has sworn it!'

"Mr. de Boots, hearing this, kicks up, jingles his spurs, and knocks. down three of the side-scenes."

"That's exceedingly charming!" cried little Anna.

"Silence! silence!" said grandpapa. "Silent approbation will show that you are the educated public in the stalls. Now Miss Glove sings her great song with startling effects:

> "'I can't see, heigho!
> And therefore I'll crow!
> Kikkeriki, in the lofty hall!'

"Now comes the exciting part, little Anna. This is the most impor- tant in all the play. Mr. Waistcoat undoes himself, and addresses his speech to you, that you may applaud; but leave it alone,—that's con- sidered more genteel.

"'I am driven to extremities! Take care of yourself! Now comes the plot! You are the Pipe-head, and I am the good head—snap! there you go!'

"Do you notice this, little Anna?" asked grandpapa. "That's a most charming scene and comedy. Mr. Waistcoat seized the old Pipe-head, and put him in his pocket; there he lies, and the Waistcoat says:

"'You are in my pocket; you can't come out till you promise to unite me to your daughter Glove on the left: I hold out my right hand.'"

"That's awfully pretty," said little Anna.

"And now the old Pipe-head replies:

> "'Though I'm all ear,
> Very stupid I appear:
> Where's my humour? Gone, I fear,
> And I feel my hollow stick's not here.
> Ah! never, my dear,
> Did I feel so queer.
> Oh! pray let me out,
> And like a lamb led to slaughter
> I'll betroth you, no doubt,
> To my daughter.'

"Is the play over already?" asked little Anna.

"By no means," replied grandpapa. "It's only all over with Mr. de Boots. Now the lovers kneel down, and one of them sings:

"'Father!'

and the other,

"'Come, do as you ought to do,—
Bless your son and daughter.'

And they receive his blessing, and celebrate their wedding, and all the pieces of furniture sing in chorus,

"'Klink! clanks!
A thousand thanks;
And now the play is over!'

"And now we'll applaud," said grandpapa. "We'll call them all out, and the pieces of furniture too, for they are of mahogany."

"And is not our play just as good as those which the others have in the real theatre?"

"Our play is much better," said grandpapa. "It is shorter, the performers are natural, and it has passed away the interval before tea-time."

THE GOLDEN TREASURE.

THE drummer's wife went into the church. She saw the new altar with the painted pictures and the carved angels: those upon the canvas and in the glory over the altar were just as beautiful as the carved ones; and they were painted and gilt into the bargain. Their hair gleamed golden in the sunshine, lovely to behold; but the real sunshine was more beautiful still. It shone redder, clearer through the dark trees, when the sun went down. It was lovely thus to look at the sunshine of heaven. And she looked at the red sun, and she thought about it so deeply, and thought of the little one whom the stork was to bring; and the wife of the drummer was very cheerful, and looked and looked, and wished that the child might have a gleam of sunshine given to it, so that it might at least become like one of the shining angels over the altar.

And when she really had the little child in her arms, and held it up to its father, then it was like one of the angels in the church to behold, with hair like gold—the gleam of the setting sun was upon it.

"My golden treasure, my riches, my sunshine!" said the mother; and she kissed the shining locks, and it sounded like music and song in the room of the drummer; and there was joy, and life, and movement.

A ROLL OF JOY.

The drummer beat a roll—a roll of joy. And the Drum said, the Fire-drum, that was beaten when there was a fire in the town:

"Red hair! the little fellow has red hair! Believe the drum, and not what your mother says! Rub-a-dub, rub-a-dub!"

And the town repeated what the Fire-drum had said.

The boy was taken to church, the boy was christened. There was nothing much to be said about his name; he was called Peter. The whole town, and the Drum too, called him Peter the drummer's boy with the red hair; but his mother kissed his red hair, and called him her golden treasure.

In the hollow way in the clayey bank, many had scratched their names as a remembrance.

"Celebrity is always something!" said the drummer; and so he scratched his own name there, and his little son's name likewise.

And the swallows came: they had, on their long journey, seen more durable characters engraven on rocks, and on the walls of the temples in Hindostan, mighty deeds of great kings, immortal names, so old that no one now could read or speak them. Remarkable celebrity!

In the clayey bank the martens built their nest: they bored holes in the deep declivity, and the splashing rain and the thin mist came and crumbled and washed the names away, and the drummer's name also, and that of his little son.

"Peter's name will last a full year and a half longer!" said the father.

"Fool!" thought the Fire-drum; but it only said, "Dub, dub, dub. rub-a-dub!"

He was a boy full of life and gladness, this drummer's son with the red hair. He had a lovely voice: he could sing, and he sang like a bird in the woodland. There was melody, and yet no melody.

PETER SINGING.

"He must become a chorister boy," said his mother. "He shall sing in the church, and stand among the beautiful gilded angels who are like him!"

"Fiery cat!" said some of the witty ones of the town.

The Drum heard that from the neighbours' wives.

"Don't go home, Peter," cried the street boys. "If you sleep in the garret, there'll be a fire in the house, and the fire-drum will have to be beaten."

"Look out for the drumsticks," replied Peter; and, small as he was, he ran up boldly, and gave the foremost such a punch in the body with his fist that the fellow lost his legs and tumbled over, and the others took their legs off with themselves very rapidly.

The town musician was very genteel and fine. He was the son of the royal plate-washer. He was very fond of Peter, and would sometimes take him to his home, and he gave him a violin, and taught him to play it. It seemed as if the whole art lay in the boy's fingers; and he wanted to be more than a drummer—he wanted to become musician to the town.

"I'll be a soldier," said Peter; for he was still quite a little lad, and it seemed to him the finest thing in the world to carry a gun, and to be able to march "one, two; one, two," and to wear a uniform and a sword.

"Ah, you learn to long for the drum-skin, drum, dum, dum!" said the Drum.

"Yes, if he could only march his way up to be a general!" observed his father; "but before he can do that there must be war."

"Heaven forbid!" said his mother.

"We have nothing to lose," remarked the father.

"Yes, we have my boy," she retorted.

"But suppose he came back a general!" said the father.

"Without arms and legs!" cried the mother. "No, I would rather keep my golden treasure with me."

BOUND FOR THE WAR.

"Drum, dum, dum!" The Fire-drum and all the other drums were beating, for war had come. The soldiers all set out, and the son of the drummer followed them. "Red-head. Golden treasure!"

The mother wept; the father in fancy saw him "famous;" the town musician was of opinion that he ought not to go to war, but should stay at home and learn music.

"Red-head," said the soldiers, and little Peter laughed; but when one of them sometimes said to another "Foxey," he would bite his teeth together and look another way—into the wide world: he did not care for the nickname.

The boy was active, pleasant of speech, and good humoured; and that is the best canteen, said his old comrades.

And many a night he had to sleep under the open sky, wet through with the driving rain or the falling mist; but his good humour never forsook him. The drum-sticks sounded, "Rub-a-dub, all up, all up!" Yes, he was certainly born to be a drummer.

The day of battle dawned. The sun had not yet risen, but the morning was come. The air was cold, the battle was hot, there was mist in the air, but still more gunpowder-smoke. The bullets and shells flew over the soldiers' heads, and into their heads, into their bodies and limbs;

but still they pressed forward. Here or there one or other of them would sink on his knees, with bleeding temples and a face as white as chalk. The little drummer still kept his healthy colour; he had suffered no damage; he looked cheerfully at the dog of the regiment, which was jumping along as merrily as if the whole thing had been got up for his amusement, and as if the bullets were only flying about that he might have a game of play with them.

"March! Forward! March!" This was the word of command for the drum. The word had not yet been given to fall back, though they might have done so, and perhaps there would have been much sense in it; and now at last the word "Retire" was given; but our little drummer beat "Forward! march!" for he had understood the command thus, and the soldiers obeyed the sound of the drum. That was a good roll, and proved the summons to victory for the men, who had already begun to give way.

Life and limb were lost in the battle. Bomb-shells tore away the flesh in red strips; bomb-shells lit up into a terrible glow the straw-heaps to which the wounded had dragged themselves, to lie untended for many hours, perhaps for all the hours they had to live.

It's no use thinking of it; and yet one cannot help thinking of it, even far away in the peaceful town. The drummer and his wife also thought of it, for Peter was at the war.

"Now, I'm tired of these complaints," said the Fire-drum.

Again the day of battle dawned; the sun had not yet risen, but it was morning. The drummer and his wife were asleep: they had been talking about their son, as, indeed, they did almost every night, for he was out yonder, in God's hand. And the father dreamt that the war was over, that the soldiers had returned home, and that Peter wore a silver cross on his breast. But the mother dreamt that she had gone into the church, and had seen the painted pictures and the carved angels with the gilded hair, and her own dear boy, the golden treasure of her heart, who was standing among the angels in white robes, singing so sweetly, as surely only the angels can sing; and that he had soared up with them into the sunshine, and nodded so kindly at his mother.

"My golden treasure!" she cried out; and she awoke. "Now the good God has taken him to Himself!" She folded her hands, and hid her face in the cotton curtains of the bed, and wept. "Where does he rest now? among the many in the big grave that they have dug for the dead? Perhaps he's in the water in the marsh! Nobody knows his grave; no holy words have been read over it!" And the Lord's Prayer went inaudibly over her lips; she bowed her head, and was so weary that she went to sleep.

And the days days went by, in life as in dreams!

It was evening: over the battle-field a rainbow spread, which touched the forest and the deep marsh.

It has been said, and is preserved in popular belief, that where the rainbow touches the earth a treasure lies buried, a golden treasure; and here there was one. No one but his mother thought of the little drummer, and therefore she dreamt of him.

And the days went by, in life as in dreams!

Not a hair of his head had been hurt, not a golden hair.

"Drum-ma-rum! drum-ma-rum! there he is!" the Drum might have said, and his mother might have sung, if she had seen or dreamt it.

With hurrah and song, adorned with green wreaths of victory, they came home, as the war was at an end, and peace had been signed. The dog of the regiment sprang on in front with large bounds, and made the way three times as long for himself as it really was.

And days and weeks went by, and Peter came into his parents' room: he was as brown as a wild man, and his eyes were bright, and his face beamed like sunshine. And his mother held him in her arms; she kissed his lips, his forehead, his red hair. She had her boy back again; he had not a silver cross on his breast, as his father had dreamt, but he had

PETER'S RETURN.

sound limbs, a thing the mother had not dreamt. And what a rejoicing was there! They laughed and they wept; and Peter embraced the old Fire-drum.

"There stands the old skeleton still!" he said.

And the father beat a roll upon it.

"One would think that a great fire had broken out here," said the Fire-drum. "Bright day! fire in the heart! golden treasure! skrat! skr-r-at! skr-r-r-r-at!"

And what then? What then!—Ask the town musician.

"Peter's far outgrowing the drum," he said. "Peter will be greater than I."

And yet he was the son of a royal plate-washer; but all that he had learned in half a lifetime, Peter learned in half a year.

THE FIRE-DRUM NOT FORGOTTEN.

There was something so merry about him, something so truly kind hearted. His eyes gleamed, and his hair gleamed too—there was no denying that!

"He ought to have his hair dyed," said the neighbour's wife. "That answered capitally with the policeman's daughter, and she got a husband."

"But her hair turned as green as duckweed, and was always having to be coloured up."

"She knows how to manage for herself," said the neighbours, "and so can Peter. He comes to the most genteel houses, even to the burgomaster's, where he gives Miss Charlotte pianoforte lessons."

He *could* play! He could play, fresh out of his heart, the most charming pieces, that had never been put upon music-paper. He played in the bright nights, and in the dark nights too. The neighbours declared it was unbearable, and the Fire-drum was of the same opinion.

He played until his thoughts soared up, and burst forth in great plans for the future:

"To be famous!"

And burgomaster's Charlotte sat at the piano. Her delicate fingers danced over the keys, and made them ring into Peter's heart. It seemed too much for him to bear; and this happened not once, but many times; and at last one day he seized the delicate fingers and the white hand, and kissed it, and looked into her great brown eyes. Heaven knows what he said; but we may be allowed to guess at it. Charlotte blushed to guess at it. She reddened from brow to neck, and answered not a single word; and then strangers came into the room, and one of them was the state councillor's son: he had a lofty white forehead, and carried it so high that it seemed to go back into his neck. And Peter sat by her a long time, and she looked at him with gentle eyes.

At home that evening he spoke of travel in the wide world, and of the golden treasure that lay hidden for him in his violin.

"To be famous!"

NEWS!

"Tum-me-lum, tum-me-lum, tum-me-lum!" said the Fire-drum. "Peter has gone clean out of his wits. I think there must be a fire in the house."

Next day the mother went to market.

"Shall I tell you news, Peter?" she asked when she came home. "A capital piece of news. Burgomaster's Charlotte has engaged herself to the state councillor's son; the betrothal took place yesterday evening."

"No!" cried Peter, and he sprang up from his chair. But his mother persisted in saying "Yes." She had heard it from the baker's wife, whose husband had it from the burgomaster's own mouth.

And Peter became as pale as death, and sat down again.

"Good Heaven! what's the matter with you?" asked his mother.

"Nothing, nothing; only leave me to myself," he answered, but the tears were running down his cheeks.

"My sweet child, my golden treasure!" cried the mother, and she wept; but the Fire-drum sang—not out loud, but inwardly,
" Charlotte's gone! Charlotte's gone! and now the song is done."

DESPAIR.

But the song was not done; there were many more verses in it, long verses, the most beautiful verses, the golden treasures of a life.

"She behaves like a mad woman," said the neighbour's wife. "All the world is to see the letters she gets from her golden treasure, and to read the words that are written in the papers about his violin-playing. And he sends her money too, and that's very useful to her since she has been a widow."

"He plays before emperors and kings," said the town musician. "I never had that fortune; but he's my pupil, and he does not forget his old master."

And his mother said,

"His father dreamt that Peter came home from the war with a silver cross. He did not gain one in the war; but it is still more difficult to gain one in this way. Now he has the cross of honour. If his father had only lived to see it!"

"He's grown famous!" said the Fire-drum; and all his native town said the same thing, for the drummer's son, Peter with the red hair— Peter whom they had known as a little boy, running about in wooden shoes, and then as a drummer, playing for the dancers—was become famous!

"He played at our house before he played in the presence of kings," said the burgomaster's wife. "At that time he was quite smitten with Charlotte. He was always of an aspiring turn. At that time he was saucy and an enthusiast. My husband laughed when he heard of the foolish affair, and now our Charlotte's a state councillor's wife."

A golden treasure had been hidden in the heart and soul of the poor child, who had beaten the roll as a drummer—a roll or victory for those who had been ready to retreat. There was a golden treasure in his bosom, the power of sound : it burst forth on his violin as if the instrument had been a complete organ, and as if all the elves of a midsummer night were dancing across the strings. In its sounds were heard the piping of the thrush and the full clear note of the human voice ; therefore the sound brought rapture to every heart, and carried his name triumphant through the land. That was a great firebrand—the firebrand of inspiration.

" And then he looks so splendid ! " said the young ladies and the old ladies too ; and the oldest of all procured an album for famous locks of hair, wholly and solely that she might beg a lock of his rich splendid hair, that treasure, that golden treasure.

And the son came into the poor room of the drummer, elegant as a prince, happier than a king. His eyes were as clear and his face was as radiant as sunshine ; and he held his mother in his arms, and she kissed his mouth, and wept as blissfully as any one can weep for joy ; and he nodded at every old piece of furniture in the room, at the cupboard with the tea-cups, and at the flower-vase. He nodded at the sleeping-bench, where he had slept as a little boy ; but the old Firedrum he brought out, and dragged it into the middle of the room, and said to it and to his mother :

" My father would have beaten a famous roll this evening. Now I must do it ! "

And he beat a thundering roll-call on the instrument, and the Drum felt so highly honoured that the parchment burst with exultation.

" He has a splendid touch ! " said the Drum. " I 've a remembrance of him now that will last. I expect that the same thing will happen to his mother, from pure joy over her golden treasure."

And this is the story of the Golden Treasure.

THE STORM SHAKES THE SHIELD.

IN the old days, when grandpapa was quite a little boy, and ran about in little red breeches and a red coat, and a feather in his cap—for that 's the costume the little boys wore in his time when they were dressed in their best—many things were very different from what they are now : there was often a good deal of show in the streets—show that we don't see nowadays, because it has been abolished as too old-fashioned : still, it is very interesting to hear grandfather tell about it.

It must really have been a gorgeous sight to behold, in those days, when the shoemaker brought over the shield, when the court-house was changed. The silken flag waved to and fro, on the shield itself a double eagle was displayed, and a big boot ; the youngest lads carried the

GRANDFATHER TELLING ABOUT IT.

" welcome," and the chest of the workmen's guild, and their shirt-sleeves
were adorned with red and white ribbons; the elder ones carried drawn
swords, each with a lemon stuck on its point.   There was a full band
of music, and the most splendid of all the instruments was the " bird,"
as grandfather called the big stick with the crescent at the top, and all
manner of dingle-dangles hanging to it, a perfect Turkish clatter of music.
The stick was lifted high in the air, and swung up and down till it
jingled again, and quite dazzled one's eyes when the sun shone on all
its glory of gold, and silver, and brass.

HOW GRANDFATHER LOOKED WHEN A BOY.

In front of the procession ran the Harlequin, dressed in clothes made
of all kinds of coloured patches artfully sewn together, with a black
face, and bells on his head like a sledge horse : he beat the people with
his bat, which made a great clattering without hurting them, and the
people would crowd together and fall back, only to advance again the

next moment. Little boys and girls fell over their own toes into the gutter, old women dispensed digs with their elbows, and looked sour, and took snuff. One laughed, another chatted; the people thronged the windows and door-steps, and even all the roofs. The sun shone; and although they had a little rain too, that was good for the farmer; and when they got wetted thoroughly, they only thought what a blessing it was for the country.

And what stories grandpapa could tell! As a little boy he had seen all these fine doings in their greatest pomp. The oldest of the policemen used to make a speech from the platform on which the shield was hung up, and the speech was in verses, as if it had been made by a poet, as, indeed, it had; for three people had concocted it together, and they had first drunk a good bowl of punch, so that the speech might turn out well.

And the people gave a cheer for the speech, but they shouted much louder for the Harlequin, when he appeared in front of the platform, and made a grimace at them.

The fools played the fool most admirably, and drank mead out of spirit-glasses, which they then flung among the crowd, by whom they were caught up. Grandfather was the possessor of one of these glasses, which had been given him by a working mason, who had managed to catch it. Such a scene was really very pleasant; and the shield on the new court-house was hung with flowers and green wreaths.

"One never forgets a feast like that, however old one may grow," said grandfather. Nor did he forget it, though he saw many other grand spectacles in his time, and could tell about them too; but it was most pleasant of all to hear him tell about the shield that was brought in the town from the old to the new court-house.

Once, when he was a little boy, grandpapa had gone with his parents to see this festivity. He had never yet been in the metropolis of the country. There were so many people in the streets, that he thought that the shield was being carried. There were many shields to be seen; a hundred rooms might have been filled with pictures, if they had been hung up inside and outside. At the tailor's were pictures of all kinds of clothing, to show that he could stitch up people from the coarsest to the finest; at the tobacco manufacturer's were pictures of the most charming little boys, smoking cigars, just as they do in reality; there were signs with painted butter and herrings, clerical collars, and coffins, and inscriptions and announcements into the bargain. A person could walk up and down for a whole day through the streets, and tire himself out with looking at the pictures; and then he would know all about what people lived in the houses, for they had hung out their shields or signs; and, as grandfather said, it was a very instructive thing, in a great town, to know at once who the inhabitants were.

And this is what happened with these shields, when grandpapa came to the town. He told it me himself, and he hadn't "a rogue on his back," as mother used to tell me he had when he wanted to make me believe something outrageous, for now he looked quite trustworthy.

The first night after he came to the town had been signalized by the most terrible gale ever recorded in the newspapers, a gale such as none of the inhabitants had ever before experienced. The air was dark with flying tiles; old wood-work crashed and fell; and a wheelbarrow ran up the street all alone, only to get out of the way. There was a groaning in the air, and a howling and a shrieking, and altogether it was a terrible storm. The water in the canal rose over the banks, for it did not know where to run. The storm swept over the town, carrying plenty of chimneys with it, and more than one proud weathercock on a church tower had to bow, and has never got over it from that time.

There was a kind of sentry-house, where dwelt the venerable old superintendent of the fire brigade, who always arrived with the last engine. The storm would not leave this little sentry-house alone, but must needs tear it from its fastenings, and roll it down the street; and, wonderfully enough, it stopped opposite to the door of the dirty journeyman plasterer, who had saved three lives at the last fire, but the sentry-house thought nothing of that.

The barber's shield, the great brazen dish, was carried away, and hurled straight into the embrasure of the councillor of justice; and the whole neighbourhood said this looked almost like malice, inasmuch as they, and nearly all the friends of the councillor's wife, used to call that lady "the Razor;" for she was so sharp that she knew more about other people's business than they knew about it themselves.

A shield with a dried salt fish painted on it flew exactly in front of the door of a house where dwelt a man who wrote a newspaper. That was a very poor joke perpetrated by the gale, which seemed to have forgotten that a man who writes in a paper is not the kind of person to understand any liberty taken with him; for he is a king in his own newspaper, and likewise in his own opinion.

The weathercock flew to the opposite house, where he perched, looking the picture of malice—so the neighbours said.

The cooper's tub stuck itself up under the head of "ladies' costumes."

The eating-house keeper's bill of fare, which had hung at his door in a heavy frame, was posted by the storm over the entrance to the theatre, where nobody went: it was a ridiculous list—" Horse-radish, soup, and stuffed cabbage." And now people came in plenty.

The fox's skin, the honourable sign of the furrier, was found fastened to the bell-pull of a young man who always went to early lecture, and looked like a furled umbrella, and said he was striving after truth. and was considered by his aunt " a model and an example."

The inscription " Institution for Superior Education " was found near the billiard club, which place of resort was further adorned with the words " Children brought up by hand." Now, this was not at all witty; but, you see, the storm had done it, and no one has any control over that.

It was a terrible night, and in the morning—only think!—nearly all the shields had changed places: in some places the inscriptions were so malicious, that grandfather would not speak of them at all; but I saw that he was chuckling secretly, and there may have been some inaccuracy in his description, after all.

The poor people in the town, and still more the strangers, were continually making mistakes in the people they wanted to see; nor was this to be avoided, when they went according to the shields that were hung up. Thus, for instance, some who wanted to go to a very grave assembly of elderly men, where important affairs were to be discussed, found themselves in a noisy boys' school, where all the company were leaping over the chairs and tables.

There were also people who made a mistake between the church and the theatre, and that was terrible indeed!

Such a storm we have never witnessed in our day; for that only happened in grandpapa's time, when he was quite a little boy. Perhaps we shall never experience a storm of the kind, but our grandchildren may; and we can only hope and pray that all may *stay at home while the storm is moving the shields.*

THE BIRD OF POPULAR SONG.

It is winter-time. The earth wears a snowy garment, and looks like marble hewn out of the rock; the air is bright and clear; the wind is sharp as a well-tempered sword, and the trees stand like branches of white coral or blooming almond twigs, and here it is keen as on the lofty Alps.

The night is splendid in the gleam of the northern lights, and in the glitter of innumerable twinkling stars.

But we sit in the warm room, by the hot stove, and talk about the old times. And we listen to this story:

By the open sea was a giant's grave; and on the grave-mound sat at midnight the spirit of the buried hero, who had been a king. The golden circlet gleamed on his brow, his hair fluttered in the wind, and he was clad in steel and iron. He bent his head mournfully, and sighed in deep sorrow, as an unquiet spirit might sigh.

And a ship came sailing by. Presently the sailors lowered the anchor, and landed. Among them was a singer, and he approached the royal spirit, and said,

"Why mournest thou, and wherefore dost thou suffer thus?"

And the dead man answered,

"No one hath sung the deeds of my life; they are dead and forgotten: song doth not carry them forth over the lands, nor into the hearts of men; therefore I have no rest and no peace."

And he spoke of his works, and of his warlike deeds, which his contemporaries had known, but which had not been sung, because there was no singer among his companions.

Then the old bard struck the strings of his harp, and sang of the youthful courage of the hero, of the strength of the man, and of the greatness of his good deeds. Then the face of the dead one gleamed like the margin of the cloud in the moonlight. Gladly and of good courage, the form arose in splendour and in majesty, and vanished like the glancing of the northern light. Nought was to be seen but the green turfy mound, with the stones on which no Runic record has been graven; but at the last sound of the harp there soared over the hill, as though he had fluttered from the harp, a little bird, a charming singing-bird, with the ringing voice of the thrush, with the moving pathos of the human heart, with a voice that told of home, like the voice that is heard by the bird of passage. The singing-bird soared away, over mountain and valley, over field and wood—he was the Bird of Popular Song, who never dies.

THE OLD BARD.

We hear his song—we hear it now in the room while the white bees are swarming without, and the storm clutches the windows. The bird sings not alone the requiem of heroes; he sings also sweet gentle songs of love, so many and so warm, of Northern fidelity and truth. He has stories in words and in tones; he has proverbs and snatches of proverb; songs which, like Runes laid under a dead man's tongue, force him to speak; and thus Popular Song tells of the land of his birth.

In the old heathen days, in the times of the Vikings, the popular speech was enshrined in the harp of the bard.

In the days of knightly castles, when the strong fist held the scales of justice, when only might was right, and a peasant and a dog were of equal importance, where did the Bird of Song find shelter and protection? Neither violence nor stupidity gave him a thought.

But in the gabled window of the knightly castle, the lady of the castle sat with the parchment roll before her, and wrote down the old recollections in song and legend, while near her stood the old woman from the wood, and the travelling pedlar who went wandering through the country. As these told their tales, there fluttered around them, with twittering and song, the Bird of Popular Song, who never dies so long as the earth has a hill upon which his foot may rest.

And now he looks in upon us and sings. Without are the night and the snow-storm: he lays the Runes beneath our tongues, and we know the land of our home. Heaven speaks to us in our native tongue, in the voice of the Bird of Popular Song: the old remembrances awake, the faded colours glow with a fresh lustre, and story and song pour us a blessed draught which lifts up our minds and our thoughts, so that the evening becomes as a Christmas festival.

The snow-flakes chase each other, the ice cracks, the storm rules without, for he has the might, he is lord—but not the LORD OF ALL.

THE SNOW-STORM.

It is winter-time. The wind is sharp as a two-edged sword, the snow-flakes chase each other: it seemed as though it had been snowing for days and weeks, and the snow lies like a great mountain over the whole town, like a heavy dream of the winter night. Everything on the earth is hidden away, only the golden cross of the church, the symbol of faith, arises over the snow grave, and gleams in the blue air and in the bright sunshine.

And over the buried town fly the birds of heaven, the small and the great; they twitter and they sing as best they may, each bird with his beak.

First comes the band of sparrows: they pipe at every trifle in the streets and lanes, in the nests and the houses; they have stories to tell about the front buildings and the back buildings.

"We know the buried town," they say; "everything living in it is piep! piep! piep!"

The black ravens and crows flew on over the white snow.

"Grub, grub!" they cried. "There's something to be got down there; something to swallow, and that's most important. That's the opinion of most of them down there, and the opinion is goo—goo—good!"

The wild swans come flying on whirring pinions, and sing of the noble and the great, that will still sprout in the hearts of men, down in the town which is resting beneath its snowy veil.

No death is there—life reigns yonder; we hear it on the notes that swell onward like the tones of the church organ, which seize us like sounds from the elf-hill, like the songs of Ossian, like the rushing swoop of the wandering spirits' wings. What harmony! That harmony speaks to our hearts, and lifts up our souls!—It is the Bird of Popular song whom we hear.

And at this moment the warm breath of heaven blows down from the sky. There are gaps in the snowy mountains, the sun shines into the clefts; spring is coming, the birds are returning, and new races are coming with the same home sounds in their hearts.

Hear the story of the year: "The night of the snow-storm, the heavy dream of the winter night, all shall be dissolved, all shall rise again in the beauteous notes of the Bird of Popular Song who never dies!"

THE LEGEND OF NÜRNBERG CASTLE.

THE custodian of the castle was conducting me through the place, repeating names and dates; and his little boy was following us, but stopping every now and then to play in a window. I should have preferred to sit confidentially with the little lad, and let him tell me truth or dreams; for, after all, most of the stories our elders give us and call "historical" are but dreams when all is done. I should have liked to stand with him, in a moonlight night, and look out over the old Gothic town, whose towers point up at the stars, as if to tell the shining specks to look down on the plain, where now the postboy's horn is sounding, but where, once on a time, Wallenstein's trumpeters sounded the charge. In the mists that float over the wide expanse I should behold the Swedish troopers who fought for the Protestant faith.

I should like to sit with the little lad under the linden tree, and repeat with him what the legend tells of Eppelin, the wild knight of Garlingen. From his castle Eppelin watched for every caravan of Nürnberg merchants who travelled to that city with their wares; and then he would swoop down like a falcon on his prey. But the falcon was caught, the wild knight languished in this castle, where the linden tree is growing still. The day came on which he was to die; and, according to the gallant old custom, it was permitted him, as a man condemned to death, to ask that a wish should be granted him; and the wish of the knight was, that he might bestride his gallant horse once more.

The good steed neighed for joy, and proudly carried his master round the narrow courtyard, and the knight patted its strong smooth neck; and the noble beast's muscles seemed to swell and its hoofs beat the pavement impatiently. And it careered round in a circle, ever faster and faster, so that the gaolers and armed guards were obliged to press close to the walls, to leave room for it. But they had no suspicion, for they knew that the castle gate was securely fastened, and that there was no escape for the knight. "But if they could have read what stood written in the horse's eyes," says the chronicle, "they would have stopped its career and bound the wild knight's hands." And what stood written in the horse's eyes? They spoke in dumb but fiery language:

"In this wretched courtyard thy knightly blood may not flow! Here may not end thy merry, active life! Shall I not further bear thee into the raging battle, through the deep defiles, and the merry green forest? Shall I no more eat food from thy gallant hand? Trust to my tremendous strength, and I will save thee!"

And the horse rose as though for a spring. The knight struck the spurs into its flanks, drew a deep breath, and bent forward over the creature's neck. Fire flashed from its hoofs; a bound, and, wonderful to relate, the horse had gained the crest of the outer wall; another, and horse and rider sprang across the deep moat, and were free!

And whenever the wind whistles through the linden tree, it tells the legend once more.

A NIGHT IN THE APENNINES.

OVER the green, flat Lombard plains rise the vine- and forest-clad Apennines. The traveller who issues from the gates of Bologna may fancy his road leads across the terraces of an immense ruined garden, like that which, as the legend tells us, the mighty Semiramis built.

It was in the middle of December. The stamp of the late autumn was upon all things. The leaves of the vines were red, the forest leaves were yellow, only the laurel hedges stood as green as ever; and the pine and cypress wood waved in undiminished splendour. Slowly we drove upward, ever upward: garlands of vine-leaves trailed down over ruined walls; we met teams of giant oxen, which had been used as a help for the horses: their white shining sides gleamed with a pinky tint in the setting sun.

Gradually, as we rose higher, the region became more desolate, and presently I went forward alone. The sun had set, and in a few moments a blue glimmer shone over the mountains; a glimmer in the atmosphere, which seemed to emanate from the hills themselves. Not a breath of air was stirring; everything was mild and still, and an aspect of majesty in the mountains and in the deep valleys attuned the soul to meditation. The loneliness of the valley gave it, I may not say a tone of melancholy, but rather an aspect of rest, as if Sleep were holding his court down there; for a feeling of rest and peace was spread on all things, heightened by the soft murmur of the river far beneath. The road wound round the mountain on which I was wandering; and presently I saw no carriage, no human being, nothing but the deep valley: I was alone, quite alone.

Night came on; the stars began to glitter. In our Northern regions they shine brightest in the frosty winter night; but here, in the mountains, the sky seems much higher; and the distant vault looked transparent, as though another immeasurable space began behind it.

A ray of light presently pierced through the rocky distance. It came from a tavern built upon the mountain. In the open alcove a lamp had been lighted to the Madonna. The *camereire* or chamberlain was ready, in his white apron and velvet jacket, to receive us, the travellers. We were ushered into a great saloon, whose whitish-grey walls were covered with inscriptions in all the languages of Europe. It was cold and lonely enough; but great bundles of brushwood were thrown into the fireplace, and set on fire, and we gathered in a circle about the blaze. Each one of our little party had something to tell, especially about the last great inundation from the river.

After the smoking supper had been dispatched, each one sought his bed. Mine was in a somewhat distant room, large and lonely—a couch as broad as it was long: there was a little vessel of holy water at the bed-head, and on the wall were inscriptions, and among the rest one in Danish, a translation of the German popular song, "Enjoy life while it lasteth!"

So a countryman of mine had been here, and had written this. May his life be an enjoyable one!

A rickety table and two rush-bottomed chairs formed the rest of the furniture.

I opened a window in front of which great iron bars had been fastened. The window looked out upon a deep valley. Below all was darkness. I could hear a stream rushing onward. Above me glittered the starry sky. I leaned my forehead against the iron bars, and did not feel more lonely than I had felt in my own little room in Denmark. He who has a home in his own country may feel home-sick; but he who possesses nothing is at home everywhere. In a few minutes my room here seemed to become a familiar home to me; but I did not yet know my neighbours.

Besides the common door, I noticed another—a smaller one, which was fastened by a bolt. Whither might this lead? What was behind this door? I took the five-wicked metal lamp, three wicks of which had been lighted. I kindled the other two, drew back the bolt, and went forth on a journey of discovery.

Beyond the door I found a kind of lumber-room. Here were chests, boxes, sacks, and great jars; and old clothes and guns hung upon the walls. But there was another door leading out of this room. I opened it, and stood in a long narrow passage; traversing this, I stood before another door. Should I go farther? I stood still and listened. Suddenly I heard two sounds like notes played on a flute, one deep, the other high and piercing; after a pause they were repeated.

The longer I listened, the more I felt convinced that these sounds did not proceed from a flute. I lifted the latch, and the door flew open suddenly, much more suddenly than I had expected. The room was dimly lighted by a lamp, and an old peasant with long white hair was before me, sitting half undressed in an arm-chair, playing the flute.

I made an excuse for my intrusion, but he did not heed me. I shut the door and was about to retreat, when it was opened again by a young peasant lad, who asked me in a whisper whom I was seeking.

The old man whom I had seen was the uncle of the landlord, and had been of weak mind since his sixteenth year.

I will tell the few particulars I learned respecting his case. His illness had come upon him as though wafted towards him by the wind. No one could give any reason for it. As a boy he had played prettily upon the flute; but since a certain night he had never tried anything but two notes, one a deep and mournful one, and the other high and piercing. These notes he continually repeated, and sometimes played them at night for hours together. They had tried to take his flute from him, but then he would become as furious as a wild animal; though, when it was returned to him, he at once became calm and friendly. The boy who spoke to me slept in the same room with the old man, and had become accustomed to the sound of the flute, as a man grows accustomed

THE OLD PEASANT.

to the ticking of a clock, or the clang of a blacksmith's hammer, when the blacksmith has been his neighbour for years.

I went back to my room and locked the door; but the two notes of the flute rang in my ears: they sounded like the distant creaking of a weathercock turned by the wind. I could not sleep; my fancy was busy about the old man. I heard the flute tones sounding like notes from the spirit world, and thought how, when the old man is dead, the people of the house will hear these notes in imagination, as they now hear them in reality. At length, towards morning, I fell asleep, and I think I was awakened within an hour; for we were to start before day-break. It was still night when we sat once more in our carriage. The mountains lay before us, covered with snow, and seemed to glow hotly in the sunshine. Near Pietra Malas nothing is to be seen but naked wild rocks of volcanic origin; and the volcanoes are not yet extinct, for to the right a thick smoke comes whirling from the rocky clefts. This morning I beheld two seas like shining bands on the horizon: to the left the Adriatic, to the right the Mediterranean Sea. A strong wall has been built here close to the road, to give the passengers protection from the storm, which comes rushing from the east. Before this wall was erected, there were often days and nights in which none might wander here, for the angel of the storm was walking abroad over the mountains.

"The old man in the tavern," said our *vetturino*, "one night crawled across this mountain on all fours, so they say. I suppose he was not mad at that time. He wanted to go down on the opposite side of the mountain."

Again I thought of the old man, and of the tones of the flute. The road wound downwards in beautiful serpentine curves, over arches of masonry, always sheltered by the mountains, where the sun shone warm, where the snow had melted, and the trees appeared decked with leaves. "Beautiful Italy!" cried all, rejoicingly. The *vetturino* cracked his whip, and the echoes cracked in reply far louder than he could do.

THE CARNIVAL IN ROME.

THE circumstance which makes the Carnival in Rome more rich and lively than the same period in any other place, is the limitation of the festivities in the streets to six days, and to three hours on each day. Only the Corso and the side streets in its immediate neighbourhood present scenes for this popular festival. Everything is concentrated, time as well as place. The celebration here is like a flashing glass of champagne—the goblet foams, is immediately quaffed, and then follows the fast.

Goethe has painted the Romish Carnival, which presents the same features year after year, so charmingly, that no one could do it better; therefore a new description would be unnecessary. Nor am I about to give one; only, to furnish a picture of Rome to a certain extent, I lay a short sketch here in my book: the particular circumstances belong to the Carnival of 1841.

Brave in purple and gold sits the senator in the Capital, surrounded by pages in tawny liveries: a deputation of Jews appears before him with the petition that the community may be permitted to inhabit for another year the quarters assigned to it in the Ghetto. The petition is granted; the senator seats himself in his state coach, the old bells of the Capitol are set ringing, and this is the sign that the Carnival may begin. The carriage proceeds at a foot-pace towards the Piazza del Popolo, and behind it throng a mass of people from palaces, houses, and taverns. But everywhere the greatest order prevails; every lady can venture out without danger, in man's clothes, and nobody thinks of insulting her, or causing her embarrassment by the slightest gesture. It is amusing to see how the poor people manage to procure a dress for the Carnival. They cover their own clothes completely with salad leaves, even to their shoes, and wear wigs of salad leaves on their heads; man and wife, and sometimes the children too, appear in a complete disguise of salad leaves. A pair of spectacles, manufactured from the peel of an orange, completes the costume, in which the poor couple may be seen marching down the Corso, with perfect gravity and quite a royal bearing.

From the Piazza del Popolo the senator and his train proceed up the Corso. All the windows and balconies are here hung with tapestries of red, blue, and yellow silk ; everywhere there is a throng of people, the majority of whom are in fancy dresses, with or without masks. In front of the houses, close to the walls, little cane seats or benches are ranged along, which are let out on hire, and on which the quieter people take up a position. One row of carriages drives up, and the other down ; and often horses and carriages are adorned with fluttering ribbons and green boughs. Frequently the coachmen, old fellows with true Italian faces, are seen disguised as women, with a poodle, dressed as a baby or a girl, by their sides. Other carriages are metamorphosed into steamboats, with a crew of sailors, or girls, in uniform. When two such vehicles happen to meet, there is a grand fight, in which *confetti*, or sweetmeats, are showered down, not flung by the hand, but poured from Horns of Plenty. On the pavement, and even among the carriages, the great stream of life goes surging to and fro. When two Punchinellos or Harlequins happen to meet, they take each other's arm, and proceed together, shouting and screaming. Masks in similar costumes associate themselves together, and soon whole bands are seen making their way rejoicingly among carriages and pedestrians, like waterspouts whirling across a slightly agitated sea. At sundown cannon-shots are heard, and the carriages turn into the bye-streets at the signal ; soldiers, who have been posted at a little distance from one another, now collect into bodies, and march down the street ; the cavalry follows, at first slowly, the second time at a brisker pace, and the third time at full gallop ; for this is a sign that the races are going to begin.

On the Piazza del Popolo lofty platforms have been erected. A rope is stretched across the road, and behind there are six or seven half-wild horses, with iron balls, garnished with spikes, dangling at their sides, and lighted tinder on their backs.

The rope falls to the ground, and away gallop the horses, the silken ribbons and the tinsel ornaments rattling and fluttering on their manes and tails. " *Cavalli ! cavalli !* " is shouted in wildest clamour by the crowd, who make way for the approaching steeds, who rush onward, maddened by the tumult : they rush past, and the dense masses of men close up behind them.

Before the horses have reached the goal, they are often so exhausted that they arrive at a gentle trot ; nevertheless, the farther end of the street has been hung with great carpets, stretched across from house to house, at a little distance from each other. If the horses came storming along in ever'such wild career, they would be effectually stopped by en-tangling themselves in these draperies.

A comic effect is produced when, just before the commencement of the race, a dog happens to slip into the space cleared in the street, and the people who are standing nearest set about hooting him ; for the whole assembly follows the example thus set, and the unhappy dog is obliged to run the gauntlet through the whole length of the course, the shouting and clapping of hands he encounters on both sides keeping him in the middle of the road. What a rejoicing is there! The poor dog must needs run a race, and if he happens to be fat and plump, he looks comically miserable; for he can hardly put one leg before the other, and is, nevertheless, compelled to gallop.

It is pleasant during Carnival-time to go into a tavern in the evening, where you may often meet a whole company of merry masks: they drink their *foglietta*, improvise a song, or dance the *Saltarello*. Large groups move through the streets with song and beating of tambourines, preceded by a mask carrying a burning torch. In their fancy dresses they visit the theatres, especially the smaller ones; and there is as much acting among the audience as among the professional mimes. I followed a group of this kind into the Teatro Aliberti. About a third part of the audience wore masquerade dresses; knights in armour, flower girls, Harlequins, and Greek gods sat among us as ordinary mortals. One of the largest boxes in the grand tier was quite filled with pretty young Roman women, dressed as Pierrots, but without mask or rouge: they were so lively and charming, it was a pleasure to look at them; but they certainly took every one's attention completely from the stage. The piece performed that evening was a favourite tragedy, called " Byron in Venice, England, and Missolonghi." It was very moving, but the audience seemed exceedingly merry. In the gallery sat a man belonging to the lower classes. He had a thick black beard, and was attired as a peasant girl; he affected great emotion at the play, and spread first his veil and then his skirt over the box in front of him, and wiped his eyes, and applauded. The eyes of the audience were fixed upon him more than upon Byron in Missolonghi.

The last day of the Carnival is always the liveliest; it closes with the gem of the whole festival, the glowing, splendid *Moccolo*. This year the scene was even more animated than usual. Here came a disguised young couple, marching up on gigantic stilts, and moving boldly about among carriages and pedestrians; yonder two men came growling along, disguised as bears, one white, the other coal-black, chained to each other, and followed by a miller fastened to a sweep. Here might be seen a man, hopping along with lottery tickets; his hat was crowned by a bladder of wind. Yonder came another, dragging an organ on a handcart: out of each of the pipes looked a live cat, who mewed piteously, for the man had a string fastened to the tail of each Grimalkin, and by pulling this string he played his organ. A carriage appeared decked out like a flowery throne, and on the throne was seated a minstrel: his harp was fastened securely in front of him, but over the harp stood a wheel of Fortune, adorned with a vast show of flags, and the wheel turned as the wind blew. Another carriage was made to represent a gigantic fiddle: on each string rode a comic figure, the first string being occupied by a pretty little girl, and all of them sung as loudly as they could, being incited thereto by the fiddler, who stood ready to draw his bow over the back of each person whose turn it was to give the tone. All along the road fell showers of *confetti* and of flowers, especially of the latter, for this spring had been very rich in violets and anemones. I saw Don Miguel of Spain, the veritable Don Miguel, striding through the crowd, in private clothes; he was received with a deluge of *confetti*. Queen Christina of Spain had posted herself on a balcony: flowers and *confetti* were her weapons.

IN THE STREETS.

And now the signal was given for the horse race. On this day one of the spectators was killed by a horse; but similar accidents happen every year, so the corpse was carried out of the way, and the sports proceeded. "*Moccoli! moccoli!*" was the cry; and in a moment from every window, from every balcony, and even from the roofs of the houses, were thrust forth long poles, sticks, and planks, garnished with little lighted candles. The occupants of the carriages, who, during the progress of the race, had been obliged to wait in the side streets, now once more thronged the Corso; but the horses, the coachman's hat and his whip, were garnished with burning wax candles; every lady in every carriage held her taper aloft, and sought to protect it from the opposite party, who made every effort to extinguish the light. Sticks, with pocket-handkerchiefs fastened to them, fluttered aloft. A shouting and shrieking, which no one can imagine who has not heard it, filled the air. "*Senza Moccolo! senza moccolo!*" Little paper balloons with lights inside them sailed down among the crowd, and it seemed as if all the stars of heaven, with the Milky Way among them, were making a progress through the Corso; the air seemed heated by the numberless candles, and every ear was deafened by the din. It was the wildest Bacchanal scene: when suddenly every light was extinguished, and as the last glimmer went out, and darkness and silence fell upon all, the church bells sounded, and the long fast had begun.

And next morning, one well-packed carriage after another drove away, laden with strangers—away from quiet Rome, where all the galleries were closed, and every altar-piece was hung with black draperies.

And we went away to Naples.

MAHOMET'S BIRTHDAY.

A SCENE IN CONSTANTINOPLE.

THE fourth of April is the birthday of the Prophet. Already on the eve of that day the celebration began; and to say the truth, the performance on the eve was the prettiest part of the festivity. I considered it unfortunate that the night happened to be moonlight, and that the Osmanli police regulations demanded that every one who went out after sundown should carry a light in a lantern; but I was obliged to submit, for the police regulation could not be altered, nor could the moonlight. A young Russian named Aderhas and I associated ourselves together, and, without a companion, but duly provided with a light in a great paper lantern, we sallied forth to behold the illumination in honour of the Prophet.

We went through a narrow street of Pera, and before us lay a scene of fantastic beauty, such as we can only see in the North in a wondrous dream. From the row of houses near which we stood down towards the bay extended a churchyard, that is to say, a cypress grove, with thick dark trees; and dark night rested upon it. Over rough hills, downwards among the tall trees, winds the path which the footsteps of men and the hoofs of horses have worn, sometimes among the tombs, sometimes among fallen grave-stones. Here and there a blue lantern was seen moving to and fro, which soon disappeared, to reappear shortly upon the black background of the picture.

In the churchyard a few ionely houses lie scattered, and the lights glimmered from the upper windows, or were carried to and fro upon the balconies.

Beyond the cypress-tops shone, blue as a Damascene blade, the Gulf with its many ships. Two of these, the largest, were richly ornamented with burning lamps, which glittered around the portholes, the masts, and the guns also, or were hung in the rigging, which shone like a spangled net. Just before us lay the town itself, the great far-spreading Constantinople, with its countless minarets all wreathed with garlands of lamps. The air was still red with the sheen of the setting sun, but so clear and transparent that the mountains of Asia, and Olympus, covered with perpetual snow, showed their sharp broken outlines like a silver-white cloud behind the glorious city. The moonlight did not deaden the splendour of the lamps, but only brought out the minarets in relief, till they looked like gigantic flower-stalks crowned with blossoms of flame. The smaller minarets had one starry wreath, the larger two, and the largest of all three, one over the other.

AT PERA.

Not a human being was to be seen in our neighbourhood, all was lonely and still. We wandered down among the cypresses; a nightingale was raising its flute-like voice, and turtle-doves cooed among the shadows of the trees. We came past a little sentry-house, built of planks, and painted red; a little fire had been kindled in front of it, among the grave-stones, and soldiers were reclining around it. They were dressed in European garb; but their complexion and features proclaimed them of Ishmael's race, children of the desert. With long pipes in their mouths, they lay and listened to a story. This story was about Mahomet's birth. The nightingale translated it for us, or we should not have understood it. Here it is:

"*La illah il Allah!*" "There is no God but God!" In the city of Mecca the merchants assembled for the sake of traffic; thither came Egyptian, and Persian, and Indian, and Syrian dealers. Each one had his idol in the temple Kabba, and a son of Ishmael's race filled the highest office, namely, that of satisfying the hunger of the pilgrims and quenching their thirst. In his piety he wished, like Abraham, to offer up his son as a sacrifice; but the prophetess declared that the handsome Abdallah should live, and a hundred camels were sacrificed in his stead. "*La illah il Allah!*"

And Abdallah grew to be a man, and was so handsome that a hundred maidens died for love of him. The prophetic flame shone on his forehead, the flame which passed hidden from race to race, until the Prophet was born, Mahomet, the first and the last. The prophetess Fatima saw this flame, and she offered a hundred camels if he would be her husband; but he married Amina, and the prophetic flame vanished from his forehead and burned in Amina's heart. "*La illah il Allah!*"

And the next year came round; the flowers had never been so sweet as they were this year, never had the fruits on the trees swelled with such abundance of juice; and the rocks trembled, and the lake Sava sank into the earth, the idols fell down in the temple, and the demons, who wanted to storm the heavens, fell from the sky like millions of shooting stars, hurled down by the mighty hand that wielded the lance; for in that night Mahomet the Prophet was born. "*La illah il Allah!*"

This was the story the nightingale translated for us, for the nightingale understands Turkish just as well as our own language.

We went forth beneath the tower of Pera, out to the convent of the dancing dervishes, and a beauteous panorama met our view. The whole Sea of Marmora lay before us, lighted up by the rays of the moon, and in the mid-distance Scutari stood forth, its minarets gleaming with many lamps like those of Constantinople. The Mosque of St. Sophia with its four, and the Mosque of Ahmed with its six minarets, stood forth in especial splendour, each pinnacle crowned with a double or a triple garland of glittering stars. They seemed to surround the garden of the Serail, which stretched down towards the Bosphorus, dark as a starless night. No light shone in the palace of the sultanas near the shore; but there where the Golden Horn ends, a sword of flame had been reared, that threw a ruddy glow over the waters. Innumerable little boats, gaily decked out with red, green, or blue paper lanterns, darted like fireflies between the shores of the two continents. All the great line-of-battle ships blazed with lamps; every ship, nay, every rope and spar, could be clearly seen, the outlines drawn in fiery colours. Scutari and Stamboul seemed united by the gleaming water with its rows of shining sparks. It was a fairy city, a city of the fancy, with a magic haze poured forth over it; and only two points were covered by mysterious darkness: in Asia the great churchyard behind Scutari; in Europe, the garden of the Serail. Night and dreams lay brooding over both spots—the dead heroes are dreaming of the maidens of Paradise, and in the night of the Serail the dreams are those of earthly beauties, charming and fair as the houris of Paradise.

The streets of Pera were filled with a throng of Greeks, Jews, and Franks, each carrying his lantern or his candle. It was an Oriental procession of *Moccoli;* but the costumes were far more correct, more rich and varied, than those in the Corso of Rome on the last evening of the Carnival. In front of the palaces of the foreign ministers lamps were burning, erected in the form of pyramids, or in a great M, the initial letter of the Prophet's name. At nine o'clock cannon were fired from all the ships; there was a thundering din, like that of a sea-fight; all the windows shook; shot after shot boomed forth, announcing the hour at which the Prophet was born.

I fell asleep amid the thunder of the cannon, and was awaked early by the same sound. Merry music of Rossini and Donizetti sounded through the streets : the troops were marching on, to be paraded between the Serail and the Mosque of Ahmed, whither the Sultan was about to proceed in state.

The Danish Consul, Romain, an Italian. came to fetch me. A young Turk, with pistols in his girdle and two long tobacco-pipes in his hand, walked before us ; an old Armenian, in a dark blue fluttering caftan, and a black jar-shaped hat on his shaven head, came after us, carrying our cloaks ; and thus we strolled through the main street of Pera, down towards Galata. The servants stepped into a boat, we two embarked in another, and now we rowed across the Gulf, darting swiftly among hundreds of others, whose rowers shouted and howled at each other, as one or other of the boats ran the risk of being swamped. At the landing-place in Constantinople the mass of gondolas formed a huge swaying bridge, across which we had to skip, to reach the firm land, which is bordered by decayed planks and beams. The crowd was great, but soon we came to a broad side street. Here were many people, but there was room enough. Great crowds of veiled women wended along the same way with us, and soon we had arrived under the walls of the Serail, which are very high towards the town, and look like the walls of an old fortress. Here and there is a tower, with a little door, which looks as if it had never been opened ; the hinges were covered with grass and climbing plants. Great old trees stretched their leafy branches across the old walls ; one could fancy one's self on the borders of the forest in which sleeps the enchanted Princess.

We chose our position in front of the Mosque of St. Sophia, between the great fountain and the entrance to the Serail. From this point the Mosque of St. Sophia, with its numerous cupolas and subsidiary buildings, has a whimsical resemblance to a great flower-bulb to which several smaller bulbs have attached themselves. The terraces in the foreground were thronged with Turkish women and children, and the shining white veils worn by the former gave the scene quite a festive air. The fountain behind us is the largest and most beautiful in Constantinople. With the name "fountain" we usually associate the idea of a basin with a jet of water plashing up from it ; but in Turkey fountains have a very different appearance ; and a more correct idea of their appearance will be obtained by imagining a square house, whose walls are quite Pompeian in their variegated richness of colour : the white groundwork is painted with inscriptions from the Koran in red, blue, and gilt letters ; and from little niches, to which brazen basins are fastened, the consecrated water ripples forth, with which the Mussulman bathes his hands and face at certain hours of the day. The roof is painted and gilt with quite a Chinese richness of colour. The dove, the sacred bird of the Turks, builds its nest here : in hundreds they flew over our heads, to and fro between the fountain and the Mosque of St. Sophia.

All around were a number of Turkish coffee-houses, all built of wood, with balconies. almost like the Swiss houses in appearance, but more gaudy and less solid: before each there stretched a little plantation of trees; and all these plantations were occupied by smoking and coffee-drinking Turks, who quite lit up the gardens and the fronts of the houses with their bright-coloured caftans: some of them wore turbans, others fez caps. Between the fountain and the great gate leading into the forecourt of the Serail, two long scaffolds had been erected of boards placed on tubs and tables. The second of these was higher than the first, and on the lower one veiled Turkish women of the lowest class were reclining. Old Turks, Persians, and a few Frankish strangers, whose unveiled women were objects of universal attention, held their station on the upper platform. Now appeared several regiments of Turkish soldiers, all dressed in European fashion, in tight trousers and close jackets, white cross-belts across their chests, and red fez caps on their heads. The guards made a very good appearance in their new uniforms, with tight stock and collars; and, as I was told, they wore gloves to-day for the first time. Some of the other regiments seemed in most lamentable plight: not only were the men of all possible complexions, white, brown, and coal-black soldiers all mingled together, but some of them were lame, and others had club feet. Their European uniforms were too tight for them, consequently the majority had ripped up the seam of the sleeves at the elbow, and many had cut their trousers at the knee, that they might move their legs with greater freedom; consequently naked elbows were seen protruding all along the line, and during the march many a red, brown, or black knee protruded from the blue trouser. Especially remarkable was one regiment, which I might almost call the "barefoot warriors," for some of them had only one boot and one shoe, while others shuffled along with bare feet thrust into slippers of different colours. Amid a din of military music, they all marched into the courtyard of the Serail, and, after defiling before the Sultan, came back and drew up in line along both sides of the way: Ethiopians and Bulgarians stood side by side, and the Bedouin became the neighbour of the shepherd's son from the Balkan.

At ten o'clock the procession was to begin; but it was nearly twelve before the Sultan thought fit to leave the Serail. The sun shone warm as in summer; cup after cup of coffee was quaffed, and once or twice the lower platform gave way, and all the Turkish women tumbled down in a heap. It was a long time to wait. Until within a few years, it was the custom to bring out to this spot the heads of those who had been decapitated in the courtyard of the Serail, and to throw them to the dogs; but everything looked peaceable enough now. Young Turks who could speak a little French or Italian began a conversation with us and with other Franks, and showed the greatest willingness to explain to us whatever they thought might excite our interest. Below us, in front of the walls of the Serail, lay spread the Sea of Marmora, enlivened with many a sail, and glittering in the sunshine; and high up, in the background, the snow-covered mountain-peaks of Asia glowed in the clear blue-green sky. I had never before seen this grassy glimmer in the air. A young Turk, who told me he had been born on the banks

of the Euphrates, assured me that yonder the sky sometimes showed
rather green than blue.

But now a cannon-shot resounded from the garden of the Serail: the
procession was starting. First came a mounted military band,—even
the drummer and the man who played the cymbals were on horseback:
the latter musician let the reins hang loose on the horse's neck, while he
clashed the brazen plates in the sunlight. Now came the Sultan's guards,
as soldierly a body of men as you would see in any Christian kingdom ;
then a number of splendid horses were led along, without riders, but all
decked in gorgeous trappings, red, blue, and green, and all powdered
with jewels. The horses danced along on their strong slender legs,
tossing their heads and shaking their manes, while their red nostrils
quivered like the leaf of the mimosa, and more than instinct seemed to
flash from their bright eyes. Now came a mounted troop of young
officers, all clad in the European costume, but wearing the fez cap ; they
were followed by civil and military officials, all clad in the same way ;
and now the Grand Vizier of the empire appeared, an old man, with a
long beard of snowy whiteness. Bands of music had been posted at
different points, and relieved each other at intervals. In general, pieces
from Rossini's " William Tell " were played, but suddenly they were
broken off, and the strains of the young Sultan's favourite march were
heard. This march had been composed by the brother of Donizetti,
who has been appointed band-master here. Now came the Sultan, preceded by a troop of Arabian horses still more gorgeously caparisoned
than those who had gone before. Rubies and emeralds formed rosettes
for the horses' ears ; the morocco leather bridles were covered with
precious stones, and saddles and saddle-cloths were wrought with pearls
and jewels.

It seemed as though we were looking on the work of a spirit of
Aladdin's lamp. Surrounded by a number of young men on foot, all
displaying a feminine Oriental beauty, as if a number of Turkish women
had ventured abroad without their veils, came riding on his splendid
Arab horse the young " nineteen-year-old " Sultan Abdul Medjid. He
wore a green coat buttoned across the chest, and wore no ornament,
except one great jewel with which the bird of Paradise feather was
fastened in his red fez cap. He looked very pale and thin, had melancholy features, and fixed his dark eyes firmly on the spectators, especially
on the Franks. We took off our hats and bowed ; the soldiers shouted
out, " Long live the Emperor ! " but he made not a gesture in acknowledgment of our salutes.

" Why does he not notice our salutes ? " I inquired of a young Turk
at my side. " He must have seen that we took off our hats."

" Hé looked at you," replied the Turk ; " he looked at you very closely."

With this we had to be content, for it was considered as good as the
best acknowledgment. I told the Turk that all Frankish princes
acknowledged the salutes of their subjects with uncovered heads, a
statement which seemed quite incredible to him.

Pachas and other grandees of the empire now came by ; then Frankish officers in the Turkish employ; and then a number of servants, male and female Turks, closed the procession. Such a crowd, such a pushing to and fro! Half-naked street boys with dingy turbans, old beggar women with ragged veils, but with coloured trousers and morocco slippers, pushed noisily through the throng.

"*Allah akbar!*" "God is great!" they shouted, when the soldiers tried to drive them back with the butt-ends of their muskets. The whole street was like a many-coloured stream of fez caps, turbans, and veils, and on both sides, like reeds along the river's banks, rose the glittering bayonets. Whenever parties of Franks wished to pass through the ranks of the military, Turkish officers came forward and made room for them with the greatest politeness, pushing aside their fellow-countrymen, who contented themselves with gazing upon the favoured Franks, and shouting once more, "*Allah akbar!*"

DAYS IN THE MEDITERRANEAN.

PEACEFULLY the wide sea lay spread abroad. No movement could be felt on board our ship. We could go to and fro as we pleased, as if on dry land; only when we looked at the wake in the water could we see that the ship was making way, as it glided farther and farther from the yellow shores of Malta.

We had seven young Spanish monks on board; they could speak a little Italian, and were all of them missionaries bound for India. The youngest of them was very handsome, with a pale melancholy face. He told me that his parents were still alive, but that since his sixteenth year he had not seen his mother, who was very dear to him. "And now I shall not see her till we meet in heaven!" he sighed. He left Europe with a bleeding heart; but he saw that he must go, for it was his duty, —he stood enrolled in God's service. Like his brethren, he belonged to the order founded by St. Theresa.

To most of those on board I was the traveller who had journeyed farthest, for I came from the North.

"From Denmark!" cried our Romish clergyman, who was going to Jerusalem. "Denmark! Then you are an American?"

I explained to him that Denmark was far distant from America, but he shook his head incredulously.

We had a Papal envoy on board, bound for the Lebanon. He was the only Italian who knew anything about Denmark. He knew a Danish Princess who resided in Rome, and had been at her *soirées;* he knew that there was a man living named Thorwaldsen, and that there had been one or the name of Tycho Brahè. I have made the observation that Tycho is the man of our country who is best known in foreign parts. Tycho is the most celebrated Dane, and we drove him away!

Denmark is great as a mother, but she has often been a bad mother to the best of her children.

In the middle of the day we could still see Malta; but of Sicily we could only discern the snow-clad summit of Etna, but that glittered clear and large, like a pyramid of white sun-illumined marble. There was not the slightest stir in the sea, we seemed to be gliding through the air. An enormous dolphin, larger than a horse, tumbled two or three times beside the ship; the sun shone on his wet smooth back. Melodies from Auber's "White Lady" sounded up to us from the piano in the cabin; and the merry sailor boys sang as they climbed the rigging. "*Quel plaisir d' être matelot.*"

THE BOSPHORUS.

The boatswain's pipe sounded, and the crew were put through their exercise. Then came the welcome sound that summoned to dinner. As we sat drinking our coffee, the sun sank down, red and large; the sea shone like fire.

And now the sun had set, and the stars gleamed forth in such splendour as I can never express in words. What a blaze of light! Venus shone like the moon herself: her rays threw a long strip of light on the surface of the water, which heaved gently, as if the sea were breathing. Low on the horizon, over the African coast, stood a star that shone like fire: under this star the Bedouin rode on his swift horse, under this star the caravans moved through the glowing sand. It must be pleasant to sit in such a night beneath the African tent. The star seemed to send flames through the blood, I sat by the ship's margin and looked out over the watery expanse. Phosphoric flashes darted through the sea: it seemed as if men were walking about with torches at the bottom of the sea, and as if these were suddenly blazing up. They gleamed and disappeared as though these flames were the visible breath of the sea.

Already at nine o'clock I was in my berth, and went to sleep at once, while the ship steered busily on through the sea. When I came upon deck next morning early, they were cleaning it; all hands were busily in motion, and soon the boards gleamed so clean and bright, it was a pleasure to see them. On the forecastle, where the anchors and ropes lay, the sailors were having their grand wash. The orthodox method of washing trousers seemed to be to lay those garments flat on the deck, pour sea-water over them, and then sweep them over and over with a worn broom, among whose bristles some pieces of soap had been inserted.

Two sharp ship-boys, small, but nimble as squirrels, and full of mischief, were killing chickens, and before every execution they held a humorous speech to the fowl that was to be the victim, always ending with the word "*voilà!*" as the knife passed over the victim's neck.

We noticed a sligh tmovement in the sea, but as the sun mounted higher it became perfectly still, as it had been the whole day before. No river passage can be compared to this for stillness : here and there in the far distance, dark blue patches on the sunlit expanse of the sea indicated that there a breath of wind was rippling the even surface. Malta was no longer to be seen; but Mount Etna stood clear and plain on the horizon. To the north-east we descried the white sails of a ship, and this was the first vessel we had seen since we left Malta.

On the fore-deck the sailors were at breakfast. Each one received a ration of wine, onions, and bread : all of them were very merry, and they had among them one who was their jester, and another who served as his butt.

A Persian, in a green turban and a white shawl caftan, sat solitary, toying with his earrings or with his sword. No one spoke to him, and he spoke to no one; but a smile played around his lips, as if pleasant thoughts were passing through his soul; or was he thinking of the return home, and of all he should have to tell of his journeyings over land and sea? As I passed him, he suddenly seized me by the arm, and spoke a few words in Persian which I could not understand; but he laughed and nodded, and pointed to one side of the deck. He rewarded me for my greeting by calling my attention to an incident which occurred on our passage. A little bird had alighted in the rigging, utterly exhausted, and now sank down to the deck. A number of spectators gathered around it, and I felt quite angry with the Roman clergyman, when he proposed that it should be roasted immediately, for no doubt it would taste deliciously. But I cried, " Our little winged voyager shall not be eaten."

One of the lieutenants took it under his protection, placed it on a sail that had been stretched out as an awning over the after-deck, and provided it with a plate of bread-crumbs and water; so the bird was our guest for the whole of the day, and for that night too; it was not till the morrow that he took his departure, when he flew away, twittering, as if to thank us for the hospitality he had experienced at our hands.

This was a great event for us all; but soon we were fain to seek occupation or amusement. One went to a piano, another opened a book, some played cards, others walked to and fro together. The Bedouin sat upon the coal-sacks, silent as a spirit, his eyes flashing out of his brown face, his sinewy brown legs protruding from his white burnouse. The Persian continued to play with his sword, to handle his pistols, or to turn the silver rings in his ears. The captain was copying a picture from my album—a peasant, a reminiscence of Christian, in my tale of " Only a Fiddler." The sketch now adorns the captain's cabin, so that the fiddler travels every year between Marseilles and Constantinople on the proud ship "Leonidas." I employed myself in giving one of the ship's officers a lesson in German. He translated Schiller's " Partition of the Earth."

The time passed away charmingly, and merriment and good humour reigned at our dinner-table. The sunset was exquisitely lovely. The stars glittered down on us in full brightness. The motion of the vessel was quite imperceptible; only on looking up at the stars through the rigging it seemed as if the sky were turning slowly around the motionless ship.

We could still discern Etna, looming like a white pyramid, in the north-west; but all around nothing was to be seen but the endless expanse of ocean. Towards noon, however, I discerned a white spot in the north-east. It could not be a ship, for it extended too far; but very possibly it might be a cloud. I thought it was the Greek coast, and questioned the captain; but he shook his head, and said we should not behold the Grecian coast till the next day, though he confessed land was to be sought for in the direction where I fancied I had seen it. Neither he nor any of the passengers could make anything out.

When, after dinner, shortly before sunset, I once more sought the point I had seen, it loomed as visible as Etna itself. No, it could not be a cloud, for it had not altered its shape, and stood in the same place it had occupied three hours ago.

The captain took his best telescope, and presently shouted, " Land!" It was really the Greek coast, a mountain summit of Navarino, gleaming, snow-clad, in the pure air. So I had been the first to discern the Grecian land.

" I have never heard," said the captain, " that any one could, with the naked eye, from the Mediterranean, at one and the same time discern Etna and the Greek coast. That's quite remarkable!"

When I talked about this afterwards, in Athens, a learned man said that he had lately read an account of such a thing in a book, but that the critics had doubted if it could occur. But it is a fact, as I can vouch from personal observation. It is the snow on Etna and the snow on the Greek mountains that render it possible, in the clear sunshine, to behold at once the Eastern and the Western land.

Greece! So now I beheld before me the great native land of intellect. Beneath yonder mountains lay stretched the beauteous valleys of Arcadia. A thousand thoughts, each differing from the rest, flew like a flight of wandering birds to the glistening mountain. But the sun sank down, and the thoughts rose from recollections of the earth, and soared upward towards the beauty of heaven.

Next morning I was up before the sun; it was the 20th of March. Blood-red as I had never yet seen it, and wonderfully oval in form, rose the beauteous orb, and the day streamed out over the calm sea; and before us, on the right, lay clear and distinct, but far, very far off, the coast of the Morea. It was the old Lacedæmon upon which we gazed. A steep precipice rose perpendicularly from the ocean, and in the interior of the country towered picturesque snow-clad hills. How my heart leapt up at sight of them!

I can see the shining air and the gleaming strand; and yonder strip of rocky coast is Greece!

THE GRAVEYARD AT SCUTARI.

The Turks consider themselves strangers in Europe; consequently they wish to rest in their native land, which is Asia. Thus in Asia, by Scutari, is the great graveyard of Constantinople. Where one corpse has been buried, the Turks never deposit another, for the grave is the dead man's home, which must be held sacred; and thus their churchyards grow very rapidly, and that at Scutari extends for miles. For every new-born child a plantain, for every deceased person a cypress is placed here; therefore the graveyard at Scutari is an extensive forest, intersected by footpaths and roads. Here are the richest monuments and the greatest variety in memorials of the dead. In the midst of the large flat stone which covers most of the graves, a hole has been dug, in which the rain-water may collect. The vagrant, masterless dogs quench their thirst here; and when the Turk sees this, he considers it a sign that the soul of the departed is happy in Mahomet's Paradise.

Side by side, like swathes of corn upon a mown field, lie beneath the cypresses the grave-stones of the dead, with a turban or a fez cap sculptured on each. It is easy to see where the dervish or the Turk of the old orthodox faith lies buried, and where one of the new half-European race has been carried to his rest. On the stone is inscribed, in letters of gold, the name and rank of the deceased; a sensible epitaph speaks of the shortness of life, or exhorts the living to pray for the dead. Where the women rest the spot is marked only by a sculptured lotus flower: no word tells of them, for even in death the woman here is veiled, and the stranger knows her not.

No fence girds round this forest of the dead men's graves; lonely and solitary is it here under the dark cypresses. The broad high road passes among the overturned stones; the Arab drives his camels past the graves, and the tinkle of their bells is the only sound that breaks the stillness of the great solitude.

Silent as the dead beneath the cypress shade lies the Sea of Marmora before us, and shows us its beauteous-tinted islands : the largest of them all yonder appears like a little Paradise, with its wild rocks, vineyards, woods of cypresses, pines, and plane trees. What a beautiful sight seen from the garden of the dead! This beauteous spot was the place of banishment of fallen emperors, princes, and princesses of the Byzantine empire : in convents upon these islands they had to sigh in the garb of poor monks and nuns. It is better here, among the dead, where the perishable slumbers in dreamless peace, and the immortal rises to God!

What silence among these graves under the cypresses! We will wander forth hither on a moonlight night. What dark trees! Night broods over the graves ; what a gleaming sky!—from that sky life streams forth !

Over the uneven road a white and a red point are moving like glowing roses : they are only two paper lanterns ; an old Turk holds them in his hands as he rides through the garden of the dead. He does not think of the dead ; no, the living are in his thoughts,—the pretty merry women in his pleasant home, where he will soon stretch his limbs upon the soft cushions of the divan, eating the *pilau*, and smoking his pipe, while the youngest of his wives sits by him, and the others perform a Chinese shadow comedy before him—a merry comedy, such as the Turks love in their houses, with a *Karagof*, or Harlequin, and a *Hadji Aiwat*, or Pantaloon. Under the dark cypresses, among the graves, the old man is thinking of life, and life with him means enjoyment.

Again all is silence. And now footsteps are heard ; no lantern gleams this time, no horse trots by, but a youth, fiery and strong, handsome as the young Ishmael on his marriage day, comes yonder. He comes full of thoughts of life : he is ready to build him a nest in every house, in every tree ; the picture of glowing life, he wanders among the graves. And the thoughts that are passing through his soul proclaim him a Turk.

Silent it is in the garden of the dead—silent in the hut by the Sea of Marmora.

THE BOSPHORUS.

THE Bosphorus is a river, transparent as the sea, a river of salt water that unites two seas ; a river between two quarters of the globe, along whose banks every spot is picturesque, every point of historical interest. Here the East is joined to Europe, and fancies itself the ruler of the latter. I know no place where strength and mildness meet so completely as here. The shores of the Rhine, in the full beauty of autumn, have not the colours which glow on the Bosphorus coast. The Rhine would seem narrow compared with the bed of this grass-green river ; and yet I was reminded of the Rhine and also of the shores of the Mälar Lake between Stockholm and Upsall, when the warm sunshine glittered among the green fir trees and the trembling branches of the ash.

The mirror of waters is not so broad anywhere as to prevent the traveller from seeing distinctly the objects on either bank. In seven windings the stream rolls on, between the Sea of Marmora and the Black Sea, and throughout nearly its whole length the European bank looks like a single town, a single street, behind which the mountains rise, if not majestically, at least high enough to deserve the name of mountains—and on their sides there is verdure like that of a garden, a true botanical garden. Here are birch trees, like in Sweden and Norway; groups of beeches that remind one of Denmark, pines, plane trees, and chestnuts such as we find in Italy, and cypresses, large and majestic, as only the graveyard at Scutari and Pera can show; and amid the rich green rises the palm tree with its broad leafy crown, like a memorial pillar, to remind us in what part of the world we are.

The whole coast appears, as I have said, like a town, and yet is not a town. Here streets and gardens alternate with each other, with grave-yards and vineyards. At one point stands a mosque, with its white shining minarets, at another a palace, such as we may imagine an Eastern palace to be, and farther on, little wooden houses painted red, and seeming to have been transplanted from the pine forests of Norway.

Turning his eyes to the Asiatic shore, the traveller finds everything just as rich, as varied; only he has not this mass of buildings which makes the European side look like one continued town; here the plains are greater, the mountains higher and more thickly wooded.

The fifth of May, the day of Napoleon's death, I was destined to spend upon the Black Sea. There are for us holidays of the mind besides those which the calendar indicates as Sundays and Feasts. Our own life, and the events in history, point out to us certain days of which the calendar says nothing. Often, in thinking of the mighty events that once happened on such a day, I have felt deeply how prosaically it had passed for me.

But in this year one of the famous anniversaries of the present became an epoch in my life, when on its morning, at half-past four, I sailed out of the harbour of Constantinople, through the Bosphorus, and into the Black Sea.

I awoke as the anchor was being weighed; I dressed hastily, and ran on deck. Everything lay shrouded in mist, but only for a moment, for the veil rose with wonderful swiftness to the top of the tower of Pera; this lay behind us, with Galata and Topschana. The great barrack buildings, the lofty mosque in the suburb Funderklu stood boldly forth, with the whole Greek fleet, which had lately returned from Egypt. We glided past close to it: Turkish soldiers and sailors were peering forth from every port-hole. Each one of these could in a few minutes have told us things truer and more poetical than are to be found in the celebrated works of Pückler-Muskau. But our steamer was gliding on, and the mist too was gliding on; now it touched the funnel of our vessel, and now it rose in wreaths, to be presently changed into rain-bringing clouds. There was such a movement and life in the sky, that one might have fancied Darius and his army were passing in shadowy mist over the

Bosphorus. Life and motion was there also around us, in hundreds of boats; those that came from the ships of war were strong and well manned, but those which came rowing out from the coast were frail little barks, in the bottom of which the Turk sat cross-legged. But on our vessel there was silence. Over the deck the Turks had spread some coloured carpets: some of the passengers were asleep, wrapped in their warm furs, others were drinking their black coffee, or puffing the smoke from their long pipes. The mist rose and fell as when the world was formed out of chaos. At times the sun burst forth, at others it seemed to have lost all its power. The ships lying in the distance looked like shadow-pictures, and reminded me of the story of the Death-ship and the Flying Dutchman.

Topschana and Pera seemed to form one continuous town with Constantinople, of which Scutari was the suburb—Scutari with its white minarets, reddish-brown houses, and green gardens, lying in the brightest sunshine, which spread over the Asiatic coast. We could see the lovely village of Kandelli, the imperial garden, and the far-spreading palaces of the Sultan. Nature appears in full splendour of wealth on the banks of the Bosphorus.

How often, when I was a boy, did not my thoughts sail away with the "Thousand and One Nights," and I saw wonderful palaces of marble with hanging gardens and cool fountains! Here I saw one of these palaces in reality: it was the summer palace, built a short time since on the European side, and in which Sultan Abdul Medjid established himself last year as the first occupant. It is built in the Eastern style, on a grand scale, with marble pillars and high terraces.

Such a scene is well chosen for the love-dream of a young monarch not yet twenty years of age: here, to speak in the style of the Turkish poets, spring comes early, and dresses the tulip in its crimson garb, which the dew fringes with pearls; and for the young Prince cypresses and plane trees lift up their hands in supplication, that they may throw their shade over him during a long life. But what is a *long* life? A happy life. And what is it to be happy? Men's ideas vary on the subject: some are for a deathless name, others for the happiness of affection. Ask the youth. Alas! not every one is an Alexander, who can win both, and doubly win them, and die in the midst of victory.

The palace garden extends downward to the village of Kurutscheme, whose peculiar wooden buildings along the water-side attract the attention of the traveller. The upper storeys project over the lower, supported by beams driven in a slanting direction into the lower wood-work, so that the path between the buildings and the water is thus in a manner roofed in by the projecting storeys. Here dwell several of the older sultanas, consequently the windows are veiled by close wooden shutters, which are, however, not unprovided with peep-holes, through which the once beautiful and powerful occupants look out upon the water and upon the foreign ships.

The beauteous Valley of Bebeh, with its pleasure palace, now opened out before us. It is bounded by the dark cypresses of a ch rchyard;

but a few words can give no picture of it,—the eye must behold this valley, which, like a park, shows in the bright moonlight a variety of green, such as no palette can reproduce; these willows must be seen, whose trembling boughs cast a shadow that seems to play upon the earth; these groups of forest trees, under whose leafy covert the turtle-dove builds her nest; these fat green meadows, where the shining white ox stands like a picture of the old time, half buried in the long grass. Here we have life, sunshine, and enjoyment; and close beside extends the boundary of all things,—the dark cypress grove with its graves, offering shade and rest.

And now we have glided past the churchyard, and rocks rise up in picturesque forms: we are at the place where Androcles of Samos built the bridge over the Bosphorus—the bridge over which Darius led the Persians against the Scythians. One of the rocks was at that time hewn out into a throne for Darius, from whence he could behold all the country round; but of this no trace remains. Osmanli saints rest at the foot of the rock: the soil is sacred now that the wild hordes once trod, and tall dark cypresses seem to keep watch over the graves.

The wandering birds of the Bosphorus,—banished souls, the sailors call them,—soared towards us here, anon wheeling round and sailing slowly away. Here are built, one on the Asiatic, the other on the European side, the strong castles Anatoli Hissari and Rumili Hissari, which were to command the passage; but the embrasures are bricked up; the buildings have long been turned into prisons, and the name of the Black Towers is given to these castles, in which thousands of Christians have languished. The castle on the European side has been strangely built. The Sultan Mahmoud desired that its outline should indicate his name as the word is written in the Arabic character: a hundred Christian churches were plundered for the materials of which these inhabited characters were built; but no joy has dwelt in the castle; sighs and groans have quivered through Mahmoud's haughty pile. Stone was firmly fixed upon stone, but the strong finger of Time will wipe out the inscription, and the earth will spread the poetry of spring on the black rock whereon it was written—the poetry that dwells in the fragrant ferns, grasses, and flowers.

The Asiatic side is the most beautiful. Behind the gloomy fortress the Valley of the Heavenly Waters stretches into the land, the valley famed as the most charming of all the dales of the Bosphorus, whose fragrant loveliness has given rise to its name; but we glided by all too swiftly, and could only see as much of its beauty as we can see of the soul within, when for a moment we glance at a pair of lovely eyes.

Kandiliche's great mosque now rose before us, looking as if Ahmed's church had been borne hither by angels, that we might once more rejoice our hearts with its view. A little village lay almost hidden among gigantic fig trees, from which it has received its name, the Fig Town.

Amid plane trees, lindens, and sycamores, rose, in the form of an amphitheatre, Sultanje, its reversed outline mirrored in the clear water of the coast. The slender white minaret, pointing upwards towards heaven, while its mirrored reflection pointed downwards oo the depths, seemed to say, "Look not only on life as it appears in the sunshine around you, look upon it also as it is shown in the driving clouds and the soaring birds ; look at it as it appears in the teeming waters between the two continents !"   And, in truth, here was enough of life and motion ! Large boats, freighted with Turkish women, wrapped in light airy veils, were passing to and fro between the opposite shores. Just by our steamer, one of the youngest women rose up in one of these boats. She glanced upwards at us, and the Persian song that tells of the growth of the cedar, and of the colours of the tulip, struck upon my ear. Who does not remember seeing, on a dark night, the whole country lit up by a single flash of lightning, after which all is shrouded in darkness once more ?   But one never forgets the picture revealed by that flash ; and here we had two lightnings, a flash from each of her eyes, and then

THE TURKISH LADIES IN THE BOAT.

night sank down upon her again. We saw no more the daughter of the East, of whom, centuries ago, the poet has sung : "When she dries her locks with a handkerchief, it is fragrant with perfume ; when she wipes the tear from her eye, a pearl falls from it ; if she touches her cheek, the handkerchief is filled with fragrant roses ; and if it passes by her lips, a fruit of Paradise is found within it."   I looked after the boat, we were already far from it : the women in the white veils looked like spirits in Charon's boat ; and there was truth in the thought, for that which we shall never behold again is numbered among the dead for us. She had flung an orange into the water, and it floated to and fro, a memento of the encounter.   Slender fishing-boats shot by the great ships that came from the Black Sea ; the double eagle of Russia flapped his wings on the proud flag. Rocking slowly to and fro on the water in front of a fishing village—I think its name was Baikos—were boat-huts, from which depended long nets, wherein sword-fish were to be caught. I called them huts, but they might be called baskets. In each of them sat a half-naked fisherman, toiling at his trade.

On the European side we passed close by Therapia, in whose deep gulf great ships lay anchored. A little boat met us here; an old negro was rowing it. He wore a woollen coat, like the Greeks, and great silver rings in his ears; on his head he had no other covering than his own frizzled locks. The boat was literally filled with roses; a little Greek girl, with black hair braided around her scarlet fez cap, and ornamented with a single large coin, stood leaning against a great basket filled with roses; in her hand she held a little Bulgarian drum. The boat rocked up and down in the increased swell caused by the swift passage of our steamer through the water; the little maiden clung for support to the rose-basket, but it turned over with her, and poured its flood of blossoms over her face and form. She jumped up again, and when she saw that we were watching her, she laughingly beat the little drum once or twice, then threw it into the basket, and held up a hand-full of roses before her face. It was a picture worth painting,—the boat, the old negro, and the little Greek maiden, with Therapia, its gardens and ships, for a background.

But when a man wanders, for the first time, through a great rich gallery with thousands of paintings, one picture obliterates another from his mind; and the Bosphorus presents a series of pictures such as only the greatest master could pourtray. I, who tell these things, have only once in my life beheld the gallery, in a rapid passage in a steamer among its inexhaustible treasures.

A larger, wider bay than any we had yet seen, formed the foreground to the next picture. Bujukdere, the summer residence of the ambassadors, lay before us. I looked among the flags of many nations fluttering there for the ensign of my native land; and, behold, there it was! I beheld the white cross in the red ground. Denmark had set up its white Christian cross in the land of the Turks. The flag fluttered in the breeze; it seemed to bring me a greeting from my home. My neighbour on board the steamer pointed out to me the great aqueduct with its double row of arches, which rose in the midst of the verdure of the green valley. Another began talking of Medea, who had wandered here, where now the seamen drew up their boats under the shadows of the great plane trees; but my eyes and my thoughts were all for the Danish flag, which I had not seen until now during my entire journey; and remembrances which make the heart soft and tender arose within me.

What new sight of gentle beauty would the shores of the Bosphorus unfold to us now? As though it had nothing more of this kind to offer, the aspect of nature suddenly changed to a stern and wild character. Craggy yellow rocks rose out of the water, and batteries that had been raised to defend the Bosphorus from the raids of plundering Cossacks were in keeping with the sterner features of this new view. The tower higher up the stream is called the Ovid's Tower, because it is asserted, though falsely, that the poet was once a prisoner here on the shores of

the Black Sea. The tower is now in ruins, and is used after sunset as
a lighthouse; great torches are kindled, whose red flames burn as a
guiding beacon to the ships in the Black Sea.

On the Asiatic side the appearance of bright verdure continues for a
little space; but, soon, when the banks approach nearer to each other,
the same stern rocky character steps forth on both sides. No road now
winds along by the water's edge; but goats are seen climbing on the
strangely cut face of the rocks. In Asia the Bithynian range of mountains terminates here, in Europe the Thracian. The Black Sea lies
before us, and at the extremities of the two coasts stand lighthouses,
with flames of welcome for the ships that arrive, with farewell stars for
those that depart.

THE LITTLE GREEK MAIDEN.

Near the shore rise marvellous rocky islands, which seem to have
been flung upon each other, each block of stone seeming riveted to the
rest. The legend tells that these rocks once swam to and fro, but
became fixed after the Argonauts had achieved the passage between
them.

The sun shone on the naked stones, the sea lay spread in all its
grandeur before us, and we sailed forth upon its bosom. The mists
that had been rising and falling alternately, the whole time of our
passage through the Bosphorus, without ever entirely veiling its shores,
now fell like a curtain, that is, rolled down over a glorious scene;
another moment, and the shores of Europe and Asia were alike hidden
from our gaze; the sea-birds were fluttering round the funnel of our
bark, and then hastening away from us, leaving us alone amid the mist
in the great sea!

ATHENS.

IT was on the third morning after our arrival at the Piræus that the hour of our deliverance from quarantine sounded. A dozen Greek boats lay waiting around our ship. I sprang into the first that offered, and was borne with rapid strokes to the shore, where a number of vehicles for hire, old coaches and open chaises, stood drawn up: they seemed to have done good service, perhaps in Italy, and to have emigrated in the evening of life, to begin a new career of work in Greece. Only a few years ago, a marsh extended between the Piræus and Athens—a marsh round which the teams of camels laden with merchandise had to make a long circuit; but now a capital road has been built, and a *khan* also, where refreshments can be had. For a trifle the traveller is conveyed along this road, a distance of about five English miles. Our baggage was packed in an old coach, which was completely filled; boxes and carpet bags peering out through the windows on both sides. The company came in three great carriages; at the back of the one in which I rode, clung a Greek, gorgeously attired, a servant of the Hôtel de Munich, in Athens; he was dressed so well and so richly, that he might have passed very well for a Hellenic prince in a Northern masquerade.

So we rolled away, rejoicing, from the Piræus. Sailors in glazed hats were sitting in front of the coffee-houses, which looked like booths of boards, and they gave us a cheer as they emptied their wine-glasses. Our way led past the ruins of ancient walls, built of a kind of yellow stone which still forms the material of the walls in these parts. So we went galloping on, amid clouds of dust; but it was classic dust.

Soon we reached the olive grove—the classic grove of Minerva. A wooden booth had been erected on each side of the road: lemons and oranges were here displayed, supported by a row of bottles containing wines and liqueurs. While our horses were being watered, there came a number of beggars holding out tin dishes; we all gave them something, for were they not Greeks?

Just as in the best days of Athens, we still drive into the city through the forest of olives. Before us lay the Acropolis, as I had often seen it on pictures, now I saw it in reality. The steep Sykabettos, with its gleaming white hermitage, stood prominently forth; and now I beheld Athens. A few steps from the town, close by the right side of the way, stands the temple of Theseus, with its noble marble pillars, tinted brownish-yellow by Time.

I could hardly realize the idea that I was really in Greece—that I was rolling into the city of Minerva. The Hermes Street, the largest in Athens, is the first traversed by the traveller who comes from the iræus; but the street commences with a row of houses, which have a

miserable appearance enough, measured by the European standard.
Gradually, better houses appeared. The Acropolis towered like a gigantic
throne above all the low dwellings, and in the middle of the street along
which we were driving, grew the tallest palm-tree I had ever seen.
The stem is encircled by a paling of red planks, to prevent it from being
injured by the vehicles of the Greeks, who gallop past with their old
coaches as if they were racing. This palm attracted the attention of

SAILORS CHEERING THE CARRIAGE.

every one of our party. I afterwards learned that when the street was
first planned, the noble tree was to have been hewn down, because it stood
in the way of carriages; but Professor Ross, a Holsteiner by birth, peti-
tioned for its life, and accordingly it was spared. Accordingly, I herewith solemnly name it "Ross's Palm," and all the compilers of guide
books are requested to make a note of this. The Greeks should remember that their country forms a bridge between Europe and the East;
therefore they must hold in honour the Oriental decorations which indicate this, among which the palm tree is chief. Most of the others in
Athens have been destroyed, only two or three survive.

We stopped in front of the Hôtel de Munich. The landlord is a Greek,
his wife a German; she is called the "fair Viennese." They gave me
the best room, which was about as good as that in a German inn of the
third class; so now I had a domicile in Athens.

I will now endeavour to pourtray the impression produced by the
city, and to tell how I spent my first day in Athens.

The terrible accounts I had received in Naples concerning Greece,
and especially Athens, proved to be ridiculously exaggerated. I dare
say that a few years ago there was terrible misery here; but it must
be remembered how much even a single year will do for such a country
as Greece, which is going through a period of more rapid development
than any other European land has experienced.

It is as if the mental progress of a child were to be compared with tne less apparent progress of a grown up-person: seven months with the former are as much as seven years with the latter. Athens seemed about as large as a provincial town of middling size, and looked as if it had been hastily erected for a fair. What they call "bazaars" here are really angular streets of wooden booths, such as one sees erected at a fair. They are decorated with scarves, coloured stockings, ready-made clothes, and morocco slippers, all somewhat clumsy, but very gay in appearance. Here are butchers' booths, yonder fruit-shops; here fez caps are displayed; yonder they sell books, new and old; even our driver bought one for himself, and what was it? Nothing less than Homer's Iliad, printed in Athens in 1839. I read the title myself.

Athens has a few Greek or rather Turkish coffee-houses, and also a new Italian one, so large and elegant, that it would make a good appearance even in Hamburg or Berlin. The much-frequented Café Greco in Rome is quite a hole-and-corner place compared with this. Young Greek men appeared here, all in national costume, exceedingly pinched in at the waist, and sporting eye-glasses and kid gloves—appeared here smoking cigars and playing billiards: there was the true look of the lounger upon them all. At every street corner a row of Maltese porters are standing in the sun.

The most populous part of Athens stretches upward towards the Acropolis, around which ruin buildings are being erected. Athens is a town which seems to grow even in the few days that the stranger passes here. The new palace of the king rises between the town and Hymettos: it is of marble, every stone having been procured from the neighbouring quarries of Pentelicon. In the hall the portraits of the Greek heroes of the revolution have already been put up. The university is being built under the direction of Hansen, a Danish architect. A few churches and private dwellings of merchants and ministers grow up out of the earth like mushrooms, hour by hour; and who are the workmen? I was told they were nearly all Greeks—soldiers, peasants, robbers, who have taken up trowel, hammer, and saw; they have watched the foreign workmen, and then set up at once for masons, smiths, and carpenters. Truly the Greeks are a quick-witted race.

The first impression made by Athens surpassed the anticipations awakened in me at Naples. When I mentioned this, Ross told me of a Greek, from Chios, the island of Homer's birth, who was now staying here. He was a man who from his position and surroundings may be considered as well educated; but he had never yet seen a large town, and accordingly was quite astonished at the grandeur and luxury he found in the capital of Greece: every moment he was expressing his surprise at something he saw, and when a friend, who met him after he had been here a fortnight, suggested that now he must know Athens by heart, he exclaimed,

"Know it by heart! there's no end to the wonders of a place like this! Always something new to hear or to see: how many amusements, how many conveniences! Here are carriages for driving, here is Turkish music every day in front of the king's palace, here are coffee-houses

with newspapers, and theatres where people sing and talk! It is a
wonderful city!"

Thus he was astounded by the modern grandeur and luxury of Athens,
while I found it simply very creditable in comparison with what I had
seen and heard spoken of. Thus it is that we all form our judgments
according to our experience and our own standard of excellence.

I had fancied that I should feel terribly strange and lonely here in
Greece, so far from my own country; and, behold, it was here that I
experienced the best feeling of home. My fellow-countrymen and
German friends approached me with kindness. On the very day of my
arrival, I was carried off to a Danish house, to that of Lüth, a Holsteiner,
the Queen's chaplain, who is married to a Danish lady, whose younger
sister lives with her. Here I met several Danes, and with them came a
Hollander, our Consul Travers, who speaks Danish very well. My first
day was to finish with a visit to the theatre.

THE SOLITARY COLUMN.

The theatre of Athens lies a little distance from the town. It has
four tiers of boxes and is prettily decorated; but the most interesting
sight to me was that of the handsomely-dressed spectators in boxes and
pit. Here sat many beautiful Greek women, but I was told they all
came from the islands, that very few Athenians were handsome. An
Italian company was giving operas here. The performance was a
mixture from various works: we heard the overtures to " Norma " and
the " Bronze Horse," an act from the " Barber of Seville," and another
from the "Thievish Magpie," and the whole concluded with a ballet.

As I have said, the theatre lies a short distance outside the city. It
made a strange impression when, at midnight, after seeing the " Barber "
and the "Thievish Magpie," the spectator suddenly stepped forth from

the building, and found himself standing under an Oriental sky, all aflame with stars, so that the whole extent of the plain, with its encircling ridge of mountains, could be distinctly seen. The magnificent scenery of nature seemed to laugh to scorn the painted canvas imitations; and here, in the solitude, a drama was being enacted, which showed how small everything within the theatre had been. The contrast from the mean theatre to this starlight night displayed the whole classic grandeur of Greece. A single marble column stood by our way, among dust and weeds; nobody could tell to what temple it had belonged. The people declare it to be the pillar to which our Lord was bound when He was scourged, and assert that the Turks threw the pillar into the sea, but that it was brought back miraculously in the night. Now it stood solitary by the wayside, pointing in the starry night towards heaven.

THE STUDENTS.

THE TOAD.

THE well was deep, and therefore the rope had to be a long one; it was heavy work turning the handle when any one had to raise a bucket-full of water over the edge of the well. Though the water was clear, the sun never looked down far enough into the well to mirror itself in the waters; but as far as its beams could reach, green things grew forth between the stones in the sides of the well.

Down below dwelt a family of the Toad race. They had, in fact, come head-over-heels down the well, in the person of the old Mother-Toad, who was still alive. The green Frogs, who had been established there a long time, and swam about in the water, called them "well-guests." But the new-comers seemed to have determined to stay where they were, for they found it very agreeable living "in a dry place," as they called the wet stones.

The Mother-Frog had once been a traveller. She happened to be in the water-bucket when it was drawn up, but the light became too strong for her, and she got a pain in her eyes. Fortunately she scrambled out of the bucket; but she fell into the water with a terrible flop, and had to lie sick for three days with pains in her back. She certainly had not much to tell of the things up above; but she knew this, and all the Frogs knew it, that the well was not all the world. The Mother-Toad might have told this and that, if she had chosen, but she never answered when they asked her anything, and so they left off asking.

"She's thick, and fat, and ugly," said the young green Frogs; "and her children will be just as ugly as she is."

"That may be," retorted the Mother-Toad; "but one of them has a jewel in his head, or else I have the jewel."

The young Frogs listened and stared; and as these words did not please them, they made grimaces, and dived down under the water. But the little Toads kicked up their hind legs from mere pride, for each of them thought that he must have the jewel; and then they sat and held their heads quite still. But at length they asked what it was that made them so proud, and what kind of a thing a jewel might be.

"Oh, it is such a splendid and precious thing, that I cannot describe it," said the Mother-Toad. "It's something which one carries about for one's own pleasure, and that makes other people angry. But don't ask me any questions, for I shan't answer you."

"Well, *I* haven't got the jewel," said the smallest of the Toads: she was as ugly as a toad can be. "Why should I have such a precious thing? And if it makes others angry, it can't give me any pleasure. No, I only wish I could get to the edge of the well, and look out; it must be beautiful up there."

"You'd better stay where you are," said the old Mother-Toad; "for you know everything here, and you can tell what you have. Take care of the bucket, for it will crush you to death; and even if you get into it safely, you may fall out: and it's not every one who falls so cleverly as I did, and gets away with whole eggs and whole bones."

"Quack!" said the little Toad; and that's just as if one of us were to say, "Aha!"

THE TOAD'S RECEPTION IN THE WORLD.

She had an immense desire to get to the edge of the well, and to look over; she felt such a longing for the green—up there; and the next morning, when it chanced that the bucket was being drawn up, filled with water, and stopped for a moment just in front of the stone on which the Toad sat, the little creature's heart moved within it, and our Toad jumped into the filled bucket—which presently was drawn to the top, and emptied out.

" Ugh, you beast ! " said the farm labourer who emptied the bucket, when he saw the toad. " You 're the ugliest thing I 've seen for one while." And he made a kick with his wooden shoe at the Toad, which just escaped being crushed by managing to scramble into the nettles which grew high by the well's brink. Here she saw stem by stem, but she looked up also : the sun shone through the leaves, which were quite transparent ; and she felt as a person would feel who steps suddenly into a great forest, where the sun looks in between the branches and leaves.

" It 's much nicer here than down in the well ! I should like to stay here my whole life long ! " said the little Toad. So she lay there for an hour, yes, for two hours. " I wonder what is to be found up here ? As I have come so far, I must try to go still farther." And so she crawled on as fast as she could crawl, and got out upon the highway, where the sun shone upon her, and the dust powdered her all over as she marched across the way.

" I 've got to a dry place now, and no mistake," said the Toad. " It 's almost too much of a good thing here ; it tickles one so."

She came to the ditch ; and forget-me-nots were growing there, and meadow-sweet ; and a very little way off was a hedge of whitethorn, and elder bushes grew there too, and bindweed with white flowers. Gay colours were to be seen here, and a butterfly, too, was flitting by. The Toad thought it was a flower which had broken loose that it might look about better in the world, which was quite a natural thing to do.

" If one could only make such a journey as that ! " said the Toad. " Croak ! how capital that would be."

Eight days and eight nights she stayed by the well, and experienced no want of provisions. On the ninth day she thought, " Forward ! onward ! " But what could she find more charming and beautiful ? Perhaps a little toad or a few green frogs. During the last night there had been a sound borne on the breeze, as if there were cousins in the neighbourhood.

" It 's a glorious thing to live ! glorious to get out of the well, and to lie among the stinging-nettles, and to crawl along the dusty road. But onward, onward ! that we may find frogs or a little toad. We can't do without that ; nature alone is not enough for one." And so she went forward on her journey.

She came out into the open field, to a great pond, round about which grew reeds ; and she walked into it.

" It will be too damp for you here," said the Frogs ; " but you are very welcome ! Are you a he or a she ? But it doesn't matter ; you are equally welcome."

And she was invited to the concert in the evening—the family concert : great enthusiasm and thin voices ; we know the sort of thing. No refreshments were given, only there was plenty to drink, for the whole pond was free.

" Now I shall resume my journey," said the little Toad ; for she always felt a longing for something better.

She saw the stars shining, so large and so bright, and she saw the moon gleaming; and then she saw the sun rise, and mount higher and higher.

"Perhaps, after all, I am still in a well, only in a larger well. I must get higher yet; I feel a great restlessness and longing." And when the moon became round and full, the poor creature thought, "I wonder if that is the bucket, which will be let down, and into which I must step to get higher up? Or is the sun the great bucket? How great it is! how bright it is! It can take up all. I must look out, that I may not miss the opportunity. Oh, how it seems to shine in my head! I don't think the jewel can shine brighter. But I haven't the jewel; not that I cry about that—no, I must go higher up, into splendour and joy! I feel so confident, and yet I am afraid. It's a difficult step to take, and yet it must be taken. Onward, therefore, straight onward!"

She took a few steps, such as a crawling animal may take, and soon found herself on a road beside which people dwelt: here there were flower gardens as well as kitchen gardens. And she sat down to rest by a kitchen garden.

"What a number of different creatures there are that I never knew! and how beautiful and great the world is! But one must look round in it, and not stay in one spot." And then she hopped into the kitchen garden. "How green it is here! how beautiful it is here!"

"I know that," said the Caterpillar on the leaf; "my leaf is the largest here. It hides half the world from me, but I don't care for the world."

"Cluck! cluck!" And some fowls came: they tripped about in the cabbage garden. The Fowl who marched at the head of them had a long sight, and she spied the Caterpillar on the green leaf, and pecked at it, so that the Caterpillar fell on the ground, where it twisted and writhed.

The Fowl looked at it first with one eye and then with the other, for she did not know what the end of this writhing would be.

"It doesn't do that with a good will," thought the Fowl, and lifted up her head to peck at the Caterpillar.

The Toad was so horrified at this, that she came crawling straight up towards the Fowl.

"Aha! it has allies," quoth the Fowl. "Just look at the crawling thing!" And then the Fowl turned away. "I don't care for the little green morsel: it would only tickle my throat." The other fowls took the same view of it, and they all turned away together.

"I writhed myself free," said the Caterpillar. "What a good thing it is when one has presence of mind! But the hardest thing remains to be done, and that is to get on my leaf again. Where is it?"

And the little Toad came up and expressed her sympathy. She was glad that in her ugliness she had frightened the fowls.

"What do you mean by that?" cried the Caterpillar. "I wriggled myself free from the Fowl. You are very disagreeable to look at. Cannot I be left in peace on my own property? Now I smell cabbage; now I am near my leaf. Nothing is so beautiful as property. But I must go higher up."

"Yes, higher up," said the little Toad; "higher up! She feels just as I do; but she's not in a good humour to-day. That's because of the fright. We all want to go higher up." And she looked up as high as ever she could.

The stork sat in his nest on the roof of the farm-house. He clapped with his beak, and the mother-stork clapped with hers.

"How high up they live!" thought the Toad. "If one could only get as high as that!"

In the farm-house lived two young students; the one was a poet and the other a scientific searcher into the secrets of nature. The one sang and wrote joyously of everything that God had created, and how it was mirrored in his heart. He sang it out clearly, sweetly, richly, in well-sounding verses; while the other investigated created matter itself, and even cut it open where need was. He looked upon God's creation as a great sum in arithmetic—subtracted, multiplied, and tried to know it within and without, and to talk with understanding concerning it; and that was a very sensible thing; and he spoke joyously and cleverly of it. They were good, joyful men, those two.

"There sits a good specimen of a toad," said the naturalist. "I must have that fellow in a bottle of spirits."

"You have two of them already," replied the poet. "Let the thing sit there and enjoy its life."

"But it's so wonderfully ugly," persisted the first.

"Yes; if we could find the jewel in its head," said the poet, "I too should be for cutting it open."

"A jewel!" cried the naturalist. "You seem to know a great deal about natural history."

"But is there not something beautiful in the popular belief that just as the toad is the ugliest of animals, it should often carry the most precious jewel in its head? Is it not just the same thing with men? What a jewel that was that Æsop had, and still more, Socrates!"

The Toad did not hear any more, nor did she understand half of what she had heard. The two friends walked on, and thus she escaped the fate of being bottled up in spirits.

"Those two also were speaking of the jewel," said the Toad to herself. "What a good thing that I have not got it! I might have been in a very disagreeable position."

Now there was a clapping on the roof of the farm-house. Father-Stork was making a speech to his family, and his family was glancing down at the two young men in the kitchen garden.

"Man is the most conceited creature!" said the Stork. "Listen how their jaws are wagging; and for all that they can't clap properly. They boast of their gifts of eloquence and their language! Yes, a fine language truly! Why, it changes in every day's journey we make. One of them doesn't understand another. Now, *we* can speak our language over the whole earth—up in the North and in Egypt. And men are not able to fly, moreover. They rush along by means of an invention they call "railway;" but they often break their necks over it. It makes my beak turn cold when I think of it. The world could get on without men. We could do without them very well, so long as we only keep frogs and earthworms."

"That was a powerful speech," thought the little Toad. "What a great man that is yonder! and how high he sits! Higher than ever I saw any one sit yet; and how he can swim!" she cried, as the Stork soared away through the air with outspread pinions.

And the Mother-Stork began talking in the nest, and told about Egypt, and the waters of the Nile, and the incomparable mud that was to be found in that strange land; and all this sounded new and very charming to the little Toad.

"I must go to Egypt!" said she. "If the stork or one of his young ones would only take me! I would oblige him in return. Yes, I shall get to Egypt, for I feel so happy! All the longing and all the pleasure that I feel is much better than having a jewel in one's head."

And it was just she who had the jewel. That jewel was the continual striving and desire to go upward—ever upward. It gleamed in her head, gleamed in joy, beamed brightly in her longings.

Then, suddenly, up came the Stork. He had seen the Toad in the grass, and stooped down and seized the little creature anything but gently. The Stork's beak pinched her, and the wind whistled; it was not exactly agreeable, but she was going upward—upward towards Egypt—and she knew it; and that was why her eyes gleamed, and a spark seemed to fly out of them.

"Quunk!—ah!"

UPWARD!

The body was dead—the Toad was killed! But the spark that had shot forth from her eyes: what became of that?

The sunbeam took it up; the sunbeam carried the jewel from the head of the Toad. Whither?

Ask not the naturalist; rather ask the poet. He will tell it thee under the guise of a fairy tale; and the Caterpillar on the cabbage, and the Stork family belong to the story. Think! the Caterpillar is changed, and turns into a beautiful butterfly; the Stork family flies over mountains and seas, to the distant Africa, and yet finds the shortest way home to the same country—to the same roof. Nay, that is almost too improbable; and yet it is true. You may ask the naturalist, he will confess it is so; and you know it yourself, for you have seen it.

But the jewel in the head of the toad?

Seek it in the sun; see it there if you can.

The brightness is too dazzling there. We have not yet such eyes as can see into the glories which God has created, but we shall receive them by-and-bye; and that will be the most beautiful story of all, and we shall all have our share in it.

THE PORTER'S SON.

THE General lived in the grand first floor, and the porter lived in the cellar. There was a great distance between the two families—the whole of the ground floor, and the difference in rank; but they lived in the same house, and both had a view of the street and of the courtyard. In the courtyard was a grass-plot, on which grew a blooming acacia tree (when it was in bloom), and under this tree sat occasionally the finely-dressed nurse, with the still more finely-dressed child of the General—little Emily. Before them danced about barefoot the little son of the porter, with his great brown eyes and dark hair; and the little girl smiled at him, and stretched out her hands towards him; and when the General saw that from the window, he would nod his head, and cry, "Charming!" The General's lady (who was so young that she might very well have been her husband's daughter from an early marriage) never came to the window that looked upon the courtyard. She had given orders, though, that the boy might play his antics to amuse her child, but must never touch it. The nurse punctually obeyed the gracious lady's orders.

The sun shone in upon the people in the grand first floor, and upon the people in the cellar; the acacia tree was covered with blossoms, and they fell off, and next year new ones came. The tree bloomed, and the porter's little son bloomed too, and looked like a fresh tulip.

The General's little daughter became delicate and pale, like the leaf of the acacia blossom. She seldom came down to the tree now, for she took the air in a carriage. She drove out with her mamma, and then she would always nod at the porter's George; yes, she used even to kiss her hand to him, till her mamma said she was too old to do that now.

One morning George was sent up to carry the General the letters and newspapers that had been delivered at the porter's room in the morning. As he was running upstairs, just as he passed the door of the sand-box he heard a faint piping. He thought it was some young chicken that had strayed there and was raising cries of distress; but it was the General's little daughter, decked out in lace and finery.

GEORGE AMUSING THE GENERAL'S DAUGHTER.

"Don't tell papa and mamma," she whimpered; "they would be angry."

"What's the matter, little missie?" asked George.

"It's all on fire!" she answered.   "It's burning with a bright flame!"

George hurried upstairs to the General's apartments; he opened the door of the nursery.   The window-curtain was almost entirely burnt, and the wooden curtain-pole was one mass of flame.   George sprang upon a chair he brought in haste, and pulled down the burning articles, and alarmed the people.   But for him the house would have been burnt down.

The General and his lady cross-questioned little Emily.

"I only took just one lucifer-match," she said, "and it was burning directly, and the curtain was burning too.   I spat at it, to put it out; I spat at it as much as ever I could, but I could not put it out; so I ran away and hid myself, for papa and mamma would be angry."

"I spat!" cried the General's lady; "what an expression! Did you ever hear your papa and mamma talk about spitting? You must have got that from downstairs!"

And George had a penny given him. But this penny did not go to the baker's shop, but into the savings-box; and soon there was so many pennies in the savings-box, that he could buy a paint-box, and colour the drawings he made—and he had a great number of drawings. They seemed to shoot out of his pencil and out of his fingers'-ends. His first coloured pictures he presented to Emily.

"Charming!" said the General; and even the General's lady acknowledged that it was easy to see what the boy had meant to draw. "He has genius." Those were the words that were carried down into the cellar.

The General and his gracious lady were grand people. They had two coats of arms on their carriage, a coat of arms for each of them; and the gracious lady had had this coat of arms embroidered on both sides of every bit of linen she had, and even on her nightcap and her dressing-bag. One of the coats of arms, the one that belonged to her, was a very dear one; it had been bought for hard cash by her father, for he had not been born with it, nor had she; she had come into the world too early, seven years before the coat of arms, and most people remembered this circumstance, but the family did not remember it. A man might well have a bee in his bonnet, when he had such a coat of arms to carry as that, let alone having to carry two; and the General's wife had a bee in hers when she drove to the Court ball, as stiff and as proud as you please.

The General was old and grey, but he had a good seat on horseback, and he knew it; and he rode out every day, with a groom behind him at a proper distance. When he came to a party, he looked somehow as if he were riding into the room upon his high horse; and he had orders, too, such a number that no one would have believed it; but that was not his fault. As a young man, he had taken part in the great autumn reviews which were held in those days. He had an anecdote that he told about those days, the only one he knew. A subaltern under his orders had cut off one of the princes, and taken him prisoner, and the Prince had been obliged to ride through the town with a little band of captured soldiers, himself a prisoner behind the General. This was an ever-memorable event, and was always told over and over again every year by the General, who, moreover, always repeated the remarkable words he had used when he returned his sword to the Prince: those words were, "Only my subaltern could have taken your Highness prisoner; I could never have done it!" And the Prince had replied, "You are incomparable." In a real war the General had never taken part. When war came into the country, he had gone on a diplomatic career to foreign Courts. He spoke the French language so fluently that he had almost forgotten his own; he could dance well, he could ride well, and orders grew on his coat in an astounding way. The sentries presented arms to him, one of the most beautiful girls presented arms to him, and became the General's lady, and in time they had a pretty, charming child, that seemed as if it had dropped from heaven, it was so pretty; and the porter's son danced before it in the courtyard, as soon as it could understand it, and gave her all his coloured pictures; and little Emily looked at them, and was pleased, and tore them to pieces. She was pretty and delicate indeed.

"My little Roseleaf!" cried the General's lady, "thou art born to wed a prince."

The prince was already at the door, but they knew nothing of it: people don't see far beyond the threshold.

GEORGE AND EMILY'S FEAST.

"The day before yesterday our boy divided his bread and butter with her!" said the porter's wife. "There was neither cheese nor meat upon it, but she liked it as well as if it had been roast beef. There would have been a fine noise if the General and his wife had seen the feast; but they did not see it."

George had divided his bread and butter with little Emily, and he would have divided his heart with her, if it would have pleased her. He was a good boy, brisk and clever, and he went to the night school in the Academy now, to learn to draw properly. Little Emily was getting on with her education too, for she spoke French with her "bonne," and had a dancing master.

"George will be confirmed at Easter," said the porter's wife; for George had got so far as this.

"It would be the best thing, now, to make an apprentice of him," said his father. "It must be to some good calling,—and then he would be out of the house."

"He would have to sleep out of the house," said George's mother. "It is not easy to find a master who has room for him at night; and we shall have to provide him with clothes too. The little bit of eating that he wants can be managed for him, for he's quite happy with a few boiled potatoes; and he gets taught for nothing. Let the boy go his own way. You will say that he will be our joy some day, and the Professor says so too."

The confirmation suit was ready: the mother had worked it herself; but the tailor who did repairs had cut them out, and a capital cutter-out he was.

"If he had had a better position, and been able to keep a workshop and journeymen," the porter's wife said, "he might have been a Court tailor."

The clothes were ready, and the candidate for confirmation was ready. On his confirmation day, George received a great pinchbeck watch from his godfather, the old ironmonger's shopman, the richest of his godfathers. The watch was an old and tried servant: it always went too fast, but that is better than to be lagging behind. That was a costly present: and from the General's apartment there arrived a hymn-book bound in morocco, sent by the little lady to whom George had given pictures. At the beginning of the book his name was written, and her name, as "his gracious patroness." These words had been written at the dictation of the General's lady, and the General had read the inscription, and pronounced it "Charming!"

"That is really a great attention from a family of such position," said the porter's wife; and George was sent upstairs to show himself in his confirmation clothes, with the hymn-book in his hand.

The General's lady was sitting very much wrapped up, and had the bad headache she always had when time hung heavy upon her hands. She looked at George very pleasantly, and wished him all prosperity, and that he might never have her headache. The General was walking about in his dressing-gown: he had a cap with a long tassel on his head, and Russian boots with red tops on his feet. He walked three times up and down the room, absorbed in his own thoughts and recollections, and then stopped, and said:

"So little George is a confirmed Christian now. Be a good man, and honour those in authority over you. Some day, when you are an old man, you can say that the General gave you this precept."

That was a longer speech than the General was accustomed to make, and then he went back to his ruminations, and looked very aristocratic. But of all that George heard and saw up there, little Miss Emily remained most clear in his thoughts. How graceful she was, how gentle, and fluttering, and pretty she looked. If she were to be drawn, it ought to be on a soap-bubble. About her dress, about her yellow curled hair, there was a fragrance as of a fresh-blown rose; and to think that he had once divided his bread and butter with her, and that she had eaten it with enormous appetite, and nodded to him at every second mouthful! Did she remember anything about it? Yes, certainly, for she had given him the beautiful hymn-book in remembrance of this; and when the first new moon in the first new year after this event came round, he took a piece of bread, a penny, and his hymn-book, and went out into the open air, and opened the book to see what psalm he should turn up. It was a psalm of praise and thanksgiving. Then he opened the book again to see what would turn up for little Emily. He took great pains not to open the book in the place where the funeral hymns were, and yet he got one that referred to the grave and death. But then he thought this was not a thing in which one must believe; for all that he was startled when soon afterwards the pretty little girl had to lie in bed, and the doctor's carriage stopped at the gate every day.

"They will not keep her with them," said the porter's wife. "The good God knows whom He will summon to Himself."

But they kept her after all; and George drew pictures and sent them to her. He drew the Czar's palace; the old Kremlin at Moscow, just as it stood, with towers and cupolas; and these cupolas looked like gigantic green and gold cucumbers, at least in George's drawing. Little Emily was highly pleased, and consequently, when a week had elapsed, George sent her a few more pictures, all with buildings in them; for, you see, she could imagine all sorts of things inside the windows and doors.

He drew a Chinese house, with bells hanging from every one of the sixteen storeys. He drew two Grecian temples with slender marble pillars, and with steps all round them. He drew a Norwegian church. It was easy to see that this church had been built entirely of wood, hewn out and wonderfully put together; every storey looked as if it had rockers, like a cradle. But the most beautiful of all was the castle, drawn on one of the leaves, and which he called "Emily's Castle." This was the kind of place in which she must live. That is what George had thought, and consequently he had put into this building whatever he thought most beautiful in all the others. It had carved woodwork, like the Norwegian church; marble pillars, like the Grecian temple; bells in every storey; and was crowned with cupolas, green and gilded, like those of the Kremlin of the Czar. It was a real child's castle, and under every window was written what the hall or the room inside was intended to be; for instance: "Here Emily sleeps;" "Here Emily dances;" "Here Emily plays at receiving her visitors." It was a real pleasure to look at the castle, and right well was the castle looked at accordingly.

"Charming!" said the General.

But the old Count—for there was an old Count there, who was still grander than the General, and had a castle of his own—said nothing at all; he heard that it had been designed and drawn by the porter's little son. Not that he was so very little, either, for he had already been confirmed. The old Count looked at the pictures, and had his own thoughts as he did so.

One day, when it was very gloomy, grey, wet weather, the brightest of days dawned for George; for the Professor at the Academy called him into his room.

"Listen to me, my friend," said the Professor; "I want to speak to you. The Lord has been good to you in giving you abilities, and He has also been good in placing you among kind people. The old Count at the corner yonder has been speaking to me about you. I have also seen your sketches; but we will not say any more about those, for there is a good deal to correct in them. But from this time forward you may come twice a week to my drawing-class, and then you will soon learn how to do them better. I think there's more of the architect than of the painter in you. You will have time to think that over; but go across to the old Count this very day, and thank God for having sent you such a friend."

It was a great house—the house of the old Count at the corner. Round the windows elephants and dromedaries were carved, all from the old times; but the old Count loved the new time best, and what it brought, whether it came from the first floor, or from the cellar, or from the attic.

"I think," said the porter's wife, "the grander people are, the fewer airs do they give themselves. How kind and straightforward the old Count is! and he talks exactly like you and me. Now, the General and his lady can't do that. And George was fairly wild with delight yesterday at the good reception he met with at the Count's; and so am I to-day, after speaking to the great man. Wasn't it a good thing that we did not bind George apprentice to a handicraftsman? for he has abilities of his own."

"But they must be helped on by others," said the father.

"That help he has got now," rejoined the mother; "for the Count spoke out quite clearly and distinctly."

"But I fancy it began with the General," said the father, "and we must thank them too."

"Let us do so with all my heart," cried the mother, "though I fancy we have not much to thank them for. I will thank the good God; and I will thank Him, too, for letting little Emily get well."

Emily was getting on bravely, and George got on bravely too: in the course of the year he won the little silver prize medal of the Academy, and afterwards he gained the great one too

"It would have been better, after all, if he had been apprenticed to a handicraftsman," said the porter's wife, weeping; "for then we could have kept him with us. What is he to do in Rome? I shall never get a sight of him again, not even if he comes back; but that he won't do, the dear boy."

"It is fortune and fame for him," said the father.

"Yes, thank you, my friend," said the mother; "you are saying what you do not mean. You are just as sorrowful as I am."

And it was all true about the sorrow and the journey. But everybody said it was a great piece of good fortune for the young fellow. And he had to take leave, and of the General too. The General's lady did not show herself, for she had her bad headache. On this occasion the General told his only anecdote, about what he had said to the Prince, and how the Prince had said to him, "You are incomparable." And he held out a languid hand to George.

Emily gave George her hand too, and looked almost sorry; and George was the most sorry of all.

Time goes by when one has something to do; and it goes by, too, when one has nothing to do. The time is equally long, but not equally useful. It was useful to George, and did not seem long at all, except when he happened to be thinking of his home. How might the good folks be getting on, upstairs and downstairs? Yes, there was writing about that, and many things can be put into a letter,—bright sunshine and dark heavy days. Both of these were in the letter which brought the news that his father was dead, and that his mother was alone now. She wrote that Emily had come down to see her, and had been to her like an angel of comfort; and concerning herself, she added that she had been allowed to keep her situation as porteress.

The General's lady kept a diary, and in this diary was recorded every ball she attended and every visit she received. The diary was illustrated by the insertion of the visiting cards of the diplomatic circle and of the most noble families; and the General's lady was proud of it. The diary kept growing through a long time, and amid many severe headaches, and through a long course of half-nights, that is to say, of Court balls. Emily had now been to a Court ball for the first time. Her mother had worn a bright red dress, with black lace, in the Spanish style; the daughter had been attired in white, fair and delicate; green silk ribbons fluttered like flag-leaves among her yellow locks, and on her head she wore a wreath of water-lilies; her eyes were so blue and clear, her mouth was so delicate and red, she looked like a little water spirit, as beautiful as such a spirit can be imagined. The Princes danced with her, one after another, of course; and the General's lady had not a headache for a week afterwards.

But the first ball was not the last, and Emily could not stand it; it was a good thing, therefore, that summer brought with it rest, and exercise in the open air. The family had been invited by the old Count to visit him at his castle. That was a castle with a garden which was worth seeing. Part of this garden was laid out quite in the style of the old days, with stiff green hedges; you walked as if between green walls with peep-holes in them. Box trees and yew trees stood there trimmed into the form of stars and pyramids, and water sprang from fountains in large grottoes lined with shells; all around stood figures of the most beautiful stone—that could be seen in their clothes as well as in their faces; every flower-bed had a different shape, and represented a fish, or a coat of arms, or a monogram. That was the French part of the garden; and from this part the visitor came into what appeared like the green fresh forest, where the trees might grow as they chose, and accordingly they were great and glorious—the grass was green, and beautiful to walk on, and it was regularly cut, and rolled, and swept, and tended: that was the English part of the garden.

"Old time and new time," said the Count, here they run well into one another. In two years the building itself will put on a proper appearance, there will be a complete metamorphosis in beauty and improvement. I shall show the drawings, and I shall show you the architect, for he is to dine here to-day."

"Charming!" said the General.

"'T is like Paradise here," said the General's lady, "and yonder you have a knight's castle!"

"That's my poultry-house," observed the Count. "The pigeons live in the tower, the turkeys in the first floor, but old Elsie rules in the ground floor. She has apartments on all sides of her. The sitting hens have their own room, and the hens with chickens have theirs; and the ducks have their own particular door, leading to the water."

"Charming!" repeated the General.

And all sallied forth to see these wonderful things. Old Elsie stood in the room on the ground floor, and by her side stood Architect George. He and Emily now met for the first time after several years, and they met in the poultry-house.

Yes, there he stood, and was handsome enough to be looked at. His face was frank and energetic; he had black shining hair, and a smile about his mouth, which said, "I have a brownie that sits in my ear, and knows every one of you, inside and out." Old Elsie had pulled off her wooden shoes, and stood there in her stockings, to do honour to the noble guests. The hens clucked, and the cocks crowed, and the ducks waddled to and fro, and said, "Quack, quack!" But the fair, pale girl, the friend of his childhood, the daughter of the General, stood there with a rosy blush on her usually pale cheeks, and her eyes opened wide, and her mouth seemed to speak without uttering a word, and the greeting he received from her was the most beautiful greeting a young man can desire from a young lady, if they are not related, or have not danced many times together, and she and the architect had never danced together.

The Count shook hands with him, and introduced him.

"He is not altogether a stranger, our young friend George."

The General's lady bowed to him, and the General's daughter was very nearly giving him her hand; but she did not give it to him.

"Our little Master George!" said the General. "Old friends! Charming!"

"You have become quite an Italian," said the General's lady, "and I presume you speak the language like a native?"

"My wife sings the language, but she does not speak it," observed the General.

At dinner, George sat at the right hand of Emily, whom the General had taken down, while the Count led in the General's lady.

Mr. George talked and told of his travels; and he could talk well, and was the life and soul of the table, though the old Count could have been it too. Emily sat silent, but she listened, and her eyes gleamed, but she said nothing.

In the verandah, among the flowers, she and George stood together: the rose-bushes concealed them. And George was speaking again, for he took the lead now.

"Many thanks for the kind consideration you showed my old mother," he said. "I know that you went down to her on the night when my father died, and you stayed with her till his eyes were closed. My heartiest thanks!"

He took Emily's hand, and kissed it—he might do so on such an

·IN THE VERANDAH.

occasion. She blushed deeply, but pressed his hand, and looked at him with her dear blue eyes.

"Your mother was a dear soul!" she said. "How fond she was of her son! And she let me read all your letters, so that I almost believe I know you. How kind you were to me when I was a little girl! You used to give me pictures."

"Which you tore in two," said George.

"No, I have still your drawing of the castle."

"I must build the castle in reality now," said George; and he became quite warm at his own words.

The General and the General's lady talked to each other in their room about the porter's son—how he knew how to behave, and to express himself with the greatest propriety.

"He might be a tutor," said the General.

"Intellect!" said the General's lady; but she did not say anything more.

During the beautiful summer-time Mr. George several times visited the Count at his castle; and he was missed when he did not come.

"How much the good God has given you that he has not given to us poor mortals," said Emily to him. "Are you sure you are very grateful for it?"

It flattered George that the lovely young girl should look up to him, and he thought then that Emily had unusually good abilities. And the General felt more and more convinced that George was no cellar-child.

"His mother was a very good woman," he observed. "It is only right I should do her that justice now she is in her grave."

The summer passed away, and the winter came; and again there was talk about Mr. George. He was highly respected, and was received in the first circles: the General had met him at a Court ball.

And now there was a ball to be given in the General's house for Emily, and could Mr George be invited to it?

"He whom the King invites can be invited by the General also," said the General, and drew himself up till he stood quite an inch higher than before.

Mr. George *was* invited, and he came; princes and counts came, and they danced, one better than the other. But Emily could only dance one dance—the first; for she made a false step—nothing of consequence; but her foot hurt her, so that she had to be careful, and leave off dancing, and look at the others. So she sat and looked on, and the architect stood by her side.

"I suppose you are giving her the whole history of St. Peter's," said the General, as he passed by; and smiled, like the personification of patronage.

With the same patronizing smile he received Mr. George a few days afterwards. The young man came, no doubt, to return thanks for the invitation to the ball. What else could it be? But indeed there was something else, something very astonishing and startling. He spoke words of sheer lunacy, so that the General could hardly believe his own ears. It was "the height of rhodomontade," an offer, quite an inconceivable offer—Mr. George came to ask the hand of Emily in marriage!

"Man!" cried the General, and his brain seemed to be boiling. "I don't understand you at all. What is it you say? What is it you want? I don't know you. Sir! Man! What possesses you to break into my house? And am I to stand here and listen to you?" He stepped backwards into his bed-room, locked the door behind him, and left Mr. George standing alone. George stood still for a few minutes, and then turned round and left the room. Emily was standing in the corridor.

"My father has answered?" she said, and her voice trembled.

George pressed her hand.

"He has escaped me," he replied; "but a better time will come."

There were tears in Emily's eyes, but in the young man's eyes shone courage and confidence; and the sun shone through the window, and cast his beams on the pair, and gave them his blessing.

The General sat in his room, bursting hot. Yes, he was still boiling, until he boiled over in the exclamation, "Lunacy! porter! madness!"

Not an hour was over before the General's lady knew it out of the General's own mouth. She called Emily, and remained alone with her.

"You poor child," she said; "to insult you so! to insult us so! There are tears in your eyes, too, but they become you well. You look beautiful in tears. You look as I looked on my wedding-day. Weep on, my sweet Emily."

"Yes, that I must," said Emily, "if you and my father do not say 'yes.'"

"Child!" screamed the General's lady; "you are ill! You are talking wildly, and I shall have a most terrible headache! Oh, what a misfortune is coming upon our house! Don't make your mother die, Emily, or you will have no mother."

And the eyes of the General's lady were wet, for she could not bear to think of her own death.

In the newspapers there was an announcement. "Mr. George has been elected Professor of the Fifth Class, Number Eight."

"It's a pity that his parents are dead, and cannot read it," said the new porter people, who now lived in the cellar under the General's apartments. They knew that the Professor had been born and had grown up within their four walls.

"Now he'll get a salary," said the man.

"Yes, that's not much for a poor child," said the woman.

"Eighteen dollars a year," said the man. "Why, it's a good deal of money."

"No, I mean the honour of it," replied the wife. "Do you think he cares for the money? Those few dollars he can earn a hundred times over, and most likely he'll get a rich wife into the bargain. If we had children of our own, husband, our child should be an architect and a Professor too."

George was spoken well of in the cellar, and he was spoken well of in the first floor: the old Count took upon himself to do that.

The pictures he had drawn in his childhood gave the occasion for it. But how did the conversation come to turn on these pictures? Why, they had been talking of Russia and of Moscow, and thus mention was made of the Kremlin, which little George had once drawn for Miss Emily. He had drawn many pictures, but the Count especially remembered one, "Emily's Castle," where she was to sleep, and to dance, and to play at receiving guests.

"The Professor was a true man," said the Count, "and would be a Privy Councillor before he died, it was not at all unlikely; and he might build a real castle for the young lady before that time came: why not?"

"That was a strange jest," remarked the General's lady, when the Count had gone away. The General shook his head thoughtfully, and went out for a ride, with his groom behind him at a proper distance, and he sat more stiffly than ever on his high horse.

It was Emily's birthday. Flowers, books, letters, and visiting cards came pouring in. The General's lady kissed her on the mouth, and the General kissed her on the forehead; they were affectionate parents, and they and Emily had to receive grand visitors—two of the Princes. They talked of balls and theatres, of diplomatic missions, of the government of empires and nations; and then they spoke of talent, native talent; and so the discourse turned upon the young architect.

"He is building up an immortality for himself," said one; "and he will certainly build his way into one of our first families."

"One of our first families!" repeated the General, and afterwards the General's lady; "what is meant by one of our first families?"

"I know for whom it was intended," said the General's lady; "but I shall not say it. I don't think it. Heaven disposes, but I shall be astonished."

"I am astonished also!" said the General. "I haven't an idea in my head!" And he fell into a reverie, waiting for ideas.

There is a power, a nameless power, in the possession of favour from above, the favour of Providence, and this favour little George had.—But we are forgetting the birthday.

REMEMBRANCES OF GEORGE.

Emily's room was fragrant with flowers, sent by male and female friends; on the table lay beautiful presents for greeting and remembrance, but none could come from George—none could come from him; but it was not necessary, for the whole house was full of remembrances of him. Even out of the ash-bin the blossom of memory peeped forth, for Emily had sat whimpering there on the day when the window-curtain caught fire, and George arrived in the character of first engine. A glance out of the window, and the acacia tree reminded of the days of childhood. Flowers and leaves had fallen, but there stood the tree covered with hoar frost, looking like a single huge branch of coral; and the moon shone clear and large among the twigs, unchanged in its changings, as it was when George divided his bread and butter with little Emily.

Out of a box the girl took the drawings of the Czar's palace and of her own castle—remembrances of George. The drawings were looked at, and many thoughts came. She remembered the day when, unobserved by her father and mother, she had gone down to the porter's wife who lay dying. Once again she seemed to sit beside her, holding the dying woman's hand in hers, hearing the dying woman's last words: "Blessing George!" The mother was thinking of her son; and now Emily gave her own interpretation to those words. Yes, George was certainly with her on her birthday.

It happened that the next day was another birthday in that house—the General's birthday. He had been born the day after his daughter, but before her, of course—many years before her. Many presents arrived, and among them came a saddle of exquisite workmanship, a comfortable and costly saddle—one of the Princes had just such another. Now, from whom might this saddle come? The General was delighted. There was a little note with the saddle. Now if the words on the note had been "Many thanks for yesterday's reception," we might easily have guessed from whom it came. But the words were "From somebody whom the General does not know."

"Whom in the world do I not know?" exclaimed the General. "I know everybody;" and his thoughts wandered all through society, for he knew everybody there. "That saddle comes from my wife!" he said at last. "She is teasing me—charming!"

But she was not teasing him; those times were past.

Again there was a feast, but it was not in the General's house—it was a fancy ball at the Prince's, and masks were allowed too.

The General went as Rubens, in a Spanish costume, with a little ruff round his neck, a sword by his side, and a stately manner. The General's lady was Madame Rubens, in black velvet made high round the neck, exceedingly warm, and with a mill-stone round her neck in the shape of a great ruff—accurately dressed after a Dutch picture in the possession of the General, in which the hands were especially admired. They were just like the hands of the General's lady.

Emily was Psyche. In white crape and lace she was like a floating swan. She did not want wings at all. She only wore them as emblematic of Psyche.

Brightness, splendour, light and flowers, wealth and taste appeared at the ball; there was so much to see, that the beautiful hands of Madame Rubens made no sensation at all.

A black domino, with an acacia blossom in his cap, danced with Psyche.

" Who is that ? " asked the General's lady.

" His Royal Highness," replied the General. " I am quite sure of it. I knew him directly by the pressure of his hand."

The General's lady doubted it.

General Rubens had no doubts about it. He went up to the black domino and wrote the royal letters in the mask's hand. These were denied, but the mask gave him a hint.

The words that came with the saddle: " One whom you do not know, General."

" But I do know you," said the General. " It was you who sent me the saddle."

The domino raised his hand, and disappeared among the other guests.

" Who is that black domino with whom you were dancing, Emily ? " asked the General's lady.

" I did not ask his name," she replied, " because you knew it. It is the Professor. Your *protegé* is here, Count ! " she continued, turning to that nobleman, who stood close by. " A black domino with acacia blossoms in his cap."

" Very likely, my dear lady," replied the Count. " But one of the Princes wears just the same costume."

" I knew the pressure of the hand," said the General. " The saddle came from the Prince. I am so certain of it that I could invite that domino to dinner."

" Do so. If it be the Prince he will certainly come," replied the Count.

" And if it is the other he will not come," said the General, and approached the black domino, who was just speaking with the King. The General gave a very respectful invitation " that they might make each other's acquaintance," and he smiled in his certainty concerning the person he was inviting. He spoke loud and distinctly.

The domino raised his mask, and it was George. " Do you repeat your invitation, General ? " he asked.

The General certainly seemed to grow an inch taller, assumed a more stately demeanour, and took two steps backward and one step forward as if he were dancing a minuet, and then came as much gravity and expression into the face of the General as the General could contrive to infuse into it ; but he replied,

" I never retract my words ! You are invited, Professor ! " and he bowed with a glance at the King, who must have heard the whole dialogue.

Now, there was company to dinner at the General's, but only the old Count and his *protegé* were invited.

" I have my foot under his table," thought George : " that 's laying the foundation-stone."

And the foundation-stone was really laid, with great ceremony, at the house of the General and of the General's lady.

The man had come, and had spoken quite like a person in good society, and had made himself very agreeable, so that the General had often to repeat his "Charming!" The General talked of this dinner, talked of it even to a Court lady; and this lady, one of the most intellectual persons about the Court, asked to be invited to meet the Professor the next time he should come. So he had to be invited again; and he was invited, and came, and was charming again; he could even play chess.

"He's not out of the cellar," said the General; "he's quite a distinguished person. There are many distinguished persons of that kind, and it's no fault of his."

The Professor, who was received in the King's palace, might very well be received by the General; but that he could ever belong to the house was out of the question, only the whole town was talking of it.

He grew and grew. The dew of favour fell from above, so no one was surprised after all that he should become a Privy Councillor, and Emily a Privy Councillor's lady.

"Life is either a tragedy or a comedy," said the General. "In tragedies they die, in comedies they marry one another."

AT THE GENERAL'S.

In this case they married. And they had three clever boys—but not all at once.

The sweet children rode on their hobby-horses through all the rooms when they came to see their grandparents. And the General also rode on his stick; he rode behind them in the character of groom to the little Privy Councillors.

And the General's lady sat on her sofa and smiled at them, even when she had her severest headache.

So far did George get, and much further; else it had not been worth while to tell the story of THE PORTER'S SON.

THE JOY OF GOOD DEEDS.

PUT OFF IS NOT DONE WITH.

An old castle stood there, surrounded by its muddy moat, with the drawbridge, which was seldom let down; for not all guests are good people. Under the roof loopholes had been pierced, through which one could shoot or could pour boiling water, and even melted lead, down upon the enemy, if he should approach too near. It was a long way up, inside the house, to the open ceiling of rafters, which was a very good thing, considering the quantity of smoke that curled up from the great fire on the hearth, where big wet logs were sputtering. On the walls were pictures of men in armour, and of proud women in heavy dresses. The stateliest of all these dames walked about, a living woman; her name was Meta Mogens, and she was the lady of the house, for the castle belonged to her.

Towards evening robbers came. They slew three of the people, and killed the yard-dog too, and then they chained Lady Meta with the dog-chain to the kennel, while they themselves took their ease in the hall, and drank the good wine and beer out of the cellar.

Lady Meta was fastened up by the dog-chain; she could not even bark.

But, behold! A boy of one of the robbers came creeping up quite

THE BOY'S GRATITUDE.

silently; for he might not let them observe him, or they would have killed him.

"Lady Meta Mogens!" he said. "Do you remember how my father had to ride the wooden horse * in your lord's time? You entreated for him, but it was no use—he was to ride the wooden horse till his limbs were crippled. But you crept down to him as I am creeping down now to you; you yourself thrust a little stone under each of his feet, so that he had a support. Nobody saw it; or, if any did, they pretended not to

---

* An ancient and barbarous military punishment.

see it, for you were the gracious young lady. My father told me this, and I remembered it, and have never forgotten it. And now I will set you free, Lady Meta Mogens."

Then they took horses from the stable, and rode away through the wind and rain, and brought friends to help them.

"That was a rich reward for the little kindness I showed the old man," said dame Meta Mogens.

"Put off is not Done with," replied the boy.

The robbers were hanged.

There was an old chateau, and it is there still. It does not belong to Lady Meta Mogens; it has to do with quite another story of noble folks.

We are in the present time. The sun shines on the gilded pinnacle of the tower; little islands are scattered like bouquets over the water, and the wild swans swim majestically round them. In the garden roses are growing; the lady of the house is the most delicate rose-leaf of all. The rose-leaf shines in joy—in the joy of good deeds; but it is not displayed to all the world; it shines in the heart, and what is concealed there is not forgotten. "Put off is not Done with."

HER WORLD ENLARGED.

Now she goes from the lordly hall to the little farm-house in the fields. Yonder dwells a poor crippled girl: the window in the little room looks out upon the north, and the sun does not shine in there. The girl can only look out upon a little space of field, which is surrounded by a high fence. But to-day the sun is shining, the warm bountiful sun of the bountiful Creator is in the room; it comes from the south through the new window which has been made where there used to be only wall.

The crippled girl is sitting in the warm sunshine looking out over forest and lake: to her the world has grown so large, so beautiful, and all through a single word of the friendly lady of the chateau.

"The word was so easily spoken, the deed was such a trifling one," said she; "but the joy which it has given me is exceedingly great and full of blessing!"

And thus she does many a good deed, and thinks of all who are in the poor dwellings, and in the rich dwellings when there are sorrowful hearts likewise. It is done in secret and concealed; but the good God does not forget it. "Put off is not Done with."

There stood an old house; it stood in the busy, bustling city. It had rooms and halls; but into those we will not go. We will stay in

THE MOURNING BOW.

the kitchen, and there it is warm, clean, and neat. The copper utensils gleam, the table is polished bright, and the sink is as clean as a newly-washed rolling-board. All this has been done by a servant girl, who has yet found time enough to dress herself as if she were going to church. She has a bow in her cap, a black bow, which signifies mourning. But she has no one to mourn, neither father nor mother, relative nor lover; she is a poor girl. Once she was engaged to be married, engaged to a poor lad; they loved each other heartily. One day he came to her and said,

"We both of us have no money. The rich widow yonder has spoken words of affection to me. She will make me rich, but you are in my heart. What do you advise me to do?"

"Do whatever you think will make you happy," said the girl. "Be kind and affectionate to her; but this you must understand: that from the hour when we part we must not meet again."

And years went by. Then one day her friend and betrothed of old times met her in the street. He looked ill and miserable, and then she could not help speaking to him, and asked him,

"How goes it with you?"

"I am rich and well off in every way," he said. "My wife is honest and good; but you are in my heart. I have fought my battle, and it will soon be over. We shall meet no more till we are both with God."

And a week has gone by. And this morning it was announced in the papers that he was dead; and therefore the girl is in mourning. Her betrothed is dead, and has left behind him a wife and three step-children, the paper says. This sounds as if there were something wrong, and yet the metal is good.

The black bow signifies mourning, and the girl's face signifies mourning much more; but the mourning is hidden in her heart, and will never be forgotten. "Put off is not Done with."

You see, here were three stories—three leaves on one stalk. Do you want some more such shamrock-leaves? In the book of the heart there are many such, for "Put off is not Done with."

THE SNOWDROP.

IT was winter-time; the air was cold, the wind was sharp; but within the closed doors it was warm and comfortable, and within the closed door lay the flower; it lay in the bulb under the snow-covered earth.

One day rain fell. The drops penetrated through the snowy covering down into the earth, and touched the flower-bulb, and talked of the bright world above. Soon the Sunbeam pierced its way through the snow to the root, and within the root there was a stirring.

"Come in," said the Flower.

"I cannot," said the Sunbeam. "I am not strong enough to unlock the door! When the summer comes I shall be strong!"

"When will it be summer?" asked the Flower, and she repeated this question each time a new sunbeam made its way down to her. But the summer was yet far distant. The snow still lay upon the ground, and there was a coat of ice on the water every night.

"What a long time it takes! what a long times it takes!" said the

Flower. "I feel a stirring and striving within me; I must stretch myself, I must unlock the door, I must get out, and must nod a good morning to the summer, and what a happy time that will be!"

And the Flower stirred and stretched itself within the thin rind which the water had softened from without, and the snow and the earth had warmed, and the Sunbeam had knocked at; and it shot forth under the snow with a greenish-white blossom on a green stalk, with narrow thick leaves, which seemed to want to protect it. The snow was cold, but was pierced by the Sunbeam; therefore it was easy to get through it; and now the Sunbeam came with greater strength than before.

"Welcome, welcome!" sang and sounded every ray; and the Flower lifted itself up over the snow into the brighter world. The Sunbeams caressed and kissed it, so that it opened altogether, white as snow, and ornamented with green stripes. It bent its head in joy and humility.

"Beautiful Flower!" said the Sunbeams, "how graceful and delicate you are! You are the first, you are the only one! You are our love! You are the bell that rings out for summer, beautiful summer, over country and town. All the snow will melt; the cold winds will be driven away; we shall rule; all will become green, and then you will have companions—syringas, laburnums, and roses; but you are the first, so graceful, so delicate!"

That was a great pleasure. It seemed as if the air were singing and sounding, as if rays of light were piercing through the leaves and the stalks of the Flower. There it stood, so delicate, and so easily broken, and yet so strong in its young beauty: it stood there in its white dress with the green stripes, and made a summer. But there was a long time yet to the summer-time. Clouds hid the sun, and bleak winds were blowing.

"You have come too early," said Wind and Weather. "We have still the power, and you shall feel it, and give it up to us. You should have stayed quietly at home, and not have run out to make a display of yourself. Your time is not come yet!"

It was a cutting cold! The days which now come brought not a single sunbeam. It was weather that might break such a little Flower in two with cold. But the Flower had more strength than she herself knew of: she was strong in joy and in faith in the summer, which would be sure to come, which had been announced by her deep longing and confirmed by the warm sunlight; and so she remained standing in confidence in the snow in her white garment, bending her head even while the snow-flakes fell thick and heavy, and the icy winds swept over her.

"You'll break!" they said, "and fade, and fade! What did you want out here? Why did you let yourself be tempted? The Sunbeam only made game of you. Now you have what you deserve, you summer gauk."*

Summer gauk!" she repeated in the cold morning hour.

---

* The Danish name for the snowdrop signifies "summer gauk" or "summer fool;" "gauk" also means "cuckoo." The German *gauch* and the English *gauk*, as seen in *Gutz-gauch*, the cuckoo, and *Gawthorpe*, have the same origin. "A notorious gull and geck."—*Shakespeare.*

"O summer gauk!" cried some children rejoicingly; "yonder stands one—how beautiful, how beautiful! The first one, the only one!"

These words did the Flower so much good, they seemed to her like warm sunbeams. In her joy the Flower did not even feel when it was broken off. It lay in a child's hand, and was kissed by a child's mouth, and carried into a warm room, and looked on by gentle eyes, and put into water. How strengthening, how invigorating! The Flower thought she had suddenly come upon the summer.

SPRING'S FLOWER.

The daughter of the house, a beautiful little girl, was confirmed, and she had a friend who was confirmed too. He was studying for an examination for an appointment. "He shall be my summer gauk," she said; and she took the delicate Flower and laid it in a piece of scented paper, on which verses were written, beginning with summer gauk and ending with summer gauk. "My friend, be a winter gauk." She had twitted him with the summer. Yes, all this was in the verses, and the paper was folded up like a letter, and the Flower was folded in the letter too. It was dark around her, dark as in those days when she lay hidden in the bulb. The Flower went forth on her journey, and lay in the post-bag, and was pressed and crushed, which was not at all pleasant; but that soon came to an end.

The journey was over: the letter was opened, and read by the dear friend. How pleased he was! He kissed the letter, and it was laid, with its enclosure of verses, in a box, in which there were many beautiful verses, but all of them without flowers: she was the first, the only one, as the Sunbeams had called her; and it was a pleasant thing to think of that.

She had time enough, moreover, to think about it: she thought of it
vhile the summer passed away, and the long winter went by, and the
summer came again, before she appeared once more.   But now the
young man was not pleased at all: he took hold of the letter very
roughly, and threw the verses away, so that the Flower fell on the
ground.   Flat and faded she certainly was, but why should she be thrown
on the ground? still, it was better to be here than in the fire, where the
verses and the paper were being burnt to ashes.   What had happened?
What happens so often :—the Flower had made a gauk of him, that was a
jest; the girl had made a fool of him, that was no jest; she had, during
the summer, chosen another friend.

RESTORED TO THE POETS.

Next morning the sun shone in upon the little flattened Snowdrop,
that looked as if it had been painted upon the floor.   The servant girl,
who was sweeping out the room, picked it up, and laid it in one of the
books which were upon the table, in the belief that it must have fallen
out while the room was being arranged.   Again the flower lay among
verses—printed verses—and they are better than written ones—at
least, more money has been spent upon them.

And after this years went by: the book stood upon the book-shelf,
and then it was taken up and somebody read out of it.   It was a good
book: verses and songs by the old Danish poet Ambrosius Stub, which
are well worth reading.   The man who was now reading the book turned
over a page.

"Why, there's a flower!" he said; "a snowdrop, a summer gauk, a
poet gauk!   That flower must have been put in there with a meaning!
Poor Ambrosius Stub! he was a summer fool too, a poet fool: he came

too early, before his time, and therefore he had to taste the sharp winds, and wander about as a guest from one noble landed proprietor to another, like a flower in a glass of water, a flower in rhymed verses! Summer fool, winter fool, fun and folly—but the first, the only, the fresh young Danish poet of those days. Yes, thou shalt remain as a token in the book, thou little snowdrop: thou hast been put there with a meaning."

And so the Snowdrop was put back into the book, and felt equally honoured and pleased to know that it was a token in the glorious book of songs, and that he who was the first to sing and to write had been also a snowdrop, had been a summer gauk, and had been looked upon in the winter-time as a fool. The Flower understood this, in her way, as we interpret everything in *our* way.

That is the story of the Snowdrop.

OUR AUNT IN HER GLORY.

OUR AUNT.

YOU ought to have known our aunt: she was charming! That is to say, she was not charming at all as the word is usually understood; but she was good and kind, amusing in her way, and was just as any one ought to be whom people are to talk about and to laugh at. She might have been put into a play, and wholly and solely on account of the fact that she only lived for the theatre, and for what was done there. She was an honourable matron; but Agent Fabs, whom she used to call "Flabs," declared that our aunt was stage-struck.

"The theatre is my school," said she, "the source of my knowledge. From thence I have my resuscitated biblical history. Now, 'Moses' and 'Joseph in Egypt'—there are operas for you! I get my universal history from the theatre, my geography, and my knowledge of men. Out of the French pieces I get to know life in Paris—slippery, but exceedingly interesting. How I have cried over "La Famille Roquebourg"—that the man must drink himself to death, so that she may marry the young fellow! Yes, how many tears I have wept in the fifty years I have sub-scribed to the theatre!"

Our aunt knew every acting play, every bit of scenery, every character, every one who appeared or had appeared. She seemed really only to live during the nine months the theatre was open. Summer-time with-out a summer theatre seemed to be only a time that made her old; while, on the other hand, a theatrical evening that lasted till midnight was a lengthening of her life. She did not say, as other people do, "Now we shall have spring, the stork is here," or, "They've advertised the first strawberries in the papers;" she, on the contrary, used to announce the coming of autumn with "Have you heard they're selling boxes for the theatre? now the performances will begin."

She used to value a lodging entirely according to its proximity to the theatre. It was a real sorrow to her when she had to leave the little lane behind the playhouse, and move into the great street that lay a little farther off, and live there in a house where she had no opposite neighbours.

"At home," said she, "my windows must be my opera-box. One cannot sit and look into one's self till one's tired; one must see people. But now I live just as if I'd gone into the country. If I want to see human beings, I must go into my kitchen, and sit down on the sink, for there only I have opposite neighbours. No; when I lived in my dear little lane, I could look straight down into the ironmonger's shop, and had only three hundred paces to the theatre; and now I've three thousand paces to go, military measurement."

Our aunt was sometimes ill; but however unwell she might feel, she never missed the play. The doctor prescribed one day that she should put her feet in a bran bath, and she followed his advice; but she drove to the theatre all the same, and sat with her feet in bran there. If she had died there, she would have been very glad. Thorwaldsen died in the theatre, and she called that a happy death.

She could not imagine but that in heaven there must be a theatre too: it had not, indeed, been promised us, but we might very well imagine it. The many distinguished actors and actresses who had passed away must surely have a field for their talent.

Our aunt had an electric wire from the theatre to her room. A tele-gram used to be dispatched to her at coffee-time, and it used to consist of the words "Herr Sivertsen is at the machinery;" for it was he who gave the signal for drawing the curtain up and down and for changing the scenes.

From him she used to receive a short and concise description of every piece. His opinion of Shakspeare's "Tempest" was "Mad nonsense! There's so much to put up, and the first scene begins with 'Water to the front of wings.'" That is to say, the water had to come forward so far. But when, on the other hand, the same interior scene remained through five acts, he used to pronounce it a sensible, well-written play, a resting play, which performed itself, without putting up scenes.

In earlier times, by which name our aunt used to designate thirty years ago, she and the before-mentioned Herr Sivertsen had been younger. At that time he had already been connected with the machinery, and was, as she said, her benefactor. It used to be the custom in those days that in the evening performances in the only theatre the town possessed, spectators were admitted to the part called the "flies," over the stage, and every machinist had one or two places to give away. Often the flies were quite full of good company; it was said that generals' wives and privy councillors' wives had been up there. It was too interesting to look down behind the scenes, and to see how the people walked to and fro on the stage when the curtain was down.

Our aunt had been there several times, as well when there was a tragedy as when there was a ballet; for the pieces in which there were the greatest number of characters on the stage were the most interesting to see from the flies. One sat pretty much in the dark up there, and most people took their supper up with them. Once three apples and a great bit of bread and butter and sausage fell down right into the dungeon of Ugolino, where that unhappy man was to be starved to death; and there was great laughter among the audience. The sausage was one of the weightiest reasons why the worthy management refused in future to have any spectators up in the flies.

"But I was there seven and thirty times," said our aunt, "and I shall always remember Mr. Sivertsen for that."

On the very last evening when the flies were still open to the public the "Judgment of Solomon" was performed, as our aunt remembered very well. She had, through the influence of her benefactor, Herr Sivertsen, procured a free admission for the Agent Fabs, although he did not deserve it in the least; for he was always cutting his jokes about the theatre and teasing our aunt; but she had procured him a free admission to the flies for all that. He wanted to look at this player-stuff from the other side.

"Those were his own words, and they were just like him," said our aunt.

He looked down from above, on the "Judgment of Solomon," and fell asleep over it: one would have thought he had come from a dinner where many toasts were given. He went to sleep, and was locked in; and there he sat through the dark night in the flies, and when he woke he told a story, but our aunt would not believe it.

"The 'Judgment of Solomon' was over," he said, "and all the people had gone away, upstairs and downstairs; but now the real play began, the after-piece, which was the best of all," said the agent. "Then life came into the affair. It was not the 'Judgment of Solomon' that was performed; no, a real court of judgment was held upon the stage." And Agent Fabs had the impudence to try and make our aunt believe all this: that was the thanks she got for having got him a place in the flies.

What did the agent say? Why, it was curious enough to hear, but there was malice and satire in it.

"It looked dark enough up there," said the agent; "but then the magic business began—a great performance, 'The Judgment in the Theatre.' The box-keepers were at their posts, and every spectator had to show his ghostly pass-book, that it might be decided if he was to be admitted with hands loose or bound, and with or without a muzzle. Grand people who came too late, when the performance had begun, and young people, who could not always watch the time, were tied up outside, and had list slippers put on their feet, with which they were allowed to go in before the beginning of the next act, and they had muzzles too. And then the 'Judgment on the Stage' began."

"All malice, and not a bit of truth in it," said our aunt.

The painter, who wanted to get to Paradise, had to go up a staircase which he had himself painted, but which no man could mount: that was to expiate his sins against perspective. All the plants and buildings, which the property-man had placed, with infinite pains, in countries to which they did not belong, the poor fellow was obliged to put in their right places before cockcrow, if *he* wanted to get into Paradise. Let Herr Fabs see how he would get in himself; but what he said of the performers, tragedians and comedians, singers and dancers, that was the most rascally of all. Mr. Fabs, indeed!—Flabs! He did not deserve to be admitted at all, and our aunt would not soil her lips with what he said. And he said, did Flabs, that the whole was written down, and it should be printed when he was dead and buried, but not before, for he would not risk having his arms and legs broken.

Once our aunt had been in fear and trembling in her temple of happiness, the theatre. It was on a winter day, one of those days in which one has a couple of hours of daylight, with a grey sky. It was terribly cold and snowy, but aunt must go to the theatre. A little opera and a great ballet were performed, and a prologue and an epilogue into the bargain; and that would last till late at night. Our aunt must needs go; so she borrowed a pair of fur boots of her lodger, boots with fur inside and out, and which reached far up her legs.

She got to the theatre, and to her box; the boots were warm, and she kept them on. Suddenly there was a cry of "Fire!" smoke was coming from one of the side scenes, and streamed down from the flies, and there was a terrible panic. The people came rushing out, and our aunt was the last in the box, "on the second tier, left-hand side, for from there the scenery looks best," she used to say: "the scenes are always so arranged that they look best from the King's side." Aunt wanted to come out, but the people before her, in their fright and heedlessness, slammed the door of the box; and there sat our aunt, and couldn't get out, and couldn't get in; that is to say, she couldn't get into the next box, for the partition was too high for her. She called out, and no one heard her; she looked down into the tier of boxes below her, and it was empty, and low, and looked quite near, and aunt in her terror felt quite young and light. She thought of jumping down, and had got one leg over the partition, the other resting on the bench. There she sat astride, as if on horseback, well wrapped up in her flowered cloak, with one leg hanging out — a leg in a tremendous fur boot. That was a sight to behold; and when it was beheld, our aunt was heard too, and was saved from burning, for the theatre was not burned down.

That was the most memorable evening of her life, and she was glad that she could not see herself, for she would have died with confusion.

Her benefactor in the machinery department, Herr Sivertsen, visited her every Sunday, but it was a long time from Sunday to Sunday. In the latter time, therefore, she used to have in a little child "for the scraps;" that is to say, to eat up the remains of the dinner. It was

THE BALLET GIRL.

a child employed in the ballet, one that certainly wanted feeding. The little one used to appear, sometimes as an elf, sometimes as a page; the most difficult part she had to play was the lion's hind leg in the "Magic Flute;" but as she grew larger she could represent the fore-feet of the lion. She certainly only got half a guilder for that, whereas the hind legs were paid for with a whole guilder; but then she had to walk bent, and to do without fresh air. "That was all very interesting to hear," said our aunt.

She deserved to live as long as the theatre stood, but she could not last so long; and she did not die in the theatre, but respectably in her bed. Her last words were, moreover, not without meaning. She asked, "What will the play be to-morrow?"

At her death she left about five hundred dollars. We presume this from the interest, which came to twenty dollars. This our aunt had destined as a legacy for a worthy old spinster who had no friends; it was to be devoted to a yearly subscription for a place in the second tier, on the left side, for the Saturday evening, "for on that evening two pieces were always given," it said in the will; and the only condition laid upon the person who enjoyed the legacy was, that she should think, every Saturday evening, of our aunt, who was lying in her grave.

This was our aunt's religion.

THE DRYAD.

WE are travelling to Paris, to the Exhibition.

Now we are there. That was a journey, a flight without magic. We flew on the wings of steam over the sea and across the land.

Yes, our time is the time of fairy tales.

We are in the midst of Paris, in a great hotel. Blooming flowers ornament the staircases, and soft carpets the floors.

Our room is a very cosy one, and through the open balcony door we have a view of a great square. Spring lives down there; it has come to Paris, and arrived at the same time with us. It has come in the shape of a glorious young chestnut tree, with delicate leaves newly opened. How the tree gleams, dressed in its spring garb, before all the other trees in the place! One of these latter has been struck out of the list of living trees. It lies on the ground with roots exposed. On the place where it stood, the young chestnut tree is to be planted, and to flourish.

It still stands towering aloft on the heavy waggon which has brought it this morning a distance of several miles to Paris. For years it had stood there, in the protection of a mighty oak tree, under which the old venerable clergyman had often sat, with children listening to his stories.

The young chestnut tree had also listened to the stories; for the Dryad who lived in it was a child also. She remembered the time when the tree was so little that it only projected a short way above the grass and ferns around. These were as tall as they would ever be; but the tree grew every year, and enjoyed the air and the sunshine, and drank the dew and the rain. Several times it was also, as it must be, well shaken by the wind and the rain; for that is a part of education.

The Dryad rejoiced in her life, and rejoiced in the sunshine, and the singing of the birds; but she was most rejoiced at human voices; she understood the language of men as well as she understood that of animals.

Butterflies, cockchafers, dragon-flies, everything that could fly came

THE OLD CLERGYMAN AND THE CHILDREN.

to pay a visit. They could all talk. They told of the village, of the vineyard, of the forest, of the old castle with its parks and canals and ponds. Down in the water dwelt also living beings, which, in their way, could fly under the water from one place to another — beings with knowledge and delineation. They said nothing at all; they were so clever!

And the swallow, who had dived, told about the pretty little goldfish, of the thick turbot, the fat brill, and the old carp. The swallow could describe all that very well, but, "Self is the man," she said. "One ought to see these things oneself." But how was the Dryad ever to see such beings? She was obliged to be satisfied with being able to look over the beautiful country and see the busy industry of men.

It was glorious; but most glorious of all when the old clergyman sat under the oak tree and talked of France, and of the great deeds of her sons and daughters, whose names will be mentioned with admiration through all time.

Then the Dryad heard of the shepherd girl, Joan of Arc, and of Charlotte Corday; she heard about Henry the Fourth and Napoleon the First; she heard names whose echo sounds in the hearts of the people.

The village children listened attentively, and the Dryad no less attentively : she became a school-child with the rest. In the clouds that went sailing by she saw, picture by picture, everything that she heard talked about. The cloudy sky was her picture-book.

She felt so happy in beautiful France, the fruitful land of genius, with the crater of freedom. But in her heart the sting remained that the bird, that every animal that could fly, was much better off than she. Even the fly could look about more in the world, far beyond the Dryad's horizon.

France was so great and so glorious, but she could only look across a little piece of it. The land stretched out, world-wide, with vineyards, forests, and great cities. Of all these Paris was the most splendid and the mightiest. The birds could get there; but she, never!

Among the village children was a little ragged, poor girl, but a pretty one to look at. She was always laughing or singing and twining red flowers in her black hair.

" Don't go to Paris ! " the old clergyman warned her. " Poor child ! if you go there, it will be your ruin."

But she went for all that.

The Dryad often thought of her; for she had the same wish, and felt the same longing for the great city.

The Dryad's tree was bearing its first chestnut blossoms; the birds were twittering round them in the most beautiful sunshine. Then a stately carriage came rolling along that way, and in it sat a grand lady driving the spirited, light-footed horses. On the back seat a little smart groom balanced himself. The Dryad knew the lady, and the old clergyman knew her also. He shook his head gravely when he saw her, and said,

" So you went there after all, and it was your ruin, poor Mary ! "

" That one *poor?* " thought the Dryad. " No ; she wears a dress fit for a Countess " (she had become one in the city of magic changes). " Oh, if I were only there, amid all the splendour and pomp ! They shine up into the very clouds at night: when I look up, I can tell in what direction the town lies."

Towards that direction the Dryad looked every evening. She saw in the dark night the gleaming cloud on the horizon; in the clear moonlight nights she missed the sailing clouds, which showed her pictures of the city and pictures from history.

The child grasps at the picture-books, the Dryad grasped at the cloud-world, her thought-book. A sunny, cloudless sky was for her a blank leaf; and for several days she had only had such leaves before her.

It was in the warm summer-time; not a breeze moved through the glowing hot days. Every leaf, every flower, lay as if it were torpid, and the people seemed torpid too.

Then the clouds arose and covered the region round about where the gleaming mist announced " Here lies Paris."

The clouds piled themselves up like a chain of mountains, hurried on through the air, and spread themselves abroad over the whole landscape, so far as the Dryad's eye could reach.

Like enormous blue-black blocks of rock the clouds lay piled over one another. Gleams of lightning shot forth from them.

"These also are the servants of the Lord God," the old clergyman had said. And there came a bluish dazzling flash of lightning, a lighting up as if of the sun itself, which could burst blocks of rock asunder. The lightning struck and split to the roots the old venerable oak. The crown fell asunder : it seemed as if the tree were stretching forth its arms to clasp the messengers of the light.

No bronze cannon can sound over the land at the birth of a royal child as the thunder sounded at the death of the old oak. The rain streamed down ; a refreshing wind was blowing ; the storm had gone by, and there was quite a holiday glow on all things. The old clergyman spoke a few words for honourable remembrance, and a painter made a drawing, as a lasting record of the tree.

"Everything passes away," said the Dryad; "passes away like a cloud, and never comes back ! "

The old clergyman, too, did not come back. The green roof of his school was gone, and his teaching-chair had vanished. The children did not come ; but autumn came, and winter came, and then spring also. In all this change of seasons the Dryad looked toward the region where, at night, Paris gleamed with its bright mist far on the horizon.

Forth from the town rushed engine after engine, train after train, whistling and screaming at all hours in the day. In the evening, towards midnight, at daybreak, and all the day through, came the trains. Out of each one, and into each one, streamed people from the country of every king: a new wonder of the world had summoned them to Paris.

In what form did this wonder exhibit itself ?

"A splendid blossom of art and industry," said one, " has unfolded itself in the Champ de Mars—a gigantic sunflower, from whose petals one can learn geography and statistics, and can become as wise as a lord mayor, and raise oneself to the level of art and poetry, and study the greatness and power of the various lands."

"A fairy tale flower," said another, "a many-coloured lotus-plant, which spreads out its green leaves like a velvet carpet over the sand. The opening spring has brought it forth, the summer will see it in all its splendour, the autumn winds will sweep it away, so that not a leaf, not a fragment of its root shall remain."

In front of the Military School extends in times of peace the arena of war—a field without a blade of grass, a piece of sandy steppe, as if cut out of the Desert of Africa, where *Fata Morgana* displays her wondrous airy castles and hanging gardens. In the Champ de Mars, however, these were to be seen more splendid, more wonderful than in the East, for human art had converted the airy deceptive scenes into reality.

"The Aladdin's Palace of the present has been built," it was said. "Day by day, hour by hour, it unfolds more of its wonderful splendour."

The endless halls shine in marble and many colours. "Master Blood-less" here moves his limbs of steel and iron in the great circular hall of machinery. Works of art in metal, in stone, in Gobelins tapestry announce the vitality of mind that is stirring in every land. Halls of paintings, splendour of flowers, everything that mind and skill can create in the workshop of the artizan has been placed here for show. Even the memorials of ancient days, out of old graves and turf-moors, have appeared at this general meeting.

The overpowering great variegated whole must be divided into small portions, and pressed together like a plaything, if it is to be understood and described.

Like a great table on Christmas Eve, the Champ de Mars carried a wonder-castle of industry and art; and around this knicknacks from all countries had been ranged—knicknacks on a grand scale, for every nation found some remembrance of home.

Here stood the royal palace of Egypt, there the Caravanserai of the desert land. The Bedouin had quitted his sunny country, and hastened by on his camel. Here stood the Russian stables, with the fiery glorious horses of the steppe. Here stood the simple straw-thatched dwelling of the Danish peasant, with the Dannebrog flag, next to Gustavus Vasa's wooden house from Dalarne, with its wonderful carvings. American huts, English cottages, French pavilions, kiosks, theatres, churches, all strewn around, and between them the fresh green turf, the clear springing water, blooming bushes, rare trees, hothouses, in which one might fancy oneself transported into the tropical forest; whole gardens brought from Damascus, and blooming under one roof. What colours, what fragrance !

Artificial grottoes surrounded bodies of fresh or of salt water, and gave a glimpse into the empire of the fishes; the visitor seemed to wander at the bottom of the sea, among fishes and polypi.

"All this," they said, "the Champ de Mars offers;" and around the great richly-spread table the crowd of human beings moves like a busy swarm of ants, on foot or in little carriages, for not all feet are equal to such a fatiguing journey.

Hither they swarm from morning till late in the evening. Steamer after steamer, crowded with people, glides down the Seine. The number of carriages is continually on the increase. The swarm of people on foot and on horseback grows more and more dense. Carriages and omnibuses are crowded, stuffed and embroidered with people. All these tributary streams flow in one direction—towards the Exhibition. On every entrance the flag of France is displayed; around the world's bazaar wave the flags of all nations. There is a humming and a murmuring from the hall of the machines; from the towers the melody of the chimes is heard; with the tones of the organs in the churches mingle the hoarse nasal songs from the *cafés* of the East. It is a kingdom of Babel, a wonder of the world !

In very truth it was. That's what all the reports said, and who did not hear them? The Dryad knew everything that is told here of the new wonder in the city of cities.

"Fly away, ye birds! fly away to see, and then come back and tell me," said the Dryad.'

The wish became an intense desire—became the one thought of a life. Then, in the quiet silent night, while the full moon was shining, the Dryad saw a spark fly out of the moon's disc, and fall like a shooting star. And before the tree, whose leaves waved to and fro as if they were stirred by a tempest, stood a noble, mighty, and grand figure. In tones that were at once rich and strong, like the trumpet of the Last Judgment bidding farewell to life and summoning to the great account, it said,

DIGGING UP THE TREE.

"Thou shalt go to the city of magic; thou shalt take root there, and enjoy the mighty rushing breezes, the air, and the sunshine there. But the time of thy life shall then be shortened; the line of years that awaited thee here amid the free nature shall shrink to but a small tale. Poor Dryad! it shall be thy destruction. Thy yearning and longing will increase, thy desire will grow more stormy, the tree itself will be as a prison to thee, thou wilt quit thy cell and give up thy nature to fly out and mingle among men. Then the years that would have belonged to thee will be contracted to half the span of the ephemeral fly, that lives but a day: *one night*, and thy life-taper shall be blown out—the leaves of the tree will wither and be blown away, to become green never again!"

Thus the words sounded. And the light vanished away, but not the longing of the Dryad: she trembled in the wild fever of expectation.

"I shall go there!" she cried, rejoicingly. "Life is beginning and swells like a cloud; nobody knows whither it is hastening."

When the grey dawn arose, and the moon turned pale and the clouds were tinted red, the wished-for hour struck. The words of promise were fulfilled.

People appeared with spades and poles; they dug round the roots of the tree, deeper and deeper, and beneath it. A waggon was brought out, drawn by many horses, and the tree was lifted up, with its roots and the lumps of earth that adhered to them; matting was placed around the roots, as though the tree had its feet in a warm bag. And now the tree was lifted on the waggon and secured with chains. The journey began, the journey to Paris. There the tree was to grow as an ornament to the city of French glory.

The twigs and the leaves of the chestnut tree trembled in the first moments of its being moved; and the Dryad trembled in the pleasurable feeling of expectation.

"Away! away!" it sounded in every beat of her pulse. "Away! away!" sounded in words that flew trembling along. The Dryad forgot to bid farewell to the regions of home; she thought not of the waving grass and of the innocent daisies, which had looked up to her as to a great lady, a young Princess playing at being a shepherdess out in the open air.

The chestnut tree stood upon the waggon, and nodded his branches: whether this meant "farewell" or "forward," the Dryad knew not; she dreamed only of the marvellous new things, that seemed yet so familiar, and that were to unfold themselves before her. No child's heart rejoicing in innocence—no heart whose blood danced with passion—had set out on the journey to Paris more full of expectation than she.

Her "farewell" sounded in the words "Away! away!"

The wheels turned; the distant approached; the present vanished. The region was changed, even as the clouds change. New vineyards, forests, villages, villas appeared—came nearer—vanished!

The chestnut tree moved forward, and the Dryad went with it. Steam-engine after steam-engine rushed past, sending up into the air vapoury clouds, that formed figures which told of Paris, whence they came, and whither the Dryad was going.

Everything around knew it, and must know whither she was bound. It seemed to her as if every tree she passed stretched out its leaves towards her, with the prayer—"Take me with you! take me with you!" for every tree enclosed a longing Dryad.

What changes during this flight! Houses seemed to be rising out of the earth—more and more—thicker and thicker. The chimneys rose like flower-pots ranged side by side, or in rows one above the other, on the roofs. Great inscriptions in letters a yard long, and figures in various colours, covering the walls from cornice to basement, came brightly out.

"Where does Paris begin, and when shall I be there?" asked the Dryad.

The crowd of people grew; the tumult and the bustle increased; carriage followed upon carriage; people on foot and people on horse-

back were mingled together;—all around were shops on shops, music
and song, crying and talking.

The Dryad, in her tree, was now in the midst of Paris. The great heavy
waggon all at once stopped on a little square planted with trees. The
high houses around had all of them balconies to the windows, from which
the inhabitants looked down upon the young fresh chestnut tree, which
was coming to be planted here as a substitute for the dead tree that lay
stretched on the ground.

The passers-by stood still and smiled in admiration of its pure vernal
freshness. The older trees, whose buds were still closed, whispered with
their waving branches, "Welcome! welcome!" The fountain, throwing its jet of water high up in the air, to let it fall again in the wide
stone basin, told the wind to sprinkle the new-comer with pearly drops,
as if it wished to give him a refreshing draught to welcome him.

THE TREE'S ADMIRERS.

The Dryad felt how her tree was being lifted from the waggon to be
placed in the spot where it was to stand. The roots were covered with
earth, and fresh turf was laid on the top. Blooming shrubs and flowers
in pots were ranged around; and thus a little garden arose in the square.

The tree that had been killed by the fumes of gas, the steam of
kitchens, and the bad air of the city, was put upon the waggon and
driven away. The passers-by looked on. Children and old men sat
upon the bench, and looked at the green tree. And we who are telling
this story stood upon a balcony, and looked down upon the green spring
light that had been brought in from the fresh country air, and said,
what the old clergyman would have said, "Poor Dryad!"

"I am happy! I am happy!" the Dryad cried, rejoicing; "and yet I
cannot realize, cannot describe what I feel. Everything is as I fancied
it, and yet as I did not fancy it."

The houses stood there, so lofty, so close! The sunlight shone on only one of the walls, and that one was stuck over with bills and placards, before which the people stood still; and this made a crowd.

Carriages rushed past, carriages rolled past; light ones and heavy ones mingled together. Omnibuses, those over-crowded moving houses, came rattling by; horsemen galloped among them; even carts and waggons asserted their rights.

The Dryad asked herself if these high-grown houses, which stood so close around her, would not remove and take other shapes, like the clouds in the sky, and draw aside, so that she might cast a glance into Paris, and over it. Notre Dame must show itself, the Vendôme Column, and the wondrous building which had called and was still calling so many strangers to the city.

But the houses did not stir from their places. It was yet day when the lamps were lit. The gas-jets gleamed from the shops, and shone even into the branches of the trees, so that it was like sunlight in summer. The stars above made their appearance, the same to which the Dryad had looked up in her home. She thought she felt a clear pure stream of air which went forth from them. She felt herself lifted up and strengthened, and felt an increased power of seeing through every leaf and through every fibre of the root. Amid all the noise and the turmoil, the colours and the lights, she knew herself watched by mild eyes.

From the side streets sounded the merry notes of fiddles and wind instruments. Up! to the dance, to the dance! to jollity and pleasure! that was their invitation. Such music it was, that horses, carriages, trees, and houses would have danced, if they had known how. The charm of intoxicating delight filled the bosom of the Dryad.

"How glorious, how splendid it is!" she cried, rejoicingly. "Now I am in Paris!"

The next day that dawned, the next night that fell, offered the same spectacle, similar bustle, similar life; changing, indeed, yet always the same; and thus it went on through the sequence of days.

"Now I know every tree, every flower on the square here! I know every house, every balcony, every shop in this narrow cut-off corner, where I am denied the sight of the great mighty city. Where are the arches of triumph, the Boulevards, the wondrous building of the world? I see nothing of all this. As if shut up in a cage, I stand among the high houses, which I now know by heart, with their inscriptions, signs, and placards; all the painted confectionery, that is no longer to my taste. Where are all the things of which I heard, for which I longed, and for whose sake I wanted to come hither? What have I seized, found, won? I feel the same longing I felt before; I feel that there is a life I should wish to grasp and to experience. I must go out into the ranks of living men, and mingle among them. I must fly about like a bird. I must see and feel, and become human altogether. I must enjoy the one half-day, instead of vegetating for years in everyday sameness and weariness; in which I become ill, and at last sink and disappear like the dew on the meadows. I will gleam like the cloud; gleam in the sunshine of life, look out over the whole like the cloud, and pass away like it, no one knoweth whither."

Thus sighed the Dryad; and she prayed:

"Take from me the years that were destined for me, and give me but half of the life of the ephemeral fly! Deliver me from my prison! Give me human life, human happiness, only a short span, only the one night, if it cannot be otherwise; and then punish me for my wish to live, my longing for life! Strike me out of thy list: let my shell, the fresh young tree, wither, or be hewn down, and burnt to ashes, and scattered to all the winds!"

THE BEAUTIFUL DRYAD.

A rustling went through the leaves of the tree; there was a trembling in each of the leaves; it seemed as though fire streamed through it. A gust of wind shook its green crown, and from the midst of that crown a female figure came forth. In the same moment she was sitting beneath the brightly-illuminated leafy branches, young and beautiful to behold, like poor Mary, to whom the clergyman had said, "The great city will be thy destruction!"

The Dryad sat at the foot of the tree—at her house door, which she had locked, and whose key she had thrown away. So young! so fair! The stars saw her, and blinked at her. The gas-lamps saw her, and gleamed and beckoned to her. How delicate she was, and yet how blooming!—a child, and yet a grown maiden! Her dress was fine as silk, green as the freshly-opened leaves on the crown of the tree; in her nut-brown hair clung a half-opened chestnut blossom. She looked like the Goddess of Spring.

For one short minute she sat motionless; then she sprang up, and, light as a gazelle, she hurried away. She ran and sprang like the reflection from the mirror that, carried by the sunshine, is cast, now here, now there.   Could any one have followed her with his eyes, he would have seen how marvellously her dress and her form changed, according to the nature of the house or the place whose light happened to shine upon her.

She reached the Boulevards.   Here a sea of light streamed forth from the gas-flames of the lamps, the shops, and the *cafés*.   Here stood in a row young and slender trees, each of which concealed its Dryad, and gave shade from the artificial sunlight.   The whole vast pavement was one great festive hall, where covered tables stood laden with refreshments of all kinds, from champagne and Chartreuse down to coffee and beer.   Here was an exhibition of flowers, statues, books, and coloured stuffs.

From the crowd close by the lofty houses she looked forth over the terrific stream beyond the rows of trees.   Yonder heaved a stream of rolling carriages, cabriolets, coaches, omnibuses, cabs, and among them riding gentlemen and marching troops.   To cross to the opposite shore was an undertaking fraught with danger to life and limb.   Now lanterns shed their radiance abroad ; now the gas had the upper hand ; and suddenly a rocket rises !   Whence ?   Whither ?

Here are sounds of soft Italian melodies : yonder, Spanish songs are sung, accompanied by the rattle of the castanets ; but strongest of all, and predominating over the rest, the street-organ tunes of the moment, the exciting " *Car-can* " music, which Orpheus never knew, and which was never heard by the " *belle Hélène* : " even the barrow was tempted to hop upon one of its wheels.

The Dryad danced, floated, flew, changing her colour every moment, like a humming-bird in the sunshine ; each house, with the world belonging to it, gave her its own reflections.

As the glowing lotus-flower, torn from its stem, is carried away by the stream, so the Dryad drifted along.   Whenever she paused, she was another being, so that none was able to follow her, to recognize her, or to look more closely at her.

Like cloud-pictures, all things flew by her : she looked into a thousand faces, but not one was familiar to her ; she saw not a single form from home.   Two bright eyes had remained in her memory : she thought of Mary, poor Mary, the ragged merry child, who wore the red flowers in her black hair.   Mary was now here, in the world-city, rich and magnificent as in that day when she drove past the house of the old clergyman and past the tree of the Dryad, the old oak.

Here she was certainly living, in the deafening tumult.   Perhaps she had just stepped out of one of the gorgeous carriages in waiting. Handsome equipages, with coachmen in gold braid, and footmen in silken hose, drove up.   The people who alighted from them were all richly dressed ladies.   They went through the opened gate, and ascended the broad staircase that led to a building resting on marble pillars.   Was this building, perhaps, the wonder of the world ?   There Mary would certainly be found.

"Sancta Maria!" resounded from the interior. Incense floated through the lofty painted and gilded aisles, where a solemn twilight reigned.

It was the Church of the Madeleine.

Clad in black garments of the most costly stuffs, fashioned according to the latest mode, the rich feminine world of Paris glided across the shining pavement. The crests of the proprietors were engraved on silver shields on the velvet-bound prayer-books, and embroidered in the corners of perfumed handkerchiefs bordered with Brussels lace. A few of the ladies were kneeling in silent prayer before the altars; others resorted to the confessionals.

Anxiety and fear took possession of the Dryad; she felt as if she had entered a place where she had no right to be. Here was the abode of silence, the hall of secrets: everything was said in whispers, every word was a mystery.

The Dryad saw herself enveloped in lace and silk, like the women of wealth and of high birth around her. Had, perhaps, every one of them a longing in her breast, like the Dryad?

A deep, painful sigh was heard. Did it escape from some confessional in a distant corner, or from the bosom of the Dryad? She drew the veil closer around her; she breathed incense, and not the fresh air. Here was not the abiding-place of her longing.

Away! away!—a hastening without rest. The ephemeral fly knows not repose, for her existence is flight.

She was out again among the gas candelabra by a magnificent fountain. "All its streaming waters are not able to wash out the innocent blood that was spilt here."

Such were the words spoken. Strangers stood around, carrying on a lively conversation, such as no one would have dared to carry on in the gorgeous hall of secrets whence the Dryad came.

A heavy stone slab was turned and then lifted. She did not understand why. She saw an opening that led into the depths below. The strangers stepped down, leaving the starlit air and the cheerful life of the upper world behind them.

"I am afraid," said one of the women who stood around, to her husband, "I cannot venture to go down, nor do I care for the wonders down yonder. You had better stay here with me."

"Indeed, and travel home," said the man, "and quit Paris without having seen the most wonderful thing of all—the real wonder of the present period, created by the power and resolution of one man!"

"I will not go down for all that," was the reply.

"The wonder of the present time," it had been called: the Dryad had heard and had understood it. The goal of her ardent longing had thus been reached, and here was the entrance to it. Down into the depths below Paris? She had not thought of such a thing; but now she heard it said, and saw the strangers descending, and went after them.

The staircase was of cast iron, spiral, broad, and easy. Below there burned a lamp, and farther down, another. They stood in a labyrinth of endless halls and arched passages, all communicating with each other. All the streets and lanes of Paris were to be seen here again, as in a dim reflection. The names were painted up; and every house above had its number down here also, and struck its roots under the macadamized quays of a broad canal, in which the muddy water flowed onward. Over it the fresh streaming water was carried on arches; and quite at the top hung the tangled net of gas-pipes and telegraph-wires.

In the distance lamps gleamed, like a reflection from the world-city above. Every now and then a dull rumbling was heard: this came from the heavy waggons rolling over the entrance bridges.

Whither had the Dryad come?

You have, no doubt, heard of the Catacombs? Now they are vanishing-points in that new underground world—that wonder of the present day—the sewers of Paris. The Dryad was there, and not in the world's Exhibition in the Champ de Mars.

She heard exclamations of wonder and admiration.

"From here go forth health and life for thousands upon thousands up yonder! Our time is the time of progress, with its manifold blessings."

Such was the opinion and the speech of men; but not of those creatures who had been born here, and who built and dwelt here—of the rats, namely, who were squeaking to one another in the clefts of a crumbling wall, quite plainly, and in a way the Dryad understood well.

A big old Father-Rat, with his tail bitten off, was relieving his feelings in loud squeaks; and his family gave their tribute of concurrence to every word he said:

"I am disgusted with this man-mewing," he cried—"with these outbursts of ignorance. A fine magnificence, truly! all made up of gas and petroleum! I can't eat such stuff as that. Everything here is so fine and bright now, that one's ashamed of oneself, without exactly knowing why. Ah, if we only lived in the days of tallow candles! and it does not lie so very far behind us. That was a romantic time, as one may say."

"What are you talking of there?" asked the Dryad. "I have never seen you before. What is it you are talking about?"

"Of the glorious days that are gone," said the Rat,—"of the happy times of our great-grandfathers and great-grandmothers. Then it was a great thing to get down here. That was a rat's nest quite different from Paris. Mother Plague used to live here then; she killed people, but never rats. Robbers and smugglers could breathe freely here. Here was the meeting-place of the most interesting personages, whom one now only gets to see in the theatres where they act melodramas, up above. The time of romance is gone even in our rats' nest; and here also fresh air and petroleum have broken in."

Thus squeaked the Rat; he squeaked in honour of the old time, when Mother Plague was still alive.

A carriage stopped, a kind of open omnibus, drawn by swift horses. The company mounted and drove away along the Boulevard de Sebastopol, that is to say, the underground boulevard, over which the well-known crowded street of that name extended.

The carriage disappeared in the twilight; the Dryad disappeared,
lifted to the cheerful freshness above. Here, and not below in the
vaulted passages, filled with heavy air, the wonder work must be found
which she was to seek in her short lifetime. It must gleam brighter
than all the gas-flames, stronger than the moon that was just gliding
past.

Yes, certainly, she saw it yonder in the distance: it gleamed before
her, and twinkled and glittered like the evening star in the sky.

She saw a glittering portal open, that led to a little garden, where all
was brightness and dance music. Coloured lamps surrounded little
lakes, in which were water-plants of coloured metal, from whose flowers
jets of water spirted up. Beautiful weeping willows—real products of
spring—hung their fresh branches over these lakes like a fresh, green,
transparent, and yet screening veil. In the bushes burnt an open fire,
throwing a red twilight over the quiet huts of branches, into which the
sounds of music penetrated—an ear-tickling, intoxicating music, that
sent the blood coursing through the veins.

Beautiful girls in festive attire, with pleasant smiles on their lips,
and the light spirit of youth in their hearts—" Marys," with roses in
their hair, but without carriage and postillion—flitted to and fro in the
wild dance.

Where were the heads, where the feet? As if stung by tarantulas,
they sprang, laughed, rejoiced, as if in their ecstacies they were going
to embrace all the world.

The Dryad felt herself torn with them into the whirl of the dance.
Round her delicate foot clung the silken boot, chestnut brown in colour,
like the ribbon that fluttered from her hair down upon her bare shoulders. The green silk dress waved in large folds, but did not entirely
hide the pretty foot and ankle.

Had she come to the enchanted Garden of Armida? What was the
name of the place?

The name glittered in gas-jets over the entrance. It was " Mabille."

The soaring upwards of rockets, the splashing of the fountains, and
the popping of champagne corks accompanied the wild bacchantic dance.
Over the whole glided the moon through the air, clear, but with a somewhat crooked face.

A wild joviality seemed to rush through the Dryad, as though she
were intoxicated with opium. Her eyes spoke, her lips spoke, but the
sound of violins and of flutes drowned the sound of her voice. Her
partner whispered words to her which she did not understand, nor do
we understand them. He stretched out his arms to draw her to him,
but he embraced only the empty air.

The Dryad had been carried away, like a rose-leaf on the wind. Before her she saw a flame in the air, a flashing light high up on a tower.
The beacon light shone from the goal of her longing—shone from the
red lighthouse tower of the *Fata Morgana* of the Champ de Mars.
Thither she was carried by the wind. She circled round the tower;

the workmen thought it was a butterfly that had come too early, and that now sank down dying.

The moon shone bright, gas-lamps spread light around, through the halls, over the all-the-world's buildings scattered about, over the rose-hills and the rocks produced by human ingenuity, from which waterfalls, driven by the power of "Master Bloodless," fell down. The caverns of the sea, the depths of the lakes, the kingdom of the fishes were opened here. Men walked as in the depths of the deep pond, and held converse with the sea, in the diving-bell of glass. The water pressed against the strong glass walls above and on every side. The polypi, eel-like living creatures, had fastened themselves to the bottom, and stretched out arms, fathoms long, for prey. A big turbot was making himself broad in front, quietly enough, but not without casting some suspicious glances aside. A crab clambered over him, looking like a gigantic spider, while the shrimps wandered about in restless haste, like the butterflies and moths of the sea.

In the fresh water grew water-lilies, nymphœa, and reeds; the gold-fishes stood up below in rank and file, all turning their heads one way, that the streaming water might flow into their mouths. Fat carps stared at the glass wall with stupid eyes. They knew that they were here to be exhibited, and that they had made the somewhat toilsome journey hither in tubs filled with water; and they thought with dismay of the land-sickness from which they had suffered so cruelly on the railway.

They had come to see the Exhibition, and now contemplated it from their fresh or salt-water position. They looked attentively at the crowds of people who passed by them early and late. All the nations in the world, they thought, had made an exhibition of their inhabitants, for the edification of the soles and haddocks, pike and carp, that they might give their opinions upon the different kinds.

"Those are scaly animals!" said a little slimy Whiting. "They put on different scales two or three times a day, and they emit sounds which they call speaking. We don't put on scales, and we make ourselves understood in an easier way, simply by twitching the corners of our mouths and staring with our eyes. We have a great many advantages over mankind."

"But they have learned swimming of us," remarked a well-educa Codling. "You must know I come from the great sea outside. In the hot time of the year the people yonder go into the water: first they take off their scales, and then they swim. They have learnt from the frogs to kick out with their hind legs, and row with their fore paws. But they cannot hold out long. They want to be like us, but they cannot come up to us. Poor people!"

And the fishes stared: they thought that the whole swarm of people whom they had seen in the bright daylight were still moving around them; they were certain they still saw the same forms that had first caught their attention.

A pretty Barbel, with spotted skin and an enviably round back, declared that the "human fry" were still there.

"I can see a well set-up human figure quite well," said the Darbel. " She was called 'contumacious lady,' or something of that kind. She had a mouth and staring eyes, like ours, and a great balloon at the back of her head, and something like a shut-up umbrella in front; there were a lot of dangling bits of sea-weed hanging about her. She ought to take all the rubbish off, and go as we do; then she would look something like a respectable barbel, so far as it is possible for a person to look like one!"

THE FISH.

" What's become of that one whom they drew away with the hook? He sat on a wheel-chair, and had paper, and pen, and ink, and wrote down everything. They called him a 'writer.'"

"They're going about with him still," said a hoary old maid of a Carp, who carried her misfortune about with her, so that she was quite hoarse. In her youth, namely, she had once swallowed a hook, and still swam patiently about with it in her gullet. "A writer? That means, as we fishes should describe it, a kind of cuttle or ink-fish, among men."

Thus the fishes gossiped in their own way; but in the artificial water-grotto the labourers were busy, who were obliged to take advantage of the hours of night to get their work done by daybreak. They accompanied with blows of their hammers, and with songs, the parting words of the vanishing Dryad.

"So, at any rate, I have seen you, you pretty gold-fishes," she said. "Yes, I know you," and she waved her hand to them. "I have known about you a long time in my home; the swallow told me about you. How beautiful you are! how delicate and shining! I should like to kiss every one of you. You others, also: I know you all; but you do not know me."

The fishes stared out into the twilight.   They did not understand a word of it.

The Dryad was there no longer.   She had been a long time in the open air, where the different countries, the country of black bread, the cod-fish coast, the kingdom of Russia leather, and the banks of eau-de-Cologne, and the gardens of rose oil, exhaled their perfumes from the world-wonder flower.

When, after a night at a ball, we drive home half asleep and half awake, the melodies still sound plainly in our ears; we hear them, and could sing them all from memory.   When the eye of the murdered man closes, the picture of what it saw last clings to it for a time like a photographic picture.

So it was likewise here: the bustling life of day had not yet disappeared in the quiet night.   The Dryad had seen it; she knew, thus it will be repeated to-morrow.

BY THE FOUNTAIN.

The Dryad stood among the fragrant roses, and thought she knew them and had seen them in her own home.   She also saw red pomegranate flowers, like those that little Mary had worn in her dark hair.

Remembrances from the home of her childhood flashed through her thoughts; her eyes eagerly drank in the prospect around, and feverish restlessness chased her through the wonder-filled halls.

A weariness that increased continually took possession of her.   She felt a longing to rest on the soft Oriental carpets within, or to lean against the weeping willow without by the clear water   But for the ephemeral fly there was no rest.   In a few moments the day had completed its circle.

Her thoughts trembled, her limbs trembled, she sank down on the grass by the bubbling water.

"Thou wilt ever spring living from the earth," she said mournfully. "Moisten my tongue—bring me a refreshing draught."

"I am no living water," was the answer. "I only spring upward when the machine wills it."

"Give me something of thy freshness, thou green grass," implored the Dryad; "give me one of thy fragrant flowers."

"We must die if we are torn from our stalks," replied the Flowers and the Grass.

"Give me a kiss, thou fresh stream of air—only a single life-kiss."

"Soon the sun will kiss the clouds red," answered the Wind; "then thou wilt be among the dead—blown away, as all the splendour here will be blown away before the year shall have ended. Then I can play again with the light loose sand on the place here, and whirl the dust over the land and through the air. All is dust!"

The Dryad felt a terror like a woman who has cut asunder her pulse-artery in the bath, but is filled again with the love of life, even while she is bleeding to death. She raised herself, tottered forward a few steps, and sank down again at the entrance to a little church. The gate stood open, lights were burning upon the altar, and the organ sounded.

What music! Such notes the Dryad had never yet heard; and yet it seemed to her as if she recognized a number of well-known voices among them. They came deep from the heart of all creation. She thought she felt the sighing of the old oak tree; she thought she heard the stories of the old clergyman, of great deeds, and of the celebrated names, and of the gifts that the creatures of God must bestow upon posterity, if they would live on in the world.

The tones of the organ swelled, and in their song there sounded these words:

"Thy wishing and thy longing have torn thee, with thy roots, from the place which God appointed for thee. That was thy destruction, thou poor Dryad!"

The notes became soft and gentle, and seemed to die away in a wail.

In the sky the clouds showed themselves with a ruddy gleam. The Wind sighed,

"Pass away, ye dead! now the sun is going to rise!"

The first ray fell on the Dryad. Her form was irradiated in changing colours, like the soap-bubble when it is bursting and becomes a drop of water; like a tear that falls and passes away like a vapour.

Poor Dryad! Only a dew-drop, only a tear, poured upon the earth, and vanished away!

THE THISTLE'S EXPERIENCES.

BELONGING to the lordly manor house was a beautiful well-kept garden, with rare trees and flowers; the guests of the proprietor declared their admiration of it: the people of the neighbourhood, from town and country, came on Sundays and holidays, and asked permission to see the garden; indeed, whole schools used to pay visits to it.

Outside the garden, by the palings at the road-side, stood a great mighty Thistle, which spread out in many directions from the root, so that it might have been called a thistle bush. Nobody looked at it, except the old Ass which drew the milk-maid's cart. This Ass used to stretch out his neck towards the Thistle, and say, "You are beautiful; I should like to eat you!" But his halter was not long enough to let him reach it and eat it.

There was great company at the manor house—some very noble people from the capital; young pretty girls; and among them a young lady who came from a long distance. She had come from Scotland, and was of high birth, and was rich in land and in gold—a bride worth winning, said more than one of the young gentlemen; and their lady mothers said the same thing.

The young people amused themselves on the lawn, and played at ball; they wandered among the flowers, and each of the young girls broke off a flower, and fastened it in a young gentleman's button-hole. But the young Scotch lady looked round, for a long time, in an undecided way. None of the flowers seemed to suit her taste. Then her eye glanced across the paling—outside stood the great thistle bush, with the reddish-blue, sturdy flowers: she saw them, she smiled, and asked the son of the house to pluck one for her.

"It is the flower of Scotland," she said. "It blooms in the scutcheon of my country. Give me yonder flower."

And he brought the fairest blossom, and pricked his fingers as completely as if it had grown on the sharpest rose bush.

She placed the thistle-flower in the button-hole of the young man, and he felt himself highly honoured. Each of the other young gentlemen would willingly have given his own beautiful flower to have worn this one, presented by the fair hand of the Scottish maiden. And if the son of the house felt himself honoured, what were the feelings of the Thistle bush? It seemed to him as if dew and sunshine were streaming through him.

"I am something more than I knew of," said the Thistle to itself. "I suppose my right place is really inside the palings, and not outside. One is often strangely placed in this world; but now I have at least managed to get one of my people within the pale, and indeed into a button-hole!"

The Thistle told this event to every blossom that unfolded itself; and not many days had gone by before the Thistle heard, not from men, not from the twittering of the birds, but from the air itself, which stores up the sounds, and carries them far around—out of the most retired walks of the garden, and out of the rooms of the house, in which doors and windows stood open, that the young gentleman who had received the thistle-flower from the hand of the fair Scottish maiden had also now received the heart and hand of the lady in question. They were a handsome pair—it was a good match.

"That match *I* made up!" said the Thistle; and he thought of the flower he had given for the button-hole. Every flower that opened heard of this occurrence.

"I shall certainly be transplanted into the garden," thought the Thistle, "and perhaps put into a pot, which crowds one in: that is said to be the greatest of all honours."

And the Thistle pictured this to himself in such a lively manner, that at last he said, with full conviction, "I am to be transplanted into a pot."

Then he promised every little thistle-flower which unfolded itself that it also should be put into a pot, and perhaps into a button-hole, the highest honour that could be attained. But not one of them was put into a pot, much less into a button-hole. They drank in the sunlight and the air; lived on the sunlight by day, and on the dew by night; bloomed —were visited by bees and hornets, who looked after the honey, the dowry of the flower, and they took the honey, and left the flower where it was.

"The thievish rabble!" said the Thistle. "If I could only stab every one of them! But I cannot."

The flowers hung their heads and faded; but after a time new ones came.

"You come in good time," said the Thistle. "I am expecting every moment to get across the fence."

A few innocent daisies, and a long thin dandelion, stood and listened in deep admiration, and believed everything they heard.

The old Ass of the milk-cart stood at the edge of the field-road, and glanced across at the blooming thistle bush; but his halter was too short, and he could not reach it.

And the Thistle thought so long of the thistle of Scotland, to whose family he said he belonged, that he fancied at last that he had come from Scotland, and that his parents had been put into the national escutcheon. That was a great thought; but, you see, a great thistle has a right to a great thought.

"One is often of so grand a family, that one may not know it," said the Nettle, who grew close by. He had a kind of idea that he might be made into cambric if he were rightly treated

And the summer went by, and the autumn went by. The leaves fell from the trees, and the few flowers left had deeper colours and less scent. The gardener's boy sang in the garden, across the palings:

> "Up the hill, down the dale we wend,
> That is life, from beginning to end."

The young fir trees in the forest began to long for Christmas, but it was a long time to Christmas yet.

"Here I am standing yet!" said the Thistle. "It is as if nobody thought of me, and yet I managed the match. They were betrothed, and they have had their wedding; it is now a week ago. I won't take a single step—because I can't."

A few more weeks went by. The Thistle stood there with his last single flower large and full. This flower had shot up from near the roots; the wind blew cold over it, the colours vanished, and the flower grew in size, and looked like a silvered sunflower.

One day the young pair, now man and wife, came into the garden. They went along by the paling, and the young wife looked across it

"There's the great thistle still growing," she said. "It has no flowers now."

"Oh, yes, the ghost of the last one is there still," said he. And he pointed to the silvery remains of the flower, which looked like a flower themselves.

"It is pretty, certainly," she said. "Such an one must be carved on the frame of our picture."

And the young man had to climb across the palings again, and to break off the calyx of the thistle. It pricked his fingers, but then he had called it a ghost. And this thistle-calyx came into the garden, and into the house, and into the drawing-room. There stood a picture— "The Young Couple." A thistle-flower was painted in the button-hole of the bridegroom. They spoke about this, and also about the thistle-flower they brought, the last thistle-flower, now gleaming like silver, whose picture was carved on the frame.

And the breeze carried what was spoken away, far away.

"What one can experience!" said the Thistle Bush. "My first-born was put into a button-hole, and my youngest has been put in a frame. Where shall *I* go?"

And the Ass stood by the road-side, and looked across at the Thistle.

"Come to me, my nibble darling!" said he. "I can't get across to you."

But the Thistle did not answer. He became more and more thoughtful —kept on thinking and thinking till near Christmas, and then a flower of thought came forth.

"If the children are only good, the parents do not mind standing outside the garden pale."

"That's an honourable thought," said the Sunbeam. "You shall also have a good place."

"In a pot or in a frame?" asked the Thistle.

"In a story," replied the Sunbeam.

MEG AT HOME.

POULTRY MEG'S FAMILY.

POULTRY MEG was the only person who lived in the new stately dwelling that had been built for the fowls and ducks belonging to the manor house. It stood there where once the old knightly building had stood with its tower, its pointed gables, its moat, and its drawbridge. Close by it was a wilderness of trees and thicket; here the garden had been, and had stretched out to a great lake, which was now moorland. Crows and choughs flew screaming over the old trees, and there were crowds of birds; they did not seem to get fewer when any one shot among them, but seemed rather to increase. One heard the screaming into the poultry-house, where Poultry Meg sat with the ducklings running to and fro over her wooden shoes. She knew every fowl and every duck from the moment it crept out of the shell; and she was fond of her fowls and her ducks, and proud of the stately house that had been built for them.   Her own little room in the house was clean and neat, for that was the wish of the gracious lady to whom the house belonged. She often came in the company of grand noble guests, to whom she showed "the hens' and ducks' barracks," as she called the little house.

Here were a clothes cupboard, and an arm-chair, and even a chest of drawers ; and on these drawers a polished metal plate had been placed, whereon was engraved the word " Grubbe," and this was the name of the noble family that had lived in the house of old. The brass plate had been found when they were digging the foundation ; and the clerk had said it had no value except in being an old relic. The clerk knew all about the place, and about the old times, for he had his knowledge from books, and many a memorandum had been written and put in his table-drawer. But the oldest of the crows perhaps knew more than he, and screamed it out in her own language—but that was the crow's language, and the clerk did not understand that, clever as he was.

After the hot summer days the mist sometimes hung over the moorland as if a whole lake were behind the old trees, among which the crows and the daws were fluttering ; and thus it had looked when the good Knight Grubbe had lived here—when the old manor house stood with its thick red walls. The dog-chain used to reach in those days quite over the gateway ; through the tower one went into a paved passage which led to the rooms ; the windows were narrow, and the panes were small, even in the great hall where the dancing used to be ; but in the time of the last Grubbe there had been no dancing in the hall within the memory of man, although an old drum still lay there that had served as part of the music. Here stood a quaintly carved cupboard, in which rare flower-roots were kept, for my Lady Grubbe was fond of plants and cultivated trees and shrubs. Her husband preferred riding out to shoot wolves and boars ; and his little daughter Marie always went with him part of the way. When she was only five years old, she would sit proudly on her horse, and look saucily round with her great black eyes. It was a great amusement to her to hit out among the hunting-dogs with her whip ; but her father would rather have seen her hit among the peasant boys, who came running up to stare at their lord.

The peasant in the clay hut close by the knightly house had a son named Sören, of the same age as the gracious little lady. The boy could climb well, and had always to bring her down the birds' nests. The birds screamed as loud as they could, and one of the greatest of them hacked him with its beak over the eye so that the blood ran down, and it was at first thought the eye had been destroyed ; but it had not been injured after all. Marie Grubbe used to call him *her* Sören, and that was a great favour, and was an advantage to Sören's father—poor Jon, who had one day committed a fault, and was to be punished by riding on the wooden horse. This same horse stood in the courtyard, and had four poles for legs, and a single narrow plank for a back ; on

LADY GRUBBE.

this Jon had to ride astride, and some heavy bricks were fastened to his feet into the bargain, that he might not sit too comfortably. He made horrible grimaces, and Sören wept and implored little Marie to interfere. She immediately ordered that Sören's father should be taken down, and when they did not obey her, she stamped on the floor, and pulled at her father's sleeve till it was torn to pieces. She would have her way, and she got her way, and Sören's father was taken down.

Lady Grubbe, who now came up, parted her little daughter's hair from the child's brow, and looked at her affectionately; but Marie did not understand why.

She wanted to go to the hounds, and not to her mother, who went down into the garden, to the lake where the water-lily bloomed, and the heads of bulrushes nodded amid the reeds, and she looked at all this beauty and freshness. " How pleasant! " she said. In the garden stood at that time a rare tree, which she herself had planted: it was called the blood-beech—a kind of negro growing among the other trees, so dark brown were the leaves   This tree required much sunshine, for in continual shade it would become bright green like the other trees, and thus lose its distinctive character. In the lofty chestnut trees were many birds' nests, and also in the thickets and in the grassy meadows. It seemed as though the birds knew that they were protected here, and that no one must fire a gun at them.

Little Marie came here with Sören. He knew how to climb, as we have already said, and eggs and fluffy-feathered young birds were brought down. The birds, great and small, flew about in terror and tribulation; the peewit from the fields, and the crows and daws from the high trees screamed and screamed; it was just such a din as the family will raise to the present day.

" What are you doing, you children? " cried the gentle lady: " that is sinful! "

Sören stood abashed, and even the little gracious lady looked down a little; but then she said, quite short and pretty,

" My father lets me do it! "

" Craw—craw! away—away from here! " cried the great black birds, and they flew away; but on the following day they came back, for they were at home here.

The quiet gentle lady did not remain long at home here on earth, for the good God called her away; and, indeed, her home was rather with Him than in the knightly house; and the church bells tolled solemnly when her corpse was carried to the church, and the eyes of the poor people were wet with tears, for she had been good to them.

When she was gone, no one attended to her plantations, and the garden ran to waste. Grubbe the knight was a hard man, they said; but his daughter, young as she was, knew how to manage him: he used to laugh and let her have her way. She was now twelve years old, and strongly built: she looked the people through and through with her black eyes, rode her horse as bravely as a man, and could fire off her gun like a practised hunter.

One day there were great visitors in the neighbourhood, the grandest visitors who could come: the young King, and his half-brother and comrade, the Lord Ulric Frederick Gyldenlöwe. They wanted to hunt the wild boar, and to pass a few days at the castle of Grubbe.

Gyldenlöwe sat at table next to Marie Grubbe, and he took her by the hand and gave her a kiss, as if she had been a relation; but she gave him a box on the ear, and told him she could not bear him, at which there was great laughter, as if that had been a very amusing thing.

And perhaps it was very amusing, for, five years afterwards, when Marie had fulfilled her seventeenth year, a messenger arrived with a letter, in which Lord Gyldenlöwe proposed for the hand of the noble young lady. There was a thing for you!

" He is the grandest and most gallant gentleman in the whole country,"
said Grubbe the knight; " that is not a thing to despise."

" I don't care so very much about him," said Marie Grubbe; but she
did not despise the grandest man of all the country, who sat by the
King's side.

Silver plate, and fine linen and woollen, went off to Copenhagen in a
ship, while the bride made the journey by land in ten days. But the
outfit met with contrary winds, or with no winds at all, for four months
passed before it arrived; and when it came, my Lady Gyldenlöwe was
gone.

" I 'd rather lie on coarse sacking than lie in his silken beds," she declared. " I 'd rather walk barefoot than drive with him in a coach ! "

Late one evening in November two women came riding into the town
of Aarhuus. They were the gracious Lady Gyldenlöwe (Marie Grubbe)
and her maid. They came from the town of Weile, whither they had
come in a ship from Copenhagen. They stopped at Lord Grubbe's
stone mansion in Aarhuus. Grubbe was not well pleased with this visit.
Marie was accosted in hard words; but she had a bed-room given her,
and got her beer soup of a morning; but the evil part of her father's
nature was aroused against her, and she was not used to that. She was
not of a gentle temper, and we often answer as we are addressed. She
answered openly, and spoke with bitterness and hatred of her husband,
with whom she declared she would not live; she was too honourable for
that.

A year went by, but it did not go by pleasantly. There were evil
words between the father and the daughter, and that ought never to be.
Bad words bear bad fruit. What could be the end of such a state of
things ?

" We two cannot live under the same roof," said the father one day.
" Go away from here to our old manor house; but you had better bite
your tongue off than spread any lies among the people."

And so the two parted. She went with her maid to the old castle where
she had been born, and near which the gentle pious lady, her mother,
was lying in the church vault; an old cowherd lived in the courtyard,
and was the only other inhabitant of the place. In the rooms black
heavy cobwebs hung down, covered with dust; in the garden everything grew just as it would; hops and climbing plants ran like a net
between the trees and bushes, and the hemlock and nettle grew larger
and stronger. The blood-beech had been outgrown by other trees, and
now stood in the shade; and its leaves were green like those of the
common trees, and its glory had departed. Crows and choughs, in
great close masses, flew past over the tall chestnut trees, and chattered
and screamed as if they had something very important to tell one another—as if they were saying, " Now she 's come back again, the little
girl who had had their eggs and their young ones stolen from them; "
and as for the thief who had got them down, he had to climb up a leafless
tree, for he sat on a tall ship's mast, and was beaten with a rope's end
if he did not behave himself.

The clerk told all this in our own times; he had collected it and looked it up in books and memoranda. It was to be found, with many other writings, locked up in his table-drawer.

"Upwards and downwards is the course of the world," said he: "it is strange to hear."

And we will hear how it went with Marie Grubbe. We need not for that forget Poultry Meg, who is sitting in her capital hen-house, in our own time. Marie Grubbe sat down in her times, but not with the same spirit that old Poultry Meg showed.

The winter passed away, and the spring and the summer passed away, and then the autumn came again, with the damp, cold sea-fog. It was a lonely desolate life in the old manor house. Marie Grubbe took her gun in her hand, and went out on to the heath, and shot hares and foxes, and shot whatever birds she could hit. More than once she met the noble Sir Palle Dyre, of Nörrebäk, who was also wandering about with his gun and his dogs. He was tall and strong, and boasted of this when they talked together. He could have measured himself against the deceased Mr. Brockenhuus, of Egeskov, of whom the people still talked. Palle Dyre had, after the example of Brockenhuus, caused an iron chain with a hunting-horn to be hung in his gateway; and when he came riding home, he used to seize the chain, and lift himself and his horse from the ground, and blow the horn.

"Come yourself, and see me do that, Dame Marie," he said. "One can breathe fresh and free at Nörrebäk."

When she went to his castle is not known, but on the altar candlesticks in the church of Nörrebäk it was inscribed that they were the gift of Palle Dyre and Marie Grubbe, of Nörrebäk Castle.

A great stout man was Palle Dyre. He drank like a sponge: he was like a tub that could never get full; he snored like a whole stye of pigs, and he looked red and bloated.

"He is treacherous and malicious," said Dame Palle Dyre, Grubbe's daughter. Soon she was weary of her life with him, but that did not make it better.

One day the table was spread, and the dishes grew cold. Palle Dyre was out hunting foxes, and the gracious lady was nowhere to be found. Towards midnight Palle Dyre came home, but Dame Dyre came neither at midnight nor next morning: she had turned her back upon Nörrebäk, and had ridden away without saying good bye.

It was grey, wet weather; the wind blew cold, and a flight of black screaming birds flew over her head—they were not so homeless as she.

First she journeyed southwards, quite down into the German land. A couple of golden rings with costly stones were turned into money; and then she turned to the east, and then she turned again and went towards the west. She had no food before her eyes, and murmured against everything, even against the good God Himself, so wretched was her soul. Soon her body became wretched too, and she was scarcely able to move a foot. The peewit flew up as she stumbled over the mound of earth where it had built its nest. The bird cried, as it always cries, "You thief! you thief!" She had never stolen her neighbour s goods; but as a little girl she had caused eggs and young birds to be taken from the trees, and she thought of that now.

From where she lay she could see the sand-dunes. By the sea-shore lived fishermen; but she could not get so far, she was so ill. The great white sea-mews flew over her head, and screamed as the crows and daws screamed at home in the garden of the manor house. The birds flew quite close to her, and at last it seemed to her as if they became black as crows, and then all was night before her eyes.

EXHAUSTED.

When she opened her eyes again, she was being lifted and carried. A great strong man had taken her up in his arms, and she was looking straight into his bearded face. He had a scar over one eye, which seemed to divide the eyebrow into two parts. Weak as she was, he carried her to the ship, where he got a rating for it from the captain.

The next day the ship sailed away. Madame Grubbe had not been put ashore, so she sailed away with it. But she will return, will she not? Yes, but where, and when?

The clerk could tell about this too, and it was not a story which he patched together himself. He had the whole strange history out of an old authentic book, which we ourselves can take out and read. The Danish historian, Ludwig Holberg, who has written so many useful books and the merry comedies, from which we can get such a good idea of his times and their people, tells in his letters of Marie Grubbe, where and how he met her. It is well worth hearing; but for all that we don't at all forget Poultry Meg, who is sitting cheerful and comfortable in the charming fowl-house.

The ship sailed away with Marie Grubbe. That's where we left off.

Long years went by.

The plague was raging at Copenhagen; it was in the year 1711. The Queen of Denmark went away to her German home, the King quitted the capital, and everybody who could do so, hurried away. The students, even those who had board and lodging gratis, left the city. One of these students, the last who had remained in the free college, at last went away too. It was two o'clock in the morning. He was carrying his knapsack, which was better stocked with books and writings than with clothes. A damp mist hung over the town, not a person was to be seen in the streets; the street-doors around were marked with crosses, as a sign that the plague was within, or that all the inmates were dead. A great waggon rattled past him; the coachman brandished his whip, and the horses flew by at a gallop: the waggon was filled with corpses. The young student kept his hand before his face, and smelt at some strong spirits that he had with him on a sponge in a little brass scent-case. Out of a small tavern in one of the streets there were sounds of singing and of unhallowed laughter, from people who drank the night through to forget that the plague was at their doors, and that they might be put into the waggon like the others had been. The student turned his steps towards the canal at the castle bridge, where a couple of small ships were lying; one of these was weighing anchor to get away from the plague-stricken city.

"If God spares our lives and grants us a fair wind, we are going to Grönmud, near Falster," said the captain; and he asked the name of the student who wished to go with him.

"Ludwig Holberg," answered the student; and the name sounded like any other; but now there sounds in it one of the proudest names of Denmark; then it was the name of a young, unknown student.

The ship glided past the castle. It was not yet bright day when it was in the open sea. A light wind filled the sails, and the young student sat down with his face turned towards the fresh wind, and went to sleep, which was not exactly the most prudent thing he could have done.

Already on the third day the ship lay by the island of Falster.

"Do you know any one here with whom I could lodge cheaply?" Holberg asked the captain.

"I should think you would do well to go to the ferry-woman in Borrchaus," answered the captain. "If you want to be very civil to her, her name is Mother Sören Sörensen Müller. But it may happen that she may fly into a fury if you are too polite to her. The man is in custody for a crime, and that's why she manages the ferry-boat herself—she has fists of her own."

The student took his knapsack and betook himself to the ferry-house. The house door was not locked—it opened, and he went into a room with a brick floor, where a bench, with a great coverlet of leather, formed the chief article of furniture. A white hen, who had a brood of chickens, was fastened to the bench, and had overturned the pipkin of water, so that the wet ran across the floor. There were no people either here or in the adjoining room; only a cradle stood there, in which was a child. The ferry-boat came back with only one person in it: whether that person was a man or a woman was not an easy matter to determine. The person in question was wrapped in a great cloak, and wore a kind of hood. Presently the boat lay to.

It was a woman who got out of it and came into the room. She looked very stately when she straightened her back; two proud eyes looked forth from beneath her black eyebrows. It was Mother Sören, the ferry-wife: the crows and daws might have called out another name for her, which we know better.

She looked morose and did not seem to care to talk; but this much was settled, that the student should board in her house for an indefinite time, while things looked so bad in Copenhagen.

This or that honest citizen would often come to the ferry-house from the neighbouring little town. There came Frank the cutler, and Sivert the exciseman. They drank a jug of beer in the ferry-house, and used to converse with the student; for he was a clever young man who knew his " Practica," as they called it; he could read Greek and Latin, and was well up in learned subjects.

"The less one knows, the less it presses upon one," said Mother Sören.

"You have to work hard," said Holberg one day, when she was dipping clothes in the strong soapy water, and was obliged herself to split the logs for the fire.

"That's my affair," she replied.

"Have you been obliged to toil in this way from your childhood?"

"You can read that from my hands," she replied, and held out her hands, that were small indeed, but hard and strong, with bitten nails. "You are learned, and can read."

At Christmas-time it began to snow heavily. The cold came on, the wind blew sharp as if there were vitriol in it to wash the people's faces. Mother Sören did not let that disturb her; she threw her cloak around her, and drew her hood over her head. Early in the afternoon—it was already dark in the house—she laid wood and turf on the hearth, and then sat down to darn her stockings, for there was no one to do it for her. Towards evening she spoke more words to the student than it was customary with her to use; she spoke of her husband.

"He killed a sailor of Dragör by mischance, and for that he has to work for three years in irons. He's only a common sailor, and therefore the law must take its course."

"The law is there for people of high rank too," said Holberg.

"Do you think so?" said Mother Sören; then she looked into the fire for a while; but after a time she began to speak again. "Have you heard of Kai Lykke, who caused a church to be pulled down, and when the clergyman, Master Martin, thundered from the pulpit about it, he had him put in irons, and sat in judgment upon him, and condemned him to death? Yes, and the clergyman was obliged to bow his head to the stroke. And yet Kai Lykke went scot-free."

"He had a right to do as he did in those times," said Holberg, "but now we have left those times behind us."

"You may get a fool to believe that," cried Mother Sören; and she got up and went into the room where the little child lay. She lifted up the child and laid it down more comfortably. Then she arranged the bed-place of the student: he had the great coverlet, for he felt the cold more than she did, though he had been born in Norway.

On New Year's morning it was a bright sunshiny day. The frost had been so strong, and was still so strong, that the fallen snow had become a hard mass, and one could walk upon it. The bells of the little town were tolling for church. Student Holberg wrapped himself up in his woollen cloak, and wanted to go to the town.

MOTHER SOREN.

Over the ferry-house the crows and daws were flying with loud cries; one could hardly hear the church bells for their screaming. Mother Sören stood in front of the house, filling a brass pot with snow, which she was going to put on the fire to get drinking water. She looked up to the crowd of birds, and thought her own thoughts.

Student Holberg went to church; on his way there, and on his return, he passed by the house of tax-collecter Sivert by the town-gate. Here he was invited to take a mug of brown beer with treacle and sugar. The discourse fell upon Mother Sören, but the tax-collector did not know much about her, and, indeed, few knew much about her. She did not belong to the island of Falster, he said; she had had a little property of her own at one time. Her man was a common sailor, a fellow of a very hot temper, and had killed a sailor of Dragör; and he beat his wife, and yet she defended him.

"I should not endure such treatment," said the tax-collector's wife. "I am come of more respectable people: my father was stocking-weaver to the Court."

"And consequently you have married a Government official," said Holberg, and made a bow to her and to the collector.

It was on Twelfth Night, the evening of the festival of the Three

Kings, Mother Sören lit up for Holberg a three-king candle, that is, a tallow candle with three wicks, which she had herself prepared.

"A light for each man," said Holberg.

"For each man?" repeated the woman, and looked sharply at him.

"For each of the wise men from the East," said Holberg.

"You mean it that way," said she, and then she was silent for a long time. But on this evening he learned more about her than he had yet known.

"You speak very affectionately of your husband," observed Holberg, "and yet the people say that he ill-uses you every day."

"That's no one's business but mine," she replied. "The blows might have done me good when I was a child; now, I suppose, I get them for my sins. But I know what good he has done me," and she rose up. "When I lay sick upon the desolate heath, and no one would have pity on me, and no one would have anything to do with me, except the crows and daws, which came to peck me to bits, he carried me in his arms, and had to bear hard words because of the burden he brought on board ship. It's not in my nature to be sick, and so I got well. Every man has his own way, and Sören has his; but the horse must not be judged by the halter. Taking one thing with another, I have lived more agreeably with him than with the man whom they called the most noble and gallant of the King's subjects. I have had the Stadtholder Gyldenlöwe, the King's half-brother, for my husband; and afterwards I took Palle Dyre. One is as good as another, each in his own way, and I in mine. That was a long gossip, but now you know all about me."

And with these words she left the room.

It was Marie Grubbe! so strangely had fate played with her. She did not live to see many anniversaries of the festival of the Three Kings; Holberg has recorded that she died in June, 1716; but he has not written down, for he did not know, that a number of great blackbirds circled over the ferry-house, when Mother Sören, as she was called, was lying there a corpse. They did not scream, as if they knew that at a burial silence should be observed. So soon as she lay in the earth, the birds disappeared; but on the same evening in Jutland, at the old manor house, an enormous number of crows and choughs were seen; they all cried as loud as they could, as if they had some announcement to make: perhaps they talked of him who, as a little boy, had taken away their eggs and their young; of the peasant's son, who had to wear an iron garter, and of the noble young lady, who ended by being a ferryman's wife.

"Brave! brave!" they cried.

And the whole family cried, "Brave! brave!" when the old house was pulled down.

"They are still crying, and yet there's nothing to cry about," said the clerk, when he told the story. "The family is extinct, the house has been pulled down, and where it stood is now the stately poultry-house, with gilded weathercocks, and the old Poultry Meg. She rejoices greatly in her beautiful dwelling. If she had not come here," the old clerk added, " she would have had to go into the workhouse."

The pigeons cooed over her, the turkey-cocks gobbled, and the ducks quacked.

" Nobody knew her," they said; " she belongs to no family. It's pure charity that she is here at all. She has neither a drake father nor a hen mother, and has no descendants."

She came of a great family, for all that; but she did not know it, and the old clerk did not know it, though he had so much written down; but one of the old crows knew about it, and told about it. She had heard from her own mother and grandmother about Poultry Meg's mother and grandmother. And we know the grandmother too: we saw her ride, as a child, over the bridge, looking proudly around her, as if the whole world belonged to her, and all the birds' nests in it; and we saw her on the heath, by the sand-dunes; and, last of all, in the ferry-house. The granddaughter, the last of her race, had come back to the old home, where the old castle had stood, where the black wild birds were screaming; but she sat among the tame birds, and these knew her and were fond of her. Poultry Meg had nothing left to wish for; she looked forward with pleasure to her death, and she was old enough to die.

" Grave! grave!" cried the crows.

And Poultry Meg had a good grave, which nobody knew except the old crow, if the old crow is not dead already.

And now we know the story of the old manor house, of its old proprietors, and of all Poultry Meg's family.

WHAT ONE CAN INVENT.

THERE was once a young man who was studying to be a poet. He wanted to become one by Easter, and to marry, and to live by poetry. To write poems, he knew, only consists in being able to invent something; but he could not invent anything. He had been born too late—everything had been taken up before he came into the world, and everything had been written and told about.

" Happy people who were born a thousand years ago!" said he. "It was an easy matter for them to become immortal. Happy even was he who was born a hundred years ago, for then there was still something about which a poem could be written. Now the world is written out, and what can I write poetry about?'

Then he studied till he became ill and wretched, the wretched man! No doctor could help him, but perhaps the wise woman could. She lived in the little house by the wayside, where the gate is that she opened for those who rode and drove. But she could do more than unlock the gate: she was wiser than the doctor who drives in his own carriage and pays tax for his rank.

"I must go to her," said the young man.

The house in which she dwelt was small and neat, but dreary to behold, for there were no flowers near it—no trees. By the door stood a bee-hive, which was very useful. There was also a little potato-field—very useful—and an earth bank, with sloe bushes upon it, which had done blossoming, and now bore fruit—sloes, that draw one's mouth together if one tastes them before the frost has touched them.

THE WOULD-BE POET.

"That's a true picture of our poetryless time, that I see before me now," thought the young man; and that was at least a thought, a grain of gold that he found by the door of the wise woman.

"Write that down!" said she. "Even crumbs are bread. I know why you come hither. You cannot invent anything, and yet you want to be a poet by Easter."

"Everything has been written down," said he. "Our time is not the old time."

"No," said the woman. "In the old time wise women were burnt, and poets went about with empty stomachs, and very much out at elbows. The present time is good—it is the best of times; but you have not the right way of looking at it. Your ear is not sharpened to hear, and I fancy you do not say the Lord's Prayer in the evening. There is plenty here to write poems about, and to tell of, for any one who knows the way. You can read it in the fruits of the earth, you can draw it from the flowing and the standing water; but you must understand how—you must understand how to catch a sunbeam. Now just you try my spectacles on, and put my ear-trumpet to your ear, and then pray to God, and leave off thinking of yourself."

The last was a very difficult thing to do—more than a wise woman ought to ask.

He received the spectacles and the ear-trumpet, and was posted in the middle of the potato-field. She put a great potato into his hand. Sounds came from within it; there came a song with words, the history of the potato, an every-day story in ten parts—an interesting story. And ten lines were enough to tell it in.

And what did the potato sing?

She sang of herself and of her family—of the arrival of the potato in Europe, of the misrepresentation to which she had been exposed before she was acknowledged, as she is now, to be a greater treasure than a lump of gold.

"We were distributed, by the King's command, from the council-houses through the various towns, and proclamation was made of our great value; but no one believed in it, or even understood how to plant us. One man dug a hole in the earth and threw in his whole bushel of potatoes; another put one potato here and another there in the ground, and expected that each was to come up a perfect tree, from which he might shake down potatoes. And they certainly grew, and produced flowers and green watery fruit, but it all withered away. Nobody thought of what was in the ground — the blessing — the potato. Yes, we have endured and suffered—that is to say, our forefathers have; they and we, it is all one."

What a story it was!

"Well, and that will do," said the woman. "Now look at the sloe bush."

"We have also some near relations in the home of the potatoes, but higher towards the north than they grew," said the Sloes. "There were Northmen, from Norway, who steered westward through mist and storm to an unknown land, where, behind ice and snow, they found plants and green meadows, and bushes with blue-black grapes—sloe bushes. The grapes were ripened by the frost just as we are. And they called the land 'wine-land,' that is, 'Groenland,' or 'Sloeland.'"

"That is quite a romantic story," said the young man.

"Yes, certainly. But now come with me," said the wise woman; and she led him to the bee-hive.

He looked into it. What life and labour! There were bees standing in all the passages, waving their wings, so that a wholesome draught of air might blow through the great manufactory: that was their business. Then there came in bees from without, who had been born with little baskets on their feet: they brought flower-dust, which was poured out, sorted, and manufactured into honey and wax. They flew in and out: the queen-bee wanted to fly out too, but then all the other bees must have gone with her. It was not yet the time for that, but still she wanted to fly out; so the others bit off her majesty's wings, and she had to stay where she was.

"Now get upon the earth bank," said the wise woman. "Come and look out over the highway, where you can see the people."

"What a crowd it is!" said the young man. "One story after another. It whirls and whirls! It's quite a confusion before my eyes. I shall go out at the back."

"No, go straight forward," said the woman. "Go straight into the crowd of people; look at them in the right way. Have an ear to hear and the right heart to feel, and you will soon invent something. But, before you go away, you must give me my spectacles and my ear-trumpet again."

And so saying, she took both from him.

"Now I do not see the smallest thing," said the young man, "and now I don't hear anything more."

"Why, then, you can't be a poet by Easter," said the wise woman.

"But by what time can I be one?" asked he.

"Neither by Easter nor by Whitsuntide! You will not learn how to invent anything."

"What must I do to earn my bread by poetry?"

"You can do that before Shrove Tuesday. Hunt the poets! Kill their writings, and thus you will kill them. Don't be put out of countenance. Strike at them boldly, and you'll have carnival cake, on which you can support yourself and your wife too."

"What one can invent!" cried the young man. And so he hit out boldly at every second poet, because he could not be a poet himself.

We have it from the wise woman : she knows WHAT ONE CAN INVENT.

IN SWEDEN.

I.

WE TRAVEL.

IT is spring, beautiful spring, and the birds are singing. You don't understand their song? Then listen to a free translation of it.

"Seat yourself upon my back," said the Stork, the sacred bird of our green islands; "I'll carry you over the waves of the Sound. Sweden, too, has its fresh fragrant beech woods, its green meadows and waving corn-fields. In Schoonen, among the blooming apple trees behind the farmer's house, you will fancy yourself still in Denmark."

"Fly with me," said the Swallow; "I fly over the mountain ridge of

Halland, where the beech trees cease. I fly farther northward than the Stork. I will show you where the arable land must give place to the rock; you shall see pleasant towns, old churches, and lonely farms, in whose interiors it is comfortable and good to dwell, where the family stand in a circle round the table covered with steaming dishes, while the prayer is spoken by the mouth of the youngest child, and where a pious song is sung morning and evening: I have heard it, and I have seen it, when I was yet small, from my nest under the roof."

"Come, come!" cries the restless Sea-Gull, flying impatiently round in a circle. "Follow me to the Scheeren, where thousands of islands, covered with pine trees, lie along the coast like flower-beds, and where the fisherman draws the full net from the ocean."

THE TRAVELLERS.

"Sit down between our outspread wings," sing the wild Swans; "we will carry you to the great lakes, to the ever-rushing, swift-flowing mountain stream, where the oak no longer flourishes, and even the birch is dwarfed. Sit down between our outspread wings—we soar aloft upon Sulitelma, the 'Eye of the Islands,' as they call the mountain; we fly from the valley green in the smile of spring, over the drifts of snow, up to the mountains, from whose tall summits you may behold the North Sea stretching out beyond Norway. We fly to Jämteland, with its lofty blue mountains, where the waterfalls foam, where the beacon fires blaze up as signals from shore to shore to tell that people are waiting for the ferry. Up to the deep, cold, hurrying waters, which in the height of summer see not the sun go down—where the evening red is the morning dawn."

Thus sing the birds. Shall we take their song to heart, and follow them, at least for a space? We will not seat ourselves on the wings of the Swan or on the back of the Stork, we will win our way onwards by the power of steam, and sometimes upon our own feet, and now and then look across the palings from the kingdom of reality into the realm of imagination, which is always a neighbour country, and pluck flowers or leaves, which are laid up in the book of remembrance, because they blossomed as we passed on on our journey. We fly on, and we sing! Sweden, thou glorious land! Sweden! whither came heroes in the old time, from the mountains of Asia! thou land still irradiated with their splendour! It pours from the flowers, with the name of Linnæus; it beams before thy chivalrous people from the banner of Charles XII.; it sounds forth from the monumental stone erected on the field of Lützen!

Sweden! thou land of deep feeling, of glorious song! where the wild swans sing in the gleam of the Northern Lights! Thou land on whose deep calm lakes the fairy of the North builds her vaulted bridges, and across whose frozen mirror the armies of spirits march to the combat! To thee we will fly, with the Stork and the Swallow; with the restless Sea-Gull and the wild Swan! Thy birch forest is so refreshing in its fragrance, that the harp shall be hung under its waving boughs and on its white stem, and the summer wind of the North shall whisper through its strings!

II.

THE BEGGAR BOY.

The painter Callot—and who does not know him, by name at least, from Hoffmann's book " In Callot's Style "?—has given us a few remarkable pictures of Italian beggars. One of these represents a lad clad in a wonderful fringe of rags; besides the bundle, he carries a great flag, with the inscription " *Capitano di Baroni.*" It can hardly be imagined that such a wandering mass of rags is to be found in reality, and we must acknowledge that we never saw one, even in Italy; for the beggar boy there, whose whole costume frequently consists of a waistcoat, has not space enough for such a display of rags in his primitive garb.

But in the far North we found it: on the canal journey between Wenern and Wigen, up on the barren, unfruitful, elevated plain, there stood, like " beauty-thistles in the landscape," two beggar boys, so tattered and torn, so picturesquely dirty, that we recognized in them the originals of Callot, unless their garb was an arrangement made by industrious parents, who wished to awaken sympathy and charity in the breasts of travellers; for nature could not have produced such a display: there was something so especially bold in this drapery of rags, that each boy at once became a " *Capitano di Baroni.*"

The younger of the two had clinging round him something that had certainly once been the jacket of a very corpulent man, and which hung down to the ankles of its present wearer. The whole structure hung upon one sleeve, and upon a kind of brace formed by the seam, which now remained as the very last relic of the lining. It was a difficult thing to define the line of demarcation between the coat and the trousers

for the rags were mingled together, and the whole costume seemed calculated to produce an air bath; there were ventilating valves in every
part and corner of it; while a yellow cotton rag in the lower regions
seemed to be a delicate hint at the presence of body linen.   A straw

THE TWO BEGGAR BOYS.

hat of vast dimensions, that had evidently been crushed beneath more
than one cart wheel, was stuck all askew on the boy's head, and did
not in the least prevent the appearance of his crop of white flaxy hair,
that peered boldly forth from the cavity where a crown had once been.
The finest thing about it all was the way in which the naked bronzed
arm and shoulder looked forth from the jacket.

The other lad boasted only a pair of trousers.   These also were tattered, but they had been fastened to the boy's limbs with string; one
piece was fastened round his ankles, another string went round under
his knees, a third above them, and a fourth round his body; so the boy
held together, and what he wore looked sufficiently respectable.

"Away with you!" called our captain from the ship.

And the boy with the tied-up rags turned round, and we—why, we
saw nothing but string, one bow over the other; and noble bows they
were.   The boy was only dressed in front, and all the rest was string—
nothing but the bare string!

III.

THE PRISON ON THE SEPARATE SYSTEM.

By separation from other men, by solitude and silence, the criminal is
to be improved, and accordingly prisons are built with separate cells.
In Sweden there are many of these, and new ones are being constructed.

I visited one, the first I had seen, in Marienstadt. Like a great villa, white and smiling, with window by window, this building stands in a fair landscape, close to the town, beside a babbling stream. But soon we notice that a stillness as of the grave broods over this place; it is like a deserted spot, or a plague-stricken building, from whence the inhabitants have fled. The gates of these walls are locked; but one of them opens to us, and the gaoler receives us with his bunch of keys in his hand. We enter the "reception-room," into which the prisoner is first introduced; then they show us the bath-room into which he is led. Next we mount a stair, and find ourselves in a great hall occupying the whole length and height of the building. Several galleries run round the hall at different heights, and in the middle stands a pulpit; on Sundays the preacher ascends the pulpit, and preaches a sermon to an invisible congregation. The doors of all the cells, which open upon the gallery on the various storeys, are half opened, and the prisoners hear the preacher, though they cannot see him, or he them. The whole system is a well-arranged machine to weigh like an Alp upon the spirit. In the door of each cell a bit of glass about an inch square is fastened; a valve covers it from without, and through this glass the warder can see all that the prisoner does, unobserved by the latter; but he must come silently and with noiseless steps, for the captive's sense of hearing is marvellously sharpened by incarceration. I silently pushed back the valve from one of the glasses, and looked into the confined space within, but instantly the occupant's eye caught mine. The cell was airy, clean, and light, but the window is so high that the prisoner cannot possibly look out. The furniture consists of a high bench, fastened to a kind of table, and a hammock, with a blanket, that can be fastened to the ceiling by a hook.

Several cells were opened for us. In one of these I saw a young and very pretty girl. She had lain down in her hammock, but when the door opened she sprang out, and immediately fastened it up. On the little table stood the water-jug, and near it lay the remains of a hard piece of black bread, the Bible, and a few hymns. In another cell sat a woman who had murdered her child: I only saw her through the little pane of glass in the door. She had heard our footsteps and our voices, but she sat still, crouched together in one corner by the door, as if she wanted to hide herself as much as possible. She sat with her back bent, her head bowed down, and her hands folded over it. They told me the unhappy creature was quite young. In two separate cells were two brothers, who were suffering punishment for horse stealing; one of them was quite a boy. In another cell sat a poor servant girl; they told me "she was without means of subsistence, and without friends or kin, and therefore had been sent hither." I thought I must have heard wrong, and repeated my question, only to receive the same reply. But still I cling to the idea that there must be some mistake. Without, in the bright sunshine, is the bustle and industry of the day; within, there rules always the stillness of midnight. The sun, which works its way along the wall, the swallow at rare intervals sweeping close by the window-pane high up in the cell, even the step of a stranger in the gallery passing by the door, is an event in the dumb, uniform life, in which the thoughts of the prisoner are ever turned inwards. We must remember the cells of the Holy Inquisition, the wretched prisoners of the *Bagnios* chained one to another, the hot lead roofs, and the dark wet abyss of the well-dungeons of Venice, before we can wander with a quiet heart through the galleries of these cell-prisons. Here at any rate are light and air; here is more of humanity. And when the sun pours its mild ray upon the prisoner, there may also a beaming ray of the Divine essence sink into his heart.

IV.

WADSTENA.

YONDER in Sweden are to be seen, not only in the country, but even in several of the smaller towns, houses built entirely of sods, or roofed with them; and some of these houses are so low that it is an easy matter to climb on to the roof, and to repose there among the fresh turf. At the beginning of spring, when the fields are still covered with snow, but the white veil has melted from these roofs, they give the first promise of the renewed year in the young sprouting grass, among whose blades the sparrows hop to and fro, and twitter, "Spring is coming."

Between Motala and Wadstena, hard by the high road, lies a turf house of this kind, and one of the most picturesque. It has but one window, and that is broader than it is long; a wild rose bush forms a sort of curtain over it from without. We see it in the spring. The roof is of green turf, green velvety turf, and close by the low chimney, almost out of its very side, a cherry tree springs up. This tree stands in full blossom, and in the soft wind the blossoms shower down their petals upon a little lamb that pastures up here, and is tethered to a cord fastened to the chimney. This is the only lamb of the house: the old mother who dwells here carries it up herself when the morning dawns, and brings it down in the evening, to give it a place in her room. The roof is just strong enough to bear the little lamb, but can carry nothing more—that is an ascertained fact. Last autumn—and at that time of the year these roofs are generally covered with blossoms, mostly yellow and red, the Swedish colours—last autumn there grew here a flower of a strange kind; it attracted the eye of the old professor who used to pass the house botanizing. Immediately the professor was on the roof, and immediately afterwards first one of his booted legs, and then the other, and then half of the professor—the half that does not include the head—broke through the roof; and, forasmuch as there was no ceiling under the said roof, the legs of the professor were waving over the head of the little old woman, and, in fact, in very close contact with her. But now the roof has been set right again, the fresh grass grows over the spot where so much learning was engulfed; the little lamb is bleating aloft; and the old woman stands beneath, with folded hands, with a smile on her lips, rich in possession of her one lambkin, on which the cherry tree strews its petals in the warm sunshine.

The background of this picture is formed by the Wettern, the lake which popular belief declares to be fathomless, with its transparent waters, its waves large as those of the sea, and its *Fata Morgana*, seen

THE OLD WOMAN AND HER LAMB.

when no wind ruffles its steel-like surface. We saw the castle and the town of Wadstena, the "City of the Dead," as a Swedish author has called it, "the Swedish Herculaneum," the city of remembrances. Let the green house be our theatre-box, whence we shall see the rich remembrances pass before us—recollections from the legends of saints, from the King's Chronicle, and the love songs that still live in the mouth of the old dame who stands in her low doorway, while the lamb feeds on the roof. We hear her tell her story, and we see what she sees. We turn our steps to the little town, to the other green houses with fresh grass roofs, in and before which sit other poor women making lace—pursuing what was the celebrated employment of the noble nuns here, in the old days when the convent was in its glory. How quiet and still it is now in these grass-grown streets! We pause before an old wall overgrown with the moss of centuries; behind this wall lay the convent; there is now only one wing of it left; there in the now neglected garden still bloom the "St. Bridget's leek," and other once rare flowers. In this garden the King John was walking one evening with the abbess Anna Gylte. The King asked cunningly if love never attacked the maids of the cloister. And the abbess answered, pointing to a bird which was just flying past over their heads, "It may well happen: we cannot answer for it that a bird shall not pass over the garden, but we can prevent him from settling there."

The old lady will also sing you a song of the fair Agda and Olaf the Dumb; and as you listen to her, the convent stands before you in all its glory, and the bells toll, and stone houses rise up, even from the waters of the Wenern, and the town is resuscitated, with towers and churches. The streets are thronged with grave, well-clad people; and down the steps leading to the old council-house that is still standing, comes, with his sword girt around him and a silk cloak on his shoulders, Michael Merchant, the most powerful citizen of Wadstena. At his side walks his young, beautiful daughter Agda, clad in velvet and silk, and passing fair in her cheerfulness and fullness of youth. All eyes, at first turned upon him, the rich man, quickly forget him for her, the fair maiden. Life smiles upon her, her thoughts soar high, her mind soars high, her future is to be happiness! So thought the crowd; and among them was one who looked at her with the feeling of Romeo for Juliet, of Adam for Eve in the Garden of Paradise. This was Olaf, the handsomest of youths, but as poor as Agda was rich, and therefore he must conceal his love. But as he lived only in her, and knew only of her, he became quiet and silent, and a few months afterwards all the city called him Olaf the Dumb.

· Day and night he wrestled with his love; for many days and nights he suffered tortures unspeakable; but at last—a single dew-drop, a single sunbeam is sufficient to make the blooming rosebud unfold itself—he felt obliged to tell it to Agda.

And she heard his words, and was frightened, and sprang away with hurried steps; but her thoughts remained behind with him, and her heart followed her thoughts, and went forth to him also. She loved him deeply and faithfully, but in all modesty and honour. And then the poor Olaf went to the rich merchant as a suitor for his daughter's hand. But Michael barred his door and his heart, he would listen to neither prayers nor tears, but only to his own will; and when Agda ventured to oppose her will to his, he shut her up in the Wadstena convent, and Olaf, as it says in the old song, was obliged to allow them to

'Throw the black earth
All over fair Agda's arm."

For him and for the world she was dead.

But one night, when the weather was stormy and the rain poured from the sky, Olaf stood beneath the convent wall, and threw a rope ladder across; and though the waves of the Wenern reared aloft their foaming crests, Olaf and Agda flew in their bark over the fathomless lake in that wild night.

Early next morning the nuns missed the fair Agda; and there was a great calling and crying, "The convent has been desecrated!" The abbess and Michael the Merchant vowed vengeance and death against the fugitives. Linkjöping's severe bishop, Hans Brask, hurled the ban after them. But they were already beyond the Wettern, they had reached the shores of the Wener, and were at Kinnekulle, at a friend of Olaf's, who possessed the fine estate of Hellekis.

Here their marriage was to be celebrated; the guests had been invited, and a monk had been brought from the neighbouring Husaby to perform the service, when a boat arrived, bearing the ban-curse of the bishop, and this was pronounced over them instead of the Church's blessing. All started back from them in horror: the master of the house, the friend of their youth, pointed to the open door, and bade them begone. Olaf begged only for a cart and horse, to carry off the fainting Agda; but they were both beaten with sticks and pelted with stones, and Olaf was compelled to carry his unhappy bride in his arms far away into the forest.

It was a bitter wearisome journey; but at last they found a shelter in West Gothland: an old couple took them in, and cherished and comforted them; they remained there till Christmas, and on the holy eve the feast was to be joyfully ushered in. Guests were invited, and the table was spread with the delicacies of the North; and now the clergyman of the parish entered to read the customary prayer; but while he read he recognized Olaf and Agda, and the prayer changed to a curse upon them, and terror and amazement came upon all present. The outcasts were driven from the house, out into the bitter frosty night, through which the wolves prowled in packs, and where the bear was no unusual guest. And Olaf felled wood in the forest, and kindled a great fire to scare away the wild beasts, and to keep Agda alive, for he thought she must die; but, behold, she was stronger than ever.

"God is almighty and merciful. He will not forsake us!" she said. "He has one upon earth here, one who can save us, and who knows what it is to wander alone in the forest among the wild beasts. It is the King—King Gustavus Vasa has also known want, and has wandered among the deep snows of Dalecarlia; he has suffered, and has been tempted. He knows what grief is—he can and will help us!"

The King was then in Wadstena, whither he had summoned the deputies of the people. He was staying in the convent itself, where the fair Agda, if the King did not receive her graciously, would have to suffer the sentence the abbess would pass upon her, and this sentence would be penance and a painful death.

And through the wild forest, over untrodden paths, in storm and snow, Olaf and Agda reached Wadstena. At their appearance some were alarmed, and others jeered at them and threatened them. The guards at the convent gate crossed themselves when they saw the two sinners, who dared to demand audience of the King.

" I will receive and hear each and all! " was the royal command; and the two suppliants fell trembling at his feet.

And the King looked down upon them graciously : in his inmost heart he had long wished for an occasion of humbling the proud Bishop of Linkjöping, and this was not a disadvantage to them. The King heard them out, and gave them his promise that the curse should be taken off them; he laid their hands in one another, promising that the priest would soon do the same, and assured them of his royal favour and protection. And old Michael the Merchant was so frightened at the King's anger, with which he was threatened, that he opened his house and his arms to Olaf and Agda, and even made a display of all his wealth on the wedding-day of the youthful pair, in honour of them and of the King. The marriage service was read in the convent church, whither the King in person conducted the bride, and where, at his command, all the nuns were present, that the celebration might have additional solemnity; and, as all eyes were fixed upon Olaf, many a young heart may secretly have muttered the words of the old ballad :

> "Heaven grant that such an angel
> May carry off me and thee."

Now the sun throws its rays through the convent gate, and we, the children of the present, stand at the open portal. Let us acknowledge the trace of the divine that was to be found also in the convent ! Not every cell was a prison, against whose windows the caged birds beat their wings despairingly : here, even, a sunbeam from God penetrated heart and bosom, and from hence went forth comfort and blessing ! If the dead could rise from their graves, they would bear witness to it; if we could see them lifting the tombstones in the moonshine and marching towards the cloister, we should hear them say, " Blessed be these walls ! " —if we could see them soaring in rainbow splendour in the sunshine, they would say, " Blessed be these walls ! "

What a change ! This is the wealthy powerful Wadstena convent, where the daughters of the noblest of the land lived as nuns, where young nobles wore the monk's gown, whither pilgrimages were made from Italy and Spain; from afar the pilgrims wandered barefoot through the snow and ice to the threshold of the convent; thither, from Rome, holy men and women bore in their hands the corpse of St. Bridget, and the bells of every chapel and church by which they passed on their journey were tolled as they went along.

We turn our footsteps towards the old convent building, or, properly speaking, towards the small portion of it that still remains. We step into St. Bridget's cell, which stands deserted but unaltered. It is small, low, and narrow : four little panes make up the window; but the eye can wander over the garden, over the beautiful Lake Wettern. The same glorious landscape which bounded the horizon of the pious saint, the same fresh smiling nature which surrounded her while the morning or evening prayer streamed from her lips, lies around us still

In the brick floor of the cell a rosary has been cut; in front of this she used to kneel, and pray a *paternoster* for every bead in the circle. Here is no chimney and no place for fire; cold and desolate it is and was here, where the most celebrated woman of the North dwelt—Bridget, whom her own genius and the spirit of the century raised to the saint's throne.

From this humble cell we step into another, yet colder and narrower, where the very daylight comes sparingly through a slit in the wall; no glass has ever covered this cleft, and the wind pours in unchecked. Who was the pious woman, or the penitent, who here closed her days?

Our time has arranged a whole row of light comfortable rooms beside the broad corridor: from these come merry songs, but also a mingled sound of laughter and weeping, and strange faces peer forth and nod at us. Who are these? St. Bridget's rich convent, to which kings once made pilgrimages, is now the madhouse of Sweden, and visitors write their names upon it by scores. We hurry past into the splendid convent church, the " blue church " as it was called, from its walls of bluestone; and here also, where the broad stones of the pavement cover the ashes of powerful lords, of abbesses and queens, only one monument appears. Before the altar rises a knightly figure of stone, the effigy of the mad Duke Magnus. From the rows of the dead he alone steps forth, as if to tell of the life that now reigns where once St. Bridget dwelt.

Tread lightly on this earth! Thy foot is on the grave of a good woman; the smooth, plain stone in yonder corner covers the dust of the noble Queen Philippa. She, the daughter of mighty England, the immortal woman who wisely and bravely defended her husband's throne, was repulsed by him with cruelty and violence. Wadstena offered her its protection, and here in the grave she found peace.

We enter the sacristy. Here under the double lead of a coffin rested the remains of the holiest person of a whole age—of her who was the glory and the crown of Wadstena—St. Bridget. The legend tells us that on the night she was born, there appeared in the heavens a beaming cloud, and on the cloud sat a majestic virgin, who said,

" A daughter is born this night, whose voice shall resound throughout the whole earth."

In the castle of her father, Brahe the knight, the strange, delicate child grew up; dreams and visions manifested themselves to her, and became more and more numerous. When at the age of only thirteen years, she married the rich Ulf Gudmundson, and afterwards she became the mother of many children. " Thou shalt be my bride and my instrument," she heard the Saviour speak, and every one of her actions was, she said, but a fulfilment of His will. At His command she went to Nidaros, and prayed by the coffin of St. Olaf; at His command she wandered to Germany, to France, Spain, and Rome. Sometimes honoured, sometimes contemned, she travelled from place to place, visiting even Cyprus and Palestine. Dying she returned to Rome, where her last revelation was that she should rest in Wadstena, and that this convent should in future enjoy in a marked degree the favour and blessing of

Heaven. The Northern Light doth not throw its beams more widely across the earth than extendeth the fame of this saint, who is herself but a legend now. In serious silent meditation we bent over the decayed remains in the shrine, the bones of St. Bridget and her daughter St. Catherine; but even from these the halo of remembrance is passed away, for in the mouth of the people there is a story that the real bones were carried away at the time of the Reformation to a convent in Poland, the name of which is unknown, and that Wadstena no longer holds the dust of St. Bridget and of her daughter.

Gustavus, the first Vasa, was the sun of the monarchical power, before whose lustre the convent star was compelled to pale. The stone walls are still standing of the lordly castle he caused to be built, with cupolas and towers, hard by the convent. From afar, on the waves of the Wettern, it seems as if the castle still stands in its old glory; and even seen quite close in moonlight nights it seems to stand unaltered, for the massive walls are standing, the carved ornaments over doors and windows stand sharply forth in the light and shade, the moats still encircle the walls, only separated by a narrow road from the Wettern, and the venerable pile is mirrored in its waters.

But let us stand before the building in the daylight. Not one of the windows has a pane left; boards and old doors are nailed up against the openings; and only over the two gates are the cupola roofs still standing, looking like two heavy broad mushrooms. The iron peak of one of the towers still rears aloft its slender point, but that of the other is bent like the hand of a sundial, and points to the time—the time that has passed away. The other two pinnacles have fallen down; sheep wander about among the fragments, and the space below is devoted to the purpose of a cow-shed.

The coat of arms over the entrance has not a spot or a blemish, it looks as if it had been carved yesterday; the walls stand fast, and the staircases look like new. Inside the courtyard, high over the portal, open the large folding doors, from which the players came forth to give a welcome to arriving guests from the balcony; but the balcony itself has been broken away. We pass through the great kitchen, on the walls of which the eye is still attracted towards pictures of the Wadstena castle, with its sheep, and the blooming nature around, portrayed in red chalk.

Here, where roasting and boiling used to go on, is now a great empty space; the chimney itself is broken down, and from the roof, where thick heavy beams are ranged side by side, hang cobwebs heavy with dust, making the whole roof look like heavy grey stalactites. We go from hall to hall, and the wooden shuttered loopholes are opened to let in the daylight. All is grand, lofty, roomy; the old chimneys are magnificent; and from each window there is a beautiful view over the clear deep lake. In this room sat through many days and nights the lunatic Magnus, whose stone effigy we have just noticed by the altar in the church: here he sat, pondering in horror over the deed he had committed, the condemnation of his own brother to death; madly in love, moreover, with the picture of the Scottish Queen Mary Stuart, for whose hand he was a suitor, and expecting the arrival of the ship that should bring her to him from over the sea to Wadstena; and he fancied that she came at last in the guise of a mermaiden, rising up out of the waves, and beckoning to him; and the unhappy duke threw himself from the window to meet her. From this window we look into the deep castle moat in which he was drowned.

We now go into the pursuivants' hall, and into the imperial hall, on whose walls warriors are depicted in strange costumes, half Dalecarlian, half Roman. In this once magnificent hall knelt Swante Stenson Sture before the Queen of Sweden, Margaret Lesonhufwnd; she had been Swante Sture's affianced bride before the will of Gustavus Vasa made her a Queen. The lovers gave each other a meeting here; the walls did not betray what they said; but the door opened, the King came in, and seeing Sture kneeling, asked what was the meaning of this. Then Queen Margaret answered hurriedly, with ready words,

"He is asking the hand of my sister Martha in marriage."

And the King gave to Swante Sture the bride whom the Queen had asked for him.

Here we stand in the royal wedding-chamber, into which King Gustavus led his third consort, Katharine Stenbock, who had likewise been the affianced bride of another, the knight Gustavus. It is a mournful story.

Only when the heavy wooden shutters are unfastened do the sunbeams penetrate those halls; and then the dust circles in the air in bright streaks. Here the whole place has been converted into a granary. Great heavy rats lurk in these halls, and the spider weaves her mourning web among the rafters. Such is the castle of Wadstena.

Mournful thoughts come upon us. We turn aside to gaze at the low hut with its turf-covered roof on which the little lamb is grazing, under the cherry tree, whence the white petals rain down. And our thoughts descend towards the turf, from the wealthy convent, from the proud castle; and the sun sinks, and its radiance is quenched upon the grass; and the old mother goes to sleep beneath the turf, and with her rest the mighty memories of Wadstena.

V.

THE ZÄTHER VALLEY.

EVERYTHING was prepared. The carriage had been arranged, and even a whip with a good lash had been provided: the dealer suggested that two whips were better than one, as he sold us a specimen, and the dealer was a man of experience, and that is more than the traveller can always say of himself. A whole bag of "Slanter," or copper coins of little value, stood before us in the carriage, for bridge money, for the beggars, for the shepherd boys, or others, who would open for us the many barriers that are thrust across the high road at every enclosure; but we had to do it ourselves, for the rain poured from the sky, and nobody thought it pleasant to turn out in such weather. The reeds on the moor bent and bowed themselves; there was a regular rain feast among them, and there came a humming voice out from the summits of the reeds:

"We're drinking with our feet, and with our heads, and with our whole body, and yet we can stand all the time upon one leg. Hurrah! here's a feast! it pours and pours, and we drink and sing our own song, and to-morrow morning the frogs will quack it out to us and declare that it's quite new!"

THE JOURNEY IN THE RAIN.

And the reeds swayed and staggered, and it poured down from the sky, splash! splash! Yes, it was fine weather, indeed, in which to visit the famous Zäther Valley, and behold its freshness and glory! And now the lash came off the whip, though it was tied on again and again, and it became shorter and shorter, till at last we had neither lash nor handle, for the shaft flew after the lash, or, more properly speaking, floated after it; the road had become quite navigable, and presented a perfect view of the commencement of the Deluge. Then one of the poor jades pulled too much, and then the other pulled too little; and now one of the traces snapped—a pretty state of things! A fine journey it was! The apron in front of the carriage had a great pool in the midst of it, with a channel leading into our lap. And now the rope bridles got entangled, and the reins were disgusted at this, and refused to hold. O thou glorious tavern in Zäther! how did I long far more to behold thee than thy famous valley! And the carriage went slower and slower, and the rain poured down faster and faster; and as for us, we were a long way from Zäther yet.

Patience, thou attenuated spider, that weavest thy web quietly in the antechamber, over the foot of the waiting suitor, spin thou my eyelids close, that I may sleep a sleep as quiet as the pace of the horses! Patience—but, no, there was nothing of the kind in the carriage that went to Zäther. But towards evening I reached the tavern by the road-side, close to the famous valley.

And everything in the courtyard was swimming in a comfortable chaos—litter and agricultural implements, broken pails and tubs, straw and hay; the fowls sat there so thoroughly soaked that they looked only shadows of themselves, or at best like feathered skeletons drawn up in rank and file; and even the ducks crowded against the damp wall, tired of so much water. The waiter was idle, and the maid still more idle, so that it was difficult to get anything from them; and the stairs were askew, and the floor was uneven, and had just been scoured and strewn thickly with sand, and the air was damp and raw; but without, scarcely twenty paces off, on the opposite side of the way, lay the celebrated valley, a garden laid out by Nature herself, and whose charm consisted in forest and birds, and especially in purling brooks and rushing fountains. There was a long opening: I could see the summits of the trees peering forth; but the rain had flung its misty veil over all else. The whole long evening I sat looking towards the valley, during this downpour of downpours; I could have fancied the Wenern and Wettern and a few more lakes were pouring down from the clouds through an immense sieve. I had ordered something to eat and drink, but I got nothing; they ran upstairs and they ran downstairs; there was a great clattering on the hearth; the maids gossiped, and the men drank brandy; and strangers arrived, who were taken in and served with roast and boiled. Several hours had thus passed away, and I read an energetic lecture to the maid, whereupon the maid very coolly replied,

"But the gentleman can't eat anything, if he goes on sitting there writing."

That was a long evening, but it passed away at length. In the inn every sound had ceased; all the travellers except myself had departed, no doubt to seek better quarters in Hedemora or Brümbäck. I peeped into the dirty parlour through the half-open door, and there sat two labourers, playing with old greasy cards; a big dog was lying under the table, glaring with round red eyes; the kitchen was empty, the floor was wet, the wind howled, and the rain plashed.

"And now to bed," said I.

I had slept an hour, I might have slept two, when I was awakened by a loud cry from the road. I started up: it was twilight, for the nights do not become quite dark at this time of the year; it was about one o'clock. I heard a great knocking at the outer gate, a deep male voice called aloud. and then there was a great beating against the panels with a cudgel. Was it a drunkard or a lunatic trying to force his way in? And now the gate was opened; only a few words passed, and I heard a woman scream loudly. Then a great confusion began. Wooden shoes clattered across the yard, the cattle roared, rough voices of men mingled in the din. I jumped up, and sat wondering on the side of the bed. Go or stay ? what was to be done ? I looked out of the window, but nothing was to be seen on the road, and it rained still. All at once heavy steps came tramping upstairs; the door of the room next to mine was opened, and now the intruder stood still. I listened: my door was fastened inside with a great iron bolt. There was a tramping in the next room, and then some one knocked at my door; and all the while the rain was beating against the window-panes, and the wind rattled them to and fro.

"Are there any travellers here ? " cried a voice. "The house is on fire ! "

I huddled on my clothes, and ran out of the door towards the staircase. No smoke was to be seen; but when I got out into the yard— the whole building was of wood, a long, straggling pile—I encountered smoke, clouds, and flame. The fire had broken out in a baking-oven, which no one had cared to look after; a traveller, who happened to pass by on the road, saw what was occurring, and called and thundered an alarm at the gate. And the women shrieked, and the cattle roared when the flames stretched their red tongues towards them.

An engine now arrived, and the fire was put out. It was bright morning. I stood on the high road, hardly a hundred paces from the celebrated valley. One may just as well jump into the water as creep in, and accordingly I jumped in! The rain poured, and the water streamed, and everything was one great pond. The trees seemed to turn the wrong sides of their leaves to the rain, and they said, as the reeds had said yesterday,

"We drink with our heads, and with our feet, and with our whole bodies, and yet we can stand on one leg! Hurrah! It rains, it pours: we drink and we sing, and this is our song, and it's a bran new one!"

Yes, but the reeds sang the same thing yesterday. I looked and looked, and all that I could see of the beauty of the Zäther Valley seemed that it had been washed!

VI.

THE MIDSUMMER FEAST AT LECKSAND.

On the farther bank of the Dal River, across which our way now led us for the third or fourth time, lay Lecksand. The belfry tower, built of red boards at a little distance from the church, rose over the high trees of the clayey declivity; old willow trees bent in picturesque fashion over the strong stream. The "flying bridge" tottered beneath us; yes, once it even sank slightly, so that the water rippled about the horses' hoofs; but that is the nature of this kind of bridge; the iron chains that held it clattered and creaked, the planks groaned, the flooring was splashed, the water gurgled and rippled, and at last we disembarked where the road leads down to the town: there still stood the maypole of last year, with its faded flowers. How many of the hands that twined those wreaths may now already lie cold in the grave!

Next morning was the St. John's Feast. It was Sunday the 24th of June, a charming sunshiny day. The most picturesque feature of the celebration is the arrival and disembarkation of the people from the various parishes across the Siljan Lake.

We drove to the landing-place called Barkedalen, and before we had left the town behind us, great crowds came flocking from thence, and also from the mountains. Near Lecksand the way is skirted on both sides by rows of low wooden booths, which receive light only through the door. They form a complete street, and are used as stables by the country strangers, and are also used as dressing-rooms. Nearly all these booths were occupied by peasant women, who were arranging their dresses in the most becoming folds, while at the same time they glanced out at the open doors, that no one might pass by unobserved. The number of arriving churchgoers increased—men, women, and children, old and young, even babies—for at the Midsummer feast no one stays at home to take care of them, so that they must, perforce, go too. All must go to church. What a blaze of colour! green aprons and aprons fiery red gleam upon us; the rest of the costume of the women consists of a black petticoat, with a scarlet jacket and white sleeves. Each one carried a hymn-book wrapped in a folded silk pocket-handkerchief. The little girls were dressed all in yellow, with red aprons, the youngest of all in gowns of turmeric colour. The men wore black coats like our paletots, with embroidery of red wool; a red ribbon with a tassel hung down from the big black hat; dark breeches, and blue stockings with red garters, completed their costume. Thus there was a great diversity of colour on the woodland path that sunny summer morning. The path led directly down to the lake, which lay there bright and blue: twelve or fourteen long boats, formed like gondolas, were already drawn up by the flat shore, which is here covered with large stones; these served as stepping-stones for landing; the boats drew up to them, and the people scrambled, and carried and helped each other ashore. A thousand persons must have been standing there; and on the surface of the lake in the distance ten or twelve more boats were seen approaching, some with sixteen oars, others with twenty, and even four and twenty, the rowers being persons of both sexes, and each boat decorated with green boughs. This adornment, together with the many-coloured costumes, gave a more lively appearance than one would have expected to see in the sober North. The boats came nearer; all were crowded with passengers, but they approached quietly, without noise or sound of talking, to the forest-crowned shore. The boats were drawn up on the sand. It was a scene for a painter, especially one spot, where the whole company were seen moving onwards between trees and bushes. The most conspicuous objects were two ragged boys clad in fiery yellow, each with his bundle on his back: they belonged to Gagnef, the poorest parish in the "Dalern." A lame man, too, with his blind wife, came along. I thought of the verse in my A B C book:

> "The lame man with his crutch gets aid
>   From the blind man, marching on;
> Thus by these two is the journey made
>   That neither could compass alone."

We, too, managed to reach the town and the church, whither all were wending. More than five thousand persons were said to be assembled there. At nine o'clock the service began. Organ and pulpit were decked with blooming elder; the children also carried branches of the birch and elder tree; the very little ones were provided with a bit of hard bread, which they amused themselves by gnawing. There was communion service to-day for the young people who had been confirmed; there was organ music and psalm-singing; but, alas! there were also ear-piercing shrieks from the children, and a continual clamping of heavy iron-bound Dalecarlian shoes upon the stone pavement. All the church chairs, the gallery, and the aisle were filled with people; in the side aisles groups of playing children were seen mingled with devout elders; close by the sacristy sat a young woman nursing her infant, and looking like a living representation of an Italian Madonna.

The first effect produced by all this was impressive, but *only* the first effect. There were too many distracting sounds, too much crying of children piercing through the singing, too much noise of walking to and fro; and, to crown all, an unbearable smell of onions. Almost all present had brought with them little bunches of onions, at which they were continually biting. I could bear it no longer, and fled into the churchyard. Here, as everywhere amid the scenes of Nature, it was calm and holy. The church doors stood open, the sound of the organ and of the hymns poured out into God's sunshine by the open lake, and many who could find no room in the church stood here, and joined in the songs of those within; while round about on the tombs, which are nearly all of iron, sat mothers nursing their children—the beginning of life in contact with death and the grave. A very young peasant stood by a grave deciphering the inscription—

> "To have lived, how sweet it is!
> To know how to die—how glorious!"

Beautiful maxims of Christianity, verses evidently selected from the hymn-book, were to be read on the various tombs: there was time to pore over them all, for the service lasted several hours, a circumstance that could not have been favourable to devotion.

At last the congregation came pouring out of the church; the red and green aprons gleamed forth; but gradually the throng became closer, and, as it pressed forward, the black head-dresses and white linen sleeves and stripes became the prevailing colours, recalling the appearance of a procession in a Catholic country. Now the path became lively once more; the overcrowded boats pushed off, one waggon after another drove away, but yet people were left behind. They stood in groups in the broad street of Lecksand, from the church to the tavern. And I must acknowledge that my Danish tongue sounded very strange to them all; so I began speaking broken Swedish, and the waitress in the hotel

declared to me that she understood me better than she could the Frenchman who talked to her in French last year.

I was sitting in my room, when my hostess's little granddaughter, a
pretty child, comes tripping in, elate at the sight of my gay carpet-bag, my

THE GINGERBREAD MODELS.

Scotch plaid, and the red morocco lining of my travelling trunk. I took
up a sheet of paper, and cut out a mosque for the child, with minarets
and open windows, and she ran out of the room delighted. Soon afterwards I heard loud talking in the yard, and gradually became aware
that my work was the subject: stepping quietly forward to the wooden
balcony, I beheld grandmamma standing below in the yard, holding up
my mosque, with a beaming countenance. Around her stood a crowd of
Dalecarlians, male and female, all in a state of high artistic appreciation;
but the dear little girl was crying and stretching out her hands towards
her lawful property, which was being withheld from her because it was

' so beautiful." Much gratified and flattered, I crept back into my room, but presently there came a knock at the door: it was grandmamma, and she carried a large plate of gingerbread cakes.

"I bake the best in all Dalecarlia," she said; "but they are cut out in the old forms of my grandmother's time. Now, as the gentleman cuts out so beautifully, I thought perhaps he would cut me a few new shapes."

So all the evening of that midsummer day I sat cutting out designs for gingerbread cakes: nutcrackers with soldiers' boots, windmills which might have been mistaken for the miller in slippers and with a door in his stomach, and dancing girls who pointed one foot at Charles's Wain. The grandmother received them all, but she looked askance at the dancers, whose legs went too high for her; she thought they had three arms, and only one leg.

"These are new fashions," she said, "but they are difficult to copy."

So I may hope that my memory lives in Dalecarlia, in the form of new fashions for gingerbread.

VII.

THE POET'S SCUTCHEON.

IF a man wanted to paint a scutcheon for a poet, the most appropriate thing would certainly be to paint Scheherazade out of the "Thousand and One Nights," telling stories to the Sultan. Scheherazade is the poet, and the Sultan is the public that wants to be agreeably entertained, otherwise he will cut off his Scheherazade's head.

Powerful Sultan! Poor Scheherazade!

In more than a thousand and one forms Sultan Public sits and listens. Let us look at one or two of these forms.

Yonder sits a bilious, ill-tempered learned man. The leaves of his tree of life are scribbled over with commentaries; industry and perseverance crawl like snails over his pachydermatous skin, but his digestion is moth-eaten, and in a bad, a very bad state. Forgive, O learned man, the rich fulness of song, the untaught inspiration, the fresh young soul! Don't cut Scheherazade's head off!—But he *does*.

Yonder sits a most experienced sempstress; she has been in strange families out of solitary rooms, whence she has derived all her knowledge of the world: she understands what is romantic. Forgive, O ancient virgin, thou that hast been yoked to the needle, and sighest for romance in the prose of thy life, if these stories are not exciting enough for thee.

"Off with her head!" says the sempstress.

There sits a figure in a dressing-gown, the Oriental garb of the North for young counts, highnesses, rich brewers, and others. It is not easy to judge from the dressing-gown, the look of command, and the polished smile, upon what tree he has grown. His aspirations are those of the sempstress—to be excited, aroused, stuffed full of mysteries such as the late Speiss knew.

And Scheherazade is decapitated.

Wise, enlightened Sultan, now thou comest in the form of the school-boy; Romans and Greeks, buckled together in the book-strap, bearest thou upon thy back, as Atlas bore the sky. Don't overlook poor Scheherazade; don't cut her head off before you have learned your task, and become a child again; don't decapitate poor Scheherazade.

Thou young diplomatist, in gorgeous array, who showest by the crosses on thy breast the number of Courts thou hast visited with thy noble

THE SULTAN AND SCHEHERAZADE.

chief, speak kindly of Scheherazade's name, speak of her in French, that she may attain a distinction beyond her native tongue. Translate a single verse of her song, as badly as thou mayest, but carry it into the brilliant saloon, and her sentence of death will be remitted by the sweet *charmant* of mercy.

Mighty thrower-down and setter-up! Thou Jupiter of newspapers, Zeus of weeklies, monthlies, and periodicals generally, shake not thy locks in wrath! Hurl not thy thunderbolts if Scheherazade sing other-wise than thou hast been accustomed in thy family to hear, or if she have no following amongst thy retainers. Don't cut off her head!

One more form we must notice, the most dangerous of all—the man with the stormy rapture of applause upon his lips, the blind enthusiast. The water into which Scheherazade has dipped her fingers is to him a Castalian spring; and the throne he builds up for her apotheosis be-comes her scaffold.

Such is the poet's scutcheon: paint upon it—

"THE SULTAN AND SCHEHERAZADE."

But why portray none of the worthy forms, the mild, the honest, and the noble? They come, too, and upon these Scheherazade turns her eyes; among them she boldly raises her proud head towards the heavens, and sings of the harmonies there, and of those here below in the heart of man.

That would have a disturbing effect upon the shield, "the Sultan and Scheherazade." The sword of death hangs over her while she tells her stories, and the Sultan's expression lets us expect that it will fall. But Scheherazade is the conqueror, and the poet is a conqueror too : he is rich and conquering, even in his poor room in his most solitary hours ; and then rose after rose bursts forth, the sky is bright with shooting stars, as if a new heaven were being created, and the old one were rolling away. The world does not hear of it, for it is the poet's own festival, richer than the costliest firework display of kings. He is happy like Scheherazade, he is a conqueror, he is mighty ; fancy adorns his walls with tapestry brighter than those in the king's chamber ; feeling strikes for him a chord of beauty from the bosom of humanity ; reason lifts him through the glory of creation up to God, while yet he forgets not to plant his foot firmly on the earth. His is a rare power, a rare happiness. We will not see him at the bar of misrepresentation, accused and pitied : we paint only his scutcheon, dip into the colours of the "wrong side" of the world, and thus receive the interpretation of

"THE SULTAN AND SCHEHERAZADE."

Look! that is it—don't cut off Scheherazade's head.

VIII.

THE RIVER DAL.

THERE were heroes before Homer's time, but they are not known—no poet gave them immortality by his songs. The same necessity exists with regard to the beauties of nature—they must be made famous in the world by books and pictures ; they must be introduced to the notice of the many, and receive a kind of world-patent attesting what they are, and then only do they become living realities. The mountain streams of the North have foamed on during thousands of years in unacknowledged beauty. The great high road of the world does not lead this way ; no steamer carries the traveller conveniently along the Dal Elf ; cascade after cascade necessitate a complicated system of locks. Schubert is, perhaps, the only stranger who has written of the wild splendour and beauty of Dalecarlia, and who has spoken of the greatness of the Dal Elf.

Clear as the waves of a sea, the mighty Dal Elf rolls onward in endless windings through silent forests and changing plains, now spreading out in its broad bed, now hemmed in, sometimes reflecting the nodding trees and the red blockhouses of the lonely towns, at others falling in cascades over great boulders of rock.

Miles asunder, on the mountain ridge between Sweden and Norway, the eastern and the western Dal Elf have their source, and above Bälstad they flow together in one bed. By this time their waters have been augmented by mountain streams and lakes. Come up hither. Here you shall find a wealth of picturesque scenery, sometimes in rocky majesty, at others in soft idyllic beauty; you will be drawn quite to the source of the stream, to the rushing brook above the huts of the Finns, for a longing will come upon you to follow the windings of every stream which this river receives into its bosom.

By the Nqrwegian boundary, in the parish of Serna, the traveller sees the first waterfall, the mighty cascade of Njupeskärs; the river falls perpendicularly from a rock to the depth of above four hundred feet.

We linger in the dark woodland waste, where the Elf seems to be surrounded by all the solemnity of nature. The stream rolls its clear waters over a prophyry bed, where the mill-wheel turns, and where the gigantic prophyry sarcophagi and vases are hewn out.

We follow the river through the Siljan Lake, where superstition represents Noke swimming as a gigantic river horse with a mane of green rushes, and where the *Fata Morgana* exhibits its wonders in the warm summer day.

We sail on the stream from the Siljan Lake under drooping branches of the willow, by the parsonage, where the swans collect in flocks; we glide slowly, horses and carriage embarked on the great ferry-boat, across the deep rushing stream, under Bälstad's picturesque shore. Here the Elf spreads out and majestically rolls its great waves through a wooded landscape, as majestic and grand as a scene in North America.

We see the foaming river under Avesta's ridges of yellow clay like liquid amber; the yellow water pours down in picturesque falls by the copper mine, where fiery tongues arise in rainbow splendour, and the hammer-strokes on the plates of copper sound in unison with the moaning of the Elf waterfalls.

And as a concluding scene of splendour in the life of the Dal Elf, before the river loses itself in the waves of the Baltic, appears the Elf Karleby fall.

Schubert has compared this cataract with that at Schaffhausen, but we must not forget that the Rhine cannot show such a mass of water at Laufen as that which pours down at Elf Karleby.

Two and a half Swedish miles from Gefle, where the main road to Upsala leads over the Dal Elf, the traveller, from the stone bridge which he has to cross, gets a view of the entire majestic waterfall. Close by the bridge is a toll-house, and here the stranger may pass the night, and gaze from his little window at the foaming waters; he may behold them in the clear moonlight, when darkness dwells among the pine trees and in the thickets of oak, and all the reflected light comes from the flying, bubbling waters; he can behold them when the morning sun builds up their rainbow, like an airy bridge of colour, from the wood-crowned rock to the middle of the fall, through the trembling spray.

We came hither from Gefle, and already from afar we could see from the high road the blue clouds of shivered water-dust rising over the dark

green tree-tops. The carriage stopped near the bridge; we alighted,
and close to us the whole mighty stream was thundering down.

No painter can give us on the canvas the true picture of a waterfall—
the movement would be wanting; and how then can we paint in words
the majestic greatness of such a spectacle, its beauty of colour and its
lightning course? It cannot be done; and yet the attempt is made:
a sketch is built up in words of the marvellous picture which our eye
beheld, and which even memory can only recall with uncertain touches.

Above the waterfall the Dal Elf divides into three arms; two of these
encircle a wooded rocky island, and fall beside its perpendicular walls;
of these falls the right hand one is the finest: the third arm makes a
circuit, and rejoins the main stream just below the united falls; it comes
rushing forward as if to meet the cataract, or to command it to stop, and
now turns away in boiling eddies with the arrowy stream, which comes
bursting against the stone pillars of the bridge as if it would crush them
to atoms.

The landscape on the left was enlivened by the appearance of a number
of goats browsing among the nut bushes; reared here, and accustomed
to the thundering moan of the waters, they ventured to the very edge
of the precipice; on the right a flock of screaming birds flew onward
over the glorious oak trees. Light waggons, each drawn by one horse,
and driven by a man who stood upright holding the reins, hurried along
the broad forest road from the mining works on the island.

Thither will we betake ourselves, to bid farewell to the Dal Elf at one
of its most beautiful spots, a spot that seems to transport the stranger
into a far more southerly scene than he can expect to encounter here in
the North. For the road here is lovely, and the oak tree grows in full
luxuriance, spreading forth its leafy crown.

The island mining works are beautifully situated. We went there—
what a life and movement reigned around! The mill-wheels were turning round and round, heavy beams were being sawn asunder, iron was
being forged on gigantic anvils, and all by the power of the water. The
houses of the workmen form a complete little town. There was a long
street, with red-painted wooden houses under the picturesque oak and
birch trees. The grass was velvety to behold; and in the master's house,
that rises like a little castle in front of its garden, there reigned in hall
and chamber what the Englishman emphatically calls "comfort."

We did not find the proprietor at home, but hospitality is always
the prevailing spirit in these parts. We were well and kindly entertained; fish and poultry, fragrant and steaming, were served up to us,
as in an enchanted castle. The garden itself was a species of enchantment; and here were planted three beech trees, which throve well.
The strong north wind had marvellously rounded off the crowns of the
wild chestnut trees in the avenue; they looked as if the shears of the
gardener had been at work upon them. In the forcing-house hung
golden yellow oranges; the windows were half opened to-day for these
glorious fruits and flowers of the South, so that the artificial warmth
and the fresh warm air of the northern summer met each other. The

arm of the Dal Elf which winds round the garden is strewn with little
islands, on which grow pleasant hanging birches and pines in northern
splendour. There are little islands with quiet green groves, and others
with rich grass, high ferns, and variegated wild flowers; no Turkey

THE HAUNT OF NOKE.

carpet could display fresher colours. The stream between these islands
is sometimes rapid, deep, and clear, sometimes like a broad meadow
with silky green reeds, water-lilies, and brown feathery rushes; sometimes it appears as a brook with a pebbly bottom, and now again it is
spread abroad like a quiet mill-pond.

The landscape here in summer about St. John's Day seems created
for the play of Noke and for a dance of elves. Here in the sheen of
the full moon the dryad must tell her stories, and Noke must seize the
golden harp, and believe that one may be happy at least so long as the
night lasts.

On the other side of the estate the chief stream rolls on, the full Dal Elf. Dost thou hear the monotonous moaning? It comes not upon thine ear from the Elf Karleby,—it is close beside thee; it is the Laa waterfall, in the midst of which the island of Ask lies: the Elf is roaring and foaming over the leaping salmon.

Let us sit down here, between the rocky blocks on the shore, in the red evening sun, which pours its golden glory over the waters of the Dal Elf. Splendid river! — only for a few seconds dost thou labour yonder amongst the mills, and then rushest foaming over the rocks of Elf Karleby into thy bed, that leads thee to thy eternity—the Baltic!

The Good Mother

SINÉAD MORIARTY

PENGUIN
IRELAND

PENGUIN IRELAND

UK | USA | Canada | Ireland | Australia
India | New Zealand | South Africa

Penguin Ireland is part of the Penguin Random House group of companies
whose addresses can be found at global.penguinrandomhouse.com

First published 2017

001

Set in 13.5/16 pt Garamond MT Std
Typeset in India by Thomson Digital Pvt Ltd, Noida, Delhi
Printed in Great Britain by Clays Ltd, St Ives plc

A CIP catalogue record for this book is available from the British Library

ISBN: 978–1–844–88351–6

www.greenpenguin.co.uk

MIX
Paper from
responsible sources
FSC® C018179

Penguin Random House is committed to a
sustainable future for our business, our readers
and our planet. This book is made from Forest
Stewardship Council® certified paper.

For Dad, we miss you

'Motherhood: All love begins and ends there'

Robert Browning

Summer

I

Kate stood in the empty hall and looked around. Nothing left but memories. She remembered moving in around ten years ago. Nick had carried her over the threshold, even though it was a long time since she'd been a blushing bride. He'd been like an excited little kid, running around, showing her the fancy fridge that churned out ice cubes, the Jacuzzi and the big garden where the kids could play football.

It was his dream house. Nick felt as if he'd 'arrived'. Big house, big garden, fancy car. Things were good, really good. Nick was doing well and finally able to have the life he'd always dreamed of living.

They'd been happy then. Luke was eight and Jess was two when they'd moved in. Jess had taken her time to arrive. After three miscarriages and years of disappointment they had almost given up, but then Kate had got pregnant and gone full-term. The longed-for and beloved Jess had arrived, like a ray of sunshine, in their lives. She had been worth the wait. Gazing at her adoringly in the hospital, Nick said they now had the perfect family.

The house had been full of laughter and fun. They'd had lots of birthday celebrations and good times there. Kate had enjoyed it all, every minute.

She knew buying the house had been a stretch for them financially. She just hadn't realized how much of a stretch. Nick had been vague about the deposit and repayments, and she'd been too wrapped up in the kids and the daily chores, and too naive to ask questions.

Or maybe she hadn't wanted to know. The truth was, she'd stuck her head in the sand on purpose. Life was good, and Kate hadn't wanted to know the details. Nick had said he had it under control and she'd gladly left him to it.

When the economic downturn had badly affected the big estate agent Nick worked for, Kate had just hoped for the best. She'd redoubled her efforts to create the perfect home, always having a meal prepared for Nick when he came in at the end of the day. She'd become a regular domestic goddess, trying to smooth over the cracks.

She'd wanted to make their home a haven for Nick, but it hadn't been enough. And then, instead of bringing them closer, Bobby's birth had pushed Nick even further away. When Nick had started to work late all the time and come home smelling of someone else's perfume, Kate had ignored it . . . until it was too late.

She looked around at her home and bit her lip to prevent herself crying. Everything was so messed up. What the hell would her life be like from now on?

'*Muuuuuuum!*' Bobby shouted from the front door, hands on his hips. 'I want to go now. It's hot and sweaty in the car.'

Kate went over and kissed his hot little face. 'I just need to get Jess. She's upstairs.'

She found Jess in her bedroom. Her daughter had her back to her. Kate knew by the hunch of her shoulders and the quiet sniffles that she was crying. She went over and put her arms around her. Jess stiffened. 'I'm sorry, pet.'

'I'm fine, Mum.'

Kate turned her daughter to face her. Jess wiped away her tears roughly with the sleeve of her shirt. 'I know this is hard, Jess, but I think living with Granddad will be fun.' She tried to sound convincing.

Jess nodded. 'It's just . . . it's just all so final. I thought that maybe Dad would come home, but now I guess I know he won't. Will he?'

Kate hugged her. Poor Jess. She was the optimist in the family. The boys knew Nick was never coming back. Even at seven years old, Bobby knew. But here was Jess, the middle child, still hoping for the happy ending that could never be. 'Your dad's with Jenny now, pet. They have a new baby and a new life, and that's not going to change. But he still loves you all very much,' she added hastily.

'Yeah, which is why he never comes to see us,' Luke drawled from the doorway.

'Luke,' Kate said, in a warning voice. 'Your sister's upset.'

Luke came in and put a big muscly arm around his little sister's shoulders. 'Come on, Jess. I know Granddad's house is a lot smaller and he's a bit mad, but we'll be fine.'

'You don't have to share a room with Bobby,' Jess reminded him.

Luke grinned. 'Yeah, it sucks for you. But I have to study for my Leaving Cert so I can't have Bobby droning on about his facts all day long. Besides, I'll probably move out next year and live close to whatever university I end up going to, so you can have my room then.'

'But I don't want you to move out. I'd miss you.'

Luke kissed the top of her head. 'You're too soft, Jess. You need to toughen up.'

'She's perfect just the way she is.' Kate smiled at them.

They both rolled their eyes.

'You always say that, Mum,' Jess said, grinning at her brother.

'It's true. You three kids are my proudest achievement. And I know the last few months have been awful and I wish . . . well, I just wish that . . .' Kate was choking up.

Luke put his hand on her arm. 'It's okay, Mum. You did everything you could. Dad's just a selfish dickhead.'

'Luke, don't speak about your father like that.'

'Daddy's a dickhead,' Bobby shouted from the door, giggling.

Kate glared at Luke.

He shrugged. 'I speak the truth.'

'You're eighteen, Luke. You should know when to zip it. And as for you, Bobby, you're supposed to be waiting in the car.'

Luke flung his arm around her and pulled her in for a hug. 'Chill, Mum.' To Bobby he said, 'Don't use bad words. It's not cool.'

'But you said it and you're cool.' Bobby frowned, trying to make sense of these conflicting statements.

Kate bent down to look her youngest in the eye. 'Bad language is not okay. You know that and so does Luke. Now, come on, all of you, Granddad's waiting for us.' She ushered them downstairs and out of the front door, telling them to get into the car and buckle up.

Once they'd left, she allowed herself a few minutes for a final walkabout. It was stupid: she should just walk out of the door and not look back, but it was so hard to leave the place. You spent all your time creating a home, but you never really knew just how much it meant to you until it was taken away. This had been her sanctuary from the world, the place she most enjoyed being, an extension of herself and her hopes for the future. Now, it wasn't hers any more, and she had no idea what her future held – stress, loneliness and financial worry, probably. Nick had taken everything from her, home, security and, most of all, her self-esteem. Leaving her for a younger model was so cli-chéd it should make her laugh. But it wasn't funny. It hurt like hell. The pain of it kept looping out and around her, drowning her sense of self and self-worth.

Slowly, she forced herself to walk towards the front door. She didn't want to go. She had a brief, crazy thought of staging a sit-in protest and forcing the bank to let her keep it, but she knew that was daft. Besides, this home and that future were gone now: the place was stripped bare, back to how it was when they'd first bought it. Just like me, Kate thought sadly. Right back to square one.

Her phone pinged and she pulled it out of her pocket. A message from Maggie. She opened it and smiled. Trust Maggie and her perfect timing! *Today must be hell for you. Chin up! I'll be over at the weekend to help you unpack and put manners on George! I'll bring wine. Lots and lots of wine! You'll be okay. Love you. M.*

She pushed back her shoulders, took a deep breath and stepped outside onto the step. As she pulled the front door shut behind her, the finality of the lock's click almost made her sink to her knees and cry. Instead, she waved to her waiting children, swallowed her grief and took her place in the driver's seat.

Kate eased her battered old car down the driveway. She saw Jess's lip quivering in the rear-view mirror and her heart ached. This was not the life she'd planned for her children. She'd never wanted them to come from a broken home. How had everything gone so wrong?

I'm a forty-two-year-old woman with three kids moving back in with my dad because I'm broke and homeless, she thought. She gripped the steering-wheel and tried to control her breathing. Now that Nick was preoccupied with Jenny and Jaden, the baby, Kate had to be even more mindful of the kids. She had to be more loving and patient and giving . . . but she was exhausted. All she wanted to do was lie down, pull the duvet over her head and cry.

*

George was standing at the gate when they arrived, wearing his navy apron with 'The Village Café' on it. His cheeks were flushed.

'Uh-oh, Granddad has a cross face,' Bobby said.

They climbed out of the car.

'Lookit, Kate, I'm happy for you to move in, you know I am, but your removal men have left boxes all over the kitchen and I'm trying to run a business here. Besides, Sarah just called to say she's not coming in today and that she's found another job. The new French girl, Nathalie, is useless, so I'm pretty much on my own. I need a hand.'

Kate took charge. 'Right. Luke, you and the others tidy up the boxes while I help Granddad in the café. Put all the boxes upstairs in my bedroom. Pile them up in the corner out of the way and I'll sort them out later. When you've finished, come down and help. We'll be busy for lunch.'

Kate followed her father through the hall into the big kitchen that served the café.

'I'll sort these out if you go and serve coffees,' George said, as he began firing homemade quiches into the big oven.

Kate went through the kitchen door that led to the café. There were two tables waiting to be served. At the other three occupied tables, people were busy drinking coffee and eating scones. Five tables were empty, but not for long. The lunchtime rush would start soon.

Kate took the orders for the two tables and went back into the kitchen. She inhaled the scent of the fresh coffee beans and closed her eyes. The familiar scent of her childhood always calmed her. Kate knew the place like the back of her hand. She'd grown up behind the counter. As far back as she could remember she'd helped her mum and dad run the Village Café. Her mum had always been more front-of-house while her dad did a lot of the cooking. But after her

8

mother's death six years ago, that had changed. George had had to engage more with the customers and he had grown used to it. It didn't come naturally to him, but he was much better at it than he had been.

Throughout her married life Kate had often received urgent calls whenever a staff member had called in sick or a big party was booked in. She liked helping her parents – as an only child she was close to both and the café was her home from home.

After her mother died, she had called in every day to make sure her father was coping. He had been utterly shattered by Nancy's death, but with Kate's help and the café needing to be run, he had muddled through. Having to get up and open it every day had kept him going, given him a purpose. Kate often wondered what he would have done if he hadn't had the business. It had been a life-saver and kept him active and busy.

Her dad had been a rock to Kate when Nick had left her two years ago. He'd stepped in and given her money to get her through, and when the bank had repossessed the house, he had immediately suggested they all move in with him. Kate had wanted to weep with relief.

She knew it wasn't going to be easy, given that her father was used to living alone, but they'd get through somehow. She'd make it work. She had to – she had nowhere else to go and the kids needed stability. As a new customer came to the counter, Kate put a smile on her face. She willed herself to be positive and hopeful for the future. Things would get better – for sure they couldn't get worse. This was the lowest she had ever fallen. The only way was up. It was a new beginning.

Autumn

2

Jess swung back and forth on the little black gate. She was bored and wanted to go back inside the house, but she didn't want to leave Luke alone.

He was leaning against the wall, looking up and down the road. Jess watched him check his phone. No message.

Maybe Dad's just late, she thought. He was always late. In fact, he had never been on time in his life. Jess was always on time. She hated being late because she knew how it made the other person feel – like they didn't matter.

Luke raised his face to the sun. He was so handsome, Jess thought. He'd got a lovely tan over the summer, even though they hadn't gone on a sun holiday this year. There was no way Mum could afford it, and Dad had said he couldn't either. But Luke had spent so much time training outside, he looked as if he'd been in Spain for a month. He was super-fit, like the professional rugby players on TV.

'I bet when you go back to school tomorrow you'll be the fittest guy on your team,' she said, trying to distract him. She wanted to make him feel better. She had a horrible feeling their dad wasn't coming and she knew it would hurt him.

Luke gave her one of his crooked smiles. 'I doubt it. I'd say Harry's been working out in Italy.'

Jess stopped swinging and leant against the gate. 'Maybe not. Maybe Harry got really fat and lazy in Italy. Maybe he spent all summer eating pizza and ice cream and lying about by the pool.'

Luke laughed. 'I hope so, but it's very unlikely. Knowing Harry's dad, he probably hired him a personal trainer to make sure he stayed in top condition.'

Unlike our dad, who doesn't give a damn, Jess knew Luke was thinking.

'How come Harry's dad is so into rugby?' she asked.

Luke put his phone down on the wall. 'He played senior cup rugby when he was in school and he's obsessed with Harry making the team. I know he's hoping I'll get injured so Harry will get picked.'

'You won't, though, will you, Luke? Get injured?'

Luke shook his head. 'No. I'm going to get on that team if it kills me.'

Jess knew that rugby was the only thing Luke really enjoyed . . . well, that and being with Piper.

Jess glanced down at her brother's trainers. Piper had handed him a box yesterday covered with shiny paper. When he'd unwrapped it and held up the trainers, he'd been over the moon. He was so happy. Jess wanted to kiss Piper for making Luke's face light up like that.

'Jesus, Piper, they're way too much,' he'd said.

'Hey, babe, it's not every day you turn eighteen.'

'I know, but seriously . . .'

'I got paid last week and wanted to treat you.'

'They're awesome.' He'd leant over and kissed her.

Jess had looked away then because her eyes had filled with tears. She was so happy that Luke had Piper for his girl-friend – she was amazing.

Jess reckoned Luke was in love with Piper. She often caught him staring at Instagram photos of her when he thought no one was looking. She prayed that Piper was as into Luke as Luke was into her. She thought she was, but it was hard to tell with Piper because she was super-nice to everyone.

14

But when Jess saw the trainers yesterday, she'd felt really good. If Piper had spent that much money on Luke, she must be really crazy about him.

Bobby came up behind them on the path.

'Hey, little guy,' Luke said, high-fiving him.

Jess loved it when Luke was nice to Bobby. Poor Bobby worshipped him and sometimes Luke kind of ignored him. Jess knew Luke didn't mean it, but when he gave Bobby attention, Bobby was the happiest kid ever. It was a bit annoying because Jess always tried to be nice to Bobby but he didn't seem to care about her. He really only wanted Luke.

'Whatcha doing?' Bobby asked.

'Waiting for Dad to pick me up and take me out.' Luke sighed.

'For your birthday?'

'Yep.'

'But it was yesterday.' Bobby frowned.

'I know, but he was busy then.'

'Dad's *always* busy.' Bobby took Jess's place on the gate and swung back and forth.

Luke checked his phone again. Still no message. It was six thirty. Their father was half an hour late.

'He's probably with stupid Jaden and his pooey nappies,' Bobby said.

Oh, God, not Jaden again, Jess thought. All Bobby ever did was bang on about poor Jaden. It wasn't his fault he was born. He was only a baby. Bobby was so mean about him. He hated him. Like, really hated him. Jess sometimes worried that he might pinch the poor baby or hurt him if he was ever left alone with him. On the rare times they saw Jaden, Jess watched Bobby like a hawk.

'Dad's probably having his balls squeezed by his stupid girlfriend,' Luke muttered.

15

Thankfully, Bobby didn't hear him say that. Jess felt her stomach turn over. Even she hated Jenny. Well, 'hate' was probably too strong a word. You weren't supposed to hate anyone. But Jess certainly didn't like her. Jenny had caused this whole mess. Jenny had made her parents split up and then her dad leave, and now baby Jaden had made him not even be around any more. Jess wished he had never met Jenny.

'I heard Mummy on the phone yesterday calling Daddy a prick.' Bobby grinned.

'Bobby! Mind your language,' Jess said.

'I'm just saying what Mummy said.'

Luke's phone beeped.

'Is it Dad?' Jess asked.

'Nope. It's Harry.'

Jess leant in and read the message. *See you tomorrow, bro, hope the summer was good. I hear you and Piper are serious now – niiiiiiice.*

Luke typed back: *Not bad* ☺ *See you 2mrw.*

'Do you think Harry will be the winger on the team or you?' Bobby asked.

'Me.'

'I hope so. You're brilliant at rugby. I know Daddy thinks soccer is the best game because he was good at it, but I think rugby is. I want to be like you, Luke.'

Luke smiled down at him and ruffled his hair. 'I bet you'll be brilliant at rugby too.'

'I don't think so. I heard Daddy say, "Bobby can't kick snow off a rope."' Bobby looked down at his bare feet.

Luke cursed under his breath. 'He was only joking.'

'You're great, Bobby. I'm sure Dad didn't mean it,' Jess added.

'Can I tell you both a secret?' Bobby asked.

'Sure,' they said, exchanging a look.

'I hate Chelsea Football Club and I only pretend to like them cos of Daddy. I think they suck.'

Luke laughed. 'So do I, but we'd better not tell Dad that – we don't want to wind him up.'

Jess smiled. It was nice being together, just the three of them, chatting. Luke spent so much time with Piper or training that they didn't see much of him.

They heard the front door opening and their mother's voice calling, 'Luke?'

They turned around. She was standing in a flour-covered apron holding her phone. She looked upset. Oh, God, Jess knew that face. She was wearing her your-father's-let-you-down-again expression.

'He's not coming, is he?' Luke said, pushing himself away from the wall and standing up straight.

'I'm sorry, love, no. He said Jaden has a temperature and Jenny's panicking so they're taking him to the doctor.'

'Why can't she take Pooey Pants to the doctor on her own, like you take us on your own?' Bobby asked.

Jess heard her mother mutter, 'Because she's a child herself,' but out loud she said, 'I don't know, Bobby. She's obviously worried.'

Bobby wandered back into the house as Kate came down the path towards them. Luke was staring at the ground. Kate put her hand on his shoulder, and Jess watched as he moved away from her touch. She knew he was struggling not to crack.

In a strangled voice he said, 'I thought this once, this one bloody time, my useless fucker of a father would actually be here. Turning eighteen is kind of a big deal.'

Jess wanted to reach over and hug him, but she knew not to. Luke's fists were clenched, and he was trying hard not to cry.

'Oh, Luke, it *is* a big deal. I'm sure he'll make it up to you,' Kate said.

Luke's eyes were full of rage. 'No, he won't, Mum, because he's a loser. When Killian turned eighteen his dad bought him a car and threw a huge party for him. My dad can't even turn up a day late with a card.' He kicked the wall. 'How could I have been so stupid, waiting at the gate like a little kid? Even Bobby knew he wouldn't show. This is it, Mum. It's over. I'm never letting him disappoint me again. If you expect nothing, you can't get hurt.'

'Don't say that.' Kate looked like she might start crying. 'Why don't you call some pals and go to the movies or something? My treat.'

Luke shook his head. 'You did enough yesterday, Mum. It's fine. Forget it.'

'Luke, your dad loves you, he's just . . . a bit overwhelmed and not very good at juggling things.'

Jess flinched as Luke gazed straight into their mother's eyes. 'Dad has let me down for the last time.' He pushed past them, walked into the house and went up the stairs.

Kate's shoulders dropped and she looked defeated. Jess reached out and held her hand. Kate pulled her into her arms and hugged her tightly. 'What would I do without my little angel?' she whispered into Jess's hair.

'It's okay,' Jess said. 'Luke'll be all right soon. He's just disappointed.'

Kate straightened. 'I'd better get back before Granddad fires me,' she said, smiling weakly.

Jess watched her mother walk up the path and back inside. She worked from morning till night now, and still there wasn't really enough money to go around. As Jess went slowly into the house, she wondered how long Kate could carry on without getting sick. If anything happened to their mother, she and her brothers would be shattered. She was the centre of the circle, the point around which they all lived their lives. They needed her.

Jess went upstairs and stood outside Luke's bedroom door, listening to the music blaring. She knew he was in there, probably crying or punching the wall. She had to do something. She couldn't let his birthday weekend end like this.

Yesterday had been so nice. Mum had made Luke's favourite dinner and bought him a lovely hoodie. Jess knew that August was a really bad month for her because it was 'back to school' and she had to pay for books and uniforms, and money was tight. But you'd never have guessed it yesterday. She'd gone all out for Luke.

Jess had helped her make a cake and they'd blown up balloons and put up a banner so the kitchen looked really nice, and her mum had said how proud she was of Luke, the 'fantastic young man you've turned into', and she'd cried a bit then and Luke had allowed her to hug him. Granddad had gone all mushy too, which wasn't like him. He'd told Luke he was a 'wonderful young man and grandson' and that he had high hopes for his future. Then he'd given him a voucher for his favourite clothes shop. Jess was delighted. Luke didn't get new stuff very often. It had been a really lovely day, but now it had been ruined.

She went back downstairs to the hall, picked up the house phone and dialled Piper's mobile.

'Hello?'

'Piper, it's Jess, Luke's sister.'

'Hi, hon, what's up?'

'It's about Luke...' Jess explained what had happened and how unhappy Luke was, that he was in his room on his own and it wasn't a good birthday any more.

'Oh, no, poor Luke.' Piper sounded upset for him. 'I'll be finished work in about an hour and I'll come straight over. Don't worry, sweetie, we'll cheer him up.'

An hour later, Jess opened the front door to Piper and grinned. 'Thanks for coming,' she said, as Piper kissed her forehead.

'Where is he?' Piper asked.

Jess brought her upstairs and Piper knocked on Luke's bedroom door.

'Go away, Jess.'

'It's me, babe,' Piper called.

'Just a sec.'

Jess and Piper could hear Luke scrambling around, opening and closing drawers.

'He's tidying up for you,' Jess said.

'That's kind of sweet,' Piper said, with a smile.

Jess walked away as the bedroom door opened.

'Hey, what are you doing here?'

'I came straight from work. Jess called me about your dad standing you up. Sucks.'

'She shouldn't have told you.'

Piper put her arms around his neck. 'Hey, I want to know when you've had a bad day. I'm here for you. I'm Team Luke.'

As Jess went down the stairs, she saw Luke pull Piper into his bedroom. While kissing her, he kicked the door closed.

Happy with herself, Jess headed into the café to see if she could help. Kate still looked worried, so Jess went over to her and told her that Piper had arrived.

'Thank goodness for that,' Kate said, clearly relieved. 'That'll put a smile back on his face. Why don't you go and ask if she'd like to stay for dinner? I'll make something nice and we'll all cheer him up.'

Jess nodded. 'Sounds good. I'll just tidy those tables over there first.'

Jess worked for the next hour, helping her mother and granddad by clearing tables and putting on the dishwasher. As the café started to empty, she went back into the house and mixed up a batch of Rocky Roads, her speciality, then ran back upstairs and knocked gently on Luke's door.

'Luke?'

'What do you want?'

'Would Piper like to stay for dinner?'

Luke opened his bedroom door. 'Yes.'

'Cool.' Jess grinned. 'Hey, Piper.'

'Thanks for the call. I think I've cheered him up.' She winked.

Luke grabbed his sister's nose and squeezed it. 'You're an interfering little mouse but I forgive you.'

'I didn't want you to be unhappy on your birthday weekend.'

'Don't give out to her. She's a sweetie,' Piper said.

Jess gazed adoringly at her. Piper was so cool and nice and pretty and just . . . fabulous. Jess hoped for the thousandth time that she'd look just like Piper when she was eighteen.

'So, are you coming?'

'We'll be there in a minute. Go on.' Luke nudged Jess towards the door.

'I made Rocky Roads for dessert. I know you like them and I thought it would cheer you up,' Jess said.

'Awww, you are too cute. My sisters would never do something so nice for me,' Piper said.

'Wouldn't they?' Jess asked. 'I wish I had sisters.'

'Never! All we do is fight over make-up and clothes and who ate whose food. Yesterday Penny came into the shop I'm working in and actually tried to pull my boots off.'

Jess giggled.

'Seriously, in front of everyone, including my manager. She said they were hers, I hadn't asked to borrow them and she wanted them back. My manager had to peel her off me and ask her to leave. I nearly got fired. You're lucky not to have sisters.'

Jess shrugged. 'I guess the boys are okay.'

Luke kissed the top of Jess's head. 'I hope we're a bit more than just okay. Come on, enough talking, I'm starving.' He led the way downstairs.

Granddad was sitting at the table, reading the paper and trying to ignore Bobby.

'How high is the tallest man ever?'

'Eight foot two.'

Jess smiled. Granddad hadn't looked up from the paper when he answered. Eye contact with Bobby was dangerous: it indicated that you were interested in talking to him, and if you showed interest, he was relentless.

'Nope, eight foot eleven point one inches. How small is the smallest woman ever?'

'Three foot.'

'Two foot. How long is the longest tongue?'

'For the love of Jesus, this is the twentieth question,' Granddad said wearily.

Kate placed a roast chicken on the table. 'Bobby has a curious mind, Dad. It's important not to discourage him.'

'How long *is* the longest tongue? *I* want to know,' Jess said.

'Three point nine seven inches.'

'It's so cool that you know all this stuff,' Piper said.

'That's one word for it,' Granddad grumbled.

'How wide is the —'

Kate cut across him. 'That's enough facts for now, Bobby. Let's eat.'

'Thank God for that.'

'Don't mind Granddad,' Kate said to Bobby. 'He's just a bit grumpy.'

Jess sat beside Piper. 'Which sister are you closest to?'

Piper sat back. 'Probably Posy.'

'Do all your sisters have names that start with P?' Bobby asked.

'Yes.'

'Why?'

'Because, for some crazy reason, my parents thought it was a good idea.'

'What are they all called?' Bobby asked.

'I'm Piper, the twins are Poppy and Penny, and then there's Pauline and Posy.'

'Five girls!' Granddad said. 'Your poor father must be demented.'

Piper laughed. 'He is. He spends most of his time in the shed at the end of the garden.'

'I need one of those, these days,' Granddad said.

'I think it's lovely to have a big family,' Kate said. 'I was an only child and I always envied people with brothers and sisters.'

'One perfect child is plenty,' Granddad said.

Kate squeezed his hand.

Even though Granddad could be a bit grumpy, Jess could see how much he loved her mum. It was good to see how a normal father behaved, she thought.

Kate kept telling them all that their granddad was an example of what a great father should be – kind, caring and generous. Jess knew she was afraid that their own dad being so selfish was setting a bad example for them, especially for the boys. But she didn't need to worry. Luke and Bobby would never be like that. They were kind and not selfish at all.

Piper was telling Mum and Granddad a funny story about work. Luke was sitting back, staring lovingly at her. He was happy. Jess smiled. Everything was better again. They had each other and that was all that mattered.

3

Kate listened to her father chatting to the customers. She heard him say in a loud whisper, 'It was a big adjustment, but I'm used to it now and we're all getting along well.'

She continued unpacking the wine cases and thanked God for her father and the security of his house.

When she'd married Nick, she'd imagined a life full of happiness and fun and children and love . . . It had been, for a while.

Nick had begun pulling away after Bobby was born. He was home less often, working more often, distracted, disengaged. Kate knew she was losing him, but she didn't know how to fix it. She'd been overwhelmed with a third baby and didn't have the energy to put into their relationship. Nick had checked out, first emotionally and then physically. Jenny was the inevitable final straw. Nick's mid-life crisis had started at thirty-five and ended up with him shagging a twenty-two-year-old. He was a walking cliché, the estate agent who sleeps with the client.

Kate pulled a bottle of Bordeaux out of the case and wiped it down. She tried to quiet her mind, but it was always turning over the same questions. How was she ever going to afford her own house? Was she going to end up living with her father for ever? Would she be alone for ever? Would the kids be emotionally scarred for life? Would they not believe in marriage, having seen their parents fail at it?

Kate knew that Bobby was the most affected. Luke had had good years with his dad and so had Jess – as the only girl,

Nick had doted on her. But Bobby had drawn the short straw. That was why he was angry all the time. He felt let down by the father who wasn't interested in him. George said she indulged Bobby too much, but Kate felt she had to compensate for Nick's lack of interest.

Nick and Bobby just grated on each other. Kate had begged Nick to make more of an effort, and when he tried, Bobby ended up driving him crazy. Bobby drove everyone crazy, but he was so sweet underneath it. Kate wished more people could see that. He was a bundle of loveliness underneath his prickly exterior.

Kate sighed. Was she enough for her kids? Everyone said boys needed a strong male presence. Since Jenny had given birth to Jaden five months ago, Nick had barely seen Luke, Jess and Bobby. Kate was glad that her father was in their lives so much now. At least he was a positive male influence, even if he had got a bit impatient in his old age. He was a good granddad and a good man, and she knew Luke and Bobby would benefit from being around him.

'Kate?' George called. 'I need you.'

She moved over from the wine section, in the corner of the café, to the counter.

'I have an order for two of those green juices you put on the menu.'

Kate smiled. 'Really? The juices you said no one would want?'

Her father put his hands up. 'Okay, you were right. I think they look, smell and taste awful, but it seems people like them. Why anyone would want to drink kale and spinach and God knows what else is beyond me.'

Kate began to make up the juices. 'They're healthy, Dad. People are into health and nutrition, these days. Even Luke drinks them.'

'Do you think he'll get picked for the team?' George asked. 'He seems awfully nervous about it.'

Kate was nervous, too. Luke was so wound up about it. When he hadn't been helping in the café he had spent every spare hour of the summer working out and training – it was almost an obsession. Kate worried about the fallout if he wasn't picked or got injured or something. After three weeks back in school he seemed even more het-up. Through a series of questions, which Luke answered with grunts, Kate was able to surmise that Harry was playing well and Luke feared his friend would replace him on the team.

'I hope so. It'd be so good for his confidence and self-esteem.'

Her father raised an eyebrow. 'That little Piper seems to have done wonders for his self-esteem.'

Kate grinned. 'She's nice, isn't she?'

'She seems like a grand girl.'

'I like her. She makes Luke happy and she's very sweet with Jess.'

'Sure how could you not be sweet to Jess? She's a dote,' George said.

Kate added wheatgrass powder to the juicer. She loved that her father was so fond of Jess. Kate didn't know what she'd do without her daughter. During the break-up and Nick's departure, Jess had been so helpful. Kate had found her crying in her bedroom a few times but Jess had never complained about anything. Luke had raged against the world and got into trouble at school. Bobby had gone around kicking everything, including Kate, but Jess had been supportive. She was twelve going on sixty.

'She has an old soul,' George had said, when Jess was little, and he was right. Jess did have an old soul, and a very big heart to go with it.

Kate sometimes worried that Jess bottled up her emotions. Over the last year she'd tried to talk to her, but Jess had just said, 'It's okay, Mum. I know you and Dad love me. I'm sad because we're not a family any more, but don't worry, I'm not going to get drunk or kick things.'

Kate had hugged her and tried not to cry all over her daughter's hair. Jess didn't even seem angry with Nick. She'd come home from spending time with him and say, 'I feel sorry for Daddy. Jenny hates being pregnant. She's always complaining. He seems very stressed.'

Kate loved hearing how much of a pain in the arse Jenny was and that Nick was stressed. It made her feel considerably better. She wanted him to be miserable. She was thrilled to hear that bouncy, sexy, fit Jenny wasn't so much fun, after all. Serves the snake right, she thought. I hope their baby never sleeps.

Kate finished the juices and brought them to the table. 'Enjoy,' she said, with a smile, then went back to the counter.

'You look tired, Kate, will I make you a coffee?'

'Thanks, Dad. That'd be lovely.'

'Did you sleep badly, pet?' he asked, and Kate suddenly wanted to weep.

She had been up half the night working out her finances. Back to school had used up all of her wages, and Luke had given her a chunk of his earnings to help with his books. But Nick hadn't paid his child support again this month. When she'd called him yesterday, he'd said he didn't have it because, unknown to him, Jenny had spent a fortune on his credit card doing up Jaden's nursery.

'Jesus, Nick, I need that money. Your three children need books and uniforms. You know back to school is a really expensive time.'

'Don't start, Kate. I've had Jenny in my ear all day. Look, I just don't have it. I'll get it to you next month.'

'I need it now!'

'Ask your father for a loan.'

Kate had felt the blood rushing to her head and thought she might explode. 'My father is housing your children, feeding your children and helping to raise your children. I will not ask him for any more. Find me the money and send it or I'll contact my lawyer.'

'You don't have to be a bitch about it.'

'Go to Hell.' She'd slammed the phone down on him, then stood there, trembling with fury. She hated talking to him – any conversation ended in an argument.

She'd spent the rest of the evening trying to figure out how to pay for Jess's horse-riding lessons. She'd paid for all of their books, but had nothing left over for riding. It was Jess's one treat. Piano lessons and dance lessons had had to go as there was simply no money, but horse-riding was Jess's favourite thing in the world. She adored animals, and was happiest when she was at the stables, riding and grooming. Kate couldn't bear to tell her she couldn't go back. She'd called the stables yesterday and they'd agreed to give her a discount, but she still had to come up with two hundred euros to pay for Jess's lessons.

'Just my mind working overtime,' Kate said.

Her father laid his hand on her arm. 'Is it money?'

Kate was afraid to speak – there was a lump in her throat. This wasn't fair. She shouldn't be living on top of her elderly father with three kids, and she shouldn't be asking him for money. She felt such a failure. 'Nick didn't pay this month,' she muttered, her face bright red with shame.

'For Christ's sake,' George cursed. 'It's not your fault. I'll help you out.'

'I just need two hundred euros for Jess's riding. I know it's expensive, but she loves it and never asks for anything.'

'Of course we can sort that out. Jess deserves a treat.' George patted Kate's hand. He opened the cash register and took out four fifty-euro notes and handed them to her. 'I'll never see you short, Katie.'

It was the use of her childhood nickname that set her off. She turned to walk out so her father wouldn't see her sobbing into her sleeve.

At twenty to three Kate hung up her apron, pulled on her coat and left to walk the short distance to Bobby's school. She stood alone at the gate, not wanting to engage in small-talk with the other parents. She was still feeling raw after borrowing the money from her father and didn't think she could fake a good day in front of the others.

As the children poured out, Kate waved at Bobby, who ran straight to her and threw his arms around her. 'Good day?' she asked, hustling him along and studiously avoiding eye contact with the teacher.

'It was okay,' Bobby said. 'But guess where the most shark attacks happen?'

'Mrs Higgins,' the teacher called. 'May I have a word?'

Kate froze. Turning, she put on her I'm-not-worried-about-where-this-conversation-is-going face and followed the other woman into the school.

'Bobby, will you be a good boy and help put those books away?' Mrs Lorgan asked.

'In alphabetical order?' Bobby enquired.

'Mmm, yes, perfect.'

While Bobby was busy sorting out the little class library, Mrs Lorgan faced Kate. She was a woman in her fifties and had the authority of a teacher who had been around a while and took no nonsense.

'Mrs Higgins –'

'Call me Kate, please.'

'Fine. Kate. Bobby is a very energetic boy with a very keen interest in facts and figures, information he's always impatient to share with his classmates. While we always try to encourage enthusiasm for learning, with a class of twenty-five I can't allow him to monopolize the time.'

'Yes, I understand. He can be a bit relentless with his facts, but it's his passion and he hasn't had the easiest of years at home. Learning facts seems to keep him calm.'

'He mentioned his father's new baby in Show and Tell. I think some of the children were alarmed to hear him describe him as an evil devil baby.'

'He's having some problems adjusting.' Kate watched Bobby through the classroom window, carefully arranging the books, a frown on his serious little face. She just wanted to go in, put her arms around him, tell him not to worry and hug all his anger out.

'There was some bad language too, I'm afraid. He described his father's girlfriend as a tart. Thankfully, the children thought of apple tart rather than . . . well, the other kind. But I did take Bobby aside and we had a word about it.'

It's lucky he didn't say 'whore' or 'slut', Kate thought, which were names Luke had called Jenny when Nick had told the kids he was leaving them to go and live with her. 'I'll talk to him,' she said, 'but please don't be too hard on him in class. I know he can take over a bit with his facts and figures, but he's very insecure and he needs attention and praise. Honestly, underneath his bluster he's an anxious little boy.'

Mrs Lorgan nodded. 'I can see that, and I'll do my best to work with him and encourage him along.'

'Thank you.'

Kate called Bobby and they headed home.

'Mummy?'

'Yes?'

'Does Mrs Lorgan not like me?'

Kate stopped and crouched down. 'Hey, now, she was actually telling me how great you are and how clever, and she wondered where you got all your amazing facts. So I told her about *Guinness World Records* being your favourite book.'

'Mummy?'

'Yes.'

'Do you think Daddy will hate stinky Jaden and come back home and love us again?'

Kate put her arms around her son and drew him in. 'Oh, Bobby, Daddy loves you, Luke and Jess. No new baby is ever going to change that.'

'What if he has more babies? He'll never have time to see us.'

'I'm not sure he's going to have any more, but even if he does, he'll still love you the same. Besides, you have me and Granddad, who love you too.'

Bobby nodded and they started walking again. As they reached the gate, Bobby threw his arms around Kate's legs. Muttering into her left thigh, he said, 'If there was a world record for best mummy, you'd win it.'

Kate's heart lifted. It was moments like these that made all the pain and worry disappear.

4

He was in a deep sleep, the kind you can have only when your body and mind are completely exhausted. When he had crawled into bed earlier, his body had felt as if it had folded itself into the mattress. They were one and the same. Sleep, these days, was Nick's favourite thing to do. It was his only switch-off.

'Waaaaaah . . . waaaaaah . . . waaaaah . . .'

In his sleep he could hear something. Ignore it, his brain said.

'Waaaah . . . waaaaah . . .'

He scrunched his eyes closed and tried to block out the sound.

'Nick!'

He felt a thump on his arm. He rolled over.

'*Nick!*' This time she walloped him.

Jesus Christ, could a man not get one decent night's sleep? He opened his eyes and prayed it was after five a.m. Please God, let it not be the middle of the night. The alarm clock said it was two thirty. *Fuuuuuck!*

'It's your turn,' Jenny whined.

'I have an early viewing. Can you do it? Please?'

'No bloody way. I've been with him all day *and* I did the ten o'clock feed. Get up.'

Nick wanted to tell her to sod off. He was tempted to remind her that she wasn't working. She got to sit on her arse all day, watching TV.

He, on the other hand, was trying to sell houses to people who had no money. Thankfully, the housing market had turned a bit of a corner, but it was still a bloody hard slog trying to get people to commit to a sale. He had to get some sales in soon. He owed the bank and he owed Kate, too.

He'd spent weeks trying to get that couple to buy the big house on Jacobson Road, but they'd pulled out at the last minute. The commission on it would have paid the rent on the apartment and the childcare costs for four months, but no such luck. The wife had decided the kitchen was too dark. He'd explained to her that with a lighter colour on the walls and cream tiles on the floor it would be transformed, but the stupid cow had had no imagination.

The stress of trying to pay everyone was killing him. He needed a few drinks after work to take the edge off, but he couldn't even do that without Jenny ringing every fifteen minutes to find out when he was coming home.

Between Jenny and Kate and the kids, he felt suffocated. Sometimes lately he'd felt like running away. Just getting on a plane to South America and never coming back. He'd live in a beach hut, spend all day lying on white sand, drinking cold beers, and not have six people depending on him all the time.

He wouldn't do it, though. He wouldn't leave his kids. Even though they hated him. Well, Jess didn't, but Luke did and Bobby was hard-going. Nick had always felt Bobby could see through him. Even when he was only four years old, he'd catch Bobby looking at him, and it was as if he knew Nick was having an affair. It had freaked him out.

He hadn't wanted another child. Kate had tricked him into it. They were just getting their lives back: Jess was in school, and she was easy anyway, and Luke was eleven and they were starting to go out again, getting their mojo back, until Kate had said she wanted another baby.

He'd told her no way. She said she'd hated being an only child and wanted three kids at least. He'd said no, one boy and one girl was perfect. Why push it? They were happy, life was good. They didn't need another baby.

'We're finally getting lie-ins,' he'd argued again and again, 'and we're able to go out, have a few drinks and stay late without having to worry about bottles and night feeds and nappies and early mornings. Come on, Kate, let's just enjoy it.'

But Kate wouldn't let it go. She'd kept banging on and on about how she wanted a big family and how two wasn't enough, until eventually he gave in and said they could try for six months, and if it didn't happen, that was it.

Of course she'd got bloody pregnant in the fifth month and their lives had gone back to her being pregnant and wanting to stay in all the time. Then Bobby had arrived, and it was night feeds, no sleep, shitty nappies, early mornings and early nights. All the fun and freedom were gone.

If he was honest, Nick had been angry since the day Kate announced she was pregnant. He'd known it would change everything and he was right: it had. Bobby was just too much. Three kids was too much.

The Kate he'd married was funny and kind. She'd asked him about work, drunk wine with him and chatted about the day. This Kate went to bed with the kids at eight p.m. and never wanted to have sex . . . ever.

After Bobby was born, she'd barely acknowledged him when he came home from work. She was always feeding someone or doing homework or washing clothes or tidying up or cooking or sewing . . . The old Kate would have laughed at his stories about annoying clients and actually have been interested in him.

He hadn't meant to cheat on Kate, but when Jenny had come to view that apartment for the second time, he'd given in to lust. The first time she'd viewed it she'd flirted with him and he'd been flattered, very flattered. She was hot and young and she was definitely giving him the eye. He'd been on a high, so he'd flirted back a bit, and it had been fun, really good fun.

When she rang to say she wanted to see the apartment again, he'd worn his favourite shirt and suit. When he saw her in her tight black dress he'd had to walk away to hide his hard-on. He'd wanted her then and there.

He'd used all of his charm and she'd responded to his flirting, making it pretty obvious she found him attractive. So he'd asked her out for a drink. One drink had led to five and they'd ended up back at her place having great sex. Nick had become completely addicted to her and the sex. He couldn't have stopped even if he'd tried. She was like a drug. He hadn't felt so alive in years. He saw her at every opportunity he could.

To be honest, Nick was surprised Jenny had gone for him. He was twenty years older than her. But she'd said she liked older guys, that he was sexy and confident. He knew what he wanted and where he was going. She'd said a lot of guys her own age were still behaving like teenagers.

'I feel protected and safe with you,' she'd said, after a few months of seeing him. 'My dad left before I was born so I never knew him. My mum was a drinker, so my home life was always difficult. I guess I've always craved security. You're so sure of who you are that I know you'll look after me and never let me down. I know you won't "borrow" money from me, like my last boyfriend, who fleeced me, or the one before that, who got so drunk that he puked on me. I'm sick of immature man-boys. I want a real man, like you, Nick.'

Nick had eaten up her adoration. It felt so good to be needed and wanted. He couldn't get enough of it.

When he was with Jenny, he felt powerful and invincible – the opposite of everything he felt in his other life, the half-life he had with Kate. Jenny thought he was wonderful. She laughed at his jokes and told him he was the best estate agent in the world. Nick felt as if he mattered again, as if he was someone's number one, rather than always coming last, after the kids.

He only felt guilty when he was at home, so he avoided being there as much as possible. But he was careless. In a way he wanted to get caught.

Kate found texts on his phone. She hadn't freaked out or screamed or broken plates. She'd just cried and cried and cried. It was as if there was a river inside her.

'I want the kids to come from a happy home, not a broken one,' she'd said, making it clear that the kids came first, even in something as personal as an extra-marital affair. She'd offered to forgive him and to give it another go, but he didn't want to. He didn't love her any more – they were like strangers. He wanted out. He wanted a new start. He wanted Jenny. He wanted sex and freedom.

He looked down at Jaden's red face. What freedom? What sex? Jenny had told him she was on the pill, but somehow she'd got pregnant. He wondered sometimes if she'd tricked him. She'd always said she wanted security: was Jaden her way of making sure Nick stayed with her and looked after her? What was it with women and babies? Why did they have to have kids and ruin everything?

Nick felt his chest contract. He gripped the side of the cot. Breathe, he ordered himself. In and out, in and out. He was beginning to panic, and his head was spinning. He needed to make more money. He needed to spend more time with his kids. He needed to sort things out with Jenny because they were arguing non-stop, these days.

He felt guilty about losing touch with Luke. He missed him. They used to play football together and joke around, but now Luke just glared at him or rolled his eyes whenever Nick tried to be funny. Jess was still her sweet self, but he knew he should go and see her horse-riding and make more of an effort with her. As for Bobby . . . He had a lot of making up to do. Bobby had had the worst of him. Nick had resented the poor kid for the first few years of his life, then he'd been tied up with Jenny and then he'd left. He'd never really got to know Bobby. He felt bad about it. He didn't know his own son. But Bobby was always angry and all he seemed to do was talk about his world records, which drove Nick mad. He'd tried to play football with him but Bobby had two left feet and he'd ended up kicking Nick's leg, hard, because it was 'a stupid game'.

Nick had to try to figure out a way to communicate with Bobby before it was too late. He was already seven years old and they had no relationship. He needed to find some kind of common ground. But since Jaden had been born, Jenny barely let him out of her sight. She panicked all the time and cried a lot and kept thinking Jaden was going to die. Nick had Googled it, and she had symptoms of postnatal depression. When he'd suggested she might have it and she should talk to her GP, Jenny had gone absolutely mad and accused him of trying to leave her. But he was only trying to help.

How the hell had he ended up in this mess? He had only ever wanted a nice life, a few quid in the bank, a wife, two kids and some drinks on a Saturday night. But somehow, he'd ended up with four kids, two families, no money and stress everywhere he looked.

Jaden let out a roar. Nick picked him up and held him against his chest. He walked up and down the bedroom singing quietly. It was the same song he'd sung to all of his kids to calm them down – Frank Sinatra's 'Fly Me To The Moon'. It had even worked on Bobby.

Jaden stopped crying and soon fell into a deep sleep on Nick's shoulder. Looking down at his baby son's peaceful little face, Nick promised him he'd be a better dad. He wouldn't mess this up. He'd help Jenny more with Jaden so she wasn't so overwhelmed. He had to make this relationship work. He wanted to – he needed to.

5

Jess looked at Chloë's many photos of her trip to Australia.

'And there's me with a koala, and there's me surfing, and look at how cute that guy is! And here's me drinking a mocktail . . .'

The holiday looked amazing. White sandy beaches, posh hotels, and Chloë had got loads of new clothes as well. Jess felt a pang of jealousy. She'd spent her summer helping to move all of their belongings into her granddad's house, then helping in the café. She'd had just one week of sports camp because her mum and dad had no money for more than that.

Being poor sucked. Her dad said he was sorry but that he had two families to support now and they all had to 'make sacrifices'. But why did they? Why did he have to leave? They used to be happy. Jess remembered their holiday in France. She was only about five, but her parents had been laughing together and going down slides in the water park. They had been a family, a real family.

Bobby said he couldn't remember anything but Mum and Dad shouting at each other and Dad never being around. Luke just said Dad was 'a selfish prick' and didn't want to discuss it further. Jess wished she had a sister she could talk to.

Her dad had messed up and it was Jenny who had got the best of the whole rotten deal. She had Jess's dad and they lived together in their own place and now they had a new baby. It felt like they'd lost everything and Jenny had won. She had taken Dad away from them, with her short skirts and her red lipstick and her fake laugh. She'd tried to be all friendly with Jess when they'd first met her two years ago, after Dad had left them to move in with her. Luke had ignored her and Bobby had kicked her, so Jess knew she was just trying to go for the easiest kid. She'd been polite for Dad's sake, but she could see through Jenny.

The weird thing was, Jenny was only seven years older than Luke and she was twenty years younger than Dad. It was creepy. At first Dad was all bouncy and happy around Jenny. He called her 'babe', held her hand and rubbed her leg. It made Jess want to puke. Jenny kept saying, 'Your dad's so amazing. He's so good to me.'

Jess had wanted to shout, 'Well, he isn't good to our mum, you horrible cow,' but she didn't.

But then Jenny had got pregnant and stopped wearing short skirts and lipstick of any colour. She was grumpy and didn't laugh any more, not even fake laughs. She snapped at Dad and he stopped rubbing her legs.

The baby was really ugly. It was mean to say babies were ugly because it wasn't their fault that they didn't have any hair and dribbled all the time, but Jess couldn't help it because Jaden really was ugly. Jenny dressed him up in dorky outfits, with ripped jeans and leather jackets, and he just looked even worse.

Jess was glad she had only seen Jenny and Jaden twice since he was born. She much preferred seeing Dad on her own. The last time she'd seen Jenny, she was on her own. Luke said he had to work and Bobby had a meltdown so Mum had given in and let him stay home. Jess ended up going alone: she didn't want to let Dad down.

When she got to the apartment, Jenny was trying to breastfeed. It was disgusting – she just pulled her boob out right in front of Jess and tried to stick her nipple into the baby's mouth. Jess didn't know where to look. It was mortifying.

When she'd told Chloë about it later, Chloë had almost vomited in shock and disgust.

Jenny kept trying to get Jaden to suck but he wouldn't, and they both started crying. Jess's dad had ended up grabbing the baby and stuffing a bottle into his mouth. Jaden had stopped crying but Jenny had cried louder. She kept saying, 'But Gisele, the supermodel, says mothers should breastfeed their babies for six months.'

'For Christ's sake, will you stop banging on about Gisele? The baby needs food. Look, he's happy now,' Dad had snapped.

Jess made an excuse to leave the room then and hung about in the small hallway, watching the clock and trying not to listen to the argument Jenny and her dad were having. After twenty-two minutes her dad had come out and asked if maybe she wouldn't mind if he dropped her home early. Jess was never so happy to leave somewhere in her life.

'OMG,' said Chloë, pointing at the next picture. 'Here's me learning to surf. Check out my pink wetsuit. Dad bought it for me.' She swiped her phone screen to show Jess more photos.

'It must have been an amazing holiday,' Jess said wistfully.

Chloë wrinkled her nose. 'You know, it was in one way but, honestly, being an only child sucks. I have to do everything with my parents and they focus all of their attention on me. I know I'm spoilt, but sometimes I wish I was like your family.'

Poor and broken up? Was Chloë mad?

Chloë put up her hands. 'I don't mean that you haven't had a terrible time with your parents separating and your dad running off with that, like, OMG, total ho. I just mean that at least you have fun with Luke and Bobby.'

'But I don't really. Since we've had to sell the house and Jaden was born, Luke is all moody. All he does is train and spend time with Piper. And Jaden being born has pushed Bobby over the edge. He was bad anyway, but he definitely has anger-management issues now.'

'Poor Bobby. He was the baby of the family and now he isn't.'

'I know but he needs to stop freaking out all the time. It's a total pain.'

'Have you seen the ho lately?'

Jess shook her head. 'No, and I haven't seen Dad much either. He's busy with work and the baby.'

Chloë applied lip-gloss to her already over-glossed lips and offered some to Jess. 'Well, my mum said she saw Jenny in House of Fraser and she looked terrible, like totally wrecked. Mum said she had big bags under her eyes and she was wheeling the buggy around looking miserable. Serves her right.'

Jess knew this was supposed to cheer her up, and she certainly didn't care if Jenny was miserable, but then again, if everyone was miserable, the whole nightmare would have been for nothing.

If Dad and Jenny broke up, there would be two broken families and four kids sharing a bit of a dad. In the beginning Jess had prayed that her dad would change his mind and come home to them. But after nearly three years apart, she didn't want him to do that. She knew Mum and Dad could never live together again. All they did was argue, so there was no point in dreaming about becoming a perfect family again: they never would be.

But if Jenny and Dad were happy, then Dad might be a better dad again. He might have more time for them if Jenny was able to look after the baby without crying or phoning him all the time. Maybe if they were happy, Dad would make more of an effort with Luke and Bobby and not seem so awkward around them, like he did now.

'*Sooooo* what will we do? Do you want to play tennis?'

Chloë had a tennis court and a swimming pool at her house. Her father was a builder, and Jess's mum said, 'He prints money.' They were the richest people in the school. When Chloë had joined two years ago, everyone had tried to be her friend because they all wanted to hang out at her house. Jess's dad had just said he was leaving them to live with Jenny, so Jess couldn't have cared less about Chloë's swimming pool.

Jess often thought it was because she hadn't tried to be Chloë's friend that Chloë had sought her out. They'd clicked pretty much instantly. Chloë was fun and funny, and she never worried about anything. Jess spent her life worrying about everything. Chloë said she had to stop or she'd end up with really bad lines on her forehead, but Chloë's mum, Hazel, said she didn't have to worry about that because Botox would sort it out.

'Shouldn't we do our homework first, though?' Jess asked.

'Seriously, Jess, live a little. It's only week three back at school, we can do it later or I'll forge a note from Mum. I can do one for you too, if you like. I've got really good at copying handwriting.'

Jess grinned. 'No, thanks.'

'I knew you'd say no. I bet you end up being, like, a doctor or a scientist and finding cures to all the awful diseases of the world.'

Jess laughed. 'Are you still planning to be a professional tennis player?'

'No. That got canned this summer. I went to see this top coach in Australia and he said I'm just not good enough. I knew I wasn't anyway. When I didn't even get picked for the club's first team, I told Mum that the dream was over. Besides, I'm sick of playing two hours every day after school. It's a pain and it's boring. I'm so over competitive tennis. Dad was a bit grumpy, though, seeing as he'd built the tennis court because Mum told him she thought I'd end up playing in Wimbledon.'

'Did he go mad?'

Chloë tied the laces on her sparkling white runners. 'He huffed and puffed a bit, but then I told him he was the best dad ever for building me a tennis court and I was sorry I wasn't good enough – I laid that on very thick and even squeezed out a tear – and then he was all, "Don't worry. You're a star in my eyes . . . blah blah blah."'

Jess shook her head. 'Your poor dad. You're unbelievable.'

Chloë giggled. 'I know! Mum said I should be an actress. But I've actually decided to invent a pill where you can eat anything you want – jars of Starbursts, big boxes of chocolates – and never get fat. I'll be a zillionaire, like my dad.'

They ran downstairs and went into the vast kitchen, which was bigger than the entire Village Café.

'Hey, Jess.' Chloë's mum looked up from her magazine.

'Hi, Hazel.'

'My God, you've grown! You look lovely. How was your summer?'

'Oh, Mum!' Chloë broke in. 'Don't start asking her loads of questions – we're going to play tennis.'

Hazel arched an eyebrow. 'Really? I thought tennis was "so over".'

'Competitions and training are. We're playing for fun.'

'Did Chloë tell you my dream of watching her win Wimbledon is over?'

Jess nodded.

'She's so selfish. I even had my outfit planned, right down to the fabulous hat.' Hazel grinned.

'The scary thing is, she's not joking.'

'Well, I do have a lovely cream Roland Mouret dress that would have been perfect. Oh, well, never mind. How's your mum?'

'Good, thanks,' Jess said.

'Have you all settled in at your granddad's now?'

'We've been there nearly four months, so it feels like home.'

'Good. I'm glad to hear it. You know you're always welcome to stay here if you want a change of scenery, and if your mum needs anything, she isn't to hesitate to ask. I mean that now. I said it to her myself, but if you feel she needs help, please tell me.'

Jess smiled. Underneath her make-up, overly coiffed hair and OTT clothes, Hazel had a huge heart. 'Thanks.'

Chloë tugged at her sleeve. 'Come on, let's play.'

They knocked up a bit, then decided to play one set before doing their homework.

It was when she ran for a drop shot that Jess's nose began to bleed.

6

Piper's father, Seamus, glared at her. 'Where have you been?'

'Luke's.'

'Who's Luke?'

'My boyfriend.'

Seamus's eyebrows flew up. 'What in the name of God? Boyfriend? You're only twelve.'

Piper grinned. 'I'm eighteen.'

'When did that happen?'

'Over the past six years.'

'What age is Luke?'

'Forty-three.'

'WHAT?'

Piper laughed. 'I'm kidding. He's just turned eighteen.'

'Is he a nice lad?'

'Very.'

'How long have you been together?'

'Five months.'

'Does he know how lucky he is to be going out with the only sensible daughter I have?'

'I think so.'

'Good. Well, thank God you're home.'

'What's up?'

'Your sister has locked herself in the bathroom.'

'Which one?'

'How the hell should I know? Poppy or Penny.'

'Why did she lock herself in?'

'Because the other twin wore her top and then she pulled it off her in front of someone and she was "mortified" so she took scissors to the top and cut the sleeve off and now the other one has threatened to kill her.'

'I bet it was Penny. Poppy probably borrowed her new Superdry top.'

'Now that you mention it, there was screaming about Superdry.'

'Where's Mum?' Piper asked.

Her dad frowned. 'Olivia is at one of her lectures. I'm all for your mother having her own life, but she's never home.'

Last year, the day Posy had gone into senior school, their mother had decided to do something for herself. She'd signed up for a course in equality and human rights.

They could hear screaming from upstairs. 'Come out of there or I'll kick this door down,' Penny shrieked.

'Help! She's a lunatic! Help!' Poppy shouted.

'Hello! Can someone please tell them to shut up? I'm trying to study here,' Pauline roared. 'Someone in this house actually cares about more than stupid clothes.'

'Shut up, Pauline. You're a bore who's going to die alone because all you do is study,' Penny yelled.

'At least I'm not one half of ridiculous twins who can barely spell and will end up stacking shelves in Tesco because no one else will hire them.'

'Oh, yeah? Well, I'd rather work in Tesco than be a nerdy, weirdo scientist freak,' Penny retorted.

'I'm studying medicine, not science, you moron.'

'Same difference. You'll end up with big glasses and a white coat, living on your own with cats.'

Seamus sighed. 'I can't handle them. They're like wild animals. I've an article to write. I'm off to the shed.'

Of course you are, Piper thought. It's your hideout. She wished she had a shed. There was nowhere to get any peace in this house.

As her dad scurried off to the shed to compose his piece for the newspaper, Piper went to see if there was anything for dinner. She opened the fridge. Empty. Damn. There was a note, though, sitting on the empty middle shelf – *It starts when you sink into his arms and ends with your arms in his sink!*

Piper sighed. She missed her mother, the one who used to be waiting for them when they got home from school, with scones in the oven and hot chocolate on the hob. Now it was all about lectures and essays, study groups and equality. Piper was fine about equality. Yes, men and women were equal and should be treated that way. But her dad had always treated her mother as an equal. He discussed everything with her, shared everything he had with her and always told her she was great. Besides, her mother had chosen to give up her job in the bank to have five kids, so why was she behaving now as if her husband had chained her to the kitchen sink?

Maybe he had taken Mum's cooking for granted and the fact that she ran the house and did most of the childcare, but he was working to support them. Wasn't that the deal? Her friend Vanessa's mum was a lawyer and Vanessa's dad stayed at home and did the cooking and childminding. Maybe it was best if you both worked. Maybe then everyone was happy. But Frannie's parents both worked and they always seemed to be in a bad mood. Piper didn't know what the answer was, but she wished her mum would stop writing silly notes and start cooking again.

Crash . . . bang . . .

Piper closed the fridge and ran upstairs. It sounded as if Penny had kicked in the bathroom door.

'Aaaaargh!' Penny screamed.

49

'What the hell?' Piper found Penny with her foot stuck in the door. 'Are you insane?' she shouted at her sister. 'You've made a hole in the door. Dad's going to go mad.'

'I don't care. I want to kill her.'

Piper pulled her sister's foot out. She had a cut down one side, which was bleeding slightly.

'You see what you've done, you stupid cow? You've scarred me for life,' Penny shouted through the hole at her twin.

'Is it bad?' Poppy asked, peeping out from the other side of the hole.

'Look.' Penny showed her. 'Actual blood.'

'Does she need stitches?' Poppy seemed worried.

Piper wiped the blood away with a tissue. 'No. It's just a small cut.'

'Small but deep. I'll have a scar for life,' Penny wailed.

'Scars can be cool,' Poppy said.

'No, they can not.' Piper was annoyed. The twins were maddening.

'Let's Google maddest scars ever,' Poppy suggested.

'Cool.' Penny struggled to her feet. 'I need help walking.'

'Hang on.' Poppy unlocked the bathroom door and went to help her twin hop back to their bedroom.

Behind them lay the top with no sleeves and splinters of wood from the bathroom door.

'I'll just clean up, then, shall I?' Piper snapped.

The twins turned. 'Well, I'm injured,' Penny said.

'And I'm nursing her,' Poppy added.

A bedroom door swung open. A red-faced Pauline stormed out. 'That's it! I've had it with this family. I cannot stay here another minute. I'm going to the library.'

'Your favourite place.' The twins giggled. 'Where all your friends hang out.'

'At least I have a brain. You clearly only got half of one each, which is why you're so inane.'

'We're not insane,' Poppy said.

'Inane, you idiot! *In-ane.*'

'Pauline, you need to lie down. You're not making any sense. Maybe your brain exploded from too much studying,' Penny said, and the twins fell about laughing.

'Boom!' Poppy cackled.

Pauline held her laptop to her chest. 'Why was I born into this ridiculous family? There must have been a mix-up at the hospital.'

While Pauline stormed off to the college library and the twins looked up scars on the internet, Piper got out the Hoover and cleared up the mess. As she was putting the Hoover away, Posy came home and flung down her schoolbag.

'Bad day?'

'I got a detention.'

'Why?'

'Mrs Pender said I was far more interested in putting on lip-gloss than reading Shakespeare, and I said she was right because lip-gloss is way more interesting than boring old Shakespeare and stupid Romeo and Juliet and their lame relationship – and that Juliet was a really bad role model for women because no self-respecting feminist would kill herself over a guy.'

Piper groaned. 'Why did you say that? You know you're not supposed to answer back. It's always going to get you into trouble.'

'Mum agrees. She thinks it's a dumb play too. She said we should be studying Gloria Steinem and Simone de Beauvoir.'

Why did their mother have to fill Posy's twelve-year-old head with all of her college stuff? She was too young and it was getting her into trouble. Piper was going to have to talk to her mother when she got home.

'Look, Posy, if you want to make your life easy in school, just follow the curriculum and say nothing. You can read what you want in your spare time.'

Posy plonked herself down at the kitchen table. 'Fine. I'm starving. What's for dinner?'

Before Piper could tell her there was nothing, the back door opened and their father walked in.

'Hello, Poppy.'

'It's Posy.'

'Right, what's for dinner?'

Why did everyone ask Piper? Why did everyone assume she was the one in charge when their mother was out? 'I don't know. There's nothing in the fridge except a quote.'

Seamus opened the fridge and slammed it shut. 'Apparently your mother thinks we can live on notes and quotes. I'll nip down to the shops and pick something up. You can come with me.' He pointed to Posy.

'Not until you say my name and date of birth.'

Seamus narrowed his eyes. 'Posy Barbara, born October 2003 in the middle of the rugby world cup, which was very inconvenient. You're the cheeky, lippy one. The youngest. The one who gets into trouble in school. Mind you, the twins do a fair bit of that too. You have your mother's hair, my eyes and your grandmother Doran's determination. God help us all.'

Posy smiled. 'Okay, I'll come.'

While they went to buy food, Piper tidied up the kitchen. As she was emptying the dishwasher, her mother sailed in, carrying a large pile of books.

'Hello, Piper, how was school?'

'Fine, but there's been a lot of drama here. The twins have kicked a huge hole in the bathroom door.' Piper scowled.

Her mother plonked the books on the kitchen table. She pushed her fringe off her face and waved her hand. 'It's just a door. There are real problems in the world,' she said, shaking a leaflet at Piper. 'Did you know that up to a hundred and forty million women and girls are thought to be living with the consequences of female genital mutilation? In Somalia, ninety-eight per cent of young girls are cut. Can you imagine?'

Piper knew she should feel desperately sorry for the girls who were suffering in Somalia, but right now she just wanted her mother to cook a bloody meal.

The twins bounded into the kitchen.

'Hi, Mum.'

'Hi, girls. Here, read this.' Olivia handed her daughters a piece of paper. 'I want you all to be aware of how lucky you are.'

'Uhm, what is it?' Penny asked.

'Female genital mutilation,' her mother replied.

'Yeah, I can read but, like, what does it mean?'

'It's when young girls have their clitoris cut in order to curb their sexual desire and preserve their "honour" before marriage.'

The twins squealed. 'OMG, did you just say "clitoris"?' Poppy was horrified.

'Yes. It's nothing to be embarrassed about,' Olivia said calmly.

'It's mortifying,' Penny said. 'You have officially gone mad. Please do not *ever* say that word again.'

'These poor girls are being mutilated because –'

'Stop,' Poppy said, putting her hands over her ears.

'You need to be aware of what's going on in the world.'

Penny shook her head. 'We're fifteen! We do not need to know about that. You're supposed to protect us, not shove all this crazy stuff in our faces.'

Piper silently cheered her sisters on.

'You can't live in a bubble. I want my girls to be strong, independent women, who help other women.'

'Can you please go back to being a normal mum?' Poppy begged. 'I much preferred you when you were cooking and ironing and watching *I'm a Celebrity* with us. You're so boring now.'

'I'm trying to teach you to be strong, independent women,' Olivia persisted.

'Stop banging on about it. Go and save the girls with the cut fannies and leave us alone,' Penny snapped.

Piper felt exactly the same but would never have had the guts to say it to her mother's face.

Olivia sat down at the table. 'I'm disappointed in you, girls. I thought that as young women growing up in a safe, peaceful Western society you would reach out to your fellow women and support them –'

Seamus and Posy came through the back door. 'Chipper chips for tea,' Seamus called out.

The twins ran over to grab the food.

'Thank God you're back, Dad. Mum's been going on about girls having their vaginas cut,' Poppy said.

Seamus dropped his bag of chips. 'What in the name of Jesus?'

'*Aaaaah!* Don't say the V-word! It's so embarrassing.' Posy blushed bright red.

Olivia picked up her husband's chips and popped one into her mouth. 'I'm just telling them what I learnt about in college today.'

'For the love of God, Olivia, stick to equal pay and subsidized childcare and leave off the genital mutilation.'

The girls clapped. 'Yes, listen to Dad.'

'I'm just interested in my subjects, that's all.'

'I know, love, but seriously?'

Olivia shrugged. 'It's happening out there. We can't ignore it.'

Piper felt a bit sorry for her mother. She was enjoying this new chapter in her life after all of the years she had devoted to raising her kids. Some of what she told them about her college course was interesting, but sometimes it was a bit too much – like today.

Olivia stood up. 'I'm a bit sticky from cycling home. I think I'll have a quick shower.'

'FYI, Mum, when you take those clothes off, put them in the bin. You're too old for jeans,' Penny said, stuffing chips into her mouth.

'What's wrong with my jeans?' Olivia looked down at herself.

'Your legs are too short,' Poppy told her.

'Are they?'

'The jeans are way too tight. They look ridiculous,' Penny said.

'Oh.' Olivia's face fell.

Piper didn't like to agree, but the twins were right. Her mother did look weird. She'd bought skinny jeans to 'blend in' with the other students, but she just looked like an older woman trying too hard. 'Your legs are fine, but your normal clothes suit you better,' she said.

'I feel so old in skirts and black trousers with all the students around me wearing jeans,' Olivia said.

'You *are* old,' Poppy reminded her.

'You're nearly fifty. You're not fooling anyone by wearing jeans,' Penny added.

'Your other clothes are just more flattering,' Seamus said.

Olivia tugged at her jeans. 'Okay. Well, thanks for telling me. I think.'

While Olivia went to have a shower and throw out her jeans, the twins breathlessly filled in their father on why they thought Zayn *soooo* hot.

7

Jess and Chloë sat on the edge of the playing fields, watching Luke's team's training session.

'That bruise really is massive. Donna must have whacked you in hockey. Cow.'

Jess looked down at the big bruise on her leg. 'It looks worse than it is. I seem to bruise easily at the moment.'

'Get a move on!' the coach roared at the players.

Luke staggered forward with one of his teammates, a big burly guy, hanging onto his back.

'OMG, Jess! That guy Luke's carrying is huge. This isn't training, it's torture.'

'Right, suitcase carries – move it!' the coach bellowed.

There was a communal groan. Luke made his way over and lifted the handle of the 'suitcase' of huge weights.

'Let's go!' the coach shouted.

Luke closed his eyes and forced himself on. Jess felt sorry for him. This was mad. The players all looked as if they were either going to pass out or vomit.

'I'm so glad I'm not a boy. Imagine having to do this all the time!' Chloë was incredulous. 'Can we go now?'

'In a minute.' Jess knew that the coach was naming the team today and she wanted to see if Luke was picked. She'd told Mum she'd try to find out after school and that she'd text her as soon as she knew.

After the suitcase exercise half the team fell to the ground. Others bent over and tried to suck air into their lungs, while two threw up.

Luke moved away from those who were vomiting and lay on the grass, close to where Jess and Chloë were sitting. He didn't notice them as he was too wrapped up in catching his breath.

'I know Jenson wants to prove himself in his first year as head coach, but he's going to kill us,' Lorcan said, lying beside Luke and gasping for air.

'I know. It's insane.'

'Did you hear he's naming the team today?'

Luke nodded.

'I reckon you're safe, man.'

'I dunno. Harry's playing well.'

'You've got the pace, though. You're class in attack.'

The coach came over to them. 'I'd like a word, Luke,' he said.

Lorcan left them to it. Jess held her breath.

Mr Jenson put his hand on Luke's shoulder. 'I've seen how much work you've put in over the last few months, and I'm pleased with your progress. I want you to know that I'm starting you on Saturday. Play well and you'll be number-one choice. But I've said it before, you need to be more aggressive in the tackle.'

Luke nodded. 'Yes, Coach. I've been working on that. Thanks for the opportunity. I won't let you down.'

'Good, because if you do, Harry will get the place. Don't mess it up.'

As the coach walked ahead of him, Luke punched the air with his fist. *Yeeees!*

Jess jumped up and whooped. Luke turned, surprised to see her. 'What the hell?'

'I was passing.' She grinned.

'Spying on me, more like.' Luke picked her up and swung her around. 'Come on. I told Granddad I'd help in the café and I'm late.'

*

58

Luke told George his good news as he and Jess helped him clean up. George clapped him on the back with a soapy hand. 'I knew you'd do it. You deserve it after all those hours of training you put in over the summer. Good to see they've paid off. If the café's not too busy, I'll be out to see you. And I'll make sure your mum's free to go.'

Luke smiled. 'Thanks, Granddad. I sent Dad a text, but I haven't heard back yet.'

George fell silent. Jess had noticed that every time her dad's name came up, he said very little.

As they put away the clean crockery, Bobby came in and kicked one of the kitchen chairs.

'Hey, what's up?' Luke asked.

'Stupid, stinky Tommy said I was a know-it-all in class and that I sound like an incyclopedian when I talk.'

George stifled a laugh.

Luke turned to his brother. 'Tommy's an idiot,' he said.

'He's probably just jealous of all of your knowledge, Bobby,' Jess said, keen to make Bobby feel better.

Bobby perked up. 'Yeah, he probably is cos he's not very clever. He actually thought that an okapi was something to do with going to the toilet, like an "okay pee"!'

George and Luke looked at each other and laughed.

'Imagine that, a boy who doesn't know what an okapi is.' George winked at Luke.

'What a dork.' Luke grinned.

'I know.' Bobby giggled.

'Remind me again of the details,' George said. 'My old mind keeps forgetting things. The okapi is the one with the –'

'Stripy legs like a zebra but is related to the giraffe,' Bobby said.

'Yes, of course. I remember now.' George patted Bobby's head.

'It lives in the Congo and is about four feet nine inches tall. It –'

'I'd better check inside, but Luke and Jess would love to hear the details about the oki-thing.' George disappeared into the café.

Bobby watched him go. 'Luke?'

'Yes?'

'Sometimes I think Granddad's mind *is* a bit old. He doesn't seem to want to know a lot of new stuff. He forgets everything I tell him, and sometimes when I tell him things, he says his head hurts from too much information. Do you think your brain shrinks when you get old?'

Luke paused. 'I think Granddad is just really busy with the café and the wine shop and looking after us. Maybe you should stick to telling me and Jess and Mum about your facts.'

'Okay.'

Jess decided now was a good time to tell them about the dinner. They were both in a good mood. 'Did you hear Dad's coming to take us out for tea?' she said.

'What?' Bobby said.

Luke's head jerked up. 'Tonight?'

'He's taking us to Arturo's for a treat.'

'I'm supposed to be seeing Piper later.'

'Is stinky Jaden coming?' Bobby asked.

'Nope, just us. It'll be great. We'll have Dad to ourselves. Come on, guys, we haven't been out just the four of us in months.'

Their mother came into the room. 'Did Jess tell you about your dad?'

'Yes. It would have been nice to get some notice. When did he call?' Luke asked.

'Only about two hours ago. He said he had a gap in his schedule and wanted to see you.'

'I don't want to go, Mummy.' Bobby's face reddened. 'I don't like Daddy.'

She crouched down. 'Hey, now, he's your dad and he loves you. Don't say things like that. I know he's been busy with Jenny and the baby and work, but he really misses you and he wants to see you.'

'He either feels guilty for being a deadbeat dad or Jenny's up the duff again,' Luke said.

'Luke!' Kate snapped.

'Does this dress look nice, Mum?' Jess interrupted.

'Gorgeous.'

The doorbell rang. Jess raced out. She flung open the door and Nick bent down and kissed her. 'Hey, Jessie – wow, you look great! All the boys are going to be chasing you.'

Bobby stood in the doorway, peeping out. Luke grabbed his jacket and, taking Bobby's hand, led him towards the front door.

'Evening, you two,' Nick said cheerfully.

His sons went by him silently, walking straight out to the car. Nick's face dropped and Jess smiled as widely as she could at him, trying to make things okay.

Kate came to the door. 'I know they might not seem it, but they're glad to get time with you.'

Nick looked towards his car, where the boys were sitting side by side on the back seat. 'They really don't seem it.'

Kate found herself feeling sorry for him. 'Honestly, they do want to spend time with you,' she said. 'Just give them time to come round.'

'I'll help,' Jess said, slipping her hand into Nick's. 'We'll get them talking about rugby and world records.'

Kate loved her daughter for trying so hard, even though at the same time she was sad that she had to shoulder all the responsibility. 'Good luck,' she murmured, as she watched Nick and Jess get into the car. 'You'll need it,' she added, under her breath, as the car pulled away.

Bobby pushed aside his plate. 'It's yucky. I'm not eating it.'

Nick's jaw set. 'You said you wanted pepperoni pizza.'

'Well, I don't like this pepperoni. It's too spicy.'

'Here, take some of mine.' Nick cut a slice and handed it to Bobby.

'I don't want your stinky pizza. It has peppers on it.'

Jess watched nervously as her father tried not to lose his temper.

'You need to eat something, Bobby. How about some plain pasta? Shall I order that?'

Bobby shook his head.

'Here, he can have some of my Margarita.' Jess handed Bobby a slice, which he accepted.

'How's your chicken, Luke?' Nick asked.

'Fine.'

'How's school and rugby and all that?'

'Fine.'

Luke wasn't going to make it easy for him. Jess knew he was still furious about being stood up on his birthday.

'He's been picked for the senior cup team,' Jess said, trying to smooth things over.

Nick was obviously impressed. 'Well done! That's great. You look very fit – I can see you've been working out.'

'Daddy, do you know what an okapi is?' Bobby asked.

'What?'

'An okapi.'

'Uhm, no –'

His phone rang. Jess saw Jenny's name come up on the screen. He ignored it.

'Guess,' Bobby said.

The phone rang again.

'I dunno, what?' Nick put the phone on silent.

'What do you think it is?' Bobby persisted.

'I . . . uhm . . .' The phone flashed. Nick cursed under his breath.

Jess touched her father's sleeve. 'Maybe you should answer it, Dad. Maybe Jaden's sick.'

Nick rubbed his eyes. 'There's always some drama with Jenny.'

The phone flashed again. He sighed and answered it.

'WHAT IS AN OKAPI?' Bobby shouted.

'Jesus, I don't bloody know,' Nick snapped. Pressing his phone to his ear, he hissed, 'What is it? I'm with my kids.'

'I TOLD YOU TO GUESS,' Bobby roared.

'Your kids!' Jess heard Jenny screech down the phone. 'What about Jaden? He's your kid too and he's got a temperature.'

'Daddy, you have to guess.' Bobby was not letting it go.

'I'm here all by myself, Nick, and I'm freaking out because I think he needs to go to hospital.'

Jess could hear Jenny crying. She actually felt a bit sorry for her.

'He's fine, Jenny. You always overreact,' Nick said gruffly.

'GUESS!' Bobby bellowed.

Nick glared at him. 'Jesus Christ, Bobby, will you shut up?'

'Don't speak to him like that!' Luke yelled.

'Come home now or I'm calling an ambulance,' Jenny sobbed down the phone.

'Jenny, will you calm down?'

'I'm frightened, Nick. Come home.'

His shoulders slumped.

'Maybe you should just go. She sounds really upset,' Jess said.

'I'm on my way.' Nick shut the phone.

They all looked down at their food. Jess could see Bobby's hands clenched into little fists. His face was red, and she could see he was trying hard not to cry.

Luke was twisting his napkin around his hands tightly. He wanted to punch the wall, she thought . . . or probably Dad.

Nick asked for the bill. 'I'm really sorry, guys, but I have to go. I had hoped I'd get a couple of hours with you without Jenny calling every five seconds, but apparently I was wrong.'

'What if Jaden's really sick?' Jess worried.

Nick ran his hand over his face. 'I don't think he is. Jenny overreacts every time he gets a bit hot.'

'I hope he is sick. I hope he's really sick and he dies,' Bobby blurted out.

'What the hell?' Nick glared at Bobby.

'He's upset! Give him a break,' Luke said tersely.

'Look, guys, I really wanted tonight to be good. I wanted to spend some time with you on my own, uninterrupted. I'm sorry. I really am. It's just . . . not easy at the moment. I'll make it up to you, I promise.' Nick paid the bill.

Jess and Luke held Bobby's hot hands in theirs. As they walked out, Jess's leg began to throb.

Bobby's Diary

I HATE Daddy. He shouted at me and I was just trying to tell him about okapis. He didn't even care. All he cares about is stupid Jaden. Jess said it was a teribel thing to say that I hope Jaden dies but I don't care. Jess said God was waching and lisening and that made me a bit scared. She said you should be nice to every one and not ever say you want some one to die. But I do.

Mummy said she was sorry the dinner with Daddy was rooined and she gave us all yummy brownees to eat and I felt better then. Granddad came in and when he hearded about the dinner his face went all red and he said 'Tipical.' But Mummy did squinty eyes at him so he stopped talking and put on a pretend smile and said he was sure Daddy was very sorry to have to go home in the midel of dinner. Then he hugged me and Jess and gave Luke a pat on the sholder.

I like living here with Granddad. He is super-nice and always gives us hugs and treets and never shouts. He is super-nice to Mummy and she is waaaaaaaaaaaaay happier now. She has a real happy face and not a pretend happy face like she used to with Daddy.

Even if I have to share a bedroom with Jess, I don't mind. Jess is a nice sister and she lets me talk about facts and actualy lisens and remembers stuff.

There is something wrong with her leg. Mummy is taking her to the doctor tomorrow. She is limping like a dog with glass in his paw.

Mrs Lorgan was cross with me today. She said I need to control my temper and that calling Sammy a 'dickhead' for knoking over the green paint onto my copybook is unaxeptabel. I told her that Luke said that word about Dad all the time. She asked how old Luke is and I said eighteen and she said that he was old enuff to know better. She said it was a very bad word and not ever to use it.

Then she asked about Jaden and was I growing to love my baby brother. I said no, that I wanted him to die, and her face went all red and her eyes were all big and she said that wasn't a nice thing to say and that I'd grow to love him.

I decided not to speak. She doesn't understand, no one does. Jenny took my daddy out of the house but Jaden took my daddy out of our hearts. That's why I hate him.

8

George stood behind Kate as they watched the women stream through the café door and up the stairs. Each one had a big bag of colourful balls of wool and long needles.

'Are they really called the Stitch 'n' Bitch Club?' he muttered.

'Yes, Dad.'

'What do they do – knit and give out?' He clicked his tongue. 'I never liked all those groups of women getting together and giving out and gossiping. Sure, half of them don't even like each other. The minute you put your knitting down to go to the toilet they'll be sticking a needle in your back.'

'I'm sure they support each other too, Dad,' Kate said, smiling.

'Nonsense. Your good friends support you, not a big group like that. Sure, Dorothy Chambers hates Nuala King. All she ever does is complain about her.'

'Dorothy wouldn't know what to do if she wasn't criticizing someone.' Kate chuckled.

'I'm not sure I like it, a bunch of women up there giving out,' George grumbled, eyeing the ceiling suspiciously.

'They're paying for the privilege,' Kate reminded him.

'You're right.' He grinned. 'They can knit and bitch and scratch each other's eyes out as long as they pay.'

Kate welcomed the women with a warm smile and directed them to the stairs that led to the room above the café.

'Hello there, Kate,' Dorothy said. 'You look well, dear. Much better than when I last saw you. You were very pale and old-looking back in the spring. I said to my Gerry, that poor girl has aged twenty years because of that awful husband of hers.'

Kate gritted her teeth and plastered on a smile. 'Well, enjoy your night. Straight on up the stairs there.'

But Dorothy was going nowhere. She heaved her balls of wool over her vast chest. 'Of course, your father always said that that Nick of yours was a bad egg. Rotten to the core.'

Kate could hear her father spluttering in the kitchen behind her, out of sight but perfectly well able to hear. 'Well, Nick is my children's father so I prefer not to speak ill of him,' she said evenly.

'A skirt-chaser. That was what George always said about your Nick. Full of his own importance, he said, and all flash with no cash.'

Kate could feel her temperature rising. 'Well, as I said, he is the father of my children, so I prefer not to speak ill of him.'

'Of course, Janice upstairs married one of those. Oh, sure he rode half the town, that fella. A philanderer, as my mother would have said. Poor Janice hadn't a clue. She was being made a holy show of, so I took it upon myself to tell her.'

'Did you? How . . .' Kate paused '. . . considerate of you.'

Dorothy placed a wrinkled hand on Kate's arm. 'I always think of others.'

Yes, I imagine you do, Kate thought, all day bloody long, peeking out from behind your twitching curtain, you nasty woman. Smiling, she said, 'Well, I mustn't keep you from your knitting.'

Dorothy dragged her large frame up the stairs while Kate turned to go back into the kitchen.

George moved quickly from behind the door and pretended to read the paper.

'I've just had a very interesting chat with Dorothy.'

'Oh, yes?' He feigned disinterest.

'She told me you've been slating Nick to everyone.'

'I wouldn't believe a word out of that woman's mouth. She's pure poison, your mother always said.'

Kate stood in front of her father, hands on hips. 'Seriously, Dad, don't criticize Nick in public, for the kids' sake. You can rip him apart in front of me, but not other people. Okay?'

George rustled his newspaper. 'Sure I barely mentioned him. Dorothy exaggerates everything. I'd never do anything to upset those kids.'

Kate ruffled his hair and kissed his forehead. 'I know you wouldn't.'

When Kate went to check on Jess and Bobby, she found Bobby fast asleep with his face stuck to the pages of *Guinness World Records*. Jess was still awake, reading.

Kate gently moved Bobby's face from the page to his pillow. Even in his sleep he frowned. She hoped he'd become less angry now that they'd moved in with George and things were calmer. But the poor little fellow still seemed full of rage, especially towards Jaden, who was an innocent victim in all this. Kate needed to spend more time with Bobby. She'd have to find it somehow.

'Mum,' Jess whispered.

'Yes, pet?'

'Am I going to be sharing a room with Bobby for ever?'

'For a while anyway.'

Jess sighed. 'Okay. It's just he's kind of annoying. I was trying to read my book and he kept going on and on about his facts.'

Kate moved over to sit on the edge of Jess's bed and hugged her.

'What's that for?'

'You're just great, and I don't tell you enough. You're so good with Bobby. I know it's not easy sharing a room with him. I'll tell you what, I'll let him sleep with me three nights a week. How does that sound?'

'Amazing!' Jess beamed.

'Was the dinner with Dad awful?' Kate asked. The kids hadn't said much about it in the two days since it had happened.

Jess nodded. 'Pretty awful. Jenny was stalking Dad on the phone and freaking out about Jaden, and Dad was getting really stressed, and Bobby kept on about the okapis, and Dad ended up shouting at him.'

'God, it sounds like a mess. I'm sorry for all of you. It would have been nice for you to spend time with your dad without any drama.'

Jess snuggled down under her covers. 'To be honest, Mum, I think there's always going to be drama with Jenny and Dad. She worries a lot about Jaden. Dad seemed kind of fed up.'

Did he indeed? Kate tried not to smile. So hot, sexy Jenny wasn't so great, after all. She actually had weak spots. Fancy that!

Jess fiddled with her hair. 'Do you think Dad will ever be able to be a proper dad again?'

Suddenly Kate felt bad for being happy that Jenny was turning into a nightmare. This wasn't about her: it was about her kids.

She pulled Jess's hands gently out of her hair. 'Yes. New babies always take up a lot of time and energy, and it's Jenny's first child, so naturally she's nervous. She'll calm down soon and Dad will have more time for you guys. This is only temporary. Don't worry. You know he loves you.'

'I suppose you're right.' Jess rolled over, yawning. 'I just hope it's soon. I miss him.'

Kate leant over and kissed her cheek. 'Sleep well. We have that doctor's appointment tomorrow. I don't like the look of those bruises. I'm worried you might be a bit anaemic. You'll be going to school late.'

Jess smiled. 'Yes! I'm missing double maths.'

Kate switched off the bedside lamp and tiptoed out of the room. When she went back down to the kitchen, Luke was tucking into a large steak.

'What are you doing? We had steak for dinner,' Kate said.

Chewing, he said, 'We were told to eat as much protein as possible.'

'You're going to bankrupt me.'

'I need it, Mum. I have to be in peak condition.'

'What's this?' She picked up a half-empty carton.

'Protein milk,' Luke said, chugging down half a glass in one go.

Kate gazed at her son. He was a man now. Tall, strong, very muscular, with a shadow of facial hair. Where had the chubby blond toddler in red shorts gone? It felt as if she'd blinked and he'd grown up. She wanted to reach out and smooth down his hair and kiss his lovely face, but she knew not to.

She sat down opposite him. 'I want you to do your best at rugby but don't overdo it, Luke. Too much protein isn't healthy. You need a balanced diet, love.'

Luke polished off the steak. 'Chill, Mum. It's all under control. I know what I need to do.'

'I worry about you getting injured. Did you see the Leinster winger got a terrible concussion in the last match?'

Luke snorted. 'He can't tackle. He goes in with his head.'

'Well, you just mind yours.'

Luke rolled his eyes.

'Did you tell Dad about the match on Saturday?' she asked.

Luke shook his head.

'Ah, Luke, call him and tell him. He'll want to come.'

Luke stared into her eyes, something he very rarely did these days. 'Mum, Dad couldn't give a flying fuck about rugby or about me. I texted him when I made the team and he didn't reply. Then at the restaurant it was like he'd never fucking heard about it before.'

'Language!'

'I'm serious. He's a tosser, and I'm not putting myself out there any more. If he wants to know what's going on, he can bloody well ask. I'm over it.' Luke stood up and slammed his plate into the dishwasher.

He was so clearly not 'over it'. Every muscle in his body was tense with rage and frustration. Kate would have to call Nick and make sure he went to the game.

George came in, looking flustered. 'For the love of God, Kate, save me.'

'What's wrong?'

'Rosemary Jacobs just pretended she couldn't find the toilet. She came into the wine shop, grabbed my backside and squeezed it!'

'Way to go, Granddad.' Luke grinned.

Kate laughed. 'What's the problem, Dad?'

'The problem is, I don't want to be assaulted by the Stitch and Bitchers. They must have brought their own wine with them – she smelt of alcohol.'

'There's no law against having wine while you knit.'

George crossed his arms. 'If I was a woman, you'd all be up in arms if someone pinched me. Because I'm a man I'm supposed not to care.'

'You should be flattered, Granddad. If some bird pinched my arse, I'd be cool with it,' Luke said, and drank the last of the protein milk.

'I'm seventy-three, too old for all that.'

'Charlie Chaplin became a father again at seventy-three. It's never too late,' Kate said.

'No way!' Luke held up his hands. 'No more babies. Jaden is enough.'

'I don't think Rosemary is in any fit state to be having children. She's seventy years old and has had two hip replacements.'

'You could be one of Bobby's facts in *Guinness World Records* – the oldest couple ever to have a child.' Kate giggled.

'You could just shag her,' Luke said. 'Treat her mean, keep her keen, you know.'

'Luke!' Kate cried.

'What? I'm just saying, if he wanted a bit of action . . .'

George tapped the kitchen table for attention. 'Thank you for your advice, but I think I'll steer clear of Rosemary. If I want "a bit of action", I'll choose my own partner.'

'That Caroline who comes into the café isn't bad. She's in good shape for an auld one,' Luke suggested.

'She is attractive, all right.'

'Not too wrinkly,' Luke said.

'She's fifty-three!' Kate exclaimed. 'She's only eleven years older than me.'

'So?' The two men turned to her.

Kate was incredulous. 'So? So she's too young for you and, no offence, Dad, you look good for your age but I doubt she wants a man twenty years older than her.'

'Loads of old dudes go out with younger chicks,' Luke informed her. 'Jenny's twenty years younger than Dad.'

'Thanks for reminding me,' Kate retorted. 'It's a man's world. Right, well, I'd better see the Stitch 'n' Bitch Club out. Maybe one of them will have a brother in his sixties or seventies who might be interested in a single forty-two-year-old woman with three kids.'

She left her father and son laughing. It might be funny for them, but was this really her future? Would only men in their sixties be interested in her from now on? It was depressing.

After showing the knitting ladies out and collecting the money – a hundred and fifty euros – Kate locked the doors and went to sit in the café, where it was quiet. She made herself a cup of frothy cappuccino and called Maggie.

'Hey!'

'Hey.'

'How are you?'

'Are the only men who'll be interested in me going to be in their sixties?'

'Hell, no,' Maggie growled. 'What gave you that idea? I was with a thirty-year-old last week. Younger guys love older women. We're not needy, we don't want to have kids with them and we're not after commitment.'

Kate took a sip of her coffee. The problem was, if she was to meet another man she would want commitment. She didn't want to sleep with random strangers. She wanted a man to love her and be nice to her. Maybe it was naive, but she liked being in a relationship. She liked sitting in the cinema with someone sharing popcorn or curling up on the sofa together and talking about your day.

Maggie had always hated the idea of commitment. Even when they were at school, she had never dated anyone for more than two weeks. She was on a mission to get the hell out of Ireland and make it big in the world, and no one was going to stop her, least of all a boy. It was as if boys could smell her indifference and it drove them wild. Kate could remember the queues of boys who had chased Maggie all over town.

But the girl was not for turning. As soon as she'd finished her business degree, Maggie had been on the first plane to London, where she'd made success happen.

'How are the kids? How's my goddaughter? Beautiful and lovely as ever?'

Kate smiled. 'Yes.'

'Actually, I know more about Jess than ever now that she's allowed me to be her friend on Facebook.'

'Good. You can keep an eye on her and let me know what's going on. She refused to let me be her friend, needless to say.'

'That's normal, Kate. No kid wants their mother spying on them on Facebook. How are the boys?'

'Good. Luke got picked for the senior cup team so he's thrilled and eating every animal he can get his hands on, alive or dead. The whole diet thing is crazy. Honestly, Maggie, he consumes cows and chickens daily.'

Kate could hear Maggie lighting a cigarette. 'He has to, Kate. All those rugby guys have to build up as much muscle as they can. It's to protect themselves from the opposition who, you can be sure, are also going around eating steaks for breakfast. How's Bobby?'

'Bobby is Bobby.'

'Still spouting facts and kicking things?'

'Yes. He's kicked a lot of furniture in the last two days.' Kate filled her in on the disastrous dinner with Nick.

'Oh, for the love of Jesus, would Nick grow a pair of balls and stand up to that moany cow? She's obviously sitting in that apartment, alone all day, with leaky boobs and a sore fanny, and wondering what the hell she's got herself into. Serves her right for shagging your husband. It's always the same. These men have their pathetic midlife crises, start screwing some young slapper, think it's all going to be sex on the kitchen table and blow-jobs, until the woman decides she

75

wants a kid and it all goes tits-up. Then they realize that the wife they had was actually fantastic.'

Kate laughed. She loved Maggie. She always made her feel better about things. It was a gift. 'That about sums it up. I was feeling a bit gloaty about it all, but the kids are upset so I'm hoping Jenny will get herself together and let Nick see them more than once every six weeks.'

'He's their father! It's up to him to stand up to her. Poor Bobby, though. Not nice to be shouted at.'

'No, and he's so sensitive when it comes to Nick.'

'I'll send him something to cheer him up. How's George?'

'He's great. It hasn't been easy for him. Mum's been gone six years and he was used to living on his own when we landed on him. I think he finds us all a bit much at times, but he's really good with the kids, particularly with Luke, and God knows he needs a positive male influence. He loves Jess, but I think he finds Bobby a bit trying, and patience was never Dad's strong point. Poor Bobby, no one really understands him.'

'Except you.'

'That's true.'

'Is George still being chatted up by the local widows and singletons?'

Kate laughed. 'Yes, but he doesn't seem interested. Anyway, enough about me, how are you?'

'Good. Crazy busy. Travelling to the States a lot since I last saw you, having good casual sex with younger guys, and spending a lot of money on Botox and fillers.'

'You don't need it. You're lovely the way you are.'

Maggie exhaled her cigarette smoke. 'No way! Kate, a woman breaking glass ceilings has to keep herself looking good. If I walk into meetings with men of my age looking old and wrinkled with black bags under my eyes, I'm on the back foot. I know it sounds ridiculous, but that's the reality. If I walk in fit, fresh-faced and ready to go, they sit up and take notice.'

'Come on! What about Angela Merkel? She's not having work done on her face.'

Maggie snorted. 'She looks like a bloke. I'm going for the Christine Lagarde vibe.'

Kate was ashamed to admit she wasn't quite sure who Christine Lagarde was. That was the problem with kids and working: there was never enough time to read the papers. Even when she did have a second to herself, she was usually so tired that she'd pick up a magazine or skim the headlines in the paper but never actually read the articles. She'd Google Christine Lagarde later. 'Well, I still think you're lovely without all that stuff.'

To be honest, Maggie's face seemed a bit pulled. Her forehead was frozen. She was like one of those presenters on American TV, glittering white teeth and flawless face. She looked fabulous but, close up, it was a little fake.

Then again, what did Kate know about anything? She hadn't even had a bikini wax in almost a year. What was the point? They couldn't afford to go on holidays so she didn't need to wear swimming togs and no man was looking at her. Half the time she didn't even bother to shave her legs. She'd only plucked her eyebrows the other day when Jess said the way they were 'meeting in the middle' was a bit strange. It was only when she'd seen herself in the mirror that she'd noticed the very obvious monobrow.

That was the problem. She never looked at herself now. Not really, not closely. She climbed out of bed in the morning, got everyone fed and off to school, then helped her dad in the café, did homework with the kids, had dinner and went to bed. She avoided mirrors when she came within their range, basically ignoring herself entirely. She just didn't want to see. She had enough going on without owning up to how terrible she looked.

When she'd been with Nick, she'd made more of an effort with her appearance, her clothes and her weight. She peered down at her stomach: too many late-night comfort muffins. She'd have to start walking again and watch what she ate. Things were better now – the kids were happier, settled into the house and set-up. It was time for Kate to find herself again.

'So, do you think you're ready to date again?' Maggie asked.

'I'm not sure. Not yet. Maybe. No. Besides, who'd be interested? I'm a broke, boring mother of three who lives and works with her dad.'

'Kate. You're a gorgeous, interesting, kind, lovely woman. Any man would be lucky to have you . . . young or old.' She laughed her husky smoker's laugh.

'How old do you think I should consider?' Kate said, curiosity now taking hold of her.

'The oldest man I've ever slept with was ten years older than I am, but he was very fit – he had a Liam Neeson vibe.'

'There aren't any Liam Neeson lookalikes in our area, I can tell you.'

'Keep an open mind – you could go younger. My youngest was twenty-eight.'

Kate giggled. 'I'll be eyeing up Luke's friends soon.'

'Why not?' Maggie chuckled. 'Oh, shoot, my plane's boarding. I'd better go. Big hi to the kids, especially Jess. By the way, she said on Facebook she's had a couple of nose bleeds. Is she all right?'

'I'm a bit worried. I think she might be anaemic. She's very pale. I reckon she needs iron. I'm taking her to the doctor tomorrow.'

'Good idea. Keep me posted.'

They said goodbye and hung up. Kate finished her now lukewarm coffee and headed upstairs to shave her legs. Tomorrow she'd book a bikini wax. It was time to move on. She needed to take control of her life and shake herself up. She wasn't past her sell-by date. She was still relatively young and, with a bit of effort, could be attractive again, maybe even meet someone. Why not? Why was she writing herself off? Maybe this was one of the blessings in disguise that her mother used to talk about, a new chapter in her life, a happier one.

9

Jess was glad they were going to the doctor because she felt awful. She knew Mum was worried – she kept asking Jess if she was all right, then got that worried line between her eyes when Jess said no.

She was fed up herself: the bruises on her legs were big and ugly and the nose bleeds were a pain. Her gym teacher said she probably needed iron. She said Jess was probably going through a growth spurt and her body needed more vitamins. Jess actually hoped that what she had was growing pains – she'd like to be taller. Chloë was five foot five already, like a supermodel. Jess was still only four foot eleven.

'Now, pet, there you go.' George put a plate of homemade pancakes in front of Jess.

'Wow, thanks, Granddad.'

'Only the best for my favourite granddaughter.'

Jess grinned. He always said that, even though she was his only granddaughter. Jess loved her granddad. He could be a bit grumpy sometimes, but most of the time he was lovely and kind, generous and funny. But, most of all, Jess loved the way he minded her mum. You could see that he adored her. Jess supposed it was because she was his only child, and the way he looked at her made Jess's tummy all squidgy inside.

It was how her mum looked at her, Luke and Bobby – as if they were the sun, the moon and the stars. It was unconditional love. Her mum had told her about it one night. Jess had been upset about her dad leaving and she'd shouted at her mum that she hated her. She'd said, 'It's all your fault! You're always nagging him! He hates being nagged. He said so. You made him leave.'

Jess had felt awful after shouting. She was sick to her stomach. When she'd gone downstairs later to apologize, Mum had put her arms around her and said, 'It's okay.'

Jess had asked her if she hated her now for being so mean and her mum had laughed and said, 'Don't be ridiculous. Nothing you can do will make me stop loving you. It's called unconditional love.'

After that Jess had felt all warm inside. But she also understood that unconditional love was only between parents and kids, not mums and dads. They did not love each other unconditionally at all.

Jess had decided to stop wishing for her parents to get back together. It was a waste of time, Chloë said. 'Your dad's had a kid with another woman. He's not coming back, Jess. I'm sorry, but it's just not going to happen and, besides, would your mum even take him back? Unlikely. My mum said that if Dad ever had an affair she'd kick him out so fast his head would spin off, and then she'd smash his sports cars with a baseball bat. She said women have to be strong and show men that they can't be messed around.'

Jess thought this was good advice, but Chloë's mum was a bit scary. She was super-nice to Jess, but Jess had heard her on the phone one day to someone who had forgotten to deliver something on time and, OMG, she'd ripped their head off. Jess decided then and there never to do anything to annoy her.

Leaving their old house and moving in with her granddad had been a good thing, after all. She felt it sort of made things clearer in her life and everyone was happier – well, everyone except Bobby, but he was never really happy.

Jess ate some of her pancakes, while her mum and granddad bustled in and out of the café. Nathalie arrived through the back door into the kitchen for her morning shift. Jess loved Nathalie – she was so cool and dramatic in a fabulous French way. Chloë thought she was like a French version of Emma Watson.

Nathalie threw her bag down, plonked herself opposite Jess and began picking at her pancakes. Jess didn't mind – she wasn't all that hungry.

'How are you?' Jess asked.

Nathalie pouted in the coolest way. Jess and Chloë had practised in the mirror but they couldn't do it like her. 'Life ees sheet,' she said, chewing a tiny piece of pancake.

'Sorry to hear that. Did something happen?'

Nathalie shrugged. 'Men. Irish men are ridiculous. They are so stupid and immature, like leetle kids. They don't want to 'ave a beautiful connection, to talk about poetry and the meaning of life, they just want to get drunk and 'ave sex.'

'That about sums it up.' Kate bustled in. 'Right, Nathalie, when you're ready you might get up and go in to help my dad. Also, please try to remember that Jess is twelve. Tone down the sex chat.'

'In France we talk about sex from a young age. There is nothing to be embarrassed about.'

Jess was bright red and utterly mortified by the whole conversation. She liked Nathalie treating her as an equal, but she did find the word 'sex' really cringey and she was totally embarrassed by her mother coming in at that exact moment. She put her hands up to her face to try to cool her cheeks.

'Well, in Ireland we're less free and easy with the sex chat – hence the fact that men can't talk to women without ten pints on them,' said Kate. 'So, if you don't mind, I'd appreciate it if you kept that conversation for people older than Jess.'

Nathalie picked up her bag. 'Fine, but you should not 'ide your children from the conversation of the beauty of sex and the satisfaction of the body.'

'Thank you, Nathalie. Off you go now. You can tell my dad all about it.' Kate grinned.

'All about what?' George stuck his head around the door.

'Sex,' Nathalie said.

'Mother of Holy God, will you keep that chat to yourself! The average age of the customers in here this morning is seventy – you'll give them heart attacks.'

'Or maybe I will wake them up from the coma they are living in.' Nathalie half smiled.

'With that bit of a skirt on you, they'll be wide awake in no time,' George grumbled. 'Didn't I tell you to wear something that reached your knees? Here, put this apron on or I'll have to invest in a defibrillator.'

Nathalie sighed dramatically. 'Once again the Irish men and the body. You are afraid of the woman's form. You are all totally suppressed.'

George held up his hand. 'I'll have to stop you there. Much as I enjoy these conversations about the uselessness of Irish men and their many failures, I've a business to run and people to serve. Now, hop it.'

Jess and Kate giggled as Nathalie and George went into the café. Jess tidied her plate into the dishwasher, while Kate rushed around looking for keys and money.

'Come on,' she said, smiling at Jess. 'Let's get going while the going's good.'

Jess watched her mother's face darken.

'What do you mean, blood tests? Why?'

Dr Willis smiled reassuringly. 'It's just a precaution. I'm a little concerned about the bruising and the nose bleeds. She might be anaemic or have a low-lying infection. I think it's worth checking out her bloods.'

Jess felt her mother relax. 'Okay. She probably is a bit low on iron.'

Dr Willis rolled up Jess's sleeve and gently inserted the needle, chatting to Jess to distract her. He was a really nice man. Jess trusted him. He was the only doctor she'd ever been to – they'd always come to him when they were sick. He was nearly as old as Granddad and very kind. Mum had been seeing him since she was a little girl, too.

The needle didn't hurt as much as Jess had thought it would. It was all over quickly and they were able to leave. Her mum asked if she should give Jess iron straight away, but Dr Willis said it was best to wait and that he'd get the results as quickly as possible.

Jess felt there was something he wasn't saying. She couldn't explain it exactly but she sensed that he was worried. She felt very tired, like super-tired. She wanted to go home and lie down. She hoped the blood tests would show what was wrong and that they could give her some pills and make her better.

Kate paid and they left the surgery. Dr Willis promised to call as soon as he had some news.

'Would you like to go for a hot chocolate before I bring you to school?' Kate asked.

Jess shook her head. 'Actually, Mum, I feel really tired. Can I just go home and rest?'

Kate frowned. 'You're very pale. You poor thing. I've been so distracted I haven't paid enough attention to you. I hope you don't have an infection, but it'll be good to find out whatever's wrong and get you better.' She put her arm around Jess's shoulders. 'Come on, let's get you home and into your pyjamas and cosy you up. It'll be nice and peaceful with no Bobby to annoy you.'

Jess leant her head into her mother's shoulder. It was nice just being the two of them. Kate kissed her. They walked home across the village green and went through the back door. Kate went to check if George needed any help in the café while Jess went up to change into her pyjamas and dressing-gown. When she came back to the kitchen, her mum handed her a mug of hot chocolate, which she gratefully drank.

'It's quiet now, the lull before lunch. Can I get you anything else, pet?'

'I'm fine, thanks. I might go up and read or watch Netflix.'

'Good idea.'

George popped his head in. 'How did you get on?'

'She had blood tests done and now she's tired so I've let her off school.'

'Good idea. You're as pale as a ghost, Jess. A good rest will help. Would you like something to eat?'

'No, thanks. I'm going to bed to read.'

Nathalie slunk in. 'I am reading a fantastic book of poetry all about love and 'ow it can drive you crazy. I read one this morning on my way 'ere about a man who sets himself on fire because the woman he loves is a lesbian. If you would like to borrow it, I can lend it.'

George threw his arms into the air. 'Just what a twelve-year-old needs to cheer her up, a book about a fella frying himself over a lesbian. I tell you what, Nathalie, you're going to make one hell of a psychologist when you finish that degree of yours. They'll be queuing round the block to listen to your words of comfort and joy.'

Jess tried not to giggle as Nathalie wagged a finger at George. 'Irish people drink all this alcohol because they are so sad inside.'

George put his hand on her arm. 'This may come as a shock to you, but some people drink for a bit of fun. Not everyone who has a pint or a glass of wine is an emotional cripple.'

Jess looked at her mum, who was smiling. It was lovely to be here with them all, listening to the funny conversations and feeling like she was a grown-up.

Nathalie shrugged. 'I prefer to talk rather than drink.'

'I noticed that. I also noticed that you prefer to talk rather than work. Now come on.'

'I am entitled to a break.'

'You haven't exactly been run off your feet, and after the double espresso you just had, I'd have thought you'd be buzzing.'

Nathalie pulled her hair into a bun and anchored it with a pen. Jess thought it looked so cool – she'd try it when she was on her own.

'You are like a . . . 'ow do you say it? Driver of the slaves,' Nathalie said.

George hooted. 'Slave driver? I'm the best boss you'll ever have. You spend most of your time drinking coffee and sighing. You need a rocket under your feet to get you moving. Now, come on, I've a business to run here.'

Nathalie shuffled in behind him, pulling a face at Jess over her shoulder as she went.

'I'm not sure how long Nathalie's going to last. She's the laziest waitress we've ever had,' Kate said, as she began to make wraps and rolls for the lunchtime rush.

Jess hoped Nathalie would work a bit harder so she wouldn't get fired. She'd miss her crazy talk so much if she had to leave. And, anyway, she had a feeling that, underneath all the giving out, Granddad liked having Nathalie around too.

Jess headed upstairs, her legs heavy and uncooperative. They felt like they were made of iron already, but if everyone thought she needed more, she'd happily take it – anything to get rid of this worn-out feeling.

Piper watched Poppy and Penny doing their homework while, at the same time, trying to eat Weetabix. A lump of the milky cereal landed on Poppy's copybook.

'For God's sake, Penny! Look what you just did!'

'It's not my fault! You nudged my arm.'

Poppy tried to wipe it off, but made the stain worse.

'Great! Now Mr Keane will think I didn't bother trying.'

Pauline clicked her tongue. 'He'd be correct, then, wouldn't he? Doing your homework over breakfast doesn't qualify as much of an effort.'

Poppy glared at her eldest sister. 'Oh, go and qualify yourself, you bore.'

Penny giggled. 'I bet you always did your homework the night before and never handed anything in late.'

'Yes, actually, I did, which is why I got in to do medicine.'

Penny snorted. 'Who wants to do boring medicine and wear a horrible white coat . . . Zzzzzzzz.'

The twins pretended to fall asleep.

Olivia, who had been concentrating on reading her college notes and not listening to any of them, suddenly looked up. 'I think you'll find that studying is extremely important and valuable. Pauline could end up finding the cure for cancer or Parkinson's.'

Pauline smiled. 'That's my plan.'

'She could end up being an adviser on *Grey's Anatomy*,' Posy said, suddenly joining in the conversation.

'I have no intention of advising some ridiculous TV show,' Pauline snapped.

Posy frowned. 'I was just saying.'

'Did you know,' Olivia said, 'that it was a woman who –'

'Mum!' Piper had sensed that their mother was about to launch into one of her long lectures about women.

'What?' Olivia said impatiently.

'Don't forget you have to help out at the cake sale this morning.'

'What cake sale?'

'The one for the St Vincent de Paul. I told you last week.'

Olivia had clearly forgotten all about it. She never forgot about her lectures, Piper thought grumpily, but she did forget about everything else.

'Well, I can only stay an hour. I have a lecture at half ten. We're covering transgender this week.'

'Oh, like Caitlin Jenner,' Poppy said. 'OMG! Is he – I mean she – going to be talking?'

'Duh! Caitlin Jenner is way too busy to come to some crappy college in Ireland,' Penny said.

'Is transgender when a man wants to be a woman?' Posy asked.

Olivia put down her book. 'It means someone whose gender differs from the one they were given when they were born,' she explained to her youngest child.

'Like you,' Poppy said to Posy. 'You're going to have to be a boy because Dad wants a son.'

Posy's eyes widened. 'I am not,' she shouted.

Seamus walked into the chaos. 'What's going on? Why is Posy shouting?'

Posy rounded on her father. 'I don't care how much you want a son, I'm not going to be it. No way. I'm a girl and that's it.' She stormed out to howls of laughter from the twins.

'Would someone like to explain?' Seamus asked.

'I'm going to college. This family is insane.' Pauline picked up her laptop and left.

'The twins were winding Posy up,' Olivia said. Turning to the twins, she added, 'It's not nice. You're always tormenting her. Besides, being transgender is not a joke. It's a very serious issue.'

Penny put her cereal bowl into the dishwasher. 'We know, Mum. We've watched *I Am Cait*. God, can no one have a joke around here any more?' The twins left to get ready for school.

'Transgender at eight a.m.' Seamus sat down. 'You've outdone yourself, Olivia.'

Olivia poured herself and Piper another cup of tea. 'I just said I had a lecture on the subject. Besides, kids need to be informed.'

'Not at twelve years of age and not before breakfast is even over. Can you please tone it down?'

Olivia bristled. 'Men telling women to "tone it down" is what got us into this mess in the first place.'

'What mess is that?'

'Men thinking they're superior and putting women down.'

'When have I ever put you down?'

'Well, obviously you haven't, but I'm talking about other men.'

Seamus folded his arms over his chest. 'What – like Muslim men?'

Olivia nodded. 'Well, some, and others.'

'Like who?'

Piper saw her mother waver.

'Like other men, ones who feel insecure and put women down to make themselves feel better.'

'In my humble male opinion, women are pretty good at putting each other down.'

Go, Dad! Piper cheered silently.

Olivia put her mug down. 'You have a point there.'

'What? Me? A mere man saying something you agree with? My God, Olivia, your equality lecturer might not like that.'

Piper watched as a smile spread across her mother's face. It was nice to see – she could be a bit serious about her studies.

Seamus spread a thick layer of butter on his toast. 'So, let me get this straight. Posy thinks I want her to be a boy?'

'Yes.'

'Excellent. With her already raging hormones, it'll make her even more difficult to live with.' To Piper, he added, 'Thank God one of my daughters is sensible.'

Olivia reached out and patted Piper's shoulder. 'You're right there.'

Piper smiled. With four loud sisters, it was rare that she got any time alone with her parents. Maybe now was the time to tell them. No, she had to tell Luke first. Oh, God. Her stomach twisted into a tight knot.

The door burst open. Posy stormed in wearing her uniform, her face plastered in make-up, with big hoop earrings and bracelets jangling from her wrists. The twins followed her, laughing.

'See?' Posy threw her hands into the air. 'I'm a girl. Not a girl who wants to be a boy. Not a girl who is a lesbian. Not a girl who doesn't want to be a girl. Not a girl who wants a willy. Just a bloody girl, okay?'

'To be honest, with all that make-up on your face, you look like a transvestite,' Penny said.

They all laughed, even Olivia.

Posy's face went bright red. 'What did you say?'

Olivia jumped up and went over to her. 'Calm down. She's only joking.'

'Transvestite!' she shrieked. 'One minute I'm a transsexual and now you're saying I'm a transvestite. I hate this family. I'm going to get a lawyer and divorce you all. Yeah, I saw it on TV. Kids can divorce their families.'

'On what grounds are you going to divorce us?' Seamus asked, trying not to laugh.

'On the grounds of you being mean and calling me names and . . . What's that word? Oh, yeah, racists and bigerts.'

'Bigots?' Seamus suggested.

'Yeah, that's it.' Posy pointed a finger at her father. 'You're all worse than the Nazis.'

'I'm not sure you can compare genocide to a bit of joking around,' Seamus said drily.

'Okay. Well, you're worse than – than – Paul Potts.'

'Who?' Olivia and Seamus looked confused.

Piper couldn't help it. She burst out laughing. 'Paul Potts was the singer from *Britain's Got Talent*. I think you mean Pol Pot.'

The twins cracked up.

'Pot, Potts, whatever. You're all just mean and cruel.'

Olivia laid a hand on Posy's tense shoulder. 'Take a deep breath, darling. You're going to have a heart attack. You must learn to handle teasing.'

'It's not teasing, it's abuse.' Posy began to cry and her mascara streamed down her face in black lines, reminding Piper of a sad clown, the red lipstick making her mouth seem droopy.

'Come on. I'll help you take the make-up off so Mrs Kinsella doesn't freak when she sees you.'

Piper took her little sister upstairs and used wet wipes to remove the thick layer of foundation. When she'd finished,

Posy, who had now calmed down, grunted thanks and went to get her schoolbag.

Piper went into her bedroom and unplugged her phone from the charger. She cursed: it was already five to nine. Posy's drama meant they were going to be late. She slid the package from under her pillow into her bag. She'd dump it in the bin outside the Spar shop on the way to school. No one would find it there. Her hands shook as she tried to zip up her backpack. She had to tell him today. No more pretending, he had to know. She couldn't keep it in any longer. The last three days had been hell. She wanted to tell him, to share the news, to have him comfort her. She wanted him to tell her what to do.

Today was the day she would tell Luke that she was pregnant.

Winter

Bobby's Diary

Mrs Lorgan was super-cross with me today. She was talking about Jesus being born in a mainger and that Mary was his mother and God was his father. But I didn't understand cos Joseph was the Dad. But Mrs Lorgan said no, God was the Dad.

So I asked her how come God gets to be Jesus father when Mary is married to Joseph? She must have had an afair like my dad did with Jenny. And so how come Joseph doesn't mind about God and the afair? How come he doesn't go over to God and punch him in the face?

Mrs Lorgan said it wasn't an afair and that God got the baby in Mary's stomach by imacoolate konsepshun — but I don't understand that. So she said it was like God magiked the baby into Mary's tummy.

But you can't magik babies. That's just rubbish. Mrs Lorgan made that up to try to pretend that God was good and not a bad man who had an afair with Joseph's wife.

When I said that Mary was a slapper for going off with God when she was married to Joseph, Mrs Lorgan went mad. She shouted at me for using bad words and for blasfeeming. I don't know what that is but it must be bad.

I said Luke used that word for Jenny all the time. Mrs Lorgan said it was a very bad word and Mary was a saintly woman who never did anything wrong in her life. But I don't care what Mrs Lorgan says. Mary must be a slapper cos she went off with another man when she was married.

In the yard, Tommy said Mary must have sexed with God to have a baby. I asked him what that means, and he said when a man and woman go in the same bed and roll around babies are made.

I know that's true cos that's what Dad and Jenny did, they rolled around in the same bed and then Jaden was in her tummy. When we went to stay with them I could hear them rolling around and Jenny was saying, 'O, O Nick. Yes, yes,' and Dad was saying 'O, O, Jenny.'

But Mummy was foorious when Dad rolled around with Jenny so I know Joseph was not happy about it. I think Mrs Lorgan is just pretending that God is a good person cos she is very religos. She goes to mass all the time. We only go on Christmas and some times Easter.

I'm surprised about God cos he is suposed to be a great man who made us and the world. I heard Mum say to Maggie on the phone that all men are week and can't keep it in there pants.

I think she means money cos Dad never seems to have enuff money to give to Mum. Dad is always stressed about money. He says kids and wimen are too expensif. If he thinks that then he should never have married Mum or rolled around with Jenny.

Luke came to get me from school wich was brilliant cos he never does. But then I saw his eyes were all red and he seemed sad. He kept huging me, which he never does, like never.

I thought maybe he got dumped from the rugby team but when I asked him he said no and then he hugged me again and said that there was bad news.

11

After the meeting Nick checked his phone. Two missed calls from Jenny and three from Kate. He knew Jenny was just calling to tell him that something was wrong with Jaden, like she did every day. Her panicking about his health was getting worse. If he had a runny nose, she thought it was pneumonia. He'd have to make an appointment with the GP and take her there himself. She needed pills. She was freaking out over every little thing and crying all the time. He couldn't cope with much more of it.

Sometimes at night he lay awake, wondering if he'd made a huge mistake. But it was too late now. He was stuck. Stuck with a new baby and a depressed girlfriend. What a bloody mess he'd made of things.

He knew Kate was calling about money. She was probably going to shout at him for not giving her enough last month. Thank God that house sale had gone through yesterday – at least he'd be able to pay her next month. He hated not being able to support his family properly, but with the debts and the rent on his apartment with Jenny, everything was just going out faster than it was coming in. He felt bad about Kate, but he had been honest when he'd told her he just didn't have it to spare.

He'd call them both later, he decided. Give himself a breather before facing the music. But then he saw a text from Kate: *Call me. Urgent, it's Jess.*

Nick's heart sank. Unlike Jenny, Kate did not panic about the kids unless it was serious. Damn, what was wrong? Nick's hand shook as he dialled.

'Kate?'

'Nick . . . oh, God, Nick . . .' Kate was sobbing so much he couldn't understand what she was saying.

'What? Jesus, Kate, what is it?'

'Jess has . . . They think it's leukaemia.'

What the fuck? Nick's heart stopped. 'Kate, did you say leukaemia?'

'Yes, the blood tests came back, and . . . It's bad, Nick. Oh, God, Jess, our beautiful Jess . . .'

Nick fell against the wall of his office. Blood was rushing to his ears. He couldn't hear. He couldn't think. When he could finally speak, his voice was faint. 'But how . . . I mean, what the hell? They must be mistaken. She's fine. I know she wasn't feeling great but it was no big deal. It's a mistake, Kate. It has to be. There is no way she has cancer. No fucking way.' He was shouting now, fists clenched, body tight.

'They think it is.' Kate was bawling. 'I don't understand either, Nick. I'm freaking out here. Come to the hospital. I need you – Jess needs you.'

'I'm on my way. I'll sort this out.' Nick hung up but his legs wouldn't move. He was frozen. His mouth felt dry and his head too heavy for his body. He dragged one leg forward, then the other.

As he was stumbling through the office a colleague approached him. 'Are you okay, mate? You look like you've seen a ghost.'

'Fine. Just have to pop out – problem with my kid,' Nick rasped. He didn't want to get into it. He didn't want everyone talking about Jess. And, anyway, it was a mistake. It had to be. This was bullshit. Kate must have misunderstood. There was no way his daughter had cancer. No way.

Nick didn't remember driving to the hospital. The journey was a blur. He threw his car into a wheelchair-user's parking spot, then sprinted through the door and up the stairs. Level three, Haematology and Oncology, Kate had texted.

He burst through the doors and saw Kate on the phone, crying. He strode straight over to her.

'I know, Maggie, thanks. I haven't said anything to Dad or the boys yet. I want to find out more first. I'll call you as soon as I know more.' She hung up, turned to rest her head on Nick's shoulder and sobbed into it.

'Where's Jess?' he asked.

'She just went to the toilet,' Kate said.

'Who's in charge here?'

'I don't know. There are lots of people involved. I've spoken to a Dr Kennedy.'

Nick went over to the nurses' station. 'I want to speak to Dr Kennedy now. Right now.'

'I'm afraid he's with a patient.'

'I don't give a fuck if he's with the president, I want to speak to him *now*.'

The nurse recoiled.

Kate grabbed Nick's arm. 'Stop it. Don't shout at everyone.'

He shook off her hand. 'GET HIM!' he roared at the nurse. He could feel the veins in his neck bulging.

A door opened and a well-dressed man came towards him. 'Is there a problem here?'

'I'm sorry, Doctor. This is Jess's father – he's just arrived,' Kate said.

'Don't apologize for me,' Nick snapped. 'Are you Kennedy?'

'Yes.'

'I want to know what the hell is going on. You've clearly misdiagnosed my daughter.'

Dr Kennedy nodded. 'I'm very sorry, Mr . . .'

'Higgins.'

'Mr Higgins, I understand this has come as a shock to you. I can assure you that we're going to run every test we can to get an accurate diagnosis of your daughter's condition. From the initial test results, she does appear to have leukaemia. We need to narrow down which type she has so we can treat it accordingly.'

'She can't have it,' Nick snarled. 'She's perfectly healthy.'

'I'm afraid it looks as though she does, but please be reassured, the rates of success with the correct treatment are extremely high.'

'She's only twelve.' Nick felt his throat closing. 'How can she . . .'

Kate reached over and held his hand.

'I'm very sorry,' Dr Kennedy said again, 'and I know it must be a terrible shock but please don't be disheartened. As I said, the recovery rates are very high. I'll be back to you later with some updates.'

Dr Kennedy went to leave, but Nick grabbed his arm. 'I want results now. Why the hell do we have to wait? I want my daughter seen to first. She's your priority. No one else. Jess is number one, okay?'

'I'll speak to you later.' Dr Kennedy firmly removed his arm from Nick's grip and walked down the corridor.

'Stop it, Nick. You're going to alienate the staff,' Kate said.

'I want answers. I'm not going to sit around being patient. I'm going to rattle the bloody cage and make sure these people know they're not dealing with doormats. I want the best for Jess.'

'So do I, but shouting at everyone isn't helping, you moron. Stop behaving like a bloody caveman. You're upsetting everyone, and if Jess hears you, you'll upset her too.'

Nick frowned. 'I'd never upset Jess.'

'Well, you will if you carry on like that.'

He looked away. 'Why the hell is this happening? Jess is . . . she's . . . Why, Kate? Leukaemia? I just don't . . .' He brushed away the tears that were welling in his eyes.

'I know,' Kate said. 'I don't understand it either. But we have to be strong for Jess and show a united front. I need you to calm down and help me figure this out. We have to listen to what the doctors say and help them make Jess better.'

Nick nodded. 'You're right, I just . . . I can't sit around doing nothing.'

'I feel the same. Here she is now. Be strong.'

Nick took a deep breath and turned to see Jess walking towards him. She was in a hospital gown. She looked so young and pale. His little girl, his only daughter, his favourite child. He knew it was wrong to have a favourite, but Jess had always been so easy to love. He'd always thought he'd bond more with his sons, but the minute he'd set eyes on Jess, he'd fallen head over heels in love. He pulled her in to his chest and held her tight.

'Ouch, Dad! You're crushing me,' she said.

'Oh, God, I'm sorry.' He let go. 'Are you okay?'

'Well, I'm a bit freaked out, but Dr Kennedy said not to worry, that I was in the best place and they'd all help make me better.'

Nick could see Jess was trying not to cry. His little girl was being so strong. He felt physically sick. He had to protect her. That was his job. He'd shout the place down, if it helped get her the best care or to the top of a queue. Whatever it took. He wasn't going to sit around doing nothing. He knew how the health system worked: you had to demand to be seen and heard. You had to make sure they knew you weren't going to wait patiently for results and treatment. It was the squeaky hinge that got oiled, and Nick wasn't going to take this lying down. He was going to save Jess, no matter what it took.

He hugged her again. 'I love you, Jess, and you're going to be fine, okay? I promise. I'm going to fix this. It's just a little blip. They'll give you some medicine and we'll all go home.'

'Well, she's going to have to stay here overnight for tests, but then hopefully we'll go home,' Kate said.

Nick frowned. He didn't want Jess in here. What if she got one of those hospital bugs? This wasn't good. He'd have to talk to that doctor and get her out of here. She could come in for tests – surely she didn't need to stay the night. Kate was way too weak: she had obviously said yes to everything. Well, Nick wasn't going to. He would question everything and make damn sure that his daughter didn't get misdiagnosed or pick up some crappy bug. Those consultants thought they knew everything – well, they weren't going to push him around. He was going to research leukaemia and tell them what to do.

He felt himself beginning to calm down. He'd take charge and it would be okay. He looked around to see if he could spot Dr Kennedy, and as he did so, a boy hooked up to a drip wheeled himself out of a room. He had no hair and his eyes seemed huge in his small head.

'Welcome, newbie. I'm Larry,' he said to Jess.

Nick grabbed Jess and pulled her away from him. He didn't want her near sick kids. Jesus Christ, they didn't need to see that – bald head, emaciated body. Nick felt fear rising in his throat. That was not going to happen to Jess. No way. Not while he had breath in his body.

12

Kate left Bobby eating his pasta and went upstairs to Jess's room to pack a bag. She put in Jess's pyjamas, tracksuit bottoms, her Kindle and her favourite cuddly toy – Whiskey. She still slept with him every night. Kate's mother, Nancy, had given him to Jess when she was born, and Jess had curled her tiny fingers around his soft paw and never let go.

Kate held the yellow-and-black striped cat in her hands and squeezed him. She mustn't cry. She'd managed to hide her tears from Bobby by turning when he'd pulled out of a hug. She could hear Luke listening to music in his room next door. She didn't want him to see her falling apart. She had to be strong.

Her father popped his head around the door. He came towards her but she put her arm out. 'Don't. Don't hug me or say anything nice. I'm hanging on by a thread here, Dad.'

George nodded. 'I understand, pet. How's Jess?'

Kate looked at Whiskey's ridiculous face and shook her head. 'She's confused and frightened. They're doing all these tests on her tomorrow to find out more but they're pretty sure she has leukaemia. Now it's a question of finding out which type and how bad it is. Cancer, Dad? How the hell can Jess have cancer? I know she was feeling tired and she had those bruises, but I thought it was from playing sport. How can she just have developed cancer? I can't get my head around it.'

George sat beside her on the bed and took her hand. 'Listen to me, there is no "why" in cancer. It just is. The good news is that the survival rate is ninety per cent. Our Jess is going to be fine.'

'Ninety per cent?'

'Yes. Piper Googled it and rang Luke to tell him. I'd said he wasn't allowed to Google it as all you find on that old internet is bad news. So Piper did it and called him.'

'Good old Piper.' Kate gave a small smile. It was great news. Ninety per cent was okay. Ninety per cent gave Jess great odds. 'The nurse told me not to look it up. She said all you get is misinformation. She said to ask her and the consultants any questions I had. But I didn't have any. I couldn't think straight. All I want to know is – is Jess going to be okay? They can't answer that.'

'The tests will give them the information they need and then they can tell you what the treatment will be and how soon she'll be better.' George patted her hand.

Kate held Whiskey to her face. 'It was bad enough, but Nick kept shouting at everyone that he wanted results *now*, why the hell did we have to wait and he wanted his daughter seen to first. He was making the whole thing worse and freaking Jess out.'

George stood up and began pacing the bedroom. 'I'll have a word with him for you.'

'No, Dad, it's fine. He calmed down after I spoke to him. In fairness, he was just upset and worried. You know how he dotes on Jess – she's always been his favourite, and he isn't subtle about it.'

'He isn't subtle about anything,' George said.

Luke came in. 'Hey, you should have told me you were back. What's going on?'

Kate looked up at him and almost broke down. 'Well, they have to run some tests tomorrow and then we'll know more.

I'm going back now with a bag for Jess and I'll be staying the night with her.'

'Can I come and see her?' Luke asked.

'Sure – she'd like that.'

'Is she freaking out?'

'She's definitely worried and frightened, but the doctors and nurses have been very kind and reassuring so she's okay.'

'Did Granddad tell you about the ninety per cent?'

Kate smiled. 'He did. Tell Piper thanks.'

Luke went over to Kate and gave her an awkward hug. 'It'll be okay, Mum.'

She held him tightly. 'I know, Luke, I know.'

'Hey!' a grumpy seven-year-old voice shouted. 'You all left me by my own downstairs. I want to know what's going on too.'

Kate put her arms out and Bobby came to her and allowed her to hug him again. 'We're just talking about Jess and how she has to stay in hospital for a bit. I'm packing a bag for her.'

'Luke told me she has lukeemia. It's kind of weird – "Luke-eemia". She has a sickness called Luke.'

Kate half smiled.

Bobby shuffled his feet. 'I know about cancer cos Kerry in my class, her mum had it and her hair all felled out and she looked weird, but then it grew back and she looked nice again.'

Kate bent down to him. 'Jess might be given a medicine called chemotherapy and it will probably make her a bit sick and her hair may fall out. But it's going to make her better after that.'

'I don't understand. Why does she have to have medicine that will make her sick? Isn't it supposed to make you better? Maybe chemotherapy is the wrong stuff. Maybe the doctor got mixed up.'

'Dude, stop annoying Mum with questions,' Luke said.

Bobby tugged at Kate's sleeve. 'Mummy, I looked up cancer in *Guinness World Records* and there was information. The highest cancer death rate is in Hungary, which is good cos we live in Ireland. So you can tell Jess that she's lucky we don't live in Hungary. Right? Right, Mummy?'

'Bobby, leave your mother be,' George said.

Kate held up a hand. 'It's okay. Yes, Bobby, it is good news. Now, don't worry, pet, the doctors will make Jess better.'

'Don't forget to pack Whiskey,' Bobby said.

Kate held up the cat. 'I have him here.'

Bobby went over and picked up his *Guinness World Records* book. 'Give her this too. I always read it when I can't sleep or if I'm scared and it really helps.'

Kate took the book and turned to put it into the bag so he wouldn't see she was crying.

George stood up. 'Right, Bobby. It's time for you to go to bed – we've all lost track of time.'

'Come on, little dude. I'll give you a piggyback in to brush your teeth.' Luke picked Bobby up and carried him off to the bathroom.

George put his arm around Kate. 'Tell Jess I'll be in tomorrow morning. I'll have my phone beside me all night so call if you need anything – anything at all.'

'I will, Dad, thanks.'

Kate put Jess's favourite hoodie into the bag, then her little washbag, her One Direction towel, her iPod, her sparkly slippers and pink hairbrush. She was looking around the small bedroom for anything else she might need when her phone beeped.

It was a text from Nick: *Can u come back asap. Jenny wrecking my head, Jaden's sick. I have 2 go home.*

He really was under her thumb, Kate thought. Who would have thought it? Nick was being pushed around by his girlfriend. But he'd have to stand up to her. He needed to be there for Jess now: she was their focus. He'd have to tell Jenny to back off. If he didn't, Kate bloody well would. It was all about Jess now and she needed her dad. No one was going to stand in the way of that. No one.

13

Jess stared up at the ceiling. Haematology and Oncology. She rolled the words around her mouth. It didn't sound awful, but she knew what it meant now. It meant cancer. It meant leukaemia. It meant tests. Many, many tests.

Jess watched as a young boy was pushed past her room in a wheelchair. He was bald and hooked up to a drip. She turned her head to look at the ceiling. It was safer, less frightening. She didn't want to see bald kids. She didn't want to hear the crying parents, the screaming children and the soothing nurses. She wanted to close the door, lock it and put ear plugs in to block out the noise. Her head ached.

How could your life change so much in just a week? She'd had millions of blood tests and then they said she needed blood transfusions ASAP. Apparently she was very low on red blood cells so they'd pumped her full of 'good blood'. She felt cold and scared. The nurses covered her with warming blankets and Mum had held her hand.

As the week went on she had lots more tests – blood tests, bone-marrow aspirate, a lumbar puncture, chest X-rays – and there were lots of hushed conversations.

A few days ago, after yet another test, Jess had pretended to be asleep and listened as the doctor told Mum and Dad that she had a rare subtype of AML.

'Acute myeloid leukaemia. We call it AML ... high-risk category ... based on cytogenetic and molecular features ... unfortunate ... chemotherapy ... activating mutations ... haematopoietic cell transplantation, more commonly known as bone-marrow transplant...' Dr Kennedy spoke quietly and Jess strained to hear what he was saying and take it in.

She didn't understand it all, but she heard Mum gasp and Dad say a really bad word. She dug her nails into the palms of her hands to stop herself crying. Chemotherapy? She knew that was bad. She'd seen the movie *My Sister's Keeper*: the girl in it had chemotherapy and she was bald and sick and . . . God, it was so scary.

Why was this happening? How did she get it? Where did cancer come from? In the first few days Luke had kept telling her that she was ninety per cent okay, and so did Piper, but when they heard it was AML they stopped saying that.

Jess wasn't supposed to Google anything. Mum and Dad had banned her from using the internet, but Jess knew from everyone's reaction that AML was bad. She also knew that 'acute' was not good. She was terrified. She wanted to know but she didn't want to know. She knew there was one person who would tell her straight. She texted Nathalie and asked her to come on Sunday night, when she hoped she could see her alone.

Bobby, who didn't understand that AML was bad, just kept going on and on about the fact that it was great they didn't live in Hungary. Granddad squeezed her hand, kissed her head and coughed loudly into his handkerchief.

Jess loved her family, but sometimes they were too much. Their worry sort of passed over into her and she felt a big weight on her chest. She preferred when it was just her and Mum, sitting quietly, watching movies, or when Mum read to her. That was when Jess felt safest.

When Dad came to see her in hospital it was always kind of stressful. He'd hug her really tightly and then he'd go out and shout at the nurses and doctors, telling them his daughter needed more attention. His phone would ring and beep all the time and he'd go in and out of the room to talk to work or to Jenny – he usually argued with her – and then he'd be back all stressed. When Dad came to visit, Mum usually left them alone. Jess would have preferred her to stay.

Dad would try to cheer her up by telling her stories about when he was a kid, the goals he'd scored and the 'funny things' he'd done in school. But Jess found it all kind of boring. She knew he was doing his best, but every time he left she always felt exhausted.

Tomorrow was D-Day. They'd put the Hickman line in yesterday and tomorrow she'd be starting chemotherapy. Dr Kennedy told her that the Hickman was 'an intravenous line that facilitated drawing blood and administering medications, including chemo'. She had nodded as if she got it, then watched as they inserted it under the skin on her chest, and the attached tube went into a vein near her heart.

They had told her that getting it in wouldn't hurt, but it did and it felt weird. Jess wanted to pull it out. It felt like an alien in her chest. When she looked in the mirror, she could see the bump under her skin. She looked like a freak. She hated it.

Her mum had squeezed Jess's hand really hard when the doctor said chemotherapy. Jess knew she was freaking out but pretending she wasn't. It was silly, really. Jess could see her red eyes and she'd heard her crying on the phone to Granddad and to Maggie when she'd thought Jess was asleep. She was getting very good at pretending to be asleep – it was the only way she could hear people talk honestly and escape from Dad's stress and noise.

On Sunday, Granddad, Bobby and Luke came to visit while her mother went home to shower and catch up on some paperwork. Granddad brought her a holy medal for luck. 'It's the medal of St Raphael, the archangel and the saint of sickness.'

'Why is he the saint of sickness?' Jess asked. She was happy to get the medal – she wanted all the help she could get. She had to beat the cancer. She had to get better. She wanted to get out of this stupid hospital and go home. She wanted it all to be a bad dream. She wanted to wake up and be normal.

'Because in Hebrew the name Raphael means "It is God who heals".'

'Thanks, Granddad.' Jess held the medal to her chest, touching it against the Hickman line.

'It'll protect you, my little pet, and keep you safe.'

'Is all your hair going to fall out?' Bobby asked. 'Mrs Lorgan said that chemotherapy makes your hair fall out but that it grows back again. She said you'll look weird for a bit but that I'm not to say anything about it and pretend that it's just normal that you have no hair. She said it's worser for girls to lose their hair cos girls have long hair. She said –'

'Thank you, Bobby, I think Mrs Lorgan has said quite enough,' Granddad said.

'It's okay, Granddad. Yes, Bobby, I will probably lose my hair but the doctor and the nurses said it grows back quickly.' Jess was amazed that her voice sounded casual when inside she was panicking about losing her hair.

'I'll love you just the same whether you look like an alien or not,' Bobby said.

Luke turned his back on them and Jess saw him wipe his eyes.

'Thanks, Bobby.'

'I miss you, Jess. I've no one to talk to at night, and when I try to tell Mummy my new facts she says, "Not now, Bobby," all the time.'

'Your mother has enough going on, Bobby,' Granddad said. 'You need to be helpful and leave her in peace.'

'You can tell me your facts,' Luke said.

'You're always in your room with your earphones in or on the phone to Piper or else training or studying or helping Granddad in the café. I've no one to talk to now Jess is stuck in here with stinky cancer.'

'Tell me something now. I'm listening,' Jess said.

Bobby went over and stood beside her. 'Well, in 2013 Belgium had 1,714 robberies for every one hundred thousand people, so it's a good thing we don't live there.'

'Yes, it is.' Jess smiled at him.

'I always knew that the Belgians were a strange people.' Nathalie walked in, holding a book.

Damn. Jess had wanted her to come when everyone else was gone.

'I brought you a book of poems.'

'Cheerful ones, I hope,' Granddad muttered.

'Yes, George. They are poems of love. When Jess is sitting 'ere she can look out of the window at the blue sky and read a beautiful poem about love and it will make her less . . . How you say? Sorrowful.'

'She's not sorrowful, she's fine,' Luke insisted.

Nathalie rolled her eyes. 'She 'as cancer. Of course she is sorrowful. Everybody is a bit sorrowful. It's part of the 'uman nature.'

She was right. Jess did feel sorrowful, very sorrowful. But, most of all, she was tired and frightened.

'Bullshit,' Luke said. 'Not everyone is sorrowful. I'm not, Granddad isn't, Bobby isn't.'

'I am, actually,' Bobby said. 'And you are too, Luke. I heard you crying in your room last night and Granddad pretends to blow his nose all the time but he's really crying into his hanky.'

Luke and Granddad glared at him.

Nathalie patted Bobby's head. 'It's okay. It's normal. Why do men always pretend everything is fine? Of course you are worried about Jess. You love 'er and you want 'er to be well. It's good to cry. It's bad to block the emotions.'

'Mrs Lorgan said I need to control mine,' Bobby said. 'She said I have *waaaaaay* too much anger inside. She said I should ask Mummy to take me to kickboxing or karate so I can channel it.'

'Mrs Lorgan needs to keep her opinions to herself,' Granddad muttered.

'Tell 'er she is wrong,' Nathalie told Bobby. 'It is very important to let the emotions out. If you want to scream, scream. Cry? Cry. Be depressed? Be depressed. Always 'aving the 'appy face like a clown is ridiculous. Nobody is 'appy all the time.'

Granddad got up from the chair beside Jess's bed. 'Well, thank you, Nathalie. It's always fascinating hearing your cheerful thoughts on life.' He raised an eyebrow at Jess, who grinned. 'However, I think that's enough French philosophy for one evening. Jess needs her rest.'

He bent down and hugged her, careful not to squeeze the port. 'Best of luck tomorrow. I'll be praying for you, my little pet.'

Then Luke hugged her. 'Hang in there, sis, you're going to be fine. Love ya.'

Bobby reached up. 'I love you, Jess. Come home soon.'

Jess tried really hard not to cry. She wanted to cling to them all. She wanted to tell them how scared she was, but she didn't. She put a clown smile on her face and pretended she was stronger than she was.

As they turned to leave, Nathalie sat down beside her.

'Come on, Nathalie, out you come,' Granddad said.

'I will stay a little bit longer.'

'No, you won't.' Granddad made his way over to her.

'It's okay, Granddad. I want her to stay,' Jess said.

'Are you sure? She's not known for making people feel better, ever.'

Jess smiled, a real smile. 'Let her stay five minutes.'

Granddad didn't look happy about leaving Nathalie with her but, thankfully, he didn't argue and the boys all left.

As soon as they were out of sight, Jess turned to Nathalie. 'Well, did you Google it?'

Nathalie hesitated. 'Yes. Are you sure you want to know this?'

Jess sighed. 'Yes. Everyone's blocking me from getting information, but that's freaking me out. The doctors have tried to explain it to me. They said that AML is where too many immature white blood cells are made. The cells are not right and can't grow into normal white blood cells. So the chemotherapy I have to have is to kill the leukaemia cells and allow normal blood cells to come back. I think that's what they said anyway, but my head hurts and I find it really hard to concentrate. But I want to know more. I want to know what the percentage chance is of me getting better. Not knowing is making me think the worst.'

Nathalie fished around in her handbag and pulled out a sheet of paper. 'Okay. So I look up the cancer websites for AML. It says . . . "As with many cancers, the AML leukaemia survival rate has increased in the last decades due to advances in medical knowledge and technology. The general survival rate for children under fifteen years of age is sixty point nine per cent" – so it's good news, basically you have a sixty-one per cent chance to be better.'

Jess gripped Whiskey's soft paw tighter. Her heart was pounding. Sixty-one per cent. It was closer to fifty than one hundred. Oh, my God, I could die. I really could die. Why had she asked Nathalie to look it up? She shouldn't have. Mum was right: she was better off not knowing. She began to cry.

Nathalie took Jess's hand in hers. 'Jess, you could die in a car crash. You could get 'it by the lightning. No one knows what is in the future. You at least understand what is wrong with your body and you 'ave the best doctors looking after you. You will get the strong medicine tomorrow and you will be well again. You will fight the cancer because you are a brave girl with a beautiful spirit. You are lucky because you 'ave a family who love you very much.'

Nathalie handed Jess a tissue to wipe her tears. It was the first time Jess had really broken down in front of someone. She sobbed and let all her fears and worries out. For some reason, she didn't mind crying in front of Nathalie. She knew Nathalie wouldn't try to cheer her up or distract her with silly stories. Nathalie was comfortable around sorrow so it wasn't awkward to be upset in front of her.

Nathalie dabbed Jess's left cheek with a tissue. 'My mother loves 'er stupid dog more than me and my father is only interested in 'is son, who is only seven but is an incredible player of the violin. So even though you 'ave the bad luck with the cancer, you 'ave the good luck with the family.'

'What about your grandparents?' Jess asked.

'Dead.'

'Sorry.'

Nathalie shrugged. 'This is life. Sometimes it ees sheet.'

Yes, Jess thought, sometimes it is 'sheet'. She cuddled into Whiskey's soft comforting face, closed her eyes and, before Nathalie had even left the room, she was fast asleep.

14

Piper watched in silence as Luke added more weights to the bar bell. He lay back on the bench, took a deep breath, lifted it and pushed upwards with his arms. His whole body trembled. His eyes seemed about to pop out of their sockets.

Piper tried not to say anything. She knew he needed this. He needed to hurt physically because it distracted him from his emotional pain. He let the bar down and pushed up again. His arms shook violently and sweat dripped down his face. He gritted his teeth and kept going.

Piper put her hand on her stomach. How could she tell Luke about the baby now? Ever since he'd called her, crying about Jess, she'd known that her news would have to wait. But for how long? She couldn't bear to add to Luke's stress, but the doctor said she was about six weeks gone. She'd have to hold off for as long as possible: she couldn't land this bombshell on the poor family – they had enough to deal with at the moment. No one knew that when Piper cried about Jess she was also crying about the baby.

Luke's whole body shook.

'Stop, Luke. Please stop. You're pushing yourself too hard.'

Luke put the bar back on the stand and gulped to catch his breath.

'You'll hurt yourself,' Piper added.

Luke wiped his face with a towel. 'Every time I close my eyes I see the word "cancer",' he said, in a strangled voice.

Piper leant down and held him tightly. 'It's just awful, babe. I wish I could do or say something to make you feel better.'

'Will you come with me to visit her today?' Luke asked. 'I want to give Mum a couple of hours off. She's not sleeping at all in the hospital and she's wrecked.'

'Of course. I'd love to,' Piper said, glad to be able to help in any way.

They walked into Jess's room and her bed was empty. Luke was just going out to ask a nurse where she was when Piper caught his arm. She pointed at the bathroom door and then at her own ear, indicating he was to listen. They both went still. They could hear someone crying behind the door.

Luke went over and knocked lightly. They heard Jess putting on the taps to drown her crying. Luke kept knocking. 'Jess, it's me, Luke. Open up.'

'Go away. I need some privacy.'

'No. Open the door.'

'Please, Luke, go away.'

'I'll break the door down if you don't open it.' Luke's hand was trembling. Piper laid a hand on his arm and whispered, 'Go easy.' Then, 'Jess, sweetie, it's Piper. Can you let us in? We just want to say hi and see that you're okay. I know chemo is awful and you must be so upset and feeling terrible, but can you please open the door just for one second so we can say hello?'

They heard the lock click and Luke pushed the door open. Jess was sitting on the side of the bath, staring at the floor. Her left hand was covering the side of her head. Long strands of brown hair lay on the bathroom floor.

'Oh, Jesus,' Luke said.

Jess's tear-stained face turned to them. 'Yeah, that's exactly how I feel.'

Piper went over and put her arm around her. 'Oh, Jess, this really sucks.'

'I knew that your hair fell out after chemo, but I didn't think it would happen so soon,' Jess sobbed. 'I went to brush my hair and big lumps fell out.'

Piper held her tight. She didn't know what to say. How do you console a twelve-year-old girl when she's going bald? What were the 'appropriate' words of comfort? *I'm sorry about the hair loss. Bald can be cool. I'll buy you a great hat.* Piper scrambled around for the right thing to say.

'This shouldn't be happening. It's just not fair,' Luke raged.

Jess gulped back tears. 'I know, but it has happened. It's real, Luke. It feels really real now. I'm going to be a bald freak.'

'No. You'll —' Luke was at a loss for words to comfort his sister.

Piper knew she had to take control. Jess needed help, practical help. 'Right. We need to give you a haircut and get you some cool headgear or maybe a wig, whatever looks best. We'll look up some websites when I've sorted out your hair.'

Luke's hand squeezed her shoulder. She patted it.

'Luke, you need to go to the nurse and ask for an electric head-shaver — someone around here has to have one. Half the kids in this unit are bald.'

Piper got Jess onto her feet and turned her away from the mirror. 'I'm going to use these scissors,' she pointed at the nail scissors in Jess's washbag, 'to cut your hair short so it'll be easier to shave. All right? It's best if you look at me and not in the mirror so you don't get too freaked out. The good news is that your hair will grow back thicker and stronger, so don't worry.'

Piper turned her back to them to pick up the nail scissors. Her hands were shaking, and she didn't want Jess to see how nervous she was.

Luke rushed off to find a head-shaver, and by the time he returned, Piper had hacked off most of Jess's hair. Piper was glad Jess couldn't see herself in the mirror. Despite her best efforts, Jess's hair was short and uneven – awful. She looked so young and helpless and . . . well . . . sick.

'Right.' Piper turned to Luke. 'You can do the shaving. I've no idea how to use those.' Piper couldn't do the shaving: there was a limit. She felt sick about cutting Jess's hair off – there was no way she could shave off the rest. Besides, her morning sickness was bad today and she was afraid she might throw up.

Luke stared at her. 'What?'

'You've used those on your own hair so you know what to do. If Jess's hair is gone, it can't upset her by falling out.' Piper was using a bright voice, but her eyes were filling with tears. She was upset, exhausted and feeling sick. It was all too much. 'Come on, Luke,' she pleaded.

He nodded. 'Don't blame me if it isn't perfect, sis.'

Piper held Jess's hand while Luke gently shaved his sister's head. Piper dug her nails into her leg to stop herself crying as the last strands of Jess's hair floated to the floor. Seeing the girl's bare scalp made her want to weep.

'It looks kind of cool, very edgy. Very kick-ass-girl.' Piper was determined to make Jess feel better.

'No one's going to mess with you now, sis.' Luke tried to sound cheerful.

'Can I see?' Jess asked.

Piper hesitated. 'Are you sure you're ready? It's a big change. Maybe take a minute.'

Jess inhaled, but as she was about to turn around, Luke shouted, 'Stop. Hold on.'

Without thinking, he took the shaver and ran it over his hair.

'What are you doing?' Jess was shocked. 'You've spent ages growing your hair long on top.'

Luke kept going. He quickly finished off and put the head-shaver down. Piper's heart swelled with pride. This was the guy she loved. Her Luke. The kind of person who would shave his head for his sister. He wouldn't let her down either: he wouldn't run away when he found out she was pregnant. It was going to be fine. All three of them were now crying and smiling.

Piper clapped her hands. 'You both look amazing.'

Jess slid her small hand into Luke's big one. 'Thanks, Lukey,' she said.

'We're in this together.' His voice quivered.

'I'm not so scared to look now,' Jess said.

Piper nodded. 'One, two, three . . .'

Luke held his sister's hand tightly as they turned to the mirror.

Piper heard the little 'Oh' that fell out of Jess's mouth. Her lip trembled as she took in her bald head.

Luke put his arm around his sister's shoulders. 'We're two bad-asses now. You and me against the world.'

Jess gave him a watery smile. 'Yeah.'

Piper came over and threw her arms around them both. 'You guys are amazing. None of my sisters would ever shave their heads for me. The twins would probably scoop up my hair and make extensions for themselves out of it.'

Jess giggled, and Luke whispered, 'I love you,' into Piper's neck. She felt her legs shake. Would he love her when she told him about the baby?

15

Kate finished the chapter and looked at Jess's drooping eyelids. 'Time for you to sleep now,' she said, kissing her cheek.

'I don't want to, Mum. I want to enjoy every second of being home. It's so good to be back. The last few weeks have felt like a year.'

'I know, pet, and you've been so brave and wonderful.'

'I don't want to go back for more,' Jess said, and Kate felt her shaking. 'I hate the chemo.'

'Jess, I know you do, and it's just horrible, but it's going to kill the cancer so in a way it's a good thing, even though I know it's rotten for you. I hate seeing you so unwell, pet.'

'I'm sorry, Mum,' Jess whispered.

'For what?'

'For being sick. I know it's terrible for you and I promise to try my best to get better quickly.'

Kate couldn't even pretend not to cry. She hugged Jess to her and sobbed. 'None of this is your fault. It's just awful luck, but we're all going to help you get better. Don't ever apologize again. You're the best thing that ever happened to me, the light of my life. I'm so sorry this has happened to you, but I will do everything in my power to help you.'

Jess nodded into Kate's shoulder. Kate gently laid her back on the pillow and kissed her sweet face. 'Love you, Jess.'

'Love you, Mum.'

'Sleep now, pet. It'll help.'

Jess turned her head, pulled Whiskey close and shut her eyes. Within minutes she was sound asleep.

The first round of chemo had made her very ill. She could barely hold down any food and was weak and exhausted. Kate hated seeing her like that. To feel so helpless was torture. All she could do was tilt the bowl for Jess to vomit into and hold her when she cried. They knew she'd be allowed home after the first round, and that had been some tiny consolation, but chemo took so much out of Jess, and Kate admired her daughter's stamina in getting through each day.

Kate kept asking questions, but although the haematologists and nurses were kind and caring, they wouldn't give false hope. They kept saying they had to wait and see if the chemo was working. It was all about waiting . . . waiting for test results, waiting for treatment to work, waiting for information. Kate hated the waiting.

She went over to her laptop and started Googling. After an hour her eyes were throbbing and her heart was pounding from information overload. The internet was a blessing and a curse. She'd always thought 'information is power', but it wasn't. Sometimes you were better off not knowing what was coming down the line. Sometimes ignorance was bliss. And yet she found herself Googling every single symptom and test result Jess had received, and it often led to frightening outcomes and stories.

She glanced at Jess, who was still asleep. She looked so peaceful when she slept. The worried frown she'd developed between her eyebrows was smooth and her frightened eyes were closed.

It was wonderful to have her home for two weeks before she had more chemo. Jess was so tired that she slept most of the time, but Kate could see that being at home was cheering her up. She had put Jess into her double bed with her so she could keep an eye on her. She also liked to hold her at night, imagining that if she put her arms around her she could hug away the cancer. She could protect her daughter with her magical mother's love. If only . . .

A mother's job was to make her child better, but Kate couldn't fix this. Neither could Nick. He was so angry. Every time he'd come to the hospital, he'd shouted at some member of staff, and usually ended up accusing them of not doing enough. He looked wretched, almost as bad as Kate. She knew he was suffering too, but he really wasn't helping with his aggressive attitude and she'd come to dread his visits.

Kate chewed her lip and tried to think of the best way to word what she had to ask Luke to do. The doctors were quite clear that it would help enormously, which meant it had to be done, but she knew she would be asking a huge amount of him. She hated to do it, wished more than anything she could do it herself, but she wasn't a match. Instead, it might fall on Luke's young shoulders. It was just unbearable.

Kate felt a panic attack coming on. She was getting them regularly now. Maggie had suggested a mindfulness course, and she was thinking about doing one. She needed to stop the terror that came over her at night and crippled her, dark thoughts consuming her.

She kissed Jess's cheek and inhaled her lovely Jess smell. Then she went to get a cup of herbal tea. She tried to control her breathing to keep the panic at bay. As she reached the kitchen she saw the light was on. She could hear voices: her dad's and Luke's. She stopped and listened.

'This is crazy,' George said. 'No one can eat this much food.'

'The coach said I'm not getting enough protein. I should be eating four to five full meals a day. The problem is, I don't feel hungry. Since Jess's diagnosis, I've lost my appetite.'

'Does your coach know about Jess?'

'Yeah, and he cut me a bit of slack at training, but I can't fall behind or I'll get dropped.'

'How about I make you breakfast in the mornings? It says porridge, eggs, nuts and/or smoothies loaded up with protein powder. We can do something different each morning.'

'Thanks, Granddad.'

'Sure I'm happy to help, Luke. You need your rugby. I'd say it's a good switch-off for you.'

'It's the one and only place where I don't think about Jess. I don't want to get dropped. I need it, Granddad. I feel good when I'm playing.'

'I understand, son, and I'll help you. We'll feed you up but you might need to exaggerate a bit on your diet sheet for the coach. As I said, no one could eat this much.'

Kate pushed open the kitchen door.

'Is she asleep?' George asked, as she came into the room.

Kate nodded. 'Peacefully.'

'Ah, good. Poor little thing is wiped out.'

Kate sat down at the table. 'So, how are things here? Are you managing in the café, Dad?'

George patted her hand. 'Absolutely. Nathalie's doing more hours for me and continuing to charm and frighten away customers in equal measure. She told Brenda Kent last week that she was an ugly-handsome woman. Apparently this is a compliment in France, but Brenda didn't see it that way.'

Kate and Luke laughed.

'She's kind of mad, but Jess loves her,' Luke said. 'She always cheers her up.'

'For that I love her too.' Kate smiled.

There was silence. Then Kate took a deep breath. No point in waiting: he was here now and she might as well bring it up. 'Luke, there's something I need to ask you.'

He looked at her warily. 'What?'

'Jess may need a bone-marrow transplant and I need you to get tested, to see if you're a match. Your dad and I have been tested already and unfortunately we aren't.'

'Sure. What is it? What does it mean?'

'Well, you'll have a blood test and they'll use it for tissue typing to evaluate how close a match you are with Jess. Siblings tend to be the best matches.'

'If I'm a match, what happens then?' Luke asked, spinning his cup around on the table, avoiding Kate's eyes.

Kate hated having to ask him to do this, mainly because the bone-marrow aspiration was supposed to be painful. But at the same time, another part of her was praying he would be a match. 'Well, I have the information here.' She handed Luke a leaflet.

He took it from her and read aloud, '"You begin by having a peripheral blood stem cell (PBSC) collection. For five days before PBSC collection, a donor receives injections of a white blood cell growth hormone called G-CSF (Neupogen). These injections last five minutes. On the fifth day, a needle is placed in each of the donor's arms. The person's blood is circulated through a machine that collects the stem cells. Then the rest of the blood is returned to the donor. This collection takes about three hours and may be repeated on a second donation day. There is very little blood loss. Side-effects may include headaches, bone soreness, and the discomfort of needles in the arms during the process."' Luke stopped reading and dropped the leaflet onto the table.

'It's a lot to take in and you might not be a match, but I think it makes it out to be worse than it is.' Kate tried to hide the desperation in her voice. 'The boy in the room next to Jess had his sister do it and she said it was okay.'

Luke gripped the table. 'If I'm a match I'll do it, of course I will, but will it interfere with rugby, Mum? I can't get dropped.'

Kate nodded. 'We'll work around it, I promise.'

'Please, God, you will be a match. It'd be the best thing you could ever do,' George said, patting Luke's arm. 'With your healthy bone marrow, Jess would definitely get better. No doubt about it.'

Luke's shoulders relaxed a little and he gave his granddad a small smile. Kate exhaled. Her dad was right. Luke's brilliant bone marrow would heal Jess and get rid of the goddamn leukaemia.

16

Chloë marched up and down at the end of Jess's bed in a gown and mask. 'OMG, I feel like I'm in an actual TV show and I'm a surgeon about to do a serious, lifesaving operation.'

Jess smiled. It was nice having Chloë visit. She'd only seen family in the last week because she'd been told to keep visits to a minimum, but Chloë had begged to come and see her so they'd said she could, but only if she wore protective clothing. Jess's blood count was so low that her risk of infection was very high so she'd been isolated to protect her.

The second round of chemo was even worse. Jess felt totally wiped out and, again, could hardly eat. She felt as if she was being blasted with poison, which was just making her sicker and sicker. It didn't seem possible she could ever feel well again. The doctors said things were going well and that the cancer cells were being destroyed, but that the 'good' white cells were being affected by the chemo too, which was why she felt so ill.

All Jess knew was that she was sick of being sick. She wanted to go back to school, to sit in class listening to Mrs Fingleton talking about wars and books and maps. She wanted to be normal again. She wanted to sit beside Chloë at lunchbreak, giggle about boys, look up cool Instagram photos, play tennis and hockey, and just be the old Jess.

She wanted her life back, the good one, the one where she didn't vomit every ten minutes and she had energy and everyone didn't treat her differently.

Chloë stopped prancing, went over to Jess and held her hand in her gloved one. 'Hey, I know this sucks for you.' Her voice was slightly muffled because of the mask over her mouth. 'But I promised my mum that if she let me see you, I'd cheer you up. She said I had to make you laugh and dis- tract you so you forget about cancer for a little bit. She said when she was in hospital after giving birth to me, she was feeling awful, so she had a team of people come in and do her nails and hair and make-up, and she felt *waaaay* better after. Obviously I can't do your hair,' Chloë said, as Jess grinned, 'but I did bring you loads of clothes for when you get out, and some cool hats.'

She bent down and heaved a large bag onto the chair beside the bed. 'This is from Mum. She is, like, totally freak- ing out that you have cancer so we both went shopping and bought loads of stuff for you. You should have seen her, Jess, she was like a crazy woman. She was charging from shop to shop and kept telling me to buy more. I hope you like the stuff. If you don't, I can take it back. We kept all the receipts.'

Jess sat up. This was fun! Lots of new clothes – cool ones, too. She felt excited for the first time in ages.

Chloë reached into the bag and pulled out a pair of pink jeans. She looked at the jeans and then at Jess's spindly legs. 'My God, Jess, I didn't realize how skinny you'd got, but hopefully they'll fit you.'

Chloë spent the next half an hour pulling clothes out of the bag and holding them up. 'Now all you have to do is put your thumb up if you like it or down if you don't,' she said. 'That way you won't use up too much energy.'

Jess gave a thumbs-up to everything, even the clothes she knew were too big or that she wasn't crazy about. There was no way she'd send any of it back. Chloë had got her three gorgeous beanie hats with diamanté across the front. Jess put one on.

'Amazing!' Chloë clapped her hands. 'It's fab on you. The blue one is the nicest.'

Jess lay back on her pillows, exhausted from the visit but happy. 'Thanks, Chloë, and please say thanks to your mum. This is just so kind. I can't believe it.'

'Hold on, there's a couple of pairs of pyjamas too – Mum wanted you to have these. Apparently she got them online and they're, like, super-soft cotton or something. Anyway, I'll leave them here for you.'

Jess smiled, then a wave of nausea hit her and she threw up into the bowl beside the bed. 'Sorry,' she said, wiping her mouth with a tissue.

Chloë sat on the chair beside the bed and handed her another. 'Don't be sorry. Is it awful?'

Jess nodded. 'I just don't understand it. Where did it come from? Did I do something to make it happen? Should I have eaten more vegetables?'

'Don't be mad. If it was cos you didn't eat vegetables, I'd have it too. I hate vegetables. There's nothing you did wrong, Jess. Cancer is just . . . well . . . cancer and it hits people for no reason. Sure if they knew why you got it they could cure it.' Chloë blushed. 'I mean cure it for everyone. Obviously you'll be cured. I know you will.'

'What if I'm not?'

Chloë jumped back in her chair. 'Jeepers, Jess, don't even say that.'

'It's possible.'

'No way. Kids hardly ever die from cancer – Mum said so and so did Mrs Fingleton.'

'Did she?' Jess thought Mrs Fingleton would be a very reliable and well-informed source.

'Yeah, totally. She said she expected you to be back in school after Christmas. I hope you are – I miss you. I have to hang out with Denise and Judy now.'

Jess smiled. 'They're not that bad.'

'They're *sooooo* annoying. All they talk about is Judy's neighbour, Jack, and how hot he is. I've seen him. He's a dork.'

Jess wished she could be sitting with them, talking about Jack. She'd gladly talk about anything, just to be out of this hospital and back to actually living.

She'd never complain about school again, ever. She'd skip in and do her homework without a grumble. Mrs Fingleton had been sending in work for her, but a lot of the time she was too sick to do it. The best part of her day was when Mum read to her. She loved that. She didn't have to talk or think, just lay back, listened and let herself be transported by the stories. She was reading *Pride and Prejudice* and even though some of the words were olde-worlde, she loved the sisters – they reminded her of Piper and hers – and she adored Lizzie Bennet and the way she stood up to Mr Darcy.

When it was just her and Mum and the stories, Jess could forget . . . for a while.

Chloë tucked her legs under her on the chair. 'What's the story with the guy who was leaving when I arrived?' She giggled. 'He was kind of cute.'

Jess grinned. Trust Chloë to spot him. 'That's Larry. He's been here some of the time I have. He's really nice. When we're allowed, we play cards together and sometimes watch a movie.'

'*Ooooooooooh.*' Chloë's eyes widened. 'Love in a cancer ward. Maybe I don't feel so sorry for you, after all.'

Jess laughed. 'He's just a friend. He feels like a brother. He gets it, you know. He understands. With Larry I don't have to explain how I feel because he feels the same. We're just buddies.'

'Well, if you don't want him, will you introduce me to him?' Chloë batted her eyelids.

'When he's feeling better I will.'

'Okay.' Chloë's phone buzzed. 'Oh, my God, look at these.' She sat up on the bed beside Jess and they scrolled through hundreds of Instagram pictures. After a while there was a knock on the window. It was Chloë's mum, Hazel. She waved cheerily and held up a sign: 'We love you, Jess. Get well soon.' Jess waved back and smiled. She was glad Chloë was going – she was exhausted. She could feel her eyelids closing. It had been wonderful to see her, but she needed to sleep now.

Chloë groaned, then gave Jess a big hug. 'I love you, Jess. Focus on getting better, then come back to school and save me.'

'I will.'

'Bye for now. I'll text you later.'

Jess watched her friend leave, envying her the freedom to walk out and go back to the real world. Hazel helped Chloë out of the protective gear, then with one last wave, they were gone. Back outside, into fresh air, walking on their strong legs, safe inside their not-sick bodies. Jess curled up tighter and cried herself to sleep.

The following morning, she was getting ready for her chemo session when she heard Larry in the room next door, screaming. He was shouting and roaring at his parents, yelling that he hated them. They were to get out and leave him alone. Jess listened, her heart beating faster. It sounded so horrible, like Larry was possessed by a demon. She couldn't understand it because he was really nice and his parents were too. They talked to Kate all the time and reassured her. Larry had had two relapses, but he was still alive and seemed to be reacting well to his latest bone marrow. Jess tried to ignore his crazy shouting, feeling sorry for his parents.

Now that she was in isolation, she couldn't play cards with him on long, boring afternoons, and she missed it. Now they just chatted on the phone and sent each other goofy photos. She decided to send him one now. Maybe it would cheer him up a bit. She found a video on YouTube of a bear dancing to some funky music and forwarded the link to him. It wasn't much help, but it might just make him smile.

Later in the afternoon, when she was back from chemo and had had a nap, she phoned him.

'Hey, you, what's going on?'

'Infection,' he said shortly.

'Oh, no. I'm sorry. Did it come on last night?'

'Yep. I'm in isolation too now.'

'Sucks.'

'Sure does.'

'I'm really sorry.'

'Yeah, me too. It's back, Jess, I know it is.'

'It's just an infection, not the cancer.'

'Jess, it's not just an infection. I know it's back.'

'How?'

'Fingernails. If the bone marrow works, the dark ridges on your fingernails disappear. Mine haven't. We get the results tomorrow, but I already know.'

Jess swallowed the bile rising in her throat. This time it wasn't the chemo making her nauseous: it was fear and sorrow. 'But you can't be sure,' she said, although she knew she didn't sound convincing.

Larry sighed. 'Jess, I've been through this three times. It's not working.'

'Maybe they just need to try something new. You're young and strong, you can fight this. The infection is making you feel low.' Jess couldn't let it go: she wanted him to say there was hope.

'I need everyone to stop saying that,' Larry snapped. 'I can't pretend any more. It's over, Jess. That's why I shouted at my parents. I want them to hate me. They have to really hate me so when I die it won't hurt so much.'

Jess could taste the salty tears running down her face onto her lips. 'Larry, they could never hate you. They adore you.'

'That's the problem.' His voice was quiet and sad, so sad. 'I need them to stop. I need them to stop hoping and trying and praying and wishing . . . I need them to stop looking as if their hearts are breaking. I can't take it. It's too much.'

Jess stayed quiet while Larry cried. Sometimes there was nothing to say. In six weeks she had learnt a lot about pain, suffering, fear, death and heartbreak. She had learnt that listening silently was often the very best thing you could do.

When she heard his sobs subside she said, 'No matter what you do, no matter how much you push them away, they'll love you just the same. Don't make your time with them awful. There's no point. Make it special.'

'I don't want to die, Jess,' Larry whispered. 'I want to grow up and be a pilot. I want to fly all over the world. I'm not ready to die – I'm thirteen. It's not fair.'

'It's just . . . cruel, that's what it is. Look, I know you don't want false hope but maybe –'

'Don't, Jess, please. I need to be honest with someone.'

'Well, then, it sucks, it really sucks.' Jess wiped tears from her eyes. 'How can there be a God who lets kids suffer like this?'

'I stopped believing in God after my first relapse. I don't believe in Heaven either. I think this is it.'

'Why us?'

'You can't ask why, Jess. It'll melt your head. We can't change the fact of having cancer, we can only fight the cancer. But I think I'm coming to the end of fighting. I want to live, but I don't think I can. I keep thinking about . . . after, you know?'

'You mean, like, the afterlife?' Jess said quietly.

'Kind of. I don't think there's a Heaven, but some people say that our energy lives on. I was thinking, you know, if I die, I'd like to send a sign to my mum and dad.'

'What kind of a sign?' This conversation was making her head throb, but she knew Larry needed to be able to say this stuff out loud.

'Well, that's just it. I can't make up my mind. It has to be something not too unusual, like an eagle landing at the kitchen table, but not something really common either, like a blackbird in the back garden. It has to be something in between.'

Jess had never thought about signs. But she knew exactly what hers would be.

'Any suggestions?' Larry asked.

'My sign would be a white butterfly,' Jess said. 'I've always loved them. They're so pure and beautiful and . . . well, white.'

'Damn, I wish I'd thought of that.'

'How about a robin on your parents' windowsill or something?'

'Nah, too boring. We'll have to think up something better. Hopefully I'll live until we figure one out.'

Jess shuddered. She hadn't really allowed herself to think about death. She'd pushed it far down in her stomach. She was sick and she was going to get better. No one ever mentioned death, except Larry and Nathalie. The first time Jess had actually spoken to Larry, she'd been throwing up into a bowl. He'd stopped at her door and introduced himself, then asked her if she was scared of dying. Just like that. After only exchanging names. Jess had lied and said no because she wasn't planning on dying.

Larry had smiled. 'New and full of hope. I need to hang out with you. Maybe your optimism will rub off on me.'

But it hadn't. Cancer had rubbed off on him, more of it, aggressive, unstoppable. Still Jess did not, would not, believe Larry was going to die. He couldn't. It just wasn't possible. Like he'd said, he was only thirteen, one year older than her. She would continue to hope that he'd come out the other side. But she knew not to say that to him now.

'I wish I could come over and hang out,' she said.

'Me, too . . . I know! How about we watch the same movie at the same time and stay on the phone so we can give out about it? I don't want to be alone, and I've chased the only visitors I've had out of the hospital.'

'You'll have to apologize to them tomorrow,' Jess said. 'Now, what will we watch?'

'How about *The Fault In Our Stars*?'

Jess giggled. 'Or *My Sister's Keeper*? That'll cheer us up.'

Larry laughed. 'Seriously, how about *The Hunger Games*?'

'Again!'

'Humour me.'

'Okay.' Jess reached for the iPad Kate had lent her and clicked on the movie. 'Ready?'

'Yes. One, two, three, play.'

Jess nestled into her pillows and welcomed the distraction of the film. For now, she wanted to be anywhere but where she was.

17

Piper studied her calendar. Nine weeks. She was nine weeks pregnant. You could have an abortion in the UK up to twenty-four weeks. But that was six months. She couldn't imagine having an abortion at six months. If she was being honest, she couldn't imagine having an abortion at all.

At first she'd thought she'd definitely get rid of it. Who the hell wanted a baby at eighteen years of age? She'd even looked up cheap flights for her and Luke to go over to London. But then Jess had got cancer and everything had gone crazy.

Meanwhile, the baby was growing. Piper put her hand to her still flat stomach. She knew she had to tell Luke, but there was never a good time, these days.

She'd tried to tell him last week, but he'd been put on the subs bench and Harry had got to play the whole match. Luke had been so upset that she just couldn't do it. The time before that was when his mum told him that he needed to get his bone marrow tested. Luke had been upset about that, too. They'd spent the whole evening Googling it and talking about it.

Piper lay back on her bed and put an arm over her face. She had to tell him, but what if he wanted to get rid of it? He probably would. How could he cope with a baby on top of everything else? How could she cope with a baby? She wanted to go to college and travel the world, not be tied down with a screaming kid. The weird thing was, in the last few weeks she'd felt love growing inside her for her baby. She knew it was dumb, it was only a foetus, but she felt protective of it now.

She pictured her dad's face when she told him. Piper, the sensible one – not so sensible now. She wasn't sure how her mum would react. Disappointed obviously, but probably calmer than her dad.

And the girls? Pauline would probably think she was a slut – a stupid slut. She'd be right: Piper *was* stupid – unprotected sex, how could she? They were drunk and Luke had had a bad fight with his dad and he'd kept saying, 'I need you, babe,' and he didn't have any condoms and ... Well, she'd given in. He'd pulled out early and she'd thought it would be okay. Stupid, really stupid.

She knew the twins, who pretended to be so worldly wise, would be shocked and that Posy wouldn't look up to her any more. Who'd look up to an idiot who gets pregnant?

Piper let the tears flow. It was a mess. Everything was a huge mess. Jess, the baby, Luke ... everything. She needed to tell Luke, she needed him to support her, but she was scared. He was so fragile right now and had so much on his plate. Could he take any more? She was afraid he'd crumble under the pressure.

Piper wiped her tears. No matter what, she had to tell him tonight. He had to know and they had to make a decision together – soon.

She sat up and fixed her make-up. She was applying concealer under her tired eyes when the doorbell rang. Piper heard the twins charging down the stairs. She ran after them, but they got to the door first. 'Hi, Luke,' they gushed.

'Penny and Poppy?' he asked, grinning.

'Shove off, Poppy.' Penny pushed her sister out of the way. 'Hi, Luke, I'm Penny, the good-looking twin.'

Poppy elbowed her sister out of the way. 'I'm Poppy, the one who hasn't had a lobotomy.'

'Scoot!' Piper ordered, pushing them both aside. 'You'll scare him off.' The twins scattered.

Piper kissed Luke and ushered him in. 'Mum got stuck in a tutorial and has only just arrived home, so Dad ended up cooking. We're having steak and mash.'

'Sounds good. I brought wine – is that okay? I wasn't sure what to bring. I'm a bit nervous about meeting your parents, to be honest.'

Not as nervous as you would be if you knew I was pregnant, Piper thought grimly. She said, 'Don't be nervous. Dad's a bit mad but nice underneath.'

'It was good of them to invite me.'

'They said I spend so much time in your house and talk about your family so much they were afraid I was going to leave home and move in. And also obviously because they know about Jess.'

Luke pulled her in for another quick kiss. 'I wish you would move in. You'd brighten things up.'

They heard a cough and Luke moved away from Piper.

'Luke, I presume.' Seamus held out a hand.

'Yes, sir, nice to meet you.'

Seamus raised an eyebrow. 'Probably better if I'd met you before I saw you with your tongue down my daughter's throat. Still, you're here now.'

Luke went bright red.

'Behave, Dad,' Piper warned him.

'I'll say what I want in my own house. Now, come on, the dinner's just ready.' Waving a spatula in Luke's direction, Seamus said, 'Piper tells me you need to eat loads of meat for the rugby.'

Luke was still standing, unsure when he should sit down. 'Yes, sir. We're encouraged to load up on protein.'

'In my day we just ate what our mother stuck in front of us, put on our boots and played. It's all protein and weights and statistics, these days. Load of nonsense.'

Piper rolled her eyes. 'Dad played rugby like a hundred years ago and claims he could have played for Ireland.'

Seamus went over and flipped a steak in the pan. 'I was a shoo-in until I broke my ankle. It was never the same again.'

'What position did you play?' Luke asked.

Piper could see him eyeing up her dad, who didn't look like he'd ever played any sport. He was quite tall and relatively slim, but he had a big belly that hung over his trousers and no muscles whatsoever.

'Fullback. I had great pace back in the day.'

Luke nodded politely, then handed Seamus the bottle of wine.

'Nice Bordeaux, thank you.'

'My granddad recommended it.'

'Ah, yes. He runs the café and wine shop up on the main street?'

'That's right.'

'Take a weight off, Luke,' Seamus said.

Luke sat down beside Piper. They held hands under the table.

Posy stormed through the door, her face red with rage. 'DO I HAVE A MOUSTACHE?'

Seamus shook his head. 'For the love of God.'

'Answer me!'

'No.'

'What's wrong, Posy?' Piper asked.

'Penny and Poppy told me I had a moustache and that I'd have to start shaving and that it was proof I was actually a boy in a girl's body and my testosterone was coming out now.' Posy was getting upset.

'When are you going to learn that they're evil twins who love nothing more than to wind you up?' Piper said.

'They said I'm gender fluid.'

Luke coughed to hide a laugh.

'You're a girl, Posy,' Piper reassured her. 'One hundred per cent.'

Posy sat down and picked up a piece of bread from the basket in the middle of the table. 'Are you Luke?' she asked.

'Yes, and I guess you're Posy, the youngest, right?'

Posy nodded. 'Yes. Being the youngest sucks. Who's the youngest in your house?'

'Bobby, and he'd say he gets a hard time too. He's quite angry and kicks things.'

'I bet you're not as mean to him as my sisters are to me.' Posy took a bite of the bread.

'I've definitely never told him he was gender fluid,' Luke said. 'And if it's any help, you definitely don't have a moustache.'

Posy touched her upper lip with her index finger. 'Good.'

'You're like a mini Piper, which is a very good thing.'

Posy grinned. 'I hope I am. I think Piper's so pretty.'

Luke leant in to whisper, 'So do I, and she's really nice too. How lucky am I?'

Piper felt her heart fill. She really loved Luke.

The back door opened and Olivia bustled in. 'Sorry I'm late. I brought wine as an apology.' She placed a bottle on the table. 'The tutorial just went on and on. It was so interesting. They had a refugee from Malawi talking about —'

Piper tried to catch her mother's attention. 'Mum, this is Luke.'

Olivia stopped talking and noticed him for the first time. She looked him up and down and proffered a hand. 'Sorry. I get a bit carried away with my new college life. Nice to finally meet you, Luke.'

'You, too, Mrs King.'

'Oh, God, call me Olivia. "Mrs King" makes me think of Seamus's mother, who was a total battleaxe.'

Seamus turned back from the cooker. 'Ah, now, she wasn't that bad.'

Olivia hung up her coat and sat down at the table. 'The first time I met her, I was probably Piper's age, and I was invited for dinner. After dessert she said, "You might think about your portion sizes. It's very easy to put on weight and not so easy to lose it. With your curvy figure, you'd need to be careful."'

'Oh, God.' Luke was grinning. 'What did you say back?'

'I smiled and said that a healthy appetite was usually considered a good thing, and that Seamus was very fond of my curves.'

Luke and Piper laughed. Piper loved that story and the way her mum had stood up for herself and answered back. Piper didn't really remember her granny – she'd died when Piper was five – but by all accounts she had not been a very nice person.

'That's enough stories about my mother and her sharp tongue. Call the lunatics down for dinner, please, Penny.'

'It's Posy!' she huffed, then poked her head out of the kitchen door and shouted, 'GRUB'S UP!'

The twins thundered down the stairs and threw themselves into their chairs. 'So, Luke, I hear you're on the senior cup team in St James,' Penny said.

'Well, yes, I'm on the squad,' Luke said modestly.

Piper put a hand on his shoulder. 'He's the winger and he's brilliant.'

'I always think it's good for kids to be into sports. It keeps them out of trouble,' Seamus said.

Not always, Piper thought.

'Sport is so boring.' Poppy groaned. 'I hate having to play stupid hockey in the rain. What's the point?'

'It keeps you fit and healthy.' Seamus popped a large piece of steak into his mouth.

'I like hockey,' Posy said.

'Good girl, keep it up. Don't turn out like these two reprobates.'

Penny rolled her eyes. 'Posy's a square.'

'Total dork,' Poppy agreed.

'Besides, girls who are into sports are lesbians,' Penny said.

'Stop that,' Olivia warned.

'What did you say? Are you calling me a lesbian now?' Posy's face was red.

'Calm down, darling. They're only joking.' Olivia placed a hand on Posy's arm.

'Big butch lesbians,' Poppy taunted her.

'I am not a bitch lesbian,' Posy roared.

'I said butch, you dork.'

'What is that? A lesbian word?'

'It means –'

'Enough!' Seamus cut across Penny. 'We have a guest here tonight and it would be nice if for once we could have a civilized family meal, without shouting and tears.' Turning to Luke, he said, 'This is why I have my shed. A man cannot live with six women without somewhere to escape to.'

Luke smiled. 'It's certainly lively.'

'"Lively" is a very polite way of putting it. Bloody mayhem, I'd say.' Seamus shook his head.

'How is your sister?' Olivia asked. 'Piper told us the poor girl has leukaemia.'

Piper watched as Luke's face darkened. 'Yes, it's been hard for her. But she seems to be reacting well to the chemo, although it's making her really sick.'

'Chemo's a blessing disguised as a curse. How's your mother coping?' Olivia asked.

Luke paused. 'She's . . . Well, she's just getting on with it, I guess. She's great. She keeps everything together.'

'Mum used to be like that for us, but now all she does is go to college and read books and talk about vaginas being cut,' Penny said.

Luke choked on his food.

'Shut up, Penny,' Piper hissed.

'For the love of God, Penny, be quiet,' Seamus barked.

Penny folded her arms. 'Fine, I'm just saying.'

'I'm sorry you feel that way, darling,' Olivia said, keeping her voice even, but Piper could tell she was annoyed. 'I spent nineteen years devoting my life to raising you all. I don't think a two-year course in university is too much to ask. Do you?'

Penny shrugged. 'I'm not going to boring college.'

'Really?' Seamus said. 'And what are you planning on doing?'

'Me and Poppy are going to start a vlog, like Zoella.'

'Who?'

Poppy squealed. 'OMG, Dad, you are *such* a loser. Zoella is the biggest thing ever. Her YouTube channel has over nine point nine million subscribers and over six hundred and sixty-three million video views.'

'She is amazing,' Posy agreed.

'Even I've heard of her,' Olivia said.

'How does she make money?' Seamus asked.

'Duh, she writes books, sells her own beauty products and people pay her to try their make-up brands.'

'She's worth millions and she does most of it from her bedroom. It's so easy,' Poppy said.

Seamus sat back in his chair. 'So you're telling me that some girl called Zooella –'

'Zoella.'

'Whatever. This lassie is sitting in her bedroom trying on lipsticks and over six hundred million people are watching?'

'Yes,' Penny said. 'And then she wrote a book – well, she didn't exactly write it all by herself. She got help to write it and it sold zillions of copies.'

'And it's all about make-up?' Seamus asked.

'And hair and clothes and stuff,' Penny added.

Seamus thumped the table. 'Well, then, what in the hell are you waiting for? We've a house full of bloody make-up and clothes lying around everywhere and two foolish girls who are obsessed with it all. Get up to that bedroom and start videoing yourselves. We'll be millionaires in no time.'

Poppy and Penny looked at each other. 'But, like, what would we say?'

'Say?' Seamus was incredulous. 'You never stop talking.'

'Yeah, but it's different when you think people are actually watching,' Penny said.

'Totally. You don't want to say anything you could get slagged about,' Poppy agreed.

'Or say a lipstick colour is cool when everyone else thinks it's lame,' Penny added.

'Besides, we don't have a cool boyfriend like Zoella,' Poppy said.

'We could use Luke.' Penny eyed Luke across the table.

'Totally.' Poppy was excited. 'He's cool and hot.'

Piper put her arm around Luke. 'Back off, witches. Luke is not going to be in any of your stupid videos. He's my boyfriend. Get your own.'

'You're so selfish, Piper. We could make zillions of euros and we'd pay Luke, obviously.'

'So you're going to pretend to the world that you share a boyfriend? Is that your genius plan?' Piper asked.

'I'm sure he has a friend who could pretend too.'

'You're being ridiculous,' Piper said.

Luke shook his head. 'Much as I'd like to help you on this mission to make millions, I'm afraid I'm out.'

Penny glared at Piper. 'Thanks a lot. You're so selfish.'

'That's enough nonsense, girls. You'd be much better off spending your time on things that matter, like equality and human rights, rather than the colour of lipstick,' Olivia said.

Penny and Poppy rolled their eyes.

'If we went on about what you go on about we'd have no friends. It's boring, Mum,' Penny told her.

'Boring and depressing,' Poppy added.

'Maybe we could ask Gavin and Roger to be our pretend boyfriends,' Penny said.

'Ewww, Roger has zits, no way,' Poppy said.

'Oh, yeah, good point.'

Seamus stood up and began clearing the plates. 'Enough of this nonsense. What the two of you need is to go running about in the fresh air. I'm signing you up for the athletics club tomorrow morning.'

The twins jumped up and shouted at him.

'Dad's right.' Olivia scraped a plate and stacked it in the dishwasher. 'You need a proper focus. You're becoming vacuous.'

'I don't know what that means,' Penny said.

'It's probably some weird feminist thing to do with vaginas,' Poppy huffed.

Luke leant in to whisper in Piper's ear, 'Your family talk a lot about vaginas.'

Piper grinned. 'Not normally. I'm sorry about this. I told you the twins were mad.'

'Speaking of vaginas, any chance I could see yours later?' Luke said, very quietly, into her ear.

Piper giggled. 'Maybe.'

Luke squeezed her hand under the table. Piper felt that tonight was the best time to tell him. He was in a good mood. After dessert, they'd go for a walk and she'd tell him then.

When dinner was over and Luke had thanked Olivia and Seamus profusely, Piper suggested a walk.

'Couldn't we just go up to your bedroom and have silent sex?' he muttered into her hair.

'Not with my parents downstairs.'

'Okay. Well, come back to my place, then. Mum will be at the hospital and Granddad will be working.'

'Can we go for a walk first? I want to talk to you about something.'

Luke shrugged. 'Okay, babe. You look serious – you're not going to dump me, are you?' He grinned, but she could see fear in his eyes.

She hugged him tight. 'Never. I love you.'

She felt his body relax into her. 'I love you too.'

They kissed, but just then Luke's phone buzzed in his coat pocket. He pulled it out. Since Jess had been sick he no longer ignored any calls – just in case.

'Mum?'

Piper could hear Kate's voice. She sounded excited. 'Hi, Luke, can you come home straight away? Maggie's here! She's dying to see you all.'

'Sure. I'm on my way.'

Luke hung up and turned to Piper. 'My mum's best friend Maggie's in Dublin. I have to go. Sorry. Call you later.'

Piper watched him stride down the path.

He turned. 'What was it you wanted to talk about?'

She waved her hand. 'Nothing. Don't worry.'

'Call you later.'

Piper closed the door. She leant against it and sighed. Another opportunity missed. Tears prickled her eyes. Damn it. At this rate she'd be giving birth before he knew.

18

When Kate answered the door, she wasn't expecting to see her best friend standing there. Maggie hadn't said a word about coming over to visit. Kate had thought she was in Dubai at a trade fair, so when the bell rang and she was greeted by the smiling face of her oldest friend, she crumbled. All pretence of bravery left her. She fell into her friend's arms and sobbed.

'Oh, Kate, you poor, poor thing,' Maggie said softly, stroking her hair. 'What a bloody awful time you're having. I'm sorry I couldn't come sooner.'

Kate took a deep breath and pulled back from Maggie's soft cashmere-covered shoulder. 'Sorry. Long few weeks.'

'Long few sodding years.'

Kate wiped her eyes with a tissue. She always had tissues in her pockets, these days. Crying was a daily, if not hourly, occurrence now.

'Right, let's get inside and crack open a bottle of vodka. I stocked up in Duty Free.' Maggie gathered up her bags and suitcase and followed Kate inside. 'This kitchen always brings me back to our childhood,' she said, glancing around. 'The amount of time we spent in here drinking coffee and smoking out of the window.'

Kate smiled. 'It's strange being back home, but nice too. Especially now. Dad's such a brilliant support.'

'Sure George was always great.' Maggie pulled the bottle of vodka from one of her bags. 'Right, let's get stuck in. I have tonic here too. We just need ice.'

Kate went to the freezer, took out an ice tray and plonked two cubes in each glass. Maggie poured the vodka.

'Jesus, Maggie, go easy! We'll be hammered after one glass.'

'You need it. It's medicinal.' Maggie shrugged off her coat. 'Cheers.' She raised her glass. 'To you, Kate, to the future being bright, and most of all to Jess getting better.'

Kate swallowed the lump in her throat and drank deeply. The vodka went straight to her toes. Oh, it was a lovely feeling. Apart from the odd glass of wine, she'd been steering clear of alcohol. She was afraid of the effects. She knew if she started drinking, she might never stop. Part of her wanted oblivion. Part of her wanted to disappear into a bottle of booze and block out all the worry and heartache, but she knew she had to be clear-headed and together for Jess, and for Luke and Bobby.

But tonight she'd allow herself to enjoy a few drinks. Maggie leant over and held her hand. 'Tomorrow, you and I are going to a fancy hotel and spa. My treat. We're going to get dressed up and go dancing.'

Kate put down her glass. 'I can't, Maggie. I have to be with Jess.'

'It's all sorted. George is going to look after her and he's getting Luke and his girlfriend to help out as well. It's one night, Kate. Give yourself a break.'

Kate picked up her glass and clinked Maggie's. 'Actually, that sounds wonderful.'

George came in. 'Ah, there she is.' Maggie stood up and hugged him. 'Good to see you, Maggie.'

'Good to be here.'

Kate wagged a finger at her father. 'I hear you and Maggie have been plotting.'

George put his hand on her shoulder. 'You deserve a night off. Besides, no one can say no to Maggie.'

Luke arrived.

'*Aaaah!*' Maggie squealed. 'Lukey! You're even more gorgeous than the last time, and that wasn't long ago!' She threw her arms around him. 'I know teenagers hate hugs, but you have to give me one.'

Luke laughed and hugged her back.

'What's going on?' Bobby came into the room holding his Nintendo. 'Why is everyone shouting?'

Maggie bent down and kissed him. 'Hi, Bobby.'

'Yuck, Maggie! You know I hate kisses.'

'Sorry, I forgot. Do you hate presents as well?' Maggie wiped her lipstick off his cheek.

Bobby shrugged. 'Not really, no. In fact, I quite like them.'

Kate watched as Maggie handed Bobby a big bag. He looked inside. 'Wow! This is so cool.' His beautiful brown eyes lit up, the way they hadn't in a long time. Kate loved Maggie just a little more.

Bobby held up a book. '*Five Thousand Awesome Facts*, cool, and . . .' He looked at Kate in shock. 'Mum, it's the Omano OM117L monocular microscope and the OptixCam Summit Series SK2 1.3MP digital microscope camera that Santa couldn't bring last year.'

Kate couldn't speak.

Bobby, forgetting his hatred of hugging, ran to Maggie and threw his arms around her tightly. '*Thank* you.'

Kate saw Maggie brush away a tear. 'I'm so happy you like it. Sure a genius like you needs to be kept busy.'

'Well, Maggie, you've outdone yourself. A book with five thousand facts for Bobby to share with us is just what we needed.' George shook his head.

'I thought of you when I bought it.' Maggie grinned. 'Now, this is for Luke.' She handed him a box. He opened it and a huge smile spread across his face.

'You legend.' He held up a black rugby boot.

'They look great,' Kate said.

'Mum, these are the Under Armour Speedform leather boots. They're the best.' Luke kissed Maggie's cheek. 'Thanks.'

'I hope they fit. I asked George for your shoe size so they should be okay. Check out the back.'

Luke's smile widened. 'No way!' He turned to show Kate that his initials, LH, were on the back in gold lettering.

'Amazing.' Kate smiled and mouthed, 'Thank you,' to Maggie.

'Now, George, don't think I forgot about you. This is your gift.' Maggie handed him a box wrapped in shiny red paper.

George opened it and frowned. 'Earphones?'

Maggie shook her finger. 'Not just earphones. These are noise-cancelling headphones, so when you want some peace, you just pop them on and the world will be quiet.'

George laughed. 'Well, now, that's about the most perfect gift I've ever received.'

'And for you, Kate.' Maggie handed her a beautifully wrapped parcel. It was heavy.

Kate opened it and under the gold wrapping paper was a box, inside which she found a bottle of pink champagne. 'Oh, Maggie.'

Maggie leant over and said quietly, 'It's to open when Jess gets the all-clear. I'll come and share it with you.'

Kate hugged her, willing herself not to cry. Having Maggie there made everything better, brighter and more hopeful.

'Now, before I have another drink, I need to see my goddaughter.'

Maggie drove Kate's car to the hospital. Even after only half a drink, Kate felt a bit lightheaded.

When they got there, Kate stopped Maggie in Reception. 'You need to prepare yourself. She's totally bald and she's lost a lot of weight. She doesn't look like the old Jess.'

Maggie nodded. 'Okay.'

'You'll have to be gowned, gloved and masked.'

'I understand.'

As they approached the room, Kate saw Maggie hesitate. With the mask on, her eyes looked huge, and Kate could see fear in them. 'Deep breath and smile. Right?'

Maggie smiled behind the mask, her eyes crinkling. 'I'm ready.'

Kate watched as Maggie put her shoulders back and marched into the room, exuding energy. 'Hello, my darling girl,' she said, throwing her arms around Jess but being gentle with the hug.

Jess's face lit up. 'Maggie! I'm so happy to see you.'

'Me too,' Maggie said, and Kate noticed her friend clasp her hands together to stop them shaking.

'Do I look awful?'

'You're the same beautiful Jess to me. What's hair? It comes, it goes. Yours will grow back even thicker and more stunning. Don't you worry. And you're lucky because you have your mother's beautiful brown eyes, which dazzle everyone.'

Jess beamed.

'So, this is shit.'

'Yes, it is,' Jess said.

'But you will get out of here and live a long and amazing life. You're a very special girl, Jess, and you'll get better. I really believe that.' Maggie tapped her forehead. 'Try and be as positive as you can, it'll help.'

Jess nodded. 'I'm trying.'

Maggie patted her arm. 'I know you are, pet. Now, in the meantime, because you're stuck here, I've got you some things to make the days pass a bit quicker.' She lifted the big bag she had brought with her and handed it to Jess.

Jess peered in and began to pull things out. A laptop. Ten box-set series. Twenty movies. A book on mindfulness. Jo Malone creams and shower gels. A neck support. Three cashmere wraps in different colours. A Mac make-up bag filled with beauty products, and a pair of noise-cancelling headphones, just like George's.

'Maggie!' Kate exclaimed. 'It's so much – too much.'

Maggie raised her hand. 'I'm allowed to spoil my gorgeous goddaughter and I will. Not another word out of you, Kate, or I'll evict you from the room.'

Jess's eyes shone. 'Oh, Maggie, it's just . . . I don't know what to say . . . Thank you. It's so generous. I'm so happy.'

Maggie blinked furiously. 'Don't say any more or you'll set me off.'

Jess held up her skinny arms and Maggie leant in for another hug. Kate knew she'd never forget this moment. She couldn't have loved her best friend more.

19

The following day, before they set off for the hotel, Kate left long lists of instructions for everyone. She ran around packing and unpacking bags until Maggie grabbed her arm and dragged her into the waiting taxi.

'I forgot to –' Kate was trying to climb out.

Maggie locked the door. 'Stop, Kate. Please, stop. Sit back and breathe. It's one night. Your dad and Luke can look after things.'

'I'm just worried about –'

'Everything and everyone?'

Kate smiled. 'Yes.'

'You always were. But you need to take care of yourself, too. That's what I'm here for. Now sit back and let me look after you.'

They started with a glass of wine. Then Maggie took Kate to a swanky hair salon to have her hair cut, coloured and blow-dried and to have her make-up done.

They added honey highlights to her light brown hair, cut layers into the shapeless style and a fringe, which made her look ten years younger. The make-up artist brought out her brown eyes with shadow, liner and false lashes. When the hairdresser and make-up artist had finished, and Kate looked at herself in the mirror, she began to cry.

'Don't cry, you'll ruin your eye make-up and you look fantastic!' Maggie said.

'I can't believe it.' Kate sobbed. 'I'd forgotten I could.'

Maggie hugged her. 'You're stunning.'

Then there was shopping. Maggie insisted on buying Kate a black dress that really flattered her figure. Kate tried to stop her, but Maggie was not taking no for an answer.

Then they went back to the hotel for more drinks, lots more. As the alcohol took effect, Kate felt her whole body begin to relax. The frown line between her eyes softened and she began to smile and laugh. 'Thank you for all of this. What a wonderful day.' She sipped her cocktail. 'I feel like a person again.'

'I'm glad. You deserve it.'

'I never thought it would be this hard,' Kate said.

'Parenting?' Maggie asked.

Kate nodded. 'I love them so much and, let's face it, they're all I have. No career, no husband, no life, really. It's just the kids. I'm a mum. That's my identity. So to have Jess so sick and not be able to fix it is . . . Well, it makes me feel like I've failed her. I've failed in my only job, to protect her from harm.'

'Kate, you can't control cancer. No one can. Your kids are amazing and it's ninety per cent down to your brilliant parenting. You're a fantastic mother. You're devoted to them. There's nothing more you could have done or can do. You're wearing yourself out looking after Jess. Give yourself a break.'

Kate put down her glass. 'I just want her to get better. I thought life was tough before this happened, but it wasn't. Money and houses don't matter. The only things that do are health and happiness. I really know that now. I don't care about Nick's affair or living with Dad. I just want Jess to be well.'

Maggie put a hand on her friend's arm. 'We all do. And she will get better. She's a fighter, just like her mum. I honestly don't know how you do it. You manage to juggle all your kids and their needs. It must be exhausting.'

'You run a successful recruitment business with twenty employees. That sounds terrifying to me. I couldn't do it.'

Maggie smiled. 'Some days at work I feel as if I'm dealing with children. But I know I couldn't be a real mother. I like my freedom too much. I guess I'm too selfish.'

Kate sat up straight. 'Don't say that. You're the least self-ish person I know. Not having children isn't selfish. It's just a choice you made.'

Maggie sighed. 'That's not how society sees it. Men especially are always telling me how I've missed out and how I'll regret it. They're married fathers, who are usually trying to have sex with me. What a joke! And I don't regret it – I know full well I'd be a bad mother. I'd hate it.'

'Well, you're a brilliant "auntie". The best. My kids adore you.'

'And I love them, but after seeing them I do love to go home to my clean, tidy, quiet apartment. It's just who I am.'

Kate smiled at her friend.

They were so different. The idea of going home to an empty apartment filled Kate with dread. Although the chaos at home was sometimes overwhelming, she loved it. She loved the coming and going of the kids, hearing about their day, watching their school plays, Luke's rugby matches, Jess's tennis games, helping them with homework, minding them, caring for them . . . being their mum. Well, she had loved it until Jess had got sick. Now things were out of her control and she was terrified.

Maggie interrupted her thoughts. 'It's really important, when you're dealing with so much stress, that you carve out a bit of time for yourself. If you get too run down, you won't be able to help Jess.'

Kate knew Maggie was being kind and considerate, but where the hell would she find time for herself? She spent most of her time in hospital, reading to Jess, holding the bowl when she threw up, cuddling her when she was upset, persuading her to eat, watching movies with her – just being with her. When she got home she had to give Bobby time: he was upset by Jess being in hospital and needed reassurance.

Luke was the one who was missing out on her attention. She'd barely seen him lately. Thank goodness he had a nice girlfriend, whom Kate trusted. Piper wasn't the type of girl to get Luke into trouble. She didn't seem to be a drinker or a messer, and she was keen to go to college. She seemed to adore Luke, too, which was exactly what he needed.

'I know what you're thinking,' Maggie said. 'Where am I going to find the time? But you have to, Kate. Otherwise you'll get sick yourself from exhaustion and worry. How about a yoga class once a week for an hour? Or did you ever sign up for a mindfulness class like we discussed? It's supposed to be amazing. There must be one in the area.'

Kate drank more wine. 'Actually, there's one starting in the room upstairs from the café next week.'

Maggie clapped her hands. 'Perfect timing. Sign yourself up and go. It's just one tiny hour a week. You need it.'

She could manage one hour a week, she thought, and everyone kept telling her how brilliant mindfulness was for 'switching off your mind' and calming you down. She'd welcome any kind of help with her mind. It raced all day and most of the night, too. Funnily enough, the only time she felt calm was at night in hospital when things were quiet and she was holding Jess in her hospital bed, watching movies or reading to her or, if Jess was too tired, just lying there as her daughter slept in her arms. Those quiet times were when her mind briefly stopped whirring. She cherished them. With her arms around Jess, she felt as if she was protecting her a little — as if she was being a mother instead of a useless bystander, watching her child being poked and prodded and pumped full of drugs.

Maggie nudged her. 'Those guys over there are checking you out.'

Kate snorted. 'They're obviously looking at you. I'm hardly a catch — a cash-strapped, separated mother of three, one child in hospital with leukaemia. How could they resist?'

'Listen to me. Tonight you're Kate, a gorgeous, sexy, thirty-seven-year-old woman.'

'But I'm forty-two.'

'Not tonight.'

Maggie waved the two men over to join them. They sat down and introduced themselves, Henk and Ewoud. They were from Amsterdam and were in Ireland for a technology conference. Kate reckoned they were in their mid-thirties. Neither was wearing a wedding ring, and while they weren't particularly handsome, they were attractive enough.

Maggie bought drinks, the men bought drinks, and soon everyone was smashed, especially Kate.

One of the men suggested they go to a club. Maggie was all for it, of course. They piled into a cab and within twenty minutes they were all dancing to Taylor Swift.

Kate came over to Maggie. 'Oh, my God! He just tried to kiss me!'

'So?'

'So I can't do that.'

'Why not?'

'Well, I . . . I . . .'

'You're single, you can do whatever the hell you want. Now will you just go for it!' Maggie shouted in her friend's ear.

'What about Jess?'

'Jess is in hospital. How is you not kissing him going to make her better?'

Kate's eyes filled with tears. 'I shouldn't be enjoying myself while she's having a terrible time.'

Maggie grabbed her by the shoulders and shook her. 'Jesus, Kate, it's one lousy night. Stop feeling guilty.'

Henk came up and pulled Kate back to dance. Maggie pushed her forward. 'Let go, Kate, just let go.'

Kate felt an arm land on her back. What the hell? She opened her eyes. On the floor beside her were the new black dress, her tights, shoes and bra. She slowly turned over.

'Morning.' Henk gave her a sleepy smile and his hand reached down between her legs.

Kate leapt out of the bed. She was stark naked. Oh, God. She ran into the bathroom and locked the door.

'Hey, what's going on?' Henk called after her.

'Go away. Please just go away.'

'Come on, Kate, we had the great time. Let's finish with one more sex.'

One more sex? Oh, Jesus, she'd slept with him! Kate began to have little flashes of the previous night. Drinking, dancing, kissing and, oh, God, sex. Yes, definitely sex. She was a slut. How could she sleep with a total stranger?

There was a knock on the bathroom door. 'How about we shower together? We can have sex in there.'

Kate pulled the towelling robe around her and sank down on the bathmat. 'Please stop talking and leave.'

'You were a lot of fun last night, now not so much.'

Kate decided not to say anything. She closed her eyes as memories flooded back. She blushed as she remembered crying out when she came. It had been a long time since she'd had sex. It was good sex, great sex. But, still, how could she?

He could have been a murderer or a weirdo or anything. And where was Maggie? Hang on, she was sharing the room with Maggie, so where was she now? Kate vaguely remembered leaving the nightclub and Maggie waving her off, telling her to have a great time. Maggie was with Henk's friend – what was his name? Ewoud. Kate began to laugh. She and Maggie had kept saying, 'He would. Would you?' while falling about laughing. Henk and Ewoud had just shrugged.

Had Maggie ended up with Ewoud in his room? Probably. She glanced around the bathroom. Her bag was there. She fished for her phone. No messages from home, good. Two from Maggie, one from last night: *Hope he was worth it!!!!! Had to book another room. Ewoud not my type. Am in room 234.*

There was another from this morning at ten o'clock. What time was it? Kate looked at her phone again. *Half past ten!* She never slept in late. Maggie's text said: *Gone for breakfast. Call when you wake up u slut!!!*

Kate could hear Henk moving around the room and prayed he was getting dressed.

He knocked on the bathroom door. 'I am going now. It was a pity that you were not so nice today. I had the good time last night. Goodbye.'

Had they used a condom? Kate thought wildly. Jesus, did I have unprotected sex? Kate opened the bathroom door and called, 'Wait, did we . . . did we use protection?'

Henk turned and nodded. 'Yes, I did. You were not asking me to, but of course I did.'

'Thank you. Thank you very much. Bye.'

Kate shut and locked the door. Thank God for that. How could she have almost had unprotected sex with a stranger? She was a disgrace.

Kate waited until she heard the bedroom door close, then exhaled deeply. Phew, he was gone. She texted Maggie, asking her to bring up some croissants and anything else portable from the breakfast buffet. Then she climbed into the shower and washed off Henk and the night before. She scrubbed and scrubbed. What was she like? A forty-two-year-old mother, with a sick child, out drunk, sleeping with strange men.

Mind you, it had been a good night. It had been fun. The sex had been pretty great, from what she could remember. Was it so terrible of her to have let go? She hoped no one had seen her. Imagine if one of the other mothers in Jess's class had spotted her falling around in the nightclub while her daughter lay in hospital. The shame! Kate closed her eyes and let the water wash away her embarrassment and her tears.

As she was drying herself, she caught her reflection in the mirror. A middle-aged woman with a thick midriff stared back at her. Who was she kidding? No amount of haircuts and make-up could change the fact that she was average-looking, with a saggy stomach and more baggage than any man would ever want.

Henk might have been the last man she'd have sex with in years, possibly decades, maybe ever. God, she might never have sex again. It was frightening but possible. She wasn't like Maggie: she couldn't just meet men and sleep with them. Well, not unless she poured eight cocktails down her neck. Could this be it? Yes, Kate thought, it could be.

There was a loud banging on the door and a shout: 'I want details!'

Kate grinned, unlocked the bathroom door and went to let Maggie in. She was holding a large napkin filled with mini croissants, *pains au chocolat* and muffins.

'I love you,' Kate said, as she began to eat one after another.

'Well well well! Let's hear it, then. Gory details, please.' Maggie lay back in the chair and folded her arms.

Kate stuffed a mini muffin into her mouth. 'Nothing to tell, really.'

'Liar.'

Kate giggled. 'Okay, yes, I did bring him back and, yes, we had sex.'

Maggie whooped. 'I'm delighted. Was it good?'

'Yes. Although, if I'm honest, it's a bit hazy.'

'You were throwing back mojitos as if they were lemonade. I'm so glad you had a blow-out. You needed that.'

Kate picked up a mini croissant and took a bite. 'Thank you so much for organizing the day. I'm afraid your makeover is ruined. I look about a hundred and ninety today.'

Maggie rubbed her eyes. 'I don't feel too young myself.'

'What happened with Ewoud?'

'He was boring and had no sex appeal. I'm not that desperate. So I waved him off and booked myself another room.'

Kate winced. 'Sorry. Our whole night must have cost you a fortune.'

Maggie sat up and patted her arm. 'I work twenty-hour days to make money and that money needs to be enjoyed. I had a great time last night and, more importantly, you got to let your hair down for once. And, boy, did you let it down!' She winked.

Kate was blushing. 'God, was I in a state in the nightclub?'

'It was kind of hilarious when you were trying to twerk.'

Kate covered her face with her hands. 'Stop.'

'I'm kidding. You were absolutely fine.'

Kate drank thirstily from a glass of water. 'My head is throbbing. I'd forgotten what hangovers feel like.'

'I can book us in for another night, if you want to flake out, watch movies and order room service?'

Kate smiled. 'That sounds like heaven, but I want to go and see Jess and spend some time with Bobby.'

'Back to mother-mode. I get it. Well, I've changed my flight. I'm not going to London until Tuesday, so I'll pop in to see Jess later this afternoon.'

Kate scoffed the last croissant. To hell with her weight, she had much bigger concerns. 'I'd better get dressed.' She stood up and began to pull on her clothes.

'I'm sorry, Kate.'

Kate looked up. 'For what?'

'That you have to deal with cancer on top of everything else. It's not fair.'

Kate sighed. 'What's fair? If I let myself think, Why me? I'd crumble. Besides, nothing that's happened so far, Nick's affair and our money problems, matters even the tiniest bit compared to this. I'm so over it. It's all about Jess now. I have to believe she'll be okay. The alternative is unspeakable and unthinkable.'

Maggie went over to her and hugged her. 'She will be.'

Kate's phone rang.

It was her father. 'I'm so sorry, Kate, I need you to come to the hospital. There's been a setback.'

Bobby's Diary

Things are terribel. Last week everyone went all crazy. Jess gotted an infection and she was really sick, like bad sick. Mummy had red and sad eyes all the time and Daddy came to the hospital and shouted and punched the wall and he had red eyes too.

Granddad had sad eyes and so did Luke and so did Maggie. It made me feel really sick in my stomak. I told Mummy my stomak hurt but she said, 'Not now, Bobby.' I told Luke my stomak hurt and he said, 'For f-word sake, Bobby, Jess is really sick.' No one cares about me or how I feel.

At home Luke is grumpy and just goes into his room with Granddad's big headphones and lissens to music or else he is with Piper. I like Piper. She gave me sweets yesterday when she sawed me in the kitchen by myself. She took them out of her poket and said they were for me becos I'm a good boy and she nows it must be hard for me with Jess being sick.

It IS hard for me and now it's worser. Jess can't have visitors except Mummy and Daddy. We have to wave at her from a window and she looks really skinny and she's tired all the time and sleeps a lot.

Yesterday I heard Mummy say to Granddad, 'Jesus, Dad, we nearly lost her.'

Granddad hugged Mummy. I cried then becos I love Jess even tho I'm cross she got sick and everyone just talks about her all the time and nothing else. I don't want her to die. I don't like sleeping in my bedroom by myself. I used to go into Mummy some nights. She put her arms around me and we sleeped cuddled up. But Mummy sleeps in the hospital a lot now so I can't.

Mrs Lorgan tried to be nice to me when Luke took me to school and told her that Jess was 'not good'. She said I could play Joseph in the Christmas play. But Tommy said that it wasn't fair and he wanted to be Joseph and he should be becos his brother has special needs and my sister was just a bit sick. He said that you can get better from cancer but you can't get better from Down Sindrum.

I got foorious then and shouted that I didn't care about his stupid brother with Down Sindrum, whatever that means, and said that cancer is really bad and really serious and all my family had red eyes and I have to talk to Jess through the telephone and wave at her through a window and he can see his brother all the time.

He said Down Sindrum is way worser than cancer and I shouted, 'NO WAY, cancer is the worst,' and then I said a bad word that Luke uses. I called Tommy a 'dickhead'. I know it's a bad word but I was very angry.

Mrs Lorgan went all red in the face and said that I wasn't going to be Joseph becos Joseph would NEVER use such shoking words. She said Tommy wasn't going to be Joseph either.

She said she was making Declan be Joseph which is so dum. Declan has a stuter and he can't even say words properly. It takes him ages to say any word that starts with M, C, F, P, S or D — which is terribel because his name is Declan! His parents should change his name to Adam or something.

Anyway he is now Joseph and his wife is Mary and he can't even say her name properly which is just stupid. When he tried to say, 'Don't worry, Mary. I'll find a place for us to stay', it took him like about a hundred minits to say don't. So then Mrs Lorgan changed the words in the play to 'It's okay, I'll find a hotel.'

Declan should be a donkey or a shepherd. I should be Joseph. But now because I said the bad word I'm a stupid inn-keeper and I only have two lines and Declan has loads of lines and he can't even speak.

The play is going to go on for hours and hours with Declan in the main part.

When I told Mummy about Declans stuter in the beginning of the year when he arrived in the school and took ages to say his name, Mummy said that I shud be especially nice to him becos it was hard to have a stuter and I shud try to imagine what it's like not to be able to just say what you want.

I did feel sorry for him in the beginning but now my problem is worser than his. Jess has stinky cancer and she's not getting better.

The only good thing that happened was when Mrs Lorgan asked Tommy to be a donkey and he said no way and he said he didn't want to be in the stupid play and anyway his mum and dad said God and Jesus were just made up and only stupid people believed in all that nonsense. Mrs Lorgan put him in the bold corner.

But then a brilliant thing happened. Maggie came to collect me and I told her about the play and everything and she stopped walking and said, 'Hang on a bloody minit' and she turned around and went storming back into the school and asked Mrs Lorgan in a loud voice if she could have a word.

They told me to wait outside the classroom but I could hear them because they were kind of shouting, but not shouting. The way grown-ups talk loudly when they are angry but trying not to be rude. They talked and talked and then Maggie said, 'This is ridikulos. Bobby is having a very hard time, give the kid a break. Let him be Joseph.'

Mrs Lorgan said, 'My desishun is final.'

'Nothing is final.'

'I will not be changing my mind. I'm very sorry about his sister, but lots of families in the class have troubles at home. He is lucky to be an inn-keeper after his behavyer and cursing.'

'So you're giving a kid with a stuter who takes ten minits to say his own name the lead part? Isn't that just a little ambishus? Aren't you just putting him under huge presure? You give the kid who stuters two lines, not the main part. It's too much presure. What kind of techer are you?'

Mrs Lorgan opened the door then and she said, 'I am a techer with 37 years experience and I will not be spoken to like this or have my desishuns questioned. Good day.'

'Somewhere along those 37 years you lost your compashun you cold cow,' Maggie said and grabbed my hand and we marched out of the school.

Maggie called Mrs Lorgan a cow!!!!!!!!!!! I can't beleeve it.

Maggie did deep breathing out her nose and then she turned to me and said, 'Stuff Joseph, he's just a doormat anyway. The inn-keeper is a good part and you get to tell Joseph to go away. Now how about we go and get a hot chocolate and a huge bun?'

I love Maggie. I asked her if she could stay with us forever. She gave me a hug and I let her and then she said she had to go to other places a lot for work but that she was going to come home as much as she could to help us. That made the ake in my stomak go away and I felt better.

20

Kate sat on the mat and peeped out from under her eyelids. There were six other people in the room, three men and three women. Thank God she didn't recognize any of them. She was surprised to see men there. Then again, men had stress in their lives, too. Maybe she should suggest to Nick that he go to a class. He was certainly stressed enough to need help.

Kate could see how hard he was working to come up with the money to look after everyone and she appreciated it, but it was making him even more difficult.

Between Jenny, the kids and now Jess being sick, Nick was like a pot about to boil over. Kate tried to avoid him as much as possible. The only time she saw him relax was when he was with Jess. She'd arrived at the hospital not long ago to find the two of them laughing together over some silly game Nick had downloaded on his phone. Kate had sat outside to give them that time together. It was so good for Jess to have her dad's undivided attention and Kate hadn't wanted to break the spell.

The lady running the mindfulness class asked everyone if they were comfortable. Kate wasn't. She moved about on her mat but couldn't find a position that felt right. She hoped the class would help her to stop panicking and allow her mind to switch off even for five minutes.

Seeing Jess almost die when the infection ripped through her body had been unbearable. Kate was waking up every night with a panic attack, gasping for breath, her whole chest rigid with fear. Sometimes she thought she was having mini heart attacks. She'd never had headaches before, but now they were a permanent part of her life. Not a throbbing in her head, but a piercing, searing pain that made her want to throw up.

Dr Willis had been so kind, calling to the house and visiting Jess in hospital. When he'd asked Kate how she was, she'd told him about the headaches. He suggested she take something but she was afraid to resort to medicine: she had to be clear-headed and keep on top of things. He had told her to call him any time, day or night, if she or Jess was in need of anything. He said Kate needed to look after herself because having a sick child was such a huge strain. She told him about the mindfulness class and he thought it was an excellent idea. Everyone seemed to think it was – but Kate knew that an hour lying on a mat wasn't going to solve anything.

At night she lay in bed, her head spinning with dark thoughts about Jess and the ever-present what-if. Before the infection, she'd kept out of her mind the possibility of Jess dying. But now that she had seen her daughter so sick and so close to the edge, she couldn't block it out. It was possible: Jess could die, and it could happen in an instant.

Panic rose in her throat. She tried to concentrate on what the mindfulness lady was saying. Maggie had made her swear she'd go to the class: 'It's upstairs from the café so you have no excuse. It'll do you good,' her friend had insisted.

It wasn't worth not going and having to explain herself to Maggie, so Kate had promised she'd give it a go. What the hell? If it helped even a tiny bit, she'd be grateful.

The lights in the room were dimmed and there were candles lit along the windowsill. It was restful, she had to admit.

The mindfulness teacher sat with her legs crossed and her back straight. Kate tried to copy her but her lower back ached. She slumped against the wall, her legs bent in front of her.

'Welcome, everyone. My name is Marie. We'll go around the room and perhaps you can tell me why you're here and what you hope to achieve from the classes.'

A woman of about Kate's age said she was doing the course because she had some health issues. Next, a man said he was going through a difficult break-up . . . Then it was just Kate and a man with a beard to her left.

'Uhm . . . well, I'm Kate and I'm here because my daughter is sick and I was hoping to get some tools to help me stop panicking.'

'Welcome, Kate. I certainly hope I can help you with that,' Marie said.

It was the bearded man's turn. He looked about sixty, with dark hair, and the beard needed a trim. Looking at the floor, he said quietly, 'I'm Liam and I'm here because my wife died almost three years ago. I'm stuck. I can't seem to get past it.'

Marie nodded sympathetically. 'Mindfulness and living in the moment will hopefully help you with that.'

'And because my daughter forced me to come,' he muttered under his breath.

'My friend forced me,' Kate whispered.

Liam glanced sideways and gave Kate a little smile. 'I've never done anything like this before. I feel like a twat,' he said.

'I tried yoga once, but I found it really boring,' Kate admitted. 'Still, at this stage I'll try anything.'

'What's wrong with your daughter?'

'Cancer.'

Liam winced.

'What did your wife die of?' Kate asked.

He looked away. 'Cancer.'

Kate bit her lip. She wished he'd said a car crash or a brain haemorrhage – anything but cancer.

'Okay.' Marie raised her voice to get everyone's attention. 'Let's start by breathing. Inflate your stomach on the inhale, pull it in on the exhale.'

Kate had to concentrate hard on the breathing as it seemed to be the opposite of the way her body wanted to behave. They lay down and did more breathing, and then they did a sort of swaying to music that Kate found a bit embarrassing. They had to stand up and shake different body parts, concentrating on each one to focus their minds. Marie said if they felt awkward in front of the others, they could do it with their eyes closed. Kate kept hers open because she was afraid of falling, but Liam closed his.

She was shaking her left leg about when Liam landed on top of her, squashing her into her mat. 'God, sorry,' he said, scrambling up hastily. 'I shut my eyes and lost my balance. I'm such an idiot. I hope I didn't hurt you.'

Kate was winded but not hurt. She waved her hand. 'No damage done.'

Liam held out his hand to help her up. 'I really am so sorry. I'm such a klutz. Dancing was never my thing. I should probably go before I injure someone. So much for calm and tranquillity.'

Kate grinned. 'Don't be silly, I'm fine, and at least you distracted me from my thoughts, which is more than I can say for the breathing.'

Liam smiled back. 'I can't get that right either. I'm not sure this is for me. I think I might be better off taking my dog for a walk.'

'I think I need a vat of wine,' Kate said, and laughed.

Marie came over to them. 'We must try to remain quiet and focus on our breathing.' She inhaled and exhaled deeply to demonstrate. 'Now if we could all lie down on our mats in a comfortable position, we're going to do a body scan.'

There was something strangely intimate about lying on a mat next to a man you'd never met before, Kate mused. But she didn't feel awkward now that they'd broken the ice. Liam reminded her a bit of her dad – he had a kind face. She closed her eyes and tried to concentrate on feeling her toes, but images of Jess's beautiful brown eyes so full of fear kept flashing in front of her.

Beside her she could hear Liam rustling about and sighing. He clearly wasn't thinking about his toes either.

Half an hour later Kate held the door as everyone streamed out onto the footpath.

'Did you enjoy it?' Marie asked.

'Yes, it was definitely nice to lie down and do nothing for a little bit, but I found it very difficult to switch my mind off.'

'Don't worry. It takes a lot of practice but keep trying. It'll really help you.'

'I will, thanks.'

Liam pulled on his coat. He was the last to leave. 'After you,' he said.

'Oh, no, you go ahead. I live here.'

'What? Here?'

Kate nodded. 'Yes, my dad owns the café and wine shop and I live with him.'

'Oh, I see. To be honest, I'm rarely down this way, but the café looks lovely. I must come and check it out.'

'You should. We do the best coffee and scones in town.'

'I love scones, as you can probably tell.' Liam patted his midriff, although it certainly wasn't big, Kate thought. Probably less obvious than hers.

'Do you think you'll give this mindfulness another go?'

Liam wrinkled his nose. 'Not sure it's for me, but my daughter's paid for the six sessions so I'd feel guilty if I didn't come to one or two more.'

'I know what you mean. My friend Maggie bought them for me. I guess one or two more can't do any harm.'

Liam had a nice smile, warm and open. 'No harm as long as some oaf doesn't fall on top of you.'

'In the scheme of my life's catastrophes,' Kate said, with a half-smile, 'that was very minor.'

Liam held out his hand and they shook. 'I'll let you go. It was very nice to meet you.'

'You, too. See you next week, maybe.'

Liam waved and walked off into the cold night.

Kate locked up and turned off the lights. When she went into the house, she went to check on Bobby. He was fast asleep. Kate bent to kiss his forehead. George was beside the bed, snoring in an armchair, his glasses halfway down his nose, his book upside-down on his lap. Kate left him undisturbed and went to get something to eat. She'd wake him later if he was still asleep.

In the kitchen she heated up some of the pea and chicken soup she'd made earlier for the café. As she was sitting down to eat it, the back door opened and Luke came in.

Kate looked at the clock – it was after ten. 'Hi. Were you in Piper's?'

'Yeah,' Luke said, walking quickly across the kitchen to the other door.

As he swept past, Kate got a strong whiff of alcohol. What the hell? 'Hold on there.' She stood up.

Luke pulled the door open. 'I'm going to bed.' He made to leave, but Kate pulled him back.

'Have you been drinking?'

'No.' Luke's eyelids drooped.

177

'Luke, you reek of booze. Where were you?'

Where the hell had he been and with whom? Kate wasn't delusional: she knew some of Luke's friends drank. She also knew he had the odd beer on a Saturday night at a party, but that was rare because he was so obsessed with sport and health. But this was Tuesday, a school night, and judging by Luke's eyes, he'd had a lot more than one or two beers.

Kate was getting angry. Why was he risking everything he cared about by getting drunk? She budged him forward into a chair.

He sat down heavily. 'What?'

'I want to know where you were.'

'I was with a few of the guys.'

'Which guys?'

'Gus and . . . well . . . Gus.'

Gus was the kind of boy you wanted your son to stay away from. He was wild and always getting into trouble. Luke was always saying what an idiot Gus was and how he was going nowhere fast. So why on earth was he getting drunk with him?

'Were you in a pub?'

Luke shook his head. 'Gus's house.'

'Were his parents there?'

'No, they're away.'

'What did you drink?'

Luke shrugged. 'I dunno, vodka, beer, whatever.'

'Whatever? Are you kidding me? Jesus, Luke, I've enough on my bloody plate without you going out and getting drunk. What were you thinking? How is this helpful to anyone?'

Luke banged the table with his hands. 'Oh, for Christ's sake, Mum, I wasn't trying to be helpful. I was trying to forget. I was trying to get away from all this shit. I'm sick of it.

Everything's so . . . so . . .' He put his head into his hands and began to cry.

Kate stopped being angry. She was so wrapped up in Jess that she was forgetting how hard this was for everyone else. She put her arm around Luke. 'I'm sorry, sweetheart, I know it's awful for you.'

'She nearly died, Mum.' Luke looked up. 'We nearly lost her.'

Kate felt her eyes welling up. She needed to be strong. 'I know we did, but she's okay now. The thing about cancer is that it's going to have ups and downs, but as long as Jess keeps recovering and getting better, she'll be all right.'

Luke rubbed his eyes. 'Do you want to know why I really went drinking?'

'Why?'

'Because I didn't want to give her my bone marrow. I was pissed off about it because it means I'll miss training and probably a game or two. I'm such a selfish prick that I was resenting having to donate to Jess. And then when she nearly died I felt sick for even thinking like that. What kind of person am I? Jess, my little sister, the nicest kid in the world, needs my help and I don't want to give it.'

Kate hugged him. 'Luke, what matters is that you never said you wouldn't do it. You stood up and said yes when the doctors said you were a match. Whatever you were thinking privately doesn't matter. It's what you do that counts. Of course you're not happy about having to donate bone marrow. It's a big deal. No one would be thrilled about it. Don't beat yourself up for how you feel. You can't help that.' Kate held Luke's hand. 'You should be proud of yourself for agreeing to donate. I'm proud of you. More proud than I've ever been.'

Luke sniffed. 'As proud as you are of me getting drunk?'

Kate smiled. 'No.'

Luke pushed his hair out of his face. 'It's all so . . . shit. I wish Jess wasn't sick. I wish Dad wasn't such a dickhead. I wish we had loads of money and that you didn't have to worry about anything. I wish . . .'

Kate stood up and tipped her now cold soup down the sink's plughole. 'If there's one thing I've learnt over the last few years, it's that wishing is a waste of time.'

21

Jess sat up, fully clothed, on the edge of the bed and listened to Dr Kennedy. She was excited and desperate to get out of the room, but she knew she had to listen.

Mum was sitting beside her on the bed, fiddling with her handbag strap.

'Now, Jess,' Dr Kennedy said, 'I want you to listen carefully. We're allowing you to go home because the infection has cleared up and the tests have shown you're in partial remission. We'll be going ahead with the bone-marrow transplant to try to get you into complete remission, which is our goal. I think it's important that you get home for a few weeks' break before we do the transplant. However,' he raised his hands, 'I need you to be very careful to protect yourself from any further infection while you're at home. This is a list of helpful hints regarding how to avoid it.'

Jess glanced at the list the doctor handed her. It was very long, and the ones that stood out to her were: 'Tell your doctor or specialist nurse immediately if you get a temperature over 38° centigrade (100° Fahrenheit). Tell your doctor or nurse straight away if you notice any bleeding or bruising. Keep as clean as you can – for instance, wash your hands before preparing food or eating. Keep away from animals to avoid infection, especially cat-litter trays and bird cages. Put pressure on cuts for longer than usual to stop bleeding. Rest when you feel tired.'

She looked up. 'Can I go horse-riding?'

'I don't think it's advisable this time, but if the transplant goes well, then we'll have you back on a horse in no time.'

'Should we wear masks at home?' her mother asked. 'Would it help protect her?'

'Unless someone has a cold or a temperature, you don't really need masks. Keep visitors to a minimum, and anyone not feeling well is best to stay away for the moment.'

Jess stood up. She'd had enough. Weeks of talking and explaining and tests and drugs and feeling better and feeling worse – she was sick of it all. She just wanted to go home and be normal for a while. They were wasting time talking.

'Can we go now?'

Her mother put her hand on Jess's arm. 'Hold on, Jess, just one more question.'

'*No!*' Jess shouted. 'No more questions! I've had enough! I want to go home.'

Her mother looked shocked. 'Okay, calm down. We're going.'

Dr Kennedy took off his glasses and smiled at Jess. 'You've been wonderfully patient and I understand how particularly difficult the last few weeks have been. Go home and have a lovely time.'

Jess felt bad for shouting. 'Thank you so much.'

Mum picked up her bag and Jess walked slowly, much more slowly than she'd have liked, out of the door and down the corridor. Her energy was non-existent, and she hated being tired all the time.

The nurses waved her off. Aideen, her favourite, hugged her. 'Have a great time. You deserve it.'

Jess grinned. 'Thanks, I will.'

She stopped outside Larry's door and went in to hug him.

'*Whooooooaa!* I don't want your infection!' he said, grinning.

'Sod off! I'm clear and you know it.' Jess laughed.

'Enjoy your time out, you lucky thing.'

'I will. Call me anytime, day or night.'

Larry winked. 'I'll leave you in peace. You don't need me moaning down the phone when you finally get out of here for a bit.'

Jess smiled and tried to remain cheerful. Now that she was dressed in 'normal' clothes, it was as if she could see Larry from a different perspective. Instead of a fellow cancer victim, she was looking at him as an outsider would and saw how utterly wretched he was. She willed herself to see past his grey, sunken face into his lovely blue eyes. 'I'm here for you.'

He held her hand in his shrivelled dry one. 'I know. I promise I'll try not to die while you're out. I'll wait until you come back.'

She shook her head. 'Don't, Larry, please.'

His blue eyes gazed into her brown ones. 'Sorry, can't help myself. You look good, Jess. Enjoy freedom.'

She squeezed his hand. 'I will and I'll send you photos to make you jealous.'

'Why would I be jealous? I have a kingdom here.' Larry waved his arm around the hospital room. They laughed.

Just before she left, Jess turned to hug him again. 'I'll see you soon. You're not allowed to die, promise?'

'Promise.' He hugged her back.

Jess was glad her mother didn't talk or ask her any questions as they walked to the car. She was upset at leaving Larry, upset and worried. It was the only fly in the ointment of getting out of hospital. She knew Larry would miss her, just like she'd miss him. They were in it together and made each other's days so much more bearable.

She vowed to send him funny pics and texts to cheer him up and so that he'd know she hadn't forgotten him.

Hospital days were so endless and any bit of distraction was welcome.

Jess expected the house to be quiet when she got home, because the boys would be in school and Granddad would be working in the café. But when she opened the back door into the kitchen, she heard a cheer. Everyone was there – Luke, Bobby, Granddad, Piper, even Nathalie.

Bobby and Luke were holding up a poster that Bobby had painted. It said, WELCOM BAK JESS. The table was full of all her favourite food, and even though she didn't feel like eating, she was touched by all the effort that had gone into it.

Jess wanted to laugh and cry. Everything felt normal and weird at the same time. The kitchen seemed so safe and warm and full of love, and she was so happy. She tried really hard not to, but she began to cry. She turned her head and buried it in her mother's stomach.

'It's okay, pet, you're home now. Safe and sound with all the people who love you,' Mum whispered into her ear. Jess heard the catch in her voice. 'We're so happy.'

Jess took a deep breath and turned. Luke picked her up gently and swung her around. 'Good to have you back, sis. I never realized how patient you are with Mr Zillion Questions here.'

'And I never realized how good you are with Mr – Mr Big Hairy Muscles,' Bobby said.

They all laughed, which broke the tension and made everything more normal.

Granddad came over and hugged her. 'So glad to have you home, my little pet. You're the sunshine in this house.' He turned away to wipe his eyes.

Piper kissed her and Jess felt more tears on her cheeks. She noticed the black circles under Piper's eyes.

Then Nathalie came over to her. She was wearing a mask over her mouth. 'I am wearing it in case of the germs. I have the leetle cold.'

'You don't have a cold, Nathalie. Nor do you have allergies or sinus or headaches or back problems. You're just a hypochondriac,' Granddad muttered.

'Another problem with the Irish men is they are afraid of the doctor. In France when a man is sick, he goes to the doctor and takes medication. In Ireland the men pretend they are "grand" and then, *poof!*, they are dead on the road of the attack of the 'eart.'

'Seriously?' Luke glared at her.

Nathalie shrugged. 'It's true. I 'ope you will not be so stupid and stubborn as the older Irish men, Luke.'

'For the love of Jesus, Nathalie,' Granddad snapped, 'will you stop barking on about death and illness?'

'I am not afraid to talk about death. It is a fact of life. We are born and we die. *Voilà.*'

'Dude, zip it!' Luke demanded.

Nathalie looked at Jess. 'Do you want everyone never to say the word "sick" or "dead" in front of you? Does that not make it like pretending? Sticking the 'ead in the sand? Of course we all pray you will be better, but you 'ave cancer, *non?* It is a fact.'

It annoyed Jess that everyone avoided words like 'ill', 'sick', 'death' and even 'cancer'. Her family never used it. They said 'condition' or 'leukaemia' but the word 'cancer' was never uttered. Jess knew they were trying to protect her and themselves, but it bugged her.

Mum took charge. 'Nathalie, I think that's enough chat about death for now. This is a celebration.'

'Do you have celebrations in France or do you just sit around reading depressing poetry and staring at your navels?' Granddad grumbled.

'We are very good at the celebrations. We know 'ow to 'ave a good time.'

'Really?' Luke looked doubtful.

'When?' Granddad asked.

Nathalie was affronted. 'All the time. We don't need to wear a green 'at and drink ten pints and fall down to 'ave fun. We drink good wine and eat good food and talk and laugh.'

'Laugh about what?' Granddad asked.

'*Jeux de lettres.*'

'What?' they asked.

'You 'ave the sentence or the word and then you twist them around and make funny phrases. It is very amusing and good for the mental gymnastics.'

Granddad slapped his forehead. 'Mother of God, save me now. Nathalie, you need to lighten up. Maybe you should try the green hat and the few drinks. You might actually enjoy yourself.'

'Green does not flatter my skin,' Nathalie huffed.

Bobby kicked the table. 'Can we stop talking about boring stuff and eat?'

'Yes!' Kate smiled at him.

Nathalie left the room to look after the café.

'Take your mask off! You'll scare away the customers,' Granddad called after her.

Jess and the others sat down. Piper put her coat on.

'Babe, where are you going?' Luke asked.

'It's your family time, Luke. I'll call you later. Welcome home, Jess.' She blew her a kiss and left.

Jess ate little bites of everything, but she really wasn't hungry. She did manage a small bowl of strawberry shortcake ice cream and saw her mum smiling as she finished the last spoonful.

They chatted about the café, Luke's upcoming match and Bobby's Christmas play, which Jess was surprised that Mum didn't seem to know about.

'Oh, Bobby, that's awful, you should be Joseph. Maybe I could talk to Mrs Lorgan.'

Bobby rolled his eyes. 'It's way too late, Mummy. Anyway, Maggie already did and she won't change her mind.'

'Oh. Well, I'm sorry about that.'

Bobby ate a piece of scone. 'You never listen to me anyway. It's only ever about Jess.'

'Bobby!' Luke snapped. 'Mum's doing her best.'

'Be nice to your mother,' Granddad said. 'She's got a lot on her plate.'

Jess suddenly felt tired. 'I think I'll lie down for a bit. Thanks for the lovely welcome.' To Bobby, she said, 'Will you come up with me and tell me some new facts while I'm putting on my pyjamas?'

Bobby's face lit up. 'Yes!' He ran to get the book Maggie had given him.

'Are you sure about that, Jess?' Kate asked. 'You look very tired. Maybe he could read the facts later.'

'No, it's fine, Mum. Let him tell me a few. I reckon I'll be asleep in two minutes anyway.'

Luke brought Jess's bag upstairs and put it into Kate's room.

'What are you doing?' Jess asked.

'Mum said you're to sleep here while you're at home. She'll sleep with Bobby.'

'She doesn't have to do that.'

Luke put the case on the double bed. 'She wants to. We all want to help, Jess.'

Jess busied herself unpacking. With her back to Luke, she said, 'I never thanked you properly for saying you'll give me your bone marrow.'

187

'It's cool. No big deal.'

Jess put her pyjamas on the bed. 'It *is* a big deal and I'm sorry you have to do it, but thank you.'

Luke said quietly, 'I'd do anything to help you, Jess, you know I would. All we want is for you to get better.'

Jess didn't trust herself to speak. She was so grateful to Luke. The infection had terrified her, but it was gone now. She had to look forward. She really believed that, with Luke's strong, healthy bone marrow, she would get better, just like her mum said.

As she lay in bed listening to Bobby spouting facts, Jess tried to visualize Luke's vital bone marrow knocking down and destroying her cancer cells. It was a nice image: it made her feel strong and hopeful . . .

'As well as having unique fingerprints, humans also have unique tongue prints. Isn't that amazing, Jess? Our tongues are all different. Look at mine and then let me look at yours. Jess . . . Jess?'

As usual, Bobby found he was talking to himself. Jess had drifted off into the oblivion of sleep.

2 2

Piper sat beside Luke and held his hand. He was pretending to be nonchalant about the bone-marrow aspiration, but his right leg was bouncing up and down. Kate sat on Luke's other side, chewing her lip, which made Piper feel a bit panicky.

Dr Kennedy explained it all to them in a calm and reassuring voice. Luke had to have a general anaesthetic, and while he was asleep, they'd take out the bone marrow. A needle would be put through his skin into the hip bone. Then they would suck the bone marrow out through the needle and into the syringe. That part didn't sound too bad, but when Dr Kennedy said they usually had to put the needle into several different parts of the pelvis and, occasionally, the chest bone in order to get the one full litre of bone marrow they needed, Piper saw the blood drain from Luke's face.

Dr Kennedy must have noticed, too, because he patted Luke's arm and told him not to worry, that his body would replace all of the bone marrow within a few weeks.

'How long will the procedure take?' Kate asked.

'No more than two hours. After the bone marrow is harvested, Luke will be taken to the recovery room while the anaesthesia wears off. All going well, he'll be free to leave the hospital within a few hours or by the next morning.'

'I've got an important rugby game four days later. Can I play?' Luke found his voice.

'I'd advise against it. You may have soreness, bruising and aching at the back of the hips and lower back for a few days.'

'Fuck,' Luke muttered.

'Luke!' Kate said.

Fuck your stupid rugby match, Piper wanted to scream. What if you bloody die? What if something goes wrong and the operation is a disaster and you die on the operating table without knowing we're going to have a baby?

Piper let go of Luke's hand and gripped her own hands together tightly to try to control her panic.

'I'm sorry about that,' Kate said to Dr Kennedy. 'We're all under a lot of pressure.'

'That's quite all right. It's a very difficult time for you all.'

'Will Jess be in isolation after the transplant?' Kate asked.

Dr Kennedy nodded. 'Yes. Until her bone marrow starts making enough blood cells, she's at risk of picking up infections. She'll have to stay in a single room with minimal visitors until her blood count improves.'

'Poor Jess.' Kate's voice shook.

Kate looked so worn out and sad. That's a mother's love, thought Piper. When you have a child, you love it more than anything in the world. She touched her stomach. Would she feel that for her baby? Would Luke? Or would he resent her and hate the baby for ruining his life? Would Luke be a good dad? Would he be like his mum, devoted to her kids, or like his dad and leave Piper for a younger woman?

Piper desperately wanted to tell someone. She felt so lonely. Walking around with this huge secret all the time was wearing her down. She needed Jess to get better soon. If Jess got better, everyone would be happy, and maybe Luke wouldn't go mad when she told him. She prayed Luke's bone marrow would make Jess better. It had to, surely.

Dr Kennedy stood up and saw them out of the room. Patting Luke on the back, he said, 'We'll see you in two days' time. Don't worry, it'll all be over in no time and we'll have you back on the rugby pitch soon.'

As they walked towards the car, Piper saw Luke's dad coming running towards them. Luke froze.

'Sorry I'm late,' Nick panted, sweat running down the sides of his face. 'I had to show a house and they were late and . . . Anyway, it was worth it because I closed the deal and it's a big one, so it'll really help with the bills.' He bent over, putting his hands on his knees and catching his breath. 'Did I miss it?'

'Yeah, you did,' Luke said, staring over his father's shoulder into the distance.

'What did he say?'

Luke's hand tightened around Piper's. It hurt. 'He said they're going to stick needles all over me, suck out ten per cent of my bone marrow and I can't play in my match this week.'

Nick frowned. 'To hell with your match, this is about Jess.'

Luke's fingers were now crushing Piper's. 'Don't you dare tell me what it's about. What the hell would you know? You're hardly ever around, and when you are, you're either late or on the phone to your stupid fucking girlfriend, who can't seem to cross the road without you.'

Nick straightened and glared at him. 'Don't speak to me like that. I'm doing my best here. I'm trying to hold down a job so I can look after everyone. I'm the one who has to come up with the funds and I'm working my balls off. Why don't you give me a break and stop behaving like a child?'

Luke snorted. 'Yeah, you're a real contender for Dad of the Year.'

'Stop it, both of you,' Kate begged. 'None of this is helping Jess.'

Nick suddenly noticed Piper. 'Who's this?'

'My girlfriend,' Luke said.

'Oh, yes, Piper. Jess has told me lots about you.'

Piper didn't know what to say. She couldn't be rude, but she knew how much Luke hated his dad and what a rubbish father he had been. Still, she had to be polite. So she put out her hand and shook Nick's. 'Nice to meet you,' she said.

'You too. Thanks for being so good to Jess. She raves about you.'

Piper blushed. 'It's easy to be nice to Jess.'

Nick smiled. 'Yes, it is. She's a very special girl.'

'So special you barely saw her all year until she got sick,' Luke said.

Piper watched Nick's face darken. He was different from how she had imagined him. She'd thought he'd be tall, dark and handsome, a ladies' man. He was fit for his age, but average-looking: brown hair, greying at the sides, and blue eyes that seemed a bit too small for his face. He had deep black rings under them, which betrayed how tired he was.

Nick inhaled deeply. 'Luke, that's enough. I don't want to argue with you. I know it can't be easy having this procedure and I'm proud of you for stepping up for your sister.'

Piper felt Luke relax slightly beside her.

'Right. Let's go. I've to pick up Bobby,' Kate said, hustling Luke and Piper towards the car.

Later that day, on her way home from school, Piper was still thinking about Kate, what a good mother she was to Jess and how she wanted to be a good mother to her baby, when she heard Posy shout, 'Piper!'

'What?'

'I just asked you three times if I could borrow your leather jacket.'

'Oh, yeah, sure.'

'Are you okay?' Posy asked.

'What do you mean?'

'Well, you seem so distracted all the time.'

Piper pulled her schoolbag higher on her shoulder. 'I guess I am.'

'Is it because of Luke's sister?'

'Yes, and other stuff.'

'Like what?'

Piper shrugged. 'Just stuff.'

'Stuff to do with Luke?' Posy persisted.

'Yeah.'

'Are you and he breaking up?'

'No.'

'Do you think he fancies someone else?'

'No.'

'Do you think he's been with another girl?'

'No, Posy, it's nothing like that. Just forget it.' Piper cursed her stupidity. Posy would never let it go now that she was convinced something was wrong with Piper's relationship.

'OMG, did you find out he's gay?'

'Jesus, Posy, no!'

'Well, then, what's going on?'

'Nothing.'

'But you said – Ouch!' Posy squealed.

The twins had come up behind her and pulled her ponytail.

'Do you have any money?' Penny asked Piper.

'No, and you still owe me the tenner I lent you last week,' Piper reminded her.

'I'm starving.' Penny groaned.

'Stop moaning, we'll be home in ten minutes.' Piper had no patience for her sisters today. She wanted to lie down and sleep for a while in peace and quiet.

'Come on, Piper, you're our older sister. You're supposed to buy us stuff,' Poppy said.

'Sod off,' Piper snapped. 'I'm not in the mood.'

'God, you're so narky, these days,' Penny moaned. 'You used to be fun, but now we can't say anything without you biting our heads off.'

'Yeah, seriously, chill, Piper,' Poppy added. 'You've got so boring. I'm never going out with someone if it turns me into a granny like you.'

Penny laughed and started hobbling like an old woman. 'I'm Piper. I used to be fun but now I'm a boring girlfriend, who's always in a grump.'

Piper's blood boiled. 'I'm sick of the lot of you. All you ever think about is yourselves. Luke is donating his bone marrow to Jess and it's a big operation and I'm worried about it and him and Jess and everything. I hope I never get cancer because I know you'd never give me your bone marrow because you're so bloody selfish.' She burst into tears.

Her three sisters stopped walking and stared at her.

'I'll give you my bones if you get cancer, Piper, I promise.' Posy was upset.

'It's not your bones, you idiot, it's bone marrow,' Penny said. 'You can't give someone your bones. How could you walk if you gave Piper your leg bone?'

'I'd give Piper my leg bone if she wanted it,' Posy said. 'Piper, you can have any part of my body that you need.'

Piper tried to smile but grimaced instead.

'Jeez, Piper, I'm sorry if we upset you. We were just joking around,' Poppy said.

'I'd give my bone marrow if you needed it,' Penny said. 'As long as they gave me loads of painkillers so I was totally out of it.'

'We could give you half each,' Poppy noted. 'Then it wouldn't be so bad for either of us. Penny'd give you a bit and I'd give you a bit. A two-for-the-price-of-one deal.'

'Perfect.' Penny pulled her scarf over her face as a cold gust of winter wind blew across the park.

'So, you see, we're not selfish,' Posy said. 'We'd all help you.'

'Thanks,' Piper said, putting her arm around Posy. 'Sorry, I'm just tired, I guess.'

'Luke will be fine,' Penny assured her.

'Totally. He's as strong as Conor McGregor and he'll bounce back super-fast,' Poppy added.

'Yeah, he's like Superman,' Posy said.

Piper shivered. 'Come on, let's go home. It's freezing.'

The twins began to argue about which organ they'd be willing to donate to each other if they needed it.

Piper let their conversation wash over her as she prayed all would be well with Luke, the bone marrow and the baby growing inside her.

Bobby's Diary

Jess has Luke's fighter cells transplanted inside her now and they're going to kick all Jess's bad cells down and punch them and kill them, and Mummy said that hopefully now Jess will go from parshell remishen to complete remishen. And now Jess will get to come home and that is very good news for me. Someone to lissen to me at last!

Everyone is happy cos we ALL know that Luke's cells will make Jess better. When Mummy came home from the hospital with Luke after they took the fighter cells out of him, Granddad hugged Luke and he haded tears in his eyes. He kept saying, 'I'm proud of you, Luke, so proud.'

When Nathalie sawed Granddad with tears she got tears in her eyes. Nathalie never cries! She's super-tuff.

Granddad says that French women are tuff cookies but that they are also very forgiving cos they turn a blind eye to their husbands wanderings. I don't realy understand Granddad sometimes, but he seems to think that the French women being blind in one eye and letting their husbands wander about is a good thing. I think it sounds dangerous. Besides, Nathalie has two normal eyes so I don't get it. Maybe French women go blind in one eye when they get married? But then why wood anyone want to get married?

Jess can come home soon wich is making everyone super-happy. Mummy is all smiley now and I hearded her singing in the shower yesterday.

Luke is super-happy too cos everyone keeps saying how great he is for helping Jess. Even Daddy said it!

He came over to Granddad's house and told Luke he was super-proud of him. Luke shrugged like he didn't care but I could tell he did cos his face went all red.

Granddad normally doesn't even speak to Daddy but he offered him a cup of coffee! Daddy said he'd love one but then his phone rang and he had to go. Jenny had some mergensy.

'She probably broke a nail,' Luke said, and me and Granddad and Mummy laughed. It was nice to see Mummy laughing. I felt all warm inside.

So, that's the good news. The bad news is that the play in school is a disaster and I don't want to be in it any more.

First of all it took Declan ages to say 'Are there any rooms free?' He got stuck on 'There' and T isn't even one of his bad letters! I think maybe he was nervous. Anyway, I decided to help him out so when we prak-tised the same lines again, I saw him begining to stuter on 'There', so I said: 'Don't bother asking for a room, Joseph. This inn is full.'

Declan got all grumpy and pushed me and said I was robbing his lines. Except it took him ages to say 'robbing', he got stuck on the R, which is one of his bad letters, so I said it for him but it made him even more crazy.

I know Mrs Lorgan said no one should finish Declan's words because it is important for him to speak for himself, but he was so red in his face I thawt he might have a heart attack so I was trying to help. I don't think Mrs Lorgan will be too happy if one of the kids in her class dies.

Declan pushed me really hard after I said 'robbing' and I banged my elbow on the side of a chair and it hurt. But Mrs Lorgan didn't even ask me if I was alrite. She said 'Let Declan say his lines and do not interupt.'

It's just so dum. Every time we practise the play, the first bit with Mary and the angel Gabriel takes about five minutes and then Declan/Joseph comes in and starts stutering and we all have to stand around and wait . . . and wait.

But Declan isn't the only problem. Tommy is being a total pain. He finaly agreed to be the donkey but today, every time I tried to say my lines he made a 'neigh neigh' sound really loud so no one could hear me.

Mrs Lorgan told him to stop but he said he was just getting into his part as the donkey. Mrs Lorgan was called out for a 'quik word' by the gym teacher and she told us to practise again. Tommy did the noise again. So I shouted at him to stop.

He shouted back, 'It's the same as you robbing Declan's lines.'

I had enuff of Tommy so I told him he was a rubbish donkey and that he was stupid becos a donkey says 'hee-haw' and a horse says 'neigh'.

Tommy said that knowing boring facts doesnt make me smart, it makes me weird. He said no one in the class is intrested in my stupid facts and that his Mum said I was 'special', like his brother with Down Sindrum.

'You're special needs,' Tommy said.

'I am not. I'm smart.'

'You're a weirdo,' Tommy said.

'Yeah,' Declan joined in, 'you're a d-d-d-d—'

'Dork?' Tommy tried to help Declan.

Declan shook his head. 'D-d—'

'Dickhead?' Tommy wispered.

Declan shook his head again. 'D-d—'

'Dumbass?' Tommy tried again.

'No!' Declan shouted. 'D-dweeb.'

I hate them all, even Mrs Lorgan, and I know it's bad to hate your teecher but I do.

I was so glad when school was over and Mummy came to collect me. I love when she comes to collect me. She used to all the time but since Jess got sick it's only some times. But when she does we have a chat on the walk home and she asks me things and it feels like everything isn't different and scary. I let her hold my hand and I don't care who sees. I like holding her hand. It makes me feel safer.

When we got home, Mummy didn't rush off to make phone calls or to go to the hospital. She made me a hot choclate and sat down and talked to me. She asked me about school and I was going to tell her all about the play but then Nathalie came in and said there was a man who wanted to tell Mummy that the coffee was the best he ever had. Mummy looked confused.

'Who is it?'

'I don't know. A hairy man who say you tell him the coffee 'ere is fantastic and he agree with you.'

Mummy went to peep out the door into the café and then she did a big smile. I looked out to see who she was smiling at.

She walked over to a man with a big beard and crinkly eyes. They had a little chat and then I heard her say about Jess and the rem-ishen. The beardy man put his arms up in the air and cheered and Mummy laughed.

'He is not perfect. *Un peu* caveman. But the beard can be fixed and he has nice eyes and a kind smile. He's not so bad,' Nathalie said.

I don't know what she was talking about. I think maybe she's in love with the beardy man. I was going to tell her about French women getting married and going blind in one eye and not knowing where there husbands went wandering off to, but it's a bit confus-ing so I'll let Granddad tell her.

23

Kate stood at the kitchen window, looking out over the small garden. There was nothing much to see on the cold December morning, but suddenly the bare tree looked beautiful, not bleak. She could hear birds twittering and a dog barking in the distance. It was as if a fog had been lifted from her. Kate couldn't remember seeing or hearing things clearly for months.

She felt lighter and younger. The constant headache had lifted and the tension in her neck was gone. Jess was in partial remission and Luke's bone marrow would get her into complete remission. Kate knew it was going to work. Jess looked better already. They had to wait four weeks until they could test to see if she was in complete remission, and Kate was determined to make those four weeks wonderful and distract them all from the waiting.

The fact that the weeks fell over the Christmas period was perfect. Another good sign that all would be well. It was a turning point. She could feel it in her bones. Their lives were going to get better. Jess would get well and they'd be happy again. She was even getting on well with Nick. Life was good right now. Kate was determined to grab the 'good' with both hands.

Recently her life had shrunk to home and hospital, but today she was taking Jess horse-riding. She was so happy that Jess was getting a chance to ride again. She knew it would give her a great lift.

Hazel had organized it. She said it was her Christmas present to Jess. She'd rung Kate and insisted on doing it.

'Chloë told me how much Jess loves riding, so please let me do this for her,' Hazel had said. 'We love Jess and we feel so helpless, so you'd be doing me a favour by letting me sort this out.'

It was amazing, really. Kate didn't know Hazel well. They had that mothers-of-kids-who-are-friends relationship – a little chat on the doorstep here and there, but that was it. They were different. Hazel lived a life of luxury, and Kate could barely pay her bills, so she felt they didn't have much in common, yet since Jess had been diagnosed, Hazel had been incredibly kind.

Aside from buying Jess clothes and treats that Chloë brought in on her visits, Hazel constantly texted Kate to check in with her. One particularly bad day during Jess's infection, Kate had come home to a big box of Jo Malone shower gels, candles and perfumes. There it was, sitting on the doorstep, with a big bow and a note that said, 'Thinking of you. Hazel.'

Kate had always liked Chloë, but she had worried that Chloë was a bit spoilt. How wrong she was. Chloë did have everything a girl could dream of, but it hadn't made her spoilt at all. In fact, she was the most generous, loyal friend Jess could possibly have had. Some of Jess's other friends had made an effort in the beginning, but they had gradually tailed off when Jess never returned to school.

Chloë, however, was ever-present. Kate had grown very fond of her. She bounded into the hospital in her bright clothes talking non-stop about things a twelve-year-old should be talking about – annoying classmates, boys, make-up, hairstyles, clothes . . . Kate loved seeing Jess giggling with Chloë about silly things. It made her worry less about Jess's childhood being stolen.

She heard footsteps and turned around. Luke opened the fridge and began pulling out mounds of food. Luke, her hero. Kate smiled at him. 'Morning.'

'Hey,' he croaked, and began to fry some eggs.

'Sit down, I'll do that for you.' Kate went over to the cooker. 'Four eggs? Seriously?'

Luke cut three big slices of granary bread. 'The coach is still saying I have to get my protein intake up. Besides, I finally feel hungry again so I'm going for it.'

'I'm really proud of you, Luke.'

'For making the team?' Luke grinned.

'Yes, and for helping to save your sister.'

Luke squirmed in his chair. 'I wish everyone would stop saying that, Mum. I didn't save her. She's not cured yet. I just helped.'

'Well, thank you.'

'Sure.'

Kate lifted the fried eggs onto a plate and handed it to Luke. 'So how are things with you? Is everything all right with school and Piper?'

Luke shovelled a full egg into his mouth and chewed. 'School is okay. Piper is good. She was so happy about Jess she cried for half an hour, like rivers of tears. We're going to catch a movie later.'

'She's lovely. I'm really glad you met her.'

Kate watched a smile spread across Luke's face. 'Yeah, she's pretty great. I'm lucky.'

'She's lucky too. You're pretty fantastic yourself.'

Luke flexed his arm. 'Yeah, I'm not bad.'

Kate coughed. 'So are you guys . . .'

Luke put his hand up. 'Stop. Don't even go there.'

'Luke, I need to know that if you're having sex you're being careful.'

Luke put down his slice of bread. 'You're ruining my appetite. Please stop talking.'

'Luke? I need to know.'

'Oh, God.' Luke looked down at his food, blushing. 'Yes, Mum, we are careful.'

'Good.'

The door opened and Jess came in. 'Morning,' she said, beaming.

Kate jumped up. 'Morning, sweetheart. How did you sleep? How do you feel? Sit down and I'll get you something to eat.'

Jess shook her head. 'I'm fine, Mum. I'll get my own breakfast. I'd like to. Let me make you a cup of coffee.'

'Don't be silly. Sit down and save your energy.'

'Mum!' Luke caught her eye. 'Let Jess do it. She wants to.'

Kate did as she was told. It felt very strange to be sitting still while Jess made her coffee. She wanted to jump up and carry the kettle for her. Jess's arms were like two little twigs and Kate was worried she'd drop the kettle or burn herself when she poured the hot water into the coffee cup, or trip or stumble or . . . Breathe, she told herself. Breathe and let Jess do this.

It was very difficult, but Kate managed to stay seated and not jump up, although she almost did when Jess made a little 'oof' sound, as she picked up the heavy kettle. As she moved to help her, Luke reached out and grabbed her hand. 'Don't, Mum,' he whispered. 'She wants to feel normal again. Stop fussing.'

Jess came over with a cup of coffee and placed it in front of her. 'There you go, Mum.' She was smiling from ear to ear.

Kate took a sip. 'Well, that's the nicest cup of coffee I ever tasted.'

Jess rolled her eyes. 'You don't have to say that.'

'It is, though, Jess, because you made it.'

'Favourite child!' Luke exclaimed. 'I always knew it.'

'I don't think so, Golden Boy,' Jess retorted.

'Yeah, right.' Luke swatted his sister with his hand, grinning. 'It's always been "Jess is so helpful", "Jess is so thoughtful", "Jess is so perfect".'

'That's such rubbish. It's all "Luke is so great at rugby", "Luke is so handsome", "Luke is such a good example to the other two".'

'Well, I am.' Brother and sister laughed.

Watching her two children bantering back and forth, laughing together, looking so happy made Kate want to jump up and down and shout, '*Yeeeeees!*' Life was almost back to normal, and it felt so good. She took out her phone and texted Maggie: *Good news! All going well with Jess. Get yourself over here later if you can. I'm opening the pink champagne tonight! x*

Kate drove towards a huge house, then followed the signs for 'Stables' around the back and down a laneway that led into a large yard.

'Wow,' Jess said. 'This is incredible. Look at that horse, Mum! It's so beautiful.'

Kate watched as it was led out of the stables. It looked like a thoroughbred racehorse, the kind you'd see at the races.

Hazel had said something about a friend of theirs who had horses and would be delighted to have Jess up for a ride. This was like a professional riding stable. Kate could see at least ten horses peeping out from their boxes.

A huge black Range Rover pulled up beside them and Chloë waved out of the window.

Kate and Jess got out of the car. Kate wrapped Jess's scarf around her neck. 'Are you sure you're warm enough?'

'Oh, Mum – yes!' Jess wriggled away from her and ran over to Chloë. The two girls hugged.

Kate joined Hazel, who was wearing a long fur coat that must have taken many animals to make.

'Hi,' Hazel said warmly, and hugged Kate, then Jess.

'Your coat is so soft,' Jess said.

'She's a murderer,' Chloë said. 'It's rabbit. Real rabbit fur. Hundreds of poor bunnies died so Mum could wear that coat.'

Hazel stroked it. 'Darling, there are far too many rabbits in the world. They're not exactly an endangered species.'

'They will be if you keep buying coats like that,' Chloë reprimanded.

'Kate and Jess didn't come here to listen to a save-the-rabbits speech. Now, come on, Julian's waiting for us.'

Julian turned out to be the stable manager. He was lovely with the girls. He introduced Jess to all the horses and told her he'd picked a very special one for her to ride.

'This place is amazing,' Kate said. 'Thanks so much for arranging it.'

'My friend Louise got it in the divorce settlement.'

'Some settlement,' Kate noted.

Hazel dropped her voice. 'She found her husband in bed with one of the stable boys – I know it sounds like a Jilly Cooper novel, but it actually happened.'

Kate giggled.

'He didn't want anyone to know, so he gave her everything she wanted in the divorce.'

'Is she here? I'd like to thank her.'

'No, she hates horses. She spends all of her time at her house in Turks and Caicos.'

Kate was incredulous. 'Why did she want the stables if she hates horses?'

Hazel raised an eyebrow. 'Because she didn't want him to have them. I'd be the same if my Keith cheated on me, I'd take the house in Portugal even though it's on a golf course and I hate golf. You've got to get them where they hurt.'

Nick didn't have anything for me to take, Kate thought. All he had were debts.

Jess and Chloë came out riding two gorgeous brown horses with shiny manes.

'Mum, my horse is called Jess!' Jess said.

'She's the best we have.' Julian winked.

Kate went over to have a word with him. 'Is she a calm horse? Jess cannot fall off – it would be a disaster.'

'Don't worry,' Julian said. 'Hazel filled me in. Jess is going to have a great time and be completely safe. If it's any comfort at all, my niece had leukaemia when she was a kid. She's twenty-seven now, got married last week.'

Kate wanted to kiss him. 'That's a huge comfort, thank you. I love hearing stories like that.'

'Come on, Julian, let's go!' Jess called out.

'Jess, don't be rude.'

'She's not rude, just keen. We like that. All right, let's go to the indoor arena and have some fun.'

To Hazel and Kate, he said, 'Ladies, I'll get one of the lads to make coffee for you. He'll bring it into the arena. It'll keep you warm while you're watching. What would you like?'

'I'll have a decaf skinny latte, please,' Hazel asked.

'Can you do lattes?' Kate was amazed.

'We have the best coffee machine in town. Louise gave it to us last Christmas.' Julian smiled.

'Wow! I'd love a cappuccino.'

Indoor arenas, coffee delivered to you by stable-hands . . . This was the life, Kate thought. She should have married a millionaire.

As she walked to the arena with Hazel, she muttered, 'I married for love the first time, but if I ever get married again, it'll be for money. I could get used to this.'

Hazel laughed. 'It's nice, all right. Not having to worry about money is a huge thing. Believe me, I know. My dad died when I was four and Mum brought me and my three brothers up on very little money. As Keith always says, "You weren't born to money, Hazel, but you certainly got used to it very quickly."'

They both cracked up laughing.

'The thing is, though, when you look at Jess and what's happened, you realize that money means nothing, really,' Hazel said. 'Health is wealth, right?'

'Yes,' Kate said. Her mother used to say that. 'It really is. It's strange, I never thought about the kids getting sick. I always worried about them being in car crashes, or drowning in swimming pools or falling out of trees, but never, ever cancer.'

'I know what you mean. When I think cancer I think older people, breast cancer or prostate, never a young girl,' Hazel agreed.

A stable boy arrived with their coffee and a plate of chocolate biscuits. They thanked him.

Kate took a sip: the coffee was delicious. She watched Jess as Julian guided her carefully over a small jump and praised her. Jess beamed.

She looked so much smaller than Chloë now. She was so thin and frail. Beside her, Chloë was a picture of health. Jess's stick-like legs clung to the saddle in jodhpurs that were once almost too small for her but now flapped about her thighs like flags.

'She's a great kid, Kate, and you're a brilliant mum. I don't know how you do it. I can barely cope with Chloë. I'd have liked more kids but . . . well . . .'

'What happened?' Kate asked gently.

'I had really bad haemorrhaging after Chloë was born and they had to do a hysterectomy.'

'I'm sorry.'

'Yeah, me too. I'd have liked her to have siblings. We thought about adopting, but Keith wasn't keen on social workers poking their noses into our lives and our finances. So we agreed that we'd stick with Chloë and give her the best life possible.'

'Well, you're certainly doing that.'

Hazel nodded, and Kate saw that her eyes were full of tears. Suddenly they had gone from idle chit-chat on the doorstep to a very intense personal conversation. It happened to Kate all the time now. Whenever she bumped into someone there was no small-talk about the weather or how the café was doing, people told her really personal things. She didn't know why. Maybe it was because her life was so serious now and they wanted to relate to her somehow by telling her their stories of struggle. Or maybe they wanted to have proper conversations about real issues but hadn't known how to do it before. Whatever the reason, in the last few months Kate had found out more about people than she ever had before Jess became ill.

Chloë cantered towards a small jump, but pulled up her horse in front of it. 'I can't do it.'

Jess cried, 'Come on, Chloë, if I can do it with cancer, you can too.'

'Maybe cancer makes you braver,' Chloë replied.

Jess looked thoughtful. 'Maybe it does. I guess when you face dying, nothing else seems very scary.'

'You see? It's easier for you,' Chloë said.

Hazel stood up to scold her, but Kate pulled her down. 'Don't. Please. It's good for Jess to talk freely about her cancer. I've never heard her do it before so she's obviously feeling very relaxed. It's great that Chloë isn't tiptoeing around her.'

Jess squeezed her horse with her legs and soared easily over the jump. 'See? It's not hard.'

Julian, tactfully saying nothing, pulled Chloë's horse back around.

'When I get close, I panic. What do you do when you're just in front of the jump?' Chloë asked Jess.

Jess patted her horse's neck. 'I close my eyes and trust the horse. A horse won't let you down if you trust it. They have to feel like you're their friend. When I jump, I feel like I'm flying. I feel like nothing can touch me or hurt me. Like I'm free from . . . well, everything, like pain and cancer.'

Kate gripped her hands together. While it was lovely to hear Jess talking freely about cancer, it was also incredibly difficult. She hated her daughter having these thoughts, that her grasp of life's cruellest lessons had been forced on her so young.

'She's amazing,' Hazel said quietly. 'She's so mature and brave.'

'I know,' Kate agreed. 'I just wish to God she didn't have to be. I wish her life was normal and carefree. Life gets so complicated when you're older. Kids should just be kids. She shouldn't have to deal with chemo and bone-marrow transplants and infections. She should just be horse-riding and going to school and having fun.'

Hazel put down her coffee cup. 'You're right. It's completely crap. But, you know, when she comes through this, Jess'll be even more extraordinary than she already is. The very first time I met Jess I said to Chloë, "There's something special about her. It's like she's been here before. She's got an old soul."'

'My mother used to say that about her,' Kate said. 'As well as that thing about health being wealth.' She felt a sudden pain in her heart. She wished her mother was there now.

She'd know what to do and say and how to reassure Kate that it was going to be okay. She'd tell her not to worry about the cancer coming back, to take the good news about the remission and trust it. She would have swept away Kate's nagging worry that it wasn't over yet.

She tried to remember the mindfulness teacher's advice: breathe and live in the moment. She focused on Jess's beaming face, not on her emaciated body. She concentrated on her daughter being in her happiest place, on the back of a horse, feeling free. She fought against the negative fears that were always there, crowded at the edge of her mind.

Please let it be over, she thought.

24

Nick handed Jenny a tissue and tried to be sympathetic. He was going to be late to pick up Jess now. Damn.

'I just feel so alone, Nick. You're always at work or visiting Jess, and I know she's sick and you need to spend time with her, but I seem to be the last person on your list of priorities. I miss you, and Jaden misses you too. I want you to have a good relationship with him. I want you to be best friends.'

Nick stiffened. 'My relationship with Jaden is fine. He's a baby, Jenny. All he wants is to eat and sleep.'

Jenny sniffled. 'You just don't get it, Nick. You form a bond with your baby from the minute they're born. It says so in all the books. You need to spend more time with Jaden and me. I hate being stuck in this apartment all day. When you do come home, you're always tired and narky.'

Nick tried to remain calm. He knew if he upset her he'd never get away. 'Look, Jenny, I know you're finding it all a bit difficult but I'm working my arse off to pay for everything for both families and I'm trying to be there for my daughter, who has cancer, and, yes, I am tired all the time. I'm tired and worried and really stressed about Jess.'

Jenny started crying. 'I just want it to be back to the way it was when we had fun and you looked after me and made me feel so special. I don't like this life. I don't think I'm made to be a mother. My own mother was shit at it and maybe I'm no good either. I find it really hard and scary. I keep panicking and thinking Jaden's going to get cancer and die, or something else terrible is going to happen to him. What if the cancer's genetic?'

Nick glanced at the clock. Damn. He was twenty minutes late. 'It's not genetic. Jaden's fine. Please, Jenny, you need to calm down. You're a great mother and Jaden is a really happy kid. Look, Jess's treatment will be over in a few months and she'll be well again, and we can all go back to normal.' He hoped he sounded more confident than he felt. Every time he looked at Jess he felt as if he was being punched in the chest. She was so sick.

He leant over and gave Jenny a hug. 'I've got to go. I promised Jess I'd pick her up. I'll come back tonight and cook you dinner and we'll open a bottle of wine. How about that?'

Jenny nodded. 'Sounds good. But be home by six. I want you to play with Jaden before he goes to bed. My dad was never around, and I want Jaden and you to be really close.'

Nick rushed out of the apartment and drove like a maniac to collect Jess. She was waiting at the front door for him, wrapped up in her winter coat.

'Sorry!' Nick said, as he hugged her. 'I'm really sorry. Did you text Larry to say we were running late?'

'Yes, it's fine. It's not like he's going anywhere,' Jess said, but she didn't smile.

'He'll be okay. He's a tough kid.'

Jess put on her seatbelt and looked out of the window. 'Not everyone gets better, Dad,' she said quietly.

Nick gripped the steering-wheel. 'But you will. Luke's bone marrow will cure you.'

Jess sighed. 'I wish everyone would stop telling me that. It might not. Some of the cancer is still in there. Luke's bone marrow may not cure me, Dad. Larry could die and so could I. That's a fact. Larry and Nathalie are the only people who actually let me say it.'

Nick slammed on the brakes to stop the car crashing into the one in front. The palms of his hands were damp with sweat. 'Please don't say that, Jess. We all just want you to get better and have the great life you deserve.'

'I want to get better too, but there's no guarantee. I can't make myself better. I'm trying, Dad, doing my best. I'm taking all the horrible drugs and praying and hoping and, well, I'm doing my best.' Jess began to cry.

Nick pulled into the car park and leant over to hug her. 'Oh, Jessie, I know you're trying, sweetheart. It's awful for you. I wish I could rip the cancer out of your body. But Luke's cells are going to cure you, I just know they are. Look at him – he's the fittest guy I know.' He tried not to get upset: he had to be strong for her. Jess's bird-like body trembled as she cried into his shoulder.

She pulled back and he handed her a tissue. Jess looked at herself in the mirror. 'I don't want Larry to know I've been crying.' She fished around in her bag and took out some make-up. Nick didn't like her wearing it – she seemed too young – but he wasn't going to stop her now.

Jess examined herself in the mirror. 'For a bald girl with cancer, I look okay.'

'You're beautiful, the most stunning girl in the world.'

She rolled her eyes. 'You have to say that. You're my dad.'

Nick smiled. 'True, but I mean it. I'm so proud of you, Jess, the way you're fighting this cancer. You've been so strong. We Higginses are warriors, and you get that from me. I know you'll be fine because you're not going to give up. None of us is going to give up until you're cured.'

Jess remained quiet. Nick was worried that maybe he'd come on too strong. But he wanted her to know that he was behind her and that it was vital she keep on fighting.

'Dad, can we go now?'

'Sure, of course.'

They walked into the hospital in silence, each lost in thought. Nick went with Jess to Haematology and Oncology and popped in to say hi to Larry. He seemed like a nice kid, but Nick didn't know him and didn't have time to get involved with any more kids. He made Jess laugh, though, and she seemed to like him so Nick was fine with that. He wanted Larry to get better, but he seemed to be getting worse. Nick didn't want Jess upset. He worried about the damage it would do to her morale if anything happened to Larry.

When Larry saw Jess his whole face lit up. 'Better late than never, I guess.' He grinned.

'Dad's fault,' Jess said.

'Sorry, I was late picking her up.'

''S okay. She's here now. So, what news from the outside world?'

Jess sat down on the side of his bed. 'I went horse-riding.'

'Did you fall off?'

'No! I was brilliant. I even did some jumps.'

'Bet it felt good.'

'Amazing. I didn't feel sick when I was riding. I was me again.'

'That's the best feeling. The longer you're sick, the harder it gets to forget.'

'I can see that. So how are you?'

'Not feeling too good. I think this chemo's going to kill me. It's the worst.'

'Yeah, but it'll make you better,' Nick said automatically. 'Stay positive.'

They both turned to face him.

'Seriously?' Larry raised an eyebrow.

Jess giggled. 'I know, they're all the same.'

'What?' Nick asked. 'I'm just trying to help. A positive attitude is important in all aspects of life.'

'It's also important to be able to be honest,' Larry said. 'I'm sorry, Mr H, but sometimes, after yet another day of puking your guts up into a bowl, feeling positive just isn't an option.'

Nick shuffled about uncomfortably. 'No, right – I mean, I get that. But in general it's good to stay focused and upbeat.'

'Is that for you or for us?' Larry looked directly at him.

'Well – I – for everyone,' Nick stuttered, unable to meet Larry's eye.

The door opened and a man came in. He handed Larry a bottle of water. 'Hi, Jess.'

'Hi, Mr Wilkinson. How are you?'

'Better for seeing you, thanks. You've come to visit?'

'Yep, can't keep me away.'

'You're some girl.' He smiled. Then, seeing Nick, he proffered a hand. 'Hi, I'm Norman, Larry's dad.'

'Nick, Jess's dad. Nice to meet you.' Nick moved towards the door, glad of the interruption and the opportunity to escape. 'I'll leave you guys to it. Is an hour enough time, Jess? I have to get back to the office for three.'

'Thanks, Dad.' Jess smiled.

Nick walked out, followed by Norman.

'She's a wonderful girl,' Norman said. 'It'll mean the world to Larry that she's come to visit.'

'Larry's a great kid. Jess is very fond of him.'

Norman smiled sadly. 'Yeah, he is. He can be a handful at times, but he's our pride and joy. He was a great footballer.'

'Really?' Nick said.

'Yep. Striker. We had every club in Dublin trying to poach him.'

'Wow. Well, I'm sure it'll take him a while to get back to form, but when he gets better he can go back to football.'

Norman shook his head. 'No, he's been out for eighteen months. His muscles are wasted. It'd take him years to get back to fitness and that's if . . . He's been in remission three times. We left here thinking it was over, but each time it came back. It gets harder to keep your hopes up.'

Nick didn't want to hear this. He wanted to hear the good stuff. He wanted to talk to the parents of kids who went into remission and stayed in remission. Kids who never came back. Kids who were back playing football and scoring goals. That was why he avoided the other parents on the ward. He didn't want to hear the bad stories. It was difficult enough to keep positive without hearing about other patients getting worse.

'Well, I'm sure he'll pull through. He seems like a tough boy.' He tried to move away.

'He is, Nick, but there are some things that, no matter how hard you try, you can't beat.'

'Well, hopefully he'll get a break this time. Kids are amazingly resilient. They're stronger than we think.'

'But not invincible.'

Fucking hell! Would this guy ever shove off? Nick did not want to listen to any negative talk. He refused to believe the worst could happen, no way. It was unthinkable.

'Well, I'm going to make a few work calls. Nice to meet you, Norman.'

'You, too, and you should be very proud of your lovely daughter.'

'I am, I really am.' Nick was choking up so he began to walk away. He *was* proud of Jess. So proud. She was his precious girl and he was damned if he was going to lose her.

25

Piper pulled at the waistband on her skirt. It wasn't going to close, no matter what. She rummaged around for a safety-pin.

There was a thump on the door.

'What the hell, Piper? I need to get my lip-gloss,' Penny shouted.

'Go away,' Piper snapped. She was in no mood for her sisters. Shit, shit, shit. Her stomach was beginning to grow and she still hadn't told Luke. She began to sweat as she imagined his face when she dropped the bombshell.

She pushed aside the twins' mounds of cheap make-up and found nothing. No safety-pin, no needle and thread, nothing to hold up her skirt. What the hell was she going to do?

'*Muuuuuum!* Piper's hogging the bathroom,' Penny roared.

'Open up, Piper. I need my hair spray.' Poppy shook the door handle.

God, this bloody house! You couldn't get a second's peace! Piper pulled her jumper down over her open skirt and flung the door open.

'There you go, you rude, ignorant pigs.' She stormed past her sisters.

'Jeez, relax,' Penny said.

'Yeah, seriously, who bit you in the arse?' Poppy said, and the twins giggled.

Piper went into her bedroom and slammed the door. Pauline was sitting up in bed with her laptop open on her knees. Piper began flinging drawers open and slamming them shut.

'What are you looking for? Maybe I can help before you tear the house down,' Pauline said.

'Don't you start! I just need a fucking safety-pin.' Piper kicked the bottom drawer of her bedside locker shut and sat down heavily on her bed.

Pauline opened her drawer and pulled out a little box of safety-pins, which she silently handed to her sister.

Piper muttered thanks and turned sideways to pin her skirt closed.

'I know,' Pauline said quietly.

'Know what?' Piper said, as she tried to close the safety-pin.

'I know why your skirt won't close.'

Piper stabbed herself with the pin. 'Ouch.' She was too distracted to pay attention to her sister's comment.

'Piper?'

'What? Jesus, I'm trying to concentrate here.' Piper snapped the safety-pin shut and breathed a sigh of relief.

Pauline got out of bed, went to the bedroom door and locked it.

'What are you doing?' Piper asked, picking up her schoolbag.

Pauline stared at her sister. 'Piper, I know.'

Piper froze. 'Know what?'

Pauline pointed to her stomach. 'I know you're pregnant.'

Piper's heart skipped a beat. 'What are you talking about?'

Pauline sat down on her bed opposite her sister. 'Piper, you can talk to me. I've known for a while, but I was waiting for you to tell me or Mum and Dad but you still haven't and you're going to start showing soon. How long are you planning on keeping it a secret?'

Piper sank down on her bed. 'I haven't told Luke yet.'

'Why not?' Pauline was clearly shocked.

'There's never a good time. Every time I go to tell him, something happens with Jess or rugby or – or – I dunno, life.' Piper pulled at a stray thread on her duvet cover. 'How did you guess?'

'Come on, we share a bedroom. I hear you tossing and turning at night and crying. I also heard you throwing up a couple of times and you keep touching your stomach.'

'Do you think anyone else has guessed?' Piper asked, her heart pounding.

Pauline laughed. 'You must be joking. The twins are far too self-obsessed, Posy is too young, Mum is too preoccupied with college and Dad probably thinks you're still a virgin.'

Piper winced. 'He's the one I'm dreading telling the most. He's going to be so disappointed in me.' She began to cry.

'I imagine he will be, very,' Pauline agreed.

'Thanks, Pauline, kick me while I'm down.' She sniffed.

'But he'll get over it. You've always been his favourite.'

Piper blew her nose. 'No, I'm not. Dad loves us all the same.'

Pauline snorted. 'No, he doesn't. He thinks the twins are vacuous, he likes Posy but finds her immature, and he doesn't get me at all. I'm far too serious for him.'

Piper felt uncomfortable because she knew Pauline was right. Piper was her dad's favourite and always had been.

Her mother was more subtle about which child she pre-ferred – Piper could see it was Posy, but Olivia was better at pretending she loved them all equally.

'How did it happen? You're a smart girl. Why didn't you use protection?'

'We were drunk and we didn't have any condoms and I thought a one-off would be okay if we were careful. I'm so stupid.' Piper covered her face with her hands and began to sob. Talking about it made it all so real. Suddenly it wasn't a little secret that she could ignore sometimes. It was real life. Piper was going to have a baby. She was going to be a teenage mother. Her life would never be the same. How the hell would she cope with a baby?

Pauline patted her awkwardly on the knee. Affection was not her sister's strong point so Piper appreciated the effort.

'Look, we all make mistakes. Well, some of us do. Anyway, the point is, what are you going to do? Do you want to have the baby? You don't have to, you know. If you want to go to London and have an abortion, I'll come with you.'

'Would you?' Piper was astounded.

Pauline nodded. 'Absolutely. Having a baby at eighteen could ruin your life, Piper. You've got to think very carefully about it. What if Luke doesn't want to know? What if you break up and you have to raise it on your own? How are you going to support it?'

Piper rubbed her eyes. She felt so weary. 'At first I was going to have an abortion, but now I don't want to. I kind of love the baby. I know I'm only about thirteen weeks gone but I feel protective of it. I can't get rid of it, I just can't.'

Pauline sighed. 'Think very carefully before making a final decision. You'll be this child's mother for the rest of your life. You may not be able to go to college or travel, like you wanted to, or have a successful career.'

'Come on, Pauline, lots of successful women have kids.'

'Not at eighteen they don't.'

'Well, I'm sure some of them do.'

Pauline stood up. 'All I'm saying is, deciding to have the baby will change your life for ever. So think carefully.'

Piper nodded. She thought about it all the time, but when it came down to getting rid of the baby or keeping it, her heart said, 'Keep it.'

'The thing is, Pauline, I saw Jess nearly die and it made me realize how precious life is. I can't get rid of this baby. I know it's going to change everything, I know Luke might break up with me, but I just can't have an abortion, even though I probably should.' Piper began to cry again.

There was a thump on the door. 'Hey, come on, narky head, you're going to be late for school. It's the Christmas carols today and I want to be on time,' Poppy called out.

Pauline went over to unlock the door. 'Before you make a final decision, Piper, you have to tell Luke. It's his baby, too. He should have a say in what happens, and at least you'll know where you stand with him. He might not react well. You need to be prepared for that.'

I am, Piper thought. I think he'll freak.

Luke hummed as he ate a huge bowl of egg noodles with chicken. Piper tried not to retch. The smell of chicken was one of her triggers. She was hoping the morning sickness would wear off soon.

'So where is everyone?' she asked.

'Mum's taken Jess and Bobby to get shoes and Granddad's working. So we have the place to ourselves for a while.' Luke grinned at Piper. 'When I've finished this, we could go to my room and hang out.'

Sex was the last thing on Piper's mind. Her stomach was twisting and turning. Now, she shouted inwardly, tell him now.

'So, uhm, Luke, there's something I need to talk to you about.'

Luke's phone pinged. He picked it up and laughed. 'Check out the photo Gavin just sent me.' He held his phone up so

Piper could see some lame photo of a donkey with a stupid sign on it. She wanted to get the phone and throw it across the room.

'So, anyway, as I was saying, I need to –'

Luke's phone rang. 'Hey, Gavin, hilarious pic, man,' he said, and began chatting about the upcoming rugby match. After missing the last one, he was hyped up about performing well this time.

Piper drummed her nails on the kitchen table and tried to resist the urge to turn the bowl of noodles upside-down on Luke's head. Yes, he was excited about the match, but what about the fact that she was sitting right in front of him, being ignored?

'Yeah, he was . . . He's a beast. Did you see the weights he was pumping? . . . I know . . . Savage session . . . I'm up for it, though. Bring on the match – we'll stuff those guys . . . No, they haven't a hope. They're not good upfront. Our forwards will kill them . . . Yeah . . . Yeah . . . I agree with you there . . .'

Piper's breathing was coming hard and fast. She'd had enough. Was Luke stupid, selfish or just immature? She'd told him she wanted to talk to him about something and he wasn't remotely interested or focused on her. Maybe he wasn't a great guy. Maybe Pauline was right – maybe he'd run a mile when he found out about the baby. Piper stared at her boyfriend. He was sitting in his school shirt and tie and he looked young. Too young to be a dad. Too young to have the responsibility of a baby.

'Dude, I know, he's class. Did you see his try last week? He was unstoppable . . . With Rocco on form, we're unbeatable . . . Yeah . . .'

Piper was wrong. She couldn't have this baby. They were kids themselves. How the hell could they possibly raise a child? They were still in school. What was she thinking? She should have had the abortion ages ago. Oh, God, it was a disaster. She must be mad thinking she could be a mum. Luke would dump her and she'd be living with her parents for the rest of her life – if they didn't kick her out when they found out she was up the pole at eighteen.

Piper stood up and rushed towards the door.

'Hey!' Luke called out.

Piper went to open the door but Luke grabbed her arm. 'Gotta go, Gavin,' he said into the phone, and threw his phone onto the countertop. 'Where are you going?' he asked.

'I have to get out of here.' Piper tugged at the door but Luke stopped her.

'What's wrong?'

'Nothing. Get out of my bloody way.'

Luke put his hands on her shoulders and made her turn to face him. 'Hey, Piper, what's going on? Talk to me.'

She looked down. She had no words. How do you tell your boyfriend that he's going to be a dad or else have to help pay for an abortion?

'Did something happen?' Luke's blue eyes were full of concern. 'Tell me. I'll fix it or help or whatever. Come on, Piper, it's me – you can tell me anything.'

Piper looked over his shoulder and tried to summon the courage and the words. Taking a deep breath she opened her mouth. 'It's –'

'Fuck, are you breaking up with me?' Luke moved away from her. 'That's it, isn't it?' Luke glared at her. 'Thanks a lot, Piper, thanks a fucking lot.'

Piper's blood pressure went through the roof. What the hell was wrong with Luke? Why couldn't he let her speak? 'WILL YOU SHUT UP AND LISTEN!' she screamed.

She had his attention now. Piper walked past him and stood at the opposite end of the room. 'I have to tell you something and I don't really know how to do it so I'm just going to blurt it out.'

'You cheated on me. Oh, Jesus, who with?' Luke's face darkened. 'Was it Harry? It'd better not be him.'

'Jesus, Luke, will you shut the fuck up!' Piper roared. 'I didn't cheat on you. I'm pregnant.'

Luke stared at Piper, his mouth hanging open like a fish's. She'd never seen anyone look so shocked. She'd wanted to tell him in a calm way, but he'd ruined it. She stood still and waited.

'Are you serious?' he eventually said.

'I can promise you this is no joke.'

'Like, how, when, what?' Luke's brow creased as he struggled to process the information.

Piper pulled out a chair and sat down. She felt exhausted. 'I guess it must have happened that night after you'd had the terrible dinner with your dad and we got drunk and you wanted to have sex but we didn't have any condoms.'

Luke sat down opposite her. 'But that was ages ago. I mean, what . . .'

'I think I'm about thirteen weeks pregnant,' she said.

'Why the hell didn't you tell me?'

Piper sighed. 'I tried. I tried to a million times, but something always happened, like Jess got the infection or you got dropped from the team or you had to donate bone marrow . . . Every single time I went to tell you, something got in the way.'

'Jesus, Piper, you should have just pulled me aside and told me. We see each other all the time. *Thirteen weeks?* You've known for all that time?'

Piper said nothing.

Luke chewed his thumbnail. 'A baby? What are we going to do? I mean, we're eighteen. We can't have a kid, can we? How can I tell Mum I've knocked you up when she's got so much shit to deal with? I can't do that to her. I just . . . What do you . . . What the hell are we going to do?'

Piper felt his fear and worry land heavily on her shoulders. She had to be calm and try to stay level-headed. She wished Luke would wrap his arms around her and tell her not to worry, that he'd fix it all or make it go away. But how could he? There was no magic wand for this.

'God, your dad! He'll kill me.' Luke's mind was racing.

Piper didn't care about her dad right now. She cared about what they were going to do. Luke hadn't mentioned abortion yet. She'd have to bring it up. Maybe he was afraid to.

'Well, my dad doesn't necessarily need to know. No one does.'

Luke stared across the table at her. Piper could almost see his mind working overtime. Biting his lip he said, 'Is that something you . . . I mean, is that what you want?'

Piper felt her throat closing over with stress and anxiety. 'I don't know what I want,' she croaked. 'I'm so confused and worried. I feel so alone.'

Luke came over and sat beside her. He held her hands. 'I'm here for you, babe. You're not alone. I'll do whatever you want to do.'

'Can we really bring up a baby?' Piper asked him.

Luke shrugged. 'I dunno. I guess technically we could, but . . . well, it would change everything. We'd be like parents and have to get jobs and an apartment and stuff.'

Piper was crying now. 'I don't want to give up my life, but I don't want to get rid of the baby either. It feels wrong.'

'It isn't, though. I mean, if we did go for an abortion, it would just be a decision. It's not wrong or bad or anything.'

'I know that, Luke, but I can feel the baby inside me. Maybe I'm imagining it, but I think I can. I'd feel so bad if I got rid of it.'

Luke rubbed her index finger. 'Well, then, we'll have it and just work it out. I can get a job and maybe study for a sport and performance degree at night.'

'What am I going to do? Sit in a tiny apartment all day with a baby?' Piper asked. She knew she was being unreasonable. Luke was just trying to figure things out, but suddenly she saw herself stuck at home, alone with a baby.

'No, you could work and study too. The baby could go to a nanny or crèche or something.'

'Do you have any idea how much that costs? Crèches and nannies are really expensive.'

'Piper, I'm trying here. Maybe your mum could mind the baby.'

'Why should she? She's busy.'

Luke was incredulous. 'Well, my mum can't. She's already looking after a sick child. There's no way we can dump a baby on her.'

Piper pulled her hands away. 'Well, you're not dumping this kid on my family to raise. It's your baby, too, and if you hadn't been so bloody insistent on having unprotected sex, I wouldn't be bloody well pregnant.'

Luke glared at her. 'Oh, so it's my fault. I don't remember you telling me to back off or pushing me away, Piper. I seem to remember you enjoying it.'

'I'm not saying it's your fault,' Piper said. 'I'm just . . . I'm scared, Luke.'

'Look, we don't need to have this stress in our lives. I can call Maggie. She'd help us, I know she would. And she wouldn't be judgemental. She'd find a clinic in London that could do the abortion, a good place, and we could stay with her for a few days. I could pretend to Mum that we'd just decided to go to London to visit Maggie. No one would find out.'

Piper paused. Now that she had told Luke, the reality of having a baby and raising it was hitting her hard. How could she bring up a baby when she was still living with her parents in an already cramped house? There was so much she wanted to do and see and experience. A baby would ruin all her plans. What if she broke up with Luke? It was possible: a baby would put their relationship under huge pressure.

Luke would get to walk away, but she'd be stuck with the baby. The woman always was. She could end up as a single mother, sitting in a bedsit all day long, living on welfare. Her stomach lurched. She didn't want that. She wanted a life full of adventure and excitement.

Maybe Luke was right. If Maggie could sort it out, then no one would have to find out and they could just do it and move on. Forget it had ever happened.

'Call Maggie. Let's see if she'll help and then we'll make a decision,' Piper said.

Luke picked up his phone, dialled Maggie's number and put the phone on loudspeaker.

She picked up after one ring. 'Is everything okay?' she asked, sounding worried.

'Everything's fine. Jess is good.'

'Oh, thank God! When I saw your number I almost had a heart attack.'

'Sorry, didn't mean to stress you out,' Luke said. 'Actually, Maggie, do you have a minute? I'm here with Piper and we need to talk to you about something.'

'Of course. Hi, Piper.'

'Hi, Maggie.' Piper twisted her fingers nervously as Luke took a deep breath and filled Maggie in on their situation. Maggie let him talk and said nothing until Luke finished. 'So we don't know what to do, but we think maybe we'll have an abortion, but we're not sure.'

'Well, I certainly wasn't expecting that. No pun intended,' she said.

Luke and Piper laughed weakly.

'Look, guys, this is a very serious decision. Luke, you've only just found out. You need to think about it for a few days. Taking some time to process the situation is important. Whatever decision you make, you must both be happy with it. If you have this baby, you will be parents to it for the rest of your lives. You don't get to walk away or change your mind. If you have an abortion, that decision will stay with you, too, but you will move on and it certainly gives you more options for your future. You are very young, and having a baby is a huge responsibility. Think very carefully about it all. But whatever you decide to do, I'll help you. I can arrange for you to be seen at a very good clinic over here, or if you decide to keep the baby I'll help you financially. But just remember, a baby is for life.'

Luke and Piper nodded. 'Thanks, Maggie,' Luke said. 'You're brilliant.'

'I'm here for you, Luke. You're the closest thing to family I have, so anything you need, just call. Now, can I talk to Piper privately, please?'

Luke raised an eyebrow. 'Uhm, sure.' He handed the phone to Piper.

He left the room. Piper switched the phone off loud-speaker and held it to her ear. 'Maggie?'

'Are you alone?'

'Yes.'

'Right, here's the deal. I'm going to be blunt with you because you seem like a great girl and I want the best for you and for Luke, who I adore. As the mother, you are going to be landed with bringing up this baby. Maybe you and Luke will make it. Maybe you'll get married and have other kids and things will work out great. But there is a big chance they might not. You need to think about that. You also need to think about your future and what you want to do with your life. Do you really want to be tied down at eighteen?'

Piper's head was spinning. Everything Maggie was saying she had thought about. It seemed that, suddenly, they were all leaning towards an abortion and it made sense. It made sense in every way but one: Piper loved this baby.

'Just put yourself first and think about it,' Maggie was saying. 'This is your choice, ultimately. Call me in a few days and let me know your decision. I'll do everything I can to help.'

'Thank you, Maggie. I really appreciate it.'

'No problem. I've gotta fly to a meeting now. Call me when you know what you want to do.'

Piper ended the call as Luke walked back into the kitchen. They stared at each other in silence. She knew he was wondering what her decision would be, and she was wondering what conclusion he'd reach. It was like that game she'd played as a kid, where someone thought of a number and you had to guess what it was. She was trying to read his mind. But this wasn't a game, and she wasn't a kid any more. This was possibly the biggest decision she would ever make in her life.

26

Chloë held Jess's hand as she led her into the classroom. Jess was shaking. Her legs felt like jelly. Mrs Fingleton had heard she was out of hospital and had invited her to come into school for a couple of hours, if she felt well enough.

Jess hadn't really wanted to go. She knew everyone would be staring at her and that it would feel weird. But then again, she did want to go because she wanted to feel normal again and going to school was what she would normally be doing.

When she'd tried on her uniform the night before, the skirt had literally slid to the floor and her shirt was like a tent. 'Try it on with this belt,' Mum had said.

But even with the belt, the skirt looked ridiculous. Her mother had turned around, pretending to look for socks, but Jess knew she was upset. Seeing herself in her uniform, with no hair and so skinny, was frightening. It was a punch in the face. The reality of what she had been through physically was plain to see. She was a different person now. The old Jess, who had filled out the uniform and sat in school with her thick hair in a ponytail, was gone.

'Just wear what you want, pet. Mrs Fingleton will understand. I'll text her tonight to explain,' her mother said.

Jess was relieved. At least now she could wear something that fitted her and she could hide her skinny arms under the cool sweatshirt that Chloë's mum had bought her.

Her mum had even let Jess put on a little bit of make-up. Just some foundation and some lip-gloss, but it had made her feel better. She knew she was as pale as a ghost and she didn't want everyone feeling sorry for her. She wore the black beanie hat with the diamanté and a pair of silver hoop earrings that her dad had bought her. She hated being bald, but the hat and the earrings were a distraction. She looked as good as she could under the circumstances. She did the breathing Mum had taught her from her mindfulness course and tried to calm her fluttering nerves.

She fiddled with the mask her mother wanted her to wear. She had promised to wear it to protect herself from germs but there was no way she was walking into that classroom with it over her mouth.

Chloë chatted away beside her. '. . . and Denise is, like, pretending she's your best friend ever. She keeps saying how much she misses you and how she's on WhatsApp to you all the time. Like, hello? I'm your best friend and Denise is just, like, a drama queen, attention-seeker. It makes me sick. Judy just sits there and agrees with everything she says. That girl has no personality, honestly. She's like Denise's lapdog. It's pathetic.' Chloë bounced along the corridor, pulling Jess with her.

Jess loved being with Chloë, who always cheered her up, but today she found her exhausting. She was so full of energy, life and chat that after the ten minutes they'd been together Jess wanted to lie down and sleep. She was wishing for the quiet of her house, sitting with Mum and just talking quietly or reading or watching movies together. She didn't want to be here. She didn't want to have to make small-talk with the girls in her class. She wanted to turn around and run.

She let go of Chloë's hand. 'Chloë, I can't . . . I just . . .'

Chloë grabbed her shoulders. 'Hey, I get it. You're worried it's going to be way too full-on with everyone crowding you and asking you about the cancer. Don't worry, Mrs Fingleton told everyone to leave you alone and just be normal.' Chloë snorted. 'Like any of *them* could be normal! Anyway, I'm your bodyguard today and I'll tell anyone who's annoying to piss off. I can be a bitch and they'll still be nice to me because of Dad being loaded. They all want to swim in my pool and play tennis and stuff.'

Jess grinned. 'Thanks.'

'By the way, how's Larry? Still "just friends"?'

Jess smiled. 'Yes, Chloë, we are just friends. He's okay. He's had a tough few weeks, but he sounded stronger yesterday. I'll see him in three days when I go back in for chemo.'

Chloë stopped outside the classroom. 'I'd say he's a super-hottie with hair. It's such a pain that you have to go back to hospital. I wish the stupid cancer would just disappear. I really miss you, Jess.'

'Me too,' Jess said.

'Are you ready?'

Jess nodded. With Chloë by her side, she'd be fine.

Jess saw her mum standing in the car park, waiting anxiously to see how she'd got on. She ran over and hugged her.

'Was it awful?' Kate asked.

'No . . . Well, kind of . . . It was just weird. I felt like an outsider.'

Jess had felt like an alien. Everyone had been very nice and welcoming, but no one had known what to say to her so she'd had to do all the chatting. Trying to be 'normal' was exhausting. She'd even cracked a joke about cancer that Larry had sent her the night before. He'd said it would break the ice if things were awkward.

'Doctor, Doctor, my hair keeps falling out, can you give me anything to keep it in?'

'Yes, here's a paper bag!'

When Larry had told her the joke, they had laughed for five minutes. Jess had laughed so much her stomach ached.

But when she told it in class, everyone was embarrassed. Well, everyone except Chloë, who laughed loudly, but it was a fake friend-helping-a-friend-out laugh, which was almost worse. Jess had wanted the floor to open up and swallow her. Then Freda had asked her how long it would take for her hair to grow back.

Chloë had stood between Jess and Freda, and hissed, 'It'll take as long as it takes, and when it does grow back it'll be beautiful, not like your fuzzy mop.'

When Laura asked her if chemo was really awful, Chloë had once again jumped in: 'What the hell kind of question is that? Of course it's awful. She's being pumped full of chemicals that make her puke all the time.'

Thankfully, it had been time to go after that. Jess had never been so grateful to get out of school.

Her mother hugged her. 'Come on, let's get you home. Maybe it wasn't such a good idea for you to go in. I'm sorry, pet. I thought it would be nice for you to see your pals and catch up for an hour this morning.'

Jess didn't want her to feel bad. 'It's fine, Mum. I'm sure after a few days it'll feel okay, but I'll need to get my energy back up before I go back to school.'

Her mother patted her arm and started the car. 'Of course you will. Please God, this next round of chemo will be the last and we can build you back up. Now, what do you fancy for your lunch?'

Jess just wanted to lie down and rest for a bit. She felt wiped out from the effort of being upbeat and chatting to everyone. But she knew if she said she didn't want to eat, her mum would worry. 'Can I have some crackers and maybe some ice cream?'

'I could make you a roast-chicken roll?'

'No, thanks, Mum. I'm not super-hungry.'

Her mother looked disappointed. 'Okay, crackers it is.'

When they got home, Jess sank gratefully into the chair and picked at some crackers. Her mum went to help serve lunch in the café. Granddad popped his head into the kitchen to see how she was.

'I'm okay, just a bit tired.'

'Not surprised, all those girls pecking about, asking you hundreds of questions, no doubt. You look worn out. Have a lie-down and rest. I've made your favourite shepherd's pie for dinner. We'll have it about six when Luke gets back from training.' George opened the fridge and pulled out some whipped cream. As he was heading back into the café, he said, 'By the way, has he said anything to you about being dropped or not playing well? He's in a fierce mood these last few days and he's not eating much, which means something must be wrong.'

Luke hadn't said anything to her but Granddad was right: he had been in a really bad mood. He had barely spoken to her, and when she'd gone in to say goodnight to him yesterday, he'd almost jumped out of his skin. She could see writing on his notepad. There were two columns and the title of one said 'Keep it'. She didn't see the other because Luke had slammed it face-down.

Jess had no idea what it meant, but she thought maybe he was fighting with Piper because she hadn't been around. 'Maybe he's having problems with Piper,' Jess said.

'That's what it is.' George waved a finger at her. 'You're a little genius. It makes sense – he's off his food and moping about. God, I hope she doesn't break up with him. He needs to be in good form and focused for the big game on Saturday. Besides, she's a nice girl, and I'd be sorry to see her go.'

A piece of cracker stuck in Jess's throat. She drank some water. She'd hate Luke and Piper to break up. 'Please, God, don't let them,' she prayed.

There was a knock on the back door. Granddad went to open it. Her dad was standing outside. 'Hi, I was passing and I thought I'd pop in to see Jess.'

Although Jess longed to go to bed she was glad to see him – she hadn't seen him all week.

'Come on in,' Granddad said, letting him past. 'I'll leave you to it. I've a big crowd in for lunch. Help yourself to tea, coffee and whatever,' he said, as he left the room.

Dad gave Jess a big hug, then went to put the kettle on and make himself a coffee. 'How are you, Jessie?'

She shrugged. 'Okay. A bit tired.'

He peered at her closely. 'You look it. You must be doing too much. You need to rest, Jess. It's not good for you to overdo it.'

'I'm not, Dad.' Jess didn't want to get into another argument with him about overdoing it. He was obsessed with her resting. If he had his way, she'd be in bed all day long and never allowed to move. He was just being protective, but it was still annoying. She needed to have a life. She was twelve! She was supposed to be running around having fun, not stuck inside, bald, with cancer.

'Were you out this morning?' he asked.

Her mother came in to say hello as Jess was finishing telling him about the school visit.

He glared at her. 'What the hell is she doing, going into a school full of germs and infections? For Christ's sake, Kate, she could have caught anything. Her bloody immune system is shot! What were you thinking? First horse-riding and now this! She needs to be kept indoors with minimal visitors. A good mother would know that.'

Jess winced as her mother thumped her hand on the kitchen table.

'A good mother? How dare you accuse me of not being a good mother? Don't waltz in here and start throwing your weight around. Jess went to school for one hour. It's important that she sees her pals and gets out a bit. She's been cooped up for weeks.'

He wasn't backing down. 'If she gets an infection it'll set her back again, and I'll blame you entirely.'

Jess's stomach twisted.

Her mother laughed bitterly. 'Well, no surprise there. You're like a child – you always blame everyone else.'

'I want Jess to be kept away from any risk of infection.'

'She wore a bloody mask! She'll be fine!'

Jess felt in her pocket. The mask was still there. She'd taken it off before she'd gone into school. She looked enough of a freak without it. She'd lied and told her mum she'd worn it. Now she started panicking. What if she did get another infection? Dad would blame Mum and it would actually be Jess's fault. What if she died because she was too vain to wear the mask? And what if Dad never spoke to Mum again because of her? She felt sick.

Calm down, breathe, she told herself desperately. She wouldn't get an infection. No one had been sick. No one had come close enough to infect her with anything. The only person she'd touched in school was Chloë. Everyone else had just huddled around, close but not close enough to come into contact with her. She'd hugged Denise, but it had been a fake hug and their faces hadn't touched. In fact, they were probably all scared of being infected with her cancer, rather than the other way round. I'll be fine, she told herself, and her stomach unclenched.

'. . . I'm with her every day. I know what she can handle.' Mum had her hands on her hips and her cheeks were red.

'Well, she looks wrecked,' Dad snapped.

Jess had had enough. 'I'm going to lie down.'

Dad pointed a finger at Mum. 'See? I told you she was tired.'

Jess spun around, eyes blazing. 'Yes, I am tired. I'm tired of you two fighting all the time. Just stop it. I'm sick of it.' She ran out of the kitchen, slamming the door behind her.

Jess was tucked up in bed reading *The Hunger Games* for the zillionth time. She wished she was strong like Katniss, not weak and sick. She loved the books: they took her away from the real world of cancer and hospital and needles, drugs, doctors and nurses and off into the world of Panem, fighting and alliances, love, danger and victory. It was all so exciting and urgent, so different from her boring life stuck in bed.

There was a gentle knock on the door.

'Come in,' Jess said.

Her mum and dad came in and stood at the end of her bed, looking guilty.

'We're sorry, pet,' Mum said, clearly upset.

'Yes, we didn't mean to argue in front of you,' Dad agreed.

'We're just worried about you and it's not fair to you to have to listen to us bickering about silly things. We just want the best for you, darling. We love you so much.' Mum came over and kissed Jess's forehead.

Dad sat down and held her hand. 'Sorry, Jess, I'm probably being overprotective, I just don't want anything to go wrong. We need to do everything we can to help you get better. I do think that, from now on, you need to stay away from crowded places, though. If you want to see your friends, they can come and visit one by one. Or maybe you can just leave seeing them until you're better. FaceTime them instead. Going to school wasn't the best idea.'

'Nick . . .'

'I'm just saying.'

'You said it already.'

He ignored her. 'I just think that for the –'

Jess held up her hands. The last thing she needed was a lecture from Dad. 'Okay, I get it.'

His mouth was set in an obstinate line. 'We all want the same thing,' he said. 'That's what's important. Even if your mother and I have different ideas about how to achieve it.'

Jess saw her mother's whole body stiffen as she didn't say all the things she so plainly wanted to yell at him. He was staring straight at Jess, not giving her mother a glance. The tension between them was unbearable.

'Everyone just wants you to be well again,' Mum said tightly. 'We're all on the same page.'

Dad nodded curtly. 'You will get better,' he said emphatically. 'It's non-negotiable. I won't let it be other–'

Jess cut across him. 'I said I get it, Dad. Now can I please be left alone to rest?'

They went out of the room, and Jess heard the harsh whispers of them arguing the whole way down the stairs.

She went back to her book to block out them and all the dark thoughts in her head.

Bobby's Diary

The Christmas play was a disaster. Mrs Lorgan is foorious with me and Tommy but not with Declan, wich is unfair as he was the kause of it.

Mummy and Luke and Jess and Granddad came to see it. Daddy was supposed to come but he didn't until it was nearly over and then he just sawed the fight.

Declan came out and asked me if I had a room. But he got stuk on a word he didn't get stuk on the day before at all. He said it perfektly. But maybe he got stage scared or something but he got stuk. He said r . . . r . . . r . . . r . . . and there was silence and I could feel all the parents staring at him and he was getting all red in the face and sweting and he looked all stresed so I saided, 'Sorry no room here.'

Then the donkey Tommy shouted, 'Mrs Lorgan said not to say his lines for him, you're a thick' and I got really cross so I told him to shut up and mind his own bizness that I was just trying to help.

Mrs Lorgan was hissing like a snake from the side of the stage to 'move on with the play'. So I stared at Declan and waited for him to say his next line but he just said,

'I hate you Bobby' and he didn't stuter one bit even though B is one of his bad letters. Then Tommy pushed me.

I saw Luke standing up like he was going to protect me so I did what he would do and I pushed Tommy back but he was wearing these clumpy shoes that were supposed to look like a donkey's hooves but they just looked really dum like they were his dad's shoes and so he wobbled and then fell over.

Mrs Lorgan shouted at me to 'behave and get on with the play'. So I went over to help Tommy to get up and he put out his hand like he wanted help and then he pulled me down and started wresling me.

Declan was shouting, 'Kill him Tommy, kill him' and he didn't stuter and K is one of his REALLY bad letters so it just shows you that aktualy he isn't such a bad stuterer when he wants to be.

Tommy punched me in my stomak wich hurts all the time since Jess got sick and I was nearly crying but I saw Dad standing at the back of the room staring up and I saided to myself to be strong.

Tommy's brother with the Down Sindrum was jumping up and down in front of the stage saying 'Go Tommy, go.' He doesn't seem sick at all, just a bit mad and obvioosly into fighting. Tommy's whole family are agro.

It all happened in about one second and then Mrs Lorgan came onto the stage and pulled Tommy off me and dragged us both off the stage.

It didn't actually matter cos our parts were over anyway. Mrs Lorgan blamed me for starting the hole thing cos I stole Declan's lines and so as usual I'm the bad guy.

But when it was over and we did our bows and everyone claped, Daddy and Mummy and Luke and Granddad and Jess came over to me and said well done. Luke said I was great and that Mrs Lorgan should have given me the best part cos I could act and the others were all 'losers'.

I told them I was in big trouble with Mrs Lorgan. Daddy saided that it was a 'farse giving a kid with a stuter the lead role' which I agreed with. But unfortunately Declan's Mummy was standing behind Daddy and hearded him say it and she got all angry and said that her son was a 'brave solider who was dealing with a disability with kourage'.

Daddy said a stuter was not a disability that it was a speech impediment and that he shouldn't get special treatment and that we all had 'shit going on' and that a kid shouldn't get a role just because it took him ten minutes to say his name.

Declan's Mummy said that Daddy was a 'very rude man with a hart of stone' and that he had no idea how dificult it was for Declan to deal with life with a stuter and that I was a 'mean boy and a bully'.

Mummy said, 'Excuse me but Bobby is a lovely boy and has a hart of gold. He was just trying to help Declan.'

Declan's Mummy said that everyone with half a brain knew that you did not finish words for stuterers.

Mummy said 'May I remind you that Bobby is seven.'

Then Tommy's Daddy came over with his brother and said that I was a 'nasty piece of work' for nocking his Tommy down.

Mummy reminded him that Tommy had pushed me first and I was just defending myself.

'He's a violent bully' Tommy's Dad said. He said that Tommy is a 'kind-harted boy who looks after his brother' and that life wasn't easy.

Daddy putted his hand on my shoulder and said that he saw the way Tommy punched me and that the only violent person was his son.

I was so happy that Daddy was on my side. It was brilliant.

Tommy's Daddy said Tommy was a lamb who minded his little brother who had chalinges.

He was going to say more but Luke throwed his hands in the air and shouted, 'Can everyone just shut the hell up. Bobby was trying to help the dude with the stuter, Tommy stuck his nose in where it didn't belong and got violent. Bobby is dealing with a sister who has cancer and nearly died a few weeks ago, so you can take your stuterers and your Down Sindrum kids and shove them where the sun doesn't shine. Bobby is the nicest kid in the world so if ever I hear

anyone call him a bully again I sware to God
I will lose it.'

Luke looked so big and tall and strong,
like a warior.

'Luke!' Mummy was shocked but she was kind
of smiling too.

Tommy's Daddy and Declan's Mummy just went
quiet and looked shoked. Granddad said, 'Time
to go' and rushed us all out of the school
before any more fighting could happen. I was
so proud that Luke was my brother. I told him
thanks and he said, 'no worries dude, don't
let anyone push you around and if they do, let
me know.'

Jess was quiet. I heard Mummy ask her if
she was alrite. Jess nodded but I could see she
had tears in her eyes. I don't know why.
Maybe she wished she had a stuter or Down
Sindrum instead of cancer.

So I asked her and she did a sad smile and
said 'A stuter maybe but not Down Sindrum
because you can't be cured.'

I thought Down Sindrum just meant you were
agro but obvioosly it's worser than that. I
feel a bit bad for Tommy's brother now and
for Tommy. A bit . . . but not loads cos he
punched my sore stomak.

27

Kate washed her hands with one of the sanitizers that were all over the house and in every bag and coat pocket she owned.

Bobby watched her from his bed. He was wearing his dinosaur pyjamas and looked very sweet and young. Kate went over and hugged him. 'What's that for?' he asked.

'It's for being a great boy.'

'Did you think I was a great boy when I ruined the Christmas play?' Bobby asked.

'Of course I did, and you didn't ruin it. It was Mrs Lorgan's silly casting of the wrong boys in the wrong roles. You were wonderful.'

'Mummy,' Bobby asked, his little forehead wrinkling, 'why does chemotherapy make you so sick?'

Kate paused. 'Well, it makes you sick but better at the same time.'

'Why can't they make a medicine that cures cancer without making you sick and bald?'

'I wish they could, Bobby, and when you grow up, maybe you can invent a chemotherapy that makes patients feel good instead of awful.'

'I will, Mummy. I'll invent that and then we can be rich and I can buy you a house and you won't have to wait for Daddy to pay you money to get us things, and I'll buy Jess a pony all of her own, and I'll buy Luke his own rugby pitch to practise on.'

'What about Daddy and Jaden and Jenny?' Kate asked. She wanted to try to get Bobby to like his half-brother at least a little. It worried her how much he disliked him.

Bobby frowned. 'I'll buy them a small house, but I'm not spending loads of money on them. I'm keeping it for us.'

'You know that when Jaden gets older he's going to look up to you like you look up to Luke?' She tried to appeal to his ego.

Bobby looked surprised. 'Will he?'

'Yes. You'll be his cool big brother and he'll want to be like you and spend time with you.'

Bobby closed his book of facts. 'But he's only my half-brother, not like me and Luke. He's not really our family, Mum. He's Daddy's family, and he's kind of stinky and stupid.'

Kate took Bobby's hand in hers. 'Listen to me. Jaden is your family and you must try to be nice to him. When he's a bit older, you can teach him your facts. He'd love that.'

'Would he? He seems dumb to me. All he does is cry.'

'That's because he's a baby, Bobby. Babies cry. When he's talking and walking you'll be able to teach him things and help him to be as smart as you are.'

Bobby seemed doubtful. 'We'll see about that. Anyway, he has Daddy to teach him stuff. Daddy's always with him.'

'Daddy's been popping in more often lately to see you.'

Bobby's big brown eyes looked up at her. 'He's been coming to see Jess, not me or Luke. Daddy cares about Jess and Jaden and Jenny. Maybe if my name started with a J he'd care about me too.'

Kate felt so sad for her little son. He was so in need of a proper father who paid him attention. It broke her heart. 'Daddy loves you and Luke just as much as Jess. He's obviously paying more attention to Jess at the moment because she's sick. He came to your play and he stood up for you. That was nice, wasn't it?'

'He was late and he missed my lines. Anyway, Luke was the one who really stood up for me.'

'Oh, Bobby . . .' Kate hugged him. 'Your dad loves you and I love you enough for a million mums and dads.'

Bobby snuggled his head into her shoulder. 'I know, Mummy, and I love you too, so don't get cancer and die. I want you here.'

Kate held him tighter. 'I'm not going anywhere and nor is Jess. We're all going to grow old together.'

Bobby wriggled out from her embrace. 'You're kind of suffocating me now.'

Kate laughed and pulled back.

'It's not funny, Mummy. Since 2000, the number of child suffocations per year has risen in the US from less than eight hundred to more than a thousand.'

Kate stopped laughing and tried to look serious. 'I doubt many of those are from mothers hugging their children.'

'Well, I don't want to be the first. Is Luke home yet?'

'No. He said he was going to study at Piper's.'

'Why is he grumpy all the time? I went into his room yesterday and he was on his computer and when I asked him what he was looking at he snapped it shut and shouted at me to get lost and pushed me out.'

Kate had noticed that Luke was short-tempered. 'He has a lot on his plate. His finals are coming up in six months, he's training really hard to stay on the team and he's worried about Jess, too.'

'So am I, you know, and I don't go around pushing people.' Kate looked at him and Bobby went red. 'Well, not unless they push me first.'

Kate leant over and put his book on the bedside locker. She kissed his forehead and tried not to mind when she saw him rubbing it off. Switching off the light, she said goodnight.

As she was leaving the room she heard Bobby's tired voice say, 'I'm really glad you're my mummy.'

'And I'm thrilled you're my little boy.' Kate smiled into the darkness and quietly made her way down to the kitchen.

She glanced at the clock. She was supposed to be at her mindfulness course but she really wasn't in the mood. She was planning on Skyping Maggie and having a drink and a chat with her instead. She was pouring herself a glass of wine when she heard a knock on the back door. She pulled it open. Liam was standing there with snowflakes on his hair and beard.

'Hi.' Kate was surprised to see him.

'Sorry,' he said, 'I didn't mean to disturb you but there doesn't seem to be anyone doing mindfulness tonight. The room is empty and I wondered if it was cancelled because of the weather.'

Kate hadn't realized it was snowing. She'd left the door unlocked for the teacher and the class before putting Bobby to bed. 'Gosh, it really is pelting down. Come on in.'

Liam hesitated. 'I don't want to come on top of your family.'

'Don't be silly. I'm here on my own. Dad's in the shop sampling the new wines that have just come in with his friend Bill. Bobby's in bed, so is Jess, and Luke is out.'

'Well, just for a minute.'

Kate offered him a glass of wine. Liam shrugged off his coat and accepted it.

'The class must be cancelled – she's never been late before. Mind you, she should have sent a text if it is.' Kate took a sip of her wine.

At that moment Liam's phone buzzed. He looked down. 'Ah! She's apologizing for cancelling at the last minute but her car won't start.'

'I wasn't going tonight anyway. Just didn't feel like it.'

Liam smiled. 'Neither did I, but my daughter called in to make sure I went. I think she knew that after the first three my enthusiasm was waning.'

'Do you think it's just us?' Kate asked. 'The others seem to really get into it. I just can't switch my mind off and the swaying to music just makes me want to laugh.'

Liam grinned. 'It's very awkward for a fella like me who has two left feet and no balance.'

Kate giggled. 'I noticed that when you knocked me over in the first class.'

'I'm still mortified.' He chuckled.

They sipped their wine companionably. He was nice in a big-bear sort of way, Kate thought. Maggie had asked her if she fancied him when she'd told her about him coming to the coffee shop and being so nice about Jess. But she didn't fancy him. He was too . . . well, hairy and squidgy. The opposite of Nick, who waxed his back and shaved every day and was fit and toned. At least, he had been before his life became one long stressful problem. He probably got very little time to work out now. Just like me, she thought ruefully.

Kate knew she should try to fall for someone like Liam, who was kind and wouldn't cheat on you, but you can't make yourself like someone when there's no chemistry. She liked him as a man friend. She wasn't remotely embarrassed about Liam seeing her tonight in her slippers with no make-up on and wearing an old baggy sweatshirt. She felt comfortable with him, and it was nice.

'So how's Jess?' he asked.

Kate put down her glass. 'She's been doing really well since the bone-marrow transplant so things are better. I'm feeling really hopeful. I'm just so glad the chemo and transplant are over. It's been so hard on her little body.'

Liam shook his head. 'It's a terrible thing. My wife was so sick on chemo – I can't imagine how awful it must be for a child.'

'I just don't understand why, with all the money and funding that is put into cancer research, they haven't come up with something less aggressive to cure it.'

'June's oncologist used to say you have to fight fire with fire. Sometimes I wanted to punch him when he said it.'

'Sometimes I want to punch everyone,' Kate said.

'It's very hard on you as the mum, with two other children to worry about. My kids were all adults when June was diagnosed. They still suffered terribly but at least they were able to look after themselves and stay with her in the hospital when I needed to go home.'

Kate nodded. 'Still awful, though.'

'Yes, it was,' Liam said quietly.

'Do you miss her?'

'Yes. It's the quietness of the house. It's been nearly three years and I still can't get used to it. I think the hardest part is when something happens, like when Grace got engaged and I wanted to talk to June about it and celebrate together, but it was just me and the dog.'

'I miss that, too. I miss sitting on the couch and talking to Nick about the kids or what happened that day. In fairness, I don't miss it right now because he's driving me crazy, but in the beginning I did.'

'I don't think humans are built to be alone,' Liam said.

Kate agreed. Before Jess had got sick and her mind had filled with tests, research and terror, she used to wonder what would happen to her when the kids left home. She was afraid of turning into a sad old lady, with cats, who lived alone, watched daytime TV and got fatter by the hour. Maggie told her she was being ridiculous, that empty-nest syndrome was rubbish, and she'd have the time of her life, that she could come and live with Maggie and shag handsome younger men, get a job and have a ball.

Kate couldn't see herself living Maggie's life, though. She didn't want to sleep with younger men: she wanted to meet a Nick who didn't cheat.

'Anyway, it's great news about Jess, with the transplant going well, I'm really pleased for you.' Liam fished about in his pocket and pulled out a small plastic pouch with something silver in it. 'I hope you don't mind, but I wanted to give you this.' He handed it to her.

'What is it?'

'It's a medal of St Peregrine, the patron saint of healing for those who suffer with cancer and other life-threatening illnesses. I thought Jess might like to keep it beside her bed or under her pillow.'

Kate looked down at the medal, tried to hold back tears and failed. It was such a kind and thoughtful gesture. She stood up and hugged him. 'Thank you.'

Liam patted her on the back. 'It's nothing really but . . . well, every little thing helps, I suppose.'

Kate pulled away and wiped her cheeks. 'Sorry, I'm a wreck. I'm counting the days and holding my breath until she has the tests to see if the bone marrow worked. I shouldn't drink alcohol at all – it makes me weepy. I'd better have a coffee.'

Liam jumped up. 'I'll make it for you. Sit down and rest.'

Kate did so. It was nice to have someone doing things for her. Liam made them both a coffee and sat opposite her. He raised his cup. 'Here's to good health and complete remission in 2016.'

Kate clinked her cup against his. 'I can't believe Christmas is only days away. I've done nothing. I'll be glad to see the back of this year, that's for sure. I'm scared, though. It's funny, you think when something awful happens that you'll assume this is your bad card in life. But now I just think, Why wouldn't I get more bad cards? Who's to say more bad luck isn't on its way?'

Liam reached over and squeezed her hand. 'It's normal to feel like that, but I really think you've had your fill. I'll light a candle for Jess on Christmas Eve and one for you.'

Kate squeezed back. 'Thank you. It's silly, we barely know each other and yet I feel as if I've known you all my life.'

Liam smiled broadly. 'I know what you mean.'

The door opened. Luke came in and threw his kitbag onto the floor. He stopped dead when he saw Kate holding hands with Liam. Kate yanked her hand back. Oh, God! It looked like something it wasn't.

Luke glared at her. 'What the hell?'

Liam stood up and took charge. He took Luke's hand and shook it. 'Hi, Luke, I'm Liam. I met your mum at the mindfulness course but we decided to skip it tonight. Nice to meet you. I hear you're a great rugby player – best of luck in the cup. Right, I'd best be off. Good luck, Kate, and thanks for the coffee.'

Luke didn't have time to react.

Kate walked Liam to the back door. 'Thanks for dropping by, I really enjoyed that,' she said quietly.

'Me too. We should skip the mindfulness class more often.'

Kate grinned. 'I agree.'

'See you in January. If we decide to mitch off, we could go for a walk, if the weather permits.'

'Sounds great. Happy Christmas.'

Liam bent down and kissed her cheek. 'You too.' Then, looking over her shoulder, he said, 'Bye, Luke.'

'Uh, yeah . . . bye,' he muttered.

Kate watched Liam go. He turned when he reached the end of the garden path and waved at her.

'Can you close the fucking door? It's freezing,' Luke snapped.

Kate spun around. 'Watch your language.'

'So who's the dude? When did you get a boyfriend?'

'He's not my boyfriend. He's a friend, a very nice man.'

'Oh, yeah? Well, if he's just a friend, how come you were holding hands when I came in?'

'He was holding my hand to comfort me, Luke. I was feeling a bit down. That's all.'

Luke shrugged. 'I don't care if you're seeing him. He seems all right, but I don't need another dad. So, if you want to go out with him, fine, but he's not to start hanging around me or telling me what to do.'

Kate stood up and washed the coffee cups. 'For the last time, I'm not going out with him and I know you don't need another dad.'

'Fine, whatever.'

'Have you eaten?'

'No.'

'Do you want me to cook you something?'

'I'm not seven. I can cook for myself,' Luke said angrily.

'Fine. Sorry for asking and being concerned.'

'Jesus, I wish everyone would get off my back.' He slammed the fridge door.

'No one's on your back,' Kate said, eyeing him. 'What's wrong, Luke? You've been really grumpy this last week.'

'Nothing. I just want to eat in peace.'

'Are you sure it's nothing? Is everything okay with school and Piper?'

Luke hesitated. 'There's actually –'

Kate heard a scream. It was Jess. She left Luke and took the stairs two at a time, her heart beating wildly. At the top she skidded left and burst through the door into the bedroom.

'What's wrong?' Kate cried, terrified of the answer.

Jess was holding her phone, sobbing. 'It's La-Larry.'

28

Her mother handed her another tissue. Jess hadn't known she had so many tears. Larry was gone. Her person, her friend, the only one who understood exactly how she felt, was dead and she couldn't come to terms with it.

'There is no God,' she said, sobbing into Whiskey's soft face.

'Jess, don't say that.'

'No, Mum, there isn't. I don't believe in God any more or Mary or saints or miracles or any of it. It was nice of your friend Liam to give me that medal, but I don't want it.' Jess handed it to her.

Her mother put it into her pocket. 'Larry was just really sick and really unlucky.'

Jess stared at her, big eyes full of tears. 'He was a good person, a great person. He didn't deserve to die. There is no God and no justice. I hate this – I hate this life, this stupid bloody cancer! I hate it!' Jess was racked with sobs.

Her mother climbed onto the bed and held her. 'I hate it too,' she said. 'But you're going to be okay.'

Jess sniffled into her shoulder. 'What if I'm not, Mum? Larry was in remission three times and it came back and he's dead. He was my best friend. He made me laugh on the really bad days.'

'I know, sweetheart, I know.' She stroked Jess's bald head.

That felt nice. Jess loved it when she did that. It reminded her of being little, when her mum used to stroke her hair before she went to sleep.

Life seemed so bleak. She felt like a black cloud was descending on her, suffocating her. Everything was dark and depressing and pointless and frightening, and her heart ached. She felt so sick and exhausted and fed up and just . . . just sad. So, so, so, so sad.

If Larry could die, so could she. No one was safe from cancer. It didn't matter about the statistics or Luke's bone marrow or chemo or anything: cancer could come back or never go away and you could die.

Jess didn't want to die. She wanted to live and become a famous horse-rider and win a gold Olympic medal at show-jumping or dressage and have a gorgeous boyfriend and be happy and healthy and never, ever see a hospital again. Why had cancer come into her life? She hated it.

Larry said you had to stop asking why and accept it. He said acceptance was the only way to stop your head melting. He said that you couldn't fight having cancer: you could only fight the cancer itself. He said you had to keep all of your energy on that fight, good against evil. You against cancer. And he had tried, he had tried so hard, to fight and be positive and not let it win. But it did. It bloody well did. Cancer had won and now Larry was gone.

As her mother gently stroked her head, Jess thought about their pact: how Larry had promised to send a sign if there was an afterlife. How she'd do the same if she'd died first. But she hadn't. Larry was dead and here she was, sick and broken. But she knew Larry would do it if he could, so she'd wait for the sign.

It had been only a few days but every morning she woke up and stared out of the window for a robin on her window-sill or rainbows or white feathers or something, but there had been nothing so far. When Jess had said that if she died first she'd send a white butterfly to sit on his shoulder, Larry had got cross and said that was silly. You couldn't be so specific, he said, because they didn't know what it was like on the other side and it might be complicated to get a sign to someone, so it was best not to be too detailed.

Jess had seen a magpie on her windowsill yesterday but Larry had hated magpies – he'd said they were a sorry excuse for a bird – so she'd known that wasn't his sign.

Her mother shifted slightly on the bed. 'You have to be strong and get well for Larry,' she said. 'He'd want you to get better and live a brilliant life.'

Jess nodded, wiping her eyes.

'It's awful to lose a friend like Larry, but don't let it knock you back. Use the sadness and anger to drive yourself forward.'

'I'll try, Mum. I'm just so tired and sad.'

'I know, pet. Will you try to sleep now?'

'Yes. I'll see you later.'

'Are you sure? I'm happy to stay with you.'

'Yes. I'm okay, Mum.'

She watched her mother walk across her room and out of the door, closing it gently behind her. Once she was alone, Jess started to cry, the kind of heartbroken tears that fill your ears and make the bedsheets wet and leave you feeling emptied out and raw. She was about as far from okay as it was possible to get.

The next morning Jess was gazing out of the window, desperately praying for a sign from Larry, when she heard a knock on her door.

'Jess, are you awake? Larry's dad's called in to see you,' her mother said.

Jess sat bolt upright.

A moment later, Larry's father popped his head around the bedroom door. 'Sorry to disturb you, Jess, but I have something for you.'

He had aged ten years and looked awful. His eyes were red and bloodshot and the skin on his face was saggy. He reminded Jess of a Basset hound.

'Hi, Mr Wilkinson,' Jess said. 'I'm glad to see you. I'm so sorry about Larry. He was such an amazing person. I . . . I'm just so sorry.'

Mr Wilkinson nodded sadly and handed her an envelope. 'Larry made me promise that if anything happened to him I'd give you this.'

'Thank you so much,' Jess croaked.

With trembling hands she opened it. Inside she found a card with a picture of a dandelion on it. She began to cry. That was his sign.

Inside was a quotation. She read it out: '"What I need is the dandelion in the spring. The bright yellow that means rebirth instead of destruction. The promise that life can go on, no matter how bad our losses. That it can be good again."'

Jess, now sobbing, looked up at Larry's father who was crying too. 'It's our favourite part of *The Hunger Games*.'

'He loved that film. He loved you, too, Jess. Thanks for being his friend and making his time in hospital less awful.'

Jess couldn't speak.

'We're praying for you and hoping that you'll get well and live a full and happy life.'

'Thank you,' she whispered. 'I'm so, so sorry about Larry.'

'Me, too,' he said, and shuffled out of the room.

Jess sat staring at the card, laughing and crying. Eventually she turned to the window and said, 'Thank you, Larry. Dandelions will remind me of you for ever. I miss you.'

She kissed the card and, holding it to her chest, lay back and fell into a deep sleep.

29

Piper tried to sneak past the twins' room without being seen, but they shouted, 'Piper! We need help – please, Piper.'

She went in reluctantly. They were sitting at the end of Penny's bed wearing Santa hats and really cheesy Christmas jumpers.

'Penny's trying to film us with her phone propped up on top of the drawers, but it looks crap. We need the camera to move around a bit. Can you do it?' Poppy begged.

The last thing Piper wanted to do right now was film her two silly sisters but she knew they'd hound her until she agreed, so she said, 'You've got ten minutes and that's it.'

'Fine,' Penny said, and she and Poppy sat on the bed.

Piper held the phone up and began to record them.

'Hi, everyone.' They waved and smiled fake smiles.

'It's the two Ps here, wishing you a very merry Christmas Eve. With only one more sleep until the big day, we wanted to talk about Christmas.'

'If you're old and you're watching this, do not buy your kids or grandkids pyjamas or socks or crappy jumpers for Christmas. They don't want them,' Penny said.

'Yeah, totally. Just give them vouchers for cool shops. Vouchers are good because then the person can buy what they actually want and not have to pretend to like the purple jumper or the pyjamas with, like, reindeer on them,' Poppy agreed.

'Don't buy vouchers for Marks & Spencer's or shops like that, buy them for, like, H&M or River Island.'

'Or Superdry.'

'Or for ASOS.'

'Do ASOS do vouchers?' Poppy asked.

'I dunno. I think so.'

'You can't say you don't know. We're supposed to be telling people what to do,' Poppy remonstrated.

'Well, you don't know either, so don't give out to me.'

'You're rubbish at this, Penny.'

'Oh, for God's sake, just take that bit out.'

'Fine. Just leave it at Superdry,' Poppy said.

'Moving on to other Christmas things,' Penny said, 'you have to give me my present and I'll give you yours and be all, like, "Wow, that's so cool," like Zoella does with her friend.'

'What did you get me?' Poppy asked.

'It's supposed to be a surprise.'

'It'd better not be rubbish, then.'

'Who cares? It's just about looking happy and pretending,' Penny huffed.

Posy had come out of her box room and was standing behind Piper. 'You can't be fake,' she said. 'People will see through you. Zoella isn't fake, which is why everyone loves her.'

'Obviously we won't look fake. We can act, Posy,' Poppy said.

'Yeah, how hard is it to look excited anyway?' Penny agreed.

'Don't underestimate your viewers. We can tell fake from real,' Posy said.

'Piss off, Posy, we're trying to film here. When we're zillionaire YouTube stars you'll get nothing because you're just being negative.'

Piper put the phone down. 'You can argue on your own time. I'm going.'

'*No!* Wait, we have to do the presents and then we're finished,' Poppy said.

'When I give the present to Poppy, you need to zoom in on her opening it,' Penny said. 'Poppy, you need to say how amazing the wrapping is and all that too.'

Piper pressed record again and Penny handed Poppy a present wrapped in silver paper with a crooked red bow.

'Wow, Penny!' Poppy said, eyes wide. 'This is amazing! I'm super-excited. The wrapping paper is so cool, where did you get it?'

Penny fake-smiled. 'It's actually tinfoil, which I used to save money and the planet.'

Piper tried not to laugh. The planet? Was Penny serious? Could she be that clueless?

'Wow, it looks like designer paper. And the bow is so awesome! It's perfect!'

Posy snorted.

Penny glared at her. 'I spent ages getting it just right. I think a nicely wrapped present is so much better than one that's thrown together, don't you?'

'Oh, yes.' Poppy opened the present – an empty St Tropez fake-tan bottle.

'Seriously?'

Penny frowned at her. 'Isn't it fab?'

'It's *my* fake tan *and* it's empty.'

'For God's sake, they can't see that. Pretend it's full and you're happy. Jesus, Poppy, you're so bad at this.'

'You can see it's been used because it has brown streaks down the side,' Posy said.

'You are so scabby. I can't believe you're giving me my own fake tan as a present.' Poppy was furious.

'We're just pretending, you freak! It's not real!' Penny shouted.

'Zoella is real. She never pretends,' said Posy.

'Can you just shut the hell up and stop banging on about Zoella?' Penny hissed.

'I thought you wanted to be like her,' Posy said, thoroughly enjoying herself now. 'You're the opposite of her. You're like the fake Zoella twins.'

'The bogus twins,' Piper said, as Posy giggled.

Poppy wasn't letting the bad present go. 'I actually bought you something with my own money and I wrapped it in actual wrapping paper, not bloody tinfoil.'

'What is it?' Penny asked.

'It's a really cool T-shirt from H&M and I'm not giving it to you.' Poppy reached behind her to grab the present and waved it under her sister's nose.

'You have to! It's for the show, for our future.'

'No way. I'm going to do this on my own without you bossing me about.' Poppy held the gift tightly.

'You can't give yourself a present, you moron.'

'Oh, yeah? Watch me.' Turning to the phone camera, Poppy said, 'So how about this? How about you treat yourself to a gift at Christmas? We all spend so much time buying things for other people and get so many rubbish presents, especially from our scabby sisters. Why don't we buy ourselves something that we actually want?'

'That's ridiculous, Poppy,' Penny said. 'The entire point of Christmas is that you give presents to others! Isn't that right, everyone?'

'Yes, but not when you know for a fact that the other person isn't going to give you one. In that case you're perfectly entitled to spend the money you were going to spend on them on yourself.'

'That makes you Scrooge.'

Poppy grinned. 'No. You're Scrooge, because you're tight, scabby and mean.'

'I am not.' Penny shoved Poppy over.

'Yes, you bloody are.' Poppy shoved her back and they began to wrestle.

'OMG, they're so lame,' Posy said.

'Somehow I don't see a big future for them on YouTube.' Piper grinned.

'No one who is actually sane would want to watch this,' Posy agreed.

They left the room with the twins still fighting.

Piper went into her bedroom and flopped down on the bed. Her head ached. They'd phoned Maggie that morning and told her their decision. She'd been very nice about it and said she'd help them.

Piper heard her mother coming through the front door, shouting, 'Merry almost Christmas,' up the stairs. Two minutes later she called them all downstairs. It was a family tradition that they sat around the tree, eating mince pies and listening to carols on Christmas Eve. Even though they all moaned and groaned about it, they secretly liked it. Piper heard the twins thundering down the stairs, followed by Posy's lighter steps. She heard Pauline coming in from college – the only student in the world who studied on Christmas Eve.

She hauled herself up and took a very deep breath. This Christmas Eve was going to be very different for her. For all of them, in fact.

Seamus put on his favourite first, Bing Crosby singing 'White Christmas'. Everyone got to choose a song and that was his. Olivia passed around the mince pies and cream.

'Yum. These are really good, Mum,' Poppy said.

'Marks & Spencer's,' Olivia told her.

'Not exactly baked with love, are they?' Poppy said, then took a bite.

'So, girls, another year gone. Where does the time go?' Olivia wondered. 'Next year Pauline will be in her second year at med school, Piper will be in college, you two rascals will be in transition year and Posy will be in second. You're all growing up too quickly. I feel as if it was only yesterday when you were babies.'

'I wouldn't go back to the nappies and the sleepless nights if you paid me,' Seamus said, polishing off his second mince pie. 'I prefer them at this age – less work.'

'Oh, I loved the baby stage – they were adorable.'

'Jesus, Olivia, we were nearly divorced over lack of sleep and dirty nappies.'

Olivia smiled. 'I don't remember that. I just remember the chubby thighs and the little white teeth poking out from pink gums, the first words and the sound of babies laughing.'

Piper watched her mother's face light up as she remembered those days. It made her want to weep.

'I bet I was the cutest,' Penny said.

'You were in your arse,' Seamus said. 'A nightmare, that's what you were. You never bloody slept. Up all night. I never saw a child with so much energy.'

'Who was the best baby?' Poppy asked.

'Posy,' Seamus and Olivia said at the same time.

'I would have thought she'd be the worst because it was your last chance to have a boy and then it was a girl and you were devastated,' Poppy said.

'Thanks a lot, Poppy, I actually have feelings, you know.' Posy's cheeks were red.

'We weren't a bit disappointed. Don't mind her. You were the sweetest baby ever,' Olivia said.

'A little dote,' Seamus agreed.

'What was I like?' Piper asked, suddenly desperate to know. Olivia and Seamus looked at each other.

'Good.'

'Yes, easy enough.'

'You don't remember, do you?' Piper said.

'It's kind of a blur. You only remember the really bad ones and the last one,' Seamus admitted.

'Thanks a lot.' Piper felt furious.

'You were lovely, darling, a lovely baby, a lovely girl and a lovely teenager too.' Olivia tried to reassure her.

Piper knew it was unreasonable, but she was raging. She wanted to know. She needed to know. What kind of a baby was she? Was she good? Did she sleep? Was she sweet? Was she . . . Oh, God, what was she doing?

She felt a cool hand on her arm. It was Pauline's. 'Breathe,' she whispered.

Everyone was distracted by Penny and Poppy arguing over their choice of songs.

'Do you want a glass of water?' Pauline asked quietly.

'No, I'm fine.'

'Have you made up your mind?'

Piper nodded.

'Are you sure?'

Piper nodded again. 'As sure as I can be.'

'No way am I listening to Mariah Carey! For God's sake, Penny, choose something else.'

'I like it and it's my choice.'

'I hate that song.'

'So do I.' Posy groaned.

The doorbell rang. Piper jumped up and went to open it. Luke was standing in the rain, soaking wet. 'What are you –'

'I can't sleep. I can't concentrate. We need to tell our parents. I know we said we'd wait until after Christmas, but it's wrecking my head. Mum knows something's wrong with me, I'm so jumpy all the time. I just can't keep it in. It's too big, it's too important. We can do this, Piper. You and me, together, we can do it. I love you.'

'I love you too.' Piper kissed him as relief flooded her body.

They laughed. It was the first time they'd laughed since she'd told him about the baby. They hugged again and kissed.

'Get a room,' Penny shouted, peeping around the door.

Luke grinned. 'Go away. I want one more kiss.'

Penny ducked back into the room.

'Now we have to tell our families,' Luke said.

'Will we do it now?'

'Let's get it over with. There's never going to be a good time. They'll be shocked, no matter what. May as well have it out there now.'

They walked into the living room where 'All I Want For Christmas' was booming out of the speakers.

Piper went over to her mother and, into her ear, said, 'Mum, Luke and I need to talk to you and Dad in the kitchen.'

Olivia's eyes widened. She shook Seamus's arm and told him to follow her.

'Where are you going?' Poppy asked.

'We just want a quick word with Mum and Dad,' Piper shouted, over the music.

'*Ooooooh!* Are you engaged?' Poppy exclaimed.

'Are you getting married?' Posy asked.

Piper's heart sank. They'd be so shocked when they found out.

'Shut up and leave them alone.' Pauline closed the living-room door.

Seamus stood leaning against the cooker. 'So, what's going on?'

Luke's face was bright red. 'I, that is, we have some news and it's . . . well . . . it's . . .'

Olivia looked right into Piper's eyes. She knew. Piper could tell. Olivia's eyes filled with tears and Piper couldn't stand it any longer: she had to say it out loud. The secret had to come out – it was suffocating her.

'I'm pregnant.'

'What the hell?' Seamus looked as if he'd been shot.

Luke stared at the floor.

It was worse than Piper had imagined. Her mother was crying silently and her father's mouth was opening and closing, like a goldfish's.

'I promise I'll look after Piper and the baby,' Luke said.

'You're only kids,' Olivia whispered.

'How the hell did this happen?' Seamus asked. He shook his head and, in a voice thick with disappointment, said, 'Piper, you're my sensible one.'

Olivia recovered. 'How far gone are you?'

'About fourteen weeks.'

'Oh, my God.' Seamus sat down heavily on a chair.

'Have you thought about your options?' Olivia asked.

'Yes, we've thought and thought and thought, and we've decided to keep it.' Piper was firm. Keeping it had always felt right to her. She knew that having an abortion seemed like the sensible thing to do – she could get on with her life and all of that – but she was having this baby and nothing would change her mind.

'But your future,' Seamus said, sounding strangled. 'You'll be tied down, you'll have no choices, you'll never do the things we wanted for you. Piper, you've your whole life ahead of you. How could you let this happen? How could you be so foolish?'

Piper's lip wobbled. She didn't want to cry. She wanted to be strong, but seeing her father so devastated was hard.

'It's my fault, sir. I'm the one to blame,' Luke said. 'It was my mistake and I can't tell you how sorry I am. But I love Piper and I promise to look after her.'

Seamus shook a trembling finger at Luke. 'You stupid son-of-a-bitch. You're eighteen, you have no idea what the hell you're talking about. Having a child is a lifetime commit-ment. You're kids. You know nothing about life. You're still in school, for God's sake. How the hell are you going to sup-port my daughter and a baby?'

'I'll get a job and we'll rent a small flat and –'

'Oh, Jesus, son, you really are clueless. Both of you are clueless and stupid, so bloody stupid.'

Olivia placed a hand on her husband's arm. 'Look, you're both very young and a bit naive. Piper is a bright, clever girl who deserves to achieve all of her goals and dreams, as do you, Luke. If you're determined to have this baby, you'll need support from us and from your family, too, and we'll help you, but ultimately you'll be tied down with this child for life. It's a huge commitment, much bigger than you can imagine.'

'We know, Mum. We've thought about nothing else and we've made up our minds that we're keeping it. We love each other, and I know we're young and I know we're naive, but we're willing to make sacrifices to look after the baby.'

Seamus put his head into his hands. 'Why, Piper? Why did you have to be so stupid? Your life is not your own any more. And as for you,' he looked up at Luke, 'you'd better stand by her side day and night, and if I ever hear that you're not pulling your weight, I'll hunt you down and wring your neck. Piper is my pride and joy and you've ruined her bright future.'

'Stop it, Dad.' Piper began to cry now – she couldn't hold in the tears. 'It's not Luke's fault, and my future isn't ruined. It's just different.'

Luke stood up and put his hands on Piper's shoulders. 'I truly am sorry, but I've been through a lot over the last few years and I know how important it is to be a good father and to be there for your kids. I will not let Piper or our baby down.'

Olivia reached over and wiped her daughter's tears. 'It's all right. We're here for you and we'll support you, no matter what. We're just a bit shocked – we need a few days to process the news.'

Piper gave her mother a faint smile. It was a relief to hear her say she'd support her because she'd need every bit of support she could get. Now that they had told her parents, it was frighteningly real. Her heart was thumping. She knew it was the right decision but it was very scary. She couldn't bear to see her father so angry and upset. It was awful to think she'd done this to him. 'I'm sorry, Dad, I know I've let you down.' She was sobbing again.

Seamus buried his face in his hands.

'Get off me, Pauline! You're a freak.' Penny burst through the kitchen door with her eldest sister hot on her heels, Posy and Poppy right behind them.

'We want to know what's going on and . . . Oh!' She stopped when she saw her father and sister crying.

'Is Jess dead?' Posy gasped.

'No,' Luke said. 'It's not that.'

'What is it?' Poppy asked. 'Why do you all look so upset?'

Piper stood up. 'I've got something to tell you. I was stupid and I didn't protect myself properly and I'm pregnant.'

'*What?*' Penny squealed.

'Oh!' Poppy's eyes almost popped out of her head.

'Poor you.' Posy came over to give her a hug.

'It's okay. Luke and I are just going to be very young parents.' Piper tried to keep calm and not fall apart again.

'You'll be great, Piper,' Pauline said. 'You've always helped with this lot – you'll be a much better mother than I ever could be.'

Piper wanted to kiss Pauline. She had never expected her sister to be so supportive, but she had been brilliant. A total rock. She mouthed, 'Thank you,' to her.

'But you're only –'

'It'll be nice to have a baby in the house again,' Pauline cut across Penny. 'And we can all help babysit.'

'Yes, I'll help you loads, Piper, I promise. I love babies,' Posy said.

'I'll do it too, but you'll have to pay me,' Poppy said.

'Don't be so mean!' Posy was shocked.

As her sisters bickered over childcare, Piper held Luke's hand and prayed that it would all work out. It would be a long and lonely road, but she had her family, mad as they were, and she knew they'd be there for her through thick and thin. She was lucky, she knew that. Very lucky.

30

Jaden crawled across the living room, which was strewn with Christmas wrapping paper, gurgling happily as Jenny filmed him. Nick reckoned she must have caught every second of the baby's life on camera. She sent him at least three videos a day when he was at work.

Still, at least she was in better form, not panicking and crying all the time. She still freaked out a lot, but it was definitely better. Whatever the GP had said to her had calmed her down. Nick was glad he'd made her go. It was the best sixty euros he'd spent. She was still very different from the fun, sexy girl he'd fallen for, but at least she was less down. Maybe, with a bit more time, she'd get back to her old self.

Nick glanced at his watch. He'd promised Kate he'd be there for Christmas pudding at six. He'd have to leave now to make it on time. He was hoping the silver and diamond necklace he couldn't really afford would make Jenny less grumpy about him leaving.

He leant over and kissed her neck. 'So, babe, I have to pop in to the kids now and give them their presents.'

Jenny stiffened. 'How long will you be?'

'An hour, tops. That necklace looks so good on you.'

Jenny fingered the diamond. 'I love it. Okay, go and see the kids and say hi for me. I hope Jess likes the mini iPad.'

'She'll love it. It was a great idea. I'll tell her you thought of it.'

'Go and hurry back. I don't want to be on my own for long.'

'Sure.' Nick grabbed his jacket and ran out.

When he arrived at the back door of George's house, he could hear loud voices chatting and laughing. He peered in. They were all sitting around the kitchen table. Maggie was there too. God, he hoped she wasn't going to give him a hard time. She was all Team Kate, and he didn't want any hassle today. Even the French waitress was there – Kate had invited all the strays in town. Typical, he thought. She was always nice to everyone. It looked like fun, the way Christmas should be, lots of people and food and wine and chat. Nick missed the Christmases they used to have. Kate had always made a huge fuss and turned the house into Santa's grotto. Jenny had barely put up a tree: she'd said she didn't feel Christmassy and she was too tired.

He saw Jess, even frailer than she had been the other day, sitting in the middle, spinning the food around her plate, but clearly happy. He took a deep breath and plastered on a cheery smile as he pushed open the door. 'Hi, guys, Merry Christmas.'

'Dad!' Jess beamed up at him. The others muttered hello. At least someone was happy to see him.

'Hi, sweetie.' He went over and kissed her.

'Did you bring presents, Daddy?' Bobby asked.

'And a merry Christmas to you too,' Nick said, squeezing Bobby's nose in what he thought was a playful way but his son pulled back and said, 'Ouch.'

'Sit down here,' Kate said, pulling a chair over for him beside Jess. 'You have to taste Dad's Christmas pudding. He's surpassed himself this year.' She handed him a bottle of anti-bacterial sanitizer.

Nick doused his hands, then sat down gratefully. He pulled his presents out of his bag and handed them out to Jess, Luke and Bobby.

'OMG!' Jess squealed. 'A mini iPad! Wow, Dad, thanks so much.' She threw her stick-like arms around his neck.

'You're welcome, Jess. You deserve it.' He held her tightly. 'It was Jenny's idea. She said to send you her love.'

Jess nodded.

'What did you get, Bobby?' Kate asked.

'A football and a book about birds,' Bobby said, as he yanked off the wrapping, seeming decidedly unimpressed.

Obviously got it wrong again, Nick thought. 'It's to encourage you to play football, Bobby. I think, if you practise, you might get into it. And you like facts, so I thought the book on bird facts would be up your alley.'

'That's great, Nick. Isn't it, Bobby?' Kate said, faking enthusiasm.

'I don't like football or birds.' Bobby kicked the edge of his chair. 'Jess is so lucky.'

Nick wanted to shout, *She has fucking cancer. Exactly how lucky is that?* He bit his lip and said nothing.

'Thanks,' Luke muttered, shoving his sweatshirt back into the bag.

Nick took a bite of the pudding. It was delicious. 'This is great, George, really delicious.'

'Glad you like it,' George said.

'I'm surprised you're eating it. I thought your body was a temple,' Maggie drawled.

'I let myself go sometimes, Maggie.'

'Oh, I know you do.' Maggie smirked.

Nick willed himself not to react. Maggie had never liked him. She'd always thought he wasn't good enough for Kate. She was one of those career types, a rampant feminist. She was all 'down with men' and 'let's break glass ceilings'. Nick found her hard to take. 'So, how's work, Maggie?' He decided to play nice.

'Good, thanks. The company is expanding and turnover is up.'

'Great.'

'You?'

'Things are on the up again,' Nick said. 'It was a tough few years.'

'It certainly was, more for some than others.' Maggie glared at him.

He couldn't win with her. Nick turned to Jess, who had barely touched her pudding. 'Hey, sweetie, try to eat a little more.'

'I'm not hungry, Dad. I feel a bit queasy.'

'Okay,' he said, rubbing her back.

'I think Jess might hit the hay soon,' Kate said, 'but you're very welcome to stay as long as you like, Nick.'

He nodded at her. 'Thanks. I have to go back, though. I'll enjoy this fantastic pudding and see Jess off to bed, but then I'll leave you all to your evening.' He felt a tiny stab of emotion, knowing that his place was no longer there. He didn't dare look at it closely enough to find out what exact emotion it was. He had to accept the new set-up and work with it, not go backwards.

They chatted about their presents and laughed about the pieces of coal George had left on Bobby's bedside locker as a joke. Kate asked politely about Jenny and Jaden and their first Christmas, but Nick knew no one was interested in hearing about that. When he saw Jess yawning, he stood up, intending to help her up to bed and then go home. Luke stopped him.

'Can you sit down, Dad, before you head off? There's something I need to tell you all.'

Nick turned to his son. His face was almost grey – as if he was about to puke. What was going on? He sat down again and looked at Kate, who frowned and shrugged. Clearly she was in the dark too.

Luke clasped his hands together and took a deep breath. 'There is no easy way and no good time to say this, so I'll just say it. Piper's pregnant.'

Nick's mouth fell open. Beside him, Jess gasped, Kate put her hand over her mouth, and everyone else looked stunned.

Nick felt the blood run cold through his body. 'What the hell!'

'Sweet Jesus,' George muttered.

'Congratulations, Luke. You'll be a cool young dad and Piper will be a great mum,' the French waitress said.

Was she stupid? A cool young dad? Jesus Christ, this was a disaster. Nick turned to Kate again, but she seemed to have frozen solid, unmoving, unspeaking.

'There's nothing cool about having a kid at eighteen,' Nick snapped.

'Well, you had me at twenty-seven, and that didn't work out so well either,' Luke retorted.

'Don't cheek me after announcing that you've got your girlfriend pregnant. How could you be so stupid?'

'Don't you dare call me stupid!' Luke's face was bright red.

'Stop. Fighting isn't going to resolve anything,' Maggie said.

'Oh, Luke.' Tears welled in Kate's eyes.

'I'm sorry, Mum.' Luke was getting upset now.

'Don't cry, Luke,' Jess said. 'It'll be okay, won't it, Dad?'

Nick felt his temples throb. The stupidity of it. The bloody-minded stupidity of it. There was only one solution to this problem. 'You need to deal with it, Luke, and fast. You're too young to have a kid. You need to go to London.'

'We are not going to London,' Luke snapped.

'Yes, you are. You're not throwing your life away because of one stupid night.'

'What's in London?' Bobby asked.

'Nick, I don't think –' Kate began, but Luke shouted across her.

'I love Piper and we've decided to have the baby and I'm going to be a good father, one who shows up every day.'

Nick felt the sting. 'Yeah? Good luck with that. Don't come crying to me when you realize your mistake six months after the kid is born when your friends are in college and you're working in some dead-end job to support it.'

'I wouldn't come to you for anything,' Luke spat.

'Luke, your dad is right,' Kate said gently. 'This is a big decision and you need to take a moment and think about all of your options before making a final choice.'

'We have, Mum. We've thought about nothing else and we're not going to London. We've decided to keep it.'

'What's in London?' Bobby asked again.

'But how are you going to support it, Luke? You're both so young,' Kate reminded him, twisting her napkin into a knot in her fingers.

'Maggie's going to help.'

'What?' Kate looked like she'd been slapped in the face. Her cheeks had two spots of red as she turned to her friend. 'You knew about this?'

Maggie nodded slowly. 'Luke called me to ask for help. He didn't want to burden you as you have so much going on with Jess. I advised him to consider London as an option, but they decided against it. So I said they could have my little apartment here. I'll get rid of my tenants. They can still go to college and pay me whatever rent they can afford.'

'WHAT'S IN LONDON?' Bobby shouted.

'Nothing,' George said. 'Nothing for you to worry about. This conversation shouldn't be happening in front of the kids. Bobby and Jess, away upstairs with you.'

'I want to stay,' Jess said.

Nick shook his head. 'George is right. This is grown-up stuff.'

'Please, Jess, would you take Bobby to watch TV?' Kate asked.

Jess reluctantly got up and ushered Bobby out of the room.

'How could you not tell me?' Kate asked Maggie.

'I'm sorry, Kate. I didn't want to upset you, not with the way things are. I told Luke that when they had made their decision he had to tell you straight away. I guess I was trying to protect you.' She gazed pleadingly at Kate, who continued to stare at her in disbelief.

'How could you?' Kate said. 'Leaving me to find out like this. Keeping it a secret. I never thought you'd –'

'Stop, Mum,' Luke said. 'Don't be angry with Maggie. She's been a rock. Her offer to give us the apartment at a low rent means we can go to college and work part-time. I think we can do it all, Mum, I really do. Maggie just did what we asked, but she also said we had to tell you as soon as possible.'

Maggie reached over and put her hand over Kate's. 'It was a difficult situation and, on top of Jess, I had to do what I thought was best. I'm so sorry.'

Kate took a deep breath. 'Luke's right. You supported them. I shouldn't be upset with you. Sorry.'

Nick was staring at his eldest son, unable to believe what Luke was willingly walking into. God, he was so naive! As if love was ever enough! Luke hadn't a clue what lay ahead of him. Having a baby with no money, while trying to study and hold down a part-time job, was going to be a living nightmare. Christ knew it was hard enough when you were forty-five and had a decent job. The plain fact was that Luke was going to ruin his life, and Nick didn't want that. He wanted Luke to have the life he himself hadn't had – to go to college, travel, work in London or New York, meet people and have wonderful experiences.

Nick had gone straight to work from school, then got married young and had kids. He'd sold houses to guys who'd gone to college and spent twenty years on Wall Street making a fortune. They'd decide to come back to Ireland to raise their kids and buy big houses with barely any mortgage because they'd made so much money on bonuses and fat salaries.

Nick wanted that for Luke. He wanted his son to be the guy buying the big house, not the guy selling it to him. He wanted Luke to have it all. Getting tied down with a baby at eighteen years of age would ruin his life choices. It was a mess. He had to try to persuade him, to make him see sense.

'Luke, please listen to me. Don't do this. You have your whole life ahead of you. Don't blow it by making a stupid decision. I'll talk to your girlfriend – I'll make her see what a bad idea this is.'

Luke bent over the table and shoved his finger in Nick's face. 'You stay away from Piper. She's the best thing in my life. We've decided together to keep the baby and no one is going to change our minds, least of all you.'

'You're making a huge mistake,' Nick said.

'He hasn't taken this decision lightly, Nick. He's really thought about it,' Maggie said.

'Does her father know?' Nick asked. 'I'm sure he'll want her to go to London.'

'We told them yesterday,' Luke said, glaring at his father. 'Yes, they are shocked, but they're offering us their support.'

'Are you absolutely sure about your decision, Luke?' Kate asked.

He nodded. 'Yes, Mum. Look, I'm sorry, I know this is the last thing you need right now. I never meant it to happen but it did and . . . well, I'm sorry, Mum.' He wiped the tears from his eyes.

Kate got up and went over to put her arms around him. 'It's okay, Luke, it's okay. We'll work it out. We'll all help you and we'll muddle through, like we always do. I love you and I don't want you to blame yourself or feel bad.'

Luke sank into her arms and buried his head in her shoulder. Nick felt a pang of jealousy. Kate was so good with the kids. He wished he could connect with them like she did. He'd have to make more effort. Kids really were hard work. Luke had no idea what he was in for. No idea at all.

31

Kate finished filling Liam in and took a sip of her hot choco-late. She had been dying to tell him. She'd just known he'd understand and be sympathetic. He was the one person she wanted to confide in when anything happened, these days.

'Wow! Never a dull moment in your house,' he said.

'I'm forty-two, and I'm going to be a grandmother.' Kate laughed bitterly.

'Not ideal, I grant you that. But if I could try to point out some positives? At least you like Piper, her parents are on board to help out, Maggie's chipping in as well, and Luke's standing up and being a responsible young man. That's something to be very proud of, you know.'

Kate raised an eyebrow. 'It's a pity he couldn't have been more responsible when he was having sex. Then he wouldn't be in this mess.'

She was sick with anxiety about it. As if worrying about Jess wasn't bad enough, now she had to worry about Luke. The awkward meeting with Piper's parents on St Stephen's Day had been made less awful than she'd expected because Piper's parents were lovely. Well, the mother was lovely. The father was quiet, clearly angry and devastated.

Luke hadn't told Nick about the meeting and had begged Kate not to. He said he didn't want Nick ruining it by trying to force them to have an abortion in front of Piper's parents.

Thankfully, it quickly became apparent that Piper's par-ents were fully on board to help out and be supportive, a huge relief to Kate. She promised them that Luke would be a good father and would not renege on his duties, no matter what happened between him and Piper.

Every time Kate saw Luke, she wanted to cry. He'd had such a bright future and now it was going to be a mess. Maggie kept saying it would be okay, that they'd work it out so he could go to college, but Kate still worried. It was a mammoth responsibility on young shoulders.

'Come on, Kate, we were all young once, and were we responsible all the time? I doubt it. Luke was unlucky, very unlucky, but it doesn't mean his life is over. With both families and their friends supporting them, they'll be fine. They sound like a lovely pair of young people,' Liam said.

Kate leant forward, so Nathalie, who was clearing up, couldn't hear her. 'Is it awful to wish they'd had an abortion and put it behind them?'

Liam shook his head. 'No, it's human nature to want the best for your kids and to protect them from struggles. But this may not be the worst thing in the world. We both have kids and we love them. Would we change a hair on their heads? No. Is there ever really a right time to have children?'

'After school would be a good start!'

Liam grinned. 'You have a point there. Will she be able to sit her exams?'

'Yes. Her due date is early July, but the poor thing will be doing them hugely pregnant.'

'Tough, but not impossible.'

Kate looked at his kind, open face. 'Are you always this optimistic?'

He smiled. 'Only when faced with someone desperate to see light at the end of a dark tunnel. You've had a huge amount to deal with, but you're strong. You've raised wonderful kids. It'll all work out.'

Kate smiled and squeezed his hand. 'Thank you for listening and for making me feel better. Thank God I went to the mindfulness class. I hated it but I met you.'

Liam blushed and focused on sipping his cappuccino.

Nathalie came over. 'I am finished with the cleaning. Are you okay for drinks? Would you not prefer to 'ave a glass of wine?'

'I think if I open a bottle I may never stop,' Kate said.

'Poor Kate.' Nathalie patted her shoulder. 'She is 'aving the very stressful time. Why Luke could not put on the condom? I understand Piper not taking the pill, it make girls fat. I say *non* to the pill, but I always use the condom.'

'If only all young people were as sensible as you,' Liam said, winking at Kate.

'It's not sensible. It's fear. I never want to be 'aving the children. I 'ate babies – crying, sheeting and doing the *pipi* everywhere. *Non, merci*. I like nice clothes and beautiful rugs and books not ruined by chocolate hands or the snotty nose.'

Liam threw his head back and laughed, a kind of joyful hooting. Kate found it infectious and soon joined in.

Liam wiped tears from his eyes. 'Nathalie, you are too much. Babies do more than just secrete all over the place. They're great fun too.'

Nathalie shrugged in her nonchalant French way. 'Maybe fun for you, but for me a nightmare.'

'I won't put you down for babysitting duties then,' Kate said.

'When the baby can go to the toilet and wash their own 'ands, I am 'appy to 'elp.'

'So, about fourteen if it's a boy, then!' Liam chuckled.

Even Nathalie laughed. 'Yes, and two if it's a girl, *non?*'

Liam nodded. 'Yes.'

Nathalie studied Liam's face. 'You know, if you cut this beard short or maybe shave it off, you could be quite good-looking.'

Liam put his hand on his heart. 'From you, Nathalie, that backhanded compliment means a lot.'

'Seriously, you should cut it and put on a shirt that 'as been ironed. This look as if your dog sleep on it.'

Liam laughed again. 'He probably did.'

'Well, if you want to impress a lady,' Nathalie grinned, 'you need to be a bit better with the grooming and the fashion.'

It was Kate's turn to blush. 'Thanks, Nathalie. That's enough advice for one evening.'

As she was leaving, Nathalie said to Kate, 'I like this one. 'Airy, but funny and kind.'

When she'd gone, Kate looked down at her cup. 'Sorry, she can be a bit too free and easy with her advice.'

Liam stroked his beard. 'You know, she's right, I should do better with "the grooming and the fashion".'

Kate laughed. 'You're fine the way you are.'

'I'd like to be more than fine.' Liam stared straight at her.

'I didn't mean it like that. You're great.'

Liam beamed. 'You're pretty great yourself.'

Kate wasn't comfortable with the way the conversation was going so she changed the subject. She really liked Liam. In the short time she'd known him he had become someone she trusted and whose company she enjoyed, but she just didn't find him attractive and, in any case, she had no space for any kind of romance. She could barely breathe with all that was going on.

'So, how's work?'

'Work is fine. I've got some very intense students eager to get firsts. It's amazing how much more focused kids are, these days. When I started out teaching Spanish, the lectures were only ever half full on a good day. Now, every lecture is almost eighty per cent full and the kids are killing themselves studying. I don't know if it's better or worse. More importantly, how's Jess?'

Kate poked at a small marshmallow that was stuck to the bottom of her hot chocolate cup. She'd have to stop drinking it or she'd put on the weight she'd lost due to stress. 'To be honest, I'm worried about her. Larry dying has really set her back. She's heartbroken, and he was so good at cheering her up and making the days less long. It's just awful that he's gone. She'll miss him so much. He was so young and a really lovely boy. It really scared me. He'd been in remission three times, but it came back and . . . Well, he's gone now. I'm trying really hard not to think about it. I'm just focusing on the fact that, in two days' time, Jess is having the tests done to see if the bone-marrow transplant has put her into complete remission. I'm sick with nerves.'

'I'll pray it all goes well. How does she seem?'

Kate tried to swallow the fear that rose in her throat every time she thought about it. Jess didn't look well. She was constantly exhausted and slept a lot. Kate didn't even want to allow herself to think about it, but Jess had seemed worse in the last ten days. The results had to be good. They just had to. 'I don't know, really. She looks so frail. I'm a bit worried, to be honest.'

Liam put his cup down. 'I know it's frightening for you. Look, I'm here day or night, so just call me. I remember nights being the worst time, when you wake up and it's four a.m., and you know you're not going to get back to sleep and you start thinking very dark thoughts. Honestly, call me anytime. I'm not a great sleeper anyway – chances are I'll be awake, reading.'

He got it, Kate thought. Only someone who had been through this could understand. That was exactly how she felt when she woke up – terrified. She often wished she could talk to someone to calm herself down. One night, in complete desperation, she'd called Nick. Jaden had been woken by the noise of the phone ringing and Jenny had gone mad. Nick had tried to be nice to her, but had hung up after a minute because Jenny was shouting at him.

She smiled at Liam. 'You may regret that offer.'

He smiled back. 'I won't.'

Kate glanced at the clock on the wall. 'Shoot! I have to go. I had no idea it was so late. I want to try to get Jess to eat something.'

'Good luck and keep me posted. I'm crossing all fingers for good news.'

Liam leant down and gave Kate a bear hug. She kissed the side of his scratchy beard and said goodbye.

32

Kate tucked Bobby into his bed and turned out the light. She went in to Jess, who was lying on her side with her eyes closed, quietly changed into her pyjamas and lay down beside her daughter in the double bed. Looking at the dandelion card on the bedside table, she said a prayer to Larry: 'Wherever you are, please help her. Please may the results be good. Please may she be in complete remission. Please, Larry, please.'

Jess had barely touched her food at dinner. She'd said she was feeling tired and had gone to bed at eight. Kate had wanted to weep. This was not a good sign. She didn't look like someone who was getting better. All of the hope was draining right out of Kate's bones.

'Mum, will you read to me?' Jess said, startling her.

'Of course I will. I thought you were asleep.'

Jess rolled over to face her. 'No, just resting.'

'How do you feel?'

'Same.'

'Would you eat any little thing now? I bought you chocolate milk. Luke said it's great for energy.'

'Gross,' Jess said.

'How about a scone? Or a muffin? Or a yoghurt?'

Jess shook her head. 'Sorry, but no. I don't feel hungry.'

Kate studied her daughter's pinched face and scrawny arms and tried not to worry. 'Will I continue with *Jane Eyre*?'

'Yes, I like the crazy woman. I want to know who she is.'

Kate cuddled Jess to her and began to read. She inhaled the smell of her daughter, the essence of her. Jess snuggled into her mother's shoulder.

As Kate was about to start a new chapter, a little voice said, 'I miss him.'

Kate put down her Kindle and held her daughter to her. She's like a broken sparrow, she thought. A tiny broken sparrow. 'I'm so sorry, sweetie. I wish it hadn't happened.'

'Me too,' Jess whispered. 'If I die, I'll send you a sign, I promise. I told Larry if I died first, I'd send him a white butterfly. I'll do the same for you.'

Kate squeezed her eyes tightly shut. She didn't want to hear that. She didn't want Jess ever to say the word 'die'. 'You don't need to think about signs or any of that, darling. You're not going anywhere.' She held her tighter. 'Please don't talk like that. I won't let you go, ever. You're going to get better. You must believe it.'

Jess sighed. 'Okay, Mum.'

'I love you so much, Jess. I just can't bear to hear you talk about signs. You can buy me a white butterfly for my birthday and give it to me. Okay?'

'Sure.'

Kate switched on her Kindle.

'Mum?'

'Yes?'

'I think it's nice Luke's having a baby. I know he's young, but it's what life's about, really, isn't it? Finding someone you love and having kids.'

'Well, I suppose so, yes. Children are the best thing in life. I just wish Luke and Piper weren't so young.'

'It'll be the cutest baby ever. Luke and Piper are so gorgeous. It'll have amazing blue eyes like them and really thick shiny brown hair. Chloë said she bets it'll look like Megan Fox if it's a girl and Zac Efron if it's a boy.'

Kate had no idea who those people were but she nodded. 'Gorgeous.'

'I wish I had blue eyes.'

'Jess,' Kate said, looking into her daughter's eyes, 'you have the most beautiful melt-your-heart brown ones I've ever seen.'

'You always say I'm beautiful, even when I look terrible, like right now.'

Kate held Jess's small face in her hands and smiled. 'You are the most wonderful, stunning creature on this earth and always will be.'

Jess giggled. 'Yeah, right! I look like crap.'

'No, you don't. You look incredible, considering what you've been through. We just need to feed you up.'

Jess laid her bald head on Kate's chest. 'Tell me about the day I was born again.'

Kate kissed it. 'There was a huge thunderstorm and a bolt of lightning struck as you were being born. I knew then that you'd be invincible. Your dad wanted to call you Storm, but I said no. Jess was always my favourite name. I stood my ground on that one. The doctor said, "This girl will be extraordinary." He'd never seen a child being born on the strike of lightning. We knew then that you were special, really, truly special, and you are, Jess. You're so special.'

Kate looked down. Jess was fast asleep. She held her daughter and prayed to the god of thunder and lightning to give Jess strength and help her beat cancer for good.

33

Dr Kennedy took off his glasses. Kate stopped breathing. If they take off their glasses, you're screwed. She knew this from all the hospital TV shows she'd watched. Whenever the doctor removes his glasses, it's inevitably bad news.

'I'm very sorry, but the bone-marrow transplant has not been successful . . . The test results showed a relapse . . . Most unfortunate.'

'Relapse' was the word Kate heard through the fog. Such an ordinary little word, but it had the ability to destroy you. She'd known. In her heart she'd known Jess wasn't getting better. In the first two weeks after the transplant she'd been full of hope, but after Christmas she'd watched Jess go downhill. She'd barely eaten, slept all the time, shrunk physically before Kate's eyes. She'd known, but she hadn't let herself know.

Oh, Jess, my beautiful Jess. Why hadn't Luke's bone marrow worked? He was so strong and healthy. They'd all been so sure it would save her. Kate had allowed herself to hope. Why? Why? Why?

Her head felt as if it was being crushed. What did this really mean? Was Jess going to die? No, no way. They'd fix her – they'd find a way. There had to be more treatment. They'd only tried one bone-marrow transplant – they could do another. Maybe with donor marrow. This was only the beginning. But Jess was so weak: could she take any more treatment? What about infections? Kate bent over and clutched her stomach. The pain was searing. There had to be light – there had to be some kind of light at the end of this dark tunnel. Please, God.

'Okay, so it didn't work, which is – is a setback. So what do we do now?' Nick snapped. 'More chemo? Another transplant? How do we fix this? How do we make her better? What's the plan?'

Dr Kennedy explained that there were some options. He said that approximately thirty per cent of children with AML experienced relapse. He spoke of re-induction regimens . . . high-dose cytarabine . . . anthracycline . . . depending on cardiac function . . . fludarabine . . . clofarabine . . . Kate's head spun. She couldn't take it in, couldn't begin to fathom what all those words meant.

Nick banged his hand on the desk. 'Can you just give it to us in plain English, please? What can we do now?'

Dr Kennedy clasped his hands together. 'I would suggest that we could try one course of chemotherapy using novel agents. I have to warn you that it is aggressive and there are risks involved. Jess is weak, and infections would be a concern. But if she reacted well, it could certainly help to get her back into remission, partial or otherwise.'

Nick stood up. 'Right, let's do it. When do we start?'

Aggressive chemotherapy? When was it not aggressive? If Dr Kennedy was saying it was going to be aggressive, it must be horrendous, Kate thought, with a shudder. Jess was so weak – could she take it? Would it kill her? Kate's head was spinning with fear and questions and worry and terror.

'Can she start tomorrow?' Nick asked.

'Wait, hold on,' Kate said, raising her head. 'Can she take it? Should we wait until she's a bit stronger? Should we build her up? Is it safe?'

'She's not getting stronger,' Nick snapped. 'For Christ's sake, Kate, she's getting worse. We have to act now.'

Kate pressed her fingers to her temples to try to help her think straight. This was Jess's life they were talking about. They had to be sure it was the right decision. It felt so rushed. At one second you're told the treatment hasn't worked, and the next you're discussing new options, aggressive options . . . There was no time to process it all. She had to be absolutely sure.

Kate eyeballed Dr Kennedy. 'If it was your daughter, would you do this?'

He looked her straight in the eye. 'I think it's worth trying.'

Kate breathed deeply. 'Then let's do it.'

'We need to discuss it with Jess. Would you rather do it or would you like me to?' Dr Kennedy asked.

'I think she needs to hear it from you. You can explain it better,' Nick said.

Kate bit her lip so hard, she drew blood.

Dr Kennedy stood up and went to call Jess in. She was sitting outside, reading a magazine.

Kate patted the empty chair beside her. Jess was searching her eyes for answers. Kate blinked back tears. Jess's face fell. She knew. Kate reached out to hold her hand. Jess closed her eyes and breathed deeply.

'How are you feeling, Jess?' Dr Kennedy said quietly.

'Not great,' Jess whispered.

As clearly as he could, Dr Kennedy explained that the treatment hadn't worked, and that they were going to try another round of more radical chemo. It was torture watching Jess's face as she took in the news. Nick put his hand on her shoulder and squeezed it tightly.

'Do you understand what I've said to you, Jess?' the doctor asked.

'Yes, I do. I knew it hadn't worked,' she said quietly.

Kate wanted to throw her arms around her, to take away her pain, but she was useless in the face of this stupid, horrible, cruel disease.

'So, you think this new chemo could help?' Jess asked.

'I think it's worth trying.'

'Is it going to be worse than the other chemo?'

'It's going to be a bit more aggressive.'

'Oh.'

Kate reached out and put her arms around her daughter, but Jess shrugged her off. She moved away from Nick too.

'We're only going to do one course,' Dr Kennedy said.

'It's only about six days and then it'll be done. It's worth it, Jess,' Nick said.

Jess glared at him. 'It's not your body, Dad. It's not you who has to have poison put into you that makes you so sick you want to die.'

Nick flinched. 'I know, Jessie. I know it's awful, but it'll make you better. What's a week against a lifetime?'

'*Might* make me better, Dad,' Jess corrected.

Kate laid her hand gently on Jess's arm. 'Why don't you have some time to think about it? It's a lot to take in.'

'There's nothing to think about,' Nick barked. 'She's doing it, starting ASAP.'

Kate frowned at him. 'Give her time, Nick.'

'We don't have time!'

Dr Kennedy stood up. 'Jess, take a day or two to think it over and discuss it with your parents. When you've made your decision you can call me and we'll take it from there.'

Nick shook a finger in his face. 'There's no taking a few days to think it over. She's doing it. Set it up.'

Dr Kennedy regarded him coldly. 'It's important for Jess to have time to consider the option I've set out before her.

292

Take a day or two to process it. Let me know when you've made a decision.' He showed them out.

They walked down the corridor in shattered silence. Kate looked at Nick, pleading with her eyes for him to let it drop for now. But Nick was like a man possessed. He arranged his face into an awkward smile and moved close to Jess. 'You have to start as soon as possible, Jess. We don't have a minute to waste. We need to get on with it.'

'Stop hassling me, Dad!'

'Leave her, Nick,' Kate said. 'She's had a shock.'

Nick rubbed his eyes. 'Look, I'm not hassling you, Jess. I just want to make you better.'

'It might not work, though, and it's going to be awful.' Jess began to cry. 'I hate this. I hate it so much.'

'Oh, Jess, it will work – it has to.' Nick's voice cracked as he bent down to hug her.

Kate watched them, and let her own tears flow. If she could have taken Jess's place, she'd have done it in a heartbeat, without a thought. She'd welcome physical pain: it would be a relief from the constant emotional torture. But she couldn't do anything. She was useless. Utterly useless. The cancer was doing whatever it wanted, rampaging around her daughter's body, and she hadn't a single weapon to use against it. The first instinct of motherhood was to protect. That was her duty. And she couldn't fulfil it. She felt a grief that took her breath away – grief for her beautiful Jess and grief for her inability to help her. Looking at Nick, she knew it was killing him too. They were failures.

Jess peered up and saw her mother crying. She held out her arm. Kate went over and the three of them held each other, each praying for a miracle, each praying for an end to the hell they were in.

34

Jess was trying not to hyperventilate. She looked in the hand mirror for the zillionth time. Piper reached over and took it from her.

'You're gorgeous.'

'Totally fab,' Chloë agreed. 'Piper did, like, an awesome job on your make-up.'

Jess smiled nervously. 'Is he definitely coming? Like, definitely?'

'Yes.' Chloë grinned. 'I've told you a zillion times. Mum told Dad that we needed to cheer you up because you were about to start the new horrible chemo. So Dad called his friend, who knows Drago's agent, and he phoned the agent and he said Drago was in Dublin for a week and he'd come to see you. The fact that he's here the week of your chemo is, like, Fate. You could be destined for each other.'

Jess giggled. Chloë was mad but in the best way. This had been such a brilliant distraction from the hell she was facing tomorrow. She was so happy to have this visit to take her mind off the chemo. She was dreading it more than anything and felt panicky every time she thought about it.

But today . . . Drago Jackson was coming to hospital to visit her! The coolest singer ever. She couldn't believe it. Since Chloë had FaceTimed her, screaming, two days ago to tell her, she'd barely slept. Drago Jackson! It was unbelievable.

She worshipped him. 'Never Let Me Go' was her favourite song ever. Larry used to make fun of her obsession and tell her she was a freak, that he was just a sixteen-year-old geek and couldn't sing, that it was all backing tracks and lip-synching. But Jess hadn't believed him: she thought Drago was the best singer ever. His voice was amazing.

'Do you know if the baby's a boy or a girl?' Chloë asked Piper.

'No. We've decided to wait. We want it to be a surprise.'

'That's cool. Are you excited?'

Piper instinctively put her hand to her stomach. 'Yes. Now that everyone knows and is being so supportive, I feel calmer and excited. Nervous, too, though.'

'You'll be such a cool mum,' Chloë said. 'I'd love to have you and Luke as my parents.'

Piper laughed. 'I'm not so sure about that, but thanks.'

'And me as their aunt,' Jess said, applying lip-gloss for the tenth time.

'Totally,' Chloë agreed. 'You'll be such a brilliant auntie, and I can be like a nearly aunt, can't I?'

'Of course you can,' Piper said.

'Your mum's like my fairy godmother,' Jess told Chloë. 'I still can't believe she organized this for me. I'm so happy.'

Chloë flicked back her long blonde hair. 'You know she adores you. She's, like, "Jess is the sweetest girl ever" *all* the time. If you weren't my BF and I didn't love you so much, it would be really annoying.'

Jess and Piper laughed. Chloë peered out of the hospital room's door. 'Here comes your mum.'

Kate came rushing in. 'He's here! Hazel just texted. They're on the way up.'

Chloë and Jess started screaming. Kate covered her ears. 'Girls, calm down, you'll scare him.'

'He's well used to screaming girls,' Piper assured her. 'It's what his career's based on.'

'OMG! It's him.' Chloë ducked back into the room and ran around flapping her arms, grinning wildly at Jess.

Jess's mouth was dry. She thought she might faint. Her mother went over and held her hand. 'Breathe, darling. He's just a boy who can sing.'

She didn't get it. Drago wasn't a boy who could sing, he was the coolest, most divine person on this earth. Jess hadn't felt this alive or excited since . . . She didn't know how long, but definitely since she'd got cancer. It was the *best* day. She'd love Hazel for ever.

Just as Jess started seeing double and was about to pass out, he came through the door.

'Ta-dah!' Hazel said. 'Jess, this is Drago. Drago, this is the wonderful Jess.'

Drago was shorter than Jess had expected. He was only a tiny bit taller than Chloë. He was gorgeous, though. Chloë was staring at him with her mouth open.

'Goldfish, Chloë,' Hazel said.

Chloë automatically closed her mouth but continued to stare.

'This is my daughter, Chloë. She'll stop staring in a minute.' Hazel nudged Drago towards Jess's bed.

'Hey, what's up?' he said, in his gorgeous American accent.

'Hi,' was all Jess could say. She felt so dumb, but she couldn't think of anything to say to him.

There was an awkward silence. Drago shuffled his feet.

'Jess is a big fan.' Piper broke the silence. 'What's your favourite song, Jess?'

'It's "Never Let Me Go". I love that one.' Jess blushed.

'Cool,' Drago said.

'What's the song about?' Kate asked.

Drago shrugged. 'You know, just about, like, never letting go and stuff.'

296

'My favourite is "I'm Hot And I Know It",' Chloë said, her eyes never leaving Drago's face. 'It's such a cool dance song.'

'Cool,' Drago said, nodding.

'What's that about, then?' Hazel asked, cracking up.

'It's about being hot.' Drago didn't get the sarcasm.

Jess didn't want them making fun of Drago. 'Are you working on a new album?' she asked.

'Yeah, totally.'

'Is it true you're dating Katie Ryan?' Chloë asked.

'Nah, we're just friends.'

'Are you dating anyone?' Chloë looked hopeful.

'Kinda, not really,' Drago said.

Jess wished she wasn't bald and skinny and sick. Maybe if she was healthy and had her hair back, he might look at her. But she had no chance now. Still, it was nice to dream. She wished she could think of something clever to ask. She racked her brains. 'Are you in Ireland for a break?' she asked.

Drago took the fingernail he was biting out of his mouth. 'I'm hooking up with a songwriter here to check out some tunes.'

'Do you like the songs?'

Drago crinkled his nose. 'I guess so.'

'Oh, for the love of Jesus,' Hazel muttered. 'Why don't you sing us something?' she asked him.

Drago looked shocked. 'No way, man. No one told me I'd have to sing. They said just come and say hi.'

Hazel's face darkened. 'Can I have a word?' she asked, dragging him outside by the arm.

They watched as Hazel yanked him out of the room and closed the door. Through the window onto the corridor, they could see her shouting at him. Jess winced as she heard her say, 'What the hell is wrong with you? There is a very sick

297

girl in there and I've paid a bloody fortune for you to come and visit her. You're a fucking singer, so sing something, you moron.'

Chloë and Jess exchanged a horrified look. Hazel was going to mess it all up. He'd walk out of there without a backward glance.

'Dude, my manager said I was to come and say hi to the sick kid and, like, talk for a bit and then I was done.'

'Your manager is a dickhead because that was not the deal. I am telling you now, get your skinny arse in there and sing something. I don't care what you sing and I don't care if it's out of tune, just open your goddamn mouth and sing. In fact, sing her that song she likes and then you can go back to La La Land and snort your millions up your nose, for all I care. But you are not going to let that girl down, okay?'

'Jeez, I did not sign up for this. I'm gonna kill Nikki.'

'Yeah, well, Nikki isn't here. He's back in the hotel charging me a fortune to put him up in that suite. So stop moaning and get in there.'

Chloë shook her head. 'My mum is so embarrassing. I am never going to get over the mortification of this. Did you hear her cursing at him? She just shouted at Drago Jackson to sing!'

Jess giggled. 'It's kind of funny.' She was disappointed that Drago wasn't nicer, but she still loved him.

The door opened. Hazel and Drago came back in.

'Drago is going to sing you that song you like. Aren't you, Drago?'

'Yeah, whatever, but, like, I don't have a track to sing to and my throat is dry, so it might not sound too good.'

'You don't have to sing if you don't want to.' Jess didn't want him to feel bad. This was hard for him. Stuck in a hospital room with five women staring at him. She felt sorry for him. It was a lot of pressure.

Hazel raised her hand. 'Drago is going to sing now.' She handed him a glass of water. 'Drink this for your dry throat and get on with it.'

Chloë was standing beside Jess. 'OMG, she is *so* bossy,' she whispered.

Drago cleared his throat. Jess clasped her hands together and waited for her favourite song.

> *My girl needs to love me the way I deserve,*
> *Else I'm gonna go.*
> *She ain't giving me what I need.*
> *I said I'm leavin' but she says, 'Never let me go . . .'*

Drago's voice was off key in parts. It sounded different – not in a good way – from the actual song. His throat must be very dry, Jess thought . . . or Larry was right, and it is all backing tracks.

He sang another verse, then stopped.

'Is that it?' Hazel barked. 'Is that the whole song?'

'No, there's more,' Chloë said.

'Sing on,' Hazel commanded.

'Dude, I can't. My voice is hurting, and I have to preserve it for my performance next week.'

'Listen here –'

'Hazel, it's okay.' Jess didn't want Hazel to force Drago to sing on. He was going to hate Jess for being the cause of all this. 'It was lovely of Drago to sing for me. I'm so grateful, but I understand he has to mind his voice.' To Drago she said, 'That was amazing. Thank you.'

'Yeah, well, you're welcome. I, like, hope you feel better soon.'

'Thanks.'

He asked Hazel, 'Can I go now?'

'Don't you have something to give her?' Hazel flared at him.

'Oh, yeah.' Drago fished around in his jacket pocket and handed Jess a signed CD of his latest album. It said, 'To Jessie, get beter soon, Drago, xx'.

'OMG! He misspelt better.' Chloë clamped a hand over her mouth.

Jess shushed her. 'Thank you so much.'

'Cool, so I'm gonna go now.' Drago scurried towards the door, followed by Hazel.

They heard her mutter, 'Thirty grand for five minutes and you can't sing.'

There was silence in the room, until Chloë said, 'Who knew Drago Jackson can't sing or spell?' and burst out laughing.

Jess looked down at the CD and began to laugh too. Then Kate and Piper joined in. They laughed until tears rolled down their faces.

When Hazel arrived back, they were still laughing. Her harassed face broke into a smile. 'Jesus, I'm glad you're all laughing – I was afraid you'd be crying. Useless, overindulged eejit of a boy.'

Jess wiped tears from her eyes. 'Thank you, Hazel. It was the best morning ever.'

'I'm sorry he was such a disappointment,' Hazel said.

'He wasn't,' Jess protested. 'I loved him, and I kind of feel sorry for him. I used to want to be famous, but now I'm not sure. It's a lot of pressure.'

'Pressure, my arse,' Hazel exclaimed. 'Pressure is having cancer, not singing out of tune.'

They all laughed again.

'Wait until I tell everyone that my mum forced Drago to sing and shouted at him. You're mad, Mum, but I love you.'

Hazel threw her arms around Chloë and kissed the top of her head. 'Well, to see Jess laughing and hear you say you love me, it was worth every penny.'

35

Kate and Olivia stood at the side of the bed, their faces turned towards the scanner. On the screen they could see Piper's baby clearly. As the sonographer moved the probe around, clicking images and measuring the child, they stood shoulder to shoulder, watching in silence.

Seeing the baby on the screen made it all very real in a new way. Kate could feel herself getting emotional. Her baby's baby. Her firstborn's child. It was insane, yet here they were, staring at this tiny new life.

She glanced at Luke, who was squeezing Piper's hand and shaking his head in amazement. They looked so young. Kate caught Olivia's eye – she was welling up too. Kate knew she was thinking the same thing: they were too young for all this responsibility. But they had made their decision and their families had to respect it and try to help.

If there was one thing Jess's cancer had taught Kate it was that you never knew what was around the corner. You could make all the plans you wanted for your children, but life would slam you in the face at any second and turn your world upside-down.

Who knew? Maybe they'd be great parents and it would all work out. Kate just had to hope for the best. She smiled encouragingly at Olivia, and Olivia raised her eyebrows and sighed. From what she'd seen of her so far, Kate really liked Olivia. She seemed down-to-earth and forthright. You knew where you stood with someone like Olivia. It would be a great help to the whole situation if the two grannies got on well. Kate winced. Granny! It was crazy.

She looked back at the screen. The baby floated around before them, oblivious to them in its dark world. It really was a miracle to think that inside Piper's stomach a child was being formed. It was what life was about, Kate thought. Life creating life. Motherhood was her *raison d'être*. She vowed to be a good grandmother and love this child as much as she did her own three.

The sonographer began talking to Luke and Piper, and showing them the measurements. Olivia leant against Kate and said quietly, 'They're so young.'

'That's just what I was thinking. God, I hope they'll be all right.'

'I think we're going to have to do a lot of minding and helping out,' Olivia whispered.

'I agree. They have no idea what's ahead.'

'None,' Olivia said. 'I hope it works out.'

'Me too.' Kate took Olivia's hand and squeezed it.

'I'm so glad you're on board, Kate. I was worried before we met that you'd want nothing to do with it all.'

'Gosh, no! I want to help as much as I can,' Kate assured her. 'This is Luke's responsibility and my grandchild. I'll be there every step of the way.'

'I really appreciate it. I know you have your hands full at the moment with Jess. We're all praying for her. Piper's so fond of her.'

'Thank you. Jess adores Piper – she's so lovely to her. She's a credit to you.'

Olivia's eyes filled again. 'She's a great girl. I just wish her father would come around – he's heartbroken. He can't handle it at all.'

'Fathers can be difficult.' Kate sighed. Nick had called her ten times to try to get her to force Luke and Piper into having an abortion. He was driving her mad. She knew he only wanted the best for Luke, but he needed to bloody well accept the baby instead of fighting it. He had chosen the path of most aggression – with the doctors, with cancer, and now with an unborn baby. It was unhelpful and bloody exhausting.

'I think Luke's going to be a great dad,' Olivia said. 'He's a really genuine boy. You've raised him well.'

'I hope so. It hasn't been easy for him with Nick leaving and all that, but he's been such a rock to me. I think he's probably more responsible than most eighteen-year-olds – he's had to be.'

'Maybe they'll make it,' Olivia said.

'We have to hope so,' Kate said.

Luke came over to them. 'I have to go. I've got rugby training.'

'I can give you a lift – I've a seminar to get to now,' Olivia said.

'You guys go ahead. I'll drop Piper home,' Kate offered.

'Are you sure?' Olivia asked.

'Absolutely.'

'Cool. Thanks, Mum.' Luke leant over to kiss her cheek. 'I'll be in to see Jess later. And thanks for being here today, Mum.'

'The baby's beautiful, Luke.'

He grinned. 'I know. It's incredible to see it growing.'

Kate watched them go as Piper wiped the gel off her stomach and pulled up her tracksuit bottoms.

She waddled over to Kate. 'Thanks for dropping me home.'

'I'm happy to. It was lovely to see the baby. It was a great distraction. Thanks for asking me to come.'

'I really wanted you to see it. I wanted my mum and dad to see it too. Dad said no, though.' Piper's cheeks flushed.

'Give him time. Nick hasn't totally come around either. Fathers can take longer to accept things.'

'I hope you're right. He seems so disappointed in me. It's hard to . . . to . . .' Piper began to sob.

Kate steered her to a row of chairs in the reception area and sat down beside her. It was the first time they had been alone together, and the first time Kate saw how hard the poor girl was struggling. 'Hey, now. I know it's hard for you, but your dad loves you and nothing can change that.'

'That's what Mum says. I'm sorry, Kate, I didn't mean to cry. I'm so emotional all the time. I just feel so bad for upsetting everyone. I know this must be hard for you. I mean, you've got so much stress with Jess – you really didn't need your son's stupid girlfriend getting pregnant.'

Kate patted Piper's hand. 'Don't you go blaming yourself. It takes two to tango. You were both careless, but it happens. The important thing is that you stay strong for each other and your baby.'

'I will, I promise. I know I'm a mess now, but I'm strong and I love Luke. I really do. He's so amazing. You all are. Jess is the bravest girl I know, and Bobby's so cute, and I'm so lucky to be part of your family. I'd never do anything to hurt you and I just want you to know that I'm sorry.' More tears ran down Piper's face.

Kate put her arm around Piper's shoulders. 'Stop apologizing. We're the lucky ones. You've been so lovely to Jess and I'll never be able to thank you enough for that. You're like the sister she always wished for. And I know you love Luke – I can see it. He loves you too. You've been a rock to him, and I'm so glad he has you, Piper. You're a fantastic girl.'

Piper pulled a tissue out of her coat pocket. 'Don't be nice to me or I'll never stop crying. I never knew you could be happy and terrified at the same time.'

Kate laughed. 'Welcome to the world of motherhood. You'll spend the rest of your life happy and terrified for your children. We mothers adore our kids, but we worry about them all the time, too. That's normal. The important thing for you to know is that we're all here for you. You're not alone, Piper. You have a wonderful family who love you and a new family who love you too.'

Piper threw her arms around Kate and buried her face in her neck. 'You have no idea how much that means to me. You're such a brilliant mother. I want to be just like you.'

I sincerely hope you have a less bumpy road, Kate thought, as she stroked Piper's hair.

That evening, Kate was sitting in hospital reading aloud when Jess began to cough. It got worse. Kate stood up and leant over her, patting her back gently. 'Take it easy – try to catch your breath.'

Jess was gasping for breath. '*Oooooooooh.*' She groaned as she coughed again. Blood splattered all over the sheets and Kate.

'Help me,' Jess wheezed, and vomited more blood. Her breath was ragged, and her eyes were wild with panic.

'Oh, my God!' Kate held her and screamed for help. Don't let her die, she prayed, please don't let her die.

A couple of seconds passed, which felt like hours, and panic gripped her. She felt sick with fear. Where were they? She didn't want to let Jess go, but she needed back-up. She sprinted to the door and onto the corridor, looking around wildly.

'Help,' she cried. 'It's Jess. Quickly!' She heard running feet and swivelled around.

Aideen, Jess's favourite nurse, was racing towards her. 'What's happened?' she called.

Kate didn't stop to talk, she dashed back into the room and grasped Jess by the shoulders, holding her upright.

Aideen burst in, then stopped short when she saw all the blood. She turned and barked instructions to a passing nurse, the urgency and concern clear in her voice. Then she walked quickly to the bed. 'It's okay, Jess, I'm here,' she said calmly.

Please, God, don't take her, Kate begged. Don't take my baby, please, please.

A moment later Kate was ushered out of the room while doctors and nurses dashed about, trying to control Jess's bleeding. After what seemed like an eternity, Dr Kennedy came out of the room. 'She's stable and sleeping now, Kate. But I'm afraid Jess has developed another infection, which is most unfortunate. We've put her on an antibiotic drip and we're going to run some tests to see if we can find the source. Often in these cases we don't discover it but the infection is dealt with nonetheless by the antibiotics. Her white blood count will hopefully reach a level soon where it will allow her to fight the infection on her own. She's very weak right now. She needs rest. I'll be back later to check on her. It's another unfortunate setback.'

Kate nodded. She felt more tired than she'd ever thought possible. It was one step forwards and three steps back. Over and over again. Why couldn't Jess catch a break? Why couldn't she just get better, come home and be herself again?

Kate sank into a chair and put her head into her hands. Why, God, why are you doing this to us, to her, to the sweetest girl in the world? Why are you punishing her? She sobbed, for Jess, for herself, for Luke, for Bobby, for her father, for the unborn baby . . . for everyone. Kate wanted to sleep and sleep and wake up when all of this was over. When life was good and kind again. When the nightmare was over once and for all.

36

Piper shuffled into the kitchen in her slippers and dressing-gown. She'd slept badly and was tired and hungry.

Her father was sitting at the kitchen table with the twins and Pauline, reading his newspaper and doing his best to ignore them.

'Morning, Dad,' Piper said, trying to sound more cheerful than she felt.

'Morning,' he said curtly.

'How are you?' Piper asked.

'Fine.'

Piper tried not to let it bother her. Ever since she'd told her parents about the pregnancy, her father had been distant and, frankly, cold. She knew he was disappointed, she knew he was upset, but she'd hoped that after six weeks of know-ing, he'd have thawed a little. She missed their conversations. She missed how he'd roll his eyes across the table at her when the twins were being annoying. She missed how his face used to light up when he saw her. Now he avoided eye contact or just looked angry when he saw her.

Her mother said he'd come around, that she needed to give him time. But Piper wondered how much time. She was beginning to think he'd never forgive her for 'messing her life up'. It really hurt. 'Would you like a coffee?' she asked him.

'No, I've had one.'

'Toast?'

'No.'

'Okay, then.' Piper filled the kettle and busied herself making toast, hiding her disappointment from him.

As her toast popped up, her father stood up and left the room, not addressing a word or even a glance in her direction. Piper buttered her toast and tried not to get upset.

Pauline put her plate into the dishwasher and said quietly, 'He still loves you. He just can't show it right now.'

Piper smiled at her sister. 'Thanks.'

One of the best things about being pregnant was how close she'd got to Pauline. She'd been amazing. So calm and measured and sensible and kind. Piper felt really bad for ever thinking Pauline was selfish. She realized now that her sister had a very big heart and was just a serious, focused person. Olivia said that from the first day Pauline had gone to school in Junior Infants, her goal was to be top of the class and nothing else mattered. She had no interest in sport or playing games or art.

But underneath her ambition and single-mindedness lay a compassionate soul. Piper hoped she could repay her sister's kindness some day. She'd already decided to ask Pauline to be the baby's godmother. No one deserved it more.

Pauline left to go to the college library and study in peace. Piper was left with the twins, who were bickering about whether Liam Hemsworth was hotter than his brother, Chris. She sat down and ate her toast.

Penny turned her attention to her older sister. 'Are you and Luke still having sex?'

Piper almost choked on her toast. 'What?'

'Are you having sex?'

'That is none of your business, you cheeky cow!'

'If you are, you'd better use protection,' Poppy warned her.

'Bit late for that,' Penny said, and they roared with laughter.

'Shut up, you freaks,' Piper hissed.

'Seriously, though, is it safe to have sex when you have a baby in your stomach?' Poppy asked.

'Why wouldn't it be?' Penny said.

'Wouldn't it poke the baby?'

'Urgh, gross! I never thought about that.'

Poppy turned to Piper. 'You need to stop having sex. You're poking your baby. You could poke it in the eye and blind it.'

'OMG, could you?'

'Yes, totally.'

'Do you think that's why Janine Oliver has a wonky eye?' Penny asked.

'Oh, my God, yes. Her dad's willy must have poked her.'

'*Grooooss*,' they both squealed.

Piper put her toast down. 'It never ceases to amaze me what idiots you are.'

'If you have sex just after getting pregnant, can you have twins?' Poppy wondered.

'Duh, of course not,' Penny said.

'How do you know?'

'Because twins are conceived the same day,' Penny said.

'I read about this woman who had twins three weeks apart. They obviously weren't conceived the same day.'

'Maybe she just had one early and one on time,' Penny said.

'Do you think Piper could be having twins? Apparently it's genetic, and if your mum had twins, you could have twins.'

'She had a scan and it was just one baby,' Penny said, talking as if Piper wasn't in the room.

'Yeah, but sometimes the twin can be hiding behind the other baby.'

'It would be so cool if she had twins.'

It would be so not cool if I had twins, Piper thought. Thank God the obstetrician had confirmed only one baby, which was quite enough of a prospect to deal with.

'Piper, are you sure it's not twins?' Penny asked her.

'Yes, positive, thank God,' Piper said.

'No need to be so rude. You'd be lucky to have twins like us.' Penny was unimpressed.

'I'd shoot myself if I had twins like you,' Piper muttered.

'You're so narky. You should be careful. If you're this narky to Luke, he might dump you.'

Piper took a bite of her toast. 'Thanks, Penny, that's just what I need to hear.'

'You should also watch what you eat,' Poppy said, pointing to the toast. 'One slice is plenty, Piper. You're not actually eating for two. Some women stuff their faces the whole way through their pregnancies and are like whales and it takes them ages to lose the baby weight. Some of them never lose it and are just fat for ever.'

Piper stood up and threw the rest of her toast into the bin. 'Thanks for making me lose my appetite and for the great advice.' She slammed the door hard on her way out.

Piper lay on her bed and tried to do calming breathing exercises, inhale for five and exhale for five. She shouldn't let her sisters wind her up, but they were so annoying. They were clueless about life. She rolled onto her side. She was due to meet Luke in an hour for coffee. She'd eat with him – at least he wouldn't comment on how much she ate. Mind you, maybe she should watch what she was eating. She had been eating way more than usual. She didn't want to be a big whale. What if she was one of the women who couldn't lose the weight? Luke would dump her for a fit girl.

*

Piper sat in the café staring out of the window. Luke was late. She was nervous: he had barely been in touch in the last four days. He'd said things with Jess were bad and he'd meet her when he could. Piper had tried not to hound him, but she was desperate for news. Two days ago, she'd even called Maggie, who'd said she'd fill her in when she could but had never called back.

Piper watched Luke walking towards the café and her heart sank. She knew by the way his head was down that something was wrong. She knew Jess had been very slow to recover from the infection and was due more test results. Maybe they weren't good.

Luke sank into the chair opposite her.

'What's going on?' Piper asked. 'What did they say?'

Luke began to cry. Oh, God. Piper reached out and held his hands. He pulled one back to wipe his tears with a napkin.

'It's bad. Really bad. The cancer is worse. Way worse. The chemo's not working and it's the strongest they can give her without killing her.'

'Oh, Luke.' Piper bit her lip, trying to hold back the tears.

'It's . . . it's . . . over, Piper. She's not going to make it.' He covered his face with the napkin and sobbed.

Piper was so shocked that she was numb. Over? How could this happen? They had all believed one hundred per cent that Jess would get better. She had to – she was twelve, for God's sake. Jess couldn't die – she just couldn't. It was crazy to say that could happen.

'There must be something,' Piper said desperately. 'Maybe she needs to go to America. They have more cutting-edge treatments over there. I can research it. We can go with her, we'll figure it out.'

Luke pulled the napkin from his face. 'We've spent the last three days with Maggie and Hazel and everyone we know looking at options. Hazel offered to charter a plane to fly us to America. Maggie got on to the best paediatric oncologist in the top cancer hospital in Boston. He looked at the test results and said the same thing. So she found the second best one, in Philadelphia, same answer, same with Cincinnati. She got the top guy at Great Ormond Street in London to talk to us. Same answer. She's dying, Piper. My little sister is dying. How can there be a God? My stupid fucking bone marrow didn't help her. I can't deal with this and Mum is . . . she's . . . she's broken.'

Piper's body was cold, as if ice was running through her veins. She was shaking. 'Does Jess know?'

Luke shook his head. 'She knows the cancer is worse, but they haven't told her yet how bad it is. But they'll tell her soon – I'd say she knows anyway. She's just so sick.'

'Look, this might not be the right thing to say, but miracles do happen.'

'Don't,' Luke snapped. 'Don't do that. I don't want false hope. Dad keeps banging on about miracles and trying more risky treatment. He read about some dodgy experimental treatment they're testing in India and he wants to take Jess there. But when Mum mentioned it, the American doctors were, like, "no way". They said it would be a really bad idea and that she would die in India, away from home and those she loved. They said the best thing to do was to try to keep Jess as comfortable as possible and make the next few months really special.'

'What did your dad say?'

'He's going crazy, shouting at everyone that they're not trying hard enough, telling them all to think outside the box, telling Mum she's quitting on her own child, shouting at

Maggie to do more, cursing, punching walls and generally having a total fucking meltdown.'

Piper wouldn't say so to Luke, but she felt really sorry for Nick. Whatever about his failings as a father to Luke and Bobby, he loved Jess madly. He'd spent as much time as he could with her in hospital, playing cards and watching goofy YouTube videos. He could probably have tried to spend more time with her – Kate was the one who was there seventy per cent of the time – but every time he came to see Jess his phone would start ringing, either Jenny or work. Jenny always seemed to need him for some drama or other or else work did . . . He always seemed stressed. Every time she saw him, and his pale, tight face, Piper worried he might have a heart attack.

Luke rubbed his exhausted eyes. 'I haven't slept in four nights. We've been up all night researching, calling people and going over and over the options.'

'What are you going to do?'

'The doctors hold out no hope. They said Jess's cancer was incredibly aggressive and unlucky and unfortunate, and all those words you just don't want to hear. They were all very sorry not to be able to give us better news or more hope.'

Piper was lost for words. What do you say to the boy you love when he's just told you his sister is dying? 'Sorry' seems so lame. But she was sorry, desperately sorry, and sad and heartbroken.

She adored Jess. She was an amazing girl. She was so brave and never complained. She'd been through so much in her short life – her parents breaking up, Larry dying, getting cancer . . . It was just so unfair. Why was life so cruel to her? Jess deserved to grow up and have boyfriends, a husband and a family and happiness and joy. She deserved more time.

Lots more time. How come bad people got to live and good people, really, really good people, like Jess, didn't? It wasn't right. It was all wrong. Everything was wrong. Piper felt physically sick. She looked at Luke's devastated face and held his hand.

Over and over again she said one little word, 'Sorry, sorry, sorry . . .'

37

Kate sat very still and tried to take in the words.

'Bacterial and fungal infection,' Dr Kennedy said. 'Her heart function has been adversely affected . . . the chemotherapy was unsuccessful . . .'

It took Dr Kennedy three minutes to tell them that Jess was going to die. Three minutes for Kate's world to be crushed by the wrecking ball of the unthinkable and be destroyed. Three minutes for her heart to be shattered into a thousand jagged pieces.

'I'm afraid the prognosis is now bad. I'm so very sorry,' he said.

Kate felt as if she was swimming under water, the words blurred. Bad? Did he say bad? 'Bad' in medical terms meant 'fatal'. She gasped for air. Her mouth was dry, her lungs wouldn't work. No air. She wheezed . . . Still no air.

'Kate?' She could hear someone calling her name, but they seemed far away, back at the shore, while she was far out to sea, sinking fast. 'Kate?'

Bad prognosis? Bad . . . bad . . . bad.

No air. Can't breathe. She tried to suck in, nothing. Breathe, Kate, she told herself. Breathe!

She sucked in air . . . Yes, air. In and out, in and out.

He said again that he was 'very sorry' . . . Oh, God.

Her chest moved up and down. She could hear now. It was Nick. He was shouting. She opened her eyes.

'Did you say *bad* prognosis?'

Dr Kennedy nodded sadly. 'The drugs have damaged her heart. Her cardiac function has been compromised. The risk of heart failure and further distressing infections is very high. The odds are stacked against her, I'm afraid. I'm so very sorry.'

Nick was stomping around the room, shouting. 'There has to be something you can do! For Christ's sake, she's twelve years old – you can't give up. There must be something, some new treatment, some miracle cure.'

'I promise you that we have exhausted every avenue and looked at every possible option. No stone has been left unturned,' Dr Kennedy assured him quietly.

'No!' Nick shook his fist in the doctor's face. 'No way. Not my Jess, not her.' His voice broke and he punched the wall violently. Kate heard a crunch. He'd broken something. It probably felt good. Maybe she should punch something too.

One word comes into your life: cancer. One two-syllable word that splits your heart down the middle. Broken. You can't fix it.

'There has to be something you can do,' Nick raged. 'There's always a solution. What about a full body blood transfusion?'

Dr Kennedy hesitated. 'We tried new agents with this round of chemotherapy and unfortunately we were unsuccessful. This treatment was aggressive. She is very weak.'

'I don't care what you think. We'll try another round of it. Let's get her signed up.'

'I would be concerned that Jess wouldn't survive any further treatment, and that her quality of life during treatment would be even worse than it is now.'

'Jess is a fighter. You don't know her. She's stronger than she looks. She's the bravest kid . . .' Nick broke down.

'I don't think her heart could take it,' Dr Kennedy said gently.

'How long does she have?' Kate somehow managed to ask.

'It's very difficult to say.'

'Try.'

'Weeks.'

'How many?'

'Four, perhaps six, possibly a few more. Children are extraordinary.'

Kate shoved her fist into her mouth to stop herself screaming. Weeks? She only had precious weeks left with her beautiful Jess. She bent over as the pain hit her again.

'You have to do something, for Christ's sake. You have to save her!' Nick yelled, his face twisted in anger and grief. Kate watched as he threw a chair against the wall, then kicked and punched it until he wore himself out. He eventually collapsed on the floor, sobbing. 'Not Jess, not my baby girl.'

Kate knelt beside him and held him. They held each other and cried. Jess wasn't going to make it. She wasn't going to grow up, she wasn't going to have the life Kate wished for her. She was going to be taken from them. Ripped away when her life was only beginning. Their Jess was going to die, and they were powerless to stop it.

Kate stood on the seafront and looked around. Where the hell was he?

A man waved at her and rushed towards her, his arms open wide. She walked towards him. When she reached him, he pulled her into a bear hug, holding her tight.

She pulled back. 'Is it really you?'

'Sorry, I should have warned you I'd shaved the beard off.'

'Liam, you look completely different, younger and . . .' Kate trailed off. He looked ten years younger, and handsome. Under all that hair was a lovely face.

'I can't tell you how sorry I am,' Liam said, his face full of concern and kindness. 'I'm not going to ask you how you are, but I am going to bring you somewhere I used to come to shout at the world. It helped a little.'

Kate followed him up a steep path and across a forested area to a clearing. She'd never been there before and it was only ten miles from her house. 'How did you know about this place?' she asked, out of breath from climbing.

'A colleague told me about it when June was sick and suggested I come here for walks to clear my head. I don't think he meant for me to come and shout my head off.' He smiled. 'It's just over here.'

They came to the edge of a cliff. The sea spread out in front of them. You could see nothing but sea and sky and, far in the distance, the faint line where they met.

'Now, I'm going to walk away and I want you to shout, Kate. Scream your head off and tell God and the universe exactly what you think of them. I promise it will help you. You must get some of the pain out or it'll kill you.'

Kate waited until he'd walked away and then she turned to the ocean. Watching seagulls dipping and diving, she thought about Jess and how she was being robbed of a future and her beautiful little family was being robbed of a daughter, a sister and a granddaughter, and now an auntie as well.

Grief and rage rose in her chest and she began to shout. She shouted louder than she'd thought possible. She screamed until she thought the veins in her neck would burst. She wanted them to – she wanted them to burst. She wanted to throw herself off the cliff and for her body to smash into pieces below. She wanted to die. She should be the one dying. Her, the mother, not the child, never, ever the child.

Kate shouted and screamed until her voice ran out. She collapsed onto her knees. Liam appeared beside her.

'Are you okay?'

'Yes,' she croaked.

'You gave it socks. Well done. All that anger will eat you up inside. I recommend you come here once a week, if not more.'

'Thank you, Doctor.' Kate gave him a half-smile, her heart breaking.

Liam put his arm around her. 'Now I'm taking you for a lemon and honey tea, fix up that throat. There's a little tea shop in the village I think you'll like.'

Kate laid her head on his shoulder. 'Why is this happening?'

'Don't ask why. It will torment you and there is no answer. You have to focus now on making these last weeks the best of Jess's life. If I can help in any way, please just ask.'

Kate looked up at him. 'You already are.' She kissed his smooth cheek. It was lovely and soft. 'You really do look so different.'

He grinned. 'Nathalie told me that no self-respecting man would go around looking like *un hobo*. She insisted on bringing me to a barber her ex-boyfriend used to go to, and before I knew it, I was clean-shaven. I've had a beard for thirty years. It took me a while to get used to it myself.'

'I like it,' Kate said.

'Good.' He smiled down at her.

A little later they sat in the little tea shop, Liam drinking coffee and Kate sipping the lemon and honey tea he'd ordered to soothe her throat. They shared a slice of chocolate cake. It was the first time Kate had been able to taste anything since Jess's diagnosis.

Most of the time she forgot to eat, and when she did, everything tasted like chalk or cardboard. But she could taste that cake.

'Penny for your thoughts?' Liam asked.

'I was just thinking that when I'm with you I feel calmer. Most of the time I either think I'm going to have a heart attack or I feel numb. But today is the first day I feel in any way calmer. It's the first time I've stopped shaking too.'

'Much as I'd like to take credit, I think letting go of some of your anger helped.'

'Yes, but don't underestimate your positive influence. I'm sorry for calling you at all hours all the time. I just need someone to get me through the nights and you're the person I want to talk to.'

Liam smiled at her. 'It's my pleasure. What you're going through is unbearable. I want to help in any way I can. I wish I could do more.'

Kate sighed. 'No one can. It's just a nightmare that I have to go through and I have no idea how to do it. How do you watch your daughter die? How do you watch her fade away, suffer and die? There's no manual for that. No *Dummy's Guide to Losing a Child*.' Her croaky voice broke and she began to cry, head bent low, shoulders shuddering.

Liam handed her a handkerchief. A proper linen one from his pocket.

'I'll ruin it,' Kate said.

'That's what it's there for.'

She blew her nose. Typical Liam to have a handkerchief on him. He was an old-fashioned gent. Kate folded it and put it into her pocket. 'Sorry.'

'How are the boys?'

'Luke is throwing himself into rugby. His big final is on Sunday. He's quiet and doesn't say much. I'm glad he has

Piper. Bobby is Bobby. Angry, kicking everything, arguing with his teacher and generally furious with the world. The poor child just doesn't understand.'

'Hard to process so much at the tender age of seven. How's your dad?'

Kate began to cry again. 'He's heartbroken. He's aged ten years. He just can't believe it. Seeing him so crushed is unbearable. He keeps saying, "It should be me, not her."'

'Poor man. He's right, too.'

Kate pushed the cake away, her appetite gone again. 'I'd better go. Maggie's back from her work trip to New York to sort us all out, as she says. She's a wonder.'

'I'm glad you have such a good friend to rely on.'

Kate took his hand in hers. 'I have another good one right here.'

Liam reddened. 'I'm glad you think so. I'll be cheering for Luke on Sunday. I hope they win. Give him a bit of a boost.'

'Thanks. It'll be a welcome distraction anyway.'

They hugged, and Kate rushed off to her car, thanking God for sending Liam to her just when she needed someone. He was so kind, so unobtrusive and undemanding, but there whenever he was needed. He really was like a gift, and she felt very grateful to have met him.

When she got home, she found Maggie sitting at the table talking to Bobby. She stood to the side of the door and watched them.

'So what you're saying is that when you grow up you're going to find the cure for stinky cancer?' Maggie said.

'Yes.'

'High five,' Maggie said. 'And, by the way, I think you're the very person who will do it because you're smart, single-minded and determined.'

'What does single-minded mean? It sounds like I only have one mind, but I don't, I have lots of minds. One for facts, one for maths, one for spelling –'

'No, it doesn't mean only one mind,' Maggie cut across him. 'It means focused, which is a good thing, vital if you want to cure cancer.'

'Well, I do. I never want other families to feel like this. It's the worst. I hate cancer. I want to kill it and smash it into pieces.'

'Me, too,' Maggie agreed, her eyes shining with tears. 'Hey, let's get something and crush it to make ourselves feel better.' She looked around and saw some bread dough on the counter. She went over, picked it up and brought it over to the table. She pushed it up into a big mound. 'Now, Bobby, smash it with your fists. Go for it. Pretend it's cancer.'

Bobby stood up and, leaning over the table, he walloped the dough. He beat it over and over again.

'Go on,' Maggie shouted. 'Punch its lights out.'

Kate watched Bobby's little hands flying at the dough, like a boxer's. His face was red with exertion, but he kept punching. Eventually he fell back into his chair, puffing.

'Good boy. Do you feel better?'

He nodded.

Kate smiled to herself. Shouting at the sea for her, punching dough for Bobby. Who knew that such simple things would help get rid of some of the agony of grief?

Maggie sat down again opposite Bobby. 'I know this sucks. No kid should have a sister who is dying. I'm really sorry this is happening to you, Bobby, and you know that Mum and Dad and Granddad and I would do anything to stop it, but we can't. I know you're sad and angry and it's important that you get the anger out. Otherwise it'll make your stomach hurt and your chest too.'

'Could I get cancer?' Bobby's eyes were wide.

'No, God, no.' Maggie went over to hug him. 'Nothing like that. It's just that worry and sadness and anger can make your stomach ache.'

Bobby twisted Maggie's long silver chain around in his little fingers. 'My stomach hurts all the time.'

Kate felt sick. Her poor little boy. He was hurting so much. She walked into the kitchen, picked him up and hugged him tight. 'I'm sorry, Bobby. I'm sorry about your stomach. I'm sorry about everything. You're such a great boy.'

Bobby hugged her back fiercely. 'It's okay, Mummy. I didn't tell you cos I didn't want you to have any more worries.'

Kate cried into his hair. 'I'm your mum. You should tell me when anything hurts. I wish none of this was happening. I hate that you're sad. I love you, and I'm sorry I've been so distracted with everything and haven't had more time for you.'

Bobby stroked her hair. 'It's all right, Mummy. When Jess is gone you'll have more time.' He jerked backwards, his hand flew up to his mouth. 'I didn't mean it like that, I swear. I didn't mean it.'

Kate hugged him closer. 'I know, angel, I know.'

For the first time since Jess's diagnosis, the long months of worry and the awful final news, Bobby cried. His little body let out all of his pain. He shook and quivered as he wept huge tears, crying with his whole body.

Maggie couldn't hold back her own any longer. She hid her face in her hands, shoulders sagging.

Kate held tight to Bobby and said over and over, 'Let it out, let it all out. I'm here for you. I'm here for you.'

Maggie silently left the room. Kate saw her punch the dough as she passed it.

38

Jess looked at the dandelion card. 'Wherever you are, Larry, I'm coming too,' she whispered. She felt awful, really awful. The chemo had been horrendous and then the infection . . . It had been terrifying. She'd thought she was going to choke to death on her own blood. She wasn't going to die like that, no way. It wasn't how she was going to leave this world. Thank God the antibiotics had cleared up the infection. At least that was some small mercy. She was hoping to go home in a few days.

Nick had just left her room, striding out in frustration. She knew he was upset with her, but she couldn't give him what he wanted. He was insisting she tried some new treatment, but Dr Kennedy said she was too weak for it.

'Come on, Jess, what harm can it do to give it a go?' he'd wheedled. 'This is a chance, a real chance. We've got to take it.'

Jess shook her head. 'I'm sorry, Dad, I can't.'

'Why not?' he said impatiently. 'You're stronger than you think, I know it.'

She shook her head again. 'Not any more. I can't do it. I feel so sick, Dad. I don't want any more drugs or pain. I can't. I just want to go home.'

Nick raked his fingers through his hair. 'Jessie, please, for me,' he implored. 'I can't be without you. What they're saying . . . we have to try.'

He was so intense, and she knew it came from love, which was what hurt most of all.

'Daddy, I need you to start letting me go,' she said quietly, looking directly into his eyes.

Nick's head was shaking, but no sound was coming from his open mouth. Jess reached over and put her hand on his, willing him to understand.

'No.' His voice trembled. 'No, Jess. I will never, ever let you go. Do you hear me? Never.'

Jess remembered Larry saying he wanted his parents to hate him, to make it easier on them when he died. She had told him it wouldn't work that way, and it wouldn't work for her and her parents either. But she could feel death upon her and she had to try to make them understand that it was coming, and they couldn't stop it.

'Dad, you have to start letting me go. I love you, and I know it's really hard for you,' her voice caught in her throat, 'but I'm not going to get better and I want to go home. I don't want to die in here. I need you to hear me, Dad, and I need you to help me.' She watched his face carefully. 'And if the pain gets unbearable maybe you could help it stop. When it gets too much for me, maybe someone could make it all go away.'

Nick stood up with a jolt, as if a bolt of electricity had shot through him. He was staring at her in horror, blinking rapidly. 'Jesus Christ, Jess, what are you saying? If you think . . .'

She knew he understood, and she also knew that he was incapable of helping. She should have known he'd react like that. Her strong, fight-to-the-end father would not help her.

'I'll never give up on you,' he said roughly. 'Never. I'm going to keep fighting until we fix this.'

Jess sank back tiredly onto her pillow. 'Okay, Dad.'

After that, there had been nothing to say. Nick gazed at her reproachfully, as if he thought she was quitting on him and life. But he had no idea how awful it was. It wasn't his fault. No one could imagine this physical hell unless they were in it. In the end, to put them both out of their misery, Jess had told him she wanted to sleep. He'd held her tight and told her to keep strong and then, thankfully, he'd left her alone.

Silent tears seeped out of Jess's tightly shut eyes. She had tried. She had given it everything, but the cancer was too strong. She didn't have anything left in her. Her dad didn't understand, no one did. It was so hard, so painful, so awful. There had to be an end to it, one way or another, because she couldn't carry on like this.

Jess loved her dad, but he was wearing her out. His constant talk of miracles made her want to scream. She was only twelve, but even she knew there were no miracles. If there were, Larry wouldn't have died.

The truth was, Jess wasn't afraid of death. She was sick of feeling ill. She watched as everyone around her suffered too, everyone she loved and wanted to protect. Her cancer was ruining their lives, too. They all looked older and sadder, exhausted and heartbroken. Cancer hadn't just destroyed Jess's life, it had destroyed theirs, too, and that was as hard to bear as her own suffering.

Everyone was worn out. Cancer had controlled her life for long enough, and Jess knew what she had to do. She was going to take control. She lay back in her bed and stared at the ceiling. 'I'm going to do this my way, Cancer, you bastard, not yours.'

It was Sunday afternoon and Jess was woken by the sense of someone moving around her room. She slowly opened her eyes, and as she blinked, Piper and Chloë came into focus, smiling down at her.

'Hi,' she said, trying to sit up but her arms were too weak. Chloë and Piper instinctively bent to help her.

'What are you guys doing here?'

Chloë and Piper smiled at each other. 'We're breaking you out.'

'What?'

'Look!' Chloë opened the door and pulled in a wheelchair.

Piper smiled at Jess's surprised face. 'I know the doctors said you couldn't go to Luke's final because you're still on IV antibiotics, but we spoke to Dr Kennedy this morning and we told him we'd look after you and bring the IV drip and put you in a wheelchair and make sure your mask was on to prevent infection and wrap you up warmly and keep you away from the crowds and all that . . . so he said yes!' Piper beamed at her.

'Piper was, like, OMG, amazing. She would not take no for an answer.' Chloë danced around the room.

'You were pretty great too. Chloë said she wasn't leaving until he said yes.'

Jess's heart jumped. 'Seriously? I can go?' She wanted to punch the air. She had been crushed when they said she couldn't go to Luke's match. It was his big day, his big final. She wanted to be there so badly. Her dad had said he'd come and watch it with her on the TV in her room, but she really wanted to see it live, and now she was going to.

'I love you, guys! I'll never forget this.'

'Stop!' Chloë exclaimed. 'I'm not crying – it took me ages to do my eye make-up.'

Nathalie strode through the door, carrying blankets, followed by Aideen, who had a mask for Jess. Aideen took Jess's temperature, then her blood pressure and checked her thoroughly before she let the others take her away. 'You have a wonderful time, pet. You deserve it. I'll be cheering Luke's team on from here. See you later.' She kissed Jess's head. Turning to the three girls, she said sternly, 'You're to mind her carefully, all right, and if it's too much or she shows any signs of deteriorating, you bring her straight back here. Is that clear?'

They nodded solemnly. Aideen winked at Jess and left them to get her ready.

They helped her to get dressed. Chloë did her eye make-up, and Piper tucked the blankets around her. Then Nathalie produced Luke's school hat and scarf. 'Luke said you 'ad to wear these for the good luck.' She gently placed the hat on Jess's head and wrapped the scarf around her neck.

'He thinks you're watching the match in here with your dad. He's going to be so happy when he sees you,' Piper said. She adjusted the hat and fixed the blankets one last time. 'Now you're perfect.'

'Fab,' Chloë agreed.

'Not too bad,' Nathalie said.

Jess was impatient to go. 'Get me out of here,' she said.

They wheeled her out of the hospital, and Jess's heart soared as she got out into the fresh air. Her mum usually took her out for a few minutes every day, but lately Jess hadn't had the energy. Now she felt wiped out from the effort of getting dressed and ready for the match, but elated from excitement too.

Granddad was waiting for them in his car. He jumped out when he saw them. Bowing, he said, 'Your carriage awaits, m'lady,' and kissed Jess's cheek.

They lifted her into the front seat and put the wheelchair in the boot.

'Does Mum know I'm coming?' Jess asked.

'It's a surprise for her and Luke,' Piper said.

Granddad drove slowly, taking great care not to hit any potholes or bumps in the road. Eventually Chloë leant forward. 'I don't mean to be rude, George, but you need to step on it or we'll be late.'

'Yes, George, why are you driving like the old man?' Nathalie asked.

'Possibly because I am an old man,' Granddad reminded her. 'I'm driving carefully so Jess won't get jostled about.'

Jess patted his arm. 'You can go a bit faster.'

He nodded and put his foot on the accelerator. They arrived with five minutes to go before the starting whistle.

As they wheeled Jess into the grounds, she could see the teams warming up. Luke was passing a ball to Rocco. He looked so strong and handsome that Jess wanted to stand up and shout, 'That's my brother.'

Chloë ran ahead to where Jess's mother and Bobby were standing beside the pitch. Bobby was swinging on the bar that ran around it. Chloë tapped Kate on the shoulder. 'Turn around, we have a surprise.'

She turned to look. 'Oh, my God . . . How?' Kate squeaked. 'She shouldn't be . . .'

'It's fine.' Piper was straight over to reassure her. 'We squared it with Dr Kennedy and Aideen checked her just before we left. They said it's okay. We just didn't want her to miss it.'

Mum threw her arms around Piper, then Chloë, Nathalie and Granddad. Finally she crouched down and hugged Jess. 'Do you feel all right?'

Jess nodded. 'Yes. The adrenalin will keep me going. I'm so happy to be here, Mum. Please don't worry, let's just enjoy it.'

Her mother kissed her. 'I'm so glad you're here.'

Bobby shouted to Luke, 'Look, Luke! Look who's here!'

Luke turned, and when he saw Jess, his whole face lit up. He ran over. 'Jess? I can't believe it.'

'I came. Piper and Chloë and Nathalie busted me out.'

Luke looked at Piper, and Jess saw the love in his eyes. 'We couldn't let her miss it.' Piper grinned at him.

'We have to win now, for you, Jess.' Luke began to choke up.

'Off with you,' Granddad said. 'You need to focus on the game.'

Luke ran onto the pitch, but turned back one last time and gave Jess the thumbs-up. She did the same back.

'Hello, gang.' They turned to see Maggie walking towards them, with Hazel.

'You made it.' Kate hugged her friend.

'I almost didn't. Couldn't get a taxi at the airport for love or money – the queue was a mile long, all the bloody tourists over for St Patrick's weekend, but Hazel here saved the day. She came out to the airport and picked me up.'

Hazel looked at Jess. 'You're a bit cold, darling. Put this over you and you'll be toasty.' Hazel took off her fur coat and wrapped it around Jess.

It felt soft and warm. Jess smiled up at her. 'Thank you, Hazel, but won't you be cold?'

'Don't you worry about me, I'll be fine.'

Nathalie gave Hazel her hat, Chloë gave her her scarf, Piper gave her her gloves and Granddad offered her his jacket.

'Stop, I'm fine,' Hazel said, shivering.

'I insist.' Granddad wrapped it around her.

'You're a gentleman, George, thank you.'

Nathalie pointed to a man in the stand behind them. 'It's Liam.'

They looked round. Jess peered to see him. Luke had told her about Liam: he'd said he was a hairy yoke and he didn't think there was anything going on with Kate, they were just pals, but this man wasn't hairy: he was clean-shaven and had a nice, kind face.

'Don't you think he looks so much more 'andsome now without the beard?' Nathalie said to Kate.

She nodded awkwardly.

'So that's Liam,' Maggie said, grinning. 'Not the older hairy hobo you described, but a very attractive man.'

'Who's Liam?' Hazel asked.

'A friend of Kate's,' Granddad said.

' 'E is a lovely man. I like this one,' Nathalie said.

'A good friend?' Hazel winked at Kate.

'A friend,' she said firmly.

Nathalie waved up at him. Liam spotted them and waved enthusiastically back.

Jess noticed her mum flushing and smiling, which made her smile too.

Chloë nudged her friend. 'She likes him.'

'I had no idea he was coming,' Kate muttered to Maggie.

'He isn't here for Luke,' Maggie drawled.

Nathalie indicated for Liam to come down. He shook his head. Then, to Kate, he mouthed, 'Good luck.'

Jess watched her mum smiling again, then Jess waved at Liam. He waved back, beaming at her.

'Who are we waving at?' Nick asked, as he joined them, rubbing his hands together against the cold.

'No one,' Kate said quickly.

'A friend of Kate's,' Maggie said, just as quickly.

'Do I know him?' Nick peered up into the stand.

'No,' Kate said firmly, giving Maggie a warning look. 'Now, come on, let's watch the match.'

Jess tugged her mum's coat. Kate bent down. 'He looks nice, Mum.'

'He's a friend, Jess.'

'I know, but he looks like a nice one.'

'He is,' she agreed. 'Now, enough about that.'

Nick came over and hugged Jess. 'You look good, Jess. I was thrilled when Piper texted me to tell me she'd broken you out for the game. Are you feeling stronger?'

Jess looked into her father's hopeful eyes and decided to lie, just for today. 'A bit, Dad, yes.'

'Brilliant,' Nick said. 'That's my girl.'

The whistle blew and the match started. It was very close. The teams were well matched. Just before half-time, Luke missed a tackle and the other team scored to go ahead by five points. Luke's head hung down as the coach gave them their team talk.

They couldn't hear what he was saying, but Jess saw him pointing his finger at Luke, and it didn't look like he was praising him.

'Poor Luke.' Piper was upset. 'He'll never forgive himself if they lose because of that try.'

'He'll come back fighting,' George comforted her.

'Of course he will, he's brilliant,' Maggie said, putting a protective arm around Piper.

'Luke's the best,' Bobby said.

Jess stared up at a passing cloud. 'Larry, if you're up there, help Luke play well,' she prayed.

Beside Jess, Kate was jumping from one foot to the other. Nick went over to her. 'Hey, calm down, you'll have a heart attack. Luke will come through, mark my words. Our son is tough. He'll bounce back.'

'I just couldn't bear it if they lost and he felt it was his fault,' she said.

'Stay calm. This is Iron Will Luke we're talking about,' he told her.

She smiled at the use of their old nickname for him. Nick had christened him that when he was about three years old – a solid lump of toddler determination, climbing on every stick of furniture and never heeding any warnings. She'd almost forgotten it – Iron Will Luke. She nodded. 'You're right,' she said. 'He'll come back out and kick up murder.'

Nick had indeed been right: Luke came out in the second half and tackled everyone and every ball. He was like a man possessed.

'I think the rugby is so violent. I prefer the tennis.' Nathalie sighed as they watched Lorcan being smashed to the ground by the opposition. 'All this running and pushing each other down in the mud is ridiculous.'

George shook his head. 'It's a very skilful game, Nathalie. One that your lot are actually pretty good at.'

'Pfff! What is skilful about 'olding another boy's legs so he fall over? Or 'ugging in a big group and trying to push the other team back? It make no sense.'

'The scrum is an integral part of the game.' George slapped his forehead.

'Integral, why? Because I think maybe they like to 'ug each other, maybe they are 'omosexual but too afraid to say.'

'Sweet Mother of Jesus, will you stop talking rubbish? They are not gay, they are just playing a game of rugby.'

'Don't wind him up, Nathalie,' Kate warned her. 'We don't need his blood pressure going any higher.'

Dad's phone rang. It was Jenny. Jess was delighted when he ignored it and put his phone on silent.

With five minutes to go, Luke's team were three points down. Their little group was quiet. Jess could hear her father muttering under his breath, 'Come on, Luke, you can do it. Give us a try.'

With two minutes to go they passed the ball to Rocco, star of the team. He came thundering down the line towards them. They all cheered and shouted – even Nathalie was screaming, 'Go, go, go.'

As Rocco got closer to the try line he glanced around. Luke was beside him. Rocco looked ahead: he could have dived and scored, but he passed it to Luke. The ball soared into the air. Luke caught it and dived to the ground. Try!

The place erupted. Jess sat in her wheelchair grinning as everyone danced, jumped, cheered, hugged and cried.

Luke hugged Rocco, then pulled him across the field to where his family was waiting. 'That was for you, sis.' Then he pushed a bashful Rocco in front of her. 'This man is a legend,' he declared, as Rocco blushed and laughed. 'He let me take the try,' Luke said, choking up with all the emotion.

'Just teamwork,' Rocco said, smiling at Jess. 'I knew it meant the world to him.' She nodded at him gratefully. 'I hope you're feeling better soon,' he said. 'I'm sorry you've been so sick.'

Jess nodded again, unable to speak, and watched as Rocco and Luke ran back to their teammates. Rocco took the kick and put it over to add two more points. Then the referee blew the whistle and the whole place erupted again. Jess was crying, laughing and cheering all at once. It felt so good to be part of normal life, of all these people happy together. She felt so happy herself.

Her mother held her hand and smiled through her tears. 'Wasn't he amazing?' she said.

'Absolutely,' Jess said.

Behind Kate, she saw Liam approaching. He gently tapped her mother on the shoulder. 'I'm so happy for you. What a try,' he said. 'I'll talk to you soon.' He turned to leave, but she pulled him back.

'Liam, wait, I want you to meet Jess.'

She introduced them. Jess shook his hand.

'I'm very pleased to meet you, Jess. I've heard so much about you. You must be very proud of your brother today.'

'Yes, I am. I'm happy to meet you too.' Jess looked into his blue eyes. They were full of kindness. 'I know you've been a good friend to Mum through all this. I'm glad about that.'

'It's been a very hard time for you all,' he said, looking straight at her. Jess felt he understood and smiled at him. 'Well, I won't keep you. You've a lot to celebrate. I'll be off.'

'Hang on there! I'm Maggie, and I want to say hello too.'

Liam stuck out his hand. 'Great to meet you, Maggie. I've heard you're the fantastic best friend.'

Maggie smiled. 'Charming to boot. You really are the whole package.'

Liam laughed and shook a finger at her. 'Kate said you were a live wire. She was right.'

Maggie threw back her head and laughed. '*Touché.*'

George came over then and introduced himself, followed by Hazel and Chloë, and finally Bobby. Liam seemed a bit overwhelmed, but he handled it with grace and good humour.

Bobby peered up at him. 'Did you used to be all hairy?'

'Yes, I did, until Nathalie here very kindly told me I looked like a hobo and to shave it off.'

'I sawed you in the café once when you were hairy. You look much better now. You were a bit scary before.'

'Well, I'm very pleased to hear that. I don't want to scare people off.'

Jess watched her mother closely. She was standing close to Liam. They weren't touching, but it was as if they were. Her father clicked his phone shut. He had been talking into it at speed for the last five minutes.

'Let's go, guys,' he said. Then, noticing Liam, he said, 'Oh, hi, I'm Nick.'

'Liam.'

They shook hands.

'Are you one of the other parents?' Nick asked.

'No.' Maggie was grinning. 'He's a friend of Kate's.'

Nick did a double-take. 'Oh, really?'

'Yes,' Maggie said. 'And we're all getting on like a house on fire.'

Jess saw that her mother was getting uncomfortable.

Liam had obviously noticed, too, because he cut in before she had a chance to. 'Well, very nice to meet you all and well done again. Luke was the star of the show today. Bye now.'

He turned to go but Kate walked to the side with him. Jess heard her say, 'Thanks so much for coming.'

'I wouldn't have missed it. Go back to your family. I'll call you.'

'Tonight. Call me tonight,' she whispered.

Jess felt warm inside. She was happy her mum had a friend or boyfriend or whatever he was. He was nice, and Jess could see that he was mad about her. It was what Mum needed most, someone to love her. It would make things easier in the future, Jess knew, and that made her feel good.

Liam left and Nick came over to Kate. 'Who's your friend?' he asked.

'Liam.'

'Yeah, I know, but who is he? How long have you been together?'

'We're not together. He's a friend who has been really supportive to me over these past months.'

'So you've never –'

'It's none of your business.'

'No need to bite my head off. I think I'm allowed to know if you're seeing someone.'

'No, you're not. You lost that privilege when you left me.'

Nick regarded her for a moment, then he nodded. 'That's fair enough,' he said quietly. 'I'm glad if you've found someone.'

Kate blinked, momentarily lost for words. She saw Maggie make an exaggerated shocked face behind Nick's back and had to suppress a giggle.

'Thanks,' she said at last. 'That means a lot to me.'

'I've got to go,' Nick said. He held up his phone. 'You can guess why.'

'No problem,' Kate said. 'We'll get Jess back to the hospital now.'

Aideen came in to check her blood pressure and smiled at Jess, lying tucked up in her bed.

'Today has wrecked you, hasn't it, sweetheart?' Aideen said. 'You're done in.'

Jess nodded. 'Yeah, I'm really tired. But I'm really happy too.'

'Well, that's all that matters,' Aideen said, stroking her forehead. 'Happy trumps tired every time. It was worth it, so.'

'It really was,' Jess said, thinking back over the day and being with everyone again. It had been wonderful.

'Hey, sis.'

Aideen and Jess turned to see Luke standing there, holding the cup. He grinned at them. 'I know you must be wiped out, but I wanted to show you the cup. I won't stay long, Aideen, I promise.'

'You certainly won't,' Aideen said briskly. Then her face broke into a smile. 'Come in! Come in and show us what you won. Aren't you brilliant? Look at that, Jess. Isn't he fantastic?'

'He really is,' Jess said, gazing up at him.

She didn't have the energy to sit up, so Luke placed the cup on her stomach and she wrapped her hands around the sides. 'Wow, Luke, it's gorgeous.'

He beamed. 'I know. What a day.'

'You were amazing, the hero of the match.'

'Right, hero,' Aideen said. 'I'm going for my tea break and you'll have to skedaddle when I get back. Otherwise you'll get me in trouble.'

'I'll go the moment you say,' Luke said.

'Good man,' Aideen said, heading for the door. 'I'll be back in fifteen minutes to settle you for the night, Jess.'

Luke took the trophy and placed it on the floor. 'Rocco was very generous to give me that pass.'

'It was Fate, your moment to take.'

'Yeah, I guess it was.' Luke looked down at his hands. 'I'm so glad you were there, Jess. It meant the world to me.'

Jess swallowed hard. 'It was the best day ever.'

'You're an amazing kid, you know that?'

'No, I'm not.'

'You are, Jess. You're so bloody brave. I just wish . . . I wish my bone marrow had saved you. I'm sorry it didn't. I feel I let you down.'

Jess felt tears rolling down her cheeks. 'Luke, you did everything you could and more. You've been my rock, always. When Mum and Dad split up, you were there for me and

340

Bobby. You've been there for Mum, too. It's been hardest on you because you're the eldest.'

'I've let her down too, you know, with the baby and all.'

Jess was angry now. 'Stop it, Luke. Stop blaming yourself. You didn't mean to have a baby so young but you took responsibility, like you always do. You stand up to things and for things and you protect people. You're going to be a great dad. That baby is so lucky to have you and Piper as its parents. It's all going to be fine, Luke.'

Luke wiped away a tear. 'How did you get to be so nice? I think all of Mum's genes went into you, and me and Bobby got a mixture of both.'

'Don't be too hard on Dad. He's trying.'

Luke sat back in the chair. 'I know, but he's never going to be Dad of the Year. He's just fundamentally a selfish person. You bring out the best in him, though.'

'It's only because I'm a girl. I think he feels he has to be harder on you and Bobby because you're boys.'

'Maybe. Poor Bobby, though – he doesn't really get a look in.'

'Since Jaden came along, the bit of attention he used to get is gone. You need to keep an eye on him, Luke. He needs you.'

'I need you, Jess. We all do. You're the glue in the family. You're the link to Dad. You're . . . you're the – the ham in the sandwich.'

Jess grinned. 'If I'm the ham, you're the bread that wraps around us.'

'What does that make Bobby?'

'Mustard?' Jess suggested, and they laughed.

'Yes, hot and spicy.'

'Spiky.' Jess giggled.

'Do you think he'll still be kicking things when he's my age?'

'Probably. He didn't lick it off a stone. Dad's kicked and punched the walls in here a lot,' Jess said.

'Well, that's different. I've punched a few walls over your cancer, too.'

'I'm sorry,' Jess said quietly. 'I'm sorry my stupid cancer's caused so much grief.'

Luke grabbed her arm. It hurt, but she didn't say anything. 'Don't you dare apologize. You're an innocent victim. This should never have happened. It's so unfair. I don't understand it, Jess. Why? Why you?' He loosened his grip.

'Don't ask yourself why, Luke. I did, and it doesn't get you anywhere. I've accepted it now and it's so much better that way. It's the only way to deal with it. When Larry died I was so angry with the world. But it didn't help. I have to accept that this is life. There is no why. There is just the life you're given and the cards you're dealt. These are my cards.'

Luke shook his head. 'I don't want you to die, Jess. I just can't handle it. You deserve a long, happy life. It's just not fair.'

'I know, Luke, but I'm going to die and you have to accept it. I'm tired. I'm tired of treatment, I'm tired of feeling like crap all the time, I'm tired of hospitals and doctors and needles and drugs and rashes and vomiting and X-rays and bone-marrow transfusions and false hope. Most of all I'm tired of that. The hope. There are no miracles. This is it and I'm okay with it. Please try to be too.'

Luke rubbed his wet eyes with the back of his shirt sleeve. 'I'll try, Jess.'

Aideen popped her head around the door. 'Time to go home, hero,' she said.

Luke bent down and kissed Jess, then pressed his forehead against hers for a few seconds. 'I love you, Jess.'

'I love you, Luke.'

She watched him leave, then closed her eyes and let sleep take her away from the pain.

39

Kate was making herbal tea in the kitchen when her phone beeped. It was a message from Nick: *I'm outside. Need to talk. Can I come in?*

Kate looked at the clock. It was almost eleven p.m. How had he managed to get out of his apartment? She felt bone tired. The last thing she wanted was to have a conversation with an overwrought Nick, but if he needed to talk, she couldn't turn him away. She went to the front door and opened it. He was sitting in his car at the kerb. She raised her hand to beckon him in.

'Would you like tea?' she asked, as they walked into the kitchen.

'No, I'm fine,' Nick said.

Kate sat down heavily on a chair, but Nick paced up and down, up and down, the nervous energy sparking off him. He was wound up and she felt exhausted just by his physical presence.

'Sit down, Nick,' she said. 'You're making me dizzy with all that striding about.'

For a second he seemed about to argue. Then he took a deep breath and sat down across from her. He began to drum his fingers on the table. Kate massaged her temples. 'What is it, Nick? What do you need to talk about?'

'She has to try it,' he said. 'She can't give up. Come on, Kate. We need to be united on this. It's the only way to get her to agree.'

Kate looked at the bags under his eyes, his pale face, his twitchy body, and she felt sorry for him. But she also felt the weight of his blind hope, like an anchor pulling them all down. How could she counter him? 'She's too weak, Nick. Any more treatment will kill her. She's begged us both to stop. She can't take any more.'

'She has to,' he said urgently, leaning forward. 'She can't give up. We can't give up. I won't, Kate, I bloody won't. She has to fight. We're not quitters, we're fighters.'

'It's not a war, Nick. Jess isn't a soldier fighting the enemy. She's a little girl with cancer,' Kate said, pleading with him to understand. 'You have to stop pressurizing her. She's so frail and weak and sick.'

'I can't, Kate.' His face crumpled. 'I can't let her go. We have to give it one more shot. It might work.'

'Nick, all the experts have told us it will cause her more pain and will probably kill her.' Kate sighed. 'You can't force her to do something she doesn't want to do. It's her body. We have to respect her wishes, Nick.'

He glared at her, the anger seeping out of him, filling the room. 'She's a child, Kate, we're the adults. She doesn't know what she wants. She told me she wanted to die. She said . . .' his voice cracked '. . . she said, "Please, Dad, I just want the pain to stop and for it to be over." I mean, Jesus Christ, Kate,' he was shaking now, as if his body was cold, 'she doesn't know what she's saying. The drugs are messing with her mind. She asked me to . . . well, she kind of suggested I or someone else help her stop the pain. She'll probably say the same to you. I told her no way. We are her parents. We are the ones who have to keep her alive and make her do treatment to save her.'

Tears ran down Kate's cheeks. 'She's not a child when it comes to cancer and pain. She knows far more about it than we do. And only she knows how much she can take. I know it's awful, I hate it too, but there comes a point when –'

'I will *not* give up on her, Kate, and you're a bad mother if you do. We have to do everything possible to save her. Even if it's only a one per cent chance, we have to seize it. I will not let her go. I need you to stand with me on this. For God's sake, Kate, this is our daughter's life we're talking about here.'

Kate could feel her own anger rising. She was struggling to remain composed. Yes, she felt for him, but why was he being wilfully blind to reality? 'Do you honestly think I want to let her go? Jesus, Nick, I love her as much as you do. She's my baby. This is killing me. I want her to try more treatment, too, but I also don't want her last weeks to be full of pain and suffering.'

'She's going to suffer anyway!' Nick shouted. 'She either dies without trying more treatment or she tries and maybe, just maybe, it works. It's a no-brainer! She has to do it! Jesus, Kate, why don't you get it? We have to try everything, and I mean *everything*, to keep Jess alive. That's our bloody job, Kate, to protect her and keep her safe and alive.'

'Keep your voice down! The last thing I need is the boys to hear you.' She steadied her breathing again. 'Please, Nick. We can't force her. It's ultimately her choice.'

'Bullshit! We're her parents. *We* make the decisions. She's just tired and feeling low. Of course she doesn't want any more treatment, but in a few days, when she's feeling better, she'll change her mind and she'll be glad we persuaded her to do it.'

'She has begged us not to, Nick,' Kate reminded him. Nick closed his eyes, as if trying to block out her words, block out their reality, but this was it. It was happening now and she had to make him see. 'All of the professionals we've spoken to said that more treatment will be incredibly aggressive and most likely kill her, Nick. I'd never forgive myself if that happened after she begged us not to do it. I won't do that to her. I can't.'

Nick opened his eyes and stared at her. 'You're being weak, Kate,' he said coldly. 'You need to grow some balls and step up to your responsibilities here.'

That was it. Kate felt a white-hot streak in her brain and lost the battle to stay calm.

'Don't you dare call me weak!' she said, her jaw clenched tight, her hands balled into fists. 'I've been there every single day, holding Jess's hand and watching her suffer, while you breeze in and out whenever you manage to get off the leash Jenny has you on.'

Nick slammed his hand on the table. 'That's crap! I've been there as much as possible. I've got more ties than you, that's all. I have to work and I have to see Jaden and Jenny, too.'

'Oh, poor you, Nick. I have such an easy life. I'm only raising Luke and Bobby basically alone, and helping Dad in the café every spare minute I have. You're no busier than me, I can assure you.'

'Spare me the martyr act, Kate, you're not raising them alone.'

'Really, Nick? How much time have you spent with your sons in the last six months?'

'Here we go! I'm the bad father again. I've seen the boys as much as I could. No matter what I do, someone's pissed off with me. I can't win.'

'Maybe if you hadn't cheated on me your life would be a lot simpler.' Kate sat back, arms folded, cheeks flushed. In a way, the fight was almost a relief. She needed to lash out and she'd gladly punch someone too. Nick wouldn't stand a chance against her. She felt like she could pick him up and break him in two. She was fearless – and that felt good in its own way.

'Don't start with that shit now, Kate. I know I messed things up royally. Believe me, I'm the one who's paying for it.'

'Poor you,' Kate snapped.

'Jesus, Kate, can we please not argue about Jenny now? I've paid for my mistake and, yes, I know you did, too, and the kids and, yes, I know I'm a selfish prick and all the other names you've called me, but please can we just focus on Jess right now? I don't have the energy for anything else. Please.'

Kate's anger began to slide away. Looking at him, she saw he was a broken man already. There was nothing she could do to him that could hurt him more. Jess had only weeks to live: that was the reality they were both facing and trying to deal with. Nick could be an idiot, but he was still Jess's father and he adored her. And Kate had loved him, too, once. When Jess was born, those were really happy times. She felt a stab of guilt at ever thinking she wanted to hurt him. What was wrong with her? This whole situation was making her crazy.

She looked across the table at her ex-lover, her ex-husband, Jess's father, and she knew the only way through this was together.

'Do you remember the day Jess was born, with the big thunderstorms?'

Nick was clearly surprised by her change of tack. Then his face softened. 'Of course I do, like it was yesterday. I knew then she'd be special.'

'Me too.'

'And she is, isn't she, Kate?' he said sadly.

'Yes, Nick, she is.'

He sighed deeply. 'I know I'm not a great father to the boys, I know I need to try harder, but with Jess I feel I did a good job.' He pulled at the bandage wrapped around the finger he'd broken, punching the wall in the hospital. 'Mind you, it wasn't hard. She was always the sweetest thing.'

Kate smiled. 'Yes, she was – she still is. She's the glue in our family. She's the one who worries about everyone and tries to fix things.'

Nick nodded. 'Your mum used to say she was an old soul, and she was absolutely right. Jess has always been mature beyond her years.'

'That's true,' Kate agreed. 'There's just something different about Jess, something special.'

They sat in the kitchen and reminisced. It was nice, sitting together, talking about Jess the way only parents can, boasting, proud, over-exaggerating her achievements, talents and all-round incredibleness.

Nick talked and talked, crying in parts, laughing in others. Kate held his hand and listened, joining in, jogging his memory, laughing and crying with him.

Finally, Nick looked up at the clock. 'God,' he said, rubbing his hand across his face. 'Sorry, I've kept you up late.'

'I wouldn't be sleeping anyway,' Kate said. 'Will you get into trouble?'

'Yes,' Nick said, with a half-smile. 'But that's nothing new.'

'It's hard on Jenny, too,' Kate said. 'She's probably feeling very left out and low down in the pecking order in your life.'

Nick nodded wearily. 'I do know. But it's just . . . times like this . . .'

Kate understood. 'Times like this, you need to talk to me?'

He nodded again. 'We're her mother and father, only we feel this same pain.'

'I know,' Kate said. 'But that's hard on Jenny, too. Even though it's just the way things are.'

'Thanks for letting me come in,' Nick said, standing up.

'Sorry I got so thick with you earlier,' Kate said.

'Me too. It's all just so . . . impossible,' he said, his shoulders sagging again.

He walked over and held Kate in a long hug. In that moment Kate realized they could be friends. With things about to get really awful, with the loss of their beautiful Jess, they'd need each other to lean on. When it came to the children, love went deeper than everything else.

Spring

40

Piper stood sideways in front of the bathroom mirror in her bra and pants. She was really showing now. At almost seven months, her bump was really growing. It was hard being in school with it. She felt like a freak. Thank God it was her final year. Once the exams were over, she'd be free of her stupid uniform and the constraints of school.

It was so kind of Maggie to offer them her apartment. She called it her pension fund. It was small but perfect and close enough to both families, but not too close. It was a one-bedroom on the ground floor, with a tiny garden.

'That means you can sit out with the baby in the summer and not be stuck indoors,' Maggie had said, when she'd shown it to them. 'Now, look, I'm not taking any rent for the first six months and that's final. After that, when you get settled in college and work out part-time jobs and childcare, we can talk about it. But for the first six months it's on me. Consider it my baby-shower present.'

Piper felt bad about Maggie being so generous, but Maggie had insisted. 'Luke is the closest thing to a child I'll ever have and I love him. I want the best for him and you. Kate needs to focus on Jess, so I'm happy to take this on. There will be no more discussion about it and no more thank-yous. It's my pleasure to do this.'

Piper's mum wasn't sure about the arrangement at first, but she'd met Maggie, and Maggie had explained she was Luke's honorary aunt, had no kids and it was a gift. She said she thought it best for Luke and Piper to be together when the baby was born and to figure it all out between them. Also, Luke might feel left out if Piper was living at home: it was his baby, his responsibility, and he wanted to be involved from the get-go. This was a way of letting him do that.

Maggie had been very persuasive and Olivia had come around to the idea. But she told Piper that if she preferred to stay at home, Luke could move in when the baby came. It would mean Pauline would have to sleep with the twins or else they'd put bunk-beds in Posy's tiny box room. Piper was grateful to her for offering, but she knew it would be a complete nightmare. Especially with her dad still barely speaking to her. She was so glad Maggie was there to save the day.

The door burst open and the twins came in. 'Oh, my God!' Penny squealed.

'Argh.' Poppy covered her eyes.

'Put some clothes on! You look like a freak,' Penny said.

'It's like there's an alien in there,' Poppy said.

'Your stomach's all stretched and gross.'

'It'll never be the same,' Poppy assured her. 'They say after you have a baby, the skin on your stomach never goes back to the way it was.'

Penny frowned. 'I dunno, Poppy. Look at Nicole Richie, she's, like, super-slim and so is Kourtney Kardashian.'

'Yeah, but they probably had a tummy tuck when they were having their babies. That's what all the celebs do.'

Penny turned to Piper. 'You should definitely do that. You don't want to be all saggy and flabby after the baby comes out. Luke is hot – you need to look good to keep him.'

'Definitely,' Poppy agreed. 'He'll totally go off with some-one else if you turn into a fat lump.'

'Thanks a lot, girls. You really know how to cheer me up.' Piper pulled on her dressing-gown.

Penny picked up her mascara wand and began coating her eyelashes. 'What's wrong? We're just helping you, Piper. We're trying to make sure you don't end up a single mum pushing a buggy around the park in a saggy tracksuit all day.'

'Everyone knows that if you look like crap, you'll feel like crap,' Poppy, the mothering expert, said.

'Totally,' Penny agreed. 'Kim Kardashian was, like, totally miserable when she had her baby because she whacked on so much weight. But she knew she had to lose it or Kanye would be humping one of his backing singers or whatever, so she focused like mad and got her figure back and started wearing all sexy clothes and everything was fine.'

Piper put her hands up. 'I can't listen to another word of this drivel.' She pushed past them.

'Oh, Piper,' Penny called after her, 'seeing as you're kind of a whale now and can't fit into any normal clothes, can I borrow your skinny black jeans?'

'No way. I love those jeans and I plan to wear them again when I'm not a whale, after my tummy tuck,' Piper snapped.

'Are you going to get a tummy tuck?' Posy asked, coming out of her bedroom in her school uniform with her bag on her back.

'Of course not. Those two are just telling me what a heifer I am and that I need one.'

Posy's eyes widened. 'They're so mean. You look beautiful, Piper. All glowy and healthy.'

Piper smiled at her youngest sister. 'Thanks, Posy. I know I do look a bit like a whale, but it's sweet of you to say so.'

'They can be right cows. As you always say to me, Piper, just ignore them.'

'Don't worry, I will.'

'Will I wait for you?' Posy asked.

'No, go ahead. I'm going to take my time today. I'll just make you late for school.'

'See you later.' Posy skipped down the stairs, followed by the twins, who were arguing over a lipstick.

Piper lay down on her bed, enjoying the peace and quiet. She wasn't feeling well and her stomach was cramping. She must have eaten her breakfast too quickly. She closed her eyes and waited for the cramps to pass. But they didn't.

A moment later she felt something trickle down between her legs. She sat up and looked. Blood. Oh, no. Please, no. She began to shake. She stood up on wobbly legs and stumbled to the bathroom. More blood ran down her thighs.

Her mother had gone to college early with Pauline. She knew she should call Luke, but he had his Irish oral exam this morning and she didn't want to ruin that for him. Oh, God. There was only one person in the house.

Piper pulled on tracksuit bottoms and a hoodie. Clinging to the banisters, she made her way carefully down the stairs. She went through the kitchen, out of the back door and across the garden to her father's shed. She could see him typing furiously on his laptop.

She knocked on the door. He frowned, stood up and opened it. 'What?'

'Help,' Piper gasped, holding her stomach as another cramp doubled her over.

'Jesus, Piper! Is it the baby?' Seamus held her up.

'I need to go to hospital, Dad.'

'Of course. Come on, we'll get you there.'

Seamus half carried her to the car, helped her into the front seat and buckled her seatbelt. He then hopped in and drove like a maniac towards the hospital.

Piper sat crouched in the front seat. Please, God, don't take my baby away. Please, she prayed.

'You're going to be all right, love,' Seamus kept saying. 'It'll be okay.'

He screeched to a halt outside A&E and ran in, shouting, 'My daughter needs help! She's pregnant and she's bleeding! Help! HELP!'

A nurse came out and helped Piper into a wheelchair. While her father went to move the car, Piper was wheeled into the waiting room where her details were logged into a computer. Then she was taken for an ultrasound.

As the gel was being applied to her stomach her dad rushed in, pulling back the curtain. 'Is she okay? Is my girl okay? Is the baby all right?'

'We're just checking now. We need you both to be calm.'

The sonographer moved the scanner probe over Piper's stomach and stopped. Piper held her breath. She loved this baby. She wanted this baby. This baby was part of her. She couldn't bear for anything to happen to it.

Then she heard it, the beautiful sound. The sound of a horse's hoofs, galloping galloping . . . Her baby's heartbeat.

'The baby's fine.' The sonographer smiled. 'Everything looks good. Sometimes bleeding can happen when pregnancy hormones cause you to develop more sensitive, expanded blood vessels. But the baby is fine and the placenta looks perfectly healthy, too, so please don't worry.'

Piper burst into tears. Beside her, her father, holding her hand and staring at his grandchild on the scanner, wiped away a tear. 'Will you look at that?' he said, amazed.

The sonographer smiled at him. 'I take it you're Granddad,' she said.

Seamus nodded.

'And this is your first time to see the baby?'

He nodded silently again, never taking his eyes off the screen.

'It's a pretty special moment,' the sonographer said, running the probe over again, so they could see the baby *in utero* from every angle. 'It won't be long now before you're holding this little one in your arms.'

'Jesus,' said Seamus, utterly gobsmacked.

'You'll need to take it easy for a few days,' the sonographer told Piper. 'It's important to get some rest after a bleed. You need to put your feet up and tell this man here to wait on you.'

Piper nodded, unable to speak. She felt suddenly exhausted after the whole drama.

Seamus patted her shoulder. She glanced up at him. He was gazing at her intently. 'We'll make sure she relaxes, Doctor.'

'Good. She needs it. She looks tired.'

'Sure the poor girl is worn out,' Seamus said. 'Between studying for her exams and the stress of the baby, and her boyfriend's sister is very sick too. Piper's always the one who helps everyone. The most selfless girl you could meet.'

The sonographer smiled as she wiped the gel from Piper's stomach. 'Your dad clearly thinks very highly of you.'

'I used to think so,' Piper said quietly.

The sonographer shot her a look. 'Okay, folks, you're free to go,' she said. 'We're here if you have any worries at all, Piper.'

They stepped outside the room and Seamus suddenly grabbed her in a tight hug. 'I'm sorry, pet,' he said. 'I've been all caught up in myself. I was just worried about you being so young and having a baby and your future and all of that. But it doesn't matter. We'll all help you. And I'm proud of you, Piper, more proud than I can say. Sure you're the light of my life.'

Piper buried her face in her father's woolly jumper and bawled. Tears that had been buried deep came gushing up. She'd been so hurt by his coldness and disappointment, and it was a huge relief to know he still loved her and would support her.

'Now listen to me,' Seamus said sternly. 'I want you to rest. Enough running around doing things for Luke and his sister and everyone else. You are coming home with me and I'm tucking you up in bed. Then you're going to sleep and relax. No studying today either. You must mind yourself, pet, for yourself and the baby.'

Seamus put his arm around her as they walked slowly out of the hospital. In the car, Piper leant her head back and smiled to herself. She'd thought her father would be angry with her for ever. She was so glad he'd changed his mind. She felt as if a huge weight had been lifted off her chest and she could breathe again.

When they got home, Seamus ordered her into bed, then brought her up a cup of tea and a plate of chocolate biscuits. 'Now, I'm going to work in the kitchen today, and if I hear you move, I'll be up like a shot to get you back into that bed. You're exhausted, pet. You need a good sleep.' He closed the curtains and kissed her forehead.

'Thanks, Dad,' she said, feeling like a kid again and enjoying it immensely. It was lovely to be looked after.

'Right, I'll leave you to it. Sleep well, and if you need anything, just shout.' As he was leaving the room, he said softly, without turning around, 'I love you, Piper.'

'I love you too, Dad.' She saw him smile as he closed the door.

Piper snuggled down in the bed and took out her phone to call Luke. But then she stopped. He didn't need to know. Everything was fine. The baby was perfect. He had enough worries. Piper closed her eyes and savoured the feeling of warmth spreading through her body and her heart. She had her dad back and it felt wonderful. Knowing he still loved her made everything so much better.

41

Jess began to cry, jerky sobs that shook her tiny body. 'It hurts, Mum, it really hurts.' The pain was getting worse by the day, and the intravenous morphine drip wasn't enough any more.

Her mother called Aideen, who appeared, like an angel, at the door. An angel of mercy, Jess thought. 'She needs more morphine. There isn't enough pain relief in the drip,' Mum said.

'No problem. We'll give the poor dote a booster.' Aideen came over and adjusted the drip. Jess closed her eyes and welcomed the relief. 'Is there anything else I can get you?' she asked.

Jess shook her head.

'All right. You try and get some sleep now.' She watched as Jess's eyes fluttered, then closed. To Kate, she said, 'She'll be more comfortable now. I'll pop back in to check on her in a bit.'

Fighting the sleep that was overwhelming her, Jess opened her eyes and looked at her mother, who was exhausted. Jess hated what her cancer had done to her whole family. It was enough, it was time. She had to tell her mother now, before it got worse.

'Mum,' she said.

'Yes, love?' She leant over, putting her ear close to Jess's mouth.

'I need to ask you to do something.'

'Anything, my darling.'

Jess took a deep breath. She'd gone over this speech in her mind a thousand times. She had to get it right. She glanced up at the dandelion card and felt Larry's presence. 'Mum, I know I'm going to die and I've accepted it. Over the last eight months I've had no control over anything. But I can control this. I can control how I leave this world. I don't want to die on a day when I get an infection and I'm vomiting blood and can't breathe. I don't want to die like that, when I'm not expecting it. I want to go when I decide to. I can't fight any more, Mum. I just don't have the energy. I've tried, I've really tried, but it's beaten me. I need you to help me, Mum. I need you to help me die.'

Jess watched her mother's face. Kate didn't move. She was completely still, bent over her daughter's body, her ear close to Jess's mouth, catching every unbelievable syllable. Jess saw the pain and sorrow in her eyes. Please say yes, she prayed. Please, Mum.

Her mother tried to compose herself, but tears streamed down her face. Jess hated seeing her so upset, but she needed this. She would not let cancer dictate to her any more. This was the one decision she could make, and she was going to make it.

The light from the lamp on the bedside locker framed her mother in silhouette. She was a blend of light and shadow, like the line between night and day. Between life and death.

'I know it's a terrible thing to ask,' Jess whispered, 'but if you love me, Mum, if you really love me, you'll help me. I know you will. I want to die in my own way. Everything has been stripped away from me. I'm just a shell, Mum. I have no life. I can't stand the pain any more. I hate it. I hate what I've become. I'm not me. This isn't Jess.' She began to cry again. Damn, she'd promised herself she'd remain calm and in control.

Her mother breathed out, and slowly found the ability to move again. She put her arms around Jess. 'But you are. You are you. You're still the wonderful, beautiful, amazing Jess we all adore. We love you, Jess. We want every second that we can get with you. I can't cut your life short. I need you, Jess. Every minute I have with you is a gift. I can't cut that short.'

Jess stopped crying and pulled herself together. She had to make her mother see. She had to make her understand that by helping her die she was doing the best and kindest thing she could do. 'Mum, please, listen. I know it's going to be hard for you, but I'm begging you. There is nothing better that you can do for me. It's what I want more than anything in the world, Mum. Please do this for me. You've always been there for me. You can do this, Mum. I know you love me enough to do it. You're the only person who can. No one loves me the way you do. That's why I have to ask you to do this. I'm sorry, but I want this more than anything. I'm ready.'

Jess waited while her mother struggled to find words. Finally she said, 'I understand why you want to do this. You've had such a terrible time. And I want to help you more than anything in the world, but, Jess, how can I let you go when the thought of it just rips me apart?' She covered her face with her hands. 'Your dad said you mentioned this to him and he flipped out,' she whispered. 'How can I possibly say yes?'

Jess shook her head. 'I said it to him to see his reaction. I knew he'd freak out. But I just wanted to plant the seed in his mind. I know he can't do it. You're the only one who can because you're the one who loves me the most.'

'Yes, I do love you the most, which is why I'm the last person who can do this. You're my only daughter, Jess. You're my baby girl. I ... You don't understand ... to lose a child. Jess, what you're asking, it's too much.'

Jess dug deep. She dug down to her toes. She had to be strong. 'Mum, it's only going to get worse. I'm going to be in more pain and sleeping all the time and slipping in and out of consciousness. And it's going to happen anyway, no matter what we do. I want to control this one last thing. I know I could possibly live for another month or so, but I can't do it, Mum. It's not a life. This isn't living. This is dying all the time, and I want to do it my way. Please, Mum, please do this for me. It's the right thing, I promise you.'

Her mother was crying now. 'But what if . . .'

'. . . a miracle happens and I get better?' Jess was getting angry. 'I'm not getting better. There is no cure. It's over and we all know it. Even Dad knows it deep down. I'm begging you, Mum, help me.' Jess's strength began to fade and she turned her head to cry into her pillow.

Her mother came over and lay down beside her, holding her, stroking her face, kissing her cheek. 'Don't get upset, sweetheart, please don't cry. You've taken me by surprise. I need time to process this. I need to think about it. Can you give me a day or two? It's such a huge decision. Can you give me some time?'

Jess nodded. 'Okay, but please don't take long, Mum. I need to know. I need to know this will soon be over. You're the best mum in the world. I know you can do this.'

As her mother's tears landed on her cheek, Jess felt herself drifting as the morphine took over her body and mind. Jess prayed as sleep crept up on her: Help me, Mum . . . If you love me, help me die.

42

Kate left the hospital, walking quickly down the quiet corridors. She went straight to her car, sat inside and bent her head to the steering-wheel. She waited for the tears to come, but they didn't. She felt emptied out, hollowed. She had moved beyond tears into some kind of shocked space where she simply couldn't believe that this was her life.

How the hell was she going to make the decision?

She picked up her phone and stared at it. She couldn't ring Nick: he'd come straight here and scream blue murder at her. He'd be disgusted with her for even considering it. A part of her wanted to hear her father's voice, but she knew this was too big to confide in him. It would be a huge burden to put on someone else, to ask them to share the decision with her. There was only one person she trusted absolutely one hundred per cent.

The phone rang at the other end and Kate held her breath.

'You've reached Maggie O'Neill. I'm not available to take your call, but please leave a message.'

'Damn,' Kate breathed. Maggie's phone beeped. 'Em . . . oh, hi, it's just me. Nothing important. Everything's okay here. Was just ringing for a chat. I'll try you tomorrow.'

She threw her phone onto the passenger seat and her stomach churned, as if she was going to be sick. She stared up at the hospital, counting the windows across on the third floor to the one she knew was Jess's. Up there her daughter lay dying. The grief of that was fathoms deep, and now Jess wanted to die early, to go sooner – and Kate was the one she'd turned to for help to do that. How can this be happening? Kate thought, her head aching. It was a nightmare there was no waking up from.

She had a sudden idea and knew where she wanted to be. She buckled up her seatbelt, turned the key in the ignition, put the car into gear and drove away from her daughter, turning onto the motorway as the stars came out and the moon rose higher in the sky.

She didn't remember any of the journey, other than the vague impression of lampposts forming a tunnel down which she drove. She drove on automatic pilot, hearing Jess's voice over and over again: 'I know you can do this . . . You love me the most . . .'

Eventually, she reached the turn-off and followed it to the little car park. Everything was silent. There wasn't a soul about. She locked the car and made for the steep path, walking fast up it, enjoying the sensation of her lungs burning with effort. She didn't stop once, just pushed on across the forested area and then to the clearing. Below the cliff's edge, the waves crashed against the rock. The grass was springy and tough beneath her feet as she walked to the edge. The moon was high enough to provide some light, but the shapes around her were still only half formed, made mostly of darkness.

Kate sat down and watched and listened, taking in the sounds and smells of the night. She breathed deeply, slowing her racing heartbeat, trying to be in the moment as the mindfulness teacher had shown them. She felt she needed to be calm now, to think clearly so that she could make the right choice.

What had really struck her about Jess was how serious and determined she had looked – it was the face of someone who had thought long and hard about their decision. She had said, 'I'm ready,' and Kate had to admit that she had looked ready. There had been no fear in her eyes, no hesitation in her voice. She had never seemed more grown-up than in that moment. She had known exactly what she was asking and why.

Kate could understand her desire to take control now. She really could. When your life is reduced to constant pain and suffering, who wouldn't want to say, 'Enough'? So was it because of Jess's age that she had been so shocked by what she had said? That was probably some of it, yes. How could a twelve-year-old be so sure they wanted to leave this world? But, then, Jess was no ordinary twelve-year-old.

It hurt, though – it really hurt that Jess was ready to give up and leave them all. When she had said she was ready to die, she was also saying she was ready to leave her family. That part Kate couldn't bear.

But was it fair? None of them could feel her physical pain. It always seemed impossible from the outside that someone could want to die, but if you were living in a body racked with pain, it was probably the case that you reached a point of acceptance and the desire to end it. And, by God, Jess had suffered. Kate had watched her go through hell, her poor body battered and bruised, pushed to the limits of pain. Who could blame her for wanting it to stop?

Kate shifted about, then lay down to be more comfortable. She gazed up at the stars.

'My daughter is going to die,' she said out loud. It was the first time she'd spoken those words. She felt the weight of them, even if they didn't feel quite real yet. Her mind kept resisting them, blocking them, arguing with them, telling her it couldn't be true. 'It's true,' she said to the stars. 'My daughter is going to die.'

But could she help her to die, hasten her death? She felt a cold lump in the bottom of her stomach at the thought of it. No matter the motive, it was still killing. Kate hadn't done an illegal or wrong thing in her life. It wasn't the way she was made. She wouldn't hurt anyone, wouldn't want to, but now her own child wanted her to kill her. That was the truth of it – and if anyone ever discovered what had happened, that was how the police would see it. Kate would be a murderer in the eyes of the law, pure and simple. Could she risk that? What about Luke and Bobby? What if she got caught? In order to fulfil Jess's last wish, she could be setting up a lifetime of pain for her sons. Was that fair?

Her phone buzzed in her pocket. She looked at it. It was 2.05 a.m., the bright screen told her. How had it got so late so quickly? The message was from Maggie: *Probably too late, but I'm here now if you need me.*

Kate stared at the words. Did she need her? Yes, it would be great to talk it over with her, but it really was too big a thing to ask of Maggie. It would implicate her as well. Kate put her phone away and tried to think of what Maggie's advice would be. She'd be shocked – the idea of a twelve-year-old begging to die was shocking – but she felt that once she'd got over that, Maggie would probably say that Jess should be allowed to choose her own way to die. She'd probably tell Kate that the grief would be the same whether it happened tomorrow or in a month, so why not allow Jess to make the call?

That's true, Kate thought. It won't actually change the aftermath for everyone else – they'll be devastated no matter what. Yes, it will be different for me, living with the knowledge of what I did, but I'll also be living with the knowledge that I did exactly what Jess wanted. I mean, if I were old and sick and asked my children to help me go, I'd be asking because I really wanted to do it. And I'd be hoping against hope that they'd have the guts to do it for me.

Kate curled up on her side, smelling the grass and the soil and the salty air. She tried to put herself into Jess's shoes, think herself out of her own body. If I were lying in a hospital bed, day after day, with tubes in my arms, vomiting, bleeding, soiling the bed, losing all my hair, the pain of mouth ulcers, watching my loved ones suffer over me, and the doctors told me death was now inevitable, how would I feel? What would I want? In her heart, Kate knew she would think just as Jess was thinking. She knew she would want to be allowed to die with dignity, by choice and before the bitter end.

She felt her mind move towards 'Yes', but just as quickly it snapped shut again, screaming, 'No!' The thought of being without Jess, of her not being in the world . . . It hurt with a jagged, searing pain that made her hunch her shoulders and curl up as if she'd been stabbed. It just hurt so much. The prospect of burying her Jess, and soon, made her want to throw herself off the cliff. She didn't want to be here if Jess wasn't. It would be unbearable. But then . . . but then . . . but then . . . it was going to happen anyway. It was now inevitable. That was what the doctors had told them. She was going to have to find a way of living without Jess. Find a way of being a mother to Bobby and Luke and of being a grandmother to the new little one. Life would go on, no matter what.

Kate rolled over onto her stomach and her whole body shook as she cried, gulping for air. She balled her hands into fists and hit the hard brown earth over and over again. Jess was going to die. She was going to be buried in this soil. She would be gone. Kate couldn't change that.

When she finally sat up, shivering with cold, her eyes sore from crying, limbs stiff from being so tensely held, she turned to face the sea and saw the dawn beginning to spread across the horizon. She watched, numb in mind and body, as the peachy pink colours became stronger, pinker. It was as if the whole heaving sea was holding its breath, waiting for the sun to come up above the horizon. Kate wrapped her arms tightly around her body and waited too.

Her tired eyes saw the moment when the rim of the sun curved above the horizon line, the sudden shot of gold, bright and hot against the pinkish wash. She was on the edge of the world, wishing she could drop over the side.

But she couldn't. She was a mother, which meant you never got to give up. It was a relentless love that wouldn't ever let you rest. She had to be a mother to Jess now, and to Bobby and Luke. And she had to help Piper be a mother in the years to come. Kate had to play her part. She couldn't step back from it. That wasn't an option.

The sun rose higher, and Kate's mind went back and forth, back and forth. I can do it. I can't do it. Pros and cons, she said to herself wearily. Let's do it that way. Okay, cons: Jess dies; maybe someone figures it out and I go to prison. Her mind drew a blank. That was it. Okay, pros: I give Jess her dying wish, which makes her die happy, with dignity and safe in the knowledge that I love her more than life itself.

Kate bowed her head and squeezed her eyes shut. She had thought about it for hours but, really, she'd known deep inside all along that there was only one option. She was Jess's mother, and her daughter needed this to make her happy, to take away her pain, to let her feel in control of her own life. Jess had asked her to love her by letting her go, and that was what Kate had to do.

She stood up and stretched out her stiff body. The seagulls were wheeling across the sky now, screeching to each other, looking for food. The day had begun.

Kate slowly retraced her steps, back through the forest, down the steep path, to the car. She reversed out of the car park, drove back to the exit onto the motorway, quiet in the early morning. Eventually she went through the gates of the hospital and parked the car. She walked slowly back inside, nodding good morning to the nurse at Reception. She went down the corridors she had passed through just hours before, feeling like a different person. She already felt like a culprit, as if they'd see it written on her face, what she was going to do. She reached Jess's room and stopped outside, took a few deep breaths, rubbed her eyes, then pushed back her shoulders and went in.

She sat on the side of the bed and watched as Jess came back from sleep. The first noise she made, before she'd even opened her eyes, was a whimper of pain. Her eyes opened and she saw Kate. She smiled at her. 'Mum.'

'I'm here,' Kate said.

'What time is it?' Jess asked.

'About six,' Kate replied. 'Early. I've been up all night, thinking.'

Hope filled the beautiful brown eyes. 'And?'

'I love you, Jess,' Kate said. 'I love you more than anyone else in the world. From the day you were conceived I felt connected to you in a way no one could understand. The day you were born was the happiest day of my life. You were so longed for and so perfect. I love you in a way that has always scared me because, even before you got sick, I knew that level of love could mean the same level of hurt one day. But I never in my wildest dreams imagined I'd be losing you.' She smiled weakly. 'It's unimaginable for a mother to lose a child.'

Jess bit her lip as tears came into her eyes. She couldn't speak. Her eyes were trained on Kate's, waiting, waiting.

'Because I love you like that,' Kate said, taking her hand, 'I'm going to do as you've asked. If you're absolutely, totally sure.'

Jess nodded, still unable to speak, but she squeezed Kate's hand.

'I'll help you die the way you want to,' Kate whispered. 'I'll figure it out, and you can tell me when.'

They sat there, unmoving, staring into each other's eyes. Kate felt a sense of exquisite understanding, as if they'd come full circle and Jess was part of her again, part of her body and mind, as she had been in the womb. It was a strange feeling, but it was as if Jess was coming home, and that home was her. For the first time, Kate felt a small sense of relief – that it was the right decision, even though it would condemn her to a lifetime of hurt and to a secret that would burden her for ever. But she was Jess's mother and that was her sacrifice, and she was going to make it because she loved her daughter enough to do it.

43

When her mother had left to go home for a few hours, Jess lay in her bed feeling a strange mix of emotions. She couldn't quite believe she had agreed. She'd felt there was a chance she would, but seeing Mum's face when she'd asked her had made her think that the chance was very small. But whatever had happened in her mind overnight, she had seen in her face that morning that she was now convinced by what Jess had said, that she would do it.

For Jess, it was a relief, but it was bittersweet at the same time. She wanted to go, and she didn't want to go. If she could live, she'd grab life with both hands and live for all she was worth. But she had accepted that death was now a fact, and she knew in her bones that this was the best way to handle it.

She asked Aideen to let Dr Kennedy know that she had made her decision, and after morning rounds, he came to see her.

'How are we this morning, Jess?'

'I'm good, thanks.'

'So you've discussed things with your parents and thought things over?'

Jess nodded. 'I don't want any more treatment. I can't take any more. I'd like to go home now and let whatever happens happen.'

Dr Kennedy nodded sadly at her. 'For what it's worth, I think you're right.' He smiled. 'You've got a very wise head on those young shoulders.'

'It's for the best all round,' Jess said.

'Jess . . . I'm so very sorry.' The poor man looked like he might cry, which was very unlike him. It made Jess feel a bit uncomfortable. 'I wish the treatment had been more successful.'

She felt for him. It must be awful to do a job where you had to watch people die all the time. Timidly, she reached out and touched his hand. 'Thank you for trying so hard,' she said. 'It's no one's fault. I've accepted that this is just the fate I've been dealt.'

He bent his head for a moment, then raised it again and smiled. 'That's the way it seems to work, unfortunately.' He stood up. 'I'll talk to Aideen and your parents, and we'll sort out palliative care for you at home. They'll make sure you're comfortable and pain-free at all times.'

'That's perfect. Thank you so much.'

Dr Kennedy left, and she lay back, staring up at the ceiling. Jess smiled. She was so happy to be going home. Her heart lifted at the thought that she'd be leaving this hospital never to return. Jess knew she'd made the right decision. It felt so right, and she loved her mother so much for helping her.

'Hello, beautiful.' Dad walked in, carrying a tall sunflower in a vase. 'Something to cheer up the room,' he said.

'Wow, that's gorgeous,' Jess said. 'It's huge. Aideen's going to kill you for bringing that in.'

Nick looked guiltily at her. 'Oh, crap, are flowers not allowed?'

Jess took a fit of laughing. 'You're actually scared of Aideen, aren't you?' she wheezed.

Nick grinned. 'Yes, and man enough to admit it too.'

'Don't worry, I'll tell her you'll take it home with you. You can share it with Jenny and Jaden.'

'Thanks,' Nick said, smiling. 'Was that Dr Kennedy I saw rushing down the corridor?'

Jess's heart sank at the sight of his hopeful face. 'Yes, it was. We were just confirming things.'

Nick sat down quickly on the edge of her bed. 'And what did you confirm?' he asked eagerly.

'I'm sorry, Dad,' Jess said. 'I know you want me to do it but I'm not doing the treatment. I'm going home.'

He stared at her for a long minute, then turned away. He bent over and Jess watched in shock as her father's body heaved with sobs. She had no idea what to do. She'd expected him to shout at her or punch the wall, but not this, not crumble in front of her. She reached out and patted his back gently, feeling awful that she had done this to him.

Nick cried and cried, shaking with grief. After some minutes the tears began to subside.

'I think you're wrong,' he said, when he could speak again. 'You're giving up too soon. We're fighters not quitters.'

'I'm sorry, Dad, but I just can't do it any more. I'm ready to go home. It's over, Dad.'

'Please, Jess.' His face was wretched. 'Just one more try.'

Jess wanted to scream at him to stop harassing her, but she held it together. She shook her head. 'No, Dad. I'm done.'

He began to cry again. 'I don't want you to die,' he sobbed.

She put her arm around him. 'Dad, I know that. And I don't want to die either. But we can't change what's inside me. The cancer is in there. At some point, we have to accept that.'

He looked up sharply at her and rubbed his eyes hard. 'And if your mother was standing here pleading with you to keep trying, would you say no to her?'

375

Jess was taken aback. 'I would say to her exactly what I'm saying to you,' she said.

'No. Kate has the power to make you change your mind. I know she does. If she'd just bloody well listen to me, I know she could persuade you.'

'No, Dad, she couldn't. No one can change my mind. Mum respects my decision. She'd love to change my mind, but she accepts she can't. She listens to me.'

Nick turned his body so that he was looking directly at her. His eyes narrowed as he watched her carefully. 'Your mother had better not be letting you make any foolish decisions, Jess. I want you here as long as possible. Every second with you counts. Do you understand? Every single second. Is precious.' He began to cry again.

Jess felt worried now. Her dad would go mad if he found out what Mum had agreed to do. What if he made trouble for her afterwards? What if he told Dr Kennedy? Or the police? She hadn't thought about that. She'd been so focused on persuading Mum to help her die that she hadn't thought about Dad causing trouble if he found out or even suspected. They'd have to be really careful. Jess's heart was beating wildly as her mind raced through the possibilities of her father's grief destroying everything. She breathed deeply and willed herself to be calm.

Nick held her gaze. She felt as if he was looking through her and could see all.

She muttered, 'Yes, Dad, of course, I know that,' and then, mercifully, his phone beeped. He cursed.

'Sorry, Jessie, but I have to go to work.' He looked at her again. 'Promise me you won't do anything silly? I want you for as long as I can have you.' His voice cracked as he leant down to kiss her cheek.

Jess swallowed. 'Okay, Dad, I love you,' she said, afraid to say anything else for fear of implicating herself or her mother.

He nodded – exhausted, and his day had barely begun. 'Take care. I'll pop in after work, okay?'

'Bye, Dad.'

Jess breathed a sigh of relief when he left. She went over their conversation in her mind again and again. She was worried now. She'd been so caught up in controlling her end that she hadn't given a thought to what might come afterwards. She had to make sure that Dad wouldn't cause any trouble for Mum.

When Aideen came on shift that afternoon, Jess asked her for a pen and paper.

44

Piper handed Luke half a cupcake.

'Should we be eating these before she arrives?' Luke asked.

'Your baby is starving and there are about five thousand more, so I think it's all right,' Piper said.

They watched Chloë and Bobby putting out the plates and napkins. Maggie was placing mountains of presents around the space where Jess would be sitting.

George and Nathalie were polishing glasses and cutlery. Hazel was shouting down the phone at someone. 'If you don't get here in the next thirty minutes, I'll come and burn your fucking place down.'

'Mum!' Chloë hissed.

Hazel's face was flushed. 'I apologize for my language. Sorry, Bobby. I'm just a bit stressed.'

Maggie handed her a glass of wine. 'Get that down your neck.'

Hazel smiled at her. 'Thanks, Maggie, you're a star.'

'That woman needs to calm down,' George grumbled to Luke. 'Turning my café into a party shop. I can't see a bloody thing with all these balloons.'

Luke and Piper grinned. When Hazel had offered to help decorate, they hadn't known she was going to hire a professional event organizer. The café was crammed full of balloon decorations, towers of cupcakes, three huge birthday cakes, a chocolate fountain surrounded by vast plates of marshmallows and strawberries. There was a tent in the corner full of dress-up clothes and Hazel had even ordered a photo booth for everyone to get their photo taken with Jess.

'Hazel's great, but everything is kind of super-sized,' Luke said quietly.

'I know, but it's kind of fabulous, too. Jess will love it,' Piper said.

Maggie came over and sat beside them. 'How are you feeling, Piper?'

'Good, thanks,' Piper said honestly. After the bleed, she'd rested for a few days and had really felt the benefit. Things with her father were great again, too, and she felt happier than she had in months.

'Doesn't she look gorgeous?' Luke said, and kissed her.

'Get a room . . . Oh, no, you already did.' Maggie grinned. They all laughed.

'Are you managing to study?' Maggie asked Luke. 'I know it must be so difficult right now with Jess being so unwell, but try to do some work – it'll help distract you.'

Luke stared at the floor. 'I know. It's hard, though, Maggie. She's so . . . so . . .'

Maggie's eyes welled. 'I know.'

'Before, I could believe she'd get better, but now she looks as if she's dying.' He wiped tears from his eyes.

Piper held his hand.

'I wish I could think of something comforting to say, but it's just so unfair. I wish there was something I could do, but I feel so useless. I'm a fixer, and I can't fix this.'

Piper leant over to hug Maggie. 'You've helped in so many ways. You've been amazing to me, Luke, Kate and everyone.'

'You're a rock, Maggie,' Luke agreed. 'A total rock.'

'Ah, stop, my make-up will be ruined. I'm glad Jess is coming home. It'll do her the world of good.'

'Yeah, it'll be really nice having her here with us,' Luke agreed. 'Dr Kennedy says we'll take it day by day, but he won't bring her back into hospital unless he has to.'

Bobby ran into the room. 'She's coming!'

Everyone got up and rushed to the front door. An ambulance was parked at the kerb, its back lowered to accommodate Jess's wheelchair. She was fixed up to a morphine drip and had a blanket tucked around her legs. The palliative-care nurse was by her side, supervising the transfer.

'Looks like some people are happy to see you, Jess,' she said, smiling at the little crowd gathered to greet them.

Chloë ran over and hugged her. 'You look gorge, Jess. Wait until you see the café! It's amazeballs.'

'I can't wait.' Jess grinned.

'Mum went totally over the top, but in a good way this time,' Chloë gushed.

Nick walked down and took charge of pushing the wheelchair. He was trying to smile, but it couldn't reach his eyes. Kate knew that while he was happy to see Jess at home, he was still cut up about her decision not to take further treatment. He looked as emptied out as she felt. It was as if he was dying, too, alongside Jess. But, still, he fixed his face into some form of a smile as he wheeled Jess up the path and into the house.

When she reached the kitchen, Kate grabbed her in a tight hug. 'Now close your eyes, darling,' she said, nodding at Nick to wheel Jess through the door and into the café.

Nick stopped just inside the door. 'Okay. You can open them,' he said.

'Oh, my God, it's *amazing*!' Jess cried, clapping her hands together with delight. 'I can't believe it.'

'It's all for you, darling. Happy nearly birthday,' Kate said.

'When is your birthday?' Nathalie asked.

'Second of July,' Jess said, 'but why wait when you can have an amazing birthday right now?'

'Amen to that,' Hazel said.

Piper went over to give Jess a kiss. 'Happy almost birthday.'

'Thanks! I'm so happy.'

She looked it, Piper thought. For the first time in ages, her cheeks were flushed with colour and her eyes were bright and shiny. She genuinely looked happy. 'You deserve it, Jess.'

'Can I feel the baby?' she asked.

'Of course.' Piper took Jess's hand, placed it on her stomach and pushed a little. The baby kicked back.

'*Ooooooh!* I love when it does that!'

'Me too.' Luke grinned. 'I reckon there's a future football star in there.'

'I hope it's a boy like you, Luke,' Jess said.

'I hope it's a girl like you,' Luke replied.

'Hey, what about me?' Piper laughed.

'A mixture of Jess and you would be perfection,' Luke said.

'Okay, I'll take that.' Piper winked at Jess.

They sat down at the table. Piper tucked in, feeling ravenous. She hoped that she wouldn't end up being a whale, but right now she needed food. The baby was obviously having a growth spurt. To hell with Penny and Poppy and their fat-pregnant-women stories! Piper bit into her cupcake with relish.

Hazel, Chloë and Maggie were wonderful, keeping the conversation light and fun, making sure there were no silences for sadness to creep in. By sheer force of will, they pushed the grief out of the room for a few blissful hours.

When Piper got up to go to the toilet for the zillionth time, she heard a noise coming from the kitchen and peered around the door. George was sitting in a chair with his back to her, weeping into a tea-towel. Nathalie was standing behind him, hugging his neck. 'Let it out, George. You must let it out.'

'Why her? Why not me? That beautiful little girl had her whole life ahead of her. I've had my life and it was a good one. Why is this happening to her? I can barely look at Kate, she's so broken. It's just not right.'

'Kate is full of sadness, yes, but she is a strong woman. She will be okay. She 'as you and Luke and Bobby and her Maggie. And she 'as Liam now also. 'E is very kind.'

'No parent should see a child die. It's not right.'

Nathalie patted him on the back. 'George, life is not always 'appy. There is a lot of tragedy as well. But you 'ave to accept it or it will kill you. Look at Jess today, just focus on that. She is 'appy. Go and be with 'er. You can do this, George, you are a wonderful father and grandfather. They are lucky to 'ave you. Now, take the deep breath and you go back and be with Jess.'

George turned around and hugged her. 'Thank you for coming into our lives when we needed you, for being mad but in a good way, and for being a bloody decent human being.'

He walked out, and Piper saw Nathalie bury her face in the already tear-stained tea-towel.

When she got back to the table, Chloë was in the photo booth with Jess, the wheelchair squeezed in sideways. She was dressing Jess up in funny hats and glasses and feather boas and they were making goofy faces and being young and carefree. It was so lovely to see Jess having fun.

Chloë waited for the photos to print. She whooped when she saw them and showed them to Jess, laughing loudly. 'I have to show them to Piper,' she said, rushing over to her.

'Look, Piper, aren't they hilarious?' she said, as tears streamed down her cheeks. 'Don't let Jess see me cry,' she whispered.

'They're brilliant,' Piper said. 'Come and show them to Luke.' She brought Chloë to the other side of the room, where she shielded her from view while Chloë mopped her face.

'She looks so sick – she's like a little alien. Oh, Piper, she's my best friend. What am I going to do without her?'

'I know, sweetie, it's unbearable. But always remember you've been the best friend she could have wished for. You really have been brilliant, Chloë. You always cheer her up. Every time, no matter what.'

Chloë fought back more tears. 'That's my goal when I see her. I have to make her laugh as much as I can, and then I don't feel so bad. Mum said the most important thing I can do is cheer her up. I'm trying, Piper, I really am.'

Piper leant in and whispered, 'You're doing an amazing job, Chloë. Really amazing.'

Chloë plastered a smile on her face. 'Come on, Jess,' she called. 'One more funny one. Let's do the wigs now.'

Nick came over to her. Piper froze – he made her nervous. He seemed so on edge all the time.

'So, how's the pregnancy going?'

'Okay, thanks.'

He smiled. 'Better than Jenny's, I'd say. She moaned the whole way through.'

'Well, some women get very sick. I've felt fine, really, just tired.'

Nick nodded. 'Kate was like you – she just got on with it. So, I hear Maggie's offered you her place?'

'Yes, she's been so generous. I hope we can pay her back some day.'

Nick fiddled with his watch. 'I wish I could have helped more. I'm just stretched so thin, supporting two families.'

383

'Oh, gosh, no, it's fine, honestly. We wouldn't expect anything.'

Nick turned to watch Luke, who was showing Bobby how to do a press-up. 'Luke will be a great dad.'

Piper smiled. 'Yes, he will.'

'A lot better than I ever was.'

Piper didn't know what to say. She remained silent.

'Maybe I'll turn out to be a great granddad,' Nick went on. 'Who knows? Stranger things have happened.'

'I'm sure you will,' Piper said, trying to be polite.

'You're a nice girl, Piper. I really hope it works out for you both. Look after Luke – he pretends he's so strong and resilient, but he needs you. And he will continue to need you.'

'I will, I promise.'

Nick left her and went over to Jess and Chloë. He let them dress him up in ridiculous outfits and smiled for the photos.

Luke came over. 'What was Dad saying?'

'Just how great I am.' She grinned at him.

'Seriously?'

'Yes! No need to sound so surprised.'

Luke kissed her. 'You know I'm your number-one fan.'

'He was nice, actually, sweet.'

'Dad and the word "sweet" do not go hand in hand.'

'He's trying, Luke. At least give him credit for that.'

Luke stroked her hair. 'For you, anything.'

Hazel shouted over everyone, 'The final surprise for Jess is here – and about bloody time too.'

They looked out of the café door, and there was a horse on the street outside.

'It's Jess the pony, and Julian!' Jess squealed. 'Oh, Hazel.'

Nick picked Jess up and carried her outside to the horse. Kate followed, clutching a blanket for her, and the others streamed after them.

'It's so good to see you again, Julian,' Jess said. 'Thanks for bringing Jess. Can I ride her?'

Julian nodded. 'I'll sit behind you and hold you and the drip. If your dad can lift you, I reckon we can go for a short walk.'

'Mother of God, the neighbours are going to love this.' George shook his head.

Between them, Nick and Luke managed to hoist Jess into position, seated in front of Julian. Kate fussed around with the blanket, but Jess waved her away happily. Julian tapped the horse's sides lightly and, very slowly and carefully, the huge animal started to move. They watched as Jess and Julian walked slowly down the road, cars slowing as they saw them. Jess was smiling from ear to ear.

Piper looked around: every single person in their little group was crying.

45

Jess hugged Hazel. 'Thank you for the best party ever.'

'I'm glad you had a good time, sweetie.'

'You've been so amazing, Hazel. You have the biggest heart. I'm so grateful for everything.'

'There's plenty more fun to come, so you just stay strong.'

Chloë nudged her mother aside. 'Bye, Jess. I'll send you all the photos I took. Some of the ones with your dad are hilarious.'

Jess kissed Chloë's cheek. 'You're the best friend in the world. Thanks for always cheering me up, even on my worst days.'

Chloë blushed. 'That's what friends are for.'

'No,' Jess said. 'That's what really special friends do. I love you, Chloë, you're the best.'

'Stop! You'll make me cry!' Chloë said.

Hazel took her daughter by the arm. 'Right, let's get you home. Jess needs some rest. See you soon, sweetie.'

Jess watched them walk down the path. Hazel put her hand out and Chloë took it. Two very special people I was lucky to know, Jess thought.

She'd miss them. She wondered what Chloë would become. She reckoned she'd be famous in some way. Chloë had pizzazz and energy and so much charm, she'd probably end up taking over the world. Jess wished she could be there to see it.

Nathalie came up behind her. 'Did you enjoy the day?' she asked.

Jess nodded. 'It was brilliant. Thanks for all your help making it so special.'

Nathalie shrugged. 'It was my pleasure. To see you so 'appy with your eyes shining makes me 'appy.'

'It was the best party ever.'

Nathalie picked up some plates. 'You 'ave a fantastic family, Jess. They love you so much. It's beautiful to see this.'

'I know I'm a lucky girl.'

Nathalie smiled crookedly. 'Maybe not so lucky with the cancer, but with the family, yes.'

Jess laughed. 'Thanks for being so great with Granddad and so lovely to me and Bobby and everyone.'

Nathalie paused. 'For me, it has been a great experience. I am honoured to be part of this family's life. It can be a bit crazy sometimes but there is so much love, it's beautiful to see.'

Love, thought Jess. It was what life was all about. When you took away everything else, it all came down to love. That was what sustained you through the difficult times. It got you through the bad news, the pain, the suffering – love was the most powerful thing in the world.

'Anyway,' Nathalie interrupted Jess's thoughts, 'I 'ave to go. I 'ave a date.'

'Ooooh! Who with?'

'A man I met at a poetry reading.'

'What's this?' George asked.

'Nathalie has a date.' Jess filled him in. 'Is he nice?'

'We'll see. He doesn't drink, so at least I know he won't be falling down after ten o'clock.' Nathalie grinned.

'Is this the poet fella?' George seemed up-to-date.

'Yes.'

'Poets are a flaky lot. You should go out with a fella with a decent job who'll look after you, not some eejit who spends three years writing five lines of drivel,' George told her.

Nathalie laughed. 'Come on, George, you know me. I like the artistic men.'

'You deserve better,' George said.

'If I don't like him and 'e is – 'ow you say? – flaky, I just move on and find someone else. Don't worry about me, George. I am a strong French woman.'

'You can say that again.' George laughed. 'Most of my customers are afraid of you.'

Nathalie punched him playfully in the arm. 'I 'ave to go. See you tomorrow.' She hugged Jess.

'Thanks for everything, Nathalie. You've been like a sister and a friend all mixed together.'

Nathalie looked into Jess's eyes. She became very still and then she whispered, '*Au revoir*, my beautiful Jess.' Her eyes filled with tears as she turned to go.

Everyone finished tidying up, and then Kate said it was time for Jess to get some rest. As Nick and Maggie were putting on their jackets, the door opened. Jenny walked in, holding Jaden.

'Oh, no.' Bobby groaned.

'What the hell is she doing here?' Maggie muttered.

Jenny smiled awkwardly. 'I'm sorry to interrupt – I'm not staying. I just wanted to give Jess a present.' She went over to Jess and handed her a gift. 'I thought you might like to have it beside your bed. I'm sorry you're having such a terrible time,' she said.

Jess unwrapped it. It was a framed photo of her dad throwing her up in the air. She must have been about a year old in the photo and she was laughing hysterically. Nick was beaming up at her, so handsome and happy. Jess felt a well of emotion building up. She crushed it down. 'Thank you, Jenny, so much. I'll treasure it.'

'Oh, it's nothing, really, but I'm glad you like it.'

'It's beautiful, Jen.' Nick beamed at her.

'It was really thoughtful of you,' Kate said.

Bobby came bustling over. 'Jaden won't let go of my leg and he stinks.'

Jenny laughed. 'Oh, God, sorry. You're right, he needs to be changed. Anyway, I'll go.'

'I'll come with you. I was just leaving,' Nick said.

'Hey, let's get a photo of me with Jaden,' Jess said.

'Great idea!' Nick looked surprised and pleased.

Jess tried to ignore the smell of Jaden's dirty nappy. She held him and smiled as the photo booth flash went off. When it was finished, Jenny came over and picked him up off Jess's lap.

Nick turned to Jess and leant down to give her a hug. 'Thanks for doing that. See you tomorrow, Jessie.'

Jess clung to him and inhaled the scent of his aftershave. 'I love you, Dad,' she whispered into his ear.

'Oh, Jess, I love you too, more than you can imagine.'

They held each other for a minute, until Bobby said, 'Daddy, you have to go before Jaden stinks the whole house out.'

Everyone laughed, and Jess watched her father leave. As he got to the door, he turned and blew her a kiss.

Maggie helped Kate tuck Jess into bed, then sat with her after Kate had gone down to sort Bobby out.

'Good day?' Maggie asked.

'The best ever,' Jess said.

'You deserved it. You're an amazing girl, Jess, just like your mum.'

'I'm so glad she has you, Maggie. You're such a support to her, and to all of us.'

'You're like my family, kiddo. You're stuck with me. It's a pity your mum and I aren't gay – we'd make a great couple.'

Jess giggled. 'Now that would be funny.'

'Anyway, you look tired and I've got a conference call with the US. I'll pop in to see you in the morning before I fly back to London.' Maggie hugged her.

As she was leaving, Jess called out, 'Look after Mum, won't you, Maggie?'

'Always, Jess, you know I will.'

Watching everyone leave was draining Jess of the little energy she had, but she knew the worst goodbyes were to come. But, as awful as it was having to say goodbye to every-one without them even knowing it, she knew without a shadow of a doubt that this was the right thing to do. It was time to go. Cancer had controlled and ravaged her life. It had come into her body and destroyed it. It was destroying the happiness of her family and friends. Everyone was at the end of their tether, worn out, devastated and unable to take much more. Jess wanted out. It was time to do things her way.

Granddad, Piper, Luke and Bobby came in to say good-night. Jess hugged them all in turn.

'I wish I could have an almost-birthday party like that,' Bobby said.

'Maybe we could organize one for you next year,' Piper said.

'Really?' Bobby's eyes lit up.

'Sure, but it wouldn't be quite the same. We don't have Hazel's bank account.' Luke grinned.

'I wouldn't want all the pink stuff, just the cakes and the people and the sweets.'

'I was pretty surprised to see Jenny arriving,' Luke said.

'The photo is beautiful,' Piper said, looking at it on the table beside Kate's double bed where Jess was lying.

'Jaden was obsessed with me,' Bobby said. 'He was stalking me and he kept grabbing my leg.'

'You used to do that to Luke.' Their mother came in, holding a cup of tea.

'Did I?' Bobby was surprised.

'I guess it's a younger-brother thing,' Luke said.

'Well, it wasn't fun cos he stinks,' Bobby grumbled.

'He can't help that,' Mum said.

'Does that mean you're not going to help change our baby's nappies, Bobby?' Piper asked.

'No way!' Bobby shouted.

Jess smiled. She'd miss this. The banter, the fun, the family time. Just her family being her crazy, beautiful family.

'Right, this poor child is worn out. Let her rest.' George kissed Jess goodnight.

'I love you, Granddad. Thanks for letting us come and live with you. It's been amazing.'

'I've loved having you, my little pet. Now sleep well.'

Piper kissed her. Jess pulled her close. 'Look after Luke. He needs you.'

Piper looked surprised at the urgency in Jess's voice. 'Of course I will. I promise.'

'He loves you so much.'

'I love him, too, sweetie, so don't worry. It's all going to work out,' Piper whispered. 'Now rest up and stop worrying about everyone else.'

'I love you, Piper.'

'I love you more.'

Luke walked Piper out and Bobby followed them. 'Hang on, Bobby, come here for a second,' Jess called out.

He came back in, reluctantly. 'What? I'm tired, Jess. I want to go to bed.'

'I just want you to give me a hug. Please?'

He rolled his eyes. 'Everyone's always hugging in this house.'

'Bobby,' his mother said sharply, 'give your sister a hug.' Then she got up and left the room.

'Okay, one hug cos it's your almost-birthday, but that's it.'

He threw an arm around her, then pulled back.

'Thanks, Bobby. You know I love you and I think you're just brilliant.'

'You always say that, Jess.'

'I mean it, though. Don't let anyone try to change you. You're perfect just the way you are. I think you're going to do something incredible with your life, I really do. There's something really special about you.'

'Are you joking now?'

'No.'

'Did Mummy tell you I want to cure cancer?'

Jess coughed to hide the sob that escaped from her throat. 'No.'

'Well, that's what I'm going to do, Jess. I'm going to cure it so no one has to suffer like you.'

'That would be amazing, and I bet you'll do it.'

'Can I go now?'

She smiled. 'Yes, love you.'

'I know. You said it already.' He bustled out of the room.

Jess lay back on the bed. Only Luke to go. He'd be the hardest. Apart from Mum, he knew her the best. She had to keep calm. She wanted this memory to be a good one for him.

'Penny for your thoughts?' Luke stood at the door, hands in his pockets.

Jess smiled. 'Hey, come in.' She patted the bed.

'Good day,' he said. 'Even Jenny didn't cause a scene.'

'It was sweet of her to do that.'

Luke wrinkled his nose. 'About bloody time she did something nice for you.'

'Come on, Luke, give her a break. It's not easy for her. She's the home-wrecker no one wants to see. It was brave and kind of her to come today.'

'All right, Mother Teresa, I admit it was a nice gesture. Maybe she's not all bad.'

Jess folded the bed cover over in her fingers. 'You'll be a great dad.'

'I hope so. I want to be, but it's kind of scary.'

'Yeah, I can imagine.'

'I just want to get the exams over, then focus on Piper and the baby and trying to figure it all out.'

'You'll be fine. You've got so many people looking out for you who want to help.'

Luke nodded. 'You're right. Even though our family's a bit mental and half the people in it aren't even related to us, they're a good bunch.'

'A great bunch.'

He bent his head. 'I wish I could fix it, Jess.'

Jess put out her hand and took Luke's. 'You can't. You tried, and I'm so grateful to you for your bone marrow, but you can't fix me, Luke. No one can. But it's okay, honestly. This is how things are, and I've accepted it now.'

'It's not okay. It's so unfair.'

Jess squeezed his hand. 'Luke, please listen to me. I've made peace with it. You have to try to do the same.'

'I'll never accept it,' he said, in a strangled voice. 'You're the nicest, bravest person I know. You don't deserve this.'

'No one does, but it happens all the time. Please, Luke, don't be angry. It'll eat you up.'

Luke rubbed his eyes. 'I'll try, Jess.'

Jess reached under the pillow and pulled out an envelope. 'I need you to give this to Dad when I die. It's important, Luke. Promise you won't forget.'

'What is it?'

'It's just something I need to say to him and it was easier to write it down.'

Luke took the envelope and stood up. 'I'll let you get some rest.'

Jess held up her arms for one final hug. 'I love you, Luke. You're the best older brother I could ever have wished for. Everything's going to be fine.'

Luke smiled. 'If you say so, Jess. Now get some sleep. Love you, sis.'

Jess watched her brother and her hero walk out of the room, and her life.

46

Kate looked down at the pills spread out on her bathroom shelf and counted: twenty-eight Xanax tablets and fourteen Tylex. This was what would kill Jess.

Agreeing to end her child's life was one thing. Planning it was another. At first, Kate had thought about stealing morphine from one of the palliative-care nurses or doctors who came every day to check Jess's morphine pump and up the dose as her pain got worse. But she quickly found that they were incredibly careful with their medications and never left any lying around.

They were very kind. They said it was important for Jess to be comfortable, but not knocked out by the morphine so she could still function 'normally'. Kate loved and hated them coming – loved them because they were so caring, hated them because of what they represented.

She'd thought about asking Dr Willis, their GP, who also called in regularly to see Jess, to get her some morphine. But she didn't want to implicate him in any wrongdoing. No, Kate was on her own. This was something no one could knowingly help her with, and no one could ever find out about. She had to be careful, really careful, or she'd end up in prison. Then Bobby and Luke would have a dead sister and a convict mother.

So Kate went to plan B: search the internet. She was shocked by what she found. If you wanted to know how to kill yourself or someone else, the internet would provide you with all the information you needed. She had spent hours trawling for ways to overdose. If anyone looked at her Google search history, she'd be locked away on that evidence alone. But she'd covered her steps as best she could, scrubbing out her search history again and again.

She had quickly found everything she needed to know. The information she'd gathered told her it would take a combination of medications to end Jess's life. She needed benzodiazepines and morphine. Benzos she could get in Xanax, and morphine by taking codeine, in Tylex tablets. It was far simpler than she'd thought it would be. A part of her actually wanted it to be harder, so she could stall and delay it, but the all-knowing internet spewed out everything in a morning.

Kate hated lying, but this was not a 'normal' situation and she was no longer afraid of anything. The worst possible thing was already happening to her: her daughter was dying. So she went to Dr Willis and told a few white lies. She said the stress of Jess's cancer was making her extremely anxious and she needed Xanax. He readily gave her a prescription. Then she said she was also having terrible migraines and needed dissolvable Tylex. She began to cry at this point because part of her wanted him to say no. Then she wouldn't be able to kill Jess.

But Dr Willis patted her hand sympathetically and said she was under terrible duress and he'd gladly give her Tylex, but that she must be careful not to take the two together. He said he'd pop into the house in a few days' time to see Jess and check on Kate.

Kate had cried harder then. If only he knew, she'd thought. If only he knew what I plan to do with these tablets. I'm a bad person. I'm a bad mother. I'm a murderer.

Her mind kept flip-flopping crazily from 'This is right, it will be okay' to 'I'm killing my own child. I'm a child-killer.

I'm immoral and unnatural.' She wanted to honour Jess's final wish, but felt like it might kill her too. She could never be the same after this act, an act of which she'd never have thought herself capable – until her daughter had looked her in the eye and begged her.

Luke was saying goodnight to Jess, not knowing he was saying goodbye. Kate leant her forehead against the cool glass of the bathroom mirror. Give me strength, Mum, she pleaded. Help me.

She stared down at the tablets spread out before her. Jess trusted her. She was waiting. She would be devastated if Kate changed her mind now.

Kate mixed the effervescent Tylex tablets in a glass of apple juice and scooped up the little Xanax tablets in her hand. She went in to Jess. Her eyes were closed. Whiskey, the cat, was tucked under her chin. She looked so peaceful and so young. Kate put the glass and the tablets on the bedside table, then lay beside her daughter and held her one last time.

A montage of memories floated through her mind: Jess's birth, her first day at school, swimming lessons, roller-skating with her bright pink helmet, smiling with no front teeth, shouting up the chimney on Christmas morning, 'I love you, Santa', laughing hysterically when Nick tickled her, hugging Whiskey in bed at night, smiling, happy, alive . . . so alive.

Kate lay holding her broken, emaciated, bald daughter, the one cancer had ravaged, and she remembered the good times, allowed herself to travel back there and take solace. She thanked God for giving her this incredible child, who had lit up her life every day for twelve years and 306 days.

Jess was a gift, a precious gift, and Kate knew she was lucky to have had her. Jess had been the light of all their lives.

Imagining a future without her was unbearable, unthinkable, yet here she was about to help her end it.

Love, Kate realized, was very complicated. She loved Jess so much that she was willing to help her die. True love meant putting your feelings aside. True love meant helping your loved one die with dignity. True love meant sacrificing your wishes for theirs. It hurt like hell, but it was love nonetheless.

Jess stirred and groaned. She opened her eyes. 'What time is it?' she asked.

'Almost one.'

'I know this is hard for you, Mum, but thank you.'

'I'm only going to ask you once more. Are you sure?'

Jess nodded. 'More sure than I've ever been. The pain is getting unbearable. Yesterday was amazing, though. I saw everyone I love. It's the perfect time to go.'

Kate pushed the tears down. There were things she needed to say. She didn't want to waste the time crying. 'I love you so much and I'm so proud of you. I can't believe that Dad and I made someone so perfect.'

Jess smiled. 'I'm proud to be your daughter. You're amazing, Mum. Through thick and thin, you've always been there for us.'

'You three kids are my life.' Kate couldn't help it, she began to cry.

Jess wiped the tears away with the palm of her hand. 'Don't cry, Mum. I'm happy to go now and, besides, Luke's baby will make it three again.'

'No one will ever replace you. I love you so much, Jess. From the very first moment they put you in my arms, such a tiny thing, I felt a surge of pure love. It's never gone away. I adore you. Every last little bit of you. You're such an amazing person.'

'I know you love me, Mum. You're going to be okay – you have so many people who love you and will be there for you. You're the best mother in the world. I love you. And I'm so sorry it has to be like this. I'm sorry that we have to say good-bye this way.'

Kate pulled her daughter's fragile body even closer, breathing in her scent, resting her lips against her cheek. 'Me too. You should have had a better life,' she whispered. 'But you must know that every second of the last almost thirteen years has been a privilege and a joy.' Kate pushed up on her elbow to look into her daughter's eyes. 'I will miss you every single day of my life.'

Jess nodded, tears starting to fall down her cheeks. 'I'm sorry I have to go,' she whispered back.

Kate pressed her forehead against Jess's. Around them, the house was silent with sleep. It was dark and warm in there, just the two of them.

'If I can I'll try to send you a sign. I told you before, remember?'

'Yes,' Kate said. 'Send me a sign so I know you're okay.'

'I'll send a white butterfly. Larry always said I'd better not die in winter or you'd be waiting a long time to see one.'

'Say hi to Larry for me, and to your granny. She'll be there to look after you,' Kate croaked.

'I will. Can you open the curtains and the window?' Jess asked.

Kate did so. It was still dark outside, but in a few hours light would begin to break its way through and another day would begin. Her first without Jess. Kate felt her resolve weaken, and fiercely ordered herself to be strong. All those wakings without Jess, one after another for the rest of her life, were going to be like little deaths every time she opened her eyes. She tried to push the thought away. Not now, she told herself.

From behind her Jess said gently, 'I'm ready now, Mum.'

Kate turned and picked up the tablets. Jess opened her mouth. Kate's hand was shaking. Sadness crashed through her, taking her breath away. 'I can't do it. I want more time with you,' she sobbed.

Jess grabbed her arm, and put Kate's hand up to her mouth. 'Please, Mum, you have to let me go.'

Kate gulped back tears and looked at Jess's determined little face, at the morphine drip, at her bald head, at her thin body. She wanted to be selfish, to hold on to Jess for every second she could, but that was what she wanted. It went against Jess's own wishes. She was going to have to find the purest love inside her and hold on to it to enable herself to do this. She focused on Jess's face, on Jess's need, and dissolved her own wishes to nothing. She could do this. She could do it for Jess.

'Sorry, sweetheart. It's okay.'

She placed the tablets in Jess's mouth and helped her swallow them with water. Then she handed her daughter the glass of apple juice containing the Tylex and Jess drank it straight down. No shaking hands, no hesitation.

Jess lay back on her pillow and sighed. Kate groaned and her legs went to jelly and she collapsed beside the bed, her knees sinking to the floor. 'What have I done?' she gasped. 'Oh, Jesus, Jess, what have I done?'

Jess took Kate's trembling hands in her small, bony ones. 'Look at me, Mum,' she ordered.

Kate raised her head and gazed into the beautiful brown eyes.

'Thank you. Thank you for saving me from any more pain. Thank you for letting me die my way. I'm happy, Mum. I'm ready to go. This is what I want. I love you so much.'

Kate looked deep into her daughter's eyes and knew she had done the right thing for Jess, but that didn't take into account how she herself was feeling. It wasn't simple for her. It was a crushing blow of emotions, all racing around her body making her feel panicked and grief-stricken. She had done the unthinkable – helped her own child to die.

She climbed into the bed, under the covers, and held Jess close. She stroked her cheek, her head, kissed her face over and over again. She told her how much she loved her, she told her how wonderful it felt to be her mother. Kate talked through life and on into death.

For four hours Kate held her precious girl and watched as her breathing got slower and slower. She breathed with her, she breathed for her. This is love, she thought. This is the ultimate act of love: letting someone go.

Never in her wildest dreams when she'd held that bonny, healthy baby girl for the first time almost thirteen years ago could she have imagined that she'd now be holding her as she took her last breath.

Kate keened and moaned, as she rocked Jess in her arms. The room steadily became brighter as the sun slipped above the horizon. Jess's breathing was very shallow now, more like gasping. She was peaceful, though, not struggling. Then there came a shuddering gasp, and she was still. Kate bent her head and kissed Jess's eyelids.

With the end of Jess's breathing, which Kate had been straining to listen to for so many hours, came other sounds she hadn't noticed before. The birds in the garden had taken up their chorus, which broke into her consciousness now. Morning song. Mourning song. They were singing the new day into being – Kate's first day without her daughter. It was over. Jess was gone.

47

Kate woke up with a start. Luke was shaking her.

'Wake up! Jess isn't breathing. Jesus, Mum, I think she's . . . I think . . .' He began to cry.

Kate pulled her arms from around her daughter's body. Jess lay still, her body still warm but her soul now far away. She wasn't there any more. The enormity of what she'd done hit Kate and she doubled over in pain.

'Is she dead, Mum? Is she?' Luke cried.

Kate nodded.

'Oh, God, *nooooooo* . . .' Luke covered his face with his hands and wept. 'Why, Mum? Why did it have to happen? I thought we had more time? Oh, God.'

Kate stroked Jess's face. What had she done? She'd cut her life short. What mother does that? She heard Jess's voice in her head: *If you love me, you'll do this.* Well, she did love her. She loved her more than anything in the world and she wanted her back. She wanted one more day, one more hour. Oh, Jess . . . what have I done? Kate began to sob uncontrollably.

Luke came over and put his arms around her. They cried together, each broken-hearted over the loss of their beloved Jess.

George came in and froze when he saw them crying. 'Oh, sweet Jesus,' he murmured. He came over to the bed and looked down at Jess. 'Oh, Jess, poor broken bird.' He put his arm around Kate. 'Come here, Katie, it's okay. At least she's at peace now. No more pain for the poor pet.'

He turned to hug Luke. 'She won't suffer any more, Luke. She was ready to go.'

Luke shook his head. 'But I'm not ready, Granddad,' he said, through his tears, and Kate's heart broke.

George patted him on the back. 'We're never ready to let go of the ones we love. There is no right time to say goodbye.'

Kate felt her throat closing. Jess, my beautiful Jess. I want you back, I need you, I can't believe I did this . . .

George bent down and forced Kate to look at him. 'Breathe, Kate. Come on now, look at me. Breathe.'

Bobby stumbled in in his pyjamas. 'What's going on? Why is everyone crying? Is Jess sicker?'

Luke went over to his little brother. 'Bobby, I'm really sorry to have to tell you this but . . . Jess died last night.'

Bobby frowned. 'Died? How could she die? She was all happy yesterday and smiling and taking photos and . . . and alive. I think she's just sleeping, Luke.'

Kate pulled herself together and gathered Bobby into her arms. 'She is sleeping, Bobby, but she's not going to wake up. She's gone to Heaven now.'

Bobby wriggled away from her. 'She is not in Heaven cos there is no Heaven,' he shouted. 'God is not real. If he was, he wouldn't have made Jess get stinky cancer and he would never, ever have made her die.' He kicked the bed violently. 'Ouch!' He began to cry.

The four of them stood around the bed, crying, each lost in their own thoughts. Finally, George wiped his eyes with his handkerchief and said, 'Kate, you have to tell Nick.'

Kate's heart sank. She was dreading it.

'I'll do it, if you like,' George offered.

'No, it should be me. I'll ring him now.'

Kate left the room and went down to the kitchen. She also had to phone Dr Willis and ask him to come over to sign the death certificate. There was no way Jess could have a post-mortem. If that happened, they'd find out what Kate had done.

Part of her would have welcomed being found out and sent to prison. She wanted to be punished for what she had done. She wanted to feel physical pain. She wanted someone to punch or hit her. She was a bad person, a bad mother. She had killed her baby. Oh, God . . .

Stop it, Mum. I wanted to die. Jess's voice sounded in her ears.

Kate pinched her arm, hard. The pain brought her back to her senses. Her sons needed her. She couldn't risk a post-mortem. She called Dr Willis.

'I'm so very sorry, Kate,' he said. 'The poor child was very sick. At least she's out of pain and at peace now. I'll be right over.'

Kate thanked him. She'd call the palliative-care team a little later. She wanted Dr Willis to get there first. Taking a long, deep breath, she dialled Nick's number. Her hands shook.

'Hi.' He sounded sleepy.

'Nick, it's Jess. She's . . .' Kate tried to get the word out '. . . she's . . .' She couldn't say it. How could she tell him? She knew that his heart would split in two and it would be irrevocable.

'What?' Nick sounded alert now. 'Is she in the hospital?'

'No, she's . . .'

'Oh, shit, is it another infection?'

'No, Nick. She's – she's dead,' Kate blurted. 'She passed away during the night.'

'*What?*' Nick shouted. 'What did you say?'

Kate began to cry. She'd done it now, she'd told him. His life would never be the same again. None of their lives would ever be the same. It would always be 'before this moment' and 'after this moment'. 'Before Jess' and 'after Jess'. There was no way to fix this or go back and change the outcome. Jess was dead. Gone. Never, ever coming back. They'd never see her smile again, never hear her voice, hold her, kiss her, love her. Kate slid down onto the kitchen floor and sobbed.

'*Nooooooo*, Kate, please. No, it can't be . . . Oh, Jesus Christ, no.' Nick broke down. Kate could hear Jenny beside him, asking him what was wrong.

'I'm sorry,' Kate said. 'I'm so sorry.' And then she hung up.

Dr Willis gently examined Jess's body. He listened for heart sounds, then for breathing sounds in the lungs and then checked Jess's pupils with a torch. Kate saw him give Jess's hand a little squeeze and heard him mutter, 'May you rest in peace, sweet girl.'

Turning to Kate, he said, 'I'm so very sorry. She went quickly in the end.'

Kate looked away from him. 'Yes, she did.'

'She was in a lot of pain, and it was only going to get worse. It's no comfort to you, but perhaps it was best that she went now and didn't suffer any more.'

Kate was afraid to speak. She wanted to tell him. She wanted to confess what she had done. It was eating her up inside. 'I killed her,' she wanted to shout. 'I'm an evil person. I cut my baby's life short.' She shook all over with guilt.

Dr Willis walked towards her, clearly concerned. 'Do you have the Xanax I prescribed? You might need to take one, Kate. Will I get one for you? Where are they?'

'*No!*' Kate gasped. 'No, I'm fine. I just need a minute.' The empty packets were tightly wrapped up in a bag in the bathroom bin.

'Well, sit down and put your head between your legs – it'll help with your breathing.' He guided her to the chair in the corner of the room.

As Kate concentrated on catching her breath, Nick crashed into the room. He ran to the bed and cried out his daughter's name over and over. He kissed her face and her hands and stroked her cheek, sobbing wildly.

Dr Willis whispered, 'I'll pop downstairs and see your dad,' then discreetly left the room.

Kate sat in the chair, silently watching Nick fall apart.

He turned to her, his eyes red and bloodshot. 'How could she go so soon? How could she just die like that? I thought we had more time.'

Kate didn't trust herself to speak.

'Our little girl. How can she be gone, Kate? How? It's not right. It's too soon.'

Kate felt her stomach twist.

'I didn't tell her I loved her.'

'You did, Nick.' Kate found her voice.

'Not enough. I should have told her more.'

'She knew you loved her.'

'How did it happen? Were you here? Was she alone?'

'I was with her. She just went to sleep and then she . . . Well, she . . . stopped breathing.'

'What did you do? Did you try to bring her back? Did you do CPR? Was the nurse here?'

'No, she'd gone home. I didn't do CPR. I just . . . well, I just knew she was gone.' Kate could feel herself blushing.

'Did she say anything? What were her last words? Do you think she knew?'

How could Kate tell him that Jess's last words were *Thank you for saving me. I'm happy, Mum, I'm ready to go?*

'She was happy, Nick. She loved the party yesterday and saw everyone and I think she was just ready to go.'

Nick knelt beside the bed, caressing Jess's arm. 'That's just it. She seemed so joyful yesterday. I said to Jenny on the way home, "I think maybe she'll get her strength up and be able to do more chemo." I honestly thought she might make it. I can't believe this has happened . . . It's all wrong. It's such a shock. I mean, I know she was really sick but I just can't take it in. Jess, my little girl . . .' He buried his face in the duvet and sobbed.

Kate went over and laid her hand on his shoulder. She felt as if she was made of glass and could shatter at any moment.

Nick looked up at her wild-eyed. He grabbed her arms. It hurt. 'Did you do something?'

She stared at him, unable to compose herself quickly enough. She shook her head. 'No,' she whispered. 'I didn't do anything.'

He stared hard at her, still gripping her arms. 'Because if you did anything to cut her life short,' he said quietly, 'I would never, ever forgive you. I want my Jess back. I don't want her to be gone. If you did anything at all, I promise you now, Kate, I'll bring you down.'

48

Nick sat in the corner of the café in a daze. People came and went, bringing food. So much food. There were cakes and buns and lasagnes and dinners on every surface. People he knew and didn't know shook his hand and told him they were sorry for his loss.

Loss. What a ridiculous word. He hadn't lost Jess, she'd been ripped from him. Fate had wrenched her from this life to the next. If she was lost, he'd be able to find her. There was no finding her now, no getting her back. He was bereft.

Bobby wandered around in circles, kicking the tables and chairs. Luke and Piper sat in the corner, holding hands. Maggie and Hazel moved around talking to everyone and making sure they all had food and something to drink. Chloë sat in a corner, staring at photos on her phone and crying quietly.

In the sitting room, in a closed coffin, lay Jess. His little girl, put inside a wooden box. Tomorrow, after the funeral, she'd be in the ground, buried six feet under. This was not how life should be. His head thumped with anger. It took huge effort not to jump up and scream, hurl the furniture through the windows and punch all of the well-meaning onlookers who were staring at the debris of his smashed-up life.

The French waitress made vats of coffee and tea and kept trying to get him to eat. 'You must keep the strength up,' she said, as she offered Nick yet another plate of food. But he couldn't eat. He felt constantly nauseous. How could people sit around drinking fucking coffee and eating cake? Jess was dead, for Christ's sake.

Kate kept wandering in and out, unable to sit still. Whenever she saw Bobby or Luke or George, she hugged them. Nick watched her, knowing she was as ripped apart inside as he was and marvelling at her ability to think of others still.

'Dad?'

Nick looked up. Luke was standing beside him, holding out an envelope.

'Jess asked me to give you this.'

'What?'

'The night she died, she told me to give this to you once she was gone.'

'My God.' Nick's hands were shaking as he took the envelope. 'Thank you, Luke.'

Luke nodded at him, then went back to Piper. Nick opened the envelope and pulled out the letter. It wasn't Jess's normal writing: it was sloping, jerky and much harder to read. It had clearly taken her enormous effort to write it. He squinted, deciphering the letters and the words one by one, a lump forming in his throat as he read her last words to him.

Dear Dad

By the time you read this letter, I'll be gone. I'll be in a place where I can be at peace. I'm not happy here any more. I can't take it any more, Dad. It's too much pain. I want to go. I'm happy to go — it's important you know that, even if it's hard to hear.

I know you wanted me to do more treatment, but I couldn't. I knew I was dying before the doctors told me. It was a feeling I had, hard to explain, but I just knew. I think I'd accepted it long before everyone else did. But I love you all so much for trying to keep me alive.

The strange thing is, I'm okay about dying. I guess I've had a while to get used to the idea. Until Larry died, I didn't even allow myself to think it was a possibility, but after he went I realized it could happen to me too.

I hoped it wouldn't, but I got sicker and here we are.

I tried, Dad, I tried really hard to beat it, but the cancer beat me. I tried to tell you I was ready to go, but you weren't ready to hear it. Dying this way, at home with dignity, is my final wish, Dad – let me go and don't blame anyone for my death. Please.

I want to die in my own way, on my own terms, just as I told you. I want to be in charge. That means everything to me. So please don't blame Mum. She only did what I begged her to do. She allowed me to leave this world with dignity. I asked her to help me die because I knew you couldn't. I made her say yes, I forced her to agree, and I love her so much for doing this.

You reacted so strongly when I mentioned wanting to let go and I understand why. You're a fighter and a warrior and someone who never gives up and wouldn't allow me to either. And I love that about you. But sometimes, Dad, sometimes you have to accept defeat and let go.

I've had a short life, but it's been a brilliant one. I have the best family in the world. I love you all so much. It was hard when you met Jenny and left, but I understand that life can be complicated and that you fell in love with her and that's okay. I want you to be happy. I want everyone to be happy. I know you worry about your relationship with the boys not being that good. But it can be, Dad. You can fix it so easily. Just spend more time with them. Luke needs you in his life. He pretends he doesn't but he really does.

Bobby looks up to you so much and he's jealous of Jaden only because he thinks he's taking you away. He's angry because he's confused and scared. Be patient with him, Dad. He's such a gorgeous boy. He just needs to know he's loved. Thanks for being a great dad to me. I love you so much. I'm so proud to be your daughter. You always made me feel like the most important girl in the world.

I'm sorry I caused everyone so much unhappiness. I wish cancer had never come into our lives but it did and I've accepted that my time is up. You need to accept it too. Remember the good times and try to look forward.

I'm sorry I'll miss Luke's baby being born, but I'll be watching. Wherever I am, I'll be watching. If you see a white butterfly, it'll be me, letting you know I'm okay. But even if you don't, please don't worry about me. I know I'll be fine.

I'm not scared, Dad. I'm not frightened of dying any more. I want to go.

Mum is letting me go, and you must too.

I love you always,
Jess

Nick's hands were shaking so much, he could barely read the last line. Rage welled up inside him. White hot, burning through him.

He stood up, unsteady on his feet, and stumbled forward. He had to find her. She wasn't in the café. He staggered into the kitchen. She was there, with Maggie. He grabbed her by the shoulder and spun her around to face him.

'You lying bitch,' he hissed, shaking the letter in her face.

Maggie stepped in. 'Jesus, Nick, calm down.'

'It's okay,' Kate said quickly.

'No, it isn't. He can't speak to you like that. She's heart-broken too, Nick.'

'You don't know what she is! She's a monster!' he spat.

'You need to calm down, Nick.' Maggie stood in front of Kate, protecting her from his venom.

'It's okay, Maggie, leave it.' Kate took hold of Nick's arm. 'Nick, come upstairs. We can talk about this in private.'

'So your dirty little secret doesn't get out?' he snapped.

Kate turned and strode out of the kitchen. Maggie looked shocked, but she let them go. Nick followed Kate into her bedroom and slammed the door.

'You bitch, you lying bitch! You killed her!' he shouted. 'It's here in black and white.'

Tears spilt down Kate's cheeks. 'Yes, I did help her die. I did it because she begged me, Nick. She wanted to die in her own way.'

'Her own way? She was twelve! She was a child. She didn't know what she was saying! She was sick. How could you do this? You cut her life short. You stole her from me, from us. Who the hell are you to decide when she should die? Who made you God?' He dug his finger into her chest.

Kate pushed his hand away. 'I didn't decide, you moron. Jess did. Do you think I wanted to do it? Do you think I wanted to cut her precious life short and lose one minute with her? She begged me, she pleaded with me – and you know what, Nick? She deserved to die her own way. She'd suffered so much. She desperately wanted that final control, and I let her have it.'

'She should have died when it was her time, not now, not before. She could have got better.'

Kate glared at him. 'No, she couldn't. She was terminally ill. You saw how weak she was.'

'Weak, yes. About to die, no. How could you do this? Why didn't you say no? What the hell is wrong with you?'

Kate sank down on the edge of the bed. 'I did say no. But she kept pleading with me. She wanted to go, Nick. She was tired of the pain and suffering. She couldn't take any more.'

'She was a child. You were supposed to talk her down, make her see that she had to live.'

'Jesus, don't you think I tried? Do you think I wanted to do this? It broke me in two, Nick. But she asked me and it

412

was what she wanted. And Jess wasn't a kid, not really, she was a very old, wise soul.'

'She was twelve!' Nick roared, his hands balled into tight fists. 'You should have told me. How could you not tell me? I would have talked her out of it. I'd have made her see sense.'

'You told me that she did talk to you about it, remember? So you must know, in your heart, that she didn't want to be talked out of it. She wasn't going to change her mind. It wasn't a snap decision. She thought it through long and hard.'

'I'm her father, for Christ's sake! How could you decide this without me? I wanted more time with her. You stole that from me. You robbed me of that. You robbed all of us. Her brothers, George, everyone. How could you, Kate? You were her mother – how could a mother do that to her own child? I mean, Jesus Christ . . .'

Kate began to cry again. 'She said, "If you love me enough you'll help me." I didn't want to do it. Don't you get it? I wanted her to keep going but she couldn't. She just couldn't go on. I tried, Nick . . . I loved her so much – I never wanted this. I'm broken, destroyed.'

'You're destroyed? Oh, poor Kate. What about me? There were so many things I wanted to say to her, to do with her, to . . . to . . . just to be with her.'

'I'm sorry. I don't know what else to say. I did what Jess wanted. I know it was wrong, but for her it was right. She was happy. She'd had a wonderful day with everyone and she was happy to go.'

'Don't try to justify this.' Nick shook the letter in her face. 'If I hadn't read it, you'd never have told me and I'd never have known what a devious witch you are. I'd have had my suspicions, but you'd never have been straight with me, would you?'

'What does it say? What did Jess say?' Kate grabbed the letter and scanned it quickly. She read aloud: '*I made her say yes, I forced her to agree, and I love her so much for doing this.* You see? She tells you herself.'

'I don't care what this says. She was my daughter and you had no right to do this. I could go to the police.'

Kate stood up. 'Go ahead, Nick. I really don't care what happens to me. My heart is broken and I'd be happy to die right now because then I'd be with Jess. But just remember, if you put me in prison, you'll be raising the boys. It'll make a nice change from me raising them on my own.'

'Don't start with that crap.'

'It's true, though. In the last three years I've been pretty much on my own with the kids while you were tied up with Jenny and then Jaden. I'm not saying you weren't there for Jess when she got sick, but you weren't there much beforehand. I'm not shouting at you for being a rubbish dad. I never went to a lawyer when you were constantly late with maintenance cheques. I let you see the kids whenever you could fit them into your schedule. I picked up the pieces when you cancelled on them or just didn't turn up. I never spoke badly of you in front of them. I bent over backwards for you, Nick, even though you treated me very badly. So go ahead, sit on your high horse, put me in prison. Ruin the boys' lives. You can't hurt me more than life already has.'

Nick picked up a glass from the bedside locker and flung it against the wall. He needed to hear something smash. He was afraid he was going to hit Kate. She winced as the glass shattered and the pieces bounced onto the floor.

'I will never forgive you,' he said, his face red with fury. 'I will never forgive you for being a *murderer*. I might even go to the police. What kind of a monster are you? I could never have done that. Never.'

'That's because you didn't love her like I did.' She raised her hands. 'I'm not saying you didn't adore her, just that I loved her enough to give her what she most wanted, even though I knew it would destroy me. I made the ultimate sacrifice because I loved her. Can't you see?'

Nick walked towards the door. 'You can try to justify it any way you want, but you cut her life short and that is wrong, not to mention immoral and illegal and completely unforgivable.'

Kate's eyes were swollen from crying. 'It was love, Nick, pure love.'

Nick walked out of the room and closed the door on the woman he'd thought he knew, the stranger who had killed his daughter.

Bobby's Diary

Mummy made me wear a scrachy jaket to the funeral. I hated it. It made me all uncomfortable. The funeral was horrible. Daddy and Mummy didn't speek even one word and Daddy was giving Mummy dagger eyes the whole time, which is really mean cos she is hartbroken about Jess.

Luke said Daddy was just acting weird cos he's hartbroken too.

Jess died exaktly ten days ago and everyone is walking around like zombies. No one nows what to say. People still keep coming to the house with food which is ridikulus cos we own a café and we have tons of food.

Everyone cries now all the time. No one hides it or tries to pretend or put on a brave face. They all just cry out loud. Even Nathalie and she's a strong French woman. Nathalie has a new boyfriend who writes poems. He has long hair and is a bit smelly. Granddad said he's a useless 'bad word' and she needs to get rid of him.

Nathalie says he is a kreative soul and she loves his mind. Granddad said she'd have to love his mind cos his body stinks. He also said that the poet isn't getting any more free cofee or food and needs to pay his way like a real man.

Nathalie said Granddad has no soul. Granddad said his soul left him when Jess died. Nathalie looked sad then and hugged Granddad and said she loved him with or without a soul.

Piper comes over every morning and makes sure Luke is up and studying and not in bed crying. Piper is ginormous now. She looks like a normal person from the back but a big whale from the front.

Mummy sleeps a lot and cries a lot and goes out a lot with Liam to a place where she says she shouts. She said she'll take me there one day but I like punching doe. I showed Granddad how to do it and he thinks it's great. He does it all the time now.

Daddy came over and took me out yesterday. He still isn't speeking to Mummy and still gives her dagger eyes.

He brawt Jaden with him and we went to the playground in the park. Daddy sat on the bench with his sunglasses on and tried to hide that he was crying but I cud see the tears coming down his face.

Jaden was kind of annoying. He folowed me everywhere. He can't get enuff of me so I tryed to be nice to him. He calls me 'Dobby', which is kind of funny. He asked me to push him on the swing so I did.

When I feel my hart getting sad about Jess and there's no doe to punch, I go outside and kick the wall. Daddy found me kicking the wall out the back yesterday and he kicked it too. We kicked and kicked until our toes hurt and our shoes were all scrached. Daddy ruffled my hair and said I was a great boy and that he was proud of me. I didn't think kicking a wall was something a Dad would be proud of but whatever.

I miss Jess a lot. It's like there's a big hole in the house where she used to be. Maggie said for a small girl she had a huge presense and made a big and beootiful mark on life.

I keep looking for white buterflys cos when I was crying really hard one day, Luke told me that Jess said she would try to send a white buterfly to let us no she was okay. But I don't see any, ever.

I sleep with Whiskey now. Mummy said I cud. If I sniff him reelly hard he smells of Jess. Mrs Lorgan is being super-nice to me now Jess is dead. Even Tommy and Declan are being nice to me because having a dead sister is way worse than a stuter or a brother with Down Sindrum.

Mrs Lorgan said time will heal my sad hart, but so far it feels the same - reelly reelly sore.

49

Kate sat opposite her father and stared at her plate.

'Try to eat something, Katie,' George pleaded with her.

'I can't, Dad. Everything sticks in my throat and I think I'm going to choke.'

George patted her hand. 'I know that feeling. But you have to keep your strength up for the boys. They need you, Kate.'

She sighed and shovelled a forkful of lasagne into her mouth, then gagged and spat it into her paper napkin.

'Well, maybe tomorrow.' George took the plate away. 'Are you getting any sleep at all?'

Kate shook her head. 'Not really. I wish I could sleep more because when I do sometimes I dream of her. It's magical. She's right there beside me. I can see her, but when I go to touch her I wake up, and then I remember she's gone. It almost hurts as much as when she died.'

George handed her a tissue. 'I had those dreams after your mother died. It's wonderful and terrible at the same time.'

Kate wiped her eyes. 'I don't know how to do this, Dad. I just want to curl up in a ball and hide and only come out when the pain is over.'

'I know, pet, but life doesn't work like that. You have to get up and keep going. It feels like torture now, it's all so raw, but if you keep getting up and living, one day it won't be such an uphill struggle.'

'She was too young, Dad. Only twelve.'

'It's unspeakably cruel.' George's eyes welled up. 'No mother should bury her child.'

'Why her and not me or Nick?'

George slammed his fist on the kitchen countertop. 'It should have been me. I wish it had been me, not that beautiful little girl.' His chin wobbled and Kate watched as her father fell apart. He sobbed into the tea-towel he was holding.

She stood up and put her arms around him. 'I'm glad you're letting it out, Dad. You've been so brave for all of us, but I know how much you loved her.'

George nodded and Kate handed him a tissue. He had been getting up every morning, cooking breakfast for the boys, getting them off to school and collecting Bobby most days when Kate couldn't face it. He'd opened the café three days after the funeral and worked from dawn until dusk.

Kate was worried he'd drop dead from grief, overwork and exhaustion. It had been three weeks now and her father hadn't sat down for a second. She knew he was going to crash at some point and she was relieved that he was finally showing his grief.

He looked old and weary, she thought. He had aged. They all had. Even Luke and Bobby had creases under their eyes from crying and lack of sleep. Kate had Bobby in her bed most nights. He'd come in to her holding Whiskey and telling her he couldn't sleep. She liked having him beside her. Watching him sleep was soothing.

She was so glad Luke had Piper. She'd been a trouper. Calling in every day to make sure he was up, walking to school with him and studying with him in the evenings. Kate loved how affectionate Piper was with Luke, constantly holding his hand or rubbing his back or resting her head against his shoulder. She knew Luke was comforted by her presence.

Olivia sent over little gifts with Piper, not wishing to intrude but wanting Kate to know she was thinking of her. Piper had delivered soothing bath salts, scented candles and calming body lotions. Olivia had been quietly kind and supportive and Kate loved her for it.

Hazel rang every day to check in and left messages offering to pay for luxury holidays for Kate and the boys, spa days for Kate, a new car, prams and cots for Piper . . . Her generosity was endless.

'I know you probably wish I'd stop calling, but I'll keep leaving messages and suggestions. One day you might feel like going out and doing something. When you do, I'll be outside, ready to pick you up and whisk you off wherever you want to go. We miss her terribly. Chloë is bereft. We're thinking of you all.'

Kate liked Hazel's daily messages. Sometimes they even made her smile.

Nathalie came into the kitchen. 'Oh, sorry. I am interrupting,' she said, looking at George's tear-stained face.

He wiped his nose. 'It's fine. I'm fine. What do you need?'

'I'm sorry to be a pain in the ear, but that woman, Rosemary, is in the café again with more casserole for you. She says she wants to make sure you are eating and she won't leave until she sees that you are okay. She is very insistent. She like you, George.'

George threw his tissue into the bin. 'For the love of Jesus, I'm going to have to get a restraining order. She's stalking me. Right, Nathalie. You come with me – I need your protection.' George walked ahead into the café, with Nathalie following behind, patting him on the back and telling him to be nice to the casserole lady.

Kate laid her head on the table. It felt too heavy for her body. Everything was wrong. The world was twisted and upside-down. The pain of Jess being gone was worse than she could ever have imagined. It was a visceral pain, like nothing she'd ever known. Even breathing was a struggle. Some days she was tempted to kill herself so she could be with Jess again. She wouldn't do that to Luke and Bobby, though, she couldn't hurt them, but if she hadn't had them, she probably would have killed herself. Her yearning to be with Jess was so strong. To hold her one more time, to tell her she loved her once more, to feel her soft cheek against her own . . . It was a crippling pain.

Liam had been a lifeline. She called him at all times of the night and he was always there. Listening, understanding, being sympathetic. She went to the cliff with him almost daily to shout. He held her when the pain was too great and her legs buckled. She relied on him more each day. She honestly thought she would have gone mad or done something stupid without him there to hold her up and support her. He was such a good man.

The kitchen door opened and Maggie's face appeared. 'Hey, I was hoping I'd catch you.' She came in wheeling a suitcase behind her.

'Did you come straight from the airport?' Kate asked.

'Of course I did. I hated being away these last two weeks. As you know, I tried to cancel the stupid Asian trip.'

'I'm glad I insisted you go. Was it worth it?'

'We got the deal.'

'That's great, Maggie.' Kate tried to be enthusiastic.

'Thanks, but it means nothing in the scheme of things. Nothing really matters any more, does it?'

'Not to me, no.'

Maggie bent down and hugged her. 'How are you? I know it's a stupid question.'

'It's unbearable.' Kate was crying again.

Maggie sat down opposite her best friend and held her hand. Tears formed in her eyes. 'I was only her godmother and *I* can barely function with the pain of it. I don't know how you're managing.'

'I miss her so much,' Kate sobbed. 'I miss her smile, her voice, her laugh, her...' The pain of a memory flooded her body. It was Jess giggling as Luke danced around the kitchen in his boxer shorts singing into a wooden spoon. She could hear Jess's laugh, her wonderful laugh.

Maggie rubbed her back. 'Breathe, Kate, breathe.'

Kate felt her heart rate slowing. 'Jesus, Maggie, how do people do this? How do they go on? What am I going to do?'

'Live, survive, struggle on. I'm here for you, and so are George and Liam and Hazel and the boys. You are surrounded by people who love you and want to support you. We'll help you, Kate, I promise.'

Kate gave her friend a small smile. 'Thanks, Maggie.'

Maggie got up and opened the fridge. 'I need a drink.' She pulled out a bottle of wine and poured two glasses.

Kate picked hers up and swirled the wine around. 'I haven't drunk since it happened,' she said. 'I'm afraid to. I'm afraid of never being able to stop. The idea of diving into the abyss of alcohol is very tempting.'

'I can see why, but one glass won't kill you.' Maggie drank deeply from hers.

Kate took a sip. The wine rushed to her empty stomach. She noticed the effect almost immediately. Her head felt light and a bit woozy.

'How are the boys?' Maggie asked.

Kate sighed. 'Bobby walks around like a headless chicken. He's completely lost. He has nightmares most nights. He's kicking the walls a lot and not saying much. I can see his little mind trying to make sense of it all.'

'And Luke?'

'Thankfully he has Piper, who is holding him up. She's so loving and kind to him, it's really beautiful to see. If it wasn't for Piper and the baby, I think Luke would fall apart. He loved Jess so much – we all did.' Kate was crying.

Maggie squeezed her hand and cried with her. 'She was a very special girl.'

'I can't bear it, Maggie. I want her back. I just want her back,' Kate sobbed.

'I know you do. It's just so cruel.'

Kate wiped her eyes with the soggy tissue her father had given her. 'I go to the cliff to shout most days, but I've run out of expletives to yell at the universe.'

Maggie drained her wine. 'Keep shouting. If it gets you out of the house and gives you even the tiniest bit of relief, do it.'

'Liam brings me. He's been so kind. He just gets it, you know. He doesn't try to make me feel better or tell me Heaven needed another angel or any of that crap.'

Maggie smiled. 'I'm very glad he's there. He seems like a gem.'

'He's a good friend in a time of need, that's for sure.'

'I think he's more than that,' Maggie said gently.

Kate shrugged. 'Maybe. I don't know. I can't think straight, but I do know that I want him in my life. I need him.'

Maggie poured herself a second glass of wine while Kate took another small sip of hers.

'How's Piper? She must be big now. It must be hard in school. Can you imagine being hugely pregnant and trying to study for your final school exams? Not easy.'

'She's great,' Kate said, 'and getting bigger by the day. But she's studying hard and getting Luke to study too. It's funny,

I was so upset about the pregnancy but now it's the only ray of light in the midst of all this horror.'

'Hopefully it'll bring you all some badly needed joy.'

Kate nodded. 'We need it.'

'How's Nick?' Maggie asked.

'Not good.'

'What was that all about the day he screamed at you?' Maggie asked.

'What?' Kate pretended not to know what she was talking about.

Maggie raised an eyebrow. 'Come on, Kate, the day he called you a lying bitch and was shaking a letter in your face. What was going on?'

Kate's hands began to shake. 'Nothing. He was just being Nick.'

Maggie reached out and put a hand on Kate's arm. 'Hey, Kate, it's me. You can tell me anything. You know that.'

Kate felt her breath quickening. 'I can't, it's too shocking. You'd hate me.'

Maggie frowned. 'What could be so bad? Come on, Kate, talk to me. I'll never judge you.'

Kate looked at her friend's concerned face. It was Maggie, her dearest pal. Could she tell her the truth? Could she tell her that she'd murdered her own child? What if Maggie never forgave her, like Nick? Could she bear to lose another person in her life? No, she couldn't, but the desire to admit what she had done was too strong.

Kate picked up her glass of wine, drank it down in two big gulps and spluttered, 'I killed Jess.'

Maggie stared at her. 'What?'

'I gave her an overdose of drugs and I killed her.'

Maggie's eyes were huge now. 'Jesus Christ, Kate, why?'

Kate looked directly at her friend. It was a relief to say the words out loud. 'Because she asked me to. She begged me to.'

Maggie's eyes filled with tears. 'Because of the pain?'

'She couldn't stand it. She wanted to go out her own way, with dignity. She was terrified of dying alone, choking on her own blood in the middle of the night when we were asleep. She was so weak and sick. She wanted to decide when to say goodbye.'

Tears streamed down Maggie's face. 'Oh, God . . . poor Jess. And poor you.'

'Poor me? I'm a murderer, Maggie. I killed the person I loved most in the world. I cut her life short. I deprived her loved ones of a few last weeks with her. I'm a monster.' Kate began to weep. 'I wish I hadn't done it. I want those weeks with her. I should never have agreed to it.'

Maggie grabbed her shoulders and shook her. 'You are not a monster! You allowed your daughter to leave this world the way she wanted to. She'd been through so much, it's no wonder she wanted it all to stop. The poor thing was shattered. You're not a monster! You're the bravest person I know.'

Kate was shocked. 'Brave? I'm weak. I should have talked her out of it. I should have said no. She pleaded with me – she wanted it so badly. But it was still wrong.'

'She asked you because she knew you were the only person who loved her enough to do it. She knew no one else could.'

Kate let the guilt and fear wash over her. She put her head on the table and wept.

'You poor thing, carrying around the weight of all this on top of your grief. I don't know how you're still standing upright. But you mustn't feel guilty. Jess was dying, and her last few weeks would have been awful. You did what she wanted. You granted her a last wish. I always thought it was amazing the way she died after that wonderful day we all spent here with her. When I left that night, I knew she was saying goodbye to me. I felt it. I remember going home and thinking, I'll never see her again. But she was happy, Kate, she was almost glowing that day. You did the right thing.'

'Nick doesn't feel that way. He hates me, and he said he might go to the police.'

Maggie's face went red. 'What? The bastard. How dare he say that? How dare he threaten you?'

'He has the right to be angry, Maggie. I didn't tell him, although he was suspicious because he knew Jess couldn't take any more. Jess wrote him a letter and told him it was her decision and he wasn't to blame me, but he does. Oh, God, he does. He's so angry he could do anything. What if he does go to the police? I could be in serious trouble.'

Maggie stood up and paced the kitchen floor. 'Nick won't go to the police because Jess begged you to do it, and he isn't going to get you into trouble when you have his two sons to look after. Besides, if he was going to do it, he would have acted by now. Of course I understand that he's angry, but he won't do anything stupid. He's not going to bring the police into it. He's just lashing out at you.'

'But what if he does?'

'He won't. Do you want me to talk to him?'

Kate shook her head. 'He'll go mad if he thinks I told anyone. I think it's best to say nothing and hope he eventually understands why I did it, although I don't think he ever will.'

Maggie sat down again and sighed. 'I suppose you'd be pretty angry if he'd done it and not told you.'

Kate smiled sadly. 'That's the thing. I'd probably never forgive him if he'd done it.'

'You didn't do anything wrong, Kate. You just loved Jess, literally to death.'

'"Loved her to death". Now that's a saying I never thought I'd truly understand.'

They smiled at each other and Maggie poured them both another drink.

'To you, Kate, a good mother, a brilliant mother, who loved her daughter enough to let her go.'

Kate drank the wine. She didn't feel like a good mother. She closed her eyes and pictured Jess's face. Wherever you are, Jess, she thought, know that I miss you every minute of every day. Know that I struggle to get up in the morning because the grief of losing you is so strong. But I promise to keep trying. One foot in front of the other. I'll keep going to the cliff with Liam and shouting. I'll keep being a mum to Luke and Bobby. I'll keep being a daughter to George and a friend to Maggie and Hazel. But, most of all, I'll keep being your mum, always and for ever.

50

Piper rolled out of bed and waddled to the bathroom. It was still dark outside. She glanced at her watch. Five a.m. She caught her reflection in the bathroom mirror. God, I do look like a whale, she thought, and I still have five weeks to go. How can my stomach possibly get any bigger?

She shuffled back to her bed and lay down on her side with a pillow between her legs. Her mother had told her to put it there and it had really helped her to find a comfortable position to lie in. Mind you, Piper wasn't getting much sleep, these days.

Since Jess had died she kept having nightmares that she was losing the baby. She'd wake up sweating and crying out. Pauline had been brilliant. She'd talk her through the dreams and calm her down. Piper was so glad she was sharing a bedroom with her elder sister. The thought of being on her own at the moment frightened her.

She was scared of everything now. She was worried the baby was going to die, that her parents were going to die, that Luke was going to dump her, that she was going to fail all of her exams, that she was going to end up alone, living in a bedsit, on welfare, with a screaming baby.

Pauline told her that the nightmares were caused by her mind being overloaded with stress and grief – that she was grieving the loss of Jess, full of baby hormones and also doing the most important exams of her life, so it was perfectly normal that she was freaking out. Pauline had helped her come up with a study plan and tested her every evening on what she'd been doing.

Piper was also really worried about Luke. He was so heart-broken about Jess, he could barely speak. She made sure he went to school and tried to study with him, but most of the time he was in a world of his own. She was worried he'd fail all of his exams and get even more depressed. He had to do well for the sake of his self-esteem and also for their future. They both needed to get into college, then get good jobs and support their baby.

Pauline said it didn't matter if Luke failed his exams. He could always get a part-time job, study at night and repeat the exams next year. But Piper didn't want that. She wanted him to go to college in September and have the life he'd always dreamed of. She didn't want his life to be ruined. She was afraid he'd blame her and the baby, get depressed, dump her and end up an alcoholic or a drug addict or something.

Pauline said it was the hormones making her crazy: she needed to calm down. Piper was trying really hard to do that, but she still worried all the time.

She gave up trying to sleep and went downstairs with her books to get a coffee and try to study. Her exams began next week and she was very nervous. She was praying the baby didn't come early. She had three weeks of exams and then, after that, about ten days before her due date. She really didn't want to go into labour during Maths Paper 1. It was bad enough being pregnant in school with everyone staring at her and talking about her, but to go into labour during an exam would be too awful.

Another thing to worry about, she thought wearily. She made herself a cup of coffee and sat down at the kitchen table. The door opened, which made her jump. It was Dad.

'Sorry, pet. Did I give you a fright?'

'Yes.'

'Couldn't sleep?'

Piper shook her head. 'Nope. You?'

'I heard you get up and I wanted to check on you.'

'Sorry, Dad. I didn't mean to wake you.'

'Ah, sure I like being up early.'

'No, you don't!'

He grinned. 'Well, not usually, but these are not usual circumstances. How are you, pet? You look exhausted.'

'I'm all right.'

'Your mother and I are worried about you. It's been a very hard time for you, and for Luke.'

Piper could feel a lump forming in her throat. Her father came over and kissed the top of her head. 'You're a great girl, Piper, and we'll support you no matter what happens. I don't want you to worry about anything.'

'Thanks, Dad,' she croaked.

'How's Luke doing?'

Piper wiped away a tear. 'He's not great. He's just so sad. He adored Jess, and they had such a brilliant relationship. It's just awful to see him so upset. He barely speaks these days and I'm trying to be supportive, I really am.'

'Of course you are. Isn't he lucky to have you? But you need to mind yourself as well, Piper. This has been hard on you too.'

Piper sniffed. 'I miss Jess, Dad. I loved her. She was an amazing girl.'

Seamus shook his head. 'It's a cruel world. You were so good to that child. Kate said you were the sister Jess never had. You're a really wonderful, kind person. I don't tell you that enough. I'm very proud of you.' Seamus's eyes filled with tears.

Piper stood up, threw her arms around his neck and sobbed into his shoulder.

Piper knocked on the kitchen door, opened it and found Bobby sitting at the table, punching a lump of dough.

'Hi.'

'Hi. Do you want to punch?'

'Sure.' Piper stuck her fist into the dough.

'It feels good, doesn't it?' Bobby said, pummelling hard with his little fists.

'Yes, it does. Is Luke up?'

'Nope. I looked into his bedroom and he's asleep in his clothes with his headphones on. Mummy's asleep too. She's holding Whiskey really tight so I couldn't bring him down with me. I gave him to her when I hearded her crying last night.'

'That was really kind of you, Bobby. Where's Granddad?'

'He had to go out to the shops to get stuff.'

'Have you had breakfast?'

'I'm not hungry.'

'Would you eat a little bit of something?'

'No, thank you.'

'If I made toast and put it on a plate, maybe you'd have a bite.'

'Maybe.'

Piper busied herself making toast.

'Piper?'

'Yes.'

'Do you believe in Heaven?'

Piper paused. 'Yes.'

'Do you think Jess is there?'

'Definitely. They're very lucky to have her too.'

'I hate God for taking Jess away.'

Piper buttered the toast. 'I know, Bobby. It's very hard to understand why.'

'Mrs Lorgan said Jess died because all the best people die young and become guardian angels. She said Jess is sitting on my shoulder now, looking after me. Tommy said that was rubbish because his granddad died and he was mean and drank too much beer and shouted at his granny.'

'What did Mrs Lorgan say?'

'She said she was talking about children dying, not old people. But then Suzie started crying and saying she was a good girl and she didn't want to die young and be a guardian angel. She wanted to be a pop star like Taylor Swift. Then Juliette started crying because she thought Suzie said Taylor Swift had died. She was, like, crying really hard and saying, "But I've got tickets for her concert." Then I got super-cross because Taylor Swift isn't dead, and even if she was, we don't actually know her and my sister is dead and it's way worser.'

Piper tried not to smile. 'They sound like silly girls.'

Absentmindedly Bobby picked up a slice of toast and took a bite. 'They are. They just don't get it. No one does. Having your sister die is the baddest thing ever.'

'Yes, it is.'

'It's worse than your dad leaving and having another baby. Way worse. It's worse than your mum not getting up to bring you to school because she's too sad to get dressed. It's worse than your brother not speaking because he's too sad to speak. It's worse than – than anything.' Bobby began to bawl.

Piper rushed over and put her arms around him. 'Oh, Bobby, you poor, poor boy. It's just awful. I know how much you loved Jess and how much she loved you. You must miss her so much.'

'I do,' he sobbed. 'She was the one who listened to me about my facts. I know people find them boring, but Jess always made me feel as if they were interesting. She listened to me when I told her about school too. Mummy and Granddad and Daddy and Luke and everyone else, they always say, "Not now, Bobby," but Jess never said it, never. She was so nice and I wish she was still here. Everything is all upside-down and I want things to be back to normal the way they used to be, when we were happy and we laughed and had fun. It's so quiet now all the time.'

Piper handed him a tissue. She tried to find the right words to comfort the lost seven-year-old. 'It's really hard for you all. Everyone's missing Jess and trying to cope in their own way, but it will get better, Bobby. I promise. You won't stop missing Jess, but in a while you'll be able to remember her and talk about her without it hurting so much. You and your mum and Luke will stop being sad all the time and it'll be just some of the time and you'll be happy again. It will probably take a while, but things will get better. You must try to believe that, Bobby. And I'm here if you ever need to talk.'

Bobby hugged her, squeezing her bump. Then he pulled back suddenly. 'Something moved!'

Piper laughed. 'It was the baby kicking, saying hello to his or her uncle.'

Bobby's eyes were wide. 'Wow! I'm going to be an uncle!'

'Yes, you are, and it's a very important role. You'll have to teach the baby all the things you know. They'll look up to their uncle Bobby and come to you for advice and help.'

Bobby frowned. 'I'd better learn more stuff before they come out then. I need to know more facts to tell them.' He ran out of the door and up the stairs, shouting, 'I'm going to get my book.'

Luke came in, hair askew, deep creases under his eyes. 'What's up with him?'

Piper smiled. 'Nothing. We just had a little chat.'

Luke slumped down in a chair.

'Coffee?' Piper asked.

'Please.'

Piper made him a cup and set it in front of him. 'You look exhausted.'

Luke yawned. 'Bad night.'

'Nightmares?'

'No, memories. Every time I think of Jess and a memory comes back, I feel as if someone's punching me in the gut. It's . . . I . . . It's just so hard.' He was bereft, she knew.

Piper held his hand. 'You loved her so much. It's just awful.'

'I wish my bone marrow had saved her. I feel as if I let her down.' Tears streamed down his face.

Piper kissed his hand. 'You did everything you could, Luke. Nothing worked. The cancer was too aggressive. You tried and I was so proud of you, but it's not your fault. It's no one's fault. You have to stop blaming yourself.'

'I wish none of this had happened. Why did it have to happen, Piper? Why Jess? Why our family?'

Piper leant over and kissed his cheek. 'There are no answers, Luke. It's just cruel and awful, and I wish I could say something comforting to you. I'm sorry about the baby and dragging you down with all this responsibility and, well . . . I'm sorry, I'm so sorry, Luke. I feel so useless.'

Luke looked up at her. 'Useless? Piper, you're amazing, you're the glue. Now Jess has gone, you're the glue in our family. Look at you talking to Bobby this morning and coming here every day to make sure I get up and go to school and study. You're the only thing that's keeping me going. And the baby! Don't you dare apologize! We both got into this and I want that baby. The baby is the one good thing in this whole nightmare. It'll give Mum something to focus on, and Granddad and Bobby and me and you. Piper, I'm so glad you're pregnant. I want our baby so much. More than ever. We need it – our family needs it.'

Piper stared at Luke. It was the most he'd said in weeks. She felt tension flood out of her. It was going to be okay. Luke still wanted the baby and he'd said she was the glue. The glue! Tears of relief flowed down her face. Luke held her and kissed her.

51

Nick sat with Jaden passed out on his shoulder. The poor kid had a rotten cold and couldn't sleep with his stuffy nose, so Nick had got up and walked him around the apartment until he'd finally dropped off. Little puffs of his breath tickled Nick's neck, comforting him. He held him close and inhaled his baby smell.

Since Jess had died, Nick hadn't been able to let go of Jaden. He needed him close all the time. When he cried at night, Nick jumped up to settle him. He liked having a baby to hold and look after. It distracted him, stopped him crying or wanting to punch the wall.

He'd gone back to work a week after the funeral. He was there in body, but not in mind. He had no interest in selling stupid houses to stupid people. When a woman complained that the house he was showing her was a bit small for her taste, he'd wanted to shout, *My daughter's dead, you stupid, shallow bitch*.

He spent a lot of time in the bathroom or his car, crying. It was like a tsunami of tears. He couldn't stop it. The pain of Jess's death was crushing. On top of that was the rage and hate he felt towards Kate for robbing him of time. Time with Jess was all they'd had. Every second was precious. How could she take that away? How could she? Every time Nick thought about it he wanted to scream. It was eating him up inside.

Jenny had booked him in to see a shrink. She said she was worried about him because he wasn't sleeping and he was so angry all the time. She didn't know why – he hadn't told anyone. How could he tell them that his ex-wife was a murderer? He'd wanted to tell the police. He'd wanted to make her pay. He'd even picked up the phone a few times to report her, but he couldn't do it. He couldn't do that to his boys. Their lives were messed up enough as it was.

Careful not to wake his sleeping son, Nick slowly and gently placed him back in his cot and tiptoed out of the room. He went into the kitchen and took out Jess's letter. He read it for the millionth time. *I couldn't take it any more . . . too much pain . . . begged her to do it . . . I love her for doing this . . .*

I love her for doing this. Nick looked out of the window into the dark night. He remembered Jess's face on the last day of her short life, how happy she'd been. She knew, he thought. She knew it was all going to be over that night. That was why she'd been so happy.

He thought back to her face when he'd tried to get her to do more chemo. How upset she'd been. Her thin, pale face crumpling and her eyes pleading, 'No more, Dad.'

But it still came back to Kate robbing him of time. Such precious time. Nick folded the letter and tucked it into the pocket of his suit jacket, which was hanging on the kitchen chair.

The sun would be up soon and he'd have to get dressed, go to work and pretend everything was fine. When he'd first gone back, most of his colleagues had avoided him. Some gave him sad smiles and a few asked him how he was doing. But soon everyone moved on. People began to talk to him about work – houses, rentals, sales, margins, mortgages. He'd sit there listening but not hearing and wonder at their ability to actually give a shit about such trivial nonsense.

My daughter's dead, was all he could think, over and over in his mind. *My daughter's dead.* He wanted to shout it out, he wanted to scream it in their faces. He wanted them to feel pain too. He wanted everyone to feel pain. Why Jess? Why her? Why his beautiful Jess? It wasn't right or fair or even human.

Jenny had been kind, gentle and caring, but she didn't get it. The only person who knew how much this hurt, how badly the pain of Jess's loss cut into his heart, was Kate.

Nick wanted to talk to Kate. He wanted to talk about Jess and tell stories and share memories, but he couldn't. He couldn't even look at her.

The words came back into his mind – *begged her to do it . . . I love her for doing this . . .*

Could he have done it? Could he have helped Jess put an end to her life? No. Why? Because he loved her too much. But Kate had said she'd done it because she loved her so much.

What was love? What did it mean? If you loved someone, you kept them close. If you loved someone, you didn't let them go. But what if they begged you? Nick's head throbbed. He laid it on his arms and closed his eyes. He couldn't go on like this. He had to see her. He had to speak to her and have it out with her. He had to understand how she could have done something so awful.

He picked up his phone and texted her: *Meet me in Café Cos tomorrow 9.30.*

She responded immediately: *I'll be there.*

Nick sat nursing his Americano, watching the door. He saw her come in. He barely recognized her: she looked old and hunched. Her hair was lank and her coat was too big for her. Her body bent forward, as if the weight of the world was pressing her down. She glanced around the café, then saw him. As she came towards him, he saw the deep black

439

pockets under her eyes. She looks even worse than me, he thought.

Kate sat down opposite him and closed her coat around her, shivering.

'Coffee?' he asked.

'No, thanks, I'm fine. I've had three already.'

'You look terrible,' Nick said.

Kate shrugged.

'Guilt will do that to you, I suppose,' he added.

'Yes, grief, too,' she said sadly.

Nick leant in. 'How could you do it, Kate? How could you?'

Kate's eyes were full of sorrow. 'Because she asked me to. I told you, Nick, she begged me. She didn't want to die alone, choking on her own blood. I was there the night she got the infection and vomited blood. It was horrifying. She was terrified. She was afraid of dying like that, and she didn't deserve to go that way. She deserved better.'

'She deserved to live!' Nick shouted.

The people at the table beside them turned to stare at them.

Kate leant closer. 'She deserved to choose how she died.'

'She was twelve,' Nick hissed. 'She didn't get to choose when to die.'

'She wasn't a normal twelve-year-old and you know it. She lived ten lives in the last few months. She was more mature than either of us. You said it yourself, Nick, that night in my kitchen. Remember? You said how my mum always called her an old soul, and you said that was right. That she was different from other kids her age, more mature. You know this, Nick, please. Jess knew she was dying before anyone else did. She knew the cancer was back. She was so broken, Nick, so frail and battered, she just couldn't take it any more.'

Nick gazed at her coldly, his whole body tense. 'Every day I wake up and feel like puking because the pain of her loss is so bad. Then I want to kill you. I actually want to kill you for what you did. I could have had a few more weeks with her. I could have told her –'

Kate cut across him. 'Told her what? That you loved her? She knew. She knew how much she meant to you. You know she did. I'm sorry you're angry, I understand why, but I did it for her, Nick. You have to believe me. I did it for Jess. Whatever you think about me, you know how much I loved her and you know I would have given my life for her.'

Nick looked down at his coffee. 'I want to know how you did it,' he said quietly.

Kate squeezed her eyes shut and took a deep breath. 'I drugged her.'

'With what?'

'Twenty-eight Xanax tablets and fourteen dissolvable Tylex.'

Bile rose in his throat. He struggled to keep his emotions in check. 'Jesus. How did you –'

'Internet.'

'You bought the drugs online?'

'No. I got them from my GP. I pretended they were for me.'

'Christ, Kate.'

'I know it sounds completely insane, but it was for Jess. I would have done anything to make her happy.'

'What was it like? What happened at the end?' Nick's voice shook. Part of him wanted to know about Jess's last hours but another part didn't.

Kate bit her lip. 'She went into a deep sleep and then, after about four hours, she stopped breathing. It was very peaceful.

Before she drifted into sleep she smiled up at me and said, "I'm happy, Mum, I'm ready to go."'

Nick cursed under his breath. 'How could you do it? I could never have done that. It's not right. You should have talked her out of it.'

'Nick, I tried, but Jess knew what she wanted. It was something she'd thought about a lot. She was determined to go out on her own terms. I know what I did was wrong and immoral and illegal. But I granted Jess her final wish and that matters more to me than anything.'

Nick ripped up a sugar pack and watched the grains bounce off the table. *You have to let me go, Dad.* Jess had said that. He could see her gaunt, sad face gazing up at him, her brown eyes pleading with him. She had wanted to go. She had wanted to do it her way.

Nick looked at Kate, who was crying quietly. She was heartbroken. She was a shell of her former self. There was nothing he could do to make her feel worse or to hurt her more. The rage he'd felt since the moment he'd read Jess's letter slowly began to subside.

'It's hell, isn't it?' he said.

Kate nodded.

'It just hurts so fucking much,' he said.

Kate sobbed into a tissue, unable to speak.

'People keep saying it'll get easier with time. I want to shout, "Good to know, because if it gets any harder, I'll die of pain."'

Kate smiled. 'I know. Or the people who say it was God's will or there's a reason for everything. Really? What possible reason could there be for a twelve-year-old girl to get cancer and die?'

'I really hate the people who say she's in a better place – to hell with you and your better place. With her family is where

442

she should be, right here, right now.' Nick banged the table with his fist, making the cup jump.

'She was the core of our family. It's so quiet and lonely without her.' Kate was crying again.

Nick wanted to reach out to her but he couldn't: the anger was still there. 'I hate that you did what you did,' he said, 'but I understand that it was what Jess wanted. I'm going to try to forgive you because the anger is eating me up inside. It's destroying me and that's not fair on Jaden and Jenny. I know you acted out of love, but it doesn't make it right. I don't think I'll ever get over it, but I will learn to live with it. And I won't tell anyone. I owe that to Bobby and Luke. I just wish . . . I just wish we'd had more time.' His voice broke.

'I'm sorry, Nick. If there was any other way of granting Jess her wish, I would have chosen a different path. It was a nightmare. I think about it every single day, but she was happy, I promise you that.'

Nick sighed. 'She was my little angel.'

'She really was special, wasn't she?'

'Yes.' Nick wiped away tears. 'We did something right. We created an exceptional human being.'

'We did. We really did.' Kate reached out to touch his arm.

Nick pulled back and stood up. 'I'm going now. I think I might be able to sleep for the first time in weeks. I'll text you about taking the boys out.'

Kate got to her feet and they walked towards the door. As she turned to go to her car, she said, 'I'm glad we talked, and I'm sorry.'

He knew she was. He was sorry too. Sorry that life had thrown them this awful fate. But what did sorry change? What did anger change? Nothing. Jess was gone and she wasn't coming back.

Nick walked to his car and took out the letter. He read his favourite line: *I love you so much and I'm so proud to be your daughter.*

Nick pressed the letter to his lips and kissed the words. 'I love you too, Jess. I hope you know how much,' he whispered into the silence.

Summer

52

The door of her bedroom burst open. Kate sat bolt upright. Luke was standing at the end of her bed holding his mobile phone, his mouth opening and closing but no words coming out.

'Oh, my God!' she exclaimed. 'Is it the baby?'

'Yes.' Luke finally found his voice.

Kate jumped up and pushed him into his bedroom. 'Get dressed – come on, quickly. Where's Piper?'

'Her mum's taking her to hospital right now.'

Kate rushed back into her room and pulled on a pair of jeans and a sweatshirt.

George came in, woken by the shouting. 'Is it the baby?' he asked sleepily.

'Yes! Piper's on her way to hospital. I'm going to bring Luke now.'

'I'll come with you,' George said.

'Me too.' Bobby appeared in his pyjamas.

'Okay. Hurry up and put some clothes on.'

A little later George swung dangerously into the car park outside the maternity hospital, jerking to a halt at the front entrance doors. Kate and Luke jumped out.

'Stay with Granddad while he parks,' Kate ordered Bobby. She wanted to find out what was going on before they all descended on poor Piper.

Luke ran ahead and Kate rushed to keep up with him. They were told which room Piper was in and took the lift up. Luke went to open the door, and Kate stood back.

'Mum, I want you here. Come on.' He pulled her in with him.

Olivia was standing beside the midwife, her face drawn and tense. Piper was lying in bed in a hospital gown, looking frightened.

Luke went straight over and bent down to gather her in a hug, kissing her face tenderly. 'Are you okay, babe?'

'I'm fine, but the baby's coming, Luke. I'm already six centimetres dilated.'

'Jesus, I can't believe it's actually happening.' Luke's breathing was ragged.

'I'm scared,' Piper said, in a small voice.

'Don't be. I'm here, babe.'

Kate went over to stand beside Olivia. 'Is everything okay?' she asked quietly.

'Yes. The baby's heartbeat is strong and the labour is coming along well, and fast.'

'Thank God,' Kate said. She needed this to go well. They all needed the baby to come out healthy. After so much sorrow, the family needed some joy.

Piper cried out in pain. Luke held her hand. The midwife told her to breathe.

Kate felt they should be alone. She tapped Luke on the shoulder and said she'd wait just outside. He nodded. Olivia followed her out. George and Bobby were there, along with Seamus and all of Piper's sisters.

Kate had met them at Jess's funeral, but it had been a blur. They reintroduced themselves, but she was sure she'd mix them up anyway – they were all so similar.

'So why *do* you all have names that start with P?' Bobby asked.

'Because our parents are losers,' Penny answered.

Bobby grinned. 'What name would you choose if you could? I'd be Dynamo.'

'Cool name,' Penny said. 'I'd be Taylor.'

'Like Taylor Swift?' Bobby asked.

'Kind of, but hotter obviously.'

'Jesus, Penny, he's seven, tone it down,' Seamus barked.

They heard Piper shouting. Kate saw Seamus wince. He was sweating profusely with stress.

'Is she all right? Should you not go in and see?' he asked Olivia.

'She's having a baby, Seamus. It hurts. I'd have thought you might remember that from the four labours I went through.'

'Piper isn't like you.'

'What's that supposed to mean?'

'She's more petite.'

'OMG, Dad! Do you have a death wish?' Poppy gasped.

'I was more petite before I had five kids,' Olivia snapped.

'What's petite?' Bobby asked.

'It's what every girl wants to be, skinny,' Poppy told him.

'I don't like skinny. When Jess was sick she got all skinny and she looked terrible.'

Kate felt everyone freeze at the mention of Jess's name. It happened all the time. She wondered if they'd ever be able to say it outside the family without people being uncomfortable. It made her furious: she wanted to talk about Jess all the time, but people didn't seem to know what to say when she did and usually tried to change the subject.

Liam said it was because they were afraid to say the wrong thing or be insensitive, so they steered the subject away from Jess. Or maybe they were trying to distract Kate with other topics of conversation.

As if Kate could be distracted from Jess. All she thought about all of her waking hours was Jess. Her face, her smile, her eyes, her . . . Just her. She watched old videos of her over and over again. She kissed photos of her, she smelt her clothes, she wore her lip-gloss – she ached to be close to her. A primal mother's yearning.

Inside the room, Piper let out a shriek, bringing Kate back to earth.

'Mother of Divine Christ, will you ever go in and see what the hell is going on?' Seamus nudged Olivia towards the room.

'I will if my fat hips can make it through the door.' Olivia shot him a look, then knocked quietly and went inside.

'Seriously, Dad, after twenty-six years of marriage do you not know what not to say?' Posy asked.

'I never said she had fat hips.'

'You implied it,' Pauline said.

'And that's as bad,' Poppy reminded him.

Seamus waved a hand at them. 'I'll never understand women.'

Bobby's eyes widened. 'How come? You've got so many of them living in your house, you should totally understand them.'

'It's not easy, Bobby,' George defended Seamus. 'Women are complicated.'

'We're not really,' Penny disagreed. 'All you have to do is tell us we're fabulous and buy us presents and we're happy.'

'Shallow women, that is,' Pauline said. To Bobby, she added, 'On the other hand, there are women who like to be told they're smart and interesting.'

'OMG, Pauline! You are never getting married, unless he's like one of those geeky professors with Asperger's,' Poppy said.

'Can you please behave for once?' Seamus asked wearily.

Olivia came out, her face flushed. 'Not long now. The baby's coming.'

They stood around the bed, all staring at the beautiful baby girl in Piper's arms. Luke sat on the edge of the bed beside her, gazing adoringly at his daughter.

The door burst open and Nick fell into the room, out of breath. 'Is it . . . Did I . . . Is everything okay?'

'It's a girl,' Luke said, holding up his baby.

'That's . . . well, wonderful.' Nick gazed at the tiny creature, his eyes welling. 'She's beautiful.'

'Yes, she is,' Kate agreed.

'Just like . . .' Nick said, looking at Kate and she nodded. Yes, she was beautiful just like Jess had been.

'Would you like to hold her?' Piper asked Kate.

Kate held out her hands and felt the little bundle in her arms. She snuggled the baby into her neck and inhaled the baby smell. She closed her eyes and remembered the same smell when Jess was born.

Life and death. So close together, so far apart. To have lost her baby girl and have another born eight weeks later . . . It was heartbreak and a miracle in one.

Kate gazed into her granddaughter's eyes, blue like the sky. She was beautiful. A precious gift in a time of such sorrow. A blessing. Kate kissed her tiny nose and closed her eyes as the baby wrapped her little fingers around her grandmother's thumb.

'What are you going to call her?' Bobby asked.

Luke and Piper looked at each other. Luke cleared his throat. 'Louise Jess Higgins.'

Kate smiled. 'Beautiful.'

'Perfect,' Nick said.

'Lovely,' Olivia agreed.

'I'm glad it's not another P name,' Bobby said, and they all laughed.

Luke came over to Kate. 'I just texted Maggie – look.'

Maggie's text back read: *Am now bawling in the middle of a meeting! Over the moon for you all. Will be in later today to see her and hold her.*

Kate smiled. 'I'm glad you told her. She's very much part of this.'

Luke nodded. 'She's been great.' Looking at his daughter, he asked sheepishly, 'Can I have her back? I just want to hold her again.'

'Of course.' Kate handed him his little girl.

Seamus asked for everyone's attention. 'I'd just like to make a little toast,' he said. He had smuggled in a bottle of Champagne and some plastic cups. Now he poured them all a thimbleful to 'wet the baby's head'.

'Mummy, look!' Bobby shouted.

'Not now, Bobby,' Kate said. 'Listen to Seamus.'

'DON'T YOU DARE SAY, "NOT NOW, BOBBY," TO ME!' he roared.

Everyone turned to look at him.

'Bobby!' Kate snapped. 'What's got into you?'

He grabbed her arm. 'Look! It's Jess. She came to see the baby.'

Kate's head whipped around. Outside, on the windowsill, was a white butterfly. It paused, fluttered its wings then slowly flew away.

Acknowledgements

No matter how many novels you have under your belt, writing a book is never straightforward. One thing I've learnt is that a writer never has it 'sussed'. You are never going to find it easy to write a novel. It's not supposed to be easy. It's supposed to challenge you and take you to places you haven't been before. This novel certainly did that for me. I sincerely hope you, the reader, enjoyed it.

Every book is a collaboration and there are always so many people to thank.

I had to do a lot of research into AML (acute myeloid leukaemia) for this book and I was helped greatly by my uncle, Michael Moriarty, oncologist supreme. Any and all mistakes are entirely my own.

A big thank-you to Paul Carroll for his help in researching the role of a GP. He was also a fount of information on medication and the GP's involvement and function after the death of a child at home.

Thanks to my godson, James Moriarty, for his insight into the world of rugby training.

Rachel Pierce, my editor, has such great insight and ideas. Rachel is a huge asset to my writing life.

Patricia Deevy, for always championing me and for her valuable input into all of my novels.

Michael McLoughlin, Cliona Lewis, Patricia McVeigh, Brian Walker and all the team at Penguin Ireland for their continued support and help.

To all in the Penguin UK office, especially Tom Weldon, Joanna Prior and the fantastic sales, marketing and creative teams.

To my agent Marianne Gunn O'Connor, for being a rock of support and so very kind and thoughtful.

To Vicki Satlow, for her support and tenacity on foreign rights.

To Hazel Orme, for her wonderful copy-editing and for being such a positive force.

To the wonderful people at the Tyrone Guthrie Centre at Annaghmakerrig, where I spent a magical five days finishing this novel.

To my fellow writers, thank you for your support and encouragement. It is a solitary life and those coffees, emails and phone calls are lifelines.

To Mum, who has had a very tough year: you are an amazing woman and have always been an inspiration to me.

To Sue and Mike who are always there for me, through thick and thin. Thanks for your unwavering love and support and for always being on the end of a phone.

To my amazing friends – your kindness, thoughtfulness and loyalty mean so much.

To Hugo, Geordy and Amy – quite simply the loves of my life.

And as always, the biggest thank-you goes to Troy, for being my rock in stormy waters.

Finally, this book is dedicated to my dad, who died very suddenly last year. We miss him.